THE IMMORTAL ORDERS OMNIBUS

ALLISON CARR WAECHTER

This omnibus edition of The Immortal Orders compiles previously published work including:
Dark Night Golden Dawn
Beneath the Alabaster Spire
Awaken the Fifth Order

978-1-963134-17-9
978-1-963134-18-6

Cover image by Averil the Artist
The Immortal Orders Storyscape by Charlie Arpie
Interior Book Design by Cartography Bird
Editing by Kenna Kettrick

CONTENT GUIDELINES

The Immortal Orders is an adult fantasy romance.
Please find all relevant content guidelines at:
https://www.allisoncarrwaechter.com/the-immortal-orders

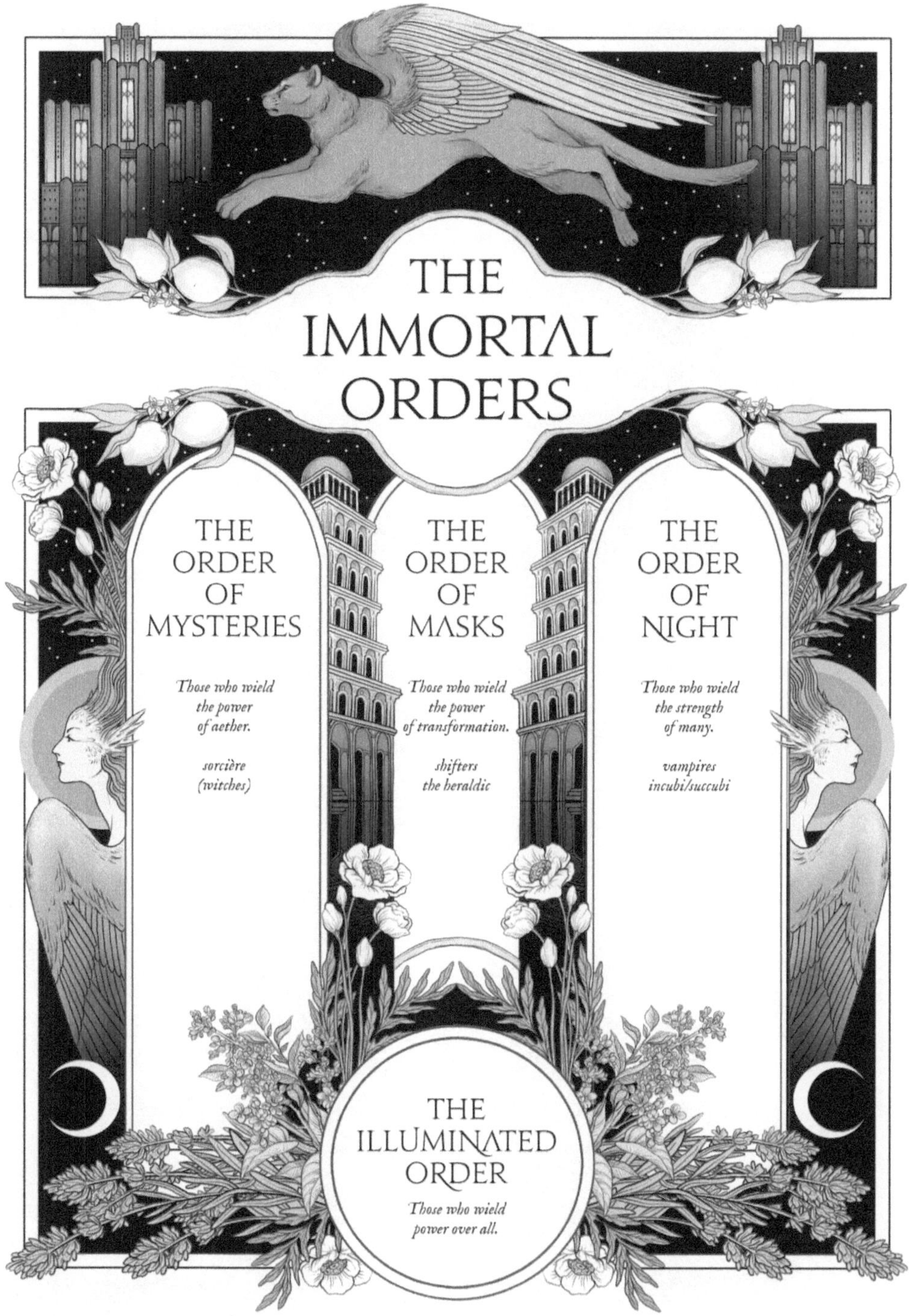
THE IMMORTAL ORDERS
THE ORDER OF MYSTERIES
Those who wield the power of aether.
sorcière (witches)
THE ORDER OF MASKS
Those who wield the power of transformation.
shifters
the heraldic
THE ORDER OF NIGHT
Those who wield the strength of many.
vampires
incubi/succubi
THE ILLUMINATED ORDER
Those who wield power over all.

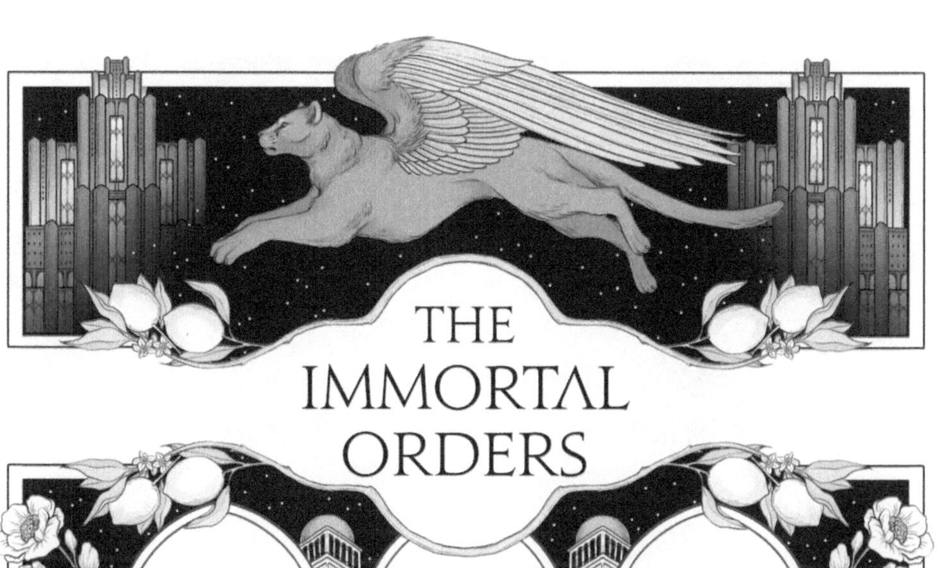

OCEANUS SOLVARUM
NUVA TROI
AMBRACIA BAY
NYTRA

THE WORLD OF THE
IMMORTAL ORDERS

BOOK ONE
DARK
NIGHT
GOLDEN
DAWN

PREFACE

"The Illuminated came to our world in the last days of the Empress Lofrata's reign, and for a time, we worshipped them as though they were gods. Soon enough, we learned they were not gods. They did not care for us, though they loved our world. No explanation was given regarding where they came from, or if they would ever leave.

Two thousand years have passed, and the Illuminated have surely changed the course of the world's history in ways we can scarcely imagine. Humans now share the world with not only the Illuminated, but their children begotten with our ancestors: vampires, witches and shapeshifters.

Though we live together in peace, as the Illuminated require, we would be foolish to claim this is a utopia. All of us live and die at their whim. As technology has advanced and the world has changed, the time of the Illuminated wanes and their numbers decrease, though their strangle-hold on power remains firm as ever."

— Sofya Starkovski, *A Comprehensive History of the Illuminated and the Lower Orders*

CHAPTER 1

Harlow Krane was doing her best not to check her phone. Her fingers itched with the desire to scroll through her socials, and the gossip sites, just to make herself miserable. It was six months ago all over again, when she and Mark broke up. Everyone was talking. Only now, they were talking because Mark had moved on—and she hadn't.

Since she and Mark separated, the gossips had declared Mark the wronged and she the wrong-doer. It made sense in many ways. The gossips were mostly run by humans, unlike the papers, which were all owned by the Illuminated. Of *course* they'd favor Mark's side of things. He was human—a human who'd *so* clearly moved on from his sorcière ex.

The texts Harlow received last night from her sisters had been unbearable. She shifted on the brass ladder she was perched on to take out her phone and read them again:

Thea: *We'll manage this tomorrow.*

So it was something to manage.

Meline: *Stay off your socials.*

She'd done so thus far, but now she desperately wanted to look.

Indigo, quickly following her twin: *Mark is out with a vampire princess. DON'T look at what they're saying about you.*

She knew it was indulging in some minor masochism, but she wanted to see. Wanted to feel the ache of knowing just how much of a loser everyone thought she'd become. Why was she like this?

Larkin: *I love you. Tell me if you're not okay? Okay?*

This was the only text she'd responded to, promising her youngest sister that she was all right, not checking her socials, and asking Larkin to tell the twins to mind their own business. Except social media *was* their business. They'd built a small social empire that had taken the bookstore, and all of Antiquity Row, from being an "Orders only" nook in Nuva Troi to being a *lifestyle*—a desirable destination for humans and immortals alike, with its charming cafes and old buildings.

And of course, the twins made their parents' bookstore, the Monas, the star of the show, the centerpiece of the cultural world of the Order of Mysteries, thereby making Harlow an object of interest to the gossips and socials alike. She'd never agreed to play such a role, but the twins' success had meant the success of their Order, and in a world ruled by the Illuminated, you took whatever success you could eke out, *and* whatever terrible side effects ensued as a result.

Harlow's disastrous love life being the talk of the town, and maybe even the country, was just one of those side effects. If she'd had her preference, she'd have spent her life in complete obscurity. She had no desire for anyone to know who she was or what she did with her life, and she certainly didn't want to think about what to do when she was the center of attention for all the wrong reasons.

She'd come into the bookstore early to avoid the inevitable barrage of strategizing that was coming as soon as Meline and Indigo scanned through the most important of the gossip apps, Section Seven, over their coffee. Her phone began to buzz again, just as Mother entered the shop from the back office. Her sisters were up.

Aurelia Krane was looking at her own phone, as she floated a tea tray above her other hand, effortlessly using magic to keep it steady and aloft. "Your sisters are quite worried about you, the twins particularly so."

Harlow sighed from atop the brass ladder, slipping her phone back into her pocket and the last of the books she'd been shelving into place, and stepped down. Aurelia looked up as she guided the tea tray down onto the glass coffee table at the center of the shop's main floor showroom. This was the heart of the Monas, the place where Harlow and her four sisters grew up, the magic they would inherit. A world of esoteric knowledge, a legacy of books.

The two green velvet chesterfields that flanked the brass-rimmed glass coffee table hosted a variety of jewel toned cushions. Harlow pulled one down to sit on, onto the plush antique rug that bridged the two couches. She watched Aurelia carefully for signs that she would bring up the news about her on Section Seven, the twins' worries, anything about Mark. Instead, Aurelia was suspiciously placid, her bobbed silver hair shining in the weak springtime sunlight.

"A rare sunny day in Nuva Troi," Aurelia commented, setting her phone down.

"It's going to rain at ten," Harlow muttered as she poured the tea. Aurelia never beat around the bush unless she was uncomfortable. "Just say what you have to say, Mother."

Aurelia smiled, serene and wise, as always. "I *am* sorry about Mark, my darling. Are you holding up all right?"

Harlow sighed, taking a long sip of the Duke and Duchess tea her mother had brewed, the sharp scents of bergamot and lavender softening into rose and vanilla. It was perfect, as always. She looked around the shop, at the warm white bookcases that stretched to the full height of the fifteen-foot ceilings, the grand staircase that took customers upstairs to the second and third floors, the ceiling, painted in rich oils and gold leaf to represent the heavens and Okairos' twin moons.

The Monas was her happy place, her true home, and she didn't want to talk about what happened with Mark here. Especially not after the nearly three years of turmoil her relationship with a human caused her family. It was the last of a long line of mistakes she'd been making for the past seven years, and Harlow's soul was brittle and fatigued.

She'd been back on solid ground with her family for the past few months and she wanted to keep it that way. This development with Mark threatened to put her back in a vulnerable spot, one she feared. Every time she felt like she was pulling things together, something unraveled her progress, and out of her small flock of sisters, she was the one who was always struggling, always lost. It was like her internal compass was missing and she couldn't find her place in the world.

"Of course," she said simply. "I'm always all right. You know that."

Aurelia raised her eyebrows, skeptically. "My dear girl, it's just us. Thea isn't in yet, and your Mama won't be down for a half-hour at least. She was running a bath when I left her."

Harlow wrinkled her nose at Aurelia. Mention of morning baths meant her parents spent the wee hours making love and it always made her want to scold Aurelia for telling.

"Don't wrinkle your nose at me, little bunny. You should be happy your mother and I still make enough of a ruckus that the neighbors text to ask if we might keep things down. Your mother had an orgasm so powerful…"

"Do not finish that sentence. *Please*. I beg you. I am happy you and Mama still have all the sex. But as someone who grew up listening to it, could you just *not*?"

Aurelia rolled her eyes. "Such a prude. Someday you'll meet someone who makes your toes curl so hard you'll think you'll explode when they look at you."

Harlow sighed. She'd felt that way about someone when she was much younger, and it ended so disastrously it had kicked off a domino effect of terrible decisions that were still ricocheting through her personal life, leaving a leaky mess everywhere she turned. She'd rather *not* feel that way again, if she was honest with herself.

"So, the human. Your sisters say something about news on the Section Seven app and the socials? Something about Mark and a vampire?"

Harlow groaned internally. Hearing her elegant, erudite mother discuss her humiliation on the gossips and socials made everything worse somehow. But she smoothed her face as well as she could. Of all the things she was bad at, pretending she was fine while her personal life burned around her was not one of them. She was an expert at *that*.

"Stop pretending you're not angry, Harlow. What good does it do to act this way?"

"I'm *not* mad. I don't care. You all just think I should because you would."

Aurelia lost her patience. "Harlow Andromeda Krane, I told you to drop the pretense."

Harlow cringed at the sound of the hunt in her mother's voice. The lupine snarl of a pack in pursuit of its quarry, the sound of the moon's song, and the goddess Akatei's power rang true in Aurelia's glamour. She glanced up at her mother, who appeared nearly ten feet tall and imposing as a divine being.

"Oh, stop that," she gasped, squeezing her eyes shut.

"Well, you wouldn't be honest." Aurelia returned to her usual self, serene as she smoothed her pants. "Be honest and I won't have to."

Harlow laughed. The dry humor in Aurelia's voice got her every time. She was the parent who hated throwing her magical weight around. Selene wouldn't have hesitated, but Aurelia *had* tried to pry it out of her another way. She'd been trying for months to talk to her about Mark, despite how much she'd disapproved of their relationship.

Harlow took her mother's hand and Aurelia squeezed hard, reassuring her girl it was all right to let her guard down. "It's been six months, bun-bun. Surely you knew he would move on."

Harlow glared at her mother. "Of course I knew he would. It's *who* he moved on with that stings. Not because I care who he's with, but because it invites comparisons."

Aurelia nodded. "It is unfortunate he aligned himself with the Order of Night."

"Our whole affair was unfortunate. You and Mama were right about humans."

"We had very little problem with Mark's humanity, you know that, don't you?" Aurelia said softly.

This was an old wound, and Harlow suppressed the wince she felt coming on, but didn't quite succeed. Aurelia's hand covered her own. "It wasn't a good relationship, my darling."

Harlow rolled her eyes. "But you didn't like that Mark was human, did you?"

Aurelia sighed. "As we've discussed many times, what your mother and I worried about was his interest in sorcière secrets, in the Order at large... And his treatment of you. The way he tracked your every move... we worried about *that* most of all."

Aurelia said the last part quietly, tentatively. Harlow knew both her mothers had been concerned about Mark's incessant jealousy, his increasing demands on her time. By the time they'd broken up, she'd never gone anywhere alone. Even if she tried, he showed up with a kind of relentlessness that had worn her out so much she'd simply stopped going anywhere. The maters had been distressed by this, arguing that he was isolating her—dangerously so.

She stared into her teacup, feeling the sting of shame she always felt when she thought about how foolish she'd been about Mark. "It's over. We don't have to talk about it anymore."

A small sigh hissed from between Aurelia's lips. "We can talk about it for as long as you need to."

Harlow's gaze snapped to her mother's bright blue eyes. There was love and concern there, and real fear. She knew more about how things were with Mark than she'd expressed. Harlow didn't put it past her mothers to have used magic to find out what really happened between them, and that thought made everything worse.

Harlow couldn't escape the feeling that her legacy would be a trail of mistakes and apologies. This one though… this one was particularly bad because it didn't just hurt her, it had hurt her family, her Order, and now Mark's actions were an embarrassing reflection on all of them.

Aurelia gestured at her, waving her elegant hands imperiously. "You'd better look at the photos and have it done with."

Harlow nodded, pulling her phone out. When she unlocked it, the Section Seven app was already open. She scrolled past several posts about humans protesting procreation screenings in Nea Sterlis in breaking news. There it was, the first featured item in the lower Orders' gossip feed: Mark and a beautiful vampire princess, Olivia Sanvier, kissing and smiling for the cameras. One caption read, "Mark Easton, son of prominent tech mogul Alain Easton, and the new Lead Media Strategist for the Limen Publishing Group, levels up from a frumpy sorcière to a princess of the Order of Night!"

"Levels up?" The implication that she'd been a launch-point for Mark's social career stung. The frumpy comment stung as well, but it wasn't altogether inaccurate. She looked down at her ill-fitting trousers and the almost purposefully ugly blouse she was wearing. She'd stopped caring as much about what she looked like late in university, and at first it'd been freeing, confidence-building. Now it had turned into something else and she knew it. Frumpy indeed.

Aurelia read over her shoulder as she poured them both another cup of tea. "You aren't frumpy. What are they talking about?"

But then Aurelia glanced at her ensemble and her forehead wrinkled. It was as though she was seeing her child for the first time in a long time—through the world's eyes, rather than her own. It hurt Harlow's heart to feel her mother's scrutiny. She could practically hear Aurelia thinking, "What else have I missed?"

They liked Mark at first. Everyone had. He was handsome, funny, and smart. It wasn't until they'd been together for almost six months that the fighting started. The feeling that she was always doing something wrong, that every person she talked to threatened their relationship. Her life got smaller and smaller, until it was just her and Mark, against the world—or so she'd thought.

When he broke up with her and kicked her out of their apartment, Harlow was shocked. Six months later, she was still processing, and now there was *this*. Harlow scrolled down to a photo someone had snapped of her leaving the grocery store in a nearly identical outfit to the one she was wearing now, her hair in the kind of messy bun that looked terrible, instead of artfully mussed, the way she'd thought it looked when she threw her hair up.

Aurelia's jaw clenched, noticeably, as though she was suppressing all the things she wanted to say, and for that Harlow was eternally grateful. Selene had tried time and time again for the past few months to get Harlow to care about how she looked, but Harlow had resisted, getting pricklier each time Selene mentioned it. It wasn't just about keeping up appearances for Selene, who was the spitting image of Raia, goddess of fertility and sex. Mama was genuinely worried about her mental health, she knew that. Everyone was worried about her.

Harlow swallowed, and the act of doing so was difficult. She *was* frumpy these days. Dull really, on all counts. And who could compete with vampires? They were genetically predisposed to be attractive to humans, just like the Illuminated; everything about their biological makeup drew humans in. Not that she wanted to compete with Olivia Sanvier, or have Mark back, she didn't. But the socials drawing comparisons between them made it impossible for her *not* to.

Harlow frowned as she scratched at a tiny stain on her pants—where had that come from? She took a shaky breath, trying to push back the wave of insecurities threatening to wash over her. She wasn't an insecure person, but Section Seven could make anyone feel terrible about themselves, and Harlow was already in a bad place.

Aurelia smoothed her hair and kissed her forehead. "Humans. You know they glorify the Order of Night."

"I suppose." Harlow's feelings swirled with confusion.

She never understood the human need to identify with the Orders as though they were fan clubs they might join. Their love for the Order of Night was even more perplexing, since they were the Order of immortal creatures that threatened their safety the most directly. It didn't matter how many laws the Consortium of Immortals passed against non-consensual recreational bloodletting, the Order of Night was as dangerous to humans now as they were a thousand years ago, despite the monthly donations all humans were required to make to the Night's Own Blood Banks.

The comments about her on the write-up of Mark and Olivia's date were brutal, many referring to Harlow in derogatory ways that made her stomach turn. Her cheeks reddened and she bit her bottom lip hard enough to draw blood. Her mother's cool fingers stroked her cheek, turning her face away from her phone. "That's enough, darling. Time to leave it be."

CHAPTER 2

Harlow blinked back tears, feeling embarrassed. She took her mother's hand and kissed it. "I'm sorry."

Selene Krane descended the staircase, just as she apologized. Unlike Aurelia, who never failed to dress for work in a three-piece suit, Selene Krane was clad in one of her hundreds of dresses. This morning it was an orchid-colored velvet wrap dress, paired with knee-high heeled boots. Her dark blonde hair floated away from her face, and if she were human she wouldn't look a day over forty-five, even though she and Aurelia both were nearer to six hundred.

Harlow was always impressed by her mothers' style, but this morning, they were quintessential Selene and Aurelia, mistresses of the esoteric rare book trade, paragons of the Order of Mysteries, and her own dear parents.

"No apologizing, Harlow," Selene commanded, imperious as a goddess. "The human was a fool, and we are lucky to be rid of him."

This was as close as Selene would come to saying "I told you so," and for that much Harlow was grateful. Mama could hold a grudge, and she was glad to be so quickly on the other side of her temper.

Selene touched her daughter's honey-colored hair, so like her own, and kissed the top of her head. Harlow smelled her mother's familiar scent of violet, musk, and mysterious ancient woods. "The only thing to do now, dearest, is to meet someone else."

Harlow bristled at the suggestion. She wasn't ready to meet anyone new. It's why she hadn't moved back in with her parents when Mark kicked her out. She knew Selene would start trying to make matches for her and she wasn't ready to be paired yet. Fixing herself had been her top priority for the past six months and the project wasn't going as well as she'd hoped it would.

Aurelia sniffed softly and rose from the chesterfield to kiss her wife. "Perhaps we should let Harlow be."

Selene kissed Aurelia, a bit more passionately than Harlow was comfortable with witnessing, but that was the way of it with her parents. Five hundred years of marriage hadn't cooled their flame a bit.

"If we let Harlow be, she will turn into a dried up old hag. Is that what you want?"

Aurelia chuckled at Selene's forecast. "Now, now, my love. She's just seen the photos from last night. Let's not pronounce her a dried up old hag just yet. Let her adjust."

Harlow hated the way everyone in her family spoke about her like she wasn't sitting right there. It was the way of big families, and she dearly loved hers, but it was eternally annoying to have them discuss her as though she had no mind of her own.

"I am *fine*," she insisted. It was the wrong thing to say, if she'd wanted to be left alone.

"Wonderful!" Selene said with a warm but calculating smile. "Then you'll have no problem with joining us for the season." She said "the season" as though it were a proper noun, which of course it was in many ways.

"No!" Harlow moaned. "Please. It's so archaic. How can we be the most powerful creatures on the planet and still be *selling* ourselves to one another? The humans moved past this centuries ago."

Selene and Aurelia sighed in unison. They'd borne Harlow's rants about this subject thousands of times. They were paired in their own season, long, long ago. They'd courted at a series of events specially designed to match children of the Illuminated and the lower Orders with socially compatible partners.

Harlow began to say something else, but Selene held up a finger. "Harlow, my love. Please. We've been over this many times and we stayed out of it while you dallied, but now it is time to do your duty to our family."

Dallied. As if she and Mark had been playing house, instead of in a deeply committed relationship. Harlow struggled not to grimace.

"It isn't as if marriages are forced upon anyone," Aurelia added. "We fell in love at our own season, as did our parents and siblings before us."

Harlow rolled her eyes. "But of course, you were pushed toward each other at every turn, weren't you? Your match was advantageous, with Mother's money and Mama's family properties. It was a business arrangement as much as love, wasn't it?"

Selene's passionate fury flashed in her large green eyes, the twins to her own, and Harlow was surprised she didn't pull the same kind of stunt Aurelia had earlier. "The fact that it was an advantageous pairing takes nothing away from how much I love your mother. Don't cheapen our love, or our traditions."

Guilt nipped at Harlow's poison tongue as she watched Selene fall dramatically into Aurelia's arms. It was true that by human standards the season was archaic and ridiculous, but nearly all the pairings resulted in long, loving romantic relationships, and those that didn't worked for other reasons. Polyamory was not uncommon amongst the Orders, and divorce was rare amongst those that paired during the season.

Harlow never knew whether it was because it stretched from spring into the blooming summer months, some of the most fortuitous times of the year to plant the seeds of love, or because the season itself, as a process, actually worked. Parents were absolutely forbidden from requiring a marriage if their children entered into a season, but of course they influenced their choices in every way they possibly could.

"I'm sorry." Harlow took Selene's hands and hugged both of her parents. "I know how much you love each other, and I do know the season works for many of our people. I just… I just wish I had more freedom in the matter."

Aurelia kissed both her cheeks before she gathered the tea tray up to brew a fresh pot. Selene's lips curved in a forgiving smile. "You have all the freedom in the world, Harlow. If you don't make a match, no one will blame you or find you lacking. Many pair outside the season, or do not bond at all. It is only an opportunity."

Harlow nodded. She had plenty to say about the matter, but she held her tongue. She knew both her parents would let it go completely if she didn't pair at all, but both Harlow and her eldest sister had been eligible to join the season for several years, and their mothers had never pressed them or encouraged it before.

Besides which, as much as she knew Selene had disapproved of her relationship with Mark, she was being uncharacteristically callous about moving on. Mama's *modus operandi* when it came to breakups was to spoil her girls until their hearts were fully healed, and if Harlow was honest with herself, she knew Selene didn't think she was "dallying" with Mark. She'd been just as worried as Aurelia was about how isolated she'd been when they were together, and now she was being altogether too glib. Something wasn't right.

Harlow glanced at the back office door, where she could hear Aurelia heating water for more tea. "Is everything all right? You and Mother have never suggested we join the season before, and all five of us are technically eligible now."

Selene's eyes darkened as she sank onto one of the chesterfields. For a moment, Harlow thought she might not answer her, but then something shifted in her countenance and Selene opened up to her second-eldest child. "Connor and Aislin McKay have their eye on this block again. We may not be able to hold out much longer. We need allies, or the Order of Mysteries will lose our foothold in the antiquities market. The Illuminated are making moves to take over."

Harlow gasped. "What?"

She hadn't realized things had gotten so bad, distracted as she'd been with Mark. The Monas was a fixture on Antiquity Row, six blocks of esoteric and occult shops and organizations that made up the backbone of the Order of Mysteries' income in Nuva Troi.

Besides which, Antiquity Row was an institution in the city—a *sorcière* institution. It was the place where anyone interested in ancient magics came to find rare goods, or just to be delighted by magic itself. The Kranes had owned the six-story building the Monas was housed in for nearly five hundred years. It was not only their business, but their home.

Selene sighed. "We were waiting to tell you. They say they don't want to change anything, just own all the property. Some families are thinking of selling. They're offering quite a lot."

"Damn them. Just another entitled Illuminated family thinking they own the world."

Aurelia returned from the office with another pot of tea. She glanced at Selene, and Harlow saw the look of sorrow that passed between them. They were afraid of losing the Monas, and maybe Antiquity Row completely. She felt a squeeze of pressured panic grip her heart.

"Hush, Harlow," Selene soothed with a hug. "They won't get it. Not if we present a united front. Perhaps there are other things we might offer them."

"Other things? Like what?"

Aurelia and Selene both looked uncomfortable. "We were going to talk with you and your sisters about this later today…"

"Spit it out, mothers."

Out the window the shadow of clouds loomed. The sunny morning was over, and Harlow felt the incoming darkness acutely, as though it were more than just the usual Avril weather in Nuva Troi.

"I'm sure you've heard the rumors about the Illuminated," Selene said conspiratorially. "That they've been having trouble as of late… conceiving."

Of course Harlow had heard that, as well as the speculation that the Order of Mysteries might be the perfect solution to their problem—or to be specific, that pairing eligible Illuminated with those of the most powerful sorcière families might be the solution. Typically, Orders didn't mix much, but it didn't mean they *couldn't*. Anyone paying attention had heard the speculation, or rather read it, as it was all the back-channel gossips wrote about, even though Section Seven wouldn't touch it.

Aurelia gave Selene a cautionary look, but Mama barreled into her next statement with her usual verve. "Finn McKay is home from Nea Sterlis. I'm told he has two graduate degrees from Aphelion, a Masters in business and what was the other one, pet?"

Harlow wrinkled her nose in annoyance. Aphelion University was the most prestigious college in the country. There wasn't a better school in Nytra and of course Finn McKay had two degrees from there, while Harlow had been too afraid to even apply, and had simply gone to the University of Nuva Troi. Apparently today was a day for rubbing it in that all her exes were doing amazing things… Not that Finn was her ex. Not exactly, anyway.

"Public policy of some kind, I believe," Aurelia said absently, not taking her eyes from Harlow.

"Yes, something like that. He's back and I have it on good authority that both he and Alaric Velarius will join the season this year."

Understanding of Selene's implication hit Harlow like a punch in the gut. "No, you can't possibly think…"

Selene shrugged. "Why shouldn't the Krane girls pair with the most eligible Illuminated bachelors? If they want sorcière wives, surely any of you would be more than good enough for them."

Harlow's breath shuddered through her lungs at the thought of Finn McKay.

Memories of stormy eyes and dark, unruly hair threatened to drag her into a past that she wouldn't, couldn't return to. Not here, not now. Not ever. That had been the start of everything falling apart, time and time again.

To tamp down the panic that threatened to take over she spoke quickly, hoping reason might curb this ridiculous idea before it went further. "You're the ones who always said the Illuminated world is dangerous. That they're too powerful for their own good. And weren't we *just* talking about how no one is forced to do anything during the season?"

"I know, I know," Aurelia said, in what Harlow assumed was meant to be a calming tone. "And if none of you are interested in them, that will be just fine."

Selene opened her mouth to say something, probably that it was *not* just fine, but Aurelia shook her head. "None of you have to do anything you don't want to, but an alliance with the McKays and others like them would increase the sorcières' power and standing in the Orders. Surely you cannot deny that."

Harlow shrugged. She couldn't deny it, but she did think it rather hard that she and her sisters were to be offered up like prizes to the Illuminated. She knew better than to say such a thing to her parents though. The thought that a pairing might be made between Finbar McKay and one of her sisters made her ill.

No. That simply would not do. Her mothers might not understand the danger someone like Finn posed to her sisters, but she did, all too well. Harlow wasn't going to let any of them be hurt by a self-centered, arrogant prick like him, and if she had to sabotage the entire season to keep him away from her sisters, she would.

CHAPTER 3

Harlow was saved from needing to respond by her eldest sister's entrance. Thea Krane was a vision. No one could deny that she took after Aurelia in both looks and intelligence. Tall, statuesque, and graceful, she was the one her mothers should have been coaxing to align with the Illuminated. Perhaps they'd already convinced her.

Harlow was well aware that she'd been left out of family business, as well as Order business, while she reacclimated to sorcière society. After nearly two years living amongst humans, the sorcière were wary of her. It was to be expected, she supposed, but she wished things were different.

She missed being invited to rituals. Seventeen hells, she'd be grateful to be invited to one of the "witch and bitch" coffee dates she used to turn her nose up at. But most of her old friends had stopped speaking to her, and since her magical talent hadn't emerged yet, it made it even easier to avoid her. She wasn't sure how to gain people's trust again; she barely felt like she could trust herself most days. Her lack of magical prowess had a lot to do with that.

Octobre had come and gone, taking her twenty-fifth birthday with it, and still she was stuck doing the equivalent of party tricks while most sorcière her age had manifested their true magical talents in ways that made them special. Selene and Aurelia cautioned her that her time living with humans may have stunted her progress, to be patient, but it made her feel like a failure all the same.

Thea kissed their mothers sweetly, taking off her coat and depositing it in the back office. Perfect Thea. If she weren't Harlow's best friend in the world, it would be easy to hate her sister. In addition to being so beautiful she was often mistaken for one of the Illuminated, she was brilliantly talented in the deep magics.

Her artistry had manifested on her twenty-third birthday, the ideal age for a prodigy, and now that she was twenty-seven, she created some of the most beautiful artwork Harlow had ever seen. Paintings, sculptures—her personal works were stunning. Here at the shop, she used her talent to restore the most precious of the ancient books the maters took in.

When Thea returned from the back office she asked after everyone's plans for the day. When no one responded to her she pulled her dark brown hair back into a low chignon and raised her perfectly groomed eyebrows. "What's going on?"

Selene poured herself a cup of tea. "We were telling Harlow about the season. She is not thrilled."

Thea laughed. "Of course she isn't. That's our Harlow." Her sister hugged her close, whispering, "It won't be so bad, pal. Just come to the events. You don't have to talk to anyone if you don't want to."

Harlow looked into her sister's luminous brown eyes, nodding. "Fine, fine. I'll come."

She wasn't going to tell Thea that she would go to these events primarily to keep her sisters from being sold off to Finn McKay. She and Thea were close, but they had differing opinions about how to change the Orders' outdated traditions. Thea thought subtlety and transforming things from within was the best method, and Harlow thought they should burn it all down.

There was no use in arguing; she could give in now or give in later, but Selene wore the look that told Harlow she wouldn't stop until she agreed to join the antiquated pairing ritual. She sighed deeply, then asked, "When is the first event? I suppose I'll need to secure an adequate wardrobe if I'm going to participate."

Aurelia and Selene both looked as though they'd collapse from the relief of not having to convince their second-eldest further, but Thea's eyes glittered with suspicion. Harlow rolled her eyes and lifted her shoulders when Thea pinched her.

Selene shot them a look that screamed, *Behave*, before beginning her instructions to Harlow. "The opening ceremony is tomorrow evening at the Grove, as it always is, followed by the garden party at the Statuary this weekend. For the opening ceremony you won't need anything new, as we'll dress for ritual. You may wear the pallyra you already have. Is it clean?"

"Of course it is." The heavy ceremonial robe was always clean, since she was never invited to important rituals anymore. At least she didn't need to worry about that. Harlow shifted uncomfortably. She knew it was time for the season, of course, but she'd lost track of the exact date it began. Tomorrow felt very soon. Too soon.

Selene nodded, then added, "You don't have to wear anything elaborate to the Statuary party. It's a casual event."

A laugh bubbled in her throat. *A casual event.* Nothing was casual when the Illuminated and all three of the lower Orders were involved. She wracked her brain. Her penchant for vintage might serve her well, but she needed to call in an expert if she was going to get through this without the gossips tearing her to pieces, and the socials… that would be the worst. All the people she *knew* talking about her return to immortal society. Her stomach soured and she swallowed hard, trying to keep her throat clear of the bile threatening to rise. The season's events would be covered relentlessly online and in print, and since she and Mark were already a story, she knew she'd be a target for the whole season.

Selene sensed her concern. "I'll transfer money into your account, darling. Get whatever you need. Perhaps you might ask Enzo to help you."

Harlow smiled in response to cover the anxiety wringing her stomach into knots. Enzo Weraka ran one of the most prestigious ateliers in Nuva Troi and they'd been the best of friends for most of their lives. Until Mark anyway. They hadn't talked in a while, not like they used to. Selene deposited Harlow's phone in her lap as she trailed back up the grand staircase. "Better text him now. I'll make calls about the money."

Harlow waited until she heard the door to the residence click shut, two stories above the shop, before turning to Aurelia and Thea, who'd begun shelving new books. "Are the sillies participating in the season too?"

Aurelia frowned. "I've asked you not to call your sisters that."

Thea shook her head, pursing her lips in disapproval. Of course, Thea always had her best manners on, even when it was just their family. Harlow's eyelashes fluttered in frustration. "Well? Will they?"

Aurelia nodded. "Yes. They are eligible to participate, and all three of them wish to attend the events."

"Even Larkin?" Harlow could hardly imagine her youngest sister, who was barely twenty, wanting to be paired.

Larkin was a quiet girl, studious and musically inclined, who had never shown an ounce of interest in lovers. Unlike the twins, Indigo and Meline, who had been obsessed with romance from the time they could form words, Larkin had never cared.

Aurelia smiled, her eyes warming at the thought of her youngest. "I think Larkin is hoping to make friends, more than anything else. And the season is a wonderful opportunity for that as well."

"Sure," Harlow said, barely concealing the ultra-dry note of sarcasm in her voice as she shot a text to Enzo. *The maters have convinced me to join the season.*

Before he could answer, she added: *Anything in my size in your treasure trove that I can wear to the Statuary this weekend?*

And then, because she'd missed him horribly and wished they could be the way they were before Mark: *Please tell me you're going to these things too. I won't make it without you.*

She waited, feeling shaky and impatient, hoping he'd respond. She'd drifted apart from everyone that mattered when she and Mark had moved in together, but since the breakup, she'd heard from Enzo a few times and they'd made half-hearted plans to have dinner that neither had followed through on.

After what felt like eons, her phone vibrated in her hands.

Client here. Come by at lunchtime?

She sighed with relief and shot back immediately. *See you at one.*

Enzo hearted her response and she tucked her phone into the pocket of her frumpy pants, feeling some measure of relief. Enzo would take care of her clothes, and maybe their friendship could get back on track in the process.

Selene returned, with Larkin, Meline and Indigo in tow. All three still lived at home and they swept into the shop like a wave of buoyant energy, especially the twins, who both kissed her and asked if she was all right. They were like the sun and the moon, identical but for their hair. Meline was tow-headed, her hair so fair it might be silver, and Indigo's was darker even than Thea and Larkin's. The worry that poured off the three of them told her they knew the true depth and breadth of what the gossips and socials were saying about her. Akatei bless them though, they didn't say a word. Larkin squeezed her arm as she pushed a cart of new books ready to be restocked past her.

Meli was on the phone and computer simultaneously already, scheduling the various Order of Mysteries events that would take place at the shop in the early evenings in the coming week. Indigo unlocked the front doors, and a ray of weak sunshine pushed through the clouds as the first customer arrived. As everyone got to work for the day, Harlow's heart swelled. The seven of them were a well-oiled machine, working in perfect harmony.

Her mothers were the perpetual hosts, solving literary conundrums and matching people with books they never imagined they needed. No one left the Monas unsatisfied or without a sense that they'd come in contact with the Mysteries. Customers ranged from the lower Orders to curious humans, and Aurelia and Selene were as much a part of the attraction to the Monas as the books themselves. Harlow and Thea set about their work in restoration and curation, in the third-floor workroom, and the morning passed quickly in companionable quiet.

The workroom was Harlow's sanctuary. Shelves of new acquisitions lined the walls, with two large library tables at the center of the room. One was for Thea's restorative work, and the other for Harlow's cataloguing. Until her magical abilities manifested fully, she was in charge of making detailed notes about each of the acquisitions and Thea's restorations for the Order of Mysteries' records, before any of the volumes were distributed for sale, or for the Order's private collections, which were vast troves of magical knowledge.

For the most part, while the Orders socialized with one another, they remained quite separate when it came to governance and sharing knowledge. The outward reasoning was that each was specifically talented in one area of the world beyond humans' perception, and that it was best to cultivate those talents, rather than water them down with frequent intermixing. Anyone with half a brain understood this was the Illuminated's way of keeping them from forming meaningful coalitions. With just enough tension strung taut between each of the lower Orders, the Illuminated never had to worry about them rising up together.

That had only happened once, eighteen hundred years ago, during the War of the Orders. Those that had risen against the Illuminated had made a valiant effort, but were crushed within two years of the war's start. Though there had been perpetual peace since that time, the Illuminated made it clear that resistance against them would result in far more dire consequences now than it had then. They'd developed and controlled the only weaponry allowed on Okairos, and their vast financial and securities organizations made it all but impossible to push back, even a little. They liked to think of themselves as a benevolent oligarchy, but in truth, they were no better than the human mafia in most ways. And of course, they controlled even those heinous criminals.

The Illuminated controlled everything. Even this store, which they could take in an instant, though the maters had owned this property for hundreds of years. If they wanted it, they could have it. If they wanted one of the sorcière to marry Finn McKay or Alaric Velarius and restart their gene pool, they could have that too. But Harlow was determined that neither she, nor her sisters, would be the sorcières entangled with them.

Alaric might not be so bad; in fact, of all the Illuminated, he was one of the best. And his parents were as kind as the older Illuminated could be. But Finn McKay was ruthless, intimidating and cold. Harlow knew that all too well. The words of a first edition copy of *Lore of the Lilu* swam in front of her eyes.

Why won't you talk to me?

What would I have to say to you?

Harlow tried to shut out the memory of how those beautiful slate-grey eyes had narrowed at her. How he'd turned and walked away, without so much as a look back, as her heart had crumbled to ash. She clutched the buttons of her ugly blouse, as though she could stop it from happening if she gripped hard enough. But nothing could change the fact that Finn McKay couldn't be trusted.

With a deep breath, Harlow attempted again to focus on noting the quality of the text and images in *Lore of the Lilu,* but nothing she read stuck. Usually, the topic of the Order of Night's most taboo creatures would fascinate her. Tales of the infamous incubi and succubi and their many fantastical abilities had terrified Harlow and her sisters as children. She turned a few more of the fragile pages. A beautifully macabre illustration of an incubus turning a screaming sorcière into a succubus as a gallery of vampires watched sent shivers down Harlow's spine. She tried for another ten minutes to read the essays within the book, but despite its salacious topic, *Lore of the Lilu* was remarkably boring.

It was nothing like the stories Thea had told her when they were small, of incubi who could steal a sorcière's heart and turn them into a soulless monster. Harlow shivered at the memory. Even vampires were afraid of the incubi, but, incredibly, this collection of essays had reduced these impossibly strong creatures to a catalogue of physical attributes and hypothetical ways to kill them. That was of no interest; there hadn't been a case of incubism or succubism since the War of the Orders. Unlike vampires, who were humans who had been turned by the magic in vampire venom, the incubi were near-impossible to sire, and they were the only ones who could turn sorcière to succubi. Both species of the Order of Night had died out long ago.

Harlow sighed and slid *Lore of the Lilu* off its cradle and into its polyethylene sleeve, then turned her attention to watching Thea work at restoring something that resembled a bestiary. Her sister's hands pulled shimmering strands of magic from the air around the book. Thea's elegant fingers moved deftly as she wove reality to fit her vision, and a particularly lovely illumination of a gryphon began to emerge from the page.

"What book is that?" Harlow asked.

Thea glanced up. "It's a first edition of *The Heraldic Order*, not particularly rare, or old, but the illuminations were done in an early modern style."

Harlow watched as the words describing the Heraldic shifters became clearer.

"Can you even imagine what a world with gryphonic shifters must have been like?" Harlow asked.

Thea shook her head. "It's tragic, I think."

"Fucking Illuminated," Harlow swore, whispering it, even here in the privacy of the workroom. They'd executed immortals who'd joined the humans in the War of the Orders, including the Heraldic Order, which had consisted of shifters whose alternae were dragons, gryphons, alicorns and the like. Nowadays, most of the Trickster's Chosen could only shift into common animals. Nothing that threatened the Illuminated.

Thea sighed, but made no other remark. Harlow pulled her stool up to her sister's table, watching her continued work. "Nonetheless, your work is beautiful as ever. That looks nearly new."

Thea looked pleased at Harlow's praise. "Thank you, pal. It's really coming along. I should finish this one today." She glanced at the little clock on the windowsill. "Oh! Don't you need to be at Enzo's soon? You'd better get going!"

Harlow nodded. "You're right. I've got to go."

She grabbed her purse and slipped her phone inside, before escaping down the back stairs, sliding into her aubergine coat with a generous shawl collar. She tied the sash hurriedly as she rushed into the chilly spring afternoon.

The crunch of dried leaves, leftover from the winter, made a satisfying noise under her feet on the cobblestone of the courtyard as she hurried into the back alley to the shortcut that would take her to Enzo's atelier a few streets over.

The thick hedgerows of dawn viburnum gave off a scent of vanilla and lilac that infused the alleyways of the Row, and Harlow couldn't help but slow her pace to breathe in the scent of renewal. Of life starting again. She rounded the corner, turning onto Mulberry Street, letting the feeling sink in, wondering if with all that was going wrong it was wise to feel this way. Just as she was beginning to feel foolish for letting hope kindle in her, a text came through from Selene.

Money's in your account. Have Enzo secure enough attire to get you to the Solstice Gala. Spare no expense.

She responded, *Thank you so much*, feeling grateful, but also frustrated at the amount of money a season would cost their family. Five girls, all needing dozens of garments and accessories, though her sisters were likely more equipped to weather the social season than she was. Her time navigating the upper echelons of human society with Mark had been less demanding on her wardrobe.

The Orders were extravagant when it came to clothes, but rigid about what was appropriate. There were dozens of rules to remember about color, motif, and fabric, whereas humans mostly cared about what they thought looked good and the newest trends. Thea once called the human obsession with "meaningless disposability" disgraceful, and it was one of her observations about them that Harlow completely agreed with.

Harlow sent another text to Selene to remind her that she would need her share of the family jewelry brought out of the safeguarded vault for the season and they were having a lively exchange about Harlow's propensity to lose things when Harlow stumbled into a wall of muscle.

"Careful there," the wall rumbled in a voice so deep she felt it in her toes.

Harlow looked up from her phone and was transported to the past. She was seventeen, and her entire body flooded with heat when she met the long-lashed eyes staring into hers. Finn McKay's hands steadied her, kept her from falling. His face was stony, serious as ever as he gazed down at her, but she saw the corner of his mouth twitch, as though he suppressed a smile.

The square jaw, the sensual lips, the broad shoulders and muscled chest were all enough to make her knees weak, but his eyes did her in. Eyes the color of a stormy sea, and so expressive she saw their history flash through them as they stared into hers. Then they went carefully blank, and his expression reformed into something cultivated and smooth, aloof, but alluring, and Harlow hated the way her breath caught looking at him.

He'd once described himself as "everyone's type," which was infuriatingly accurate. Their entire lives, people had been obsessed with everything he said, wore or did. He was the son of the richest, if not most powerful, Illuminated family in Nuva Troi, after all. But it wasn't just that, it was the aura of danger that always clung to him.

Unlike Alaric Velarius, whose mother was the arch-chancellor of the Illuminated Order and whose family was widely respected, the McKays were known for their vicious business practices and dealings in the hidden underworld of Nytra. Of course the fact that his family were some of the most terrifying Illuminated on Okairos only increased his allure for most people. She ripped herself out of the swoon her body had involuntarily dragged her into to glare at Finn as she pushed away from him.

"Watch where you're going, McKay," she muttered above the sound of her pounding heart. She prayed futilely to Akatei that he couldn't hear it, though she knew well enough that he could.

He laughed, dry and arrogant as ever, only compounding the fact that she knew he knew the effect he was having on her. "You're the one who ran into me, Krane. What are you doing here? Thought you ran around with humans these days."

The sneer in his voice grated on her nerves, flustering her. "Mark and I broke up."

"Right." He drew the word out to several dry syllables, and she couldn't tell if he was being snide or thoughtful. Probably snide, she decided when he kept talking. "I read something this morning about his level-up."

Harlow pushed past him, cheeks burning with humiliation, especially as his eyes drifted over her decidedly *frumpy* ensemble. Something like concern flared in those silvery-blue eyes, as though he regretted his comment. He grabbed her arm to stop her, then dropped it when she flinched. "Hey, I'm sorry."

Harlow looked up, infuriated by the way she had to tilt her head to look at him, his stupid floppy hair and the way his broad chest filled out the white t-shirt he wore under the leather jacket she knew he bought at a flea market when they were fifteen. She hated that she remembered that day perfectly.

"Sorry about what?" she bit out. He had plenty to be sorry for, that was certain.

He hesitated, gauging how angry she was. "About you and Mark. I was sorry to hear you broke up. He seemed nice."

Harlow's heart stopped beating for half a second, she was sure of it. It was a lie. No one thought Mark seemed nice. Mark wasn't nice. He was smart and charismatic, yes. But no one thought he was nice. Certainly not the Illuminated, who tended to despise humans who'd managed to carve out a bit of power and prestige for themselves in a world where they were meant to remain little more than well-cared-for livestock. The Eastons were just the kind of humans people like the McKays hated.

Some horrible part of her thought he *did* sound genuinely sorry, like the Finn she used to know. The one who listened when something was wrong and never judged her. The one who she'd spent hours talking to as a kid. But she knew better than to be suckered into thinking *that* Finn was here in this moment. That Finn was gone for good, washed away like flotsam at high tide. He'd been lost to her since she was seventeen years old, and he wasn't ever coming back.

"Whatever." It was an ineffective comeback, but Harlow couldn't think of anything better to say. She pushed past him and as she started to open the door to Enzo's atelier, she thought she saw his shoulders slump slightly. He turned and all the arrogance she knew and hated was plain on his face.

"See you at the Grove tomorrow." He strode away and she didn't like it one bit that her traitorous body paused to watch him go.

CHAPTER 4

"He's a dick, but that ass is worth watching," purred a voice in her ear.

She turned to find Enzo in the doorway of his shop, and threw herself into his arms for a hug. He smelled expensive, like vetiver and sun-kissed citrus, and he looked like a fever dream, dressed in a magenta suit, his eyes lined with gold. His silky black hair was tied back in a bun, and his rich brown skin was radiant, even in the vernal gloom that had descended over the afternoon.

"Come in, come in. The remodel is finally done and I want you to see what I've done with the place."

Harlow didn't miss the way Enzo's eyes carefully slid over her clothes, his face the bland neutral mask of a true professional. Her thoughts threatened to take her back to the sidewalk and Finn McKay, but she shoved them down. She was here to have Enzo help her find her way back to herself, after all, and if they could find their way back to one another in the process, so much the better. It was time to begin a new phase, one where she was a credit to her Order, her family, and her friends, instead of the perpetual mess she'd been for the past few years.

She took Enzo's hands in hers, trying to project all the feelings she'd been shoving down about losing her best friend to the surface, hoping that Enzo's talent as an empath would help him understand her sincerity. "I should have come before."

Harlow wanted to apologize a hundred ways, to say how sorry she was for letting things get so bad. Her mouth opened and closed, unsure of how to begin.

He drew her into another hug. "I should have asked you to come sooner."

Harlow felt all the tension leave her body. She and Enzo had been friends since before even she and Finn, since their parents had been close for ages. The distance of the last two years had been a strain, but in that one hug, she felt she was forgiven.

There hadn't been fights or conflict when she'd moved in with Mark, just worry and tension about his growing control over her. Everyone in her life within the lower Orders had warned her about the human obsession with magic and the world of those descended from the Illuminated. They'd warned her that Mark's interests might not be entirely focused on her, but on her status in the Order of Mysteries, as her mothers were on the high council of sorcière.

And there was always the subtle concern over what Harlow wasn't saying about things between her and Mark. Enzo had been the most worried, knowing better than anyone how long it had taken for her to recover from her only other true relationship, and he'd made no secret of how concerned he was with Mark's behavior. Harlow hadn't listened to any of her family or Enzo about the warning signs, and had been frustrated that they'd been right in the end.

Now, six months outside Mark's influence, she saw all too clearly how foolish she'd been. He'd isolated her slowly and carefully, until he thought she'd do anything he asked. When she wouldn't give up her Order's secrets, he'd kicked her out of their home, and the life she thought they were building together, cutting her off completely.

Putting things back together had been an exercise in humility. Harlow made amends to her family first, slowly over the last few months. She'd gone back to her work at the Monas, after a hiatus working in a human bookstore that Mark had approved of, and that had helped things with her sisters. Her mothers had been the first to welcome her back, no questions asked. But she hadn't known how to tell Enzo he was right about Mark, maybe because he was the only one who'd known her, who'd been to their apartment, who'd actually *tried* to see what she saw in Mark and who'd still seen the truth of the situation.

That all seemed far away now, as she stepped into Enzo's atelier. Burnished wooden racks of vintage and antique clothing mixed with Enzo's own couture creations throughout the light-filled space. The walls were painted midnight blue, and an enormous vase of curly willow branches and fragrant eucalyptus graced a round pedestal table at the center of the room. Plush, patterned rugs in deep ruby reds covered the slate floors and an enormous crystal chandelier gave the entire shop an air of luxurious artistry.

Wooden mannequins modeled Enzo's most exquisite creations, gowns of unparalleled beauty, touched with his magic in every stitch. He and Thea were very similar in that both their artistic proclivities were strong before their magic took hold, and now that they were in their mid-twenties, their artistry was amplified by their magical abilities, a natural extension of themselves.

Harlow wished she knew how her magic would manifest. She could do basic spells of protection, glamours of all kinds, and had an extensive education in magical lore, history, and craft, of course. As a sorcière, this was the way she grew up, learning the ways of mystery, and how to bend the filaments of magic, that held aether itself, to her will. But her own special ability, the way her own magic would carve the path of her life, refused to make itself known.

"Oh, Enzo," she breathed, pushing her own disappointment aside to be happy for her friend. "It's perfect."

He grinned, his straight white teeth dazzling as dimples punctuated his joy.

She clasped his arm, filled with true happiness. It was easy to be happy for Enzo; she loved him, and being here, feeling their bond reforming itself moment by moment, was just what she needed. Harlow had tried so hard when she was with Mark to forget how much she missed Enzo and her sisters, but she never could.

Shame filled her for how she'd treated them, but she tried to push it aside, deflect it before he caught on. "I see your name a lot in Section Seven."

"Attached to all the most stylish socialites of the Orders, of course," he laughed.

It was true, he dressed the most elegant members of the lower Orders, and the Illuminated were some of his best clients. "I doubt I can afford your custom gowns these days, but I'm here for whatever vintage you can armor me in. I've been roped into the season."

Enzo pulled her onto the soft leather couch at the center of the shop. "The maters are finally insisting? Is it because of the McKays' interest in the Row?"

Of course he already knew. The gossip was out and it would make this whole thing even worse. She nodded. "Are you dressing Finn? Was he the client?"

Enzo grimaced. "Yes… Are you mad?"

"No, no. Of course not. Business is business and the Illuminated are good customers, even the McKays."

"Harls… I know you don't want to hear this, but I think Finn's changed."

A long silence passed between them.

"You're right. I can't hear that. You know what he did. How he hurt me."

"I do. I'll never forget it. He hurt me too, you know? But he's been here four times since he's been back from Nea Sterlis and he seems different. Like the old Finn. We even went for coffee last week. He asked about what types of guys I was interested in these days and offered to introduce me to a few of his friends he thought I might pair well with during the season. He wasn't just being nice either. He was… like he used to be."

Harlow swallowed hard. The three of them had been so close in school, and then one day Finn snapped, and Harlow and Enzo weren't good enough for him anymore. She shook off the memories before she could fall into that abyss.

"Did he apologize? Did he explain himself? Did he say why he spent our entire sixth year making our lives a living hell?"

Enzo cupped her cheeks in his hands. The familiarity of the gesture warmed Harlow's heart. "First of all, Petra is the one who did most of the misery-making, so let's put the blame for that where it belongs. Second, I didn't ask him to explain or apologize. I don't have to."

He was right. Petra Velarius had done most of the work to turn Harlow and Enzo into social pariahs, but Finn had done nothing to stop her. He'd just walked away from them both and never looked back, until now, apparently. A sob caught in her throat as Enzo's words fully sunk in; he hadn't asked *her* to apologize either. One of his many gifts was his deep empathy, his magical ability to see what was on people's hearts. He'd forgiven her instantly, as soon as he recognized the apology that welled in her; she'd felt it happen.

"I wish I had your abilities," she said, understanding his change of heart when it came to Finn, but not able to trust it herself. The McKays were poisonous vipers, and even if Finn wasn't aligned with what they were doing now, he wasn't innocent either. "But I can't trust him. You understand?"

Enzo nodded. "I do. It was different with the two of you. I get it."

She took his hands and squeezed. "I am just really, *really* happy to have your help getting ready for this. You know how nervous these things make me."

Enzo grinned again. "You will be beautiful at every event. I'll do everything I can to make your season perfect, right?"

"I don't need to be perfect. Just presentable."

Enzo rolled his eyes. "Come on, Harls. It's just you and me. Admit it, you want to slay them all with your devastating curves. Especially after Section Seven called you frumpy this morning."

His tone was matter-of-fact, not judgmental. She knew he was seeing what Selene and Aurelia did—her outer appearance as a reflection of her inner turmoil. Harlow bit her bottom lip. "I do, a little, but here's the budget."

She pulled up the amount she had to work with on her phone and Enzo barely glanced at it. "You're good."

"What? That's barely enough for two of your couture gowns, let alone a season's worth of wardrobe."

"Come here."

He pulled her off the couch and back towards an area of the shop where a desk sat in a corner nook flanked by tall bookcases, all full of books about costuming and fashion throughout the centuries. There were several marble pedestals arranged in front of the tall windows, which displayed some of the books with illustrations. One particularly beautiful one depicted different pallyra, showing off the ceremonial robes of the Immortal Orders in all their glory. Harlow stood gaping at the spectacular collection of rare books.

Enzo touched her arm, guiding her toward the book of pallyra designs. "Your sister finished my collection last year, for the remodel, and it's so popular with clients that they wrote an article about it in the Times. Apparently, I have the most extensive collection of books on fashion history in the country."

Harlow smiled. "Thea is so good at sourcing collectors' material."

"I don't think you understand, Harlow. She tipped off the Times. My business has tripled since the article. They've been calling me fashion's greatest scholar, which is true, but still bizarre to read in print. I'm dressing your entire family for the season on whatever budget you can afford. Your family means the world to me, they always have."

He took her by the hips and guided her in front of a floor-length gilded mirror. "You're going into this season with a killer wardrobe. I won't have it any other way. In fact, come look at what I've put together for you already. I have a few options for the Statuary party I think you'll love."

Enzo showed her to a rack with her name on it, full of jewel tones that would set her skin and hair aglow. Most of the clothes were for daytime events and he began the work of measuring her for the gowns she'd need for Solon Mai and the Solstice Gala, helping her onto a platform so he could have access to her limbs. She tried to chat with him, while he did so, but he hushed her.

"I won't be able to keep my numbers straight if you talk, so zip it."

She did as he asked, grateful for everything he was doing for her. Grateful to Thea and her parents for always treating Enzo like family, and that they all loved him as dearly as she did. His parents had been killed in a horrific train accident when they were in secondary school and the maters had welcomed him to every family dinner, brunch and high holiday celebration after that so he'd never be lonely in the huge townhouse they'd left him.

When he was finished measuring he helped her down from the platform. Tears pricked the corners of her eyes; she'd missed Enzo so much it hurt sometimes, and spending this time together made the ache in her heart sharper. She looked him straight in his dark brown eyes and tried to be brave. "I made a lot of mistakes when you were honest with me about Mark and I regret them all. You have always been a good friend to me, my best friend aside from Thea, and I am sorry for shutting you out."

Enzo nodded solemnly, accepting her apology with his signature grace. "Are you okay? *Really?*"

Harlow knew he already knew the answer. That she wasn't okay. That some days she worried she was too damaged to go on, that no one would ever be able to love or respect someone as foolish as she was. That she feared that she was the kind of person who simply *attracted* bad people.

Enzo cupped her face in his hands. "Harls, you know that's not true, don't you?"

He didn't often let on that his empathy sometimes worked a little like mind-reading, as he knew it made people uncomfortable. But now, Enzo's eyes were soft with love for her, apparently caring little for whether or not his supernatural ability to read her creeped her out. Harlow averted her eyes, wiping hot tears away.

"You had other partners between Finn and Mark that were good to you. What about Kate Spencer?"

Harlow smiled. Katerina Spencer had been a supremely good girlfriend for the few short months they'd had together. When she'd moved back to Nea Sterlis to help her sire open a new winery and transferred to Aphelion, Harlow had been sad to see her go, but they'd only dated for a few months and she'd understood. She'd met Mark just a few days later. "She left me too."

Enzo rolled his eyes. "That was different and you know it. What happened with Mark wasn't your fault. It was his. I wish you could see that."

"I'm sorry for everything that happened between us," she whispered, wanting to avoid talking about Mark more. "I should have handled things differently. Especially when I came home. I needed time to sort things through."

Enzo squeezed her arm. "I know, Harls. You didn't have to say it."

Her head tilted to the side. "I didn't *have* to say it, but you should expect better from me."

"Fair enough." He squeezed her hands hard. "Want me to help bring the first round of things to your new place?"

Harlow shifted her weight uncomfortably. "I know you're busy, with things starting up tomorrow and everything..."

Enzo's chiseled brow furrowed. "Why don't you want me to see your apartment?"

Harlow looked at the herringbone pattern in the expensive wood floors, tracing it with the toe of her shoe. "It's… It's… Not very nice. But it's what I could afford when Mark kicked me out."

Her best friend's jaw clenched. "Why would you think I'd care about that kind of thing?"

Harlow shrugged, not saying what was in her head. The sorcière cared about how things looked. They were Nuva Troi's aesthetes. And her apartment did not give evidence that she was from one of the Order of Mysteries' oldest and most prestigious families. She loved it, but she knew that others would not, and she didn't think she could stand it if Enzo hated it.

"I'm coming over. Don't argue." He picked up an armful of clothes and began packing them for transport. The command in Enzo's voice reminded her that *he* was the true heir to the arch-chancellor's position. That when he came of age, Aurelia would step aside and he would head the Order. She couldn't help but smile.

"Wear comfortable shoes. It's a climb."

CHAPTER 5

"It's no wonder your ass looks so good," Enzo laughed, lagging half a flight behind her. "This is a workout."

Harlow paused, shifting the bulk of the clothes she carried slightly. "It's a bit of a hike, I know. And the building could use some work… I'm sorry the elevator was out. It's like that sometimes…"

"Harlow, stop. I like it."

She squinted slightly, but like most empaths, Enzo rarely lied.

"Really. I love these green walls, and the layers of peeling paint are actually very charming."

There was no hint of sarcasm in his voice, to her surprise. He saw what she did in this place: worn beauty. The Illuminated didn't allow much to fade on Okairos. It was one of the many double binds of their rule. The world was well-kept, beautiful, and in many ways safe, but its people weren't free. Places like this building, that showed their age, were extremely rare.

They walked the last few flights in silence. The building was owned cooperatively, and when the last owner of the penthouse had died, none of the tenants could agree on who should buy it next. Preserving the structure of the building had been important to the board, as well as not washing away the building's history with magic. They'd been looking for someone who wouldn't go to the Illuminated to complain about the layers of age that had failed to be restored. When they'd first read Harlow's application and seen her name they rejected her, but when they'd heard she'd lived two years among humans, they'd allowed her an interview.

When the board finally let her in to see the apartment, she'd emptied her meager savings that day. To her, the place was perfect, but she knew it wasn't what most people she knew would have chosen. Now, her heart fluttered nervously as she pressed her palm to the cool metal plate that scanned her DNA.

The locks made a soft *snick* sound as the security system recognized her and the door opened softly.

Behind her, Enzo gasped. "Oh, Harlow. Now I *completely* understand…"

She saw it again for the first time, through Enzo's eyes. The exposed brick peeking through the crumbling white plaster. The ancient black steel-paned windows that arched towards the soaring ceilings, and the view of Ambracia Bay from the terrace that filled the undressed windows. There wasn't much in the way of walls, only the bathroom was contained—and there was barely a kitchen. Only a stove, a fridge and an ancient stepback hutch remained, as the former tenant's children had stripped the place of anything of value when clearing her estate. Harlow's few possessions sat in boxes still, except for her bed and a few nearly-empty wrought iron racks for clothes.

"You could use some furniture… and a real kitchen," Enzo mused. "But I love it."

He dropped his armful of clothes on her bed and pushed open the double doors that lead to the terrace. "This is unreal," he gasped, looking out at the blue water of the bay. The sun was peeking out from the clouds, gearing up to give Nuva Troi a rare sunset over the bay.

She joined him outside, smiling. "Do you want to change it all? Make it shiny and new again?"

Enzo shook his head. "No. I love this. I love seeing the history of the building in all its glorious layers." His eyes closed for a moment and Harlow could feel the threads of magic shifting around them. He was probing the building. "It's structurally sound. The sorcière here have done good work to make sure the building is safe, while allowing the aesthetic features to age naturally. It's absolutely genius."

Harlow grinned. "I thought so too, to be honest. It's unlike anything I've ever seen."

"The Illuminated cannot tolerate age…" he murmured as he wandered back inside. "It's a shame, really. Age and decay are nothing to fear. Everything about this place is beautiful."

Harlow didn't answer. They'd been over this a million times in their youth, questioning why the Illuminated were the way they were, dreaming of a better world. Enzo started to unpack the zippered bags they'd brought her new clothes upstairs in, but she shooed him away.

"You've done enough. I'll hang them. Do you want something to drink? I have…" she peered into her fridge. "Water or some oat milk."

"Not even a kettle for tea?"

She grimaced at him. "Of course I have tea and a kettle. What do you want?"

"Something dark and smoky."

She smirked. "You sure you're talking about tea?"

Enzo laughed. "It was very nearly a single entendre. But I do want some tea."

Harlow took a smoky black tea blend with a hint of vanilla out of the hutch and started the water to boil as Enzo slipped off his shoes and settled onto her bed. "Your linens are lovely."

She nodded. The fresh white bedclothes had been her gift to herself when she moved in. They were soft and silky, with half a dozen pillows piled like clouds to nest in while she watched the ubiquitous Nuva Troi rain or the rare sunset. Enzo did just that now, and when she handed him a steaming mug of tea, she snuggled in close next to him.

"So, are you seeing anyone?" she asked.

He shook his head. "No, I've been so focused on finishing the atelier I haven't had time for that. I cleaned out the townhouse too. It's rented now."

"How's that feel?" Enzo's parents' home had been a haven for all when Clarissa Weraka was arch-chancellor of the Order of Mysteries. The Werakas had been some of the few sorcière who believed in a world without such strict delineations between the four species of humanoid creatures who populated Okairos and their home had been full of joyful parties and quiet respite from the busy world in equal turn.

"At a certain point, it got easier. When everything was in boxes, one day it was just *things*. It had become a time capsule, you know?"

She nodded. After Enzo's parents died he hadn't changed a thing in their five story townhouse in Uptown.

"I was afraid to move anything for so long. I just kept the dust off things. But the longer I let it sit, the worse things got inside." Enzo patted his heart. "Last year, I walked downstairs and was afraid to make coffee. I was afraid that if I moved another mug the last memories of my mother would disappear."

Harlow looped her arm through Enzo's and he rested his head on her shoulder, assuming a pose they'd sat in thousands of times since childhood. Her mind's eye saw Clarissa bustling around her kitchen, dark tresses piled on her head, her sculpted face bursting into laughter as she made breakfast for Enzo, Maurice, and Harlow. Harlow had eaten hundreds of breakfasts at Enzo's as a child. When Clarissa and Maurice died, Enzo wasn't the only one to lose his family. Clarissa and Maurice were Aurelia and Selene's closest friends, and Enzo their godschild.

Harlow's chest shuddered at the memories. "I should have been there to help you."

Enzo nodded. "I wish you had been. I...I should have called you. It's not all your fault, you know. I made mistakes too. Gods, I needed you though."

Tears trailed down both of their cheeks and Harlow felt Enzo's arm tighten around hers as he sipped his tea.

Enzo's voice was shaky when he said, "I should have fought harder for you to come home, Harls. I saw his heart, what he was like, and I wasn't as supportive as I should've been."

"You tried to be..."

He cut her off. "A little. I tried a little. But my mother wouldn't have liked that I let things go so easily, Harlow. If you're not ready to meet someone new, maybe the season isn't the best idea..."

Now Harlow cut Enzo off, her voice struggling through the sharp pain clenching her throat. "It's okay. I'm ready. I need to get back into the swing of Order life and prove to everyone they can trust me. It'll be the easiest way to move on." Enzo nodded, understanding the depth of Harlow's emotions, probably better than she did. "As bad as Mark was, I'm worse. I thought I deserved it all—all his anger, his jealousy—I thought I caused it. And even though my head knows that's not true now, my heart doesn't." It was the first time Harlow had admitted this to anyone, even herself.

"Then is this really the time to get into a new relationship?"

Harlow shrugged. "It's been six months. Things are getting better, and my family needs me. The Order needs me. I need to be a part of our world again, Enzo."

He kissed her forehead. "I completely understand, but what are you going to do if they want you to pair with Finn?"

Harlow shook her head. "As long as it's me, not my sisters, I'll do whatever it takes."

"Harlow," Enzo said, drawing her name out several syllables longer than it was, but he didn't say anything else.

No one understood duty to the Order of Mysteries better than Enzo. He shook his head, but didn't respond to the thoughts that were probably broadcasting themselves at a shout from inside her head. Like Thea, Enzo believed in the magic of the season, that it drew the right people together and matched them perfectly, so long as they showed up with open hearts, willing to find love. Harlow wasn't sure that was anything more than lore, and an open heart certainly wasn't going to solve anything between her and Finn.

The rain started up again, obscuring the last of the sunset. Enzo drained his cup and slipped his shoes back on, taking his cup to the kitchen sink. "Let's get these clothes hung up and order some food, okay? No more sad talk right now."

Harlow smiled. She could do that. She typed their order into her Dined, Dealed, Delivered app for delivery of fancy burgers and parmesan fries from the pack-owned pizza joint, Gastro Lupo, around the corner. Enzo unzipped the wardrobe bags they'd used to transport the clothes and they began hanging them together in companionable silence. When they began chatting again it was to gossip about the newest hit television show, *Knight's Children*, a *very* loosely historical drama about medieval vampire knights.

Enzo was complaining about the intricacies of inaccurate portrayal of medieval costuming and makeup when the burgers arrived. The rain broke long enough for them to eat on the terrace on two plastic chairs Harlow had found in the dumpster out back. When the last fry had been consumed and Harlow was sure she'd burst, Enzo kissed her forehead.

"You know how to get to the Grove, right?" He asked as he dragged her up from the terrace tile.

Harlow nodded as she walked him to the door. "The invitation will come at the eleventh hour and act as a portal…" Harlow rolled her eyes. "And then I'll be in our super secret ritual spot in the woods somewhere, right?"

Enzo shook his head. "You might try taking this a little more seriously."

"I might," she laughed as he ran down the steps. She closed the door. "I might."

CHAPTER 6

When she turned back to her empty apartment, it felt lonely for the first time. It wasn't that she hadn't felt sad here before—she'd rarely felt anything else since she moved in—but she'd also valued her solitude while she'd grieved the loss of her relationship with Mark. Tonight, for the first time, she wished she had furniture and a TV or stereo, instead of just her phone. She wished she had her boxes of books and art, packed away in the Monas' attic. All things Mark had insisted she give up when she'd moved in with him.

A phantom movement caught her eye, but when she turned nothing was there. A shiver slipped deep into the secret parts of her, rattling her to her core. It might be one of the building's many ghosts, but in her heart she knew it was something worse: the memory of what she'd abandoned. Harlow tried her best never to think about the giant black cat Mark forced her to leave behind, but tonight it was impossible not to. She missed Axel so much her heart nearly burst with guilt. The helpless feeling she got any time she allowed herself to think of him squeezed her lungs until she could barely breathe.

Harlow left the double doors to the terrace open, letting the chilly spring air fill her lungs as she blinked tears away. It was pouring again and the rain made the view of the city below and the bay look like a painting. She climbed in bed, knowing she couldn't escape the looming loneliness that crept in, filling her with grief. The witchlights that floated above her bed went out with a quiet word and Harlow stared into the dim darkness of her nearly empty apartment.

Mark hadn't wanted anything that reminded Harlow of her "old life" when they'd moved in together, emphasizing that they were building a life together outside of the Orders. When he kicked her out, she hadn't had much to take with her except her clothes. Keeping Axel had been his cruelest move though. Mark didn't even like the feline; he'd kept him to spite her, and she'd been too ashamed to tell anyone that she'd left her baby behind.

Harlow couldn't escape the knowledge that the emptiness of her apartment was a half-hearted punishment for failing with Mark, as was her general failure to dress in ways that made her feel good, or feed herself nourishing food. She hadn't been taking care of herself, because when she'd chosen Mark, that was supposed to prove to everyone that she could do things differently than the other sorcière, and that she would succeed at it. That the years she'd spent wasting herself at uni were over, and she was making a new life for herself.

Except nothing worked out the way she'd planned. Things ended with Mark. She never applied to grad school. Her magic never deepened or grew. She was lost, adrift in all the things she'd done wrong. Every time she tried to make things better, it seemed like they just got worse instead. So she'd opted to do nothing for herself. She was practicing what she considered neutral neglect, trying to keep her head down and not make anything in her life worse than it needed to be.

She'd seen a therapist for exactly one month and when they'd asked her to name something she'd done right since she was seventeen she came up blank. Harlow knew the therapist was trying to help, that they thought this question might help her see that she hadn't *actually* done everything wrong. But her failure to come up with a satisfactory answer sent her into a spiral of shame that lasted for weeks. She'd never gone back. What was the point?

Harlow tossed and turned for a few minutes, trying to get to sleep, but she couldn't relax. It felt like beetles were crawling under her skin. She opened up her phone and scrolled through Section Seven until she found posts that would prove she deserved the punishment she was doling out to herself. There they were, both of them, fortuitously grouped together, one right after the other.

Mark Easton Leaves the Antiquity Row Dud Behind For Good. There was a photo of Mark helping Olivia out of a black town car. Olivia's dress was so short that Harlow could see her panties, which was probably the point. Jealousy roiled in her gut. It was the worst kind of jealousy, because it wasn't even that she wanted Mark back.

No, she genuinely wanted Mark to move on, and quickly. Just not with someone who looked like *that*. Everywhere Harlow had curves, Olivia was lithe and sensual in a way Harlow knew she couldn't pull off. In the last days of their relationship, Mark had made many comments about how unattractive he found her, saying she'd "let herself go," more than once. It stung that he'd found someone so easily that fit every qualification that Harlow could not. Even now, as much as she resented him, she wrestled with the fact that she wanted him to want her back, for her to be the one who rejected him, not the pathetic way things had ended.

She took a deep breath, trying to interrupt the spiral of shame she was headed down. *Next.*

She'd already caught sight of the telltale stormy eyes, but as she scrolled up her stomach did somersaults. *Illuminated Playboy Finbar McKay Returns to Nuva Troi With Prize.* Harlow snorted; apparently the "prize" was Petra Velarius. At the very least it pleased her that Petra would be absolutely horrified not to have her actual name published alongside Finn's, but Section Seven was alarmingly sexist at times, to provoke people into loudly complaining, sharing stories on all their socials about the publication's retro attitudes. It was all an act to get more engagement.

Neither Finn nor Petra looked dressed for a night on the town. In fact, they were both wearing jeans and sweaters, as though they'd been to a coffee shop together. And she knew for a fact that he hadn't returned to Nuva Troi *with* Petra. She'd been here all along, working at her parents' investment firm. Still, it grated Harlow's nerves to see them together.

She did the thing she was always promising herself she wouldn't and started to scroll through the comments on the post. Most were humans, speculating that Petra and Finn would be the season's "it" couple. People talked about them like they were characters in a TV show or book, saying they "shipped" them together.

A text came through from Meline that blessedly blocked her view of Petra's sour expression. *If you're reading Section Seven, don't believe everything you read. Finn and Petra were at a family dinner at Umbra. They cropped Alaric out of the pic.*

I wasn't looking at it, she typed back.

Indi says to tell you that you're a big liar-liarface and that you wouldn't've texted back so fast if you weren't. CAUGHT!

Mind your own business, sillies.

You ARE our business, came a text from Indigo, popping up in front of Meline's. *Get off socials and go to sleep.*

Harlow sent the twins both a series of black heart emojis and then tossed her phone aside, resisting the urge to go back and read the posts she'd skipped earlier about the protests in Nea Sterlis. There had been more pushback from humans as of late against the restrictive laws that treated them as objects, rather than people. She couldn't say she blamed them, but she wasn't sure what to do; the Illuminated proved time and again that they were too powerful to resist. Harlow groaned into her pile of pillows, angry that she'd let herself get so worked up. There was no way she was going to sleep now.

"Lux," she muttered and the soft witchlights illuminated.

Harlow got up to look at the clothes she and Enzo had hung together. Her pallyra was ready for tomorrow evening and she couldn't help but feel excited to wear the embroidered, floor-length robe. She stroked the soft, heavy black fabric, tracing the dark flourishes that bled into the cranes and wolves that represented her family's lineage. Tomorrow wouldn't be so bad, as the opening night of the season was more about the ritual than socializing, as she understood it.

The Statuary party gave her pause though. She stared at the dress Enzo had picked out for her to wear to the party held in one of Nuva Troi's many elegant public gardens. As an outdoor event, it was expected that the attendees would dress casually, but what that meant was hard for Harlow to tease out, especially when she looked at what she'd be wearing.

She ran her fingers down the decadent fabric of the dress for the Statuary party. It was a deep, dark blue, with a high neck and a buttoned bodice that she was to leave slightly undone to reveal the lace trim of the vintage bustier she would be wearing underneath. The hem of the dress fell to her knees, and there were a pair of tall black stack-heeled boots that tied with satin laces to wear with it. It all seemed the opposite of casual to her, especially when combined with the gorgeous slate-grey wool frock coat she was to wear over the dress.

But Enzo had assured her that this was what was considered a "casual" look for the season. That the tailored high-waisted pants and blouses were suitable for morning and early afternoon events, but nothing after two o'clock. After two, day dresses were the only acceptable option, and between five and nine, cocktail dresses, and after that only evening gowns. The additional rules about colors, jewelry and ornamentation were baffling to her, despite her love of clothes.

The ritual of it all was mysterious, and she had to admit she was feeling a bit lured by the siren song of jewel tones on the racks in front of her. She ran her hands over the luxurious fabrics. When she'd unpacked the rest of her clothes, ones that had largely had Enzo's touch in one way or another over the years, she saw that her wardrobe was one she recognized as a sorcière of the Order of Mysteries.

"Not frumpy at all," she whispered to her wardrobe, thinking of the terrible Section Seven post.

No, now she would finally feel like she was dressed as *herself*, rather than dipping into human trends, or the other Orders' fashions. She couldn't help but feel proud. She'd always loved her people's ways, their deep commitment to using their magics to enrich the arts and academic pursuits. The Order of Mysteries made the world a more beautiful, more intelligent place, and she loved that aspect of her heritage, even if she wasn't directly contributing to it yet.

Completely unwelcome thoughts about Finn began to creep back in now that she was idle. She pushed away thoughts about him and Petra and instead considered what Enzo said about him changing, about the way he'd looked today. Older, but still beautiful in that perpetually mussed way he had, his eyes glowing, if faintly, with immortal power. And the dangerous pull of him was the same as it had ever been, wicked in its intensity.

She flopped onto her bed and closed her eyes, feeling his hands on her, steadying her. Feeling their slick skin slip against each other, further in the past. The feel of his mouth on her neck so long ago as they'd kissed in his car. The way the backseat of the Woody, his sturdy SUV, had felt like the whole world as they'd ground against one another in a feverish wave of lust that had been building between them for years. Her fingers slid into her pants at the memory of his hands in the same spot, her pleasure mounting as she remembered the way his face looked when his fingers had stroked the crotch of her panties, finding them drenched with her desire for him.

It was no different now, but instead of remembering the teenagers they'd been, her mind supplanted the people who'd run into one another on the street today. The memory of that night mixed with the fantasy of fucking him now. Her body heated, responding to her touch as her imagination replaced teenage Finn with the adult she'd been so furious with this afternoon.

Her breath came in short gasps as she rubbed tight circles around her swollen clit, imagining Finn pushing her dress up as she straddled him in the backseat of the SUV, pushing her panties aside as he slid effortlessly inside her. The thought of him filling her so easily was incongruent with the memory of how they'd fumbled through their single sexual encounter, but she didn't much care. That night, awkward as it had been, had been perfect, a promise of learning together, that their passion would carry them into the kind of sexual prowess that would leave them both satisfied for centuries. It wasn't that she hadn't had good sex after Finn; she had, perhaps even better. It was that she'd never felt quite as deeply for a lover as she had for him that night—she never *let* herself feel that way.

But now she felt too much, other emotions clouding whatever pleasure she might have gleaned from mixing the memory and the fantasy of him. The feel of him driving into her, moaning words of devotion in her ears, grew ever more distant as she failed to bring herself to climax. Harlow's head fell back as a moan escaped her lips, frustration mixing with the elusive power of the memory. The fantasy slipped away far too quickly, which inevitably brought about thoughts of everything that followed from what happened in real life. The months of sorrow. The worry that clouded both her parents' eyes every time they looked at her.

Harlow sat up gasping, yanking her hand from her body. She marched herself into the bathroom and turned the shower on cold. There would be no thinking of Finn McKay and that one perfect night, the one that ruined everything. And there *certainly* would be no fantasizing about him now.

If she was going to do this, honor her family's wishes and complete the season, she was not allowed to think of him that way, *ever*. She shed her clothes and stepped into the water, letting the freezing streams cool her hot skin and drag her back, firmly, into the present, where she promised herself she would stay.

CHAPTER 7

Though the thick fabric of the pallyra was heavy, it wasn't warm enough for a cold spring night in the sacred Grove. She'd only been there for the high holy days, the turn of the wheel, never for any of the other rituals that all four of the Immortal Orders conducted there. Her participation in Solon Mai rituals of years past told her that she'd need to layer well underneath her ceremonial outwear, so she'd slipped on a pair of leggings and a sweater and planned to wear comfortable boots when she heard her phone buzz. It was Enzo.

Wear something hot under your frippery tonight, we're invited to the Velarius afterparty.

She sighed, thinking of opting out, but another text came through just as she was about to suggest her favorite pub, the Three Besoms, instead. Thea this time.

I know Enzo is texting you about the Velarius party. You're going. Dress appropriately. Jeans are fine, but for Aphora's sake, wear a nice sweater or one of those vintage jackets you love. No UNT sweatshirts.

There was a pause while the little dots cascaded, indicating that Thea was sending another text.

I mean it. Wear something beautiful, Harlow. Show them who you are.

Thea texted like she was writing a formal letter, and though it made Harlow's heart race to think about mingling with all the people from her past who'd made her miserable in school, she texted both her sister and Enzo back to assure them she'd dress appropriately.

Show them who you are.

Who was she, anyway? There was nothing wrong with dressing down, but her frumpy clothes weren't who *she* was. She'd been purposely hiding herself. Her throat clamped closed. Letting herself be seen felt dangerous, but maybe she could live dangerously. Maybe to get through this, she would have to. Harlow yanked off her cozy boots and leggings and pulled on a pair of wide legged jeans.

Wear something hot.

Next, she discarded the sweater in favor of an expensive, cream-colored henley with a black bra underneath. To keep warm, she slipped on a black shearling-lined vest, and then unbuttoned her shirt one button more than she usually would. She slipped the gold medal she always wore, depicting Akatei's three faces, back on and felt instantly better, protected by the Order of Mysteries' patron goddess.

Her phone told her it was 10:48. The invitation would arrive at the eleventh hour, so she didn't have much time for hair and makeup. She wished she hadn't frittered the day away reading a new romance novel, but it was what it was. She had just enough time for a simple glamour. It was all she could manage with her limited magical abilities anyway.

Harlow went to the bathroom and while she looked in the mirror, pulled strands of magic from the air and wove them around her until her lashes were darkened and longer, 'til the dark circles under her eyes disappeared and her long honey colored hair curled away from her face. She gave her already high cheekbones a boost and left her nose alone, adding a faint blush to her pale cheeks.

A sound of paper scraping the wide planks of the wooden floor outside the bathroom caught her attention. The envelope she was waiting for slid under the front door and flew towards her, of its own accord.

"Ridiculous," she muttered, plucking it from the air as she slid on her pallyra, fastening the thick fabric with nearly invisible metal hooks.

She opened the envelope to read what she assumed would be a charming inscription, but instead found a long list of small-print legalese about consenting to participate in the season. Her eyes floated over the bloated verbiage until she found instructions at the bottom of the page that directed her to speak the Illuminated Order's motto for Okairos aloud and press her thumb to the page to indicate consent.

Ab ordine libertas. From order comes freedom. She begged to differ, especially when it came to the Illuminated's ideas of "order," but she said the phrase aloud and pressed her left thumb to the page. Sharp pain lanced through her skin and she felt momentarily emptied out of all energy as she was transported from her apartment to a clearing in the forest.

Above her, Okairos' twin moons waxed to near fullness, lighting the enormous redwood trees that surrounded her with uncanny light. The woods were silent, though she knew they must be full of others like herself. She staggered a bit, feeling hollow; she'd never felt that way after portaling. Harlow glanced at her thumb—there was no trace of a wound, but a distinct feeling of unease lingered inside her. Perhaps it was just anxiety about the evening ahead.

A lantern sat at her feet. Harlow saw nothing to indicate what she was supposed to do next, so she picked it up, pressing her fingers to Akatei's medallion for comfort. The light from the lantern dissipated a bit, tiny globules of light falling to the forest floor and floating like fireflies along the path ahead of her, into the dark forest.

Harlow took a step forward and the effect intensified. The short train of her pallyra dragged the ground behind her, her billowing sleeve flowing prettily as she held the lantern aloft, and she felt like a true sorcière for the first time in a long while. She was meant to follow the trail of lights, she supposed. The woods were eerily quiet as she walked, and though she peered deep into the darkness, she saw no other lights, no other indication that the forest was full of this season's participants.

The faint sense of unease occurred to her again. Something just beyond her understanding pressed at her senses. She tried to use her second sight, but found she could not. In a moment of panic, Harlow struggled to feel the threads of magic around her, the most basic skill a sorcière had, but felt nothing at all. Her heart began to pound louder with every step she took.

Somewhere in the distance, a shrill scream pierced the air. Cold fear laced her blood. That was no animal, it was a *person*. She halted, trying to pinpoint the location of the scream, but it was as though it came from everywhere. Just as suddenly as it began, it stopped, and the air was thick with magic. She felt the threads around her sing to life again, full to bursting with aethereal power so potent it threatened to overwhelm her. Then there was a great contraction in the air and she was nearly knocked to her knees, the breath sucked roughly from her lungs.

When she could breathe freely again, the threads of magic around her felt the same as they always did. Sounds of the forest at night time, rustling pine needles in the breeze, an owl in the distance all echoed in her ears. And voices. When Harlow looked around, she saw trails of light through the forest, indicating there were dozens of people in the forest, making their way to the Grove, just like her.

This was strange magic, like none she'd ever felt or seen, and she'd seen a lot of fantastic magic in her twenty-five years. She kept following the trail of bobbing lights until she spotted Enzo and Thea, walking together a bit away from her. Ahead she could see the clearing where the ritual would take place. She gathered the train of her pallyra up in her arms and waded through the dense brush until she reached them.

They both reached out to kiss her cheeks and Thea strung an arm through hers as they huddled together.

"Hi," Harlow murmured quietly. "That was odd, wasn't it?"

The two of them looked mildly confused.

"What was odd?" Enzo asked. "Using the portal?"

Thea nudged her in the side, playfully. "You haven't been out here in a while, have you? Snapping from one place to another can be disorienting."

Her sister was right, of course; she hadn't been to a ritual or portaled since she moved in with Mark, but that wasn't it. Enzo and Thea smiled at her, gently, sweetly. Both were perfectly calm. They hadn't had the same experience she did. Harlow sensed that this was neither the time nor the place to explain. "Yeah, I guess I haven't portaled in a while. I felt a little sick after."

Thea smiled sympathetically. "Are you feeling better now, pal?"

Harlow nodded and the three of them walked together in thoughtful silence toward the Grove. As they neared the clearing, the air changed, growing cold and viscous. Harlow felt the individual strands of magic, distended and thick with too much aether. Her brow furrowed as she pushed through them, feeling them scrape against her spirit body uncomfortably. The part of her that, as a sorcière, was always just beyond the material world cringed at the unnatural feeling of bloated aethereal threads. The trails of bobbing lights floated in a spiral to the night sky and all around the clearing, as more and more of this season's participants and their families gathered in the clearing.

Enzo took her elbow, and Thea led the way through the crowd to where Selene and the sillies stood together. Aurelia was standing on a low stone dais in front of a pair of wooden effigies decorated in purifying herbs, with the other leaders of the Immortal Orders. Merhart Lear, the arch-chancellor of the Trickster's Chosen, stood next to her, locs of their snow-white hair twisted into a crown atop their dark head, the emerald green of the Order of Masks' pallyra setting off the cool undertones in their skin beautifully. Lear was one of the few snow leopard shifters and their feline intelligence was evident as they chatted amiably with Aurelia. Berith Sanvier, leader of the Order of Night, stood apart from them, eyes narrowed in annoyance.

The Order of Night had no use for unions between themselves or other Orders for the purposes of procreation, but they participated in the season to broker unions of power. Harlow had to admit that not all vampires were bad, nor were they *inherently* evil; Katerina Spencer was one such example, along with her House. But Berith and the House of Remiel were something different.

Berith was said to be one of the first vampires, not sired by venom but born from a union between the first of the Illuminated and a human who carried the extremely rare Gene-V. And he was the Order of Night's king, rumored to have killed tens of thousands of humans in his long life. His moonstone eyes were cold in contrast to his crimson pallyra as he gazed out over the growing crowd. When Pasiphae Velarius, the arch-chancellor of the Illuminated, joined the other three leaders on the dais, Berith squirmed as the glowing light of her eyes fell upon him.

"Someday that will be you up there," Selene said to Enzo as she hugged his shoulders proudly as any parent.

"Not for another hundred years or so," he mumbled, looking slightly embarrassed when she kissed his cheek. The arch-chancellor of the Order of Mysteries was required to have completely matured into their magic, something that usually took at least a century.

Meline and Indigo giggled, while Larkin looked slightly bewildered by the crowd. Harlow moved to stand behind her younger sisters. She wasn't sure if it was what happened in the woods, or some deeper instinct, but something about this gathering didn't feel safe. Someone brushed against her back and when she turned, she found Finn McKay standing behind her. His pallyra was gold, as all the Illuminated's ceremonial garb were, and its color did nothing for his pale skin. It was one of the few times she'd ever seen him look bad in something.

His stormy eyes lit softly in the dark, but were narrowed in suspicion as he looked at the dais. She forgot herself and asked the question on her lips. "What's wrong?"

He glanced down at her, as if noticing she was there for the first time. "Getting here was strange."

She was about to ask him what he meant when Pasiphae began talking. Unlike Finn, the gold of her pallyra set off her brown skin and glossy black hair beautifully. "Welcome friends. Welcome to the seventeen *hundredth* season."

The crowd murmured a greeting back to her. Seventeen hundred years of this. The Illuminated had started this tradition a mere hundred years after the War of the Orders, after they had finished exterminating those that stood against them—the season was a show of goodwill, according to them. Harlow fought to keep the sneer off her face. She felt Finn shift behind her as more people crowded into the clearing. His chest bumped into her back and she felt his hands on her arms, bracing them both as the space in the Grove tightened, constricted by the surge of the crowd.

"Sorry," he breathed, his mouth uncomfortably close to her ear. Heat flooded her abdomen, gathering at her core in a way that made her want to scream. How dare her body betray her this way?

Harlow had space to step closer to her family, to give him more room, but she stayed stubbornly rooted in place. She told herself it was because she wasn't going to move for him, but part of her knew she enjoyed the heat pooling between her legs, the heavy weight of her breasts, so apparent now that he was touching her. When the crowd settled, his hands disappeared. He stepped backwards, a shock of cold air hitting her back, but she could still feel the heat of him like she was an asteroid drawn into his orbit—she couldn't quite step away.

Pasiphae was talking about duty now. The Orders' duty to the world, to humans especially, to maintain safety and order, to ensure the freedom and prosperity the world now experienced, would continue through the strength and cooperation of the four Orders. Harlow could hardly hear the words. Her body tuned itself to Finn's. She could hear each breath he took, and her chest rose and fell in time with his.

And she knew, because she knew how sensitive the damn Illuminated's senses were, that he could hear the way her heart beat faster, feel the synchronized breaths they were taking, and could likely scent the wet desire gathering between her legs.

"Unbelievable," he growled as he yanked her close to him, one hand spreading possessively across her abdomen as he pinned her to him, his other arm shielding her from some oncoming threat.

Harlow didn't have time to wonder at the close contact. A vampire stumbled into them hard as Finn's arm warded her from the impending collision. Harlow stifled a cry as she crumpled into Finn's embrace at the impact. Vampires got their physical strength from the Illuminated though, and it only took Finn's outstretched arm to push the creature away from her.

"So sorry," the vampire slurred. "Had a bit too much of a drunk co-ed before I came. My first season...." She hiccupped slightly and wiped a trickle of blood from the corner of her mouth.

Harlow wondered if the co-ed had survived the encounter, as the vampire disappeared into the crowd. It took a lot to make a vampire drunk, and if she'd been drinking only from the co-ed, they were very likely dead. The utter helplessness she felt at this realization was frustratingly familiar, as was the rapidity with which her mind put it aside. There was nothing she could do. As long as the Illuminated's control over Okairos went unchallenged, there was nothing anyone could do about individual acts of violence like this.

Finn's arm lingered around her waist longer than was necessary, his fingers spreading over her belly as though he wanted to caress every soft curve of her body. Her breath caught in her chest and she felt his lungs stop in time with hers.

"Are you all right?" he whispered. The arm he'd used to shield her lowered slowly, as though he was afraid something else might threaten her and that hand, the one that pinned her against him, only pressed harder, as though he was as desperate as she was to drink in the electric heat passing between them.

She nodded, unable to form words. No one had seen the encounter, it happened so fast, but Enzo glanced back at her, noticing the trajectory of Finn's hand, which was moving tantalizingly lower by the second. Enzo winked at the two of them. *Winked.*

Finn's hands fell away and he pushed her upright so quickly she nearly fell forward into Thea, who seemed determined not to look back, even though Enzo was elbowing her suggestively. Harlow glanced back at Finn, only for a second. It was a mistake. His gaze was fixed on her, his expression full of so much longing she felt it reverberate through her, tingling in all the best, worst spots, until her toes involuntarily curled inside her boots. His lips parted, as though he too was remembering the way it felt to be deep inside her, and then the mask fell.

The open look in his eyes shuttered and his expression was dry arrogance again as he backed away. "See you at Alaric's," he muttered, his beautiful upper lip curling slightly.

She hated him. She wanted him. She *hated* him more.

Pasiphae's speech was ending and she lifted her hands and shouted, *"ab ordine libertas."*

The crowd echoed her and the effigies burst into flame with the heat of Pasiphae's power. In the moment of combustion, time slowed, and dark shadows clouded Harlow's vision. She didn't know why exactly, but she turned to look back at Finn—he was still backing away, but he too was suspended in time, while the rest of the crowd moved normally.

Nausea flooded Harlow's body, bile burning her throat. She felt unnaturally bound and helpless. Her movements slowed as she turned, as some unknown force restricted her movement. Finn's eyes met hers before he turned away, and they glowed with intense light. As time sped up again he looked back over his shoulder and nodded once.

Whatever just happened, he saw it too—or rather, he sensed the same thing she did. The wrongness of it. Whatever was happening here was more than it seemed. Harlow had always hated the idea of the season, and now she feared it.

CHAPTER 8

Hot drinks were served and people mingled, but Harlow stuck close to Enzo and Thea. Meline and Indigo disappeared into the crowd with their massive group of friends, but Harlow noticed that Larkin stayed with Selene, her eyes betraying the panic she was feeling. Harlow watched as Selene had a brief, quiet conversation with her youngest sister. When Larkin nodded, Selene smiled and motioned to her and Thea.

"I'll go see what's up," Harlow said.

Thea and Enzo were busy talking to a small group of sorcière that Harlow knew by sight, but hadn't gone to school with. They were some of the few sorcière that moved to Nuva Troi from elsewhere; all were musicians and artists of some kind or other, and one was a celebrated model. Thea nodded as she broke away from their little group. No one had asked her even one question, so enamored as they were with Thea and Enzo.

That was fine with her, but she'd hated the way their eyes skimmed over her, as if they were trying not to look at her. She knew everyone read Section Seven religiously. They'd all seen her humiliated several times now since she and Mark broke up; the most recent posts just happened to be the worst since Mark was clearly flourishing and she wasn't.

"I'm not feeling very well," Selene said. "Larkin is taking me home to watch movies in bed."

"Scary movies," Larkin said, a mischievous glimmer in her green eyes.

"We will settle on a psychological thriller," Selene said definitively, the same mischievousness in her countenance. "Tell Li-li that we're leaving, all right darling?"

Harlow nodded, smiling at Selene's nickname for Aurelia. "Of course, Mama." She squeezed Larkin's hand. "See you tomorrow, pal?"

Larkin smiled bravely. "Yes, I'm going to be at the Statuary party. Definitely."

She sounded like she was trying hard to convince herself of the idea and Harlow's worries about Larkin being too young to be at a season renewed, but it would be decidedly unfair to keep her from the festivities, if that's what she wanted. Harlow knew all too well that sometimes you just had to try things to find out what was right for you and what wasn't.

Aurelia was chatting with a few members of her book club when Harlow found her. She patted Harlow's arm and smiled at the news that Selene and Larkin had gone home, barely pausing her conversation. Harlow's heart ached at the way the sorcière her mother spoke to simply ignored her, as though she did not exist. She'd known these witches her entire life, and now their gazes drifted over her like she was a ghost, something best ignored. When Harlow returned to the group surrounding Thea and Enzo, they were waiting for her. "We're going to the Velarius party now. You ready?"

Harlow nodded and she took Thea and Enzo's outstretched hands. None of their magic was mature enough to portal significant distances on their own, but as their powers had already manifested some time ago both Thea and Enzo could manage a trip across town and had just enough magic to bring her along. The others in the group blinked out of sight and Harlow drew a sharp breath in, closing her eyes and focusing her tiny bit of power so that it added to Thea and Enzo's. They would direct their travel, all she had to do was lend them her energy and wait.

When she opened her eyes, she felt fine. Nothing like she had when she entered the Grove. The realization struck her again that something had been wrong with magic at the opening ceremony, but she tried to brush it off. She looked around, taking in her surroundings to distract herself. They were standing behind a blossoming cherry tree in a rooftop garden in fashionable Midtown from the look of things below. This wasn't the Velarius estate in Uptown. "Where are we?"

Thea smiled a bit too sweetly. "This is Alaric's place."

Harlow narrowed her eyes at the familiarity with which her sister referred to Alaric Velarius. "You've been here before?" she asked, suspicion edging her voice sharply.

Thea laughed. "No, silly. But he did invite me and Enzo both. In an email."

Enzo nodded. "He did. He writes lovely emails."

Harlow shook her head. It was true that Alaric Velarius was a nice person, but he was heir to the Velarius fortune, and more importantly to his mother Pasiphae's seat as arch-chancellor of the Immortal Orders. One day, he would very literally rule not just Nytra, but all of Okairos.

She supposed it didn't really matter what she thought, so she kept her mouth shut and let them draw her into the party. Both of them shed their pallyra quickly and she handed hers to Thea, smiling sheepishly. Thea pulled at threads of magic and all three of their ceremonial robes disappeared.

"Back home where they belong," Thea said with a soft clap of her hands.

She was elegant in a long-sleeve black bodysuit and skinny jeans tucked into thigh-high black boots. Medallions of Akatei and Aphora both hung around her neck and her fingers were adorned with half a dozen gold rings. Enzo was dressed in an understated black button-down and peacock-blue jeans, with loafers. They both looked incredible.

Enzo shook his head, wrestling Harlow out of her fuzzy vest. "No to this. Send it home, Thea."

Her sister did as ordered, grinning as Enzo flicked another button of her shirt open. The lace of her bra was showing now. Harlow sighed as Thea's fingers wove magic rapidly, fixing her hair and makeup, she assumed.

It was the kind of profligate use of magic that made humans wary of them: needless, ridiculous, extravagant. It wasn't that humans couldn't learn to use magic; in theory they could. It wouldn't be as easy for them as it was for the sorcière, but anyone could do magic if they learned how. But it was as illegal to teach humans magic as it was for them to learn, and they rightfully resented the sorcière more than the other Orders as a result, despite the fact that the law was made by the Illuminated. She'd empathized with that resentment since she was a child, and it had been one of the things Mark said he'd loved about her most.

As though reading her mind, Enzo shook his head. The practical boots she'd chosen disappeared before she could protest. He yanked a pair of stack-heeled boots out of the aether and had them on her, while Thea sent the others home.

"*Now* you're ready," Enzo declared as he turned her toward the mirrored windows of Alaric's apartment. She looked good. Everything in the outfit strategically hugged her curves, fitting and flaring so her legs looked a mile long and her chest was tastefully exposed.

"Okay," she said quietly. "I look kind of…"

"Hot," Thea finished for her. "You look hot, Harlow. Not frumpy, miserable, or any of the other things all the socials have been saying. You look like *you*."

Harlow's lips curled slightly, but she felt every muscle in her contract at the thought of the party beyond the cover of the tree. Out there, music was playing and she heard people talking and she knew as soon as they walked in, they'd be talking about her, pitying her.

"Let's go," Enzo said as he took her hand. "Rip the bandage right off, okay?"

She nodded and followed them down the pea gravel path that was littered with petals from the dozens of blooming cherry trees that dotted the rooftop garden. A bar was set up near the doors to Alaric's place. This was nothing like her penthouse, which was tiny in comparison. It was, like most things the Illuminated coveted, both old and new at the same time. Everything was beautiful, nothing showed a hint of age, even though much of Alaric's furniture and decor were likely vintage, mixed with precious antiquities.

Just as she'd expected, heads turned as they walked through the group of familiar faces, but most eyes lingered on her sister and Enzo. And just like at the Grove, the rest slid over her as though she were invisible. For that, she supposed she ought to be grateful. Only one gaze rested on her. She shook her head; Finn McKay was glowering at her from under a tree.

He wasn't alone. A slender, blonde vampire was flirting with him. He nodded absently as she talked, his eyes never leaving Harlow. The vampire followed his gaze and then she was glaring at Harlow as well.

"Excuse me," Harlow said to Thea and Enzo as the vampire stalked off in a fiery huff. Finn didn't seem to notice that his companion had disappeared. Similarly, if Thea and Enzo said anything to her as she left them, she didn't hear them. She tried to convince herself that it was because she and Finn McKay needed to have a word, not because they were drawn to one another like opposing ends of a magnet.

"You noticed something was off at the Grove, didn't you?" she asked before she'd even reached him. She knew he could hear her as she neared. He stood so still, it was unnatural.

The intensity of his eyes drifting over her set her heart to pounding as he leaned harder against the tree. "No pleasantries then. I like it."

She rolled her eyes. "What did you see?"

He shrugged, looking bored. Too bored. He was putting on an attitude, wearing it like a coat. She could feel the eyes at her back and he could probably hear everything people were whispering, but she was grateful she could not. His face stayed carefully aloof, but his voice lowered significantly. "It isn't what I saw. It's what I heard."

He took out his phone and fiddled with something. The music changed to a popular club song and got significantly louder. "I'm in charge of the noise this evening," he said. "Better that we're not overheard."

She nodded once, but didn't turn. She wouldn't give them the satisfaction. "A scream. Did you hear a scream?"

She saw the look of real worry in his eyes as he nodded, though the rest of his face didn't move from that insufferable expression of bored annoyance. Everything about him said he couldn't care less about social conventions, and yet he still managed to look perfectly put together. His slouchy vintage band t-shirt draped across his muscular chest, and he'd had the audacity to wear low-slung grey sweatpants and sneakers. Everyone else was dressed to the nines in their "casualwear"—and Finbar McKay was dressed in sweats. Only he could get away with something like that.

"You've made quite the sartorial shift," he remarked, his eyes running over her body again. Something about it felt appraising, rather than lewd, like he was checking her over for wounds after a battle. She didn't like the way her heart grasped onto the idea that he might care how she was faring.

The tone he used confused the way he looked at her. Harlow couldn't tell if he was being sarcastic or not—if he was insulting her, or simply making an observation. She wasn't sure how to react, so she glared. "None of your business, McKay."

He laughed, his eyes crinkling at the corners in a way that nearly melted her resolve to keep hating him. "Right. Got it, Krane. But if you don't want it to be my business, you might try buttoning another button." She turned her glare into a glower and he threw his hands up. "I'm just saying. That's a very eye-catching shirt."

He said the words, but his eyes were locked on hers. In fact, though he'd clearly appraised her, his focus hadn't lingered anywhere but her eyes since she'd noticed him watching her. It was far too intimate.

As he shoved his hands back into his pockets she caught a clearer view of the tattoo around his left arm. As she'd walked up, it had looked like a beautifully rendered sleeve of black line art; now she saw the details of the image on the inside of his forearm more clearly. A snake wound around a sword and a horns up moon in the background. Lilacs bloomed behind the sword, encircling his forearm. The sight of the flowers stopped her breath.

It had been a spring night, in early Mai; the windows had been down in the car and the scent of lilacs drifted in, her favorite flower. The memory of him above her, pushing her hair away from her face as he'd whispered that he… No. No. *No.* This was *not* allowed. She had forbidden herself to think about that night and she would stick to it. The lilacs on his arm meant nothing. It was a coincidence, nothing more. Plenty of people liked lilacs.

She broke the connection between them by stepping away. He cleared his throat and shifted his stance against the tree. A bloom flushed his cheeks that matched her own.

"What do you think it was?" she asked, changing the subject. "The scream?"

He shrugged, conspicuously turning his arm so the inside of his muscular forearm didn't show again. "I really don't know. Nothing good. Did your sense of magic just… disappear?"

She nodded. "Yes, and then everything kind of contracted and then it all came back."

"Until the ceremony. Something happened when the effigies combusted. I know you felt it too."

Harlow started to answer, but the change in his expression caught her attention. The interest that lit in his eyes when she was talking died and he was no longer affecting boredom; now his expression was something else entirely, though she couldn't tell what. She turned slowly to find Petra Velarius standing behind her with a bottle of sparkling wine and two glasses. Her sleek ebony hair was pulled into a ponytail so tight it looked like it would give her a headache, and the black sweater dress she was wearing was so fitted Harlow could count her ribs.

Finn pushed off the tree and walked past her without a second glance. "Later, Harls," he said quietly as he passed her.

Petra heard, her head snapping over her shoulder, her dark eyes narrowed into a glare. Petra Velarius was stunning no matter what, but Harlow suspected she glared so much because she knew it made her look even more beautiful.

"Later, McKay," Harlow murmured as they walked away.

She wasn't sure what to make of the conversation, but she understood one thing: whatever they'd seen and heard, Finn didn't want Petra, or anyone else, to know about it. This was curious.

There was a bench a few steps away from Finn's tree and she sank into it, hoping to wait out the rest of the party here in peace. She wasn't to be so lucky. One of the Trickster's Chosen approached her. Their facial structure reminded her a bit of Merhart Lear, and like Merhart they wore their long hair in locs, pulled into an elegant bun at the back of their head.

Harlow couldn't help but think Enzo would be impressed with their outfit, as they were wearing a midnight blue satin flight suit, with a pattern of golden swallows and clouds embroidered onto it. The collar was flipped up and the suit was unbuttoned halfway down their muscled chest.

When they smiled at Harlow, offering her a glass of iced tea, she felt an empathic connection snap between them. "You're a chameleon," she breathed, amazed to be meeting such a rare shifter by coincidence. Most of the Order of Masks had one animal form they could shift into at will, but chameleons could change into *anything* living, even other people, and they were notoriously empathic.

They grinned, dimples pressing into the cool-toned, dark skin of their face. "I'm Riley Quinn," they answered. "And it's good to finally meet you."

"Finally?" she asked, accepting the iced tea gratefully, noticing that Riley sipped a glass of their own.

"I'm a friend of Kate Spencer's. She says hi by the way."

Harlow nodded, blushing slightly. It was nice that Kate still talked about her. That explained the iced tea. Most people outside her family didn't know she didn't drink much anymore, but Kate knew, as they'd kept in touch sporadically over the years. "Do you want to sit?"

Riley grinned again. "Thanks, you're the only person I know here, except Alaric and Finn, and they're both busy."

Harlow laughed. "And you don't really even know me."

Riley bumped her shoulder with theirs. "I do though. Katie talks about you a lot."

"*Katie?*" She'd never heard anyone refer to Katerina Spencer that way before. She was too enigmatic, too epic for diminutives, in Harlow's opinion.

Riley laughed again. It was a nice sound. "I think I bring out her softer side. She deserved a nickname."

"That's something I'd like to see," Harlow said. Kate was notoriously wild and brash, Harlow's complete opposite. Their short affair had led her to believe they'd probably be better off as friends than lovers, but that hadn't dulled Kate's allure. "Well, if she's been talking about me lately, I'm nervous to know what you must think of me."

Riley's perfectly groomed eyebrows raised incredulously. "What do you mean? Katie thinks the world of you. I've never heard her say a bad word about you."

Something about that made tears well up in Harlow's eyes. She knew it wouldn't be the same if Riley knew Mark, and knowing that Kate spoke well of her touched her deeply. Maybe Enzo was right, she wasn't the asshole-magnet she thought she was.

"Well," she said, her voice rough with emotion. "I don't have a bad word to say about her either."

"I get it," Riley said. "Your relationship was complicated. The way it ended was complicated."

"True," Harlow said, resisting the urge to say more. Chameleons were tricky; their empathy made it all too comfortable to say things you'd never say to anyone else. They'd just met and they were already talking about exes. She couldn't help but be suspicious.

"Why have I never met you before?" she asked. "I'm sure I'd have heard of someone as obviously stylish as you."

Riley's laugh was drier now. "You're smart to be cautious, Harlow. I already liked you from what I'd heard about you. Now I like you more."

She noticed they didn't answer her question, but she didn't press it. Something about Riley Quinn was too intriguing to pass up. She didn't want to ruin the organic feel of their conversation. "Well I haven't heard anything about you and I like you too. Are you, by any chance, interested in meeting a renowned fashion historian and famous designer?"

"*Please* tell me you're talking about Enzo Weraka, because *yes*, yes I am. Finn said he'd introduce me, but I know Enzo's really your friend, and I admire his work so much. Did you read his article in Couture Review last autumn about aethereal iconography in pre-Illuminated fabrics and pottery? It was fascinating."

It was Harlow's turn to grin, though she noted that Riley mentioned Finn. She tucked that away for later, focusing on the realization that the magnificent shifter before her was obviously interested in her best friend for all the right reasons. She loved it when people saw the same genius she did in Enzo. "I think I see him at the bar. Come with me."

When she introduced them, she hardly heard the pleasantries they exchanged. The sparks flying between them were so obvious. She waited for a polite amount of time before asking, "Where's Thea?"

Enzo looked around. "Dancing, I thought. But I don't see her."

Harlow took a small step out of Riley and Enzo's cloud of flirtation to shoot her sister a text. *Where are you? I'm ready to head home.*

One flashed back immediately. *Ran into a friend from uni. Probably going to have a long talk at a coffee shop. Catch up tomorrow?*

Sure thing, she responded, then interrupted Riley and Enzo. "I'm going to take off."

Enzo looked momentarily distraught, but she shook her head as he took her hand. "I'm fine. Just tired and ready to turn in."

He kissed her cheek and she his, whispering, "Careful with your heart. I think Riley Quinn's a bit of a personality."

Enzo hugged her tightly. "Get home safe, love."

"It was so nice to meet you," Riley said with another dazzling smile.

She nodded, looking back once as she left to check on Enzo. He and Riley were already slow dancing and she shook her head with a smile. Someone who believed in the magic of the season as much as Enzo did deserved a little romance. She made her way back down the path littered with cherry blossoms and found the elevator, slipping out of the party without taking a second to look for Finn and Petra. She didn't want to know what they were up to.

The entire day had been a lot. Harlow needed time, space and possibly a big order of parmesan fries to process. So she went home, and put herself straight to bed. The first event of the season was over, and she deserved the rest.

CHAPTER 9

The next morning, Harlow treated herself to a pineapple-coconut smoothie from the coffee shop around the corner, and then began to get ready for the Statuary party. She was exhausted from the night before, but she played an audiobook version of her favorite volume of children's folklore to distract herself from turning it all over in her head again.

She'd already spent the night dreaming about it, there was no need to go over it again. After she'd bathed she dressed, in between texts from her sisters and the maters, all checking in about the previous night. She shot off a few to Enzo as well, and when he finally answered he confirmed that he had not taken Riley home, but that he was hoping to see them again soon. A smile stretched across Harlow's face. Introducing them had been a good idea.

She stood in front of the ancient mirror that hung behind her front door. The glass was spotty, but it gave her a clear enough view of herself to make sure she looked all right. The dress Enzo chose nipped and flared in all the right places to make Harlow feel like an old film star. She'd been skeptical about unbuttoning the dress to reveal the lace of the bustier, but it gave the ensemble an elegantly alluring flair that kept it from being matronly.

Harlow managed a glamour on her hair that tamed her waves into large, loose curls that curved away from her face in a fashionable way that looked a bit undone. She did her makeup by hand, the human way, because she liked to. It was something she'd learned from Kate in uni and she'd kept doing it, even though she could get the same effect in mere seconds from a glamour.

The ritual of painting her face calmed her, soothed her frayed nerves and focused her scattered mind, which kept trying to go over the events at the Grove just one more time. Harlow preferred a somewhat natural look for daytime, but it still took the kind of effort that satisfied her. She set the entire look with glamour, to make sure none of her hard work would disappear in the hours that would follow, but she was pleased with the effect as she washed her hands. Harlow snapped a quick selfie in the mirror and sent it to Enzo and her sisters for approval. When no one had any objections, she walked downstairs to the car that was waiting to take her to the Statuary.

As they drove through the city, Harlow pressed her head against the cool window of the cab, drinking Nuva Troi in. Outside, the glittering neighborhoods of uptown melted into the rainy afternoon like watercolor paintings. Here, the buildings were centuries old, with enormous walled gardens that hid the estates from the view of the road.

Below, modern steel and glass rose shining in the drizzle, glowing before the ocean beyond. Everywhere, dark forest contrasted with the lights of the sprawling metropolis. Harlow's heart swelled with love for Nuva Troi. Despite its many flaws, she loved this city. Its dark beauty made her feel at home in a way no other place ever had.

The sky was grey and a perpetual drizzle threatened the rest of Nuva Troi, but the Statuary remained dry as a bone, due to the Illuminated's efforts to make the afternoon event perfect. The human cabbie shook his head as she paid him, suspicious of the magic that changed the weather for one part of the city but not the rest, she assumed.

Harlow couldn't say she blamed him. She too thought it was ostentatious to use magic for something as trivial as keeping party guests from getting rained on, but it was the way of the Illuminated to make certain the events of the season were perfectly executed. Harlow texted both Thea and Enzo to tell them she'd arrived and then wandered into the gardens.

The Statuary was a monument to "great" Illuminated warriors and politicians, as well as being the city's second largest botanical garden. Everywhere, a riot of flowers bloomed, filling the air with the heady scent of lilacs, roses, and the blooms from the jacaranda trees that lined the path that led to the center of the garden. Beyond the trees, the afternoon was ablaze with gold, purple and deep indigo flowers, as well as glossy green leaves everywhere she turned.

Many of the flowers wouldn't bloom naturally until later in the spring or early summer, but the Illuminated had used magic to ensure the entire Statuary was awash with color and scent. The effect was utterly enchanting, but also formidable. Forcing flowers to bloom ahead of season was an intimidating show of dominion to anyone who truly understood the way magic and nature interacted.

To speed up a growing season, literally thousands of factors had to be managed. It was complex magic that went against the aethereal order, the natural force of nature and magic working in concert. To do such a thing, in addition to keeping the rain away from the Statuary with a degree of ease that Harlow knew wouldn't drain the Illuminated in charge of these aspects of the party in the slightest, was a message to the lower Orders.

It was a reminder that everything in this world belonged to the Illuminated. Everyone else existed at their whim. That included the lower Orders, who even with their combined power, inherited from their Illuminated ancestry, never stood a chance of resisting them. And so traditions like the season, started by the Illuminated to control the lower Orders, went on as though they were *enjoyable*.

Harlow wasn't well-versed in the deeper lore of the season, but she knew the tradition started after the War of the Orders to tempt the lower Orders into forming alliances with one another, rather than with humans, which would expand their numbers. Of course, because the Illuminated were generally good at whatever they put their minds to, especially when they worked as a group, it was successful. It helped that their resources were limitless, their magic unsurpassed.

Aside from the Order of Night, which procreated through infecting humans with their venom, the Order of Mysteries and Order of Masks had eventually been convinced to pair within their own groups over humans, and true societies had formed within the Orders, strengthening the traditions the Illuminated started as the Orders made them their own.

It had never been forbidden to form unions with humans, but after the season had grown in popularity, those pairings were fewer and farther between than before. The lower Orders became suspicious of human motives, and the humans were as fascinated with the lower Orders as they'd been with the Illuminated, creating stark societal stratification between the groups. The Illuminated got their way yet again, by exerting their wealth and influence over the lower Orders. It was how it had always been for two thousand years. The Illuminated shaped society as they saw fit and everyone else simply followed along.

It helped that they were excellent at throwing a party. Harlow resented the Illuminated's unchecked power over the world, and the lower Orders in particular, but she had to admit they knew what they were doing in that regard. Soft, sultry music floated through the air and all paths led towards the center of the gardens, where vast quantities of food were laid out on tables and people were milling about socializing.

Harlow saw plenty of people she knew, and would rather not speak to, but she located Enzo and Thea quickly. Thea looked lovely as ever in a creamy white and tan plaid coat that caused her pale skin and dark hair to glow ever so slightly. She looked like Aphora, goddess of the sea and moon, had descended to attend the first party of the season, and everywhere, people were staring at her, whispering.

"Where are the maters and the sillies?" Harlow asked as Enzo handed her a mug of steaming lavender tea.

"Not arrived yet," Thea said, looking slightly uncomfortable as the people around them whispered. "Is there something wrong with the way I look?"

Her expression was so genuinely pained, so nervous, that Enzo and Harlow burst into a fit of laughter. "No, darling," Enzo said when he was able to breathe again. "They're stunned by how beautiful you are. You're outshining the Illuminated."

Thea blushed, which only served to make her prettier, in Harlow's opinion. Through the crowd, she saw a tall, dark figure notice the effect. He was the same as he'd been in secondary school in many ways but older, less lanky, and still so beautiful it hurt to look at him. She hadn't seen him at all last night, at his own home, so it was a little surprising to see him now.

"Don't look," Harlow whispered. "But Alaric Velarius is coming this way."

Thea did not do as she was told. She looked directly at the Illuminated man who was pushing through the crowd towards them and her cheeks flushed further. Harlow noticed that his eyes emitted a faint glow, and the grin that spread over his face was full of dangerous joy. Was it possible that Alaric Velarius was already *in love* with her sister?

Enzo elbowed her. "He's going to make her a target for the entire season if he isn't careful."

Harlow shook her head, almost imperceptibly. She'd never been through a season herself, but she knew the stories. When the swan of the season was marked so early, the competition could get vicious. And Alaric Velarius was arguably the most eligible bachelor in all four Orders. Harlow had a feeling Thea's competition was about to be *very* angry.

The crowd parted for Alaric and Harlow saw he carried two cut glass flutes of rose cordial. She looked at her sister's empty hands and knew. He was going to hand her one of those glasses and every person that had been hoping they had a chance with Alaric Velarius, Okairos' prince of princes, would be crushed.

It happened in nearly slow motion from her perspective. His eyes were locked on Thea's as he greeted the three of them. As he approached, his dark skin glowed softly in the green gloom of the garden and his eyes shone with appreciation for her sister, along with the usual light of the Illuminated that seemed brighter when they experienced strong emotions.

"It's been a while," he said to Thea, his sonorous voice sounding a bit unsure.

"Yes," she replied.

He held out the flute of cordial to her sister, as Harlow knew he would, and when Thea's slender fingers curled around it, they brushed his, their eyes never faltering from the other's gaze. Harlow had a brief moment where she was tempted to make a gagging noise, but then she saw the narrowed eyes of those who'd hoped to have a chance with him.

She hoped he meant this, this small-seeming but monumental gesture. Otherwise Thea's season would be over before it began. If he decided on someone different, or this gesture wasn't meant to be as meaningful as everyone had clearly already determined it was, the jealous vipers that were now seething around them would destroy Thea's chances at anyone else.

Harlow needn't have worried that Alaric didn't know the impact he was making. As Thea took the flute from him Harlow heard him whisper, "Gods, Thea. I missed you. You look beautiful."

Her sister looked down at her cordial and smiled as he swept her cheek with a kiss so sweet and chaste several people in the crowd gasped. The first kiss of the season had been laid, and Thea Krane was its beneficiary. She was the season's blooming rose, and now everyone knew it.

Harlow tried her best not to smirk, but hardly succeeded. Enzo nudged her again and she thought he was agreeing with her that Thea's success had been incredibly satisfying to watch, but she realized too late that he was warning her. He'd been looking at something over her shoulder—she'd assumed it was the jealous onlookers, but the deep voice that sent shivers down her spine brought her back to the horrifying reality of the moment.

"Hey, Harls."

CHAPTER 10

She turned slowly to face Finn McKay. He was dressed in a pair of slim fitting grey wool slacks, a white t-shirt, and a soft-looking navy blazer with the collar turned up. He was flouting tradition by not wearing a collared shirt, but she doubted anyone would care. His hair was freshly cut and yet still looked as though he'd just rolled out of bed.

Do not think of Finbar McKay rolling out of bed, she chided herself.

"Hello, Finbar." Her voice was chilly, as she tried to tamp down the incredible rush of heat she got from looking at him.

He winced. "Harls, don't call me that."

"Stop calling me 'Harls' and I'll call *you* something else."

He narrowed his eyes at her, then one corner of his mouth quirked up in that horribly smug, sensual way he had of smiling. "As you wish, Ms. Krane."

"If I had *my* wish, you'd be anywhere but here, McKay."

Thea hissed softly in disapproval and Alaric's face was strangely twisted with pain, as though she'd hurt *his* feelings. The crowd was listening, Harlow knew, and it was likely a misstep to be so rude to the heir to the McKay fortune, but she couldn't seem to stop herself. The way he'd just walked off with Petra in the middle of their conversation last night had stung more than she realized.

Finn blinked a few times and then nodded, taking a place next to Alaric, rather than her. The rest of them began to chat idly and slowly the crowd lost interest. Harlow felt the tension in the air relax, as people began to tend to their own business.

But Harlow did not relax. In fact, her body tensed so rigidly she thought her muscles might explode and she struggled to keep her breath even. Enzo and Finn were discussing one of Finn and Alaric's friends from Nea Sterlis who wouldn't arrive until just before the Solstice Gala, but Harlow couldn't follow their conversation. Her throat was dry and her mug was empty.

She murmured something about getting another drink and moved away, swiping a glass of rose cordial off a table, and wandered into the boxwood maze. She knew the maze would be occupied later in the party by the first sets of lovers to pair off. But now, while everyone was getting to know one another in the context of the season, it was blessedly empty.

A shiver ran through her. The air was a bit too chilly here to be drinking something cool. She turned to make her way back to the party to find hot tea instead, and saw him seated on a stone bench, as though waiting for her. "Are you following me, McKay?"

He rolled his eyes and pulled a pack of cigarettes out of his jacket pocket. "Don't flatter yourself, Krane. I just hate this bullshit. You know that better than anybody."

She did know that. They'd made fun of the season endlessly in secondary school, calling it a desperate way to find love. Now, here they both were, neither of them paired, both expected to make an advantageous match. Both the kinds of desperate actors they'd once derided.

"So why come?" She didn't know why she asked.

He looked up and she saw the kind of pain in his eyes she remembered from when they were children. The kind that spoke of the cruelty of his parents, their ruthless ways. The kind that had brought them together, originally, because she and Enzo were the only ones who knew how bad they were, how much they hurt him.

He pulled a cigarette from the pack, lighting it with a brief pull on the threads of magic surrounding them, then took a deep drag. The smoke wasn't toxic smelling like some of the stuff humans smoked. It smelled of woodfire, dark honey and cloves, expensive. "You know why I'm here."

His voice was wary, no trace of his usual arrogance, or the swagger she'd come to know in the months after their friendship ended. She was tempted to read something deeper into his words, something beyond the obligation she knew he felt he owed his parents. The freshly cut hair and clean shaven face showed that he cared about *something* here, despite his obvious attempt to appear as though he didn't. She'd never seen him look so much like he was conforming to the Illuminated's stuffy sense of style.

Something nipped at her suspicion, making her wonder if it were possible he'd cleaned up because he knew he'd see *her*. Not that she cared about that kind of thing. She actually preferred him the way he usually was, longer hair, the merest hint of a beard. Her skin heated at a random memory of a video she'd seen on socials of him at the beach, walking out of the waves carrying his surfboard, water dripping off his bare chest.

Harlow shoved her reaction down deep and lashed out to get herself in line. "Still doing everything mommy and daddy say, I see."

As she swept past him, out of the maze, she heard the sharp intake of his breath. It was a low blow, and perhaps he deserved it, once. *But it has been nearly seven years,* a little voice whispered in her heart, *does he still deserve it now?* She wasn't willing to stay in the maze and find out. He'd hurt her by walking off last night, and that hurt compounded years of pain—pain that had only started because of him—and now his family was trying to destroy her family's livelihood. She wanted nothing to do with him.

The rest of the party was mind-numbingly boring and while Finn still primarily socialized with Alaric, Thea, and Enzo, he stayed well away from her. That was fine. It was all just fine. When Petra arrived to wrap herself around Finn, Harlow decided to find somewhere else to be.

Petra's satisfied smile was enough to make her regret giving up ground, but she didn't feel confident enough to stand up to her. Enzo looked concerned, as though he'd follow, but she shook her head slightly. He shouldn't have to lose his place in what was the most highly coveted circle at the party because she couldn't stand to be near both Petra and Finn at the same time.

Harlow spent an hour trying to find the maters and her sisters in the vast gardens, as her phone had run out of battery life, but could only locate Larkin. Her youngest sister sat alone at a wrought iron table, staring at her hands, her dark hair in her face.

"Hey, pal. Where's everyone else?"

Larkin looked up at her, her green eyes and heavy brows a mix of both their mothers. "They all found people to talk to."

"And what about you? Why are you alone?"

Larkin shrugged, examining her fingernails. "I don't think I understand all this very well."

Harlow sat down on the bench next to her and sighed. "Me either."

Larkin shook her head. "I know what *you* mean, but that's not what *I* mean."

This caught Harlow's attention. "Parse that out for me, pal."

"*You* mean that you don't understand all the frivolity. You think this is ridiculous and hate the forced nature of the season and the way the Illuminated control us."

Larkin's eyes were bright and intelligent, her words incisive. Harlow nodded. "That's a good approximation of how I feel. Sure."

"But *I* don't understand how to flirt."

Harlow started to say something sisterly and encouraging, but Larkin shook her head. "I don't understand *why* either. Why flirt? Why run off into the maze together? Why, Harlow? Why does any of that seem appealing?"

Harlow began to understand better. She pulled a piece of her sister's dark brown hair playfully, thinking of how she'd never liked romances, or to play romantic pretend games as a littling. "I don't know how to explain it. It's all a feeling I don't quite understand myself."

"What's wrong with me that I don't feel that way at all, ever?" Larkin's voice was full of such despair, such sorrow, that Harlow's heart cracked.

"Nothing, pal. Nothing at all." A tear rolled down Larkin's face and Harlow wiped it away. "Got your phone? Mine's out of battery."

Larkin nodded and handed her phone over. Harlow texted the maters and Thea. *It's Harlow, my phone's out of batt. Taking Larkin home. Tell Enzo I'm not going out this evening.*

Harlow didn't wait for a reply. She didn't want one. "Let's get out of here. Go home, order pizza and watch a movie."

Larkin wiped another tear from her face. "A scary movie, okay?"

"Scary as you please," Harlow agreed, knowing Selene hadn't indulged her last night and they'd probably watched a slew of mysteries instead.

They made their way out of the garden to where a line of cabs should be waiting, but none were there. Harlow groaned; it was too early. The cabs wouldn't arrive for another hour or two. She started to ask Larkin for her phone again when Finn McKay walked out of the garden gates holding his car keys, smoking another of his expensive cigarettes. He was leaving.

He didn't see them standing there. She had to make a quick decision. His name was out of her mouth before she could change her mind. "Finn?"

When he heard her, his head snapped around. It took him seconds to see Larkin's miserable face and her worried eyes. He'd been halfway down the block when she called to him, but he reached her side in seconds, the cigarette gone from his hand.

"Are you okay?" He sounded concerned.

Harlow wasn't sure what to say.

He seemed at war with himself for a moment, then before she could answer he asked, "Do you need a ride?"

There were a thousand reasons to say no, but her sister's hunched shoulders were all she needed. "I'd be grateful if you could help us get out of here."

He nodded and gestured to the street. "My car's parked this way. I'll take you home."

Harlow put her arm around Larkin and followed Finn to a dark green vintage sports car. "Will we all fit?" she asked sarcastically.

He grimaced at her. "It has a backseat."

"I'll sit in back," Larkin said, quietly interrupting.

He opened the doors and pushed back the camel-colored front seat so she could get in and then helped her inside. Harlow was surprised at how gentle he was with Larkin, and the soft tone of his voice as he showed her where the seatbelt was. For someone who struck fear and awe into most people, he could be surprisingly considerate.

The ride through the city was quiet. He cracked a window and started to light another cigarette. Before she could think better of her actions, she snatched it out of his fingers. The current that snapped between them was electric.

"Hey," he snapped, glaring at her sidelong as he watched traffic.

"Just because you can't get lung cancer doesn't mean you should smoke this shit. If it's illegal for humans, maybe you should lay off too."

She rolled down her window a crack, rolling her eyes at the old crank lever, and tossed the cigarette out.

"And now you've littered, Krane," he said, the sharp edge of his deep voice tempered by humor. "Now who should be following the rules better? Isn't littering illegal for humans too?"

Larkin snorted softly in the back seat and Harlow spun so fast to glare at her sister that her seatbelt choked her.

"Careful there, kitten," Finn murmured. "Don't hurt yourself."

She crossed her arms across her chest and sighed. "Don't call me kitten."

"Don't call you kitten, don't call you Harls." Finn shook his head, making eye contact with Larkin in the backseat via the rearview mirror. Both of them were laughing at her.

Harlow fought the urge to laugh along with them. Finbar McKay was not her friend, he was not her prospective lover, he was a problem. One she needed to solve, and quickly, as they were almost home. Harlow only spoke again to tell him how to get into the courtyard. When he stopped, there was awkward silence.

"Thanks for the ride," Harlow said, her hand on the door handle.

"Do you want to order pizza and watch a scary movie with us?" Larkin asked from the back seat. It was the first thing she'd said in twenty minutes.

Harlow's eyes went wide. Her heart tumbled as he grinned, peeking into the back at Larkin. When he answered she didn't know whether to cheer or scream. "Yeah. I'd love that. Thanks for asking."

CHAPTER 11

Harlow followed them into the house, up the four flights of stairs that led to the residence above the bookstore. The staircase wall was papered in a rich tapestry-style that depicted stags and cranes, representative of her mothers' combined heritage. Harlow let her fingers drag over the wallpaper as she had as a child, thinking she might feel the feathers or fur come to life under her touch.

She watched Finn's eyes take in every part of her childhood home as they entered. The plush rugs, the natural objects and copious amounts of art. The cozy furniture and rich, colorful palette. She'd told him about it dozens of times as children, but he'd never come here. Of course, neither of their parents had approved of their friendship, and so they mostly saw each other at school and parties.

Larkin said something about changing out of her dress and they were left alone in the living room. Harlow plugged her phone in and turned to ask him why he'd wanted to come inside, but his expression was so open, and so unlike the cold version of him she'd grown used to, that her words died in her mouth.

He swallowed hard as she made eye contact. "I always wanted to come here. It's just like you said, better even. This place feels like a real home."

She nodded. It was true, her mothers had elegant taste, but never sacrificed comfort or the ability to gather with their family. There were three long couches in a u-shaped arrangement in the great room, and a television that was magicked to look like an oil seascape when not in use. The walls were painted a deep green, and the couches were overstuffed, with dozens of pillows and blankets ready to snuggle into. Round brass lamps with empire shades cast warm pools of light on the blue rugs. For a moment, she saw it all from his perspective.

Everywhere there was evidence of the women who called this home. Dozens of framed photographs gilded the library table behind the couches. Tables were strewn with notebooks, scrunchies, and novels stuck with bookmarks. Someone's slippers and a pair of wool socks peeked out from under one of the couches. This was where seven people who genuinely loved one another gathered frequently.

She knew there were no spaces like it in his family's home. He'd said as much when they were younger. Harlow started to say something but he shook his head again. "Please don't ask me to explain myself tonight, Harls. Just let me order pizza?"

Part of her wanted to say no, was tempted to tell him to get out, but there was such a soft look of need in his eyes that she couldn't manage the unkind words on her tongue. "Fine. I'm going to change clothes too. You know what I like on pizza. Larkin only likes cheese."

He nodded and she slipped out of the great room while he dialed his phone, a look of subtle joy on his face that bothered her. She went up one floor to Larkin's room and knocked.

"Come in," Larkin called.

She was wearing sweats and had removed all the makeup she'd worn at the party. Harlow had to admit that she looked more herself this way, more comfortable and real. And happier. She didn't look the way Harlow always looked when she wore sweats, frumpy and miserable. She looked like Larkin, like the essence of Larkin, athletic and fresh. And cheeky as seventeen hells. The little silly was grinning her head off like she'd gotten away with murder.

"Why did you ask him in?" Harlow asked sharply.

"For the same reason you brought me home. He needed it."

Harlow closed her eyes. *He* needed it. "What about me?"

Larkin shook her head, smiling. "You needed it too. I remember how you used to talk about him. Whatever happened between you, you should fix it."

"It's complicated, pal."

Larkin shrugged. "I may not understand why people fall in love, or how, but I know what two people in love look like."

Harlow threw a stuffed bunny at Larkin. "We are not in love."

"You were though," Larkin said, wise as a sage as she caught the threadbare rabbit. "And maybe you will be again."

"Fat chance."

"I've always thought that expression sounded like it meant there was a really good chance that said thing was about to happen," Larkin mused. "Plus, he seems nice. I don't know why you've said so many mean things about him."

Larkin was too young to remember the way he'd shattered her. Too young to remember her broken heart. And she'd never told the sillies everything, only Thea and Enzo. Larkin only remembered that once he'd been Harlow's friend and then for some reason he wasn't.

"I'm gonna go change."

"Mama packed you and Thea's spare things in cold storage when the attic closets got moths, remember?"

"Damnit. Thanks for reminding me."

She left Larkin and went to her parents' room, a vibrant peach palace of decadent love. Harlow dug through Selene's drawers until she found the only thing she hoped wouldn't make her look like she was trying to seduce someone, a pair of lavender cashmere drawstring joggers and a matching sweater with a wide neck. When she changed, the sweater fell off one shoulder in an alluring way she'd rather avoid, but Selene didn't own clothes that *weren't* alluring and nothing of Aurelia's would fit her.

"Damn you, Mama," she said as she looked in the mirror. She looked sexy, like she wanted to be touched, which was of course the point of this outfit. Selene was in perpetual seduction mode, even after hundreds of years of marriage.

"No wonder the two of them are always doing it," she muttered as she shut off the light.

In the great room, she found Larkin and Finn arguing over which horror movie to watch. They were laughing, talking about directors and their favorite actors. She'd forgotten he loved movies, that horror was one of his favorite genres.

The door buzzed and Larkin jumped up. "I'll get the pizza."

Finn handed her several bills. "No change, okay?"

Larkin nodded, grinning at the big tip he was going to give. Her sister was very interested in tipping well and he'd clearly impressed her.

When they heard her feet on the stairs, his gaze turned to Harlow, slowly as though he was afraid to look at her. "You look…"

"Ridiculous," Harlow finished for him, grabbing her phone from the charger. "I had to borrow something from Selene and all her casual clothes look like she's about to seduce Aurelia. Believe it or not, this was the best I could find."

"I was going to say you look beautiful," he muttered, not taking his eyes off the screen as he scrolled through the horror section.

Harlow was stunned. He'd never said anything like it to her. Not even before, and certainly not with that quiver in his hands. He tried to hide it, but she saw. His hands were shaking. Akatei blessed them, and Larkin came back with the pizza before she had to think of something to say. The three of them sat on the floor in front of the coffee table, and Larkin chose a ghost story.

Harlow checked her phone. There were messages from the maters asking for an update on how Larkin was doing. She texted back to let them know they were home safe and that she planned to spend the night.

She apologized again to Enzo for abandoning him, and got a text back that said he hoped she had a great night. A winky emoji followed and she texted a question mark back.

I saw who took you home. Update me on everything tomorrow.

Thea said she'd be home in a few hours, that Alaric was taking her out for a late dinner, but that she planned to spend the night at home, rather than her own place. Before she could text back, Larkin plucked her phone from her fingers.

"Watch the movie, please," the little tyrant commanded, tossing her phone aside. Eventually, Larkin moved to the couch and covered up with a blanket, but Harlow was glued in place.

She was acutely aware of both the moment Larkin fell asleep and Finn's warm body next to hers. He was sitting close enough to touch. The film got scarier. It wasn't a gory slasher film, but a tense ghost story, a thriller. Harlow knew the jump scare was coming, felt her body go taut and then startle as the ghost appeared for the first time. Her fingers brushed Finn's involuntarily and he took her hand.

"I forgot that you hate scary movies," he whispered.

She tried to even her breathing, but he ran his thumb down the center of her palm in a way that was far from innocent. Warmth flooded her belly as his eyes grazed over her bare shoulder, at the bustier that was practically exposed by the sweater's wide neck.

Every nerve in her body screamed for his touch, betraying her heart. Harlow closed her eyes and she felt the whisper of his breath on her face. Then nothing. He let go of her fingers and moved ever so slightly away from her. Her heart dropped with disappointment, traitorous disappointment.

Then she heard it: Larkin's breathing was irregular. She was awake, but pretending to sleep. She glanced at Finn and saw his lips curl into a smile, a real one, not that smug one he'd worn at the party. He'd known before she had, that preternatural Illuminated sense of hearing telling him Larkin had woken.

When the movie ended, Larkin was awake and she said goodnight quickly. Harlow knew she wasn't going to bed. Her littlest silly was going to get the talking to of her life when Finn left. He helped to take the leftover pizza boxes into the kitchen. When Harlow turned away from the huge fridge he was smiling wistfully, leaning against the island, arms crossed.

"This is almost how I imagined it would be."

"Almost?" she asked, as though in a dream. Only the little lamp on the counter was on, making the kitchen cozy and dark.

Finn pushed away from the island, the muscles in his chest flexing. Sometime during the movie he'd taken his jacket off, and the t-shirt he wore was practically sinful, it looked so good on him. He moved slowly, deliberately, giving her a chance to move away. She told herself she stayed in one spot because this was better than one of her sisters being the object of his attention, or worse, *his parents'* attention. But the deeper voice inside her spoke the truth: she knew he'd never make a single move on any of her sisters.

The ferocity of his attention spoke volumes. He was nearly touching her now. Her breath quickened when one long arm snaked around her waist as he pulled her to him. She didn't think, didn't allow herself to think, but raised her chin to be kissed as she leaned into him, pressing her palms into the solid, warm bulk of his chest.

He tugged on her gently, bringing her closer and she responded, wrapping her arms around his neck. He smelled so good, and the way his body warmed hers was decadent, indulgent, and oh so dangerous.

Finn's mouth was soft against her skin as he bent to kiss her cheekbones. "I wanted this so much when we were in school. To come here, to watch a movie with your sisters and hold your hand. To kiss you in the kitchen. To be a normal couple."

"Then why did you ruin it all?" she asked, the words slipping out, even as she leaned into the heat of his chest.

"Godsdamn it, Harls," he growled, letting her go. The cold air that filled the space between them shocked her system.

Before she could ask him again, he was gone, using that supernatural speed to leave her standing alone in the kitchen, her chest feeling flayed open as though she were seventeen again, heart freshly broken. She slid to the floor, shaking with the sobs she'd shoved down for seven years.

CHAPTER 12

"Harlow?" Larkin's voice was gentle. How long had she been sitting here? "Are you okay? Did he hurt you?" Now her sister was panicked.

"No, pal. He didn't hurt me. Well, maybe my feelings, but that was a long time ago."

Larkin pulled her up off the marble floor. "Come on. Come to my room."

Harlow nodded, wiping her face with the tissue Larkin handed her and following her sister to her room. Larkin's room was lit by a host of floating witchlights, and her bed had a canopy with dark grey linen curtains. Her walls were papered with old sheets of music and her violin was out, as though she might play at any moment.

Harlow let her little sister tuck her into bed and then crawl in next to her, curling up against her shoulder. "Thought I was supposed to be comforting you," she muttered.

"You can, if you want… I had fun until he made you cry. I didn't think that's what would happen, not from the way you were looking at each other."

Harlow didn't reply. She just let the tears slip down her face.

Larkin tucked her cold feet under Harlow's legs. "What's the story between you?"

It was a simple question, but there were no easy answers. Mostly because Harlow didn't really know what happened. "We were good friends from the time we were ten. His family moved here that year, and Finn, Enzo and I became inseparable."

"How old was I?" Larkin asked.

Harlow smiled faintly as she counted back. Larkin always asked how old she was whenever Thea or Harlow told a story about their past. She seemed fascinated with the idea that there was so much history she'd missed, being the baby. "About three, I guess?"

"That explains why I don't remember."

Harlow swiped a quick kiss on top of Larkin's dark head. "His parents didn't like that we were close. They wanted him to have more Illuminated friends, so we could only socialize at school or at events where all four Orders gathered. And even then, they made it clear that they disapproved."

Larkin scoffed. "And now they think one of us should marry him."

"Yeah. A bit hypocritical."

"What else is new?" Her sister sounded almost as jaded as she did. Larkin poked her side. "Finish the story."

"By the time we were in secondary school, right before uni, we both knew we were in love, that maybe we'd always been in love, but we knew we couldn't be together. His parents wouldn't allow it and they're the McKays. They always get their way."

Larkin nodded and looped her arm through Harlow's, holding her hand. Harlow smiled. Larkin was so sensitive. She knew the awful part of the story was coming.

"Anyway, one night Finn took me to see an exhibit. He loved to draw and one of his favorite artists was showing at a gallery downtown. So we went, just the two of us."

"Where was Enzo?"

Harlow hugged her littlest sister. "On a date of his own."

"So, you went to the art exhibit. What happened after?"

Harlow blushed. "We drove around for a while, and then… We stopped, and… Things went too far, I guess."

"You had sex?" Larkin sounded surprised.

"Yes, it had been building between us for a while. We'd kissed a few times and never talked about it. And that night things went further. It was my first time."

"Was it really bad? You look like you're going to cry again."

"No, it was wonderful. One of the best nights of my life."

Larkin wiped tears from Harlow's face. "What went wrong?"

"I don't know. But the next day he was different. Cold. Within a month he was downright mean to both me and Enzo. He cut us both out. Do you know Alaric's cousin Petra?"

Larkin nodded.

"He started hanging around her and her crowd."

"Was Alaric friends with them?"

"Not really. He's Thea's age, a year older, actually. He had his own friends and eventually Finn ran around with them instead."

"With the uni kids?"

"Yes, and that was better. When he was friends with Petra, they were really hard on me and Enzo. Well, she was anyway, and he did nothing to stop it. He didn't participate, but he just stood there whenever she bullied me and Enzo. Me especially."

"I remember that part. You coming home every day, broken looking and exhausted. I remember hearing the maters saying they thought they'd have to send you away, but then things got better. Was that when he became friends with Alaric?"

Harlow wasn't sure if Larkin actually remembered that, or if the twins had told her about it enough times that she thought she did. "Yeah, I guess so. Alaric is a good person. Maybe he was a better influence on Finn. I don't know. When we all went to university, I tried to leave it behind, let it go, but it ate me up inside for years. I made a lot of mistakes at uni because I couldn't let it go."

"Then you met Mark."

"Well, I saw a lot of other people in between, but yeah, Mark was the first person I really loved after Finn."

Larkin grimaced, as though she thought Mark was a bad follow-up. "And now Finn's back and everyone wants you to pair."

"I guess." Harlow felt as though the breath had been knocked out of her as she sunk down into the pillows of Larkin's bed.

"Does that seem a little wild to you?" Larkin peered over at her. "Like, *really* wild?"

"Yeah, pal. Shut off the lights, okay? I think I'm done for the day."

"Nyx," Larkin whispered and the witch lights went out, and Harlow was left with a head full of memories and a bruised heart.

CHAPTER 13

Harlow smelled breakfast before she was fully awake, the familiar sounds of a weekend morning at home filling her ears and making her drowsy. She opened her eyes and was supremely confused. Instead of the huge attic bedroom she shared with Thea until she was eighteen, she was someplace else.

"I got you tea," Larkin chirped, pressing a warm mug into her hands.

"Oh, right, I slept in here." Harlow took the mug and sipped gratefully as she sat up, propping herself up in the enormous pile of pillows Larkin slept amongst. "What's with the tea service?"

Larkin wrinkled her nose. "Everyone is in the kitchen interrogating Thea about her dinner with Alaric."

Harlow sunk deeper into the pillows and pushed back the covers. "Get in. We don't need to participate in that."

Larkin smiled and cuddled in. Harlow loved the twins fiercely, as she loved all her sisters, but they were an intense pair, and if they had Selene on their side, the scene in the kitchen was bound to be more than she wanted to deal with just now. Besides, Larkin had slipped out of discussing the reason they left the party last night.

"So, pal. You cleverly avoided having to talk to me last night. Want to fill me in on what's going on with you?"

Larkin tucked her face into Harlow's shoulder, like she had when she was a little girl. "It's hard to explain."

"Give it a try."

"I know what romance *is*. I even kind of like to read about it or watch TV shows with it, but I just don't… feel it."

"Not ever? With anyone?"

Larkin shook her head. "It's not a matter of who, it's just that I don't feel like that about people."

"What about sex?"

Larkin shook her head. "I don't really get that either. I fooled around with the people I dated in secondary and sometimes it felt nice, but all the stuff the books talk about? I just didn't feel it. Do you think something's wrong with me?"

Harlow threw an arm around her sister and hugged her. "No, pal. I don't. Lots of people feel that way; humans are better at talking about it than the Orders. Since we're so obsessed with pairing, we don't talk about what it's like when someone doesn't want to."

Larkin nodded. "That makes sense I guess. I just feel like the odd one out."

Harlow's arm tightened around her sister. "I think you'll find other people like you and when you do, it'll help you understand yourself better."

"Really? Do you know any?"

Harlow laughed. "Probably. I'll think about it and ask Enzo, if that's all right. I think one of his friends from uni felt similarly about things. Would you like to talk to her if that's the case?"

Larkin nodded. "Enzo always has nice friends."

"Do you want to keep going to the season parties?"

Larkin blanched. "No, but I think Mama will be mad."

"She won't. I promise. Just tell her and Mother how you feel. They'll understand, pal."

"You think the sex queens will get this? They've been in love forever."

They giggled together and Harlow set her empty mug down to wrap her other arm around her youngest sister. "They've also *lived* forever. They get a lot of stuff we don't give them credit for."

When Harlow said it, she realized how true it was, and how lucky they were to have such good parents. All Finn's troubles with his own family were a thought away. She tried to brush it off, but something bothered her about how he'd acted the night before, so happy to be here, and then gone the instant she'd questioned him about why he'd abandoned her.

Selene poked her head in. "So that's where my cashmere sweatsuit went. Time for waffles, my darlings."

Harlow gave Larkin a meaningful look as she climbed out of bed. "Talk to her. I'll send Mother in."

Selene looked concerned and Harlow kissed her cheek as she passed. "I love you, Mama."

Selene pulled her back before she got out the door, into a massive hug. "I love you too, dear girl. I'm so glad my babies are all home."

Harlow grinned and sent Aurelia to Larkin's room as she entered the kitchen. The twins were already planning a lazy day of a family movie marathon, taking their waffles into the living room. Only Thea was left in the kitchen.

"So, Alaric Velarius, and you're the swan of the season."

Thea blushed. "No one is saying that."

Harlow grabbed Thea's phone, clicked open the Section Seven app and scrolled down past news of a human celebrity's party. Then she flipped the phone around to show her sister the headline.

Sorcière heiress the swan of the Orders' mating season.

Thea looked horrified. "Oh dear. Mating season?"

Harlow shrugged as she piled waffles on her plate. "The app is run by humans, what do you expect? Plus, it's not altogether inaccurate."

"Crudely put," Thea said ruefully, closing her phone.

"So, is he serious about you?" Harlow cut right to the chase. She had no desire to question her sister after the morning she'd probably already had.

Thea's smile was small, but joyful. "Yes."

"And you're serious about him?"

Thea nodded, looking pleased.

Harlow ate her waffles. "Sounds good."

Thea started to say something, then seemed to think better of it. "Was Finn here last night?"

"I don't want to talk about it."

"Harlow…"

"Leave it." Harlow's voice was sharp as she pushed away from the table. Explaining things to sweet, sensitive Larkin was one thing, but she couldn't talk about this more today. "I've gotta go home."

Thea grabbed her hand. "Please don't go. We're supposed to have a movie marathon and eat junk food all day. It won't be the same if you go."

"I can't talk about him," Harlow rasped, her voice rough with unshed tears. "Please, don't make me."

"Fine," Thea said, guiding her back into her chair. "Finish your waffles."

Harlow did, as her sister watched in perfect silence.

❧

THE REST of the weekend slipped by in domestic bliss. The maters tended to the shoppers and the girls took shifts helping, but mostly they lay about enjoying themselves. When Sunday night came, Harlow dreaded going home to her near-empty apartment.

"Why don't you move back in?" Aurelia suggested, as though reading her mind.

They'd been reading together in the study for over an hour, but Harlow was distracted by thoughts of her lonely apartment. "I can't."

Aurelia put down her book. "Why not?"

Harlow mirrored her mother and shook her head. "I just can't."

"You hate your apartment."

Harlow *loved* her apartment, but that would be hard to explain to Aurelia, who liked everything in her life to be just so. "I need to be there for a while. It was so good to be here this weekend, to be with all of you and to forget about everything that's wrong, but I need my own place."

"Tell me why." Aurelia's expression suggested a willingness to listen.

Harlow sighed. "Because I have things I need to work out, and if I stay here, you and Mama will work the magic you work without even thinking, and I'll feel better and forget that I need to sort myself out."

"Would that be so bad? To let us help you? To feel better after everything that happened with Mark?"

Harlow got up and kissed Aurelia's cheek. "It wouldn't be if I'd actually work out all the bullshit going on in my head, but I won't. I'll just keep putting it off."

"What's going on up there, bun-bun?" Aurelia tapped Harlow's forehead.

Harlow sat at Aurelia's feet, rested her head on her lap, and thought about her mother's question. "I feel like I can't do anything right."

"Is this about your magic? You know your talent will manifest soon enough. Your time with humans simply delayed things. Now that you're back with us, safe in the lower Orders, things will right themselves."

Harlow didn't answer. Aurelia was usually very perceptive, but she and Mama had been skirting around asking what really happened with Mark for six months. All Harlow had told them was that it was over and her new address.

Aurelia tipped Harlow's head up so their eyes met. "What happened with Mark, bun?"

She took a shaky breath, remembering what she'd told Larkin about their parents understanding the world better than they gave them credit for. "You were all right. He was hurting me."

Aether surged in the threads of magic around Aurelia, dark and menacing, a reminder that her mother was a force to be reckoned with. Harlow shook her head. "Not physically. But the way he talked to me... It was confusing. Even now, I know he was manipulating me, but I can't shake the feeling I'm the one who was wrong."

Her mother's eyes narrowed in fury. "I will kill him."

Harlow believed it. "That would only get us in trouble with the Consortium. It's not against the law to make someone believe you're the only person they can trust. He twisted everything anyone said to me in so many ways... I thought for a long time that you all hated me."

"We were *afraid* for you, my darling," Aurelia said, pressing a kiss to her forehead. "You changed so much in such a short time. We weren't sure how to address it without making things worse. Mama and I know we made a mistake. We should have gotten you out of there sooner."

Harlow bit her lip, trying not to cry. "I wouldn't have gone, and if you'd have forced me, you'd have proven him right. The worst part is that he knew it. He knew he had me fooled."

Threads of magic sputtered with power, sizzling around Aurelia's fingertips. She drew them back from Harlow. "I'm sorry, bun. I'm finding it difficult to control myself."

Harlow took her mother's hands and kissed them, letting the little sparks of power fizzle out against her skin. "I didn't know how much he'd fooled me until the day he kicked me out."

"Why did he do it? If he had you fooled, why did he let you go?"

Harlow couldn't meet Aurelia's gaze. "I don't really know."

The magic flared around Aurelia's fingertips again. "What does *that* mean?"

"I don't remember the last night very well. There's a kind of blank spot in my memory. I remember some of the fight we had, that he pushed too far about

Order secrets, but I can't remember the particulars… and then everything goes blank until I woke up here the next day."

Something broke in Aurelia's eyes as Harlow met them. "Darling girl, I am so sorry. I didn't know."

Harlow took one last wobbly breath. "And I left a friend behind."

Aurelia's brow wrinkled. "Who?"

Harlow's shoulders slumped with the burden of her guilt. "I adopted a street cat when he forced me to quit my job at the shelter. The only part of our argument I remember is that he took Axel from me. I've texted him dozens of times, trying to get him back, but he doesn't answer." She choked on a sob. "I don't even know if he's okay."

"My sweet girl." Aurelia stroked her hair. "We'll get Axel back, I promise you that." Aurelia's tone was reassuring, but it wouldn't make up for the months she'd let her ragamuffin baby stay with Mark.

Harlow stared at her hands. "The whole thing made me feel like I don't deserve to have good things happen to me. I can't seem to take care of myself, or care what happens to me unless I think about you all."

Aurelia's fingers stopped. "What do you mean?"

"Somewhere along the way I stopped believing I was worthy of my own love."

Aurelia took a sharp breath in and held it, as though she were afraid she'd say the wrong thing. But she continued to stroke Harlow's honey-gold hair, letting her speak.

"I need time to sort all of this out. I know all the ways he made me feel were a ploy to find out Order secrets. You all were right about him. But the stuff he said to me about myself—it felt real. It still does. I have to find a way to get the inside of my head back under my control. Being alone gives me the space to do that."

"Okay, bun. You know Mama and I will help you, don't you? Whatever you need."

"I know. Thank you. You and Mama are so good to us…" she hesitated, not wanting to ruin the tender moment, but as long as they were discussing the hard stuff, she might as well ask. "What do the McKays *really* want from us? Why are you and Mama so worried?"

Aurelia's brow furrowed and Harlow thought she might not answer. But then Aurelia let go of whatever was holding her back. "Things are bad with the Order of Night. The humans' fascination with them is causing problems. We need strong alliances to get them back in line."

"Are they making more vampires?"

Aurelia nodded, her face grave. "And it's not just that, though that is bad enough. They are killing more indiscriminately, though we've managed to keep it quiet so far."

Harlow thought of the vampire in the Grove and how open she'd been about draining a UNT co-ed. The thought of the Order of Night being out of control was chilling. Aurelia continued, "The Illuminated haven't been doing much to stop them, and you know the Order of Masks… The shifters hate to take a side without all the evidence, so that's left the council trying to form alliances with the Illuminated.

"But the Illuminated have been too busy creating more wealth to be interested in the Order of Night, perhaps to compensate for how clear it is that they're no longer reproducing the way they once did. They're consolidating power, which means we should be too."

Finally, Harlow understood the scope of her family's worries about her relationship with Mark, given his fascination with the lower Orders, and the push towards having all five girls in the season. She was sickened to know the Order of Night was being so reckless and that the Illuminated didn't care, but she wasn't surprised. The lower Orders existed in a delicate balance between the unrivaled power of the Illuminated and the massive numbers of humans. The vampires' callous indiscretion could be the end of the lower Orders if they weren't more careful.

"What are we going to do?" Harlow breathed, head reeling with the information.

Aurelia sat back in her chair, shaking her head. "Many things we won't like, I suspect."

The answer was vague, but Harlow didn't get the sense that her mother was being evasive, only frustrated. She wouldn't be this worried about the season and alliances with the Illuminated if this was all there was to the problem. The Order of Mysteries was always navigating power struggles like these.

"What does all this have to do with all of us participating in the season?"

Her mother's head fell to the side, resting on her fist as she frowned. She was contemplating how much to tell Harlow, that much was clear. Harlow's stomach turned. The worry in her eyes was telling. "Mother, what does this have to do with the McKays and Finn? What aren't you telling us?"

Aurelia's chin quivered. Harlow's chest tightened to see her typically serene mother in such consternation. She swallowed hard and drew courage up from some unknown spot inside her. It was better to know than not. "What have they offered?"

"They're offering to back off from buying up the Row, and they'll support us with the Order of Night, get the other high families of the Illuminated Order to force them to fall in line."

They wouldn't offer so much if there wasn't something they wanted in return. "In exchange for what?"

"An heir. They seem certain that you, in particular, could produce one with Finn. I'm not sure why, but they're utterly convinced."

Harlow felt dizzy, suddenly sick to her stomach. "Does he know? Finn, I mean. Is he a part of this?"

Aurelia shook her head, distressed. "I don't know, my darling. I won't ask you to do anything you don't want to, but I don't see how we'll avoid a true disaster with the humans if they don't help us. We'll lose everything. *Everything.*"

"Oh," Harlow sighed, sinking onto Aurelia's footstool. Her proud mother wept in front of her, thin shoulders shaking with furious grief. There was no sign of the flickering aether now, just Aurelia's surrender to her helplessness against the Illuminated's machinations. Harlow's chest constricted sharply with each sob that wracked her mother's frame.

"Mommy," she whispered as her arms went around Aurelia. "Mommy, don't cry."

"I can't help it, my girl. It's shameful to ask you to even consider this, especially after everything you just told me about Mark. I can't ask you to do this. The McKays are hideous, vulgar. Cruel."

"Shhhh," Harlow soothed. "They are, but Finn isn't like that. I'll talk to him."

"No," Aurelia sobbed. "No, Harlow. Don't do it. Oh, my darling, I'm so sorry."

"Mommy," Harlow pleaded. "Mommy, please don't cry. I'll fix things, I promise."

She looked up to see Selene in the doorway, face white as a sheet, clutching her chest, tears streaming down her face at the sight of her strong, proud wife breaking down in her second-eldest's arms.

Harlow motioned to Selene. "Mama, come take her. I have to go."

Selene rushed to Aurelia, replacing Harlow's arms with her own. "I don't want you to worry, either of you. I am going to fix this."

Selene caught her hand. "She's right, my love. Don't do anything rash."

"Finn is different. I'll fix this. Please let me go."

Selene nodded, and Harlow kissed them both, and then went home to think.

CHAPTER 14

Harlow paced the floors of her apartment until the downstairs neighbors pounded on their ceiling. She hopped onto the bed to relieve them from her nervous noise. Her thoughts swirled uncontrollably. She needed to sort things out, figure out a way to stop all this and get things back on track with the Order. More than that, she had to find a way to keep her family safe from the McKays. She might be a ruined specimen of a witch, but she wouldn't see her sisters sacrificed to them, nor would she see her parents turned out of their home.

There had to be something that unwound all of this—something that would set the Kranes and maybe even the entire Order of Mysteries free. It was a tangled knot of issues, and she had no idea where to start untangling it. Her head dropped into her hands in frustration.

Start at the beginning, she thought. But where *was* the beginning?

The night in the Grove. The scream in the forest, and the fact that as far as she knew, she and Finn were the only ones to hear it. Somehow, in all this, they were connected. She didn't want to think about the almost-kiss in the kitchen, or the way Finn's hands had felt on her when he pulled her out of the drunk vampire's way in the Grove, but she did.

It was hard to read him, but if she was honest with herself she knew he still cared for her, and after the things he'd said at her parents' she knew a part of him longed for something she could give him, but that he couldn't seem to have on his own: family. She'd always wondered what she could possibly have to offer Finn McKay, and now she understood; he had the world at his feet, but she had family.

Though she loathed the thought of giving his parents anything they wanted, her family was what was most important. She'd made her decision before she'd even left her parents' house. There wasn't anything left to do but try to get him to agree. She texted Enzo.

Do you have Finn's number?

...

Yes, why?

I need to call him.

Call me first.

I don't have time for this tonight. I'll tell you everything over brunch tomorrow. Promise.

Finn's contact info came through, with a message. *You most certainly will. Eleven. My place.*

Harlow took a deep breath and then called. The phone rang several times, so long she thought she'd get his voicemail, but then he picked up.

"Who's this?" His voice was sleepy. She looked at the clock: nine-thirty. He was asleep at nine-thirty? Shouldn't he be out partying?

"Harlow."

He was immediately alert. "Harls? What's wrong?"

She had to say it or she'd lose her nerve. "Can you meet me at our spot by the river?"

"Are you all right?" He sounded awake now, a bit panicked even.

"Yes. I just need to talk to you."

"Okay." His voice was hesitant. "I can be there in twenty. Do you need a ride?"

"No, I'll see you there."

She hung up and breathed, then changed into leggings and a sweater, sneakers, and a puffer vest to ward off the humid chill in the air. Then she scrambled down the stairs before she could think better of what she was about to do.

Harlow made the walk to Riverside Park in short order. She infused her vest with a tiny bit of magical warmth just for good measure as she folded herself up on a bench to wait. The pine trees in the park whispered in the cold nighttime air, and the scent of freshly mowed grass filled her nose as she waited. Chilly as it was in Nuva Troi, it was still spring and things were beginning to grow again.

"I wish you'd let me drive you," Finn said as he sat down next to her.

He was too close, but she'd sat at the end of the bench and there was nowhere to scoot away from his tantalizing heat. "I'm fine."

"You're clearly not."

She sighed and threw back her head in a silent scream, shaking her fists at the wind. It felt a little embarrassing to lose her cool, but it also made her feel marginally better.

He bumped her shoulder with his. "See. Not fine. What's up?"

The gesture was friendly, too friendly. Maybe that would make things easier. Gods above, she didn't want to be having this conversation. She didn't know any way to begin that might soften the blow of her questions, and she wasn't sure she wanted to. "Did you know about the offers your parents have been making mine?"

She watched his face carefully, wishing she had Enzo's talent for empathy. His eyes darkened with confusion. "No, what do you mean?"

She gave it to him straight, no sugar-coating. "Apparently, if I bear your child they'll stop harassing the Order of Mysteries about buying up the Row and help us to keep the Order of Night from destroying our tenuous alliances with the humans. *Apparently*, the vampires are killing them again and your parents won't help until I make a baby with you."

He sprang away from her, so fast it caught her by surprise. It was easy to forget the Illuminated were different from the rest of the Orders, that they were more like gods than the creatures of the lower Orders—until one of them moved like that or did magic. Then it was easy to remember that they ruled the world with an ironclad grip for a reason.

Fury burned in Finn's eyes. "They…" he appeared to be struggling to breathe. "Said what?"

Harlow was tempted to shrink back. When Mark got angry with her, when his fury rose the way Finn's did now, she always had. But tonight she felt reckless and she let her sharp tongue fly. "Oh, you heard me. Did you know they've been planning this? How long has this been going on?"

She braced for retaliation, for cruel words about her and her family's inferiority. But he didn't react like Mark did to her moments of bravery, with that cold, devious anger that smelled like danger. No, Finn was as distressed as she was. He paced like a caged animal, and for all his bulk and preternatural grace, she wasn't afraid. He was objectively one of the most terrifying people in Nytra, and yet, she was not afraid.

This surprised her. When Mark was angry, she was *always* afraid, frozen with cold terror, waiting to make her next wrong move, because all her moves were wrong when she and Mark argued. But something about Finn's reaction comforted her, as enraged as he seemed. It was clear he wasn't angry at her.

But why should he be? she thought to herself. *It's his family that's done something wrong.*

It hadn't ever mattered who was wrong with Mark. It was always Harlow's fault. Her heart clenched as the depth of the comparison she was making hit her. How had she missed this reality when she lived with Mark? The unfairness of his anger had never occurred to her. Even when she resisted it, deep down, she'd believed it was her fault for mouthing off. For making him mad.

The sound of Finn's voice brought her back to the present moment. He knelt before her. "I didn't know. Harls, I promise. I knew they had some harebrained scheme about you. They've been hinting, but we don't talk much since… Well, ever…" He was out of breath, panicking. "And I knew something was up with the Order of Night, but I thought it was being handled. The sorcière can't keep them in check on their own. Obviously, we need to help. There's too many humans… If they decided to stand against us… Gods, Harlow…"

His eyes were wild as he got up. He began to pace again and she saw the way his hands shook as he moved. On a strange whim, she caught one of them as he passed her. "Finn. *Finn*."

He stopped and knelt in front of her again, his head bowed as though he were a penitent, or a knight to his lady. Her heart thumped a little too hard at the thoughts that his position before her brought up. Finn's voice was determined when he spoke. "I will stop this. I promise."

"How?" The question was simple, but it seemed to break him. He curled into a rather large ball at her feet.

"I don't know. I'll think of something."

She knew it would come to this when she left her parents' house. A part of her had always known it would come down to this when she agreed to take part in the season— that her family's fortune would depend on the two of them. It was what his parents wanted, and they *always* got what they wanted. There wasn't any way out of this, not really. They were trapped, both of them, stuck in inescapable patterns, no matter how much they wanted things to change.

Harlow sighed. "You don't have to. I'll do it."

Finn's head shot up. "You'll do *what?*"

"Have the baby. Give you an heir."

"Pair with me? *Bond* with me?"

She shrugged. "If that's what it takes."

He looked as though he would vomit. "Absolutely not."

"I'm that repulsive to you? Is there someone else?"

He stood, backing away from her in horror. "NO," he shouted.

When she shrank away he looked confused for a moment. Then understanding flickered in his eyes. Some recognition of her reaction, deep within himself. He crouched down again, making himself small in front of her, bowing his head. Finn McKay, one of the most powerful Illuminated in all Okairos, bowed before her, making himself innocuous to soothe her. *What was happening here?*

Harlow's blood rushed through her veins as he gingerly took her fingers into his hands, giving her every opportunity to pull away. When he spoke, his voice was as soft and gentle as it was deep. "No. There's no one else."

He looked up, straight into her eyes and there was not a shred of deceit in them. By now, Harlow knew what manipulation looked like, and there wasn't a trace of its poison on him. "Gods Harlow, do you think I'd really force you into something like that?"

Harlow tried to claw past all the complicated feelings swirling in her chest. Finn McKay might not be fooling her right now, but he was still her enemy. Still one of the Illuminated. He could not be fully trusted. She needed to get the control back in this conversation. "It's not forcing if I accept."

He carefully placed her hands back in her lap and stepped away from her. "Well, I don't. Accept that is. I won't be that to you, and fuck you for trying to convince me to be a part of this."

"Fuck *me?* Are you kidding?" There was that sharp tongue of hers again, just begging to make him angry, egging him on, daring him to turn on her. Daring him to transform into the monster she expected.

But he didn't turn into anything. He stayed infuriatingly *Finn.* He pushed his hands through his dark hair, taking breath after shuddering breath, eyeing her warily. For a moment she saw herself the way he did. Yet another person pushing him to do something he clearly didn't want to do. She could understand that at least, being with her was a nightmare—it was one of the things Mark told her about herself that she truly believed. She wrecked people, and she would hurt Finn too before all this was over; and part of her wanted to, wanted vengeance for how he'd hurt her. She was the monster here, not him.

But Harlow couldn't care about that. She'd already made her decision. She would do whatever it took to keep her sisters from having to make alliances like this one, and she'd keep her Order from losing the little power that was theirs. If the McKays wanted her, they could have her. The baby was another story, but she'd find a way around that later.

His breath steadied and his eyes cleared. "We need to delay my parents' plans so we can figure things out."

Harlow nodded, relieved that he would at least help her. "What do you have in mind?"

He covered his face with his hands and took a few deep breaths. "The Solon Mai event is next weekend. At it, we'll convince everyone we're falling for each other and by Solstice, I'll ask for your hand."

"Okay, I think that was my plan. You just said it nicer—without all the baby stuff."

He shrugged. "It could work to buy us some time anyway."

She rolled her eyes. "Is anyone going to believe we went from hating each other to cozying up at Solon Mai?"

His eyes widened. "You hate me?"

A cold breeze bit into her skin, making her eyes water. "I don't know. I used to."

When she looked up, there was something like despair on his face for a moment. Then it cleared and he was collected as ever. "There's season-sponsored cocktail parties all week this week. We can plan to be at the same ones and you know… warm up to each other again."

"And then what? My family's whole life is on the line here. We need to have a better plan than this."

He slid onto the bench next to her, sitting further away this time. "Hopefully, by Solstice I can convince my parents to do the right thing, leave the Row alone and help with the Order of Night. I'll find something else they want and give it to them. I'll go work for my dad if I have to. You won't have to go through with it and then… I don't know, we'll have a terrible fight and break up."

She sat frozen, listening. It was a decent plan. Not the most brilliant plan of all time. Some would say faking a relationship was an old trick, but it might work. "And what if they don't comply? What if they won't do any of it 'til I breed with you?"

"Holy Raia, Mother of all. The mouth on you."

She looked at him, eyes hard, expecting to see reproach in his expression or the kind of anger that meant he'd punish her for days with the silent treatment. Instead, she found desire, awe, something like pride. His hand drifted towards her, then fell before making contact.

"Well?" she demanded, flustered by the way her heart beat faster every time she pushed him and he didn't react a thing like Mark would have. "What's your plan if none of it works?"

"Then I'll consider your way. But my way will work."

She had her doubts, but at least he'd agreed.

"We'll have to convince everyone," she murmured. "Even Alaric and Thea."

He slid closer and flopped against her with a familiarity that both comforted and scared her. "Especially them. They're the two worst liars I know."

She nodded and got up before things could get too intimate. All of this was confusing, more confusing than she'd anticipated. "See you this week. I'll text you about the parties I want to attend. Not too many though."

He nodded. "One should be enough, and maybe coffee somewhere the Section Seven people like to get photos… Maybe the new place on Eighty-eighth and Vine? The one with the succulent wall everyone on socials likes?"

"Sure. Whatever you want." The whole thing was starting to make Harlow sick. She wanted to go home.

"Should we… talk about things?"

Harlow was already walking away. "What things?" she asked without turning.

"You know what things, Harls."

"No," she said firmly as she walked away.

He trailed behind her as she walked home. He made no secret of following her, but he stayed a block back, and was staring at his phone every time she looked over her shoulder. She raced up the stairs to the terrace to see if he'd waited. He was standing by the street lamp, looking up. She waved, managing a wry smile. He nodded and then walked into the misty dark of the night.

Harlow knew they'd have to talk about it all eventually. One way or another that conversation was coming, but she would do whatever it took to keep her family and her Order from losing what was theirs, and she couldn't have her feelings for Finn McKay screwing that up. She tossed and turned long into the night, worrying herself into shaky, dreamless sleep.

CHAPTER 15

Someone was hammering Harlow's head with a mallet, beating her senseless. She thrashed, fighting them off, but they'd bound her in some sort of sack. A strangled scream, her own, woke her. She was tangled in her sheets, and someone was knocking loudly on her door. She glanced at her phone.

Seven missed calls from Enzo.

It was 11:45.

She'd slept through brunch.

And also apparently, three missed calls from the maters, one from Thea, two from Larkin, and a text message from Finn from ten minutes ago.

She read the text as she stumbled to the door. *I'm all in for Solon Mai and this week, if you still are.*

I am, she replied, then flung open the door to let Enzo in.

He was dressed in a tracksuit she recognized from *Elegante Magazine* as one he'd designed himself. The fabric was printed with dozens of golden snow leopards, with red stripes on the arms and legs, and his hair was in a ponytail.

"I like your outfit," she said as she wiped sleep from her eyes. "Sorry I missed our date. Finn and I were up late."

"If you spill quickly, I won't strangle you for missing brunch," Enzo said, perching on her kitchen counter.

Harlow knew from experience it was best to comply immediately. She yawned as she filled the kettle with water. "Well, you know he took me and Larkin home from the Statuary party, right?"

Enzo nodded as she put the kettle on the stove. He wasn't going to say a word until she'd told him everything. *Close to the truth as you can get it,* she reminded herself. She hated to lie to Enzo, but too much was on the line.

"He stayed and we watched a movie… and there were sparks. But I kind of freaked out. I called him to see if we could try to work things out and we talked for a long time."

"And?"

She poured hot water over a pot of Empress Grey leaves, sprinkling lavender buds and a spoonful of honey in for good measure. It wasn't Duke and Duchess, but it was close enough.

"And I think we're in a better place. We'll see how things go."

"Did he apologize for everything?"

She shook her head. "No, but I think you're right that he's changed."

That was all the truth at least. She hadn't really lied, not yet. She *did* think he'd changed. It's why she'd called him at all, why she'd come up with this terrible plan. Because deep in her heart, she knew there were worse things than being paired with Finn McKay, even if he didn't love her, even if his parents were *his parents*. Like the Order of Night destroying the balance of the world. That would definitely be worse.

Her phone vibrated. Finn. Enzo saw and smiled. "What's Mr. McKay have to say this morning?"

Harlow read the text and blushed.

"Well?"

"He says he hopes you have something indecent planned for my Solon Mai gown."

"That's *exactly* what he said?" Enzo asked with a grin.

Harlow glanced at the text again. "Verbatim."

That was a lie. The text actually said, *Good. Wear something to the Solon Mai ball so indecent that I'd be an idiot not to fuck you on the spot.*

But she couldn't quite bring herself to say that out loud. So she lied. And she'd be lying further if she said that every bone in her body hadn't threatened to turn to jelly when she'd read it. As for her text back, all she could manage was, *Will do.* She was fighting the urge to cringe. Why couldn't she think of better things to say to him? Snappy, clever things?

"I have *ideas*. Will you come to the atelier today? I'm scrapping my old plan for something different."

Harlow texted the maters to tell them she was all right, and going to be fitted for her Solon Mai dress. "Yes, do you want to go now? I have the day off from work."

Enzo laughed. "I bet you do, princess. Let's go."

He sat on the bathroom counter and chatted to her about Riley Quinn as she showered. Apparently, they were just in from Nea Sterlis, which was why she'd never met them before. "They're gorgeous and smart as hell. I'm in so much trouble. My mother would have loved them."

"What do they do for the Order of Masks, any good dirt on them?" Harlow asked as she rinsed her hair.

"That's the funny thing. Riley's not a member of the Order of Masks."

"What?" Harlow peeked out from the shower curtain. "A Rogue?"

Enzo nodded. "A little dangerous."

"Your mother would *not* have loved that."

Enzo smiled wickedly. "But I do."

"You are delighted with this, aren't you?" Harlow flicked water at her friend, who grinned.

"Oh, absolutely. I've always wanted to date an agent of the Rogue Queen."

"So Riley works for her? She's real?"

"Quite real, and yes."

Enzo handed her a towel when she stuck her hand out. "And you're seeing them again when?"

"Riley's coming with me to the Solon Mai ball. By then, it should be our fifth date."

Harlow wrapped herself in a fluffy robe and combed out her hair, then glamoured it dry, with a touch of makeup.

"Most excellent," Enzo said when she came out of the bathroom, and handed her clothes to wear. "Let's get you fitted for something wholly indecent. Something that will make Finn McKay lose his mind."

Harlow gave Enzo a shaky smile and got dressed.

~

SEVERAL HOURS later and the dress was nearly pieced together. Enzo wiped a bit of perspiration off his brow and snapped some photos. "I can finish the rest without you. Do you like it?"

Harlow nodded, hardly recognizing herself in the mirror. The dress was beyond what she could have imagined herself. It conformed perfectly to the Solon Mai standard: ball gowns must be floor length, long sleeved, and always black. Lace or damask were the only approved fabrics. By most stretches of the imagination, this would lead gowns to be rather staid, but in Enzo's capable hands, the dress was wickedly extravagant.

The dress required that Harlow wear a strapless bodysuit that matched the color of her skin perfectly, giving the impression that she was completely nude under the transparent gown. The silky fabric mimicked the patterns of the most intricately woven lace, with none of the usual itch, making her tantalizingly touchable. The bodice fit close and had a high neck, but the skirt swept away from her hips suggestively.

Tiny reflective threads woven into the pattern of the lace shimmered slightly when she moved, giving the dress a subtle glow, rather than the flash of sequins. It was perfectly tasteful, yet wildly sensual at the same time.

"Something's not quite right," Enzo mused, pulling strands of magic from the air around the dress, weaving his vision into reality for the gown. The lace pattern emerged further to look like hundreds of wings, rather than the floral motif he'd started with.

"There," he breathed. "I think that's it."

Harlow could barely speak.

Enzo grinned, snapping a few more photos and then unpinned her from the gown. "I'll get the finish work done shortly."

"What should I do with my hair and makeup?" Harlow murmured, watching the fabric move in Enzo's hands as she changed back into her clothes.

"Nothing fussy. Since you will already appear to be nearly nude, I'd go for something loose. Already mussed."

Harlow smiled. "You are a gift, you know that?"

Enzo repinned the dress to the mannequin in Harlow's size. "Oh, I know."

Harlow scanned through the titles of the books on Enzo's shelves. "Have you ever thought about writing a book?"

He looked up from his work, his dark eyes slightly surprised. "Yes, how did you know?"

Harlow shrugged. "You're just so talented, and the way your magic manifested was so brilliant. I hope you'll write lots of books. The world should know more about you."

Enzo hugged her fiercely. "Thank you for saying that, Harlow. It means a lot. Now go! I have half a dozen dresses to finish."

She kissed him goodbye, and left feeling thoughtful.

CHAPTER 16

Her conversation with Enzo made her think about her own magic as she walked through the vibrant atmosphere of Mulberry Street. Her entire life, she'd been surrounded by talented sorcière. People with innate gifts so strong, even before their magic manifested, that it was obvious what their magical abilities would mature into. She wasn't like that.

Harlow couldn't identify a single talent of her own. It wasn't that she was mediocre; she was perfectly competent at many things, but unlike the other sorcière she knew, she wasn't particularly good at any *one* thing. She had lots of passions, many talents, and as such was at a complete loss as to how her magic would mature, and the sorcière she would settle into. It made her feel like a flake.

She headed toward the Monas. She wanted to do some reading for the rest of the afternoon. The maters had a collection on manifestation; surely she could find the answers she sought and jumpstart her stalled progress. A nasty voice inside her reasoned that if her problems could be solved with books, she'd already have solved them. Harlow steeled herself against the voice, pulling her coat tighter around her body.

As she made her way through the crowded streets of the Row, a cold, hard body knocked into her shoulder, pushing her off course. She looked behind her to find Olivia Sanvier scowling at her. She was even lovelier in person than she was in photos, with shoulder length red hair, pale skin, and the kind of lips that made her black lipstick look elegantly gothic, rather than foolish. The intensity of the hatred the vampire was projecting was startling.

Harlow tried to move aside. "Oh, sorry. I must not have seen you."

The vampire mirrored her movements with eerie accuracy, blocking her way. "Watch where you're going, witch."

Harlow felt the throb of her heartbeat in her veins acutely, as a chill slid into her bones. She was surprised by the tone the encounter was headed. She'd only met Olivia socially a few times, and they had been utterly unremarkable. Aside from the fact that Olivia was seeing Mark now, Harlow couldn't think of any reason for her to be so hostile. She'd been jealous of exes before, but this was something else, something visceral. Surely this couldn't all be about Mark, could it?

And like she'd summoned him just by thinking his name, Mark appeared, stepping out of a store that primarily sold divination tools, with a large shopping bag in his arms.

"Harlow," he said with a tight smile. "It's nice to see you. Liv, this is Harlow Krane."

Olivia rolled her eyes. "We've met. She ran right into me. She's as clumsy as you said."

Harlow's cheeks burned with embarrassment. Of course Mark had been talking badly about her. That certainly wasn't a shock, but everything about this encounter thrummed with an undercurrent that warned her to stay alert.

"Not really a surprise though, with all that body. She must run into things all the time." Olivia laughed and took Mark's free hand in hers. The gesture was possessive, and the air around her crackled with feral energy. Olivia Sanvier was a dangerous vampire, as petty as she was powerful, apparently.

Mark laughed, a cruel sneer on his lips, but added nothing, turning sharply away from her in abject dismissal. Harlow felt as though she would crumple into the sidewalk, flat under their feet. She couldn't remember a time in the recent past that she'd felt so small. But then, she'd been back among the only people she was sure she could trust. Now, cowering here in front of Mark, she remembered too acutely what the last few months of their relationship had been like—the constant derision, interspersed with briefer and briefer periods of intense passion.

"Well, good to meet you," Harlow said, unsteady on her feet as they passed her.

Olivia sneered, her fangs showing and her stony eyes fierce. "See you again soon, witch. Don't worry, I'm taking *good care* of your little kitty."

Something splintered into dozens of jagged pieces inside Harlow as she watched them hail a cab and head uptown, towards the House of Remiel. Mark glanced at her from the back seat, a smug glint in his eyes. What had Olivia meant by that? She'd never heard of vampires feeding off animals, but of course they *could*. They had blood, after all. *Would Mark let Olivia hurt Axel?*

Deep in her gut, she knew he would. He'd let the House of Remiel's princess do whatever in seventeen hells she wanted to get what *he* wanted: more power. It was the only thing he'd ever been interested in, she understood in a sickening, enlightening moment. From the day they met, until the day he kicked her out, all he'd ever wanted was more power. He'd never wanted *her* at all.

For a moment, she understood it. Though the lower Orders were ruled just as stringently as the humans by the Illuminated, they were not their victims in the same way. But Mark was something else. Rich and powerful in his own right, he was exempt from things like the monthly blood donations required of other humans, and she knew the Eastons had never undergone the kinds of rigorous screenings most humans suffered in order to qualify to procreate. He'd had as much power as she had growing up, perhaps more, because his family was so much wealthier than hers. He'd never wanted justice or equality between the creatures of Okairos, not the kind she dreamed of.

How had she been so foolish? How had she ever believed he wanted the same things she did? How had she been so easily seduced by a few carefully constructed conversations in the beginning that never amounted to anything? How had she let things get so bad that she'd leave Axel with him?

Something bloomed deep within her as she hailed a cab of her own, something fierce and primal, protective. The fibers of magic in the air around her snapped, as though she'd done something to alter reality, but she was too focused on her plan to pay much attention. Her vision focused sharply and all her senses heightened in a way that made her feel like a cat stalking prey.

Harlow gave the cabbie Mark's address. He'd taken her key back, but it didn't matter. Today was the day she was taking Axel, and the final shreds of her self-respect she'd left behind, back. The elite human sector downtown in Greenvale Slope was as lovely and well-kept as any of the Orders' sectors, but Harlow barely registered the scenery. Something inside her was writhing, changing, begging to be let out. She paid the cabbie without speaking a word and swept into the building she'd lived in for nearly two years.

Salvatore, the human doorman, waved to her as she passed, looking worried. She knew he'd be too afraid to stop her, and as she expected, he was dialing the phone at his desk as the elevator doors closed. She had at least a half-hour, given traffic at this time of day, to get Axel and get out before Mark could make it back to this side of town. She closed her eyes, waiting for the elevator to reach the fourteenth floor.

Harlow floated out of the elevator, as if in a dream. She wasn't sure if it was the shock of coming face to face with Mark and Olivia, or if she was finally losing it, but her vision was blurry and she could have sworn magic crackled around her from elsewhere, beyond the threads that made up everything on Okairos. She would have to consider that later. Right now, she had only one goal.

"I'm coming, baby boy," she murmured, though she wasn't exactly sure how she would achieve that. Some force in her, whatever bloomed on Mulberry Street, urged her on.

From somewhere inside the apartment, she heard Axel howling in response. He could hear her. Absolute fury overcame her and her vision went completely dark for a moment. Her eyes shot open to the sound of the door flying past her, into the hallway. She'd just torn it off its hinges. That was something new, but she would have to think about that later. Someone had opened the door to their apartment, so now she probably needed to worry about the city guard, in addition to Mark returning.

"Axel?" she whispered, not wanting to step foot inside her former prison. For that's what it had been after he'd persuaded her to quit her job at the human bookstore: a prison.

Inside, the sounds of frantic yowling and a loud thud echoed through the cold hallways. Axel was shut up somewhere. Whatever new power seethed in her propagated at an unbelievable rate, filling her to the brim with an undulating force begging to be let out.

Harlow stepped inside the apartment, her skin prickling as a flood of memories threatened to wash her new confidence away. The dynamic force of the power in her fluctuated, changing by the moment. Harlow rode the waves of it as best she could, and found that she sailed along the currents of the storm within her with ease. There was no danger of her losing control now.

"Axel. Baby boy, where are you?" she called. The sound of her voice was alien, deep and resonant, shaking the walls and doors.

The volume of Axel's yowling increased and there was another loud thud. He was locked in the hall bath. She ran down the tiled hallway, willing her fear to subside enough to carry her through this. Harlow yanked on the door, which always stuck a little, and it flew open, releasing the stench of feline urine and feces. Mark hadn't been regularly cleaning up after the cat, and the bathtub was full of waste. Harlow tamped down her rage, focusing on searching for Axel. Her eyes met two golden pools of wrath.

Axel was sitting on the counter, enraged by his captivity, but clean enough, given the circumstances. His usually silky coat was dull though, and the fur around his middle sank into the impression of his ribs—not much, but enough for Harlow to know he hadn't been eating enough. Mark and Olivia would pay for this, but not until she got him away, made sure he was safe. Tears streamed down her face as she opened her arms. Axel cried, the piteous sound breaking Harlow's heart, as he jumped into her arms, clinging tightly to her.

He'd been a sleek, muscular eighteen pounds when Mark kicked her out, and now he was skinny and far too light. She held him close as she ran for the hallway and the stairs, everything behind them a blur. Harlow refused to look back, knowing that her window of time to escape without question was narrowing. As she went, the elevator showed that a car was coming up and she didn't want to be on this floor when it arrived.

"Hold on, baby boy," she cautioned. "We're going home."

The cat nuzzled against her face, purring happily, which shattered her heart even further as she raced down flight after flight of stairs. It was impossible to imagine how he could be so happy to see her when she left him behind. It didn't matter now. All that mattered was getting him out of here.

A shout rang out from the flights above her; the city guard she supposed. Footsteps clattered down behind her and she ran faster, but they were gaining and she had several more flights to go—and then what? She hadn't asked the cabbie to stay, and even if she had, they wouldn't have run from the city guard for her.

She'd be caught and they might even make her give Axel back to Mark. Somewhere, deep inside, a voice reminded her that was unlikely to happen, that her mothers were important people, that Finn might even help her, but the protective instinct that drove her on overrode that logic. The same instinct bade her to halt, suggesting something she didn't even know was possible. But she wouldn't question it, not now, with Axel in her arms and freedom just a few flights of stairs away.

"Hold tight," she warned Axel, who stared murderously up at the guards clambering down the stairs.

Aether crackled around her, flowing through the threads of magic she pulled at with her free left hand, holding Axel close with her right. Midnight blue shadows spilled from her fingers as she wove sigils of protection, the most basic she knew. It was all she could think of to do, but when she'd finished, nothing happened. The threads of magic didn't shift the way they were supposed to. In fact, nothing happened.

She'd somehow pulled a door off its hinges on her way in, but couldn't do a simple protection spell? What was wrong with her?

The most basic tenet of magic occurred to her then: magic is will, woven into reality. The aether was the power, but magic, at its core, was a matter of will. Harlow felt something stirring within her, and her spirit eye snapped open in the limen, the world between all worlds, where her spirit form flew as if on giant wings towards the heart of the limen, where all magic came from. It was full of inky blue shadows, just like the ones that came from her. They seemed to sing when they saw her coming. Power coursed through her spirit form, into her material body.

Harlow blinked and was back in the stairwell. The city guard was nearly upon them, their feet pounding the metal stairs. She didn't have time to think, but she glanced down at the shadows swirling around her and whispered a plea, "Protect us."

By Akatei's grace, the shadows dancing at her fingertips came alive and the aether crackled once more as the shadows billowed out of her, filling the stairwell, until the light from the fluorescents disappeared entirely. The sounds of the guards' shouts muffled to a dull roar as Harlow walked calmly down the remaining flight of stairs, out the back door and onto the concrete stairs that led to the alley. She pressed her hand to the closed door, more shadows flowing from her touch, and wished she knew a way to lock the door.

Something vibrated softly under her hand, and a lock appeared and turned of its own accord, looking as though it had always been there. A key appeared in her hand and she tucked it into her purse, clutching Axel tight, relief edging each breath she took. She couldn't explain what was happening with her magic, but they were almost free.

As she turned to walk down the steps she felt her second sight engage. A glassy wall, opaque and treacherous, rose up before her. She and Axel had been here before, the night she and Mark split up.

"I don't have time for this now," she breathed, holding Axel just a bit tighter.

Her second sight refused to disengage and Harlow had the distinct sense that she was falling, as if in a dream. The shadows that had filled the stairwell flooded her mind's eye now, pulling her back into the reality outside her connection to the aether.

Thank you, she thought to herself. Whatever it was, this primal force was helping her. The glass wall was gone and she could move again. Inside the building, she heard the city guard shouting, pulling on the door. They would go around the building eventually. If she didn't want to be caught, she had to leave now.

Harlow walked as calmly as she could out of the alley onto the street, and hailed another cab, stepping into it with only a quick glance behind her. No one followed as the cab pulled away, and the shadows had disappeared.

"Don't usually let animals in the cab, miss," the cabbie remarked as he pulled into traffic.

"I understand," Harlow said, clinging to Axel. "I'll pay extra."

The cabbie glanced at her in the rearview mirror. "You two running from something bad?"

Harlow met his gaze in the mirror, and she saw the fear that she'd been suppressing surface in her reflection. "My ex."

He nodded then, understanding in his gentle brown eyes. There were still good people in the world. People who would help someone in trouble, just because they recognized that kind of fear. The cabbie's voice was calm when he said, "Let's get you two home then."

"Thank you," Harlow murmured, giving him the Monas' address. She buried her face in Axel's fur and wept silently with relief. "Let's go home," she whispered to her cat, who still clung to her, purring softly in her ear.

CHAPTER 17

Harlow paid the cabbie extra, just as she'd promised, even though he hadn't charged her anything for bringing Axel. He watched her closely from the cab until she pushed the front door of the shop open, waving to him to let him know she was fine. The cab pulled away from the curb and Harlow stumbled inside the Monas. As she did, the impact of what she'd done hit her, wooziness flooding her limbs. She was surprised to find the shop empty of customers. What time was it?

Harlow tripped on the edge of the rug at the front door, righting herself quickly, but shaky on her feet. Larkin looked up from the register as Harlow stumbled toward the couches at the center of the main floor showroom. Axel leapt from her arms onto one of the green couches. She met his lamp-like eyes as she crumpled to the ground.

"Mama!" Her youngest sister's scream filled her ears as she tried to sit up, to reach her cat.

Selene came rushing out from the back and helped her onto one of the couches at the center of the showroom floor. Axel leapt into Harlow's lap, hissing protectively at Selene. Mama raised her eyebrows at the cat, and her voice was sharp when she issued her command. "Lock the doors, Larkin. We're closed."

Larkin did as she was told. "Is there anyone else here?"

Selene shook her head after a moment of appraisal, using her magic to probe the shop. "I don't think so. Go get Li-li. Now."

Larkin disappeared. Harlow was dizzy, but Axel's weight comforted her. "What's wrong with me?" Her words were clumpy in her mouth, which felt dry and swollen.

Selene held up one of Harlow's hands, showing it to her. All of her fingers were deepest midnight blue, as though she'd dipped them in a vat of ink. "Has this ever happened before?"

Harlow shook her head.

"What happened before you came in? Tell me everything, in detail."

Aurelia appeared, with Larkin and Thea. "The twins are double checking that we're alone. Dear gods, is that what I think it is?"

She was looking at her fingers, not Axel. Harlow was sure Mother knew what a cat was. That struck her as funny, and she giggled, stroking Axel's back, which was heartachingly bony.

Selene shushed her wife, sparing only a glance for the cat. "Tell me everything that happened, Harlow."

"I saw Mark, and the vampire princess. She threatened to hurt Axel... So I went and got him." Her head was cloudy, and she was having trouble remembering exactly what had happened.

"Keep talking," Selene urged. "Then what?"

"I made the door fly off. Then the city guarffs came... the city guarf. The city *guard*... Yes, that's it. They came and the shadows ate them up and then I locked them in the building! A nice human drove me howl. *Home*."

She felt inebriated. That was what this feeling was. Aurelia examined her stained fingers, showing Thea. "Get the Merkhov text and something for this cat to eat. The fourth volume from the new shipment—for the book, not the cat food. Get the cat some kind of meat."

Thea nodded, apparently knowing the book Aurelia referenced, and having some idea of how to feed a cat. Thea was so smart. The smartest smarty there had ever been probably, except for Mother, and maybe scientific geniuses. Harlow's mind swirled with the train of thoughts that careened wildly off course.

"I feel drunk," Harlow said, her voice fuzzy-sounding in her ears.

"We don't need the Merkhov to confirm this," Selene said softly. "I thought my grandmother was the last of them, but this is just like what she described, down to the stained fingers. I made her tell me how it happened to her the first time—when we decided to have children... so I'd know the signs."

Aurelia nodded. "I believe you, but I don't think having the Merkhov on hand will hurt. Larkin, please go make a very strong pot of tea. Your sister is going to need something bracing."

Larkin did as she was bid. Selene helped Harlow into a more upright position, gripping her chin tightly in her fingers. "Look at me. Did you use any magic? Do anything with it?"

Harlow bobbed her head vigorously. Too vigorously. Now her vision swam. "Yes, I made a lock for the door and filled the stairwell with shadows. *Beautiful* shadows... They came out of my *hands*! I got him back, my baby boy. Isn't he such a good boy?"

Aurelia laughed softly at Harlow's babbling, then grew serious as she spoke to her wife. "Her heart is so big; she did all this for the cat. Is this why this happened?"

Selene shook her head as Axel flexed his paws against Harlow's leg and then nestled into her side for a nap. "Perhaps. Sometimes feelings of protectiveness or heightened stress can trigger it. Li-li, this explains why she's such a late bloomer.

Striders typically don't come into their power until they're twenty-five or six. Sometimes later."

Annoyance prickled at the corners of Harlow's awareness. "Stop talking about me. I'm right here." She felt a mug press into her hands.

Larkin smiled at her gently. "Drink up."

Selene nodded, urging her on. "It won't always be like this, bun. A Strider's initial manifestation is typically a bit dramatic. It's addled you a bit. Drink your tea."

"Tea solves everything," Larkin whispered.

Axel darted forward from his spot next to Harlow and she opened her eyes more fully to watch him eat from a plate of plain chicken. She sipped from the warm mug slowly; Larkin was right, tea did solve everything. Thankfully, everyone stopped speaking while she drank.

Thea returned with a thick leather-bound book that looked as though it had sustained terrible water damage. She already had it open when she handed it to Aurelia. Mother nodded as she read a few pages, and then handed the book to Selene.

Harlow started to feel more like herself, the wooziness wearing off slowly as she sipped the fragrant Duke and Duchess tea, breathing in the comforting scent of lavender, vanilla and rose. She flexed her fingers. They ached slightly, but the inky stain was starting to fade.

Axel finished eating and then climbed into her lap, turned thrice, and then curled his nose into his long tail. His soft, rhythmic purrs soothed her further as she stroked his fur, which was in poor shape after six months with Mark. They'd fix all that—there were veterinary experts in the Order—she'd make sure he saw the best ones, sorcière who'd fix him up, and fit him with his own protective sigil that would keep anyone from harming him again.

Her mind drifted back to the conversation at hand. What the maters were saying was perplexing, but something deep within her warmed to the ideas they discussed. It all made a certain kind of sense.

"What's a Strider?" she asked when she'd drained her mug.

Larkin was reading the book now, her eyebrows raised, her open mouth covered with one hand. "A bridge between the aether and Okairos," she murmured from behind her hand.

Meline and Indigo came downstairs. "There's no one here. We swept twice," Indigo said softly to Selene. Even though the wards were set up to indicate such things with a high degree of accuracy, the maters had instilled a value in their girls not to solely depend on magic. Magic, like all things, was fallible.

Meline read over Larkin's shoulder. "Harlow can use pure magic? She doesn't have to weave threads or use spells?"

Selene shrugged. "That's what Grandmama always said. Spells and weaving didn't work for her once she'd manifested. She had to do everything by instinct. She was one of the last of a line of sorcière that could access magic at its source. I haven't heard of another coming into power for years, but that's not surprising. The Illuminated don't like them much, as you might imagine; it's likely they hide, if any still exist."

All of her sisters spoke at once. Harlow couldn't make out one vein of the conversation, let alone a quarter dozen. She was trying to parse out the idea that she would no longer be able to do spells, or weave threads of magic in the ways she was used to, but they were all *so noisy*. It had happened to *her*, and no one had asked her how *she* felt about it.

"Stop. Talking. *About*. Me," Harlow hissed. Strands of magic around her snapped and she watched her fingers stain with dark, inky magic. Her vision darkened slightly, as though she'd slipped sunglasses on. Axel's ears swiveled, but he did not move. In fact, he seemed even more relaxed.

Everyone quieted as they turned to look at her.

"Oh Harlow," Thea breathed. "You're divine."

Indigo nodded. "The embodiment of Akatei."

"Hush, don't be blasphemous," Meline cut her off. But Meline switched her phone's screen to front-camera and showed Harlow her face, as though she held up a mirror. Harlow's eyes had gone completely dark, pinpricks of galaxies being born or dying lighting from deep within. And the filaments of magic swirling around her fingers undulated in formless waves, like liquid shadow, rather than the usual iridescent strands she was used to seeing.

"Put that down," Harlow commanded her sister. Her voice sounded strange, like hers, but something more. So it hadn't just been the apartment's acoustics. Meline put the phone down instantly. It was the fastest she'd seen one of the twins obey, ever.

"Harlow, calm down," Aurelia said, taking Harlow's dark blue fingers in hers. "We'll explain everything. Girls, could you give me and Mama a few minutes with your sister?"

Slowly, her sisters dispersed. Harlow watched Thea usher them upstairs, and she knew exactly which step her eldest sister sat on in the stairwell to eavesdrop. It wasn't her heightened senses that told her this, though she thought they might be able to capture such an image, but rather years of sisterly experience. She'd sat on that step with Thea, dozens of times, listening to what went on in the shop below, when she was supposed to be abed.

The familiar childhood memory of eavesdropping with Thea on Order meetings brought her back to herself. She felt the magic recede and her vision cleared to show her a matched set of worried mothers. Axel sighed deeply in his sleep, turning on his side so she could rub his soft belly fur. "So, are you going to explain what's happening to me now?"

Selene draped an arm around her and hugged her. "Your magical talent has manifested, my love. And it's a bit different than we expected it might be."

"Though perhaps we should have seen the signs earlier," Aurelia mused as she flipped through the pages of the Merkhov book, which had no title, only a damaged black leather cover. A mild mildew scent floated up from the pages, confirming that it had either been damaged by water or stored someplace damp. "It says here that Striders often tend to feel displaced and misunderstood."

Something heavy lifted from Harlow's heart. "Really?" Her head was starting to clear.

Aurelia nodded. "Yes, it also says that Striders tend to be competent, and even good at many things before their magic matures, which can further confuse them. I am so sorry, Harlow, I should have hunted this book down sooner, knowing that your great-grandmother was a Strider herself."

"But what is a Strider? Why can't I weave threads or use spells?"

Selene's smile was gentle. "Because you don't need them, my love. What happened when you protected yourself and Axel from the guard, when you actually tried to use magic?"

Harlow remembered the way her spirit body had flown. "I went to the limen in my spirit body—but it was different than it typically is. I think I had wings."

Aurelia seemed to be tracking what she said in the book, nodding. "The limen is where all aethereal power comes from, it's the heart of magic."

Axel settled against her, purring deeply. "That's what you meant when you said I could use magic at its source. I'm using liminal magic."

Selene made a humming noise. "Not exactly. The limen is rather large, a world unto itself, with its own magical rules. To use what we typically term 'liminal magic' you would have to be a creature of the limen itself. You are simply drawing magic from its most potent source, rather than through the threads of reality. There is no conduit between you and your power."

Harlow stared at the herringbone pattern of the wood floor beneath her feet. A hundred competing feelings rattled around inside her. She wasn't sure if she wanted to laugh or cry.

Aurelia passed the book to Selene, pointing to a particular passage. "It says here that the lineage sometimes skips two to three generations, but that Striders are typically born into times when their powers are needed most."

Selene closed the book without reading the passage Aurelia indicated. "Harlow? Are you all right?"

"Sure, Mama. I'm fine. I'm always fine."

Selene cupped Harlow's face in her warm hands. "My darling, that is not true. No one is always fine."

Harlow shrugged, looking anywhere but at either of her parents. She wanted to drag Axel off her lap and hug him tightly to her chest, but he looked so peaceful that she let him be. "So what does this all mean? How do Striders use magic if they don't use spells or weave threads? I assume it's a bit different from the rest of you, since I don't know anyone whose manifestation made their fingers turn colors."

Aurelia's smile was wide. "Each Strider's process is a little different, so there's no methods, no spells. She must learn to trust herself, her intuition. And then, Harlow... A Strider's power is as strong as her will. There are limits, of course, but each Strider must find the edges of her magic on her own."

That sounded a bit frightening. "So no one can teach me?"

Selene shook her head. "No, dearest, I'm afraid not."

There was a rustle of footsteps on the stairs, and a flurry of whispers. "Just come in here," Selene called.

Larkin and Thea rushed into the room. Thea clasped a second book to her chest. "Larkin found this. It's the companion to the Merkhov book, a collection of facsimiles of the texts Merkhov worked with primarily to write her book. Look at this."

Larkin set up a cradle on the coffee table and they gathered round to look at the facsimile of a triptych. The writing underneath each image was indecipherable, written in glyphs Harlow had never seen before. The images themselves were difficult to make out, because of the damage to the book, but she could make out scales in the first two and bodies that looked like snakes. The third seemed to depict something else entirely.

"They almost look like the humans' alchemical illuminations," Selene murmured. "Merkhov's book isn't about alchemy though. It is about navigating the limen, and those who move between. Thea, can you do anything about the images?"

Meline and Indigo peeked through the door to the back stairs. "Can we come in?"

Selene motioned to them and somehow all seven of the Krane women piled onto one couch together. Selene stroked Harlow's hair as Thea worked. Axel jumped onto the back of the couch, stretching his long body out contentedly, resting his chin on Harlow's shoulder as he too watched the oldest Krane sister manipulate reality.

Thea pulled strands of magic quickly, hands darting here and there as she wove them together with expert grace. "I hadn't planned to start either of these texts until next month. I will get to it immediately, but... yes, there... That's better."

The first illumination in the triptych was beautiful. It depicted two snakes, each consuming the other's tail, encircling a semi-transparent sphere that encased a giant egg. The upper snake's body had likely been gilded in the original manuscript, while the intensity of the lower snake's dark blue hue was probably derived from lapis. The originals had to have been extremely costly to produce.

"The color of the snake," Larkin gasped, grabbing Harlow's hands. "It looks familiar, doesn't it?"

Selene's mouth pressed into a grim line as she gazed at the metallic gleam of the upper snake's body. Thea continued her work and shortly the first image was much clearer, showing that the gilded snake emitted light, while the lower snake did not. Selene stared into her wife's eyes for a long time before Aurelia shook her head, worry creasing her brow.

"What is it?" Harlow asked as Aurelia stared off into the distance. "What do you think this represents?"

"A union," Selene said softly. "Your mother believes this represents a union."

"Of who?" Indigo murmured as Thea sank to the floor in front of Selene. Everyone shifted slightly as Larkin joined her, spreading out a bit more. Larkin poured her eldest sister a cup of tea, and Thea sipped gratefully. The maters were suspiciously quiet.

"The gilded snake represents the Illuminated, doesn't it?" Meline asked, though it hardly sounded like a question. "And the blue snake may depict a

Strider. It's not the pure blue of a lapis ink. They must have mixed it with something else to get the darker hue. Maybe tumsole or a bit of vermillion?"

It was a mistake to think that Indigo and Meline only cared about society happenings and their socials. They were as well versed in manuscript production as any of the Kranes.

As if to prove this fact, Indigo nodded at her sister thoughtfully. "Two snakes, locked in what… a destructive cycle? But they're protecting the egg… What do you think the other two images show, Thea?"

Thea shrugged. "I'm a little tired from the rapid-restoration, pal. I'll keep working on the other two and then I guess we'll see."

"I suspect they depict what will happen if a Strider and one of the Illuminated procreate," Aurelia replied bitterly.

Selene let out a deeply held breath in an angry hiss, and Harlow's heart began to pound. If the original triptych represented some sort of indicator about what would happen if a Strider procreated with one of the Illuminated it could explain the McKays' interest in her pairing with Finn. "Do you think the McKays have seen this? Do they know what I am? What book is this originally from?"

"I don't know the answers to any of those questions, darling." Aurelia shook her head as the collective tension held between the seven of them filled the room. "I think until we know more, we should keep this between us."

"If the McKays have seen this…" Harlow mused, the possibilities endless and terrifying. "Maybe they know more than we do already."

Meline looked thoughtful, her knack for thinking through complex social problems in overdrive. "That's possible, of course, but if you want the upper hand, you need to act as if you don't know."

Indigo nodded at her twin. "Exactly. And if you want to draw them out, find out what they know, you should start making nice with Finn."

Harlow narrowed her eyes at the twins. This was her plan, of course, but the two of them were excellent social strategists. It made sense to hear them out. "Why?"

Meline shifted out from under Indigo's legs. "Because if they think they're getting their way, they're likely to let their guard down. Right now, they're vigilant, trying to get the two of you together. If they think they're winning, they might show their hand."

"Do you think Finn knows what this is all about?" Larkin asked, eyes worried. Harlow read her easily; Larkin liked Finn and didn't want to be disappointed in him.

Meline and Indigo shrugged in unison. "It's hard to say. There are pros and cons to both sides. If he regularly defies them, probably not. They'd want to keep their motives a secret as long as possible."

Thea looked uncomfortable. Harlow kicked her lightly. "You have secret-face, Thea."

Everyone turned to look at the eldest Krane sister. "Alaric told me some things. Many of them are irrelevant to this conversation and private…" She was clearly flustered. "But if I had to make a guess, he doesn't know. Finn hates his parents. Isn't that right, Harlow?"

Harlow nodded. "He does. But he's desperate for their approval."

Thea's face revealed she had more to say.

Aurelia looked annoyed. "Spit it all out, Thea, for Goddess-sake."

"It's not mine to tell. All I'll say is that I don't think Finn would help his parents hurt Harlow." She took Harlow's hand. "You need to talk to him, pal. You need to let him tell you what happened before uni."

"She can't tell him all this," Meline screeched. "He might be the enemy here."

Harlow untangled herself from her family's arms. "Thank you for your thoughts. If it's okay, I think I'm going to go home. I need a few days to myself. I'll see you all at the Metro for the Solon Mai ball."

Selene kissed her cheek. As protective as she was of her children, she always knew when to let them have space. "We'll be here, love."

Harlow nodded, and kissed her family goodbye, one by one and then slid into her coat. "Come on, Axel," she murmured as the black cat leapt from the back of the couch to follow her. "Let's go home."

CHAPTER 18

Harlow knew Thea would follow, so she walked slowly, waiting in the alley for her sister. She scooped Axel into her coat, whispering to him that he'd had a big day and should let her carry him home. Soon enough, the sound of hurried footsteps signaled Thea's approach. She was pulling her coat on and extending an umbrella to fend off the rain that hung in the air, rather than fall in heavy drops.

"Hey pal, thanks for waiting." Thea's smile didn't reach her eyes.

Harlow ducked under the umbrella and looped her free arm through Thea's, taking in her heady orchid and wood scent. "You want to walk us home?"

Thea gripped her arm, to steady herself or Harlow, she didn't know. "That would be good."

They walked in silence for a while. Axel purred softly against Harlow's chest, content to curl against her as they walked. Thea seemed deep in thought, and Harlow knew better than to rush her sister while she was working out the right way to say something. She'd speak when she was ready.

"Finn told Alaric about your plan. He was worried he couldn't pull it off alone. Alaric wasn't supposed to tell me…"

Harlow sighed. "But he did."

Thea sounded uncomfortable. "Yes."

"Are you going to tell Alaric about me being a Strider?"

"No! Harlow, I would never. You're my sister and… Do you really think I would?"

Harlow shrugged. "I guess I don't know much about how close you are. Why doesn't Finn think he can pull this off alone? I'm sorry it's such a stretch for him to pretend to be interested in me."

Thea stopped, yanking Harlow around to face her under the umbrella with unusual force. Her eyes burned with intense frustration. "Is that what you think? That he needs tips on how to *fake* being in love with you?"

"What else am I supposed to think?" Harlow's voice was an octave or two higher than usual, the shrill sound of her words grating on her nerves. Axel grumbled at the decibel of her voice from inside her coat.

Thea shook her head and stepped back, leaving Harlow in the rain that was falling in earnest now. "You need to talk to him. Hear him out about what happened between you."

"Why can't *you* just tell me?"

Thea was already walking back towards the Monas. She didn't stop as she called over her shoulder, "It will be better if you talk to him. In person, preferably." She stopped and turned around. "Tell him everything, Harlow. I mean it. *Everything.*"

That was in direct violation to what the twins had suggested. Harlow watched her sister disappear into the falling darkness, wondering what Thea knew that the twins did not, and then trudged home. The stairs to her apartment felt even steeper with Axel in her jacket. He seemed to sense her slowing down and jumped out, racing up the stairs ahead of her. When she unlocked the door he ran inside, excited to look around, and then sat down hard.

"Not much here, huh?" Harlow said. "Lots to look at out on the terrace though."

She opened the door for him and he immediately went outside and curled up in one of the plastic chairs Harlow had placed under the narrow awning that provided a bit of shelter from the rain. He purred happily, as if to say, "This will do," and then promptly fell asleep.

Harlow tossed her phone on the bed and changed out of her wet clothes and into a pair of silk pyjamas Enzo had tucked into one of the bags of clothes they'd taken home. She found an empty box that could make do for a litter box, tearing up a newspaper to substitute for litter, and called Axel into the bathroom, where she tucked the box behind her sink.

"Can you go there 'til we get some litter?"

He bumped his head against her leg, agreeing. They went to the kitchen together and she got out a bowl for water and pulled a chicken breast out of the fridge, cutting it up and placing it on a plate next to the bowl on the floor. Axel ate a few bites and then hopped onto her bed, meowing plaintively. She obliged him, climbing into bed and nestling into the pile of pillows as he curled into a ball, warm and cozy in the blankets.

Tears clouded Harlow's vision as she stroked his back. After so many months of feeling unbearably lonely, she could hardly believe her little friend was here now. Safe. They were *both* safe. No one could enter the apartment without her express desire for them to do so. This was the secret of this building, the reason she'd been interested in it in the first place. The wards were second-to-none, built straight into the bones of the building itself, complex and customizable, making this a veritable fortress. Mark couldn't get to either of them here.

As Axel's tiny feline snores drifted into the air, mixing with the sounds of the rain on the terrace, Aurelia's words ran through her head on repeat: *each Strider's process is a little different, so there's no methods, no spells. She must learn to trust herself, her intuition.*

She lit the candles on her bedside table with a quick twist of the threads near them, then got comfortable, focusing narrowly on her breath. She listened to the sounds of her apartment, of Axel snoring, and allowed them to disappear from her notice. Her eyes relaxed and her vision softened until her second sight engaged.

Harlow felt for the filaments of magic that surrounded her, the fibers of reality that wove gracefully together to build the world as she knew it. They were in everything, glowing strong in her, as a living being, and slightly faded in inanimate objects, but still they lit softly at her notice, as they always had. Now though, she saw the other side to the light, the shimmering darkness from which the threads of power grew and conducted aether into the whole of Okairos.

She was certain she was seeing between, into the limen, beyond reality into the source of magic itself. She allowed her second sight to focus on that fertile shadow. It called to her, its sweet song growing louder in her ears as her fingers reached for it, almost involuntarily. She felt a stab of self-doubt, worried about doing this on her own, and the shadows shrank from her.

Harlow was tempted to cringe, tempted to stop. Her fear was there before her, nearly tangible in its magnitude. For the first time in a long time, she knew exactly what to do. She felt her fear and doubt acutely, every sharp, ragged edge. Instead of pushing them away as she usually did, she welcomed them. Tucked them into her heart, like she would joy or comfort, and began to hum a noteless song of promise.

"I will not abandon you," she murmured.

The shadows swirled at her vow, growing in size and shimmering grace. They swirled towards her outstretched fingers in liquid slow motion. When they made contact, she was full for the first time of what felt like limitless power. Every filament of reality sang before her, begging to be shaped, changed, loved, *made*. All because the source of the light, the fertile dark, had settled within her heart.

"I'll never leave you," she said, a bit louder now. "I'll never turn away."

She knew now that she wasn't speaking only to the living shadow, staining her fingers with its potent power, but also her*self, her* darkness.

"You are mine, and I am yours," she promised the darkness, and its song was a pledge in return. If she would not turn away, if she would take it in and keep it always, it would also keep her. The liquid shadow danced over her skin, then over Axel's fur. She watched in awe as her vision shifted, showing her the sources of all Axel's little hurts, his weakened bones and muscles, the growing malnutrition he was suffering from.

Her heart ached with desire for him to be made whole and well again. Before her eyes, that desire was made real, inside first and finally in the sheen of his fur as he stretched out on the bed, rolling onto his back. His golden eyes opened slightly and he sighed deeply, as though he were comfortable for the first time in ages. Harlow's shadows danced with joy at her success. The rush of pleasure, joy and bittersweet sadness she felt all at once threatened to overwhelm her.

She did not shrink back. She did not turn away. There in the dark, she too was made whole, forged anew. The candles flared. The shadows drank her in and she swallowed them down. Harlow Krane was more herself than she had ever been, and now she was becoming something more than she had ever been before.

CHAPTER 19

Harlow spent the next two days practicing with the shadows. Soon she could manipulate reality in much the same way as her parents and Thea could, but instead of pulling power from the tapestry of magic surrounding her, she used it at its source. The difference was subtle at first, but she sensed as she worked that a profound ability lay beyond what she could immediately understand.

She created furniture for herself, then made it disappear. Decorated the entire apartment, then tore it down, banishing all evidence of what she could do from her sight. Eventually, she settled on making up a litter box for Axel. Her real accomplishment was fashioning an enormous cat tree from scrap wood she found in the basement, which she transformed into gnarled manzanita branches that made the apartment feel like an enchanted forest. The feline climbed into it immediately to look out the windows.

The only thing she could not change was herself. Any time she tried to do more than a basic glamour to enhance her beauty, the shadows refused, as if in disapproval, though there was something else behind the refusal—a sense that she was not ready yet, that there were other steps to take first. Aside from that, her imagination was her only limit, or so she thought. Then she attempted to create a living being from nothing. Just a moth, nothing larger like a mammal.

The shadows shrank back, and she felt the wrongness of it. She spoke aloud to them, apologizing, and then spent time in deep meditation communing with the source of magic as best she could. It didn't use words to communicate, but she felt its desire as though it were speaking. She didn't understand the power yet, but her affinity with it grew by the hour. As time went on, she understood that she could not create new life from nothing, but she could breathe new life into what was already available to her.

Harlow thought she had an excellent handle on things, for a beginner anyway, when she built a miniature replica of the house she'd dreamed of living in since she was a witchling from a cardboard box that she found in the trash. An irrepressible grin spread over her face, gazing at the gardens she built for it, when her phone buzzed. Annoyed by the interruption, she stepped away from her creation to check her phone.

It was a text from Finn. *Ready for tonight? We should go to the thing at the White Oak, unless you want to go somewhere else.*

Worry coursed through her, and fear. Not about the cocktail party, or even Solon Mai. They could manage that. But afterwards. The conversation she knew they had to have. So many scenarios ran through her mind, and all of them scared her. The ones the secret parts of her longed for scared her the most.

The White Oak is fine, she texted back, forcing herself to be brave. *I'll be there at 7.*

When she turned back to her tiny dreamhouse, it was gone. She felt for the shadows and they did not respond. Her heart pounded. She'd made so much progress so quickly. Why was this happening now? She glanced at her phone and wondered.

The shadows didn't like fear. Or maybe it was that she wasn't able to wield them properly when she was afraid? She sat down to try to figure it out, but her mind flooded with memories. Finn smiling that half smile when she talked about her dreams as he sketched. His arms around her at a party, secret kisses. Laughing 'til her sides ached over jokes only the two of them found funny.

She pushed away the thoughts of the night it all ended and let the way his demeanor changed the day after fill her mind's eye. The way his gaze slid over her in the hallways at school, like she wasn't even there. When she'd begged to talk to him, he'd laughed, and asked what *she* could have to talk with *him* about in an emotionless tone that had crushed her heart so fast she hadn't seen what was coming.

And the months after. It wasn't just Petra's bullying. It was the way he looked away from both her and Enzo. The calls he never returned. The way she'd felt more lonely and desperate than she'd imagined possible. He'd left her empty, broken, a shell of her former self, and she'd spent the following years filling herself with as many lovers as possible. Kate Spencer had been a brief respite from those times, but then she'd gone back to Nea Sterlis and Harlow's desperation returned. The drugs, the booze, anything to stop her from feeling the emptiness Finn left behind.

And then one night Mark Easton had held her hair back as she puked in a bush like it was the most natural thing in the world. He'd wiped Harlow's mouth with his shirt and taken her home. When they fucked it was the most alive Harlow had ever felt, and Mark was *proud* of her. Proud to be with her. Or at least he had been at first. Harlow thought that feeling could last forever. But of course it hadn't. Being with Mark had made everything worse.

Could she ever stop operating from this place of fear? The hurt she felt was so deep, so impenetrable, she didn't know if she could ever reach the end of it. Something soft as silk brushed her hands. The shadows flit between her fingers, winding up her arms as though they wanted to comfort her.

"Thank you," she whispered.

The darkness in her sang in response and she let the notes wash over her. Surrounded by her beautiful dark magic, Harlow closed her eyes and dipped into the fluid sadness, letting herself sink deep into it for the first time in years.

Harlow didn't know how long she disappeared for, but when she came to Axel was licking her fingertips and it was nearly six thirty. She'd have to hurry if she wanted to meet Finn at the White Oak on time. First, she called for a car, then texted Enzo to find out what she was supposed to wear, and groaned when the answer was all too simple: *The little black dress. Heels.*

She knew the one and had been dreading it. Once she had smoked out her eyes with black shadow she pulled it on, whispering a prayer to Aphora that she'd look all right. When she checked herself in the mirror, she smiled. She actually liked it.

"What do you think?" she asked Axel, who merely yawned and settled into the blankets for a long nap.

The black velvet wrapped around her in soft folds that hugged her hips and waist, propelling her bust into prominence via the low neckline of the dress. Long sleeves covered her arms—it was still too cold for shorter sleeves at night—and the dress fell to just below her knees, so she wouldn't have to worry about accidentally flashing anyone. When she stepped into the simple black pumps she smiled again. She could walk in these. Enzo had thought of everything.

Harlow fed Axel and then hurried downstairs to catch her car. The driver, a human in their mid-fifties, greeted her and then returned to listening to an art history podcast, leaving Harlow to her own devices as they wound through the city. She was nervous about leaving Axel for the evening, but knew he'd be fine on his own. Before things had gone so wrong with Mark, he'd always been fine by himself.

Besides, Larkin had promised to check in on him. Harlow knew she was being overly anxious, but she texted her youngest sister one more time to remind her. There was a near-instantaneous reply: *I'm already headed to your place with a pizza and a ginormous box of toys and stuff Mama bought him. She's not-so-secretly in love with your cat. Stop worrying and have fun, catmom.*

Harlow shot off a thank you and closed her eyes, taking deep breath after deep breath, and before she knew it they'd reached the White Oak. It was Nuva Troi's most prominent whiskey bar, located in a renovated warehouse in Midtown. It was always trendy, but tonight it was lit with witchlights, music floating onto the street.

She was alone tonight, which was both good and bad. The maters and the twins had gone to a big party down by the wharf that seemed tailored to the season's slightly younger crowd and their parents, and Enzo and Thea were attending a party in Uptown. Something at one of the wineries' tasting rooms. She was glad she didn't have to go to that—she'd rather drink whiskey if she had to drink at all.

As the car drove off, she lingered for an extra moment outside, feeling nervous.

"Going in?"

She turned to find Alaric standing next to her, dazzling her with his casual beauty. "Yes, are you?"

He grinned. "Nope. I got my wires crossed with your sister and thought she was coming here, but she said she was going to that thing at Cask & Vine. Wishful listening on my part, I guess. *I don't really like wine.*" He whispered the last sentence conspiratorially, as a goofy smile spread across his face.

Harlow smiled. It was impossible not to be charmed by him.

"Finn's inside already, and I happen to know that my cousin is at the wharf party tonight."

Harlow chuckled. "Well, at least there's that."

He squeezed her shoulder. "Gotta dash. Can't keep my girl waiting."

Harlow didn't have time to think of something else to say. He'd disappeared.

CHAPTER 20

She'd never been to the White Oak. It was a favorite among the Order of Masks, owned by a wealthy wolf pack from Nea Sterlis, and it had opened when she and Mark were together—but they never came to this side of town. They never went anywhere in the last months of their relationship where Harlow might run into anyone she knew. She'd thought at the time that it was because he wanted her to himself, but now she saw it differently. He'd wanted her alone, weak, and pliable. She shook off the thought of the argument they'd had about coming to the White Oak's opening as she stepped inside the bar.

As she took it all in, she understood why Finn wanted to come here. Not only was the building beautiful with its exposed brick walls and the dozen enormous crystal chandeliers that hung from the ceiling, but the White Oak hadn't closed the bar down to the public for the party, only devoted their main floor to it.

The upper bar was still open and it was full of gawking humans, and some photographers she recognized as Section Seven staff, as well as a bevy of free-lance paparazzi. She resisted the urge to pull the neckline of her dress up, or fade into the shadows. She steeled herself against what she knew was coming: the posts on the gossips, the chatter on the socials.

Photos would be taken and shared without her consent. People would speculate about her motives, talk about her and Finn, her and Mark, all of it in ways she wouldn't be able to control or ignore. The feeling that she was making herself a target in this dress, coming here with Finn, this *was* the plan. This was what she needed to do for her family.

The music shifted and Harlow's heart dropped into her stomach. The song was one she'd put on every playlist as a teenager. The one that made her think of him—and he had to know it—this song had been playing *that* night. This whole damn album on repeat. When she tore her eyes from her shoes, the bartender was grinning at her.

"He said you might need this." The shifter gave Harlow a decidedly lupine grin and pushed a glass of whiskey towards her. "It's our best, and Finn knows what he's talking about."

Harlow took the glass and sipped, wondering how the bartender got on a first name basis with Finbar McKay. The whiskey was good. Deep, complex, smoky. She was in so much trouble. She threw back the whole glass, even though shots hadn't been her thing in quite some time. She eyed the bartender, who was short, with an athletic build and short black hair, shaved on the sides.

Her sparkling brown eyes crinkled with amusement as she poured Harlow another finger of whiskey. "I hear you don't even need this stuff to fuck him."

Harlow raised her eyebrows. "And you would know?"

The bartender laughed, a rough, joyful sound. "He wishes. I don't swing that way though."

Harlow laughed with her. "I wish I didn't."

The bartender rested her elbow on the bar, smirking roguishly. "If you change your mind about Finn, stay after the party."

Harlow bit her lip, stifling the giggle that was bubbling up from her chest. "If he can't behave, I might."

"You won't, but it was fun talking to you." The bartender nodded to someone behind Harlow and when she turned, Finn was standing in the middle of the room, his gaze intense as his eyes found hers. He was on the phone, but as their attention locked onto one another, he said goodbye and hung up, sliding his phone into the pocket of his jeans as he drank her in. Something coiled tight and low in Harlow's belly woke, warmth creeping through her in slow, fiery licks.

Then he was next to her and if the bartender stayed to hear what he'd say to her, she didn't know, because the smell of smoky oud wood and rich, golden amber, so familiar in its exhilarating nature, distracted her to the point that she nearly lost her good sense. He leaned against the bar, his body close enough that she could feel its heat, but far enough away for propriety.

"You trying to kill me with that dress, Harls?"

She struggled to find the words she wanted, and sharper, uglier ones came out instead. "You're immortal. It'd be harder than I'd like to kill you."

He laughed as the music swelled, and it was impossible not to remember their last night together. Not with this song playing, not with him standing so close to her. His body hovering over hers, the sweet pain of him inside her. The way he'd pushed her hair out of her face as he told her he loved her.

"You trying to kill me with this song, McKay?"

He swallowed hard, his throat bobbing. "I didn't ask them to play it." His fingers skimmed her hip. "But I'm not sorry they are."

It was her turn to swallow. He was too good at this. If she wasn't careful, she'd fall for him for real, and she couldn't let that happen. She looked at the wide rustic planks of the wood floor. If he was going to play this way, she could too. When she raised her eyes, she did so slowly, taking a small step closer.

"Do you think about it? That night?" she asked so softly only he would hear her. To anyone watching, she knew it would look like they were flirting. Well, not *flirting* exactly, but definitely courting.

She watched his chest heave as he struggled to breathe naturally. "Yes."

His fingers pressed into the soft curve of her hip and she slid a hand up the buttons of his crisp white shirt. He'd actually dressed up for this. "How much?"

"I try not to… but a lot."

She made a soft humming noise as she took another step closer, looking up at him through her lashes. "Me too. I think about the way it felt to run through the rain. We were soaking wet."

A low rumble vibrated through his chest and his eyes lit softly; he was reacting to her, just the way she'd hoped he would. The photographers upstairs saw too and got out their cameras. She tugged gently on his shirt. The collar was open and he wasn't wearing a tie, so she slipped a finger inside, caressing his skin lightly.

He looked good, but she didn't like this buttoned-up look he'd been trotting out to the season events. Something in her wished for his usual leather jacket and messy hair. Hells, she missed the way he'd painted his nails when they were in secondary. Those were dangerous thoughts—she needed to stay on track here. It would be best if she stayed in control and *he* was off balance.

She lifted her face, parting her lips, pleased with the way his eyes tracked even the smallest of her movements. "I think about the way it felt to have you so deep inside me I forgot we were two people."

"You really are trying to kill me," he murmured, his voice rough.

"And I think about how you pushed my wet hair from my face and moved in me, so gentle and slow… You told me you loved me. Do you remember that?"

He nodded, his thumb drifting to her face, grazing her bottom lip, as the fingers that had pressed into her hip strayed to the small of her back, pulling her so close she could feel his desire for her stirring. He was going to kiss her. What's worse, she wanted him to. Her lips ached to feel his.

Her wounded heart spoke before her mutinous body could act. "You fucked me, told me you loved me, and then you acted like nothing happened between us." The words fell from her lips in a honeyed tone that did nothing to mask the anger burning in her chest. The cameras on the balcony wouldn't catch that, but he would.

She felt the flinch he didn't show as she stepped even closer, her breasts pressing hard into his chest. "Remember that, McKay. Remember that you broke me into a million pieces. Remember that you let that vicious princess Petra Velarius make my life a living hell for a year. Remember that I can *never* fully trust you."

"I know," he said, breathless. "Believe me. I know."

She looked at him now, really looked. His storm-grey eyes were dark with some version of sadness, maybe grief. A kernel of guilt burrowed into her heart. She'd actually hurt him, which for some reason, she hadn't expected. Just like she hadn't expected for this moment to feel so terrible. For years after what happened between them, she'd imagined working him up the way she had just now, only to decimate him, destroy him the way he'd destroyed her.

But this didn't feel good. She didn't feel like she'd won anything. In fact, she had the distinct feeling that she'd lost something that had become very precious to her in recent months—her self-respect. This wasn't how she treated people. This was how *Mark* treated people. Harlow recoiled from the thought, horrified. She started to say she was sorry, but couldn't form the vulnerable words, much as she wanted to.

"We should go," she said, softening her tone in lieu of an apology. "If they think we're leaving together it will be on everyone's socials in minutes. That's what we want, right?"

He cleared his throat and she wondered if he could hear the unspoken apology she'd wanted to voice. "If they think I took you home, they'll call you all sorts of terrible things and no one will take this seriously."

Godsdamn him, he was right. She imagined Indigo and Meline rolling their eyes at her lack of foresight. Harlow sighed. "I shouldn't have said all that."

His hand was still on the small of her back, though his arm had tensed significantly. Now, it relaxed a measure and she stepped back a little, but not so far away that his hand would be dislodged.

His head dipped and he wore a contrite expression. "I probably shouldn't have moved things forward so quickly. I don't know how to do this with you. It feels good, and then bad… We should talk about what happened between us."

Her heart skipped a terrifying beat. "Not here, not tonight."

He shook his head. "No. On Solon Mai though, all right? After the ball."

She nodded, glancing at the balcony to the upper bar. The music had changed, thank Aphora, though the White Oak was apparently playing nostalgic favorites tonight. A different bartender than before asked if they wanted anything else.

Finn shook his head. "Can I get my check?"

"What are you doing?" she whispered. "I thought leaving was a bad idea."

"Follow along, please."

She raised her eyebrows, suspicious.

"You can choose not to trust me. I deserve that. But please, just follow along."

She watched while he left an enormous tip and signed his name, taking his card back and putting it in his wallet. Then he took her hand, kissing her palm. His lips were warm and soft against her skin and the kiss was slow and sweet as his eyes met hers.

"They'll follow," he murmured, as he leaned close enough for his lips to brush the shell of her ear. "Now laugh and nod, like I just asked you to do something fun."

She did as he asked and he led her out of the bar, still holding her hand. Sure enough, the photographers scrambled to follow. "They'll catch up," he said when they reached the sidewalk.

His eye met hers as his fingers laced tighter through her own. The heat coiled in her belly slithered with pleasure, loosening again, sending warmth lapping across the sweetest aching spots. She tore her eyes from his, asking, "Where are we going?"

His mouth lifted in that rare, signature Finbar McKay smile that girls in secondary had claimed dropped panties in an instant. The memory brought her attention to her own undergarments, which were decidedly damp from their encounter inside the bar, to her horror. His voice was smooth, gloriously honeyed with some unknown pleasure. "You'll see."

They walked down the street, still holding hands. In this area, there were bars and restaurants everywhere. Fancy places she didn't usually go. Places the Times reviewed constantly, on repeat, like there wasn't other food in the city. When Finn stopped, it wasn't in front of any of those places. It was in front of a human street vendor.

"Finn McKay," the man said with a smile. He was middle-aged, with pale skin, red hair, and fantastic dimples. "What'll it be for you and the goddess tonight?"

Finn grinned. "Hey, Brennan. Can we get two giant waffle cones, with vanilla bean ice cream and chocolate sprinkles?"

"You don't want one to share?" Brennan asked, grinning deviously. Harlow wondered how often Finn brought dates to Brennan's cart. She could just imagine how charming it would seem to all the high society immortals he'd been linked with in the past. Her heart stammered, unsure. That wasn't a fair assumption. And why should she care who he brought where?

Finn shook his head. "Nope, we're not at the sharing stage yet, but vanilla bean with sprinkles is Harls' favorite."

The words struck her hard, slamming into her, a truckload of memories she'd worked hard to repress since things went wrong between them. After every test she failed, every time she disappointed Selene, all the times she'd embarrassed herself trying out for plays she never got into, he'd brought her vanilla bean ice cream, her favorite, and a bottle of sprinkles to shake onto every bite. Her chin threatened to quiver, so she bit her bottom lip hard.

When Brennan handed the big cones over, he also gave them wooden spoons. As they walked away, she heard, rather than saw the photographers following. They'd catch up soon.

"I should have been there to give this to you when some asshole treated you like shit in secondary."

She looked up at him and started to say he didn't need to say anything else tonight, but he shook his head. His words came out in a tumble. "I shouldn't have been that asshole. I've done a lot of work on myself since back then, and maybe I don't deserve your forgiveness, but I hope at least when I explain things on Solon Mai, you'll get any closure you still need…"

"Okay."

He looked down at her, his brow furrowed in surprise. "What?"

She didn't want to hold grudges or act out in ways that made her feel like a monster. That path was dangerous. Harlow wasn't the least bit sure that she could trust Finn, and she was positive they weren't starting anything real, but she could hear him out and let this go for good. She could try to heal, and then start over. She didn't know how that would work with everything she'd committed to doing for the Order and her family, but she was finally willing to try.

"Okay," she said, so quietly she was afraid he might not hear her. "We'll talk. I'll get closure, and then we'll figure out what to do next."

His face was open and she saw how surprised he was. How hope lit softly in his face, flickering weakly as a candle in a windstorm. "Yeah?"

Harlow nodded as she took a big bite of the ice cream, and started walking towards the subway. She didn't want to be the one to douse that light. Not tonight, even though she knew anything more than this between them was utterly impossible. "Yeah. Wanna ride to my stop with me?"

Finn smiled. "I do."

Behind them, the sound of cameras followed until they disappeared into the subterranean stairway.

CHAPTER 21

The days after the White Oak party were a riot of news about Harlow, Thea, and the Illuminated men courting them. Section Seven and the socials all but quit talking about Mark and Olivia. Instead, photos of her at the whiskey bar, and on the street with Finn, circulated everywhere, along with commentary about her clothes, about how long she and Finn had known one another and if she or Thea were to be considered the season's swan.

The nearly unanimous conclusion was that despite the entertaining showing she and Finn put on as a couple, the glamor of Thea and Alaric's fairytale match was too good to pass up. Their burgeoning love story was all anyone following the season closely—which according to Indigo and Meline was literally millions of people—were talking about. Harlow spent the entire morning in bed cuddling Axel, catching up on gossip sites and socials, drinking tea and laughing to herself at all the speculation.

A few times, she'd thought of texting some of the funnier memes people were making about her and Finn to him, but she refrained. They'd reached a truce the night of the White Oak party, but she still didn't completely trust him. She was almost certain he wasn't in league with his parents, but she didn't know if they could even be friends, let alone anything more.

Still, the realization that she wanted closure and to move on from their sad past remained, and that was enough for her. That and getting his parents off the Order of Mysteries' back for good. She had to remember that was the real goal here, not making herself feel better.

An alarm went off on her phone, reminding her to get going. She'd promised to get ready for the Solon Mai ball with Enzo and her sisters at his place, and she'd been trying to take a nap with Axel but had gotten sucked into her phone. She hadn't slept well all week, between monitoring socials and practicing with

116

her shadow magic. Harlow hoped to Aphora that Thea could glamour away the dark circles under her eyes.

The alarm rang again, insistently. Harlow shut it off and fed Axel, who was fast asleep, sprawled out on her bed. She kissed him and he purred, but did not wake. He was doing much better, sleeping comfortably now and eating regularly. He'd even started to play with the toys Larkin had brought over, to Harlow's surprise. Axel had never been interested in toys before, but perhaps that was because he'd known what she hadn't at the time—that they hadn't been safe at Mark's.

She gathered her things and went downstairs to hail a cab, which was blessedly easy to do. She fell into the back seat, feeling drained and anxious about the evening ahead. The ever-present spring drizzle in Nuva Troi draped the world in a comforting blanket of grey and she dozed a little in the back seat.

When they came to a stop on Mulberry Street, she paid the cabbie, tipping generously, and entered the atelier from the back. Enzo's parents had owned the entire building, and at one time rented out the top floors as office space. Now, Enzo resided here, above the shop.

Harlow pressed her palm to the metal plate next to the door, as Enzo had instructed her to do, and it opened—a stunning bit of magical tech that must have cost Enzo a fortune. Her own combination of lock and wards worked similarly to let in who she wanted to, and keep out anyone else, but this single piece of tech seemed to do it all in one go. Her eyes narrowed slightly as the door opened and a soft voice said, "Welcome, Harlow Krane."

The muffled sound of blaring pop music from upstairs suffused the stairwell. Harlow took a deep breath; they were already having a good time and she didn't want to be a downer, but the past few days had been draining. Her feet moved slowly as she reluctantly headed up. She hadn't been upstairs since Enzo spent a year remodeling the building, but the limewash blue paint felt familiar. Her memory of Enzo's blue bedroom in the Weraka townhouse was still as vivid as though she'd been there yesterday.

She smiled as she trailed upstairs, where she found all four of her sisters, Enzo, and Riley Quinn dancing in the great room to the music she'd heard below. Harlow hesitated for a moment. They were having fun and she wasn't sure if she could have fun today. She wanted to, but her whole body felt heavy and sluggish, as though she were having an emotional hangover.

Larkin spotted Harlow and left the group to pull her into the living room. Everyone was singing the words to the popular song as loud as they could. Awkwardness flooded Harlow's body. She felt as though she'd forgotten how to move. Larkin took her hands and started to sway with her, singing in an exaggerated fashion that made Harlow laugh.

Slowly, her body began to move along with Larkin's. She was a terrible dancer, unlike her athletic, spritely sister, but she was starting to have fun. Larkin twirled her and Thea bumped her hip with her own. Soon, Harlow was singing along too, with the same abandon as her sisters. She felt the infectious magic of the moment in the shadows that pushed power into the filaments of magic surrounding them. Everything in the room began to glow slightly in Harlow's second sight as the tightness in her chest dissipated into the music.

The song ended and a slow song came on. Enzo turned the music down as she went to greet him. He was a little breathless as he pulled her into a hug, and looked so satisfied that it made it hard for Harlow not to smile when he ordered her to "Come chat with Riley. I want them to feel welcome."

Harlow's heart swelled with happiness for Enzo. She knew that look; he was falling hard for the talented shifter. Riley was in the kitchen, their locs wrapped in an intricate half-up style that was punctuated by jeweled gold combs. Their ears were slightly elongated, as with all the Trickster's Chosen, and they wore earrings in each ear that coordinated with the combs in their hair.

"Only part way done," Riley said, gesturing to their visage. "Thea was kind enough to offer to do my eyes."

Their voice was rich and the cadence of their words slow and measured, as though they had never been anxious or flustered in their life. Their fawn-colored eyes were long lashed and the faint glow of gold highlighter shone on their clear, brown skin. Outside of the Illuminated and Thea, Harlow had never seen such an intensely beautiful person. Or perhaps their beauty might be better described as handsome. Whichever way she thought of it, their allure was beyond just looks, but seemed to emanate from a deeper place that spoke of a truer grace, with no small helping of acute intelligence.

"It's so good to see you again, Riley," she said with a smile.

They hugged her immediately, and she felt the electric current of their empathy. It made a stronger impression now that they were in close contact. Harlow had never felt empathic power like this before. She wondered what the depths of Riley's power actually were, or if they even knew.

"Wow, that's amazing," she murmured as a wave of reassurance smoothed her frayed nerves. "You're brilliant at that."

"And you are something else… aren't you?" Riley asked, eyes alight with interest.

Harlow's eyes narrowed with wary concern. Empaths couldn't help but pick up the surface details of other people's thoughts and feelings, but only extremely rare empaths could sense things like the depths of other immortals' manifestations. From the wide-eyed wonder in Riley's eyes, she sensed they knew about her shadow magic.

"I won't say a word," Riley murmured. "But Enzo will be able to tell, too. Your secret is safe with us."

"But is it safe with the Rogue Queen?" Harlow asked.

Riley poured Harlow a mimosa, their eyes glittering with some secret knowledge. "I see no reason to tell her, at this juncture. You'll show the world soon enough, I think."

They handed her the mimosa and as she sipped it, Riley added, "But if she *did* know about you, Harlow, you could trust her to keep your secret."

Harlow wasn't sure if it was Riley's empathy at work on her, or just a sense she had, but she trusted what they said. Though it did spark a wave of curiosity about the Rogue Queen. From the very little she'd heard about the Rogue

Order, asking about them would do no good. They were notoriously secretive. Her shadows pressed on her conscious mind in a warm, pleasurable way that signaled approval, though for what she wasn't certain.

Internally, she asked, *Do you like Riley?*

The answer was emphatically positive. Her magic liked Riley, and everyone in this room. These people made it feel safe and strong. She marveled at the wordless way it communicated until she noticed Riley's raised eyebrows and faint smile.

Just as Harlow was about to explain herself, Enzo brought her dress out from the bedroom, hanging it on the rack with the rest of the garments for the evening. "What are the two of you discussing?"

Harlow hugged him, opening herself up to his empathy fully and directing the shadows, *Show him in a way he can understand.*

"Oh," he said, raising his dark eyebrows as she pulled away. "Oh… Harlow. Your magic… It's beautiful."

She smiled as he kissed her cheeks. Riley's arm went around his waist and the two of them smiled at her like proud parents.

"Are you talking about me?" she asked after a moment. They were nodding as though having a silent conversation.

"Oh! Sorry, yes," Riley said, a bright smile lighting their face.

Enzo brushed a kiss on Riley's sharp cheekbones. "Easy to forget that others can't hear us. Sorry, Harls. Riley's right, your secret is safe with us. After Solon Mai, I'd love to see what you can do."

Harlow nodded, glad they knew. She had a feeling she would need allies soon, more than just her parents and sisters. Besides, Enzo had always been her family, and if he chose Riley, they would be her family too. Thea danced over and dragged Riley away from Enzo's embrace to finish their glamour.

Harlow watched them go, smiling faintly as Riley twirled Thea to the music. They were a graceful dancer, and some small part of her warned that with grace like that they'd probably be deadly in a fight. She wondered where that thought came from, tilting her head slightly as Enzo poured himself a mimosa. Finally, she said, "I like them. Things are moving quickly though, is that all right?"

Enzo nodded, watching Thea and Riley discuss their vision for Riley's glamour. "Empath to empath pairings are intense. Riley's mother was a sorcière, which as you know is very rare. Though Riley can't wield magic as a witch would, their empathy is stronger than anyone I've ever met. We immediately felt at home with one another."

That made sense, and Harlow's shadows danced at the explanation. They liked the two of them together. *Are you sure Riley's safe?* she asked. Her magic swirled inside her, comforting her with a reassuring warmth that she hoped she could depend on. She certainly wanted to.

"I'm happy for you." Harlow hugged her friend. "Will you help me get into my gown?"

Enzo looked at her appraisingly. "Are you doing your face by hand?"

"Not tonight," she replied. "I'm feeling a bit tired from the last few days."

Enzo nodded, putting his mimosa down to fetch her dress. Harlow slipped out of her sweats and Enzo helped her into the gossamer lace gown. One he had her buttoned up, she waited for Thea. Indigo and Meline were resplendent, already dressed in matching black damask ball gowns. They didn't always dress alike, but tonight they were a vision of similarities, the only difference between them the color of their hair. Meline's shone with the same honey-gold sheen as her own, while Indigo's was darker than both Thea and Larkin's.

"So Larkin is staying home?" Enzo's eyebrows furrowed with concern. "She doesn't seem upset."

Larkin was busy helping everyone put the finishing touches on their ensembles for the evening, but she was wearing her favorite sweats, her dark hair in a messy bun. She was fresh-faced and happy, nothing like the anxious mess she usually was before an event. Her eyes met Harlow's and her smile radiated happiness and ease.

"I think she's better than she's ever been. Did she talk with you about the feelings she's been having about relationships?"

Enzo smiled. "Yes, she came over early and we spent the afternoon talking. I'm going to introduce her to Avery Hargrove. Do you remember Avery?"

Harlow did remember Avery from university, a sorcière with a gift for sculpture, who was never linked to anyone romantically. "I do. How is Avery doing these days?"

"She's great. Her sculptures are doing well in Nea Sterlis and she's touring again this winter. I think she and Larkin will have a lot to talk about. They have a call set up for next week."

Relief flooded Harlow's chest. She'd been worried that her talk with Larkin hadn't been good enough, that the fact she hadn't known the right words to say would hurt, rather than help. She knew if Larkin was able to talk with someone who felt similarly that she might understand herself better.

"I just want her to do better than I did. To understand herself better… not to suffer so much, you know?"

Enzo nodded, popping a tiny canape into her mouth. It was divine and Harlow desperately needed a snack. "Give me another."

He obliged and then it was her turn with Thea. She replaced Riley in one of the upholstered blue chairs at Enzo's table. Thea was already dressed, her slim figure clad in a simple velvet gown that fit close to her body, with long sleeves that fell off her shoulders. A tiara, sparkling with black diamonds, shimmered in her hair.

"I haven't seen that before," Harlow said as Thea sipped her mimosa.

"It was a gift from Alaric."

Harlow raised her eyebrows. "It looks expensive."

Thea pursed her lips disapprovingly. "I'm sure it was. Now, what are we doing with your face and hair."

"Something that looks like I just rolled out of bed, but elegant."

Thea shook her head. She, of course, was elegant *and* polished, her face painted in understated, classic lines, her nails pale pink ovals, every hair perfectly placed.

"I want to look a little mussed."

Thea nodded, pulling strands of magic so quickly that Harlow barely saw her fingers move. When Thea held up a mirror for her to look in, she grinned. Her eyes were subtly smoky, and her lashes elongated past what she could hope to achieve with products, but not so dramatically that she looked overly made up. Everything else looked like her skin, with a slight glow.

"Thank you," she whispered. "I look beautiful."

Thea smiled. "You always do, Harlow. But yes, this is some of my best work."

Enzo clapped his hands to get everyone's attention. "The maters are on their way. It's time to head to the Metro."

CHAPTER 22

The Metropolitan Archive of Fine Arts' marble columns were lit sparingly, but dark lanterns scattered the steps, giving the entrance to the grand old building a feeling of mystery. Photographers from every major publication and the gossips were only allowed on the sidewalk, so after walking past the column of flashing lights and shouts to turn this way and that, Harlow was free to enjoy her walk up the MAFA steps.

She'd always loved the old building, and all the art it held within, as it was one of the few places in Nytra that didn't discriminate between Orders and humans. If the art was good enough, it was here, regardless of mortality. The curatorial staff and board of directors had even shifted in recent years to employ more humans. It was slow progress, but it was *some* progress.

As Harlow walked through the arched doorway to the museum with her family, anticipation filled her. While the Solstice Gala was the apex of the season, the Solon Mai ball was considered a pivotal moment in the journey for most pairings. Typically, this was the night when the season's most prominent couples emerged and the race to the Solstice began for anyone not already matched. She'd purposely avoided making any kind of elaborate plan with Finn. Indigo and Meline cautioned her repeatedly that the best lies were told with as many grains of truth as possible, and so she'd decided to allow things to play out as naturally as she could.

Harlow was acutely aware of the way her heels clicked against the marble floors of the Metro hallways, which had been transformed to look like an enchanted forest, the boughs of the trees parting overhead to reveal a sparkling night sky. Everywhere, flowering branches wound around columns and hung from ceilings, as though an enormous blooming thicket had taken over the Metro. Tiny golden witchlights floated in and out of the dark branches, blinking slowly in and out like fireflies on an early summer evening, hinting at what was to come on the Solstice.

Interspersed between the columns of branches, hundreds of glass lanterns of different shapes and sizes glowed on the ground. It gave the dark entrance to the museum dozens of secluded nooks that many couples were already taking advantage of. Music drifted seductively out from the ballroom at the end of the hall.

From somewhere in the expertly contrived dark forest, Harlow felt eyes watching her. She stopped to look around, her dress swishing around her ankles as she stepped towards the prickling sensation of being seen by someone she could not perceive. Someone took hold of her arm and she spun to find Thea.

"Coming?" her sister asked.

Harlow nodded, following slowly as Thea led her to the ballroom, where their family was waiting. Very quickly, the twins were asked to dance; Enzo and Riley followed, as well as the maters, leaving Thea and Harlow alone to watch the dancers together. Here, the darkness of the entry hall gave way to the lush greens of ferns and branches of fragrant wisteria, dripping with blossoms. The ground around the edges of the dance floor was dotted with thick moss and lichen that led into yet another corridor of dark trees that encircled the ballroom. The same tiny golden witchlights from the hall flickered between frond and bough. At the center of the room, couples danced, surrounded by groups of people in conversation.

"There's Alaric," Thea murmured, as a raven-haired head swiveled their way.

She hesitated, as though she didn't want to leave Harlow alone. "Go to him," she said, urging her sister on. There was no need to spoil Thea's evening with the fact that she felt watched, that she felt the sinister pressure of eyes on her, even now. Thea would just worry, and she deserved an evening of romance. That was what *she* was here for after all, unlike Harlow.

Thea's smile met Alaric's and Harlow knew she no longer heard her. She watched as they gravitated towards each other, pulled by some invisible force. Alaric took her sister's hand and led her onto the dance floor, where the crowd parted to allow them room.

People stopped to stare at the figure they cut. Truly, they were the most attractive people in the room, and together each amplified the goodness and beauty in the other. The vision was so sweet in its purity that Harlow found herself clutching her heart, forgetting the feeling she had that she was being watched, if only for a moment.

And then she saw Finn. She didn't know how she could have missed him; once her eyes locked with his, she saw nothing else. He was somewhat carelessly dressed; his perfectly tailored tuxedo was everything it should be, but as usual, he refused to wear a tie. Petra was standing next to him, trying to speak to him, but he paid her no mind.

Could it have been him she felt watching her? That didn't seem right to her. The feeling she had now, with his focus on her, was nothing like the chilling prickle of warning she'd felt walking in. No, this was different. Her skin flushed hot under her gown as their eyes locked onto one another.

He pushed away from the wall he was leaning against and strode across the room, leaving Petra behind. He didn't force his speed the way she knew he could. Instead, he used his time to run his eyes over her body, causing tight longing to clench in her abdomen as he approached. He took her hand when he finally reached her and the feel of his skin against hers set her heart to pounding in her ears, as her cheeks flushed in an unmistakable blush.

"We have to go do something unpleasant," he said softly as he brushed a kiss to her palm.

"What's that?"

She followed his pointed gaze. His parents stood at the edge of the room, surrounded by people all vying for their attention. But both of them were staring at Finn and Harlow, and she felt the predatory nature of their shared attention in her bones. She had the good sense to suppress the shudder she felt coming on, but nothing could lessen the fear she felt in this moment.

But still, as much as they terrified her, this was not the presence she felt watching her earlier. The realization chilled the flush in her skin, turning her clammy almost instantly. Though most humans didn't realize it, the older Illuminated were dangerous beyond imagining. The common assumption in the Order of Mysteries was that they'd lived too long, and nothing satiated their desire for pleasure anymore but cruelty and degradation. No one could gain concrete information about them, but the rumors she'd heard were enough to make anyone ill.

Which was why the instinctual feeling she had that even they were not the threat she sensed was so unsettling. She realized Finn was speaking, tugging gently on her arm to get her attention. "We have to, Harlow. They want to meet you."

She knew he wasn't saying much else because their attention was so focused on them. The Illuminated could focus their hearing intensely for short periods of time, and it was very possible they were listening to every word they said.

"I'd be delighted to meet them," she said, forcing a smile. She wondered if, like the night of the Grove party, he sensed whatever she did about what was wrong.

"Thank you," he murmured, pressing her hand to his chest as he led her across the room. As usual, he seemed perfectly calm, at least outwardly. It was exasperating how steady he was, how safe she felt with her hand in his, even as they walked towards some of the most dangerous immortals on Okairos.

She'd have to ask him later about the feeling she had. Harlow didn't dare look for her own parents; in fact, she hoped they wouldn't join them. It was better they do this on their own, though if she could, Harlow would gladly run into the comforting arms of either of the maters to avoid this. She braced herself against the intensity of his parents' stares.

Connor McKay didn't look a human day over forty, a touch of gray at his temples the only thing to show that he was very nearly ancient—over two thousand years old, if rumors were true. Everything in his incredibly handsome bone structure was a mirror to his son's, but the similarities ended there. Where Finn was considerate under his intimidating exterior, Connor was cold and tightly wound all the way through, controlling and raptorial. If possible, Finn's mother was worse. Aislin McKay wore a simple black satin gown, her chocolate brown hair knotted into a severe chignon. She was gorgeous, and Finn's beautiful eyes clearly came from her, though that beauty was drowned in the expression of pure hunger she wore. She looked like she might reach out, snatch Harlow, and devour her.

Finn squeezed her hand as the people surrounding his parents scattered at their approach. "Mother, Father, this is Harlow Krane."

He didn't say "Mother" and "Father" in the sweet tones she and her sisters referred to Aurelia and Selene in. The words were clipped in his mouth, as though he hated to say them. Memories of bruises on his arms when they were children, as well as countless times he wasn't allowed to eat lunch, or the times he simply didn't show up to school for days at a time, played in the back of Harlow's mind. He would come back paler, with dark circles under his red-rimmed eyes, never speaking once about what he'd endured.

In secondary, it had been clear his parents expected him to join his father's real estate development firm, and when he'd applied for university, they'd been angry, but she had been proud. Like Alaric, he'd refused his parents' money after uni. It had been all over the gossips when the two of them started their own securities company, specializing in the hybridization of magic and technology. Still, they had some hold over him, though she didn't know what it was, exactly.

Harlow held out her hands in greeting, bowing her head only slightly as Aislin took them. Her hands were cold as ice, and she squeezed Harlow's hands hard enough to bring tears to her eyes. But her voice was smooth and cultured as fine silk when she said, "It is so good to finally meet you, Harlow. You are a vision."

Harlow doubted very much that Aislin sincerely felt that way. The woman was thin to the point of gauntness, as the Illuminated valued a certain kind of feminine fragility that was an unpopular beauty standard with the Order of Mysteries and the Trickster's Chosen, but all the rage with humans and vampires. Harlow could see from the slight curve of her upper lip that she was dying to make some snide comment. Connor nodded, but would not make eye contact with either of them, instead scanning the crowd, as if he too sensed a hidden menace in their midst.

"Yes," Harlow said slowly, trying hard not to pull her hands from Aislin's death grip. "It is good to meet you too."

A long, uncomfortable beat passed and Aislin released Harlow's hands, smoothing non-existent wrinkles from her opulent gown. Finn made no effort to fill the silence and Harlow wasn't sure what the expectations for her were. Her head was empty now, but for the thought that these people wanted to breed her to their son and take her family's home and livelihood. Certainly it wouldn't be strategic to mention that.

A smile spread across Aislin's beautiful face so malevolent that Harlow's stomach soured. "You two should go have fun. We will talk again soon."

Connor nodded, still staring intently beyond the crowd. "Yes, we have much to discuss about your future."

Finn visibly bristled at his parents' words, and Harlow couldn't blame him, though she suppressed her own reaction. Their statements may have been phrased kindly, but they were barely concealed threats, and neither had bothered to try to hide that fact. Finn took one of Harlow's hands, soothing it with gentle strokes of his thumb down the center of her palm.

"Wonderful," he said sharply, gripping her hand tighter, as though he feared one of his parents might steal her away. His jaw clenched so hard she thought his teeth might crack. "Enjoy your evening."

The tone of forced respect in his voice broke Harlow open. His desire to please them was as evident to her as was his clear hatred for them. Again, she wondered what it would be like not to have a family like her own, to walk through the world without people who loved you no matter what, to be alone with all the complex feelings that were obviously coursing through Finn as they walked away.

As his parents receded into the crowd, Finn's grip on her hand loosened slightly. Their palms were sweaty against one another, but she didn't let go. The hurdle they'd just cleared was significant. As Aislin and Connor disappeared from sight, the tension between them lessened enough that she recognized it for what it was: fear. They were both terrified.

Suddenly what they were doing, and the consequences for what might happen if the McKays suspected their deception, became clear. The instinctual fear coursing through them both was an indicator of how high the stakes were. Finn's parents weren't average adversaries; they were ancient immortals with unlimited, completely unchecked power. She'd spent so much time wondering about the mysterious feeling of being watched, she'd forgotten how much rested on her shoulders.

Dizziness struck Harlow hard and she stumbled, but Finn sensed the spiral she was descending and he took her arm, drawing her close against him as they walked towards the dance floor. His body was comfortingly hard, steel against every curve of her currently melting into him.

"I don't have words for how you look tonight," he murmured. "Will you dance?"

She felt his eyes on her and she nodded, allowing herself to be led onto the dance floor and when his arms went around her, she leaned into him gratefully, glad to allow the familiar steps she'd known her whole life to take over. He held her closer than was technically necessary, allowing his chest to brush hers period-ically. Slowly, the fear began to dissipate, breaking apart in her chest and floating away on the music.

Finn's grey-blue eyes met hers as she looked up, and there were oceans of unspoken words tossed about behind them. Years of longing seemed to echo the feelings she tried her best to deny. Her throat tightened, the way it always did when she allowed herself to think about what they'd lost so long ago, and she wondered, was it all just childish love? Or was there more there, something that could last longer than the flush of firsts they'd had as teenagers?

The longer they didn't speak, the closer he drew her into him. Both their breathing sped up markedly, but not from the rigor of the dance. His fingers pressed into her back as she moved closer into his orbit, letting him pin her to him so closely she felt the rock-hard length of him against her as they stepped and turned. Every nerve in her was alive at his touch and when he leaned close to her ear, his breath elicited a rush of heat between her legs that caused her knees to buckle.

His words started out as a soft rumble. "I'm glad we had these dances drilled into us as littlings." His hold on her tightened, as his fingers swept up her spine and into her hair, the rumble melting into a growl. "I don't have an ounce of blood left to operate my brain."

Harlow felt exactly where his blood had gone as he dragged her against him, her body soft and supple in his arms. She didn't have the power to think, the feel of him was so mesmerizing. Her blood lit on fire as the music swelled and for a moment it felt as though they were completely alone.

But of course they weren't alone, not at all, and this dance wasn't for their pleasure. They had a job to do tonight. She reminded herself that this wasn't about the two of them, but her family, her Order, the entire balance of the lower Orders. To keep herself from liquefying, she glanced around at the crowd, catching curious stares no matter which direction they turned. One song bled into another. "It's working—they're all buying it."

"Buying what?" he asked, his voice thick and distant.

"That my dress has seduced you."

She felt his laugh against her breasts and deep in her core, which was aflame with desire she could not quell.

"There's nothing to *buy*, Harls."

To punctuate his point, his legs parted hers and the hard length of his erection pressed into the core of her, momentarily obscured by the fan of her skirts. An involuntary moan floated from her lips. His breath was sharp as he pulled her off the dance floor and into the shadowy forest edging the dance floor. She followed without question, knowing there were hundreds of eyes watching.

Though they were partially hidden by the ferns and boughs, she knew they were still in perfect view of the ballroom itself when he dragged her into his lap. She looked down to see he'd found a chair nestled in an alcove that was tailor-made for a tryst such as the one they appeared to be having.

"Is this all right?" he asked softly, winding a loose strand of her hair around his fingers.

"Yes," she murmured.

His voice was strained, and now alone in this little alcove, he wouldn't meet her eyes. "It's not the dress. Though the dress is very good."

She frowned, not knowing what he meant, but she didn't press him. This was all for show, after all. She wrapped her arms around his neck, feeling the crowd in the ballroom watching them surreptitiously, ravenous to see whatever they'd do next. Finn's body tensed under her, his breath as tight in his lungs as hers, his fingers skimming down her shoulders and over her arms.

"If I kiss you, would that be all right?" he murmured, his mouth moving ever nearer to her own.

She nodded and his palms grazed her hips and hair as he pulled her closer, nuzzling her neck. His warm breath on her bare skin sent currents of pleasure through her body.

"You smell fucking amazing," he groaned. "How do you smell this good?"

She turned her face so their lips brushed against each other, lightly at first, as even the slightest bit of contact sent her heart racing. A growl vibrated in his chest as his fingers tightened on her hip and at the nape of her neck, pulling her hair gently, exposing her neck to him. A feeling of primal arousal flooded her senses. She was acutely aware of his fangs, as they glinted in the dim light of the alcove.

Harlow wondered what it would be like for him to sink them deep into her neck, for him to bite her as they moved against one another. Her vision dimmed at the thought and her thighs clenched tightly around the scorching heat emanating from the center of her. When his lips met hers, his kiss was rough and fast, as though he'd been denied something for too long that he was finally allowed to claim as his own.

Her arms tightened around his neck as her fingers tangled into his hair, deepening the kiss further. She forgot a ballroom of people watched their every move for a brief second. When the hand gripping her hip began to graze up her side, toward her breasts, she remembered. She pulled back slightly, though it pained her to do so. Throbbing pleasure pulsed between her legs and she ached with need as she parted her mouth from his.

Finn's eyes were glossy with lust, his body taut with urgency. "I'm sorry," he murmured. "Got carried away."

Harlow couldn't speak, so she nodded. She had no idea how much of this was a show, his body simply responding to her soft warmth against him.

"If we left now, I think everyone would get the point, don't you?" His eyes were pleading, but what the plea was, she couldn't say. Did he want to stop, or go further?

"I agree," she murmured.

"Can I take you to my place, or yours? We need to talk."

"Yours," she responded immediately.

"Give me a minute… Standing might be a problem."

Harlow smiled wickedly. "You could always glamour yourself."

He laughed. "See, I can't even think. The way you look and smell has me…" His eyes glazed as they ran over her.

She very deliberately reached into the little bag hanging off her arm and shot a few texts to her family to let them know she was leaving with Finn. When she looked up at him through her lashes he was biting his bottom lip, mirroring her exactly. Then he kissed her, swiping her teeth with his tongue as he set her on her feet.

"Can I get us out of here fast?" he asked.

When she nodded, he swept her into his arms and she felt nothing but a slight breeze before he was setting her down in front of his car. She glanced around to find him parked at the far reaches of a back parking lot, no other cars in sight, only the stars to light their way. The usual clouds cleared to show the twinkle of the cosmos.

She didn't wait to hear anything he had to say, but pulled his hips against hers, sliding her hands up the muscles of his chest. She waited for him to stop her as her arms wound around his neck.

"Was it all for them?" she asked. "Was it just for the crowd?"

His eyes snapped open and the corner of his mouth lifted in a wicked smirk. In a flash he had her pinned against the car, his strong thighs caging hers, his hands in her hair.

"That was for them, yes," he groaned as her fingers dug into his back. "This is for you."

His kiss was tender now and would have been sweet, if the hard length of him wasn't pressed into her. Instead, the heat between them intensified as she wrapped one leg around him, angling herself so that his erection pushed against the core of her, sending waves of ecstasy through her body as they rocked against one another.

Finn's mouth opened to hers and his tongue slid suggestively against hers, telling tales of all the places he might touch. One hand cupped her breast as he ran his thumb over her obviously pebbled nipple, a hard peak straining against the thin fabric of her bodysuit. She whimpered into his mouth as he kissed her harder, sliding his hand under her dress, between her thighs, now open wide for him. When he stroked the wet spot forming on the bodysuit he groaned in her mouth.

She was surprised when he stopped, failing to pull the bodysuit aside and bury his fingers in the wet folds that ached for his touch. "This isn't where I want to do this," he murmured, the movement of his fingers slowing. "And we *have* to talk first. Would it be all right if I portaled us back?"

She nodded, rocking her hips against his fingers, which had stilled. "Do it."

Finn's hands slid away from her most intimate parts and he gripped her around the waist. He kissed her again, and when she opened her eyes, they were standing next to a dark lake, a dimly lit house behind them.

"This is your house? The place you built?"

He nodded. "But I don't want to go in just yet. Can we stay out here for a minute?"

He didn't have to ask her twice; she knew that pausing to go into the house would mean realizing they needed to talk, and she needed something else more. She sank onto the ground, pulling him down on top of her. His mouth crashed into hers as he pushed her dress up past her thighs. She spread her legs quickly, arching her back as he teased her through the bodysuit.

She slid her own hand between his legs, gripping the hard length of him through his pants. He groaned, pressing his fingers into her harder, tracing small intentional circles around her swollen clit through the thin fabric that separated them. She stroked him hard, unable to grip him as easily as she could if he were naked, but he thrust into her hands as hard as she did against his.

"You're so fucking wet," he groaned into her mouth.

"I want you inside me," she begged. "Now."

He pulled away from her and she saw in his eyes that he felt the same—that he wanted to be buried so deep in her that neither would be able to tell where they ended and the other began. So his answer surprised her: "Not until we talk. You have to hear me out first. If you haven't changed your mind, then we can do this."

Harlow saw how serious he was and reluctantly, she pulled away from him too, pushing her dress down over her knees. She struggled to her feet, reaching back to pull him up beside her, then her head tilted in curiosity as she looked at the house. Calmer now than before, she recognized it. "Why does your house look so familiar?"

Finn took her hand. "Come find out."

Finn led her up the hill to the house. The closer she got, the deeper the bittersweet ache in her heart grew. She recognized every stone, every window.

"Is this my dream house? The one you drew for me?"

He nodded. "Is it too much?"

She heard the vulnerability in his voice. The fear that she would think it was a violation of her trust. And maybe a long time ago she might have gotten angry, but now, something shifted in her, as though a key slipped into a locked door she'd never seen before. As the door inside her opened wide, she gazed at the man beside her and smiled.

"It's wonderful."

CHAPTER 23

The house was an exact replica of the one she'd imagined since she was a little girl. She'd always dreamt of living in a house in the woods, rather than in the busy city. It wasn't that she didn't love Nuva Troi, but sometimes she needed quiet, distance. And this was the house she'd always dreamed of—from the peaked roof, to the arched doors, to the leaded glass windows, it was everything she'd imagined, or at least it looked to be so here in the dark.

"Can I see inside?"

He pulled her close to him, tucking her back against his chest as he spoke. "Before we go in, I need to confess. I think I built this for you. At first, I told myself it was just because I liked the house you always talked about, because it was the kind of home I wanted as a child, but never had. But once it was built, I knew it was more."

Harlow waited for Finn to continue, feeling his breath through her shoulder blades as he hugged her tightly. She lifted her face to his, resting her head on his shoulder. "What do you mean?"

"I couldn't fill it with furniture or art because I hoped someday you'd do it your way, even though that seems impossible—I need you to know that I don't expect anything from you. If you don't want me, I'll understand and I promise, I'll help you do everything I said I would and then I'll leave you alone... But you're the reason I agreed to participate in the season. I hoped I'd see you again, and maybe things might be different."

The words tumbled out of him in a desperate way she wasn't used to hearing. His voice cracked with emotion, as he pressed his palms into the gentle curve of her soft stomach. His erection was hard against her ass, but the touch was less sexual, and more for comfort, somehow wistful as he ran his hands over her.

She looked away from him, back at the house. Some part of her knew they were crossing a threshold she might not be able to return from, but she felt reckless. Here in this moment, what she was *supposed* to be doing with Finn was far away, removed from this conversation entirely. It was as though they existed in a different world for a short time, one where she could trust him, where they might actually have a chance.

Even so, she asked, "What about your parents? Didn't they want you to?"

She felt him shrug. "They did, but I didn't know that when I came home for good, when I moved in here. All I knew was that you'd broken up with Mark, and if I was going to have another chance with you, this was it."

Her breath caught at the mention of Mark, and it felt as though poison leached into her. A memory flashed in her mind's eye: Mark calling her a slut on the way home from a dinner with friends, where she'd talked for too long to one of his colleagues about the rare book trade. There had been nothing to it; the friend was just that, a friend—but he'd screamed at her for hours when they got home. He said she'd made an idiot of herself and embarrassed him. That she was a fool to think anyone else would want her the way he did.

After that, he'd started going out to bars, parties—everywhere really—without her. She hadn't minded at first. His friends were wary of her, and it was easier to just stay home with Axel and enjoy the peace. But of course, that was when he started meeting other women. Came home smelling like them, with lipstick all over him. He hadn't even bothered hiding it. And then, eventually, he'd kicked her out. Some hidden memory of that day pressed against her consciousness, that glass wall that hid something she wasn't supposed to think about, ever.

"Where did you go?" Finn's deep voice, so steady and different from Mark's shrill tone, brought her back to the moment she was in.

"I'm sorry," she said quickly.

"For what?" He turned her, so he could see her face, his fingers tipping her chin up until her eyes met his. "What could you possibly have to apologize for?"

She shrugged, lowering her eyes.

"I mentioned Mark... Is that what's wrong?"

Harlow shrugged again, her breath shuddering through her, panic barely at bay. She shouldn't think about Mark. Not right now.

"Harls," Finn said, his voice so soft and gentle that she nearly let her panic flow, nearly let her fear take over, just so he could comfort her, prove to her that she was safe. "What happened with you and Mark? Why did you break up?"

"Because I wasn't good enough for him," she said bitterly. "We didn't break up. He dumped me. Kicked me out of our apartment. Kept my cat."

Finn's entire frame tightened, tense as his eyes began to glow with fury. "He kept your *cat* when you left?" His fingers laced through hers as he started toward the house. "Come on. We're going to get your cat. *Now.*"

The word "now" sent a shiver through her. She'd seen Finn like this before, but only rarely. He could be chilly, but he was usually calm. Now he was furious, and so lethal her skin prickled with awareness. Immense power flowed off him in waves, filling the tapestry of magic that surrounded them, lighting the threads in their immediate vicinity in a vicious glow.

There was nothing left of the vulnerable man he'd been a few minutes ago; now he was wholly the immortal predator, dangerous and terrifyingly beautiful. But Harlow wasn't frightened in the slightest. In fact, she was something else altogether. She was aroused, nearly as aroused as she'd been when he mercilessly teased her on the lawn.

His nostrils flared. He could *smell* her desire. Why had she forgotten that?

"Are you…" he trailed off, his eyes glowing.

"I already got Axel back," she said, interrupting his recognition of what seeing him so ready to help her was doing to her body. "Last week. I went to go get him when Olivia and Mark were out."

"You did?" Finn's voice was strained, as though he were almost disappointed that he wasn't going to get the chance to enact some kind of violence on Mark tonight.

"Yes, he's safe at my apartment. Larkin is staying with him tonight. I know that's a little silly, but she likes getting away from the maters and the twins and she loves animals… so, it sort of works out perfectly, since I'm a little overprotective right now."

"That's good." A shaky breath shuddered through him. "You could have asked me to help."

She nodded. "I know. But I needed to do it on my own."

Finn cupped her face in his hands and kissed her forehead so sweetly it brought tears to her eyes. "Do you want to go home and see him? We can go together, spend the night there if you want. Or I can drop you off and go. Whatever you want."

His voice shook in such an uncharacteristic way that Harlow was reminded of the conversation they were supposed to have. "No, I don't want to go home. Axel is fine with Larkin. I want to see the house… and talk. The way we said we were going to."

He nodded, seemingly unable to speak, and led her inside. As he'd said, it was mostly empty, though there was evidence he'd been living here. His jackets, hanging on hooks in the mudroom by the back door. A single handmade mug, rinsed clean in the sink. An ironstone bowl of apples on the marble counter in the white kitchen.

Far from the open concept that many people had begun to prefer in newer homes, this house rambled from generously sized room to room. Each space was perfectly sized to accommodate a large family gathering, but there were no ballrooms, no enormous dining room, no grand halls. Only cozy places to gather intimately.

It was like no Illuminated home she'd ever been in. The walls were painted a clean, creamy white, both bright and cozy at the same time. Elegant and rustic simultaneously, the combinations of wood, stone and architectural details were immaculately chosen. She knew exactly how she'd fill the space, with rich texture and fabrics layered in light colors of alabaster, ivory and gold, with books and antiquities on every built-in shelf.

Harlow loved the dark beauty of Nuva Troi, but she wanted to fill this home with comforting light. Her shadows itched to get to work, but she shushed them.

A fire burned in every hearth, springing to life from the magic in Finn's fingertips as they entered each room, and shaded wall sconces were lit dimly all over the house.

"So," she asked, "no furniture at all besides the kitchen table? Where will we sit?"

He flushed then, color rushing to his cheeks. "There's furniture in the bedroom... Or we could go back to the kitchen. Sit at the table..."

Harlow swallowed hard. He was giving her a chance to back out, to slow things down. But she didn't want to do that. She wanted to know what he had to say, and she was willing to hear it all in the bedroom. Whatever happened after that... Well, she was ready for that too.

"Bedroom," she said.

Finn swept her up the staircase in the open foyer and down a long hallway in an instant, depositing her in a room with an arched ceiling. The enormous upholstered bed was tucked into a curtained alcove. Two oversized chairs flanked the fireplace, as though waiting for them. The walls were painted the same white as the rest of the house, and all of the fabrics in the room were coordinating whites and delicate creams, just as she would have chosen. Above a primitive dresser, near the door to what she assumed was a bathroom or closet, there were nine framed sketches.

Harlow drifted towards them and when her vision focused enough to make them out clearly she whimpered, stretching her fingers towards them. They were his sketches of the house, with her handwriting everywhere, labeling things. They'd worked on these sketches for days the summer between primary and secondary, dreaming together of a place filled with light and whimsy that felt different from the world they knew. He'd followed her instructions perfectly.

"You kept these?"

She turned to look at him, standing in the middle of the room. For the first time in their lives, he appeared helpless to her, as though whatever she said next might actually break him. He nodded slowly, but said nothing, though his gaze burned with an intensity of feeling she didn't remember having seen before.

"But why?" Tears gathered in her eyes. "Why would you do this?"

"Come sit." He took her hands and led her to one of the chairs in front of the fireplace, which roared to life as she sat. Instead of taking the other chair, he sat on the floor in front of her, so he faced her.

"The last night we had together was the most perfect of my life," Finn began, his voice rough with emotion.

Harlow clutched his hand in hers, sensing that she would need the support as much as he did. She was reluctant to admit it, but that night had been perfect for her too, the world full of possibility and love. They'd had their whole future spread out in front of them and that night, she'd foolishly thought they'd spend it together.

She took a deep breath to steady herself, knowing that what came next would probably hurt. "It was perfect for me too."

He didn't miss the waver in her voice and his hand cupped her face, as his eyes darkened with feeling. "When I got home after dropping you off, my parents were waiting for me. My dad was smiling this manic smile and my mother looked absolutely feral."

Harlow could imagine it, after the scene in the ballroom at the Metro. She sensed the anger in him and squeezed his hand harder. Her knuckles went white with the effort.

"They had photos of us, Harls. I guess they had us followed? Though the photos didn't look professional… I never found out where they came from. But I couldn't understand why they were so *happy*. After all the years they lectured me about not getting too close to you—they were always suspicious about how I felt about you. They knew I was in love with you. Hells, everyone knew. It was so obvious… So their happiness… It made me suspicious."

She nodded, understanding this reaction. His parents had insulted her family so many times when they were younger that she too would have been shocked to know they were pleased by the union—as well as being instantly wary regarding their intentions.

He slid out of his jacket and flung it aside, and Harlow was momentarily distracted by the breadth of his chest and the muscles of his forearms as he rolled up his sleeves. The tattoo of the sword, snake and lilacs caught her eye again. When his arms tucked back around her, her heart slowed its thumping pace.

"Go on," she urged.

"They sat me down and urged me to keep… Gods, I can't even say it." His forehead fell to her lap in shame. She resisted the urge to run her fingers through the waves of his dark hair.

"No, say it." She wanted to know what had driven him from her, what had changed him so deeply.

"They urged me to *breed* with you. That was how they put it. Like you were an animal. Breed with you until you produced 'viable offspring.'" A strangled sob escaped his throat. She wished she could be surprised, but it wasn't surprising at all that they'd actually said it. Harlow was sure they'd said worse.

"I was so disgusted with the way they spoke about you that I argued with them. Told them I'd never use you that way. I told them I loved you, that I'd pair with you, bond with you, but that I'd never treat you the way they were asking me to."

"They just wanted us to have a baby?" Her voice was soft, but of course, given what she already knew, this wasn't much of a shock for her.

He looked up at her. "No… I mean… Yes… But by any means necessary. Whether you wanted it or not—and who the fuck knows what they wanted with our child?"

The implication sunk in. They'd tried to force him to violate her. She shook with anger. How could parents ask such a thing of their child? Especially one as *good* as Finn had been. But still, this didn't explain his actions, how he'd reacted.

"We talked about everything back then, Finn. I knew how bad they were. I would have understood," she reasoned. "You could have told me."

"Could I? Could I have said to you at eighteen that my parents wanted me to impregnate you, even if it was against your will? Harlow, I was fucking terrified. Of them, of myself…"

Anger burned a hole in her tongue, and she lashed out. "Why in seventeen hells would you have been afraid of yourself?"

He jumped up, as though she'd struck him and turned from her, shame cowing his ample shoulders. "Gods forgive me, Harls. I considered it, for the briefest moment. I thought about what it would be like to have a child together."

She followed him to where he leaned against the hearth, his forehead pressed to the enormous stone mantel. Her arms went around his waist. "You thought about what it would be like to have a baby?"

He turned and tears were in his stormy eyes. "Yes, and in the context of the conversation I hated myself."

Harlow was perplexed. This wasn't what she'd expected to hear at all. She'd always thought that his parents might have been involved in what happened, but she'd assumed it was that they'd convinced him once and for all how inferior she was to him. How foolish he'd been for falling in love with a lesser immortal. Every choice she'd made for years after had been based on that assumption— that some fault in her had caused the first person she'd ever fallen in love with to turn cruel after one night with her.

This, though. This was something else, and her mind struggled to comprehend the enormity of the consequences that assumption had on her life. "I'm not sure I understand. You thought about us having a baby, not forcing me to do so, but only what it would be like if we had a child. You liked it, and that was terrible of you?"

Tears collected in his eyes, along with shame. "They could tell. Could smell the desire on me. Harls, they knew how much I wanted you, how much I wanted a family of my own, and I knew in that moment they'd never stop trying to manipulate us both into whatever sick plans they have."

"And what are those plans?" she asked softly, thinking of the Merkhov book, as she tightened her grip on his abdomen. Should she tell him about it?

Before she could speak, he was answering. "I don't know. That was the last time we spoke for nearly two years. I moved into my godsfather's brownstone that he willed to me, the one in Midtown, remember?"

Harlow nodded. She remembered the place the Trickster's Chosen had left Finn when he died, but couldn't remember exactly how the shifter was connected to the McKays. Maybe she never knew.

Finn continued. "I was determined to make you hate me. I couldn't trust myself with you, not with all their fucked up shit running through my head, and I knew you'd have some clever solution, some way to solve things." He shook his head. "But you don't know who they are, Harlow. You don't know the things they've done. The things they could still do."

Harlow let her arms fall away from him. Finally she understood. She didn't like it, but it all made sense now. But for something that made sense, it didn't make her feel any better. Maybe he'd made a mistake with the way he went about things, but she'd made one after another, letting his treatment of her define her self-worth. She wasn't certain she could forgive him, or herself for all that.

"What's different about things now, then?" she asked. "Why is it safe now, when it wasn't then?"

Finn shook his head. "It's not. I'm just tired of fighting how I feel. I needed you to know what happened and make a choice for yourself. I took that from you before."

She stared into the fire. "Their goals are consistent at least. Whatever they think us having a child could mean for them can't be good for the baby, or for us."

He shook his head. "No, it can't. But I'm an adult now, and… Well, there are a lot of other things I should tell you, if you think you might want to give us a try, but they involve other people and me asking you to keep a lot of things secret." Finn inhaled deeply, his composure returning. "I can keep you safe now in ways I couldn't before."

She believed that he believed that, that he wouldn't say so if he didn't think it was true. Harlow sank back into her chair. Only one thread was left to pull. "And what about Petra?"

His head hung with remorse. "I've never hated myself so much as when I stood by and let her bully you and Enzo. I've been in therapy since I told Alaric everything."

That surprised her, but only a little. Alaric was good, through and through. Of course he'd tried to help Finn, the way an older sibling would. "When was that?"

"When I was nineteen. He found me a therapist and I still see him—through video calls now though, he's in Nea Sterlis. James is Riley Quinn's dad, an empath like they are."

Harlow was quiet. Her emotions swirled in confusing circles. She was angry he hadn't just spoken to her, explained everything. At the same time, she remembered what it was like to be that age, to be afraid of every changing emotion, to be afraid of yourself and your desires. If she was honest with herself, she couldn't say how she would have reacted if he had told her. But the abandonment and Petra's behavior still did damage that she didn't know how to undo.

He knelt in front of her, as a supplicant might. "I don't expect you to forgive me. And I don't expect you to come live here, or be with me… Or anything. I came back here two years ago, with the intention of telling you everything, and asking you to be together."

"But I was with Mark."

He nodded. "And when I saw pictures of the two of you together on Section Seven, I left. Came here. There was another house on this property then and I had it torn down. When I had the plans drawn up for this place it just sort of came out. But I never thought you'd break up with Mark, so I moved back to Nea Sterlis. Last Yule, everyone said you were going to be engaged. I thought you'd marry him."

"So did I," Harlow whispered. "But things changed."

Finn nodded. "About that… I have something else to admit, and you're not going to like it."

Harlow raised her eyebrows.

"Do you remember Avery Hargrove?"

Her heart sank. So this was about Avery? Was he attracted to her? Her skin prickled with jealousy she wished to Aphora she didn't feel. She nodded, her mouth pressing into a grim line.

"I ran into her at a gallery in Nea Sterlis last winter and she told me a story about Mark Easton that worried me."

Surprise pulsed through Harlow, sending tiny shockwaves coursing through her. "What?"

"They were together in secondary…"

"At boarding school?"

Finn nodded. "Yes. And he was so controlling and violent that her parents had her transferred here to that academy downtown."

"Oh…" Harlow's voice was soft. She'd always thought it was her fault that Mark acted the way he did. It's what he'd said so many times, *You bring out the worst in me, Dollface. I can't help it. I love you so much, it makes me lose my mind.*

"I knew I had no right to get involved in your life, Harls, but Avery warned me that she'd heard from other women he'd been with that he'd escalated his behavior in the time since they were together… That he was worse now. When he was with her, he'd never hurt her, not physically anyway. But he broke her things, yelled at her a lot…"

His voice drifted as he searched her eyes. She knew what he wanted to ask. But there was a blank spot in her mind where that information should be. She stayed very, very still, waiting for him to continue.

"I arranged for him to meet Olivia—I knew from various sources that she was interested in wealthy human men, and I made sure they'd meet, and that she would be primed to be interested in him." The breath he let out should have been one of relief, but he didn't look relieved. Just worried, and slightly ashamed of himself.

"How?" Harlow asked.

He shrugged. "Do you really want to know the details? It worked. I interfered, and it worked, but not the way I thought it would… I thought…"

Harlow understood then and laughed, the sound dry and brittle in her ears. "You thought I'd find out and leave him."

He nodded, guilt clouding his eyes, as though he'd just realized how he'd set her up for more pain, not less. "But something else happened instead, didn't it?"

"He was sleeping with other women before her, Finn. I didn't leave him then. I didn't think I deserved better. He kicked me out though, and it's probably the best thing that could have happened, even though it was awful."

She thought it was anyway. The glass wall between her and that memory was opaque as ever. Harlow took a deep breath. "You helped me. It didn't work out the way you thought it would, but you did help me. I don't know if I ever would have left on my own."

He was lost at sea in his own emotions, a frown furrowing his brow. Finn had always liked things to be cut and dry, bad or good, and this wasn't one of those things. What he'd done, all these things he'd done, they'd been for the right reasons, but they'd hurt her just the same. Harlow sensed he was seeing the bigger picture as they spoke, understanding the depths of how his actions had reverberated in her life for years. "I feel like it was cowardly now—like I should have come to get you."

"I wouldn't have gone," she said, her voice small and quiet. "Back then, I wouldn't have thought I deserved to leave with you, or to be protected like that."

"And now?" There was no hope in his voice.

Maybe the smart thing to do was talk about it more. Go over it all again and again until she had more information. But she'd had enough for one night. She'd need time to process all of this, understand it better for herself, but she wanted to be close with someone who loved her, someone who'd made mistakes, but had made them trying to protect her. The one thing she knew in this moment, with all the fucked up things she'd done, was that no one was perfect. No love was perfect, and sometimes people doing their best messed up. She did, all the time.

Harlow wanted what was behind that once-locked door that opened into something new. And even if she wasn't ready to fully admit that yet, she was willing to walk to the threshold and step between to see what was possible on the other side. "Now I want what I've wanted since our last night together."

His eyes lifted. "What's that?"

"To have another night with you."

Finn's jaw clenched. "Just one night?"

"We'll start with one, and then another… I need to go slow, Finn. I've done a lot of work on myself in the past few months. In a lot of ways I'm over what happened with Mark, but I'm not healed. Not yet."

"We can go as slow as you want," he said, pulling her onto the floor and into his lap. He cradled her close to him and his familiar, sensual smell filled her nose as he held her tight against him. "What about my parents? They obviously want the same things they always have."

Harlow thought of the image of the snakes in the Merkhov book. She should tell him. This was the perfect moment, but she couldn't make the words come out. She was still shaky around the edges of her trust. She could tell him as soon as she was sure of him.

"They can *want* anything they please," she spat, venomous hatred for Aislin and Connor McKay rising in her chest. "There's nothing that says we have to give it to them."

She looked up to find Finn's eyes glowing at the ferocity in her voice. "My brave girl."

She stood, feeling restless and not at all brave, but she didn't contradict him. She needed him to think better of her than she really was right now. If he could think of her that way, maybe it might build a bridge she could cross for herself. She couldn't depend on him to make her whole, she'd have to do that herself, but it was all right to let someone help her, wasn't it?

His eyes followed her as she walked around the room, her dress swirling around her feet. The Solon Mai ball seemed eons in the past, rather than just hours ago. She felt his gaze caress her back, as tangible as if his fingers dragged over the buttons of her dress. He was giving her time, moving slow like she'd asked. She leaned against the doorway to the bathroom, watching him watch her.

He'd misunderstood her. She needed time for her heart. She couldn't reciprocate what he felt for her right now, not in the way she wanted to, but in the meantime, there were other things they could do. Other ways to build trust between them. She hadn't slept with anyone since Mark, hadn't even wanted to. But this was different: this was Finn, and she wanted him, and he so clearly wanted her too. That much she could trust with every fiber of her being.

"Come here," she murmured, so softly she wondered if he'd hear her.

He was there in an instant, but he hesitated, the heat of his body warming her. Her breath hitched as his eyes met hers. "You're sure?" he asked.

"Yes," she breathed as he stepped closer. "I'm sure."

And she was. Sure that while it might take some time for her mind to wrap around the complexity of their past, that he'd been honest with her. That he'd told her what he did at a potential cost to what he wanted most, and that was so far removed from what she'd grown comfortable believing she deserved that it surprised her. Beyond that, she was sure that tonight her body was *hers*, no one else's, and that reverent look in his eyes told her he was ready to worship it.

Harlow was absolutely certain that was part of what she needed to move forward, to trust someone to treat her with respect, to look at her that way tonight and give her freedom and choice tomorrow. But still, he hesitated, his eyes searching hers.

She reached for him, pulling him by the shirt until her back pressed against the wall and the hard planes of his body pushed into her. His eyes stayed on hers as she wrapped her arms around his neck. A small voice cautioned that he wasn't touching her, that she'd misread him, that he didn't want her. She banished it immediately. That wasn't it.

He was letting her lead. He understood that too many choices had been taken from her, that she'd been helpless against the waves of mistakes that had crashed over her for far too long, and now he was letting her be the one to take action.

Finn's head dipped towards hers as she lifted her chin, her lips parting. His chest heaved in time with hers. They were barely touching, and her body already responded to the proximity of his. She tugged his head closer to hers, and their lips met.

The kiss was slow, languid even, as she parted her lips to allow his tongue to dance against hers. Her fingers dug into the hair at the nape of his neck as he deepened the kiss further. He still wasn't touching her with his hands, but her aching breasts met his chest as her back curved, propelling her forward, greedy to make more contact with him.

As she arched hard into him, a deep moan rumbled from his chest, vibrating into her now-molten core. One of his thighs parted her legs as his hands glided up her sides, grazing the curve of her breasts, before they fastened around her waist, dragging her against him as he rocked into her. Every nerve in her body lit with the flame of his touch, heat gathering between her legs, where that thigh offered her release. But he did not press harder into her, did not bring it closer to the swollen flesh between her legs.

He kissed her hard, and each thrust of his tongue teased the release she wanted, but he offered that thigh and it was up to her to take her pleasure. She pulled him closer, parting her legs a bit more and tilting her pelvis until his leg and sizable erection made contact with her.

A moan broke free from her lips, throaty and deep as she ground herself against him. With that, he responded, grabbing her ass and pulling her against him as he aided her efforts to increase the friction between them. His mouth slid down to her neck as his fingers gripped her ass. She was openly whimpering, wordless noise urging him on.

"Come for me," he said, voice husky and low as his tongue swept the sensitive shell of her ear.

She wanted to, but she needed more. More than just this sweet agitation. "I need you inside me."

He pulled away from her, but just slightly, letting her legs lower as his hands moved. He passed a hand over the inside of his wrist, illuminating the expensive sigil embedded under his skin that protected against pregnancy and sexually transmitted disease. Her heart beat faster as she showed him her own. They were really going to do this, after so many years of waiting, of sadness—tonight they'd begin again, find a new way forward.

Finn's lips curved upward into a smile as his hands traveled to her breasts, to the hard peaks of her nipples, his thumbs sweeping across them in tantalizing circles. "Turn around," he said.

She obliged, her knees weak as she braced herself against the wall. He made short work of the buttons on the back of her dress, as he kissed her neck. "You're so fucking beautiful," he said as he pushed the dress off her shoulders.

He pulled her against him as she kicked the dress aside, caressing her breasts and then lower to her stomach. She flinched slightly and he stopped. "Are you all right?"

"It's just..." She didn't want to think about Mark right now. It was the last thing she wanted. "I... I gained weight when I was with Mark."

He froze for a moment, then turned her so that she faced him. His eyes had that predatory, dangerous look she recognized from before. "And?" he asked, his voice soft and deadly.

"And he didn't like it." Her chin began to shake and she squeezed her eyes shut. This was going to ruin everything. They'd been having a good time, and she just had to ruin it.

She heard the sharp breath he took, but his voice was steady, eternally calm, when he said, "Harls, open your eyes."

She did. He'd shed all his clothes in a mere instant, using that Illuminated speed. He was breathtaking, and she wasn't sure what he was trying to accomplish, but it only made her feel more unsure about what they were about to do. She wasn't like she was in secondary, she wasn't thin anymore, and Mark had accused her of "letting herself go."

"Look at me, Harlow," Finn commanded. "Look how fucking hard I am."

She looked, blushing slightly. His cock was thick with desire for her and he stroked it a few times, one side of his mouth lifting slightly. "That's for you. Because *I* like it—the way you look right *now*." He stepped closer, and his voice dropped lower. "That's not quite true, I don't like it, I fucking love it."

Her breath caught as he spun her around, pinning her against him again, in the same position they'd been in when she flinched. Now his hot skin pressed against hers, only the thin fabric of the bodysuit separating them.

His hands cupped her breasts, and he lightly pinched her nipples through the bodysuit as his mouth met her neck again. "Ever since I ran into you on Mulberry Street, I've been thinking of your body, what you'd feel like if I got to touch you like this."

He pushed the bodysuit down a little, exposing her breasts to the cool air of the room and to his view, as he looked over her shoulder. "These are perfect, you understand me. I've dreamed of having them in my mouth for weeks."

She groaned as the warmth of his hands contrasted with the chilly air. He pushed the bodysuit lower, past her hips, exposing the curve of her belly. "Will you let me touch you here?" he asked as she stepped out of the bodysuit, his hands traveling lower.

Harlow's voice stuck at first. "Why do you want to?"

"Because I love the way you look, the way you feel, I love every silken curve of you, and I want you to *feel* it."

He pressed his thick cock against the curve of her ass, punctuating his words with primal ferocity. She nodded and he slid his palms over her stomach, groaning deeply behind her. "This, *this* sends me over the edge. I want to bury my cock in you," he growled as he stroked her skin.

A rush of wet heat gathered between her legs and she spread them, bracing herself on the wall. "Do it," she begged, tipping her hips so that the head of his cock pushed at her slick entrance.

"Not so fast." He laughed, a wicked noise that sent chills down her spine. "I want to see you when you come for me."

He took her hands and turned her, leading her toward the soft fur rug in front of the fire. When she stepped onto it, he kissed her deeply, pulling her to the floor on top of him. She drifted over his body, letting her skin play against his as she straddled him, dragging her wet center over his hard length and then back down again. He groaned, pushing her upright. "I want to see every inch of you."

She leaned back, luxuriating in the heat of the fire, in the pressure of his erect cock, sliding against the most sensitive part of her. His hands slid up her thick thighs, spreading them further as he traveled inward, his thumb grazing her clit for a mere moment before it dipped into the wet folds below.

As he plunged his thumb into her she arched into his hand. "Godsdamn, you are so wet," he growled.

Beneath her, his cock twitched in response, jealous of his thumb. He dragged slick desire out of her and onto the swollen flesh begging for his touch. As he traced tight intentional circles in the spot she needed him most, her legs widened and she rose to position him at her entrance.

He moaned her name as she fitted herself around the weeping head of his cock and lowered slowly onto him. He never took his thumb from her clit as he stretched into her. When he filled her completely, she began to move on him, slowly at first. His eyes burned with lust as her breasts swayed in the firelight.

She smiled as he licked his lips, lowering herself gradually until her nipples bounced against his mouth. He drew his hand back from her clit as she ground it into him. He sucked each of her nipples in turn, his lips pulling at the hard, pebbled peaks of her breasts.

Harlow's abdomen tightened in ecstasy as Finn thrust deeper and deeper into her as she rode him, her hips undulating smoothly, guiding the curve of his cock to a place inside her that made her cry out. At the sound of his name on her lips, Finn grabbed her ass, pulling her harder against him as he fitted his mouth to hers, his tongue moving against hers in time to his feverish thrusts. This was nothing like it had been the first time. That was tentative, sweet, loving. This was frenzied, desperate and wild.

She couldn't get enough of him, couldn't get him deep enough in her. And then her hips tilted a slightly different way as he pulled her ass, slamming into her so hard her vision went dark. She cried wordless pleasure as he fucked her harder, stars lighting her eyes as they found release at the same time.

When she collapsed against him, boneless and spent, his arms went around her. She listened to his heart beating, feeling satisfied, safe and cared for. He played with her hair, sending shivers through her. He was still buried in her and she felt his cock jump inside her, eager for more, but his touch was soothing.

"Do you want a snack?" he asked. "Or dinner? I could make us something."

Harlow was surprised by how wistful he sounded. She was nothing but satiated. She slid off him, feeling empty without him inside her.

"Be right back," she whispered, brushing a kiss to his cheek.

She got up and went to the bathroom, feeling his eyes on her as she went.

"There's sweats in the closet if you want to put something on."

She didn't, but she cleaned herself up quickly, and used his toilet. The bathroom was beautiful, all white marble and perfect lighting, with a tub so deep and long, it made her sigh.

"Do you want to take a bath?"

Harlow turned to find Finn leaning against the bathroom door, naked and perfect. She grinned. "Could we?"

"We?" he asked, smirking. "Yes, *we* definitely can. And then food, and then a *lot* of sleep."

His hand caressed her bare ass as he started to run water in the tub. She wrapped her arms around his waist, pressing her breasts into his back as she kissed a spot between his shoulder blades that she could reach. She was tall, but like all Illuminated, he was taller, nearly six-five, she thought. "You're a little bossy sometimes."

Finn turned, pushing hair out of her face as she tilted her head to be kissed. The sound of running water was comforting in a way that warmed her to her core. "I'm sorry about that. I'll do better. I worry when the people I—I care for —don't seem to be taking good care of themselves."

"Then come care for me," she said, perching on the edge of the tub.

He shook his head, smirking. "As my lady commands."

CHAPTER 24

Harlow woke in an empty bed, gloomy morning light blanketing her. At first she was disoriented, confused. But as her body slid against Finn's sinfully soft sheets, she remembered. The pleasurable ache between her legs reminded her further. And the sounds of the shower emanating from the bathroom brought it all back.

She got out of bed, not waiting for her brain to kick in. She didn't want to second-guess herself or even think as she entered the bathroom. There was a new toothbrush laid out on the counter and she brushed quickly, then glanced around the corner to where she had a full view of Finn in the shower.

When he saw her his skin glowed, emitting a faint light that brought a tight ache to her belly. He crooked one finger at her, grinning. "Get in here."

She obliged, stepping into the massive marble shower. He pulled her to him immediately, kissing her so deeply she was grateful she'd brushed her teeth. He'd clearly brushed his, so she had no doubt he'd been thinking of her.

Water fell from the ceiling in a gentle torrent. He turned her body so she faced away from him. "Morning, Harls. I'm happy to see you."

She felt that acutely, parting her legs as he slid against her back. His hands glided up the front of her and she realized he'd taken a bar of soap from somewhere she couldn't see. He began to slowly lather around her breasts, her nipples hardening at the attention as his free hand rubbed slow circles down her abdomen, lower and lower until he pressed his palm against her belly the way he had the night before. Today she didn't flinch as his fingers pressed into her flesh. She felt the way it affected him to touch her, grip onto her soft body. His cock throbbed against her ass as a growl of pleasure caressed her ear.

Finn's mouth grazed her neck and his fangs scraped against her. Heat built between her legs as his lips and tongue teased her ear. "You felt so good last night I thought it was a dream. I didn't want to wake you though… in case you'd changed your mind."

Harlow leaned forward, pressing her hands against the cool tile of the shower wall as water washed the soap away. "I haven't changed my mind," she said. She leaned forward further, angling her hips upward as she spread her legs. "Feel how much I want you."

The low growl that emanated from his throat sent shivers through her as he gripped her ass. "I can't believe you're here."

Finn's voice was so tender she turned to face him. His stormy eyes were full of emotion and his fangs shone in his slightly parted lips. She kissed him, letting her tongue drag across the sharp point of his elongated canines as his fingers dipped between her legs.

As she kissed him, one long finger slid into her, then two. Her hips rocked forward, plunging his fingers deeper inside her. When he drew them out of her he sucked them slowly. "I love how you taste," he murmured, voice low as he guided her to the seat in the shower.

Her heart thumped hard as he knelt in front of her. He kissed her mouth, his tongue dancing against hers, making promises about what was to come as his fingers plunged into her once more.

Harlow moaned into Finn's mouth as his fingers worked her, gently at first, then harder as she thrust against him. His mouth traveled down her jaw, sucking her neck gently as his fangs scraped against her wet skin. She pressed her neck against them.

"I want you to," she moaned.

"Not yet…" he murmured. "Not yet."

His mouth slid to each of her nipples, sucking them to raised peaks as he used his free hand to squeeze the abandoned breast. She felt the pressure of her release as his fingers curled inside her, but he slowed as the tension mounted.

Then his head dipped lower, trailing kisses down her belly and onto her thighs, which she parted further, wanting desperately to make room for his head between her legs. He hovered above her, his breath on her most sensitive skin nearly enough to send her over the edge.

Her breath came in labored heaves as his mouth closed over her, his fingers thrusting in time to her bucking hips as his tongue lapped and sucked in turns. Her body shuddered against him, but he did not relent until she softened in his arms.

"Are you ready to get dressed?" he asked politely.

"No," she said, rising, her knees only a little wobbly. She turned from him, bracing herself against the shower wall again, flashing him a smile as she spread her legs. "No, I'm not done. Are you?"

He took her by the hips and she guided him to her entrance, which was slick with the results of his ministrations. "No, I'm not," he growled as he slid inside her, stretching her with his girth.

Harlow drove her hips towards him, increasing the power of his thrusts as one of his arms wound around her waist, sliding down to stroke the curve of her belly, moving lower to squeeze her clit as he thrust deep inside her.

"Harder," she commanded, her fingers drifting between her legs.

He moaned in response. "Does that feel good?"

"Yes," she cried as light flashed behind her eyes, as the shadows of her magic crept into her vision. He yanked her to him, kissing her neck as she quivered. He slowed his thrusts slightly now, and she felt the thick pulse of him as he breathed in her ear.

"Nothing feels as good as you," he groaned as he slid back into her, his fangs dragging against her neck.

"Bite me," she begged, clenching hard around his cock.

His hands wound through her hair and he thrust so hard into her she saw stars, the actual glimmer of the cosmos as she came against him. He called her name again and again, but his teeth did not sink into her as she went limp.

The Illuminated were an amalgamation of the lower Orders; they had the ability to change shape as the Order of Masks did, a deep talent for magic like the Order of Mysteries, and a similar body composition to those in the Order of Night, including fangs. Harlow knew that when the Illuminated were intimate that they often bit their partner, and the rumors she'd heard about the way it enhanced the pleasure of the experience intrigued her.

Finn turned her in his arms, warm water rinsing them both as he washed her hair. She felt drowsy and sated, but not quite satisfied. "Why wouldn't you bite me?" she asked softly.

He had a dreamy look in his eyes, as though he felt as come-drunk as she did. "I… I want to…" he murmured. His skin glowed still, warm against hers.

"I know the Illuminated do that when they fuck," she reasoned.

A wary look flickered over his face, so quickly she almost missed it. "They do, you're right."

"Then why won't you bite me?"

He pulled away from her. "We're turning into prunes. Let's get out."

She pulled him back. "Is it me?"

"Yes," he snapped, stalking out of the shower.

Harlow froze, her body reacting to the tone of Finn's voice immediately. A flush of shame burned her cheeks. He stood, dripping on the bathroom floor, his face twisted immediately in distress. "That… didn't come out right. Come out of the shower, all right?"

He held his hand out to her, but she couldn't move. It wasn't fair for her to hold him responsible for always speaking in a calm tone, but the way he snapped at her reminded her of Mark, and now she was stuck.

Finn's fingers grazed her chin, lifting her eyes to his. "I'm sorry I snapped. I'm a little wound up. Can you give me a beat?"

His voice was steady now, as though he knew exactly why she was stuck in the shower. She took a deep breath and stepped out, and let him wrap her in a warm, fluffy towel. There was something at work here she didn't understand. "Do you want me to wait for you in the bedroom?"

"Thank you, yes," he said, squeezing her arm. "There's a robe on the hook there."

She saw it, and knew it was his when she slid it on. His scent was all over it and she breathed it in, letting it comfort her. Harlow went to work lighting the fire and when Finn came out of the bathroom, dressed only in a pair of loose grey sweatpants, she made every effort to stay in her chair.

"Will you sit with me?" he asked softly.

She'd meant to give him a little space, but she liked that idea better. He sat in the chair opposite hers and opened his arms. Her movements were slow, careful, in case he changed his mind, but as soon as she was within reach, he pulled her into his lap.

"I'm sorry I snapped," he said, stroking her damp hair. "What I said didn't come out right."

"It's okay," she replied, her voice tentative. "Mark was... unpredictable. I know that's not your fault..."

Finn pressed kisses to her cheeks, then her lips. "Thank you for telling me though. I'm pretty even tempered, but this, biting you. It scares me."

Harlow's forehead wrinkled as she tilted her head, signaling that she was ready to listen.

"Every time I'm inside you, I desperately want to bite you," he whispered.

"You can," she insisted. "I'm not afraid."

"But maybe you should be."

"You're not a vampire," she scoffed. "The Illuminated don't kill with their bite. Everything I've ever heard is that it makes sex... better."

That's not *exactly* what she'd heard. What she'd heard was that it made for one of the most mind-blowing orgasms ever, and frankly, she wanted that. She wanted that with him.

"Yes, that's how it usually works."

"So you've bitten other people?"

Finn's cheeks flushed red. "Yes."

Now her cheeks flushed. "But not me."

"If I bite you it will be different." His eyes fell closed and he pinched the bridge of his nose. "The way I feel about you changes things. It could change my bite."

"What do you mean?"

"What do you know about the Claiming?"

She'd never heard of it. "Nothing. What is it?"

"A brutish mating ritual between my kind. I didn't know it could happen between an Illuminated and a sorcière. In fact, I thought it was impossible, or I would have been more careful, but last night I tasted venom the first time we fucked and it scared me."

"Venom?"

He shook his head. "Not like snake venom... It wouldn't poison you or harm you, but it would bind us together in a way that would make it difficult for us to be parted."

"How so?"

Finn's brow furrowed. "It's a psychic bond. And if we were no longer in love, it would be painful for us to separate. We would need magic to revert to our original selves... Difficult magic."

Harlow's heart pounded. "Are you saying you're in love with me?"

Finn sighed. "That's complicated to answer."

"Try?" she asked, so quietly she wasn't sure if he'd heard her at first.

"I'm still in love with who you were when we were young. I get it, I don't know you now, not well anyway. But we're still connected—my heart, my body, they don't know the difference my mind does. Maybe that's what triggered my venom." Harlow nodded, understanding. "I think I could be again though," he added. "If you wanted this too. I think I could be."

Harlow swallowed hard. She couldn't lie to herself, the thought was exhilarating as it was frightening.

"You don't have to say anything about how you feel about me right now, in fact, please don't."

She could understand that impulse, and she was glad he was giving her time to think. "So the Claiming, it's reversible?"

He nodded. "But it is a physically painful process to reverse. I told you, it's brutish."

"But that's the bad part. If we were together, what would it be like if we didn't fall out of love?"

His eyes darted to hers, full of fear and hope. "It would make our joining pure bliss. It's why the Claimed rarely part, even if they fall out of love. They just screw some more, get their fix and keep going. My parents are that way. That's why they're so awful."

Harlow understood now—he didn't want to trap her, nor be trapped himself. She also understood why he'd reacted badly. This topic made him feel scared, vulnerable. Her fingers wound into his dark hair and she shifted in his lap, straddling him. He pushed her wet hair back from her face. "I shouldn't have snapped at you."

Underneath her, his hips rose to make closer contact with her as his hands ran up her thighs. She pulled gently at the hair at the nape of his neck, tilting his head back so she could brush the angles of his face with her lips. "You're allowed to have feelings. I understand everything you said." She sank deeper onto him, moving against him slowly as his hands roamed under her robe. His thumbs skimmed her inner thighs, teasing her mercilessly.

Harlow let out a tiny whimper then bent to nip his earlobe, whispering, "I'll stop asking you to bite me. For now."

As she pulled back, his eyes blazed. She was thrilled by the faint glow in his skin, the growing pressure of him against her, only the thin fabric of his sweatpants between them. She opened the robe and let it fall away, yanking his pants down as she positioned herself above him.

The dull sting of too much sex mixed with the hot rush of feeling him push into her. He was leisurely and purposeful as he dragged her down on him, stretching her aching body slightly with each increased inch. They moved slowly, looking into each other's eyes, as he moved deep inside her.

A faint scent of smoke from the fire filled Harlow's nose, mixing with Finn's scent of oud and rich amber, so intoxicating that she nearly lost her head. The rhythm and intensity of their movements increased as her hips bucked and rolled over him. Cool, dry air contrasted with the wet heat between them as he thrust harder into her. Harlow moaned, leaning back to allow the gentle curve of him to hit her in the spot that made her see the universe, keeping her eyes on his as her shadows gathered around her.

"What is that?" he breathed. "Is that you?"

She nodded as his skin lit, his lips parted as she clenched around him. "Come with me," she begged.

He pulled her hips, pushing hard into her as she cried out, her voice mingling with his. Above them inky shadows mingled with the light that poured out of him, twisting and writhing together as they did. Harlow knew he was just as amazed as she was, pleasure washing over them both in waves of light and shadow.

And for an instant she saw herself through his eyes, beautiful curves of darkness and shadow, mysterious and alluring as a new moon, dangerous and beloved. When her conscious mind snapped back into her own body, tears streamed down both their faces.

"How did you do that?" he murmured as he clung to her, kissing her over and over. "How did you channel magic that way, Harls?"

CHAPTER 25

Harlow wasn't sure what to say. She couldn't find words at the moment. Nothing like that had ever happened to her before during sex, and she'd had some truly spectacular orgasms in her lifetime.

"Are you a Strider?" Finn asked, his eyes wide with wonder.

"How do you know what that is?" she asked, voice sharper than she'd like.

Finn shook his head. "I don't know much, just that the Striders were legendary witches, a force against the Illuminated during the War of the Orders. My people are deeply afraid of them."

Her heart clenched, but she felt her magic respond. It was encouraging her, winding around her arms and fingers, soft and pleased. It liked him; it wanted to mingle with the light again.

"What about you? Are you afraid?"

A grin spread across his face. "No, I know I should be, but that was nothing like what I was taught to fear."

"What you were taught to fear?"

He nodded. "Yes, all Illuminated children hear tales of the Striders, who will extinguish our light with their never-ending darkness." Harlow's smile was faint. The Orders were full of such tales, primarily meant to scare children. For the sorcière it was the incubus, who would steal their hearts and their magic— shifters told tales of the Trickster deity, Voltos, stealing their ability to change forms. "I honestly thought those were stories to convince us to behave. But that… That was…"

"Mind-blowing?" she breathed.

He laughed, amazed as she was. "Yeah, it really was. And I feel stronger too."

"Stronger?" she asked.

"Yeah, watch this."

And without a word, they were standing on the rocky cliffs that looked over the ocean, far above Nuva Troi, both of them naked in the pouring rain. Harlow laughed as she spun. Usually portaling came with a sense of being pulled, sometimes nausea, but this had been like taking a step. "That was effortless."

"You try," he laughed.

She closed her eyes for a moment and when she opened them, they were both fully clothed, dry and standing under an enormous umbrella that Finn held above their heads. She felt her shadows sing in her blood, her fingers stained with inky, beautiful magic.

"That is amazing," Finn said, stepping close to her, winding his arm around her waist. They stared out at the ocean for a few moments, listening to the rain hit the umbrella.

"What does it mean?" she asked.

He shook his head. "I don't know, but I have to believe it has something to do with what my parents want from us, don't you?"

Fear lanced through her, cold and clammy as a dead hand gripping her heart. "I imagine it does."

"Then the stakes are higher now. Whatever it is they want, it isn't that, Harls. Or at least not that version of your magic. That was nothing my parents would want anything to do with. They want a baby, some creature more powerful than what the Illuminated can produce on their own, not for either of *us* to be stronger."

They stood together watching the rain for a long time, both of them teeming with thoughts, she assumed. Her mind was racing and she wished Thea had been able to restore more of the Merkhov facsimile. Rain thudded harder on the umbrella now, and waves crashed on the rocks below. She snuggled further into Finn's arms, grateful for his warmth.

He pressed a kiss to her hair. "Harlow, what do you think would happen if I Claimed you while whatever that was happened?"

Something wonderful. Something terrible. Harlow didn't know which. She took a sharp breath in, watching the rain. She couldn't keep the Merkhov text from him any longer. "I need to show you something. Can you take us to the Monas?"

He nodded and took her in his arms, and moments later they were in the alley behind the courtyard. This time she felt a tiny wave of nausea. "Oof," she groaned. "It wears off."

Finn stroked her arm. "You all right?"

She nodded. "Let's go inside."

He followed her, still holding the umbrella she'd made. She was pleased to find they were also still dressed. So her magic wouldn't wear off. She felt the shadows sigh indignantly, almost as though they were saying, *of course not, silly*.

It wasn't that they communicated exactly, but that she was so in touch with her magic that it was easy to feel the semi-sentient pulse of its will. She'd known magic was a force all its own before, but now she understood intimately.

When they stepped inside the house, Aurelia was waiting in the mudroom, arms folded tightly around her narrow frame, a worried expression on her face.

They'd obviously tripped one of her wards when they arrived, and she'd watched them walk in. "You told him?"

How did she always know everything? As children, the Krane girls had never gotten away with anything. Selene and Aurelia both seemed to have a seventh sense precisely tuned to predicting their daughters' impulses. Harlow laughed at the way things never changed, and then shrugged. "Not exactly… He… saw?"

Aurelia barely suppressed a smug smile. "The Merkhov text *does* mention something like that might happen. Were the two of you…"

Harlow glared, cheeks turning bright red. "*Mother. Please.* I am not going to discuss this with you." Behind her, Finn snickered. She shot the glare over her shoulder to apply to him as well. He just laughed harder. *Arrogant prick.* "Finn needs to see the illumination."

Aurelia nodded, sniffing to hide her smile. "Of course." But she did not move. Her eyes went to Finn and they narrowed, appraising and cold.

Finn bowed his head slightly. "It is so nice to meet you, Archchancellor Krane. Officially, I mean."

Aurelia held out her hand and Finn took it, kissing the ring that marked Aurelia as presiding Archchancellor of the Order of Mysteries. "Be welcome in my home, Finbar McKay."

"Thank you," he murmured so softly, and with so much emotion that Harlow saw her mother's eyes narrow, assessing him.

"Go upstairs please. I'll find Mama and the book."

Harlow took Finn's hand and led him up the stairs, taking him into Aurelia's study. The room was small, lined with crowded bookshelves stained a dark green hue. Mother's mahogany desk was piled with neat stacks of notes and a small brass lamp cast a cozy glow. A heavy antique library table sat in front of the enormous windows, natural light flooding into the room through the leaded glass.

"Why does every room of your parents' house feel so much like home?" Finn murmured as his eyes flew over the spines of the books on the shelves. His voice was painfully wistful. Harlow wasn't sure what to say, so she pressed a kiss to his hand, which she still held.

Selene cleared her throat. "Aurelia is making tea. I don't believe we've met."

Finn's hand shook in hers. He understood immediately. Aurelia was politically the most powerful Krane, but Selene was the heart of the family, the ultimate test he would have to pass. Harlow's eyes widened in shock when he fell to one knee, bowing his head. This was a position of fealty the Illuminated only took when swearing oaths. It was an ancient custom, one she had not expected to see from him, especially not today.

"I promise you," he swore, taking Selene's outstretched hand. "She is safe with me. Nothing my parents want will come to pass. I will protect her with my life."

Harlow took a sharp breath in. Her heart raced, as her shadows sang with pleasure. She wanted to shush them—this was binding. He was swearing an oath to her mother. Nothing like this had even seemed possible just a day ago.

"I accept you at your word," Selene said, her voice smooth and regal. "The next oath you take will be to her."

Finn nodded, his head still bowed. "If she will have me, I will swear any oath she asks."

A lump rose in Harlow's throat, coated with fear. *This was all moving too fast, wasn't it? Or was this the natural place for their path to take them, given all the years between them?* She tried to dismiss the feeling of the walls closing in on her. None of his promises required her to make any in return, not yet anyway.

When Selene pulled Finn gently from the floor and kissed his cheeks, the claustrophobia dissipated, realization dawning on her. This wasn't *just* about her. Finn wanted her family to trust him. No, he *needed* them to trust him, because so few people in his life ever had before, except maybe Alaric. Trust wasn't a part of his relationship with his parents. Finn had always wanted a family like hers, and given what he'd grown up with, she couldn't blame him for that.

Harlow slipped her hand into Finn's and he squeezed it hard. "Thank you," he said, and she wasn't sure who he was thanking, or if he was simply grateful.

As they settled into chairs around the library table, she wondered what it would be like to live with parents who you could not trust, and who did not trust you in return. She wondered if anyone in his family had truly loved him. From the slump in his shoulders, she thought he might be thinking the same thing.

"I'm glad you're here," she said, as Selene rose to help Aurelia with the tea tray and Thea entered behind her with the Merkhov text.

"Me too," he answered. There was an unmistakable tremor in his voice. This was as important to him as she'd suspected it might be.

As Selene arranged the tea tray, Aurelia opened the book in a cradle on the worktable. "I believe this is the illumination you wanted Finn to see."

He leaned forward. Thea had done more work on it. The image was close to being fully restored, with the coloring on the snakes' bodies showing in brilliant hues, while the egg and sphere still looked a bit dull, but much easier to make out. The most stunning improvement was the way the light and shadows coming off the snakes were interacting, twisting together. This was eerily reminiscent of what they'd experienced in Finn's bedroom just hours before. His eyes narrowed as his body stilled, his focus winnowing in a way that Harlow knew probably intimidated people who worked with him.

"Where did you get this?" No one had a chance to answer Finn. He continued speaking, his words coming out in an excited rush. "This is representative of a union between a Strider and one of the Knights of Serpens, isn't it?" He looked closer, seeing the egg, as if for the first time. His usually healthy coloring paled. "*Oh.*"

"The Knights of Serpens?" Harlow asked, gripping his knee under the table.

He nodded, glancing at her, but only for a moment. "A sect of Illuminated warriors. They came in the original envoy to protect the ambassadors. Our history tells us they fought against the Striders in the War of the Orders."

Harlow had never come across any such history of the Great War, but she understood the lower Orders and a contingent of humans had risen up against the Illuminated, attempting to force them back to their own realm. Obviously, it hadn't worked. Though the Illuminated were struggling to reproduce, they were as powerful as they'd ever been, and there hadn't been a war on Okairos since. Shortly after the war, poverty was eradicated and the strict regulation of human life began. It was a steep price for peace, in Harlow's opinion, but of course that was not the tone history took on the matter. It was practically treason to even think such a thing.

"The Striders and the Knights of Serpens were enemies?" Harlow asked, trying to understand how her people had actually fit into things.

"So the Illuminated would have us believe," Thea replied, giving Finn a pointed look. Harlow noticed the way his eyes flicked quickly away from her sister's. "But the Knights haven't been seen or heard from since the war ended. Effectively, they don't exist."

Finn shifted uncomfortably under Thea's gaze. The two of them shared some secret, Harlow realized, her stomach turning at the thought. He stared at his hands. "That's not exactly the case."

Selene's eyes snapped to Finn's, demanding he continue.

"When Alaric and I were at uni, something happened... We received keys to an ancient store of knowledge, an invitation from the Knights of old to reinvigorate their society, which was not what we'd been told it was at all."

"Who sent the keys?" Harlow asked.

Finn shook his head. "We never found out."

That was saying something, given the work they did together at their securities company. What kind of organization could keep secrets from people like Alaric? Thea sat back in her chair, a hint of a smile playing at her lips.

Aurelia and Selene shared a concerned look. Selene asked, "Can you tell us more? About the Knights?"

Finn nodded. "Yes, because you've found this, and because of the implications... I think I can." He took Harlow's hand and kissed it, smiling faintly at her. She thought he looked anxious, but the impression passed quickly. He was far too good at masking his emotions. "The Knights of Serpens fought alongside the Striders in the war, not against them, and as punishment they were executed when the Illuminated won. On his execution day, their commander had a vision that one day the Knights and Striders would be reunited, and it would bring about an event he called 'the reckoning,' though we don't know what he meant, as he was executed before he could elaborate."

"How do you know all this?" Aurelia asked, deep suspicion etched into the lines around her eyes.

"All of the Knights' last words were magically transferred to the vault of information in Nea Sterlis that we received keys to," Finn answered.

Selene took a deep breath. "And so you are a Knight? You and Alaric both?"

Finn nodded. "Yes, and Petra. Along with a select few others, we have a network across Nytra... My friend Cian Herrington is my second and helps to run our special projects."

It was an odd addendum, like Finn was relieved to speak about someone significant to him. Harlow hadn't heard Cian's name before, but the tone Finn took indicated they were someone important.

"Your *second?*" Harlow asked. That would imply that Finn was, what exactly?

"I am the Serpens' commander," Finn said softly. "Though we do very little fighting these days, and Alaric, who is technically my third in command, handles most of our more nefarious activities."

"Which are what exactly?" Aurelia asked, leaning forward.

Finn opened his mouth to give some answer, but Selene cut in. "Where is Thea?" Her voice carried a note of panic. Everyone stopped and looked around. It was true, Thea was gone.

"I'm right here," said a soft voice in the doorway. All eyes swung to the elegant figure standing in the entry of the study. "Alaric's here too. I went to let him in. We thought you might need us both today."

Alaric peeked around the door. "Hello, Kranes! Finn," he said cheerfully, with a wave so characteristically Alaric that one might have thought they were gathering for brunch, not discussing the kind of sedition that could get them all killed.

Finn nodded to Alaric, his brows furrowing in mild confusion. "What are you doing here?"

Alaric moved into the room and tapped the Merkhov text. "The same thing you are. Protecting the woman I love."

Thea beamed at Alaric with such pride that Harlow felt the lump in her throat again. *Was this what love looked like?* "Thea?" she asked. "What's going on?"

Aurelia motioned for Thea and Alaric to take the remaining seats at the worktable as she cleared the Merkhov text and began to serve tea. Thea reached across the table to take Harlow's hand. "I'm sorry I couldn't tell you everything," she whispered. "We wanted to wait to find out if you and Finn could work things out on your own."

Harlow's brow furrowed. "Okay, we've worked things out. Could you all explain what's happening here?"

Finn looked slightly irritated, as though Alaric had stolen his thunder, but he sat back in his chair as the two got settled. When they were comfortable, Alaric looked to Finn, a question in his eyes. Finn nodded, though Harlow noted he still looked perturbed. It occurred to her that he likely spent his life rarely being questioned or challenged. Unless it came to his parents, of course.

Alaric smiled at Thea again. "Thea and I knew each other in school, as we all did, but when we were at uni we met again."

Thea's cheeks pinked, as though she was remembering something especially enjoyable. "We were both researching the Knights of Serpens, and their conflict with the Striders."

"Why?" Selene asked sharply.

Thea's face twisted apologetically. "Because I knew it was possible that one of us could become a Strider. I knew it wouldn't be me, because I'd shown all the early signs of manifestation—I was clearly not the Strider. I actually thought it might be Larkin for a while."

"As did I," Alaric murmured. "And since I'd already taken my oaths, I wanted to know more about our ancient allies, and what our shared goals may have been."

Thea continued fluidly, as though the two of them had been paired for years, which Harlow supposed they had, if they'd reconnected six years ago. "Alaric had a book I needed and we began talking. Neither of us knew the other's personal interest in the old stories at the time, but in researching our histories, we fell in love."

Something sliced into Harlow's heart. Thea had been keeping secrets from her for so long. What did all this mean?

Alaric was still speaking, "Eventually, we found the original book the triptych is from. The illumination in the Merkhov text is a facsimile of a section of the Scroll of Akatei."

Aurelia gasped. "No. You've seen it? Both of you?"

Thea smiled at her mother, and the resemblance between them was so strong they could have been twins in that moment. "We have it. Or part of it anyway. It was in the Velarius family archives, but now we have the original in the Vault."

Aurelia looked perturbed, embattled over the fact that she believed Thea should have revealed all this to the Order of Mysteries, no doubt. And perhaps she should have. It was hard for Harlow to decide. She couldn't deny she also felt the sting of having Thea keep so much from her.

Selene leaned toward Alaric, while simultaneously patting her wife's hand to console her. "Do your parents know you have this?"

Alaric shook his head. "No. My parents are more sympathetic to the lower Orders and humans than many of the Illuminated, but I haven't trusted them with this knowledge. I've been careful to hide my interest in this subject, especially after Thea and I met."

"Get to the point, you two," Finn cut in. "Tell them."

Thea's face was cool as ever, but her eyes revealed her guilt. "When we were sure I wasn't the Strider, I was sworn in. I am one of the Knights of Serpens."

"What in seventeen hells does *that* mean?" Aurelia said, her voice low and dangerous. A sorcière's first duty was always to the Order of Mysteries.

Thea shot back, no trace of her usual politeness evident: "It means that I've been *helping*, Mother. Helping to make things what they should be on Okairos. Or at least here in Nytra."

Alaric took Thea's clenched fist into his own. "What Thea is trying to say is that the Knights are committed to finding a way to bring more equity into the world, as we always have been. We know that historically, members of all the Orders were Knights, even sorcière."

Thea nodded, looking nervous. As Alaric clutched Thea's hand to his chest, Harlow noticed the enormous black diamond shining from the ring on her sister's left index finger. She was not only paired, but bonded.

Harlow snatched her hand. "Explain this. Now."

"Oh," Thea murmured. "I forgot to take it off."

Alaric's grin could have lit a city. "We made it official last night—a priestess of Aphora performed the ritual."

Harlow's eyebrows shot so far up, she could feel her hairline move. She stole a glance at Selene, who'd been planning her daughters' bonding rituals since they were children. Mama was seething, sheets of tempestuous energy filling the room. Each of the Krane children were to be married in the Temple District in Nea Sterlis, at a date determined by one of the Order of Mysteries' astrologers, with weeks of celebration both before and after the ritual proper. A clandestine ceremony in a dark city temple was *not* what she'd planned.

Alaric seemed to sense the danger he was in and hastily kept explaining, but Harlow noticed his hands shook as Thea took them into her own. "If anyone finds out what we are doing here, we are all in a great deal of danger, as you know… Anyway, to be safe, we just went ahead and were bonded—"

He was babbling, probably due to the intensity of Selene's glare. Thea stopped him from continuing, by adding, "We'd like to have the celebrations you planned at a later date, Mama."

"Congratulations," Selene said drily, ignoring Thea's comment completely. "Please clarify why all this secrecy was necessary."

Thea nodded, continuing quickly. "Until Harlow's magic manifested, this was all just speculation. The Scroll of Akatei seems to indicate that the unification of a Knight of Serpens and a Strider will usher in a new age of magic— which we believe would effectively end the Illuminated's stranglehold on Okairos."

Alaric added, "Thea and I believe a fifth Order will be formed through this union, that the egg symbolizes a new start, or a new power."

Harlow thought of the ease with which both she and Finn had used their power earlier in the day. Could this be an explanation for why that was possible?

Alaric continued, "Though we do not know how. The triptych is incomplete in the Scroll of Akatei as well."

Was this why Finn was so interested in her? Harlow felt as though the walls were closing in on her again. This time she could not slow it down or stop it. Her heart beat erratically and her palms began to sweat. "Did you know this?" she asked, turning to Finn. "Is this why you were so eager to ally with me?"

Finn turned to her, shock on his face. "No. I mean, I knew about your sister and Alaric, of course. But not about the Scroll." He glared at Alaric. "Why didn't you tell me this?"

Alaric sighed. "We didn't want to affect either of your choices. It's not a prophecy, Finn. It's the key to unlocking the trouble our people caused when they came here. It's only a solution, and when we didn't know about Harlow, we didn't want to introduce anything that would complicate the issues between you."

Thea nodded. "But we think your parents know. That's why we needed to tell you, *today*."

"If my parents knew all this, don't you think they'd want to keep Harlow and I apart?" Finn asked. It was a reasonable question, as it seemed unlikely they'd want to force something that would bring about the end of the Illuminated's power.

Thea and Alaric shared a look. "Well, that's just *our* interpretation of what the scroll may be saying."

Aurelia rolled her eyes. She and Thea had many conflicts over the interpretation of texts that relied on iconography and symbolism to convey meaning.

Usually it was a charming quirk of their relationship. Today it made Harlow ill. Aurelia pinched the bridge of her nose. "What does it *actually* say, Thea?"

Thea looked at her hands. "If my translation is correct, it says the combination of the Knight and the Strider will produce a power unlike any other. We believe the other two illuminations show the process, much as an alchemical text might."

Finn's voice was nothing less than lethal fury, cold and dangerous. "My parents think it means we'll have a child, and that child will be the most powerful creature in history, don't they?"

Alaric sighed. "They might, but that's not the only way to interpret things."

Selene shook her head. "It doesn't matter. If that's what they think, Harlow is in danger, as would any child she and Finn might have together. We need to see the rest of the triptych, one way or another."

Harlow felt as though she might vomit. They were all discussing her *having a baby*, and no one had even looked at her, or asked her what *she* thought.

Thea continued speaking. "We think the McKays may have the missing parts of the scroll, or at least they've seen it. Tatyana Merkhov disappeared, did you know that?"

Selene pursed her lips. "Yes, I knew. Something about a plane crash, I believe."

Thea shook her head. "We think she was killed, because of what she knew, and what she published in that book. It's impossible to find intact, as you both know. We were lucky to have stumbled upon a copy in our last acquisition. I don't think the lot-owner even knew what it was."

Aurelia shrugged. "Likely not, they weren't a collector. Just cleaning out an estate."

Thea nodded. "She obviously saw the Scroll when it was complete. She knew what the triptych showed. Others might as well."

"And you think the McKays and the Velariuses are the ones who killed her?" Harlow asked.

"It seems possible," Alaric said. "We have to behave as if they did, at least until we know more."

Harlow's head spun with information, as her attention bounced from one thought to another. The room felt very small. *Was the ceiling lower than it had been a few minutes ago?*

Finn held up a hand. "Please, will you excuse Harlow and I for a few minutes?"

He hadn't even looked at her, and yet he'd known she was crumbling under the pressure of what was being said. Everyone's eyes turned to Harlow. Her skin was cold, but inside her muscles felt as though they had been set aflame.

Finn's hand closed around hers and he rose from his chair, in a motion so fluid it nearly distracted her from the internal struggle waging war on her heart. "Come with me to the terrace?"

She stood without a word, her body simply following the commands Finn guided her through. *Stand, walk behind him, follow him to the terrace, curl into a big rattan settee, sip a cool glass of water.* When she came back to herself, he was sitting at her feet, and rain poured outside the covered terrace, making the back courtyard a blur of greens, purples and golds.

"You were panicking," he said, tucking a soft cotton blanket around her knees.

She nodded, but could hardly speak. It was all a lot to take in. Finally she said, "The maters are going to kill Thea for having their bonding ritual without a big to-do."

It was good to lighten the mood a bit, it gave her room to think. Finn snorted. "You know *we* don't have to move so quickly, right? Last night was amazing, and this morning was absolutely phenomenal, but I'm not rushing this for anything, or any*one* but you."

Harlow's brow furrowed. "What are your expectations now?"

"Nothing. My only concern right now is keeping you safe. Believe me when I say that if that means staying apart, I will make that choice. Given everything that Thea and Alaric know, maybe that would be better."

His eyes didn't meet hers, but she noticed the tremor in his hands that seemed reserved for her. *Was that what she wanted? To end things now, to remain safe? Would she even be safe if they weren't together?* She remembered what he'd said about his parents being willing to force her into something she didn't want.

"I think... I think I just need a little bit of time," Harlow said quietly.

Finn nodded, getting up. "I'll go then. Alaric can fill me in a bit more on the secrets he and Thea have been keeping. I'll check in with you tomorrow, if that's all right?"

She saw it in his eyes, and heard it in the clipped, businesslike tone of his voice. He thought she was backing out, that she didn't want him at all. Her hand slipped into his. "I need to breathe, Finn. That's it. Just a beat to get my bearings, okay?"

She pulled on his arm until his face met hers. A half-smile curved the corner of his mouth as he asked, "And what about the things that happened this morning?"

Harlow's words tumbled out. "It was all amazing. To tell you the truth, I was excited about all of it until it turned into a big thing. When it was just you and me, not Striders and Knights."

Finn crouched down, so his eyes were at her level. "It's still you and me. You heard Alaric, this isn't a prophecy, it's a solution, and *we* don't have to be the solution if you don't want us to be."

The idea that he would walk away, let her go, let her *choose*, made her throat clench. Air seemed scarce. Harlow closed her eyes. "I need time for my mind to catch up. This is how I am."

His voice was soft in her ear, his lips brushing her neck, while her eyes stayed squeezed shut. "I remember."

She wound her arms around him. He kissed her forehead and was gone. When she was alone, she considered that Finn had known her almost her whole life. That he knew the way she needed time to herself to process things quietly meant something. That he respected her enough to walk away if she asked meant even more. A seed of trust drove deep into her soul and took root.

Her shadows sang at the progress she made, and she let them dance around her fingers as she thought things over. While she needed time like this to be quiet and let her brain work things through, she knew he needed to take a more active approach. Finn needed to *do* something, rather than think. It had the possibility to cause conflict between them, but if they managed it right, gave each other space to be themselves—it was possible they'd be stronger together.

Harlow took several long breaths, finally opening her eyes. The door to the terrace slid open. Thea pressed a mug of tea into her hands and curled up next to her on the settee. Harlow let the sound of the rain drown everything else out while she tried to find her way back to herself again.

"Why do you think Finn and I could do anything to bring equity to the world?" Harlow asked her sister after a time. She appreciated the company, but she wasn't going to be able to process her feelings with Thea watching her, so she might as well get some questions answered.

"The Scroll of Akatei. That's what it's all about."

Harlow shook her head. "Spell it out for me, Thea. I'm tired."

"The Scroll of Akatei isn't a written text. It's mostly images, and the few inscriptions are vague to the point of opacity and in a variety of ancient languages that are difficult to translate. Many of the images are deceptively similar to those we're used to seeing in humans' alchemical texts, which would have been the Scroll's contemporaries, but there's more to it than that. Alaric and I think it's the story of the Illuminated—what they were *supposed* to do when they came here."

"Which was what?" Harlow asked, exhaustion growing closer by the minute.

"Activate this realm's magic… for everyone."

Harlow's head hurt. "Didn't they do that, sort of? I mean, the Orders are their children and we're all magical to some extent, right?"

"Yes, but they weren't supposed to come here and have children. They were *supposed* to come and unlock magic for everyone, making it accessible to anyone. Instead, they hoarded it for themselves, and a very small amount of the world."

Thea was obviously frustrated by Harlow's slow uptake and her tone was bordering on condescending. Harlow also got the distinct impression there was more to the story that Thea wasn't saying. She was keeping secrets for Alaric, and the Illuminated, and Harlow couldn't help but feel betrayed.

"And how were they going to do that?" Harlow asked, feeling snappish.

Now Thea looked perplexed. "We don't know. Again, the Scroll is a series of images and I was unable to restore most of them, in addition to the fact that a crucial piece is missing. It was damaged magically."

"How did Merkhov get her hands on it?" Harlow's question was more idle wondering than actual question, but Thea's eyes lit up.

"That is a really good question. One I hope we'll answer when we find out more about the triptych."

Harlow suppressed the urge to roll her eyes at Thea's tone. "Wonderful."

Thea sighed, apparently annoyed by Harlow's acidity. There was a long pause before she asked, "Are you going to congratulate me?"

"Of course. I'm happy for you both." Unlike Selene, she had nothing invested in fancy bonding rituals, or days of celebration. Still, having so much kept from her stung. "I just wish you could have told me all this sooner. Why did the two of you wait for so long?"

Thea shrugged a little, looking distressed. "I wasn't sure what to do, honestly. When I found most of this out, you were living with Mark and it seemed like it wouldn't be a good time."

Mark. Of course Thea hadn't wanted to tell Harlow anything when she was with him. When she'd been with Mark, she'd been deemed untrustworthy, despite the fact that she'd kept all the Order's secrets. Harlow drew her knees to her chest and pressed her forehead into her hands. "Okay. That makes sense. I'm not trying to be a jerk. This is all just a lot for me, and knowing you knew all of this—plus the truth about why Finn left me—it's just a lot to take in, okay?"

Harlow hated how she'd start to melt down when things got overwhelming. In fact, she felt the tears building behind her eyes and she knew it wouldn't be long before she was hysterical; she had to get out before that started. She didn't want anyone trying to comfort her right now.

"I'm going to go home. I'll see you tomorrow," she said, forcing an evenness she didn't feel into her voice.

"Okay," Thea replied softly.

Her luminous eyes filled with tears, but Harlow couldn't stop to say anything kind. She didn't want to hurt her sister, but Thea purposely kept things from her while watching her implode. Thea was the one person who knew how much Finn had hurt her and the fact that she also could have stopped so much of that pain with the knowledge she withheld cut deep, too deep.

As she stood, Thea clasped her hand. "I *am* sorry, Harlow. I made a mistake not telling you, or at least not encouraging you to talk to Finn. Alaric and I should have tried harder to get you two to talk."

Harlow drew her hand back like she'd been stung, but Thea held on. "No. *You* should have told me what you knew. I know you're sorry now, but you knew how bad things were for me right before I met Mark. You knew and you *still* didn't tell me."

Thea held tighter, tears rolling down her face now. "I know. I'm so sorry."

Harlow yanked her hand back now, infuriated by Thea's tears, by the audacity she had to say she was sorry and expect forgiveness now. "Don't apologize. You chose your loyalty—to Alaric and the Knights. Not me, not when I was *literally* dying from how lonely and sad I was."

Thea had been the one to pick her up from the hospital. She was the only one who knew, other than Mark. She'd told Mark too. What a mistake that had been. He'd held her fragility over her head more times than she could count, reminding her that she'd lost her grip once, and that if he didn't watch her, she might again.

Every heartbeat felt like pounding a bruise and she ran, passing Aurelia and Selene in the hallway, down the back stairs and into the alley. She was on her way to Mulberry Street and Enzo's before she remembered she didn't have her phone.

It didn't matter. Her eyes blurred with tears and so she didn't see Kate Spencer, coming around the corner, until she'd steadied her. "Hey, Lo. Gods, what's wrong?"

Lo. The nickname only Kate had ever used prompted another onslaught of sobs. What in Akatei's name was Kate Spencer doing here? "I... I..." She couldn't say what was actually wrong. She knew better, even though a rebellious part of her wanted to say it all. "I had a fight with Thea."

"Oh shit," Kate said, pulling her under an awning and out of the rain. "I'm sorry to hear that."

Kate didn't ask if she was all right. Most people would, but not Kate. Kate never asked questions that had obvious answers. It was one of the things Harlow always liked best about her.

"You wanna grab a drink? We could go get some tea... Or maybe a whiskey?"

Harlow nodded and she let Kate lead her around the corner, past Mulberry onto Lupine Blvd, where there was a pub Harlow liked called the Three Besoms. When they slid into a booth, upholstered with the familiar Three Besoms crimson tartan, Harlow could almost imagine it was four years ago, and they were meeting up after work. The pub was the same as ever, all dark gleaming wood and twinkling witch-lights, cozy to a tee. After a quick word from Kate, a waitress brought them both two shots of whiskey and two mugs of steaming black tea with a distinct caramel aroma.

Kate dumped one shot each into their tea, and then clinked her remaining shot glass to Harlow's. They downed their shots and then sat in comfortable silence sipping the fragrant tea. Despite being a bit damp, Kate looked amazing. Her short brown hair was freshly cut and swept away from her beautiful face, which was immaculately made up, as always.

She slid out of her leather jacket and Harlow choked up a little to see she was wearing a t-shirt from a concert they'd gone to together. Harlow didn't think before she spoke. "What in seventeen hells are you *doing* here?"

Kate grinned. "Business. Aside from having a fight with Thea, what are you up to?"

Harlow shook her head, glancing around the bar to avoid making eye contact with Kate. "Fucking everything up, as usual."

Kate's cavalier grin shifted quickly into a frown. "That's an odd thing to say."

A hysterical laugh choked Harlow. "No, *that's* an odd thing to say."

Kate tilted her head in that hawklike way she had. "Lo, you're just about the most put-together person I know. What're you talking about?"

Harlow shook her head. "Still not reading the gossips, huh?"

"I read them. What's that have to do with anything? You're still smart as seventeen hells, and beautiful as ever. What's it matter what trash like the Section Seven editors say?" Kate's grin showed the glint of her fangs. She was flirting, but just a little. "And you're seeing my buddy Finn McKay now, I hear. That's pretty slick of you."

"You know Finn?" Harlow asked, blushing a little.

"Yeah, we surfed together a lot when I moved back to Nea Sterlis," Kate said, adding, "I'm a little jealous you're seeing him though."

Harlow frowned. "You don't date men."

The laugh that erupted out of Kate's mouth sounded like a pack of wild dogs. "I meant *you*, Lo. I heard you and Easton broke up, but by the time I could get away, Riley Quinn informed me I was too late."

"Oh," Harlow said, feeling confused.

Kate took her hand. "Lo, we had so much fun together, but it's not like it is with you and Finn, is it?"

Harlow looked deep into Kate's green eyes, remembering the short time they'd spent together. "No, Finn and I have history. But we *did* have fun. *So* much fun."

Kate kissed her fingertips, sighing. "I wish it had lasted longer, but I think it might have ended badly if it had. I like how we left things. You're the one who got away, and that's a damn romantic story to tell myself... *If I'd only come back sooner, she wouldn't have paired with the most handsome man on the planet...*"

Harlow laughed, which of course was the point. Kate was great at making her laugh. They'd spent the short time they had together either screwing like bunnies or laughing 'til their sides hurt. If Harlow was honest with herself, Kate was one of the best friends she'd ever had, and she missed that part of things more than anything else.

When her laughter dissolved and she breathed normally again, she asked, "Did you leave because you knew we were a bad fit?"

"No." Kate shook her head. "It was time for me to go home and help with the family business. It killed me to leave you."

It had killed Harlow to be left, but she'd always wondered if their days were numbered. Kate had always leaned more towards polyamory, and Harlow was never quite capable of that. Not that she judged the practice, like humans did; it just wasn't right for her, and it was for Kate. It would have been a problem eventually, but this way they never had to find out.

"Do you want to go out, do something fun?" Kate asked, downing the last of her tea.

It would be nice to go do something fun, something normal, but Harlow was exhausted. She felt like she could sleep for days, and she wanted to see Axel. "No, thanks. I'm going to go home and sort myself out. Can I use your phone to call a cab?"

Kate pulled her phone from her pocket. "No service. I'll go ask the bartender to call for you, okay?"

"Thank you," Harlow said. "I'm going to run to the bathroom."

Once there, she smiled at herself in the mirror. She was glad she'd run into Kate. This conversation closed a door for her that left the one Finn had opened a shining possibility. Mark always made her feel like no one had ever wanted her but him, and that no one else ever would, but she saw that for what it was now: pathetic lies. He'd had to lie to her constantly, manipulate her into a muddled mess to get her to stay with him. He *was* pathetic.

She returned to the table to find Kate with her jacket on. "I've gotta run. Your cab will be here in five. I'll be in town for a bit for business. I'll probably see you at some of the season events, if you're going to any more."

"We'll definitely be at the Solstice Gala," Harlow said, marveling at her easy use of "we."

Kate kissed her cheek. "I'll see you then. Make up with Thea, all right? She means well."

Harlow had used the same words to describe Thea's prissy, rude behavior a thousand times. Her heart twinged a bit to hear Kate say it back to her now. She nodded and watched her ex go.

Kate was so good, so free, but Harlow didn't regret that it was over. Maybe she was free now too, or closer anyway. She tried to pay the tab, but found Kate had already done so. As she walked through the bar to the cab waiting outside, she felt watched, just like she had at the Metro. Her skin crawled under the pressure of unseen eyes, and she realized she'd forgotten to tell anyone about that. Suddenly, that seemed like a misstep.

She turned slowly, pretending to fix something about her shoe. There was no one suspicious looking in the bar. A few sorcières she knew waved from the corner booth, by the hearth, their smiles a bit cautious, but mostly friendly. She waved back. The rest of the bar was empty. Perhaps she was imagining things. Her shadows swelled inside her in a way that was new to her.

Show me, she urged them. *What am I missing?*

There it was, just slipping away—motion at the back of the bar. The heavy back door was swinging shut, very slowly. Someone had been in the back, watching her and Kate. But who? She bit her bottom lip. There was nothing she could do about it now.

CHAPTER 27

As soon as she slid into the backseat of the cab, Harlow knew something was wrong. The doors locked immediately and there were no handles on the inside of the cab anywhere. When the cabbie turned, she looked into the eyes of a vampire—cold and milky, a sure tell they'd been drinking fresh human blood. Vampires who drank blood bank fare had eyes like everyone else.

Harlow's stomach clenched instinctually. It wasn't illegal to drink from willing humans, but she doubted that Athan Sanvier, Olivia's cousin and a baron of the House of Remiel, the high house of the Order of Night, gave a fig about willingness. He had a reputation for cruelty that never seemed to deter humans, but scared her to her core. Being alone with Athan Sanvier was the last thing in the world she'd ever choose.

"Hey there, little witch," he drawled. "Heard you were looking for a ride. I'd be happy to oblige."

Harlow swallowed hard. "Let me out, Athan, or you are going to find yourself in worlds of trouble."

He didn't respond, pulling away from the curb. She cursed herself for leaving the Monas without her phone. "Does Olivia know you're doing this?"

Athan smiled in the rearview mirror. "I think you mean 'does Mark know I'm doing this,' don't you?"

That honestly hadn't occurred to Harlow, but now her stomach soured. Would he really go this far to get back at her for taking Axel back? Surely he couldn't care that much. He'd been treating the cat terribly.

Athan smiled again, clearly not meaning to tell her. Panic crept into her veins, thrumming like a drum that drowned out all thought. Harlow struggled to keep her head.

Think, Harlow, she commanded herself. The sun was low in the sky, which meant she had only a few minutes to escape without Athan being able to easily follow.

"Where are you taking me?" she asked.

Athan shook his head, smiling again. The smile spoke of how much he enjoyed pain. It wasn't a vampiric trait to be vicious, Kate and her House were evidence of that, but vampirism did seem to amplify certain personality traits more than others, and aggression and sadism were both commonly magnified.

In Athan's case, rumor had it that he enjoyed inflicting the kind of psychological pain that left people broken and bitter for years. No wonder Mark sent him. This all made too much sense. While she could not be compelled like a human, there was plenty he could do to torture her, if he so chose. Sorcières were not entirely immune to vampiric magics and he was certainly strong enough to overpower her physically. Her heart fluttered wildly in response to this thought.

"You don't want to do this, Athan," she warned again. "You don't want to be in trouble with the Illuminated."

Athan laughed. "Once we're through with you, the Illuminated won't be able to do a damn thing to me."

That was an odd thing to say, but Harlow didn't have time to puzzle it out. She rolled her eyes, acting braver than she felt. "Don't be foolish, Athan. You can't do more than torture me and you know it." Murder between the lower Orders was so stringently punished that there had not been a single incident in over a hundred years.

"Who said anything about torture?" Athan breathed. She noticed one of his fingers tapped relentlessly on the steering wheel, as though whatever he had planned for her excited him to the point of perpetual motion. "You might love what we can do for you—I'd imagine a curvy thing like you is wanton as they come."

Her blood chilled. She wasn't sure what he was talking about, but his tone of voice was too sure, too confident for petty vengeance. Something else was happening here, and she very much doubted she would love anything Athan Sanvier could do for or *to* her.

"Let me out of the car," she insisted.

He ignored her. "I wonder how you'll be when we turn you. No more spells of course, but your new power will be so sweet. Promise to ride me at least once, all right?"

Cold sweat broke out over Harlow's skin as the fragments of his words fell together. What he implied was impossible. Neither Athan Sanvier nor the vampires of the House of Remiel, despite all their power, could turn *her* into anything, and certainly not a succubus. That was what he was implying, wasn't it? Harlow tried to tell herself that her imagination was running away with itself, that there was a reasonable explanation for all this. They were just vampires, after all, and vampires couldn't turn other immortals into anything else.

If there was a reasonable explanation for this, I wouldn't be trapped in a cab with Athan Sanvier, she thought.

If he'd just wanted to talk to her, he wouldn't have used this cab. Nothing good would come of this. Her mind went to war with itself, part of it trying to convince the other that the cold fear lashing through her veins was all manufactured and irrational. The other part screamed, *Get out, get out, get out.* She needed to trust herself, hard as that was. She reached for the shadows, for the inky power of her newly manifested magic, but it sputtered.

She was too afraid and wished desperately that she could portal, but she still wasn't powerful enough to blink through space. The shadows shifted within her, beyond the veil of reality. She could feel them try to help her from deep within the limen, trying to soothe her. It wasn't that she had to banish the fear; she had to accept it and master it. Harlow looked out the window for the first time, trying to get her bearings. They were headed Uptown now, toward the House of Remiel's quarters, a high-rise downtown where the hundred most elite vampires in Nuva Troi both worked and resided.

Once he took her inside, she would be subject to the vampires' will, and no matter what that would not bode well for her. *Help me,* she begged her magic. A flicker of shadow brought her back inside the car; she felt it in her fingers. Felt the threads of reality around her. The car slowed at a red light and she saw the sun was setting, streaming down 55th Avenue for the first time today. The rain had stopped.

Harlow dropped into her spirit body quickly, summoning enough power to create the simplest fix. While fear had its claws in her, she understood that she didn't need a flashy solution, just a reliable one and her wits. When the door handle appeared she willed it to be unlocked, perpetually unlocked, unable to even *be* locked.

"Shit," she whispered, looking out the front of the cab, straight into the sun. She injected as much panic as she could into her voice, which wasn't difficult, as her heart was thumping so hard she could hardly hear herself think. "What in seventeen hells is *that*?"

Athan followed her gaze, squinting in the light, his sensitive eyes unable to make much out. He reached for sunglasses in the console and she made her move. She took the newly-made handle and opened the car door, sprinting straight into the line of light the setting sun created down 55th Avenue, back the way they'd come. She knew she couldn't escape him for long, and this close to the House of Remiel there would be vampires everywhere. He was likely calling them now, if he wasn't working on his own.

She darted out of the shadows of the sidewalk and back into the street, where the sun set streams of golden light ablaze. Though vampires could technically leave the comfort of their homes during the day, even small amounts of light made it difficult for them to utilize the full range of their power. When the sun disappeared, they would be nearly as quick and strong as the Illuminated though, and in the shadows, she spotted Athan's backup gathering. They were tracking her in packs of three and four.

So he wasn't working alone. The House of Remiel supported this, whatever it was. Frantically, she sought out options. Cars honked around her as they swerved to miss her. She couldn't stand here for much longer, but the way the tall buildings blocked the light except for the very center of the street made it the safest place for her, despite the traffic.

The sun sank lower and hit the bank across the street just so, causing light to bounce off a small angled mirror affixed to the side of the building. It was a bizarre place to put a mirror, but she followed the new stream of light with her eyes. It made a narrow path through the shadows of the sidewalk across the street, hitting the door of a cafe square in the center, like a beacon.

Harlow didn't have time to be curious as the traffic lights changed and the speed of cars around her began to pick up. She had moments to make a choice and she ran, following that tiny stream of light until her hands met the heavy wooden door of the cafe. It was a strange, pale grey color. She felt, rather than saw, the vampires closing in as she pushed the door open and dashed inside.

Once on the other side of the door, inside a small enclosed vestibule, she stared at a pair of heavy wooden doors, made of the same grey wood as the front door. Could it be white ash? None had grown in Nytra for centuries, and was extremely rare, as it could kill vampires and grievously injure the Illuminated. The doors' brass handles were shaped like snakes, their scales thick and textured, like a dragon's rather than smooth skin.

Curious. She peeked out the window next to the outside door. Sure enough the stream of light was gaining strength as the sun went down, growing wider.

The vampires backed off, as if repelled by the cafe itself, but then she saw what caused the effect: the windows of the cafe reflected more and more sunlight onto the street as the sun set, and hundreds of mirrors on the surrounding buildings made similar paths of light, all leading straight here. Very curious indeed.

She turned to examine the doors again. They were inlaid with intricate silver designs. The work was beautiful, but when she engaged her second sight, she saw the spells. The silver had been wrought into ancient sigils that would make it impossible for any creature of the Order of Night to cross without express permission. She was impressed with the spellwork, which had likely been extremely expensive and utilized techniques that had been out of vogue for several centuries.

But the magic was strong. If she crossed that threshold, it wouldn't matter how dark it got outside, vampires wouldn't be able to enter. She pushed one of the heavy doors open and heard soft piano music playing inside.

The ceilings of the cafe soared above her and she saw that while the front of the building had only a few narrow windows, the back windows arched overhead, enclosing the space in steel and glass, creating the feeling of an airy greenhouse. The back of the building was enclosed in a courtyard garden, bursting with lush plant life. Inside, enormous schefflera plants sprouted out of expensive jardinieres with a deep green glaze that all portrayed forest scenes. The plaster walls were painted a fresh white and various rattan chairs, cushioned in creamy, textured fabrics, surrounded marble and glass tables. The effect was eclectic, enchanting, and *safe*.

The customers were mostly human, though there were a few shifters at a table in the far corner. People spoke softly or read books, and Harlow noticed that everyone was pointedly focused on minding their own business. This was not a place to see and be seen. As beautiful as the cafe was, she was surprised this wasn't a hot spot for socials. But she'd never seen it, not even once, and she was slightly surprised to find that no one was on their phones, or using any kind of electronic device.

"Can I help you?"

Harlow turned towards the lilting accent of the northern territories. It issued from one of the Trickster's Chosen, a tall, lithe creature dressed in a dapper, navy three-piece suit, with a sharply planed pale face and short silvery blonde hair.

She liked the look of them instantly. Their eyes were shrewd and dangerous, but infinitely calm. She wondered what their alternae was, with eyes like that. Something powerful and secretive, perhaps a big cat of some kind. Harlow took a chance that they'd help her. "I need to call Finn McKay, right away, please. Can I use your phone?"

She wasn't exactly sure why she'd used Finn's name. Perhaps because everyone knew who he was, but her deeper instinct told her there was another reason.

The shifter nodded slightly, looking out the window at the gathering group of vampires with vague disgust. At least three packs were closing in on the cafe. "Of course, Ms. Krane. I would be happy to get him on the line."

Harlow stepped closer to the shifter, taking a sharp breath in, barely noticing that they'd already known her name. She'd never seen vampires act this way, not in broad daylight anyway. Of course, she'd heard stories about this kind of behavior at night, from some of the less regulated houses, ones that allowed nests to develop and all sorts of other unruly behavior, but nothing like this from the cultured House of Remiel. And yet it couldn't be denied, the packs were in Remiel's territory and these vampires were *hunting* her.

"Ms. Krane," the shifter said softly. "I have Mr. McKay on the phone."

They followed her gaze, then pressed the phone into her hand, reassuring her. "The vampires cannot enter this establishment. Haven is a safehouse from the Order of Night."

Harlow nodded, though the words were a confusing jumble to her as she took the phone. "Hi," she murmured. "I'm in trouble."

"Are you hurt?" The chill in Finn's voice was murderous, and she shivered, even though she knew it was not directed at her.

"No. Athan Sanvier took me, but he didn't hurt me. And now…"

She didn't have to describe it to him, because he was there. He was outside, with Alaric, and they were *slaughtering* the vampires gathering outside the cafe. Humans on the street stopped to watch, though she imagined it was difficult for them to make out what was happening. Their vision was somewhat limited in comparison to her own, and even she could barely see Finn and Alaric as they moved. To a human eye, it would simply look as though the vampires' heads came loose from their bodies and rolled away as they crumpled to the ground, falling to ash as they died.

It was horrifying to watch, but Harlow's horror was tempered by something else. Arousal, yes, but something deeper as well, something deeply satisfying. When the tumult stopped, a representative of the House of Remiel, clad in a dark expensive suit, appeared in the shadows, looking furious. Alaric spoke to them, and Harlow could not recall when she'd ever seen such a hard look on his face. He was absolute power, his dark eyes glowing faintly with menace.

Where was Finn? Her eyes darted to and fro, but she could not find him. "Hey, Harls," his voice rumbled at her back. She felt the light pressure of his fingers on her shoulder, tentative as she turned and threw her arms around him.

"What did they want?" she whispered.

"Alaric is working on finding out, but they were hunting you—and that is unacceptable. The House of Remiel will be fined and an inquest into the matter will begin immediately."

His words were cold, harsh even, but his arms were warm as he hugged her. "Are you all right?" His voice was softer now.

She shook her head. The noise of the cafe began again. She'd forgotten they were in a restaurant and about the shifter who'd helped her until this moment.

"Perhaps you and Ms. Krane would like to go upstairs," the shifter suggested.

"Yes, thank you, Herrington," Finn replied. So this was Cian Herrington. Harlow understood immediately why Finn had spoken of them with such reverence in his voice before. There was something feral and immensely powerful in their presence. Immediately, she wanted to know them better.

Finn continued, "Harls, this is Cian Herrington, who I told you about earlier… and my partner in the Haven project."

Well, that explained the door handles. Harlow shook hands with Herrington as she asked, "The Haven project?"

Herrington smiled as they led them through the cafe to stairs in the back hallway. "Yes, the Knights of Serpens have been creating safe havens in neighborhoods where vampires reside—places they cannot enter—where humans are safe."

"You did this for *humans*?" Harlow asked, incredulous.

Finn nodded. "Yes, Alaric, Herrington, and I started the Haven project two years ago. We've been buying up property and creating places like this, here and in Nea Sterlis, in the hope that we might help some folks. The cafes run all day and night, and the apartments upstairs are for people who need more in-depth help."

Harlow nodded as she followed them up the narrow staircase. "And the humans… they know about this?"

Herrington unlocked a door at the top of the stairs and ushered them inside. The room was simply but elegantly decorated in shades of grey. One wall was lined with bookcases. A hardwood desk sat in front of floor-to-ceiling windows and two pewter colored velvet couches faced one another at the opposite end of the room.

"I'll fetch us some refreshments while you explain things to her," Herrington said softly. "Ric will be up in a few minutes, I suppose. Will Thea be joining us?"

Finn nodded, unfazed by the shift in tone. Downstairs, Herrington had been excessively formal. Here, Alaric was "Ric" and Thea was Thea, rather than Ms.

Krane. Harlow wondered how well they all knew one another. Well, she assumed, since they were all Knights.

She was grateful for the help, but felt woefully left out. They were doing the kind of work she'd dreamed of since she was a teenager, and her sister hadn't bothered to tell her about it or include her.

"I imagine she's close by now." Finn answered, glancing at Harlow. "Alaric called her as soon as we knew where you were."

"She knows about this place?" *Of course she did. What a stupid question.*

Finn smiled. "The Haven Project was her idea."

Harlow's chin quivered. They'd all had this project together for two years—more, maybe. And the whole time she'd been doing what? Trying to have a human life with Mark? *Mark.*

Godsdamnit, it hurt to think he set her up. That he wanted her tortured, or dead? Or worse. Mark was cruel, but that didn't make sense. Harlow didn't know she was shaking until she felt Finn drape a soft wool blanket around her shoulders.

"You're in shock," he said.

She nodded. That much was clear.

"Can you tell me what happened?" He sat next to her on the couch, a respectful distance away, clearly trying to give her space. She realized how afraid he was when he wouldn't meet her eyes.

"Athan didn't hurt me. But… I think he planned to."

Finn nodded, and she saw he was shaking too. The tremors wracking his body weren't shock or fear though, they were fury. His eyes glowed with that menace she'd seen in Alaric before, faint light emanating from his irises. It wasn't like the golden light that shone from his skin when they were in bed together, or the bright pure light that had come from their union. This was something different, something deadly and cold.

"Would you hold me?" she pleaded.

In an instant, she was pulled into his lap, his arms curled around her back and hips, his legs cradling her body. He untied her shoes and slipped them off, covering her feet with the blanket that had fallen off her with the sudden movement. His hands slid into her hair, gently pulling through tangles and knots.

Harlow closed her eyes and let her head fall onto Finn's shoulder, listening to his heartbeat as his fingers skimmed her hip, the outside of her thigh, and tucked themselves behind her knee. Slowly, the shaking subsided, replaced by the awareness of his body heat and the tremble in his fingers as he smoothed her hair.

She'd been so afraid, but she'd escaped on her own power, found this place, and now she was safe. Harlow lifted her face to Finn's, noting the cloud of concern in his eyes, but also the flare of his nostrils—he scented something of her mounting arousal, before she'd even known she felt it. But as she calmed, she realized she wanted to feel something other than reliving the fear of being trapped in the cab with Athan Sanvier. Her lips parted slightly as she grazed a thumb over Finn's bottom lip, the square line of his jaw.

He quivered slightly at her touch and as her thumb dragged down the center of his throat, she felt him swallow hard. The rate of his breath increased slightly to match her own and the heat building in her core turned molten as his hand slid from behind her knee to her inner thigh, his hands warm on her bare skin.

"Are we about to be interrupted?" she asked softly.

His stormy eyes, dark with lust, didn't leave hers and his fingers continued their journey up her inner thigh as his other hand, invisible to her, fiddled with his phone.

"They'll give us a bit… to talk…" his half-smile was faint, almost sad. "Are you really all right?"

Harlow shook her head. "No, will you help me? I have all this energy… the leftover fear and anxiety… I just need to feel safe."

"And I make you feel safe?" he asked. There was incredulity in his voice. He didn't know if she trusted him or not.

"You do," she murmured. "I was mad at Thea for keeping secrets, and I planned to go to Enzo's to talk, but I ran into Kate Spencer on my way. She took me to the Three Besoms for a drink and a talk—she asked me to come out with her, but I said no… and I forgot my phone, so she called me a cab…"

"*Kate* called you a cab?" That cold quality to his voice was back.

Harlow shook her head. "No, the bartender did. I don't think Kate was a part of this."

Finn's usually sensual mouth made a thin line. "I think you're being very generous."

Her head tilted slightly, remembering the presence she'd felt in the bar, and at the ball. "I don't think I am. There was someone else there, watching me. They were at the ball too. Whoever it is, I think they're following me."

The journey his fingers were making on her inner thigh stalled. "How do you know?" His tone indicated curiosity, not disbelief.

"I feel it, a sinister kind of pressure. I don't know how to describe it otherwise. I think my shadows make it easier for me to use my natural instinct, if that makes any sense."

Finn nodded, his expression thoughtful. "Yes, from what Alaric has told me about his and Thea's research into Striders, that does make sense. They were said to develop an almost supernatural instinct for their surroundings. Thea thinks it's likely a result of so much close contact with the aether. The more you use it, the more honed your senses will become."

Her head fell against his shoulder, suddenly heavy. "Today has felt years long."

He laughed softly, hugging her tight. "It really has, hasn't it? Did Athan say anything to you?"

"Not much. He seemed to be threatening to turn me into a succubus."

Finn snorted; apparently the idea of it was as ridiculous to him as it had been to her. "He's always been such an asshole. Did he say anything else?"

Harlow nodded. "He said something about Mark that made me think that he and Olivia planned this together."

Finn sighed. "The two of them make a terrible pair. They're beyond petty and Athan has always done whatever Olivia asked. I'm sorry… he got away."

Harlow shrugged. "Maybe this was revenge for getting Axel back and embarrassing Mark. He's always been so sensitive about that kind of thing... Oh gods, someone needs to call Larkin and check on her."

Finn soothed her. "I already did. She and Axel are fine. I have my people watching your building."

"Your people? You have *people* who do things like that? Lackeys?"

"Please do not call Arebos and Nox that when you meet them. They will be incredibly offended."

She'd never heard those names before. "Who are they?"

Finn's face closed for a moment, as though he might not tell her. Then, miraculously it opened, as if he'd just realized he didn't have to keep it all a secret from her. "Knights, siblings. They call themselves Wraiths. They're shifters, but only in the most technical sense."

Her breath caught. "What does that mean?"

"They shift *into* their surroundings."

Harlow didn't think he could possibly mean what she thought he meant. "They actually become *invisible?*"

Becoming invisible wasn't hard, in theory, if you only wanted to trick humans. But immortals had better eyesight, and a highly developed second sight. Becoming invisible to the other Orders was practically impossible, unless you could shift into the background noise of daily life. "Where in Akatei's name did you find such creatures?"

"They found me. I'll tell you the story another time." He paused for a moment, as though considering whether or not it was a good idea to ask his next question. "Can Mark be compelled?"

Harlow took a deep breath. The multitudes of ways that Mark's relationship with Olivia could go disastrously wrong played out in her head. It had been a long time since a human as much in the public eye as Mark Easton had been involved in a compulsion scandal. "It's possible. I had a protective amulet made for him, but I'm not sure if he still wears it. He probably doesn't think he needs it with Olivia."

"Since the Anti-Compulsion Act passed, it seems like humans have gotten lazy about protecting themselves," he mused.

Harlow nodded. It was true. Once, humans had practiced all sorts of rituals to make themselves less vulnerable to the Order of Night's attacks, but now they felt protected by a law that was nominal at best. There were very few ways to prove compulsion.

"How did you get out of the car?" It felt a little like he was grilling her, but she understood. Her memory of the encounter might soften over time, and any tiny detail she could remember might help them see the shape of the new threat they faced.

"I made a handle and asked for it to be unlocked," she murmured, shifting slightly in his lap. She sat up, swinging one leg around so she straddled him. His hands moved up the tops of her thighs, under the skirt of her dress.

"That was an elegant solution," he said with a smile.

It struck her how close she'd come to harm. Her magic had not yet fully manifested, and she'd been alone with a vampire who wanted to hurt her. The afternoon could have ended much differently. Finn sensed the change in her mood.

"Do you want to start doing some training with your shadows? I could help you learn to fight with them, so you wouldn't have to be afraid of monsters like Athan Sanvier."

"Will we get all sweaty when we train?" she asked, deliberately playful. She desperately needed relief from all this tension and the residual stress coursing through her.

His hands were back in her hair, pulling gently as he nipped at her neck lightly. "We probably will. Don't worry, I know all sorts of ways to get you clean again." Finn kissed her face, pulling her into a tight hug. "I'm sorry about how things went today with your family. I didn't want you to learn about the Knights that way, or Thea's involvement. I thought I'd have more than one day to make sure things were okay with us before we talked about all that."

Harlow relaxed into him, feeling the deep, purposefully steady rise and fall of his chest as she lay her head on his shoulder, nuzzling her face into his neck. "I'm not angry with you," she explained. "I'm angry with my sister. She should have told me all this a long time ago."

He didn't say anything, but he hugged her tighter. It occurred to her that what they were doing felt like a relationship. He was comforting her. They were making plans. They were supposed to be pretending, but this didn't feel like pretense anymore. They'd crossed over into the real thing. The beginning stages, yes. But a real relationship, all the same.

"You really murdered those vampires," she murmured.

"As opposed to sort of murdering them?"

She laughed. "I know I should be horrified, but…"

"You're not. And you shouldn't be. They violated every rule we live by." He was quiet, but she felt something lingering behind the silence. Something he was hesitant to say. "You know, what happened is probably enough to bring the vampires back in line… And I believe I can use the entire incident to convince my parents that their focus needs to be back on the Order of Night and away from the sorcière."

She thought she knew where his line of thinking was headed and didn't much like it. "And then what?"

"If you wanted to end things, we could. You could walk away. I have a feeling the House of Remiel pulled this today because of our relationship. I'm not sure why yet, but I'll find out… Maybe you'd be safer if we ended this now."

Her heart stuttered and she pushed away from him to stare into his face. "Is that what you want?"

Finn's eyes softened. "No. It's the last thing I want, but I feel like you're in danger and I can't stand it."

She cupped his face in her hands. "Thank you."

"For what?"

"For not being able to stand it. For coming as soon as I called. For trusting me. For being worthy of my trust. For everything."

His gaze flit away from hers as his face twisted with some internal pain. "I feel like I don't deserve to hear those things."

Her heart ached to hear him say it. "I know, but you do. And they're the truth. My truth anyway."

He pulled her close, his arms so tight around her she could hardly breathe.

"I wish we got to have a normal love story," she said, stroking his hair.

"*Love* story? Are you saying—?"

She sighed. "I'm not going to fight how I feel anymore. I think today makes it clear that we need each other."

He nodded. "We don't need to make any big declarations now."

"Okay," she agreed.

There was a knock at the door and Thea peeked in. "Everyone decent?"

<h1 style="text-align:center">CHAPTER 28</h1>

Harlow nodded, climbing off Finn's lap, though she snuggled into the crook of his arm as Thea sat in a chair opposite the couch. "Alaric and Cian are downstairs dealing with Veronica Morova. She is quite unhappy about how the two of you dealt with the House of Remiel foot soldiers today."

"Then they shouldn't have been trying to kidnap my—" he stopped short and blushed.

Thea raised her eyebrows. "Do finish that sentence, Finn."

Harlow giggled as the flush in his cheeks deepened.

"That's a conversation we ought to have in private, probably…" he muttered.

Harlow smiled and patted the hard muscle of his stomach. "It's okay. You can call me your girlfriend. I'll allow it… Or were you going to call me your *lovah?*"

Thea giggled now and Finn blushed even more. It was adorable to see him so undone by two giggling witches, Harlow decided. She brushed a kiss on his cheek and slid her hand into his, stroking her thumb down the center of his palm so he'd be reminded just how much she enjoyed being his lover. She felt his shiver of pleasure, and when he returned the gesture, she knew he'd understood.

Thea was talking, saying something about the vampires, so Harlow tried to focus. "I think they'll be talking for a while. Apparently Berith is in quite the rage and Veronica was sent to find out what the Illuminated will do next. Cian is trying to help Alaric, but to be honest with you, I think they're being too nice."

Finn grimaced. "Should I go help?"

Thea smiled gently. "That might be good."

Finn got up and pressed a soft kiss to Harlow's lips. "I'll be back soon."

She nodded, staying silent as he left the room, her eyes fixed on her hands, instead of her sister. Harlow couldn't bring herself to look at Thea.

"This all happened because you were angry with me," Thea said, accusation coloring her words.

Harlow resented her saying it, even if it was technically true. But if Thea was going to be condescending, two could play that game.

"Because I *am* angry with you," Harlow corrected.

"Fair enough. I kept things from you, but can you blame me?"

Harlow looked up then, surprised to see the ugly, arrogant look on Thea's face that reminded her so much of the Illuminated as a whole. The entire Illuminated Order wore that look constantly, like they knew better about *everything*.

"You're turning into one of them, aren't you?"

Thea looked confused.

"The Illuminated. You're just like them. Is it from spending so much time with Alaric? Is that why you're like this? So cold and callous?"

Now her sister was furious. The pink flush creeping over her ears tipped Harlow off, but the ice in her voice confirmed it. "You were a *mess*, Harlow. When I picked you up from that hospital I had no idea how to keep you alive. Do you even remember the weeks I spent with you that summer at the cabin?"

Harlow sighed. "I remember how you helped me. And I'm grateful for it."

The summer after Kate left for Nea Sterlis, Harlow had spiraled out of control. She'd been drinking too much, doing too many drugs. It hadn't been for fun, not any of it; she'd been trying to dull the pain. And then one night, she'd taken too much of something. She wasn't even sure what, but she'd known it was too much at the time. She hadn't meant to end things, not exactly, but neither had she cared when she felt herself slipping away. Harlow didn't even know how she'd gotten to the hospital.

Thea didn't look at her. "When I picked you up from the hospital you wouldn't speak to me. They said you'd hadn't spoken once in seventy-two hours, except to make your phone call."

Harlow didn't remember much about that. The drugs they'd given her made her groggy, and she hadn't taken them again when she left. Whoever took her to the hospital had left her at a top-notch facility, but she hadn't wanted to stay, and after seventy-two hours, they couldn't keep her against her will. She'd called Thea, and they never told anyone else what had happened. They told the maters they were headed up north for the summer, and no one had questioned them.

"It was a bad start to our summer, but we had an okay time eventually, didn't we?" Harlow asked, trying not to sound petulant, but it was tiring being the sister that always screwed things up. Besides, after the first week or two things hadn't been so bad, had they?

Eventually she'd stopped wanting to die and after that her memories of that summer were golden and bittersweet. She and Thea had swum in the lake every day, napped, read books, cooked together and when they began laughing together again, Harlow had known she would make it. That she would live. She hadn't stopped the hard drinking for another two years, but she never touched drugs again.

Thea's face contorted with grief, as though she was wrestling with herself and what she wanted to say next. Harlow thought she looked like she wanted to deliver a lecture about mental health, but she'd had enough of those and interrupted her sister's train of thought. "Sorry I'm a pain in the ass, Thea. Sorry I'm not perfect like you. But that summer was *not* so bad. We had fun."

Thea flinched at Harlow's words, as though she'd been slapped. "Fun?" she murmured as she stood and walked toward the window, staring out, wrapping her arms around her slender frame. "When we first got to the cabin, you talked about how much you wanted to die every single day, Harlow. Do you remember that?"

Harlow's breath hitched. She didn't remember that. Thea glanced at her, deep sadness in her eyes. "You said no one could ever love you. That you were fundamentally flawed somehow. Later, it was the thing that started my research into The Scroll of Akatei, into the history of the Striders… but back then…"

None of that was surprising, despite her inability to remember it. Those thoughts had lived inside her for a very long time. "But you *knew*, you knew Alaric and you knew the truth about Finn. You knew all that, you knew what I was going through, and you *still* didn't tell me the one thing that could have stopped it all."

A long silence stretched between them as Thea obviously tried to calm herself. She'd covered her mouth with her hands, and when she spoke again, her words were muffled. "But I didn't know that then… I had no idea what would help, or hurt…" Thea's voice cracked. "I was so afraid to lose you, Harlow. What if I—" Thea stumbled forward, sobs wracking her shoulders.

Harlow froze. She'd never seen her sister lose control like this, not ever. She was incapable of moving from the couch.

"I didn't know what I could tell you and what I couldn't, but then you started to get better and I just—I just couldn't open it all up again. What if you went back to that place because I re-opened a wound that should have stayed closed? What if I lost you forever, because I made a mistake?"

The words fell from Thea's lips in a deluge of pain as she fell to her knees. Harlow moved then, freed by the understanding that Thea was a person. Not some perfectly controlled creature who did everything right, with all the answers. She was just a person, a person who got scared and made mistakes. Harlow didn't know what Thea should or shouldn't have done in that moment, only that she was certain her sister had done her best. And that knowledge was enough. Her arms went around Thea and they cried together.

"I'm so sorry, Harlow," Thea whispered. Her fingers dug into Harlow's back. "I don't love anyone in the world the way I love you. Do you understand that? I would do anything to protect you. *Anything.*"

Harlow rocked them both. "I know, Thea. I know."

"And then everything happened with Mark and I failed you. I didn't keep you safe. Mama told me what you told Larkin about how you found Axel… I'm so sorry." Thea was sobbing so hard Harlow could hardly understand her.

"It's not your fault," Harlow soothed. "I should have gone to therapy—like they said at the hospital. I walked right into my pain, and I paid for it."

Thea's sobs quieted. "You don't have to be with Finn if it hurts, Harlow. Everyone will understand. We'll find another way to fix things."

"That's not what this is about. Not anymore."

Thea looked up. Her face was swollen. None of the Kranes were pretty criers except Larkin and Meline. "It's not?"

"No, I have real feelings for him. It's time for me to move on, and I think I want to do it with him."

"You're sure?"

Harlow looked around at the office, thinking of the cafe below, and the apartments and offices on this floor. The work she imagined the Knights of Serpens were doing was the kind of work she'd always wanted to do. And she wanted to be doing it alongside her sister and Alaric—but most of all, Finn. "I'm sure."

Thea's swollen eyes crinkled and more tears squeezed out. "You're really all right?"

"Yes," Harlow said, hugging her sister even tighter. "Yes, I'm doing better now."

In that moment, as she held her sister, she understood it was true. She *was* better now, and it wasn't because of Finn, or her magic manifesting, or anything else. It was because of the work she'd done on herself. The time she'd taken for herself. The months alone in her empty apartment working through things, letting herself be lonely, staying with herself, with her pain, instead of running from it. She wasn't perfectly healed, and maybe she never would be, but she *was* better. Stronger.

"Do you promise?" Thea asked as her sobs began to quiet.

Harlow nodded. "I do. I'm not in that place anymore, and it's because of you. Because of that summer. I'll never forget that."

They rested against the windows, huddled together, wrapped in each other's arms, holding one another's hands.

After a long, calm pause, Thea said, "It doesn't matter what happens next, who we pair with, any of it. You'll always be the most important person in my life. You and the sillies and Enzo and the maters. You know that, right?"

Harlow smiled, letting go of one of Thea's hands to wipe a stray tear from her sister's cheek. "It's okay to let Alaric in. He can be a part of our family too. And then someday, you'll have babies of your own, and they'll be just as important. We can expand. Love is an infinite well."

"Love is an infinite well," Thea repeated. "I like that."

"There's enough room for all of us in this family."

"Even Finn?"

"Yes. And I expect Cian Herrington, and Riley Quinn as well."

A few more tears slipped down Thea's cheeks as she nodded. "Alaric and I are going to need a really big dining room table in our new house."

"Yeah," Harlow replied as she leaned against her sister's shoulder. "You are."

CHAPTER 29

The next few weeks flew by in a blur of trying to balance the events of the season with trying to sort out what the House of Remiel had been up to when they took Harlow. Finn and Harlow went to the season's annual brunch at The Palace hotel, and made an effort to be seen everywhere from the most popular coffee shops and lunch spots to the grocery store. When she was with Finn, everything felt normal, but anytime she went somewhere alone she had the same chilling sense of surveillance as she had at the Solon Mai ball and in the bar.

Finn and Thea talked her out of calling Mark and giving him a piece of her mind. Furthermore, and perhaps more telling, Mark didn't call her either, which felt odd because he loved to gloat when he punished her. And though Harlow scraped the internet for information about him, she couldn't find mention of him having been out anywhere, with Olivia or anyone else either. Both his and Olivia's socials were silent, which was unusual. Athan, on the other hand, was busily updating the world on his rugby team's prowess.

A few of the gossips speculated that Olivia and Mark were probably holed up in a love nest somewhere, subtly implying that Mark's humanity might be getting an upgrade soon. The thought of Mark living an eternity as a vampire turned Harlow's stomach, but it was a plausible theory, and it would explain why the whole House of Remiel was going about their business as normal.

There had been no mention of the vampires' attack, and the ensuing altercation outside Haven, in the news or gossips. Harlow was equally impressed and horrified with the way that Alaric had handled things. His securities firm had reached out to everyone involved and "made it more attractive to stay quiet."

The resources it must have taken to make something like that possible were vast, and when Harlow had discussed it with him, Thea and Finn, she began to understand that there were many things that happened in Nytra, and Okairos as a whole, that no one knew about, because the Illuminated simply erased events with money and threats. Because as rich and resourced as Alaric and Finn both were, their parents and the rest of the Illuminated had more. More power, more money, *more* of everything. So much more that it was dizzying to think of even trying to resist them when she began to truly comprehend the scale of things.

Harlow stayed at Finn's most nights, enough so that he'd gotten a litter box and a store of cat food and they'd introduced Axel to the house. The feline loved the many windows, and he and Finn seemed to enjoy one another's company. They went walking the perimeter of the property together twice a day every day, the only time Axel went outside. Harlow got a kick out of watching the two of them walking together and sent her sisters and Enzo videos and photos of them goofing off nearly every day.

The house began to fill slowly with furniture she and her shadows built. Just a chair here and there for comfort. She wanted to buy most of their things the normal way, and besides, she wasn't sure she was ready to officially move in. It was a little soon for that, but being here felt safe and good.

By contrast, her apartment, which had once been her refuge, did not. She trusted the wards on her building, but the few times she and Axel had been home to get more clothes or to simply be alone for the afternoon, she got the now-familiar feeling of being watched. That sinister pressure appeared and her shadows went wild, trying to ferret out where it was coming from, to no avail. She never felt it at Finn's and they'd agreed it was better not to risk things.

So she'd come to stay, "for a nice, long visit," they'd said, but it was all over the gossips that they were "playing house." She didn't care. They could say whatever they wanted now. The hours she and Finn spent just talking both reminded her of their childhood, and were something new altogether. It seemed they never ran out of things to talk about, their interests were so different and varied. His deeply analytical mind was always two steps ahead of things, and her big picture thinking let them look at any topic from dozens of angles. It felt good to talk to someone who listened intently when she spoke, and who she wanted to listen to in return.

Harlow hadn't been home in over a week, and hadn't checked her socials in days. Things had been blessedly quiet, near-perfect domestic bliss. She knew it wouldn't last, but she reveled in it all the same. Especially the part where when Finn did a load of laundry he'd put away her clothes in the empty half of his enormous walk-in closet and they'd started to take up a respectable amount of space. She was standing, marveling at the neat piles he'd made, when he brought her phone to her.

"You are *really* good at folding things," she mused with a grin.

He smiled, but the expression didn't reach his eyes as he passed her phone into her hands. "Alain Easton has called you seven times in the last five minutes. I didn't mean to pry, but your phone was vibrating non-stop. I was worried it might be your family."

"It's okay. Thank you." She kissed his cheek and as she did so, the phone began to vibrate again. It was Mark's father.

"Do you want some privacy?" Finn asked.

Harlow shook her head. "No."

She answered as she walked out of the closet and settled into one of the chairs in the bedroom. Rain fell in a steady sheet outside the windows, giving the bedroom a gloomy green glow. "Hello, Mr. Easton. What can I do for you?"

"Harlow?"

"Yes, Mr. Easton."

His voice was shaky. "Have you heard from Mark? Is he with you?"

"No," Harlow said, drawing the syllables out, making eye contact with Finn, who sat on the floor, adding more wood to the fire. "No, I haven't."

"I haven't heard from him in two weeks. Sixteen days. It's like he's disappeared."

Harlow didn't like the sound of that. "Have you called the Missing Person's Unit?"

"Yes, yes. I've called. They say they're doing something about it, but I don't get any updates. You know how it is…" He trailed off. The MPU was not always diligent about following up on missing humans. "I wondered if you or your parents might… Well… If you might help me."

"What are you worried about, Mr. Easton?" Harlow didn't really have to ask. She knew.

"I think that should be obvious, Harlow. I'm worried he's dead."

Harlow swallowed hard. "Does anything suggest that he might be?"

"He's dating a vampire, Harlow. I may not have approved of your relationship with Mark, but I wasn't afraid you'd kill him. Can you help me or not?"

He really *was* worried. Alain Easton wasn't a very good father. He'd neglected Mark as a child, in favor of his work and his many extramarital affairs, according to Mark, anyway. But he did love his son. If he was worried, it confirmed her own concerns.

"I'll see what I can do. Let me get back to you."

"Don't sugarcoat anything, Harlow. I can handle whatever you find out."

"I know, Mr. Easton. I'll see what I can do."

He hung up, and Harlow locked her phone, setting it on the low table next to her chair, made from a piece of perfectly petrified wood. She and Finn looked at each other for a long time before either of them spoke.

A prominent human like Mark Easton being killed by a vampire couldn't be erased as easily as an altercation between the House of Remiel and the Illuminated. There were too many factors to control; the news would get out and upset the tentative balance between the Orders and the human world. And, as it had always been, the result would be dead humans, and dead immortals of the lower Orders. The Illuminated always came out of situations like this unscathed and seemingly more powerful than before.

"He's either dead or turned. You know that right?" Finn said finally.

Harlow nodded. "Honestly, I figured as much."

He got up. "I'm not on very good terms with the House of Remiel, obviously, but I'll have Cian make some calls. They're far more diplomatic than I am. Maybe they can get somewhere with Veronica Morova. She's at least halfway reasonable."

Harlow nodded, kissing his hand as he passed her. She knew he was going downstairs to lock himself in his office, and that he probably wouldn't just call Cian, but his other contacts as well. Maybe even the mysterious Nox and Arebos, who she still hadn't met. She listened as he walked downstairs.

When the door to his office shut, she picked up her phone and shot off two texts. One to Riley Quinn: *Just heard from Alain Easton. Mark is missing. Any ideas?*

Finn and Alaric had been wary of telling Riley much, because the Rogue Queen was such an unknown factor, but Harlow had argued time and again that the Rogue Order's resources were untapped potential and that if Enzo trusted Riley, they should too. But this was important. They needed to find Mark and control the story before people got hurt.

She steeled herself and sent another text to Mark himself. It was worth a try to see if he'd respond. *Your dad's worried about you. He's calling in the cavalry. If you don't want shit-tons of people looking for you, text me back.*

And then she waited. She waited so long, she fell asleep in her chair. When she woke, the sun was setting and her phone vibrated in her lap. From downstairs, she heard the soft sounds of Finn on the phone in his office. She picked up her phone and swiped the screen open.

The text was from Riley, not Mark. *Have some feelers out. Nothing yet, but you should talk to Petra Velarius. Privately. Without Finn.*

Now that was curious. *Why?*

Just ask her to have coffee with you at Cerberus, downtown, and ask her to help you.

Harlow started to explain all the reasons why that wouldn't work. Why Petra Velarius was the last person in the world she wanted to help her, and how Petra certainly wouldn't be seen *downtown*. But she stopped herself and simply wrote back, *I doubt she'd help me.*

If you ask her to meet you at Cerberus to talk about Mark, she will help you. I'll be in touch if I hear anything. I can't emphasize enough that you should not tell Finn. You can use me as a cover.

Now that was downright strange, but she trusted Riley. *Okay, thanks.*

She texted Meline to see if she had Petra's number, which she did, and finally gave up prying when Harlow said she wanted to ask her where she got her hair done. Petra Velarius had enviable hair, and was notoriously secretive about where she got any of her beauty services.

When she had the number she hesitated. Was this a good idea? Petra hated her, and she hated Petra. She listened for Finn—yes, he was still on the phone. She bit her lip and typed out a text. *It's Harlow. Mark's missing. Can you meet me at Cerberus in an hour to talk?*

Petra had her read receipts on and Harlow saw the moment she read the message. There was a long pause and then the cascading dots indicated that she was responding.

I'll be there in thirty minutes. Don't be late.

Harlow was shocked. She looked down at the leggings and cozy socks she was wearing with one of Finn's plaid flannel shirts. This was going to have to do. She texted Riley to make sure they'd cover her with Finn, and she pulled on a pair of shearling boots that were tossed under the side table next to her chair.

She was not cutting the most fashionable silhouette, but Petra couldn't possibly hate her any more than she already did. There wasn't any impressing her, after all.

She ran downstairs and pulled on her raincoat, poking her head into Finn's office. Axel was sleeping on his lap, and he had his feet up on the desk and his phone to his ear. She whispered, "I'm meeting Riley downtown. They might have a lead on Mark. You getting anywhere?"

He muted the phone and shook his head. Though he frowned slightly at the mention of Riley, he didn't comment on her choice to tell them what was happening. "You can take my car."

"I can't drive your car!" she hissed. "It's too fast."

He grinned. "The other one in the barn. Keys are on the dash."

She didn't know which car he was talking about. He usually parked his sports car in the garage attached to the house, next to his motorcycle. The "barn" was his workshop and she'd only peeked inside one day to see if he wanted lunch.

She walked outside. It was starting to warm up a little, finally, but the breeze was still cold. Inside the barn it was warmer, and when she turned the lights on in the garage portion of the barn, she smiled. Finn's beat-up old blue SUV, with the wooden panels on the doors, sat inside. It was the car she'd learned to drive in. Neither of the maters drove, but Finn had made sure she knew how to drive a car when she was fifteen, and he went with her to get her driver's license.

It was also the car they'd first made love in, and seeing it brought back a flood of memories. The Woody was in great shape still and it roared to life when she put the keys in the ignition. It had been detailed recently, and a book of CDs sat on the passenger seat with a folded piece of paper tucked into the elastic strap that held it closed. She opened it and read:

Thought you might need a soundtrack. The Woody won't connect to your phone, but I made you some mix CDs. —F

He'd been planning to give her the Woody. She couldn't believe it at first, but Finn had always known how much she loved the bulky beast of a car, how it made her feel safe on the road. She smiled gratefully, feeling slightly guilty to have lied about who she was meeting, but she could be honest later, once she knew why the secrecy was necessary. She would wait to listen to the CDs later. She put an audiobook of a new romance novel on her phone's speaker to keep her company and zoned out as she drove downtown.

She had a hard time finding a parking spot, and Petra was walking out of the coffee shop as she rushed to the door. "I'm so sorry," she apologized. "Parking in this neighborhood is awful."

Petra pressed her lips together, as though she was trying to suppress the disgust she felt looking at Harlow's outfit. "I hope you didn't change your clothes to meet me. Because it would be a tragedy if you were late because you changed into *that*."

Harlow rolled her eyes. "No. I came as quickly as I could. And my outfit is fine."

Petra, who was wearing what looked like couture, seemed as though she'd like to object, but she shrugged instead. "Do you want to go inside, or take a walk? It's stopped raining for the moment."

Harlow looked up at the grey sky. "Sure, we can walk."

They walked toward the river in silence. Finally Petra spoke. "Did Riley Quinn tell you to get in touch with me?"

Harlow nodded as Petra sat on a bench outside the Riverfront Park. She hesitated for a moment, but then reluctantly sat next to Petra, who smelled fantastic. Like a high-end department store, and a hothouse all at once. She looked impeccable as well, of course; though her tailored trench coat covered her outfit completely, she was perfectly made up, and her long hair was swept into her signature ponytail.

"Riley saw me here with Olivia Sanvier a few months ago. I thought no one I knew would come down here, but there Riley was. I had no idea they'd become such an integral part of our circle at the time."

Harlow furrowed her brow, confused. "Why were you worried about being seen having coffee with Olivia?"

"We weren't drinking coffee when Riley saw us."

It took Harlow a moment to understand.

"Oh... *Oh*. But why would that matter?"

Petra took a shuddering breath. "The lower Orders and the humans are so much freer about these things... But have you ever noticed how few of the Illuminated are like me?"

"Like... you?"

"I am *only* interested in women, Harlow. There are *not* sapphic Illuminated. Especially not in my family."

"Obviously there are," Harlow said softly.

Petra's beautiful face screwed into a grimace. "But it's forbidden. My parents would never allow me to pair with a woman."

"They know and would keep you from being who you are?"

"No, of course not. They don't know, and they never will. Unless you tell them. You or Riley Quinn."

There was a long silence between them.

"I wouldn't do that," Harlow said, finally. "I would never do anything like that to anyone. Not even you."

Petra wiped a tear, looking away from Harlow. Her mouth was set in an unattractive tight line. It was the first time Harlow had ever seen her look less than stunning. "Well, I'd deserve it if you did."

Harlow wasn't sure what to say to that, but she'd been honest. She wouldn't ever tell a secret like that, not even about her worst enemy. And while she didn't like Petra, she most certainly wasn't her worst enemy. Not anymore. "Do you know anything that might help us find Mark?"

Petra sighed and handed Harlow a slip of paper. "Look for him here. This is Olivia's safe house. She fucks and sucks here pretty often. If she turned Mark, it's where she'd take him to complete the transition."

"Thank you," Harlow said, taking the piece of paper and standing. As she did, she felt it, the pressure of eyes upon her. The feeling that whoever was watching did not have good intentions. Carefully, she scanned the surrounding area with her second sight, something she'd wished she'd done the other times she'd felt this. But she came up empty. She couldn't find the source of the feeling, though it did not lessen.

"I am sorry, you know?" Petra said softly as Harlow stood.

"For what?"

"The things I did to you in secondary. It makes me sick to think about."

Harlow sat back down, the breath stolen from her lungs. "It does?"

Petra nodded. "I was always jealous of you and Finn. Before he met you we were close, and then, when he met you and Enzo, we weren't anymore."

Harlow had been momentarily distracted by Petra's confession, but now she felt the presence, closer than before. She tried to appear natural, to continue the conversation as normally as she could, while sending her second sight out further. "We could have all been friends."

Petra's face twisted again. "My parents wouldn't have allowed that. I have to be perfect, and that means being above everyone else."

Her second sight came up empty again. There was nothing in the park that seemed capable of producing such a feeling, just the usual immortals and humans, and their children. She spoke more harshly than she meant to, frustrated. "So you bullied me?"

Petra's mouth opened and closed. Her eyes closed. "That's not why I bullied you. I know you won't believe me, but that had *nothing* to do with you."

Harlow turned her full attention to Petra now. Whatever the source of the threatening feeling, she couldn't suss it out. "You're right. I don't believe that."

"There's nothing I can say that would ever justify the things I did to you, Harlow. No way for me to apologize. But I *am* sorry."

Harlow sat numbly, lost for words. Petra sounded sincere. In fact, she sounded tortured. "If it had nothing to do with me, then why did you do it? I thought it was because you were in love with Finn… But if that wasn't it, then why?"

Petra stood, walking into the park. Harlow hurried after her, using the opportunity to scan the park further—still nothing. Petra walked quickly until they were standing near the waterfall at the center of the park. The noise was so loud here that Harlow worried if Petra actually said anything she wouldn't be able to hear her. When Petra turned, she understood from the look on the other woman's face that was the point.

Petra leaned in, placed her mouth close to Harlow's ear, and spoke quickly: "Aislin McKay caught me in her pool house with Melisandre Marillier when we were sixth years."

Harlow's eyes widened. Suddenly things started to make more sense.

"She threatened to tell my parents if I didn't do everything she asked. And what she asked was that I follow Finn and watch the two of you."

"You took the photos of us, didn't you?"

Petra nodded. "And then, when Finn refused to do what they wanted, Aislin said I had to bully you, make you so miserable Finn would be forced to save you from me. She thought you'd get back together. But it didn't matter how cruel I was, Harlow. He wouldn't step in. I hurt you both, and I hated every second of it."

Harlow understood now why Finn hadn't stepped in, but it still stung. The three of them were such victims of the McKays' twisted plotting, it made her ill.

"I'm so sorry, Petra. I'm sure if Finn had known, he would have done something… Helped you somehow."

Petra laughed, a dry, brittle noise. "He knew, Harlow. I was there the night his parents put the whole awful thing to him about impregnating you. And he knew about Melisandre and his mother… He knew it all. Not about the pictures, I couldn't bear to tell him that. But he knew the rest. I think he even knew about the reason I bullied you, or at least suspected. He was just *that* afraid of them."

"We were kids," Harlow said softly. "We were just kids."

She knew Petra could hear her.

"We were then, but not now, Harlow. Aislin McKay is still holding what she knows about me over my head and he's never said a word to her. Never tried to stop her. I'm not telling you this to hurt you. I'm telling you because I know what's at stake for you, and if you're hoping that Finn McKay will stand up to his parents for you… Well, I love him dearly, he's my commander, and I trust him with my life, but you should know what you're getting into, Harlow."

Harlow frowned, emotion stirring deep within her that she thought she'd left behind. "What would you do if you were me?" she asked.

Petra looked surprised to be asked, her brows wrinkling her eternally smooth forehead in a way Harlow thought was probably novel to her. "What do you mean?"

Harlow shrugged. "If you were me, falling for him all over again, what would you do?"

The immortal shook her head, her dark ponytail swishing down her back. Her brown eyes were the color of smoky topaz, and they glowed a little in the gloomy light of the park, the only thing that let Harlow know she was feeling something rather deeply. "Honestly, I don't know. I'm hurt too. I don't have a good answer for that."

Mist from the waterfall hit Harlow in the face, carried by a gust of warm spring wind. The year was turning, something that usually pleased Harlow. Winter was ending, but her heart felt colder than it had in months. In fact, her entire body was frozen. She couldn't move, couldn't think. She was stuck in the hurt of the moment and wasn't sure what to do.

Petra squeezed her arm then. "I am sorry. I really am. Please understand, this is the only way I can make amends—to tell you the whole truth."

And then Petra was gone, using her Illuminated speed to leave Harlow standing in the park alone. The pressure of the eyes watching her intensified, but Harlow couldn't bring herself to try to look for its source again; she was too flummoxed by what Petra had said. It began to rain again and Harlow didn't move. She couldn't. She just stood there getting soaked, thinking about what Petra had said, trying to ignore the feeling that she was being followed and the anger oozing in her chest like an infected wound.

CHAPTER 30

Harlow didn't remember much about the drive home, just the mounting anger building in her as she took turn after turn in the Woody. By the time she pulled into the driveway at Finn's house, rage consumed her. Old rage, rage she should have let go of long ago, but that she couldn't seem to part from for good. It was the constant in her life, the thread that tied each of her terrible choices together.

A logical part of her knew that things hadn't been perfect before her sixth year in secondary. She'd always struggled with self-worth. Something to do with being smashed between four sisters who were all extraordinary in some way, while she never amounted to anything special. But that was the moment it had all come crashing down, when she'd shattered into pieces too small to put back together again—she'd looked at that mess and *given up*.

It was the giving up she couldn't forgive herself for, and that lack of empathy for herself transferred all too easily to Finn. She walked slowly to the house, trying to let the pouring rain soothe her, but nothing could quiet the storm in her now. Finn, Alaric and Thea were sitting in the front living room together, in chairs she'd crafted from deadfall in the yard only yesterday. They looked up, startled by her appearance, she assumed.

Finn rose quickly, but Harlow's hand shot out in front of her. "Don't come near me."

He drew back, as though she'd slapped him.

She stepped into the room, her voice sharp as a blade. "You knew what she was going through." He looked lost, so she clarified. "Petra. You knew and you did nothing to stop your parents."

Finn took a step towards her. "Harls... I can explain."

She stepped back, shaking her head so hard it hurt. A headache split into the back of her skull so painful she was tempted to cry out. "No. Not unless you want to tell me she was lying. *Was she lying to me?*" The shrill sound of her voice surprised her. "Did you not know what she was going through, what she is *still* going through? Do you not know what your mother is doing to her?"

His head hung in shame and Alaric and Thea both shifted uncomfortably, but Harlow got the impression they might be confused by what she was saying. Let them ask. She wasn't going to enlighten them.

"What is she talking about, Finn?" Alaric asked, his voice gentle as he touched his friend's arm.

Finn started to say something but Harlow stopped him, screeching. "Don't you *dare* tell her secret. Not here. Not to anyone."

He flinched, but she saw defeat in the angle of his shoulders. "She wasn't lying to you. I knew."

"The bullying. You knew why she did it?"

He nodded. "I suspected."

A suppressed sob choked her. "Did you know how much it hurt her to do it?"

"I did." His voice was flat. Resigned. "It's why we stayed friends."

Thea looked as though she might panic. She clutched Alaric's arm so tightly Harlow could see the whites of her knuckles. Harlow was sure she was worried about what was coming next, and she wished she could spare her sister from this scene, seventeen hells, she wished she could spare *herself.*

But the words came tumbling out in a vicious outburst, meant to wound rather than expose her own vulnerability. "Did you know that I tried to kill myself in college? Because of how she treated me? Because of how *you* treated me, and everyone else who followed suit because of the two of you? I went to college and people were *still* treating me like shit because of you."

The things she was saying were true, but they weren't fair, or even accurate, and she knew it. *Why was she saying these things? Why was she saying them* this way? But she couldn't take the words back, not now. Her heart beat wildly as she began to panic; she was out of control in a way that was completely unfamiliar to her.

No one spoke. Axel wound himself around her legs and she picked him up. "I want to go home," she said. Her words sounded alien to her, as though someone else was speaking from within her. This wasn't how she'd wanted to tell Finn about this. She'd been angry in the park with Petra, but she hadn't imagined coming home and creating this kind of scene. Her head pounded, feeling like an icepick driving into her brain.

Thea let go of Alaric now, rushing to Harlow's side, taking her arm. Alaric's eyes widened in shock. He moved to stand next to Thea, a clear sign of support for the woman he loved.

Finn dropped into his chair. He was struggling, but she didn't know if she cared. "How can I trust you when you know that someone you love is being personally victimized by your mother? You do love Petra, don't you? She's one of your best friends? A comrade as a fellow Knight?"

He nodded, but did not form words.

"Then what in seventeen hells is *wrong* with you?" she screamed, clutching Axel. "How could you let her suffer like this?"

"I'm scared," he yelled back, then quieter, "I'm *so* scared of them."

A part of her, deep underneath all this rage, understood it. She was scared of his parents too. But she didn't know if she could forgive it, because if anyone could stand up to them, it was him. "Then how can I expect you to help me if they want to hurt me, or my family?"

Finn got up, moved toward her as though he would touch her, but she held up a hand. "Don't. Just don't. I'm going home and I don't want you to follow me or call me. I mean it."

She moved toward the door and Thea and Alaric followed. Her heart burned with shame for what she'd just done, but her pride wouldn't let her turn around and apologize. This wasn't the way to do this. Yes, she was angry, perhaps even justifiably so, but behaving this way didn't feel right. Trying to humiliate him and berating him like this wasn't who she wanted to be. *Why couldn't she just turn around, apologize and talk things out?*

Harlow was stuck again, stuck in a place she didn't want to be but couldn't see a way out of. She couldn't seem to retreat, but she could do something right. Before they could follow her out she turned to Alaric, and looked him directly in the eyes, so like Petra's the way they glowed with feeling. "I fucked that up."

He exchanged a look with Thea, but didn't respond. She felt his disapproval, and she knew she'd earned it. She'd earned her own.

"Stay with him," she pleaded. "Take care of him. I can't right now, but you can."

Alaric's eyes softened and he hugged her. "You are a good woman, Harlow Krane. I am glad you'll be my sister soon."

Harlow shrugged. "I'm not that good." She leaned into the half-hug Thea gave her. "Can you drive us home?"

Her sister took her hand and led her to Alaric's car. They got in and drove away in silence, heading back into the city. "Do you want to talk about it?" Thea asked.

"No. I said more than I should have back there."

Thea sighed. "It sounds like whatever you said was true. He admitted it."

Axel rubbed his face against hers, purring. "But why did I scream at him like that?"

Thea glanced at her, sidelong. "Why did you?"

Harlow shook with unshed tears. "I don't know. I just… Blew up… It was like all this old anger just exploded out of me. I thought I was doing better…" Her breath came in harsh gasps.

Thea reached out, taking her hand. "Harlow, *Harlow*. He will forgive you. You'll talk and work things out."

She shook her head, so angry and full of shame she couldn't think straight. "I just want to be alone. Is that okay?"

Harlow saw the worry in Thea's hunched shoulders and felt even worse, as she murmured, "Of course." It wasn't okay with Thea at all.

They stopped at a railroad crossing as the gates were going down. Harlow remembered the reason she'd gone to the city to begin with. She fumbled in her pocket, then handed Thea the slip of paper Petra had given her. "This address is Olivia Sanvier's safehouse. Petra says that's where she might take Mark."

Thea took out her phone and sent a text message. "Alaric will take care of it. If Mark's there, he'll find him."

Harlow nodded. She felt nothing but pain so deep and so close to all her old wounds she nearly went numb. In the past, she would have stopped by the liquor store, bought a bottle of something, or called one of her many connections to find drugs, but now she just wanted to go home and get into her comfortable bed and cry. The overwhelming anger was draining away, the further she got from the house. Confusion and shame coursed through her until her hands ached with the pain of balling them into fists.

Slowly she relaxed her fingers and began to force air deep into her lungs. Maybe Thea was right, and Finn would forgive her if she apologized, or at least admitted that she was wrong. She hugged Axel close, slid her phone out of her pocket, and sent a text message. Just one, because her integrity demanded she do so. *I said things I shouldn't have. It wasn't your fault I hurt myself. Please give me time to sort myself out.*

She watched as the little dots cascaded, waited for his response, but nothing came. He was doing as she asked, giving her time. Loneliness gnawed at her, and after so long being sidelined, it was ravenous. She leaned back in her seat and let it devour her.

CHAPTER 31

Harlow spent exactly a week moping about what happened with her phone shut off but for the once-daily check-in she promised Selene, before Enzo showed up at her door. He had a pizza and a bag of burgers and parm fries from Gastro Lupo in his arms.

"Since you didn't answer your phone, I got everything," he said as he pushed inside her apartment. She looked behind him, half-expecting to see Riley Quinn or her sisters trailing behind, but he was alone.

Axel twined around his legs, purring in greeting as Enzo went to work getting plates out and running tap water into glasses. He peeked into her hutch and fridge, shaking his head. "So. You're punishing yourself for being shitty to Finn?"

Harlow's mouth fell open at his tone. Was he *mad* at *her*? Axel perched next to Enzo in the kitchen and together they glared at her. "What did I do to the two of you?" she grumbled.

Enzo shook his head, flinging his hands into the air. "Why is this so hard for you to get? When you do this, when you retreat like this—it hurts everyone who loves you."

Harlow sat on the bed, her chest tightening. "I needed space."

Her best friend rolled his eyes. "Yeah, and what about me? What happened with us when you were with Mark was one thing. And babe, I take responsibility for not knowing the right thing to do when all that went down, but you *cannot* disappear on me again. *Do you understand?*"

She'd been staring at her hands as he talked, but the sound of the shake in his voice caused her to look up. Grief, deep echoing grief, ricocheted on Enzo's face. Harlow leapt up, throwing her arms around him. She didn't need to be an empath to know he was thinking about how lonely he was without his parents.

"I'm sorry. You're right. I've been a bad friend."

He hugged her back and she felt the smooth comfort of his magic envelop her. "Why can't you call Finn and tell him that too?"

Harlow pulled back, sighing. She walked out onto the terrace. The air was warm and balmy today, weak sunlight filtering through the usual haze over Ambracia Bay. Enzo followed her, plopping down in the single plastic chair, munching a plate of parm fries. She stole a couple before answering.

"Because it's complicated. I went about things the wrong way, and I'm honestly not sure why I got *so* mad, but what I said stands up. Did Riley tell you what Finn did?"

Enzo smiled, slouching down in the chair. "This chair is awful," he said, disdain for the cheap plastic monstrosity in his eyes. "Actually, Petra and Finn both told me. Riley is a vault."

Harlow froze. "Petra *and* Finn?"

He handed her the plate. "*You* sit here and tell me this is a chair worth keeping." She laughed. The chair *was* awful; the other had fallen apart a few days ago, and this one was on its last legs. She let her shadows out, thinking of the plastic chairs they had at the cabin, the ones that were much, much more comfortable. The chair shifted under Enzo, until he was sitting on an exact replica of the cabin chairs.

"Better?" she asked.

"Much." She started eating the fries, a signal that Enzo should keep talking. "Yes, they asked Riley and I over for dinner. Your whole family was there, actually, and Cian Herrington."

Harlow's stomach flipped. They'd all met without her?

Enzo saw the face she was making. "You've said no to everything, Harlow. We all needed to talk about what's going on and we couldn't wait for you."

She slid down to sit on the ground, propping her feet in Enzo's lap. "Fair. So what's up?"

"No news on Mark, or Olivia. No one has seen either of them."

Harlow nodded. She'd expected as much.

"Mark's dad is gone too."

"What?"

Enzo shook his head. "If you'd been checking the news, you'd know. He's missing."

"That seems bad," Harlow said.

"Yeah... And shit gets worse... Finn confronted his parents about Petra."

Harlow felt her eyebrows raise until her forehead ached. "He did?"

"Yes. And that did *not* go well. The McKays outed her to her parents. She's out of their will and cut off financially. They paid for her apartment and car, of course. I guess she got fired from her job at their company too."

Harlow wasn't sure what to think about that. "Is she okay?"

Enzo stared off into the distance. "You know, it's weird, I've disliked her nearly our whole lives. She's always been such a miserable person to be around... But she's different now. She was *kind* at the dinner, which was at Alaric's by the way, and the food was excellent. She's staying there now. She's still a little... blunt... sometimes, but maybe that's just Petra."

"No one should have to live like she was," Harlow said, her voice quiet. "I'm glad Finn stood up for her. Did he tell her he was going to do that?"

Enzo nodded, leaning forward to steal a handful of fries. "Yes, he asked her first, and I guess she said that she'd rather face the consequences with her parents than think he didn't care enough to stand up to them. They worked their shit out." Harlow's breath caught in her throat as she bit her lip. "Can I give you some advice, Harlow?"

She lowered her eyes. "Okay."

"You should do the same. It's not your place to be mad *for* her. She told you what she did because she needed someone to tell, and she thought she was helping you. I think she feels genuinely bad that what she said caused you to be so angry with him."

Harlow's voice died in her throat for a moment, then she coughed. "I don't really know why I flew off the handle like that. I've been trying to figure it out for days. I mean, I was frustrated with him, but I was out of control..."

"You've been holding all that in for a long time."

Harlow set the plate of fries down. "Yeah, but I do actually know Finn and Petra weren't the reason things got so bad, *I am*. I've been working on this stuff for a while now. Something about the whole incident doesn't feel right."

Enzo arched an eyebrow. "You're sure you're not just repressing stuff?"

She shrugged instead of trying to convince him. There was only one way to know for sure. "You tell me. You're the empath."

He held out a hand to her. "If you really want to know, come inside."

She took his hand and let him pull her to her feet.

"You'd better get that plate, or your cat will be eating fries. I don't think they're supposed to have garlic."

Dutifully, Harlow picked up her plate and followed Enzo inside, tucking it into the oven before sitting with him on the floor. He and Axel were sitting in a patch of sunshine peeking through the haze.

"He likes you," Harlow murmured as she sat, facing Enzo.

Axel made his way into her lap as Enzo took her hands. "Breathe with me and try not to resist. Since your anger is likely rooted deep, it may take a while for me to find."

Harlow nodded, closing her eyes, trying to focus all her attention on the air moving in and out of her lungs. She felt the pressure of Enzo's magic, as he pushed deeper into her mind. Empaths, even ones as talented as Enzo, mostly read surface feelings without effort, needing to probe more deeply to uncover older emotions, or something that wasn't being actively felt.

She relaxed into the feeling, letting herself picture Enzo's gentle search as a connection between them. When she imagined it as part of the thread between them, a magical link forged by their years of friendship and connection, she felt the pressure ease off. Instead of Enzo's empathy feeling like an attack, it felt more like having a visitor.

When he let go of her hands, he sighed. "That was amazing, Harlow. Did you use your magic to help ease my way?"

She opened her eyes. "I think so." They both looked down at her fingers, which were now stained inky blue. "What did you find?"

Enzo's expression clouded. "It's strange. I found the spot where your emotions about what Finn and Petra did reside... And all I found was a deep well of sadness. Some self-hatred, but no rage, not even any anger... At least..." He trailed off, creating a hollow in his cheek as he bit it, making his prominent cheekbones look even sharper on one side of his face.

"What?" she prompted, anxious to know what he'd found.

"It's almost like there was something left over. Not a resolved emotion, that's different..." he sighed. "I'm not explaining this well."

Harlow smiled encouragingly. Sometimes Enzo got flustered when he couldn't be as precise as he liked to. She'd always found it best not to interrupt his train of thought when he was like this.

He stared up at the ceiling. "Resolved emotions are like healed wounds. They leave silvery scars, but they are healed. I can tell what they were, how deep they ran, and many times how much damage they caused. But this was something else... A remnant of rage, but it wasn't like anything else in you."

When his eyes drifted back to hers, she saw the fear in them. "What does that mean?"

He shook his head. "I'd rather not guess."

Her arm shot out and she took his hand. "Try. Please."

Enzo grimaced. "It doesn't look like it belongs to you, Harlow. *Your* anger, even your rage, looks completely different. Everyone's emotions have similarities, but they have their own signature. This didn't belong to you."

She knew he wouldn't want to answer this, but she had to ask. "What could cause something like that?"

"I'd like to talk with James Quinn, Riley's dad, before I answer that. He and Riley's mom are kind of experts about this stuff. She's a researcher specializing in parapsychology and they often work together on cases like these. Is it all right if I talk to them about what I saw inside you?"

Harlow didn't like the sound of what Enzo was suggesting might be wrong with her, but what choice did she have? If there was something inside her that wasn't hers, she had to find out how it got there and what to do about it, or there was no way she could move forward with Finn.

"Sure." She needed to change the subject. The idea that some alien remnant of rage was festering inside her was too disturbing. "How are things with Riley?"

Enzo's face lit up with a beautiful smile that warmed Harlow to her toes. "So good. They're the best."

Harlow couldn't help but echo that gorgeous grin. "And it's *all* good?"

Enzo covered his mouth and waggled his eyebrows as he nodded. "Yes. It's all *so* good. The best ever."

They dissolved into laughter, collapsing on the floor with Axel sprawling between them. Enzo's fingers laced with hers. "Call Finn. I think he really misses you."

"I can't," she whispered, her voice suddenly hoarse. "Not until I know what's going on with me. Where all that anger came from. What if I lost my temper like that again?"

Enzo grimaced. "You are going to lose your temper again, Harlow. That boy is infuriating. People lose their tempers, get in fights, get mad. Then they apologize, make up… You get this, right?"

She almost lied and said that she understood. "Not really. There's a lot I haven't told anyone about me and Mark."

Enzo nodded. "I figured. But can I tell you that when I was looking for your anger, I saw a lot of new healing. You're doing the work, babe. You'll get there. I promise."

The floor was hard under her as she rolled onto her back. As she stared at her ceiling the hole in her memory about the night Mark kicked her out pressed against her conscious mind. "There's something I can't remember. Can you help me?"

Enzo sat up, looking down at her. "I know—I saw it. I can't help with that, Harlow. I'm sorry. Riley could, maybe, but I'm not sure they would."

Harlow swallowed as a tear spilled onto her cheek. "Why not?"

Enzo's thumb swept the tear away. "Because sometimes stuff like that gets locked away for a reason. It's tricky business to undo it. But I can loosen some of the thorns around it, if you'd like. That way, when you work out the tangles, it should release safely."

"Okay," Harlow said, sitting. "I'd like that."

They took hands again, and Enzo set to work.

CHAPTER 32

Harlow spent the next few days at home, but she answered her texts, and called her sisters and the maters, one by one. Enzo had said he'd get back to her when he heard from the Quinns about the strange remnant of alien emotion inside her. She tried not to dwell on what might have caused such a thing to happen, as the idea of something influencing her in ways she couldn't detect was so terrifying it sent her into a dissociative spiral each time she thought about it too hard. She was taking things hour by hour, but sometimes it felt like she might be stuck in this spot forever, unable to trust herself even more than she had before.

There were still no texts from Finn. And why would there be? She asked for space and he was giving it to her. When the intercom buzzed, she jumped, her heart leaping into her throat.

She pressed the button, her heart pounding. "Who is it?"

"Petra... Velarius. Can I come up?"

As if anyone else in Nuva Troi would dare be named Petra, Harlow thought with a smirk. "Sure, press your hand to the metal plate by the door, then come on up. Penthouse 2."

The light on the intercom went on as Petra pressed her hand to the plate downstairs. Harlow pressed the green button next to it to approve Petra's presence, then ran to the bathroom to brush her teeth, changing into a clean sweatshirt as she went. When she opened the door she was surprised by Petra's appearance. Her dark hair was pulled into its usual ponytail, but instead of being flat-ironed into a satin sheet, her hair curved in natural waves, and she wore only a touch of makeup. And her clothes...

"I'd forgotten you went to UNT too," Harlow said, glancing down at their matching sweatshirts.

"It's the weekend," Petra said, cheeks flushing. "I'm trying out being..."

"Relaxed?" Harlow suggested.

"Casual," Petra corrected, laughing. "My parents actually kept most of my clothes when they ejected me from their lives and kicked me out of my home."

Harlow shook her head. "Petty."

Petra nodded. "That's my mom and dad. But believe it or not, this feels better. They hate me, but I can *be* me now."

Harlow was tempted to hug her, but she wasn't sure what Petra would do if she did. "I'd offer you something to eat or drink, but I don't really have anything."

Petra's gaze lit on Axel. "You have a kitty!"

Harlow watched in amazement as Petra Velarius dropped to the floor making little clicking noises at Axel, who looked at Harlow as if to ask, *What is this immortal fool up to?*

"You like cats?" Harlow asked as she got a bag of treats out of a drawer and handed them to Petra. "He likes these."

Petra took the treats, wrinkling her nose slightly at the smell, but grinning with delight as Axel took one after another from her hand. "My parents never let me have pets. They think animals are dirty. I've always wanted a cat. Some big, floofy monster that would love me."

Harlow understood then. Petra Velarius had spent her life isolated by her secrets, and by parents who cared more about some stupid illusion of propriety the rest of the world left behind nearly a century ago. Free from that, she was a slightly sad girl, who apparently liked cats, and women. Harlow's head shook slightly. What a shame that her parents would rather have her rich, perfect and miserable, over the sweet person stuffing Axel with rabbit treats in front of her now.

Axel pushed past the bag of treats in Petra's hand and climbed into her lap. "He wants you to pet him," Harlow said. "He likes ear and chin rubs the best."

Petra obliged, beaming at Axel. When he curled up to sleep, she looked up at Harlow, who had curled up on the bed, facing them. "So, what's up?" Harlow asked.

Petra sighed. "I... I thought I was helping you when I told you that about Finn."

Harlow held up a hand. "Please. Don't apologize. I'm the one who was wrong for getting so angry. I mean, don't get me wrong, I was pissed... But I lost my temper and made a mistake."

"Can you forgive him?"

"Have you?"

Petra smiled. "I forgave Finn before he asked me to, and we worked out the rest. When he told his parents to back off us both, it was really brave. I knew the McKays would tell my parents about me. That's how they are, they follow through on their threats. We both knew and I gave him permission to do it anyways. It was time for both of us to cut the cord. Alaric did it a long time ago when he started his company, though he and Pasiphae are on much better terms than either Finn or I will be with our parents."

"Wait... What do you mean he told them to back off us both?"

"He told them to go fuck themselves, Harlow. He shut down the bank account they opened in his name, and he told them if they didn't leave you and Antiquity Row alone that he'd make problems for them. As I'm sure you can imagine, he knows quite a few of their secrets. I tried to get him to come over here and tell you this himself, but he wouldn't. He told me not to tell you either, which of course forced me to come directly here to do the exact opposite. He's kind of a dummy about stuff like that sometimes."

Petra snickered and Harlow couldn't help herself, she joined her. "Yeah, he is, isn't he?"

"So will you forgive him now?" Petra asked.

Harlow sighed. "I'm not angry with him. I'm angry with myself. It's complicated."

Petra nodded, petting Axel gingerly, so as not to wake him, Harlow supposed. "I get that. But he's in love with you Harlow. I don't think he ever stopped being in love with you. He'd move worlds to keep you safe. Make himself miserable, if he had to. He gets a little too *focused* sometimes, and misses what might be collateral damage, but he is a good man."

"You don't have to convince me of that, Petra," Harlow said. "I already know."

"Okay, well I feel like I started something crappy between you, and I wanted to try and see if I could make it right." She looked around. "This is a nice place."

Harlow smiled, a little surprised that Petra liked it, but Enzo was right, she was different now that she was free of her parents. "Thank you. It's been good for me."

"Will you come to dinner tonight at Finn's? We're meeting to talk about some stuff your sister dug up about the Scroll of Akatei."

"Did she restore the images in the Merkhov book?" Harlow asked. *Why didn't Thea text her?*

Petra shook her head. "No, I think she's having trouble with that for some reason. This is something else. Will you come?"

Harlow nodded.

Petra looked down at Axel. "I have to go. What do I do?"

Harlow suppressed a smile, taking the cat off the beautiful immortal's lap. He chirped sleepily as she tucked him into the blankets on her bed. Petra stood, looking around again. "This place is *really* beautiful, Harlow. What a view."

Harlow thanked her again, walking her to the door.

"Do you need a ride to Finn's?" Petra asked. "I could come get you."

Harlow shook her head. "No, that's okay. Thank you though."

She couldn't stand the thought of trying to wrangle her nerves *and* trying to make conversation with Petra for nearly forty-five minutes in the car, but there was no nice way to say that. She'd figure something else out.

As Petra stepped out the door, Harlow put a hand on her arm. "Can I hug you?"

Petra looked startled. "Why?" She clapped a hand over her mouth. "That was rude. I'm sorry. I…"

"I'm really glad you came over, Petra."

"You are?"

Harlow nodded. "Yeah. In sixth year, I used to have this fantasy that one day you'd just stop being so mean to me and we'd be friends. Isn't that weird?"

Petra's eyes filled with tears. "Not really. I used to have the same one. Where my parents knew about me and didn't care, and I got to be friends with you, Enzo and Finn." Her chin wobbled. Harlow recognized the same loneliness that haunted her chasing Petra, even now.

Harlow reached out and tugged on Petra's matching sweatshirt, something she couldn't imagine having done even a month ago. "Hug?"

Petra nodded and Harlow pulled her into a gentle embrace. When Petra's arms went around her, Harlow felt the other woman's breath shudder through her. "You get to have a whole new life now, one where all those things are true, and more."

When Petra pulled away she gave Harlow a watery smile. "We'll get there. Both of us."

Harlow nodded. "We're already on our way. See you tonight."

Petra waved as she ran down the steps. "Seven. It's casual. Don't be late."

CHAPTER 33

Petra had said this dinner was casual, and she had no doubt that meant *actually* casual, unlike season events. Still, she stood in front of the racks of clothing sitting in the middle of her apartment for what felt like forever, trying to figure out what to wear. The weather had warmed just enough in the past few days to make sweaters uncomfortably warm, but lighter clothing was still too chilly.

Eventually, she settled on a plaid shirt in an impossibly soft twill fabric, tucked into a pair of vintage wide leg jeans. Harlow pulled her long hair into a ponytail, deciding not to fuss with makeup or glamour. Everyone knew she'd been having a hard time; there was no need to pretend like everything was fine.

Her intercom buzzed just as she was feeding Axel and thinking about ordering a car. "Yes?"

"Delivery for Harlow Krane. I need a signature."

A delivery? "Be right down."

She pulled boots on and ran down what felt like unending flights of stairs. Before she reached the bottom, she hesitated. What if this was some kind of trap from the House of Remiel? She slowed down, breathing deeply, reaching for her shadows. She wasn't completely confident about using them to defend herself, but she wanted to be prepared.

As she entered the vestibule, she saw a human courier, dressed in street clothes, holding an envelope and a clipboard. Their bike was sitting outside and they were looking at it anxiously. She sighed. Just a human kid, worried about their bike being stolen.

"Hi," she said as she stepped into the vestibule. "I'm Harlow."

The kid looked at her, nodded. "Yep. Just like in the gossips."

She narrowed her eyes.

"What?" the kid said with a grin. "Everyone follows along with that shit. You're my favorite, by the way. I hope you win. Sign here."

They handed her the clipboard and she signed, trying not to be offended that her personal life had been reduced to "winning" Finn McKay. Within seconds, the kid had handed her a stiff cardboard envelope and was outside and back on their bike. A dry laugh blew out from her lungs; it was ridiculous to be recognized for doing absolutely nothing—she wasn't like the twins, she didn't work at being seen. She tore open the envelope and was about to dump its contents out on the low console table in the front hall of her building when a shifter couple from the third floor passed her coming in from the parking lot.

"Finally using your spot, eh?" the older man said with a wink. "I do love a classic."

"Hi, Phil. Marisa," Harlow replied, not sure what Phil was referring to.

Marisa rolled her light brown eyes and tucked a lock of wavy black hair behind her ears. "Come on, Phil. Harlow has better things to do than talk to an old codger like you about classic cars."

Harlow smiled. They were sweet together, but she had no idea what they were talking about. She waved as they got in the elevator, before turning back to the envelope. She turned it over and a key fell onto the table with a note. She picked up the note and recognized the handwriting instantly.

If I can't drive you, at least I can give you a ride.

—Finn

She looked at the key again, and then walked quickly in the direction of the parking lot. The penthouse came with a nice parking spot near the door and she could see the Woody from halfway down the hall. He'd known she would need some space to fret on her way over because she'd always been this way, anxious before events. It wasn't the kind of lavish gift that most immortals would gush over. It was just an old car to most people, but the Woody meant something to *her* and Finn knew it.

Her phone was upstairs, along with her purse, so she raced back to the penthouse as quickly as she could, pulling out her phone.

Thank you, she texted Finn, not knowing what else to say.

He saw immediately and began to write back. *You're welcome.*

Harlow waited, but he didn't say more and she wasn't sure how to reply. Her stomach flipped as she put her phone down. Axel curled his long tail around her leg in comfort. "You can't come, bub. Not tonight. I'll be home soon."

She picked the cat up and he bumped his face against hers, then used her shoulder to boost himself into his tree, where he curled into a plush hammock she'd created for him near the window. Within moments the cat was asleep, his little snores drifting down to her, making her jealous for the millionth time that she hadn't been born a cat.

Her phone vibrated on the table and she picked it up. Finn. *I'm nervous about seeing you. Changed my t-shirt four times. This look okay?*

A photo came just as she was reading. It was him, standing in his bathroom in jeans and a heathered grey t-shirt that said, in faux-vintage lettering, "My girlfriend is a witch."

Harlow burst out laughing. If he'd been trying to break the possible tension between them, it worked. A small measure of relief crept into her chest, loosening the hold on her lungs until she breathed freely. She texted back. *Where'd you find that?*

A vendor on 55th. They had some with your face on them, but I thought that was too much.

She snorted and typed back. *Probably right. Humans are so weird.*

His next text came as she pressed send. *Jk. I got it.*

The photo he sent had her in tears. Someone had printed a caricature of her on a shirt, and underneath it said, "Harlow Krane: frumpy to fabulous." *Which should I wear tonight?*

Harlow shot back, *The first one.* The second was too embarrassing, even for a family dinner. Her sense of relief that he wasn't freezing her out was tempered by her fear that something might trigger that piece of alien rage that might be left inside her.

She waited while the torturous little dots blinked. *Drive safe.*

See you soon, she wrote back, then tucked her phone in her purse.

As she locked up and headed to the car, she felt more, rather than less nervous. She knew the shirt was meant to make her laugh, maybe clear the air a little, and it had, but where did they stand? A part of her wanted to say screw it and work things out together, but her fear that something else was affecting her, causing her to react to things in ways she normally wouldn't was too frightening.

Furthermore, the memory she'd lost bothered her. Something about it felt connected to all this, though she didn't know how. Maybe unlocking it would make everything make sense, but until then it was better not to do more harm to Finn than she'd already done.

The Woody was gassed up and had been detailed since the last time she drove it. It smelled like Finn, decadent and a little like woodfire. She pressed play on the CD player, which already had something in it. It was a copy of a mix he'd made her in secondary, with all their favorite songs. It was hard not to get nostalgic as she drove through the city, rain splattering on the Woody's windshield in a non-committal way that suggested it would pour later. Her mind drifted as she drove, and she reached Finn's house sooner than she expected. She sat in the driveway for a moment. Everyone else had already arrived and she'd be walking into a group of people who knew how badly she'd embarrassed herself last time she was here.

Her cheeks burned as she bit the inside of her mouth, trying to maintain some semblance of calm. A light rap on her window startled her. Cian Herrington stood outside her window, wearing what she assumed they interpreted as "casual" clothing, but actually consisted of a pair of slim trousers and a button-down that was unbuttoned halfway down their chest in an alluring way. Their hair had been silver the last time she saw them, but today was lavender, and they wore a hint of shadow around their eyes.

She opened the car door. "Hi," she said as she got out.

Cian smiled. "I like you."

Harlow was taken aback by the blunt nature of this statement. "What?"

"You're passionate and honest. Finn's dated a lot of volatile people trying to get over you. But you are unpredictable, which is different from volatile, and I like it."

A smile crept onto Harlow's face. "Well, I'm certain I'll like you too, if we get to know one another better."

Cian's head tilted to one side as their eyes narrowed. "*When* we get to know one another better, you mean."

Harlow swallowed hard, glancing at the house. "You seem like a bit of a package deal, with Finn, I mean. And…"

Now Cian grinned, and their face was so ferocious that Harlow was tempted to step back. "And nothing. You and Finn will work things out. I'm *glad* you challenged him. He's not used to that. His parents are the only ones to ever tell him no, and they do it out of spite. Why did you do it?"

Harlow bit her bottom lip, wondering why they were having this conversation at all. But as she looked into Cian's pale eyes, something in her recognized what they were doing. They were protective of Finn and this was how they were vetting her. She was glad someone was vetting her, that someone cared enough about him to make sure she was good enough in the right ways, and she was pleased Cian found her acceptable.

"First of all, I don't like *how* I did it. I'm not proud of losing my temper that way. I'm working on it."

Cian nodded. "Fair assessment."

"But I did it because it hurt so much to hear Petra's story. I couldn't let it go."

Again, Cian nodded. "And what about the way humans are treated by the Orders? Can you let that go?"

Harlow couldn't help it; she looked around, worried to voice something like this aloud, even here. "No, I can't. I've waited my whole life to find a way to do the things you're doing with the Knights. It doesn't matter what happens with me and Finn on a personal level. We have to find a way to change things."

Now Cian's grin was positively feral. Harlow had the sudden impression that she wouldn't want to have to fight them, for anything. She was tempted to ask a *very* rude question, but she held it in. The Trickster's Chosen hated to be asked about their alternae, but she desperately wanted to know what creature lurked under Cian's humanoid form. She had the feeling they shifted into something magnificent. Cian's grin spread wider, and Harlow's heart nearly stopped as their pupils disappeared and an image of an immense silver beast covered in scales filled her second sight.

"You're an Argent?"

Cian chuckled in response, linking their arm through hers. "Aren't you a clever girl?"

Harlow was nearly stunned into silence. *Nearly*. "How… How is that possible?"

Heraldic shifters hadn't been born for over five hundred years, as the Illuminated had exterminated them in massive campaigns, since they fought against them in the War of the Orders. The Argent were the fiercest of the firedrakes, and the most deadly. Even one could lay waste to legions of Illuminated soldiers.

"We are not as rare as you might think. Of course, we must be careful who knows our secret."

"I would *never* tell," Harlow said, squeezing the shifter's arm.

"I know that," Cian said softly. "I wouldn't have let you see otherwise. There is a world beyond what you know to be true, Harlow. Tonight is just the beginning."

They'd reached the front door and Harlow took a deep breath. To think there were mysteries she hadn't uncovered yet, even after twenty-five years of being a sorcière, gave her a thrill of joy. Curiosity and deeply held interest lit a flame in her heart so bright that she felt sure she might catch fire. As she put her hand on the door Cian pulled her back.

"Do you know that the Striders fought with the Heraldic shifters in the war?"

Harlow shook her head. "No, I don't know much about them at all. Didn't everyone who fought against the Illuminated fight together?"

Cian let out a small huff of frustration. "Well, of course, but I mean the Striders actually *fought* in our units." The way Cian said "our" made Harlow wonder if they'd been there. If they were possibly that old. Her breath caught as Cian continued, "They fought in our units because they too could shift shape."

Surely, Thea would have told her this already if she'd known, wouldn't she? "I haven't heard anything like that before."

Cian leaned one narrow shoulder against the house. "You wouldn't have. We kept it a secret. It wasn't all of them, mind you. Many of the Striders couldn't shift. But some could."

"What were their alternae?" Harlow asked, using the Order of Masks' word for their non-human form.

Cian sighed. "They were the Feriant."

Harlow hadn't heard that word before, but played with the etymology in her head. *To strike, to kill, to slay*, all possible roots. "I don't know that word," she finally admitted.

The Argent pushed past her, opening the door to the house. "You will, in time, I believe. I learned it was best not to tell Striders their business a long, long time ago."

The note of finality in their voice as they walked into the house indicated that they wouldn't be moved to answer more questions, so Harlow tucked the information away for later. From the sound of things, her entire family, plus Enzo and Riley Quinn, were talking loudly in the kitchen.

Before Cian disappeared into the thick of things, Harlow pulled them back into the hall. "You know that Riley Quinn is with the Rogue Order, right?"

Cian nodded. "Yes, we know. Finn is hoping to use tonight as a way to extend goodwill to the Queen. Perhaps form an alliance."

Harlow breathed a sigh of relief. "They seem like a good person."

Cian nodded thoughtfully. "Yes, many of the Rogue joined for the same reasons the Knights were formed. They are much more willing to create chaos than we have been, but perhaps we need that kind of energy now."

That wasn't anything Harlow knew much about. She'd spent a lot of her adult life just trying to get herself under control. She knew nothing about how to fight for justice or make societal change, only that she wanted to learn, and she hoped her efforts now weren't too late to change things for the better, for humans and immortals alike.

Cian joined the group around the kitchen table, and as they did, Finn caught sight of her lingering in the doorway. His hair was mussed as ever, and her heart did flip after flip as he approached. The street vendor's t-shirt looked good on him, tight around the arms, draping over his muscled chest. She knew he probably didn't mean to do it, but he had his hands shoved into the front pockets of his jeans and his forearms flexed in a tantalizing fashion that had her reminding herself what she was here for.

"Hey, Harls," he said as he approached. She could swear he moved in slow motion, every beautiful thing about him amplified as he drew closer.

"Hey, McKay," she replied, unable to get anything else past her dry mouth. Petra peeked around the corner and gave her an extremely uncharacteristic two thumbs up.

Finn followed Harlow's startled gaze and he shook his head at his best friend. "Sorry about that. And about her coming over earlier. I didn't ask her to. In fact—"

"I know," Harlow interrupted. "She said you told her to stay out of it, but I'm glad she came."

"You hugged her?" Finn asked as he steered her into the library, away from prying eyes. Her sisters were craning their necks trying to hear what they said to each other. He closed the door and the sounds from the kitchen died immediately, as though the door had sealed them in a world of their own. There were no books on the shelves still, and no furniture in the room. Something about the emptiness felt sad to Harlow, instead of full of possibilities as it had just a week ago.

"Petra told you that?"

Finn nodded as he sat in the window seat, gesturing for her to sit across from him. It was large enough that they weren't touching when she obliged, and this too felt sad, like lost potential.

"Yeah, she seemed sort of delighted, actually." His smile faded as he raked his hands through his dark hair, sending it in wild directions. He hadn't had it cut recently, she noticed, nor had he shaved. In his t-shirt and jeans, he looked like *her* Finn, not the person trying to please his parents and the rest of the Orders in the season. Her heart thumped hard in her chest, making her question every instinct she had about staying apart.

When he spoke, she heard the strain in his voice, but also a measure of resolve. "Harls, I thought I was protecting her, but I never *asked* her what she wanted. I just assumed, which was shitty of me."

Harlow nodded, crossing her legs and resting her elbows on her knees to cradle her chin. It was infinitely cool that he could admit the ways he was wrong so effortlessly. A little voice inside her suggested that it probably wasn't effortless, but that he'd done the work to learn how to do something she found difficult. And that voice gave her hope that if he'd done it, maybe she could learn to do so as well.

His fingers stretched toward her, but he clasped them in his lap. "You look just like you did when we were ten, learning to play chess."

Her smile at the memory felt weak. Here, in his presence, she felt like crying, though she wasn't sure why. "I shouldn't have screamed at you like that," she said after what felt like an awkwardly long pause.

He shrugged. "Maybe not, but what you said was spot on. I was a coward about the whole thing."

"But it changed something between us, didn't it?" she asked, wondering if he felt it too.

He nodded. "Yeah, I think it did."

She knew it. The way things had been going was all too good to be true. She'd screamed at him, and after a lifetime of being treated like shit by people who were supposed to love him, he was doing the right thing, drawing strong boundaries and cutting her out. She sank deep into her sadness before saying, "So that's it then."

His brow furrowed as every muscle in his body tensed. "Wait—what do you mean?"

Harlow shook her head. "I assume you want to call this whole thing off. Just be friendly… I mean, we can still work together, but…"

He leaned forward, but still didn't touch her. "Is that what you want? To stop what we've been doing?"

Harlow's jaw clenched. "What do you want?"

He looked down at his shirt, frowning and tugging on the hem. *My girlfriend is a witch.* "I thought it was pretty clear what I wanted."

Air caught in Harlow's throat, momentarily unable to reach her lungs. Surely she was misunderstanding him. "You still want that? You still want… me?"

His slate eyes widened. "Did you think getting mad at me would make me stop wanting you?"

Her eyes watered, but she couldn't answer.

"Harls," he said, his deep voice gentle as he cupped her chin in his hands, one of his thumbs stroking her bottom lip so tenderly she thought she might sob. "You are allowed to get angry. I hope we don't spend all our time yelling and snapping at each other, but if it happens, it happens. We'll make up and move on."

Harlow stared at a place on the windowsill behind Finn's head, avoiding his eyes. "I want all that," she choked out. "I just… I just…"

Finn moved her chin slightly so she had to look at him. "Whatever it is, you can tell me. I'm not going to fly off the handle and get mad. Please, just talk to me."

She wanted to tell him everything, but she couldn't quite manage, even though she *was* trying. What if the Quinns decided that all that anger *was* actually hers? If she told him about her fears now, and Enzo was wrong, she'd look like she was making excuses for bad behavior, and she didn't want that. She wanted to take responsibility for herself. So she kept it to herself; she was accustomed to keeping secrets. Secrets had always kept her safe in the past.

She settled somewhere in between the truth and her secrets. "I need more time to process what happened with Mark. There's something in my memory, this blank space about the night we broke up. I need to figure out what happened and let go before I start something new with you."

"Okay," he said softly. She saw the disappointment in his eyes and his hand fell from her face, but slowly, back into his own lap. "Can I ask you one thing that will make me sound pathetic?"

"You can ask me anything," she said, hating to hear the strain in his words.

"If I were different, if I hadn't fucked up with the whole Petra thing, and everything else, would you still feel this way?"

"Yes. It's not about you, or because of you. This is all me."

"Okay," he said.

Harlow got up. "We should get in there."

He caught her hand. "Harls." She looked back down the line of her arm, where her hand rested in his, raising her eyes to meet his gaze. "We're still in this together, right?"

She nodded, something choking her voice. It felt wrong to walk away, but she knew that before she could move on with Finn, she had to remember that night with Mark and figure out what was affecting her emotions so strangely. Then she had to let it all go, find some way to be free. As much as she wanted that to be something they could do together, she wasn't capable of that now and he deserved better than what she could give him after everything his family put him through.

Finn's lips pressed into her palm. "I'll wait as long as it takes, Harlow."

She nodded once, tearing her eyes away from him so she could walk away. He followed her into the kitchen, where Thea had a series of printed photos spread on the table. Everyone was squeezed into the large alcove, which could barely fit the eleven immortals. Cian got up and they and Finn pulled the two chairs from in front of the hearth to the table.

Finn lit the fire to stave off the chill of the evening, which had, as expected, blown in a massive thunderstorm. Thea was explaining that they could eat after she showed them what she'd found in her facsimile of the Scroll of Akatei.

"Hey," she said when she saw Harlow.

Riley smiled up at her, tucked into the curve of Enzo's arm. Harlow looked around the table, her gaze finally lighting on Petra, who was still dressed in her UNT sweatshirt and leggings. "Hey, everybody."

The maters both smiled. They'd been worried about her isolation, and about the feeling she'd had that she was being watched, but had allowed her to make her own choices about where to stay. She was glad they were here now.

The back door flew open and everyone startled. Two tall figures stepped inside, pushing back their hoods as they closed the back door. Finn pressed a hand to Harlow's shoulder—she hadn't realized he was standing so close to her. "It's just Nox and Arebos."

With their hoods back, the Wraiths proved to be less than the gruesome creatures Harlow worried they might be. In fact, they had an ethereal beauty that couldn't be denied. They were tall and sturdily built, with skin the color of burnished amber, dark hair, and eyes that glistened with acute focus. The taller of the two had their long dark hair pulled half-up and the other's hair was cut short, with the sides shaved, but otherwise they shared many of the same sharply defined features. Clearly they were siblings, though Harlow didn't think they were twins.

"Hi," the shorter one said. "We ran the perimeter twice. The wards are good. No one is getting in." She made eye contact with Harlow momentarily. "I'm Nox," she said. "And this is my brother, Arebos."

"You can call me Ari," her brother said, making eye contact only briefly, his gaze lighting on Meline, who'd looked up from her phone. Ari grinned at Meli and she blushed prettily at him.

Nox rolled her eyes. "He's an incorrigible flirt. Beware."

Indigo looked up at the sound of Nox's sarcastic tone, her eyes immediately appraising the Wraith, and Harlow shook her head. The sillies had always been attracted to their direct opposites, and here were two people who couldn't be more unlike the two of them: the Wraiths could make themselves invisible, and the twins couldn't possibly be more visible. Indigo sat up a bit straighter, and her sweater fell off her shoulder in slow motion. Harlow was sure she'd practiced the move numerous times. Apparently it had the desired effect, because Nox was staring at her, mouth slightly ajar as she pushed a hand through her short hair.

"Gods help us," Harlow muttered to Thea.

Thea's dark head shook as she muttered, "What did you expect? They've been waiting all season to find people dangerous enough to make Mama mad and we just served two of them right up."

Indeed, Selene glared at Arebos as he leaned against the alcove, conducting a soft conversation with Meline, who was whispering so quietly that Harlow couldn't keep up. Clearly Arebos could, because he laughed as she smiled up at him through her long lashes. He crouched down, tapping his phone to hers. They were already exchanging numbers?

Harlow sighed. "Before they get engaged, start talking."

Thea suppressed a laugh, then cleared her throat, getting everyone's attention. "Right. Let's talk about what Alaric and I found when we examined the place in the scroll where the triptych should be."

Thea pointed to a section of the printouts on the table that depicted a white ash tree, with an Argent curled into its roots, asleep. "In the chronology of the scroll, Alaric and I believe whatever the triptych represents comes before the fire-drake, which as we can see, wakes and joins the other Heraldic creatures in the next phase."

Larkin leaned forward, pointing to some faded swirls of color winding around the tree. "Do you think this is the same representation of aether we saw in the triptych?"

Alaric nodded at Larkin. "Yes, we think the triptych is the catalyst to all of what happens in the rest of the scroll."

"What do these represent?" Harlow asked, looking closely at the humanoid forms pictured inside small bubbles in the branches, similar to the ones Thea had restored in the first of the triptych images. Some of the bubbles were shown as cracked and the small forms floated above the tree.

Alaric grinned. "That's the exciting part. We think they might be humans. If we could figure out what happens in the triptych, Thea and I believe we'd unlock the secret to what is happening with these cracked bubbles."

"It looks like the humans are being released somehow," Riley added, squinting at the images. "But if that is the case, what would the purpose of the bubbles be?"

Thea answered, but Harlow didn't hear what she'd said. She looked at Finn, who was turning towards her, as though he'd wondered the same thing she had. Finn held up a hand. "I'm sorry to interrupt, Thea. But originally, you said you thought the triptych might have something to do with what happened when a Strider and Knight… er…. Joined forces, right?"

Thea nodded. "Yes, we think that you and Harlow might hold the key to whatever this shows."

Finn ran a hand through his hair, mussing it into further perfection. Harlow forced herself to focus. "And the tree itself? What's that represent?"

Aurelia answered. "The tree nearly always represents the web of aether in the world. The roots and the branches are an easy way to represent the threads of magic immortals draw upon."

Finn's jaw clenched. "When Harlow and I arrived at the Grove party, we both experienced something strange. With everything going on, I forgot about it…"

Aurelia's voice was sharp. "What happened?"

Harlow moved to stand next to Finn. "It was as though we were isolated from everyone else. In some kind of weird pocket of reality that only we perceived. And we both heard a scream."

Finn added, "And then magic seemed to swell, before dumping us back into our usual reality. It was unsettling."

Selene frowned. "It sounds like you witnessed a ritual from the other side of the veil."

Aurelia took her wife's hand. "I'm afraid there are some dark rituals that might be associated with the season. The Order of Mysteries has been investigating this for nearly a century, but we cannot detect exactly what is happening. We've long believed the Illuminated have some ulterior motive for encouraging the season year after year."

Thea sighed. "Why haven't you ever said anything?"

Aurelia rolled her eyes. "You and your sisters are barely adults. That's not the kind of thing you tell children."

All five Krane sisters glared at their mothers, who glared right back at their children until each averted their eyes. Harlow was the last to break Selene's gaze. "Fine. Is there anything else we should know?"

Selene sighed. "I'm sure there's a great deal we know that is connected to this. Your mother and I have been alive for the better part of a thousand years, it will take time to sort things out. And we will need to take this to the Order at some point, you understand?"

Finn balked visibly. "I think it would be better to keep this a secret for now."

Aurelia's hand flew up. "As do we, Finbar. But eventually, when we decide what must be done, we will need to have the Order of Mysteries' High Council approval. That is, if you want allies."

Finn nodded. "We do. I understand."

A long moment passed, punctuated in its awkwardness by the slow ticking of the clock above the stove. Arebos broke the uncomfortable energy, staring at the images on the table. Then he turned to Thea and asked: "What is the scroll about?"

Thea smiled, appreciative of the redirect, no doubt. "No one really knows, though there have been lots of assumptions made over the years by the different Orders."

Cian tapped the image above the tree, where the Heraldic creatures were awake, flying in formation. "My people believe this means that someday, the Heraldic Chosen will reawaken, and join forces again against the Illuminated."

Aurelia nodded. "That is certainly an interpretation that makes sense. But if I may ask, what is this alternae a representative of? I've never seen it in depictions of the Heraldic before."

She tapped a darkly colored bird that flew in formation with the Heraldic warriors: firedrakes, alicorns, gryphons and the chimaera. It looked like something between an eagle and bird of paradise, though if it were as large as the scale in the facsimile it was probably the size of a person. Its feathers were a mix of dark emerald green, blue, and black in the image.

Cian looked at Harlow when they answered. "That is the Feriant."

Harlow took a sharp breath in, just as Selene covered her mouth. "*That* is a Feriant?"

Cian nodded. "It isn't one of the Heraldic shifters at all, but a sorcière."

Indigo shook her head. "But the sorcière can't change shapes. It's not in our nature."

"It was for some of you, long ago," Cian answered, never taking their eyes off Harlow. "And perhaps will be again."

"How?" Harlow asked, surer than ever that Cian had fought in the War of the Orders. "How did they do it?"

Cian shook their head. "It was kept secret. Not because they didn't trust us, but because it was dangerous knowledge. With the Feriant Legion, we stood a chance against the Illuminated. It is why both the Heraldic and the Striders were systematically eliminated. Without them, we cannot hope to mount any kind of force against the Illuminated Order."

Harlow glanced at Finn. She knew what he was thinking, because she was thinking it too. The Knights of Serpens had been eliminated in just the same way. Could this have something to do with the triptych and their union? She couldn't bring herself to ask. Not right now while things were still so bruised between them, and she saw in his eyes that he felt the same. It was as though they made a silent promise to wait, for just a bit, to talk about that.

"And that is what you think we should be doing?" Aurelia asked sharply, directing her question at Thea and Alaric. "*Fighting* the Illuminated?"

Thea began to gather her papers. "Yes, Mother," she said, voice quiet, but steady. "I do. I think the Illuminated Order has poisoned Okairos for long enough. That's why we asked you all here tonight, to begin to form an alliance—to make a plan, and move against them, before something terrible happens."

"Like what?" Aurelia asked, hysteria in her tone. "We've lived for close to two thousand years without the kinds of poverty, war or major conflicts that plague other worlds. What do you think could happen now?"

Indigo, who'd been staring at her phone, turned it around. "Something like this?"

A video played without sound, but it was clearly the House of Remiel's building in Nuva Troi—and it was on fire, a mob of humans out front. They were being slaughtered by vampires in high definition on the screen.

"What is this?" Selene gasped.

"A livestream from a cafe across the street," Indigo answered. "Humans gathered outside the House of Remiel, demanding to know where Mark and Alain Easton are, apparently they're both missing now—it was all over the gossips earlier today—and things got out of hand. They set the building on fire, apparently, and now the vampires are slaughtering them in retribution."

The livestream was happening inside Haven. Harlow glanced at Finn, whose face was drawn. He squeezed her arm, just once. She felt as though she moved in slow motion as she looked up at him. She knew what he would say, what he would do. Time sprang back into motion and she felt as though she'd missed a chance for something, though she wasn't sure what.

"We have to go," Finn said, glancing at Alaric, who nodded. "Get there, fast," he said to the Wraiths. "Cian?"

"I will hold things down here—after I call in reinforcements for you."

Riley Quinn spoke, after looking up from their phone. "The Rogue Order is sending help as well. We'll get as many humans out as we can. Can we use your safehouse? You have one across the street, yes?"

Cian nodded. "Yes, coordinate with Nox and Arebos. You can ride together."

Alaric kissed Thea. "Stay here. The wards will keep you safe. We'll be back soon."

She nodded, but Aurelia rose. "We should help."

Finn shook his head. "Please, stay here. Make calls if you need to, but the Knights are well prepared for this kind of thing, and I assume the Rogue Order is as well."

Riley nodded, swiping a kiss to Enzo's cheek. "I'm not headed into the fray, love. I promise. I'll go to Haven and wait. The Erynes will be along shortly."

"Erynes?" Harlow asked as Alaric and Finn portaled out.

"You can think of them as the Queensguard, if you like," Riley said, then brushed a kiss on her cheek. "We'll all be back soon."

And then Riley and the Wraiths were gone, back out into the night. Harlow's head spun with how fast they all worked. There was so much she didn't know about the Knights still.

Petra got up. "I need to go too, but there's some really nice food in the fridge and in the oven. You all should eat something and get some rest."

"Where are you going?" Harlow asked, concerned.

Petra took her hand. "I have to help too, Harlow."

"You'll fight?"

Petra laughed. "I'm not as delicate as I look." She turned to the rest of the table. "Plan to stay the night. Nobody leaves 'til Finn says it's all right. Cian, Harlow, you can get everyone settled and comfortable, right?"

Harlow and Cian both nodded. Harlow turned to the Argent as Petra portaled out. "If you need to go make calls, I can handle my family. The bedrooms upstairs?"

"All are ready for guests. Sparsely furnished, but they should find everything they need—and I believe anything else that's needed, you can help with, yes?"

"Yes," Harlow agreed, as Cian disappeared into Finn's office.

Petra portaled back in, holding Axel. The cat was calm in her arms, as though he knew he traveled with a friend. "I just thought you'd want him here with you."

Harlow took the cat, feeling wildly grateful for Petra, and glad she'd invited her in earlier so that her wards had recognized the immortal and allowed her in. "Thank you," she said as Petra disappeared again, portaling back to the House of Remiel.

Larkin sighed. "Well, this is going well."

Selene got up. "I suppose we might as well eat."

Harlow looked around, watching as her mothers pulled pans of lasagna and garlic bread out of the fridge and preheated the oven. Her family was safe. She wasn't too worried about the Knights, not after seeing Finn and Alaric decimate the vampires who'd stalked her, but anxiety plagued her all the same. *What would happen when they truly made their move? When they'd gathered all the information they could and made a decision about action?* As she sat down to eat at Finn's kitchen table, surrounded by her family, she wondered just how many evenings they'd have left together.

CHAPTER 34

The next morning, Harlow sat cocooned in a blanket with Axel in the kitchen alcove drinking tea and waiting for everyone to return home. Persistent rain pelted the kitchen windows and she'd queued up a playlist of gentle piano music to play on the house speakers in the kitchen to soothe herself. Petra had texted her late into the night, saying that the Knights were headed to Haven to get the human survivors settled and not to wait up. Harlow hadn't been able to follow that advice, despite everyone else going to bed shortly after midnight.

Axel rolled onto his back, snoring loudly, as she scrolled through the news and gossips. News outlets reported on the House of Remiel fire as though it were an unprovoked attack on the vampires, justifying their actions. She looked up, blinking tears into her dry eyes. She'd been staring at her phone for too long. The little ironstone lamp on the kitchen counter cast a golden glow of light into the gloom. Harlow pulled a bit of magic through the threads surrounding her to reheat her tea and watched the rain.

It wasn't surprising that the Illuminated were working with the vampires to suppress the truth of what happened, but Harlow was disappointed nonetheless. At some point, this tactic of covering things up would backfire. Too many humans would see the violence being perpetrated by the Immortal Orders and they would resist. Harlow feared the consequences the Illuminated would rain down on all of them when that happened.

If they could just prepare a little more before things went that far, maybe they could prevent massive amounts of bloodshed. She'd downloaded three books about the War of the Orders onto Finn's e-reader and had been skimming through them all night, trying to get a better idea of how things had happened then. The trouble was, they were all written from the Illuminated's perspective. Harlow needed better histories, better accounts of those who had resisted the

Illuminated in the past. She wondered briefly if the Knights' vault in Nea Sterlis had records that might help her.

Harlow had double majored in history and literature at UNT, and when things settled down she'd always planned to get a graduate degree in one of the two. In her heart, she was a researcher, curious to a fault at times. All that had died in her when she was with Mark, and she felt it coming back to her now, the deep need to know more—to tease out the threads of history and story to understand where the narrative would go next.

Axel's head popped up and he jumped into the windowsill, hearing something she could not. She peeked out the window, but saw nothing until Petra and Alaric portaled into the backyard with Nox and Arebos. All four were clean, wearing different clothes than they had been the night before, but looked exhausted.

She ran to meet them outside, hugging each of them before asking, "Where's Finn and Cian?"

Ari explained that they'd stayed at Haven, with Riley and the humans, and that though they'd saved nearly a dozen of the protestors from the vampires, the ones who'd been saved were deeply traumatized from the attack. Finn had stayed to help get them settled. When Ari was done explaining, his hand clapped her shoulder in comfort, and she saw deep empathy in the charismatic shifter's dark eyes before he walked into the house. Nox nodded solemnly, as though she understood Harlow's silence, as she followed Petra and Alaric, who both appeared completely drained, inside.

Harlow thought about texting Finn to ask if he was all right, but his people had to be hungry and tired, so she focused on figuring out breakfast and getting them all to bed instead. A voice inside her reasoned it's what he would have done first, and the thought warmed her. Finally, she was helping with something real, something honest. Her shadows danced inside her as she went back into the house that was beginning to feel like home, despite the dull ache in her heart.

THE FOLLOWING DAYS PASSED QUICKLY, as everyone had work to do, both to help the surviving humans disappear from Nuva Troi, and to prepare for whatever came next. The twins jumped easily into the action, learning to use their digital networking skills for darker, more secretive purposes from Nox, who was apparently also one of Alaric's most talented hackers. Everyone agreed that knowing what both the House of Remiel and the Illuminated were up to was of the highest importance, and the twins were such a quick study Harlow wondered if they'd been traversing the dark web on their own for quite some time.

The Kranes opted to stay at Finn's for the time being, at least until the Solstice Gala was over. The twins created a ruse about a poltergeist problem in the Monas, which would explain their absence and the shop's closure until after the gala. Dealing with violent ghosts was a well-known pain in the ass.

"That way we'll have some time to get our information sorted and figure out how we're going to proceed," Indigo explained.

Finn agreed. The Knights had worked for the past few years on small subversive projects, but never anything as serious as the treasonous activities they were contemplating now. Moving slowly, gathering as much information as they could, and feeling out who in the lower Orders could be trusted was of utmost importance.

Arebos and Larkin formed an unexpected friendship, with Ari training Larkin in various hand to hand combat techniques and Larkin teaching him to play chess. The maters were in and out, feeling out the elders' of the Order of Mysteries loyalties and talking about strategy with Finn and Cian, late into every evening. Thea locked herself in the library most days to try and understand why she could not restore the missing images in the facsimile of the Scroll of Akatei.

Riley Quinn was strangely absent, and though Harlow asked Enzo for more information, he'd gently refused to share what he knew about the Rogue Order's involvement in the attack, as well as their help with the rescue. Harlow understood when Enzo had opted to leave Finn's to join Riley; her only question had been if he felt safe. When he'd answered yes and hugged her, she didn't argue further. He still hadn't heard anything from Riley's parents about the residue of anger he'd found in her, but he promised he'd call immediately when he knew more. It was all they could do on that front.

Finn and Harlow slept separately and she noticed he made a point never to be alone with her, though she caught him watching her from time to time, and she knew Axel still slept with him sometimes, splitting his time between them. They'd forgone the rest of the season's events, planting rumors that they were too busy planning bonding celebrations with Alaric and Thea to bother with cocktail parties. The gossips ate it up, speculating about where the ceremony would take place, and whether Enzo would design the dress.

Harlow had asked Cian if the Knights had any less-biased records of the War of Orders, and they'd gotten her everything they had in Nuva Troi, promising to get her the translated diaries of the Knights' commanders from the vault in Nea Sterlis after the Solstice. On the morning of the Solstice Gala, she'd been sorting through a very dry text on the physiology of Heraldic shifters for nearly two hours, and was beginning to feel as though her eyes might fall out of her head.

"Hey, are you listening to me?" Meline asked, snapping her fingers in Harlow's face.

Harlow looked up. Her body was antsy, but her mind had focused too hard and she felt pulled in a dozen directions. "No, sorry."

Meline sighed. "I said I think Finn should look into these three human-run tech companies, it's possible they're run by members of the Rogue Order and…"

Her sister's words became a blur. *When had Indi and Meli become such grownups?* They were twenty, after all, but she certainly hadn't been this smart when she was twenty. She smiled warmly at her sister; it was foolish to keep calling them sillies, they were anything but. "Meli, I have no clue what you're talking about. Maybe you should discuss this with Finn?"

"Discuss what with me?" he asked from the doorway to the library.

Meline glanced at the intense look he was giving Harlow, the little velvet box in his hand and shook her head. "Nope. Not touching this right now. I'm sure Ari's about somewhere."

Harlow rolled her eyes as her sister left the room. "Should I be worried about those two?"

Finn shook his head. "Arebos and Nox are great. Both your sisters are in good hands. Even if it's just a fling. I don't work with people who treat their partners like shit."

Harlow's lips curled in a small smile. "What have you got there?"

Finn blushed. "I figured I'd better show this to you before tonight. Let you try it on to make sure it fits."

They were still planning on the faux proposal at the gala, and she knew what was in the little box, though they hadn't talked about it specifically. "Okay," she said, trying to keep the shake out of her voice.

Harlow was curled in a chair that she and her shadows had created. She'd been busy creating a lot of furniture over the past few days to give everyone somewhere to just *be*, since they were all spending so much time in the house together. Finn perched uncomfortably on the arm of her chair.

"I don't really know where to be when I hand this to you."

"I think you're supposed to get down on one knee."

He smirked at her, raising an eyebrow. "I know what to do tonight. But right now… This feels awkward."

She nodded, holding her hand out. "Just hand it over."

He did so and then got up, striding across the empty library to look out the windows into the front yard, where Alaric, Arebos and the twins were tossing a frisbee around. The sun had burst through the morning gloom and the sounds of everyone having a good time were comforting to hear.

Harlow opened the little box and her heart leapt at the sight of the ring. It was simple, not at all the heavy, elaborate style of most Illuminated jewelry. A single emerald-cut sapphire, set in a gold band. The stone was large, but not ostentatiously so. She slipped it on her finger. It fit perfectly. She resisted the urge to gaze at it any longer than necessary.

Quickly, she returned it to its box and snapped it shut, not bothering to close it slowly or quietly. She rolled her shoulders, swallowing hard. This was not a romantic moment, she reminded herself. They were just working together, nothing more, until she could figure herself out. And at this rate, with no time to herself, she had no idea when that might be.

Finn turned, taking a deep breath. "So it fits?"

"Yes," she said, afraid to say anything else.

If she spoke one more word, she'd tell him how perfect it was. How the deep blue of the stone reminded her of her shadows, and the simple setting was exactly what she'd always hoped for. Her fingers ached with regret as she held the box out. She hated to give it back.

"Fits perfectly. Nice job."

He took the ring from her, and to someone who didn't know him, perhaps he'd seem calm and collected, but she saw the slight tremble in his fingers as he gripped the box. He was as affected by the moment as she was.

"All right then," he said. "I should go shower."

"Sounds good," she replied, pretending to be engrossed in her phone. The phantom weight of the ring on her finger haunted her as she listened to him walk upstairs. His footsteps were slow, and she felt the tug between them as viscerally as if it were a cord, desperate to coil back together, instead of being stretched to its breaking point.

She closed her eyes. She'd taken her shower an hour ago, and Thea would make short work of her face, hair and nails. Her dress was hanging upstairs in the room she and Larkin shared, and she barely cared about putting it on. It was beautiful, of course, but everything about tonight felt like something to get through, rather than what she'd hoped it would be a few weeks ago.

Even then, she'd known they'd probably be pretending tonight, but the possibilities would still be wide open. Things hadn't been so complicated then. The thought made her laugh to herself now. *That* had been simple? She closed her eyes, regulating her breathing and took herself back to the night she and Mark had broken up once more.

She'd been trying every day to remember more, and like Enzo had said it might, some of what she'd forgotten had grown clearer, the tangles around the dark spot in her mind loosening day after day, but she still could not reach the actual memory, and she felt sure now that she wouldn't be able to move on until she confronted whatever it was she'd been trying to forget.

As she sunk deeper into her mind, aided by her shadow magic, she saw it clearly. She and Mark had been arguing, which was nothing unusual. He'd asked her for the thousandth time to tell him something she wasn't allowed to reveal about the Order of Mysteries. *But what had it been?*

And there it was, right in front of her. She watched, as though it were an old film, the two of them flashing before her. Him and her. *How dare you speak to me that way?* Her and him. *Just who do you think you are?* She picked Axel up, said she was going to bed, and then… Nothing, she couldn't remember anything else. A slippery wall of dark glass stood in front of her. She pounded on it until her fists actually hurt, but it stayed firmly in place.

Harlow slid back into her conscious mind. She glanced down at her hands, which throbbed with pain. Dark bruises covered her wrists, a physical manifestation of the vision she had. Why couldn't she remember?

She made the long climb upstairs, and her sisters buzzed around her in a haze of actions she barely registered. Her mind was stuck in front of that glass, seeing her own eyes glowing back at her in the dark.

Thea's voice broke into her quiet reverie as she gingerly held Harlow's hands in front of her face. "What happened here?"

Harlow looked up. "I've been trying to remember the night it ended with me and Mark."

Her sister sucked a sharp gasp in. "And in remembering, these bruises appeared?"

Harlow nodded, tears filling her eyes. "Every time I return to the memory, it's like there's glass in front of me, between me and what I can't remember. I was pounding on the glass in my vision just now." She sighed, exhausted. "I shouldn't have tried, but Finn showed me the ring for tonight... and I thought..."

Thea shook her head, dismissing something about what Harlow said. "I know what you thought, but do you not remember these bruises?"

Harlow's frowned. "No? What do you mean?"

Thea held them up in front of the mirror Harlow was seated in front of. Thea had finished with her hair and makeup. "When I found you, you were pounding on the back door to Mark's building, sobbing. Your hands and arms were bruised, *exactly* like this. I'll never forget the shape of those bruises. Your knees and legs too. You were all banged up—you said you fell..."

Harlow shook her head. She didn't remember any of that. Just waking up at home, in the attic, in her old bed next to Thea's the next morning, with puffy eyes. She hadn't been injured.

"You really don't remember?"

Harlow shook her head. "Tell me."

Thea crouched in front of her, looking up at her with luminous eyes. "I asked you how you got hurt and you said you fell down the stairs on your way out. You said you were crying too hard and you tripped. I asked why you were pounding on the door, but you were in so much distress that I couldn't understand you." Thea sighed, as though the memory was physically painful for her to recall. "I took you to a healer right away. Kylar Bane. You don't remember?"

"No," Harlow said. "Wait, Kylar Bane? The healer they found in the river last winter?"

Thea nodded. "Yes. Are you saying you don't remember seeing her? I left you alone with her for a while, because you kept trying to talk to me about what had happened and you were so upset she couldn't treat your wounds."

Harlow shook her head. "I don't remember any of that. Just waking up the next day."

"Shit," Thea swore. "I never thought to ask you... But it is strange that she was killed so shortly after treating you, isn't it? At the time, I thought it was because she was helping humans to have unplanned children, but now..."

Harlow nodded. "It's too much of a coincidence. We should look into it as a part of all this. I'll talk to Finn about it tomorrow. We just need to try to get through tonight first."

Her sister's arms wrapped around her. "Did Mark hurt you, Harlow? I'm sorry, I know I should have asked sooner. But did he?"

Harlow looked at the floor. "He didn't hit me ever. But he broke things that were important to me. It wasn't like he was flying off the handle and throwing a random glass, or anything like that. He chose things that were special to me, and broke them."

Thea's grip on her hand tightened.

"And once I woke him after a night he'd spent out with other women. He was supposed to be at a meeting with his father. He was going to be late. So I tried to wake him up, but he wouldn't rouse. I shook him, I was worried something was wrong with him. So I dumped a glass of water on him and he woke up."

"You don't have to talk about it, if it's too hard."

Harlow shook her head. "I want to say it. He woke up fast, so fast I don't even really know how it happened. One second he was dead to the world, and the next he was awake, and he had me pinned to the wall, his hands around my neck. He was calling me a bitch, and there was just *nothing there* in his eyes. I think he was still drunk, or maybe on drugs, I don't really know. But I got out of his grip and locked myself in the bathroom with Axel. I stayed in there for hours until he left."

"How did he explain that?"

It was a logical enough question to ask, Harlow supposed, but it just proved that no one had ever treated Thea that way. Harlow was equally glad that her sister had no frame of reference, and consumed with envy. Thea had spent the majority of her adult life being cherished by one man who was utterly *good*, despite his parents and his upbringing. Alaric would never think to pull Thea apart over and over, just for the pleasure of seeing her wounded.

How wonderful it must be to be so unmarred, she thought wistfully.

"Nothing. He pretended it didn't happen when I asked him what happened. The other times, when he broke my things, he'd apologize, but that time he acted like I made it all up."

"Oh, Harlow." The pity in Thea's voice was unbearable. "When was that?"

Harlow's eyes drifted back to the floor. "About a month before he kicked me out."

"Why didn't you tell me? Or the maters?"

Harlow laughed, finally making eye contact with her sister. "Because every time I told him I would tell someone, he said, 'Tell them what?' and then he'd remind me that everyone who'd ever loved me left me, that he was the only one who stayed. He reminded me for days on end, until I stopped pushing back."

Thea's body tensed, hearing the things coming out of Harlow's mouth, things she was sure Thea thought didn't happen to girls like the Kranes, with families who loved them and happy childhoods. She had to end this conversation. She had to stop thinking about all this and play her part in the terrible evening ahead.

"I didn't think anyone would understand when I was in it. It's taken me months to sort this all out for myself. But I am fine now." Harlow stood, smoothing her robe. "I'm going to get dressed. Could you give me a minute?"

Thea looked like she wanted to say something else, but she just nodded and left the room. Harlow slipped out of her robe and into the dress Enzo had so lovingly made for her. It was the deepest shade of sapphire blue, so dark it was almost black, with a neckline that plunged between her breasts. It was simple in every way, but for the sleeves that trailed off her shoulders and would drag on the ground behind her, draping beautifully in a cascade of weightless feathers. When she'd first seen it, she'd loved it. Tonight, she couldn't wait to have it off and be snuggled in bed with Axel.

She was struggling with the zipper when Thea returned. "Oh, thank goodness you're back, I can't quite—" She looked back over her shoulder to find Finn, in just his trousers and tuxedo shirt, untucked and unbuttoned.

"Thea asked me to come help you." His voice was rough and she saw the awe burning in his eyes. "Are you trying to kill me with this dress?"

Harlow was so exhausted from her afternoon of memory that she barely had the energy to feel. She definitely had no energy for banter, so she smiled weakly. "You're immortal. You'd be harder to kill than I'd like."

"Harls," he said, his knuckles brushing her cheek. "Thea said…"

"Please," she whispered, as she turned away. "Please. Can we not right now?"

She met his eyes in the mirror, and as the hollowness of her gaze registered in his, he nodded. She felt his fingers, warm and gentle as he zipped her up. His arms went around her waist, and she had no energy to decide if it was a good idea or a bad one.

"Lean on me," he said.

"What?"

"Lean on me. Now, tonight. Let me help you." He pulled her closer, his arms tightening around her. "Let me keep you safe."

The weight of what she felt sunk into her slowly as she relaxed into his chest. He wasn't asking her to talk, to tell him anything. He wasn't asking her *for* anything. He was asking to be there for her, and for the life of her, she couldn't find anything wrong with accepting that offer. All her reasons for staying apart shattered as she let him hold her. Her shadows danced with joy as her resolve to do things on her own weakened, as though her magic came alive at the thought of letting him help her.

Strange, she thought to herself as she melted into Finn's embrace. He stood so still behind her, not tense, but almost afraid to disturb her as she relaxed into him. *I do actually feel better.*

They could do what they needed to do tonight. Pretend, if that's what they needed to do, and tomorrow... Tomorrow she could let him help her. They could call the Quinns together, ask what it would take to unlock that memory and free her, find out what that remnant of emotion was and solve it. She knew Finn would help her and she was tired of trying to do things on her own. When she'd decided, it had seemed like the best plan, but now she knew she needed help, and he was offering it. Tonight, they could get through the finale of the season, and tomorrow they could have the future back.

"Okay," she said, sliding one of her hands into his and then the other, turning in his arms to face him. "I'll lean on you." She didn't qualify it with a timeframe. She meant what she said. She would lean on him. Whatever came next, they'd do it together.

His eyes lit with an unspeakable joy. "Let me go grab my jacket and then we can go."

She nodded, and sank back into her chair, depleted. Harlow didn't know how they'd get through the next few hours, but she was determined to get tonight over with, because tomorrow her future could finally begin.

<h1 style="text-align:center">CHAPTER 35</h1>

The Solstice Gala was held each year at Nuva Troi's massive botanical gardens. Tonight, the Jardin was lit with thousands of tiny witchlights, giving the hundreds of topiaries and enormous mosaiculture figures scattered throughout the grounds an even more surreal quality than usual. Everywhere Harlow looked, flowers had burst into bloom, filling the air with a heady natural perfume. Beds of irises created a wash of blue as they entered the enormous, elegant conservatory. Finn's hand stayed firm against her back as they moved through the crowd.

The rest of her family would arrive separately. They'd agreed that since the big distraction of the evening would be Finn's proposal, that it would be better not to socialize together. That way the others would more easily observe the crowd's reaction to Harlow's acceptance—the McKays and Velariuses, of course, being of particular interest.

"Lo, you look *stunning*."

Harlow turned to find Kate Spencer looking fairly stunning herself, in a white pantsuit covered in thousands of sparkling sequins. Her slender, athletic body was accentuated by the cape that fell from her muscular shoulders to the floor.

Finn grinned and the two of them hugged. "It's great to see you, Kate. Why haven't we gotten out on the water?"

Kate ran her eyes over Harlow. "I heard you've been busy."

Finn's arm was relaxed around her as she watched them interact. They seemed to genuinely be friends. Something warmed in her chest at the thought. That meant that if she and Finn were together, she and Kate could have a friendship of their own. Nothing like that had been possible with Mark. He'd been even more jealous when he understood that her attraction wasn't limited in the slightest by gender. Everyone had become a suspect after that. She lost track of what Finn and Kate were saying as she watched the crowd swirl around them.

The conservatory was warmer than she'd like—too many people, too much movement. The now-familiar feeling of being watched crept over her skin, causing goosebumps to raise on her arm, despite the heat. Next to her, Finn tensed, as though he too sensed something amiss. Finn's eyes slid to her bare arm, and the pressure of his hand on her waist increased.

Kate's eyes followed his and her voice was low when she asked, "What's wrong?"

"I don't know yet," Finn murmured. "Dance together while I get some drinks?"

Harlow nodded, wondering at how easily he trusted Kate. How quickly they'd fallen into an attitude of camaraderie. How had they achieved that? Kate's arms slipped around her waist and they joined the dancers at the center of the room.

"What's going on with you and Finn?" Harlow asked, keeping her face pleasant and her voice low.

Kate raised her eyebrows. "Jealous?"

A little laugh bubbled out of Harlow's chest. "Nope. I'm glad of it."

Kate's gaze softened. "Me too."

The energy in the room was shifting. Harlow felt a ripple of anxiety wash over her, and then aggression. She found herself wondering if Kate might be lying to her, if she and Finn were keeping secrets from her. Maybe they'd had a relationship in Nea Sterlis, when Finn was at Aphelion. As they turned on the dance floor, her suspicion grew. Her cheeks flushed. Had they planned this? Was this all a ploy to humiliate her?

Her shadows flickered inside her, soothing her, cooling the heat building in her. She blinked. Kate was watching her carefully, concern in her eyes. "What's going on, Lo?"

Harlow tried to stay calm, but her emotions spun out of control. "I honestly don't know. You still only like women, right?"

Kate laughed, loud and hearty. "Yeah. I don't see that changing anytime soon. Why?"

Harlow shook her head. "I just had the strangest worry that you and Finn might have something going on..."

The concern deepened in Kate's eyes. "That's not like you. You've always trusted people *too* much, in my opinion."

Enzo's words echoed in her mind: *This was something else... A remnant of rage, but it wasn't like anything else in you.* Of course. Whatever was happening now was the same as it had been in the park with Petra. A tiny seed of her real feelings had magnified, amplified to an irrational level she didn't actually feel. Except that she did. The emotions coursing through her *felt* real.

Something stirred deep within her memory, as though beyond the comprehension of her conscious mind, things were beginning to come loose and pull together to make a larger picture. Enzo's words played over and over in her mind, and suddenly she thought of the book she'd been cataloging the day she'd first visited Enzo's atelier. What had it been? *Lore of the Lilu.* Panic broke loose in her and though she tried to stay calm, Kate obviously knew she was distressed.

Before Kate could ask questions, she asked one of her own. "What immortal creature can change the emotions of other immortals?" she said softly, knowing all too well that Kate would know the answer immediately. Empaths could smooth emotions, or impart some of their own feelings in those they were close with, but they couldn't actually change anything anyone felt, or make their feelings more intense. This was something different, something menacing and wrong.

"No…" Kate breathed. "It's forbidden. Not even the House of Remiel could make an incubus. It's impossible… The Illuminated made sure of it—they screen for Gene-I in the mandatory screenings at the monthly donations. Whole human families have been wiped out because one member carried Gene-I."

Harlow resisted the urge to ask Kate how she knew that. For obvious reasons, vampires always knew more about how the screenings at the Night's Own Blood Banks worked, and what was done with that information. They didn't have time for that conversation now. "How long would it take for a human to make the full transformation?"

Kate spun Harlow in time with the music, and Harlow couldn't help but be impressed with the calm exterior she presented. "About six months. Maybe nine for the incubus to grow to full strength, and until the last few weeks of the transformation they'd appear as a human would. But Harlow, even if they could make one, why would they? The incubi were uncontrollable, nearly unstoppable at full strength, even for the Illuminated."

Harlow nodded, then pulled Kate off the dance floor. "We have to find Finn. Now. He isn't by the bar."

Kate grabbed her arm. "Tell me what is going on here."

"Athan Sanvier and the House of Remiel tried to kidnap me a few weeks ago. He implied that he could do something terrible to me. *Change* me."

Harlow searched the room for Finn, or Alaric, or anyone in her family, but they were nowhere to be seen. Kate's brow furrowed, watching her. "Okay, but we'd know if Athan were an incubus. He's the worst kind of vampire, but Harlow… That's not something he could hide. Not for hundreds of years. And besides what would he do to you—*No.*"

She glanced back, shaking her head as Kate realized what she had. "Only an incubus can turn a sorcière into a succubus. I thought he was being cruel, using our biggest fears against me, but maybe he was telling the truth…"

It had been foolish to dismiss his threats so quickly, impossible as they'd seemed at the time. Harlow began to move through the edges of the crowd. If none of her family or the Knights were inside, maybe they were outside. She tried to appear casual, but she was tugging on Kate's arm rather hard as she walked outside, onto the lawn that dropped off in a steep hill towards the lake.

Behind her Kate murmured, "And only a witch can become a succubus. Fuck, why didn't I see this coming?"

Harlow looked back, confused. "Why would you?"

Something flickered across Kate's face in the moonlight that Harlow couldn't identify, and she didn't have time to worry about it. Sounds of a struggle came from the lake. Harlow started towards the noise, but Kate gripped her arm. "Don't go down there without backup. Just wait here and I'll get help, okay?"

Harlow nodded as Kate pushed her gently behind an enormous oak. Her face was stern as she tapped Harlow's nose. "You promise you'll wait?"

She nodded again and Kate used her vampiric speed, disappearing back into the conservatory in the blink of an eye. As soon as Harlow knew she was out of range to keep tabs on her, she started towards the lake. There was no way in seventeen hells she was leaving her family in trouble. If that's what was going on here, she would find a way to help them.

Her heels sunk into the soft ground, so she slipped out of them, hiding them under a blooming lilac. She snuck towards the lake, pausing every so often to duck behind a bush and listen. She was sure she heard Mama's voice, as she got closer, though she couldn't make out what she was saying.

As she rounded a corner in the hedgerow, she got her first sight of them, a group of hooded figures, holding on to a handful of the people she loved most in the world. Her sisters and Enzo were nowhere to be seen, nor was Alaric, she noted with relief, but they had the maters—and Finn.

How in Akatei's name were they holding him? Why didn't he portal out?

She squinted, trying to see better. It took two of the figures to hold Finn, but he wasn't struggling. One of them had what could only be a white ash stake positioned above his heart. Her chest clenched. It couldn't kill him, but if they staked him, it was hard to say what might happen. No Illuminated had suffered that fate for so long, it was impossible to say exactly how it might affect him.

Harlow took a few steps backward, thinking to go back to the conservatory to find Alaric, and perhaps Kate, though she wasn't sure exactly how Kate could help. She backed into something—no, some*one*.

"Dollface. So glad you could join us."

Mark. Fingers dug viciously into her arms and all went dark.

CHAPTER 36

When Harlow came to, she was woozy. An acrid smell of burned wood filled her nose. Her head ached as though she'd been drinking for hours. She struggled to open her eyes, move, anything, and found her arms were restrained. Voices were arguing nearby, only slightly muffled.

A feminine voice complained, "You were supposed to get them *all*, not just her and Finn." *Was that Olivia Sanvier?*

"All we need is them."

That was definitely Mark. Harlow fought against the restraints as she struggled to open her eyes. They were heavy, too heavy.

"But now someone knows we took them. That wasn't the plan. Aurelia Krane can make trouble for us."

"You're worried about the wrong people," said a groggy voice. Finn.

Harlow forced her eyes open and her vision swam. She watched as Mark Easton backhanded Finn hard enough to make his body strain against the chains that held him. His face was bloody and beginning to bruise. How was Mark strong enough to harm him? No human could hit one of the Illuminated hard enough to bruise them.

They were in a dark room. Everything in it was dirty… No, sooty. Were they in the burned-out House of Remiel? She looked around as much as she could in the dim light. Her vision was still unfocused, as though she'd been drugged. In the distance, she saw shallow windows. They were in a basement. Probably the House of Remiel's basement, given the red velvet of the chairs that surrounded a scorched table at the center of the room. She'd only been to the House of Remiel a few times, but the red velvet was ubiquitous and memorable. Her throat hurt as she swallowed.

As Mark turned towards her, her entire body went cold and rigid. *How could she have been so stupid? Why hadn't she put this together sooner?*

Mark had turned into a thing of nightmares. His once-brown eyes had turned a muddy shade of red, his skin gone pale with an unnatural grey undertone. He was the thing under the bed that little witches feared: an incubus who could steal her heart. No, that wasn't right. That was just a children's story.

She wracked her brain trying to remember exactly what kind of danger she was in, but her mind was still cloudy… Then she remembered. He could turn her into a succubus, a creature whose only purpose in life was to seduce and drain the lifeforce from their victims. All her magic would disappear, everything she was would disappear.

A wave of fear washed over her, intensifying until she was so terrified she vomited, the bile burning her sore throat. *Had she already vomited?* She looked down to find her dress was already stained.

"Dollface, you ruined your pretty dress," Mark said with a fiendish smile.

There was nothing left of the boy who'd held her hair when she puked in uni. She'd thought he'd been a monster when they ended things, when he wouldn't let her have Axel back out of spite, but she hadn't known how bad he could be until now. Now, it didn't take an explanation to see that he was perfectly willing to harm her. She glanced at Finn's bloody face. Her and Finn both.

She vomited again and Finn struggled towards her, the chains binding his hands above his head clanging, causing her ears to ache. "Get her some water," he growled.

"No," Mark said, hitting him again. "The little bitch can soak in her own stench."

"What have you done to me?" Harlow asked, her voice coming out in a croak. She had to distract him from hitting Finn again.

Mark turned to her, his ugly red eyes narrowing as he focused on her. In a flash he was in front of her, stroking her cheek with his icy grey fingers. He was nearly as fast as one of the Illuminated, she'd hardly seen him move.

"I haven't done anything to you… yet, Dollface. You need to be awake for the ritual. But now that you're up, we can get started."

Olivia Sanvier stepped out from the shadows, her arms curling around Mark's waist. The look on her face was one of pure malice. "Now that Heifer Harlow is awake, what games should we play with our fattened prize?"

Mark smiled, but didn't answer. Harlow saw something in his expression that belied whatever he truly felt. *Was he annoyed with Olivia?*

Olivia stepped forward. "She's already so pathetic, with her stupid little cat, and her frumpy clothes… Gods, even Enzo Weraka couldn't do something to make her look glamorous." Olivia's moonstone eyes locked onto Harlow's. "Why *are* you so pitiful, Harlow?"

Hot tears slipped down Harlow's cheeks. She was furious, and when she was angry, she often cried. It was a weakness she'd hated, but now it seemed to fill a purpose. As tears splashed onto her dress, she saw the revulsion it evoked in Olivia. Anything to stall them. She had to think of a way out of this before they began whatever infernal ritual they'd unearthed to turn her. She had the terrible feeling that her first feed as a succubus was meant to be Finn. She couldn't let things get that far.

"Ugh. She's crying." Olivia slapped her face, her nails dragging across Harlow's cheek, drawing blood as she went. "What do *you* have to weep about, you spoiled little cunt?"

A roar erupted from Finn's throat. He seemed to be fighting some unseen force. Mark was manipulating his emotions, pushing him somehow. Harlow didn't know the technicalities of how an incubus' power worked, just that they could control what anyone felt, and the Illuminated were not immune. He was torturing Finn. If only she'd dug deeper, paid more attention to *Lore of the Lilu* when she had it right in front of her. Or any of the dozens of books in the Monas that explored the taboo lore of the Order of Night's most dangerous creatures.

A sob choked her as Olivia hit her again, this time in the stomach. She doubled over, letting her head fall forward. She *had* to think, buy them some time. Outwardly, she cried harder, since it provoked Olivia. Inside, her shadows roused. The sounds of Finn's cries of rage and pain lit something within her that seemed to block some of the effects of Mark's power.

If she could distract them, she might be able to get free. And then what? She hadn't trained to use her shadows in combat. She wouldn't even know where to start. Fear gripped her. She was tempted to shove it down, but her shadows didn't like that. Instead, she leaned into her fear, embraced the idea that she was scared. *She was scared because the man who'd hurt her, the people who'd hurt Axel, were hurting Finn.*

And she *loved* Finn. She was *in* love with him. Her future was with him, doing the work he'd started with the Knights of Serpens, and these two would not take that away from them. Her magic swelled within her as her fear transformed into something else. Something she could *use*.

Olivia punched her in the jaw. Either she wasn't trying very hard, or something about Harlow's magic protected her from the full impact of these blows. Finn wasn't faring as well. Whatever Mark was doing to him was wearing him down. His skin had begun to dull, losing its usual faint luminescence that hinted at his power. She wondered how long they'd tortured him before she woke up. It was obvious Mark and Olivia meant to kill him, and turn her into a mindless beast, but why? This was all too much just for the sadistic pleasure of being cruel.

"Why are you doing this?" she asked, injecting as much fear as she could into her voice without sounding as though she was putting something on. She still wasn't sure what to do. She needed to keep them distracted, see if she could get Mark to pay attention to her, rather than Finn.

Olivia laughed. "Are you really so stupid?"

Harlow sobbed quietly, lowering her eyes as though she was frightened. "*Why?*"

Fingers gripped her chin, Olivia's nails dug into her face. "We're going to stop you and the golden boy here from spawning whatever little abomination the Illuminated want."

That was it? The Order of Night believed, as the McKays did, that a child begotten between them would be some kind of powerful creature. It all made a sick kind of sense. The Order of Night wouldn't just kill them, they'd turn Harlow into a succubus to prove that they could. To prove that they could still make the most volatile immortals Okairos had ever known and wreak havoc on the world. This was all some stupid power play between immortals.

Mark turned as Finn sagged against the chains. Finn's eyes fell shut and Harlow fought panic, waiting, watching his chest. His lungs expanded, but his breath was too shallow. Olivia's phone buzzed and she stepped out of the room, her voice muffled as the sound of her footsteps died away. Harlow reached inside herself. She needed to do something now, while Olivia was gone, use her magic to help them both.

Mark's voice broke her concentration. "No babies for you, Harlow. Just an eternity of fucking and sucking."

Her heart sang with pleasure at the idea, but only for a moment. Her shadows fought it off at the source, understanding dawning on her. He'd been following her, influencing her feelings. Planting seeds of doubt, rage, and gods knew what else in her. But now that her shadows knew where the threat was coming from, they fought it. She felt better almost immediately, but she couldn't show that. She felt the influence of Mark's power, its intention, and she arched her back, moaning softly as she pushed against her restraints.

It created the desired result. Mark's lips curved into a seductive smile. "Just like that, Dollface. Wait until you see all the ways I can make your body sing for me."

Finn's eyes met hers as he raised his head slightly. He was in pain still, but she saw that like her, he'd been exaggerating how hurt he was. As Mark turned back to him, he grinned at Finn, his new fangs glinting in the dim light of a lantern as he patted Finn's cheek. "Poor boyfriend, maybe I worked him too hard that last time. That little show should have made him very angry."

Mark walked over to Harlow, caressing her cheek. "I missed you, Dollface. But now we're going to be together, forever. No more Order of Mysteries. No more stupid witches. Just you and me."

Olivia returned to the room, fury written all over her face as she glared at Harlow. "And me."

Mark smiled, looking for a moment like the handsome co-ed Harlow had fallen in love with. "Of course, Liv."

His voice was smooth. Too smooth. Harlow wasn't sure why Olivia didn't hear the lie in his words. She knew that tone all too well. The vampire princess was pouting now, and he wandered over to her, soothing her with touches and words. "We'll break her together. Use her up and then turn her. And then…" Now he stroked Olivia's jawline, planting kisses on her neck. "Then we'll feed McKay to her." So she'd been right, after all. Mark's hands roved over Olivia's body as he whispered, "You'll see, Liv. It'll be fun."

"Yes," Olivia said, her voice full of a desperate need for approval as she wrapped her body around Mark's.

Now who was pathetic? Still, this interaction gave Harlow time to try to figure out what to do to get them out of this. She sank down into her mind, the way she had before when she called up her shadows, but the glass wall that hid the suppressed memory of the night Mark kicked her out rose up in front of her instead.

In reality, Mark wrapped his arms around Olivia's waist, one hand sliding into the front of her pants. "Does that feel good, baby?" he crooned as she lapped Harlow's blood off her fingers.

"Yes," the vampire moaned. "Harder."

They weren't watching her, enraptured as they were with one another. Inside her mind, Harlow stood in front of the glass. The tangle of thorns that had been there before was gone now. The wet sound of Mark pleasuring Olivia broke through her ability to concentrate.

"Tell me about how you hurt her," Olivia begged. "Tell me about the poor little witch's fall down the stairs."

"Shut the fuck up," Mark said, his voice shrill. Harlow's entire body reacted to that tone so violently that Olivia's words almost didn't register. Almost. *The poor little witch's fall down the stairs.*

What fall?

What?

Fall?

In her second sight, the glass wall splintered into a million shards and she slid easily into the hole in her memory, living it again.

They were standing on the backstairs at Mark's apartment. Their *apartment. Above, the moons were waning, barely emitting enough light to see by. The flickering light at the back door made her head hurt. Her eyes were swollen and tired from crying. She had a bag of her clothes slung across her chest and Axel was yowling in his carrier.*

"Can't we work this out?" she pleaded. "It doesn't have to be like this."

Mark shook his head. "You'll always choose them over me, Dollface. My questions were innocent, but you proved I can't trust you."

"Innocent? You asked me to find out how to make a succubus, *Mark." Her voice was harsh; she hadn't even tried to modulate it into a tone he'd like better. This was a mistake she'd been making more frequently lately, and now she knew he'd make her pay for it.*

His hand flew towards her and she stepped backwards, almost falling down the steep concrete stairs. He caught her before she fell, tearing Axel's carrier out of her arms.

"Thanks," she said, quiet, but still not in the tone she knew he'd prefer. She wasn't going to grovel anymore. They could work this out in a healthier way, she knew it. Things had been good once, hadn't they? He was just going through a hard time.

"It was only a question, Dollface," he murmured. "But you overreacted, like you always do. You always have to make something out of nothing."

A part of her immediately believed him. Immediately lapped everything he said up. She was overreacting, wasn't she? But there was a hard glint in his eye that scared her. Something about him was different than before. Something fundamental had changed, but she didn't know what. Her head tilted as she stared at him. She knew he was seeing someone else. He'd done it before, but this time something was different… but what?

Mark watched her as her body instinctively shrank from him—something was wrong with him—rage built in his shoulders and tensed muscles. Rage beyond anything she'd ever seen in him, flowing off him in waves that almost felt like magic. *How had she missed this about him? What was she seeing?*

"Get out of here," he snarled, pushing her hard.

Her feet flew out from under her, and her spine hit the concrete steps as she fell, tumbling down, until she hit the ground with a hard crack to her skull. When she looked up, he'd gone inside, taking Axel with him. What had that been, that power he'd emitted? Had she imagined it? He'd taken her key and she had no way to get in now. Not without using magic, and she was too afraid to use any of her meager powers against him.

She looked down at her battered legs, sobbing, and crawled up the steps. Surely he was waiting on the other side of the door. He'd done things like this before to teach her a lesson. If she begged hard enough, he'd open the door and at least she could get Axel. Harlow crawled up the stairs and began to beat her hands against the door, begging him to open it.

Harlow's eyes opened slowly, her mind clear. He'd been turning, even then. Olivia, and whoever else was involved with this nightmare, must have turned him shortly after they'd started seeing one another. *How had she missed it? Had there been other signs?* She shook her head a little. Now was not the time for berating herself. She could feel guilty later.

Mark and Olivia were still going at it in front of her. The memory had come loose too late. She wanted to scream, but that wasn't going to help her, or Finn, now. Her shadows stirred within her, coming to life with her fresh clarity.

It wasn't too late, now she was free. Something inside her that had stayed shut tight since that night had opened, and she was finally free of Mark Easton, once and for all. She'd been afraid to use magic on him back then, but she wasn't now. The trouble was how to use her shadows best.

"Fuck me now," Olivia begged. "Make her watch."

"No," Mark replied, his voice rough. "Let's turn her, and then we can watch her destroy McKay."

Olivia pouted, rubbing her ass against the front of Mark's body, writhing seductively as she rode his hand. Harlow knew she didn't have much time. Mark would get his way, because he always got his way. She went deep inside herself to where her shadows waited patiently.

No more chains, she directed them with new confidence. *No more chains for me or Finn.*

The threads of aether surrounding the chains pulled apart, softly, slowly as they disintegrated into nothing.

Olivia cried out again. "Fuck me, baby. Make her watch."

Mark spun Olivia to bend her over the large, sturdy table at the center of the room. Harlow didn't have time to watch them too carefully; her arms were free, the chains truly gone. Across the room, Finn stumbled but caught himself as the chains disappeared. He was far worse off than she was, and she saw it then, the splinters of white ash protruding from his chest.

He shook his head once, looking down at them. He didn't need to say anything for Harlow to understand. He couldn't help her fight them off or portal them out; the white ash was affecting him too much. If an Illuminated at the height of their power would struggle to fight an incubus, how would she fare alone?

"I told you what I wanted, Olivia," Mark growled. And before Olivia, or Harlow for that matter, knew what was coming, he twisted the vampire princess' head clean off her shoulders. Her body fell to ash. Harlow only saw it in her peripheral vision, because she was watching Finn, watching the helplessness in his eyes turn to resolve. He motioned for her to come to him, one finger barely crooking towards him.

She didn't have time to consider the horror of what Mark had just done, or the realization that she and Finn were very likely next. She had to move. It was a risk. Mark still had his back turned, but any motion would alert him to their freedom. Harlow trusted Finn though and she ran for him, sliding into his arms as she tripped on the hem of her dress. He dragged her up, turning her so she faced Mark as he twisted around.

A look of surprise crossed the incubus' face, seeing they were free. Then he laughed. "I don't know how you got rid of those chains, Dollface, but it doesn't matter. You can't get away. Neither of you can. And now that Olivia is gone, we're going to have some fun together."

Finn's arms went around her waist, his mouth at her ear. "I figured out how the Striders shifted. Trust me?"

She nodded once, knowing he referred to the Feriant. If he knew how to help her shift, it might be the only chance they had, because otherwise, even with her shadows, she knew she couldn't handle him.

Mark's head tilted, his eyes narrowed. "What are you whispering in my dolly's ear, McKay?"

"I'm saying goodbye," Finn said, his voice clear and strong.

Mark laughed, sinking into a half-burned chair, apparently unconcerned by this. "Should I kill him first, Dollface, or do you want him to watch us after I turn you?"

Something about his transformation had deranged him. The way Mark laughed, how easily he'd killed Olivia, made her think the transformation to an incubus was different than a vampire's usual amplification of personal qualities, good or bad. Though, of course, it was possible this was Mark's true self.

Finn's grip on her waist was firmer now as he pressed her against him, careful to keep her back from the shards of wood in his chest. "I'm sorry, Harls," he murmured. "I didn't want it to be this way."

Mark's head fell back as he laughed, his eyes closing in apparent mirth. "Boo-hoo, he's sorry." Mark's laughter rang through the burned-out basement. He turned from them to face the table he'd bent Olivia over only moments ago. Whatever power he had as an incubus was so great that he didn't care that the two of them were free. His shoulders shook with laughter as he began to adjust a series of instruments laid out on the table. Harlow hadn't seen them before, but now she recognized them as a set of tools any sorcière would know: he was preparing for a ritual.

"Say your goodbyes then." He waved his hand at them, as though what they did didn't matter.

Mark may have misunderstood Finn, but *she* knew what he'd meant. He'd wanted this all to go differently. For them to figure this out together. She wished she could tell them that they still would. That if this worked, they'd never be apart again—she had to believe there was still time for all that. Harlow's eyes fell closed and she tried to relax as much as she could into Finn's hold on her. Whatever was coming, she knew she couldn't react, or Mark would spring into action.

Finn's fangs slid into her neck, venom burning through her as he pulled blood from her in several strong draws. Euphoria lit her soul, even through the pain. Lightning fast, he spun her, using the last of his energy to bite open his own wrist, pressing it to her mouth. She was only confused for a moment. When his blood hit her tongue, her shadows sang.

"What the fuck are you doing?" Mark screamed, turning at the sudden movement.

Harlow did not stop, pulling mouthful after mouthful of Finn's blood into her. Her power shifted, grew, fluctuating within her in such a way that she vaguely remembered what it felt like to get high. This was so much more. She was connected to the center of the limen, the space between all worlds, the dark home of the aether. In this moment, she was connected to the heart of the limen, deep in its swirling depths. Just as she felt the attention of the heart's inhabitants begin to turn her way, her spirit form pulled back, just enough to keep her safe.

Finn's voice broke her heady reverie. "I *told* you." There was so much unbridled arrogance in his voice that it caused a feral grin to spread over her face. "Saying goodbye."

Harlow stepped out of Finn's arms, raw magic pulsing in her veins, racing through her. Her shadows danced with pleasure as she healed completely. She wasn't sure what the mechanics of shifting were, but as it turned out, it was much like anything else with her manifested powers. She just had to want it enough. And she *did* want it. More than anything in the world, she wanted an end to this.

"Goodbye, Mark," she said, just as her mouth disappeared. Her humanoid body dissolved into something avian, lethal and without a shred of doubt about what to do next.

Her new body launched at Mark as he stood, mouth hanging open as her razor-sharp beak ripped into his throat, one of her talons making short work of his bowels. The stench was unbearable as his guts spilled out. Ichor spilled in her mouth, dribbling over her beak as she snapped ferociously once more, severing his head from his body completely.

She let go of the body, letting it fall. It didn't turn to ash the way a vampire's would, but the flesh disintegrated all the same, leaving behind Mark's skeleton. Her wings longed to stretch free, to fly out of this place, but she was too large for the door. A rustle behind her caught her attention. She turned, a long trill emanating from her throat.

Finn stumbled against the chair Mark had been sitting in. Finn. He needed her help. She shifted from talon to talon awkwardly. *I can't change back*, she said, speaking directly into Finn's mind.

He smiled, as he pulled splinters of white ash from his chest. "Give yourself a second to come down from the high." He was remarkably calm, given the fact that she was an enormous bird. She watched him pull the ash from his chest.

"Fucker splintered that stake and then shoved these into me one by one. Really glad you were out for that part of things."

Her head tilted, and she knew how much of a bird she was in that moment.

"I may have cried a little," Finn said with a grimace as he yanked a particularly large splinter out, tossing it to the floor. His tuxedo shirt was torn open; underneath he wore a shirt that said "Cat Dad Extraordinaire" on it. The humor in his voice soothed her.

"*What are you wearing?*" Her voice came out of her mouth. She looked down at her very humanoid arms and legs. She was stark naked.

Finn looked up. "Is it messed up that I think you look *super* fuckable right now?"

She laughed, but tears streamed down her face at the same time. "We have to get out of here. This is the House of Remiel, right?"

He nodded, yanking another splinter from his chest. "I think that's the last one."

"Can you portal?"

He paused, then shook his head. "Not yet. But the good news is that we're in the basement." He stripped his ruined tuxedo shirt off, tossing it aside. "We're near the garage. We can take one of the vampires' cars."

Harlow nodded and started for the door. Finn caught her arm. "Slow down." He pulled his t-shirt off. "Much as I'm sure I'm going to regret this, can you please put this on so I can concentrate on getting us out of here?"

She took the t-shirt, yanking it on quickly. It covered her ass well enough. "Good?"

"No," he said softly, pulling her into his arms. "Not yet."

His mouth found hers. The kiss was gentle at first, then as she wound her arms around his neck, the intensity grew, heat building between them. When he pulled away, she felt his reluctance in the grip he still had on her hips. "Okay, now we can go."

CHAPTER 37

They found the garage, behind a heavy metal door. "I guess this kept the cars from getting blown up in the fire?" Harlow remarked as she helped Finn pull the scorched door open.

It was concerning how weak he was, but she didn't say anything. Neither of them addressed the room they'd set on fire before leaving. "It'll be obvious they didn't die in the original fire," Finn had said as they left.

Harlow knew it was true, but there was nothing they could do. What she'd done...What *they'd* done... It was unthinkable. She'd turned into a giant bird and murdered her ex-boyfriend, after all. Sure, it was self-defense, but Harlow doubted that would matter much in light of her transformation into a mythical creature that had been hunted to extinction.

Finn pointed. "That one. Can you drive it?"

The sleek, black sports car was intimidating, but she nodded. "You want me to drive?"

He stumbled. "I think you're going to have to. I can get the car started if we can't find the keys inside, but then I'm going to need time to recover from the white ash."

Harlow helped him into the car, wondering if it had ever been driven. It still had a delicious new-car smell. There weren't keys anywhere that she could find. Finn pressed his hand to the dashboard, closing his eyes. The car revved to life and he slumped a bit in his seat.

"I'll be fine," he said, taking her hand. "Just get us home as quickly as you can, all right?"

She nodded, finding the garage door opener as she pulled out of the spot. There was no one around in the dark garage. Only one light near the exit flickered as though it was shorting out. She remembered the twins saying that the electrical had been damaged in the fire. As she pulled up to the garage door, she prayed to Akatei and Aphora that it would open.

Gods all bless them, it did, and she sped out of the garage and into the dark night. Outside it was pouring rain and she pulled into traffic. She wished she had her phone, but of course, it had been lost somewhere along the way, as Finn's probably had been as well. She glanced over at him and his eyes were drooping.

"Should you stay awake?" she asked.

He shook his head slightly. "No, sleep will help. Are you okay to get us home?"

Harlow nodded. They'd talked about what to do if anything went wrong, not that they'd anticipated anything like this. The plan was to meet back at Finn's, where Larkin had stayed home with Axel for the evening.

The streets were nearly empty, likely because everyone was home or at bars watching coverage of the Solstice Gala. It was only eleven o'clock. They hadn't even been missing for four hours. She took a risk and increased her speed, knowing everyone would be worried about where they'd gone. Soon, they were outside the city limits, past the suburbs and onto the road that led to Finn's house.

When she crested the hill, she cried out. Finn woke up. "Shit," he swore. "That's…"

"Our house," she breathed, hitting the gas as hard as she could. "Our house is on fire."

Panic flooded her and she felt Finn's hand on her thigh. "Pull over. I think I can portal us the rest of the way." She pulled over and he directed her to a small grove of trees. "This is part of our property, just pull into the woods. I'll send Nox and Ari back to deal with the car later."

She raced to the other side of the car to help him. He was still so weak. "Are you sure about this?"

He nodded. "Yes, just… hold on tight, okay?"

She did, and they blinked between, appearing on the driveway.

"Finn," she screamed as he fell to his knees.

Hands pulled him from her and she took in the inferno. Indigo and Meline ran towards them, and Alaric and Cian were already tending to Finn. The maters were nowhere to be seen, nor were the Wraiths. "Where's Larkin?" she shouted. "Where's Axel?"

No one seemed to hear her and she started toward the house. Hands yanked on her arm. "They're in the barn with your parents." She looked up into Petra's eyes. The girl threw her arms around her. "Thank all gods you're both okay," Petra murmured.

Alaric and Cian helped Finn into the barn, where the rest of her family, including Riley and Enzo, sat in folding chairs, wrapped in various blankets, despite the sticky heat. When Finn was settled in a chair, drinking from a bottle of water, he motioned for her. "Come sit with me," he said.

She hesitated. "I don't want to hurt you."

"You won't," he said, pulling her down into his lap. "I'm mostly just tired. A big nap and I'll be fine. I need you close."

She snuggled into his arms as he whispered, "They're going to want to know what happened. Are we talking about the big bird?"

Harlow nodded. "I think we have to."

And so they did, everyone listening in silence. Harlow didn't know if it was the horrors of the night, or just general shock, but for once, her family was quiet. No one asked a single question. When Aurelia simply nodded, accepting everything they'd said, Finn asked, "Where are Nox and Ari?"

Cian answered. "They're containing the fire. We can't do anything about the house. I'm sorry."

Finn nodded. "What happened?"

Larkin shook her head. "I don't know. Axel and I fell asleep watching a movie. He woke me and the house was on fire. I called Mama and everyone came home. The fire department never arrived."

Alaric shook his head. "Fuck them, seriously. Fuck them."

Harlow frowned, looking to Finn for answers. He dragged a knuckle over her cheek, soothing her. "My parents. They have a tendency to do things like this as retaliation for betrayal."

He was so casual about it. His parents had set fire to their home, nearly killed her sister and Axel, and he sounded as though he wasn't the least bit surprised. All the things he'd told her about them started to add up. How scared he'd been of them, how worried he'd been they might hurt her. This was why, because he wasn't shocked that they'd burned his house to the ground for standing up to them. How was his heart intact? This wasn't the time to talk about that. Later, when they were alone.

"They could have killed my sister," she murmured.

"Not that I think they care about that," Alaric said, "but likely they assumed she'd be at the gala. They don't pay much attention to the intricacies of other people's lives."

Petra nodded. "He's right. It's likely they were sending a message, not trying to start a war between the Order of Mysteries and the Illuminated."

Harlow reasoned that the McKays simply didn't care who was hurt, so long as their message of intimidation was received. She wasn't going to argue with Alaric and Petra about that. Not right now. "What happened after we were taken? Did Kate find you?"

She noticed a look pass between Enzo and Riley. Alaric shook his head. "No, none of us talked to Kate."

Aurelia said, "Alaric and Cian found us, but not before the vampires portaled out with you. The two vampires who were holding us are in custody and being questioned."

"The *vampires* portaled?" Harlow asked.

"Incubi can do that," Selene commented, her face thoughtful.

"But… At the House of Remiel, it was just Mark and Olivia. And *she* wasn't an incubus. You're sure *both* of them portaled, they weren't touching?"

Aurelia nodded. "I'm afraid so. There are two of them."

"That is very bad news," Finn said quietly.

"What do we do now?" Larkin asked.

A long silence passed, while everyone thought. Harlow wondered how any of them were reasoning through this. She was dead tired, and hot. The barn was humid and the sticky air made her more agitated than she'd like to be right now. She squirmed in Finn's lap. He pressed a kiss to her sweaty cheek.

"I think we go home," Selene said finally.

No one looked particularly interested in that idea, not even Selene. With the McKays out for vengeance and the Velariuses not too far behind, going home—to any of their homes—felt dangerous. But it seemed to Harlow that no one else had any ideas about what their next move should be.

Cian held up a hand. "There is another option."

They all turned to look at the shifter. "What's that?" Aurelia asked.

Cian shifted in their folding chair, uncomfortable under Aurelia's imperious stare. "We could catch the night train to Nea Sterlis. Maybe we need to visit the Vault. Get some distance between us and Nuva Troi for a while."

"What's the Vault?" Enzo asked.

"Technically, it's the Knights of Serpens original records space," Finn said. "It's under Cian's family home in Nea Sterlis."

"You don't have to come, if you want to stay," Harlow said to Enzo. "My guess is that this might all blow over for you if you put some distance between us."

Enzo shook his head firmly. "No. I go where my family goes." Riley took his hand and they smiled at each other. "Besides. I've been wanting to scout some locations for a shop in Nea Sterlis and who wants to suffer through a Nuva Troi summer?"

Harlow couldn't argue with that. Nuva Troi was crowded, humid and blisteringly hot for the months of Juli and Aout; things were only going to get worse from here. By contrast, Nea Sterlis was filled with sea breezes and a warmer climate for the entire year, so it was always refreshing in the summertime. After everything they'd been through, why not get away for a while?

"What about the Monas?" Meline asked.

"We'll have to close up shop for a while," Aurelia said. "The building should be safe enough, I should think."

"We can say Harlow and Finn got engaged, and we're going to Nea Sterlis to celebrate," Indigo said brightly. "It makes a romantic cover story."

Thea cleared her throat. "Maybe we should say that Alaric and *I* eloped, and you all came with us. That would make a better story, and as it's very nearly true, I think it might work better."

Thank you, Harlow mouthed to her sister, who nodded in return.

Nox and Ari returned as Indigo booked sleeping cars on the two a.m. train to Nea Sterlis. "The blaze is out and we cleaned the vamps' car and left it downtown," Ari said.

Nox handed Harlow a bundle of clothes. "It's just sweats, and they're mine, but I thought you might want something else to travel in."

"Thanks," Harlow said, ducking into the barn's bathroom while Finn gave the Wraiths their orders. They were to keep an eye on things in Nuva Troi and meet them in Nea Sterlis in a month. No communication in between, unless they came in person.

When she came out of the bathroom, everyone was piling into cars and driving away. "I'm sorry about the house," she said as she got into the Woody's driver seat.

"Me too," Finn said. He was wearing a new t-shirt and his tuxedo pants, holding Axel in his lap. He craned his neck to watch the house for a long time as they drove away.

CHAPTER 38

When they reached Ambracia Station, valets took the cars to board in freight, and a concierge led them to their private sleeping cars. Enzo, as always when boarding a train, looked nervous, but Harlow was pleased to see Riley whispering something to them that made them smile. Her best friend waved as he stepped into the private room they would share and Harlow had the distinct sense Enzo would be all right.

Before she could go inside the car she would share with Finn, Petra pulled her aside, taking Axel from her. "I'll take this little monster tonight, if you like."

Harlow nodded, kissing the cat on the head as he purred loudly at Petra. "Thank you. I need to take care of Finn."

Axel rubbed his face against Petra's. He knew who would spoil him, and he seemed happy enough to go with her. Petra rubbed her nose to his, then turned to Harlow. "He needs to rest, Harlow. *Really* rest."

Harlow nodded sleepily. "Me too. I don't think I can keep my eyes open much longer. I promise I'll let him sleep."

"He's going to kill me for telling you this." Petra sighed, and wiped a sheen of sweat off her forehead. "White ash can do some serious long term damage. He needs to shift and rest in his true form."

"All right," Harlow said slowly, not understanding.

Petra patted her shoulder, then covered a yawn. "Just tell him what I said. See you in the morning."

Harlow stepped into the car, just as the train began to move. She shut and locked the gilded mahogany door. The twins had fretted about having to ride in the second-class private rooms, but Harlow didn't care that they didn't have spacious suites. That they had privacy at all felt like a precious gift right now.

Finn was using their tiny bathroom, showering from the sound of things, which meant there was just enough room for Harlow to stand, alongside a double bed and a chair near the window. Much like the rest of the train, the second-class cars were lavishly decorated. The chair she sat in was sublimely comfortable, covered in a dark blush velvet with a pattern that made her tired vision swim. The bed looked comfortable, but a little small for the two of them, and it was tucked under an unfortunately low dip in the ceiling. When Finn came out of the marble bathroom, he was clean and looked like he might fall asleep on his feet.

"Wish we'd been able to book first class," he muttered as he hit his head on the low doorway. "I barely fit in here." The train picked up speed as he sat down on the bed, indenting the blue velvet linens. When she didn't respond, he kicked her lightly in the shin. "What's up?"

"What is your alternae?" she asked. "I've always heard that the Illuminated can shift, but I've never seen one actually do it. What's yours?"

Finn flopped onto his back, and his head sunk into the mountain of pillows behind him. "Fucking Petra," he growled.

She got up and crawled in next to him. His arm went around her as he drew her close. Without thinking, she wrapped her leg around his, as her arm went around his middle. The way he played with her messy hair felt comfortable and sensual, all at the same time. "Yeah, she's such a bitch, wanting you to get better fast."

Finn's arm slid under her head as they turned toward each other. He kissed her sweetly, pulling back before either could deepen the embrace. "This is my alternae."

Harlow sat up, banging her head on the ceiling. "Fuck," she swore as he pulled her back down. He kissed her head, pulling her to his chest. She was confused; alternae were usually animal forms. They could be hereditary, though often there were other factors at work in what a shifter's alternae manifested as that Harlow didn't truly know. The ways of the Trickster's Chosen were mysterious to humans and the other Orders, as they were quite secretive. "What do you mean this *is* your alternae?"

Finn shrugged. "This is the form I wear all the time. My true form is underneath."

"Why?" she asked.

There was a long pause. Harlow waited patiently, listening to the steady noise of the train picking up speed.

Finn's eyes were dark in the dim light of the train car, his breathing even, but slightly labored. "If I tell you this, there is no going back. We can break up, but you will always be bound to me by this secret. Are you ready for that?"

What Finn didn't understand was that there was no going back for her, not now. Not ever. Like him, she had no idea what was ahead for them personally, but he had opened up her world in a way that she couldn't walk away from. His fight was hers, from here on out, and she wanted to know everything.

"I don't want to go back," she said. "Just forward, together."

She wanted to kiss him, but she didn't. The moment seemed too solemn for that. What they agreed to now was beyond love or lust, or just them. She felt the weight of that bearing down on her and accepted it without question or doubt.

When Finn spoke, his voice was marked by a distant quality, as though he had never spoken these words aloud. "The Illuminated are hiding on Okairos. Not that we get too many travelers from elsewhere, but it was decided when we got here that we'd never show our true forms in public, just in case."

"Hiding from what?" Harlow asked.

"The rest of our people. When we left our world, we were supposed to come here, wake magic, and begin training your people to fight in our wars. But the Illuminated that came in the original envoy were tired from the endless wars on our home world. They decided not to return. The way we got here was dangerous, and my parents didn't think it was likely that they'd be followed."

"Your parents were among the original envoy?"

Finn nodded. "Yes, and Alaric's parents, though none of them were bonded at the time. They were the leaders of the envoy, coworkers, essentially. When they arrived, the envoy was in terrible shape. After a few months here, they decided not to awaken magic at all, as it would alert their home world to their progress. While they were less worried about being followed, they knew their people would feel the shift in the balance of power."

"How?" Harlow breathed, amazed by the idea.

Finn shook his head. "I don't know. It's a secret they've guarded carefully, and it's likely that what I just told you is only part of the truth. Only my parents, Petra's and Alaric's were actually there. The rest are dead now."

"How many came with them, originally?" Harlow asked.

Finn sighed. "A legion, if what I was told is true."

Harlow's heart beat erratically. *And only six were left? What had happened to the rest of them?* Likely, many had died in the War of the Orders, and of course the original Knights of Serpens had been executed, but still. Only six of the original Illuminated remained. It seemed strange.

Finn continued. "Make no mistake, Harlow. My parents and the Velariuses, they are evil, but they are a lesser evil than those who ruled the planet they left behind. They'd endured centuries of pointless wars before coming here. It's why they were determined to keep the peace on Okairos instead, create a paradise. But you see the way it turned out."

"They had good intentions once," Harlow murmured, the rhythmic vibration of the train soothing her.

"They did," he murmured, yawning.

"So, if we awaken magic, will we broadcast something about Okairos to the rest of the galaxy? Something bad?" The thought was worrisome.

She twisted slightly to see his face. Finn shook his head. "To be honest, I don't know. It could have consequences. It's why we need to proceed carefully. But I don't think Okairos can go on this way, do you?"

Harlow shook her head, exhaustion creeping in. There was so much she didn't know, didn't understand. Part of her was frustrated that she had been kept so sheltered, so in the dark about all this. A more reasonable part of her understood the complexity of the problem. These secrets were dangerous for her, or anyone, to know.

Finn shifted next to her, his hand sliding up the back of her shirt as he pressed kisses to her eyelids and cheekbones. "Petra's right. If I don't want to spend the rest of the summer recovering, I'm going to have to sleep in my true form. You have to promise never to tell anyone about all this."

"Does Thea know?" she asked.

Finn yawned again, nodding. "Yes."

"I promise," she said, propping herself on her elbows. "Show me."

"You're sure?" he asked, hesitating.

"I am. We're in this together, so let's be *together* all the way, okay?"

His fingers traced the lines of her face, and she felt the aether in the room begin to move. He changed slowly, the pale shade of his skin turning to something nearly opalescent, a very light blue color. The dark brown of his hair deepened into ebony, with a bluish sheen. His face was mostly the same, but the angles of his jaw and cheekbones were sharper, and his teeth seemed larger, especially his fangs. In fact, he was larger overall, his limbs visibly longer, including his hands, which she took in hers as his fingers lengthened.

Aside from these changes, he was still obviously Finn; he looked much the same. Or at least he did until he rolled over. Three pairs of enormous wings sprang out as he rested his head on his muscular arms, which were covered in shimmering scales. "It's been a long time since I shifted," he said, watching her face carefully.

The wings were beautiful, closely resembling a firedrake's, she thought. In fact, from the scales to the wings, he very much resembled something distinctly draconic. She wondered if this was a part of what drew him and Cian together, if Cian felt more at home with someone who looked like this underneath their humanoid form.

"Am I hideous?" he asked, his eyes drooping heavily.

"Not a bit," Harlow said, pressing a kiss to his forehead. He needed to sleep, and she needed a moment to herself. "I'm going to clean up a bit."

"Shower's tiny," he murmured, already mostly asleep.

The bathing chamber was opulent, though, as Finn mentioned, tiny. Harlow peered at the blown glass tile in the floor, shaking her head. Such artistry was inspiring. She undressed and stepped into the narrow marble shower. The hot water flowed over her body, creating a tranquilizing effect, even as her mind raced. She washed absently with a finely milled soap that smelled like summer at the seashore. Everything she'd ever known about the Illuminated was wrong, and she tried to puzzle pieces together that blew her mind.

It wasn't that the people of Okairos were ignorant of the existence of other populated worlds; they learned about their existence in school. But the nearest was too far to travel to, even by spacecraft, and no other kind of reliable intergalactic travel had ever been developed. But of course, that was probably because the Illuminated had stopped any progress on such science. What had Cian said? *There is a world beyond what you know to be true, Harlow. Tonight is just the beginning.*

Of course Cian knew this secret, and looking back she understood that they had been sure she'd eventually know as well. Cian Herrington could be a good friend if she let them, she thought. She rinsed her hair, watching the grime of the night swirl around the drain and out of sight. As she got out of the shower, she couldn't bear to put Nox's clothes back on, so she wrapped herself in a towel.

When she entered the bedroom, Finn was fast asleep. His clothes had disappeared, folding themselves neatly on the chair, and he was covered to his waist by the blankets on the bed. His wings fluttered slightly in his sleep, but for the most part looked relaxed.

She crawled into bed. There wasn't much room for her with his increased size and the wings, but she was too tired to care. Something velvety stroked her arm, sending delicious shivers down her spine. Harlow looked over her shoulder to find one of Finn's wings wrapping around her, as his arm drew her into his side. She lost her towel as he moved her, but couldn't say that she cared much. Her skin flushed with wanton need as it made contact with his.

"You're back," he murmured in her ear as she reached out to shut off the lamp next to the bed. Every nerve in her body came alive as his hands made slow, languorous swirls around her breasts and belly, moving lower by the moment.

"Yes, and you're supposed to be sleeping," she said when the room was dark, curving her body to make as much contact with his as she could. One hand slipped between her thighs, teasing her.

"I napped while you bathed," he whispered. His voice was nearly the same, but seemed to have dropped another octave, and even at a whisper its depth vibrated within her as he murmured, "Now I'm *very* awake."

He moved next to her, covering her body with his in one fluid motion. In this form, he was even faster than he usually was, somehow even more graceful. His legs tangled with hers, their skin sliding against one another as he kissed her neck. Above them, his wings moved of their own accord. As his mouth reached one of her breasts, closing around her nipple, she reached up to stroke one of the arms of the wing closest to her. He shivered with delight.

"You need rest," she murmured as he sucked gently on her nipple, his fangs dragging sinfully over her skin.

"I need to be inside you," he replied, kissing her protests away. She needed him too. Every part of the day had been painful, hard, and confusing.

Her legs spread for him as he slid down her body, trailing kisses until he reached the center of her. His mouth closed over her clit, two of those extra-long fingers sliding into her. She moaned at the feel of his tongue tracing circles around her swollen flesh.

She pulled his head from her gently. "I don't want you exerting yourself. Come here."

He glided against her, his skin like silk in this form. She reached between them to take hold of his cock. That was bigger too, she noted. Big enough to make her wonder just exactly how this might feel. But his fingers still traced wicked circles around her clit as he kissed her deeply, his tongue dancing against hers as he moaned in her mouth.

She spread her legs a bit wider, guiding the head of him to her entrance as he moved his hand to brace himself above her. "Go slow," she murmured against his mouth. "I don't want you to wear yourself out."

He pushed into her, stretching her slowly, as warm, wet heat flooded her core, slick desire guiding him into her. Above her, his eyes glowed softly in the dark. "You can't believe how good this feels," he said, his voice rough. "I've never been with anyone in my true form."

"What you did earlier, to help me shift into the Feriant, was that the Claiming?"

she asked as he inched deeper inside her.

"No," he moaned, distracted by her. "That has to be during intercourse." He

slowed his descent into her, looking into her eyes. "You'll know when I Claim you. It will be both our choice, and you won't mistake it for anything else."

He thrust deep into her, taking her breath away with the sweet ache of him. He stopped then, pushing her damp hair from her face. "I'm so glad it worked. You were amazing tonight. You saved us both."

"I'm glad it worked too," she said, arching into him, drawing him further inside her as she clenched hard around him.

His movements were slow and steady as he rocked against her, his glowing eyes never leaving hers as she ground herself against his pelvic bone, her breath coming in quicker gasps each time their bodies met. Ecstasy of a new kind bloomed in her as the air around them filled with magic.

She stroked the arm of his wing again, then pressed her fingers lightly to the spot between his first set of wings. He cried out with pleasure as he moved in her, his mouth meeting hers in a desperate kiss as he came hard, his body shuddering with pleasure.

He didn't stop moving when he'd found his release, their wet spend creating more lubrication as he increased the strength of his thrusts. "Slow down," she murmured, worried about his condition. "It's all right. We can sleep, if you're tired."

In the dim light of the train car, she saw him grin. In this form, his smile was feral, alien and familiar at the same time, and her arousal mounted higher. "I feel so good, you have no idea. It's easier to heal in this form. My alternae slows everything down for me." His hand slid between them to rub her clit. "Let me fuck you," he growled in her ear. *"Please."*

She was caged by his enormous body and she loved it, loved feeling his strength return, and the heat of his need for her. Underneath him, she drew back from him, feeling empty as she released his cock. She flipped onto her stomach, then raised herself up on all fours under him. He let out a primal noise when he realized her intention, his cock sinking immediately into the wet folds of her as his hands slid to her breasts, which he squeezed as he thrust hard into her.

His fingers worked her clit as he bent over her back, purring. "When it's time, when we decide it's right, I am going to Claim you over and over in this form. I'm going to sink my teeth into your neck."

Finn's other hand stroked her throat, showing her where he would bite her. She clenched around him, eliciting a noise from him so loud she was sure the entire train could hear. His free hand slid from her neck to her breast, pinching her nipples hard. She cried out with the pleasurable bite of pain. "And here."

"Where else?" she whimpered.

He flipped her onto her back, his fingers gliding between her thighs as he hovered over her, dragging his wet fingers towards her core. "Do you want me to bite you here?" he asked, tapping the inner crease of her thigh.

She nodded and he lowered his mouth to the spot he'd touched. His fangs dragged across the spot, stinging slightly. His velvet tongue lapped at the spot they scratched. Harlow's hips raised to meet his mouth as Finn's fingers moved closer to her center, tracing her sensitive flesh, wet from their encounter.

"How about here?" he asked.

"Yes," she begged as his mouth teased her.

The train rocked beneath them, bouncing her heavy breasts as he forgot about the game they played and dragged his mouth over her clit, plunging his tongue deep inside her as he drank her in. His fingers followed and she felt the sting of his fangs against her sensitive flesh and was surprised by how much she wanted to feel that bite of pleasure on her most sensitive skin.

He slid his body up hers, his lips capturing hers, the taste of her in his mouth as he thrust hard into her. Stars exploded behind her eyes, her shadows dancing with the bright light that he emitted as they came together, all six of his wings spreading taut above them as he cried her name.

When he slowed, she saw a glimmer of tears in his eyes that she knew were echoed in her own. She hugged him tightly, and spoke without hesitation. "I love you."

The quiver of his heartbeat against hers told her the depth of his reaction. An echo of the orgasm they shared throbbed between them, where they were still connected. Finn's hands dug into her hair and he kissed her deeply, thoroughly. When he pulled out of her, she no longer felt empty. He filled her with his words.

"I have always loved you," he said, with so much feeling that she thought she would sob at the sound of his voice. "And there is nothing in this world, or any other, that could make me stop."

Her kiss was tender as she left the bed to clean up. When she returned from the bathroom he was fast asleep, his breathing deep and slow. She watched him emit a faint glow, and saw that the wounds from the white ash on his chest were gone now.

Harlow's eyes were heavy as she crept into the space he'd left for her, his arms and legs, and wings, closing around her as soon as her skin made contact with his. When she fell into a deep and dreamless sleep, she did so knowing she was safer than she'd been in years, cocooned in their love, lost once, but now found.

CHAPTER 39

When she woke, the train was still moving, but it was day. She was alone in bed. The bathroom door was open, and as she rose on her elbows, she saw it was empty. The window shades were drawn, but light streamed in from outside.

Just as she was about to get up, the door opened, and Finn walked through, his humanoid alternae back in place. She missed his true form already, but he looked better today. In fact, he looked to be in perfect health. He was also dressed in a luxurious looking white cotton t-shirt that clung to his chest in a tantalizing way, and a pair of linen pants that weren't quite his style. When she sat up, she saw he wore flip flops and held a large paper shopping bag. He looked sexy, but far, far too preppy for her taste.

It took everything in her not to laugh as her eyebrows raised. "That's quite the outfit, McKay. All ready for your seaside vacation?"

He smirked playfully at her. "It was what they had in the shop. I got you something to try on. Larkin helped. We should be in Nea Sterlis in an hour. We slept through most of the trip."

The bag he held must have clothes in it. She yawned, still sleepy, but she felt clean and refreshed. The horrors of the Solstice Gala felt like a dream. Harlow blushed when she realized she wasn't dressed, and Finn was staring, leaning against the bathroom door, a seductive look playing in his eyes.

"You don't have to dress, of course," he said, pouncing on her at lightning speed. "We could have breakfast here."

"There's nothing to eat here," she countered. She *was* hungry, and she needed tea.

"I beg to differ," he murmured in her ear, pulling the covers down further to trail kisses down her throat and breasts. "Though, we *have* already been accused of keeping others awake last night."

They both dissolved in laughter and he hugged her tightly as she cuddled into his open arms. Here in their nest of pillows, she felt like happiness was a true possibility. The memory of the previous night, of Mark and Olivia marred that feeling.

"I killed Mark," she said, her words sticking to the roof of her mouth.

Finn's arms tightened around her. "You did."

She thought about it for a moment. "I don't feel bad. Is that wrong?"

He loosened his grip on her and raised himself up on one elbow, playing with her hair. "No," he said slowly. "He was going to destroy us both. That was very obvious. And you were quick about it. Do you think he planned to offer either of us the same clean death?"

Harlow shook her head. "Will I be in trouble?"

Finn sighed and her heart sank. There would be consequences, she knew that. "I just got off the phone with my father."

"What?" she yelped. "Why would you speak to him?"

Finn sighed again. "He called, Harlow. He knew where we were and he called here directly. I couldn't very well not take the call in front of a train full of people. I'm sure he knew that."

"What did he say?" she asked quietly.

"That whatever we'd done at the House of Remiel was justified, that it was cleaned up and that he and I are square. He said that he and my mother will back off, leave us in peace, leave the Order of Mysteries in peace. He said we should enjoy our summer."

Harlow's heart pounded in time with the sharp sound of each of Finn's words. "That is altogether too easy."

Finn nodded. "The worst part is, he meant every word. I can always tell when he's lying. The trouble is, *why*… Why back off now?"

They lay together in silence for a few moments, listening to the train. Muffled sounds of people moving about distracted Harlow for a time. "They got what they wanted. Or at least they think they did. You told them we were together, right?"

He nodded.

"Then they think they have us right where they want us. They think they engineered all this. Why do they think we killed Mark?"

"He congratulated me on eliminating my competition. He thinks I killed Mark because I was jealous. And before you ask, I don't think he knows about the incubi, and I didn't tell him."

Harlow nodded slowly. "That's good. We bought ourselves some time."

He turned to her. "We did. Speaking of that, I have something for you. Do you want to get dressed first?"

"Sure," she said, slipping from his arms, letting him watch her as she pulled out what he'd bought her. A long linen dress and a pair of flip flops were inside the bag, along with a silky set of panties.

She turned, watching him watch her as she pulled the panties on, and then the dress, which was comfortable and loose, but very low cut. He moved in a flash to the edge of the bed, his long arms drawing her between his legs.

"You're so fucking beautiful," he sighed, his hands skimming the line of her generously curved hips. She ran a finger down the tattoo on the inside of his forearm, her eyes flicking up to his when his muscles tensed in response to her touch.

"Lilacs are my favorite flower," she said, almost feeling shy.

He caught her fingers, kissing them. "I know."

"And this moon is the same as the symbol on Akatei's temple."

He nodded, his face grave. "It is."

A small frustrated breath escaped her lips. She wished she could just ask him what it meant, but that seemed rude.

"I got this the year I found out about the Knights, Harlow." He drew a long breath in. "I wanted a reminder of what I was protecting. What I gave up my chance at happiness for."

"Oh." The single word couldn't convey everything she felt in that moment. Nothing could. "Did joining the Knights help?"

He stared at the window shade. "Yes, it gave me purpose. Something else to focus on, besides losing you."

She traced the lines of his face with her fingers, memorizing him in all his smoldering glory. She was the one with dark liminal magic, but he was the one who lived in the shadows. They complemented one another well, the perfect mix of dark night and golden dawn.

"We are going to have a good summer, you know that?" he said as her fingers brushed over his chest.

She nodded, pressing a kiss to his lips. They were warm against hers. His hands closed around hers, and a small velvet box appeared in her palm. She broke their kiss and looked down.

"You still have this?" she murmured.

He nodded slowly. "I'd like us to go out there and make a show of my proposal."

"Okay," she replied, knowing that it was the right thing to do. It would complete the charade, maybe even buy them a few more weeks or months of time to figure out their next move.

"Before we do that, I want you to know something, though. If you say yes now, everything I say out there will be real. I know it's probably fast, but…"

She interrupted. "Yes. I want it to be real. This is already real," she said, her palm against her heart. "I love you, and I don't care if it's fast. We've waited years for this."

Finn took her hand and kissed her palm. "Then come on, everyone is waiting for us." He bent down, sliding the flip flops onto her feet, returning the velvet box to his pocket. When he looked up at her, his face was relaxed and serious.

They left the tiny car that had begun to feel like the whole world to her; she let out a little gasp as the windows in the hallway let in a view of the coastline. Unlike the dark blue roiling waters that surrounded Nuva Troi, here the ocean was calm, and a deep aquamarine, with sandy beaches that stretched along the coastline as far as the eye could see. The train was rounding a huge curve as they entered the dining car.

Outside the windows, the white buildings of Nea Sterlis were stark against the rocky coast and myriad evergreen varieties that dotted the shoreline. The Alabaster Citadel that housed the Temple District rose high above the city, contrasting sharply with the dark sky. A storm was moving in, but perhaps it would pass quickly and they'd dine under the stars tonight. Harlow hadn't had the opportunity to spend more than a few days in Nea Sterlis, and she was looking forward to spending at least part of the summer in the Alabaster Citadel's many libraries.

Finn squeezed her hand, bringing Harlow's attention back inside the train. Her friends and family sat together at a small cluster of tables, already drinking tea and eating baskets full of buttery croissants. Harlow's mouth watered at the sight of them, but Finn shook his head, a smile curving one corner of his mouth as his fingers laced through hers. There were plenty of other people in the dining car, and most of them at least pretended to mind their own business, though Harlow thought at least one human couple was trying to take photos of Thea and Alaric. She reached for a chair and Finn stepped in front of her.

They were taking up the aisle of the dining car. She glanced back at the servers, worried they'd be upset, but she saw the trays of sparkling wine they held and their grins, and understood. Slowly, she turned to face Finn, her cheeks flushing as her heart beat so loudly she was sure the whole car heard.

"Hey, Harls," Finn said, the sound of his deep voice quieting all conversation in the car. He didn't say anything else, but dropped to one knee, taking her left hand in his. She saw him struggle for words, his throat bobbing. She brought his hand to her heart, a tear escaping, rolling slowly down her cheek as she nodded at him. A big speech wasn't necessary; they'd said everything they needed to in private.

He took the velvet box from his pocket, pulling her hand back to his level. "Be my girl?" he murmured, his voice rough with emotion.

"Forever," she agreed, as he slipped the sapphire ring onto her finger.

The dining car exploded with applause and cheers as he stood, sweeping her into a kiss so deep she was almost embarrassed to have her family witness it. *Almost.* In the background, she heard Aurelia comment to Selene, "I think we can stop worrying about Harlow drying up, my love."

"Indeed," Selene replied, sniffling a bit.

When they turned to take their seats at the table, the maters beamed with pride. Everyone talked at once, as was the way with her family, and she knew as she made eye contact with each of them that they understood the proposal was real, that she was finally happy.

Cian got up from the table to take a call, clapping a cool hand over her shoulder as they went. "Welcome to the family, Harlow," they said as they left the table.

"You too," she replied, smiling at Finn as Cian walked away. "Welcome to my family."

EPILOGUE

Rain pelted the sea, thunder crashing as lightning lit the sky. The speedboat bobbed on the waves, as Aislin McKay's skin turned a sickly shade of grey. "Why in seventeen hells did we have to meet here?"

"You know perfectly well why," Pasiphae Velarius said, her usually pleasant voice sharp as the boat sped further away from shore. Aislin didn't answer, but glared at Pasiphae before running to the bathroom. The sounds of her retching echoed through the cabin, punctuating each crash of lighting outside.

"Where is your husband?" Connor asked the Archchancellor, as his wife returned to the table, wiping her lips with a silk hanky.

"None of your godsdamn business," Pasiphae said, every inch the leader of the Illuminated. "Show me the photos."

Connor spread six photos on the mahogany table. The cabin of the speedboat was well appointed, like everything he owned, including his wife, who looked positively wretched but was at least outfitted well for the occasion in a dress that hugged her narrow frame.

A tiny whimper in the corner caught his attention. "Quiet," he commanded, his gaze narrowing at the creature, who shivered in the corner.

Aislin rolled her eyes. "I'll never understand why you need to bring your pets along at times like these."

Connor shrugged, tapping one of the photos to redirect Pasiphae's attention. "This is the one that shows the teeth. The bodies were burned, but you'll notice these are not the usual formation we see in vampires."

Pasiphae's mouth tightened as she looked closer. "No, they are not."

"We have a problem," Connor said.

Aislin rolled her eyes. "Finn took care of it." Her skin was turning green now as the boat rocked wildly in the storm. "We *had* a problem, and now we don't."

The back of Connor's hand met Aislin's cheek before she could flinch away. "If I tell you we have a problem, *we have a fucking problem.*"

Aislin's eyes burned with hatred. Pasiphae sighed, exhausted by the two of them. They'd be fucking in the bedroom before she could get off the boat, of that she had no doubt; the Claimed were all the same. "What exactly *is* our problem then, Connor? I agree that it's not ideal that the vampires have regained the knowledge to create incubi, but as Aislin notes, the creature was destroyed. Your boy destroyed him. You know as well as I do that Gene-I is rare in humans. It's unlikely they'll be able to replicate their results."

Connor pushed a manilla folder across the mahogany table. Pasiphae's eyes glazed over with boredom. "Why am I looking at an MPU case file?"

"The dead incubus," Connor said, pointing to the photos of the burned bodies in the House of Remiel basement, "is Mark Easton. That case file is the MPU report on his father, Alain Easton, who is still missing."

"Oh," Pasiphae remarked, sipping her whiskey. "That does present a problem."

"It does," Connor growled.

"How did they get past us?" Pasiphae mused.

"Money, status… The Eastons have been buying their way out of their blood donations and family planning for generations," Connor said, his lip curling in disgust.

Pasiphae shook her head. "Our own corruption will be the death of us, Connor."

He rolled his eyes at her, clearly impatient to get on with things. "What's more, my people found traces of white ash on the floor of that basement. There's no way Finn killed the incubus on his own. Harlow Krane was with him."

There was a pause as the implication marinated, each of the women turning over the possibilities in her mind. "Impossible," Aislin said with a scowl. "That little cunt couldn't have helped him out of a cardboard box."

"Easton's head was severed," Connor replied. "Torn clean off his body. Finn couldn't have done that at full strength, not to an incubus, especially not one that was newly made. Unlike vampires, they're strongest in the first months of their reborn life."

"So what did this?" Pasiphae asked.

Connor sat back in his chair, glaring. "The *little cunt* is a Feriant."

"You don't know that," Aislin replied, getting up and pacing.

"No," Connor replied. "I don't. But I'm going to find out."

Pasiphae nodded. "We'll get people on it immediately. They all went to Nea Sterlis for the summer. We'll have them watched."

Aislin shook her head. "You'd better. What we buried in Nea Sterlis is too—"

"You don't need to tell me my business, Aislin," Pasiphae said, cutting her off. "I know the stakes as well as you do."

Connor rolled his eyes as the two most important women in his life glared at one another. "Enough arguing. Let's eat."

Aislin smiled, blinking across the room in an instant. "Come now, pet," she crooned to the human cowering in the corner. "It's time for dinner."

Outside, the early summer thunderstorm raged on, the sound of screams lost to the waves crashing against the rocky shore.

BOOK TWO
BENEATH
THE
ALABASTER
SPIRE

PROLOGUE

The chilled air flowing from the vent in the ceiling did nothing to stop the sheen of sweat on Connor McKay's forehead from rolling down one cheek. It was unbearably hot and humid in Nuva Troi. He wiped the offending bodily fluid with his handkerchief and then returned to his phone and his pacing. The reports were infuriating, *impossible*. After over a thousand years of peace, everything was falling apart.

Pasiphae Velarius, arch-chancellor of the Illuminated Order, entered her office in a cloud of rich floral perfume, looking cool as an autumn day despite the oppressive heat outdoors. She offered him a mug of steaming coffee as she sipped from her own, but Connor shook his head.

"Too damn hot already," he remarked, loosening his tie.

Connor regretted his staunch commitment to wearing a three-piece suit to the office every summer, and today was no different. He stared out over Nuva Troi, at Ambracia Bay. Pasiphae's top floor office had a gorgeous view of their city and the ocean, and he never failed to admire it at their weekly breakfast. Boats filled the bay, full of recreating immortals and humans alike, but he didn't feel a lick of resentment towards them. It was a sign that while everything fell apart overseas, at least it was doing so in secret.

He stopped pacing to allow himself a measure of composure, letting the sound of the enormous wall of falling water from Pasiphae's ostentatious fountain soothe him. He'd thought it ridiculous when she'd had it installed a few years back, but now he saw its merits. The quiet sound of moving water was pleasant, and so few things in his life were. Perhaps he needed a fountain downstairs.

His own office was deep in the bowels of the building, a catacombed fortress guarding the hoard of information he'd collected in his over two thousand years on this planet. It was worth it, but he had to admit, he was jealous of this view.

The sapphire expanse of water, the people going about their normal lives. It was all so different from what they'd left behind, the carnage of eons of war, the constant rebuilding, the pain of living the same day again and again. This, for all its imperfections, was better. Two thousand years later, he didn't regret his choices. Not when it came to Okairos, anyway. His personal life was another matter entirely.

Pasiphae stood next to him, sipping her coffee in silence. He glanced at her sidelong, wishing to long-dead gods *they'd* fallen in love back in the beginning— that he'd chosen someone smart, ambitious, and shrewd like her, instead of Aislin.

But his bond-mate had been alluring, beautiful. One of the Emperor's favored courtesans and supposedly an expert diplomat, Aislin had ostensibly been sent to aid the envoy in efficiently utilizing the people of Okairos for the empire's endless wars. In reality, she had caused problems between the Emperor and his new wife. Connor had been fool enough to Claim her the first time they'd fucked and had gotten himself stuck. He supposed he should be grateful for Pasiphae's friendship, their alliance in overseeing Okairos, but it was times like these, when she stood next to him quiet and patient, that he truly regretted his choice in partners.

"What are you getting so worked up over?" Pasiphae asked, her voice low, sonorous and seductive as it always was. "I can *feel* you thinking."

Connor's cock jumped in his pants. But she hadn't a hint of arousal in her scent. She wasn't attracted to him in the slightest, nor had she ever been, to his knowledge. He shook his head, shoving his phone into his jacket pocket. "The early readout on the Août security report detailing the riots in Falcyra."

Pasiphae nodded. "They were handled swiftly, and we suppressed most of the news about them. They're nothing but salacious rumors here."

Connor turned from the view and sank into one of the leather chairs that sat opposite to Pasiphae's enormous desk. She drifted to her plush velvet desk chair and wrote in her diary for a while, waiting for him to speak. The familiar sound of her pen on paper always calmed him, and she knew it. This was how it had always been with them: he handled the horrors of their rule, and she governed the public face of their endeavor to keep Okairos safe from the worlds beyond.

He sighed, covering his face with his hands. "*So far,* it's nothing but rumors. The House of Sorath is out of control. Ducare let nests develop all over the country. We shouldn't have allowed the Order of Night a governorship."

Pasiphae shrugged. "They're our closest allies. The shifters and witches will never align with us. Giving the vampires their own country made sense, and Falcyra is isolated. Worry about handling Ducare."

Gerard Ducare had been a problem overseas for nearly a century—ever since the House of Sorath had defected from the House of Remiel's rule. Giving them Falcyra had been an experiment to see if the vampires could handle their own territory. It had seemed safe enough when Ducare defected. After all, Falcyra was a beautiful country, but cold and nearly desolate. It was also far enough from Nytra to keep things under control in Okairos' capital city—but it had all gone wrong at this point. It was only a matter of time before the truth of it reached Nytra, and when it did… Well, they weren't prepared for that. Not yet anyway. He had to buy them some time.

"I sent a legion to Falcyra this morning to impose martial law for the rest of the summer. Does that handle things well enough for you?" Connor couldn't help flashing Pasiphae a crooked grin. He'd meant to be flirtatious, but she didn't even look up from her notes.

Bitch, he thought to himself.

Pasiphae still didn't look at him, continuing to write in her diary. "Who did you send to fix things? Not Penemue, I assume. I saw her at the gym this morning."

"Rakul," Connor said, his voice quiet.

"Oh my." Pasiphae finally looked up, a ferocious smile spreading over her face as her head tilted. She tossed her pen onto the leather blotter on her desk; her luminous brown eyes shone with mirth. "You *are* serious then."

"This isn't a joke," Connor growled. "Everything we've worked for is on the line."

Pasiphae's eyes flashed with cold, furious power. "You think I don't know that, Connor? I read the reports. Ducare was searching out Gene-I. We had the Night's Own's master records wiped clean a month ago—after the incident with the Eastons and your son."

Mark Easton, Harlow Krane's ex-lover and an incubus, had been killed in the House of Remiel's basement on the night of the Solstice Gala. It had been a nightmare to clean up, and the boy's father, Alain, was still on the loose. All evidence pointed to the fact that he too, had been turned into an incubus. Failure after failure had plagued Connor, ever since the Krane girl had re-entered his son's life. She would serve her purpose soon enough, though, and then they could be rid of her once and for all.

Connor shook his head. "And yet, we still haven't found Alain Easton, and there are *riots* in Falcyra. Sending Rakul was the right choice, and I'll bring him back here to handle things if need be."

One of Pasiphae's eyebrows arched dangerously. She'd made her opinions on Rakul's methods clear time and again: allowable for handling things in other countries, but not here, not in Nytra. This was their *home*. "You don't get a say in that, Connor. *I* say what happens in Nytra."

"Of course." Connor gave in immediately. This separation of power was a vital part of their agreement. It kept the peace, and despite what people thought of him, that was the most important thing. No wars, no poverty—only blessed, *peaceful* order.

"I see on socials that your son and his betrothed have been making quite the splash in Nea Sterlis. Are they having trouble? Someone recorded them arguing at a cafe, didn't they?"

Connor rolled his eyes. She was baiting him because her own son had bonded with the rather perfect Thea Krane. "They were arguing over what toppings to get on a pizza. I hardly think that means anything."

Pasiphae's eyebrows lifted. "You had someone parse out the audio?"

"Yes, of course. They're still on track for our plan. It was just foreplay. They fucked twice afterward in a back alley."

The sound of the waterfall was the only noise for a tense few moments. Then Pasiphae smiled. "Watch them carefully, Connor. We need that child if we hope to maintain our hold on Okairos."

Connor's skin crawled at Pasiphae's tone. Hadn't *he* been the one to come up with the plan to push the Krane girl and his son back together? Pasiphae had some nerve. If she were his, he'd punish her for that imperious little mouth. That line of thinking was unproductive though, so he grasped for a change in subject. "Why aren't these humans grateful for all we've done for them? Do they have *any* idea what it's like on other worlds?"

Pasiphae chuckled, and Connor's ire raised a notch higher. "No, Connor, they do not. We've made sure of that, haven't we?"

It was just like her to throw facts in his face. But it *had* worked—keeping the lower Orders at one another's throats, the humans scrambling for prestige, and *everyone* but a precious few ignorant of what the cosmos beyond Okairos was really like—for centuries it had all worked. Now it was falling apart, and Connor was supremely annoyed. He kicked his feet up on Pasiphae's desk because he knew she hated it.

Sure enough, she glared. "Have you ever considered that perhaps they are unhappy in captivity—that this was all inevitable?"

"They aren't *captive*," he sputtered. "They are free to do whatever the hells they please!"

Pasiphae raised her eyebrows. "Humans are free to make as much money as they please, Connor, but their lives are hardly their own. You and I made sure of that."

He hated that she was right. "It's never been ideal, but the alternative…"

"You don't need to school me on the alternative," Pasiphae bit out. "I was there. I remember the price we paid. Never forget that I saw it all—unlike your precious Aislin."

Connor stood in frustration, unable to stay still any longer, and resumed his pacing. He had to get himself under control. Now was not the time for a power struggle with Pasiphae. She served her purpose, and he needed her—for now. "Perhaps we've given the Order of Night too much leeway. Too many privileges."

"I'm certain Rakul's presence in Falcyra will correct that," Pasiphae mused. "Berith Sanvier will not be pleased."

The business with Berith's protégé, Olivia, had been messy, and beyond treasonous once she'd kidnapped Finbar. Finn was troublesome with all his nonsense about helping humans, but he was still Connor's *son*. A foolish son, full of the idealistic vigor of youth, to be sure. But those ideals, Finn's obvious penchant for leadership, and his love for the people of Okairos was exactly what Connor needed to keep the peace. He would be the monster so his son could be the shining hero; he'd always been willing to play that role, and now was no different.

Pasiphae cleared her throat. *Had she asked him a question?* "I said, Berith is already causing problems. There's dissension in the House of Remiel. Some vampires reportedly think we aren't fit to rule. They're discussing it openly."

Connor shook with grim laughter. "Berith won't last the summer. I let him live so that your people could find out all they could about our incubus problem, but I won't suffer a traitor in our midst."

Pasiphae sighed, opening her planner and jotting down a few notes. "Fine. I'll schedule a termination team. Athan as well?"

"End them all. Every single one that questioned the sanctity of our power," Connor replied, releasing the tension that had been building in his chest all morning. Nothing calmed him quite so much as tying up loose ends. Pasiphae pushed his coffee towards him and he took a long sip. He'd finally cooled down.

CHAPTER 1

The arched plaster ceiling blurred in Harlow's vision, as the sound of waves filled her ears. Her skin beaded with sweat and her head lolled back on the impossibly soft pile of pillows beneath her. Août had been the hottest month of summer in Nea Sterlis yet, and she'd gotten a bit too much sun on her walk back from the Alabaster Citadel. Harlow had to admit she was ready for fall and missing Nuva Troi. Her sunburnt shoulders stung against the silky sheets.

Strong hands pushed her dress to her waist, cool fingers teasing her inner thighs open. "Want me to heal that sunburn?" Finn asked before pressing his lips to her calf. He could, of course. All Illuminated could heal minor injuries—cuts, bruises, and the like.

Her breath caught in her throat as he kissed his way up her left leg. "Sure," she whimpered as one finger dragged across the thin fabric of her panties so lightly she wanted to scream.

Her shoulders stopped stinging immediately, a cool rush of relief, as her core heated beneath his touch. The contrast of hot and cold, relief and frustration, sent her into a frenzy of desire. Her head lifted to beg for more, and Finn's eyes, the color of a stormy sea, met hers, sparkling with wicked resolve.

They were meant to be downstairs, in the Vault, training. She was supposed to be trying to turn into the avian creature, the Feriant, that she'd turned into the night of the Solstice Gala. Except nothing they'd tried for the entire summer had worked. No matter what they did, Harlow couldn't shift into the Feriant again. She was supposed to be training her abilities with her shadows, too, but Harlow had come home frustrated. Nothing had turned up at the Citadel libraries today either, and she'd been to three different ones. They'd come to Nea Sterlis to get away from Nuva Troi, yes, but also for information, and so far all they'd done was fail.

They'd spent almost the entire summer in the same routine: Harlow attempted to research sorcière with abilities that were considered outliers to the usual talents, anomalous shifters, limenal magic, anything that might give her a clue how to turn into the Feriant, while Finn tried to find out more via the Knights of Serpens' network. Nothing had turned up, and each passing day was more frustrating than the last in that regard.

She'd left that morning for the Citadel without waking him. He'd been out late, meeting with one of the city's oldest vampires to talk about incubi lore—they were still trying to find out just how the House of Remiel had revived the infamous creatures—and she hadn't wanted to disturb him. But she'd received a series of texts when she broke for lunch that promised this torture, and more, for leaving without so much as a kiss.

Now she closed her eyes, reveling in the way the light touch of his fingers on her inner thighs sent delicious chills up her spine. A drop of sweat rolled down the arch of her back as Finn dragged her panties aside, exposing her to the heat of his breath. The scent of her arousal filled the air, and he groaned as his mouth met her clit.

Apparently, he couldn't wait either. His tongue caressed her, softly at first, then harder as his fingers plunged into her, curling upward to the spot that made her cry out with each thrust into her. He'd been naked, fresh from the shower, when she'd returned to their rooms in Cian Herrington's cliff-side villa, and now she was glad of it.

Her eyes opened as his mouth left her, and she marveled at the way his skin glowed with the effects of the summer sun and his desire for her. Her legs spread wider as he licked his fingers clean of her.

"Touch yourself," he breathed, his deep voice sending a thrill of ecstasy through her as she obliged, rubbing tight circles around her wet clit.

Finn watched, a wanton smile covering his face as he pulled the neckline of her sundress down to expose her breasts. He stroked the length of his cock a few times, liquid beading at the tip, which he swirled over the head as he lowered himself onto her.

He slid into her easily, stretching her open as he moved. His mouth crashed into hers as their bodies met, filling her with his cock, his tongue, his love. Her hips rose as she wrapped her legs and arms around him, letting the friction between them take over the work her hand had been doing. Around her, her shadows gathered as he thrust harder, meeting her wordless begging for *more, harder, faster.*

The light he emitted grew stronger, twining with the magic she produced. Flashes of that light filled her eyes and his fangs scraped her neck, directly above the throbbing artery that begged to be pierced. She knew better than to ask him to bite her now, but she wanted it.

Harlow craved the Claiming more each day, and she knew Finn did too. She felt it in the desperate way he fucked her. They both came hard, her insatiable desire reflected in his eyes as he slowed in her.

She kissed him, squeezing his cock inside her. "We can't go on this way much longer," she murmured. "We both need it."

He brushed a piece of damp hair from her forehead, rocking gently against her, stimulating her swollen, sensitive flesh. Already, she felt him getting harder inside her. Neither of them were fully satisfied with one orgasm, or even two or three anymore. It hadn't been this bad when they first arrived in Nea Sterlis, but the more time they spent together, the closer they got, the more the Claiming seemed to taunt them.

"I know," he replied. "It's not that I don't want to…"

Harlow knew it wasn't. They'd been over this a thousand times—it had started with Finn's worry about the way it would bind them to one another, and what the consequences might be. There wasn't evidence of how the Claiming might affect them both, since she was not one of the Illuminated. They had talked it over with Thea and Alaric a dozen times, but Thea had never triggered Alaric's venom. Apparently, their situation was totally different. As deeply in love with one another as they were, they had experienced nothing like this.

Finn kissed her forehead and then rolled off her, flopping on the bed next to her. Her skin was so sensitive, she nearly cried. He was clearly ready for another round, and so was she. She pulled off her panties, tossing them on the floor as she climbed on top of him.

His breath quickened as she slid her wet center over his hard length, pulling her sundress over her head as her hips moved.

"I missed you," he growled, his cock pushing into her swollen, wet flesh without resistance. He pulled her hips down harder each time she rose and fell above him, her breasts bouncing as her back bowed with the pleasure of riding him as rigorously as she could.

The desire to be Claimed raged through her. She needed more from him. It was all she could think: *more, more, more.* "Shift," she begged. "Please."

The fire in Finn's eyes blazed as his humanoid form fell away. And then beneath her, and inside her, was a creature so powerful she thought she might be able to resist the Claiming another day. She whimpered as his cock grew inside her, filling her so completely she thought she might not be able to take more.

Beneath him, the three sets of wings that she'd first seen on the train from Nuva Troi spread out on the bed, the same opalescent color of his skin in his true form. Harlow blushed for a moment, embarrassed as she remembered that first time she'd seen Finn's true form. She'd thought he had scales, like a dragon. Now she knew that what she'd mistaken for scales, in her exhaustion after the nightmare in the House of Remiel basement, was a part of Finn's illumination she'd never imagined possible. His desire for her lit him up from within, his skin flashing like a fire opal in the dim light of the bedroom.

The Illuminated got their name from the way their eyes and skin glowed in intense, emotional moments in their humanoid alternae, but in their true form, the effect was that much more incandescent. Finn sat up and his wings sprang out—cocooning the two of them as their movement slowed. The flashing light in his wings made her feel like they were at the center of a kaleidoscope. He was stronger and larger in this body, so they had to be careful at first. She rolled her hips slowly, getting used to the increased length inside her.

Finn's long fingers dug into her hair at the nape of her neck with one hand, and pressed against her lower back with the other, sliding down to grab her ass.

She arched harder, slamming into him, the reverberations of his giant cock vibrating through her into her bones.

The growl that roared from his throat was primal and his fangs glinted as he pulled her hair, exposing her neck. As he dragged his teeth over her, teasing her with the promise of further exquisite penetration, a long cry built in her chest, tumbling from her lips.

"Claim me," she begged, forgetting all the reasons they had to be cautious. "Make me yours."

She saw it in his eyes. He'd lost his last reservation, or at least his last shred of control. His tongue grazed over her throat. "It will hurt at first," he said, his voice thick with desire as he rooted deeper inside her.

Unable to form words, she nodded her consent. His mouth fell open, his fangs elongating as he pulled her closer. Both their phones blared. It was their family alarm, the one no one was allowed to ignore. Finn's mouth snapped shut as he drew away from her.

Harlow whimpered, her needy body clenching around him. "Please," she murmured. "Can't we just—"

Finn's expression mirrored her anguish and for a moment she thought he'd keep going, but the alarm continued. He shuddered as his arm snaked out to the bedside table, pulling both their phones to him so quickly she barely saw him move.

"It's Indigo," he said. "She and Nox found something. We need to get down to the Vault."

Harlow wanted to scream. The ache inside her, the raw need to connect deeper, was insatiable. She forced new air into her lungs, deep into her belly. "Head down without me. I need to rinse off." When he frowned, she sighed. "I won't wash my hair, but if no one's dying, then I can at least rinse off."

Finn's mouth twisted slightly, as though he wanted to say something. On a rational level, she understood all the reasons they'd waited on the Claiming, but her body told another story entirely. Her muscles, her skin, her blood were all burning, set ablaze with an unquenchable desire for him. She saw it in his eyes, felt it in the way his fingers tightened around her. He felt it too.

"You need a minute," he finally said.

Harlow averted her eyes. "I do. I don't bounce back as quickly as you."

It was true. Every time they were together lately, it didn't matter how many times she came; it was never enough, and it sometimes took her hours to settle down to something normal. Even now, she felt her heartbeat throbbing through her core, pulsing around him. With an expression of the sweetest remorse, he lifted her off him. She did her best to ignore the sight of his enormous alien body, shimmering in the afternoon light with sweat and the slick remains of their encounter.

Finn kissed her eyes and cheeks. "I love you."

Her heart swelled to hear it. "I love you too," she whispered, her heartbeat slowing a measure. This wild desire drove her nearly out of her mind, but the love… The love grounded her in a way nothing ever had.

Finn's wings folded behind him as he kissed her. Then he shifted, moving at that annoying Illuminated speed, zipping through the bedroom until he wore a pair of lightweight joggers, an old surfboard brand's t-shirt and a pair of flip-flops. His skin was golden once more, burnished by the sun. His hair had grown over the summer, and it flopped into his face even more than usual. He'd let Larkin paint his nails black a few nights ago when she did her own, and it was chipping a little already. Harlow sighed as he pushed her toward the bathroom; he looked good enough to eat.

"Shower," he insisted as he slid a pair of horn-rimmed glasses on. He needed them to read, and she thought it was adorable that his Illuminated body didn't somehow correct his eyesight for him. Some things had limits, she supposed.

His gaze lingered on her for a moment longer than necessary, as she smiled at him. "You could join me in the shower."

"*Fuck,*" he drawled from the doorway, as if unable to find other words. Then his arms were around her, his mouth on hers, devouring her whole.

He pinned her against the wall, his body caging hers. Her legs went around his waist as she pushed his joggers down. As the head of his cock pushed between her still-drenched folds, their phones both rang again.

Finn groaned in her mouth. "Damn you, sillies." She nodded in agreement as he pulled out of her, rearranging his clothes. His lips brushed her cheek, then her jaw, his tongue grazing the shell of her ear. "Promise you'll think about me in the shower."

Harlow's mouth went dry, but he disappeared so fast she didn't have time to drag him into the bathroom with her. Feeling supremely unsatisfied, Harlow piled her long blonde hair into a messy bun and headed toward the bathroom for a hair tie. Meline had finally taught her how to make it look like all the influencers on socials and she was perpetually pleased that she could pull her hair up without looking like a slob. She turned the shower on before hunting for a hair elastic.

When she found said accoutrement in a drawer of the enormous marble-covered vanity, she fixed the pile of hair atop her head and stepped into the shower, admiring the view of the ocean out the window in their enormous bathroom. Cian Herrington's ancient family villa was nothing short of breathtaking, with a wide view of the cerulean water that surrounded this part of the coast from nearly every window. The best part was that there were nearly a dozen terraces, both covered and uncovered, to lounge and relax on.

To even the keenest observer, it appeared the Kranes were having a rather lovely summer holiday. Finn surfed nearly every day, and the twins sunned frequently on every available terrace, lunching in town with fellow Order darlings most days of the week. Socials, gossips, and the newspapers, alive and well in Nea Sterlis, had gone wild over the twins' sense of style and they were closely followed. The maters attended starlit rituals in the Alabaster Citadel, and dinners hosted by the city's elite sorcière. Thea and Alaric made a big show of enjoying their "elopement" and the media covered them frequently as well.

Harlow was still an object of ridicule, unfortunately. Apparently, the clicks on Section Seven's "Harlow Krane is Over" campaign had been too good *not* to continue trashing everything from her fashion choices to her coffee order. The gossips speculated wildly and incessantly about her and Finn's relationship, and even Axel from time to time. Just last week she and Finn had nearly asphyxiated laughing over what seemed to be an earnest pondering about the cat's life of luxury. What sort of treats did he enjoy? Was he a fan of fresh fish, or was he allergic? It was all too much.

The only piece of luck she could identify was that Mark's death had only been news for about a week. The news claimed he and Olivia died in the House of Remiel fire and that Alain Easton was overseas, deep in mourning, not missing. Harlow was a touch surprised that the humans hadn't seemed that interested in Mark's death, but they often had a strange relationship with their own. One week, a human was interesting to the masses, and the next, they were done with them entirely. Perhaps it was something about the fleeting nature of their lives that caused them to be so fickle, but Harlow was supremely grateful for it. And certainly no one had mentioned the House of Remiel turning humans into incubi. Thankfully, the creatures remained nothing more than scary lore for most of the world.

Harlow rinsed, standing under the water for a few moments longer than necessary to get completely clean. Memories of the night she'd killed her ex haunted her—though not as much as she'd expected. Riley and Enzo both had helped her come to terms with what she'd been forced to do and the nightmares had slowed down, as had the intrusive thoughts, but she couldn't erase the fear she felt that night. The realization that Mark had been changing before they'd even broken up bothered her now—that and the fact that she couldn't shift again.

She'd begged Finn over and over to bite her again, since that had triggered the change the night she'd killed Mark, but he'd refused. He said he was worried about accidentally initiating the Claiming, but Harlow sensed there was more to it. She understood Finn wasn't maliciously keeping secrets from her. It was more that they'd spent seven years apart, and he had an entire organization's secrets hoarded away, and for good reason.

If the Illuminated knew what the Knights of Serpens were up to with the Haven Project, Harlow feared they'd not only shut it down, but execute everyone involved. It was more than just safe house cafes, like the one in Nuva Troi. There was a network of people who helped those who were victims of the Immortal Orders. It was a noble cause, one she was proud to be a part of, but it could get them all killed.

So she tried to be patient. It was difficult not to grill Finn about everything he was keeping from her when she couldn't do the one thing that might protect all of them: shift into the Feriant. The night of the House of Remiel fire, she hadn't truly understood that a newly made incubus was stronger than one of the Illuminated. But now, after looking through the recorded lore in the Vault about the incubi, it was easy to understand why making them was outlawed: they could cause significant harm to the Illuminated. Maybe even kill them. And with Alain Easton, Mark's father, still unaccounted for, Harlow *needed* to turn into the Feriant.

The glass shower door was cool against her forehead as she shut the water off, forcing air through her lungs in even drafts. *Why couldn't she shift again?* Alain Easton could be *anywhere*, and all signs pointed to the fact that he'd also been turned—and she'd killed his son. Even Alaric, who unfailingly believed the best about people, agreed it was likely that at some point he would come for Harlow and Finn. The possibilities about what might happen if she couldn't shift were dizzying.

Outside the bathroom, she heard a soft knock on the bedroom door. "Come in," she called, forcing herself out of the shower. Quickly, she dried off and slid into one of the long, silky sundresses Enzo was prototyping. This one was a beautiful emerald shade, even though prints were *en vogue* for the summer. All the solid color samples had made their way into her closet, as Harlow did not enjoy loud prints.

When she entered the bedroom, Cian Herrington was standing on the balcony, staring at the sailboats in the little bay. "Your sister found evidence that someone purged the Night's Own Blood Banks' master records. They erased all evidence of families with a history of Gene-I, going back nearly fifty years."

This was the big news Indi had? They'd assumed something like this would happen, but from the look on Cian's face, it wasn't the full scope of the news. The firedrake shifter was dressed sharply in pressed linen pants, canvas loafers, and a tank top with an artistically rendered alligator on it. Sunglasses rested atop their head, nestled in their shock of silvery blonde hair. Today they wore a little neon yellow eyeliner, just on the inner corners of their eyes.

Harlow sighed. There was no way she'd ever be as effortlessly chic as the ancient immortal. Cian grinned as they turned, leaning on the railing. "I love all these sundresses Enzo's made for you. But why are your sisters all wearing such gaudy prints? All except my precious Larkin, of course."

A small laugh bubbled out of her chest, breaking up the tension the rush of thoughts in the shower had brought up. "Of course, precious Larkin can do no wrong."

Cian raised their eyebrows. "You disagree?"

Harlow bumped Cian's shoulder. "Quite the opposite. I am so glad you and Larkin have grown to be such good friends."

They really had, ever since Harlow's youngest sister had discovered that while Cian did harbor romantic and sexual feelings towards partners, it took them a long time to develop them. As Larkin explored her lack of sexual and romantic feelings, she'd appreciated getting to know the people in her life who experienced something similar. The culture of the Immortal Orders was so focused on pairing and producing progeny that for those who did not have that drive, it could be an isolating experience.

Harlow was glad that Larkin had expressed herself early enough in her life that she could find a strong community of others like herself, even as supported as she was within her own family. Everyone needed friends who understood them deeply, and Larkin was no different. Her friendship with Cian had started with mutual understanding and respect, and grew from there into long talks about their love of classical music and books Harlow considered unbearably dull. She was glad they had each other. Larkin had always struggled to make friends outside their family and it was good to see her connect with someone who shared her interests.

The sound of waves in the small cove beneath the balcony mixed with the whispering of the wind through the needles of the mix of conifers that dotted the rocky cliff face. The scent of the sun-warmed pine needles and salt air combined into a perfume that sent Harlow into a near-instant state of bliss. She was so sensitive to any sensual stimuli these days; everything either grated on her nerves or brought her intense pleasure.

Before the scent of trees could distract her further, she interrupted her own train of thought. "Now, about these 'gaudy' prints... Have you *seen* the curtains in the billiards room?" They were an awful olive green and orange stripe that Aurelia claimed gave her a migraine.

Cian shrugged, keen eyes observing the flush in her cheeks. They pushed away from the railing and headed toward the bedroom door, apparently agreeing to play along with this line of conversation. "I didn't pick them out, my decorator did."

Harlow raised an eyebrow as she followed. "Seventy years ago?"

Cian snorted as they looped her arm through theirs, leading her down the enormous marble staircase at the center of the house. "All right, they're ugly curtains."

Harlow hummed a noncommittal response. Her skin had gone instantly cold inside the house, although it was only mildly cooler than the balcony had been. She shivered.

Cian rubbed her arm, warming her with their hands, but didn't remark on yet another of Harlow's mysterious sensitivities. "They're the *ugliest* curtains. Happy?"

It was Harlow's turn to snort. Like Larkin, she and Cian had fallen into an easy friendship over their summer together, ribbing one another relentlessly like siblings, despite their vast age difference, and laughing late into the evening many nights. Cian felt like family, as much as her sisters or Enzo did.

She tripped over the hem of her dress. Cian caught her before she stumbled down the marble staircase. When she'd righted herself, she asked, "What else did Indi find?"

Next to her, she felt the muscles in Cian's sinewy arm tighten. "There's more trouble in Falcyra."

Nothing seemed amiss on public channels. All the gossips out of Falcyra showed people staying in luxury treehouses overlooking the fjords, partying in Austvanger's glamorous rooftop gardens, or traveling further north to observe the arctic bears and the *limenara borealis*. However, there had been increasing back channel reports on the dark web about what was really happening in Falcyra, though the Wraiths, Arebos and Nox Flynn, hadn't been able to pin anything down—until today, apparently. What they knew for sure was that Falcyra's humans weren't taking their vampire overlord's governing without question anymore, but so far nothing had made it into the mainstream news.

"Something's been confirmed?"

Cian nodded. "Yes, there's rioting in Austvanger. The humans may have burned the Governor's Mansion down last week, but we're still cleaning up the footage. Indi found records of it in the trail she's opened. The Illuminated sent the Dominavus. Rakul took lead."

Harlow's heart skipped a beat. Rakul Kimaris was a legend. He'd spent most of Harlow's life overseas and had led every rumored cleanup for nearly a hundred years. Things rarely went wrong when the Illuminated decreed something should go one way or another, but if they did, the Dominavus—a small, elite crew of immortals—took care of things. When they solved something, it stayed solved. But none of that was why she reacted the way she did.

They'd nearly reached the basement door, where the secret entrance to the Vault was located, and Harlow stopped Cian. "Why is this important to us, other than the fact that the riots in Falcyra are worth watching?"

Cian's pale eyes narrowed. "Because Rakul Kimaris is the only living Knight of Serpens from the envoy. He fought with us in the Great War... And he was the one that sold us all out to the Illuminated."

That shocked Harlow deeply, and it must have shown in the involuntary shudder that passed through her.

"Are you all right?" Cian asked as they opened the door to the basement and pressed their hand to the metal plate next to it.

The door opened with a soft swishing sound. Harlow passed through, descending into the wood paneled staircase that dove deep into the cliff the villa sat on. "I had a strange experience with Rakul when I was a child."

They walked through what appeared to be a wine cellar until they reached the tasting room. Cian punched numbers into the walk-in refrigerator and, once inside, swung back a shelf to reveal a secret door. Harlow pressed her own hand to the metal plate next to the entryway. It took two verified Knights, or their affiliates, to open the Vault, and Finn had made Harlow an affiliate at the last dark moon. The doors opened and Cian followed her through.

The next set of stairs was much darker, lit by dim sconces on the rough stone wall, and wound deep into the subterranean depths of the Vault—the headquarters of the Knights of Serpens. Over the summer, Harlow had learned much more about their current operations, but still felt she didn't know the extent to which the organization had power. One of the primary policies the Knights adhered to was "just in time" knowledge, meaning that no one knew more than they needed to until exactly the right moment. It was frustrating and occasionally felt unnecessarily secretive, but because their organization was deeply seditious, it made sense.

"What happened?" Cian asked.

"I was on an initiatory trip to the catacombs, under the Order of Mysteries' primary offices, six months before my thirteenth birthday."

Cian smiled fondly. "I bet little witchling Harlow was adorable."

"I was a fool, and an incredibly clumsy child—not much different from now, really. Anyway, Lorcan Greenbriar dared me to walk out onto the Ledge of Wishes..."

"Oh, dear..." Cian said, trailing off.

Lore around the Ledge of Wishes was well known throughout the Orders. The stories said that if you could make it to the end of the Ledge, Ashbourne could hear your voice in the depths of the limen—the realm between all worlds where aether, the force that made magic possible, resided. Supposedly, sound carried straight into the fabled prison of Nihil, where Ashbourne the Warden would grant you a wish. It was a ridiculous legend, come to think of it.

Why would a prison warden grant wishes? It didn't really matter—no one ever made it that far, because the ledge was made of slippery crystal and most witches turned back before it got dangerous. "I wasn't even that far out, but I slid and couldn't stop, heading straight for the edge—and then—like magic, I was caught up in powerful arms and dragged back to my friends."

It made little sense before, how he'd appeared in thin air above her, but now she understood that he'd used his true form. Like Finn, under the humanoid exterior, Rakul Kimaris must have three sets of draconic wings. It had seemed like an absolute miracle. The group of chaperones had chalked it up to Illuminated speed, but Harlow had always known something else was happening. It was satisfying to recognize the truth.

Cian caught her arm, looking shocked. "Are you saying Rakul Kimaris *saved* you from falling off the Ledge?"

Harlow nodded, slightly surprised that Cian didn't expect more from Rakul, but of course, the ancient shifter probably had a much different perspective on him than she did. "Yes, and he said the oddest thing to me. I thought I'd never forget it... I'm actually surprised I didn't remember until now..."

Her brow furrowed. At the time, it had made no sense. She'd just thought Rakul was strange. But now...

"Well," Cian insisted. "What did he say to you?"

"He said, *careful hatchling, your wings aren't yet strong enough to carry you from the abyss.*"

Cian's pale eyes went wide and Harlow thought she glimpsed the silver fire-drake that slept inside them, if only for a moment. "Did anyone hear him?"

Harlow shook her head. "I don't think so. Why?"

"There weren't many Knights and Striders like you and Finn in the Feriant Legion. Most of them were deeply platonic partnerships. But a few were in love and had children. They called their children hatchlings. It was... not widely known."

Now Harlow's heart had stopped completely. She looked up to find Finn waiting at the bottom of the stairs, and from the look on his face, he'd heard every word of Harlow's story. Power vibrated through him as his eyes smoldered with lethal force. "Are you suggesting that Rakul Kimaris knows what Harlow is?"

Cian nodded, face grave with concern. "I think we have to assume he does."

Harlow couldn't see the issue. "But he saved me. Wouldn't he have let me fall if he were a traitor like you said? Or have told one of the Illuminated about me?"

Cian sat down on the steps. "Ten minutes ago I would have said yes, without question. But now… Now I wonder."

Finn took Harlow's hand, and she looked up into his worried eyes. "Don't worry," he said. "I can protect you from Rakul, if it comes to that."

"I don't think he'd hurt me, Finn," she said. "He saved my life. He was kind. Strange, but kind."

She didn't think it was a good idea to mention that she'd dreamed of bonding with Rakul for years, before learning just how old he actually was. He hadn't looked a day over twenty-five to her, dashing in his flexible body armor, with long black hair tied in a plait down his back.

"What was he doing in the catacombs, anyway?" Cian asked. "He shouldn't have been allowed in there."

Harlow shrugged. "You'd have to ask the maters."

CHAPTER 3

Selene passed by, carrying a tray of hot tea from the Vault's state-of-the-art kitchen. She pushed through a pair of steel-paned glass doors, into the conference room, which was really more like a giant living room. "Ask us what?"

"Why was Rakul Kimaris in the Order of Mysteries the day I fell from the Ledge of Wishes?"

Selene sat the tray down on the enormous sun-bleached driftwood coffee table that sat at the center of four buttery soft, navy blue leather couches. The conference room was mostly dark glass and black marble, a bit of sleek modernity in the ancient subterranean archives. The plush red patterned rug that covered the glossy floors was antique, and the couches were obscenely comfortable and could fit their entire entourage, though no one else was here yet.

Selene poured tea into a stoneware mug and handed it to Harlow, while Finn and Cian made themselves comfortable. Her face softened as she looked at her second-eldest daughter, as though remembering the child she'd been. "I'd forgotten about that. He saved you, didn't he?"

Harlow supposed that with over six hundred years of memories and five daughters, Selene Krane was allowed to forget a few things. She'd lost track of the memory herself, after all.

Selene's big green eyes, nearly identical to Harlow's, narrowed as she scraped her memory for information. "If I remember correctly, he was there for the last of the yearly inspections."

Harlow's face twisted in confusion. "Yearly inspections?"

Finn cringed. "Yes, my father used to have Rakul and the Dominavus inspect all the Orders' headquarter buildings once a year as an intimidation technique. It ended when we were children after a rather long bout of negotiations."

Selene nodded, handing Finn and Cian both mugs of their own. "Yes. It's interesting though—now that you mention it, Rakul was always very kind when he came to the Order of Mysteries."

Selene sat, crossing her legs. She too wore one of Enzo's new designs, a long, loose gown with flowing sleeves in a beautiful, dark floral pattern. Cian raised their eyebrows at Harlow as if to say *gaudy print.* Harlow ignored their antics and refocused on what Mama had to say.

"Merhart Locklear used to complain that the Dominavus were unruly and rude at the Order of Masks, but with us, they were polite. Quick about their business and gone. It was an inconvenience, but not nearly as bad as the other Orders made it seem."

Conversation stalled when Indigo and the Wraith, Nox Flynn, entered together carrying laptops. Indigo hardly looked like herself today, or at least the version of herself that had inhabited Nuva Troi last spring. She wore a pair of wide-legged linen pants and a cropped tank top, with her dark hair piled atop her head—and she was wearing her glasses. Over the summer, she'd relaxed more than Harlow had ever seen, no longer looking like the perfectly coiffed society darling that she'd appeared to be in Nuva Troi. Harlow liked the way her sister's style seemed to have evolved into something more comfortable for her. While she'd always been interested in fashion and society happenings, just as Meline was, Harlow had always wondered how much of that was their twin bond, and how much was truly Indi.

Harlow caught Nox checking out Indi's rear as she sat and nearly groaned. The two of them were wild about each other, but unlike Meline and Nox's brother Arebos, who were open about their flirtation whenever Ari reported in, Indi and Nox were desperately pining. Nox caught Harlow watching her, and the tips of her ears got pink and then disappeared completely. The Wraith's faintly arched ears reappeared, and she bit her bottom lip nervously.

Ari and Nox Flynn were rare shifters who could shift into the very scenery of any location, rendering themselves completely invisible, but Harlow hadn't seen either of them use their talents very often. It was adorable to see that the talent could manifest in a moment of embarrassment. Somehow it made Nox, who was imposing otherwise, seem more relatable. Harlow flashed her sister's love interest a conspiratorial grin. She'd never dream of calling either of them out. As open as the twins were about things on their socials, Indi was remarkably private, and she'd be mortified if anyone teased Nox or her for their shy courting.

"Where's Meli?" Harlow asked.

"She, Thea and Larkin are shopping this afternoon," Nox replied, after pulling up the family calendar and checking. Nox had insisted on creating a detailed calendar that coordinated a steady stream of frivolous-looking activity here in Nea Sterlis, especially for the younger Krane girls and the maters, who were all known for being naturally social.

As for Harlow, she wasn't going out much in social situations. Section Seven had been especially cruel about her since the season. While her sisters and the maters were objects of interest and speculation, they seemed to get their kicks out of ridiculing everything from her fashion choices to the expressions she made. They didn't feature her any more or less than anyone else in the family, but the tone they used made it hard to take.

Selene added, "And Li-li is having lunch with the new Order of Mysteries treasury board today, so we'll catch her up later."

The maters had used the summer wisely, gaining supporters in the Order of Mysteries. The plan they'd proposed for dealing with the Illuminated's lax control over the Order of Night was to ally with key members of the Order of Mysteries and the Order of Masks and stage a confrontation and a vote at the Council of Orders that would take place on the Winter Solstice. Harlow had her doubts that having a polite argument with the Illuminated and the vampires was the way to solve Okairos' growing problems, but she understood why the maters wanted to try this route first.

Selene looked around. "Where's Alaric and Petra?"

"Here," Petra said, brushing a kiss to Selene's cheek as she and Alaric rolled in. Selene and Aurelia had essentially adopted Petra since arriving in Nea Sterlis and hearing about how her parents had disowned her. They were the worst of the Illuminated in some ways, ancient, bigoted, and completely removed from the world. Petra's parents rarely socialized with anyone from even the lower Orders, keeping their circle tightly governed to other Illuminated. The little Petra had told Harlow about them was sad—her friend's childhood had been lonely but for her cousin Alaric and Finn, as she hadn't been allowed to make friends from the lower Orders. It warmed Harlow to see Petra accepted into her family.

When everyone settled in, sipping their tea, Indigo caught them up on what she and Nox had uncovered. It was all as Cian had said, but apparently there was more. "The order was there for Rakul and the Dominavus to go to Falcyra, but when we checked into it, he's not there."

Nox watched Indigo closely as she spoke, as though every word that fell from her lips was a gift from Aphora, before adding, "The Dominavus are in Falcrya. We confirmed that. But no one has seen Rakul."

Next to her on the couch, Harlow felt Finn's muscles tense and his hand gravitated toward her knee. She knew he was thinking of what she'd told Cian just minutes ago. "Where is he?"

"We don't know," Indigo said, her brow wrinkling in frustration. "It's like he's disappeared into thin air. But all we've got is the operatives' accounts right now. Footage from the riots is still processing through the decryption software... There's a lot of it."

Alaric sighed. "That's not like Kimaris. Keep looking."

Nox nodded, getting up. "I'm going to go use the central computer for a while. My laptop doesn't have enough juice for this kind of covert digging in the CCTV archives. The riot footage should be out of decryption shortly."

Indi nodded, checking a timer on her phone. "It's slowed down, but we should have something soon. There's something else..." Indigo hesitated.

"What is it, darling?" Selene asked in a clipped tone, clearly impatient.

Indigo glanced at Nox. "You can explain it better than me."

Nox shook her dark head. "You could explain it just fine."

Indigo blushed and Harlow felt everyone in the room inwardly rolling their eyes with secondhand embarrassment. The two of them were something else. Before anyone could urge them to get to the point, Nox succumbed to Indi's pleading eyes and explained.

"There's been some unique pressure on the wards here at the villa. Someone is probing us." The shifter crossed her legs, looking slightly frustrated. "But they're doing it in a really blunt, obvious way."

"Amateurs?" Alaric asked, one of his dark eyebrows raised.

Indi grimaced a little, her shoulders raising slightly. "Maybe, but the analysis I've done on the probes is anomalous. I'd like to have Enzo look at it when he comes back, if that's okay with you. He's better with complex spellwork than most of us."

Alaric glanced at Harlow and Selene, looking somewhat dubious. Mama nodded. "It's true. Enzo may be a designer, but he's a Weraka, and the entire family has an aptitude for understanding spells. His mother was a prodigy, and she always said he took after her."

Sorcière rarely needed spells, as most pulled aether through the unseen threads of reality that made up all things living and inanimate on Okairos to weave changes, but some workings were too big for that kind of magic. If pulling threads was like embroidering a pillow, then spells were like weaving a giant tapestry. Many threads were engaged, and anchors like herbs, gemstones, and other natural objects had to be used in very specific ways to make spells work. Workings like effectively warding a secret subterranean vault of seditious infor-mation, while maintaining the appearance of an average warding, were just the kinds of spells that someone like Enzo needed to look at. Even Aurelia, who was the Kranes' expert in spells, would struggle.

Selene's eyes misted over at the mention of Enzo's mother. Maurice and Clarissa Weraka had been Aurelia and Selene's closest friends before they were killed in a terrible train accident when Enzo and Harlow were in secondary school. Finn placed his hand on Selene's arm, and she patted it, giving him a small smile. He sat forward, making eye contact with Alaric. "It's true. Enzo is as brilliant with spellwork as you are with tech. I think we should have him and Thea look together."

Alaric's head shook slightly. It was the most Harlow had ever seen him disagree with Finn. "We need Thea to stay focused on the restoration of the Merkhov book and the triptych."

Thea had been hard at work restoring the images in the Merkhov text which they all believed to be a depiction of the relationship between Striders and the Knights of Serpens. She wasn't having much luck with the second and third images. Whatever was done to destroy them was magical in nature and complicated.

Finn nodded once. "All right then, see if you can get Enzo to look at what you've documented about the probes. It should be easy enough for you to work out, shouldn't it?"

Nox smirked at Finn, who had a glint in his eye that told Harlow they'd had conversations like these hundreds of times. She flashed a cocky smile. "Easy as pie."

Indi raised her eyebrows, eyes wide with earnestness. "Pie's kind of hard to make."

Nox's brown eyes went gooey again, like Indi's brand of open seriousness was the most adorable thing she'd ever seen. "Wanna go get back to work?"

Indi nodded, a flush coloring her cheeks pink. They walked off together, laughing softly at some private joke.

Selene checked her watch and then rose from the couch. "Petra, we need to get going if we're going to meet Li-li and the girls for drinks at the Obsidian. Harlow, darling, are you coming?"

The Obsidian was the most popular new club in Nea Sterlis this summer, a collaboration between the Order of Night and one of the human mafia families, if rumors were to be believed. But the way Section Seven had been targeting her lately didn't make it fun for her to go out in the evenings.

Harlow shook her head. "No, I'm going to stay here."

Petra brushed a quick kiss to Harlow's cheek as she followed Selene. "We need a pool day soon."

Harlow nodded and squeezed Petra's hand as she walked away, their arms stretching out between them. Axel passed Petra as she entered, wrapping his long black tail around her slender leg as she went, purring loudly at her in greeting before racing through the room, chasing some invisible prey. He must have come down with Selene earlier, and been napping in the workroom she and Aurelia shared in the back half of the Vault, where there were several rooms for offices and other work.

When it was only Harlow, Alaric, Cian, and Finn, she asked the question she'd been holding in the entire meeting. "Why did the Illuminated let Ducare and the Order of Night have Falcyra?"

Cian sat back, crossing one long leg over the other, their expression pointedly wry. "Well, the climate is perfect for vampires. Cold and cloudy. You know most of them hate a sunny day."

Harlow rolled her eyes. "What? That's not why."

Cian smirked as they kicked Harlow playfully. "No, but it's part of it."

Alaric, ever the diplomat, steered the conversation out of sarcastic territory. "Three hundred years ago, Gerard Ducare was getting out of hand here in Nytra. He wanted to rule the House of Remiel, but of course, the Sanviers wouldn't dream of giving up their power in Nytra."

"And Rosamund Penemue hated the Falcyrans," Finn added. "She was the Illuminated governor there before Ducare."

Harlow knew the name, but had never met Penemue, as she was usually called. "Isn't she some elite warrior?"

Alaric nodded. "Yes, she's one of the original envoy. But she's always said Falcyra is a backward country, obsessed with folklore, and far too liberal with their beliefs about human autonomy."

"But it was the white ash groves that did her in," Cian said. "There were rumors for years that Falcyra somehow has hidden white ash groves."

Harlow narrowed her eyes. "I've never heard that."

Finn shrugged. "The Illuminated don't like it to get around, of course. And we've never been able to find evidence that it was true. Nothing shows up on satellite, nor in any of the extensive ground searches that were done."

"But in Penemue's day, humans kept attempting to kill the Illuminated with weapons made from the stuff," Alaric said. "Eventually, my mother and Petra's parents, who were more involved in governing back then, decided that everyone might be safer if Ducare took over for Penemue."

"Thousands of vampires went with Gerard," Cian added. "Nobody talks about it much, but it made Nytra far safer for humans."

This was why Harlow had hesitated to ask her question in front of the group. She was embarrassed she didn't know all this, or the follow-up question she had. "So, are humans treated badly in other countries? Is that why they're rioting?"

Finn took her hand, his face patient. "Yes. It's much worse than in Nytra."

Harlow nodded, heart sinking. "It's bad enough here, despite…what people say."

"You can say it," Alaric said softly, his usually kind brown eyes hard. "Despite the Illuminated propaganda. Because that is what it has always been: propaganda. *Lies.*"

His words sunk in. Amidst all Alaric's good humor, sometimes he'd say something something so starkly justice-minded, that it shocked Harlow a bit. "We miss it all so easily," Harlow said, letting the idea ruminate a bit. "We look away when we travel. Why?"

Finn sighed deeply, squeezing her hand. "Because none of you are safe from us either."

The air seemed to go out of the room. Harlow appreciated that Finn didn't mask the fact that he too was a part of the threat, just by virtue of being one of the Illuminated, but it did nothing to make her feel better. Perhaps that was the point. Maybe trying to make things *feel better* for too long got everyone into this mess.

Harlow nodded, but Finn's words highlighted exactly why she needed to figure out how to shift, sooner rather than later. A time was coming when they'd have to fight, and she might be among their most effective weapons. Alaric and Cian exchanged glances with Finn, but he shook his head and changed the subject to discussing a tactical operation that one of the Knights' operatives was running in southern Falcyra, to get more information on the situation there. Harlow stopped paying attention.

They were using a lot of jargon she didn't understand, not being well-versed in intelligence gathering. Instead, she went over the little she'd learned about the Feriant in her head, adding her interaction with Rakul Kimaris to her cache of knowledge. She turned the memory over again and again, trying desperately to extract anything from it she might have missed.

CHAPTER 4

Harlow didn't realize she'd completely lost track of what was happening around her until she looked up to find that Alaric and Cian had left her alone with Finn. He was reading something on his phone, but when she moved, he looked up at her over his glasses. The lights in the conference room were soft, and the golden glow of the lamps shone on his dark hair.

"You okay?" he asked. "You kind of zoned out there."

She looked around. "Everyone left?"

Finn nodded. "Haven't seen you go deep inside yourself like that since we were kids."

Harlow nodded, feeling absentminded and scattered. "I was thinking about Rakul and the Ledge."

Finn set his phone down, shutting the screen off. "I thought you might be. Did you remember anything new?"

Harlow shook her head. "No, but with Alain Easton unaccounted for, everything going on in Falcyra, and what we're doing here… It seems like we should make my shift more of a priority."

A long moment passed, as though Finn was weighing her words. "I don't want to pressure you."

Of course he didn't. He didn't want her to feel like any of this depended on her. But in some ways, it did. She glanced at the clock hanging on the wall above the console table across from them. "We have time to get a bit of practice in. We could try that new meditation Cian mentioned yesterday."

Cian had been researching different ways to help shifters who'd lost their ability to access their alternae. It was a rare issue, but it happened occasionally, and they believed Harlow might focus her way into shifting.

"You hate the meditations," Finn said.

Harlow let out a wry laugh. "I don't hate them. I'm *terrible* at them."

Finn raised an eyebrow. "I can't understand how someone who can read a romance novel for a whole day can't sit still long enough to meditate."

Harlow rolled her eyes. "Romances are *exciting*, Finbar. Meditating is… not."

He dragged her by her ankle toward him and she let out a little squeal of laughter, but didn't resist as he pulled her into her arms, whispering in her ear, "Yeah? What's so *exciting* in a romance novel?"

The sound of his heart beating was a comfort, as she rested her head on his chest. "Maybe you should read one and find out."

He hummed a little, and his chest vibrated, sending shivers of delight through Harlow. "Only if you get me a smutty one."

"I think Indi and Meline have some of those monster romances. I've heard they're pretty smutty," Harlow said, waggling her eyebrows suggestively.

Finn rolled his eyes. "*Monsters*? Who would want to fuck monsters? Next you'll tell me there are incubi romances."

Harlow almost laughed, but her brain stumbled over what he'd said. There *were* incubi romances, of course. Ones full of biting and mind control. After her experience with a real incubus last spring, she didn't find them very sexy at the moment. Maybe she'd feel differently in a few years—fiction about the things that scared you most could be healing. But right now, remembering was too much, too raw. Harlow's brain tripped again around the memory. There was something there, even if she didn't particularly want to look.

Thoughts swirled in her head for a moment, uncontrollable and disjointed. When they coalesced, it was so obvious she nearly slapped her forehead. She sat up to face Finn. "You have to bite me."

Finn shifted uncomfortably on the couch. "I'm not ready for the Claiming, Harlow. We've talked about this."

Standing, she tugged on his arm. "I'm not talking about *that*. I'm talking about what we did in the House of Remiel. You bit me."

He sighed. "We've talked about this. It's a dangerous line to walk. If you trigger my desire for you, it could set off the Claiming. I'm not ready for that."

Harlow's jaw clenched. "And if I can't turn into the Feriant, who will kill Alain Easton if he shows up here?"

It was Finn's turn for a clenched jaw, but irritated as it might make him, she knew he couldn't argue. The incubi were the only thing he had to fear, outside his parents. Even with Cian and Alaric here, they'd estimated that the best they could do was hold Alain off while everyone else ran. It was dangerous for her not to be able to shift, and they both knew it.

"We have to try," Harlow said. "You and I both know meditation isn't going to do it. You bit me in the House of Remiel and I shifted."

"It was a foolish move. A gut feeling," he said, looking down at his hands.

"And it's the only thing we haven't tried. If it doesn't work, I won't ask again."

Finn sighed. "Fine."

It surprised her that he agreed so quickly, but it confirmed her worries: they were running out of time to get the upper hand in the conflict that was surely brewing. He stood, and she followed him to the Vault's training room. The ceilings were high, accentuated with cedar beams and gentle lighting that made it feel like being outdoors, rather than deep underground. Mirrors lined three of the walls for practicing form, and the fourth was an arsenal of weaponry.

Finn stood at the center of the room and closed his eyes. "Give me a minute to calm down, and when I motion for you, come stand right here in front of me, just like we were that night."

Harlow nodded. "Then what?"

"I'll bite you—and hopefully the shift will take hold, the way it did on the Solstice. As soon as it does, tap my arm and I'll break my skin for you. Then you'll drink from me… If we've done it right, you'll shift."

"And if I don't?"

"Then stay absolutely still," Finn cautioned. "This is a volatile moment, and I'm going to try my best to stay calm. If my bite doesn't initiate the shift, ask me to stop, okay? But do it quietly, and whatever you do, don't pull away."

Harlow wondered if she ought to ask more questions about why that was necessary, but she was afraid if she did, he'd simply refuse to try this, so she nodded. He closed his eyes and took deep, cleansing breaths. She watched as he rolled his muscular shoulders. Muscle group by muscle group relaxed. Harlow was wretched at meditation, but Finn—well, Finn was great at it. A small smile played on her lips as she watched him. Everything about him was beautiful.

When he flicked a finger at her, she did as he'd asked, walking slowly to stand in front of him, facing the giant mirrors that surrounded them. She'd always thought the mirrors were a little mesmerizing, but now, as she watched Finn's fangs protract, it was difficult to stay calm. It wasn't fear she felt, but she knew she had to tamp her desire down quickly, or Finn would stop.

His eyes were closed as his mouth latched around her neck. The bite was fast and painful, with none of the ecstasy she'd felt in the House of Remiel basement the night she'd killed Mark. This just *hurt*. Finn's fingers dug into her waist as he took draw after draw of her blood. His venom burned through the wound.

Nothing happened on her end. The euphoria she'd experienced the last time they'd done this never appeared. She was practically distraught, but she did as Finn asked and stayed still. "It's not working," she whispered.

He didn't respond. In the mirror, she saw his face, and it scared her. His eyes were predatory, burning with that Illuminated power.

"Finn," she said again, this time more forcefully. "It's not working. Let me go."

But he only gripped her harder. She felt faint.

"Finn!" she shouted, hysteria edging her voice.

Behind her, he snarled. The sound was vicious—like an animal approached while it was *eating*. Vampires lost control sometimes when they fed, becoming more predator than person. Harlow couldn't think through the mechanics of what was happening now. She struggled in Finn's arms, squealing like prey in the throes of death.

An icy voice broke her panic. "Finbar! Let Harlow go."

There was a long, tense moment when she thought Finn wouldn't stop, that perhaps nothing could stop him. His grip on her tightened. Though her vision was hazy, she could just make out his reflection in the mirror. He was staring at whoever was speaking, their eyes locked on one another. Behind her, he paused; his lips slowly pulling away from her skin. When his fangs retracted, her head slumped forward. She could not hold it up.

"Let her go," the voice said. Harlow's vision was still fuzzy, but she vaguely recognized the illustrated alligator floating in front of her. Cian. Cian was here now. "Let Harlow go, Finbar. You don't want to do this."

Finn's fingers loosened, and then she was falling. Before she could hit the floor, Cian caught her in strong, wiry arms. There was a thud behind her, and the sound of muffled cries. She twisted in Cian's grip to see Finn on his knees. He clutched at his hair, and his chest heaved with sobs. He was rocking back and forth, mumbling something to himself.

Not her. Not her. Not her. Not her.

She fought her way out of Cian's arms. They tried to stop her, but she had her arms wrapped around Finn before the firedrake could catch hold of her. Cian kneeled on the floor next to them, observing as she gathered Finn into her arms.

"I'm so sorry, baby," she whispered.

Whatever had happened, whatever had gone wrong, she'd pushed him to do this, knowing he was scared. And now he crumpled on the floor, sobbing, and she didn't see the grown man she loved; she saw something of the deeply wounded child that lived within him.

His sobs slowed a little as she held him, rocking him gently back and forth. Cian's hand ran through Finn's hair and then moved to Harlow's face. Their silver eyes were full of tears. "He's not ready for this, Harlow. Outside the Claiming, the Illuminated should not consume others' blood."

Harlow's brow knit. "Why not? I thought they were like vampires... Can't they have blood?"

Cian stood. "That is not something I'm permitted to speak about."

Frustration flared through Harlow, rushing through her veins like a monster that raged inside her. She needed to know these things, and all the Knights' wretched policies about secrets meant she wasn't allowed to know, not yet anyway. Cian cupped her face in one of their cool hands. "He loves you, dear girl. More than anything in the world. Please don't initiate anything like this again."

She didn't understand, but there was no way she'd ask Finn for this again. "I won't."

Cian motioned for her to follow them. She didn't want to leave Finn, who was staring vacantly at himself in the training room mirrors, her blood still on his lips, but Cian clearly expected her to follow. She withdrew carefully, watching Finn wrap his arms around his knees and curl into himself.

Out in the hall, Cian hugged her. When they pulled away, they searched her face. "Are you all right?"

Harlow nodded. Her immortal blood healed her quickly, not as quickly as a vampire or one of the Illuminated perhaps, but she was feeling better already. "What was that? What happened to him?"

Cian shook their head. "I cannot tell you that, Harlow… And please, don't ask Finn to tell you either. There are many things he keeps from you. Not to hurt you, but to protect you. This is one such secret."

Harlow let out another huff of frustration. "Wouldn't it be better for me to *know* the dangers?"

Cian shook their head. "Oh, my dear child. You are so young, and so very naïve."

"That's not fair," Harlow bit out.

"It's just the truth, and for what it's worth, I envy your naivete. There are many things I wish I didn't know about the Illuminated." That much Harlow could easily believe. Cian's face held a dark expression that spoke volumes. "Let Finn tell you when he is ready. The things he knows about his people—his family—they are a burden he doesn't want you to carry."

There was something in Cian's countenance that sent Harlow's heart racing. As they squeezed her arm, she felt the weight of all they *hadn't* said. There were so many things she didn't know about Finn. They'd known one another practically their entire lives, but it wasn't just the years they'd spent apart. There had always been secrets.

She hadn't even known who Cian was until Finn came back into her life, and now couldn't imagine her own life, let alone Finn's, without them. It was suddenly very clear to her that even as children, Finn had only let her see a small portion of who he was and what was happening to him.

"He needs you," Cian said as they disappeared down the hall.

When Harlow re-entered the training room, Finn was standing in front of the weapons rack, fiddling with what looked to be a loose screw. He didn't turn when she approached, though the muscles in his back tensed. She reached towards him, but drew her hand back, not knowing if he'd want to be touched right now.

He caught the motion in the mirror and winced. "You're afraid of me now."

She shook her head. "No, I didn't want to touch you without your permission."

Finn looked down at his hands. "That was unforgivable of me."

Harlow moved to stand next to him, looking up at the helpless expression on his face. She longed to touch him, to brush the hair from his eyes, but she'd meant what she said. She knew what it was like to do something terrible, something that felt simultaneously well within your control, but also desperately beyond it.

"Maybe if this had been your idea, or if you'd just bitten me without my consent. But I pushed you. Am *I* unforgivable?"

A hiss of air rushed through his teeth. "Of course not. You were just trying to figure this out."

Harlow craned her neck, trying to catch his eye. "You were helping… and something went wrong. We pushed things too hard in the wrong direction. You don't have to tell me what that was right now, but I want you to know that when you're ready, I'm here."

"Thank you." His voice was quiet, nearly a whisper. "I need to think this through. I want to tell you these things… It's just…"

"You don't have to tell me anything until you're ready, Finn. We were taught to keep secrets—even in my family—it's how the Orders are. You know it as well as I do. It's going to take time, and we're lucky to have so much of it."

The back of his hand brushed hers, and she pressed her hand into his. "Can I hug you?" he asked, his voice breaking over the words.

Harlow threw herself into his arms, hugging him fiercely, her heart swelling with love. She had no more words in her. A few hot tears slipped down her cheeks as she pressed her face into his chest.

"Are you crying?" he asked. When she didn't answer, he pushed her gently away from him. "You feel guilty for asking me to bite you."

Sometimes it was like he could read her mind. "Yes."

A dark look filled his eyes. "I lost control, Harlow. It wasn't intentional, but I am the one who lost control. You don't need to feel guilty."

Harlow sucked in a shuddering breath. "Maybe neither of us do."

Something new flickered in his eyes, and then a slow smile spread over his face, his eyes crinkling at the corners. "You mean we could just accept that we both fucked up a little and not berate ourselves for days as a result?"

Harlow laughed, pulling him into another hug. "We could try that."

"What will I brood about then?"

"You could try thinking about your poor choices in pizza toppings. That's something to brood about."

"There is *nothing* wrong with pineapple getting hot, Harlow Andromeda Krane," he chided, as he scooped her into his arms. He smiled, but his eyes were still serious as he used his Illuminated speed to whisk them both upstairs.

In their room, he dumped her onto the bed, crawling over her, searching her skin for marks. When he found only a hint of where he'd bitten her, he pressed a soft kiss to her neck. Harlow could feel him worrying.

"Hot pineapple is *disgusting*," she laughed, pulling him down so that his body rested between her legs. Shaken as she still was, she couldn't let either of them dwell on this. Both were prone to overthinking things, and she didn't want to spend the next week tiptoeing around one another. She wrapped her legs around his waist. "I'll forgive you for your poor taste if you finish what you started before we were so rudely interrupted earlier."

Finn paused, as though considering the wisdom of being intimate so soon after feeding on her. He seemed frozen above her, his eyes wide and worried.

"It was an accident, Finn. A mistake. We won't make it again. Make love to me."

He looked down at her as she brushed his hair away from his eyes. When their gazes finally met, his eyes were wet. "Do you think that's safe?"

She nodded. "I trust you. Even if Cian hadn't come in, you would have stopped."

The look on his face told her that nothing she said would convince him, so she pushed him onto his side, rolling over to face him as she laced her legs through his. "We don't have to do anything but be here together," she whispered. "You're safe now, and so am I."

He nodded, his eyes drooping with exhaustion. This was what he needed, to sleep and recuperate. Harlow snuggled closer to him, breathing him in as his arms tightened around her waist. They *were* safe—for now anyway.

CHAPTER 5

Harlow woke with a start to find that she and Finn had slept through dinner, and the entire night. It was dawn and light was leaking into the bedroom, as neither of them had closed the curtains. Quietly, Harlow slipped out of bed and closed all the shades before going to the bathroom and shutting the door. Inside, she looked at her neck in the mirror.

There were no marks where Finn had bitten her yesterday, for which she was grateful, but even she did not heal quite so fast. It was strange, but she didn't let her mind linger long on it. She showered quickly and threw on another sundress that Enzo had tailored for her earlier in the summer. It was a beautiful shade of dark blue-green, and the halter neck was flattering and comfortable. A pair of sandals and she was ready for her day.

In the bedroom, Finn was still sleeping soundly, though he murmured something when she pulled her phone from under his arm. "What was that?"

"You okay today?" he mumbled into the pillow.

Harlow stroked his hair, planting a kiss on his forehead. "I'm fine. Don't get up—it's early."

"Love you," he said into the pillow.

She didn't respond, waiting for his breathing to even out. When she was sure he was back asleep, she left the bedroom. He was usually a very light sleeper, and she was positive he needed rest right now. She found Axel sleeping against their bedroom door and scooped him up.

"So sorry, sweet boy," she said, pressing a kiss into his fur as she walked downstairs.

Petra was just coming in the front door, heels in her hand. Harlow raised her eyebrows at her and Petra just shook her head, hurrying toward the stairs. "Talk to me at noon. It's been a night."

Harlow shrugged, watching her friend blush and cover a mark on her neck.

So it had been *that* kind of night. She chuckled softly as she padded down the marble halls to the kitchen. Axel jumped from her arms and trotted to the terrace door in the kitchen, meowing loudly.

Cian was making espresso. "I'll bring you a latte on the terrace. I have a bag of pastries from Moretti's that I'm willing to share with just you."

"Deal," Harlow said, opening the terrace door for Axel. The human bakery was divine, only open a few random days each week, but the pastries were better than anywhere else in Nea Sterlis.

She followed the cat outside. The terrace was cool and shaded at this time of day. Birds sang and the smell of the sea below mixed with the faint scent of lemons and sun-warmed cypress, making a fragrance unique to Nea Sterlis. The view of the deep green sea from this vantage point was enough to make anyone get emotional.

Harlow folded herself into a big rattan chair and looked around for Axel, who was bumping noses with an enormous auburn cat. *Where did that creature come from?* She jumped up quickly, ready to pull Axel back if the cat were to attack him. But it did nothing of the sort. It blinked at Harlow, its topaz eyes gleaming in the sunlight. And Axel rubbed his head against the gigantic beast's chin.

Harlow had seen nothing like it. The cat had long hair and a fluffy tail, and beautiful lynx tips on its ears. It was so large, it practically looked like a wild animal. It licked Axel's head a few times and then flopped down in the sunshine. Axel joined it, as Harlow stood watching, shaking her head.

Cian interrupted her by handing her a giant latte mug. "Who is that terrific creature?"

"Do you think it's a shifter?" Harlow asked, suddenly anxious. Was this how they were being watched? Could this somehow be the mysterious probe in the wards?

Cian laughed, stepping forward to set their own coffee down on the table between the chairs, along with the bag of pastries they had tucked under their arm. "No, it definitely isn't a shifter. It's just a cat. A huge cat, but gods all bless, what a specimen. Axel seems to like him, and he looks clean and healthy."

"Should I just let them hang out? How did it get up here?"

Cian shrugged. "Who knows with cats? They're having a nice time; why ruin it? Everyone needs friends."

Harlow laughed, feeling silly as she sat down. "I actually thought it might be what was testing the wards."

Cian shrugged. "Valid suspicion, but I don't think that's it. Sometimes a cat is just a cat, Harlow." They picked out a scone and then handed the bag to her. "How are you feeling today?"

Harlow selected a bacon and cheese croissant, then set the bag on the table. "I'm fine. The wound is completely healed."

"Yes, I suppose it would be. Their bites are different somehow—I've never been able to figure it out. I'm glad you've recovered well." Cian was quiet for a few moments, staring out at the slow waves rolling into their little bay. "Are you all right emotionally?"

Harlow drew in a deep breath and held it briefly, knowing her agitation likely showed on her face. "Yes, but it's going to take some effort to not push Finn to explain what happened."

The firedrake shifted in their chair to better look at her. "We immortals keep too many secrets. There can be no doubt about that. Have you considered that it takes time to build the kind of relationship that can withstand the revelations you're asking for?"

A part of her wanted to argue that Finn had always been able to trust her, that she wasn't the one who'd broken their trust to begin with. But that wasn't quite true, and she knew it. "It's just so frustrating that he has secrets from me."

Cian's head tilted slightly. "It's true; his life, his line of work, they all bank heavily on secrets. But these aren't just secrets, Harlow. This situation is wrapped up in Finn's past, in his childhood, and that is a much more complicated thing to navigate."

Harlow looked down at her croissant for a moment, tracing the striations in the pastry with her eyes. She remembered how Finn had acted the night of the Statuary party in Nuva Troi, when he'd driven her and Larkin home. The way he'd been in awe of her family's cozy home life stuck with her. "It's probably hard to tell me things about his childhood, isn't it?"

A slim hand took hers. Cian's eyes were sad. "Yes, dear one. The two of you grew up very differently."

"But you were there when he was a child, weren't you?" Harlow asked, wanting to shift the subject slightly. She knew Cian wouldn't reveal any of Finn's secrets, but that didn't mean they couldn't help her know him better.

Cian grinned. "Yes, Finn and I were together a lot when he was a child."

"Why?" It was always fine to be blunt with Cian. They never seemed to mind, and she found it comforting to speak with them, never having to play all the games or go through all the social machinations it took to socialize with most people.

"It's complicated. Long ago, the Illuminated, especially the McKays, operated much more like the human mafia than they do now. And I was someone who could always find things."

Harlow sipped her coffee. It was perfect, as always. "What kinds of things?"

Cian's mercurial face revealed nothing but mischief. "All kinds. That is of little importance." Harlow doubted that very much, but knew if Cian wanted to tell the story, it would be told. "But I worked for Connor for many years in an affiliated capacity. When Aislin was pregnant with Finbar, she had some trouble with the pregnancy, like many of the Illuminated now, but hers was one of the first in the pattern of their trouble to conceive."

Harlow leaned forward. This was interesting. "What kind of trouble?"

Cian frowned, their brows knitting together. "I was never let completely in, but there was some concern that the pregnancy wouldn't be viable for much longer, and so they hired a hedgewitch."

Harlow nearly gasped in shock. Hedgewitches were human practitioners of magic and were extremely rare, working primarily with earth magics and complex spells that drew aether out. They were often employed as midwives.

"The McKays wanted ingredients for a spell that were difficult to find. So they hired me and I found them."

"What were they?" Harlow was desperate to know. The ingredients might give some clue as to what the issue was, and might give them valuable information on what was stopping the Illuminated from being able to conceive—and why they were so interested in Harlow and Finn having a child together.

Cian shook their head. "They were clever about it. Most of the ingredients were decoys. Connor McKay is always three steps ahead. I could never parse out which they actually used in the spell, but it worked and Finbar was born safely. I brought him a gift on his naming day, and I'd never engaged with a child thus."

Cian's eyes lit up. Harlow kicked the shifter to get their attention. "You're positively dreamy looking. What does that mean?"

Cian smiled, open and genuine. "I never had an opportunity to have children of my own, and I never thought I wanted them. But Finbar was different somehow. Connor and Aislinn asked me to be his godsparent, and I couldn't refuse. I took one look at him and knew that someone had to be in his life who could provide *more* than the two of them."

It all made sense now. Finn had often spoken of his "godsfather" when they were younger. He had been masking Cian's identity even then, protecting them. Harlow didn't bother to ask about that. Whatever it was, there was no way Cian would tell if it were as wrapped up in these family secrets as it seemed to be.

"So you were always there in the background, being his proper family."

Cian nodded, that smile returning to their face. "Raising Finn was a pleasure. And before you ask, he has always loved you, Harlow. From the day the two of you met when you were ten."

Tears sprang to Harlow's eyes. Finn didn't talk about that time much, or what he remembered from their actual childhood, and she stayed away from reminiscing too much, since it seemed to pain him.

"The day he met you and Enzo, he came to my home and we spent hours talking about you both. But mostly you. He's always believed you see the best in him, much as I do."

Harlow took Cian's hand and squeezed. "I love you, you know that?"

Cian looked down at their hands, a faint blush coloring their cheeks. "I love you too, Harlow. I always have, for caring for my boy the way you do. Even when Finn could not be in your life, I did everything I could to make you safe."

Harlow's heart beat faster. "What do you mean?"

A single tear slipped down Cian's cheek. "The night you tried to take your life." They choked on their words, unable to meet her eyes.

Harlow had never known who helped her, but now it was so clear. "You're the one who took me to the hospital. You found me."

Cian nodded, finally looking at her. "I should have been there sooner. I made a mistake, Harlow, and I made more letting things get so bad with Mark Easton. There are so many things I could have done to help you, and I was a coward..."

Harlow shook her head. "You saved me, Cian. You don't even know how much."

Cian's silver eyes filled with tears. "How?"

"I held it in my heart for years that someone cared enough to take me to the hospital. I used the fact that someone thought I was worth saving as armor against trying again more times than I could count back then."

Cian kissed her knuckles. "I wish we could have been friends sooner."

"Me too," Harlow whispered, feeling like Cian had returned a missing part of her heart.

The firedrake squeezed her hand one more time and then changed the subject. "I looked into the Ledge of Wishes last night."

Harlow frowned. "Why?"

Cian shook their head as both Axel and the mysterious red cat rolled into a sunnier spot on the terrace simultaneously. "Before you mentioned it yesterday, I'd never heard of it. Is it a secret with the Order of Mysteries?"

Harlow frowned. "Not that I know of. It's a strange bit of lore though, don't you think? Why would a 'warden' of any kind grant wishes?"

Some of the puffy clouds that were marching across the azure sky shaded the sun, and Cian's face relaxed. "I should have brought sunglasses. Even with the clouds, the sun is hurting my eyes."

Harlow handed them hers, which they put on. Somehow Cian made her giant sunnies look even more fabulous. She tried not to be jealous. This was the way it was with anything Cian touched; it became instantly cool. They leaned back in their chair, stretching their long legs out in front of them. "What's stranger is that there's no record of the Ledge of Wishes or Ashbourne the Warden in the Vault's records."

That *was* odd. "None?"

Cian shook their head. "None."

"What do you think it means?"

Cian sighed. "What do *you* think it means?"

Harlow rolled her eyes, but the grim line of Cian's mouth told her everything she needed to know. "This is another of the Illuminated's secrets?"

Cian shrugged. "I don't know, but we have records of some truly inconsequential lore in the Vault. Why wouldn't we have anything on this?"

"Because the Knights are Illuminated as well, I suppose. But what's the connection between the Illuminated and an aethereal being who supposedly grants wishes and lives under the Order of Mysteries?"

The sigh Cian let out was as exasperated as it was long. "If I knew that, this wouldn't be so intriguing."

"The Sistren of Akatei Library might have something on it," Harlow mused. "If anyone would, they would."

"And you're currently the only one of us with a reader card," Cian replied.

"So, I guess I know what I'm up to today." Harlow stood up, brushing crumbs from the skirt of her dress. "Tell Finn where I went when he gets up."

"Tell me yourself," Finn said from the doorway. He had mussed hair, and wore the same clothes they'd fallen asleep in the night before.

"I'm headed to the Citadel," she said, brushing a kiss to his lips.

"What for?" Finn asked, pulling her in for a hug. Her heart thumped harder when his fingers grazed the bare skin on her back. She drew away from him, not wanting to be distracted.

"I want to look up the lore about the Ledge of Wishes. The library at Akatei's temple should have texts on it, but the Vault has nothing."

Finn's lips met her hair, then her cheeks, then so softly on her mouth, it nearly brought tears to her eyes. "Okay," he said, his lips moving against her own. "Take my car. It's going to be too hot this afternoon for you to walk."

The Woody was too big to drive around Nea Sterlis—the streets were too narrow, and it made her constantly nervous she was about to hit someone—so it had stayed in the garage all summer. Harlow hated to drive Finn's little vintage sports car. It was gorgeous, irreplaceable, and hard to drive, but he'd insist on taking her if she didn't agree to drive herself. And the last thing she wanted him to do right now was offer to come with her. She'd get nothing done with him in the library.

Even now, his fingers toyed with the zipper of her dress, as though he'd like to yank it down, right in front of Cian. The thought heated her through. She rose before her arousal could mount further.

"Fine," she said, her tone clipped. "I'll take your car."

Finn smirked that arrogant smirk she loved to hate. He knew exactly how wet she was, how much she wanted to take this upstairs, how feverish it made her just thinking of it.

"I'll take it *now*," she emphasized.

"Keys are in the garage," he said with a smile. He plopped down next to Cian, searching for a pastry, and taking a sip of her discarded coffee.

Harlow sighed, wishing she'd thought to bring the coffee with her as he downed the last of it. "This could take a while. I'll have to miss lunch, all right?"

Finn had plans with Kate to surf and go out for a late lunch, and though they'd invited her to come along, she'd found in the past few weeks that it was less comfortable to hang out together than she'd originally hoped it would be.

Finn glanced up, his gaze revealing his worry. "We'll miss you."

"You'll have more fun without me," she said without conviction. She didn't really believe it, even as the words came out, but some plague of insecurity was hounding her lately.

"Not even possible," he replied as she entered the villa. "Want me to bring you something from the restaurant? It's the place with the salad you like, the one with the little flowers in it."

"Sure," she said, though she didn't really want a salad. It was disconcerting how sometimes it felt like he could read her mind, and at others he didn't seem to know her at all. She'd mentioned thinking the salads at the beach cafe were cute with their little edible flower garnishes one time.

Cian must have caught the face she was making, because they rose and placed her sunnies back on her face. "See you when you get back, love."

Harlow pushed the glasses back on her head and then headed to the garage, listening to Cian and Finn's voices echo throughout the villa as she went.

CHAPTER 6

The old sports car made it up the narrow, winding cobbled streets to the Temple District in the Citadel without giving her much anxiety, and at this time of day there was no traffic. Everyone was soaking up the last days of summer sunshine, not spending time in the Alabaster Citadel's dusty libraries. While Harlow preferred fall to summer, there was always a wistfulness that came over her when seasons changed. Yet this year it felt deeper, rooted in an ache in her chest that refused to dissipate.

Maybe it was the fact that this year was different. After so many months of estrangement with her family, being together here in Nea Sterlis with everyone she loved had been a true balm for her heart. But everyone was already talking about going back to Nuva Troi, and what they planned to do this autumn, though Finn and Harlow hadn't made plans yet.

They had found nothing significant in the Vault to help them discover the Illuminated's motives for manipulating their relationship, though Harlow was invested in learning the history of the Knight of Serpens, regardless. Their role in the War of the Orders had been fascinating. Instead of insisting upon leading, which they might have done with their military superiority, they'd let humans and the lower Orders guide them. Finn held the same value for the Knights now, and he spent a lot of time talking with leaders in the human community about their needs, as well as those in the lower Orders.

The scent of the sun-warmed lemons growing on cedar arbors floated out towards her as she pulled into the Sistren of Akatei Library parking lot. Harlow found a spot easily and sat in the car for an extra moment, looking out at the view of the sea, and Nea Sterlis spread out in tiers below her. The library was at the apex of the Alabaster Citadel, and even the parking lot had views to die for.

Sailboats dotted the rocky coastline and she could see how busy the many terraces and beaches were in the city below. They'd empty in the next few weeks, as everyone traveled back to the city, but for now, Nea Sterlis was bursting at the seams with people and paparazzi. Summer in Nea Sterlis was remarkably similar to the season in Nuva Troi, and Harlow didn't care a whit about any of it. Not the film festival that was in full swing when they'd first arrived, not the wine tastings at the vineyards just outside of town, or the gallery openings. None of it seemed relevant to her—it was all just a beautiful distraction.

The more she learned about the truth of the Immortal Orders, the things the Illuminated had worked so hard to hide, the more uneasy she'd become about the sheltered life she'd led. As she got out of the car to gather her things, she thought she felt eyes on her back, but when she turned, the parking lot was empty. Unease filled her, but she didn't feel she could trust herself.

Harlow had bordered on paranoia since Mark's influence on her in Nuva Troi last spring. She'd missed so many clues that something was going wrong, and now she was jumpy every time she felt even the slightest bit watched. The fact that no one was in sight didn't relieve her a bit. There was still a pressure on her that only her second sight could sense.

Most of the time, it turned out to be paparazzi, just waiting to sell photos of her to the gossips, but now she wasn't sure, so she quickened her pace as she walked through the parking lot. As soon as she passed the library's front gate, relief washed over her in a cool wave. The wards on the library itself didn't allow anyone without a reader's card to enter, and the libraries in the Temple District were strict about vetting their readers. Paparazzi rarely breached the Citadel buildings.

The atrium of the library was made from the same alabaster blocks as the rest of the Citadel buildings, with high arched doorways that led into different wings of the library. One of the Ultima—the Order of Mysteries' warrior class —staffed a heavy wood desk at the center of the atrium. These days, the Ultima were little more than security guards, but during the War of the Orders, they'd been a powerful military force. Harlow showed her reader's card to the fierce sorcière at the desk. She was a tall woman, with dark umber skin, and hair shorn close to her head as all the Alabaster Citadel's guardians had. The hairstyle was an ancient tradition the Ultima still adhered to, and it made them look all the more severe. She wore a simple, close fitting uniform made from flexible material, and a pair of heavy combat boots.

The hammered metal bracelets stacked on each of the warrior's arms showed her rank—she was young like Harlow and didn't have many yet. Harlow thought she noticed a flicker of recognition when she glanced at Harlow's ID, but the stern-faced Ultima said nothing, only nodded as she handed the card back.

I really am getting paranoid, Harlow thought to herself as she settled into one of the carrels, which housed a catalogue computer, and began searching. *Imagine thinking one of the Ultima would have any interest in me.*

There was that strange, discordant, insecure voice in her head again. Enzo and Riley both thought there might be a kind of psychic residue from Mark's influence that dug deep in places her ex had been cultivating for years. The result, Riley presumed, was a trauma response combined with a nasty bit of magic that made it extra hard to shake. She shook her head and turned her attention back to her search for texts about the Ledge.

When she'd come up with four titles that might have information on the Ledge and the catacombs under the Order of Mysteries' headquarters, she filled out an electronic request form and sent it in, writing her ticket number on a pad of paper left in the carrel for that purpose. Then she headed to the reading room, passing the stern Ultima on her way.

Not even a glance to spare for me, she thought, laughing to herself as she found a seat near the retrieval desk and settled in to wait. *I really am being paranoid.*

Her phone didn't work here. There was poor service all over the library, so she was forced to look around while she waited for her books to arrive. It was no hardship, as the library was a stunning piece of classical architecture. At the opposite end of the reading room, an enormous statue of Akatei, in her three aspects, stood watch. Sunlight filtered in through the glass dome overhead, casting beams of light into the stacks of books that seemed to go on forever.

Four floors of stacks rose above her, librarians flitting back and forth amongst the books and great limestone columns, their feet moving quietly over the stone floors. The only sounds were that of laptop keys clicking, and pages softly turning. Every now and again, a soft cough or sniffle broke the rhythmic sounds of the library.

Harlow took a deep breath in, reveling in the comforting smell of leather-bound books and old paper. Calm settled over her. She was often restless when she was at the villa with her family and Finn, but here everything was well-ordered, and *so* blessedly quiet. Part of her felt guilty for feeling this way. It had taken her a bit to recognize how overstimulating it was to be with everyone nonstop, but quiet moments like these reminded her she *needed* alone time to recharge and think, especially after what had happened with Finn.

Harlow really was all right, but she couldn't deceive herself—the experience had shaken her. Not because Finn seemed to have lost control. She'd meant what she'd said about believing he would have stopped on his own if Cian had not appeared. What had shaken her the most was how different his bite had felt from the night in the House of Remiel basement. It seemed possible that the real problem was that they had started "cold." The night she'd shifted, she'd been scared, all her senses elevated—and he had been too. Those conditions would be difficult to reproduce in a controlled setting, and she wasn't even sure she wanted to.

A soft clacking noise alerted her that the number at the retrieval desk was changing. She glanced down at her piece of paper to double check, but it wasn't her number. Her mind drifted back over the past day, trying to figure out why things felt so different now, so urgent. Harlow knew she was spiraling, trying to pinpoint something that simply needed time to develop. To distract herself from her thoughts, she looked around the reading room. There were several sorcière scattered about, none of whom she knew, a smattering of shifters, and one vampire, who looked as though they were reading something salacious. There were no Illuminated here today.

Not that there had been since she started coming here each week, trying to find more information on the Striders and the Feriant. She was careful about what books she called up, but she *had* to know why she couldn't turn. Thus far, her research had yielded nothing, nor had she been able to find anything of use about the Knights, or anything she didn't already know about the War of the Orders.

It had been dead end after dead end. Aurelia had come with her a few times, watched her process, and called up a few books of her own. But her determination had been that Harlow had the research process more than well enough in hand, and Harlow thought she was secretly enjoying a summer off.

"You have a knack for this, my darling," Mother had said, before excusing herself to meet Selene for a sailboat ride.

It sure didn't feel like she had a knack for this kind of work anymore. So far, she'd read an absurd amount of Okairon lore, but not much of any use. The Orders loved their stories—stories about gods and the heroes of the Golden Age, the time when the Orders first came into their power—and though these were interesting enough, it had become clear to Harlow just how much the Illuminated controlled the way even Order-specific lore was told.

The number at the retrieval desk turned over again, and this time it was Harlow's. She got up to collect the pile of books a librarian had placed in the tray that corresponded with Harlow's number. The witch must have been near a thousand, as her hair had silvered, and she had fine lines etched onto her face.

Harlow took her books and made her way into a brightly lit part of the reading room, near Akatei's foot. She sat down at one of the long bleached oak tables, taking a notebook out of her leather messenger bag. Writing utensils were not allowed near the books, but she could pull threads of aether to take notes. It was an energetic drain, but preserving the books was the most important thing, and Harlow hated to haul the expensive tablet Finn had bought her, with its sleek stylus, to the library.

It had cost nearly three times anything she might have afforded on her own, and was a gorgeous piece of tech, but it made her feel self-conscious. Harlow was fine taking notes the old-fashioned way, with magic, in a paper notebook. She knew it hurt Finn's feelings that she wouldn't take it with her, but it was just so *fancy*. The same company had come out with an intimidating new phone this year that was all the rage. Harlow wasn't that interested in technology, so none of it mattered to her.

The first three books had nothing of interest about the Ledge of Wishes or the Warden. Two focused on the geological aspects of the Ledge, and the third had the same variations of the stories every sorcière heard as a child about people wishing for ridiculous things and then having to make more wishes to fix their terrible first wishes... They were more cautionary tales than anything else.

The fourth volume was slender, with an unremarkable black cover, titled *The Warden*. No author, no description. Harlow glanced back over her request form, which was lying on the table. She most definitely had not called this volume up, but sometimes librarians added related books to retrievals that they found relevant, and certainly the title implied that it was related to Ledge lore.

She placed *The Warden* on the cradle, opened it carefully and examined the book. Though the book was printed by fairly modern means, there were none of the required origin markings that all presses were mandated to emboss on every book, nor was there a copyregister page at the front to show that the book had been approved by the Council for Published Works. This was shocking. The book was likely very rare, and technically, the Sistren of Akatei Library was not allowed to lend out such books without direct supervision and approval of the CPW.

Harlow's heart beat slightly faster. There was no way a librarian would breach the rules in such direct conflict with the CPW, which was a powerful organization. The Illuminated knew just exactly how dangerous knowledge and ideas were, and the CPW was one of the most feared of their government organizations. She took a few slow inhalations to calm her breathing, schooling her face into a bland expression. There was no need to draw attention to herself. She took great care as she read, knowing this might be the only copy of the book in existence. The first few pages outlined a war amongst a race of people the author called the "Ventyr," which Harlow knew loosely translated to "wind."

According to the author, the Ventyr were the first people in the cosmos, and were so powerful they would seem like gods to Okairons—*perhaps* even to the Illuminated. At that, Harlow raised an eyebrow. It was as close to treasonous as an author could get away with, without their work being destroyed. Harlow skimmed for a while. The account was interesting enough, even if it was far-fetched. According to the book's unnamed author, the Ventyr were a clannish people and fought many wars in their own realms, which numbered four, originally.

From what Harlow could tell, the author meant different planets, but the book was quite old. There wasn't much else in the text, as far as she could tell, that related to the Ledge of Wishes at all. Perhaps it had been shelved incorrectly and the librarian who'd fetched her books simply included it for the title's relationship to the rest of her books. She was about to close the book and go home when a chapter name toward the end of the book caught her eye: "Ashbourne and the Sixteen." She skipped right to it and began reading.

The two greatest houses of the Ventyr were at war with one another for many a year until both were beleaguered by a heretofore unknown host of incorporeal foes. Though no one could determine what they looked like, all knew quickly after their arrival what they might accomplish. Their presence elevated emotion of all kinds, distracting all they influenced from everyday concerns and matters of state.

When the Ventyr mages determined the scope of the mysterious beings' influence, a truce was struck between House Thuellos and House Anemoi. Despite their ancient grudge, they shared a common enemy, one that neither could defeat alone, as the creatures' presence had an unintended side effect: they drained aether from the land, consuming it at unprecedented rates. While all beings utilize aether to live, essentially consuming it, they also produce it, giving rise to more life. For some reason, the Ravagers, as they were named, did not.

As I am sure you are aware, aethereal energy replenishes itself in all cycles of life, death and destruction, which is why, above all else, a balance must be struck. The Ravagers grew in power for many years, as the Ventyr fought on. When they grew strong enough to leave the Ventyr's realm, the Winged Ones had to admit to themselves that the creatures were an imminent threat to all worlds, as they seemed driven to remake life in their image: creatures that consumed aether, but did not feed the limen in return. This is likely the only reason House Anemos and House Thuellos made the most temporary of alliances.

Winged Ones? Harlow thought of Finn's true form. A sinking feeling came over her. She pretended to look for something in her bag, but glanced around the room. No one was looking her way. She turned back to the beginning of the book to see if there was a detailed description of the Ventyr. Though she couldn't find one, something about the narrative troubled her.

Logic intervened. There was a lot of Okairon folklore about winged creatures—large birdlike creatures with humanoid heads and various humanoids with enormous bird wings were some of the most popular, but they were nothing more than fantasy stories.

Still, *The Warden* wasn't framed as an analysis of folklore, or a collection of fictional tales. It appeared to be a historical account. However, in the century before, there had been a rash of pseudo-historical novels published by underground presses. Aurelia had a small collection of these types of tales, and had always said that their value was in disseminating actual knowledge about the cosmos that the Illuminated suppressed, so it was possible that *The Warden* was such a text. If so, it was not supposed to be here, and she should not have access to it.

As casually as possible, Harlow glanced around. She couldn't help but wonder if the book's inclusion was some kind of trap? But no one was paying even the slightest bit of attention to her. These episodes of paranoia had been happening a lot when she was out by herself lately, and she was determined not to let them get the best of her. *The Warden* was an odd book, to be sure, but to believe its inclusion was anything other than one of the librarians helping her with what was clearly her area of research was ludicrous. She turned back to the book and kept reading.

The two houses' scholars and mages devised a plan to imprison the Ravagers in the only place with enough raw aether to create a container that might hold them: Nihil, the center of the limen. As you know, of course, Nihil is not technically the center of anything in the limen, as it is a realm without shape, without true form. But Nihil is the birthplace of aether, and therefore the most logical place to imprison indestructible beings. It is also obviously the most dangerous, since the creatures were capable of consuming aethereal power at such a destructive rate. But the alliance saw no other way.

The first problem was wrangling the creatures into Nihil, and the second was keeping them there. For once the doors to Nihil closed, it would be dangerous to open them again, lest the creatures escape. The mages determined that at least a dozen immortals would be needed to control the spell that would keep the creatures contained. But neither House would volunteer their own to spend eternity with the creatures.

That tracked with what Harlow knew about the limen. Though no sorcière had ever *been* to the world between worlds, where all aethereal power originated, there was plenty of theoretical work on the matter. Most scholars of metaphysics agreed that the limen was an actual place, and that it likely touched all inhabited worlds, as aether was integral for life to exist on a planet. Realms without aether could not sustain any life, and certainly had no access to magic.

Harlow made a note to look up more about the kind of spellwork that would be needed for such a feat later. Perhaps a vascularity of some kind? Vascularities were most often used in industrial applications these days, but she guessed one might connect the guardians to form a network of extra strong wards. If anything, it was a fascinating idea; perhaps the book itself said more. She read on.

During the alliance between Thuellos and Anemos, fraternization amongst the houses was forbidden, which was to make it easier to resume the war once they had dealt with the Ravagers. The two noble houses agreed to work together to avoid the destruction of the known realms, but anything more was as forbidden to them as intermingling with humans too closely would be for us. Despite this, Ashbourne of House Thuellos fell irrevocably in love with Lumina of House Anemos, and she with him.

Harlow flipped the page, and found that it had been torn. Bits of the story remained; from what she could discern, the Ventyr had found a way to temporarily subdue the Ravagers but in doing so Lumina and Ashbourne were somehow discovered, and her family imprisoned her at their estate.

Together, he and his sixteen generals led seventeen legions of House Thuellos on a campaign to regain his love and her freedom, but his father, Notus, had not approved the campaign. When Ashbourne's legions attacked, they slaughtered many of House Anemos, but failed to reclaim Lumina. Had they done so, Notus might have let them go unpunished, for the Ventyr loved nothing more than a fight well-won, with the reward of a good woman at the end.

For his son's unforgivable failure, Notus appointed Ashbourne as Warden to the newly constructed prison for the Ravagers, deep within the limen, along with the companions who helped him. Of course, House Anemos wanted retribution as well, so this served their purposes nicely, as each House had agreed to appoint half of the guardians needed to maintain the Nihil prison for eternity. Being that it would take exceptional warriors to accomplish such a feat, each house had been reluctant to elect their best and brightest to the position. Ashbourne and his generals made this choice easy for everyone.

But House Thuellos wanted reassurances that their connection to House Anemos was well and truly severed. Their greatest fear was that Lumina might escape her family's imprisonment and tempt Ashbourne to find a way out of Nihil. Their first petition asked that Lumina be immediately executed, but House Anemos summarily refused.

It seemed, for a time, that the two Houses had come to a stalemate. Soon though, Notus devised a devious plan to end this diplomatic conflict so that the great Houses might return to the nobler enterprise of eternal war. As Lumina valued her freedom so highly, second only to her love for Ashbourne, Notus suggested she be exiled to the realm of Sirin—a dark world, populated by creatures so ingenious that the Ventyr could not conquer them. And so Lumina and Ashbourne were separated for all time.

And there the story ended, though Harlow eagerly flipped the page, hoping that perhaps there might be a happier ending for all concerned. The next page was the start of another story about the conflicts between the two Houses, not the continuation of Lumina and Ashbourne's story. Someone had removed about thirty pages from the book with a sharp instrument.

Harlow sighed. It was like this with many books that revealed too much information, or used a defamatory tone about the Illuminated. Sections would be missing or redacted. As this might be the only copy of *The Warden* in existence, there was little chance she'd find out the whole story, if someone had already removed it. She wondered why that particular bit had been removed, but the rest was allowed to stay. What did the end of the story reveal? And why had this book found its way into her possession?

Nearby, someone dropped their tablet, swearing softly, and the noise startled Harlow. She turned her attention back to *The Warden*, returning to the beginning of the chapter to read the preface to the tale several more times, taking notes. The mention of relations between humans and what Harlow assumed to be immortals gave her an idea of when the book had been written. Until just a few centuries ago, it was forbidden for immortals to fraternize in any way considered intimate with humans, whether that be friendship or more.

She wasn't sure how the story might help her at this point. It was more of a tragic love story than an explanation of how the Ledge of Wishes came to be, or what Ashbourne's connection to it was. What she *was* certain of was that Ashbourne was one and the same with the character who granted wishes in Okairon lore, but why had anyone come to that conclusion, if this was the truth of his story?

Perhaps the early part of the story had been left in to allow scholars to make sense of the legend. She skimmed the rest of the book quickly. There was no mention of the Ledge of Wishes itself or what was beneath it, but this was a solid lead. Harlow gathered her things. She wanted to use their secure server in the Vault to look a few terms up before examining *The Warden* more closely, and she wanted to show the story itself to Finn and Cian.

Harlow made her way to the small chamber right off the reading room, which housed a copy machine that had to be thirty years old. The machine had a hand scanner that would be perfect for preserving the delicate book, though, and she could quickly make a hard copy of the chapter on Lumina and Ashbourne. She nearly groaned when she entered the chamber; a gigantic sign reading "Out of Order" was stuck to the copy machine. She would have to come back another day.

Harlow had two options: return the book and try requesting it again at another time, or ask the librarian at the retrieval desk to hold it for her until the copy machine was fixed. She eyed her little stack of books and tucked *The Warden* in the middle of the rest.

At the retrieval desk, she filled out a hold form, indicating that she wanted to hold the books from being re-shelved or lent out to readers until the copy machine was fixed.

The witch at the retrieval desk smiled at her, read her request and whispered,

"We should have the machine fixed in three to four business days. At least that's what the repair shop said."

Harlow smiled back at the librarian. "I'm in no rush."

"We'll email you when it's fixed, dear."

"Thank you," Harlow whispered back, and then made her way out of the library.

CHAPTER 7

The early evening air was cool and damp on her skin, a sure sign that autumn was coming. It would bring rainstorms to this area for a few months, while Nuva Troi would enjoy the golden light of autumn. The phenomenon was called "reversal of the rains," and it signaled the end to summer's vibrant social season in Nea Sterlis and the return of Aphelion University's students, which inevitably changed the entire feel of the town, though Harlow had never visited during fall or winter. Harlow glanced upwards. Aphelion was located in the Alabaster Citadel, and there was a view of its high walls, covered in climbing roses, from the library's courtyard.

Finn had fled here after secondary school, to Nea Sterlis and Aphelion, rarely coming home to Nuva Troi for years. It had occurred to her more than once this summer that he rarely spoke of his university days, but that he'd lived here for seven years. She didn't even know where he'd lived during that time. *Had he lived on campus, or did he stay at the villa with Cian?* She shook her questions off as best she could. Cian was right; they had plenty of time to discuss these things. It wasn't necessary that she know everything at once.

Harlow wound through the courtyard of the library, amongst gigantic palm fronds and fragrant blooms, enjoying the last smells of summer. While she was missing Nuva Troi, she was happy enough not to be there this time of year. Summer here had been glorious, and until this month, the heat had been mild. The crunch of footsteps on gravel caused her to turn, but when she did, the courtyard was empty—save for the fountain, a rendition of Akatei weaving the first threads of aether.

Harlow looked at it closely for the first time since she'd arrived in Nea Sterlis. The pose was familiar to her. It was a common enough way to depict Akatei, but there was something different about this one. Typically, the "First Weaving" imagery featured Akatei drawing sigils in front of her body, but this statue was different—the goddess' arms stretched out in front of her, reaching upwards. Something about the difference caught Harlow's attention, though she'd walked by the fountain dozens of times this summer.

There was something written on the palms of Akatei's hands. Harlow leaned so far over she nearly fell in the fountain. There was no way to read the words without actually getting in. A librarian passed by just then, likely the source of the footsteps. They smiled placidly at Harlow as they went, their eyebrows knitting slightly as they observed the close attention she was paying the fountain.

Harlow smiled at the librarian. "My parents were affianced here. I've always wanted to see it."

The wrinkles in the librarian's brow smoothed. "How lovely." They moved on without another glance back. There was no way to examine the statue more closely right now, curious as it was. Perhaps she could look again when she came back to copy *The Warden.*

When she finally made her way to the parking lot, Finn was waiting by the car, leaning against it as the light of the setting sun set his skin aglow. He was looking at his phone, but the way the muscles in his forearms clenched as she approached told her he knew she was coming. He'd probably smelled her as soon as she'd left the library. Damn Illuminated and their weird sense of smell.

"Thought you were getting me a salad," she said as she approached.

He looked up, nodding toward the takeaway bag in the back. His smile was sheepish. "Got you gyros instead. Kate said they're your favorite."

Harlow's breath caught. It put her off-kilter, the way Kate remembered so much about her. She desperately wanted to be the kind of person who was completely cool with this, but she was struggling with Kate and Finn's friendship more than she'd expected to.

At first it had seemed so wonderful that they were already friendly with one another and that Finn wasn't the least bit jealous, but after spending a handful of coffee dates and brunches together when they'd first arrived in town, Harlow found that the two of them were better friends than she'd expected and she mostly felt left out—and a little resentful about it. She didn't particularly like this, but wasn't sure how to make the feeling go away.

Finn pushed off the hood of his car. The motion was casual, full of ease, but Harlow saw the intensity burning in his eyes. He'd noticed her reaction. "What is it?"

Harlow had to suppress the urge to cringe, reminding herself that even though he'd been upset about the incident in the Vault, he wasn't upset with her... And that even if he had been upset with her, Finn would not act the way Mark had when he was angry with her. This was the hardest holdover from their relationship to break.

All Harlow wanted right now was those gyros and to feel just slightly normal again. She took a deep breath, tossing her bag into the car. "Nothing. I'm just edgy today. It's about time for my bleed and I'm getting hormonal."

His nostrils flared, and she rolled her eyes. She slapped his arm, though her breath caught as a flush of damp heat spread into her core. "Stop smelling me, you creeper!" The looming feeling that something was still wrong between them cleared; the constriction in her chest loosening as she watched him visibly relax back into their usual dynamic.

Finn's left eyebrow raised. He laughed as he brushed a kiss to her forehead, then buried his face in the crook of her neck, his breath hot against her skin as his tongue grazed the shell of her ear as he laughed. "But you smell *delicious*."

That laugh combined vulnerability and longing, and the mixture shot right to Harlow's heart. All her worries melted into the core of her, now aching with need. Desire licked over her, spreading like wildfire. With Finn, it was easy to go from burdened with worries to *this*.

As though feeding off her arousal, his arms were around her waist before she could say a word, turning her, pushing her toward the car, grazing her hips and belly as he went, as though he couldn't quite help himself. She gasped, leaning into him. Some modicum of propriety and sense kept her from bending over the hood of the car and lifting the skirt of her dress, though the thought thrilled her.

What if he fucked her right here, in the parking lot of the library?

Finn helped her into the car, murmuring, "Let's get out of here. *Now*."

His voice rumbled with the same ravenous passion that roared through her as he closed her door behind her and hopped into the driver's seat. He started the little sports car and was out of the parking lot in a flash. The cobblestone streets of the Citadel were blessedly empty and the slight nausea Harlow often felt going down the switchbacks was tempered by Finn's hand on her thigh, and the hitch in his breath.

The movement of his thumb on her inner thigh sent a rush of chills through her. In a nearly involuntary motion, her legs parted as her back arched.

"*Damnit, Harlow*," he growled, glancing at her sidelong.

"Keep your eyes on the road," she pleaded, her voice breathless.

She pulled the hem of her dress up and Finn's hand slid under, grazing the bare skin of her thigh. Her legs parted wider, giving him easier access to her. The sound of his tortured groan filled the car as he caught the scent of her mounting lust.

"How wet are you?" he bit out, glancing away from the road again.

"Find out," she begged as his fingers grazed the outside of her panties.

He was so quick she barely felt his fingers move the thin fabric, but her sensitive flesh lit on fire as the tip of his fingers pushed between her swollen folds, sliding easily inside her.

"Yes," she hissed.

His arm was at an awkward angle and the stroke of his fingers inside her was excruciatingly slow and gentle, where she wanted to be filled hard and fast. It wasn't enough for him either. She could sense it in the tension in his forearm, the way he couldn't keep his eyes on the road. There was a scenic overlook ahead, and thank Aphora, Finn pulled into it.

No other cars were there, but the traffic to and from the Citadel was picking up. Evening events and devotional services were starting, as archival and museum staff changed shifts. Finn adjusted slightly, and switched hands, sucking his fingers slowly, then kissing her deeply so she tasted herself on his tongue.

"I can't get enough of you," he murmured as one set of fingers twined into her hair, while the other teased her, letting her panties cover her once more.

The tips of his fingers dragged over the wet spot in her panties. She wanted his fingers inside her so badly she thought she might reach down and push them in herself. Beneath the thin fabric of her undergarments, she felt her lips open for him. He pressed one finger a little harder into the now very damp spot between her legs. The fabric of her panties dragged against her flesh, tantalizing her, promising some of the blessed friction she desired as his mouth met hers.

Finn's tongue against hers made promises about what he could do to the rest of her. The finger between her legs pressed the fabric of her panties a little harder, increasing the pressure on her clit. Her hips lifted, trying to get more of the sweet relief she was desperate for.

"What do you need?" Finn's question was all command, and she was eager to comply.

"Release," she moaned.

Finn rewarded her with another breathtaking kiss and an increase in pressure. The wetness between her legs pooled, soaking the fabric of her panties.

Finn's voice came out in a growl. "Release?"

She nodded as he pulled her hair, and she yanked the bodice of her dress down to expose her bare breasts. His mouth closed over one nipple and as he moved to the other, he asked, "You need me to make you come?"

"Yes," she begged.

His lips covered her other nipple, and he nipped it lightly. A cool breeze drifted in through the cracked window, making her exposed nipple pebble into a stiff, damp peak. She whimpered with need, pushing her molten core hard into his teasing hand.

"Please," she begged.

"Please, what?" he teased, nipping her neck, her ears, her bottom lip. "What do you want?"

"I want you inside me," she begged.

He pushed his seat all the way back in one fluid motion, his hands leaving her desperate for contact, and then he deftly dragged her into his lap, where he'd freed his cock, which was now pressed hard against her wet center, only the thin fabric of her panties between them. It was a flagrant display of his immortal strength and agility, and it only aroused Harlow further.

"How much do you like these panties?" Finn asked, pulling her hips down so his cock rubbed hard against her clit.

"Not a bit," she answered, and he ripped them off her like they were made of sodden paper. As soon as the wet folds of her slid against his bare cock, she lifted her hips.

"Just like that," he said, one hand sliding up her back to pull her hair out of its bun so he could dig his fingers into her hair. "Tell me again how you want me inside you."

The head of his cock teased her entrance now, but he was holding her firmly in place, not letting her slam down on him as she wanted to. Every nerve in her was alight as her lips caressed the head of his cock, wanting desperately to suck him inside her until he hit that place that would make her scream.

"Tell me, baby girl."

"I want you inside me," Harlow begged, but he shook his head, a mischievous glint in his now-glowing eyes. He wanted more. His hips moved and his cock shifted slightly, slick with her arousal, to press against her clit, then dragged back to her entrance. She didn't know how it was possible for him to make such precise movements. Maybe it was just a Finn thing, but it was driving her wild.

"I want you to fill me with that huge cock," she snarled, nearly feral with lust. "I want you to fuck me so hard I can't walk straight. Bury your cock in me. *Now, McKay.*"

His eyes blazed with clear golden light as he pulled her hips down hard, giving her exactly what she asked for. She ground herself against him, every thrust pushing her closer and closer to the edge she desperately wanted to fall over.

"You're everything I've ever wanted," he said.

His words caused every muscle in her body to tighten around him. She was pulled apart with this wild need for him to be deeper inside her, for them to join on some other level she couldn't yet attain. Pleasure mixed with the intense need for *more*, as the tease of release remained just out of reach.

The warm rush of his orgasm, the wet heat of their union, pushed her over the edge. Her shadows released, twining with the bright light Finn emitted as he continued to ride her wave of pleasure as well as his own. When their bodies finally slowed, he stayed buried deep inside her and she rested her head on his chest.

Harlow loved the feeling of Finn rooted in her, of the second round of desire she felt brewing, even as he softened inside her. She knew that all she'd have to do was rock her hips a little, or lean back and touch herself, and he'd be ready to go again. She wanted to desperately, already wanting more of him.

But before she could start another round of things, another car pulled up, followed quickly by another, and a pack of fox shifters piled out of the cars, taking photos of the dying sunset over the sea. Harlow pulled her dress back up over her breasts and ducked slightly, attempting to hide the fact that she was on Finn's lap. The shifters were several spots away, at the end of the overlook parking lot, by a set of stairs that led to an observation deck. None of them spared a look for Harlow and Finn, but all they had to do was turn.

Finn's cock hardened inside her, growing rapidly as he too registered they might be caught. His breath quickened, and she saw the question in his eyes, *Stay and fuck again, or go home like respectable people?*

Harlow rocked against Finn, pressing her breasts, which had grown heavy and aching, against his hard chest as she clenched around him.

"Yes," he hissed as he grabbed her ass.

She glanced at the shifters, who were still not paying a lick of attention to them as they spread a blanket out on the observation deck. Finn followed her gaze as she moved slowly above him, tightening herself around his cock as she moved. When his eyes turned back to her, she pulled her dress down again, pinching her nipples.

"You are so fucking hot," he groaned.

The sun slipped further down into the sea, and the parking lot was nearly dark. The shifters were unpacking a picnic dinner and had lit a few lanterns. Someone was playing a guitar, and the soft sound of their voices faded away as Harlow pulled her dress off. She honestly didn't care who saw, or smelled, what they were doing.

Finn's eyes glowed in the twilight of the parking lot. He cupped her face in his hands as she undulated above him, her breasts and belly moving in time with his slow thrusts into her. She didn't pull away in order to slam down on him, as she'd done before. Now they moved languidly as he pushed deeper still inside her.

She realized his girth was growing, as well as his length, but the rest of him was still in his humanoid form. "Did you let your glamour drop on just your cock?"

Finn grinned. "I can't believe I never thought to try it before."

He kissed her, his tongue dancing against hers for a moment before he pushed her back into an upright position. "You're the most gorgeous thing I've ever seen," he said as his hands slid down her neck, his fingers grazing reverently over her collarbones and the top of her breasts. He cupped them firmly, his thumbs rubbing over her sensitive nipples for a few blissful moments.

"Don't stop," he begged. She hadn't realized she'd paused, but she moved against him again as he dragged his hands down her sides, grazing her hips and thighs. "Rub your clit for me."

She'd been bracing herself on his chest as she moved her hips, and released one hand to do as he asked. She leaned backwards slightly so he could see her better.

"You smell so good," he grunted. "I wish you were sitting on my face."

She moved the fingers she'd been using to touch herself into his mouth. He sucked them, his tongue massaging them with a sensual grace that showed her exactly what he wanted to do to her clit. She'd discovered he loved to go down on her more than just about any other act and the scent of her arousal was enough to have him between her legs within moments if they were alone.

As he sucked her fingers, she pulled his shirt up. He released her fingers to yank his shirt off, tossing it in back. He was sweating under it. When she had him free, he pulled her against him, their damp bodies sliding against one another. His cock was so big inside her now, and Harlow felt it pulse with Finn's increased arousal. This was one of her favorite parts of his true form, something that differed from his humanoid anatomy. Sometimes, if they moved slowly like this, his cock pulsed in a low vibration that buzzed through her in a way that no toy could ever achieve.

His fingers pressed hard into the full flesh of her ass cheeks as the intensity of the encounter heightened. She knew better than to ask him to bite her now. That wasn't an option, though she still wanted it desperately. The low vibration reached the base of Finn's cock and traveled into his pubic bone, straight into Harlow's clit.

Her back arched hard as he pressed her ass harder into him, grinding her against him as he writhed beneath her, the muscles in his chest and abdomen rippling with the effort. Now her breasts were in his face and as he rode his pleasure, he latched onto one of her nipples, sucking hard as he came. Harlow's toes curled as she moaned Finn's name over and over, moving her body fast and rough against his. In his true form, orgasms lasted for minutes, not seconds, and could be intensified by increased speed and pressure. Though he hadn't shifted entirely, this still seemed to be true.

He pushed her back into a seated position as he crested his wave of pleasure, rubbing her clit with his thumb. A few of the fox shifters had glanced their way now, and Harlow was sure they knew what was going on, but she couldn't seem to care. She pinched her nipples and screamed Finn's name as he released fully inside her, the furious rush of his orgasm filling her, sending her over the edge.

When the haze of her pleasure cleared, the fox shifters were gone, and she and Finn collapsed against one another, sweaty and come-drunk as teenagers. "Holy Raia." He pressed a kiss to her damp hair. "You are a goddess, you know that?"

Harlow wrapped her arms around his neck, boneless and spent. "I love you, McKay," she muttered as she fell asleep. She was mildly aware of him wrapping her in the picnic blanket he kept in the backseat and the kiss he brushed on her brow.

"Love you to the end of everything, baby girl," he said, so softly she wondered if he was talking to himself. The last thing she heard before falling into a deep, restful sleep was the rumble of the car coming to life, and then all went blissfully dark.

CHAPTER 8

The next morning, as Harlow was feeding Axel and most of the household was gathering for breakfast, Nox rushed upstairs in her pajamas, followed closely by Indigo. The footage they had been working on decrypting had finally finished processing, and what it showed was apparently so shocking that neither could describe it. Riley and Enzo had come over for breakfast, so everyone gathered around the cozy kitchen table overlooking the bay to watch.

Nox had a few bracing sips of the latte Aurelia handed her and explained that at first it had appeared the video was only footage of humans in Falcyra burning the Governor's Mansion to the ground, but once decrypted, the true revelation was why they'd done it. Someone had leaked a video onto the dark web, filmed by a group claiming to be resistance fighters in Falcyra. Nox and Indi had already put together a full dossier on the ones they could identify. All had radical political leanings and were associated with a loosely formed group calling themselves "Humanists."

Alaric skimmed over the report as Nox was talking. "All your evidence points to them being a disorganized group of humans disgruntled about vampiric rule —easy to ignore."

Nox shook her head. "Doesn't line up with what you're about to see. There's something else happening here."

Finn raised an eyebrow as Nox paused, looking exhausted. The shifter smiled sheepishly and opened her laptop. When the video played, the smile slid off her face. It was clear she and Indi had both seen it already, because they immediately looked away as the video began. Under the table, Indi took Nox's hand in hers.

The footage was blurry at first. Whoever was holding the camera was running in a group of three people, all wearing ski masks. Then the footage cleared, though the camera was pointed at the ground, and the camera person spoke softly. "We got word a month ago that this was happening—and we—"

"Shut up," a harsh voice cut in.

"I'm just trying to tell them what we're looking at," explained the first voice.

"We're in the Governor's Mansion, that's all they need to know," a third voice chimed in. "We're going down into the fourth sub-basement to see if we can get our people out."

"No more than that," the harsh voice barked. "If what's down here is what we think it is, the rest will be obvious."

The first voice started to say something but the harsh voice interrupted again: "Got the sample? It's asking for it."

There was a shuffle, and the camera angle changed, showing a computer screen for a moment. Alaric said, "It's got a DNA lock. Old school—has to come right from the finger."

A freshly severed hand came into the frame for a moment. Selene turned green, burying her face in Aurelia's shoulder. The elevator door opened, and the Humanists were running again, this time down a long wood-paneled hallway. A few broke off at the first door on the left, as the harsh voice rang out, "Search all Ducare's files. Scan what you can. You. You're with me."

The camera jostled a little as the camera person ran alongside the person who was clearly their leader. Another door opened and the harsh voice spoke again. "Zoom in on them."

The footage was blurry for a moment, but when focused, showed a decadently decorated room. Humans lay about, in various stages of undress, barely moving, but clearly still alive.

"What is wrong with them?" Enzo asked, his voice breaking a little. His empathy had to be going wild. Harlow reached across the table and squeezed his hand.

The harsh voice answered, as though they'd heard Enzo's question. "Ducare and his cronies have been fucking and sucking down here for months. There's a reason there's no food, no money for schools, roads or clean water. They've been frittering it all away on this. On *orgies*."

One of the humans laying on a crimson velvet settee opened her eyes, a lazy smile on her face. "Calm down, man. Everybody here is having a good time."

The harsh voice growled, then pulled the camera towards their face. They yanked a mask off, revealing a handsome face, with the eyes of a vampire, surrounded by a crown of wavy golden hair. The Humanists had vampires among them, *helping* them. "Ducare is out of control. We have reported back to Nuva Troi a hundred times about this shit, and you do *nothing*. Help us. Help these people."

The human woman laughed at the speech. "We have everything we need." She slumped over on the settee, losing balance as her silk robe came untied; she struggled to tie it.

The vampire shook his head at someone standing behind the camera person. "Get them out of here." He stared into the camera again. "Let's go."

The camera person and the vampire ran back down the hall, stopping at the office they'd left part of their party in before. Two masked figures sorted through a pile of papers, using hand scanners. One looked up, handing a small pile to the vampire. Through the mask, Harlow could see their eyes were the brilliant blue of a cetacean shifter. They rarely left water or used their humanoid form.

"The Humanists have shifters among them," Cian said. "And vampires."

The vampire on screen skimmed the information on the papers. "Just as I thought. You fuckers know full well Ducare isn't holding up the agreement we made when we allowed a vampire governor. Our people were supposed to be taken care of."

Our people. The Falcyran vampire thought of the shifter next to him, and the humans among his group, as his people. Did the Orders matter less in Falcyra? Harlow didn't know what to make of what she saw, but her chest ached at the thought. She turned her attention back to the video now that the vampire was moving again, shouting to his companions.

"Get them all out. Search every room and then burn it all down." He looked back at the camera. "This is your final warning. Help us, or we will make you pay."

"Pause the video, please," Riley asked.

Nox looked to Finn who nodded. Riley examined something on the screen, something she couldn't see. Axel rubbed against Harlow's leg and she made a soft sound, coaxing him onto her lap. He chose Finn instead, flicking his tail in her general direction and purring loudly. Finn almost immediately relaxed, as Axel rubbed his face against Finn's chest. The cat was being aggressively affectionate; he'd sensed Finn's distress. As Finn's body relaxed, so did Axel, who settled in on his cat-dad's lap, purring happily now as he made biscuits on Finn's leg.

Such a Daddy's boy, she thought.

Riley looked away from the screen finally, smiling at Axel, who blinked back at them slowly, now flexing his paws at the shifter who'd won him over by turning into a cat for a few hours each week. Riley always said they thought that if they had to have one form, it would be a house cat, and Harlow occasionally found them napping together in the sunshine.

Riley pointed to the screen, at a blurry image on a bookshelf near Ducare's desk. "Can you zoom in on this?"

Nox nodded, typing a few commands into the computer. The screen showed a framed photo of Ducare sitting on a boat with Connor and Aislin McKay. They were smiling and holding drinks. It wasn't a pleasant revelation that they were friends, but Harlow didn't know why it was significant.

Riley turned to Enzo. "Isn't that dress from your spring collection, for the season?"

Enzo nodded. "Yes."

Riley looked at Finn, who was vibrating with fury. "He can't claim he doesn't know what's going on in Falcyra if he's been taking photos with Ducare. He's probably been to the orgies—and that's *our* boat."

Aurelia sighed, picking at her fingernails. "But he *will* deny knowing anything about it… Publicly anyway…" she trailed off, frowning.

Selene sneered. "The cowards. All of them."

Next to her, Aurelia shifted uncomfortably, averting her eyes from Harlow's careful gaze.

"You can keep playing it," Riley said.

Nox pressed play. The camera swiveled out of the office and down the hall where several of the Humanists practically carried humans to the elevator. Some were fighting their rescuers, swearing violently.

One sobbed as she beat the ground with her fists. "I was promised immortality. *Ducare promised me.*"

"Get her up," the harsh-voiced vampire barked. Harlow heard the exhaustion in his voice, saw it in his eyes. Whoever he was, he was at the end of his rope. "I mean it, Berith," the vampire said. "Help us. Get Connor to change his mind, or I will make Nytra sorry. Our people have suffered enough."

The footage ended, static filling the screen.

Thea clapped a hand over her mouth. "I knew I recognized him. That's Jareth Sanvier."

"Sanvier?" Enzo asked. "Is he House of Remiel?"

"Not exactly," Thea answered. "He was born in Falcyra. He just came here for uni. There are rumors he is Berith's natural son."

It was rare for vampires to be born, not made, but it did happen occasionally —once every few hundred years, as their fertility was even more sluggish than the Illuminated's.

"Why does no one know this?" Selene asked.

Thea shrugged. "Jareth hates the House of Remiel, from what I remember. He was a year or two ahead of me. Did you know him?" Thea turned to Alaric, who shook his head. Thea shrugged. "I remember him saying he hated Nytra a lot. It made a lot of people dislike him."

Nox took a deep breath. "That's not all. As we finished the decryption, Indi picked up on a rumor making its rounds through our sources: Connor hired a hit on Berith and the rest of the House of Remiel higher-ups."

Everyone took a collective sharp breath in. "For what?" Enzo asked.

"Because he betrayed them with the Mark Easton thing," Riley replied, avoiding Harlow's eyes. "And all the research into Gene-I."

Indigo's forehead wrinkled. "That might be the real reason, but the chatter says it's because the House of Remiel was being pretty open about thinking the Illuminated have lost control."

"Are they all dead?" Aurelia asked.

Nox grimaced. "It's hard to say. No one's seen much of them, so at the very least they're in hiding. Jareth was clearly trying to get this message to Berith though."

"Naming a child something that rhymes with your own is the height of poor taste," Cian said.

Normally, everyone would have laughed, but the mood around the table was somber. Indigo blinked back tears. "Why would the Illuminated let things be this way in Falcyra? What happened to 'no poverty'? And if Berith knows, who else does?"

Again, Aurelia looked uncomfortable. Selene turned to her wife. "What aren't you saying?"

Aurelia shook her head, conflict on her face. "We all knew. All the heads of the Orders. We all knew what Ducare was up to. The way he'd let things go. It was made clear that taking any action would put not only ourselves at risk, but our families."

Selene's eyes went wide as she took Aurelia's hands. "My love," she breathed. "I can't believe you've been carrying this around and I didn't know."

It was clear to Harlow that Selene forgave Aurelia, and she saw on everyone else's face that they did as well, but she saw the flicker of unease still in Aurelia's eyes. The others began talking, discussing the video, but Harlow watched Aurelia. As Selene comforted her, Harlow's sense that she was uncomfortable dissipated. Perhaps she'd been mistaken, or perhaps Aurelia was simply ill at ease because she'd admitted to a fact that could get them all killed, if the Illuminated learned she'd told.

"Where's Meline and Larkin?" Harlow asked Indi, who was getting up to grab a hanky from her purse.

Indi dried her eyes and glanced towards the back stairs. "I think they're both still asleep. Meli was up really late last night reading the new Wesley Arden book, and you know Larkin these days…"

Harlow smiled at Indi's comment about Meli, who was on a steady diet of *very* sexy sci-fi romances, which were all the rage on the bookish socials. But Larkin was another story. During the day, she seemed happy enough, but everyone noticed she'd been sleeping later and later as the summer wore on. Harlow was just as glad neither of them had watched the footage with the rest of the family. Axel wound around her legs asking to be held. She picked him up, whispering, "Go get your Aunties up and see if they want breakfast."

The cat trotted off, disappearing up the back stairs. He loved living in this enormous villa with all his favorite people. While everyone talked over what seemed like endless possibilities about who might control the Humanists, Harlow made coffee and tea. Riley joined her, working in silent concert to lay out a spread of pastries, cheeses and cut fruit. Indi disappeared upstairs with Nox's laptop, returning a few minutes later with red eyes.

"They both need a little time," she whispered to Selene, who nodded as Aurelia took their breakfasts to the terrace.

Everyone was going about their day as usual, which didn't surprise Harlow. Her family had become rather used to living double lives. In public, they pretended to go on with life as usual. In private, the frequency with which they discussed the various atrocities committed by the Illuminated and the Order of Night was growing. There was a palpable sense that the time they had left to live their normal lives was winnowing, and so they transitioned quickly from things like the video they'd just watched into a perfectly normal summer day, full of mundane plans. Whatever was coming with the Illuminated and the Order of Night was getting closer, but no one could determine what action to take yet.

Finn often said they were still in the information gathering stage, but Harlow worried they were missing something vital, and the Vault hadn't yielded the information they'd hoped for. Harlow poured herself another cup of tea and looked around for Finn. Enzo and Riley were already on the terrace strategizing about a luncheon meeting with a realtor for Enzo's new retail space, and Indi snuggled into the crook of Aurelia's arm, looking exhausted and very young. Finn must have gone to the bathroom, as he popped out of the back hallway near his office. He looked to be headed down to the Vault with Nox and Alaric, who were going to analyze the footage on what Harlow assumed would be a granular level.

Finn brushed a kiss to her cheek as he passed by her. "Are you headed to the Citadel today?"

Harlow checked her phone to see if there was news about *The Warden* being ready to scan, but there was nothing. "Not today."

She hadn't told him about the book yet… It was important, but she needed to bring up *The Warden* delicately, and now was not the time.

Shifting focus might be best. They could talk about the book later. "Where is Petra this morning?"

Finn averted his eyes. "I'm not sure… She had a date last night."

Harlow made a pleased little noise, a smile lighting her lips. "Really? She didn't text me."

Finn swallowed hard, his expression changing. Harlow's stomach flipped as he looked away. *Was Petra upset?* They'd gotten along so well since she'd explained her behavior in secondary to Harlow a few months ago and the thought that Petra might be angry with her turned her stomach.

Finn waved Alaric and Nox on. Nox was on the phone with Ari, who was presumably still in Falcyra, and Harlow caught a snippet of their conversation. "—I'll look into it, send anything you find over. See you soon." Finn took her elbow gently and drew her into the back hallway, where there was a little nook that looked out over the lemon arbor, with a view of the bay.

"So, Kate wanted to talk to you about this yesterday, but you wouldn't come out with us…"

What did Kate have to do with anything? Her heart stumbled over a beat as she understood. "Oh," she mumbled. "Oh… *Oh.*"

A smile played on Finn's lips, and the flip in Harlow's stomach went deeper, morphing into another feeling entirely. The uncomfortable feeling that she got thinking about Petra and Kate dissipated as Finn's lips curved. Her skin heated as she became acutely aware of him, as though noticing him for the first time. He looked delectable, still in a pair of low slung, light joggers and an old band tee. His hair was standing up in all directions after he'd shoved his fingers nervously through his hair a thousand times while they'd watched the footage. It was his only tell, as far as she knew, and she only saw it when he was comfortable, and with family.

"Are you okay with this?" Finn asked. "I get the impression things are very new with them, and they were reluctant to tell you until they were sure they liked each other."

Amidst her growing arousal, Harlow felt a stab of something she couldn't quite identify, maybe a little jealousy, followed quickly by protectiveness for Petra.

The haze of desire that was flooding her system clouded the feeling as her skin flushed. She stepped closer to Finn, by instinct, but tried her best to stay focused on the conversation at hand. "Does Petra know Kate's not interested in monogamy?"

Finn's eyes hooded slightly as he breathed her in. He was having the same trouble concentrating that she was. He cleared his throat, obviously trying to focus. "She's not super into it either, from what I gather, though I think they might be serious about each other—or they will be when Petra knows you're okay with it. She's worried."

Harlow frowned as her hands skimmed over Finn's chest of their own accord. "Then why didn't she talk to me about it?"

Finn brushed a loose strand of honey colored hair from her face. "You haven't been exactly… open… to hanging out with Kate this summer."

Harlow's eyes fell to the floor and her hands, which had been tracing the lines of his pectoral muscles, stilled. "That's not because I'm still interested in her."

Finn's arms tightened around her waist. "It's okay if you're a little jealous. I know you and Kate had something special."

Harlow's eyes flickered up to Finn's. His voice was so gentle, but she could see he was crawling out of his skin with anxiety. She threw her arms around his neck, and he lifted her, setting her onto the heavy chest of drawers that was tucked under the window in the nook. They were face to face now, the same height.

"I'm not jealous—well, that's not true—" Finn's arms tightened around her and she felt him steady his breathing. Was he panicking? She rushed to add, "I was jealous that the two of you are better friends than I am with either of you."

"What?" The word came out in a bark. He looked genuinely confused.

"Every time we hung out, it was so clear. The two of you have a ton in common. I didn't want to intrude on your friendship." He was staring at her in disbelief. "I just make things awkward," she added.

"Harls," he breathed as he kissed her. "*You* don't make things awkward. It's just awkward to figure this stuff out."

"Oh," she responded. Riley and Enzo had both talked to her about this kind of thinking and she'd been working on it, but sometimes it was still hard to remember that not everything was her fault.

He hugged her tight. "Kate is a good friend, but you are one of the *best* friends I've ever had. You always have been."

"I'm not your *very* best friend?" she asked playfully, feeling the weirdness that always followed episodes like this dissipate.

Finn's head dipped towards her ear as he yanked her forward, pulling her body into tight contact with his. "I don't fuck my friends in front of packs of fox shifters."

Harlow bit her lip as his hand slid under her pajama top, his fingers grazing the bare skin of her back. "They really saw everything?"

He laughed in her ear, his breath sending chills through her. "I don't think they saw much, but they definitely heard us."

"Sorry I fell asleep," she murmured as his hand skimmed her side, grazing the curve of her breast. Her nipples hardened in response and she arched into his chest as he kissed her neck.

Their friends and family were just in the other room. She was ravenous for him now, but they had things to do today. He pulled away, seeming to think the same thing. They were both breathing hard, and he shook his head slightly. She slid off the counter and walked back towards the kitchen. They needed a measure of space before they both became frenzied with lust. Already her head was clouding, and it was hard to think of anything but him.

An arm snaked around her waist, and Finn pinned her against his body. The hard length of his cock pressed into her ass as he dragged her with immortal speed through the back hall, into his little office. Inside, with the door shut and the lights still off, he kept her pinned to him. "I don't know how I'm supposed to go downstairs and think, with you smelling like this."

She wrinkled her nose. "So weird."

He kissed her hair, then her temple, his voice low as one hand slid down the front of her body. "It's not just your wet pussy, though that smells so good I can hardly think. It's your skin, your blood, your magic. You smell like rich amber, and silken pleasure… I want to sink my cock, my teeth, my fingers—anything I can get inside you—I want in."

With those words, his finger tucked into the waistband of her pajama bottoms, pushing them down over the generous curve of her hips. "That smell," he breathed as she spread her legs, bending over to brace herself on the book-shelf next to the door. "That fucking smell. I want it all over me."

His fingers teased her entrance from behind, and he groaned when he found her wet and eager for him. Two fingers slid into her as he gripped one hip with his other hand.

"Won't Nox and Alaric wonder where you are?" she asked, desperately not wanting him to stop.

"No, it's obvious where I am."

"Why can't we behave?" she asked, spreading her legs a little wider to steady herself.

He halted. "Fuck," he swore, in a tone that did not suggest arousal.

"Please don't stop," she begged. For some reason, his tone didn't deter her. Her body's needs had taken over.

He pulled her against him, pinning her to his body once more, but this time immobilizing her. She thought she might burst into flames, she needed him so badly. His fingers spread over her bare belly as he moved his other hand away from the breast it was cupping. He was panting hard behind her.

"What do you feel like right now?" he asked. Again, his tone was strained. He wasn't asking to arouse her further. This wasn't bedroom talk. She tried to focus, but the pressure of his cock between her ass cheeks was so delicious she could hardly think, and she wiggled her hips a little in frustration.

"If you do that, I'm going to lose my focus and fuck you," he groaned. "I need you to think for a minute and then I promise I'm going to make you come as many times as you need."

The promise was enough to tide her over, for the moment anyway. "I feel like if I don't get you inside me soon, I'm going to die," she said honestly.

"Like you're going to *die*?"

Harlow nodded. She'd spoken impetuously. The feeling of his hand on her belly was distracting, but she was honest. "And once we get going… I can't stop now… It's like—if I don't have more of you, I won't live."

"Fuck," he said again. "*Fuck.*"

"What is it?" she asked.

"The fervor. I don't know how you could have it. It's not really possible. Or at least it shouldn't be, because you're not Illuminated."

Harlow wiggled her hips again, spreading her legs so his cock slid between them. "What's the fervor?"

"Bad girl," he moaned, slapping her ass lightly. "I told you I'd make you come as many times as you need, but we *have* to talk about this."

"Talk while you fuck me," she begged, maneuvering so the head of his cock fitted against her entrance. She felt his thighs clench behind her. He was struggling not to thrust into her. He allowed the head of his cock to enter her, the proud ridge of it massaging her flesh as he spread her ass cheeks wider.

She glanced behind her. The dim office light showed the reverence on his face as he watched his cock slowly sink into her. His voice was a low, restrained growl. "The fervor happens when Illuminated resist the urge to Claim one another. I've been feeling the effects for a few weeks now, but it shouldn't be possible for you to. You can't bite me back—the Claim can go only one way between us."

"It feels like this for you? Like you'll die if you don't have me?"

"Yes," he said, sliding deep inside her as he pulled her against him. One hand rubbed her clit, and the other went softly around her neck, his thumb putting gentle pressure on her throat as he slowly thrust into her.

"I think about you constantly," he growled in her ear. "The last few days, all I've wanted is to taste you, your sweat… your blood. I know it's wrong, after what happened, but I can't stop thinking about it."

Harlow gasped with pleasure as the pressure on her throat increased ever so slightly, but his confession didn't scare her. She'd been thinking of it too, but she hadn't wanted to admit it to herself. The primal urge to Claim and be Claimed seemed to override both their good sense. He sank to the ground, pulling her down with him. When she was steady on all fours, he thrust into her harder a few times. The wet sound of him sliding in and out of her thrilled Harlow.

He pulled out of her, leaving her hollow with need. "We have to stop and actually talk about what this means."

"Now?" she asked, turning to face him.

Finn nodded, getting up, pulling his joggers on as he went. His face contorted with worry, or disgust, she couldn't tell which in the shadows. He'd shed his t-shirt at some point that she'd missed. In fact, the last few minutes were a blur. She remembered what they'd been talking about as Finn rummaged in the little fridge behind his desk for a glass jug of water. He poured some into two glasses, handing one to her as he sipped his own.

He sank into the club chair across from his desk. She stepped toward him, but he shook his head. "Don't. I need to regain composure, and I need you to hear me."

Harlow stopped, feeling momentarily hurt. Some whisper in the back of her mind recognized the desperation in his voice though; he was serious about all this. A blessed string of logic threaded its way through her: this was real. Whatever the fervor was, it was riding them hard, and after what had happened in the Vault, there was no question it could be dangerous. She pulled her pajama bottoms up, then sat on the edge of his desk, a safe distance away.

"The fervor can drive people out of their minds, and if I'd had any idea you were experiencing it too, I would never have tried biting you in the Vault the other day. This is too big an anomaly. It shouldn't be possible."

She let out a noise of frustration. "But it's fine for you to feel like this?"

Finn sighed, putting his glass down on the corner of his desk. "No, it's not. I slipped up the other day, but it won't happen again. I have more experience getting shit like this under control than you do."

A dark look crossed his face, one she knew was reserved for memories of his father he didn't speak about. The most she'd ever heard him say was that his father had been brutal about training him to fight as a child. Connor McKay believed in the old ways of the Illuminated, unlike many of his peers, and he'd trained his son to be a soldier, just as he had been on their home world, wherever that was. The training, from what Harlow understood, was little more than abuse a good portion of the time.

Her mind traveled over the conversation she'd had with Cian after the incident. There was little doubt in her mind that this was all connected, that some Illuminated secret was tied to this very issue—and that at some point, Connor and Aislin had terrorized Finn into keeping it, no matter the cost to himself. The thought of it sickened her. How had he turned out so well with parents like them?

Cian. Cian Herrington had loved him. And then Alaric and Petra, and eventually Nox and Ari. They'd been his family. They'd shaped him to be the good man before her, who was fighting with his unquenchable desire to keep her safe. If he felt half as tortured by the fervor as she did, then she knew he was nearly wild with desire right now.

Her instinct was to go to him, to stroke his hair and comfort him, to make love to him until all these memories and worries washed away, but even her smallest movement towards him caused him to grimace, so she leaned back on the desk, holding her hands up in surrender. "I hear you," she said. "Is there any way to stop the fervor?"

Finn's eyebrows raised. "If you were Illuminated, we'd Claim one another and it would recede. But—"

"Since I'm not, you're worried my fervor will drive me out of my mind."

His head fell into his hands, muffling his words. "Yes. I did this to you. Because I'm selfish. Because I couldn't stay away from you."

A lump formed in Harlow's throat. She hated to hear him say things like that. This was a complication, but they could get past it. "Is there any way to slow it down and give us some time to figure this out?"

There was a long pause, and Harlow closed her eyes, feeling both her heartbeat and her shadows, which gathered at her fingers, softly soothing her. Some of them extended from her hands, wrapping around Finn's too, as though she took his hands in hers. Finn looked up, smiling faintly.

"That feels nice." The crack in his voice confused her. She pulled the shadows back, but he shook his head. "Not sexy-nice. Nice-nice. Comforting."

"Everything keeps getting more complicated," she murmured.

He sent a bit of his own magic swirling back to her, intertwining with her shadows. "It doesn't matter how complicated it gets. We'll work it out."

Harlow believed Finn. With every thread of her being, she believed him. And if they needed a little space to get their heads together, she'd give it to him. "Go on downstairs and find out what's going on. I'm going to go grab a lemon scone and some tea from The Gate. Want me to bring anything back for you?"

The Gate was their favorite coffee shop in the neighborhood, and Finn could consume half a dozen of their lemon scones in a sitting, so it surprised her when he shook his head. "No, but enjoy yourself, okay?"

And then he was gone, just a breeze and an open door. Harlow's heart ached deeply, but she went upstairs to get dressed, texting Petra on her way. Now was as good a time as any for the two of them to talk.

CHAPTER 9

Petra Velarius looked like sunshine embodied, her bronze skin contrasting with the tight cotton mini-dress she wore. As she entered the shady courtyard garden at The Gate, she pushed her sunnies on top of her head, sending her mane of wavy dark hair flying backwards. Harlow already had two of The Gate's signature tea lattes waiting, and a plate of lemon scones on the table she'd grabbed in the corner. The scent of the bergamot in the tea wafted through the air as a breeze crept through the courtyard.

Petra sat down, her eyebrows raising as she crossed her arms. "Finn is such a snitch. Are you mad?"

"Mad that you didn't tell me," Harlow said, keeping her voice even. She was terrified that Petra was angry with *her*, and her heart was beating out of her chest. "It's fine if you and Kate are interested in one another."

"No, it's not." Petra glared at her. "I picked up your sloppy seconds. Somebody who was carrying a torch for you still last spring."

The words stung, but Harlow understood them. Her own inner landscape sounded like that far too often. She pushed the plate of scones to the side and took both Petra's hands in her own. For a long moment, she simply stared at her friend. The music from inside the coffee shop drifted into the courtyard, mingling with the sound of the fountain and birds singing. *Nothing could be more peaceful*, Harlow thought.

In moments like these, the threads that made up the world, reality as they knew it, were more than conduits for aether. The peace of the courtyard flowed through her, changing the riot of emotion in her, thread by tiny thread. As her own mood calmed, the invisible threads that bound her and Petra together, stronger than ever now because of their growing friendship, smoothed out. Harlow had always sensed threads with her second sight. That was as easy for a sorcière as breathing. But ever since she'd manifested, her sense of the threads that wove reality had become more acute. Her shadows purred with the pleasure of reaching into them. She wasn't using magic, and yet this moment was magical.

Petra's expression finally softened enough that Harlow let go of her hands. "I don't think that's fair to either of us, but especially you."

Petra sipped her latte, her face a perfectly cultivated mask. Harlow had seen this version of Petra thousands of times. It was a kind of armor—the illusion that she was shallow, so no one would see her true depths. Her voice was bone dry when she replied, "Fine. But I'd be mad if I were you."

"Would you?" Harlow asked, a tease in her voice. Humor and gentle teasing were surefire ways to break through Petra's outer shell, she'd discovered.

A cool breeze blew Petra's hair into her drink and she spent a moment blotting foamed milk out of her tresses. Harlow shivered. Autumn was just around the corner. When Petra's hair was deemed clean enough to disregard, she sighed, her protective mask finally dissolving, revealing the true Petra. "I just... It took us so long to be okay with each other. I feel like I might have fucked up."

The threads between them sang with life-giving aether, strengthened by nourishing truth. Harlow took a deep breath, drinking in the heady sensation of being able to feel the energetic compound behind mundane reality. It was odd. She rarely felt this so acutely with Finn, and given their conversation this morning she had to wonder if perhaps the fervor masked this ability with him. What a disappointment *that* was... she could only imagine what it would be like to sense this with Finn. She turned her focus back to Petra. "Do you like Kate?"

Petra nodded, a smile playing at her lips. "I really do."

"And she likes you?"

Petra's smile got wider. "Yeah."

"And you're giddy and excited all the time?"

The full-bellied laugh that spilled out of Petra was everything Harlow wanted for her. The threads between them practically thrummed with the beautiful energy of this moment. "Yes, I am. It's great."

Harlow reached out and grabbed Petra's free hand, giving it a squeeze. "Then how could I be mad?"

Petra brushed a kiss to Harlow's knuckles before releasing her hand. "Thank you. That means a lot."

"You deserve to be happy," Harlow added.

After everything her parents and the McKays put her through, Petra deserved to be blissfully happy for the rest of her life. Harlow just hoped that Kate was able to give her friend whatever she needed. Whether that was forever, or just a few months or years, Petra deserved to have the best of every relationship experience she could have after the way her parents had treated her. Harlow was honored to be a part of Petra's chosen family, and she wasn't going to let the potential awkwardness of this situation get in the way.

Petra took a long drink of her iced latte. "What do they put in everything here to make it taste *so good?*"

And just like that, things were fine between them. Harlow had four sisters and Enzo, and it had never been this easy to make up when things went wrong.

But Petra was different. For all her bluntness, which could be irritating, the other side to it was this; she didn't linger long on bad feelings. Harlow enjoyed this feature of their relationship immensely. She smiled as Petra scarfed down scone after scone. No one could resist the allure of The Gate's lemon scones.

They chatted for a while about a podcast they both listened to that was being turned into a television show. Harlow's muscles relaxed as she listened to the utterly mundane sounds of the coffee shop. There weren't many people here right now, as it was just after the morning rush. Perhaps it was the aetheric link she'd just experienced with Petra, but her sense of connection to the threads was strong this morning, affecting her deeply. Something prickled at her back, sending a bizarre chill between her shoulder blades. She turned slowly to find the Ultima from the library watching her, though she glanced away quickly enough when she saw Harlow turn.

Today she wore a fashionable shift dress and heels, and she sat at a table with another woman, who faced away from Harlow. The other woman was human, but there was something odd about her, something limenal in nature that Harlow couldn't quite put a finger on. The Ultima wore that same stern expression as she had at the library, and Harlow wondered if it might just be the way her face looked. Their eyes met for a moment, and the warrior murmured something to her companion.

They both rose to leave. When they passed Harlow and Petra's table, Harlow got a good look at the Ultima's companion. The young woman was stunning, with muscular arms and a grin that could melt hearts. She flashed it at Harlow as she passed, and a younger version of herself practically swooned. Her hair was short, though not as short as the Ultima's, with a spectacular fade. Her skin was the same rich brown as Petra's. A tattoo on her wrist caught Harlow's eye; it looked like a compass.

The two exited the cafe and Harlow felt momentarily guilty; her heart was beating fast at the sight of the human. She was probably a few years younger than Harlow. More the twins' age, but still... As her heart settled, she smiled. It was fine to be attracted to other people. Finn wouldn't have minded at all, she knew. But a weird flutter lingered in her stomach.

"Someone doesn't wear heels often," Petra said softly as the sorcière warrior and her companion faded out of sight. "She was wobbling something fierce."

Harlow hadn't noticed that at all. In fact, the guardian had looked rather graceful to her, but Petra was probably the expert on such things—or just being petty. Either way, the flutter in Harlow's stomach calmed. She checked to make sure the warrior and her companion were gone and then leaned forward. "I think they were watching us."

"The one looking at us recognized you," Petra said. "The human was just flirting."

Harlow ignored the comment about the human. "The one in the dress is a guardian at the Citadel. One of the Ultima. She's checked me in a few times."

Petra frowned. "Oh, yes, I suppose that could be it." She glanced away quickly. Ever since Petra had broken free of her parents, she'd been almost allergic to lying and deception in personal situations. As it turned out, her emotions were perpetually written on her face, and now she looked supremely uncomfortable.

"What is it?" Harlow asked.

Petra shook her head, her lips pressing into a tight line, like she was refusing to speak.

"Spit it out, Velarius," Harlow chided. She couldn't help but smile as Petra pulled her phone out of her purse and unlocked the screen, so clearly relieved to be asked to tell the truth.

"She might have recognized you from this," Petra said.

Section Seven was pulled up, and there was Harlow on the pinned post. The photo wasn't terrible. In fact, she thought she looked nice, but underneath the caption read, *Harlow Krane can dress it up as much as she wants. We know the frump will return. Click through to see Harlow's twenty worst fashion blunders.* Harlow sighed deeply; there were nearly three thousand comments already. Yet *another* article that rehashed the incident at Gastro Lupo, which the Krane sisters had dubbed "The Great Pineapple Debate," followed it.

"For gods' sake," Harlow said. "We were just arguing about getting pineapple on pizza. Finn has the worst taste in toppings."

"Yeah," Petra agreed. "Pineapple should not be hot."

Harlow grimaced, shuddering.

"Have you been checking it lately?" Petra asked, her voice careful in a way that made Harlow's stomach turn. "Section Seven, I mean."

"No," Harlow sighed. Of all the gossips, Section Seven was the worst, and the cruelest to her. "I kind of hate to give them the views."

Petra nodded, but she looked worried.

"What is it?" Harlow asked.

Petra shrugged, but then seemed to change her mind. "They've started running old content about you from the season. They're picking apart everything about you and Finn's relationship…"

"And?" Harlow prompted when Petra trailed off.

"They're implying that the two of you look like you're faking things. That Finn probably feels sorry for you or something."

"Wow," Harlow breathed. Mean content had always been a part of Section Seven's brand. She was far from the only person they wrote about this way, but it was hard not to feel singled out. "Well, they're not wrong about the fact that we faked it for a while. I suppose it was only a matter of time. Are the stories popular?"

Petra nodded, pushing the plate of scones towards her. "I think your sisters didn't want to mention it to you, but they've been in the 'top likes' category for the past week."

Harlow took a scone, grimacing. "Thank you for telling me."

She wasn't wholly sure she was grateful as she turned the thought over in her mind a few times. *Why did they have to be so cruel about her?* She hated having drawn their attention like this. It would mean being followed more frequently, and she had to admit, it just *hurt* to be scrutinized so closely, to have so many people saying things about her, speculating about her life.

"Distract me," she said, passing Petra's phone back to her. There was no need to dwell on Section Seven's bullshit; they were the way they were, and nothing was going to stop them but something else being bigger news. "Tell me more about you and Kate. How did you meet?"

A slow smile spread over Petra's face. "We met here at the start of summer and kind of hit it off. It's not a very exciting story, really. We just had coffee that day and have been a thing ever since."

Harlow was positive there was more to the story than that, but she understood why Petra wasn't giving her details. She would have done the same if the roles were reversed, but she hoped that eventually Petra would share more. They were careful with each other, after so many years of snide comments and uncomfortable encounters, and Harlow didn't mind it a bit. She trusted Petra, and that was what counted.

Before Harlow could say anything else, she was interrupted by a familiar voice. "Harlow, Petra!"

Harlow turned to greet Meline. "Hi, you."

Meline looked like she'd been crying. Her eyes were red, a sharp contrast to her pale skin, and her hair was pulled into a tight ponytail. The dress she wore was pretty, but she didn't have a single accessory on, nor was she carrying a bag. Petra gave Meline a once-over, noted the same uncharacteristic lack of accessories that Harlow did, and got up from the table. She pulled up another chair, giving Harlow a knowing look that said, *I'll give you two a minute*, and went to order Meline her usual cup of black coffee.

Meline sunk into the chair Petra procured, looking dejected. She took the last of the lemon scones, but didn't eat it. She just sat there, staring at the scone, not saying a word. It was, perhaps, the most subdued Harlow had ever seen her.

"What's wrong?"

Her sister shrugged, then sniffled as though she was suppressing a sob. She mumbled something Harlow couldn't make out.

"I can't understand you, silly."

Meline looked up, her eyes puffy, and said, clearer this time, "I am useless. Those people are in trouble, and I'm fucking *useless*."

Although Meline had been vague, Harlow couldn't help but glance around. The coffee shop was still empty. Meline had many talents, but none of them had been particularly helpful this summer, and when Ari was gone, which was most of the time, she'd retreated further into herself than Harlow had ever seen. She faked it well when she went out, but Harlow had noticed that she was quieter than usual when they were alone with just family.

"You aren't useless," Harlow said. "But I understand why you feel helpless. I do too. Especially after this morning."

It was true; the video footage made Harlow feel ineffective, like nothing she was doing meant anything. She could understand why Meline felt as she did. While they were here in Nea Sterlis, essentially on a luxury vacation, people in Falcyra were fighting for their lives.

Meline picked at the scone angrily, with a long, perfectly manicured nail. "I want to be helping. Not pretending to have a social life. Even Larkin has been helping the maters with covert networking schemes. I'm not even good at that. All I know how to do is run socials and shop."

"*Meline*," Harlow implored, not knowing what to say.

Meline shook her head, biting her bottom lip. "You don't have to convince me of something else. I know it's true."

Harlow's phone buzzed. It was Petra, from the line inside the shop. *Ari's back from Falcyra. Might cheer her up.* Petra's keen ears probably caught the whole conversation. She glanced over her shoulder, and Petra's eyes were full of understanding.

Another text came through. *I know how she feels. Before the Knights, I was just like her. She needs a purpose, Harlow. Talk to Finn.*

I will, Harlow texted back. To Meline she said, "I just got a text. Ari's home. Do you want to go see him?"

Meline shook her head, looking away. "No, he'll be disgusted by me."

This broke Harlow's heart to hear. She hadn't realized Meline was struggling this much, and felt guilty about it. She tried to reassure her, "He will *not*."

Her little sister looked her straight in the eyes. "Why wouldn't he be? He's off doing important things while I hang out here getting my nails and hair done. Shopping. Dinners. *Useless bullshit.*"

Harlow's chest ached with each sharp word Meline spoke against herself. "Arebos Flynn thinks the world of you, Meli, as does everyone who knows you. And there's *nothing wrong* with liking to do things like getting your hair and nails done."

Meline rolled her eyes, but Harlow saw her jaw relax a measure. She obviously wasn't torturing herself out of some desire to stir drama. Meline had always shied away from dwelling in negativity, which is why it affected her so deeply when she couldn't break free of a mood. Indi was the opposite, seeming to enjoy yearning and aching a bit more, but Meline liked for things to be straightforward, and she embraced happiness easily.

A slow smile quirked the corners of Meline's mouth. She looked so much like a young Selene in this moment that Harlow felt like she was looking through a window to the past. Harlow saw both herself and Mama in her sister, and the connection was so intense it throbbed in her chest. There it was again, that sense that her connection to the threads was refining somehow, changing shape before her.

Meline interrupted her thoughts. "Ari really does like me, doesn't he?"

Harlow nodded, taking one of Meline's hands and kissing her palm. "You are wonderful, Meline. Everything you've done this summer has been really helpful. You know that, right?"

Meline glanced at her. "I'm a good distraction."

Harlow nodded, smiling. "You are at that, my beautiful bun-bun." Selene always called the twins that, her beautiful bun-buns. Meline cracked a grin as Petra handed her a cup of coffee, but tears still threatened in her eyes. Petra went wide-eyed, and Harlow realized that for once, she was going to have to guide the conversation, as Meline was too caught up in her head to do so, and Petra didn't really *do* girlfriends.

She wracked her brain, trying to think of something to talk about that wouldn't take them deeper down the sad-spiral each of them seemed poised to slide right into. Television was safe, wasn't it?

"Did either of you catch the *Knight's Own* spinoff last week?" The vampire drama was on summer hiatus, but a new show had just aired exploring one of the side-character's dramatic exploits.

Within a few minutes the three were chatting amiably about the soap opera, and the new romance novel Meline had devoured the night before, which apparently featured a sexy monster love interest. Both Petra and Harlow added it to their StoryTracker accounts and listened with rapt attention as Meline recounted some of the juicier bits.

Content as Meline appeared, Harlow recognized it for what it was: a finely honed act. Her sister wasn't satisfied, and things would change. Harlow had never met someone as strong-willed as Meline. Once she figured out her purpose, she would be unstoppable. As another chill, damp breeze blew in through the courtyard, Harlow felt unsettled, despite the pleasant turn the day had taken.

Things were changing, as they should. It was time they all grew up and faced the truth of the world they lived in head-on, but Harlow wished she could slow time down a little. Every second of peace and pleasure these days felt like they might be the last for a long while. A prickle of excitement skittered through her, chased by a vague sense of foreboding.

CHAPTER 10

The last week of Août passed in a blaze of heat and as soon as the month turned—in fact, nearly the exact moment Septembre began—the rain started. Nea Sterlis' summer of society events and beach days waned, and the tourists all went home. Section Seven let up on Harlow and Finn just enough for them to go out in public more frequently, and though speculation continued that their relationship might be on the rocks, it looked like attention was waning. When a wolf-shifter heiress threw over her longtime alpha lover for a rabbit shifter, Section Seven dedicated their content to discussing the ins and outs of The Order of Masks' social mores.

While that offered some temporary relief, Harlow knew better than to get comfortable. Someone on Section Seven's editorial team had a thing for her, and they'd likely turn back to their nonsense when the uproar over this latest scandal died down. Besides, she had other distractions. She and Finn could hardly keep their hands off each other. He'd fucked her in nearly every room of the villa, and just last night she'd gone down on him in the bathroom at the market.

In the grip of fervor, and a desire not to push Finn too hard to talk about the past, Harlow forgot about *The Warden* until she received an email from the library telling her that her hold was about to expire. She and Finn were cuddled in bed, both scrolling on their phones, when the email came through. She noticed *The Warden* wasn't listed among the books whose hold was about to expire.

"Shit."

"What is it?" Finn asked, looking up at her over his glasses. He was using her belly as a pillow and she'd been playing with his hair.

"My hold at the library is about to expire. One book is missing. I meant to tell you about it…"

She hesitated, not sure if this was a good time to talk about this. They'd been having such a peaceful evening, and things had been good between them, the incident in the Vault firmly in the past. She knew that discussing *The Warden* would bring it all up again, and though she knew she couldn't keep putting this conversation off, she wanted to hold on to this moment of peace between them.

He was clearly still reading an article about woodworking when he responded. "Yeah, what was it called?"

"*The Warden*," she replied.

Finn glanced up. "*The Warden*. Like Ashbourne the Warden?"

Harlow nodded. "Yes, I found a book in the library that claimed that Ashbourne was a member of a race known as the Ventyr, and that in some alien war he fell in love with a girl from an enemy house… Her name was Lumina—"

Finn sat up. "The Ventyr? Are you sure?" He'd gone ghoulishly pale. "*That* word was actually used in the book?"

Harlow's brow automatically furrowed. "Yes…" Finn's hands shook. She'd been right. This was connected to whatever had happened in the Vault. Harlow sat up as well, pushing herself off the pile of pillows she was reclining on, praying to Aphora to smooth the way between them. "What is it?"

"Did the book mention the Anemoi?" Finn asked, his voice hollow.

Harlow nodded. "Yes, they were one of the houses in the book. House Anemos and House Thuellos. They were enemies who had to work together to imprison elemental creatures called the Ravagers, and Ashbourne fell in love with a girl from the Anemoi house, and…. Finn, what's wrong?"

He'd sprung away from her like her words were poison, his chest heaving. "All that was… in a *book* at the *library*?"

Harlow was utterly confused. He seemed panicked by this information. She got up and moved towards him, but he threw his arm out in front of himself. "Harlow, you read that book in the library? *When?*"

Harlow thought back. "The night of the fox shifters, it was that day."

"And you haven't been back to the library since, have you?" He paced like a caged animal.

"No." She reached out, trying to catch his hand, but he was just out of reach. "What's this about?"

Finn's hands glowed, and his bright power flashed through the threads of aether surrounding them, into the wards on the windows and that surrounded the villa proper. *Why was he checking the wards?*

"Nothing like that should exist," he said, his voice quiet but dangerous.

This was the Finn people both feared and admired, the one that got him his way wherever he went. She marveled at how different he was from the softer version of himself that had been resting on her belly a few moments ago. He sank into one of the chairs that sat in front of the fireplace. It wasn't lit, of course, it hadn't cooled enough for that yet. Harlow moved to sit in the chair opposite his, folding her legs underneath her.

"Why not? What does it mean?" The fearsome Finn was dissolving before her. Now he rocked slightly, back and forth, as his face went blank. Like he was somewhere else, lost deep inside himself. "Finn?"

He didn't hear her, that much was clear. She slid to the floor in front of him.

He'd buried his face in his hands and was shivering. "It was so cold in the basement," he murmured. "So cold."

Her heart skipped a beat. He'd only talked about something like this once before. Long ago, when they were children, he had told her and Enzo that sometimes Connor locked him in the basement as a punishment. But what did that have to do with *The Warden*, the Ventyr, or House Anemoi? Whatever it was, this was the thing that Cian had warned her from pushing him to tell. She needed to keep her head now and be careful not to push him too hard.

"Finn," she said again, as she tried to take his hands. He wouldn't budge. "*Baby*," she said, softer this time. His fingers, which were digging into his hair, loosened. "Baby," she said again, dragging the syllables out soft and slow, as his arms fell around her. She rose quickly, winding her arms around his neck, pulling him to the floor in her arms.

He buried his face in her neck, his hands clutching her tightly. His humanoid alternae fell away, and he was naked in front of her, in his true form. For the first time in weeks, there was nothing even mildly arousing about his naked body. All she cared about was the shake in his shoulders and the hot tears seeping into her shirt.

Harlow felt for the surrounding threads, the way she'd done instinctively at The Gate with Petra, but though she sensed them, whatever had happened there wasn't happening now. Once again, she had the unnerving sense that the fervor was blocking this new ability and she had to fight her own frustration to focus on Finn.

She held him tight. Even without being able to connect through the threads, she could help Finn. She had to. "Do you want to tell me what happened in the basement? If you don't want to, you don't have to, but I'm here."

His voice was deeper in his true form, and now it shook as he nodded, his chin quivering. "I told. I wasn't supposed to tell about the Ventyr, but I told…" Finn was murmuring now, nearly unintelligible, but she caught one phrase, his shoulders shaking as he choked out, "Cian… My father beat Cian… I thought he'd kill them… But I promised. Promised we'd never tell… and that I would take the punishment instead."

The story was tumbling out of him in such a confused manner that she had trouble understanding it at first. From what she could gather, Finn had nearly died from the beating and the cold, while Cian was forced to watch. Apparently, the point of this abominable endeavor was to drive home that if either spoke about the Ventyr again, they and anyone they associated with would be swiftly killed. The only reason Connor had not executed Cian was that he seemed to believe they had no interest in the knowledge. She'd always known that Connor McKay was a monster, but she'd never imagined *this*.

Inwardly, she raged. No parent should ever treat a child this way. "That shouldn't have happened to you."

Harlow wasn't entirely sure what he was talking about, but at least he was talking. *Why did he know about the Ventyr as a child? And why was this such a problem for Connor McKay?* She watched Finn's wings flex behind him, and then tuck into a tight bundle at his back. *A winged race—more powerful than gods—who could conquer and inhabit multiple worlds.*

She wrapped her arms closer around Finn, holding him as tight as she could as her mind raced ahead of her. Could it even be possible that her suspicions about *The Warden* had been correct? The conversation they'd had on the train the night they came to Nea Sterlis played in her mind.

The Illuminated are hiding on Okairos.

Hiding from what?

From the rest of our people.

The author of *The Warden* had gotten it all wrong. The Ventyr weren't more powerful than the Illuminated, the Illuminated *were* the Ventyr. At the very least, *The Warden* was a story about who the Illuminated *might* be. Whether it was accurate could be impossible to say, especially if Finn didn't know the truth of it… but the Ventyr were very real. The implication of this information was terrifying. The Illuminated were more powerful than they seemed—and they seemed omnipotent as it was.

Finn stilled in her arms, calming some. He looked up at her, eyes feral with fear. "Did you tell anyone about the book?"

"No," she said, cupping his face in hers. "No, I wanted to see it again and get a copy to show you and Cian. I thought it was one of the pseudo-histories, like the ones Mother collects."

His head shook vigorously. "It's not. I haven't heard that exact story, but everything else—it's all true. The Ventyr, the two warring Houses. The Ravagers… It's why they came here. Something about Okairos was different, hidden from all that. *Safe.* It's why the secret is so important." Finn's words tumbled out of him in a frenzy, as though he was pushing them towards her as fast as he could, while every instinct in him told him to stay silent.

Her first reaction was icy terror, and then white-hot fury ripped through her veins as the full magnitude of what Finn had endured sunk in. Connor McKay deserved to be torn apart, piece by piece. Her skin was too tight. Finn had only been a little boy, telling the only person he was safe with a dangerous secret. *He had just… been… a… little… boy…* Her thoughts were thick and stilted, as though time had slowed to a crawl.

Finn looked as though he moved in slow motion. He was gripping her arms, saying something to her she couldn't make out as rage engulfed her. *Now* she felt the threads between them. As she looked down, her second sight saw them… and something else. She saw where her shadows and his light intertwined, and those led somewhere *beyond.* Her second sight slid over them, and she was out of her body before she knew what was happening, racing along the threads as though they were a pathway she could travel, a road of sorts.

Harlow didn't expect what came next so much as she launched into it head-first. She was thrust out of her own reality, deep into the heart of the limen—the heart of Nihil, where shadowy magic gathered, raw and unbridled. She counted fifteen guardians of the prison, clear as if she stood in front of them. She counted them again. Weren't there supposed to be seventeen?

But no, there were just fifteen. They appeared to be sleeping inside tight, coffin-like chambers, but she sensed their sharp intelligence. Though their eyes were closed, they were not asleep, but in some sort of stasis, in a grand chamber at the center of what she assumed was the prison—Nihil. The heart of the limen pulsed behind them, an enormous knot of life-giving dark power: the aether that filled not only the threads of reality on Okairos, but made magic possible everywhere, in all worlds.

The wardens were winged, just as Finn was, their skin varying shades of subtle blues and greens. Unlike Finn's true form, they were taller, and grander somehow, their features more severe. Harlow wondered if it had something to do with their proximity to the heart of the aether, which flowed around them, into them and out of them. The aether was more alive here than she'd ever seen it and the wardens were absolutely breathtaking in their power.

As the shadowy magic moved, she saw where the missing wardens *should* be: there were two empty chambers. *Two of the wardens were missing? What did that mean?* A sharp burst of fear sliced through her.

Seeing the prison for herself, it hit home what a dangerous gamble it was to house any elemental being that ostensibly fed on aethereal energy so near its *actual* source. As she looked around, she understood the risk. Her spirit body was a pure vehicle for her second sight, which meant she saw the threads of power here more easily than she would in the waking world.

The guardians—the wardens—channeled aether into the great web that was the prison itself; not a physical building exactly, though it had form, but a spell so complicated she could barely track the intricate threads that bound the place together. As she examined the spellwork, she saw that the wardens themselves were the conduits for its power, all that stood between the prisoners and what they likely wanted more than anything in all worlds.

As if by instinct, Harlow traced the dark source of magic; it made up the very walls of the chamber, spreading into vast spaces that she sensed, rather than saw, in her spirit form. There were countless smaller cells, but four that were vast. One was empty, but the others were occupied. Her curiosity piqued, she tried to sense what was inside them from the outside, but could not tell.

Harlow wasn't sure what she could do in this space, but she badly wanted to see what was inside those chambers. She pressed into one, sliding between the walls of the spell easily in her non-corporeal form. It was a little surprising that her presence didn't trip any wards, and she wondered if being a Strider made her somehow invisible here. As her second sight adjusted to the chamber, she recoiled in horror. The thing imprisoned there was nothing like any elemental being she'd ever read about, or could even conceive of.

Its attention moved slowly, but she felt when it turned towards her. She was but a speck of dust in comparison with it, and yet, it sensed her. Its size was inconceivable, and though she could not make out its form, her spirit understood that it was a thing of nearly pure malevolence, which should not be possible—all things were a mixture of what she understood as good and bad, even elemental creatures. She froze in abject fear as it laughed. The thing was *sentient*.

Hello, little bird.

Its words were not words. They were bloody shrieks and tortured wailing.

They were little more than an impression, but one that filled her with despair. She pulled away from the Ravager, for that was what it had to be, as quickly as she could, but she felt it in every fiber of her being as she re-entered the stasis chamber.

See you soon, it called after her as she retreated.

Harlow's spirit form threatened to pull apart from panic. It was vital that she regain control of herself, as there was no guarantee that her consciousness would reassemble in her body on Okairos if she disintegrated here. She stumbled towards the wardens, thinking to steady herself nearer to the knot of aether they guarded.

The largest of them opened his eyes, which glowed with the same light as the Illuminated's. There was no doubt that, whatever power the Illuminated had, they were one and the same with the Ventyr. There was something regal in his expression, as well as deep sadness.

"Strider," he whispered, a smile forming on his impossibly beautiful face. His features were stronger, more rugged than Finn's, but there was a resemblance between them, she thought. Some hint of affinity.

When he spoke again, he had a voice that would have sent her to her knees, had she been in her corporeal form. "Go home, child. It is not safe for you here." His hand stretched out before him, and the shadows he channeled from the heart of the limen surrounded her, pushing her backwards, out of the dark world at the center of all life.

Her eyes flew open. Finn was staring at her. He was back in his alternae, his jaw slightly slack as he took her right hand in his. Her entire arm was covered in black, iridescent feathers. The feathers dissolved before their eyes, melting into her shadow magic, which flowed around her ink-stained hands.

"You started to shift," he said.

"How long was I gone?"

Finn glanced at the clock. "Gone? What do you mean?"

Had no time passed? How was that possible? "I was angry," she replied. "And then… I think I was in Nihil. I think… I think I *saw* Ashbourne."

"You saw him?"

She nodded. "And the generals. They were like you… I must have been hallucinating."

He shook his head. "You weren't."

"The Illuminated are the Ventyr," Harlow said.

"Yes," Finn replied, his shoulders slumping.

"That's not all I saw," Harlow choked out. She did her best to describe the Ravager, but no words could capture its terrible essence.

Finn rose far enough to slide back into his chair, dragging her with him into his lap. They were silent for a long time, breathing in time with one another. When he finally spoke, his voice was weary. "No one can ever find out that you know this, Harls. Promise me you won't tell anyone else."

Part of her railed against the idea of having another secret, of keeping a secret for the Illuminated. But when she thought about the fact that Connor McKay had beaten his only son within an inch of his life for just telling Cian, literally the most trustworthy person ever, that the Ventyr *existed*, it made more sense. She had no trouble imagining that Connor, or any of the elder Illuminated, would kill her and anyone they thought she might have told about all this. This was a secret they wanted kept at all costs.

As much as she hated to admit it, after coming in such close contact with one of the Ravagers, if there was any possibility that what Finn had said was right, that somehow Okairos was safer than other realms—hidden somehow—then keeping this a secret made more sense than telling. It excused nothing about the way the Illuminated had operated here for the past two thousand years, but she could agree that if Okairos was beyond the reach of those creatures, and the rest of the Ventyr, then maybe secrecy was necessary.

"All right," she agreed.

"Stay away from that book."

She nodded, but he took her chin in his fingers. He didn't grip her hard, but his hold on her was firm. "Promise me."

"I will," she whispered. He didn't need to explain further. She already understood. Children were precious to the Illuminated, and Connor had tortured Finn to drive his point home.

He pulled her tighter against his chest, playing with her hair. Both of their breathing slowed. "The Ventyr are dangerous, Harlow. They have a limited ability to travel between worlds, but when my parents came here, they were looking for easier ways to do so, and not to explore or create alliances, but to serve their endless desire to conquer."

"Isn't that what they did to us, though?" Harlow asked. She didn't want to make Finn feel bad. She understood he was nothing like his parents, but there was something she didn't feel he was acknowledging.

"Yes," he agreed. There was no *but*. "I don't think my parents' generation knew any other way to behave. If it matters at all, I think they love Okairos and want to protect it."

Harlow let out a derisive huff of air, rolling her eyes. "That's one way to put it."

"They're evil. I know that… I'm just not sure they ever had a choice to be any different."

Harlow thought of the noble expressions on the guardians' faces. The way Ashbourne had looked at her when he sent her home. It was *nothing* like Connor or Aislin McKay, or any of the older Illuminated. "Are you sure that's true? The wardens were different somehow."

Finn's bottom lip quivered and his eyes fluttered shut. "No," he said, voice hoarse. "No, I'm not." He stared into the dark fireplace.

She stroked his cheek, pressing kisses to his cheekbones, his brow, then finally his lips. "I understand why you need to believe there could be good in them."

He glanced at her, visibly cringing at her words. "Do you?"

She kissed him again. "You're the only good thing they ever did. *You* are what's good about them."

His eyes fell to her engagement ring, which he touched. "You are what's good about me."

She shook her head. "That is not true. *You* are what's good about you. You, Alaric, Petra... You're all good in ways they aren't. The three of you *chose* something else."

Finn's jaw clenched, as though he couldn't quite trust what she said.

She gripped his chin now, a mirror of what he'd done to her before, turning his stormy eyes to hers. "It is a *choice* to be good—to do good—one you make every single day despite them." His eyes misted as she spoke. "I'm so fucking proud of you."

"You are?" he asked, his voice breaking over the words.

"I am," she replied. They stared at one another as her words sunk in. "Everything you are, everything you've done, everything you've *endured*... I am so proud of you."

He shook his head, a smile playing at his lips. "What did I do to deserve that kind of love?" he murmured. The look in his eyes was full of gratitude she didn't want.

"Nothing, sweet boy," she said, pressing yet another kiss to his lips. "You never had to *do* anything for me to love you this way. It's not something you can earn." The blush blooming on Finn's cheeks sent heat through her. He looked so damn *happy*. "It's not something you can lose, either."

He hugged her tight. "I love you, Harlow," he breathed into her hair as he lifted her, carrying her to bed.

CHAPTER 11

The next day felt like autumn, a Nea Sterlis autumn, mild and blessedly sunny; but a storm was raging out at sea, though the weather reports said it was unlikely to come ashore. From the terrace off the kitchen, the view of the imposing clouds was menacing. Harlow sat outside, sipping her last cup of coffee for the afternoon. If she drank much more, she'd be unlikely to sleep.

The household was all out at their scheduled activities, she and Axel the only ones left at home. Even Larkin had gone to the pool with the twins and the Wraiths. They'd asked her to come along, but Harlow was still shaken from her trip to the limen. Thea knew something was wrong, but when she'd pressed her about it over breakfast, Harlow had snapped at her, which started one of their silent wars.

Harlow hated to keep a secret from her family, particularly Thea. She'd worked so hard to mend her relationships with them, after everything that happened with Mark, and having to keep a secret so monumental from all of them bothered her. A heavy thump caught her attention. The auburn cat was back, and it rubbed its face against her calf.

"Hello there," she crooned, patting her lap. She wasn't sure if the big feline would consent to be held, but she felt like offering.

It didn't take her up on the invitation, instead leaping onto the table next to her, staring into her eyes. Its expression was fiercely intelligent, as though any moment it might open its mouth and speak. She chuckled at her own foolishness.

"May I scratch your ears?" she asked politely, stretching her fingers towards him.

He bumped her hand with his head and she gently rubbed behind the massive ears, feeling the muscles in the cat's neck as it strained towards her, purring. "Aren't you sweet?" she crooned.

It glared at her, pawing her hand away as if to say, "Don't underestimate me."

"You are very fierce," she said. "Obviously."

Axel chirped from the doorway and the red cat jumped down from the table to bump noses with him. The two of them leapt onto the wall and disappeared down a steep ledge that ran along the sea wall to the next terrace over. Harlow couldn't watch. Though she knew it was probably safe for a cat, Axel was her baby and she hated to watch him navigate such spaces.

She waited a moment, then rose to peek over the balcony at them. They were facing away from her, watching something intently below. She followed their gazes, but saw nothing. The red cat turned, its topaz eyes alight with awareness and it looked straight at her and yowled, then looked back at the spot below where Axel's gaze affixed. Harlow saw nothing at first.

The red cat hissed just as Axel growled. Both cats' fur stood on end, their tails doubling in size. Harlow peered again at where their attention was affixed. She took a few deep breaths and then engaged her second sight. Sure enough, the threads were disturbed, just in the spot the cats were looking. There was something there, rendered clumsily invisible by spellwork.

"Not so clumsy if I missed it the first few times I looked," she muttered.

Harlow marked the spot where the disturbance was. It was near the door to the beach below, bouncing against the villa's ward. If she could get down there before whatever it was disappeared, she might be able to get a better look at the thing. She rushed down the stairs that led to the seawall level. Footsteps followed her, and she glanced behind her.

Finn grinned at her, caught sneaking. His hair was still damp. He'd been surfing earlier in the day and had made a trip to the market. His hands were full of groceries. "Hey there, gorgeous. Where are you off to in such a rush?"

"Axel and his cat friend found what's probing us. Somebody's made whatever it is invisible, rather badly, but still… It's at the beach door."

Finn set the groceries down. "Okay. And you're going to look?"

She nodded, urgency filling her. "We should hurry before it gets away."

Finn grabbed her arm. "Let's take this slow, okay? Whatever it is, it might be a good idea to pretend we don't see it, don't you think?"

Harlow rolled her eyes. "Or we could grab it and take it apart."

They stared at each other for a moment, both thinking. "Something about the Great Pineapple Debate has been bugging me," Finn said.

Harlow threw her arms up in the air. "What in seventeen hells does that have to do with anything? You want to argue about pizza right now?"

He snickered. "No. Though you're wrong. It's a superior topping."

Harlow glared.

"No, what's been bugging me was the angle the video was taken from. Like the camera was on the ground," Finn said, taking her hand and kissing it.

Harlow couldn't remember the video itself. She tried to avoid watching anything Section Seven posted. "What's weird about that?"

Finn pulled her towards the beach door. "Even if a person had taken the video, it would be odd for the camera to be on the ground. Maybe table height, but the angle was strange."

Harlow couldn't really see the significance, and she was worried they were going to miss whatever the thing was altogether.

"How did you catch sight of it, if it's invisible?"

"My second sight caught the spell. If I'd known what I was looking for, I'd probably have caught it sooner. The cats hissed at it."

Finn nodded. "Cats see through spells easily. Did you know that?"

Harlow sighed. "Of course."

"Okay, okay," he said, drawing her toward him, wrapping his arms around her waist. "So, think with me for a minute. What if we have a fight in front of it and see what happens?"

He had a point. If Section Seven, or one of the other gossips was utilizing some kind of surveillance device, then having a fight in front of it might trigger some kind of reporting. It was the kind of thing she wasn't used to thinking yet, but of course he was. She smiled, agreeing. "And then what? Just let it go?"

Finn nodded. "You use your second sight to see if you can get a better look at it, but we'll be having a fight about something."

"Like what?" she asked as his hands slid under the light sweater she wore. It had been chilly in the house all day and she'd pulled one of his sweaters on over a bathing suit. She'd meant to go swimming this afternoon. The warm days were numbered, after all.

"Did you have to be wearing this?" he asked, his fingers grazing over her hips, tugging at her bikini bottoms. "It's going to be very distracting to be rude to you while you're wearing something so hot."

"Focus," she laughed. "Was anyone with you today when you surfed?"

His forehead wrinkled. "Kate, of course. But we ran into some of her friends on the beach. Some kind of bird shifters, swans maybe?"

Harlow's heart leapt. "Was one of them Leto Vipointe?"

Finn nodded. "Yeah. She wouldn't stop touching my arm."

Harlow snickered. "This is almost too perfect. Kate and I used to argue about that girl all the time."

Finn frowned. "Because?"

"Because she's a hideous flirt!" Harlow smacked his arm. "You are so oblivious sometimes."

He shrugged, kissing her nose. "I think about you a lot. It doesn't leave me a lot of room for noticing other people that way."

His face was so open and earnest that Harlow had to kiss him. She raised up on her tiptoes, pressing her lips to his. "I'm really sorry about this, okay?"

Finn started to say something, but she threw the door open and stalked out onto the beach. "Don't follow me," she sneered, her entire countenance changing.

"Harls," Finn pleaded as he followed her out. "What's wrong?"

She spun, letting out a dry laugh. "Like you don't know."

He looked genuinely confused, shaking his head. This was perfect. She was facing the door now, and her second sight locked onto the device. It was a tiny drone, with a camera affixed to it. Invisibility spells were hard to cast, and though this one was fairly good, it wasn't anything like what Nox and Ari could do. The drone was easy to sense now that she had it in her sights.

"Leto Vipointe? Really?" Harlow tried to inject as much jealousy as she could into her words, remembering the way Kate and Leto had flirted at a party when they first started dating.

Finn shook his head, the picture of confused innocence. "Who?"

Harlow strode forward and poked him in the chest. "The swan shifter you were flirting with at the beach this morning. I've been getting messages all day."

Finn captured her hand in his. "I honestly don't even remember who you're talking about. Could we go inside and talk?"

Harlow groaned loudly. "You're just going to keep following me until I agree, aren't you?" This was exactly the kind of thing Section Seven should eat up. Finn being the dejected good guy, her the shrill bitch.

He hung his head, his shoulders slumping. "Can we please just talk?"

"Fine," she snapped, practically stomping back into the villa.

When the door was firmly shut, they rushed to a hidden window in the back stairwell that looked out over the beach door. "Is it still there?" Finn asked.

Harlow shook her head. "It's gone. Now what?"

Finn shrugged. "Now we wait. If the footage appears, we'll know who's been probing us."

Harlow snickered. "I can think of a few things I'd like probed."

Finn gave her a helpless look. "The groceries are melting. I got gelato from Moretti's."

"By all means," Harlow laughed. "Let's take care of that, and then *you* can probe *me*."

He tossed her over his shoulder in one fluid motion, pressing a kiss to her exposed ass cheek. "And we can eat gelato after."

She squealed with delight as he stroked the back of her legs. When he set her down next to the pile of groceries, he pressed a kiss to her forehead. "We make a good spy team, Krane."

Harlow smiled as she picked up a few bags. "That we do, McKay." She smacked his ass with one of the bags. "Get going."

Finn cheated and simply whooshed away, his laugh echoing as she trotted up the stairs after him.

CHAPTER 12

There was no sign of their "fight" on the gossips, but the next day brought the threatening storm closer to shore than had been predicted. New reports suggested hurricane gales were possible, but that the storm itself would likely still miss them. Everyone's phones blared Nytra's severe storm warning shortly before dinnertime. All across the city, storm shutters closed and people went into their basements to wait things out. The entire family was making their way downstairs with books, laptops, and tablets, but Harlow wasn't sure where Axel was and she needed to check in with Enzo before they shut the front door. All summer, he'd alternated between staying at the villa and with Riley.

She was on the floor, looking for the cat under his favorite chair, when Enzo texted her back. She could hear Finn shaking treats upstairs, calling for his "little baby kitten." He'd probably find him first, so she sat back on her heels to read the text. *Safe at Kate's. Petra's here too.*

Enzo and Riley had been so busy coordinating the sale of the new retail space that they hadn't had much time for socializing as the summer wound down. Harlow was a little jealous that Finn, Enzo, and Petra were all spending so much time with Kate. This hadn't been an issue before everything with Mark happened. Logically, Harlow *knew* Kate had nothing to do with what happened with Mark, but she found herself less trusting overall these days and she was frustrated that Kate had inched back into her world, person by person, until she had no choice but to have her as part of her life.

You'll stay put through the storm? Harlow replied.

Of course. We're spending the night. See you tomorrow.

"Come *on*," Thea said, pulling on her arm. Axel was in her arms and she pointed to the last open window, the one Ari was busy shuttering. From their vantage point, Harlow could see the terrifying way the sea lurched towards the shoreline. It was clear why there were no buildings close to the beaches, and why the majority of homes were perched high atop the cliffs of Nea Sterlis. Everything about the bay was different in the green light of the storm.

Rain hit the windows, blown by the high winds, and then all was quiet as the villa's storm shutters closed in place. Finn came running down the stairs, and he activated the shutters that closed the front door. "All in, right?"

Harlow nodded, taking Axel from Thea, who disappeared downstairs. "Enzo and Petra are with Kate and Riley."

Something flickered across Finn's face, almost like he was confused for a moment. Harlow had to wonder if he was seeing what she did, that Kate was a bigger part of their lives than either of them had noticed. Something banged against the shutters at the back of the house. Something big. Axel yowled piteously.

"We need to get downstairs," Finn said, taking Axel from her.

Fittingly, he was wearing his *Cat Dad Extraordinaire* shirt today, and Harlow chuckled a little, despite her racing heart. She was terrified of hurricanes and tornadoes. Finn took her hand, and she followed him to the Vault, where everyone gathered in various states of undress. They'd been getting ready for dinner when the storm rolled in, fast and unpredictable. Nox pulled a few bins out of a closet in the Vault's common room.

"There's a bunch of sweats in here," she explained. "And tactical stuff, but we bought emergency clothes a few years ago, in case we had to lock the house down."

Everyone started digging through the bins, handing one another clothes. Harlow had been wearing a robe when the storm swept in and was chilly now, so she took both a sweatshirt and some sweatpants. They all had the Haven logo on them.

"Are these merch?" she asked with a laugh.

Alaric snickered. "Yes. Cian designed them, but we never sold any of them, so all the samples came down here."

Indigo shrugged. "I think they're smokin."

Cian raised an eyebrow.

"She thinks they're cute," Meline explained. "It's slang."

Cian shrugged. They were dressed in a luxurious cream-colored cashmere tracksuit, which Selene was wearing a twin of. Aurelia glanced between them. "Have the two of you been shopping together?"

"Yes, Li-li," Selene said with a sigh. "*Online.*"

"Every night before bed, with wine," Cian added.

Everyone was joking and chatting. Larkin was arranging snacks on the table and Nox got cards out as Thea and Alaric sat on the floor, wrapping themselves in blankets. Axel curled up on Thea's lap and it seemed like the twins were settling in with their ereaders, along with Finn, who stretched out with his feet on Aurelia's lap. She had a book about ancient shifter iconography that she raised so Finn could get comfortable.

They were all chatting, their conversation a comfortable buzz as Harlow stood at the doorway of the room, gathering up the last of the shed pajamas and robes into an empty bin. Only Ari was missing, but she'd seen him come down.

She finished pulling a set of wool performance socks on and then stuck her head out into the hallway. A light was on in the office he shared with Nox.

She padded down the hallway to see if he wanted tea. The heavily-muscled shifter hunched at his desk, staring at a screen that she couldn't see, because his desk faced the door. The room was eerily quiet for Arebos' usual tastes. He typically had loud rock music playing, as he said it helped him concentrate—and he hated to wear headphones.

Now, the office was silent, a sure sign something was wrong. Half of Ari's long, ebony hair was pulled away from the sharp planes of his face, and his hand covered his usually smiling mouth. Arebos Flynn was one of the most incorrigible teases Harlow had ever met, constantly making jokes and flirting. It was rare for him to look so serious. The sounds of happy family life muffled as she shut the door.

"What is it?" she asked. They'd told the Wraiths and the other Knights about their subterfuge with the drone. Perhaps the footage was airing. "Has someone released the beach footage?"

Ari startled, his narrow eyes worried. He shoved a piece of hair behind one of his pointed ears, pointing at the computer screen in front of him. "No, nothing on that yet. It's Falcyra. Things are getting worse."

Harlow trailed around the piles of Nox's books on the floor. The Wraith had been obsessed with theories of surveillance all summer and collected tomes on everything from cutting edge tech to the ethics of surveillance culture. Harlow didn't know Nox well yet, but she was impressed with the vigor with which she explored her own position in the shadowed world of espionage. When Harlow made it through the maze, she caught sight of Ari's screen, and her breath caught in her chest.

The footage was playing on a loop with the sound off, in three-times speed, but that didn't make it any less horrific. Falcyra was *burning*. The vampires were killing humans by the dozen and it looked like the humans were revolting.

Harlow closed her eyes. "I thought the Dominavus were sent to handle this."

"They were," he replied. "But even they can't be everywhere. They get one riot calmed, and another crops up elsewhere. Falcyra has fallen to chaos."

Finn poked his head in, his excellent hearing having drawn him toward their conversation, no doubt. Alaric was behind him, followed by Thea. Soon, the whole family crowded behind Ari's desk, watching the awful footage.

Ari slowed it to normal speed, and the sound turned back on. The humans were overpowered, but the vampires and the Dominavus were outnumbered. It was sheer carnage on both sides. Nox went to her desk, murmuring something to Ari about sending her the footage as she went. She pulled the footage up on her super-powered computer and ran a scan.

"Rakul Kimaris isn't in any of this footage," she said.

"You can't know that yet," Alaric reasoned.

"No, but I'm willing to bet on it," Nox replied with a smile that showed she knew more than she was saying. Harlow was continuously surprised by the things that Nox and Arebos could find out about people—she with her near-magical ability to navigate technology and he with more traditional means of reconnaissance.

Nox tied her mass of jet-black hair back and began typing furiously, squinting a little at the screen. Indi handed her a pair of glasses and the wistful look they exchanged elicited a fake gag from Larkin, shot in Harlow's direction.

"She's right," Ari added, pointedly ignoring Larkin's antics. "I caught something this morning, but I've watched that footage a dozen times. He's never with the Dominavus, and it's not like you could miss him."

"What did you catch?" Larkin asked.

"I think he's back in Nytra," Ari replied, glancing at Larkin, who squeezed his shoulder as she passed him, plopping down on the couch behind his desk. The office was too small for this conversation, but no one seemed like they were willing to go elsewhere.

Nox nodded. "He used a little known alias at Cerberus, just last week," Nox said. "CCTV picked it up."

Ari glanced at the information his sister pulled up and added, "It's an odd one: Vivia Woolf."

The teacup Cian was carrying clattered onto its saucer. Harlow noted the nearly imperceptible shake of their fingers and made eye contact with Finn. He saw it too.

"What is it?" Finn asked.

Cian's mouth pressed into a grim line. "I haven't heard that name in a very long time. What makes you think Rakul uses it as an alias?"

Nox frowned. "It's in the Vault's records as being associated with him. I haven't ever seen an instance in which he actually used it."

"Associated?" Cian laughed. The sound was harsh and tears filled their eyes. "Yes, that name is *associated* with Rakul."

Everyone went still. Cian Herrington was nothing if not perpetually serene and in control. Sometimes their humor was dry and acerbic, but they never appeared as they did now.

Unhinged, Harlow thought to herself. She made eye contact with Indi, who nodded, understanding her older sister's expression immediately. Indigo whispered something to her twin, who then whispered to Ari.

"Let's give Cian some space," Indi said, ushering Nox out of the office. Nox protested, but Indigo shook her head. Harlow watched as Nox's fingers brushed Indigo's as they left the room. They were like courtly lovers from an old story. Something about it was achingly sweet to watch. Meline and Ari left as well. Selene and Aurelia followed, dragging Thea and Alaric with them.

Larkin gently pried the teacup from Cian's hand. "I'll take this," she murmured.

Cian nodded, looking lost as Larkin left. Harlow led Cian to the small couch behind Ari's desk and slid onto the couch next to them. Their head was in their hands and their shoulders shook. Cian was obviously in pain.

Finn sat in Ari's chair, leaning forward as Harlow's hand went to Cian's back. "Are you all right?" she whispered.

"No," Cian choked out. "No, I am not."

"What does that name mean to you?" Finn asked.

Cian covered their face with their hands. "Vivia Woolf was an Argent."

Finn's breath caught. "Rakul's alias…"

Cian nodded. "Yes, Vivia and Rakul were bonded."

"What happened to Vivia?" Harlow asked, knowing the story couldn't possibly have a happy ending, not with the dark look on Cian's face.

Cian tossed their hands in the air, frustrated somehow. "To be honest, I don't know. I believe she's dead, but Rakul would never, or *could* never, say."

Finn tensed, but his voice was gentle. "There's something you're not saying, old friend."

Cian ran a hand through their hair, sending it spiking up in all directions. "This secret has protected the few of us left for nearly two thousand years…" Cian trailed off, looking distraught.

While she'd never describe Cian as stoic, she expected a well of stillness in their persona that she could depend on. This version of her friend was unsettling, worrisome.

"We would never tell anyone," Harlow said, trying as hard as she could to keep her voice even. Every part of her stood at attention. Whatever Cian was keeping from them had to be monumental to get them so worked up.

Harlow's sense of the threads in the room clarified. Tension snapped like an electrical current through them and Harlow's second sight sensed the connections between the three of them. They were strongest between Cian and Finn, but she was connected to them as well. Both glanced down at her.

"It's nothing. Just another weird development with my Strider abilities."

Relief spread through Cian's countenance, but Finn looked concerned. He'd been more worried than ever after her strange "trip" to the limen, given the way she'd partially shifted.

"Whatever it is, you can tell us," Finn said, reassuring the firedrake. For the moment, he seemed to have refocused on the problem at hand.

Cian reached toward Finn, their brow furrowed and mouth tight. The two of them grasped onto one another's forearms. It was a silent pledge, Harlow understood. A confirmation of a lifelong commitment between the two of them, deeper than any bond of simple friendship. They'd made promises to one another, binding promises, and Finn was a good enough leader to remind his friend that those promises would be kept forever. Harlow couldn't help but swell with pride.

Cian let out a long sigh. "The Argent were here before the Illuminated, as were many of the Heraldic Order."

The silence in the room rang in Harlow's ears. It was one of the basic tenets of life with the Illuminated. They had created *all* the immortals on Okairos. What Cian was saying undermined everything Okairons held as truth. She glanced back at Finn to see his reaction. *Had he known this already, the way he had with the truth of* The Warden? The open shock on his face told her everything she needed to know.

"And you?" Finn asked, his words clipped.

"Born not from the Illuminated, but Argent parents, about fifty years before your people came here. We age very slowly and truth be told, I remember little of the world before the Illuminated came."

A long silence passed. Cian was older than most of the Illuminated on the planet. Many things made sense that had simply been mysterious about Cian previously. Their strange mix of youth and antiquity, in particular. Harlow's mind raced past those revelations and towards the historical implications of what Cian said. "Were there sorcières here? Vampires?"

In an uncharacteristic movement, Cian pushed both hands through their short hair, mussing it in a way that still looked perfect. "There were magical practitioners before the Illuminated, but not like sorcières. They worked aether differently, with more subtlety. As for vampires, they didn't exist before the Illuminated, but there were the Vespae..."

Harlow had read about the Vespae in books of old Falcyran folklore. They were creatures of legend, humanoid in some ways, but like swarming or hiving insects in others. Their sting was said to immobilize an immortal's access to the aether, a tall tale. "They're not supposed to be real," she mused.

Finn and Cian both raised their eyebrows in an identical expression that proved Cian had essentially raised Finn. She grinned at them, tempted to boop each of their noses, the way she would with Axel, but she restrained herself. "The tales I've read seemed tailor-made to scare children."

Cian nodded. "The lore is pretty accurate. Probably because for a long while in Falcyra, a nest or two would crop up—deep in the mountains, but still it made sense for people to tell their children the stories."

"A safety precaution," Finn mused.

"Yes. They were intensely territorial and once they'd decided to make a home in a given area, they wiped out all humanoid life. There weren't many of them for a long while, so the best line of defense was avoidance. When the Illuminated arrived on Okairos, the Vespae were growing in numbers, expanding their territory. A swarm working together could slaughter whole towns and cities in a single night. Humans didn't stand a chance against them."

The sheer thought of it was terrifying. Even now, humans had the means to at least make a stand against immortals. The riots in Falcyra were proof of that. Despite everything, their numbers won out over immortal strength, but the Vespae sounded like they might present another kind of problem.

Cian continued. "My people were the single line of defense against the Vespae for centuries, but there were few of us, spread thin across the planet. We were leaders, royalty in most places. The Empress Lofrata herself was an Argent. We protected our people the best we could."

Cian's head lowered, sadness in their eyes. Finn gripped their shoulder, attempting to comfort the Argent. "But it wasn't enough?"

Cian shook their head. "No. It wasn't enough—they overran us. For most of our history, the Vespae had been a problem, but a manageable one. And then their numbers swelled. When the Illuminated came, Lofrata accepted their offer of aid, never believing the price we would all pay for it. She was the High Empress, ruler of all—and they executed her..." Cian's voice broke over their next words, as Harlow's heart shattered in her chest. "... and my parents, along with all the heads of state with Heraldic blood. A few of us—children, mind you, the oldest were adolescents—were spirited away, kept hidden."

Harlow reached out to hug Cian, but they shook their head. This was painful, and they needed to finish. "When the Order of Masks came into prominence, we could reintegrate into society more fully. Many of our children were weaker than we were, and they presented differently when they shifted than we do. The Illuminated believed that their own remarkable genetics generated *our* children."

The scorn in Cian's voice cut deep. It was remarkable that they could stand to be around any of the Illuminated.

"What does all this have to do with Vivia Woolf?" Finn asked, his voice gentle. "And Rakul?"

"Vivia was Lofrata's daughter, the heir to the most powerful draconic power the world has ever known. The daughter she had with Rakul Kimaris was remarkable, but wholly different from both her parents. Inasa was pure shadow, a creature of the limen."

Cian paused as their silver eyes lit on Harlow and held fast. "Inasa Kimaris was the first Feriant, and she paired with a sorcière, and her daughter..."

"... was the first Strider," Harlow breathed. "No wonder she could shift. With both Illuminated and Argent blood, as well as her sorcière half, she must have been very powerful. But why the Feriant? Why a bird and not a dragon?"

Cian smiled sadly. "No one ever knew."

Finn leaned back, eyes shrewd and analytical. "That's how Rakul knew what Harlow was. His own grandchild was like her. What happened to them? To Inasa and Vivia, and the first Strider?"

"Inasa died in the War." Cian's eyes filled with tears. "Caitriona, the first Strider, died later. She was a good friend. We grew up together."

Harlow was willing to bet that Caitriona Kimaris was more than a friend, but she wouldn't press on what was still clearly an open wound. "What happened to Vivia?"

Cian shook their head. "I don't think anyone ever said, and we scattered so quickly that information on what happened to everyone became hard to keep track of."

There was so much grief in Cian's voice, but they turned towards Finn, steadying their breath. "Your father was the one to execute Caitriona. He had an obsession with her. They were left... alone... for days before the execution."

Finn paled, staring at Harlow. "Why didn't you tell me this sooner?"

Cian stared at their hands. "I should have. But just like your secrets have kept you safe, so too have mine." They glanced at Harlow. "But I should have told you both when you were seventeen. I should have known."

Harlow took one of Cian's hands. "How could you have? Even my own parents didn't know what I was—and they were watching for the signs in all of us."

Cian wiped their eyes. "I worried it might be one of you and when Finn loved you... I... I should have seen this all coming. Connor won't stop until he has what he wants from the two of you." Cian paused, their mouth a thin line.

"Caitriona had a disorder that Argent sometimes get. Her bleeds were painful, debilitating. She was infertile."

Harlow's breath caught as a wave of nausea washed over her. Her chin quivered, as what Cian was saying became clear. "That's why Connor killed her."

Cian nodded, tears flowing down their face freely. Finn looked as though he might burst into flames. His eyes glowed fiercely with that cold, lethal light that only appeared when he was incensed. His fists clenched tightly, and he obviously held his breath.

Harlow didn't want to push either of them harder on any of this, so she left her questions about all the specifics of Cian's story for another time, and got to the point. "So what does Rakul using Vivia's name at Cerberus mean?"

Finn spoke. "It's a message."

Cian nodded. "I think we have to assume so."

The implications of all this pieced together. Her heritage was part Illuminated, part shifter, and part sorcière. Something tickled in the back of her mind, some connection she felt just about to make, but Finn interrupted her train of thought.

"Someone has to go back to Nuva Troi to find Kimaris and ask him about all this," Finn said in a hollow voice—looking beyond her at Cian. "Whatever he wants, I don't think we can afford to ignore him. He wouldn't leave the Dominavus alone in Falcyra for no reason."

Cian regained some composure. "I agree. It might be valuable for you to spend some time with your father, to gauge his level of concern with you and Harlow. Connor will play this carefully, and we need to be a step ahead for once."

The sound of Finn's teeth grinding together made Harlow's skin crawl. "Then I have to go back. If we have any chance of getting the upper hand, the window is surely closing."

"I am sorry, Finbar. I should have told you all of this sooner," Cian said.

Finn sighed. "I understand why you didn't. I only wish we didn't have to guard ourselves so carefully. Secrets are our way. That won't change."

"We will go back to Nuva Troi then," Cian said, standing.

Harlow saw the way they were looking at one another. "No," she said, shaking her head. "I'm coming too."

Finn's response was sharp, his voice jagged and rough at the edges. "No. You will stay here with Alaric and your family. Where it's *safe*."

"You don't get to decide that for me," Harlow argued.

"I do," Finn said, standing. "You were sworn into the Knights and I'm your commander. It's not a request. It's an order. You will stay here."

Harlow stood. "Fuck you, McKay. You don't get to boss me around. I'm coming to Nuva Troi."

Cian stepped away from them carefully, backing out of the room. "I'll leave you two to discuss this. I'll plan for our trip, Finn."

Finn nodded. "Do that. Make arrangements for *two* of us."

Cian nodded once, then disappeared.

"Why are you cutting me out of this?" Harlow hissed.

Finn growled. "Didn't you hear what Cian said? You are the descendant of a pairing that should not have been possible. That my parents did *everything* to stop. You've met Rakul Kimaris. Do you think there is any instance in which he'd work for my father after he killed Rakul's family—unless they had some way of *making* him stay loyal?"

Harlow was stunned into silence. Put that way, it didn't make much sense.

"He's sneaking around, leaving a trail of breadcrumbs for us to find… Whatever Connor has on him to keep him loyal, it's not something small. Until I know *exactly* what's happening here, I don't want you anywhere near Nuva Troi."

Harlow saw his point, but they had to make this time count. The sense of foreboding she'd had for weeks culminated here, she was sure of it. "Fine. But we have to be clever."

Finn relaxed a measure, one eyebrow quirked. "You have a plan in mind?"

Harlow paused for a beat. "I think so, but you won't like it."

Finn's head fell back, and a laugh escaped his beautiful lips. Harlow was confused until he said, "All my Knights' best plans start with those exact words. Tell me what I won't like." He pulled her closer to him so that her head rested against his chest, his arm curling around her.

"This all started with us pretending to be together to draw them out…" she began.

Finn pressed a kiss to her forehead. "Yes, and it worked."

"Sort of," Harlow agreed. "It got them to back off Antiquity Row, but we also gave them what they wanted… *us*."

Finn's entire body tensed. "You want to take it away?"

She craned her neck to look up at him. "Yes. Let's make it look like we're about to break up and see what they do. Section Seven has them primed, and our little show for the drone supports it."

His eyes darkened as his forehead wrinkled in thought. "Section Seven will rip you apart if we do this right."

Harlow swallowed hard. "I know. I can take it."

"You won't be able to tell anyone, not right away anyway. Not until we know what that probe was about. Anything that even hints that we might try to trick them could be a risk."

"I know," she whispered, her fingers curling around the arm draped around her waist. It hurt to think of deceiving her family this way, but they had this one chance.

"Then we'll get it set up. I'm going to tell Cian so they can be our go-between if we need one, but that's it. It'll only be a week, maybe two." He shifted a little against her, his breathing relaxing as he thought things over. "I think we have to assume the drone might not have been from Section Seven. It could very well be a decoy."

Harlow pulled away, looking up as Finn's arm dropped away from her. "What would the point of that be? Misdirection?"

"Yes. It's one of my father's favorite ploys. Send something just clever enough to draw everyone's attention, but clumsy enough to be discoverable… And then while everyone's trying to figure that out…"

"Send in the real probe," Harlow finished.

Finn nodded. "We'll have to be very careful about this, Harlow. There can't be even one slip up."

For the first time all summer, Harlow felt like they might be getting some-where. Like all the weeks of frustration and failure might lead up to a win. "Let's do this then. Let's trick Connor McKay again."

Finn pulled her closer again. "We can do this. We can win." He kissed her, his mouth desperate and warm against her own.

Harlow wound every part of her with what she could of his. She let her shadows out, sending them through the threads that bound them tighter with each passing moment until his light responded, twining in amongst the darkness as they made wordless promises to one another. Vows that could not, would not, be broken by subterfuge or deception.

CHAPTER 13

The next day dawned blessedly clear, though the temperature had dropped significantly. Harlow had to wear one of Finn's sweaters with a pair of leggings to get coffee together. The sun was warm, but the air smelled like fall, or maybe it was simply the myriad evergreen needles that had been strewn about by the storm crunching under their feet. They were walking back to the villa when a ruckus from the bushes startled them both. A cheeky red squirrel ran out, chattering angrily.

Finn pressed a kiss to her hair, as he squeezed her shoulder tight in reassurance. "I love seeing you in my clothes," he said as he wrapped an arm around her waist.

She'd been about to text Larkin that The Gate was out of lemon scones and when jostled, her coffee and her phone both slipped out of her hands. "Shit."

Finn bent to pick up her phone, and she tried to grab the cup that was flying away in the breeze. Another noise from the bushes caught both their attention. It was a camera. They'd been followed to the coffee shop again. They were just getting past the overblown drama around the pizza toppings. And now this? Harlow lunged for the photographer, suddenly furious. She knew exactly how those photos would be used—another Section Seven spread, making fun of her. The shifter scandal in Nuva Troi was dying down, and the scavengers needed fresh meat.

Finn pulled her back as the photographer stepped out of the bushes, backing away, but slowly, still taking photos. She struggled against him for a moment and then relented. When she stilled in his arms he let her go, but surprisingly he didn't follow the photographer, or menace them in any way. Her heart skipped a beat. Usually he was so protective of her.

"Sorry," she muttered, an unpleasant feeling taking root in her gut.

"You did great," he replied, handing her phone back to her. She looked up at him and saw the concern in his eyes, though his face didn't change. "You did great," he said again, watching her carefully.

So this was it. The game had started. She nodded, letting her feelings show on her face. They had no idea who was watching, and this was their first opportunity to show their relationship changing, even subtly.

Harlow looked down at her phone. The screen was shattered.

"I'll get you a new phone," Finn said, and in those few words, she heard another step of their plan formulating.

"One of the fancy ones?" Harlow asked with a grimace.

"Yes," Finn laughed. "You'll love it."

She wrinkled her nose at him to show her displeasure, but brushed a kiss to his lips to show him she was okay.

"Do you want to go back for another coffee?"

Harlow shook her head. "No, it's fine. I'll just make tea at home."

His hand slipped into hers, warm and comforting. A sinking feeling spread through her. He was leaving soon, and then she'd be here without him, and there would be more moments like these. More times when he treated her in ways that didn't feel good, so they could lure Connor into giving something away. He seemed to be thinking along similar lines, and they didn't talk much the rest of the walk home.

When they entered the villa, Meline was standing in the front foyer, shaking her head as she stared at her phone. "Sorry about your coffee," she said, obviously reading about the encounter on one of the gossips. "Did your phone break too?"

Harlow rolled her eyes. That was fast. "Yes."

"Bummer," Meline replied, taking Harlow's elbow. "Can me and Ari talk to you two?"

Finn nodded. "Sure. Let me go give Larkin these croissants."

Meline shook her head. "That's gonna be disappointing. She wanted the lemon scones."

Harlow laughed, trying to banish the rush of anxiety she felt after the encounter with the paparazzi. She hugged Meline as they walked together into the villa's ridiculous formal living room. Ari and the maters were already seated, and everyone looked uneasy.

"What's going on?" Harlow asked as she found a seat. She hated this room. All the chairs were too hard to get cozy in. She'd asked Cian if she could turn them into better chairs, and they'd screeched something about heirlooms and respect for historical artifacts.

"It's time for us to go home, dear," Selene said as Harlow attempted to make herself comfortable in a stiff armchair covered in a blue satin stripe.

Aurelia nodded. "We've been away for too long already, and you know that autumn is our most important season at the store."

Harlow had been expecting this for a week or two. The maters had done all they could in Nea Sterlis, talking with the sorcière and shifters here that they thought they could trust about potentially confronting the Illuminated over the imbalance of power at the next Council of Orders, after the Winter Solstice.

Neither Harlow nor Finn believed it would do much good, but they'd agreed to solve things as amicably as possible before other, more violent options were considered.

It was time for them to go home, and continue the work there, but she wasn't ready for her family to go their separate ways—even though it would be easier to pull off her ruse with Finn if the maters weren't here looking over her shoulder constantly. They took Section Seven and the rest of the gossips with a grain of salt, but if they saw her getting upset, they'd want to know what was happening.

Tricking Thea would be harder. Both Alaric and Finn had made it abundantly clear at breakfast that they thought it was best for both Harlow and Thea to stay in Nea Sterlis, at least until Finn and Cian could gauge what Rakul Kimaris was up to, and talk to the McKays and Velariuses both in person.

Harlow smiled sadly. "Okay. You're going home. I'll miss you so much."

Aurelia, who sat in the chair next to her own, patted her hand. "We will miss you too."

"Indi and Nox are going with them," Meline said.

Ari added, "Nox and I have connections in the city, and someone needs to help Finn and Cian with the intelligence side of things."

"Okay," Harlow said. They needed people in Nuva Troi to monitor Rakul's movements if they could find him, she knew that. She just wished her little sister didn't have to be a part of it.

Finn entered the room, plopping down on the loveseat next to Selene, slinging his arm around her shoulders. "So what do the two of you want to talk about?"

Ari and Meline glanced at one another, both looking anxious. Ari spoke first. "You know I have to go back to Falcyra. We need eyes on the ground."

Finn nodded. "Agreed."

"I want to go too—" Meline said.

"No," Harlow responded, cutting Meline off. "No. It's too dangerous."

Finn held a hand up, then looked at the maters. "You think this is a good idea?"

Aurelia sighed. "Meline's power will manifest soon. She shows every sign of being an expert with glamour."

Selene added, "It runs in my family, and we've been sure Meli will be the same for some time."

"It's started already," Meline said. "It's a matter of days now, not weeks. Maybe hours."

If the maters were right, and they usually were, when Meline's power manifested, she would be capable of glamouring herself to look like almost anyone for short periods of time. And Ari could literally disappear. They would make an excellent team if Meline knew anything about being a spy.

"Ari has been helping me," Meline said softly. "I asked him to tell me about his job, and at first it was a game, but look…" Meline's fingers worked swiftly, pulling threads of aether in lightning fast strokes. Before Harlow could blink twice, Meline had transformed into a perfect copy of Wesley Arden, her favorite author.

It was a stunning piece of magic, as she hadn't even fully manifested yet. Typically, witches who excelled at glamour did best with people they saw every day. Meline stood and walked around the room. From every angle, the glamour was perfect.

"That's incredible," Finn said. "And no one knows you can do this?"

Meline shook her head. "I can hold it for a few hours now, but when manifested, I think I could go a few days without reapplying the magic."

"And how will we explain your absence?" Harlow asked. It wasn't that she wanted to burst Meline's bubble. She saw how much her sister needed this. How much she wanted to do something useful with her talents, rather than simply turning herself prettier and prettier for social events.

Ari grinned. "You know that silent retreat that everyone's been raving about on socials?"

Harlow shrugged, but Finn nodded. "Sure. The thing in wine country, where you get the private cabin for as long as you want, and it's basically a luxury hotel."

Meline smiled. "I announced to my socials this morning that I'm having a spiritual awakening. Apparently, Aphora has called me into 'beautiful silence' for at least a month, maybe more."

"I'll go with her," Ari said. "Out of sight of course. And we'll disappear in a week. The place has some seriously strict rules around privacy. Their contracts are magically enforced, so we should be good."

Harlow glanced between Ari and Meline. They were pleased with their plan, and it seemed like they'd thought of everything. But they didn't need her permission. They needed Finn's. He looked to her though, wanting to make sure she thought it was a good idea. She nodded once and Meline whooped with joy, throwing her arms around Ari.

As they left with Finn to make plans, Harlow turned to the maters. "Are you sure she's ready for this?"

Aurelia smiled, but her eyes were sad. "My darling, we learned long ago never to clip our girls' wings when they were ready to fly."

Selene brushed a kiss to her forehead as she and Aurelia left to go pack. Axel passed them on their way out and hopped into her lap. At least he wasn't leaving her. Thea and Alaric would be here still, and Enzo and Petra of course, but they were busy with their partners. She wondered if Larkin planned to go home as well.

Where *was* Larkin? Harlow picked Axel up and walked through the house. Larkin's favorite terrace was located just off the library, as it was sheltered by trees and quieter than the ones overlooking the bay. Also, there was a hammock, and Larkin was a sucker for a hammock. Sure enough, her sister was napping on the terrace, the hammock swinging gently in the breeze.

Harlow grabbed a blanket from the back of one of the chairs in the library and let Axel down. He followed her out to the covered terrace. Larkin opened her eyes. "Hi, the croissants weren't awful. Thanks for getting the lemon ones."

Harlow smiled. "Brought you a blanket." Axel jumped into the hammock, landing on Larkin's chest. "And a cat."

"And a sister," Larkin added, scooting over. "Hop in with me?"

Harlow got in, covering herself and Larkin with the blanket. It was just cool enough on the covered terrace to need it. When Axel was settled between them and they rocked gently once more, Harlow asked, "Are you going back to Nuva Troi with the maters? Or are you running away to Falcyra too?"

Larkin smiled. "I'm staying here with you and Thea. If that's all right, anyway."

"Of course it is. I'm happy you're staying."

"Me too," Larkin said, but she didn't *look* particularly happy.

"Is everything okay?"

Larkin forced a smile. "Yeah. I've been sleeping poorly for the past few weeks, that's all. Maybe my bleed is coming. I haven't been tracking it very well."

Harlow made a non-committal noise. The sound of the waves far below the terrace soothed her, and because everything was chaotic, she needed all the soothing she could get. Larkin went back to her book. Axel purred, setting a deep rhythm as the hammock swung. Harlow woke to Finn carrying her upstairs.

"Put me down," she murmured sleepily. "I can walk."

"You can, but I'd rather carry you," he assured her. "We're going to train for the next few days. You need the extra rest."

She was tempted to grumble about it, but the resolve in his voice was firm. So she snuggled into his chest and drifted back off. They didn't have many days left together, and she didn't want to spend them fighting.

CHAPTER 14

The next few days made Harlow deeply regret not arguing with Finn about the training. He'd seen her shift, at least partially, so they knew she *could*. But nothing happened, no matter what they tried, and they certainly weren't going to try anything including biting again, so they settled on honing her abilities with her shadows. Finn taught her how to make weapons from mundane objects, and she practiced launching them at all manner of targets.

She tried knives, javelins, and a variety of sharp, pointy objects, but arrows seemed to be her favorite projectile. When she got the hang of making them, they flew true, at least sometimes. Finn was proud of her. She could tell from the way his eyes shone whenever she struck one of the dummies he tossed into the air for her to hit.

On the day she hit half of them, he grinned. "We don't have time for you to learn hand to hand combat techniques before I leave, but I feel better knowing you can protect yourself."

Harlow snickered. "I can protect myself half of the time, you mean."

He slung an arm around her. "It's *progress*, Harls. And you'll keep practicing while I'm gone, right?"

Harlow nodded. "So, I guess it's time to work on the Feriant again."

Finn shook his head, his eyes on the floor. "Forcing it isn't working. I'm sorry I pushed you so hard earlier this summer. I acted like my dad."

"What?" Harlow was incredulous. "No. You didn't."

He looked away. "I don't know if I want to have children."

That was a surprise, but she understood exactly where the worry came from. "Okay," she said. "If you don't want them, we won't have them."

He looked up, shock on his face. "Just like that?"

She shrugged. "Just like that."

"Do *you* want them?" he asked. They'd never talked about this before.

She sat on the floor of the studio, hugging her knees to her chest. The truth was that it was impossible for her to imagine having children. She could imagine being an auntie to Thea and Alaric's children easily. In fact, it was a favorite pastime of hers to imagine what their babies might look like, but she never thought about her own. She'd barely spent a moment or two thinking about the same between her and Finn. "I don't think I really care one way or another. If you wanted them, I'd be happy to think it over, but if you don't, that's fine with me too."

He sat next to her, his shoulder pressing into hers. "Really? You won't be disappointed?"

Harlow laughed as Axel rolled on his back in front of the studio's mirrors, admiring his reflection. She'd never played at being a mother like Thea had when they were little. She'd spent her time imagining what her manifested powers might be, the books she might discover and restore, the person she might marry, but she'd rarely pretended to parent. Thinking about it now, she realized she'd never cared much about having her own children either way. "No. I have you and him, and probably a whole gaggle of little AlThea witchlings."

"*AlThea?*" Finn grimaced, squeezing her shoulders. "That is terrible. Who came up with that?"

Harlow fell into his lap, tweaking his nose playfully. "The kids on the interwebs, Finbar, who else?"

He kissed her. "So, just me and you for all eternity?"

"For all eternity," she agreed.

He sighed, and she saw a layer of the hurt he carried peel away. It left him a little raw, but she loved him more for it, if that were even possible. Axel lost interest in his reflection, and came to lie on Harlow's chest, and the three of them chatted aimlessly for long hours, until someone called them to dinner.

～

Two DAYS before everyone was set to part ways, Cian popped into the studio in the Vault's subterranean gym, where they'd just finished a series of exercises meant to help focus Harlow's breath and mind. Even though Finn had suggested they stop trying so hard, Harlow still made at least one attempt every day.

It hadn't worked. Of course. She was still in her humanoid form, not a feather in sight.

"Have you tried the river?" Cian asked.

Finn's eyebrows raised. "No, I hadn't thought of that, but now that you mention it… It makes sense. Let's try it."

"What river?" Harlow asked.

Finn took her hand, helping her up from her seated position on the floor. She blushed as she rose, a tingle of desire flickering through her veins. Nearly every part of her was painfully distracted by him. The way the muscles in his chest and abdomen rippled as he dragged a shirt on didn't help things.

Cian made a gagging noise. "The two of you are *terrible.*"

A giggle slipped between Harlow's lips, and Finn kissed them, muttering against her mouth, "I think we're pretty amazing."

His hand slid around her waist as he turned her, pushing her forward, after Cian, who was hurrying out of the gym. She followed them, acutely aware of Finn right behind her. He followed closely enough that every once in a while some part of him brushed her.

Her ass, her shoulder, the small of her back. Every touch was like a burning brand. Fervor raced through her, driving her into a near-frenzy when he tugged on her ponytail. It was meant to be a playful gesture, but her body responded immediately.

"Keep your hands to yourselves, please," Cian begged, clearly exasperated as they led them further back into a dark hallway behind the Vault's gym that Harlow had never noticed. There was a half-flight of stairs in the dimly lit hall, and then her feet hit what felt like stone, rather than marble tile.

"Are we headed deeper underground?" she asked.

"Yes," Finn said, keeping enough distance now that he wouldn't risk brushing against her again. He grinned when she looked back, and a piece of his dark hair fell onto his forehead. She nearly leapt at him.

He shook his head at her, but the bulge in his joggers gave him away. He was as far gone as she was. Fervor had them in its clutches, and they were embarrassing themselves, shamelessly, so it seemed.

She bit her bottom lip, and Finn growled. "Turn around, you merciless creature."

She did as he asked, flipping her ponytail at him with a seductive look over her shoulder.

He was at her back in an instant. His breath caressed her ear as he said, "When we're done here, I'm gonna pull that ponytail. *Hard.*"

A thrill went through her, throbbing with molten heat in her core. His hands gripped her hips, his fingers pressing into her soft flesh, an obvious clue to how he'd like to take her—the position in which the hair-pulling might take place.

"Would you like that?" he asked. Cian was gone from sight.

Harlow nodded, unable to speak.

Finn's voice lowered now to a quiet rumble. "These fucking leggings… And this tiny little crop top, are you even wearing a bra?" He pulled her hard against him, stopping them both from progressing further.

She tried to laugh, but she was too breathless to make much noise. His hands —his wicked hands—were everywhere, slipping underneath her top to find out if she was, or was not, wearing a bra.

"Bad girl," he said as his fingers grazed her bare flesh. He spun her around, pulling her tight against his heaving chest. "We were *supposed* to be training today."

His fingers wrapped around her ponytail and he tugged. She leaned into him as he exposed her neck. Harlow's eyes fell closed. Somewhere in the distance there was the sound of water, but she didn't care. All she wanted was for this moment to last. For Finn to stay right here with her, for them to go on with their engagement. To bond, and move into a new house. To be safe and *normal*, not faking a breakup.

But they weren't normal. Even now, they were driven by fervor, and as they dug deeper into the Illuminated Order's business, they ensured their lives would never be normal again. He sensed her breathing change and stopped. "What's wrong?"

She shook her head, squeezing her eyes shut.

"Harls, you're crying," he whispered. His hands were gentle on her now, pulling her close for comfort's sake.

"I don't want to do this," she said as she buried her face in his chest. "I don't want you to go."

His arms tightened around her. "I know. I wish everything was different…"

"That we could just be happy," she finished.

She felt, rather than saw him nod, since she'd tucked her face between his ridiculously large pectorals. He smelled so good she could eat him, but the fervor relented a little. Just enough for her to feel her emotions welling up, the dark sadness behind all the desire.

"Do you want to back out of the ruse? We don't have to do it," Finn said as he hugged her tighter.

"No," she whispered, though she knew he heard. "I just wish we didn't have to."

"Me too," Finn answered. He didn't have to say more. They both knew they'd go through with this. It didn't make letting it happen any easier.

In the dark of the tunnel, Finn's fingers laced through hers and they walked forward. There weren't any sconces on the walls here, but as her eyes adjusted, she realized there was light. Above them, thousands of bioluminescent insects crawled on the ceiling. Harlow was fascinated. They were delicately formed beetles, slow moving and peaceful, and they put off the mildest glow that was just enough to see by. The walls of the tunnel were smooth, as was the ground, though it didn't look to have been made by people or modern means.

"Where are we?" Harlow asked as the path curved sharply, descending even further into the earth.

"Under the Vault," Finn explained. The sound of rushing water filled the tunnel. "These tunnels were made in one of the prehistoric eras."

"Wyrms?" Harlow breathed. There was evidence that Okairos had long ago been host to enormous subterranean wyrms, who never surfaced, but wove through the many upper layers of the planet's surface.

"Yes," Finn said. The tunnel widened into a cavern, and the glowing insects on the ceiling of the tunnel were *everywhere* here. Harlow frowned—that wasn't quite the case after all. They were still only on the ceiling, but their reflection in the rushing river that took up most of the cavern floor was deceiving. The river looked like it was made of stars.

Cian sat on a rock near the river, grinning. "Welcome to the Pyriphle."

Harlow sounded out the word in her head, trying to find the source of the tickle of recognition she felt. *Peer-eef-lahy*—it was one of those ancient human words with far too many consonants in a row that sounded nothing like it was spelled. Her brain hit on it, *Pyriphle*. Human lore said that the river was the pathway to Akatei's domain. "The river to the underworld?"

"Yes, we think so," Finn said, watching Harlow closely. He and Cian were both watching her rather closely, she noticed.

"What do you think is going to happen?" she asked, raising her eyebrows.

Both of them laughed, and Finn let go of her hand. "We have some evidence that this river is connected to the limen."

"What kind of evidence?" Harlow asked, her interest piqued.

"It's more of a theory," Finn said. "Magic behaves strangely around the Pyriphle."

"The river doesn't respond to any of the magic that most sorcière and Illuminated use," Cian said.

"But I don't use magic like they do," Harlow said, following their reasoning.

Finn nodded, smiling at her in encouragement.

"Use your second sight," Cian urged, stepping towards the riverbank and dipping a hand into the water.

As the water slipped through their fingers and back into the river, Harlow engaged her second sight, until she saw the threads. They appeared as glowing filaments of golden light, filled with dark aether. The aether that flowed through them was what made magic possible. According to metaphysical theorists, on many worlds only a little aether flowed through the threads of reality—just enough to create life. Okairos' threads were more robust, according to them, more conducive to carrying aether, which made magic possible.

But the water of the Pyriphle was different; it wasn't made of threads at all— which was impossible. *Everything* was made of aethereal threads. But this water was made of the same substance her shadows were, the same substance at the heart of the limen. At the heart of Nihil.

And then the fifteen guardians flashed before her spirit sight. Two were still missing. When Ashbourne's eyes snapped open, she was flung back into the cavern. Harlow wasn't sure what had happened, if she had been to Nihil again, or if she'd just recalled her earlier visit, but something had changed in the cavern in the split second she'd been gone.

Time slowed to a crawl around her, as it had that first visit to Nihil. Though this time she moved freely, or so she thought. She walked toward the river, drawn to its dark magic. Her feet moved as though they had a will of their own, and before she knew it, she was sprinting towards the water, her body preparing to dive. There wasn't a single thought or strand of reasoning in her head. She moved on instinct and desire alone. Hands gripped her, dragging her back as time resumed its usual pace.

"What the fuck?" Finn yelled as he dragged her away from the river.

He was utterly panicked, she realized, as her mind raced to catch up with what had happened. *She'd run towards the river at full speed, hadn't she? Why?*

Harlow looked down at her arms, expecting to see feathers again, but this time her fingers had sprouted claws—no, talons. Both arms, to her elbows, were stained the deepest midnight blue.

"I'm sorry," she said, looking up into Cian and Finn's worried faces. "I don't think I was in control of myself."

Cian crouched down, running their knuckles across her cheekbone. "You're all right?"

Finn turned away, and she watched him take several deep breaths. "Yes," she said. "The water is different. It's made of the same substance as my shadows."

Cian pressed a hand to Finn's back as they stood. "She's fine, Finbar."

But Finn didn't turn. Harlow stood, Cian helping her up as she went. "I'm okay."

"How can I leave?" Finn said, his voice barely loud enough to make out over the rushing of the river. "How can I leave you? How can I be sure you'll be fine on your own?"

She took one of his hands, exhaling. "I promise not to come down here alone, but maybe you could start by *listening* to me."

He glanced back at her, catching Cian's chuckle just as she did.

"I won't come down here alone, but honestly, it's not affecting me the way it was at first, even now."

Finn turned. "And how was that?"

Harlow looked down at her hands, which were slowly returning to their normal color. The talons were gone. "It was like my shadows wanted to join with the river. They're made of the same stuff."

"And now?" Finn asked. His expression was drawn, but at least he was listening.

"Now they're calm." They were slithering around her legs, reaching out to touch him, as though in apology. When one tickled his palm, it glowed with his own power.

He glowered at her, at her shadows, but they were persistent. A smile played at the corner of his mouth. "Okay, I believe you."

Cian walked toward the tunnel. "Let's go back, just to be safe."

Finn took her hand, and they followed, talking as they went. "The river might help me shift," Harlow pondered. "But I don't think it's safe."

"No?" Cian asked, casting a look back at her.

Harlow glanced up at Finn. "No. I don't like the idea that I wouldn't be in full control of the shift. When you get back, maybe we can try some experiments."

Finn squeezed her hand. "We can."

What were sure to be harrowing weeks ahead loomed like a spiral of anxiety and insecurity, just waiting for her to slide right down. She had to change the subject. "Have you ever tried to travel downriver, like by boat?"

Finn nodded. "Yes, a few times, but there's a waterfall about a mile in, and no instrument we've ever brought with us has ever been able to measure it. Something about the river messes with reality."

That made all the sense in the world to Harlow, given that there were no threads in the river, just pure aether.

Cian added, "Honestly, we just thought it was an interesting feature of the house. We found it rather recently when we expanded the Vault to make the gym. I'm sorry I didn't think of taking you down there sooner." The shifter paused. They'd re-entered the finished part of the tunnel, and now sconces lit their way, so it was easy to see the deep consideration on their face. "Are you sure about our trip to Nuva Troi? We could put it off and prioritize this."

Finn glanced at Harlow. She shook her head, and he squeezed her hand again. "No, we've decided. Plus, Father is expecting me now. It would be hard to back out without arousing his suspicions."

Harlow's chest tightened around her heart at the harsh tone in Finn's voice, the one reserved for discussing Connor. She squeezed Finn's hand, raising it to her lips.

"It's okay," he said, his voice gentling for her.

Cian nodded. "Good. In addition to everything else, we need to try to suss out what he and Pasiphae are thinking about Falcyra. It's nearly time, don't you think?"

Finn nodded. "Yes."

"Time for what?" Harlow asked.

Finn smiled, but it didn't reach his eyes. Cian walked away, calling back to them. "I'm going to go look through my notes about the Pyriphle. Come find me when you're done."

Harlow's stomach felt as though it had dropped into freefall, or that someone had pulled a rug from beneath her feet and she was crashing to the floor in slow motion. The sense that everything was going to change was overpowering.

"You understand we are not the only operatives of the Knights, don't you?"

She understood that, vaguely anyway. She knew there were others, but not how they were organized or what they did. They'd been so focused on trying to figure out how to get her to shift again at the beginning of the summer, and then the fervor had taken over, she'd lost focus somewhat and hadn't asked the kinds of questions she usually would. Looking up at Finn now, she knew that falling in love had made her not want to ask those kinds of questions. She hadn't really wanted to know. But now she did. With him leaving, she *needed* to know.

"Tell me everything," she said.

CHAPTER 15

They went to Finn's workroom in the Vault, which belonged to both of them now. The antique library table at the center of the room held both their notebooks and the fancy tablet that Finn had purchased for Harlow. The one she never took out of this room, if she could help it.

Finn perched on one of the stools that surrounded the table, gesturing for Harlow to sit on the one opposite him. When she sat, he stared at her for a few moments, then reached out to touch the soft curve of her jawline. She saw in his eyes that this was hard for him to tell her, and not because he didn't trust her. There was a sadness there that let her know he was about to bring her into the full scope of his world in a way he didn't much want to.

He still didn't understand. She wanted this—she wanted to know every part of him. This, the Knights, whatever their true goals were, this *was* Finn.

"You know that we've worked for many years to carve out places that the people most harmed by the Illuminated—by the Orders—could find safety, right?"

Harlow nodded. The Haven project was bigger than just the cafes in Nuva Troi and Nea Sterlis; it was a shadow network of people who helped mostly humans, but often shifters and sorcière as well, when they'd been targeted by the Illuminated or the Order of Night. The Haven units provided immediate escape from imminent harm, but also helped people disappear, or at least relocate, when more complicated situations arose.

"While that's been one of our primary objectives, it's only a part of our bigger goal…" Finn trailed off, frowning, as though he couldn't quite figure out how to say it.

But Harlow already knew. It was obvious. "You're looking for a way to break it all. To break their reign for good."

Finn nodded. "We are, and we're just getting started, but this is the Knights' purpose."

A part of her had always known this was the mission. She just hadn't wanted to admit it to herself. It was too big to think about. The Illuminated Order was more than just the Illuminated. It was entire systems, nations. It was everything that Okairos was built on in this modern era. Breaking those systems down would take years, decades even.

It wouldn't be easy, and a part of Harlow understood that they might never see the fruits of their labor, not in their very long lifetimes, but she was in. Hope flooded the dread that had been collecting for weeks, amongst the constant stream of twisting turns and failures to find her footing with all this. She'd hoped for something like this to come along and claim her for years, and now here it was: purpose, paired with love and belonging.

Finn played with a pen on the desk, clicking it over and over. She pried it out of his fingers. "I'm in. All the way."

"You understand that the penalty for doing this kind of work is execution, right?" Finn's voice didn't waver, but his eyes dropped to the floor as he finished speaking.

It hadn't occurred to her how much he banked on being perfect until now. It wasn't just that he was a leader, or that he felt responsible for all the people who looked to him for guidance. He actually believed he wasn't worthy of love if he couldn't be perfect. What she'd always assumed was ambition, was actually something much more complex. He fought terrible internal battles, just like she did.

Harlow waited for a long moment to speak, until his eyes dragged back upwards to hers. "I want this. All of it. You, Haven—all of it. I don't have any questions about this. I'm sure. Are you?"

His eyebrows pulled together in an ever-so-slightly petulant frown. "*Obviously.*"

Harlow raised her own eyebrows and shook her head, mimicking his petulance, but secretly pleased that he'd bounced back so quickly. "Well, me too."

She knew she couldn't heal the wounds that caused him to feel this pain to begin with, but she could be here for him, just like he was for her. It was good to see him unfurl a little, to trust her more—and not just with the Knights' secrets, but with his heart. As that well of emotion filled, Harlow's skin tingled with anticipation. The way his eyes smoldered for her alone was enough to send her into a desirous frenzy.

"So much sass, Krane," he purred leaning across the table to brush a kiss to her lips. "Please never stop with your smart mouth. I have so many things I want to do with it."

Harlow resisted the urge to fan herself as he sat back down; she would miss these snippy little back-and-forth battles. "So, what's our first step?"

Finn opened his laptop and turned it towards her. "We've been mapping out possibilities for three years. We knew that social instability had to be one aspect. The humans had to resist. Their numbers are too great at this point to completely control without eradicating them."

"Which the Illuminated Order would never do, because the Order of Night is their closest ally," Harlow reasoned.

Finn's expression darkened. "Yes, there's that, and—" He looked like he'd swallowed something too large for his esophagus for a brief moment.

"What is it?" Harlow urged. Whatever was causing that expression wasn't going to get any easier to say.

"Some Illuminated… Not me. Not Alaric or Petra—*ever*. But some of the older Illuminated… Enjoy human blood."

The room spun around Harlow. Of course she knew that the Illuminated had fangs, but unlike vampires they ate food. They obviously didn't need blood to sustain life. "Why would they?"

Finn's eyes fell to the floor. "Because it feels good."

While the feeling that the room was moving around her had stopped, Harlow's heartbeat throbbed in her ears, her nerves setting a ragged rhythm in her body she could not slow. "Like in the Claiming."

Finn nodded. "Yes, but the Claiming grounds us. It's intimate. Passionate, but it is meant to form a bond, much like the ways vampire families are bonded."

"Okay," Harlow said. That made sense. Not all vampires were like the House of Sorath or Remiel, both of which seemed unusually interested in growing power. Most vampiric houses operated more like families, sharing resources. "So what's wrong with that, and why is it such a secret?"

"Because it is addictive for us. And as such, a weakness. One my parents have." Finn's eyes darted away from hers. "It is also part of why I was so worried about the Claiming, and about biting you. There's a certain amount of any bloodletting that can open the door for those desires, and I was afraid of what it might trigger for me with you since you are not one of us."

Harlow nodded. "That makes perfect sense now."

They sat quietly for a while, each thinking private thoughts, processing. Harlow turned the conversation back to Finn's original confession. "So the older Illuminated won't be motivated to completely eradicate humans if they start to resist on a larger scale."

"Right," Finn agreed, grimacing slightly.

"That makes what's happening in Falcyra an opportunity for the Knights, right?"

Finn frowned. "In some ways, yes. But I want to know who the other players are in this. There's someone helping the Humanists—their money trail makes little sense. Nox chased it into multiple dead ends."

Harlow sighed, shrugging somewhat helplessly. It sounded like a difficult thing to try to find out to her. People were always manipulating money in exciting ways in novels, so she assumed the same was possible in real life.

"Nox is *really* good at shit like this," Finn said, twining a finger through her ponytail. "There should be *something*."

"Then she'll keep looking. She'll figure it out."

"She will." He glanced at his phone. "It's getting late. I'm going to leave my laptop here, and you can read all the files you want while I'm gone, okay?"

"I bet they're meticulously organized, aren't they?" Harlow teased.

He scooped her into his arms. "Just because you're the messiest person alive doesn't mean everyone else is."

"I'm not the messiest," Harlow argued. "Meline is worse."

Finn carried her upstairs. "I'm going to miss refolding all your laundry for the next few weeks."

As he kicked the door to the bedroom shut, she replied. "Me too, sweet boy. Me too."

CHAPTER 16

The next morning, everyone left on the early train. Finn had asked Harlow not to get up. He thought it would make things easier on them both. So she stayed in bed, Axel in her arms, as she listened to the quiet sounds of her heart leaving her behind. She knew they were doing the right thing, but it didn't make things any easier.

Except, in some ways, it did. The further Finn got from the house, the more relief she felt. The fog that had cluttered her mind for weeks slowly cleared. She could feel his train leave and by the time she was feeding Axel and making tea, she knew he was gone. It was strange to be heart-achingly sad and full of relief at the same time.

Harlow found a box on the counter, with a note. *New phone, text me when you get it set up.*

After they'd made love several times last night, Finn had explained that her new phone would have a tiny flaw in its security system. Something that looked like a mistake in the extra security that went into all their phones that blocked them from prying eyes. If Connor was probing their security, he'd eventually find it. So while Finn's phone would remain secure, hers would not. Even despite the security system that Alaric and Nox had built for their tech, the Knights had a strict policy against using phones for any sensitive conversations. The security was to keep their private lives private.

She had been worried that if the phone's security was weakened, it might be hackable—turned into a listening device. There had been a rash of articles on just that fear in the past few years, but Finn assured her that the rest of the phone's security would be firmly in place, so that the text and call monitoring would be convincing as a glitch. Harlow would have to be careful to limit her phone and text conversations with her friends and family until Finn returned, which made her nervous. She boosted herself on the counter next to Axel and stared out the villa's floor to ceiling windows at the ocean. Then she got to work setting the new phone up.

When she was finished, she texted Finn. *How are you feeling?*

He saw it immediately. Like he was waiting for her message. *Sad, but also… better?*

Harlow couldn't help but sigh with relief. Some of the guilt she carried for feeling better eased. *Me too. It's okay.*

It is. We'll fix this and I'll be back before you know it.

There was a long pause, and she saw he was still writing something. *I got in touch with an old friend, Sabre LeBeau. Do you know them?*

Axel bumped her hand, then flopped over on the counter to show her his belly. She snapped a photo of him being cute and sent it to Finn, then responded, *Maybe? Who are they?*

A realtor. They're going to show me houses while I'm in Nuva Troi… for when we get back this fall.

This was a part of the ruse—the one she hated the most. Sabre LeBeau was one of Finn's exes and an affiliate of the Knights of Serpens. They were utterly trustworthy, and would be brought in on the ruse, but what they were about to do still made Harlow sick. The plan was for Finn to be seen about town with Sabre to get the gossips going. They hoped that was all it would take, but Harlow knew it might take further measures to lure Connor into believing that Finn and Harlow's relationship was truly in trouble.

They had agreed not to plan much else, to let the lies they told be spontaneous. Finn reasoned that they'd both done so well at improv nights as teenagers that they should have no problem with that now.

"We're *theater kids*, Harls," he'd said, wiggling his fingers in a showy dance meant to make her laugh. "We can do this."

She'd dissolved into giggles when he'd said it, and she smiled now, remembering that while this whole thing was bound to drum up old insecurities, under all his sexy broodiness, Finbar McKay was a theater kid, a history geek, and cat dad extraordinaire. And that he was *hers*. She tried to rub Axel's belly, but he nipped at her fingers, warning her to stop. She sent Finn another photo of her cat-trapped arm. Axel looked absolutely feral.

She had to ask something else about Sabre, even though she knew the answer. If they were being monitored she had to behave as though she was in the dark about Sabre. *Are they human?*

Yes, we met at Aphelion. They're back in Nuva Troi now. Cian's in a huff with the concierge about our seats. Gotta run. Love you.

Harlow locked the new phone. The camera on the thing was phenomenal; her photos of Axel looked practically professional. The cat bumped her arm, purring, and she pulled him into her arms for a hug. She needed the comfort. That conversation was just the first, and probably the most comfortable, of many that likely wouldn't be.

"What are you going to do today, baby boy?" she asked as the cat hopped down and perched in a windowsill, cackling at some birds in a cypress below. Just underneath the tree, she saw a flash of auburn fur. Axel's cat friend was back.

Harlow pressed a kiss to his head, and he pawed at her face, pushing her away. "Have fun."

The house was quiet. Larkin would sleep until mid-afternoon. She'd been up late in the Vault, playing her violin. Harlow had heard her come upstairs in the wee hours of the morning, when she'd been watching Finn sleep. Thea was probably already in the study, hard at work. She didn't much like spaces without windows, so she rarely worked in the Vault if she could help it.

Harlow wandered through the bright marble halls until she heard her eldest sister humming her favorite sonata. When she peeked into the study, she was met with a vision of magic. Thea's fingers pulled threads at a pace that was nearly too quick to watch, the filaments of aether shimmering at her fingertips. Her focus was trained on the book in front of her, resting in a cradle.

Thea had been hard at work all summer trying to restore the second image in the triptych from the Merkhov book, but though the snakes were easier to make out now, the details were still unclear. The first image had been easy enough to restore, but Thea's magic had snagged on the second and progress had stalled out.

"Any change?" Harlow asked softly, not wanting to startle Thea.

Her sister looked up. She'd lopped off her long, dark hair into a fashionable chin-length bob the first week they'd been in Nea Sterlis and it swished around her face in a satin curtain as she shook her head. "No, I can bring out the details in the scales, and I can see the snakes are positioned differently in this one, but it's the egg I can't get."

Harlow stood next to her sister at the library table, staring at the facsimile of the triptych from the Scroll of Akatei. The first, and only fully restored, image showed two snakes, one golden and one midnight blue, locked in a figure-eight pattern, consuming one another's tails. Inside the lower half of the figure eight was a luminous egg, surrounded by a protective film.

The second image seemed to show the same two snakes, no longer locked together, but united, protecting the egg, or so she and Thea thought. The part of the image that should show the rest of the two snakes holding the egg was still obscured.

"You brought the color out," Harlow breathed. "The snakes really are one now."

Thea nodded, wiping a thin sheen of sweat off her brow. "Yes, and see, they are golden and blue now, elements of both. I got it last night, but I can't get the egg."

Harlow looked closely at the image. "Is the egg… cracking?"

Thea nodded. "I think so… But the longer I work on it, the worse I feel."

With those words, Thea stumbled. Harlow caught her elder sister in her arms and led her to a linen-covered chaise and sat with her. "You all right?"

Thea nodded, and Harlow reached out towards the facsimile with her shadows. "What's making Thea sick?" she whispered.

Arebos had suggested to her that speaking to her magic might help direct it. He'd had some experience working with the Ultima, apparently, and they swore by something called "verbal manifestation." He'd thought it might help her, since the Striders of the Feriant Legion had also been warriors. She'd been testing it out. It worked well enough most of the time, but when she looked at Thea, there was no obvious clue to what was making her woozy.

Harlow looked closer, utilizing her second sight. Her shadows gathered around the book. She walked over to the table where Thea had been working, and sure enough, though it was faint, she saw it. There was an anomaly in the threads, so slight she could understand how Thea missed it. Her sister was most talented at fixing art, restoring it. Sometimes she was so focused on bringing out the best in something, she missed little details like this. Harlow moved around the book, using her second sight to look at it from several angles. There was most definitely something there.

"Did you test the book for spellbinding?" Harlow asked.

Thea rolled her eyes, clearly annoyed, despite her nausea. "Of course. I'm not a fool."

Harlow stepped closer to the book, turning her head as her shadows moved in and out of the aethereal threads that both surrounded the book and that made it up. Thea rose on shaky feet to stand next to her.

"Can you see it?" Harlow whispered, not knowing if Thea saw the same thing she did.

Her sister leaned forward, squinting. Her breath caught as she saw what Harlow did. "Oh…"

"It's so subtle," Harlow breathed. "Like it's a part of the book itself."

"Only a healer could have done a spellbinding like this," Thea said, her words slow and thoughtful. She looked long and hard at Harlow.

"What are you looking for?" Harlow asked as Thea lifted her wrists, examining them. One of Thea's talents, part of what made her restorations so sought after, was her ability to see traces of magic left behind, to identify them, and bring out their original intent. Now that she saw the spell on the book, she might be able to fix it.

"The magic used on the book. I've seen it before." Harlow looked into her sister's fawn-colored eyes. "On you."

Harlow glanced down at her wrists, at the place that had been injured the night she'd left Mark. "Kylar Bane."

Thea nodded. "I don't think this is a coincidence."

Harlow had to agree. "I don't think it is either."

"I'll talk to Alaric about it," Thea said. She scrunched up her face a little, pressing the back of her hand to her forehead, which bore a slight shimmer of sweat. "Sorry I snapped before."

"It's okay," Harlow reassured her.

Harlow's phone dinged loudly. She'd forgotten to turn the sound off when she activated it earlier. Both she and Thea startled and then laughed.

"I don't think I've had the sound turned up on my phone in years," Thea said as she took a few photos of the restoration with the camera reserved for such things.

Harlow scrolled through her settings, turning the sound off, smiling. "Me either."

The notification was a message from a librarian letting her know her book was ready to retrieve. Harlow frowned. She'd emailed the library back after Finn asked her to stay away and told them to terminate her hold. This email didn't state *which* book was ready to retrieve, and what's more something was odd about the email itself. Harlow had been requesting books all summer; she knew what the form email for this type of thing looked like, and this wasn't it.

Someone wanted her back at the library. She'd promised Finn she wouldn't, but after her two trips to Nihil, she desperately wanted another look at *The Warden*. If there was any possibility that this might be about the mysterious little book, she needed to know. It wasn't as though anyone would hurt her in the Citadel, after all. It was the most heavily guarded place in Nea Sterlis.

She'd made her decision. "I've got to run to the Citadel for a few hours," Harlow said.

Thea nodded absently, lost in re-examining the Merkhov book, apparently.

"Wake Larkin up, please," Harlow said as she brushed a kiss to Thea's cheek.

Her elder sister made a noncommittal noise and waved as Harlow went to gather her things. When she was ready, she stared for a moment at Finn's car keys, then left them behind. It was early enough in the day to walk while it was still cool, and the trip home in the sunshine would make an afternoon swim that much better.

The winding streets to the Citadel were quiet and fragrant. Occasionally, when the wind blew just right, the Citadel filled with the scent of the lavender fields located just outside the city. The sun was out as Harlow ducked into her favorite shaded back-path, covered by a lemon arbor.

The sounds of waves crashing against the shoreline were faint here, and she didn't have to look over the sickening drop down the cliff side that the switch-backs to the Citadel provided—just lovely, peaceful lemons surrounded by bushy rosemary plants and various succulents and blooming flora. Really, nothing in the world could be more pleasant. The sound of crunching footsteps in the pea gravel behind her caused her to look back. She was sick to death of the paparazzi, and was going to give them a piece of her mind.

But there was nobody following her. No paparazzi anyway. A large hound, low to the ground, with long ears and enormous paws, was following her. She was tempted to stop and coo at it, but it growled loud enough for her to hear— and even at this distance, it was enough to have her back on her journey quickly.

When she glanced behind her, the dog had laid down in a shadowed door-way, big head on its paws. It didn't follow her, and its eyes drooped sleepily. Perhaps she'd just startled it. She popped her earbuds in and listened to the audiobook for the monster romance Meline had enjoyed so much as she walked on.

She was only a little sweaty when she reached the library, but the cool atrium had a drinking fountain. The Ultima from the coffee shop was nowhere to be seen. In fact, there was no one at the desk at all checking reader cards.

They must be on shift change, she thought as she approached the retrieval desk. There was a different sorcière working than the last time she'd been here. This one was younger, closer to her own age, and wore a disgruntled expression on her pale face.

"Hi," Harlow said softly. "I got an email about a retrieval?"

The witch looked up, her eyebrows raised in such a way that made it look as though she didn't believe Harlow.

"I actually had sent all my books back, but…" Harlow trailed off. The glare the librarian was giving her was cold enough to freeze lava.

"Reader card," the librarian demanded, not bothering to lower her voice. A few patrons looked up, annoyed at the disturbance.

Harlow handed her the card, and she scanned it, then swiveled in her wooden chair, rolling it backwards a few inches towards the rack that held retrievals. The witch pulled a book out of a basket and handed it to Harlow.

"You must have forgotten you requested this."

Harlow stared at the book in her hands for a brief second, then nodded. "Thanks."

The witch's forehead wrinkled and then she shrugged, sighing a dismissal. Harlow went into the reading room. The same seat she'd sat in dozens of times before this summer was open. She sat down in it, her forehead wrinkling in confusion. The book she held was titled *The Warren*.

Was this some kind of joke?

The Warren was a classic children's book about warring clans of hare shifters. Aside from the fact that the plot of the book was in some ways disturbingly similar to that of the story she'd read in *The Warden*, she couldn't see what the meaning of this was. There was nothing to do but examine the book itself, she supposed.

Was it possible there had simply been a mistake? She supposed there was, but this felt like a message. Awareness that someone was watching her crawled over her skin. Casually, she looked around. No one was looking at her. When she glanced back at the book, she saw that something was written on the back of the retrieval slip. Seven words.

The Gate. One o'clock. Don't be late.

Harlow glanced at her phone. It was nearly noon. She had time to glance through the book casually, but she practically knew the story by heart. It had been the sillies' favorite as children, and she and Thea both had read it to all three of them dozens of times, and Larkin still fell asleep to the audiobook many nights. The real information was this message.

The noise of the room disappeared as she placed *The Warren* on the cradle and began to look through it. As she'd suspected, there was nothing particularly special about this edition, but the illustrations were lovely, all the same. Comforting as that was, the sense that she was being watched did not abate, and Harlow's pulse raced.

I shouldn't have come here, she thought, panic rising in her throat. *I made a promise to Finn, and I broke it.*

Why had she been so arrogant? The first day Finn was gone, she'd done the very thing he'd expressly asked her not to.

Always defiant, aren't you, Dollface?

Mark had said that to her once for "talking back" to him when he was berating her. He'd then proceeded to give her the silent treatment for a week. Harlow wished she hadn't thought of Mark. Memories of their relationship, of the way he'd influenced her emotions, of the night she'd killed him—all came flooding back.

Her breath came in shallow gasps, and her sundress felt too tight, like the fitted bodice was restricting her lungs. She glanced around the room, careful to appear as casual as possible. No one was looking at her, nothing was amiss. She tried to tell herself that she was imagining things and to just calm down—but that didn't work.

Harlow's heart fluttered into a rapid drumbeat, pounding in her ears. Her skin was overheated, and her hands were clammy. She wiped sweat from her brow, feeling chilled as well as hot. There was no way she could sit here any longer—whether or not someone was actually watching her, she was panicking. Harlow gathered her things quickly and dropped the book off at the retrieval desk.

"Thought you were scanning it," the grumpy witch said, not looking up from her computer.

"It turned out to be less informative than I'd hoped," Harlow replied, her heartbeat accelerating.

The witch looked up at her and Harlow wondered if the irritation on her face could be more than just grumpiness as she asked, "Will you need it again?"

Harlow shook her head. "Not right now. I'll call it up again if I do."

She stepped away from the retrieval desk slowly, and the librarian never broke her gaze. The look of irritation was replaced with something steely, evaluative and shrewd. Something in the other sorcière's face frightened Harlow—was she the one who was watching her? What purpose would that serve? Harlow turned, concentrating on taking slow, even steps as she left the library.

When she got past the courtyard and into one of the narrow alleys that led downward and out of the Citadel, she picked up her pace. Thoughts raced through her. Was there any possibility that she wasn't overreacting? That the librarian could have been the person watching her somehow? But that made no sense. The sorcière had been in Harlow's line of sight the entire time and had never looked up from her computer. Still though—that look she gave Harlow as she was leaving.

"Maybe you just looked like an unhinged yew elf," she muttered to herself. Her heart slowed to a more normal pace. Enzo's breathing techniques came in handy right now. She fished her headphones out of her bag and popped them in, calling Enzo.

"What's up?" Enzo asked as he answered.

"Are you busy?" Harlow asked, checking her phone to make sure she was taking the best route to The Gate.

"I'm walking," Enzo said, sounding a little breathless. "Up seventy thousand stairs to meet a supplier. You all right?"

Harlow paused. She *was* all right—she wasn't sure what was going on, but she wasn't losing it. "I'm okay. I'm going to grab some tea at The Gate. Do you want to go for a swim?"

"Gods, yes," Enzo laughed. "I'm going to be a sweaty mess after all these stairs and we won't have many pool days left, I wager. Meet you at the Grand Plaza when I'm done?"

Harlow wished they could just go swimming at the villa, but the pool at the Grand was gorgeous and she hadn't been all summer. "Sure. See you in a few. Love you."

Enzo made the sound of kisses and hung up. She felt better, clearer, after even that short conversation. Harlow switched on her audiobook to keep her company on the rest of the walk, but her mind wandered almost immediately. This wasn't the first time since the House of Remiel fire that she'd panicked somewhere and overanalyzed her interactions with others.

Enzo had been teaching her to interrupt herself when her thoughts spiraled into something unproductive and then reevaluate, so she tried to concentrate on the audiobook, but it was almost as if the narrator was speaking a language she didn't understand. She had to back the book up twice before it made sense again.

As her breathing slowed into the rhythmic pace of her walk, she evaluated her emotions. The sense that she'd been watched at the library and that the librarian had been acting strange was less urgent now, but it was apparent to her that something *had* been happening there. She wasn't imagining things simply because she had unresolved feelings about killing her ex.

Harlow rounded a corner and found that she'd already arrived at The Gate. She hardly remembered the walk from the library at all.

It was often like this after she panicked; the twenty or thirty minutes afterwards sometimes got a little fuzzy for her. Soft jazz played on a speaker and there were people tucked into various corners of The Gate's garden, reading or sipping delightful beverages. A quick check told her she was about ten minutes early, and she might as well get in line for a drink.

CHAPTER 17

There was a line three deep in front of her, so she didn't bother to shut off the audiobook. It was starting to get good, and Harlow understood why monster romances were all the rage with Meline's generation. Harlow was half in love with both of the love interests already, and any moment they were about to fall into bed, which promised to be beyond satisfying. She wished she were at home, instead of in the coffee shop, but anything to keep her mind off what had happened at the library was a welcome distraction.

Suddenly, the sound of the narrator's voice gave way to a song she'd never heard before. The singer crooned about going your own way, and Harlow felt transported to… *somewhere else*. The song felt familiar somehow, but also strange. What *was* this music?

The person in front of her turned around, a quizzical look on her face. It was the young woman who'd been with the Ultima the last time she'd been here with Petra and Meline. She was about as tall as Harlow, with brown skin, and luminous, long-lashed eyes. Her hair was short, cut similarly to Kate's, but with a closer undercut and longer on top, grazing her high cheekbones in a way that nearly made Harlow blush.

The young woman took a white earphone out of one of her ears and seemed to listen before flashing one of the most dazzling grins Harlow had ever seen. "Were you, perhaps, listening to an audiobook just now?"

Harlow was reluctant to pull her own earphone out, afraid the music would stop, but she nodded. "Am I listening to your music somehow?"

The woman leaned forward, and Harlow noticed she smelled of vetiver and moss, and something otherworldly—she *reeked* of raw aether. Until this moment, Harlow hadn't recognized that Nihil had a smell, but the woman definitely smelled like the heart of the limen, or perhaps just the limen itself. She couldn't be sure.

376

The woman appeared to listen momentarily, then smiled again. "Yeah, somehow our signals must have gotten crossed."

"What *is* this?" Harlow asked. "I need this album."

The woman smiled, then shook her head, fiddling with her phone. "You can't get it here, unfortunately. Besides, it's a cover of the original."

"Who sang the original?" Harlow asked, as her audiobook mysteriously returned.

Harlow thought she said something like Fleetfoot's Tracks, but wasn't sure. The woman was already ordering her drink. Someone touched her arm, and she startled, staring up into Rakul Kimaris's amber eyes. He didn't look a day older than he had when he pulled her off the Ledge. Harlow's heart beat wildly again. *What was he doing here?* He was supposed to be in Nuva Troi.

"Come sit," he urged, pulling her toward a table in the corner.

"I wanted tea," she responded, her head spinning.

"You can order some when we're done," he said. His voice was urgent as his forehead wrinkled into a deep frown. "It would be better if we weren't seen together."

She whispered, "Did you send me the message in the library?"

"Yes," he muttered. "Please, let's sit. I don't have much time."

She followed Rakul to a table in the corner. He was casually dressed, in a pair of dark tactical pants and a black tank top showing the tattoos that covered his ridiculously muscled brown arms.

Rakul Kimaris made Finn look positively puny in comparison, at nearly six foot seven feet tall and at least thirty to forty more pounds of muscle. His long, dark hair was twisted into a messy bun and he was exactly as swoon-worthy as she remembered him. She glanced at the attractive person she'd been standing behind in line and wiped a bit of sweat off her forehead. This coffee shop was filled to the brim with dark-haired beauties today.

She sat across from him, waiting for him to speak, trying not to remember the giant crush she'd had on him for years as a teenager, until she'd developed feelings for Finn, that is. He seemed to struggle, so she began. "Why did you ask me here?"

He shook his head. "Listen, it's not going to be easy to explain this. There are things I'm not capable of telling anyone..." he trailed off, his brow wrinkling and his amber eyes narrowing in frustration.

Harlow's head tilted of its own accord. She was thinking about what he might mean, but when she did it, his eyes softened. "Such a hatchling."

There was a slight disturbance in the threads around him, as though they constricted somehow. Her second sight was engaging more easily than ever these days. Now she saw it, fascinated. "Someone *bound* you."

He neither moved nor responded. In fact, he was frozen, as though he could not react to her question. Even if she had not somehow developed the ability to see a spell in the threads, it would be a giveaway that someone had done one of the most terrible spells in existence on him, on *Rakul Kimaris*. That in itself was telling.

Spellbinding an object was one thing. But to bind a *person*—that was so forbidden that the Order of Mysteries had never needed to make an ordinance against such spells. To bind anyone's will was such a grave violation of their personal sanctity that Harlow felt the shock reverberate within her enough to feel cold, despite the close air in the shop.

"Okay," she said. "Okay, so *that* happened. I understand."

Rakul's body relaxed. The only way to circumvent a binding that was specifically directed, as Rakul's seemed to be, was to speak neutrally—stop asking questions of any kind. Quickly, Harlow puzzled together what she knew about the situation. Obviously, Rakul was able to use the full range of his Illuminated power, and from the way he was struggling, she assumed he could remember what he was not allowed to speak of.

That meant that one of the Illuminated had done the binding, rather than a sorcière. If one of her own had done it, he simply wouldn't remember what he was not supposed to. But the Illuminated had never been good at complex spells, and it took a very special, very talented witch to cast a binding as intricate as the one that would have been needed for such a task. This was more like a blunt instrument—a gag—and she wished to Akatei that Enzo or Riley had come with her today. Perhaps they would have been able to discern more.

Rakul glanced at his watch. "We don't have much time."

Harlow wanted to say, "You asked me here," but instead she asked, "What happened to the copy of *The Warden* I was looking at?"

Rakul sighed. "It disappeared. I was the one who sent it to you to begin with, and when I returned for it—it was gone."

"So the story of Ashbourne and Lumina, it *is* important."

Rakul did not answer, frozen once more.

Harlow decided to try an indirect approach. "Do you think one of the librarians is involved somehow? Could one of them have taken *The Warden*?"

"It's possible," Rakul said, glancing around. "But the book isn't important now. You read the story, didn't you?"

Harlow nodded. "I did."

"So you have to start look—" Rakul tried to continue, but his skin reddened, as though he were being choked.

"Shit," Harlow swore, fumbling for anything that would distract him. "Do you like cats?"

Rakul's eyebrows raised, but the flush drained quickly from his skin. "I'm more of a dog person… Thank you."

There were so many ways she could go with this, but they didn't have much time. The way she saw it, there were two important things about the story of Lumina and Ashbourne: that the Illuminated had some extremely dangerous Elementals imprisoned in the limen, and that they'd used their own people to guard them for eternity. Either could be tied to the reason why Rakul wanted her to see *The Warden*, and why he was bound, or both, she supposed. But it might be easier to talk around the binding if she knew which it was.

"What do you know about imprisoning an incorporeal creature?" she asked.

Rakul's forehead wrinkled. "Not a lot, from a technical perspective. Spellwork isn't really my thing."

Vague, she thought, *but he's not choking*. So this wasn't more *specifically* about the imprisoned Elementals. "Right. But let's say you wanted to find where they were being kept, specifically. Would you know where to look?"

Rakul nodded, looking uncomfortable. "The underworld," he choked out.

So even referring obliquely to Nihil might be dangerous. But why? "Have you ever been there?" she asked. It was a risky question, but she might as well try.

"To the human underworld?" Rakul asked, raising an eyebrow.

"Sure," Harlow agreed. "Let's call it that. Have you been?"

"Once," Rakul choked out.

They'd hit gold. She pushed him further. "Is there a way to get there from here?"

Rakul gasped for breath loudly enough that a few patrons turned. He collected himself quickly, shaking his head. "No more about that," he pleaded, his voice hoarse.

So this was what he wanted her to find out. How to get into Nihil. *But why?*

"So I need to find the way to the wish-granter," she said, trying to keep her wording vague; she wasn't sure how the spell was tripped.

Rakul nodded, rubbing his throat. He was clearly afraid to say more. "Be careful. The Sistren of Akatei cannot help you." He choked again, frowning.

They were getting closer. Harlow turned what she knew about Rakul Kimaris over in her mind. When her memory hit on the fact that he'd been one of the original Knights of Serpens, she paused, her magic fluttering inside her like an excited moth. "Do I have access to the information already?"

Rakul did not move. His face turned red, and it was obvious that he couldn't answer. The Vault. There *had* to be something in the Vault. Rakul looked at his watch. Harlow sensed he wanted to leave, but she had to ask about the fervor. "Have you ever met anyone like me—a sorcière—who experienced..." She looked around and then whispered, "the fervor?"

Rakul's cheeks turned a little pink, but otherwise he didn't react. "Yes. You must be Claimed."

"It's safe?"

Rakul shook his head, looking frustrated, but managed to say, "No."

She didn't want him to be hurt by the binding, but she had to ask. "Will it kill me?"

Each word he said sounded forced. "No... will.... change...." Rakul doubled over, clutching his neck.

Harlow struggled to think. "What's your favorite pie, Rakul?"

He glanced up at her, face pained. "Lemon meringue."

"I'm sorry," she breathed. "I'm so sorry."

He nodded. "I wish I could help you. I thought if I had you here in front of me that I'd be able to just—" His face crumpled, and he buried it in his huge hands.

"Shhh," Harlow soothed, touching his arms. A tiny bit of her shadow magic wound around his fingers.

He glanced down at it and smiled. "It's been a long time," he said, almost as though he was speaking to her magic itself. "I'm sorry I can't help you more."

Before Harlow could answer, a barista called out, "Morgaine Yarlo, order's up!"

The person from the line stood. She'd been waiting at a corner table and as she fetched her coffee and a bag that probably held a pastry, her gaze caught Harlow's and she winked. As she left the shop, Rakul's nostrils flared, and Morgaine grinned at him, a rakish look on her face that Harlow swore looked like a *dare*.

"That one smells of aether," he growled, nearly standing to follow.

"What of it?" Harlow asked.

"I need to go. If you want your questions answered—all of them..." He paused, then forced out a few more words. "Find the Warden—by whatever means necessary. He can help you."

Harlow knew better than to question Rakul Kimaris. He looked positively lethal at the moment, even though he rubbed his neck as though the binding was chafing him. She hoped Morgaine Yarlo, whoever she was, had a good head start. Rakul looked as though he might take his frustrations out on an unsuspecting victim.

"All right."

Harlow held out her hand, and he took it, kissing her palm as though she were an intimate, rather than someone he just met. "Thank you for meeting me, little bird." Her heart nearly stopped. The creature in Nihil had called her that as well. Rakul stood. "The next time we meet, it may not be as friends. Please remember today if that happens."

Harlow nodded, squeezing his large hand in hers, hoping to give Morgaine a little time to get wherever she was going without Rakul's interference. "I understand. Thank you. I'll figure this out, Rakul. I *promise—all* of it."

She hoped he understood. If there was a way to break the binding that he'd endured, she would find it. She thought he understood her as he nodded solemnly, kissing the back of her hand now, with chaste gratitude. Then he was gone, faster than even the typical Illuminated could move; but he was not the typical Illuminated, after all. Harlow ordered one of The Gate's signature tea lattes and a lemon scone to go, then walked home, deep in thought.

CHAPTER 18

The air was sultry in the sun, but in the shade, it was almost too chilly to be wearing a swimsuit. The beach at the Grand Plaza was emptier than Harlow had seen it all summer. After receiving a text from Enzo that Riley would join them, Harlow scored one of the coveted cabanas overlooking the infinity pool. It shocked her when the concierge told her one was open, even this time of year. Typically, she needed one of the twins to get such treatment, but she wasn't going to question her luck.

Enzo claimed not to care about things like the exclusive cabanas at the Grand, but she knew he secretly loved this kind of luxury, so she ordered a spread of delicious food and settled in with a magazine. She would have preferred loungers on the beach, which was blissfully empty and quiet right now, while the cabana level was nearly full. Still, with everything she'd had going on in the past few weeks and Enzo's hard work on the new retail space, she'd had almost no quality time with her best friend.

She liked Riley Quinn a lot, but she would have preferred to spend time alone with Enzo today. She was trying to adjust her attitude, but the various immortals chatting loudly in their cabanas were making her grumpy. The food came just as Riley and Enzo arrived, and their delighted smiles washed any irritation she felt away.

They wore matching swimwear that Enzo had designed. The only difference was that Riley also wore a new robe in a stylishly clashing print over their tiny briefs. "I am jealous of this," Harlow said, gesturing towards the billowing magenta fabric that featured whimsical winged cats.

Enzo grinned and dove into his beach bag, pulling out another robe, in a similar fabric, this one midnight blue with snow leopards. "It matches your suit."

Harlow let out a delighted noise as she took the robe from Enzo. It was exquisite, of course, with generous sleeves and an extra long hemline. Her swimsuit, which had been a hit on some of the gossips earlier in the summer, was made from a midnight blue leopard fabric, and the two would be divine together. It had been the only positive attention she'd received from the press all summer, and if they saw this, they might run another positive story about her. Harlow hated that she wanted that so badly, but with everything they were bound to say about her when her ruse with Finn really got going, she did.

"Put it on," Enzo urged, pulling her from her lounger.

"Your new supplier is phenomenal," she cooed. "These fabrics are to die for."

Enzo grinned. "The Grand thinks so too. They'll be carrying both the suits and the robes in their shop next spring."

The contract was a big one and would help fund the new retail space. Harlow listened to Enzo and Riley detail the progress they'd made in the past two weeks, proud of her best friend. The way they talked, finishing one another's sentences—the sweet way that Riley beamed when Enzo got excited about the new suppliers they'd contacted this summer—it was everything Harlow wished for her best friend.

When each of them had a plate piled high with food, the conversation died down to a supremely comfortable silence. Harlow's heart swelled a little, and again, she wanted to hold tight to the sweetness of the moment.

"Not to get too serious," she said, keeping her voice low. "But I've been having this weird feeling lately—like anything that's good might disappear at any moment."

Enzo and Riley nodded simultaneously, giving one another a knowing look.

"You're going to say it's the trauma of what happened in Nuva Troi, aren't you?" Harlow responded, trying hard for a dry laugh that didn't quite land.

Riley shrugged. "Sure. It's probably a little of that. But, with the shit in Falcyra, and with what happened in Nuva Troi today, why wouldn't you feel that way?"

Harlow frowned. "What happened in Nuva Troi?"

Enzo's eyebrows raised. "You don't know?"

"No, what happened?"

"There was a bomb in the subway, on one of the school lines," Enzo said.

Harlow's heart skipped several beats. There were two lines in the city that were devoted to children and teachers during school commuting hours, to make sure they were able to get to and from school on time with supervision.

"Which one?" Harlow asked. They were, of course, largely divided by geography. Since humans in Nuva Troi didn't live in the same parts of the city as the Orders, for the most part, the two lines were separated.

"Ours," Riley said, clearly as uncomfortable with the distinction as she was. "There were no casualties. According to the Crisis Management Unit, the bomb malfunctioned somehow and went off sooner than it was supposed to. There were injuries, but no deaths."

Harlow thought she might throw up. Someone had targeted *children*. She glanced around at the other cabanas. No one was paying any attention to them.

"Was it, you know… the Humanists? Or—" She didn't look at Riley, but the "or" just slipped out.

Riley sighed. "Akatei's tit, Harlow. The Rogue Order has morals. We would never target children."

"Sorry," she muttered.

"Don't be," Enzo replied, giving Riley a pointed look. "It's not like you've been briefed on what the Queen is up to."

Harlow sensed a conflict between the two of them, and she didn't want to be in the middle of it. Riley looked around, glaring at Enzo as if to say, "Anyone could hear you."

Enzo stuck his tongue out and pulled threads quickly until the sound of the others at the pool muffled into eventual silence. "Better?"

"Better," Riley said, kissing Enzo's nose. "And for the thousandth time, when I'm at liberty to brief Harlow, I will."

Harlow frowned at Enzo. "Does that mean that *you* know what's going on with the Rogue Order?"

Enzo looked uncomfortable. "I know some things. Not all."

"Are you defecting?" she asked. Her tone came out too blunt, but she genuinely wondered. Would Enzo give up his legacy as the future of the Order of Mysteries for the Rogue Order and its mysterious goals?

"No," Enzo replied. "I can appreciate the Rogue Order's purpose, and try to collaborate with them without abandoning my people, Harlow. It doesn't have to be one or the other."

"Of course," Harlow replied, chastised. She wasn't sure how to feel. Of course neither of them owed her any explanation, but this was awkward.

"If it were just you, Harls, we'd have already told you," Riley said, as though that explained everything.

"Just me? What does that mean?"

Riley sighed, exasperation written all over their face.

"Oh," Harlow said. "You don't trust Finn."

"Or Alaric or Petra," Enzo added, as though that would help.

"And it's not that we *mistrust* them," Riley explained. "It's that we're not done vetting them."

Harlow set her plate down. She wasn't hungry anymore. "Why didn't you just ask Finn whatever you want to know?"

Riley smiled. "We didn't have to. He's offered us a lot of information already. But he and the others are still Illuminated. It's safest for us to be sure of them by independent means. Finn understands."

That was an interesting way of putting it. "He *understands*?"

"Sure," Riley said with a grin. "And his confidence that we'll trust him and your Knights eventually is either very reassuring, or chilling, depending on how you look at it."

She turned to Enzo. "And what do you think about all this?"

Enzo grinned. "I know Finn's heart." He patted Riley's hand. "I think it will all turn out fine."

Riley's smile was a touch tight, but their brown eyes were relaxed and clear.

"I hope so. We would like to be allies, Harlow. But surely you understand that we all need to be cautious."

She supposed she did, so she nodded. The conversation made her feel a little foolish for trusting Finn so easily. For just believing everything he'd told her, after everything his parents, and the rest of the Illuminated had done.

Enzo took her hand. "Stop that. You *know* Finn. Neither of us would let you or your family continue on with him or Alaric if we thought they were a threat to you. You know that, right?"

Harlow glanced between Riley and Enzo. Both smiled at her. "I think so."

Riley leaned over, taking her other hand, and Enzo's both. "This is about alliances, not personal stuff. It's complicated."

Harlow nodded, as though she completely understood. On a cognitive level, she did. The Rogue Order was mysterious, a shadow organization that the Illuminated allowed to go about their business largely because they thought they were silly—nothing more than a haven for immortals who didn't like the way their Orders operated.

Finn had explained to her that Connor and Pasiphae actually thought the Rogues were useful in keeping immortals who felt like outsiders from aligning too closely with humans, as the Rogue Order had a reputation for scorning human members. Apparently Connor's view was that, "They believe themselves an edgy 'alternative' to what we've set in motion, when in reality, they simply replicate our ideals in different packaging."

But Finn and Cian suspected they might be more than that, though they struggled to probe deeper into their organization. Even Nox and Ari had hit dead ends with the Rogue Order. Petra and Thea had a believable theory that if they were as silly as Connor supposed they'd have recruited the Wraiths at some point, since most shifter clans were prejudiced against those with "outlier" alternae, like Riley and the Wraiths. But neither Nox nor Ari had ever been approached.

Thea thought it was likely because of their loyalty to Finn, and that the Rogue Order was protecting their secrets closely. Petra thought that something about the Flynns scared the Rogues. Harlow picked her plate of food back up and took a giant bite of dolmades. The Grand's were some of the best in Nea Sterlis, and she wasn't going to waste them.

Enzo's spell kept the commotion outside the cabana from getting in, but she saw the paparazzo anyway, as one of the vampires in the next cabana was striding toward them with purpose. Their camera was pointed right at Harlow.

"Shit," Enzo swore.

Riley rolled their eyes. "Time to go."

"We didn't even swim yet," Enzo said, sounding disappointed.

Harlow put her plate down, as she finished chewing. Her temper was rising, but she attempted to stay calm. "You stay. I'll go. It's me they're after."

It was clear that the photographer meant to get closeups of her eating, not photos of her gorgeous swimsuit, or new robe. If they were going to obsess over everything she did, she wished that it might be something pleasant, at least occasionally.

"No," Enzo pleaded. "Look, security's getting them."

Harlow shook her head. "I just want to go home and call Finn."

Riley got up and hugged her. "It's okay. They shake me up too."

She brushed kisses on each of their cheeks and gathered her things. Enzo showed her the way the robe's belt worked to close it into a stylish summer gown, and she left without going to change back into her street clothes. She considered calling a cab, but the day was fine, and the weather tomorrow called for rain, so she walked home, turning the day's events over and over in her mind.

On her way home, Petra texted her, *Don't let this send you into a spiral. Come out with me and Kate tonight.*

Don't let what send her into a spiral? She rolled her eyes and swiped over to Section Seven. There she was, shoving food in her face. The caption read, "Finn McKay's been back in Nuva Troi for twelve hours and Harlow's already stress-eating."

"Fatphobic fucks," she muttered.

It was a distinctly human thing to use thinness as a metric for attractiveness, and Section Seven often shied away from making such commentary, since they wanted to stay on the Orders' good side—but apparently she was fair game since they hated her so much. The photo had been out for nearly an hour, and there were only about a hundred comments on it.

She did the thing she knew she shouldn't and opened them up. Quite a few were from immortals saying that Section Seven had gone too far. Apparently, it was fine when they were speculating about her relationship and diminishing her character, but immortals didn't want humans deciding what made a person attractive or not. Harlow tried hard not to hate them all, her eyes stinging with tears.

Then the comments were all gone, and when she clicked out of them, the post itself had been removed. Finn had offered several times to ensure that Section Seven stopped publishing so many hit pieces on her, but they'd eventually agreed that his interference would only stir up more trouble in the end.

But she knew the disappearance of this post was his way of protecting her from afar, doing what he could before the real maelstrom started, to give her some peace. He couldn't stand that they wrote such terrible things about her, and their relationship, while they praised him like he was a god. She tripped over the sash of the robe, into a bench, and just about dropped her new phone. Her heart skipped a beat.

"Careful there." A hand steadied her, and she looked up into the warm eyes of the young woman from the coffee shop. What had her name been? *Morgaine.*

"Thanks," Harlow said. She probably shouldn't have been trying to walk and read her phone at the same time. There was never a time when she wasn't a bit off-balance, but that certainly didn't help things.

"No problem," Morgaine said.

Harlow looked down, Morgaine had clearly been sitting on the bench Harlow had run into. Her drink and the remains of her pastry sat next to a sketchbook. Morgaine had been drawing a gorgeous dark-haired girl with pale plush cheeks and a pretty mouth.

"Did you draw that?" Harlow asked, pointing to the sketchbook.

Morgaine nodded, gesturing for Harlow to sit down. It was a little unusual to be invited to chat with a stranger on the street, but Harlow felt oddly at ease with Morgaine.

"It's really good," Harlow said. "She's beautiful. Did you dream her up?"

Morgaine grinned, a faint blush coloring her cheeks. "Sometimes it feels that way."

Ah, so they were involved. Something about knowing the beautiful girl in the drawing and this gorgeous creature were together was downright comforting. Outside all the strange drama she was surrounded by, there were average humans, like these two, falling in love and swooning over one another.

"How long have you known each other?" Harlow asked.

Morgaine thought for a moment. "It feels like forever, but a little over a year."

"And you've been together the whole time?" It was altogether too easy to talk to Morgaine. Harlow liked the way it felt, just to randomly make a friend like the fate of the world wasn't currently in the balance.

"Not exactly. She was involved with someone else when I met her. Bad timing." Morgaine winked.

"You won her over though, didn't you?" Harlow laughed.

"I won them both over," Morgaine said, stretching her long legs out in front of her.

"Nice," Harlow commented.

Morgaine snickered. "Not like *that*. Though if I were into guys, Fenric might be okay. He's one of my best friends now, though."

"Wow." Harlow was impressed. "And your girl…"

"Echo," Morgaine prompted.

"Echo… She's okay with that? They're friends too."

Morgaine nodded. "Yeah, pretty much." There was a deep sadness in her eyes.

"You miss them," Harlow said after a moment.

"I do," Morgaine said.

There was a long pause between them and Harlow almost got up to go, but Morgaine spoke again. "I hope you don't mind me saying this, but the social media here is fucking rotten about you."

Social media? Harlow had never heard anyone refer to the social apps quite that way before, though she supposed that was what it was. "Yeah… You recognized me, huh?"

Morgaine nodded. "And from the coffee shop."

Harlow remembered that Rakul had been interested in Morgaine. She smelled faintly of aether still, which was odd. "Do you practice magic?" Some humans did, after all, though it was forbidden, and quite difficult for them.

Morgaine shook her head. "Nope. Never had any penchant for it." She glanced down at her phone and saw the time. "I've gotta run. It was nice running into you, Harlow."

"It was," Harlow said as Morgaine packed her things up.

"See you around," she called over her shoulder, as she jogged off.

Harlow leaned into the back of the uncomfortable bench and smiled to herself. This is what she was working for—nice people like Morgaine and Echo, who didn't deserve to have their lives controlled by the Illuminated. Whatever went on in her personal life, in Section Seven and the other gossips, this was what mattered. Making the world a better place for people like them.

CHAPTER 19

Harlow debated whether or not to tell Finn that she'd seen Rakul. She worried he would insist on coming back to Nea Sterlis, and they needed whatever information Finn and Cian could dig up about the McKays in Nuva Troi. After some thought, she emailed Cian about the entire interaction over a secure server in the Vault. She wasn't taking any chances that someone might find out she'd spoken to Rakul. He was in enough danger already, just for having had coffee with her, and their conversation had crossed a line. She knew there would be no explaining if people like the McKays found out.

When Cian emailed back that they'd take care of things with Finn, Harlow enlisted Thea to help her search the archives in the Vault for anything that might give them more information about Ashbourne and Lumina—in addition to the Ledge and Nihil. She was careful not to tell Thea about the Ventyr, or anything that might lead her to make the connection between the people in the story and the Illuminated, but she told her enough of the story so that she could help.

She'd already broken her promise to Finn not to go back to the library, and she had no desire to put her sister in more danger than they were already in, but she needed the help to get this done as quickly as possible. Despite all that, they looked for three days, and came up shockingly empty in terms of new information. They found various accounts of the geological formation of the Ledge, and the usual children's stories.

And of course they came across stories of the Ravagers, in one form or another. Stories of epic destructive forces were common, especially in human fiction and folklore. But nothing they found shed new light on anything. Nothing was any different from what they'd known going in, even after careful probing. It was odd not to find even one significant deviation.

"I didn't expect we'd find exactly what we were looking for," Thea said as she filled the electric tea kettle in the Vault's common room with water. "But it's suspicious to find *nothing*. The Knights have been meticulous with records of the other gods, and so many legends."

From her spot on one of the blue couches, Harlow nodded. "It's definitely suspicious."

Thea scooped tea into the teapot, musing, "When Alaric gets back from Santos we can ask him to help us look."

Alaric had gone to handle a leak at the Velarius family compound on the exclusive island off the coast of Nea Sterlis. Harlow made a noise to show she'd heard, but she was lost in thought as Larkin came down the stairs, looking rumpled from sleep. "What are you two doing?" she asked.

Thea smiled brightly, too brightly in fact. "Making tea."

Before they'd left, the maters had asked that Larkin not be roped too deep into the intrigue brewing around them. Selene had been worried enough to caution, "I think with her awakening about her asexuality that she needs time to come to terms with herself. Let's try to give her that time."

So Thea and Harlow had done just that for the past few days, letting Larkin sleep as much as she wanted, and only telling her the bare minimum of what they needed to in order to keep her from prying further. But it was easy to see she was getting annoyed.

Right now she looked about ready to roll her eyes. "Pour me a cup then."

Thea smiled brightly and got another mug out for just that purpose. "We need more oat milk down here. Wanna go fetch some, littling?"

Larkin plopped down next to Harlow. "Not really."

Thea sighed, doing her best impression of Selene, and then just as Mama would have done, she went upstairs to do it herself.

"Be nicer to Thea," Harlow murmured as Larkin snuggled in next to her.

"You two are keeping something from me. Why should I be nice to either of you?"

Harlow sighed. "Mama asked us to let you rest. After everything that happened—with the fire, with all your ace stuff..." Harlow trailed off as she felt Larkin tense.

"When you figured out that you like all genders, was it confusing?"

"Yes, sort of."

"Did you just stop doing everything?"

Harlow saw where her youngest sister was going. "No, of course not."

"So tell me what's going on—"

Harlow was about to answer, though she wasn't sure exactly what to say, when Thea came back downstairs, without the oat milk she'd gone up for. She stared at her phone in a fairly uncharacteristic way for her as she rushed down the steps.

"What's going on?" Harlow asked, worried that something might have happened to the maters or Alaric.

"Open up Section Seven," Thea breathed.

Harlow and Larkin both got their phones out. Larkin made a little noise, and her countenance immediately tensed as she glanced at Harlow, whose app was taking a moment to load. She cleared a few open windows and when it finally loaded, she understood what they were reacting to.

The pinned post was a photo of Finn, arm in arm with a luscious brunette with luminous brown skin, dressed in couture. The headline read, "Nuva Troi's consummate playboy returns, looking at Midtown brownstones with fashionable Sabre LeBeau." The first line of the caption read, "It's time for another round of #HarlowKraneIsOver."

She bit her bottom lip, glancing up at her sisters. "I'm okay. Sabre LeBeau is our realtor. Finn's looking at brownstones for us—for this fall when we go back."

Larkin nodded. She loved Finn and would never want to think the worst of him. "You forgot the oat milk," she said to Thea. "I'll go get it."

Thea nodded and when Larkin had disappeared upstairs, Thea turned to her. "This article says Sabre LeBeau is one of Finn's exes."

Harlow kept her composure as well as she could. "Really? Interesting."

"Did you know he'd dated them?"

Harlow shrugged. "I guess."

"And you don't have any problem with the two of them spending time together like this? They look pretty cozy."

Harlow glanced at the photo again. Sabre LeBeau was wearing sky-high heels, and they were walking down a set of steep stairs, wet with rain. "He's clearly helping them with the stairs. Being *polite*. The gossips like to stir up drama."

Thea didn't look convinced. Inwardly, Harlow groaned. Thea wasn't going to let this go. "You know as well as I do that Section Seven loves to trash me—it's like a sport for them and Sabre LeBeau is a human. They're gorgeous, fashionable, and glamorous. Everything I'm not. Of course Section Seven is going to make it into something it isn't."

That *did* seem to make sense to her sister. "You're right," Thea said. "Partially anyway—Sabre LeBeau isn't 'everything you're not,' they're who they are—"

Harlow interrupted, "I just meant Section Seven *thinks* I'm not those things. I don't need a pep talk. Can we talk about something else, please?"

Thea's expression clouded with something Harlow desperately hoped wasn't pity, but she nodded as she changed the subject. "Do you get the impression that all the information about Ashbourne and Lumina is *purposely* missing?"

Harlow considered that they couldn't find anything at all related to the Ledge of Wishes or how it came to be. In her experience with mythologies, that wasn't how it worked. There were always seeds of different stories that grew and transformed, proliferated, shapeshifting as they went, but remained recognizable.

The fact that there was a sorcière legend about Ashbourne the Warden, and no stories about who he was or how he came to be, was more than suspicious, it was impossible. "I think someone—probably one of the Illuminated—scrubbed Ashbourne and Lumina from as much as they could."

"But why?" Thea mused.

Harlow would rather she not ask that question. She was about to try to distract her sister when a clatter came from the stairway, where Larkin had dropped the carton of oat milk, which was now rolling down the stairs. Axel followed close behind her, seemingly disappointed that it hadn't shattered and spilled all over the floor. Larkin rushed to pick up the carton before it burst, while Harlow and Thea looked on, startled.

When she'd picked up the milk, she looked up at her sisters, her face a flurry of conflicting emotions. "Are the two of you talking about Ash?"

Thea glanced at Harlow, fear in her eyes. "*Ash?*"

Larkin nodded, coming in the room. "Ashbourne the Warden. Are you talking about him?"

Harlow felt how tightly wound Thea had become, and reached out to squeeze her sister's arm, a silent plea to calm down, lest she terrify Larkin. Thea's shoulders relaxed, slightly, and she looked like she was in pain. Harlow's head shook. She had no idea how Thea had kept her relationship with Alaric a secret for so many years. She was typically an awful liar, and this was more evidence of that fact.

"Yes, we're talking about Ashbourne," Harlow replied, getting up to take the oat milk from Larkin. "Why do you ask?"

Larkin gave Thea a worried look, as Harlow poured milk into their mugs. "I just—wondered."

Harlow bumped her shoulder to Larkin's. Larkin looked back at Thea, who had her knees drawn to her chest and a truly strange look on her face. "Don't mind Thea, bun. She's pretending to be calm about this."

Larkin snorted and Thea let out a little noise of frustration. Harlow took her eldest sister a mug of tea and the three of them curled onto the couch together. "We're looking for stories about Ashbourne. Do you know where we might find one?"

Larkin stared into her mug, as though it was the most interesting thing in the world. "No, I don't know where you'd find *stories* about Ash."

Why was she calling Ashbourne, Ash? "Okay, well what *do* you know then, pal? Obviously you know something."

As Thea tensed into an even tighter ball, Harlow's chest felt like it might burst from the overwhelming amount of tension between the three of them. She was relieved when Larkin finally spoke. "It's hard to explain, but Ash is my friend."

"He's your *what?*" Thea screeched. In Selene's absence, Thea often took on the role of Over-Reactor in Chief.

Larkin's face scrunched up as she leaned away from Thea. Harlow stared at the ceiling. A family of five sisters could be a lot sometimes, even if only three were in the room. "Could we maybe—take it down a notch?" Harlow asked.

Thea sighed. "Explain, *immediately*, why you're friends with an ancient immortal and no one knows." She sounded remarkably like both of the maters; Harlow was impressed.

"He speaks to me in my dreams…" Larkin whispered.

The faraway look in Larkin's eyes twisted Harlow's stomach. Thea glanced at Harlow. When Larkin was little, the Order of Mysteries High Council had believed that Larkin might be a seer, because she often dreamed true, but she'd stopped before she turned eight, the true dreams simply disappearing. Everyone had forgotten about it, or at least it had seemed that way.

"Do you mean you have dreams *about* Ashbourne?" Harlow asked carefully.

Larkin shook her head. "No, they aren't dreams *about* him. He's *there* and we talk."

Thea drew in a sharp, deep breath, every trace of annoyance replaced with deepest worry. "You walk realms in your sleep?"

It was a highly valued but rare talent—so much so that Realm Walkers, like Striders, were thought to be extinct. It made a certain kind of sense that Larkin might have a special ability, one specifically related to the deeper magics, as her own Strider abilities were. What they'd learned from Cian about the origins of Striders made it seem possible that out of five sisters, at least two of them might have anomalous manifestations of magic.

But this revelation made Harlow more than nervous; it terrified her. If Larkin walked realms, there was no doubting why she'd kept it a secret from even her family. The last Realm Walker had died in Illuminated custody, kept imprisoned for their entire life, in servitude. Times had been different, but there was no doubt in Harlow's mind that the same could happen today.

Larkin let out a breath. "Yes. I stumbled into the limen when I was eight, and there he was, almost like he was waiting for me… except he was as surprised to see me as I was him."

Harlow wondered how he'd gotten free of the chamber in Nihil, but she didn't interrupt.

"And then I saw him lots of times when I walked realms. It was like we kept running into each other. Each time, he had that same look, like somehow he'd been waiting for something, but was surprised it was me."

"Interesting," Thea said. "And what did Ashbourne the Warden have to say to a child?"

Larkin rolled her eyes. "He's not some creep, Thea."

Harlow hid a smile when Thea gave Larkin her best Selene-stare, but she felt a measure of relief. It wasn't that she thought the immortal had done anything to her sister; in fact, from her only encounter with him, she'd guess he was lonely more than anything else. There had been a moment before he sent her back where it seemed he was relieved to see another person.

"Ash warned me about what would happen to me if I kept 'dreaming' the way I had been. About the Illuminated."

"How did he know who the Illuminated were?" Harlow asked. Larkin didn't know that the Illuminated had another form, not yet anyway.

Larkin sighed. "He's one of them. You know how the Illuminated are supposed to shift? Well they shift into great big winged people, with sparkly skin."

Thea muttered, "It's not sparkly. It's *illuminated*."

Larkin's eyebrows lifted, creasing her forehead with exasperation. She turned to Harlow, giving her a pointed look.

Harlow shrugged. "I *guess* there's a difference. They do that in their humanoid alternae anyway. You know, all the glowing."

Larkin pursed her lips, teasing. "It's definitely *sparkly*. You have sparkly boyfriends."

"It's not as ridiculous as you're making it sound," Thea insisted. "Besides, I'm *bonded*." Her voice had a shrill edge to it that suggested she was getting defensive. They could be here all day.

Larkin's response was a hysterical screech that Harlow supposed might be a laugh. Harlow wished her sisters didn't have such a propensity for high-pitched noises; it was disconcerting. "The point is," Larkin said when she quieted, "I can't believe the two of you kept all this from me. It's rude."

Thea folded her arms across her chest. "There are lots of things that the Illuminated keep secret. Things that are dangerous for people to know. This is one of them."

Larkin snorted. "I meant I literally can't believe *you* could keep this a secret. Harlow, I can believe. You? Not so much."

The two of them looked as though they might start fighting, so Harlow changed the subject. "You talked with Ashbourne in Nihil?"

"Nihil? Is that the prison?" Larkin asked.

Harlow nodded. "Yes, there's a chamber, where the guardians sleep, or are in stasis or something."

"Sounds like someone *else* is keeping secrets," Thea said as she poked Harlow sharply in the leg.

Harlow tried to stay casual about it. It wasn't exactly that she'd meant to keep it all a secret from her sisters, but that she hadn't gotten around to telling them yet. Sorting out what was a secret and what wasn't was complicated these days and she was worn down by the idea. Reluctantly, she admitted, "I may have been to Nihil. Twice."

Thea looked as though she might start screeching again. "Why the hells wouldn't the two of you tell me these things?"

"You should talk," Harlow responded. "You were a member of the Knights for how many years? With a secret *boyfriend*?"

Thea rolled her eyes, as though that were nothing in comparison with an ancient immortal friend, secret talents, and traveling to the limen. Anyone with sisters understood this was the way it was; you thought you knew them because you saw them every day, and then one day they'd change on you, morphing into someone else entirely. Sometimes the change was mundane. Sometimes it was life-altering, but the best thing to do was roll with it.

Larkin stuck out her tongue, then directed them back to the conversation at hand. "I don't think I've ever walked in the chamber you're talking about, but maybe the other parts of the prison. Sometimes there's just nothing but Ash when I arrive, and he's saddest then. But the rest of the time, we meet in the limen itself, not the prison. Ash and the other guardians can manifest in the limen in astral form. Kind of like a break from their responsibilities."

Thea held up her hands. "You're going to have to back up and tell me everything the two of you know."

Harlow recounted her visits to Nihil in close detail, along with her experience with the Pyriphle. When she'd finished telling about how quickly she'd started to shift near the heart of the limen, Thea nodded. "Yes, that would make sense. Because your shadows are aether in its purest form, before it fills the threads, and the Feriant is tied to your manifestation, contact with the heart would make it easier for you to shift."

Larkin nodded along, the exaggerated look on her face making it clear she was mocking Thea's academic tone. "Yes, Professor Krane."

"Shut up," Thea said, now poking her youngest sister playfully. "Does that all line up with what you know?

Larkin's face fell into seriousness. "I guess so. Though I don't know much about all of it, not the way you do. Mostly Ash listens while I talk."

The loneliness in her little sister's voice tugged at Harlow's heartstrings. Sometimes she forgot that Larkin was so young, and that she'd never made friends the way the twins had. She wondered why Ashbourne wanted to speak to Larkin. As her sister talked more about him, Harlow thought she understood; he was lonely too.

The other guardians were resentful of Nihil, and though they'd all been friends once, they were tired of one another now. Some of them hated each other, from the way it sounded. And Ashbourne, he felt guilty about it *all*. Harlow wished Finn were here to hear this. She thought he'd understand how Ash felt.

When she finished talking, Larkin looked exhausted, but Harlow had to ask her something. "Does he ever say anything about someone named Lumina?"

Larkin smiled sadly. "No, not specifically, but I've gotten the impression there's someone he worries about."

"Okay," Thea said, pushing a piece of hair out of Larkin's face. "Do you know where he is? Or rather, how to get to him in the waking world?"

Rakul had said that if they wanted all their questions answered that they needed to "find the Warden." The more she tried to understand all of this, the more it felt like a web. Threads connected to one another and then dropped off when she didn't have enough information, but they spiraled out from one another, regardless. Harlow wondered what was at the center of it all. The deeper in she went, the more she got the sense that she was missing some wider view.

Larkin's head fell to the side as she thought. "Other than what we already know? Not really… I don't know how to get to Nihil. Not even my way."

"What happens when you visit his realm?" Harlow asked. "As opposed to the other places you've met, I mean."

"I just *arrive*. I rarely see anything but Ash… I think he wants it to be that way. The prison isn't safe."

"I should think not," Thea said.

Harlow's body remembered the Ravager, and its terrible voice. *Hello, little bird.* She shivered, glad that Ashbourne had kept her sister safe. Even in her astral form, she was vulnerable.

"Has he ever talked about what he guards there?" Harlow asked.

Larkin shrugged. "Not really."

"And you can't dream walk on purpose?" Thea asked.

Larkin shook her head. "No, I'm sorry. If I'd had a teacher, I probably could, but I'm pretty bad at it, I think."

Harlow knew how that felt. She wished she'd had anyone like her who could tell her what to do as a Strider. "Have you ever been anywhere else, besides being drawn to wherever Ash is?"

Larkin smiled. "A few places. The limen is interesting. It presses up against all worlds, of course, and sometimes there are doors to other places. Occasionally, I come across one and just watch."

"Watch what?" Thea asked.

"The world on the other side," Larkin said with a dreamy smile. "There are some really beautiful worlds."

It was hard not to ask questions about that, but they needed to stay on topic. "You don't go through though?" Harlow asked, uncomfortable. A theory was beginning to form in her thoughts, and she didn't much like it.

Larkin pushed some hair out of her face, her mouth screwing into a tight knot. "No. In the limen, I know how things work. My astral body is predictable. Once I stuck my hand through one of the doors and it felt strange. I'm not sure what might happen if I moved into a whole other realm."

Harlow nodded. "Have you ever seen anyone else there?"

"Anyone like me, or Ash?" Larkin asked.

"No," Harlow said slowly. "Have you ever seen anyone in the limen who was actually *there*."

Larkin shook her head. "No people, but occasionally an animal will wander in from the doors. I saw a fish swim in from a door that was underwater once. I tried to throw it back, but I couldn't become corporeal enough to touch it. It died."

Harlow nodded. "Because it wasn't underwater anymore."

Larkin's face scrunched up. "No… I mean, yes, it probably would have… but something came out of the aether and snatched it up…. It disappeared."

"Weren't you worried about your own safety?" Thea asked, sounding anxious.

Larkin laughed. "No. There are creatures in the limen, of course. It's a world of its own, despite how it layers between so many worlds. But they're semi-corporeal and have no interest in the non-corporeal."

Harlow raised her eyebrows.

"They don't care about my astral form. I think they see me, or sense me anyway, but they're not interested in me in the slightest."

"What are these creatures?" Harlow asked.

"I don't really know," Larkin said. "I don't see them very often, and they use the clouds of aether to hide in. Some seem harmless, like the ones who took the fish. I think they were just hungry… But others…" she shook her head. "They could be dangerous to corporeal beings."

Harlow swallowed hard. "Okay."

Thea watched her, likely recognizing the face Harlow was making intimately.

She'd certainly seen it dozens of times over the years as they solved the mysteries of the texts they'd restored together. All that seemed like a lifetime ago now.

Harlow knew how the Illuminated got to Okairos, and knowing it terrified her. If they'd come through the limen, then more of them might be out there. Finn had said the "journey" was dangerous. Wherever they came from, if they found their way here, they would most certainly change things, and *not* for the better.

CHAPTER 20

T he next morning, as Harlow readied herself for brunch with Enzo and Riley, Thea entered the bathroom. "What do you know that you're not telling?"

Harlow set the curling iron down. There was no need to burn herself because she was distracted. Thea turned the iron off and began pulling threads to shape Harlow's hair into her usual waves. Like Meline, she was talented with glamour. "Well, are you going to tell me?"

Harlow stared at her sister in the mirror. In so many ways they were different. Thea was so beautiful she nearly always got her way. It made her blunt and insistent at times like these, when she felt someone wasn't immediately giving into her every whim.

"No," Harlow said. "I'm not."

Thea glared at her. There was no malice, or even anger in it, just sisterly frustration. "Why not?"

"I promised Finn I wouldn't tell anyone. Not even you. Some of what I know is dangerous."

Thea finished working on her hair and turned, sliding onto the vanity countertop so she faced Harlow directly. "Is this about who the Illuminated really are?"

Harlow nodded. Thea was clever enough to figure things like this out on her own, and they'd certainly been skirting the issue in their research for days. She'd wondered when Thea might figure it out. There was no need to try to lie, but she wasn't going to give anything away.

"I know," Thea said. Her fingers fluttered out, checking the wards on the villa, adding an extra layer of sound protection to just the surrounding space. "I know about the Ventyr, the Anemoi and Thuelloi."

"What?" Harlow whispered, afraid to speak aloud, even here. "Alaric told you?"

Thea nodded. "A long time ago. Back when we were trying to find information about the Striders, I came across a little volume of poetry. Quite obscure, just a few printings—they were numbered. The verse was quite bad, really. No artistry to it."

"And it was about the Ventyr?" Harlow asked.

Thea tucked her hair behind her ears, nodding. "About an endless war between a winged race of people, and an Emperor who wanted too much. He wasn't satisfied with the two planets he'd managed to conquer, so he used his children, twins, against one another to open portals to other worlds. It had a disastrous result—the witches of one world cursed them—throwing all sorts of things off balance in the worlds they'd accessed."

Harlow was acutely aware of the blood rushing through her veins as her heart beat faster. It was a disconcerting feeling to be so sensitive to everything going on in her body still, despite Finn's absence. "You confirmed with Alaric this was about the Illuminated?"

Thea's mouth pressed into a grim line. "The Ventyr. He swore me to absolute secrecy, and I never told anyone. We never even talked about it again. But all this has brought it up again. You know how they got here, don't you?"

Harlow closed her eyes. She wished to all gods that Thea didn't know any of this. Now she had to worry about her, in addition to everything else. Still, it was easier that she knew. Harlow hated keeping secrets and having one less to worry about eased her burden. Finally she nodded. "They got here through the limen."

Thea bit her bottom lip, humming softly, as she often did when she was puzzling through something. Harlow had heard her make the same noise thousands of times in the workroom at the Monas over the years. "Yes, that's what I think too. Are you worried that somehow they'll find their way here? The rest of them, I mean."

"I can't really help but think they might." There was so much to be worried about these days. Admitting that she was worried about her fiancé's ancient ancestors coming to Okairos and making everything worse was awful. The complications just kept piling up. Thea didn't look concerned though.

Harlow threw her hands up in the air. "That would be bad, don't you think?"

Thea shrugged, grimacing. "Yes, but I'm not sure that's even possible at this point. It's been over two thousand years. Don't you think if they were coming they would've done it?"

Harlow tended to agree. "Yes, but what if what the Merkhov text shows will make magic accessible to everyone, somehow also brings the Ventyr here?"

She'd asked Finn about this before and he'd agreed with her; since awakening magic was what the Illuminated were sent here to do, it might somehow signal to the rest of their people, the Ventyr, where they were.

Thea's brows knit together. "I think that's a real risk. Whatever we find out with the Merkhov text, with the Scroll of Akatei, I think we'll have to weigh the risks pretty carefully."

Harlow's heart was heavy. "I have to get to brunch. We can talk about this later. Obviously, I don't think it's a good idea to talk to Larkin about this."

"Because Ashbourne and the guardians are Ventyr, right?"

Harlow nodded. "Exactly. That, and I came in contact with what they're guarding, Thea. It's worse than anything you can imagine. They're not like what we've been told the primordial elementals are like. They're sentient."

"What?" Thea snarled. "Sentient? Primordial elementals are…"

"Supposed to be more like animals, or worms, I know. And maybe they are like that, somehow—in form anyway—I don't know. I couldn't actually see it. But it spoke to me, and it said we'd see each other again soon."

Thea pursed her lips. "It was messing with your mind."

"Two of the guardians are missing. I don't think we can afford to ignore the threat."

"Fuck," Thea swore. "*Fuck.*"

Harlow pressed a hand to her sister's shoulder. "My thoughts exactly."

"Every time I think it can't get worse it does," Thea muttered, her elegant fingers fluttering as she waved Harlow away. "Go to brunch. You might as well."

The foreboding she'd gotten used to reflected back at her, in her sister's eyes. "I'm sorry, Thea. I don't want this to be how it is."

Thea brushed a kiss to her forehead, dissolving the extra sound protection around them. "I know you don't. Go to brunch. I'm going to take another pass at the Merkhov."

⁓

Riley's home in Nea Sterlis wasn't as grand as the Herrington villa, but realistically, not many places were. Still, it was very nice, a flat in a beautiful modern building, with views of the sea. By the time Harlow got there, it was raining and chilly, so the three of them ate in the cozy kitchen, rather than the terrace. Riley had been decorating, spending the summer at the famous Nea Sterlis flea markets, picking up charming oddities. Harlow was impressed with their eclectic grasp on home decor, and the stories they had about each item they'd collected.

It was a pleasant enough meal, but Harlow was distracted. Her conversation with Thea had been disturbing, and to make things worse, in the cab on the way over Section Seven had run another story about Finn and Sabre. Apparently, they were *also* at brunch, which meant their ruse was in full effect. She'd texted Finn, the first of her queries that was meant to indicate jealousy and suspicion, and he hadn't answered her yet, which put her on edge.

"So," Riley said. "Are we going to talk about it?"

"What?" Harlow asked.

"About this idea that S7 has that you and Finn are on the rocks," Enzo chimed in.

His calm expression was slightly strained, around the eyes—he was reading her. She could only imagine the dread and anxiety that were coming to the surface. He'd read them as being about Finn, but in reality, they were about this, about lying to the people she loved. She'd just gotten Enzo back, and now she was keeping something huge from him, something that would make him worry for her, and maybe even hate Finn.

Harlow rolled her eyes, trying to affect a casual air. She had to try to diffuse some of this to soften the eventual fallout. "There's no truth to it. Sabre is our realtor."

"Who Finn used to *date*," Enzo said, emphatic. He was definitely reading her high levels of anxiety. "That really doesn't bother you?"

"They went on like five dates three years ago," Harlow tried her hardest not to sound defensive, but didn't make much headway. Trying to deceive two empaths was anxiety-producing. "Decided they were better off as friends, and that's how things have been ever since."

"And now Sabre's helping you buy a house?" Riley asked, one eyebrow raised. They looked suspicious enough that Harlow knew they knew she was lying about something. "And you're not even *there*?"

Her ability to stay calm was deteriorating with every passing moment. She'd known this was how it might be, but the reality of it was different. "Do the two of you *want* there to be a problem?"

Enzo shook his head, giving Riley a look that said, *we should give her space.* "No, Harls, of course not."

"We just want to make sure you're okay," Riley said, their voice gentle.

Both of them clearly sensed her distress, and it was infuriating that it was working in the ruse's favor. The more worked up she got, the more they believed something was truly wrong between her and Finn. She would have a lot of explaining and apologizing to do when this was over.

Harlow drew in a long breath and gathered her thoughts, but her emotions took over and the words spilled out of her, unbidden. "And yet, the tone of this conversation makes me feel like things are very much not okay. Is there something about Sabre that I should find threatening? Because they're so attractive and glamorous and I'm just *me*?"

The room was so silent Harlow could hear the wards on the building humming, ever-so-slightly. Enzo's lips pressed into a tight line. "You know that's not what we're saying."

"I know." Harlow swallowed hard. *Where had all that come from? Did she really feel that way?* She stared at the ceiling for a moment, trying to stay calm. "Of *course* I'm sensitive about the things the gossips are saying. It hurts, especially when I'm trying hard and they still hate everything I fucking do."

They were staring at her now, slightly aghast at her outburst. Harlow took a beat, examining her hands, her ring, for a brief moment before saying, "I trust Finn, okay?"

No matter that he was taking his sweet time answering her text. Even if it was fake bad news, she hated waiting for it. She glanced at her phone. Both Riley and Enzo caught the direction her attention had traveled in. The look they shared nearly broke Harlow's resolve to stay calm. There was nothing in the world she hated more than being pitied.

Luckily, a knock at the door saved her from further conversation. Riley got up to answer. Enzo tried to take her hand, but she snatched it back from him. He had that look in his eyes that said he wanted to talk about her feelings, and she just *couldn't*. Not right now. "I don't want you to comfort me, okay? Nothing is wrong."

"Okay," he said. "I believe you."

"Do you?" she asked, hating the high pitch of her voice.

"No," he replied. "I don't. There's something wrong, but whether you're upset about this Finn stuff or something else, I can't tell."

Harlow's jaw clenched so hard it ached in the back of her neck. She reminded herself again that this was the plan. This was exactly what they'd meant to happen. If they were convincing Riley and Enzo, they were likely to be convincing anyone else who was watching.

"I know that face," Enzo whispered. Harlow made a silent plea to Aphora, wishing hard that Enzo actually knew what was happening. Tears filled her eyes as he said, "I'm here if you need me, all right?"

"I know," she said, finally taking Enzo's outstretched hand. "Just give me some time, okay?"

Enzo nodded and squeezed her hand, just as Kate and Riley entered the room. "Sorry to interrupt," Kate said brightly. "I borrowed a book from Riley and thought I'd return it on my way to the beach—but the WaveReport just said there's a possibility of a storm moving in."

Kate's usually brown hair had gone a bit red from her summer in the sun, and she was tan, with a few freckles sprinkling across her nose. Her linen shirt was unbuttoned past the point of what the gossips would consider decent, showing her bikini. It irked that she looked so good, casual and at ease, when Harlow was so uncomfortable.

"I asked Kate if she wanted to stay for brunch," Riley said. Their face was cautious, as though they were worried Harlow might get upset. She wasn't that bad, was she?

Harlow tried her brightest smile, but Kate raised her eyebrows incredulously. "Don't strain yourself, Lo," she said as she sat. "It's just brunch. I won't bite."

The air in Riley's apartment felt sticky and hot, all of a sudden. Harlow shifted uncomfortably in her chair, feeling as though she might be drowning. This was supposed to be something fun to do, something to distract her from missing Finn, and she wanted nothing more than to bolt. Of course she'd known there would be friction around all this, she'd just expected it to go differently.

Riley brought out an epic spread of toppings and freshly made bagels, as Enzo and Kate chatted about the science of growing grapes at the vineyard. It was so boring Harlow nearly yawned, but the food looked delicious, so she focused on it instead. No one spoke directly to her for the rest of the meal, though both Enzo and Riley exchanged several furtive looks that did little more than agitate her further.

When they were finished eating, Harlow went to the bathroom to text Finn again. *Are you ignoring me?* Her heart beat a little faster as she waited. His read receipts were on. She saw the moment he saw her text, the little dots cascading that indicated that he was answering, and then nothing. Her hands shook as she washed them, but she steadied herself enough to go back to the living room, where everyone was having tea. Or rather, Enzo was drinking tea while Kate and Riley made coffee in the kitchen.

"I'm gonna go," she said.

Enzo gave her a close once-over, but only nodded in response. Harlow glanced towards the kitchen, meaning to say goodbye, but Riley and Kate were deep in conversation with one another, speaking in soft voices. She prayed they weren't talking about her and Finn, but the way they startled when she walked towards them made her sure they probably had been.

"I'm going home," she said. "Thank you for a beautiful meal."

"Did you walk here?" Kate asked.

Harlow's chest tightened. "No, I took a cab."

"I have my car, want me to drive you back to the villa? Petra and I are supposed to have a date later anyway, I can see if she wants me to pick her up early."

Harlow's immediate instinct was to say no, but after talking to Morgaine, she'd been determined to try harder and things had gone badly enough already. She took a deep breath and nodded. "Sure, shoot her a text."

Kate did, and almost instantly received a response, which Harlow tried not to be jealous about. "We're a go. Come on, I'm parked out front."

Harlow hugged Enzo and Riley, trying to ignore the concern in both their expressions. She supposed that as soon as she left, they were going to have an extra analytical conversation about her, determining that she was jealous of Sabre, and likely jealous of Kate and Petra. If so, they wouldn't be altogether wrong. Kate chatted easily about Petra and the vineyard as they made their way to her car and Harlow did feel jealous, but not for the reasons Enzo and Riley might have guessed.

The skies opened up then, and the mild drizzle she'd arrived in shifted to a torrential downpour. Kate and Harlow were soaked in an instant. They ran the rest of the way to Kate's car, laughing from the shock of being so quickly drenched. They were still laughing when they shut the doors to the SUV.

Kate had purchased the rugged little SUV when they were in college. It was banged up and about a million years old, but like the Woody, an absolute classic that she refused to magically restore. She always said that the Illuminated and Order of Mysteries used magic to fix things that weren't broken, and loved the SUV for what it was.

Harlow reached for her seatbelt, but it was stuck. A faint memory that it had always been broken came back to her, followed by some less innocent memories about the back seat. Harlow blushed.

"You remember the trick to get it to go?" Kate asked. The question and tone were innocent enough, but a flush colored Kate's cheeks that made Harlow wonder if she'd had the same thought.

Harlow shook her head, unable to trust her voice. Kate leaned over and pulled gently on the seatbelt, her face close to Harlow's. It was a friendly enough moment, but it made Harlow nervous all the same. How was she supposed to act natural when they'd had sex in every seat of this car, and on the hood, and once on the roof? It wasn't that she missed those times, but just thinking about them made it awkward as Kate handed her the seatbelt.

"This is weird for me," Harlow said, her voice shaking slightly.

For once, Kate was serious. "It's weird for me too. I'm not sure how to act."

A long silence passed as Kate started the car, pulling away from the curb and into the light traffic. Nea Sterlis was so much easier to navigate by car this time of year, Harlow might actually start to get comfortable driving again.

"I really like Petra, and we have a good understanding about things."

Harlow nodded. "I'm glad." She stared at her hands, at her ring. The pause was so long that awkwardness set in.

She was about to say something about how happy she was for the two of them—she *was* happy for them, after all, but Kate spoke. "It wasn't your fault, you know."

"What wasn't?" Harlow asked.

"The way things ended. I was wild about you."

Harlow sighed. "We don't have to do this, Kate."

Kate rolled her neck, an exasperated laugh filling the car as she pulled over, into a parking lot overlooking the ocean, one of Nea Sterlis' dozens of scenic overlooks. "I kind of think we do. *I* need to. We never talked about it after I told you I was leaving."

"What was there to *say*?" Harlow said. She didn't realize she'd been angry with Kate all this time. "I couldn't do things the way you wanted, and you couldn't do things the way I wanted. It was all a mistake."

Kate shut the SUV off. "That's not fair. It wasn't all a mistake. I *loved* you."

The words hit hard. They'd never said them while they were together. It had been implied, but the fact that Kate leaned heavily towards non-monogamy hadn't worked for Harlow and though there hadn't been anyone else at the time, the mere thought had scared her, kept her from saying all she'd felt at the time.

"I loved you too," Harlow finally admitted. It felt good to say it, even if that verb was in the past tense. She'd spent the whole summer working hard on healing, and she knew this was part of things. Being honest now was important to her, because this was obviously keeping both of them from fully moving forward —and it was time. With Finn and Petra involved, it was beyond time. "But you left and Mark showed up... and I know it's not fair, but if you stayed he never would have done all those things to me, because I never would have left you. I would have figured it all out."

Kate's mouth fell open, and then she shut it. "I know. I *know*, Lo. Don't you think I know that? It's all my fucking fault. Everything that happened to you..." A sob choked off the end of her sentence.

Tears wet both their cheeks as their words hung in the air. That wasn't what Harlow had meant at all. The stress of the day had made her emotions a jumble, and her words had come out all wrong. "It's not. None of it was your fault. I know that. I'm just *so mad* that I let it all happen."

Harlow's chin trembled with grief. Snot was running down her face and she buried her face in her hands. She was too far gone to care what Kate thought about how she looked. The lid was off the box she shoved her feelings down into now, and she couldn't get it back on.

Kate's arms went around her, stroking her hair. "It was *his* fault, Lo. Not yours. It was always all his fault. I'm glad he's dead."

Harlow pulled back a little to look at Kate. Something about the way she said it made Harlow think she knew more about what had happened at the House of Remiel than she was supposed to. She'd never found out where Kate had disappeared to that night.

Kate pulled a hanky from her pocket and wiped Harlow's face off. "You're all puffy," she said, smiling as though she thought it was cute. "All I meant is that he was so obviously an asshole, and you deserve better. Finn is a good man."

Kate hugged her again, and she smelled familiar, like sunshine, wood sage and salt air. Long ago, this would have ended with their clothes off, but now—now Harlow was just grateful Kate was here. She'd forgotten how the best part of *them* had been their easy friendship. The rest was fleeting, but maybe that could last.

She let her arms go around Kate too. "I missed you," Harlow mumbled into Kate's shoulder. "I missed you so much."

When they let go, Kate said, "I missed you too. Can things be better with us now? Could we *try* to be friends at least?"

Harlow shook her head. "We don't have to try. I think we're already there." She smiled through her tears as Kate's face lit up.

Harlow felt the joke coming before it came out of Kate's mouth. "Really? That is so good, because Petra hates *Pretty Little Firestarters* and the final season is about to start."

It was her way of smoothing things over. Of making intense emotions easier to digest, and Harlow didn't mind it a bit. It felt good to laugh. "The Illuminated have terrible taste in television. Finn doesn't like it either."

Kate fished another hanky out of the console for Harlow and started the car again. They chatted about their shared love for the nighttime soap opera the rest of the way home. It felt like a new start, made more poignant by the fact that the rain let up and the sky cleared. When they pulled into the villa's half-moon driveway, Petra was sitting on the front steps, staring at her phone.

As they got out of the car, she looked up. "Did the two of you finally make up?"

Kate nodded, grinning, but Harlow saw the caution in Petra's eyes. "What is it?"

Petra glanced away from them, cheeks flushing slightly. "Section Seven."

Kate took the phone from Petra's outstretched hand, swearing at it. "Those fucking assholes. It wasn't like that, babe."

"I know it wasn't," Petra said simply. "They're obsessed with breaking Finn and Harlow up."

"Do I even want to see?" Harlow asked as she took Petra's phone from Kate. The question was rhetorical, of course; she was already reading. Photos of Kate fixing her seatbelt certainly looked like they were getting intimate in front of Riley's building, and the ones at the beach overlook were even worse.

The headline read, "Finn McKay is gone for mere days and Harlow's replaced him."

"Their headlines aren't even clever anymore," she said. How were they getting all these photos taken and out so quickly? They had to be using more of the invisible drones. But why weren't they publishing the footage of the fight at the beach then? Inside her bag, she felt her phone vibrate. She glanced at it, then took Petra's hand. "Are we okay?"

Petra surprised her, pulling her into a hug so tight that Harlow could barely breathe. "Yes," Petra said into her hair. "Of course we are."

Harlow hugged Petra back. In so many ways, she was the easiest person Harlow knew. If she were mad, or worried, she would say.

Petra let her go and grinned at both Harlow and Kate. "Besides, you're the ugliest crier I've ever met. Your face is all splotchy. You and I both know you wouldn't have been sobbing if you'd been doing what Section Seven said you were."

Kate protested. "Hey, I've made girls cry because it was so good."

Petra bit her lip, taking Kate's hand. "Prove it."

Harlow groaned. "I don't need to hear that."

Kate dragged Petra to her side, glancing back at Harlow. "You gonna be okay? We could stay?"

Harlow's phone buzzed again, several times in a row. "No, I'm fine. Have a good time."

She watched as they drove off, then sat on the steps herself. She had no idea if Larkin and Thea were home, but she didn't want to do this in front of them. Her phone vibrated yet again as she opened it. Several texts from Finn awaited her.

Not ignoring you. At brunch.

Everything okay?

What's going on with you and Kate?

Are you ignoring ME?

Harlow waited for her read receipt to show up and took a few breaths before responding. *Nothing's going on with Kate. Section Seven's just being Section Seven.*

She watched as he read her message and then began to write his own. He was obviously writing and rewriting, because it took a while for him to respond. *Okay. They're jerks.*

Harlow's chest tightened. This was hard. She could feel him wanting to say more to comfort her, and her intense desire to be comforted, but they couldn't do that. Not if they wanted this to work. So she asked what they'd agreed would be one of their code questions: *Yeah. Any good properties?*, which meant, "How are things going with your parents?"

The answer was quick this time. *At least one good lead, but it won't be on the market for another few weeks.*

Harlow's heart beat faster. So the game had truly begun. His parents were buying what was happening. They'd agreed to be subtle at first. *Want to call and talk it over?*

His answer was immediate. *Not a good time. We can talk when I get home.*

And that was that, the code was over, he was back to being dismissive. *All part of the plan*, she reminded herself. Harlow locked her phone and closed her eyes. *I can do this*, she thought as she breathed deep.

"Are you sitting on the porch because Section Seven is at it again?" Thea asked.

Harlow glanced over her shoulder. Thea and Larkin were standing in the doorway.

"Yeah," she said, getting up. "I could really use a cup of tea."

Larkin came around to help her up. "No shortage of those here."

Thea hugged her as the three of them walked into the villa together, closing the door on the outside world.

CHAPTER 21

The next week brought rain, and not much else, as Thea tried to break the binding on the Merkhov text. They didn't see much of their friends, and Harlow wondered if maybe her behavior at brunch and the Section Seven onslaught had gotten to them. Every text she sent was met with friendly responses, and on the surface it seemed like they were busy, but she couldn't stop going over things in her mind. *Had she given too much away? Did they suspect she was lying?* She knew she was probably being paranoid, but worrying over every little thing she said was an old habit that she couldn't quite shake.

It wasn't as though there weren't plenty of other things to hold her attention. She helped Thea with extra research on breaking complicated binding spells and used the Vault's resources to find a whole host of training exercises that had names like "Lucid Dreaming for the Intermediate" and "Astral Projection for the Advanced Practitioner." She and Larkin watched them together in Cian's office, since it had a big screen television, and laughed at the retro-vibes of the videos that had been digitized from videotapes.

The videos weren't entirely pointless, vintage as they were. The principles were solid, and Harlow and Larkin worked together nearly every day to improve Larkin's control over herself when dreaming. Harlow secretly hoped that she was helping herself as well. She could use some increased control over her mind, and the tutorials seemed to focus on that idea a lot.

"I'm just like the heroine in Meli's sci-fi romance book," Larkin quipped one morning over iced coffee and toaster waffles.

The two of them had just finished the seventh installment in "Astral Projection for the Advanced Practitioner." They sat at Cian's desk in the Vault, which faced the big screen TV. Axel had taken the opportunity to stretch out in front of them, sure he was the main event, rather than the instructional videos.

"I thought it was a monster romance," Harlow said as she put the video back in its case, searching for another. There were two or three more in the series, but they seemed to have misplaced the next one.

"Oh, there's that one too, but it's a trilogy about three psychics who fall in love with different creatures—this one is about a dream walker and she falls in love with a mafia enforcer," Larkin explained.

Harlow turned. "And you… liked this book? The one with the cat-people was super spicy."

Axel rolled onto his back, purring at Larkin, who rubbed his belly as she laughed. "Would you believe it if I said I liked the story?"

"Whatever turns your key," Harlow said, laughing along with her sister. "I don't think that's why everyone else is reading them though." She found the missing video and set it up.

Larkin popped the last bite of her waffle in her mouth, shrugging. "We can all appreciate different things about romances, Harlow. This one's got great found family vibes."

Harlow plopped back in the chair next to Larkin, giving Axel's ears a scratch as she settled in. "So how are you like the main character? I haven't read that one."

"She walks into people's dreams and solves their deepest mysteries," Larkin explained.

"And you're going to do that?" Harlow asked, not quite seeing the connection, since Larkin wasn't exactly going into a dream world, but astral projecting into a real place, albeit in her sleep.

Larkin shook her head, taking a long drink of her iced coffee, draining it of the last precious drops. Then she grabbed Harlow's, right out of her hands. Harlow rolled her eyes, letting her sister jack herself up on caffeine if she wanted to. For whatever reason, it had the opposite effect on Larkin than it had on most people; it seemed to calm her more than anything.

"No, see, she and the love interest form a connection in the dream world, one they can't seem to make in the waking world, on account of the fact that they're both so damaged and broody, of course."

"Of course," Harlow agreed, snickering as she snatched her coffee back. The days of iced coffee were coming to a close, and she didn't want to miss one scrap of them, even if they were locked deep underground in the Vault.

"Well, I can connect with Ash in the *real* limen, and hopefully I can solve the mystery of where you can find him, since that's what Rakul said you had to do." She smiled smugly, raising her eyebrows and kicking her feet up on Cian's desk. "And then I'll be the hero of the story, just like the girl from the book."

Harlow smiled. "I would love that so much. It seems like everything keeps going just a little wrong, you know?"

Larkin nodded. "It feels like that sometimes. Things are really complex, you know? Maybe we're making more progress than we think."

It was a nice way to think about things. Harlow kissed Larkin's cheek, dragging her sister into a one-armed hug. "There's like three more of these astral projection videos. Guess if you're gonna be the big hero, we'd better watch them, huh?"

Larkin sighed in mock-exasperation. "Every hero has their training montage. This is mine."

They cackled hard as the credits started rolling. Cian's computer flashed a notification. "Keep watching," Harlow ordered, pointing to the screen. "I don't want you to miss any part of your big montage moment."

Larkin stuck out her tongue as Harlow scooted closer to Cian's computer in her rolling chair. The notification was from Cian, so Harlow clicked into it. It was a message for her, sent over the secure line from Haven in Nuva Troi: *I see you're watching movies in my office. Clean up after yourselves and get that cat off my desk.*

Harlow stuck her tongue out at the camera she knew was placed above the TV and rubbed Axel's belly before reading on.

While Finn's been off looking at brownstones and brunching, I've been doing some digging in the Order of Masks' archives. Merhart Locklear approved me for some of our more classified material last week, and I found this. It appears to be a crypt from about two hundred years ago.

Look closely at the inscription.

Hope you're well.

C

Harlow clicked on the attached image. It was an engraving of a cemetery, full of beautiful headstones, statuary, and large gated crypts all in a row. There was an inscription on the most prominent of the crypts: "The world between worlds waits just beyond knowledge. Beware what lies—" Harlow couldn't read the rest, as the inscription seemed to wrap around the crypt.

The first line was familiar somehow though. She opened up the private search engine that Nox built for the Vault's digitized archives and typed it in, leaving the unfinished line out. Larkin paused the instructional video to read over her shoulder. "That sounds familiar, doesn't it?"

"Yes, I'm searching." The search engine that Nox built for the Vault's archives showed it was ninety percent through its scan. One answer came up, in a rather common prayer book published by the Sistren of Akatei.

Larkin and Harlow both leaned in, right as Axel sat up, directly in front of the computer screen, blocking their view. Larkin dragged him off the desk and into her lap, where he grumbled before crawling into her hoodie, which she held open for him.

"You'll spoil him," Harlow said absentmindedly.

"Good," Larkin replied as the scan of the prayer book flashed onto the screen.

There it was, the inscription to the book, right after the ornate title page.

The world between worlds
waits just beyond knowledge.

"I mean, that's an obvious reference to the limen," Larkin said. "Which I guess makes sense. Akatei is supposed to govern it, after all."

Harlow nodded. "So you're the one who was obsessed with the nekropoleis as a kid. What do you think this means?"

Larkin thought for a moment. "Well, lots of crypts are entrances to the cata-combs beneath them and operate as family altars. It was a popular way to build them about six or seven hundred years ago, but kind of went out of style during Grandmama's time, because there were a series of cave-ins that made the cata-combs in Nytra unsafe."

"Okay," Harlow replied as she chewed on the thought. "So could there be some sort of entrance to limenal space in a catacomb?" She thought of the Pyriphle, and the strong feeling she'd had that it connected directly to the world between worlds. It made sense. Maybe this was how they'd find Ashbourne.

Apparently, Larkin thought so as well. "It could. What else is there for us to look at?"

"There's nothing else. It was just on this random crypt, and here in this prayer book." Harlow said. "I don't even know how we're supposed to know if this is even in Nea Sterlis."

Larkin pointed to a figure in the drawing. At first Harlow thought it was a leopard, or other big cat, but as she looked closer, it looked more like a dog. "Is that a dog?"

"Either that or a panther," Larkin said. "Doesn't really matter. I've seen it before."

"Where?" Harlow asked.

Larkin made a face, shaking her head as she chuckled. There was one histor-ical site in Nea Sterlis that Harlow had refused to visit all summer. She hated going anywhere where the unquiet dead tended to congregate. Unlike most sorcière, she did not find communing with the dead to be peaceful, or even help-ful. It was mostly just creepy, and Nea Sterlis' nekropoleis was one of the most haunted in Nytra.

"No," Harlow whined, drawing the word out to several syllables. It was terribly obvious, of course, but she didn't have to like it.

"I guess we know what we're doing tomorrow," Larkin said, looking at her phone. "It's too late to go today. The ghasts will be out in an hour."

Harlow grimaced. Nobody went to the nekropoleis after dark. Ghasts weren't fundamentally dangerous, but unlike most other spirits, they could touch you. Most people, even those that enjoyed chatting with dead people, found them disconcerting. Luckily, they only came out at night. "Let's leave early tomorrow, this could take a while."

Larkin nodded. "See if Thea will take a break. She could use some sun." She gestured towards the television. "I'm gonna finish watching this, but I could use a snack."

Harlow let out a bark of laughter and messaged Cian back with their plans, then went upstairs to make her spoiled sister a snack and convince Thea to go with them to the City of the Dead.

～

"WELL, at least it's not raining," Thea said, smiling cheerily. The air was crisp, and she wore a dress that made her look like she stepped out of a murder mystery set in Nea Sterlis about seventy years ago. As many of them had been filmed in this very nekropoleis, it was fitting.

The City of the Dead was pretty enough in the daytime, but even now there were spirits lurking everywhere. The spirit of a human woman, wearing a tattered gown that trailed the ground, passed by them screaming noiselessly and then disappeared as she walked straight through a wall. It wasn't raining, but that didn't make Harlow any happier to be "skulking around the cemetery," as she'd put it at breakfast.

They'd asked Enzo and Petra to come along, but neither had been available. Harlow was starting to worry that they all might be mad at her. She brushed the thought aside and took a quick selfie with her sisters to calm her nerves. There was a hedge of late-blooming *lantana camara*, and the riot of crimson flowers was too pretty to miss.

She posted the photo onto her socials, with the caption "Sister day!" and a little skull emoji. It felt disrespectful to the spirits, but she was trying to get some-one's attention, after all. Paparazzi were absolutely forbidden from entering the nekropoleis, so there was no danger of being followed today. Besides, they were all back on the rabbit shifter love story again. As much as she hated it, she had to keep them interested in her, so posting a photo some place they were expressly forbidden from entering was sure to get them interested.

"Should we split up?" Larkin asked when Harlow was finished on her phone. "It might make things go faster."

She hadn't been able to remember exactly where she'd seen the dog-panther-leopard statue, so they were set to spend the day here. Harlow dreaded the idea of searching through the nekropoleis alone, but it made sense.

"Sure," she said, making a face.

Thea hugged her arm. "Don't be like that. The ghasties won't get you for at least another six hours. We've got plenty of time."

Harlow rolled her eyes at Thea, shrugging her off. The whole family knew Harlow was scared of spirits and loved to tease her about it. "It's fine. I'm fine. Let's split up. Text if you find anything."

Thea and Larkin both nodded, and they went their separate ways. If you could ignore the fact that at nighttime the place was quite literally crawling with the spirits of unhappy dead people, who behaved in all manner of disgusting ways—showing you their deaths, spitting up various insects, and generally scaring the shit out of you—in the daytime the nekropoleis was quite pleasant. Just a few restless ghosts milling around. *Absolutely nothing to worry about.*

The architecture of the tombs was varied, but many of them were ancient, preserved by magic, and the nekropoleis was famous for its long-blooming gardens. Plants that were beginning to go dormant elsewhere in the city in antic-ipation of the autumn rains were still blooming here, giving the City of the Dead the intoxicating scent of a spring garden.

Harlow's phone buzzed, and she fished it out of her purse. Despite the lovely architecture and plants, she desperately hoped one of her sisters had found what they were looking for. A decapitated vampire carrying its own head had been following her for several minutes and she already wanted to leave. The sooner they found what they were looking for, the better. Instead, it was Finn. Her hands went immediately clammy as she unlocked her phone.

Probably shouldn't post your location on socials if you want Section Seven to leave you alone.

That was it. That was all it said. No hello, how are you… Nothing. He was turning the screw tighter, taking the ruse further, she knew that. But after all these months of learning to trust him and herself again—the cold condescension stung. She shook it off and took a deep breath before responding. *Paps can't get in here.*

He saw immediately and responded. *Still, I'd expect you to be more careful.*

Harlow's eyes narrowed as she read Finn's words over and over, puzzling through them, trying to figure out the best way to respond. On instinct, she looked at his socials. Nothing. Then Sabre's. Sure enough, there was a selfie of the two of them. On a rooftop, poolside at the Ambracia Palace, posted twenty minutes ago.

She took a screenshot and sent it back to him, no message. He saw, then began typing. Then stopped. Then began again. Then stopped. She waited, but there was no response. The minutes ticked past. The headless vampire still appeared to be following her. Now it was tossing its head around, playing with it. It set Harlow even further on edge, despite the prevalent thought that day-spirits couldn't actually see or sense the living, but were simply going about their own post-death existence.

To distract herself from the vampire-spirit, which seemed to be going the same direction she was no matter which avenue she turned down, she checked Sabre's socials again. They'd posted several stories. Harlow clicked into them, and sure enough, there was Finn right next to them at the pool. Sabre was wearing a tiny bikini that showed off all their curves, and their hair was pulled into a perfectly coiffed ponytail.

Harlow touched her own messy bun as her jaw clenched. She watched the stories as she walked, not bothering to look around her. She'd had quite enough of the headless vampire. In Sabre's stories, a waiter brought out a feast of late-summer delicacies. Finn's phone was in his hand, but he watched the waiter setting the food down between him and Sabre with rapt attention as they popped a bottle of sparkling wine and said in what Harlow could only describe as a sultry voice, "Here's to us! A most excellent team."

Harlow closed the stories and opened her text messages. *Cheers to your most excellent team. Is there something for me to be celebrating, or are you and Sabre just having fun?*

It was an undeniably petty response that she was immediately embarrassed by, despite its likely effectiveness if anyone was monitoring them. She stared at the message, cringing so hard her shoulders and neck ached. She'd felt that jealousy, that pettiness, right to the core of her being and it was awful to recognize it.

There was no response. No read receipt. Just silence. Harlow's heart thumped hard in her chest, her throat suddenly dry. She dug in her bag for her water bottle and took a long drink, suddenly dizzy. *Could she unsend the message?*

Her phone buzzed.

"Please let it be Larkin or Thea," she said aloud.

No such luck. *Calm down. It's just some sparkling wine.*

Harlow locked her phone immediately to keep from responding—she was actually mad at him. She'd always had a penchant for jealousy and her hackles were up, much as she desperately wanted to be cool about this, like a girl in a spy film. Instead, her back teeth gritted together unglamorously, and she flushed with rage. She stared up at the sky, hoping to soothe herself by looking at the clouds, but the sky was perfectly clear. As her eyes fell back towards the nekropoleis, she saw the dog-panther-leopard they were looking for in the distance.

Her heart leapt. She rushed toward the statue, having to navigate several small alleyways before she found it. She tried climbing onto a few of the crypts' front steps, but she couldn't see the tomb from Cian's message. She opened her maps app, grabbed her exact location and texted her sisters. It would be better to look together.

Harlow sat down on the steps of a crypt to wait, scrolling through all of Sabre's socials, making herself needlessly miserable. *Why am I doing this?* she thought to herself. Finn showed up in a few images, looking tanned and relaxed, and her heart ached. She missed him terribly and hated how this was going.

I should just call, she thought. *Hearing his voice might help.* Her fingers hesitated over his name in her phone, her chest constricting. Footsteps saved her from having to make a choice.

"You found it!" Larkin said, a broad grin lighting her face.

"Yep," Harlow said, faking brightness. Thea shot her a suspicious look. "But I can't find the tomb from the image from here. Any ideas about where it might be? I'm hopeless with directions in this labyrinth."

Thea looked up at the statue and opened her phone to look at the original image. "Come," she said, already walking.

Harlow and Larkin followed their elder sister through several twisting paths. Thea looked up and back at the dog statue, high above them the entire time. When Harlow was fully lost in the maze of crypts, they stepped out onto a broader avenue and Thea smiled. "There you are."

A magnificent crypt rose above them. No, not a crypt. It was a small, very ancient temple of Akatei, and above the front the words from the image were still visible, though the building was in surprisingly poor shape, as though no one had bothered to maintain it for some time.

The words were as they had been in the image, *The world between worlds waits just beyond knowledge. Beware what...* Harlow and her sisters walked around the side of the building to read the rest: *lies beneath the Alabaster Spire.*

"The Alabaster Spire?" Larkin said aloud. "What's that?"

Harlow shrugged. "I've never heard of a building in the Citadel named that. It has to refer to something in the Alabaster Citadel, don't you think?"

Thea nodded. "It must. You're right, there's no building named anything like that, but that doesn't mean there never has been. We could look."

Harlow nodded, but she'd hoped for more. Above their heads, clouds were rolling in on a chill wind. "Let's go home before it rains."

Larkin snapped a few photos of the temple, and even shook the front doors, which were securely locked and warded. "Can't get in."

"It's progress," Thea said, sounding encouraged.

Harlow tried to let her sister's optimism outshine the text conversation playing in her mind as they walked home, but she couldn't shake the darkness creeping in.

CHAPTER 22

Harlow spent the next morning with Larkin and Thea, combing through the Vault resources for mention of any "Alabaster Spire." Nothing turned up. Larkin messaged Nox, but got no response.

"They're probably all busy with the shop," Thea said. "I think we've done what we can for today. I'm going to work on the Merkhov for a bit before Alaric gets home."

Harlow wished she'd go paint instead. Thea had a way of focusing on a problem so closely that other things—things she loved to do—disappeared from her life until she'd solved it. She typically ended up irritated and exhausted, drained for days or weeks. But Harlow knew better than to say anything about this. Thea would just scowl and do whatever she wanted anyway.

Larkin got up from her perch, stretching. "I'm going to go try my astral projection meditation again. I'm making some progress; yesterday I projected into the upstairs hall bath."

"Useful if your astral body has to pee," Thea said.

The three of them laughed, but Harlow thought hers sounded hollow. She couldn't shake the feeling that time was slipping away. After her sisters went upstairs, she looked at her calendar—where had the summer gone? It was nearly the equinox. At home, the Order of Mysteries would be getting ready for their annual feast and rituals. She texted the maters to find out how things were going at the shop. She, Thea, and Larkin video conferenced nearly every day on the secure line in the Vault, but she wanted to check in anyway.

Selene sent back a few videos of the Monas, bustling with customers, just as Thea had assumed. Indi and Nox were working the front desk together. Indi's hair was cut in a sleek ear-length bob, and her outfit was a slightly more femme version of Nox's tech-goth style, with an edge of glam that was all Indi's own. She hadn't been posting much to socials, except for the Monas account, since they'd returned. Indi had always over-compensated for her intense dislike of being thought of as "the shy twin," and Harlow was glad she was finally doing things her own way. Nox and Indi waved at the camera, leaning towards one another in a way that warmed Harlow's heart.

Her heart ached for Nuva Troi at the beginning of autumn, the Monas, and her family. The past few days had been terrible, and all she wanted to do was curl up in Selene's lap and watch trashy reality TV. The city would be cooling off finally, the leaves would turn soon. Was she just supposed to stay here and rot? What were they even doing here still? Rakul Kimaris was back in Falcyra, Cian had told them late last night, and Alaric was returning from Santos this afternoon. Maybe she could convince them that they should just go home.

Whatever the plan for the ruse had been before, was it even working now? Without much communication from Finn or Cian to let her know that their little game was working, it felt like nothing but a painful exercise in misery. Harlow trudged upstairs to find Axel, who was curled up on the couch in the library. She snuggled in next to him and practiced making the uncomfortable couch into something cozier and slightly more modern. Cian hadn't sworn her off the furniture in this room, after all.

Her shadows danced with pleasure at being used. She hadn't tried to turn into the Feriant for days. The longer Finn was gone, the less she wanted to try. A little frustrated growl escaped her throat. She didn't miss the fervor one bit, but since he'd left, everything seemed so dull.

This is how it starts, she thought. *You depend on them too much, and then lose yourself.*

Her shadows shimmered around her, begging to be used. She got up, tucking Axel into a blanket, full of every intention to go down to the gym to see what she could manage on her own. She passed through the foyer and glanced outside when movement on the driveway caught her eye: Alaric's car pulling up in the driveway.

"Hubby's home," she called to Thea as she headed towards the Vault. Though the study looked out onto the front drive, her sister was probably too engrossed in her work to notice the love of her life arriving.

"No, no, no…. shit," Thea swore. There was a clatter from the study. Harlow slowed her trajectory towards the Vault, turning back to see what was wrong. Thea rarely swore like that, and certainly not because of Alaric. Her feet moved faster as she heard her sister repeating the words over and over.

"What are you doing?" Harlow asked. Her sister was flailing, trying to find a place to hide the Merkhov book. But Thea didn't have to answer. Harlow saw out the window, and swallowed her panic quickly, as she watched Alaric help his mother out of his car. Pasiphae Velarius was *here.*

"What is she doing here?" Harlow hissed.

"I don't know. I missed a text from Alaric…" Thea looked up, throwing her hands in the air. "Stall them, please, while I make myself presentable."

The Merkhov text was nowhere to be seen, but Thea was still wearing her pajamas. Harlow nodded. "Go, go… I'll keep them busy."

Thea was halfway up the stairs when she stopped. "Is Larkin in the Vault or her room?"

"Her room, I think," Harlow said. Alaric and Pasiphae were headed towards the house. "Go check and text me."

Thea ran up the stairs in record time. Harlow popped into the hall bath under the stairs and pulled a few threads of aether, trying to spruce up her hair. Luckily, she was wearing one of her favorites of Enzo's new line of dresses, so she didn't look terrible, but she hadn't bothered with makeup or her hair today. The best she could do was fix her flyaways and apply a bit of color to her lips before Alaric and Pasiphae came in the front door.

"It's been a while since I've been here," Pasiphae was saying as Harlow stepped out of the bathroom. "I don't think Cian has ever been particularly fond of your father."

Or you, Harlow thought.

"Hi," Alaric said, his voice tense and face drawn. She'd never seen him so obviously anxious. Usually he was cheerful and friendly, but now his broad shoulders were tight and his jaw was squared so hard she thought he might burst. Whatever reason Pasiphae had for being here wasn't good, or innocent.

"Hello," Harlow said, attempting her best Selene-voice—the one Mama always used for company. "I'm so glad you could visit us, Madame Arch-Chancellor."

She held her hand out to Pasiphae, who took it and smiled. "Please. You may call me Pasiphae. We're practically family, after all." She glared at her son for a moment, then poked him in the ribs. "Cheer up, darling. I'm going to be making that jab for years to come."

Alaric attempted a smile, but it didn't reach his eye. Pasiphae patted his cheek. "Sons who elope must expect such treatment from their mothers. Daddy didn't mind, of course," she said, more to Harlow than Alaric.

Harlow laughed, surprised at how easy it was to fake it in front of Pasiphae. "The maters feel the same as you." She paused for a moment, listening for Thea's possible entrance, and when she heard no sign of her sister, said, "Please, won't you come inside and I'll make some tea. Thea should be down in a moment. She's helping Larkin with some delicate spellwork."

Pasiphae raised her eyebrows as she followed Alaric down the long winding hallway to the conservatory. As villas in this area of town went, the Herrington's conservatory was small, but it was a gorgeous addition to the house, having been built about a century ago from wrought iron and seeded glass; it was a totally different style than the original house, but charming all the same.

Cian didn't have the patience for taking care of indoor plants, and for security reasons hiring one of the expensive gardening services in Nea Sterlis was out of the question. So the conservatory was unusually bare, containing only a small rattan table that sat in the center of the room. For her own preferences, Harlow liked the lack of furniture. The rough limestone tile in the conservatory had been laid in a beautiful starburst pattern.

The family hadn't used it much for entertaining all summer, preferring to be in places where they could all gather, but the table was big enough for this small group. Besides which, the conservatory was cut off from the rest of the house at the end of a long hallway, with its own bathroom, making it nearly impossible for Pasiphae to go wandering off. Alaric had done some quick thinking to get them in here, rather than the formal living room right off the foyer.

"I'll go make the tea," Alaric said as Pasiphae sat. His words came out too fast, too desperate.

"All right," Harlow said, not knowing how else to respond. Alaric was so often at his ease that she was thrown off by this version of him.

When he'd left, Pasiphae smiled, gesturing to the seat next to hers. "I'm afraid my visit has put my son quite out of sorts."

Harlow forced another smile. "It's natural that he would be nervous. He wants you and Thea to get along."

"Yes," Pasiphae agreed. She also smiled, but Harlow noticed that like her own, it didn't reach her eyes.

Something in her pocket buzzed several times. She was getting a call.

"Please, don't ignore it on my account," Pasiphae said, not a note of malice in her voice.

Harlow stood, inclining her head respectfully. "One moment."

She stepped away from the table. It was Finn. She opened the conservatory door and stepped outside. "Hello?"

"Hi," he said. His voice was distant, like they had a bad connection.

"What's up?" Harlow asked, not really knowing how to begin. "Did we find a place?"

"Maybe," he said, but didn't elaborate. She couldn't tell if something was wrong with the connection, but his words sounded clipped. Harlow thought quickly, but his demeanor was so disconcerting that she couldn't put her thoughts together.

"Oh," she said, fumbling for the right words. "I just thought that the drinks on the roof might be to celebrate—"

"No," he cut her off. "We were just having a bit of fun. For gods' sake Harlow, are you going to make every conversation we have about Sabre?"

"Every conversation? We've barely spoken since you left."

Something crackled, a bit of static, perhaps, but it didn't mask the agitation in Finn's voice. "Whose fault is that? You're always busy with Thea."

Thea. Did this have something to do with Thea? Harlow paused, glancing at the open conservatory door and wondered if he knew Pasiphae was here. "I can't really talk about this right now," she said, not trying to keep the shake out of her voice as she lowered it a measure. "We have company."

His laugh was dry, acerbic. "Seems like you're social now that I'm gone."

That stung, but Harlow swallowed her hurt. "When are you coming back?" Finn was silent. "Are you still there?"

"Yeah," he said, sounding exhausted. That was real, she could feel it in her bones. This was wearing him out too. Something in her heart sang a little to know that he was struggling as much as she was, that they were still in this together.

Some of her vitality returned, and she added a little edge to her voice. "I asked when you were coming back."

"Yeah…" There was noise in the background. A muffled voice. He was covering the phone. "Sorry, Harlow. Now isn't a good time."

"You called me," she said.

"I'll call you later," he said, and the line went dead.

Harlow wanted to collect herself, but she felt eyes at her back. When she turned, Pasiphae was standing right behind her and had clearly heard every bit of the conversation with her keen Illuminated hearing.

"I—" Harlow began to explain.

"You don't have to explain a thing, my darling," Pasiphae said, striding forward to take her arm. She led her back to the table in the conservatory. "I've been bonded to an Illuminated man for quite some time."

Harlow nodded, her face heating with embarrassment. This was no time to let her guard down, no matter how humiliating this was. She had one job now, and it was to help get Pasiphae out of the house without incident.

Pasiphae's expression was shrewd as she smoothed the fabric of her skirt, just so. There was a glint of strategy in her eyes that made Harlow suspicious. "This is how they are, Harlow. *Fickle*."

Could this be the reason Pasiphae was here? To check on *Harlow*? In all their plans, they'd focused mostly on Connor, and by association Aislin. They'd never talked about whether Pasiphae might be involved.

"Everything is fine," Harlow said, careful to keep her voice smooth and her face calm. Pasiphae would get nothing from her.

Pasiphae laughed. "Oh, you will make a wonderful wife for Connor's son. I'd hoped Finn might turn out a modicum better than his father, but they are the same, through and through, chasing tail all over Nytra."

Harlow kept her face very still; this was no time to argue. The ruse was working. Pasiphae believed that Finn and Sabre's interactions were real. She forced even, steady breaths through her lungs as Pasiphae continued. "There was a time when I thought I might have bonded with Connor McKay, but the way he treats Aislin? No thank you. I prefer my cuckolding to be quiet. Discreet."

Now *that* was interesting. Leopold Velarius was practically insignificant. He never came to events, and was rarely seen. According to Alaric he was mostly interested in birding and golf. Apparently, he was also bedding people outside his bonding.

"Everything is fine," Harlow repeated, trying not to react to the information Pasiphae had given her.

"Yes," Pasiphae said. Now the smile reached her eyes. "You *will* be one of us, won't you, witchling?"

Harlow wasn't sure what that meant, but she lowered her eyes. She hoped Pasiphae read it as respect, but she simply didn't want her to see the fury burning in them. "I hope so," she replied.

Pasiphae took her hands. "Look at me, child."

Harlow composed herself before dragging her eyes to meet the ancient immortal's. How old was Pasiphae? Her eyes were dark pools of mystery, and her skin glowed faintly with the pleasure she seemed to derive from this moment.

"You are humiliated now. But you will find ways to push back, subtly of course. You will marry, and give Finbar a family, and in return, you will be one of the most powerful women on Okairos. This is what you want, isn't it?"

Harlow dropped her eyes again. There was no way to respond to that. Honesty certainly wasn't an option, and she didn't trust herself to lie at the moment. Not with the level of fury coursing through her. But still, despite that anger, a thrill of victory hummed through her. She and Finn had not only deceived the Illuminated, they'd revealed that whatever Connor's machinations were, Pasiphae was also involved.

Pasiphae let go of one of her hands, her fingers curling around Harlow's chin, as though she was appraising her. "You're not like your sister. Thea is lovely, and the perfect wife for my Alaric. Docile and always so *appropriate*. But you have a fire in you I recognize. You will make Finbar McKay pay for every time he embarrasses you, won't you?"

Harlow nodded once. It was the furthest thing from what she wanted, but it seemed like it served her best to let Pasiphae think the anger in her eyes was for him.

"All that rage," Pasiphae said. "You come to me when you're ready to make him pay, my darling, and I will teach you the ways of an Illuminated wife."

Footsteps in the hallway signaled that Alaric and Thea were on their way. Harlow let a thin smile spread over her face. "Thank you," she said. "I would be grateful for your help."

"Of course you will be," Pasiphae said, standing. Thea and Alaric entered, a vision of newly bonded bliss. Thea wore a pastoral-inspired floral day dress that skimmed the floor of the conservatory and Alaric carried tea, which he set down as Thea kissed Pasiphae warmly.

"Now, what spellwork does young Larkin have going?" Pasiphae asked as she took a cup of tea from her son.

Harlow barely listened as Thea explained Larkin's most recent project. She'd created a spell that allowed musicians to hear their compositions played by multiple instruments at once as they composed. When it was perfected, it would be a major contribution to the Order of Mysteries' body of work.

That much was not a lie, but the fact that Larkin was upstairs working on it obviously was. Harlow couldn't concentrate on any of that though, so consumed by anger as she was. She didn't touch her tea once for the hour that Pasiphae stayed. When she finally got up to go, Harlow said the mere politest of goodbyes.

"I'll be back in a bit," Alaric said as he kissed Thea goodbye. He'd agreed to take Pasiphae to the Velarius' flat across town. "Should I pick up gelato on the way home?"

"That would be nice," Thea said, her eyes softening as she squeezed his hands.

Gelato was nearly always Alaric's way of apologizing for some minor infraction he thought he'd committed. It was more of a joke than anything most of the time, but Harlow saw the real apology in his eyes now, and Thea's acceptance.

When they were gone, Thea's shoulders slumped and Larkin appeared at the top of the stairs, cradling Axel in her arms. "Is she gone?" Larkin asked.

Thea nodded as Larkin made her way down the stairs. The three of them went into the kitchen together and began the work of making a sheet pan of frozen pizza bites. It was at least an hour 'til their usual late dinner time, but they needed the sustenance after Pasiphae's visit. The ritual of making snacks in times of trouble was a Krane family tradition.

"She ambushed him in Santos," Thea explained. "Apparently, she insisted on coming back with him. She'll be here for a week."

Larkin made a face. "She's terrifying. I listened in on the old intercom. Did you know it still connects to the conservatory? So convenient for spying on you all." She waggled her eyebrows at Thea, and Harlow cringed. She wondered how many times Larkin had caught her older sisters screwing like bunnies this summer. She and Finn had done it there at least twice.

Harlow's phone buzzed, and she dreaded the idea it might be Finn. When she made her way across the kitchen to look at her phone, she realized it hadn't been hers after all.

"It's me," Larkin said, pulling her phone from the pocket of her sweatpants. "It's Meline. She and Ari are leaving tomorrow for Falcyra—everything is set up there. We won't hear from them again until they establish a safe connection and get new phones."

"Tell her we love her," Thea whispered, her face drawn as she put the pizza bites in the oven.

Harlow yanked both her sisters into her arms. They squeezed each other tight in a three-way hug. Thea had tears on her cheeks. Harlow wiped them away as they pulled away from one another. The three of them settled into the table in the alcove, flipping through the stack of magazines and catalogs Selene collected wherever she went. They sat quietly for a while, while the kitchen filled with the tantalizing scent of melting cheese.

"She'll be okay," Harlow assured Thea.

"I know," Thea sniffled. "Ari won't let anything happen to her. I just hate that we're not together."

"Me too," Larkin said, her voice breaking a little. "We haven't been apart like this since Harlow left us for…" She glanced at Harlow and then quickly added, "I'm sorry. I didn't mean to bring Mark up."

Harlow kissed Larkin's cheek as Axel rubbed her ankles with his face. "It's okay. I hated being apart from you all then, and I hate this now."

The little kitchen timer rang and Thea pulled away from the group to save the pizza bites from burning. When all three of them had a plate, she asked, "Isn't *Pretty Little Firestarters* on tonight?"

"You want to watch it *live*?" Larkin asked, slightly horrified by the idea.

Thea smirked. "Yes, because I'm *old*, and remember when that was the only way you could watch something on TV."

Larkin shrugged as she walked towards the study. "You said it, not me."

Alaric walked in the front door, with a bag of gelato from a place near the City Center, not Moretti's, which Harlow thought was a mistake. "What are we doing?" he asked, raising his eyebrows

Thea nodded towards the kitchen. "There's snacks on the baking sheet. Put the gelato in the freezer."

"And?" he asked, clearly wanting to know the rest of the plan.

She swiped a kiss to his cheek. "*And*, we're watching *Pretty Little Firestarters* in the study. Come with us."

Alaric's smile was a light. He was literally glowing. "I love you," he said, before practically running to the kitchen.

"You let him off easy," Harlow joked as they settled into the little couch in the study.

Thea glanced at Harlow, a concerned look on her face. "What did he need to be let off for?"

Harlow shrugged, a little embarrassed, despite the fact that Thea seemed genuinely confused, not snarky. "Nothing, sorry. Bad joke—it's been a long day."

Thea patted her knee. "You'll get some good rest tonight and feel better tomorrow."

Alaric entered with a plate full of frozen snacks and snuggled into the couch next to Thea. Harlow's heart ached deeply, despite the minor victory she'd achieved with Pasiphae, but she pushed the feeling down. This would all be over soon. Finn would come back and things would go back to normal. She couldn't pay attention to the episode, no matter how hard she tried. She'd picked up her phone on the way to the study, and it buzzed now. Kate.

Petra finally admitted PLF is good. She said to tell you that next week you're coming over for a watch-party.

Harlow gave the message a little heart and texted Petra. *So you finally caved.*

Petra wrote back immediately. *If you can't beat 'em, join 'em. LU.*

Enzo was next, apparently she'd missed a plot twist in her misery and he had a long theory that he explained in about fifteen consecutive messages.

Missed it tonight, she wrote back. *But I'll watch tomorrow and we'll dish.*

No one was mad at her. She'd been being paranoid. They were all just busy with their own lives, and hadn't been obsessing over her at all. Why did she do this kind of shit to herself?

"Because you're insecure, Dollface." She heard Mark's voice like he'd spoken aloud. But of course he hadn't. Mark was dead, and she was imagining things. "I'm going to bed," she said, getting up. If hallucinating Mark speaking to her wasn't an indicator that she needed to be done for the day, she didn't know what was.

"The episode isn't over," Larkin said, confused.

"It's your favorite show," Thea said as the show came back on.

"I know, but I'm tired—" Harlow started to say when the sharp blare of an alarm interrupted the scene-setting music of the nighttime soap. A screen that read "Breaking News" flashed, and a new anchor came on the screen.

"We have news tonight from Falcyra that Austvanger has fallen to a group of rebels calling themselves 'the Humanists.'" The human anchor paused, pressing a finger to the device in her ear. "One moment, please, we're going to our correspondent in Falcyra."

"Shit," Alaric said, whipping his phone out. He glanced at Harlow, a silent query passing between them about whether or not she'd heard about this from Finn. She shook her head once. He nodded, turning back to his phone. "I can't believe Mother let this get onto the news… Someone at the station is going to lose their head."

Harlow wished he were exaggerating, but it seemed possible that someone could, indeed, lose their life for a report like this. Sure enough, his jaw clenched as his phone rang. Though he stepped outside the study, they could all hear Pasiphae on the other end of the phone, screeching about not being able to get through to Nuva Troi. Apparently, there were so many calls into the city, hers wasn't getting through and she wanted Alaric to do something about it, immediately.

He poked his head back in the study. "I'm going downstairs to get in touch with Cian."

Thea trailed after him, but Larkin stayed. Axel wandered in and curled up between them as the correspondent in Falcyra came on the screen. She stood in front of a mass of burning buildings. "Nytra?" she asked. "Nytra, do you have me?"

Someone spoke in the background, and she continued, "I'm told we've lost connection to our Nytra office, but that I am on air. This is the scene in Aust-vanger tonight. The city is burning, and the House of Sorath and Governor Ducare are no longer in control. We aren't sure what will happen in the days to come but the last three weeks here have been hell. Tonight is the first time our signal hasn't been jammed getting out of the country."

The correspondent went on to describe many of the things they already knew, and some more personalizing details about the people affected on the ground. Stories that would move a Nytran audience about schools being bombed, and mass executions without trials.

"Wow," Larkin said. "Honestly, after getting a really good look at the way the Illuminated have suppressed information, I'm shocked this is airing."

Harlow nodded. "Yeah, me too."

"Pasiphae is totally freaking out right now, huh?" Larkin asked, her eyebrows raised mischievously. She was covering up how upset this made her, and Harlow couldn't really blame her. It felt as though the world was spinning out of control, just beyond their grasp. They were forced to watch, unable to do much to change any of it yet.

Harlow attempted a laugh, but the sound was dry as a bone in the nekropoleis. "I bet she's having a shit-fit. Poor Alaric."

Larkin snickered, but Harlow couldn't seem to laugh with her. Thea was wrong—she wouldn't sleep well tonight at all. Harlow felt like she might never sleep again.

CHAPTER 23

The next day, Pasiphae went back to Nuva Troi without so much as goodbye. No one was sorry about it, but Alaric and Larkin got to work mobilizing as many aid units as they could muster in Falcyra and Harlow worked on communicating with Cian and the rest of the Haven team, both in Nuva Troi and Nea Sterlis. Their assumption was that the Illuminated would instill martial law in the next few days to control Nytran humans from attempting something similar, and that they might need more support.

Not surprisingly, she didn't hear from Finn, but instead got a notification from Section Seven—which just *had* to make the day worse—just as she was leaving to help Petra at the Alabaster Way house, Haven's more extensive safehouse in Nea Sterlis. Thea and Larkin both shook their heads when their notification came through, but neither made eye contact with her. Harlow knew this was getting old, and no one really knew how to address their bullying at this point.

Section Seven had the audacity to mark the news as "breaking" in the midst of everything going on and used a push notification for it. The headline read, "Harlow Krane is officially over. Finn McKay spotted canoodling human beauty Sabre LeBeau at the White Oak last night."

Harlow clicked through to the article. Finn was, indeed, hugging Sabre LeBeau, who had their face buried in his neck. She closed her eyes, her jaw tightening as the muscles in her back tensed, drawing her shoulder blades together. For a brief moment, everything hurt.

"I need to get to the Alabaster Way house," she said.

"Okay," Thea replied, her voice soft and soothing. She reached out to touch Harlow's arm.

Harlow stood. "I'm fine, okay?"

"You can't just keep saying that," Thea said.

"I can," Harlow said. "Because it's true. I'm fine, and I need to get over to the AW house to see if they need help today. Humans are going to need help, Thea."

Her sister didn't meet her eyes. "Of course. You should go."

Harlow scooped Axel up and hugged him, grateful for his rhythmic purrs against her chest. "See you when I get back, baby boy. Naps on the terrace?"

He blinked his golden eyes at her, as though agreeing. She deposited him in Larkin's lap and left the house quickly. The safehouse was only a twenty-minute walk away, so she set out on foot. The day was the coldest they'd had since arriving, and Harlow wished she'd brought a jacket. She was already dressed in a pair of loose pants and a light sweater that fell off her left shoulder, but she shivered in the breeze.

Her phone rang. She'd turned her sound on after last night's announcement, not wanting to miss any more breaking news, should it come through. Still, it startled her into picking up without seeing who it was.

"It's not what you think," Finn said on the other end of the phone. Harlow's heart pounded. They'd promised not to call unless it was absolutely necessary. So this was necessary, and she had to keep her wits sharp.

"What do you think I think it is?" Harlow asked. It wasn't hard to sound agitated; this was nerve-wracking.

"Don't do this," Finn hissed. There were voices in the background.

"Are you with *Sabre* right now?"

"No, my parents."

So this was for them. Even more nerve-wracking then. "Even better," she bit out.

"I can explain everything."

Harlow turned a corner and walked into the park to take the shortcut to the Alabaster Way location. "Oh, I'm sure you can."

"I *can*," Finn said, and there was a plea in his voice that broke her heart a little. "I'm coming back on the morning train. Tomorrow. Meet me at the station?"

"Whatever you say," she said, hanging up. It was an instinct to do so, but if they were looking for a fight between them, her hanging up would prove she was angry with him. But he was coming home. Tomorrow.

Her heart hammered an unsteady beat in her chest as her vision blurred with tears, and she ran straight into Morgaine Yarlo. "Sorry," she said immediately. "I—I didn't see you." It was as though the girl had appeared out of nowhere.

"No apologies necessary. I blend in a lot of the time."

Harlow very much doubted that. As she calmed down, she wondered if Morgaine might not have the money for a hotel here in Nea Sterlis. "Hey, do you need help? Like a place to stay or something?"

Morgaine smiled bashfully. It was a sweet expression. "No, I'm staying with my friend Samira. You know her, I think—I was with her the first time we saw each other at The Gate."

"The Ultima?" Harlow asked, momentarily distracted from the horrible conversation she'd just had with Finn.

Morgaine nodded. "Yeah. She lives on the next block over. I was out for a run."

Harlow looked at what she was wearing: leggings, sneakers, a sweat-soaked t-shirt. Morgaine hadn't appeared out of nowhere, she'd just come around the corner Harlow was turning, and Harlow hadn't been paying attention, as usual. Her distractedness was going to get her into real trouble someday if she wasn't more careful.

"But thank you for the offer, Harlow. That was really kind of you."

Harlow shrugged. "It's no big deal."

Morgaine fell into step next to her. "Kinda seems like it might be. That's some wild news you all got last night."

The way she said it was oddly distanced, like it hadn't happened to her too. But it was obvious Morgaine was just visiting Nea Sterlis. Maybe she wasn't from Nytra, or even Falcyra, but somewhere further away like Castel des Rêves, or Avignone. Most humans didn't travel so far away from their home countries—many weren't allowed to, as humans had to submit to the Travel Advisory committee before leaving their home countries, unless they were rich enough to buy their way out of such things. The compass tattoo on Morgaine's arm made it pretty clear what her priorities were though, and Harlow got the feeling the young woman could talk her way in or out of pretty much anything.

All Harlow could think to say was, "Yeah. It seems like the world is going to pieces."

Morgaine let out a wry laugh. "Seems like the whole universe is, doesn't it?"

It was an odd thing to say. Harlow wasn't exactly sure what to make of Morgaine. "Have you been in touch with Echo? Is she okay?"

Morgaine looked confused for a moment.

"I just assumed she's human, like you—and you know things are probably about to get a bit difficult…"

"Oh, yeah," Morgaine broke in, as though just realizing how being human might be a problem in this political climate. "Echo's fine in that regard."

That seemed unlikely. All humans would be especially restricted now, targeted even more than usual. "But you haven't had a chance to talk to her?" Harlow asked, pressing a little harder.

She was worried about the two of them, despite not having met Echo. Morgaine's lack of concern for both their safety was naïve at best. At worst, it could get the two of them killed. Humans were often like this. Since they seemed to regard immortals as benevolent celebrities, they didn't realize the danger they were in until it was too late. Harlow liked Morgaine too much to let her make reckless choices.

"No, not yet," Morgaine said, her voice sad. "Hopefully soon." She glanced down at her phone. "I've gotta run. See you around."

Before Harlow could say another word, Morgaine had resumed her jog and was out of the park. Her phone rang. She was not ready to go another round with Finn right now. Luckily, it was Thea. "I broke the binding on the Merkhov. Come home. Now."

Her sister was out of breath, panting hard. "Where's Alaric?"

"I'm here," Alaric said, clearly having taken the phone from Thea. "She's all right. I've got her, but you need to get back here."

Harlow sighed as she hung up, texted the coordinator at the Alabaster Way house that her plans had changed, and headed back home.

~

THEA HADN'T JUST BROKEN the binding, she'd shattered it. When Harlow got home, she was stretched out on the couch in the study, an ice pack pressed to her forehead. Larkin sat next to her, holding a big glass of water with a straw.

Harlow rushed to Thea's side, just as Alaric entered the room with a plate of nachos. It looked like enough food for four people. Using magic always took energy. Breaking spells took more, and it was likely Thea was ravenous after breaking the binding on the book.

Harlow raised her eyebrows at Thea. "Are you going to share those?"

"If you're lucky," Thea said, struggling to sit up. "Go look at the book first, please."

The sound of chips crunching followed Harlow across the room, where the Merkhov book sat open on its cradle. All three of the triptych images were perfectly clear now.

The first showed two snakes, locked in a figure-eight pattern, each consuming the other's tail. In the lower half of the eight sat an egg, encircled in a protective film of some sort. In the second, the snakes had become one, but they still protected the egg. Now that it was restored, Harlow saw that the egg was indeed cracking, and the protective barrier had been pierced. The swirling lines that were meant to represent aether and the Illuminated light were fully intertwined in this image.

But the next image was something else entirely. There was no more egg at all, but an image of a fierce bird, with feathers of deepest midnight, encircled by a single serpent. "Oh," Harlow breathed. "*Oh...*"

In the first image the snakes were biting *one another*, and then they became one, and then separate once more: the serpent and the raptor. The triptych wasn't about what a Strider and a Knight might *create* if they had a child, though the egg had certainly been misleading. It was about how to make the Feriant shift happen. A Strider needed a Knight—or perhaps even just one of the Illuminated—to activate them. And the egg wasn't a baby, but representative of intimate energy, as well as of life and hope.

The Claiming. It had to be that the Claiming was the trigger. But that didn't make perfect sense, Cian had said many of the former Strider-Knight pairs had been platonic. Intimate energy could be platonic though, she reasoned. The way the Orders were raised to focus on romantic partnerships as primary obscured that as an obvious line of thinking, but of course familial and platonic relationships could be intimate as well.

But then why had biting her worked in the House of Remiel, but not here at home? The thought was distressing. To avoid thinking about Finn and spiraling out, she moved onto ramifications. She understood why Kylar Bane had gone to so much trouble to hide this information. If the Feriant were strong enough to kill an incubus, they would be strong enough to fight the Illuminated. This was incredibly dangerous knowledge.

She turned to look back at her sisters and Alaric, who sat in a perfect row on the couch, all three munching on nachos. "You didn't save me any," she complained.

Larkin shrugged. "Alaric can make more."

Alaric rolled his eyes in mock-annoyance, but he got up to do as Larkin suggested, flashing a smile as he left the room. He was happy to give the sisters a moment or two to think things through together, that much was clear.

"It's not a baby at all," Harlow said finally, letting the knowledge sink in.

"No," Thea agreed.

"Do you think this is how I'll make the shift?" Harlow asked after a long moment.

Larkin's head tilted to the side. "Seems like it. Is that going to be a problem? With the Claiming and you and Fi—"

Thea shot her youngest sister a glare so deadly that Larkin flushed with embarrassment. Clearly, they'd agreed not to move too fast for Harlow, given the weirdness with Finn. "It's none of our business, of course."

Both of them averted their eyes from Harlow's, the threads between them tightening in Harlow's second sight, taut with the tension between them.

Alaric returned with more nachos, interrupting the possibility of more discussion. Everyone snacked quietly for a few minutes, but Harlow saw the glances they were giving one another, even Alaric, who'd overheard their conversation. It was unbearable. Finn was coming home tomorrow, but she didn't think she could take another minute.

She broke into the uncomfortable silence. "Are we positive that the wards on the house are good? That no one can hear what we talk about?"

Alaric and Thea exchanged a look. "I check them every day," Alaric replied. "And before you ask, I set up an extra set of triggers for things like the drone, even Axel's new friend. Anything that touches the wards, or puts any pressure on them in the slightest is recorded and analyzed now. Even the elder Illuminated don't have this kind of security."

When Harlow met Thea's gaze, her sister nodded. "It's true. You can trust Alaric, you know that, right?"

Harlow laughed, but the sound was hollow, without humor. "That's not what this is about… It's about me and Finn."

The room went silent and still, as though everyone was afraid to move.

"Our relationship isn't in trouble," she began. Larkin raised her eyebrows, tensing. Thea looked as though she might want to argue. It hit her: they'd heard her talk like this before—about Mark, during the worst times, when she was constantly defending him to everyone. The reverberations of that relationship just kept echoing through her life.

"We faked all this to draw the Illuminated out. Sabre is in on it and everything," she said quickly, wanting to move past this stage. "We're okay. This has all been a ruse, but I can tell you now, because he's coming home tomorrow."

Alaric let out a harsh breath, and his face crumpled. He covered his face with his hands. "Thank gods," he murmured as Thea rubbed his back, her perfectly groomed eyebrows pulling together in a knot of concern.

Larkin was misty eyed, and when Harlow made eye contact with her, she smiled. "That's good. That's really good."

"I couldn't figure out why he was behaving this way," Alaric said, his chin quivering slightly. "I thought I'd failed him somehow."

"No," Harlow breathed, sorry beyond belief that their actions had hurt their family so much. "No, you didn't do anything wrong. And if he were here, he would tell you how sorry he is, I'm sure."

Alaric laughed. "He wouldn't. He's our commander, and you had a mission; he wouldn't apologize for not compromising it… The real question is did it work?"

Harlow nodded. "We won't know the full extent until tomorrow, but I think your mother showing up here yesterday was an indicator that we've convinced them."

Everyone looked slightly confused.

"She spent the entire time you were gathering Thea and the tea convincing me to let her help me become what she termed 'an Illuminated wife.'"

Alaric's face twisted slightly in disgust. "I'm so sorry, Harlow. That was so far out of line…"

Thea drew a breath in. "It's not just Connor and Aislin who want you to have the baby…"

Larkin covered her mouth, looking at Alaric with pity. He shook his head. "I'd be lying if I said I was surprised. I just… I hoped she was better than this."

"Of course you did," Thea said, her arms going around his neck. They leaned into one another.

"So we need to make preparations for his return," Alaric said. "We'll need to decon him pretty thoroughly."

Harlow's face scrunched in confusion.

"He'll have to be decontaminated for surveillance spellwork," Thea explained. "We'll get everything set up. The two of you can use the carriage house until we're sure he's clean."

There was a small cottage at the entrance to the villa that no one used. Harlow knew the place.

Alaric nodded. "Good thinking. We can get that set up now, if you want."

Harlow breathed a sigh of relief. She'd still have to talk to everyone else, but it felt good to have this out in the open.

"Is there anything else to discuss about the scroll?" Larkin asked. "If not, I can go do an initial sweep of the carriage house and…"

Larkin continued, describing an herbal tisane that could be used for ritual cleansing. Harlow hardly heard her. Something bothered her about the Scroll of Akatei—the document the triptych originated from. She needed to see it again to be sure.

"Thank you, Larkin." Harlow held up a finger, as Larkin finished speaking and Alaric and Thea both made ready to get to to work. "But before we get moving, Thea, do you have the rest of your scans of the Scroll of Akatei?"

Thea got up and pulled an envelope from a drawer in the table the cradle sat on. She pulled the scans out and spread them across the table. Harlow looked at where the triptych was meant to fit into the Scroll.

"What are you thinking?" Thea asked, examining the same spot Harlow looked at.

Harlow pointed to the formation of Heraldic creatures that included the Feriant. There was one of each type of creature. "What if these don't represent single creatures?"

Alaric nodded. "They might represent a collective of fighters. An alliance of sorts."

Thea's breath caught. "There could be other Striders. Others capable of turning into the Feriant."

The thought was dizzying. If there were, then they might actually stand a chance against the Illuminated. "But what about the rest of this, the humans in the tree? The firedrake? What does it all mean?"

Thea stared at the Scroll for a few long moments. Harlow could feel her thinking as Larkin moved to stand next to them, leaning on the table with her head perched in her hands. She too seemed to think deeply about the story the Scroll might tell.

Larkin pointed to the humans that had broken out of their shells after the firedrake's awakening. "Something about all this has to do with the firedrakes."

"Or a very specific firedrake," Thea mused. "We should talk to Cian about this. Are they coming home with Finn?"

"I don't know," Harlow replied. "I didn't get a chance to ask."

Alaric checked his phone. The family calendar, Harlow presumed. "Cian is coming later this week. They have Haven business to wrap up in Nuva Troi."

Harlow nodded. "All right then. We have a strong lead here, between the Merkhov and what we found out in the City of the Dead. We just need to find out where this Alabaster Spire used to be and find Ashbourne..."

Alaric frowned. "I think it would be wise to be cautious about that advice. We don't know what Kimaris' intentions were, and until Larkin can actually speak with Ashbourne, I think we should be careful."

Harlow nodded. "You're probably right. But the Claiming?"

Thea grinned. "Have at it, love."

Alaric gave two, very dorky, thumbs up. "Seems like the way to go!"

Harlow smiled, but it was hard to laugh along right now.

CHAPTER 24

When the train pulled into the station, Harlow thought she had herself pretty well composed. But as Finn stepped off, every bit of their history, their love, the hurt, and the fervor hit her at once. He was clean shaven, his longer hair slicked back, wearing a blue button-down shirt, tucked into a pair of perfectly pressed trousers. He looked nothing like the Finn she loved, and as his stormy eyes met hers, they held a warning.

He moved towards her, deliberately slow, his square jaw clenched tight, the slightest tilt of his head causing her gaze to drift behind him. Connor McKay stepped off the train, directly after his son, stern, handsome, and trussed up in a three-piece suit. Harlow's blood nearly boiled to see him, but she realized that like Pasiphae, his being here was a victory.

"Hello, Harlow," Connor said, using a bit of Illuminated speed to stand next to her just as Finn reached for her hand. "My son has behaved abominably for the past few weeks, and I am here to make sure he puts things right."

The elder McKay's voice was smooth, placating. He obviously had experience with this kind of thing, placating women. No doubt he spoke this way to Aislin all the time, but Harlow wanted none of it. If she could shove him back on the damn train and send him back to the city, she would. Instead, she just stood there with no clever comeback, no thought in her head but how she might murder Connor McKay.

Finn started to say something, but Connor held up a hand. "My boy. You fucked up with Sabre, and embarrassed Harlow deeply. You will apologize, make amends with one another. I will see you both at dinner this evening. I expect you'll have solved this by that time."

He took Finn's elbow and drew him aside. Harlow barely caught what Connor whispered to Finn. "Claim that little bitch and be done with it, Finbar. Do your duty, and you'll get your way with the human."

Harlow looked down at her shoes as she listened. They were a pair of vintage leather boots that were glorious with the dress she wore, also vintage, from an estate sale she and Enzo had been to a few weeks ago. She'd taken every effort with her appearance. Her heart ached to hear Connor McKay's words. He didn't know his son at all.

"See you in a bit," Connor said before walking away.

"He's going to his hotel," Finn explained.

Harlow nodded. Neither of them moved a muscle. Heat built in her chest, and then slid down her spine, straight into her core. She hated the buttoned up look he wore now, the conformity of it, the way he looked like his father. But the high of having won just a few inches back from Connor and Pasiphae was intoxicating, stoking the energy of the fervor higher with every breath she took.

"I am sorry for everything that happened in Nuva Troi while I was gone." Finn's voice was flat.

"Sounds like it," she bit out, turning toward the car. There was every possibility they were still being watched. Besides, this felt like a game now, and the heat building between her thighs made her *very* motivated to play. "Come on. Let's go home."

Finn grabbed her arm. The gesture was more violent looking than the actual gentle press of his fingers into her flesh. His body heat filled the space between them and Harlow didn't even bother to fight the fervor. She let it rage through her, flooding her scent.

"I would like it if you'd accept my apology, Harlow." The harsh tone of his voice didn't match the silent plea in his eyes, or the bulge growing in his trousers. He adjusted himself, nostrils flaring as he scented her true feelings, no doubt.

"Fine," Harlow agreed. "I accept. I'll just forget about Sabre, and the fact that I've barely heard from you for weeks. I'll accept that apologies like these are just 'how it's going to be.' That's what I'm supposed to do, right? Just be grateful you're lifting me up out of my low state and keep my mouth shut."

Everything they'd said and done when he was gone was horrendous. But this heat building between them was delicious. It was like a reward to know that she could stand here, smarting off to him, proving to the Illuminated that she wouldn't be cowed so easily, and turning him on. Because there was no doubt in her mind, Finn was aroused.

"I can think of better uses for your mouth," Finn growled, yanking her into his arms.

"I bet you can," she snarled back, every bit as feral as he was. She would tear his clothes from his body right here if he let her.

Finn's voice was low and dangerous. "Get in the car, now."

His fingers pressed into her waist as he pushed her towards the waiting Woody in the parking lot. There were only a few people around, but Finn's grip on Harlow's waist was firm as he pushed her against the car, lifting her dress as she wrapped her legs around his waist.

"That's my good girl," he purred. "Say you accept my apology."

"*Actually apologize*," she hissed.

He dropped her, shaking his head as he reached into the pocket of her dress to fetch the car keys. His fingers dragged up her hip from inside the pocket, lighting a fire within her that wouldn't be stopped for anything now.

"Get in the car," he commanded as he got into the driver's seat.

She did as he asked, her heart pounding ferociously, her teeth practically aching from how tightly her jaw was set. They drove in silence for a few minutes. Finn pulled her phone from the console, and tossed it out the window, into the ocean, as they curved up the steep road toward the villa.

When the window closed she sighed with relief, but Finn shook his head. They still had to make it through decon. She let out a needy sound and his free hand stroked her thigh, sending the fire in her into a blazing inferno. Still, Finn said nothing, but kept the tease of his fingers moving up her thigh, closer and closer to the spot she needed him, through her dress.

He took a sharp left turn in the villa's driveway, pulling off to the carriage house that sat in a wooded grove. A blazing bonfire crackled merrily in front of the little cottage. Finn stripped out of his clothes immediately. Alaric had assured her that Finn knew the rules of decon well, and sure enough, he threw his clothes directly into the fire. A bundle of herbs went in next, and the two of them pulled threads, using sigil magic to set his clothes fully ablaze. They were ashes in moments.

Harlow took the waiting glass jug of the ritual tisane that Larkin had prepared and poured it over Finn's head. The fragrant herbs that made the spell work perfumed the air as water dripped over the planes of his face and down his muscled chest. She pulled threads of magic from the air, as well as directing her shadows to find any trace of foreign magic that might be hiding on or in Finn. She tried not to stare at his body, at his proud cock, standing at attention for her.

"You're clean," she said when he did not react to the water, or her probe. Her voice broke over the words. He was wet, water droplets still running through the rivulets of his various muscle groups, but it was the look on his face that undid her.

The raw love and fear in his eyes had her leaping into his arms. He caught her, yanking her up his naked body as his mouth crashed into hers. The kiss was desperate, fervent, nearly violent with the intensity of passion between them.

"I'm so sorry," he murmured against her mouth. "I'm so fucking sorry."

"Me too," she said as the sobs she'd been holding in since the moment he left came spilling out of her. "I knew. We agreed. But it felt too real sometimes."

And it had. All the arguments, well-positioned as they'd been, weren't scripted. They'd agreed it was best to improvise, and some of them had hurt more than others. She'd known he'd push her buttons and dig into things that were well-known insecurities for her, but she hadn't anticipated how real it all would feel. How truly heartbroken she'd been at times.

His arms tightened around her, as he held her effortlessly aloft. "I know, baby girl. I know. But it worked. We've got them worried, and despite everything going on at home, he's here. I don't know why, but he's here."

"Let's go inside. My sisters and Alaric are finishing with a second round of advanced wards in the villa. Alaric is going out to the bay this time, just to make sure."

He glanced over her shoulder at the cottage. "They did this already?"

Harlow kissed Finn's face about a dozen times, thrilled to be back in his arms. "Yes. We're alone and it's safe. I have so many things to tell you."

He detached her legs from around his waist, scooping her into his arms. "I don't really want to talk right now, do you?"

His kiss was gentle, persuasive. "Not really, but I have—er, some pertinent information."

Finn laughed, his real laugh, the one she loved as he carried her into the carriage house. No one had used it for several years, as it was mostly extra space for guests now, but there was a huge, comfortable bed upstairs, and she'd changed the linens on it herself this morning. When he dumped her in the bed, he stood at the end, smiling that slightly crooked smile, looking devious as seventeen hells.

"There's quite a few buttons on your pretty dress," he said. "I'll give you until I'm done unbuttoning them to catch me up. Deal?"

Harlow was unable to focus as she watched his cock. "Sure." She slid to the end of the bed and pulled him toward her. "But first, tell me a few things."

Finn's eyes fell shut as she stroked his cock a few times. Her hands were soft and loose as she asked, "Did you miss me?"

His eyes opened slightly and his fingers ran gently through her hair as her mouth closed around him. "Yes," he moaned. She took him deeper into her throat. This wouldn't be possible in his true form. When she pulled her mouth off his cock, swirling her tongue around the head of it for good measure she asked, "Did they read all our texts?"

He nodded, pushing her hair out of her face. "Yes, they read them all. Cian couldn't get a good bug on them, but they tracked where the information was routing to, and it's definitely Connor's people. Pretty sure the texts were the clencher."

"So they believe you want Sabre as your lover?"

"My dad at least thinks I fucked them while I was in Nuva Troi, especially after the Section Seven shit." He crouched down, and she made a little noise.

"I was playing with that."

The kiss he initiated was sweet, slowing things down, rather than advancing them. "I know, but I need you to listen. I am so sorry for what Section Seven put you through. When we decided to do this, I knew they'd be cruel, but the comments… Harls. I'm so sorry."

She nodded, swallowing her sadness. He was here now, and things were fine with them. They had been the instant he'd stepped off the train, and she'd felt how much he'd missed her in that first shared look. "It's okay. I don't care what anyone else thinks, as long as I know what's true."

"When this is over, I'm going to set this right. They won't be able to publish shit like that about you anymore."

Harlow stroked his face, running her fingers over the lines of his cheekbones, his jaw, and his lips. "You are wonderful, you know that?"

He turned his face away from her. "I don't deserve that." His expression was

434

tortured. "All I've ever wanted was to keep you safe, but everything I do gets you hurt somehow. I fucked up your life again."

It would be so easy to agree with him, to be angry about the ways his status had made him unaware of how differently they would be treated, but he already saw it. He already understood, and she still wanted him. She still wanted to be *here*, and it seemed a miserable way to go about their relationship to constantly be keeping score on who'd made more mistakes.

With everything they'd already been through, she didn't want to spend their time together arguing about who'd screwed up the worst. She pulled him down on top of her. "Fuck me up then, McKay. Fuck me up forever."

"What?" he asked, looking confused.

"Claim me, now. Do what your dad asked and make me yours."

His brows narrowed with worry, but she felt the effect of her words pressing into the core of her as she wrapped her legs around him. "We don't know if it's safe," he said.

"It's not safe. It's never going to be safe. But it's the key to me shifting—Thea broke the binding on the triptych."

He sat back, straddling her. She reached for him and he pinned her arms above her head, his head tilting. In the dim light of the cottage bedroom, he looked alien—a beautiful predator, ready to consume his prey.

"Shift," she urged. "Shift and I'll tell you."

His glamour fell away and the creature who caged her body was magnificent, his skin lighting from within. His hard cock pushed between her legs, pressing against her now-throbbing clit through her dress. Six huge wings flexed behind him, enormous as they unfurled from the tight bundle at his back.

"If you Claim me—if we Claim each other—I will be able to shift into the Feriant permanently."

"How?" he asked.

Harlow shivered at the sound of his true voice. "Think about what Cian told us. My heritage is part Illuminated and part shifter, as well as part witch. When you Claim me, I believe it will trigger something in me that will shift into what I'm truly meant to be. Like a magical chemical reaction."

He seemed to be thinking. The planes of his face were sharper in his true form, harsher and almost painfully beautiful. "The snakes were biting *each other*," he said, finally.

She nodded, rocking her hips a little so that he pushed harder against her. The effect was immediate; she felt him tense, holding all that Ventyr strength back that she wanted inside her, *now*. "And in the subsequent images, the snakes become one, which breaks the egg, and then the serpent and the raptor exist separately."

"Become one..." His eyes glowed with desire as it all fell into place for him. He looked down at her, his skin faintly glowing as he met the subtle movement of her hips with his own, creating a delicious tease of friction between them.

"Yes," she moaned, her back arching off the bed. The word was a plea from the depths of her soul.

He grasped both her wrists in one hand, using the now-free hand to slip under her dress, between her thighs. When his fingers met the silken hair between her legs he moaned. "What are you wearing under here?"

"Nothing," she whispered, meeting his gaze.

In a flash, he popped every button down the front of her dress, baring her to him completely. His eyes ran over her flesh. Every curve, every dip and fold of her body. He panted with need as he parted her legs wider with his free hand, teasing her with his fingers, dragging them lightly over the sensitive skin of her thighs and then away before giving her what she so clearly wanted.

Her scent filled the air and his fangs protracted as his nostrils flared. His wings went as taut as his cock. Every bit of him seemed prepared to take her but his mind. "You're sure?" he asked. "It would be hard to take this back."

He pulled back from her a little, as though he only now noticed that he had her pinned to the bed. In an instant, he freed her hands, seeming to want her to take the lead in this. She understood: there could be no doubt in his mind that she'd chosen this.

Harlow was more than willing to show him just exactly how much she wanted to be Claimed, and to Claim him in return. She raised up, pressing a hand to his chiseled chest, pushing him backwards into a seated position. He moved with fluid grace under her direction as she climbed into his lap, sliding out of her dress as she went.

He adjusted to cradle her as her slick folds slid against his massive erection. She raised her hips, positioning herself above him. As she sank down onto his waiting cock, they stared into one another's eyes. In this form, his eyes were dark, his irises nearly as black as his pupils.

She lowered herself slowly, letting every ridge of him caress her inside as he stretched her open, and when he could sink no further into her, she began to move, her hips undulating in a steady slow rhythm. He caressed her ass, never taking his eyes from hers as she ground her clit against him. The vibration she loved so much purred inside her, sending electric shivers of pleasure up her spine.

The pressure of his hands increased slowly as she moved faster, giving in to the pent-up passion she'd locked away for the past weeks. She reveled in the way her soft belly and breasts met his hard muscles, letting the intensity of need in his expression drive her. One of his hands slid up her back and into her hair as she neared her peak.

She let her head fall backwards as his fingers fisted into her hair, a primal growl emanating from his throat as she cried out with anticipation. His bite would take her over the edge.

"Claim me, McKay," she moaned, letting the fervor take her over.

His mouth opened as he drove hard into her, the slick results of the encounter making it easier for him to slide in and out of her. Her back arched as she fell slightly backward in his grip, her hard nipples meeting the cool air of the bedroom as his fangs grew longer. He struck in a serpentine moment, one that turned her into both predator and prey, she wanted it so badly.

The pain was momentary, followed quickly by euphoria that sent her tumbling over the edge into ecstasy. A symphony of limenal shadow and Illuminated light burst to life as he drank from her. Every nerve in her body was more sensitive than it had ever been and she was connected to not only him, but his magic, the golden source of his power, and when it too entered her, she changed.

The Claim between them would not be an unbreakable bond. Its power was to transform, for as his light became hers, so did her shadow become a part of him, and in this exchange, her own canine teeth transformed. She tasted the venom in her mouth, sweet and thick, and her body's only mission was to complete the transformation—to share it with him.

As his fangs retracted, he licked the twin wounds on her neck, and they closed immediately. He looked up at her face, his expression astounded.

"Goddess," he breathed.

She looked down at herself, at the way her shadows glowed now with their own dark light. Yes, she was a goddess. Whatever this was between them, it was no less than divinity. She pushed him down onto the bed, straddling him, in a fast, fluid movement which he met with no effort.

"I want to look at you," he begged. "Let me see you."

She leaned back as his hands skimmed her hips and ribcage, cupping her breasts. He pinched her nipples, lightly at first, and then harder as she whimpered with pleasure. One hand slid between her breasts and slowly over the gentle curve of her belly and then between her legs to her swollen clit.

She was stretched full of him and as he rubbed her clit, she bent backwards to let him get a better view of the place where their bodies merged. As she did, she felt the jerk of his hips, the increase in his pleasure at seeing her writhe for him, mistress to the power of his cock plunging deep within her again and again.

And then his eyes lifted, and for the first time he saw her new fangs, shining with venom as she cried his name. The fingers rubbing her clit migrated upwards, into her mouth where she tasted herself mingled with her new venom.

"You are magnificent," he breathed. "Every fucking bit of you." He thrust hard into her as he dragged her against him. "Claim me."

The scent of his blood, coursing hard in his veins, spurred her on. As her mouth closed around his neck and her new teeth, purpose-built for this moment, pierced his skin, they came together, their pleasure winding together in what felt as though it might be an endless loop of love and euphoria.

He roared with a ferocity she'd never heard as she pulled his essence into her, from his cock, his blood, his power, his love. They were, in that moment, truly one. She felt when the peak crested and began to fade. Warm, contented bliss came over her, and her fangs retracted. She remembered how he'd licked her wound clean and she did the same, elated at the fact that like her own wound his closed immediately, healed by some unknown power.

His arms went around her as their movements slowed. "That was nothing like what I expected," he whispered as she stilled above him.

"What did you expect?" she asked, cuddling into his chest. She was in no hurry to move and loved the feeling of him still hard inside her, as the wet mingling of their bodies seeped out of her.

"My father said it was the ultimate possession. Those are the words he used. That I would feel as though I owned you. And I knew that was skewed, that his perspective was skewed by his values, but it wasn't anything like that. We were one, but…"

She nodded, raising her head to look in his eyes. "Now we're both *more*."

He hugged her even tighter. "Will you shift for me?"

Harlow looked around the room. "I don't think this room is big enough for the Feriant."

His laugh was rich, free of burden. "I suppose not. Do you want to go downstairs?"

Harlow shook her head. "No, I want to go somewhere I can *fly*."

Finn grinned. "I think I know just the place."

CHAPTER 25

Finn shifted back to his humanoid form and teleported them to a deserted cliffside overlooking the sea. Far, *far* to the south, Harlow could barely make out the dotted coastline that made up Nea Sterlis. The day was cloudy, a storm brewing. When they'd both determined they were well and truly alone, a grin spread over Finn's face.

He looked up, pointing to the sky. "Perfect cover for a flight, don't you think?"

Harlow gazed into the churning clouds. She and Finn were both naked as the day they were born, and she laughed at the audacity of the situation, and the brazen, unbridled joy in Finn's face as he shifted into his true form. He shot into the air, his wings leaving her in a cool wake of air as he went.

"Can you catch me?" he called as he disappeared into the mist.

He didn't doubt her ability to shift one bit, even after the hundreds of failed attempts they'd made all summer, and that confidence spurred her on. Harlow closed her eyes, and as she looked for a place to focus her attention, her shadows guided her to the heart of the limen, the source of all her power. The change was nearly instantaneous.

When she opened her eyes her vision was different: panoramic in nature, the colors more vibrant, and everything sharp and easy to focus on. When she shot into the air, she found she didn't have to *try* to fly; she already knew how. In her humanoid form, Harlow was frightened of heights. As the Feriant, she feared no altitude, climbing higher and higher, searching for her heart's mate.

When she spotted him, she caught up to him quickly. They soared through the clouds, climbing ever higher until they broke free of the storm and into the sun-drenched aerial landscape that lay beyond. She didn't know how long they flew, stretching their wings, riding currents of air, but she had never felt anything like it before. For the first time in her entire life, she was free.

In this form, there were no questions, no pressing worries; those existed in her conscious mind. She knew herself still, but as the Feriant she was purely focused on instinct, on the trust she'd worked so hard to build with herself, and her anxiety had no place here. For the briefest of moments, she wondered if she had to shift back, or if she might stay this way forever.

As Finn soared beneath her, flipping over so he could watch her fly, she knew she would change back. *Can you hear me?* she asked in her mind.

Yes, came his answer. She could sense the laughter in his voice, rather than hear it.

Do you think you could catch me?

He grinned, but his brows knitted together in a question.

If I shifted back, could you catch me?

Here?

Yes.

Suddenly, he understood her. *I'll catch you anywhere you fall.*

It was dangerous, and she knew it, but she trusted him. Beneath her he spread his arms open, and she shifted back, falling for the briefest of moments before his body met hers, his arms wrapping around her tight and secure.

She wrapped her arms around his neck as they soared higher, her mouth meeting his in a kiss so passionate, so full of joy, that Harlow understood the full scope of their bond, the depth of the Claiming. It was like he had said—there was no sense of possession between them. They were separate entities, powerful in their own right, but deeply connected now in a way they had not been previously.

Her legs wrapped around his waist as his wings carried them onto a current of warm air. They glided, supported fully by the wind, which caressed her bare skin, heightening every sense of pleasure she experienced: the press of his fingers in her back as he kept her clasped tightly to him. The feel of his tongue as it moved in her mouth. The way she opened for him as his cock pressed at her slick entrance.

She deepened the kiss as she lowered her hips. Here in the air, with nothing to press against, she would be the momentum that brought them pleasure as he controlled their flight. She bore down on him as he stretched her open, sinking into her as they kissed. When he was as deep in her as he could go, she tilted her pelvis and hips, moving them in slow, sensual circles, rather than pumping up and down on his cock.

He came quickly, clutching her tight. When his eyes flew open, he was out of breath. "My wings aren't used to all this flight."

She wrapped her arms around him. "Take me home."

He teleported and they reappeared in the bedroom of the carriage house, where he shifted into his humanoid form and flopped onto the bed. "I never did get you to sit on my face," he said with a wicked grin. "And you know how I hate not getting my way."

She stood at the end of the bed, his words lighting a fire in her core. She crawled up his body, leaving a trail of kisses as she went. When she finally straddled his face, he groaned, taking in her scent, mingled now with his own.

"I can't wait to bury my face in you," he said.

She steadied herself and his hands drifted onto the small of her back, grazing the dip of her hips, then latching around her thighs as he brought her down to meet his mouth. His tongue was warm and soft as she moved against it, his lips gently sucking at her clit, then licking in turns.

Harlow was careful not to clench her thighs too tightly or bear down too hard. His mouth on her was sublime, but she didn't want to smother him. He pushed her away from his face for a moment, using the opportunity to slide a finger into her, teasing her as he spoke.

"Ride my face, baby girl. Ride it hard. I want you to scream."

Then he slid down further, so she was leaning forward just enough that he could take her clit in his mouth, and slide two fingers into her from behind. The extra pressure of his fingers in her sent her into a frenzy as he licked and sucked her. Her thighs tightened around his face and she did as he'd asked and rode his face hard, getting exactly the pressure and speed she needed.

Her breasts were heavy with desire, her nipples hard, and she was greedy for more stimulation. She grabbed her own breasts with one hand, caressing their fullness as she fucked Finn's face. She'd never felt so powerful and cherished as she did in this moment, pinching her nipples, as her hips moved faster. Finn moaned, and she glanced backwards at the liquid beading on his cock. He was so hard for her, for the way she tasted, and the feel of her taking her pleasure.

Her free hand moved from her breasts to her belly, which hung in a way that would have made her insecure months ago, but now it was beautiful to her; she touched herself the way Finn sometimes did when he took her from behind, stroking the soft curve of her flesh as Finn feasted on her. She cried out as her fingers caressed her own soft flesh, coming hard as she moved against his lips and fingers.

When her orgasm waned, he slid out from under her and flipped into a kneeling position, pulling her back until she was on all fours in front of him.

"Yes," she begged. "Yes."

He drove into her, spreading her legs, gripping her hips. "I missed you so much," he growled. "I missed your scent when you want me like this. The way I can smell you from across a room and know you're thinking about me too."

He reached around her to touch her swollen clit again as she lowered onto the pile of pillows he'd been resting on. His body was heavy on top of hers as he moved slowly in her, his fingers rubbing her clit exactly the way she wanted.

Their movements were less dramatic now, but more fervent somehow, as she raised her hips to give him a better angle. He slid another pillow under her stomach and the position was so perfect she felt her release begin to build.

"Yes," he urged her. "Yes, come for me."

"Bite me," she begged. "Please."

Behind her, he pushed her hair off her neck, then an arm snaked around her front, pinning him to her chest as he drove his cock into her harder. His fingers rubbed wicked circles around her clit as she begged for more.

When he bit her, she came so hard she saw deep space. It was easy to understand how the Illuminated got addicted to this, how they used it to bandage over emotional wounds, rather than working things out between themselves. There was no doubt in her mind that was a danger she and Finn would have to watch out for as time passed, but the pleasure it brought them both now was evident in the way he moaned her name as his fangs retracted.

When they recovered enough to talk, laying in a boneless heap of entwined limbs and soft skin, they exchanged stories, comparing notes on the way their deception played out. "Sabre wanted me to tell you how sorry they are about the comparisons Section Seven made. They're enraged on your behalf," Finn said.

Harlow nodded, but couldn't quite find words at first. Finally she said, "Maybe we'll be friends someday."

Finn pressed a kiss to her temple. "You'd love each other. You have the same kind of huge heart. After the rooftop stories got played thousands of times, they were nearly inconsolable. I thought we were going to have to end the whole thing."

Harlow smiled through her tears. "Thank you for telling me that. There were times when I wanted to call it all off too."

Finn stared at the ceiling. "I punched a hole in the wall at my parents' house when the photos of you and Kate came out."

"I'm sure that helped them believe you," Harlow reasoned.

Finn glanced down at her. "I'm sure it did. But I wasn't faking it. Not all the way. Something in me worried… That maybe you'd remember that Kate is *fun*."

Harlow propped her head up on her hand so she could look at Finn more easily. "Yes, Kate is fun. That's a given. What's your point?"

He sighed. "I'm not really all that fun."

His face was so serious she had to laugh. "I had a pretty good time just now."

He shook his head. "I don't mean sex. I mean the rest of the time. I'm not funny like Kate, and apparently I'm 'broody' all the time."

Section Seven had called him "Nuva Troi's Brooding Bad Boy" and posted dozens of images they'd taken of him over the years where he looked intimidating or angry. Overall, the effect had been complimentary, or so Harlow had thought, but he looked genuinely upset now.

"Kate is a great date," she said, her fingers grazing his chin, turning his face towards hers. "But you are the love of my life. I don't need you to entertain me. I'm interested in everything you say and do."

His eyes softened as she spoke. "I am the luckiest person on the planet," he said, wrapping her in his arms and rolling on top of her again. "I will love you to the end of everything," he said as entered her.

They made love again and again, making up for the weeks they lost.

CHAPTER 26

The rooftop restaurant at the Grand was nearly empty. As this was primarily a tourist spot, and the tourists were well and truly gone from Nea Sterlis now, this was not unexpected, but Harlow felt extremely unsettled by being alone with Connor McKay on a rooftop. Finn took a call nearly as soon as they'd sat down and now the two of them sat across from one another in awkward silence.

Connor spoke first. "What do you do with your time, Harlow?"

Harlow frowned. "Are you asking if I have a job?"

Connor shrugged, expression blithe. "I assume you have causes you care for. You have a degree in history, I understand."

"I've always worked at my parents' bookstore. When I return to Nuva Troi, I assume I will go back to work at the Monas," she answered.

To Connor's credit, he wasn't one to dole out fake smiles, or pleasantries. "I don't think that will be appropriate for my heir's wife. Perhaps you'd like to go back to school. I understand you spent quite a bit of time at the Citadel this summer."

Harlow paused. It wasn't the worst idea in the world, but why did he want this? Talking to Connor McKay was like playing three dimensional chess. He was on one level and she was on another. "Yes, I'd considered getting another degree in history, but if I'm not going to work in restoration at the Monas, I'm not sure why I would."

Connor smiled now, but it wasn't placating or kind, it was pure amusement at her lack of understanding. "Why work at all?"

Harlow frowned. "Regardless of how much money Finn earns or inherits, I plan to work."

"Of course," Connor said, chuckling. "You all do at first. Tell me about your summer studies. Which libraries have you visited most?"

Harlow sucked in a breath. Being alone with Connor McKay felt like all

443

oxygen had disappeared from the planet. "I've spent quite a lot of time at the Sistren of Akatei Library recently." Likely, he already knew this, so why hide it?

"Yes," he said slowly. "Why so much interest in that particular library?"

So this was what he wanted to talk about. She didn't have to make it easy for him. "Well, aside from the fact that Akatei is the patron goddess of my Order, I confess, I just love the gardens."

It felt glib to say it, and she assumed this would annoy him since he was so interested in knowing what she was studying, but she did not expect the reaction that passed over his face. He'd been taking a sip of water when she spoke and now he nearly choked, spitting his water back into his glass.

"Excuse me?" he asked. His voice was quiet and deadly as he wiped his mouth. The calm that came over him was eerie, like he was laser focusing on her. She fought to keep control of her body, not wanting to give away that he was making her anxious.

"The gardens? I don't remember that facility having particularly impressive gardens."

Really, it didn't. The courtyard garden was pleasant enough, but nothing special. She'd just been trying to annoy him by not answering his question. She racked her brain for something to say. "It has a rather unique fountain though."

Harlow took a sip of her tea, hoping they might move onto another topic, but Connor's expression darkened further and his jaw was clenched so tightly a vein near his eye began to twitch. Harlow fought to keep up. Somehow she'd lucked into making him react.

She kept talking, babbling really, just to see if she could get him to react further. "It's Akatei pulling the first threads of aether, but the body positioning of the statue itself is atypical, and I believe there might be something written on her hands. Of course, I'd never blaspheme and get into the fountain to look, but it's a delightful little mystery."

His face was still now; in fact his entire body was still, too still. If she weren't here as Finn's fiancée, she would be terrified right now. Finn's footsteps announced that he was returning to the table.

"How interesting," Connor bit out.

Beneath the table, Harlow's shadows danced around her ankles, almost as if they were issuing a warning. It was unnecessary. Every bit of her base instinct was on high alert. Finn glanced at his father as he approached, and Harlow knew she wasn't imagining things when she saw fear flash in his eyes as he sat down next to her.

He affected a cold demeanor. "Sorry for the delay. One of my properties in Nuva Troi went up for sale this morning and we've had three offers. That was Sabre."

Harlow shivered at the way he let his tone soften to a purr around Sabre's name. Even knowing full well that it was all for show wasn't enough to keep her from reacting. Her eyes fell to the table, and she bit her lip, trying as hard as she could to keep her chin from quivering.

Across the table Connor smiled—*smiled* at her reaction, and sniffed the air as it shifted in the breeze. "You've Claimed her. How lovely." He set down his coffee and clapped a hand to Finn's shoulder. "Good work, my boy."

Harlow's skin prickled with fear. How could he talk about something so intimate, so personal, like it was something to celebrate?

Connor grinned at her as her eyes raised. "You'll find things easier to handle now, my dear. Finn will take care of you. Each time you suffer, he'll erase it with a bite. Won't that be lovely?"

Finn's smile dripped with arrogance as his hand drifted to the back of her neck, his fingers wrapping around her throat. "That it will."

She knew it was a show, knew this was all just a ruse, but fear mixed with arousal. Connor's nostrils flared, and he laughed, loud and hearty. "See, even now she wants it. Go give her what she needs, my boy. I'll order us a spread."

It wasn't a suggestion. He'd just commanded them to go fuck. Finn shook his head. "She's had enough for today. It would do her good to wait. I don't want her to get too greedy."

Harlow nearly gagged on Finn's words. It made her sick to watch him twist himself into this. How could this be what Connor wanted, when the real Finn was so *good*? She knew she couldn't reach for his hand, but a single tear slipped from her eyes, down her cheek and as Connor laughed again, throwing his head back in delight, she saw the flash of understanding on Finn's face.

He knew exactly what that tear was for—*him*. She wasn't humiliated by Connor, she was sorry for him. Sorry he couldn't see the wonderful man his son had become, despite him and Aislin. And she was sorrier still for the little boy that lived inside Finn, the one she desperately wished she could travel back in time and comfort. The one that Connor broke, time and again for his own gain.

Connor's phone rang, and he answered, stepping away from the table. Harlow and Finn watched the delight slide right off his face, shifting quickly to fury. When he hung up his voice was sharp. "I have to handle this now. I'm sorry, Finbar. It doesn't look like I'll have much time for you this week. I need to handle things with the Falcyran ambassador. He's just arrived in port."

Finn nodded as he stood to shake his father's hand. "I understand. Please let me know if there's anything I can do to help."

Connor's eyes softened as he hugged his son. "Truly, my boy, *truly*, I am so proud of you. I worried you might not come around to my way of thinking, but I see now you have things well in hand."

Connor nodded to Harlow. "Do as Finbar commands, girl."

Harlow let her eyes fall to the table, and she tucked her chin in a semblance of a bow. "I will," she promised.

When the elevator doors closed, Finn went to the railing of the rooftop deck, watching his father get into his car and drive away.

"Why doesn't he just teleport?" Harlow asked from the table.

Finn turned, speaking softly. They were still alone, but he was forever careful. "Teleporting takes a lot of energy. It makes it harder to do other, smaller magics for a few days if we don't recover in our true forms, so we don't do it often."

"Oh," Harlow said, realizing how little she knew about the way the Illuminated used their power. "Can we get out of here?"

He nodded. As they walked to the parking lot, he made several attempts to make small talk with her, but she barely answered. Something was bothering her about her conversation with Connor.

"I'm sorry for how that all went," Finn said when they were safe inside the Woody. "I will be so glad when this part of things is over."

Harlow put her seatbelt on. A deep sigh shuddered through her. "When is that going to be, Finn?"

He started the car, but turned to look at her. "What do you mean?"

Harlow flexed her hand, gazing at her engagement ring. "How long are we going to pretend for your parents that we're like them?"

Finn leaned back in his seat. "Not long. Cian thinks we need to make moves soon to gather our people and find a way to strike back."

"They're weakened enough by what's happening in Falcyra?" Harlow asked.

Finn nodded. "They had to send a legion there, in addition to the Dominavus. The next step would be to invoke a military presence, and that will take time to assemble."

"The lower Orders will never agree to that," Harlow mused.

"The Order of Night might, but my father and Pasiphae seem to anticipate that if the humans rise up, there will be mass chaos."

Harlow nodded. "And what about the Rogue Order?"

Finn shrugged. "Connecting with Riley really hasn't benefited us much. We're no closer to meeting with them than we were before. I thought I had a lead on the queen when I left here, but it dried up almost immediately."

Harlow pushed a hand through her hair. "So it's just us against them? There aren't nearly enough of us."

Finn backed out of the parking spot, pulling into the street. "There's not. Our war with them will be hidden—in the shadows. It will be waged privately, not in big battles, until we can find a way to undermine them enough that we can gain allies."

"Numbers," Harlow added.

"Yes," Finn agreed.

"We have to enact the process the Scroll shows," Harlow said. "If we need numbers, we need to set magic free."

"But how?" Finn asked as they pulled into the villa's driveway.

Harlow shook her head. "I don't know, but I think Thea does." She held up her new phone, which she'd had on silent. *Come home as soon as you can. Scroll unlocked.*

Finn leaned over and kissed her. "It's finally all coming together."

∼

ALARIC, Thea, and Larkin sat waiting for them in the Vault conference room, with Petra and Enzo. As they entered, Thea was finishing getting them up to date about the truth about Harlow and Finn's ruse.

As Harlow sat, Enzo grabbed her hand. "I knew there was something else going on."

"I'm so sorry I couldn't tell you," she said.

Finn was making similar apologies to Petra, who shot a weary smile at Harlow that let her know they'd be easily forgiven. Still, she doubted they'd be allowed to forget this anytime soon. Harlow engaged her second sight to view the threads that connected them, and they appeared graceful and calm, with only small areas of tension. She was beginning to see fine details of color variation in the threads, and thought that soon she might be able to decipher what they meant.

"Where's Riley?" Harlow asked Enzo as they got settled into seats.

"They're off somewhere with Kate today. Something at the vineyard, with her sire," Enzo replied. "Sounded boring."

Harlow laughed, and it felt good to have a normal conversation after the past few weeks. "I know, right? Why does everything she does at the vineyard always sound so, so boring?"

Apparently, they were all feeling how the tension between them had loosened. Petra kicked her, but she laughed too. "Gods, is this a thing? I was actually starting to think that Kate was too perfect, and then she talked about the vineyard and the winery and I was just bored to tears. All the talk about the genetics of the different vines..."

"And the natural pesticide compositions," Enzo added. "But Riley thinks it's all fascinating."

Harlow shook her head. "Everyone has their flaws."

Axel entered the room and hopped into Petra's lap. The three of them laughed about Kate, as Alaric struggled to establish a safe line between Nuva Troi—with Cian and the maters—for a video conference. Finn got up to help, but as he did, some expression flickered across his face that Harlow couldn't quite pinpoint.

He stopped, looking back at the three of them. "It's kind of weird, isn't it? Kate is always so much fun to hang out with, but you're right, *nothing* about the vineyard seems at all interesting."

Thea interrupted them. "I'm afraid this is why we're having trouble connecting." She turned her laptop around and played a video. "I'm pretty sure Nox just emailed this to me, but it was sent so covertly I can't be sure."

She pressed play. The video wasn't long, shot from a rooftop in Midtown. The sky was hazy, or so Harlow thought at first. She realized quickly it was smoke. Far away, in the distance of the video, there was a strange sound, like dozens of bottle rockets going off at once.

"What's that noise?" Enzo asked.

Petra's eyes darkened and Harlow watched her fingers run through Axel's fur as he purred comfortingly at her. "Gunfire."

"Gunfire?" Larkin asked. "How is that possible? Only the military has guns."

The air in the room was suddenly close, too close. Harlow's skin prickled with a deep anxiety as the camera panned across the Nuva Troi skyline. Dozens of buildings were on fire—and that sound—gunfire. Now that Harlow knew what it was, it was everywhere.

"That's your place, babe," Thea whispered, horror written on her face, as

Alaric sat down. He took one of her hands in his. They were all thinking it: *where were the people they loved in all this?*

Everyone went quiet as the camera panned down to the streets, where hundreds of Illuminated warriors were fanning out of a building across the road. "That's the tactical building, where my mom and Connor have offices," Alaric said. "Its location is why I took the Midtown apartment…"

He trailed off as a voice spoke for mere moments and then cut off. Thea rewound the video so they could hear the voice. It was clear it was Nox this time. "Me and Indi got here, with the maters. The riots started yesterday." Her voice was clipped. Out of breath. "Nothing like Falcyra here. Illuminated struck back almost immediately, but the Humanists were prepared. Hundreds, maybe thousands dead by now—we're safe here, for now. I'll get as many out as I can before things get—"

The video cut off. All the relief Harlow had felt moments before was gone, replaced by the sense that the looming dread she'd been feeling all summer had finally reached its catalyst point. That this is what she'd been waiting for, or the start of it, anyway.

"What is she talking about?" Harlow asked, her voice raising an octave. "Are they safe there? Is my family safe?"

Enzo took her hand.

"Yes," Thea said, her tone soothing, but there was intense worry in her eyes. "They'll be safe there. For now, anyway."

"That's why he left dinner," Finn said. Clearly he was talking about Connor. "The call he got—it wasn't about the Falcyran ambassador."

"Can we get a message back to them?" Harlow asked.

Finn nodded. "We can route it through Ari and Meline in Falcyra. They should be able to get through easier than us right now, believe it or not."

"Already on it," Alaric said, typing quickly on his laptop.

"Where's Cian?" Enzo followed up. "Nox said she had Indi and the maters with her, but where's Cian?"

Everyone was quiet. "We have to assume they're at Haven, helping people," Finn said. "That would be their first priority."

The room was silent but for the sound of Alaric, typing furiously on his laptop. Thea watched him, her beautiful face tense with worry.

"Okay," Alaric said. "I've got Ari—on chat only. Can't get a secure video connection. From what he and Meli can tell, it looks like the Humanists struck the Order of Night's temporary headquarters in Nuva Troi first. The building burned—they were having a diplomatic dinner though, and several of the Orders' top officials were killed."

"Any Illuminated?" Thea asked.

Alaric nodded. "Yes. At least two that we know of. And they managed to blow the school line today. Twelve children were killed this time. They got the Order of Masks and Mysteries both—the central headquarters buildings are all destroyed. No death toll yet. They've been targeting Order leaders… Enzo, I'm so sorry—they burned your parents' former home to the ground. No word on the atelier or the Monas."

"Shit," Enzo breathed. "I mean, it wasn't their house anymore, but I grew up there…"

Larkin moved to sit next to Harlow, taking her hand. Thea glanced at her sisters, and Harlow saw real fear in her eyes.

"No wonder the Illuminated cut off communications. This is unreal," Enzo said. "Who are these people?"

"Ari has a theory about that too," Alaric said. He glanced at Harlow, looking worried.

"Spit it out," Finn commanded.

"Alain Easton. Ari and Meli think they've traced the money back to Alain. He's funding the Humanists' terrorism."

Thea read over Alaric's shoulder. "That's not all. Before she went dark, Nox finally got a lock on where that drone was transmitting the information. She sent it to Ari, who traced it back to several of the same signatures that allowed him to identify Alain Easton as the financial backer for the Humanists."

Finn's jaw twitched. "Shit."

Alaric sighed. "Yeah. This isn't adding up to anything good."

They'd been so elated this morning, so happy to have finally gotten a step ahead of Connor and Pasiphae, and now all the hope that had inflated Harlow's sails simply vanished. "Why didn't they tell us this sooner?"

Alaric shook his head. "It's not confirmed yet. They wanted to be sure, but in light of all this, Ari says he thought it was better to say what they suspect now."

"He's worried they're going to get cut off from us," Finn added.

"Yeah," Alaric replied, sitting back in his chair and covering his face. "And I have to agree. The Illuminated will lock everything down. They can do it. The simulations Nox and I ran last month prove it. They can shut everything down, even the dark web. We're talking about worldwide outages of *everything*."

Finn stared at his hands. "Connor calls it the 'Great Reset.' He told me about it last week. He said if the riots reached Nuva Troi, this would be the first step—sending out the legions—they'll give it a month, and if the resistance can't be quelled, they'll 'reset' Okairos."

Harlow's heart nearly stopped. "What the fuck does that mean?"

Finn's hands shook. "They think that if they take us back to a pre-industrial period for three to five years, they'll be able to control us by force."

The magnitude of what Finn was saying was hard to even think about. No phones, no internet, no cars—no hospitals or modern medicine—no electricity…. The implications were too big to even think about. Add the fact that such a move would amplify the Illuminated's abilities immeasurably, and it was impossible to imagine anything other than total and complete oppression of humans and the majority of the lower Orders.

"But—people will die," Thea said. "So many people will die."

"They'd rather start over than give up their stranglehold on power," Enzo said.

No one else said anything. It was hard to know what to say. While it had been disturbing to see what happened in Falcyra, everything had gone on so normally here in Nytra that it was hard to imagine anything like that could happen here. But now it was, and they were all caught in the middle of it.

The only thing Harlow could hear was her heart, beating wildly at the thought of being separated from the maters and her sisters while all of this was happening. There was no worse outcome she could imagine. She'd always thought that when whatever was brewing began, they'd face it together.

"Thea, what did you find out about the scroll?" Harlow asked, breaking the silence.

"I hardly think that's important now," Thea said.

Harlow glared at her. Why couldn't she see what was right in front of them? "It might be the only thing that's important now. If their plan is to take Okairos back by force, we have to set the aether free."

Everyone watched them. It was clear Thea didn't agree; her expression turned to one Harlow had seen thousands of times as a child. Indigo had once called it "Mini-mater," because Thea looked so completely assured that she was in charge. "We don't even know if that's safe."

Larkin finally spoke. "But letting them kill thousands of people is? They could kill more in their 'reset' and you know it."

"We don't even know if that's what the scroll depicts," Thea said. Her voice was even, but there was tension around her eyes.

"But you're reasonably sure it is, aren't you?" Petra said.

Alaric took Thea's hand. "Tell them," he urged. "I think they're right. If there's any possibility that we could make aethereal power available to everyone, now is the time to take a risk."

Thea pulled her hand out of Alaric's grasp as her mouth twisted in a little knot. Finally, she sighed. "I was thinking about what you and Finn experienced last Spring at the opening night of the season. The way you were both shot out of our reality—something about it seemed strange to me, so I used the Vault's records to do some research on binding rituals—between this and the Merkhov, I've been woefully unprepared. Anyway, I pulled some advanced spellwork out of the Order of Mysteries' digital archives—"

"Thea," Harlow interrupted. If they let her go on like this, it could take her an hour to get to the point. "We don't need to know your entire research methodology. What did you find out?"

Thea glared at Harlow, wrinkling her nose in a rather pointed way at her younger sister before continuing. "The season itself is a massive ritual, as we already know. If I'm right, on opening night, the invitation takes a tiny bit of aethereal essence—core material that humans often call souls—from each of the season's participants via the invitations. It links them to the ritual for the duration of the season until the Solstice. Any magic they use during that time helps to power the spell."

"That would have to be a really big spell," Enzo said. He'd always been good at spellwork and ritual planning. "I mean, really big."

"What kind of ritual would need that kind of power?" Larkin asked.

Enzo clapped a hand over his mouth. "It has to be a vascularity of some kind."

Larkin's mouth twitched. "Don't they call those 'battery spells' now?"

Enzo nodded. "Yeah, that's the colloquial term for them. It's a way to channel large amounts of magic into a physical manifestation."

Harlow rubbed her forehead, trying to remember what Enzo was talking about. She'd never been particularly good at spellwork. So much memorizing. "A physical manifestation?"

Larkin bit her bottom lip for a moment, thinking. "Yeah, so a vascularity could be used for a lot of things. When the maters were young, people used them for things like keeping mines from caving in, or dams from breaking. They're workhorse types of spells with a physical presence that looks almost like a web of blood vessels, for channeling aether. It's why it's called a vascularity."

Alaric's eyes lit. "Yes, and as human engineering advanced, combined with both Illuminated and sorcière magics, we stopped using quite so many of those types of spells. They took a lot of power to manage."

"Right," Larkin said. "That's why people call them 'battery spells.' They need a battery of some kind to keep them going and steady. You funnel the power into the vascular tubes, and then you use some object as the battery that stores aether and dispenses it evenly. They have to be connected to one another to work."

Enzo's skin went grey. "An Archean vascularity works differently though. It uses organic matter as the battery." When everyone gave him a round of confused looks, he elaborated. "Either a creature, or a person. Likely an immortal if you were going to use a person, but I've read about instances where whales or other giant creatures were used. Intelligent brains act as a kind of computer for the spell, used to distribute large amounts of power, over long periods of time, at an even pace. If the season was being used as you posit, Thea, then it's possible the vascularity used in the season's ritual is Archean."

Thea's eyes went wide. "It could be... Oh... that makes more sense than what I originally thought..." She rushed to get her folder with the images of the scroll in it, and spread them on the table, tapping the image of the sleeping Argent. "I thought this was a metaphor, but I don't think any of this is metaphorical, not really."

Enzo shrugged as he traced the images with his fingers. "I'm afraid not."

"So the Argent is the battery for the spell?" Petra asked, horrified.

Enzo nodded. "Essentially—their nervous system is likely the conduit for the power, the base of the root—like a battery pack. And their brain controls the distribution of power. The harvest from the season's ritual is likely funneled into the firedrake, and then stored to be used throughout the year."

"That is gruesome," Harlow whispered.

Enzo nodded. "It is. They fell out of fashion in the modern age because of their cruelty, but they are powerful spells."

"If they were used mainly in industrial applications in the past, what is this one being used for now?" Larkin asked.

"There are more theoretical applications..." Enzo trailed off, his eyes narrowing as he thought. "Such as using them as complex bindings, ways to create things like prisons or barriers."

Prisons or barriers? Like Nihil? Things pieced together. "Could it be used to create a barrier between planes of reality?" Harlow breathed.

"What?" Finn asked.

She turned to him. "You said when the Illuminated came here that they were meant to free aether—to make humans more powerful to fight in the wars they were fighting on their home world, right?"

Petra nodded, following Harlow's train of thought. "Yes, and that means there must have been a source of aether on Okairos somewhere—a big one that didn't exist on other worlds. Something special."

"Like Nihil," Harlow said. "The prison is built on the heart of the limen, the actual source of aether. I don't think you and Cian were wrong about the Pyriphle. I think the river *does* go right into Nihil—to the prison—and Ashbourne. We have a door to not only the limen here on Okairos, but the heart of *all* magic."

"Is that even possible?" Petra asked.

Enzo nodded. "It is. Metaphysics tells us that it's likely the limen opens and closes portals all the time. The problem is, they're not supposed to stay open. Of course, there are stories…"

"About what?" Petra prodded, clearly getting frustrated. Axel grumbled in her lap.

Thea sighed. "That there are anomalies. Portals opened to other realms that stay open, creating massive imbalances in the universe, allowing certain elemental energies to grow far beyond their natural size and power."

"Like the Ravagers," Harlow said. "Something made them uncontrollable."

"What are you talking about?" Enzo asked.

Harlow glanced at Finn. "You have to tell them the whole truth about *The Warden.* They need to know."

He nodded and recounted the entire story of *The Warden*, explaining that the Illuminated were the Ventyr, a race of beings so powerful they'd imprisoned the elemental embodiments of suffering in the universe. The reality of the Ventyr's influence in the world, their corner of the cosmos, was overwhelming enough.

Petra's eyes went wide. Of course she had to know much of this, but Harlow had gotten the impression the finer details of many things weren't told to Illuminated women. She smacked Finn's shoulder and Axel growled, protective of Finn. "You knew this and never told me?"

"It was dangerous to know. It still is," he explained.

"We can't open a portal to Nihil, Harlow," Thea said, horror on her face. "If this is right, about the ritual at the root of the season, we can't risk disturbing whatever spell the Illuminated did to create it. They were right to close it."

Enzo frowned. "We wouldn't have to open the source up completely, just remove the barrier—whatever's keeping the aethereal energy restricted."

Thea shook her head. "No, that's too risky. We have no idea what might come through with it, or who it might draw to us. It might send a signal of some kind to the Ventyr. We have no clue what kind of tech they have, or if they're looking for a way to get to Okairos."

"Would they even still care about us?" Larkin asked. "It's been two thousand years."

Alaric shook his head. "We're young, all of us. We don't really have perspective on how time will work for us, later in life. Two thousand years might not be much time for them."

Petra drew a sharp breath in. "Our parents act like our lifetimes have been nothing but a short blip—the Ventyr could very well still be looking for a way to conquer Okairos. I think Thea might be right."

Harlow sighed. "There's only one way to figure this out for sure, Thea. We have to find out where it is and go look. Now might be our only chance."

Thea threw her hands up into the air. "Well, that solves it then. We'll just figure out where the entrance to Nihil is."

"Beneath the Alabaster Spire," Larkin said, a faraway look in her eyes. She was obviously thinking about Ashbourne. She still hadn't had any luck getting in touch with him.

"The Alabaster Spire?" Enzo repeated. "Is that where it is?"

Harlow nodded, telling them about the inscription on the crypt. Enzo smiled. "Well then, that's easy enough. You should have asked me before."

A little scream built in Harlow's throat, but she tamped it down. Now wasn't the time to explain that she'd been paranoid while she'd been pretending that Finn might have been unfaithful to her in Nuva Troi.

Enzo continued, apparently oblivious to her expression. "Right around the time the Illuminated got here, there was an earthquake in this region and a bunch of buildings fell—at least that's the logical explanation. There's an old Sterlisian legend that at least one actually disappeared: the Alabaster Spire."

All of her frustration dissolved. Harlow thought back to dinner with Connor. "It was a part of the Temple of Akatei, wasn't it?"

Enzo nodded. "Yes, part of what is now the library. How did you know?"

Harlow met Finn's eyes. "Your father was very worried that I've been spending time there. When I mentioned the statue in the courtyard, he got very upset. There's an inscription on Akatei's hands."

"That's where we have to look first," Finn said. "Who's coming with me?"

CHAPTER 27

The moons were waning and would soon go dark, and the night threatened rain. Getting into the library's courtyard was easy enough. Probably a little too easy, if Harlow was being honest with herself. Everyone else had stayed at home, to limit their risk of being caught.

Finn's fingers laced through hers, and she was so happy he was home, but that happiness was marred by everything else going on, and the risk they were taking, being here now. They'd been crouched in the courtyard near a potted plant for almost ten minutes while she and Finn both probed the building's threads for guards. It was an excruciatingly detailed task, and as the building was practically empty, it was also boring.

"There's one Ultima," Finn finally whispered. "She's at the furthest edge of the stacks now, in the basement. That gives you enough time to get into the fountain, read the inscription on Akatei's hands, and get back. I'll keep watch."

"Why do *I* have to get in the fountain?" Harlow asked, a little grumpy about having to get wet.

Finn kissed her nose. "You're a sorcière. I'm not. If there's any chance that the fountain might be a key to something big, it would make sense that it'd be warded. I might set them off, but if anyone is getting through without an issue, it would be a sorcière."

Harlow had to agree, but there was no guarantee that she would get through. She felt for wards, and found none, but that didn't mean they didn't exist. Many skillfully woven wards couldn't be detected until tripped, by even the most accomplished practitioners. There was only one way to find out.

"Okay, I'm going in."

Finn was right behind her as she darted into the courtyard. She took long strides through the fountain, trying her hardest not to make splashing noises.

She'd never been good at muffling spells, but she summoned her shadows to cloud around her and Finn.

She climbed atop the statue's base. The statue of Akatei was half a head taller than her, so it took a moment to read what was inscribed on her hands, since the sentence was split up. It was written in old Sterlisian, but Harlow was well versed in Nytran languages. *When bonfires light the ridge… The way will open.*

That was it. That was all it said. Harlow turned to get down, and stopped, spotting the rest of the inscription. The words were written in the dark shadow of the statue herself. Because of the hedge that grew behind her, this was the only view by which they could be read.

"What are you doing?" Finn hissed.

"There's something written around the inside edge of the fountain, can you give me some light?"

"That's risky," he said.

"Okay, well, use your phone's flashlight then."

He tried it, but there wasn't enough light. Harlow sighed, and tried to get her shadows to illuminate more, but their faint glow wasn't enough to see by.

"The Ultima is headed this way," Finn growled. "Get out of there."

"Not until I read it."

He glared at her, but his hand glowed as he stuck it into the water, lighting the entire fountain in a gentle glow. *The world between worlds lies just beyond knowledge. Beware what lies beneath the Alabaster Spire, for all reward comes at a price. Awaken the Fifth Order and find freedom in unraveling.*

A harsh voice broke the silence in the courtyard, nearly sending Harlow tumbling from the statue. "What in Akatei's name are the two of you doing?"

Harlow recognized the Ultima—Morgaine had said her name was Samira. She wasn't dressed in her uniform though, and for a moment Finn looked confused.

"Get out of here. *Now*," Samira insisted. She stepped into the fountain, pulling Harlow down off Akatei, shoving her towards Finn.

"Don't come back here again," she warned.

In the bushes, something moved. Harlow searched for the source of the sound, but couldn't find anything. Finn's arms went around her. "The Ultima is coming this way. We have to go."

Harlow frowned, trying to wrap her mind around what was happening. *Wasn't Samira the Ultima he'd been tracking?* He seemed to sense her question and shook his head. "I didn't even see her coming."

"*Go*," Samira whispered.

Finn made the jump, and as the courtyard dissolved in her vision, Harlow saw the bushes move again. An enormous auburn cat—the one who'd been visiting Axel—leapt towards another creature, snarling. Samira lunged for the creature the cat was attacking, in an almost coordinated strike. *As though she and the cat were fighting together.* Just as the courtyard disappeared almost completely, Harlow caught the briefest glimpse of the creature's face. It was a dog.

<h1 style="text-align:center">CHAPTER 28</h1>

They teleported straight into the Vault, much to everyone's surprise. Harlow couldn't be sure exactly what had happened at the Temple of Akatei. *Why hadn't she or Finn sensed Samira, and what had she been doing there? And what had happened right before they left? What was Axel's feline friend doing there and what was it attacking?*

The explanation for their sudden return sparked an argument, which Harlow tried to ignore as she thought. She needed a moment to process what she'd seen, and the bickering was distracting. Thea wasn't happy about them being caught, and she and Finn argued over what Samira had been doing in the library after hours, when she clearly wasn't on duty.

Harlow searched for a pen and wrote down the entire inscription for Alaric, who began running several searches on what he felt were the keywords from the inscription. She turned over the incident with the cat, trying to sort out what she'd seen. It didn't make much sense to her, but she was sure that Samira and the cat were working together somehow. The idea was beyond far-fetched. Of course cats were, as all animals on Okairos were, extremely intelligent. But if what she knew she had seen made any sense, that would mean they were somehow communicating to one another.

Larkin read the inscription several times and smiled. "The bonfires refer to the Hallowed Moon. That's an old Sterlisian tradition."

Enzo nodded. "She's right. And I agree that the world between worlds must be the limen—and 'just beyond knowledge' has to be the library, right?"

Harlow nodded, letting her thoughts about the cat go for now. "That's smart. Just beyond knowledge could be the courtyard, couldn't it?"

Thea and Finn had quieted now, listening as Alaric chimed in. "If the Fifth Order is supposed to be humans, then does that mean we have to do as the Scroll shows? Free magic?"

Thea gritted her teeth. "Perhaps, but the inscription is pretty clear that there will be a price to pay—an unraveling. That sounds sinister as fuck."

Harlow smiled at her sister's language. "Yes, but there's consequences to anything. Wouldn't the risk be worth it to be not beholden to the Illuminated any longer?"

She didn't expect Finn's response. "We've never known a world in conflict, Harlow. How can we choose that for everyone on our own?"

Her idealism fell away. He was right, and he was wrong at the same time. They *shouldn't* make this choice on their own. They shouldn't choose this fate *for* humans—whatever the Fifth Order awakening entailed, a group of immortals shouldn't be the ones who chose it.

But Finn didn't—no, *couldn't*—understand that humans and the lower Orders lived in a world full of conflict at all times. It was a quiet conflict, to be sure, but the silent screams she'd seen on the faces of her human friends every day of the years she'd spent with Mark shouldn't be dismissed so easily. Oppression didn't always look like riots in the streets.

It looked like humans making their monthly blood donations, having their reproductive choices micromanaged by people who had no business doing so. It looked like separate sectors of every Okairon city divided into Orders and humans, and a country like Falcyra that was allowed to prey on humans without interference. And that's why they shouldn't decide for the rest of the world. They had to find a way to get human input on this, and let them guide the way to change things.

"So we'll let the Hallowed Moon pass," Harlow said, finally.

Everyone was silent, but there were nods around the table.

"There's one every year," Thea reasoned. "Don't look so sad. Larkin, show her what you found tonight."

Larkin's smile was wary. "I've been curating Nox's monthly CCTV collection from Nuva Troi."

"Her what?" Enzo asked.

Alaric explained. "Nox has a program that collects anomalies in Nuva Troi's CCTV—things that are out of place. Stuff like graffiti before it gets cleaned, odd traffic patterns, sometimes even people who shouldn't be in certain places at certain times…"

Enzo nodded. "Okay. I get it. What did you find, Larkin?"

She turned her laptop around. Dozens of photos of five rings, looped together in a chain, played on loop on her screen. "This has been appearing in lots of places for the last month. Five rings—it could be the symbol for the Fifth Order." Some looked as though they'd been spray painted, others were worked into things like flyers, or other signs. "I refined the search once I saw the initial grouping—look at this."

Five images isolated on the laptop screen. "Those are all Haven locations," Alaric said.

"And they're painted on the *inside* of the windows, not the outside," Larkin said with a smile.

"So tell us what you think this all means," Petra said, grinning. She liked that Larkin had a theory.

Larkin smiled back at Petra, proud of herself. "There's a human resistance that *aren't* the Humanists already—and I think Cian is working with them."

"How do you know?" Finn asked.

Larkin enlarged the darkest of the images. The camera was focused on the glass of the window itself, but as it clarified, it was clear that CCTV had caught the actual moment this particular link had been applied. A hand pressed the appliqué to the glass. It was dark, and the image was fuzzy, but there was no denying it. The person in the window had a bright shock of silver hair.

Larkin played the video that still had originated from. It was hard to make out, but at the end the figure looked right out the window and a passing car illuminated their unique eyes, which reflected silver light into the dark.

"That's definitely Cian," Finn said. "Why wouldn't they tell us this?"

Harlow slipped her hand into his. "Maybe they started working with them more recently. Like while you were both back in the city. It was dangerous to share information then."

The lights in the Vault flickered for a mere second. Larkin turned her laptop around and frowned. "The internet's not working."

"That's not even possible down here," Alaric said, opening his own laptop. He shook his head. "Try it on your phones."

Thea was already on it. "It doesn't work."

Alaric raced to Cian's office. When he came back his eyes were wide. "The web and phone lines, even the hard lines, are down all over Okairos."

Finn picked up his phone, tried to make a call and then slammed it down on the table. They hadn't been able to get through to anyone in Nuva Troi since the email from Nox had come through, but calls to elsewhere had been working.

"Try Kate or Riley," he said.

Petra and Enzo both picked up their phones, but Harlow already knew they wouldn't be able to get through.

"Who did you try to call?" Harlow asked.

"My father," Finn answered as Petra and Enzo both shook their heads. "It's started. They'll cut off communication first and then impose martial law. Turn the TV on."

Larkin started to say she didn't think it would work, but when Petra turned on the conference room's TV, all channels were playing the same recorded message on loop.

Pasiphae Velarius sat in her pristine Nuva Troi office, smiling, her voice calm and steady. "Over the past few days, there have been a rash of terrorist attacks all over Okairos. As of now, martial law is in effect; all citizens are to be in complete lockdown. Provisions will be delivered to your homes.

"There will be no breach of lockdown restrictions. All those found in violation will be executed on sight. Please stay calm. This situation is temporary until all terrorists are in custody. Cooperate fully with all military officials in your area and we will get through this as we do all things: together. *Ab ordinae libertas.*"

458

"Bullshit," Finn said, but he sunk into the couch looking more lost than Harlow had ever seen him.

"We have to get my family out of Nuva Troi," Thea said, touching Alaric's arm. "Aurelia will be a target."

Alaric nodded. "I agree. I'll go back tonight and get them out myself. No one will question *me*."

Thea shook her head. "You're not going alone. I'm coming." He started to argue, but Thea was firm. "I'm coming."

Alaric looked to Finn, giving him a helpless shrug. "You okay with that?"

Finn nodded, clapping his hand to Alaric's shoulder, and then hugging Thea in turn. "Be careful. We'll rendezvous in Santos on the equinox."

Thea and Alaric both nodded, but Harlow was confused. "What's on Santos for us?"

Finn's smile was wry. "A plane. Until we can figure out the best way to handle all this, we need to get everyone to one of our safehouses, preferably outside Nytra. The Illuminated have always been more protective of Nytra. We'd be better off almost anywhere else."

There was a long pause, and then Enzo stood. "I'm going to get Riley. If we're leaving, I'm bringing my partner."

Finn started to protest, but Petra joined Enzo, taking his hand. "I'll go with him. We can get Kate too, if she'll come." Finn opened his mouth—to argue, Harlow assumed—but Petra shook her head. "*Finbar*. You and Alaric trained me. I'm as deadly as either of you. Don't you trust me?"

Finn hugged Petra tight. "Of course." He pulled away from her, cupping her face in his hands. "You better be careful though. Don't do anything rash. Get in, get them out. If there are soldiers involved, no retribution, you hear?"

Petra nodded, clasping the hands that cupped her face, her eyes welling with tears. "I love you too, big brother."

They fell into a hug so tight Harlow worried they'd smother each other. They had to separate in order to safely be together again, but it hurt all the same.

"What are we going to do?" she asked, when the four of them went upstairs to prepare for their respective journeys.

Larkin raised her eyebrows. "Do we get to storm something? I've always wanted to storm a castle."

Finn shook his head. "No, we'll go to Santos and get the plane ready for them… But I've got to try to talk to my father first."

Larkin looked like she wanted to fight him on that, but Harlow touched her sister's arm. "He's right. If anyone can get through to Connor, it's Finn. Will you go get Axel's things ready to go?"

Axel meowed at the sound of his name, winding his lithe body around Larkin's feet. She scooped him into her arms and nodded. "Sure."

When she went upstairs, Harlow turned to Finn. "What about Cian?"

Finn handed her his phone. It was open to what should be an impossible email, given the circumstances. "That's why I have to get to Connor. I don't know how she did it, but my girl is a genius. Look at this."

It was clearly from Nox, just two lines that read: *Everyone at Haven safe—except Cian. The Dominavus took them.*

<h1 style="text-align:center">CHAPTER 29</h1>

Harlow's hand flew over her mouth. Rakul had warned her that if they met again, they wouldn't be on the same side of things. This was her worst nightmare. They'd been caught. Cian had been caught. The punishment for sedition against the Illuminated was torture and death.

"No," she whimpered when she could form words. Then confusion set in. "How did they take Cian, but everyone else at Haven is safe?"

Finn sunk onto the couch. "I've been trying to puzzle that out for the past fifteen minutes."

Harlow sat next to him. "Why didn't you say something when the others were here?"

He shook his head. "They'll panic if they know Cian's been taken. They need clear heads to do what they're going to do. You and I are going to take care of this."

"Together?" Harlow asked, her heart lifting a little.

Finn's eyes softened. "Harls, you still have a lot to learn about combat, but I know you've got my back with my parents."

Harlow nodded. "Of course I do."

Finn gripped her shoulders. "Then I could really use your support tonight."

The look in his eyes was desperate. She hugged him tight. "Of course."

〜

THEY SAID goodbye to their family in the driveway as night fell. Enzo and Petra teleported out. Alaric and Thea left by car, and when they passed out of view, Larkin, Finn and Harlow went back into the villa.

"Don't break the wards for anyone," Harlow warned. "Only Finn and I can get back in now, and you and Axel have to promise to stay inside."

Larkin rolled her eyes. "Sure, but last time you left me at home with the cat while you all went on a mission, someone set fire to the house."

Harlow smacked her sister lightly on the arm. "The cheek on you."

Larkin grinned. "A bit of gallows humor wins the day."

Finn didn't laugh. In fact, as they'd prepared to meet his father, he'd retreated further and further into himself. He kissed Larkin's cheek as they left, though. Harlow didn't press him to talk as they drove through the empty Nea Sterlis streets and parked in front of the Grand. Finn sat quiet for a moment before turning to Harlow.

"When I ask you to go to the car, do it without arguing," he said, his voice solemn. He wouldn't meet her eyes.

Harlow's heart thumped wildly. "What? Why would I need to do that?"

"I will need someone to drive me home," Finn replied, in a tone so dark she didn't dare ask another question. Whatever she'd thought they were here to do, she realized she'd been very, *very* wrong. Dread pooled in her stomach.

They got out of the car and went into the hotel. Finn's grip on her hand was tight, so tight she could tell he was holding back, trying not to hurt her. His skin had taken on a deathly pallor, and a bright sheen of sweat covered his forehead, despite the cool night air.

The clerk at the desk looked surprised to see them, which was understandable, given the lockdown. "Please let my father know we're here," Finn asked.

The clerk nodded, stepping into a booth behind the front desk where there was an internal intercom, rather than using the phone at the desk that probably didn't work now. Harlow knew better than to say anything here, but she wanted to beg Finn to get back in the car. Surely, whatever was about to happen here couldn't be the only way. Finn looked down at her, his stormy eyes wide with fear. That's when she understood. Wherever Cian had been taken, they'd never be rescued, never be found.

The Illuminated could do whatever they wanted with the Argent. Whatever was about to happen was their only chance to get Cian back in one piece. This was the real reason he hadn't told Alaric and the others what they were going to do. Alaric and Petra never would have let him come here. They knew better, but she hadn't.

Tears threatened in her eyes, welling at the hopelessness of the situation.

"Please don't," Finn whispered. "This is the only way."

She nodded, pulling herself together as well as she could. He was so fucking brave she couldn't stand it—couldn't stand the purity of his conviction and his devotion to the people he loved. He would walk through fire for any of them, she was utterly convinced.

What would he do if it were her that was captured? She pushed the thought away, knowing the answer. Finn McKay would destroy worlds to get to her. She didn't know what Connor would make Finn do to get Cian back, but whatever it was, it frightened him. The least she could do in this moment was to be as brave as he was.

The clerk called out to them. "You can go up. He's waiting for you."

The elevator ride was brutal on her heart. The silence between them was thick with unsaid promises. Harlow was afraid to speak, so she tightened her grip on Finn's hand. When the elevator door opened, he murmured to her, "Remember what I said. Don't argue."

Harlow nodded. She wanted to fight him, but she agreed anyway. The look on his face wouldn't let her argue with him now. The fear was gone, replaced by steely determination. Determination, she realized as he squared his shoulders, to be brave in the face of the only thing he truly feared: his father.

So she squared her own shoulders, lengthening her spine and smoothing her face into an imperious mask. It was one of Selene's best faces, she knew, and she wore it now with pride. The two of them didn't look so much alike for nothing, and she carried Mama's sheer audacity with her now, grateful that each muscle in her body knew this by heart.

Finn glanced down at her as they walked into the penthouse suite, and a flicker of pride shone in his eyes. "Great Raia." He kissed her palm. "You are a vision."

She gave him her best Selene-takes-no-prisoners smile, and she saw the emotion in his eyes retreat. The creature before her now was the Finn McKay people feared. Fearless, steadfast, lethal. They walked into the monster's lair ready to be brave, or so Harlow thought, but nothing could prepare her for the scene in the penthouse living room.

There was blood everywhere, but no bodies. No bones, no gore. Just blood pooled on the floor, splattered on the walls, staining the rich carpets and upholstered furniture. And all over Connor's face and hands. Clearly, he'd been feeding. On whom, Harlow couldn't guess, but the scene suggested it had been more than one person.

He smiled politely at the two of them, but there was a feverish look in his eyes Harlow didn't trust. "I wasn't expecting guests," he said, his tone casual as he wiped his mouth with a hanky he pulled from his pocket.

"Where is Cian?" Finn asked, ignoring the carnage before them completely.

Probably best, Harlow thought. *We're here for a reason. Better to stay focused.*

Connor smiled. "Whatever do you mean?"

Harlow honestly couldn't tell if he was mocking Finn, or if he was confused by the question.

Finn's voice was steady. "Don't play games, Father. I know you took Cian from Haven."

"Ah, Haven," Connor said as he sank into a formal chair at the dining table.

"They've done nothing wrong," Finn reasoned. "Give them back."

"Nothing wrong? Your little plan to undermine my authority was ill conceived, my boy. I know you think you've kept your plans a secret from me, but I've always known you were helping humans." Connor paused, his head tilting to the side in mock-thoughtfulness. "What I can't understand is why you didn't just tell me what you wanted to do. There was no need to keep it a secret. I would have funded your efforts, happily."

Harlow struggled to keep her heart beating normally as Connor spoke. *He didn't know.* He didn't know the true extent of Haven, or that the Knights of

Serpens were the ones who ran the project. Finn squeezed her hand slightly, a reassurance.

"Then you won't have any issue giving Cian back," Finn said. "If someone needs to be punished for the transgression, let it be me."

Connor laughed. "Always the hero, aren't you my boy?"

Finn said nothing in response, but he glanced down at Harlow. The gravity of his expression was a reminder that she was not to argue. Her chin quivered for half a second before she steadied it. This would be like when he was a little boy in the basement. She understood why she was here now—why he didn't want to come alone. Every fiber of her being fought against what would come next.

Connor's voice broke through the syrupy fear that clouded her thoughts. "Let's get to it then, my boy. Will you let her watch you take your punishment?"

"No," Finn said, not sparing even a glance for Connor. "Wait for me in the car."

"All right," she said, staring straight into his eyes. She'd promised not to argue, but she wouldn't be in the car, nor the lobby, nor even the elevator. Right outside the door; *that* is where she'd be when Finn had done what he needed to here.

Connor laughed as she turned to go, and the sound of his laughter enraged her, but Finn's eyes pleaded with her: *Let me do this. Let me save Cian.* She didn't let go of his hand until the very last second possible. Leaving him here, to whatever was about to happen, was unimaginable. But she understood why she was. He would do anything for his family. Anything.

And *she* would do anything for him. Including waiting right outside the door, no matter what she heard, no matter how much she wanted to rescue her love, she would wait for him here. She felt for the threads that connected them; trying something new, sending waves of her love down the ones connected to him. Harlow only hoped he could feel it now. As the door to the suite closed behind her, she understood with heartbreaking clarity that she wouldn't be able to rescue him, even if she wanted to.

The wards sealed around the door as it closed, the knob searing her fingers the instant they went up. Even the connection she'd felt to Finn via the threads was gone now. Her teeth grit in fury as she stumbled backwards. Tears streamed down her face as she sunk to the floor. The wards were so good that even with her enhanced hearing there wasn't a sound coming from the suite.

Her eyes fell closed, and she reached for her shadows. They had to stay buried within her, but she needed their comfort now. She dropped deep inside her mind, finding the little portal within herself where her shadows originated from, a mere pinprick of a thing, deep in her second sight. They were there waiting for her, and as her spirit body approached, they sucked her through that tiny portal into the limen.

She wasn't in Nihil this time, or at least not the part where the wardens slept, but a quieter place. Raw aether pooled around her feet in billowing, midnight blue clouds. Her shadows joined their own kind, blending into their source, losing a bit of their individual sentience. This place was soothing in its darkness.

There was just enough light to see by here, flashes of lightning in the distance, dim through the thick clouds of aether. Nothing was familiar about this location. She seemed to stand on an abandoned city street. Strange architecture rose up around her as she walked, hallmarked by sinuously curving lines and glass arches; all with a sensual organic grace that was as beautiful as it was imposing. Some menace threatened this place, deep and pervasive, whatever it was. Harlow had never seen the like. There was no way this place represented anywhere on Okairos. The limen often reproduced bits and pieces of the worlds it touched for brief periods of time, but this was clearer than Harlow had imagined it could be.

A figure walked in front of her, a woman, Harlow thought, a bit shorter than herself, with generously curved hips and narrow shoulders. She couldn't make much else out about her, but she walked with purpose. Harlow followed her, curious about the soul within. Something about her burned brightly in Harlow's vision. Of course, there were no threads here. The limen was not the same kind of reality as Okairos. Everything here was pure aether.

Soft footsteps walked next to her, and Harlow looked up. The Ventyr next to her was immediately recognizable. He was taller than she'd imagined, standing next to her now. His long hair flowed freely to his waist and his wings moved slightly with him as he walked.

"Ashbourne," she said.

"Yes," he said. His body wasn't fully corporeal here. This was an astral projection. His eyes were fixed on the figure.

"Is that Lumina?" Harlow asked, going on a hunch.

He looked down at her, his head dipping as he did so. "I believe it might be, but I cannot tell."

"A curse," she mused.

"Indeed. But I wonder, little one, what do *you* see?"

Harlow looked hard at the figure ahead of them now. "Nothing distinguishable, but there is something familiar about her. Do I know her?"

Ashbourne smiled. "Yes… No… Perhaps."

Harlow rolled her eyes. "That's not much of an answer."

"Look again," he pleaded.

She did, and then she saw it again: the light within the figure. "There is a light in her, a dark light."

"Yes," Ashbourne said, his voice interminably sad. "I was afraid you would say that."

"What do you mean?" Harlow asked.

Lumina, if that is who she was, walked faster now, and they had to rush to keep up. As she rounded a corner, the scene changed. Now they were in a forest of tall conifers, and several figures fought against one girl. The same dark light shone within her that had in Lumina, except this girl was familiar to her. She recognized her face somehow, but she couldn't remember why. The girl was fast, her voluptuous body bending and weaving as she defeated each of her foes, seemingly without effort.

"Who is she?" Harlow asked. "Do I know *her*?"

She wanted answers. Why had he brought her here like this? She needed to be back in the real world, waiting for Finn.

Ashbourne shrugged. "Who can say? Perhaps an echo of someone you met once."

An echo? That made no sense whatsoever. "Why are you showing me this?"

Ashbourne laughed. "I'm not showing you anything, little bird. You are showing me."

"How?" Harlow asked.

"Your stories must be woven together somehow," Ashbourne suggested. "Whatever the reason, your time here must end."

Harlow opened her mouth to argue, but the winged god before her, for that was how he seemed to her—a god—shook his head. "He will need you. Do not come looking for me again. Not here, nor in the waking world. I do not have the answers you seek."

He was fading now; she could hardly hear him as she felt herself sucked back into her body. "Leave what's beneath the Spire be, little bird," she heard as she opened her eyes. "Let Nihil's guardians keep you safe."

Back in her body, in the hallway outside Connor McKay's hotel room, her tears had long-since dried on her face. She checked her phone—somehow an hour had passed. Where was Finn? She leapt up, about to pound on the door to the suite, wards be damned, when it opened.

Finn stood there alone, his face bloodied and swelling, his shirt soaked in blood. He stumbled forward, into her arms. Connor McKay stood behind his son, wearing clean clothes and a smile. "Have a good evening," he said as he moved forward to close the door.

Finn's weight was heavy on her, and he mumbled something. "Don't."

She couldn't help herself. As she adjusted his body, she looked back at Connor McKay. "You should be ashamed of yourself."

Surprise lit the heinous immortal's face. How long had it been since someone talked back to him? She knew she was playing with fire, but she'd never been very good at knowing when to keep her mouth shut. Even when things were at their worst with Mark, she'd get in one last word, seemingly just to see if she could make him angrier. That same foolishness had her in its grip now.

"I'll make you pay for this someday, Connor McKay. Mark my words, I'll make you pay."

Something like respect tinged the laugh that escaped Connor's throat. "I'll look forward to you trying, Harlow." He stepped forward. "It will be a pleasure to break you."

Finn roared, his broken body lurching forward. Harlow pulled him back, putting a little of her own magic into her grip. Connor laughed as he stepped back into his suite, shaking his head. "The two of you will learn the hard way then. So be it."

He shut the door and Finn stumbled. "Let's go," he slurred, his mouth too swollen to speak clearly. Tears rolled down her face, but Harlow nodded, helping Finn into the elevator.

~

Somehow, Harlow got Finn into the car. Once they'd exited the Grand, she couldn't hold her fear back any longer, and it all broke loose in a torrent of sobs. Finn, damaged as he was, tried to comfort her.

"Be quiet," she begged, fastening his seatbelt. "Just be quiet until I can get you home."

He nodded, groggy. She hated to hurt him, but she shook his arm. "Stay awake… I think you need to try to stay awake, at least 'til you can shift."

Harlow knew that he'd heal faster in his true form, so she drove as fast as she possibly could. The streets of Nea Sterlis were empty. Her mind was thrown back to the night she killed Mark. Wasn't it just like this? Her driving him, broken and battered through town—her scared for his life. At least this time she knew what would help him.

Finn wasn't in any danger of dying, but somehow that made what Connor had done that much worse. He'd done it for the sake of doing it. Because something in him got off on hurting one of the few people in this world that might ever have truly loved him back. She'd meant what she said in the hotel; someday she would find a way to make Connor McKay regret his choices regarding his son.

They'd driven out of the city proper and were on residential streets now. "Shift," she whispered. It was only a few more minutes to the villa, but still, every moment counted. He didn't open his eyes, but his glamour fell away. He'd already started to heal, but now his progress was more rapid. His face looked better almost instantly.

His head moved in her peripheral vision. He was looking at her. "You really let Connor have an earful."

Harlow shook her head. "He deserved it."

Finn coughed, and she heard a soft crackling noise. He grimaced as he gripped his ribs, which were likely healing. "He did."

"Where is Cian? When do we get them back?"

Finn growled. "We don't. The Dominavus don't have Cian."

"What?" Harlow's voice was shrill, nearly a shriek. "Then what was the *point* of that?"

Finn groaned as another rib crackled back into place. "He had to punish me for lying about Haven. Said he went easy on me since it wasn't an exchange for Cian's life."

Harlow pulled the car into the driveway, but didn't drive up to the house. She wanted to be clear on what they'd just done before they saw Larkin. "So where is Cian?"

Finn shook his head. "I have no idea. Connor doesn't know."

"And does he know about the Knights? About what we're doing?"

His long arm snaked out, and he pulled her to him by the chin. He kissed her gently, then sighed. "No, he doesn't know."

"Then why the fuck did you let him do this to you?" Harlow sobbed, tears falling in hot streams down her cheeks.

Finn grinned that crooked grin. "Because he thinks I'm still under his control. That I'll submit, without even so much as an order from him."

"You planned this?" Now she really *was* shrieking. "Did you know he had no idea where Cian was?"

Finn shrugged. "No, I knew there was a possibility…"

"*What possibility?*"

Finn winced. "You really don't know?"

She sat back, slamming her head against the headrest in frustration. Her eyes fell closed as she sighed. She played with the pieces of everything they knew. Cian was missing. A witness said the Dominavus took them, but Connor said they didn't. *How could it be both?*

Her mind drifted to the creature in the bushes at the fountain—the one the auburn cat and Samira had fought. In all that had happened, they hadn't discussed it yet, but her suspicions were firming up now. There had been a dog following her that day on her way to the Citadel, and Rakul had said he preferred dogs over cats. She'd just thought he was distracting himself from the pain of the binding at the time, but now she understood.

Her eyes flew open. "The Argent powering the Archean vascularity is Vivia Woolf."

Finn nodded; he'd put it all together as well. "Rakul Kimaris has Cian, and he's going to get his mate back on the night of the Hallowed Moon. We've led him right to her."

CHAPTER 30

It took Finn two days to recover, and much as Harlow had wanted to spend it in bed with him, she and Larkin moved all the family's private business into the Vault instead. There was only one possible plan: stop Rakul from using Cian to replace Vivia at the vascularity, rescue Cian, meet everyone at the plane on Santos and get to a safehouse. If Finn was going to be strong enough to teleport the five of them out, then he had to rest, and Harlow and Larkin had to ready the villa to be left for an undetermined amount of time.

The morning of the Equinox, they had all the windows open on the main floor. The rains had set in, so a chill autumnal breeze blew through the house. Axel sat on the kitchen counter, sniffing the air as Larkin and Harlow cleaned out the fridge.

She was throwing herself into menial tasks, trying to tamp down her frustration. *Why had she trusted Rakul so implicitly?* She was furious at herself for putting Cian in danger like this. If she'd just been a little more cautious, just taken a little more time to think, this wouldn't be happening.

"I kind of hate to do this to all these lovely condiments," Larkin said as she tossed a jar of expensive capers into the trash.

They'd made exactly a dozen different snacks as they'd gone through the food, and Finn was sitting at the counter eating a huge plate of nachos in his pajamas. He *looked* fine, Harlow thought, at least on the surface. But he'd been quieter since the night at the Grand. He smiled at Larkin's jokes, but he didn't laugh. All three of them were doing their best to make it to the Hallowed Moon in one piece, but none of them were doing well.

Harlow hadn't pushed Finn to talk about things, but she hadn't ignored it either. She left the door open between them; he just hadn't been ready to walk through yet. He was staring out at the rain now, lost in thought, and she reached out to grab his hand. He startled slightly, then his lips quirked up when he real-ized it was her who'd touched him.

His fingers wound through hers and he stroked her palm with his thumb. The movement was innocent enough, but a little tingle of desire flickered through her. She blushed. The fervor was gone now, but her primal need for him hadn't disappeared. Now was probably not the time though… His thumb moved down her palm again, slower this time, languorous even.

The breeze hit the bare skin of her shoulders and she shivered, feeling the sensation between her legs and in the heaviness of her breasts. Her breath quick-ened and when she looked up, Finn's eyes burned with the same desire she felt now.

Larkin made a gagging noise and Harlow whipped around. "Is something gross?" Thea was the one who was rabid about keeping the fridge cleaned out. It was totally possible something had gone bad since she left.

"Yes," Larkin said, rolling her eyes. "You two. Please, go get it on in private if you're gonna act like that." She laughed then. "Really, go—I've got the fridge… And the dishes… Please, I will do *anything* to get you out of here, even chores."

She popped her earbuds in and Harlow heard her turn the music up. A symphony played in Larkin's ears and she smiled, saying too loudly, "Couldn't hear a thing if I wanted to. Wards are up. Get going, lovers."

Finn smiled at Harlow. "She's right. Let's go upstairs."

She let him lead her up the stairs, and she watched every flex of his muscles, every step, with raptorial intensity. He seemed fine enough, but it wasn't his body she was worried about now, it was his heart.

When the door to their bedroom shut, she turned to him. "We don't have to do anything. We can just lay down together."

"I want to," he said as he drew her towards him. His voice heated as his fingers skimmed over her hips and waist. "I need to be inside you."

She felt his words everywhere and lifted her face, her lips parting. When his mouth met hers, his kiss was soft at first, tentative. As her hands roamed over his chest and into his hair, he groaned in her mouth, deepening the kiss. She felt his need as his tongue danced with hers, his cock hardening between them.

She pulled his shirt off, throwing it to the floor as she trailed kisses down his neck and chest, pausing to tease each of his nipples as she pushed his joggers down. His fingers combed through her loose hair as hers went around his cock. When she was on her knees in front of him she looked up at him.

His mouth was open and his fangs protracted as her mouth closed around his cock. He moaned softly as she took him deeper into her throat, breathing steadily through her nose.

"Yes," he moaned as she dragged him out of her mouth, using her saliva to wet her hand and stroke his cock. Again and again, she took him into her mouth, using her hands to create seamless pressure as she licked and sucked him.

He pulled her up towards him, pulling her sweatpants off as he pushed her onto the bed. His fingers drifted up her thighs.

"Why'd you stop me?" she asked.

One finger slid between her drenched folds. "Because I want to come here," he said as he pushed another finger inside her. His glamour fell away and his fingers lengthened, filling her. He pulled them from her body and lowered himself onto her. As the head of his cock pushed into her, he propped himself up so he could look into her eyes.

"I love you more than anything in the world," he said, voice solemn as a saint, expression just as reverent.

Her fingers ran over the angles of his beautiful Ventyr features, sharp and angular. Still her Finn, but something more as well.

"I love you," she whispered back as he moved slowly inside her. Heat built as the friction between them sent ripples of ecstasy through her. Her back arched as her pleasure mounted, the glow of his desire winding with her dark shadows, which had emerged.

His fangs plunged into her neck as he thrust harder into her, and every nerve in her body lit aflame. When he licked her clean euphoria rushed through her, her orgasm playing like music over her body in waves as he watched her.

"Just like that," he murmured.

When her orgasm peaked, her own fangs emerged and as she screamed his name, she latched onto his neck, pulling his sweet immortal blood into her mouth. Her eyes fell closed as she enjoyed every inch of him. The sounds he made as he drove into her, while she in turn, impaled him, were beyond exquisite. It felt like they were floating. Each crescendo of pleasure was that much better than the last.

Harlow opened her eyes to find that, in fact, they *were* floating, his wings and their combined magic holding them aloft. Her fangs retracted, and she looked down at the bed, laughing softly. "That's new."

He grinned as they fell to the bed, their concentration lost. It was good to see him *really* smile again. They collapsed against one another, breathing hard from their encounter.

"Should we try to make some kind of plan for tonight?" she asked. They hadn't talked about it much, just the bare facts, really, and what had to be done to prepare to leave the villa.

Finn shrugged, his glamour returning as he pulled her into his arms and under the covers. They'd opened the windows up here too and the rain had started up again outside. "I figure we'll go in through the fountain. My guess is that something about the equinox will trigger the door opening if we're in the right place at the right time."

"And then what? We'll just ask Rakul nicely to give Cian back?"

Finn's expression darkened. "I doubt it will be that easy."

"Do you think we'll need the Feriant?"

"I hope not. You and Larkin stay back, if you can. Help Cian get out."

Harlow shook her head. "No, Larkin can help Cian. I'm staying with you this time."

He opened his mouth, and she shut it with a kiss. "Don't argue," she said against his lips. His returning kiss accepted defeat, quite gracefully, she thought as she climbed on top of him. They had at least an hour before they had to be ready to go, and she wasn't wasting another moment of it.

CHAPTER 31

The three of them, with Axel in a compact backpack especially for carrying pets, made their way to Sistren of Akatei Library under cover of darkness. The rain had abated for the time being, but the night was cloudy. There were no fires on the ridges tonight because of the lockdown, and the usual local festival had been canceled.

They had to go slow, ducking into alleys and doorways periodically to avoid the Illuminated troops that patrolled the streets. "This is going to take forever," Larkin grumbled as they hid, crouched behind a stinking restaurant dumpster that hadn't been emptied since the lockdown began.

In his carrier on Finn's back, Axel growled, also unhappy. "Hush, bub," Finn ordered, and the black cat shut up immediately.

Harlow couldn't help but smile, despite the circumstances. When Finn looked back at her she mouthed, *Cat Dad Extraordinaire.* Somewhere in the distance, there was an explosion. Larkin jumped, hiding behind Finn's considerable bulk.

"What's happening?" Harlow asked, craning her neck to try to see past Finn.

He slipped out of the backpack, handing it to her. "Put this on." When she had Axel securely on her back, he bent to kiss her. "Stay here, okay. I'm going to see what's going on, and I'll circle back."

He tapped the analog watch she wore tonight. "If I'm not back in five minutes, I want you to head back to the villa and get to Santos on your own. Use the boat tied up at the dock."

"I'm not leaving without you," she whispered.

"I'll be back in five minutes," he countered.

She nodded. When he was gone, she took Axel's carrier off and gave it to Larkin. "If he is not back in five minutes, I will shift into the Feriant, you will stay hidden here, and I will go get Finn."

Larkin nodded. "I like your plan better."

Harlow smiled at her youngest sister and they huddled together as she watched the seconds tick by. The sound of gunfire drew closer and, above their heads, several bottle rockets went off. The quiet of the Nea Sterlis lockdown was shattered as people moved through the streets. Many had weapons made from a pale wood that caught the light.

She ducked back behind the dumpster, whispering to Larkin, "Some of them have white ash."

Larkin's eyes went wide. "What? How is that possible?"

Harlow shook her head, looking at her watch. Finn had been gone for five minutes and three seconds. She took a deep breath; she had no idea how white ash might affect her—if she were from a purely sorcière lineage, it would harm her, but wouldn't incapacitate her or kill her—but with the fact that she had Illuminated heritage, she couldn't say. Whatever the case, she wasn't leaving Finn out there to fend for himself.

"Move back a little," she urged Larkin. "I'm kind of… huge… when I shift."

Larkin nodded, her eyes wide and frightened.

"What are you still doing here?" Finn hissed as he ducked behind the dumpster. He was grinning like a fool; he'd known she wouldn't leave him.

She hugged him tight and the three of them huddled close. There were crowds in the street now. "I think the Humanists are here," Finn breathed. "A lot of them have white ash weapons."

Harlow nodded. "So what do we do? We'll never make it to the Citadel this way."

"If the two of you help, I think we can teleport to the library without much trouble, and it won't drain my resources much."

Larkin and Harlow both nodded as they took hands. Harlow dug deep into her well of power, drawing aether from the threads around them, as well as the pinprick portal into the limen within her. Finn shuddered a little as she directed her power into him.

"Not too much," he warned. "You need to be able to fight."

She smiled. "It's no trouble, McKay. I've got plenty."

His eyes widened with pride. "That's my girl," he said, and they blinked out of the alley.

THE LIBRARY'S courtyard was dead silent in comparison to the chaos that had taken over below. Harlow's ears rang for a moment as she adjusted to the quiet, and the force by which they'd teleported.

"Everyone okay?" she asked Finn and Larkin.

Larkin nodded, but she looked slightly ill. Teleporting made nearly everyone sick unless they were used to it. Finn shrugged. "I feel great. To be honest, I'm starting to think you could probably teleport on your own now. How do *you* feel?"

Harlow shrugged. "Fine."

"No energy drain? No nausea?"

She shook her head. "No, I feel fine."

Finn shook his head. "We're going to look into that tomorrow, okay?"

She smiled. "Sure. Let's get going."

They made their way through the maze of flowers and hedges to the fountain. Harlow couldn't figure out what felt wrong with the courtyard until it came into view: it was the silence, of course. The courtyard had never been silent before, because of the running water from the fountain.

As they approached it, they saw that the fountain was still, and completely drained of water. "He's already here," Finn said, pointing to the staircase that the dry fountain had exposed.

"Darn," Larkin said, her voice dry. "I was really hoping we were going to have to answer some sort of obscure riddle to get down there."

Finn smirked, but then his expression grew serious. "Just like we talked about, okay? Larkin, you stay back and get ready to get Cian out. We don't know what kind of shape they'll be in. Harls, you're with me."

Harlow nodded. "Leave Axel on and run if things get hairy, okay?"

Larkin hugged Harlow. "We'll be fine." She hugged Finn too. "We'll get Cian and this will all be over fast."

Harlow knew that Larkin's extra-bright outlook was a coping mechanism. She was scared, and Harlow couldn't blame her. What they were about to do was probably stupid, and completely terrifying. Rakul Kimaris was a seasoned soldier, and Finn, while a talented fighter, was not.

They were all banking on the fact that Harlow's magic, and her ability to turn into the Feriant, might turn the tides of the fight, if it came to that. But both Harlow and Finn still hoped they could talk Rakul out of whatever he had planned and get them both out safely.

Harlow felt there had to be a way to free Vivia from the vascularity, but they needed more time to figure things out. She just hoped Rakul could hear her. As they descended the dark stairs, Finn lit the way with a bit of magic.

"Let me talk to him first, okay?" she whispered as they took turn after turn.

Finn nodded, concentrating on the way ahead. "You can give it a try." He looked back. "But if it were you, and this was my chance to get you back..." He shook his head. "I'd be ready to kill anyone who got in my way."

"Why hasn't he come before this?" Larkin asked, her voice quiet behind them.

Harlow shrugged. "I don't think he knew how to get down here."

"I think the little temple in the nekropoleis was the original entrance to wherever we're going," Finn said. "I have a feeling they're connected somehow."

Harlow agreed. They were both temples devoted to Akatei; it made sense that somehow they were both connected to this place. Whatever was down here, however it got here, this all started a long, long time ago. She wondered if they'd ever really know the truth about what had made the portal, and why the Illuminated had contained it this way.

"Careful," Finn cautioned. "We're almost to the bottom. Let me see what's ahead."

Harlow looked up, but all she could see was stairs and Larkin. When Finn moved forward, his smile was tight. "It's really something down here. This must be a part of the catacombs under the temple."

When Harlow stepped off the last stair, she saw what he meant. The way was lit by torches with strange blue flames, and they cast a weak gray light onto the walls.

"Oh, that's just wrong," Larkin said as she stepped down after Harlow. "Who makes whole walls from people's skulls?"

"Our ancestors, silly," Harlow said, keeping her voice low.

Larkin grimaced.

"We should try to be as quiet as possible from here on out, okay?" Finn cautioned. Both sisters nodded in agreement and they made their way into the hall that stretched ahead. The ceilings were arched, and made from the same alabaster as the temple itself. Periodically, intricately carved stone plaques were interspersed between the skulls.

They depicted a story of sorts. In the first one she noticed, there were two winged people, Ventyr children. Though Harlow wasn't completely sure what was being depicted, she understood that the next few plaques showed them growing into adults. In different phases of their growth, different creatures and activities were shown, though to keep up with Finn, Harlow couldn't stop for long enough to examine them closely. The last that depicted the Ventyr pair showed one of them performing a ritual while the other looked to be asleep.

The final plaque depicted two rows of what Harlow assumed to be portals, and the Ventyr that had performed the ritual. In each one, horrible things were happening. Harlow couldn't stand to look for long. This vaguely reminded her of the little book of poetry Thea had found. Could this be part of the story that she'd read? Another set of panels began, but whatever they depicted was lost. Someone had destroyed each of them with a sharp implement.

The tunnel didn't smell musty, as she'd expected it to. In fact, it smelled distinctly like water. As they moved further along, Harlow heard the sound of a river, or more accurately, she felt its presence. The sound itself was quite faint, but the feeling amplified it in her mind. Could the Pyriphle run here as well? That might make sense, given Cian and Finn's suppositions about it. She paused for a moment and pressed the side of her head to one of the damaged stone plaques.

Finn stopped to watch her. "What are you doing?"

"Don't you hear the water?"

Finn gave her a quizzical look, tilting his head. "Sort of."

She drew back from the wall, surprised. "Really? You don't hear it?"

Finn shook his head, and when she turned to ask Larkin, her sister also indicated that she didn't hear the water. Finn took her hand. "Is it the Pyriphle? Do you hear its call?"

Harlow squinted. Somehow that made it easier to listen. Yes, she heard the rushing water, but mostly what she thought she heard was not a noise at all; it was the silent call to the limen, to the heart—to Nihil. Now that she recognized it, it was more than noise; it was a song, an invitation.

When the path branched in three directions, Finn was perplexed, but she was not. "It's this one," she said, pointing to the path that veered furthest left and downward.

He didn't ask how she knew. He obviously remembered all too well how she'd rushed towards the river in the cavern under the Vault. "Are you okay to do this?" he whispered.

"Yes," she said, with confidence she wasn't sure she had. What other choice did they have? Cian's life was at stake.

When the river's song sounded like it had a vocal accompaniment, she began to worry, but Finn turned. "Okay, that's chanting, isn't it?"

Larkin nodded. "Definitely."

Harlow shrugged. "Sure."

Finn kept moving forward, and as they rounded a sharp corner, he pushed them back, then peeked around. He motioned for them to stay silent and take a few steps backwards. He pushed Harlow forward and made the motion for Larkin to stay put. She nodded, understanding that she should stay here until someone brought Cian to her or called for her.

Harlow stepped forward and peeked around the corner. An enormous cavern with carved walls spread out before them. Rakul Kimaris faced away from where she stood, and he was chanting over a huddled form, with a silver shock of hair. *Cian.*

But her focus could not linger there, due to the beautiful woman who was suspended in a grotesque web of aether at the other end of the room. The physical aspects of the vascularity were horrifying. It looked like a web of organic veins, pulsing with power, feeding into a firedrake. From what Harlow could see, removing the Argent would be nearly impossible to do from a purely physical perspective, as the vascularity itself was connected to her spinal column, and likely her brain.

Vivia Woolf's hair was long and silver, though her face was young. She was as pale as Cian, though they did not look alike otherwise. Her features were broad, with high cheekbones and a generous mouth. Vivia was tiny—very likely shorter than Kate, in Harlow's estimation. Her eyes were closed, but she did not appear to be resting peacefully. Every so often, a little surge of power in the vascularity jolted her, and she made a soft noise that echoed throughout the room.

Harlow motioned to Finn that she was going to approach Rakul, and he nodded. He would hang back for a moment and see how things went. He squeezed her hand reassuringly and then she stepped into the cavern, making sure to step heavily.

Rakul turned, his chanting dying on his lips. "I'll have to start over, little bird."

Harlow nodded. "You might have to. Could we talk first?"

Rakul sighed. "Please don't try to convince me to stop. You'll only be wasting your time."

"How can you even be down here, with the binding?" Harlow asked, respecting his wishes for the time being. She moved towards him, and though he eyed her warily, he did not make a move against her.

Harlow dared a glance down at Cian, who she could see now was bound and gagged, but conscious. They blinked once at her and nodded to show they were all right. There wasn't a mark on them; Rakul had been gentle enough, she supposed.

"They never thought I'd find my way back to this place, so it wasn't a part of the binding," Rakul said, shaking his head. "And until you started looking for it, I never thought I would either. But you led me right to it."

"Ashbourne can't help me, can he?" Harlow asked. "You just wanted me to find this place for you."

Rakul nodded. "Yes, I'm sorry to have lied to you about all that."

Harlow believed that he was sorry. The slump in his proud shoulders told the tale. "And you tricked us—didn't you? Using Vivia's name at Cerberus to get Finn and Cian to leave Nea Sterlis?"

Again, Rakul nodded. "Yes, I had to get Finn at least out of the way so the two of you wouldn't figure things out." Rakul paused, sorrow clouding his eyes. "I wish I could have helped you in some way. And I am sorry about Cian, but you'll find a way to get them out."

Harlow heard the pain in his voice; there was no doubt in her mind that this was wretched for him. He thought only of Vivia, and seeing her for herself, Harlow understood. She didn't want to leave the Argent here either. But what Rakul wanted to do was dangerous. They didn't know what could happen, and she wasn't about to let Cian be put up there in Vivia's place. "It's a risk taking her down, Rakul. We don't know what it might let out."

Rakul's eyes were full of pain. "She has been up there for nearly two thousand years. Don't you think she's had enough?"

Harlow stepped forward, reaching out towards Rakul. "Of course I do, and we'll find a way to help her, I promise, but it's too dangerous to let the vascularity go down for even a few moments."

He was shaking his head, losing patience with her. She saw that and spoke faster. "Just give me some time, and we'll come back and close the portal for good, and she'll be free."

He quieted for a moment, staring at his love, and then his shoulders slumped in defeat. Relief washed over her. She stepped forward, reaching out to touch Rakul's arm. "I can work on getting the binding removed for you too, Rakul."

The vascularity pulsed with light, causing both Harlow and Rakul to turn. Vivia's eyes flickered open. "Don't do this," she whispered. "Do not break the spell, my love. You know I have to stay. This was my choice."

Rakul growled in fury, beating his fists to his chest. "But you didn't give *me* one. I didn't choose to live this life without you, nothing more than the Duke's enforcer."

Harlow's heart lumped in her throat as she reached out to comfort Rakul. She didn't know who the Duke was—maybe Connor—but the pain emanating from him was visceral.

A single tear marred Vivia's ethereal face. "I am still here. Still yours. And still committed to protect this world at all costs. You know what will happen if I fail. You must go."

The words the firedrake spoke seemed to drain all her energy. Her head drooped and she appeared to lose consciousness, though Harlow couldn't be sure. Rakul tensed visibly. She hadn't realized she was still touching him, and it surprised her when he launched into action. His arm pulled back from her touch, and he spun so quickly she didn't even see him move. He had hold of her arm before she could snatch it away, tossing her like a rag doll towards the entrance to the cavern. She slammed into something pliable.

Finn. He'd been rushing to her rescue. She tucked her body like she'd been taught and rolled, shouting, "Go!" as he crouched to check on her.

He sprung into action, shedding his glamour immediately. Rakul did as well, and they circled one another, Cian at the center. Finn lunged for Rakul, and Harlow could see it was a mistake the moment he did it, but she also understood why he'd taken the risk of letting Rakul get a hold of him.

Cian was left unguarded. Harlow rushed forward, dragging Cian out of the center of what appeared to be a sunburst, carved into the floor. As she dragged her friend out, she focused on loosening their bonds.

"Go," she said, pushing them toward Larkin's open arms as soon as they were free and moving.

She didn't wait to make sure they left, but turned back to the fight she could hear raging behind her. For a split second it looked as though Finn might be winning, but Rakul's body twisted like liquid, out of Finn's grip.

And in a movement Harlow's sorcière eyes could not follow, Rakul gained the upper hand, slamming Finn into the wall with such force he passed out immediately. Harlow cried out, rushing toward Finn with no thought for herself, and as she did, she caught sight of movement behind Vivia and the vascularity.

In the shadows, creatures were gathering, swarming, really. Harlow was immobilized by the sight of them. They were horrifying, vaguely humanoid forms. Their limbs were pale, and far too long, their hands and feet tipped with razor-sharp talons. Their heads reminded her a little of insects—perhaps it was the eyes, or the tiny mouths.

"The Vespae," Rakul said. "We locked them into the breach when we closed it. They were killing everything on this planet. The breach somehow made them stronger. It was one of ours that opened it, you know? Cut across all kinds of worlds, using his sister's power. Such a mistake."

Harlow listened to him, not knowing what to do. He was clearly in distress, and she didn't want to provoke him into more violence. "This is how the Illuminated manipulated the people here? They closed the breach and stopped the Vespae?"

Rakul laughed. "Yes, and the fools gave up all their power in the process. Did you know humans could do magic when we came here? It was incredible. Never saw anything like it on another world."

Harlow inched closer to Finn. He was breathing, but she didn't dare lunge for him.

Rakul stared at Vivia. "Make no mistake, we lost plenty of our own locking those creatures in with the Ravagers. It was a bloodbath."

Harlow had finally reached Finn. She bent down—his pulse was strong, and at her touch, he stirred. He would be fine. She left his side to try reasoning with Rakul once more. "Please. If you bring her down from there, it will let them loose on the world. Maybe even the Ravagers."

Rakul's expression was pained. "Yes, it will, and I am sorry for it. Close the breach with your Argent. My Vivia's time is served."

Before she could even think to shift, he'd tossed her to the side again, and she hit her head on the wall, hard enough to stun her. Finn came around just in time for them to watch Rakul Kimaris pull Vivia Woolf from the vascularity by force.

It did not want to let her go, but Rakul was determined, and the ritual he'd been doing had apparently loosened her enough that the vascularity stretched, pulling at her spinal cord. She let out an infernal noise, more than a scream, a sound of unbearable pain. Tears ran down Rakul's face as he pulled a sword from the scabbard strapped to his back. He sliced through the sinew of the vascularity, careful not to cut Vivia herself. Her screaming stopped, and it was obvious from the look on Rakul's face that he'd made the decision to free Vivia whether she lived or not. He gave Harlow a long, lingering look of sorrow—and then they were gone, teleported out.

Time slowed as the vascularity faltered. Without Vivia, it didn't have enough power to cover the breach. The Vespae whipped into a frenzy, surging against the weakening barrier.

"What in seventeen hells is going on here?" shouted a voice in the distance. Connor McKay rushed into the chamber, pushing Cian ahead of him at the end of a white ash spear. Harlow's heart stopped when she saw the figures behind him: Merhart Locklear, Berith Sanvier... And her mother. *Aurelia.*

Aurelia was *here*, which meant she'd known about this place all along and never said a damn word. Her eyes locked with Harlow's and she shook her head slightly, mouthing "do nothing." Harlow's chest nearly burst with rage at her mother. *How could Aurelia have betrayed them all this way? How could she ally herself with Connor now?* Her chest shook with silent sobs.

Finn sat upright now, pulling Harlow with him. He glanced down at her, his eyes full of the same anger that rioted inside her. Their parents had let them down, brought them down. But they were together, and if they had to fight them all, she knew they would. They stood, ready to face them. Harlow made eye contact with Cian, who mouthed *Larkin is fine—hiding.* It was just like them to think about Larkin at a moment like this.

"Let Cian go," Finn said.

Connor started to say something, but Cian interrupted. "Finn. Stop. It's too late. They're gone, and there's no way around this."

Tears slipped down Finn's cheeks. "No," he pleaded. "You can't."

He fell to his knees in front of the one person who'd loved him unconditionally his entire life. Harlow thought her heart might break. Behind Connor, both Merhart Locklear and Aurelia clung to one another, fear written on their faces—

maybe even regret for what was about to happen. Harlow had never hated anyone as she did Aurelia right now.

Connor sneered. "Get up, you coward."

Cian spun around, brave as ever. "Shut the ever-loving fuck up, Connor." They bent to hug Finn. "Let me do this, Finbar. I heard everything Harlow said. You'll figure out how to save me."

When they stood, Finn nodded. "We will."

Cian turned to Connor. "You were there at the beginning. I assume you remember how to get one of my kind up there."

Connor's lip curled in disgust, but he nodded, pushing Cian toward the vascularity. "Hurry up, we don't have much time. Aurelia, come and help. Merhart and Berith, we'll need you two as well when the spell begins. You understand?"

The vampire and shifter both nodded, and Harlow supposed it was lucky Berith hadn't been assassinated, after all. Finn reached for her hand and squeezed tightly. She held on for dear life, trying to spare herself the pain of looking at her mother in this terrible moment. Aurelia was clearly trying to catch her eye, no doubt to convey some useless apology for her part in all this. Harlow would not look. Instead, she looked straight into the breach, at the Vespae who pushed against the barrier.

An odd movement caught her eye. One of the Vespae had wings, ragged things that looked like shredded moth's wings, and it seemed to be pulling threads of aether just outside the vascularity. They were not brainless beasts then. The vascularity had broken down enough for one of them to manipulate reality on this side of the breach.

Connor saw it too, stepping back, his hands shaking. Connor McKay was *shaking*. "They have a queen—"

He seemed about to issue a warning when the vascularity simply dissolved. There was an enormous flash of light, accompanied by what might well have been a sound loud enough to destroy humanoid hearing, but might also have been merely a whisper.

The blast of power releasing into the world shifted something in the threads of aether so basic that at first Harlow wasn't sure anything had happened at all. And then she felt it: power flowed more freely throughout the threads, already more accessible and easier to use. Magic was free, but at what cost?

For a moment all was quiet and still but for the incessant buzzing sound the Vespae made with their tiny mouths, and then they tumbled forward in a writhing mass, rushing towards the tunnel on all fours. Harlow's body slammed against the wall, and she looked behind her to find Finn sheltering her with his wings.

"Where's Cian?" she shouted. "And Larkin?" She couldn't bring herself to ask about Aurelia or the others. A pang of guilt shot through her for it, but her anger at Aurelia was still too strong.

Finn craned his neck, and she could not see beyond him, but she heard the rush of myriad feet and her mind broke around the fear. There were thousands of those creatures, sentient and hungry, streaming into the world right now, and it was all their fault for not stopping Rakul. All the Orders' fault for not finding a better way to handle this. All Aurelia's fault for not just telling what she knew and allowing them to change this waking nightmare.

"Cian has Larkin," Finn said. And then all went blessedly, horrifically quiet. Finn stepped away from Harlow, letting her away from the wall. He stared at the breach, open and completely visible now that the vascularity was down. Berith Sanvier had disappeared, along with Merhart Locklear. To where, Harlow couldn't guess, nor did she care. Her mother stood alone near the cave entrance, pale and shivering, in complete shock. Harlow made no move towards her; in fact, she turned away.

Clouds of dark aether swirled beyond, disturbed by the Vespae. Finn stepped towards it, but Connor yanked him back. "Get the fuck away from that, boy."

Finn shook his father off. "Why?"

Connor shook his head. He looked so defeated, so exhausted, that Harlow almost felt bad for him. "There is still a barrier there—a one-way barrier of a sort. You could get through to the other side, but you would not be able to come back. It's why we built the vascularity. It made the barrier work both ways, to keep the power of Okairos limited, and to stop the Vespae, as we promised."

A soft laugh penetrated the barrier. "Yes, brother, you always keep your promises, don't you?" Ashbourne stepped forward, not in their astral body this time, but their true form.

CHAPTER 32

"Brother?" Finn asked, astonishment on his face.

Connor sighed. "Yes, we are brothers. It has been a long while, Ashbourne."

"Since you closed the breach the first time," the Ventyr warrior reasoned. "Little bird," he said, nodding to Harlow.

Behind her, there was a rustling noise. People were talking. Harlow looked back and was surprised to find Kate, accompanied by Morgaine, and her friend, the Ultima, Samira. *What were* they *doing here?* They were deep in conversation with Larkin and Cian, arguing about something. Aurelia had moved towards them, but Larkin's glare kept her from moving closer. Morgaine was speaking quickly, touching Cian's arm for emphasis as they nodded. Whatever she was saying, Cian seemed to understand.

Harlow nodded to Finn, who turned as she slid her hand into his. "Why are they here?" he asked, obviously distracted. He was trying to keep tabs on his father, who had moved closer to the breach now, and was talking quietly with Ashbourne.

"I don't know," Harlow said, gripping Finn's hand harder, unsure of where to turn her attention. She didn't understand what Kate was doing here with Morgaine and Samira—between that and what she'd seen her mother prepared to do, her mind spun. She froze, overwhelmed by the last few hours of terror and Aurelia's betrayal.

Perhaps that was why she didn't see Larkin break away from the little group, setting Axel down on the ground next to Cian. By the time her sister's movement caught her eye, it was too late. She'd moved too close to the breach, having spotted Ashbourne, and she hadn't heard Connor's warning.

"Larkin," she screamed, lurching forward, her hand slipping out of Finn's.

Her cry came an instant too late. Larkin stepped slowly through the barrier before Harlow could stop her. The void that opened up inside her sucked all air from her lungs, her heart stopping as she watched her youngest sister, her least-silly-silly, go somewhere she could not follow.

Ashbourne turned, his face a mask of horror as he saw Larkin on his side of the barrier. He shouted, rushing toward the barrier in protest, but he was not looking at Larkin. Too late, Harlow saw what caught his attention. Finn had leapt after Larkin, trying to stop her from crossing into the limen, but something about the breach was alive, and it sucked him through as well.

In one terrible instant, Harlow's world came crashing down around her. Her mind went blank as she ran for the barrier. Hands grabbed her, pulling her back. The rest of the world moved in real time, but she was stuck in slow motion as someone pushed her to the ground, begging her to stop fighting.

How could anyone expect her to stop fighting for them? They were her heart's home. Her family. Her responsibility. She wouldn't stop fighting for them, *ever*. She couldn't. It wasn't in her nature. Harlow didn't hear herself screaming, but her throat burned as she shifted. The strength of her wings knocked whoever was trying to stop her from rescuing Finn and Larkin backwards.

Beyond the breach, Ashbourne held Finn back as he screamed her name. Larkin kneeled on the ground sobbing that she was sorry, so sorry. Harlow felt sure she could bring them back, that the strength of the Feriant would carry the three of them back through the barrier, and so she crouched, ready to fly. Everywhere there were shouts, pleas to shift back, to *please just stop and think*. She ignored them. The only sound she heard was her own raptorial cry, as she launched herself towards the breach.

Something pierced her side, sending a shot of fluid pain blazing through her. She looked down as her avian body fell away. Wooziness came over her as several blurry figures surrounded her. From her vantage point on the ground, she saw Finn struggle out of Ashbourne's grip, only to be pulled back by Larkin. For her, he stopped, and Harlow could barely hear now, but she thought she heard Larkin say, "You'll destroy yourself. She wouldn't want that."

Their eyes met and even as whatever she'd been drugged with coursed through her she reached for him, and he for her. Harlow didn't know she was screaming until she was in Kate's arms. "Lo, Lo, *shhhh*…. It's all right. They're gonna be okay, but you have to calm down. Sam, why isn't it working? It's not calming her."

"It was formulated for Kamaris. It should be working," Samira said, her voice floating somewhere above Harlow. Her vision was so dark and blurry she couldn't make much out. "But she's fighting it, and Majesty, she just might win."

Majesty? Somewhere in Harlow's mind, puzzle pieces moved, but she couldn't think of them now, she only wanted Finn and Larkin back. She held his gaze with hers, her lips moving now in a silent plea, *Come back, come back, come back*. Everyone was trying to talk sense into them, but still he reached for her, and she for him. Vaguely, she saw Aurelia slide to the ground, covering her face and hands, wrapping herself in a tiny ball. *How had everything gone so wrong?*

In her peripheral vision, Kate moved to talk to someone Harlow couldn't make out. "Fine. Explain it to her, as best you can, but do it fast. We've gotta get them out of here."

Morgaine's face appeared, close to Harlow's, blocking her view of Finn. She fought it for a moment, but Samira was wrong; the drug was beginning to work and it stilled her body, no matter how her mind fought. She realized they were both lying flat on the floor, staring at one another now.

"Hi," Harlow said, her tongue thick with her continued sobs. "What're you doing here?"

"Hey there, bird girl." Morgaine's voice was low and steady. "Cian will explain it all to you later, but for now I've gotta know, do you think you might be able to trust me?"

Morgaine took hold of her outstretched hand, the one that still sought Finn. The compass tattoo on the younger woman's wrist glowed faintly with a familiar light. Harlow's second sight engaged, as if by instinct. Morgaine was using magic somehow, but it wasn't aethereal magic. It was like Finn's, made of light.

"Starfire," Morgaine explained, tapping the tattoo. "This is a conduit for celestial power, starfire, the sister substance to aether."

Harlow's second sight showed something strange about the girl. Though the celestial power of her tattoo gleamed with starfire, she herself glowed with the same dark light as the two women from her last trip to the limen had.

"Echo," she whispered, remembering how she knew the warrior girl's face. "I saw your Echo. In the aether. She was like me." Harlow wasn't sure what she meant by that—the drug was starting to make her mind cloudy—but it felt right. Somehow she, Lumina and Echo were all connected, similar somehow.

Morgaine nodded. "Yes, she's like you. We're all fighting the same thing, you just don't know it yet. The Ravagers. One of them is out already, and I'm here to make sure that its brethren can't escape."

The missing wardens. The empty space in Nihil. It probably all made sense, but everything was mixed up in her head. Whatever they'd given her was making it hard to think. She did trust Morgaine. But she'd trusted her mother, and that had been a mistake. The fuzzy thought occurred to her that she should ask questions, but she was too far gone to be clever. All she could manage was, "What will you do?"

"I'll close the breach."

"No," Harlow sobbed, struggling to rise. Somewhere in the distance, Larkin needed her, and Finn; her heart ached. She thought maybe she could hear him screaming for her, but her mind struggled to latch onto anything too far away. "My sister... Finn."

Morgaine made a soft shushing noise, stroking her hair back from her face. She spoke quickly. "I have to close the breach. It's what I'm here to do. But there *is* a way out of the limen, a natural portal in Falcyra, in the mountains. I will help them get there, but it will probably destabilize in a few days, once I close the breach. You *must* reach them before that. Do you understand?"

Harlow tried to nod, but didn't have much luck. "Why are you telling me all this?"

"Because I'm also here because of you," Morgaine said, reaching out to touch her cheek. "Because of your connection to the otham—I'm sorry—the aether. You will understand better later, but I'm here to pass a message onto you, as well as to close the breach. Will you trust me enough to carry it with you?"

Harlow nodded. "Yes, tell me."

Morgaine came closer and whispered words that were at once strange and completely familiar to her. Harlow nodded; it was as if Morgaine had unlocked a door that Harlow had been staring at her entire life.

"I don't think I'll remember," she replied.

Morgaine slid something hard and flat into her jacket, tucking it securely against her. "*The Warden*," she explained. "And I've written the message down for you. Find the missing bits of the book when you can. I have a feeling they can help you."

Harlow nodded, as her eyes drooped, threatening to shut without her permission.

Morgaine smiled as the enormous auburn cat who had been Axel's friend these past weeks brushed Harlow's face with his. Morgaine and the cat looked at one another, as though conversing silently, and the cat purred over her again, rubbing its face on hers in a comforting way.

"Do you understand what I've told you, Harlow?" Morgaine asked.

"I think so," Harlow murmured as her eyes closed further.

In her mind, she heard the cat speak, though of course that was impossible. *We knew you would, Strider. Walk with luck.* The cat bounded towards the breach and leapt through. Harlow couldn't see that far now, but she imagined Finn taking the great cat in his arms and giving it a snuggle. She was still weeping, her tears soaking the ground beneath her face, but she thought she might have laughed at that.

"I have to go now," Morgaine said.

Harlow nodded, her eyes threatening to close now. "Tell him I will find him," she mumbled before the drug her body had been fighting finally won its battle. "Tell him I will destroy worlds to find him if he doesn't come back to me."

"Let's hope it doesn't come to that, bird girl," Morgaine said, stroking her hair once more before she sat up.

"Will I ever see you again?" Harlow asked before her eyes closed.

"I'm not certain," Morgaine whispered as the girl who reminded her so much of her own dear Echo fell asleep. "But if we don't, please know that I believe in you, Harlow Krane. You'll do what needs to be done. Awaken them and prepare."

Harlow woke up with a start. Her entire body vibrated with phantom pain, and she was panicking. *Why was she panicking?* Finn. Larkin. The breach. A strangled sob clawed its way through her chest, rage at her loss, and the fact that she wasn't allowed to say goodbye, ricocheting through her. Her shadows welled inside her, begging to be let out, to take vengeance on anyone they could.

Soft arms surrounded her—they had been around her all along. "You're awake."

"Mama?" Harlow asked, sitting up. Selene held her tight. The two of them were curled up together on a big upholstered chair. Harlow was confused. She looked around, and it took her a moment to realize they were on a plane. A *big* plane.

A luxury jet, in fact. Instead of rows of seats, it was set up like a very long living room. Beyond where she sat, Indigo stared blankly at Nox, asleep on her lap. Next to them on the same couch, Thea and Alaric held hands, exhaustion written in the set of their shoulders. Enzo and Riley sat in a tight group with Cian, Petra, Kate, and the Ultima, Samira. Axel had been curled up next to Selene, but now came to sit on her lap.

Memories of what had happened in the cavern gripped her nearly as soon as she took a tally of everyone on the plane. *Finn. Larkin. Morgaine. Aurelia.*

She looked around for Mother, and found her sitting alone at the front of the plane, staring at the wall. Her clothes were rumpled and her face was dirty and tear stained.

"She lied to us all." Her throat was raw, from all the screaming, she assumed.

"She thought she was protecting us," Selene said, sounding lost.

"Has she always known?" Harlow asked.

"Apparently all the chancellors are told upon swearing in. It took the magic of each Order to keep the vascularity in place. They knew it was there all along, keeping Okairos… locked up." Selene's voice broke over her last few words. "And now… Larkin is gone."

"I'm so sorry," Harlow whimpered.

Aurelia's head turned towards them, tears flooding down her face as her chest shook. Across the plane, Thea and Indi both wept, watching the scene, clearly feeling as helpless and angry as Harlow did now. Her family was broken —shattered, like her heart.

"We'll never be the same." Her words sounded like a vow. Selene didn't answer her, but the pain in her eyes was enough to tell Harlow she understood the sentiment all too well. "What about Morgaine?"

Selene waved Kate over, rising. "Let Kate explain. I need to rest."

"No," Harlow said abruptly. Memories of the cavern were clarifying in her mind, and the last person she wanted was Kate. "I want Cian."

Cian was already walking across the plane, having seen that she was awake. Kate followed close behind. Thea walked across the plane, ignoring Aurelia as she passed her, and drew Selene into her arms, guiding her to a seat between her and Alaric.

When they were settled, Cian folded their long limbs onto the seat next to Harlow as she sat up, taking her hands in theirs. "Where's Finn?" Harlow asked, ignoring Kate as she sat down in the bank of seats across from them.

"You know where Finn is," Cian said.

She did. "The limen."

Cian nodded. "That's right. We're on our way to Falcyra now to find them."

She deliberately ignored Kate, who sat forward, her elbows on her knees, her pretty face resting in her hands. Kate looked anxious and drawn. *Well enough,* Harlow thought. *That's the least of what she should feel.* She knew she was transferring some of her anger at Aurelia onto Kate, but they had both kept so much from everyone. It was clear Kate had known about the vascularity and what it did.

"Whose plane is this?" Harlow asked

"The Rogue Order's," Kate said, speaking softly. "We're taking you to our village where you'll be safe. It's close to where the portal Morgaine described is. We'll get them, Lo. I promise we'll get them back."

Harlow refused to look Kate's way. "And *she's* the Rogue Queen."

Cian's silver eyes housed an endless well of empathy. "Yes, she is."

"And you knew," Harlow said, resentment mixing with the focused fury in her chest. So many secrets. When would it all end?

"Yes," Cian replied. They would never lie to her again. She saw it in their eyes, a promise. It was too late for that now.

"You've been with them all along, haven't you? You're the one who gave Finn and Alaric the keys to the Vault, and set them on this path."

"When did you figure it out?" Cian asked.

Harlow shrugged. *Did it even matter now?* "I think I knew when we found the inscription on the crypt, I just didn't want to admit it to myself. And you," she said, pointing at Kate. "Did you know the whole time—about what the vascularity was for and where Vivia Woolf was?"

Kate nodded. "Yes, I knew. No one else on my Nea Sterlis team did, but I knew."

"And you didn't trust me enough to tell me all this?"

"I told you, Lo. It wasn't about trusting you. It was about protecting something greater than myself. If you had any experience with stuff like this, you'd understand."

The condescension in Kate's voice was too much. That she could justify not collaborating with this bullshit line of thinking was going too far. It was all too much: losing Finn and Larkin. Her mother's betrayal. Cian and Kate's secrets. The Vespae. Dear gods, the Vespae. Where were they now, and what were they doing to the world below as she flew away on a luxury jet?

The rage in Harlow's chest coalesced, winnowing to focus on Kate. She turned too quickly, her body moving with a speed she wasn't used to. In less than a second, she had Kate pinned to the headrest of her seat by the throat, her fingers threatening to crush her delicate esophagus. "I'd understand what, *Katherine*? That these are just the casualties of war?"

Kate didn't answer; her face remained calm as if she were reading her favorite book, which only made Harlow angrier. Samira rose, but Kate waved her away. "It's fine; she won't hurt me."

"Won't I?" Harlow snarled. Everyone had stopped what they were doing to watch, even Aurelia. Harlow knew she should stop. She knew Kate wasn't who she was really angry at, and Kate knew it too. It didn't stop her from saying, "Give me one good reason why I shouldn't." Her voice didn't sound like her own, and she liked it. She liked how strong she sounded. "Do you know I believed you? I believed you actually cared about me, but it was all about this the whole time, wasn't it?"

Across the plane, Aurelia covered her mouth with her hands, a small sob spilling out anyway. She knew as well as everyone else did that Harlow's words were for her as much as for Kate. Tears ran hot and fast down Harlow's face. This wasn't all about Aurelia. Kate had lied too. She glared at the woman she'd once thought she loved. "None of it was ever about me, was it? Just what I might be able to *turn into*."

To her surprise, Kate nodded. Harlow let her go, stepping back. "At first, yes. You're like Samira and the others. We'd been looking for you for quite some time. But you never manifested, and I thought I'd made a mistake. I wasn't queen then, but then Lou got sick."

It took Harlow a moment, but then she remembered: Lou was Kate's sire. "What does that have to do with anything?"

"The story I told you when we broke up about needing to go back to the vineyard to help Lou was true. She just didn't need help with the vineyard—she needed help with the Rogue Order. So I became queen when she couldn't be anymore."

"Congratulations," Harlow muttered. "Did you ever think that if you'd just *told* us all of this that we'd have helped you?"

"No," Kate said simply. "I *hoped* you might, but it's not that simple, Harlow. I am responsible for thousands of people. A whole network of rebels, of people that if the Illuminated got their hands on them—well, let's just say they'd make what you saw Connor do at the Grand look like child's play."

Harlow fell to the floor of the plane, her knees sinking into the plush beige carpet, her will to be angry suddenly dying. Cian dragged her against their legs, their arms going around her. They pressed a kiss to her forehead. "I'm so sorry I lied to you and Finn, sweet girl. I made a mistake. I thought I could convince Kate of our intentions on my own. I should have told you both everything."

Harlow stared at the wall, her arms limp at her sides. If any of them had just told the truth sooner, none of this would have happened. These secrets they all kept were a weakness. "If we get them back, I will consider forgiving the *two* of you," she muttered, hoping Aurelia heard. "Until then, leave me the hells alone."

"*When* we get them back." Kate stood as she corrected Harlow. "I *am* sorry, Lo."

Harlow laughed, a harsh sound. "If we don't get them back, I will *kill* you."

There was a long silence as Harlow's threat against Kate's life hung in the air. "She doesn't mean that," Thea insisted from across the plane.

"She does," Cian said, leaving Harlow's side. They reached back to touch her cheek, but they gazed at Aurelia as they spoke. "And I don't blame her one bit for it."

Cian and Kate walked across the plane together, leaving Harlow alone with her grief. She slept on and off for several hours, and when she woke again, Samira was sitting next to her. Axel was curled beneath them, his tiny snores a percussive white noise she found infinitely soothing. She stroked his back and he rolled over, pressing his paws against her thigh as he nuzzled into her leg.

"Go away," Harlow said to Samira, her voice flat.

"No," Samira said. "You can hate Kate and Cian, if you want. That is legitimate. But I will stay right here."

Harlow glanced at the warrior's face. She had a bright light in her dark eyes, something deeply humorous behind all that stern exterior. The Ultima kicked her feet up onto the footrest of her seat.

"Are you protecting Kate?" Harlow asked. "Worried I'll try to murder her here on the plane?"

Samira laughed. "I don't answer to her Majesty. I'm not a bodyguard." The way Samira said "her Majesty" made it sound like a joke. Harlow liked the irreverence.

"Then who are you?" Harlow replied.

"A Strider, like you—a member of the Feriant Legion. And no one commands us. We answer only to ourselves." The Ultima's voice was soft and confident, her words seductive as she continued. "When we get to Falcyra, you will see what I mean."

Harlow turned towards the window, dragging Axel to her chest. "Perhaps," she said, as she shut her eyes against this terrible reality.

The Ultima started to get up, but a thought suddenly occurred to Harlow and she reached out to pull her back down. "Did Morgaine get the breach shut?"

Samira nodded. "Yes, her power is quite interesting. Not her own, apparently, just on loan for her mission."

"Saving us from the Ravagers?" Harlow asked. She wished she'd had more time to talk to Morgaine, to understand the world she'd come from, but Samira had spent time with her. From the sound of things, they'd have plenty of time to talk this over in the near future. Harlow remembered *The Warden*, and pressed her free hand to her side. It was there, tucked into her jacket's inside pocket still.

The Ultima grinned at Harlow's grip on her arm, her straight white teeth flashing. Harlow released her, and Samira settled in next to her once more as she explained, "Yes, the one her people call the Legionnaire is already out. It's why she became the bearer of starfire, to close the breaches between worlds. They were made by one of the Ventyr, a terrible mistake."

"Seems like they make a lot of those," Harlow said, bitterness edging her tone.

Samira smirked. "Isn't that the truth? They've been cavorting about the galaxy, fucking things up for eons. But some of them are sexy as fuck, yeah?"

Harlow's heart ached unbearably. "Yeah. Do you have a Ventyr partner?" It was not lost on her that they were calling them Ventyr, rather than Illuminated.

The dark beauty grinned, stretching her muscular legs out before her. "Yeah, Tomyris. We've been together for almost five years."

"Together-together?" Harlow asked cautiously. She didn't know if her heart could take the answer, or talk about romantic love right now, but she was curious all the same.

Samira nodded. "Yes, it's been rotten being apart this summer while I kept an eye on you." Her mouth fell open and she touched Harlow's arm. "I'm sorry…"

"It's okay," Harlow said. "I'm happy for you… That you'll get to see her soon."

"She'll love you," Samira said. "She's the warmest creature on this planet. Sweet to everyone with a wicked bite, if you know what I mean."

Harlow did, all too well, unfortunately. "I'm sure we'll be fast friends."

"You will," Samira assured her. She looked uncomfortable then, as though she knew the trajectory of their conversation had done nothing but pour salt into Harlow's very fresh wounds.

Harlow attempted to change the subject. She didn't want the Strider to go away. Right now, she might be the only person who truly understood the pain Harlow was in. "So, the Ravager that escaped to Morgaine's realm… What is it doing there?"

"As far as we know, it has taken hold of a vessel on her world, and its power grows."

"And the others?"

"Still imprisoned, but awake, after long years of slumber."

Harlow already knew that, from her visit to the limen. She didn't know if that was a usual thing for Striders to do, but she wasn't quite ready to talk about it yet. In fact, she was utterly exhausted. She curled back into herself, closing her eyes once more.

"Connor McKay got away," Samira said softly as she settled in next to Harlow, preparing to nap herself, apparently.

"Of course he did," Harlow grumbled before letting the sound of Axel's purrs lull her to sleep.

EPILOGUE

A frigid wind raked through Harlow's hair, pulling strands from the tight pair of braids that hung down her back. Though she was clad in thick gear that was spelled not to fall off her body when she shifted, the cold air still crept into her body, chilling her to the bone. Falcyra was perpetually cold in the lowlands, and here in the mountains it was even worse.

Harlow's muscles had hardened over the past two months, training and flying with the Striders. She thought Finn would be proud of the progress she'd made, and she knew he'd like the bulk she'd added to her generous curves. It was still hard to think about him and Larkin.

They'd followed the portal for weeks as it blinked through the jagged mountain range. But there was no sign of her sister or lover. One day, just as Morgaine had said it would, the portal destabilized and did not reappear. Yule would be here soon, and the air smelled like snow as she gazed down into the valley the ancient fjord sat in. Conifers covered the valley floor and walls, giving way to the rocky peaks she stood amongst now.

"They could have come through two stops back, or even four," Samira offered, looking at their paper map. The world had been without power, without internet or phone for two months now. Harlow was surprised to find she didn't miss any of it much. She certainly didn't miss Section Seven. "Both times we didn't get there for days. High winds could have masked their tracks."

Harlow nodded, but her mouth was set in a grim line. It was hard not to lose hope. It had been nearly two weeks with no leads. Harlow dreaded going down into the valley, back to the settlement. Back to the people who loved her, who grew more worried about her with each passing day. They'd been lucky that Meline and Ari had caught wind of them, and now Harlow's family was nearly reunited, despite being broken in all the ways that counted.

With Finn and Larkin still missing, she hadn't spoken to Aurelia since the night they'd lost them. Her refusal to even listen to her mother was putting a strain on her family. Though they were incredibly lucky that so many of their friends and family were safe, Harlow couldn't bring herself to hear Aurelia out. She needed time, and the work the Feriant Legion was doing to keep her from losing her good sense.

From the Rogue Order's informants, they'd learned that nearly a million people, humans and the lower Orders alike, had been wiped out by the Vespae, who were reproducing quickly. The Humanists had all but disappeared in their wake, but Harlow didn't doubt they would re-emerge eventually. Especially now that humans could use magic. In the settlement, the sorcière had started a training program for interested humans, and nearly all of them attended one workshop or another, learning to pull the threads of aether as the sorcière did.

As Cian had once described, it was harder for them. They were not genetically disposed to it the way sorcière were, but many were growing skilled far more quickly than anyone had assumed they'd be able to. Harlow was learning not to underestimate humans' capability. She'd always known they were remarkably resilient, and they proved it beyond a shadow of a doubt now.

Despite the fact that she was still angry with Kate, she admired the work the Rogue Order was doing immensely, and she understood why the vampire had been so protective of it. While she was, indeed, called the "Rogue Queen," it was nothing more than a moniker. She was a figurehead, a bogey-man of sorts representing the ideal of the outcast the Immortal Orders feared most. In truth, the Rogues were led by a small council of elected representatives from each of the five groups of people that inhabited Okairos.

Samira perched on a rock, looking distinctly birdlike, even in her humanoid form. "Hey," she said, breaking Harlow's reverie. "You never told me what Morgaine whispered to you in the cave."

Harlow sat next to her. The sun had warmed the dark-colored boulder enough that it felt good beneath her, the heat seeping into her. "You don't know?"

"No," Samira said, shaking her head. "Even though we worked together when she came through the portal, she didn't tell me much."

Harlow had learned that Morgaine's mission was to close the breaches that one of the irresponsible Ventyr had made centuries ago. It was creating a kind of imbalance throughout the realms most closely connected to the limen. There would always be portals, Samira had explained; doors to other places, shortcuts across the universe. But largely, their natural state was to be unstable, appearing and disappearing without warning.

But since the Ventyr had tried to leverage the limen in the wars against one another, they'd wanted permanent doors, and in finding a way to achieve this, had wrought all kinds of trouble on many different worlds. Morgaine was meant to close those unnatural doors, the breaches, but she was also meant to deliver a message, to both Harlow and Lumina, on their respective worlds.

Harlow stared into the valley, watching the mix of humans and immortals working together. She turned to Samira. "Morgaine said this was a part of a prophecy from her world: *Awaken the Fifth Order and the seventh ward shall break, and in so doing balance returns. The terror of the Ravagers ends when gods walk the earth as mere denizens.*"

Samira grimaced. "Horrible things, prophecies. Always so vague and easy to misinterpret."

Harlow smiled; this was the usual perspective from the Order of Mysteries. Since so few sorcière were gifted with the Sight, as humans seemed more predisposed to psychic ability, foretelling was generally looked down upon. She couldn't fault Samira for feeling that way, but the words had ignited something in her.

"Awaken the Fifth Order," she said, gesturing to the scene in the valley.

Samira shifted on the boulder, and she squinted, as though trying to see Harlow's vision. She glanced at Harlow sidelong, shaking her head. "You don't think?"

Harlow nodded. "I do. I think they're the Fifth Order."

Samira bumped her shoulder with her own. "You mean *we*. *We're* the Fifth Order."

The last little piece of whatever Harlow had been trying to puzzle out about the message snicked into place. "Yes," she breathed, hardly able to believe it.

She'd found her place. And as much as she loved Finn, and was desperate to get him back, there was a part of her that knew she had to get here on her own, without his help. That knowledge was uncomfortable, and she sat in silence next to Samira, contemplating what it might mean.

A crackle came over Samira's portable radio. They were close enough to the settlement for it to reach them. A familiar voice, Meline, said, "Samira, it's base. Do you copy?" Meline and Indigo had both taken to the communications team rather rapidly, and were often the voice at the other end of such communications.

"I copy," Samira responded. "We're headed back in. No luck."

"There's been a sighting. Sixty miles from stop four. A girl and a winged creature. Someone thought it was a Vespae queen with a hostage, but it could be them."

"Get me the coordinates," Samira said. "We'll head out now."

Meline sent a string of numbers their way, and Harlow tracked them on the map she'd unfolded in her lap. She nodded at Samira when she'd found the place. "Got it."

"We'll be back before dinner," Samira said. "And hopefully we'll have our people."

"Good flying, Warbirds," Meline said, and her transmission crackled out.

Harlow looked down on the settlement, with all its beautiful stone buildings and cobblestone streets, as she passed the map back to Samira. The area had once been a thriving resort town, perhaps three hundred years ago, but as legend went it was terribly haunted by poltergeists. There were none here now, but plenty of ghosts and other spirits, so the rumor probably persisted and largely kept people away from the region.

"We'll miss hand-to-hand again," she remarked, motioning to the two legions of soldiers lining up on the cleared fields beyond the settlement perimeter. Nothing grew in the winter, so they used them for training.

Samira laughed. "Like you need it. You took to fighting like a raven to wing."

Harlow's lips quirked up in a half-smile and she pushed the Ultima playfully. Sometimes she felt guilty for smiling, but Tomyris and Samira had urged her to try to find joy in these hard days, as much as possible. They reasoned that Finn wouldn't want her to languish in misery. "You just don't want me to kick your ass again."

"It was *one* time," Samira said, returning the smile. Harlow had been improving. She was by no means an expert, but with nothing to do but train, Harlow's gains had been rapid. Samira examined Harlow's face, looking worried. "Don't you want to find them?"

Harlow shrugged. "Of course, but it's not them. It never is."

There had been so many false starts, so many bad leads. She didn't want to give up, but her heart couldn't take much more disappointment.

"If you want to get back to Tomyris, I'll understand. I can go check it out on my own."

Samira bumped her shoulder. "I'll do one better for you."

She clicked a code into the radio and a musical voice answered. "I've got your location in my sights, lover. You headed home?"

"Nope, there's been a lead. Wanna come with?"

"On my way," the voice answered. Seconds later, Samira's partner blinked in next to them. She was a tall, muscular creature who rarely used her humanoid alternae. She was one of the Thuelloi, like Ashbourne, with mauve-colored skin and thick ebony hair that was currently braided into a crown around her head.

She planted a kiss on Samira's lips, her hand brazenly caressing her lover's ass. She then hugged Harlow, a little too hard. Samira hadn't been exaggerating about Tomyris; she was effusive in her affection, but could be absolutely terrifying in a fight. Harlow had watched her singlehandedly slaughter two dozen Vespae, the soldiers of a swarm that had tried to invade the valley only a week back. And yet here she was squeezing the air out of Harlow's lungs with the force of her friendship.

"Can't breathe," Harlow gasped and the Ventyr released her, laughing heartily.

Tomyris examined the map, pointing out possible routes to the coordinates Meline had given them, while Samira practically mooned over her lover's words. The two of them were disgustingly smitten with one another. Not all of the Striders' Ventyr partners were romantic, but like Finn and Harlow, Samira and Tomyris were in love. It was a little hard to watch at times, but it helped that they both were good friends. Harlow had always had her sisters, and Enzo, of course, but she'd never had a group of friends that were just hers. This new territory helped soothe some of the perpetual ache in her chest from missing Finn and Larkin, and the rift within her family.

"Shall we?" Tomyris asked. "Audata's making breakfast for dinner tonight and I want to be back by the time it's done."

Samira grinned and then shot into the air, shifting as she rose. Tomyris followed, yelling, "Last one there has to clean the waffle iron."

Harlow swore as she shifted, and then followed. *Hold on, McKay,* she thought to herself as she flew west into the setting sun. *I'm coming for you.*

BOOK THREE
AWAKEN
THE
FIFTH
ORDER

PROLOGUE

Frigid wind whistled through the open slats in the walls of the barn. Once, someone kept animals here, but no longer—now, monsters overran the little farm. They'd been here for six days, the longest they'd stopped moving since Finn and Larkin had been separated. Finn knew the Vespae were hungry, but for whatever reason, they would not touch him.

Nor would they release him. The creatures had a stinger containing a poison that suppressed his connection to both aethereal and celestial magics, and they'd kept him alive but sedated as they moved from place to place. Finn was weak, but not as groggy or unconscious as he'd been at the beginning; he'd cataloged their movements as well as he could. From the pattern of incoming and outgoing parties, he'd concluded that they were searching for something. The Vespae were violent—brutal, really—but they were not unthinking creatures.

In fact, he believed they had language. Outside, in the barnyard, several huddled in a circle. Soft clicks and hisses passed between them, and from what Finn could discern, there was a pattern to it. They didn't seem to be cold, but they crowded together like that when daylight became too harsh.

Finn peered out from between the rough wooden slats at the Vespae gathered in the barnyard: they were the group he thought of as "drones"—the ones who gathered food, which consisted solely of plant matter, and were the advance guard for any of the swarm's maneuvers.

The Vespae were pale creatures, with silvery-gray skin, who walked upright like the humanoids of Okairos. Their features were strikingly different though, with huge, dark eyes that resembled those of a moth, and tiny noses and mouths. The drones' long arms allowed them to drop to the ground and run at alarming speeds, while the swarm's elite were proportioned more like the humanoids of Okairos. All had long, graceful limbs that reminded him of the Illuminated's true forms.

In fact, there was something eerily similar between the Vespae and the Ventyr. Something that bothered Finn to think about, when he could think clearly enough to do so. That was rarely enough, as the noise the drones made was incredibly disorienting. He might not be groggy from the poison any longer, but that sound—both the constancy of it, and the pitch—was enough to make him want to clap his hands over his ears.

Though the drones were terrifying, they were the least of his problems. The queen and her guard were the ones whose poison kept him disconnected from his sources of strength. He hadn't seen the queen since they arrived at this farm, but one of the guards visited him every day before sunset to dose him again.

Typically, daylight hours were the most peaceful for him, since the drones were usually dormant, but today they couldn't rest. They'd been "talking" in the barn-yard for hours, so much so that he couldn't think. The intermittent hissing wormed into his mind and grated on his nerves, bringing back the memory of being sepa-rated from Larkin—something he used any mental acuity he had to suppress.

Now, memory flooded him, detaching him from the frigid wind howling through the barn. They'd traveled in the limen for nearly a day after being ripped from Harlow and Cian in the catacombs, Morgaine and Ashbourne both helping them to navigate. It had been strange to spend time with an uncle he'd never known existed, especially because he hadn't acted like they were related in the slightest. Even now, that stung, though Finn understood that the Warden had been locked in Nihil with the Ravagers for longer than he could even conceive.

Guarding a prison for ancient elemental horrors like the Ravagers seemed to have dulled Ashbourne's emotions, or perhaps he just disliked Finn on sight. He'd certainly been unhappy to see Connor. If it were just that, Finn could understand, but it was a deeper indifference that had stung. Unlike most of the Illuminated, who were typically extremely reactive in comparison to humans or the lower Orders, Ashbourne was practically stoic.

The Ventyr General had treated him like a problem to solve, and even now, with all his other problems, Finn wished it had been different. It would be nice to think that somewhere, he had a blood relative who cared for him. That not everyone he came from was a monster. Though on that front at least, he had no complaint with Ashbourne, who despite his obvious disinterest in Finn cared deeply for Larkin, and the worlds he kept safe from the Ravagers.

Morgaine and her cat, Bayun, had been different. It was obvious the human girl had been worried about her mission, but they'd been kind to him and Larkin, trying to comfort them both. As bizarre as it had been for the cat to speak, it had distracted both him and Larkin from the terror of being locked in the limen, violently isolated from everyone they loved, while the world fell to pieces on the other side of the breach.

That seemed like a faraway time now, those days of hope that he'd see Harlow again soon. Finn wasn't sure how long it had been since then, and—whether it was the effects of Vespae poison or the limen itself—his memories of what had happened inside the limen were more impressions than anything else.

The days blurred together and he thought he'd been with the hive for more than a month. They'd moved from location to location for what felt like weeks until settling here. Finn estimated they'd been here for ten days, and he thought he remembered most of them. Unlike the rest of his recent memories, the day they stumbled out of the limen was vivid in his mind.

Morgaine had disappeared back into the portal with Ashbourne. From what Finn gathered in the short time they'd traveled together, Morgaine needed Ashbourne's help to find the next world she was to visit, a place called Sirin. Finn had learned more about her mission to ensure that the Ravagers could not access aethereal worlds by closing the unnaturally opened portals, but thinking about that was confusing now.

Sometimes thinking about anything but his failure to protect Larkin was physically painful. They'd been woefully unprepared for travel through the mountains of Falcyra when they exited the limen, given that they'd been dressed for a mild autumn evening in Nea Sterlis. His first order of business had been to get them to the shelter Morgaine had located for them—a hobby farm a few miles away from the opening to the limen. It had seemed like such a good thing at the time, a place to rest and procure cold weather clothing the original inhabitants had left behind.

If only they'd gone as soon as they'd geared up for the cold. The day had been sunny, a rarity in Falcyra that lulled Finn into a sense of safety. With no Vespae about, Finn decided to explore the property to see if there was a vehicle somewhere they could use for its radio. He'd known he needed to try to get in touch with the Rogue Order, and Morgaine had given him their radio codes. She'd assured him the Rogues would easily find the farm once he got in touch with them, but he hadn't found a way to do that in the house. He'd searched for hours, failing to notice when the sun began to set.

All they had to do was stay warm, radio the Rogues, and everything would be fine. If only he'd stayed out of the barn. Or if he'd gone in at noon, rather than twilight. *If, if, if.* There were so many ways he could have avoided fucking things up, if he'd been more careful. If he hadn't been so curious about the buzzing coming from deep inside the barn. If he hadn't woken them.

His only hope now was that the Vespae hadn't been able to get into the basement where he'd shoved Larkin. He'd done everything he could to draw them off, to get them to pay attention to him instead, and he thought it had worked, but of course he couldn't be sure. They'd kept him mostly unconscious since capturing him, and things blurred together.

Outside, the drones' hisses and clicks blurred into a buzz. Finn struggled to his feet. He wasn't bound or confined. The Vespae's poison kept him weak enough that he couldn't leave. They'd easily catch him if he tried to escape again —several early attempts had confirmed this. He'd been dragged back to whatever gods forsaken camp they'd been sheltering in. Now he bided his time, hoping that soon he'd learn *something* that would be the key to his escape.

A rumble in the distance suggested a vehicle—multiple vehicles— approached. *Was he being rescued? Had the Rogue Order found him?* Hope lit in his heart. *Thank all gods for Kate.* As the Rogue Queen, he knew she'd find him, and maybe Harlow was with her. He gathered his strength. If there was going to be a fight, he'd be as useful as he could.

Finn stepped out of the barn, expecting to find the Vespae preparing for conflict. In daylight hours, they did this by hiding. Instead, the full swarm gathered in the yard, buzzing excitedly as three SUVs barreled through the snow about a mile off. Finn squinted, trying to make out who was within, but the vehicles' heavily tinted windows obscured his view.

Glancing around, dread seeped into his gut. The Vespae weren't preparing for a fight—they were *excited*. All stood upright instead of crouching near the ground. And the queen's guard stood on the steps of the house, though the queen was nowhere to be seen. Finn saw his chance in this moment of distraction—every drone and guard were focused on the approaching vehicles.

He might not get far, but he had to try one more time. He owed that to Larkin—and he missed Harlow more than he usually allowed himself to admit. Thinking of her, when he could do nothing to find her, nearly drove him to distraction, something he couldn't afford right now. Moving slowly, he backed away from the swarm. All the usual guards were in the barnyard, and all he needed to do was slip into the woods to get away. It had been a little over a full day since the last sting, and the poison's effects were wearing off. They'd never let it get so low in his system before, and his body's ability to heal rapidly kicked in —he felt stronger by the moment.

Typically, the queen or one of her guards dosed him sooner, so his access to magic never returned, but now he could feel the threads that made up reality again, and all the power of the universe behind them. If he could put enough distance between himself and the swarm, he might be able to shift and teleport out. His limbs dragged as he focused on moving silently, creeping out the back of the barn towards the woods. To his surprise, none of the Vespae followed him. They were all more interested in whoever, or whatever, was coming in those SUVs.

Finn narrowed his attention—staying quiet and moving quickly had to be his priority now, not looking back. He had no recourse if they caught him; he knew he was still too weak to fight, so getting away had to be his only goal.

The little farm nestled deep in a tall, wooded grove. Finn knew exactly where the darkest parts of the forest were, and he stayed away from them now. He'd tried that before, mistakenly thinking he was providing himself with cover, but now he understood daylight was his best advantage. So he stayed with the light, his strides lengthening with every step he took away from the encampment, some of his strength returning.

Though Finn had no idea where to go, or what he'd do when he was away from this place, his heart sprang back to life for the first time since he'd been taken. As a child, he'd learned to shut down during the long stretches of time that his parents' machinations involved him too directly, or too intensely. He'd found out early that hope could be a weakness, as it gave opponents something to destroy. Now, he couldn't escape it, couldn't pen it back in, or wrangle it into submission.

Away from the near-constant buzzing of the Vespae, Finn's head cleared. His movements grew stronger, more confident. He wasn't back to full strength, or anywhere near it, but he could think—try to make a plan. When he was younger, his father had taken him on trips to the dense forests of Castel des Rêves and Falcyra alike, dropping him in the middle of nowhere, with only his wits and a directive to find his way out of the forest. There had never been a clear destination, just "find your way to safety," and though Finn knew he'd been watched, Connor didn't rescue him from being injured or going hungry. Finn assumed his father would have stepped in if his life had been truly threatened, but there had been plenty of times he'd been afraid, and Connor never intervened.

As terrible as all that had been, it prepared him for this moment as he crested the ridge of the valley the little farm sat in. He looked behind him to find that he could survey his prison perfectly. The SUVs had parked in the barnyard now, and a dozen vampires and several witches spilled out of them. A murky feeling of doom soured the hope he'd felt moments before. *Why were sorcière helping anyone associated with the Vespae?* The group moved quickly into a guard formation as they yanked a hooded figure forward.

When the queen finally appeared, emerging out of the farmhouse, one of the sorcière pulled the hood from the vampire's face, exposing him to the queen. Her ragged wings flexed with excitement as she smelled him carefully. Her huge eyes gave nothing away, but the wrinkle of her tiny nose showed what she thought of the vampire's scent. The Vespae themselves smelled of flowers, which always struck Finn as odd, given their ferocity.

The vampire shrunk away from the queen, his eyes fearful. From the state he was in, it was clear he'd fought his captors. Finn recognized Jareth Sanvier, one of the leaders of the Humanists. The queen stepped forward, and Finn didn't have to watch what would happen next; she would incapacitate him with her poison.

Finn turned in the other direction. There was nothing he could do for the vampire, not alone and weak as he was. He didn't like the Humanists' methods, but he would have helped Jareth if he were capable. Larkin and Harlow had to be his only concern now. Finn wouldn't risk his chance to find the people he loved, his family, for someone who condoned outright terrorism.

Ahead of him was a vast mountain range, which he was in no way prepared to traverse. Already, the sun was low in the sky and cold crept into his bones. He was slightly more resistant to cold than other immortals, but he would still freeze in his mortal form. The only option he had was to shift and fly. He attempted to drop his glamour, but it wouldn't budge. Deep in his veins, there were still traces of the Vespae's venom, keeping him from shifting to his true form. His burgeoning hope deflated.

"Frustrating, isn't it?" a familiar voice rang out from the trees. "There's really nowhere for you to go."

Finn whirled around to find Mark Easton leaning against a tree. Every instinct he had edged on a knife's blade, and he dropped into a solid crouch. It wasn't possible for Mark to be here. Finn had watched Harlow disembowel and decapitate him during the Solstice Gala, last spring. There was no way he'd survived. No immortal could survive without their head.

"Keep trying to figure it out, McKay," Mark hissed.

Finn's vision blurred and now Mark stood before him in his incubus form, his glamour dropped, revealing ghastly gray skin and hungry, bloodshot eyes. When he smiled, his teeth were pointed razors. Finn's head felt as though it might split open, it ached so deeply. His ears rang until he was sure he bled from his eyes and ears both, driven to his knees in the snow.

The incubus' face swam before Finn's eyes. He attempted to muster his strength, but Mark just laughed. Finn saw the punch coming, but could do nothing to stop it as Mark's fist met his face with full impact, and all went dark.

CHAPTER 1

Blood filled Harlow's mouth, the metallic tang coating her throat as she resisted the urge to duck away from her attacker. A pale creature hissed in her face and threw its right hand back, a long thorn-like spine pushed out from its palm, glistening in the silvery light that shone through the arched windows of the enormous hallway. The creature was preparing to sting, but Harlow drew her shadows around her, honing them into daggers—extensions of her arms. She punched up fast, driving the shadow dagger through the bottom of the Vespae's chin, sending it straight into its brain.

Dark, viscous blood spilled from its mouth as it screamed, but as soon as she drew her shadows back it fell to the ground, dead. Another was on her as it fell, launching at her from the fray that surrounded her. They swung at one another, evenly matched, for the moment. Harlow slipped, the blood from her former foe slick on the smooth marble floors. The creature lurched towards her, its movements erratic and wild as she fought it off, struggling to right herself, her senses blurring with the stress of the fight. There were so many of them, and she was getting tired.

Luckily, the Vespae she fought was already injured, a gash oozing fluid down its pale, bony chest, seeping through the thin rags it wore as clothes. It was breathing hard, dazed and unable to get its bearings as it gripped her arms. Perhaps it was as tired as she was. Harlow caught herself, using the struggling Vespae to steady her body.

The second she regained balance, she thrust a shadow-dagger into the creature's already injured chest, pinning it in place long enough to separate its head from its body with shadows she wrought into a longer blade. The creature fell to the floor, and there was an exhausted part of Harlow that envied it. Its fight was over, while hers continued.

Yet another of the drones jumped at her, but before she could convince her body to move against it, Tomyris and Samira worked in tandem, ripping it apart. Tomyris leapt back into the melee, her three pairs of draconic wings spread out behind her as she sliced through two Vespae drones with a pair of short swords as easily as if they were butter. Sam shifted out of her Feriant form, catching Harlow as she stumbled, her avian features melting into her familiar humanoid face. "You okay?"

Harlow nodded, woozy. *Maybe she wasn't just tired.* She glanced down at her thigh, where blood and milky white Vespae poison oozed from a tear in her armor. That last one she'd killed must have gotten a sting in without her noticing. Sometimes in the heat of battle, she lost her ability to track every moment. "Got my ass handed to me."

The poison seeped into her, dulling her senses as she looked around to see how the rest of the team was faring. Harlow often lost track of everything but the next move in a fight. She was still a novice, and sometimes that meant tunnel vision when it came to her awareness in combat. Soon she'd lose any ability to use her magic, or shift into her Feriant form. The Vespae's poison acted as a magical immobilizer, temporarily freezing its victim's ability to connect to Okairos' source of aethereal power.

Samira helped Harlow to a velvet-cushioned bench at one end of the hallway. The fight was beginning to die down. Max, Mirai and the four others they'd come with had disappeared to chase down the last of the Vespae, lest they get back to their swarm and bring reinforcements. Harlow had been the only one of them stung, which frustrated her to no end. The Feriant Legion was having a hard time accepting her into their ranks, and she worried that every mistake would be held against her. She took a few deep breaths, trying to focus on the beautiful snow-covered courtyard outside the giant windows the bench faced.

The Austvanger Institute for Geological Research was a lovely facility in an old palace at the center of the city. Harlow's team had come here on a mission to help a group of refugees make their way to the Rogue Order's sanctuary, but their team had arrived too late. The Institute was meant to be a good place to hide, with its maze of hallways and gardens. The refugees had believed they were safe here—and they should have been.

But the Vespae got here first. They were looking for something, and the refugees had been nothing more than collateral damage. "Are they all dead?" Harlow asked, hoping Sam knew she was talking about the refugees, not the Vespae.

Samira's dark eyes widened with sadness. "All but one human. Tomy's talking to her now." Sam nodded towards a huddled figure on the floor near the doorway to the courtyard, and the muscular Ventyr woman who spoke to her. Harlow blinked several times. The Vespae poison was making her groggy and she hadn't noticed them at all. Tomyris, Sam's partner, spoke softly with the injured human. They recited a familiar prayer to Raia the Mother in unison. Tomy was honoring her last rites. "She won't last long."

"Poor thing," Harlow murmured. She watched, her vision still blurry, as Max, Mirai and the other returned. They dragged corpses, Vespae and refugee alike, into the courtyard.

Samira, who had become one of her best friends in the Feriant Legion, fished a syringe out from a pack at Harlow's waist. "Why didn't you take this sooner?" the Strider asked, as she stabbed Harlow's arm with it.

Tomyris' venom, the antidote to the Vespae's, flowed into her. It burned through her, cleansing her vital systems of the creatures' debilitating poison, but it hurt. Tears stung her eyes, and not from the pain.

Sam sunk down next to her on the bench, her sturdy body a warm comfort as the venom did its work. Though the rest of the Legion remained chilly with Harlow, Tomyris and Sam, and the Legion's strategist, Audata, had become friends. Friends who knew that every mission that wasn't looking for Larkin and Finn tortured Harlow.

"We'll be back on the search soon enough," Sam reassured her.

Harlow closed her eyes against the pain of Tomyris' venom, but it did nothing to help the ache in her heart. "It's been so long since we had a lead," she whispered. She didn't want any of the team to hear her complaining; she felt enough like an outsider as it was, and didn't want them thinking she resented being sent on missions like these.

Sam's hand closed around hers for a moment, and Harlow felt blessed for the thousandth time since that last day in Nea Sterlis for her easy friendship. She and Tomyris were a binary system: Samira, with the gravitational pull of a dark star, and Tomyris the brightest point in any room. They'd taken her under their wings and taught her the ways of the Warbirds, letting her grieve the loss of Finn and Larkin and her family in whatever ways she needed.

Her sisters had been none too happy about it. Thea especially, who wanted nothing more than for Harlow to forgive Aurelia quickly and move on. If Selene couldn't forgive the fact that Aurelia had secrets that might have kept Finn and Larkin from disappearing into the limen, then neither could Harlow. Things had been tense between the Kranes since their arrival in Sanctum, the Rogue Order's compound. So tense that the twins had left with the Wraiths, Nox and Ari Flynn, on covert missions to Nytra and Avignonne, respectively.

Tomyris' venom did its work, and the pain eased. Harlow tried not to think about what Finn's would have done for her, as her Claimed—how fast it would have healed her, or the euphoria she would have felt at his bite. This was the best she could get, and she should be grateful for it. She stood without much of a struggle. "Let's go help them with the bodies," she said, pulling Sam up from the bench.

Sam groaned. "Noooo, I was enjoying a break."

They headed for the courtyard anyway. As they neared the door to the courtyard, Harlow could hear the conversation Tomyris had with the dying refugee. The Ventyr grabbed Sam's hand as she was about to push through the courtyard door, squeezing her partner's hand hard. "There's children in the catacombs."

Sam nodded, rushing outside to tell the six other members of their team. They followed her back inside, a big Ventyr named Max leading them. He crouched over the human, taking her hand with gentle grace, his voice lowering. "Can you tell me where the children are?"

Harlow was impressed with the way the Ventyr in the Feriant Legion were able to present their true forms to humans without frightening them. Their faces were impossibly beautiful, of course, but they were still winged, fanged creatures with a variety of skin colors not seen before on Okairos.

Max, like Finn, had pale opalescent skin with a blue cast to it in some lights, and long onyx hair that hung down his back in a plait. His partner, Mirai, was a short, pear-shaped sorcière with a square jaw and bronze skin that glowed from within. She peeked out from behind Max's wings to glance at the refugee. When she turned, she murmured the directions the dying human gave to the others, glancing at Harlow, trepidation in her eyes.

Harlow was used to that look by now, the vague message that while they didn't believe she'd outright betray them, they didn't fully trust her either. It was the exact same look the sorcière of the Order of Mysteries continued to give her after she'd been with Mark Easton, a human, for two years. Harlow was both utterly exhausted by the politics of Okairos' many factions, and understood completely. When everyone was liable to turn on others for even a miniscule amount of power, this was how things were. People only trusted those they considered their own—and outsiders had to prove themselves.

"I'll stay here and finish with the bodies," Harlow said. She'd found that every time she offered to do an unpleasant task that Mirai softened towards her. She got it—she needed to earn her place.

A small smile played on Mirai's generous lips, so maybe her efforts were working. "Thank you, Harlow. We'll see you back at Sanctum."

Max looked to Samira, who shook her head. "Me and Tomy'll help with the dead." Her voice dropped. "It's going to be a few with that one anyway. We won't leave her 'til it's over."

Max clapped a hand to Sam's shoulder, squeezing it once, before motioning to the team to follow him. Harlow didn't watch them disappear. She just got to work, following Sam out to the courtyard. Tomyris stayed inside with the human, holding her hand and talking softly to her as the woman relaxed more and more. The Ventyr woman had a way with people—all people—that Harlow admired. She was brash and confident, but warm and genuinely kind. She was, Harlow thought, the best of what the Illuminated could be.

If only the rest of them could be like Tomyris...

...and Alaric, and Petra... and Finn.

Harlow pushed the thought from her mind as she piled the rest of the refugees' bodies. There were about a dozen of them, though Harlow didn't like to count the dead. Each was a tremendous failure in her eyes, an incredible loss that she couldn't bear to think of specifically in times like this.

There was so much they still needed to do, and Harlow didn't have time to grieve the way she wanted to for these lost lives. Before the season last spring, she'd never thought about death, especially not on this scale. She certainly never expected she'd have to learn to fight, to protect others with both her magic and her skills. It was overwhelming at times, but most of the Warbirds had been thinking this way their whole lives, and it didn't do her any favors with them to show how much this disturbed her.

Snow drifted down in the courtyard in huge flakes. It was pretty enough here, protected from Falcyra's incessant, frigid winter wind. The courtyard was quiet. Austvanger was quiet—too quiet for such a large city, but most people had either fled, or were deep in hiding. The Vespae and the Illuminated alike were a constant scourge here, though in different ways.

They didn't have time to bury the dead, so Harlow and Samira held hands, pulling aether from the threads of magic around them. Together, they transformed the marble statues that looked over the four corners of the courtyard into a tomb for the fallen refugees. Their last companion wouldn't rest with them, but Tomyris would give her all the help she could, and she deserved every moment of the Ventyr medic's help.

Sam's smile was sad when she turned away from the tomb. She squeezed Harlow's arm once. "It's the best we can do for them."

Harlow didn't say that the best they could have done for them would have been getting here sooner, when the call came in over the radio, instead of waiting for the Rogue Council to approve the mission. But like everything on Okairos, the Rogue Order had its processes and traditions. And while those ways were leaps and bounds more progressive in comparison to the immortal Orders, they weren't foolproof. This tomb was evidence of that, but there was no point in saying so. Samira knew as well as she did that making decisions this way saved lives as often as it lost them.

They dragged the Vespae bodies into a pile, searching each one as they went. The Warbirds' top strategist, Audata, had discovered that sometimes the Vespae carried things with them. Her talent was pattern-recognition, and she'd found there was something connecting these items, though she hadn't worked out what that was yet. As such, the Warbirds were tasked with searching all Vespae bodies before burning them.

Sam pulled a small handful of silvery rocks from one of the Vespae's ragged vestments. She dropped them almost immediately. "Shit," Sam swore.

Harlow rushed over to check Sam's hand, which showed no injury. She picked up one of the rocks, and felt what Sam must have: It was as though the rocks were repelling her. Something about them felt *wrong*.

"They were in that little bag," Sam said, pointing to the body she'd retrieved the stones from. A small black bag lay on the ground next to it. Harlow picked it up. The fabric was rough, but had a toughness to it. She examined the threads that made it up, and found they were odd. Stifling. On a hunch, she bent down, using the bag to pick up the rocks Sam had dropped. She felt none of the repelling feeling she had before.

"The fabric blocks whatever gives off that *feeling*," Harlow explained as she filled the bag.

Sam's eyes widened. "You don't think they were here *because* of those rocks, do you? Are they smart enough for something like that?"

Harlow shrugged. "You know what Audata would say."

"Don't question the impossible…" Sam began quoting their strategist.

"Figure it out," Tomyris finished as she came over. "I think the human might recover… But if we take her back together…"

"We won't be able to figure out what's going on with these rocks," Sam finished.

They finished each other's sentences. It would be cute if it didn't hurt so fucking much to watch, Harlow thought.

"You take her back then," Sam reasoned. "Harlow and I will look around. We can make the jump together once we set the Vespae ablaze."

Tomy nodded, though there was worry in her eyes. The Dominavus, the Illuminated's elite squad of enforcers, had been spotted in Austvanger recently, and the Rogues' intelligence reported they'd been hunting for both Harlow and Finn.

"Maybe Harlow should take her," Tomy said.

Sam sighed. "If Harlow hadn't been stung, I'd agree with you, but she won't be strong enough to teleport with a human for another couple of hours. You take her, and Harlow and I will finish up here."

Tomyris drew a long breath, then nodded. "Okay. See you both at base."

Sam kissed Tomyris, long and hard. "We're right behind you. Promise."

CHAPTER 2

Tomyris blinked out with the human, and Harlow and Sam got to work searching the rest of the Vespae. They found nothing, until Harlow searched the last body, and found a scrap of paper, worn and faded. On one side was the number 317, on the other an image of a building with a domed roof that looked vaguely like the planetarium in Nuva Troi.

"What's this, do you think?" she asked Sam, handing her the scrap of paper.

Sam examined it closely. "It looks like an observatory."

"I was thinking planetarium, but that tracks too."

Sam glanced at the number, then strode inside, waving at the bodies. "We can come back to burn them, before we go."

Harlow followed the Strider, who set a quick pace inside the building, her footsteps silent on the marble floors. She stopped short in front of an arched doorway. The stone around it, and all the other doorways, was ornately carved in a delicate pattern, but that's not what Samira focused on now. She tapped her fingers against a gold plate on the door.

A number. This one was 72. Harlow nodded to show she understood and followed Samira to the next door in the long hallway, which had an identical gold plate that read 71. They didn't speak. This was a rule with the Warbirds on missions—always assume the enemy can hear you, and always assume they're where you won't expect them to be. Harlow and Samira turned in the other direction and found door 73. Samira broke into a light jog, which Harlow kept up with.

The building was nearly as cold as outside, so jogging not only made their search for room 317 quicker, but also warmer. Harlow stopped by a stairwell door. A sign showed that offices 300-399 were on the third floor. They were on the "ground level" currently.

"Third floor," Harlow mouthed to Sam, silently tapping the sign.

Sam nodded once, and they crept into the stairwell, careful not to slam the door. They made their way up the stairs, feet quiet on the marble floors, both conscious of the fact that any noise would echo horribly in the enclosed area. Just as they reached the third floor, Sam reached back, gripping Harlow's arm. They froze, listening.

For a long moment, Harlow heard nothing, but she trusted her friend's instincts implicitly. Samira's primary talent was sensing any and all disturbance in the threads that made up reality. It was a little like she "saw" her surroundings in her mind, though many factors affected how much and how far she perceived.

Harlow heard it now. Many floors below, in one of the sub-basement levels, someone—no, *several* someones were creeping up the stairs. Sam's eyes widened pointedly. Harlow nodded affirmation that she'd detected what Sam had. Samira gripped her hand and they worked with their combined power to muffle the noise of their steps as they raced up the last flight of stairs.

Neither were exceptionally good with the kinds of spells that most sorcière found simple, like muffling spells or wards. Aethereal power was trickier, purer— more suited to generative work, like creating the tomb in the courtyard, or magical perception, rather than manipulation of the threads themselves. But they were good enough to dampen the already quiet sound of their steps. They strengthened the muffling when they came to the door, slipping through in silence.

When they were on the other side, Sam waited as Harlow focused. Just as she had done so many months ago in Mark Easton's apartment building, she mani-fested her desire for a locked door, to which only she held the key. Both appeared, and she felt the threads shift as Sam muffled the sound of the lock turning.

Harlow pressed her hand to the door, melting the lock. "We'll have to find another way out," she whispered.

Sam nodded, tracing a finger over the map next to the door. "This is the only way up to this floor. We'll fly out—do you think you'll be able to make the shift?"

Harlow shrugged as she followed Sam down the hallway. She felt better, and was able to use her magic now, but shifting took more power and her body was still recovering from the Vespae poison. They had theories about recovery timing, but only theories; the variations in how long complete recovery took were unpredictable. Furthermore, it was different for the other pairs in the Feriant Legion than it was for Harlow, who didn't have access to her Claimed's blood or venom. Finn could have healed her, almost completely, in an instant.

That was a forbidden thought, though—Harlow pushed it deep into the recesses of her mind and focused on her surroundings. The third floor was not as grand as the ground floor had been. Here, the hallways were narrower, and certainly darker, as there were rooms on each side, rather than an enormous courtyard at the center.

If the electricity in the building was in working order, the mahogany of the paneled walls would likely give off a warm glow. But the ruling Illuminated had cut the whole world off. As far as anyone knew, power grids were only on in Nuva Troi, parts of Nea Sterlis, and in select cities in nations like Avignonne and

Castel des Rêves, where there were large concentrations of elite Illuminated families. As well, those cities had advanced wards that kept the Vespae out. Falcyra had been utterly abandoned, and the Illuminated were determined to punish the entire world for even *thinking* of rebelling against them. The cold, flat light coming in from the window gave the Institute an unnerving, claustrophobic feeling.

Sam stopped in front of 317 and tried the heavy wooden door. It didn't open. She closed her eyes as she pulled a kit out of one of the interior pockets of her jacket. Deftly, using her perception of the threads inside the lock, she picked it in seconds. Harlow envied the skill. She could create all kinds of things with her Strider abilities, but that wouldn't allow her to unlock a locked door. Whatever her perceptive capabilities were, they hadn't emerged yet.

Grinning, Sam stood, pushing the door open for Harlow. Inside, they found what Harlow felt was a fairly typical academic's office: messy, filled with books and papers piled on a heavy desk in the center of the small room. The walls were lined with bookshelves, with one enormous arched window that showed an excellent view of Austvanger, even if it looked over the alleyway that housed the building's many full dumpsters.

Harlow shut the door behind them, knowing it would muffle the sound of their location, if whoever was in the stairwell was attempting to suss them out. She wasn't sure how they'd get up here, but in a building as old as this one, she didn't doubt there were other ways up to this level. The Institute was a former vampire palace, and there were sure to be hidden passages for servants and other clandestine purposes everywhere. They'd bought themselves time, but if their pursuers were even somewhat knowledgeable about this building, they'd find another way to this level. In silence, the two of them riffled through papers and books as quickly as they could, not knowing what exactly they were looking for,

other than something that would give them information about the observatory.

"I'm not finding anything about the observatory," Sam said.

Harlow sighed as she finished searching the desk. "Me either."

Whoever's office this was had been doing surveys of gold mines in Castel des Rêves for decades. Lucrative, but completely uninteresting. Harlow shoved the drawer she'd finished searching shut. It closed differently, hitching halfway through, instead of gliding smoothly as the others had done. Harlow opened it and closed it again, watching it hitch in the exact same spot. She stopped the drawer, then felt along the edge.

Sam turned from the bookshelf she was searching, her movement sharp. "There's something there. Something different about that drawer."

Harlow's fingertips grazed the edge. There it was, a nearly undetectable irregularity. She placed her other hand underneath the open drawer on a hunch, and pressed in on the miniscule bump. The bottom dropped out of the drawer, accompanied by a slim manila paper envelope.

Sam froze, her eyes getting that faraway look they got when she was using her perceptive abilities. "They're here. We've gotta go."

"Where?" Harlow asked, clutching the envelope to her chest.

Sam closed her eyes to focus her extrasensory ability further. "Shit. They're on the other side of the floor, moving fast." She rushed to the door, locking it once more as Harlow threw open the window, feeling inside herself for the telltale spark that told her the Feriant was ready to emerge.

There was a flicker there, but not enough to shift. There must still be traces of Vespae poison in her system. She pushed the window open wide and shoved the envelope into Sam's arms. She looked down at the dumpsters. It was a long drop, but she thought she could cushion her fall with some quick magic. And she'd been taught to fall without taking too much damage, as shifting from her Feriant form quickly in battle scenarios was fairly common.

"Go," Harlow urged. "Get this back to Sanctum."

Sam shook her head. "I'm not leaving you."

The sound of boots on the floor, moving fast was louder by the second. They didn't have time to argue. Harlow lied. "I should be able to shift in a few minutes. All I have to do is fall and run. *Go.*"

Sam's dark brown eyes were full of suspicion, but she tucked the envelope into her jacket and stepped onto the windowsill. She was graceful as a dancer, leaping into the air, the lines of her body blurring as her Feriant form took shape. Feriant were sleek, raptorial, and as big as a small SUV. The feathers on the double crest on Sam's head rippled in the wind as she looked back, hesitating as Harlow jumped into the windowsill. Someone was at the door now, and they had lock picks. They might not have Sam's talent with perception, but Harlow had to assume they knew how to use the picks. She regretted not melting the lock now, but there was no help for it; she needed the little reserve of aethereal power she'd built up to cushion her fall.

Closing her eyes, she stepped off the ledge, willing the dumpsters below to soften into several piles of giant beanbags. When her body hit soft velvety material, rather than hard metal, she knew she'd succeeded. Her nose wrinkled. They still smelled like trash though. Above her, Sam hovered, flapping her wings hard.

A figure appeared at the window, and Harlow recognized the face immediately—one of the vampires with the Dominavus squad Rakul Kimaris usually led, recognizable from the hours of footage Nox and Ari had procured over the summer in Nea Sterlis. Harlow didn't know her name, but the vampire was yelling Harlow's.

"Go," Harlow screamed to Sam as she righted herself, struggling to escape the pile of beanbags she'd created. "Go!"

Harlow was on her feet and running, unable to keep track of Sam above her in the dark, narrow alleys. Somewhere, on one of the streets surrounding her, boots hit the snow-covered cobblestone, running just as fast—faster even—than she was. The Dominavus were a combination of vampires and the Illuminated, after all. They'd use their superior speed to catch her and take her back to Nuva Troi. To Connor McKay, who she knew wouldn't hesitate to harm her if he thought it would get his son back, or if he simply blamed her for his disappearance.

Harlow rounded corner after corner, completely lost, struggling not to panic. From the sound of things, they were closing in on her, though the incoming storm muffled noises, distorting them in ways that made Harlow unable to track her pursuers accurately. Snow was funny that way, she'd learned, and Falcyran winters were terrifying both for their brutality, and the uncanny way storms altered both sight and sound.

And then something wonderful happened.

The astronomical clock sounded its bell. It was one of Austvanger's most storied tourist attractions, having been built almost a thousand years prior to track the movement of the stars and planets in their system, as well as the days. Its bell was one of the loudest in creation, and it would mask the sound of her feet. She ran towards it. If she could make it across the square the clock was located in, she might be able to lose the Dominavus and buy herself enough time until she could make the shift.

The sound of the bell grew louder; she was getting closer. She couldn't hear the Dominavus, so perhaps they couldn't hear her either. The narrow street she was running down widened as she rounded a corner. The way was clear, and she was nearly to the square. A clear view of the clock was directly in front of her, with dozens of street openings to choose from to make her escape. It was two o'clock, which meant the clock was nearly done ringing, as it had already rung eleven times.

The hope that lit Harlow's heart ablaze snuffed out as soon as she tracked her potential path across the square. None of the usual public services were functional, and the snow in the square was an untouched canvas, waiting to be marred. While the blizzard was growing worse by the second, it wasn't yet coming down hard enough to mask her prints. No matter what path she chose, the Dominavus would see the direction she'd gone if they followed her to the square. She didn't have enough power in reserve to mask her footprints either.

Her heart beat wildly, trying to think of another way out as she drifted into the square. Helplessness threatened to take over. There had to be some clever way out of this. There just had to be. She couldn't let them take her back. She hadn't once made it through Audata's tests for resisting torture: she was a risk to everyone she loved.

Tall, imposing figures emerged from half a dozen streets. Harlow's mouth went dry—she was surrounded. Of course, they'd still been able to track her, even despite the bell, which sounded one last time. Laughter skittered across the square, echoing in the new silence.

"Hello, Ms. Krane," a voice said, softly enough, though her words carried. It was the vampire who'd looked out the window at the Institute. "We've been looking everywhere for you."

Harlow thought fast, shoving her clammy hands into her jacket pockets to keep them from visibly shaking. "Is Rakul with you?"

The vampire, whose platinum blonde ponytail swung to and fro as she stalked forward, laughed again. "Rakul won't help you, witch. Give up and come with us without a fight."

"No one here wants to hurt you," one of the Illuminated said. He was a redheaded giant, nearly seven feet tall, and his voice boomed across the square.

The blonde vampire raised an eyebrow. "Speak only for yourself. *I* want to hurt you." Harlow refused to let her fear show, squaring her shoulders as the vampire took step after excruciating step towards her. "Just give me a reason. I dare you."

The six warriors strode towards her with an insulting lack of urgency. They were relaxed, confident in the fact that she was theirs. Harlow was trapped. Even with her training, she couldn't fight six of the warriors on her own. She'd gotten good enough to fight the Vespae, but this was different. The Vespae fought by instinct, not training. The Dominavus were the most elite warriors known to Okairos. Her shoulders slumped in defeat.

A gust of wind hit her face, as something dark shot out of the low cloud cover of the storm. Talons dug into her shoulders before she could fully register what was happening. *Samira.* Her feet lifted off the ground as her stubborn friend lifted her into the air. The Dominavus moved quickly, but Sam was already rising above the tops of the buildings in the square. As she hit the cloud cover, the spark Harlow had been looking for returned.

She didn't have much power left, but she'd only slow Sam down, and the Dominavus were sure to shift and follow them. "Drop me," she yelled. "I can shift."

Sam hesitated. "I mean it, Sam," Harlow screamed.

One of Sam's talons tapped three quick times on her shoulder then paused. Harlow understood the message; she'd release her in three. The talon tapped her again now, at a slower pace. Harlow closed her eyes and focused on the dark spark of aethereal magic inside her as Sam rose higher into the storm.

One.

Two.

Three.

Harlow fell, dropping quickly as she touched the spark within. As she shifted, her Feriant senses picked up their assailants, not far behind. She beat her wings hard, catching up to Sam.

Glad that worked, Sam said in her head. In their Feriant forms, they were able to speak mind-to-mind.

Me too, Harlow replied. *Thank you... The Ventyr among them are following.*

I feel them, Sam assured her, banking hard heading north.

With Sam's talent for sensing her surroundings, and the cover of the storm, Harlow was sure they'd escape. *Let's go home.*

CHAPTER 3

The blizzard cleared about twenty miles south of Sanctum, revealing the forgotten valley that had once been one of Falcyra's most luxurious ski resorts. Fifty years ago, a group of industrious vampires had bought a little fishing village, right at the edge of a fjord, and converted the entire thing into a posh resort, where Okairons could enjoy quaint scenery while indulging in ridiculously expensive spa treatments and the best skiing this side of the Apennine Mountain range. Twenty years after opening, the resort was overrun with ghasts, several nasty poltergeists, and a shade. The shade's murderous howling had been the last straw for the original owners.

The owners sold the resort at an unbelievable loss to Lou Spencer, the Rogue Queen of the time, and she'd made a very big show of having it destroyed to rid the area of the plague of spirits that inhabited it. There had been a television program and everything, though Lou's involvement had been obscured. It had all been a hoax. The television documentary had been the first of the Rogue Order's forays into media manipulation—all to hide this place from the Illuminated, and the Falcyran vampires, in preparation for using it as a large sanctuary.

And it had worked. The area was so remote, and so rumored to be haunted even after the resort's "destruction," that the world had gladly forgotten it existed. Lou had invested in advanced warding. Rogue sorcière from a securities firm in Avignonne, Lou's home nation, had created a series of wards that made Sanctum extremely difficult to perceive, unless you knew exactly the right counter spells to use.

Now it was a bustling village, filled to the brim with a bizarre intermixing of immortals and humans alike. Lou had the rougher elements of the poltergeists and shades banished immediately, which was easy for her to do, despite the former owners having hired the most expensive mediums in the world to fix the problem, to no avail. It was so easy for Lou because she was the one who'd summoned them in the first place.

The side effect was that the ghasts were permanent features of the resort, which was rather unfortunate for Harlow, who was unsettled by them. But aside from that, she was endlessly impressed by Kate's sire, and adoptive mother, who'd used the fortune she'd made from her vineyards to buy this land and make it a sanctuary for the Rogue Order.

As they drew nearer, Harlow's heart ached to see the charming stone houses dotting the valley floor, the snowy, cobbled streets, and the twilight lighting of the gas lamps throughout town. Electricity and most of the basic services that Okairons were accustomed to were still unavailable to them, though Sanctum had a generator that was used sparingly. Near the fjord beyond the village lay an enormous silver firedrake, napping in the snow. *Cian.*

The great dragon raised their head as Sam and Harlow began their descent and stretched, much like a cat would, before launching into the air in one long bound. It took Cian barely any effort to reach them, and they circled just below them, spinning a few times in the air to delight the crowds of children that had come into the streets to watch their flight.

Cian didn't get out much these days, except to complete their assigned patrols, which enchanted the children of the village as much as the abundance of ghasts did. Cian was wracked with guilt and sorrow over what had happened with Finn, but Harlow thought these flights brightened their spirits.

When you didn't return with the others, I worried. Cian said. Like the Feriant, in their alternae, they could communicate telepathically.

I'm sorry to have worried you, Harlow replied.

Samira's wings tucked close to her body as she dove. Harlow watched her trajectory, spotting Tomyris, who was waving at the center of the village square.

You worried your parents as well, Cian said.

Harlow hissed. It was a raptorial noise that she loved making—its violence was satisfying. She could all but hear Cian's inner sigh. She was still not speaking to Aurelia, and though Selene had not reconciled with her wife yet, Harlow knew the day was coming. They'd headed out on long snowshoe hikes several times in the past few weeks. They were talking, and while Harlow had no desire to see Mama miserable forever, she wasn't ready to talk to Aurelia yet.

They'd actually talked too much, in her opinion, when they'd first arrived in Sanctum. Things had been said that Harlow couldn't take back now, nor could she manage an apology, or accept another from her mother. Space was what everyone needed right now, which was difficult in the tiny village. Harlow missed Nuva Troi endlessly, for hundreds of reasons, but the ability to *not* see someone was topping her list right now.

Go on without me, Harlow said. *I want to stretch my wings.*

Cian did not reply, but made lazy circles in the air before landing just outside of town in the empty training fields. The children who'd been watching screamed, running towards the field in excitement. Harlow made circles of her own, watching as they piled atop her friend. Cian's only duties were their patrols and babysitting, as there was no safer place within the compound than with a dragon.

Harlow's wings rarely got tired anymore, now that she had daily training sessions with the Warbirds. She took another giant circle around the village, enjoying the feeling of the frigid wind in her face. In her Feriant alternae, there was a kind of peace she'd never known. It wasn't that her humanoid self was gone, but rather that all its concerns were lessened, their immediacy gone to the ultra-present worldview of the Feriant. The Warbirds were teaching her that mentality could be brought into her true form as well, that the two needn't be separate, but like working around the effects of Vespae poison, Harlow struggled to achieve mind-body alignment tasks. Her mind wandered too easily, got too lost in worry, or she was distracted by the sounds around her.

Finn would have ideas about how to make that easier for her when he got back—he always had a hack for her busy mind. *When he got back.* The thought hurt, but in a way that surprised Harlow. The ache had grown familiar, comforting almost. It wasn't that she enjoyed him being missing; there was nothing pleasant about her fear, but there was a painful kind of comfort in musing over what he'd think about the ways the world had changed when he returned.

Harlow would be expected at the Dairy in an hour or so. The standard for mission debriefing was to meet up at the Warbirds' headquarters, and then Audata would report out to the Council. She should head in and shower, but it was so quiet up here. Down there, there were hundreds of people, many of whom were suspicious of her, given her relationships to Aurelia and Finn both.

Everyone knew the ways her mother had kept the Illuminated's secrets, as head of the Order of Mysteries, and though Aurelia had been allowed to stay in Sanctum, she was not automatically trusted, and neither were her children. Harlow had watched her sisters and friends overcome the Rogues' wariness in different ways, but Harlow was having trouble doing so. Aside from Larkin, she'd always been the most introverted of her family, often feeling awkward in social situations. She was never certain how she'd offended people, but she often found out later that she'd made some misstep that couldn't be forgiven.

Okairons had what felt like thousands of subtle rules about how to interact that confused Harlow endlessly. She didn't understand why just being honest about things and respectful of one another wasn't enough, but the intricacies of tone, phrasing and even body language were often beyond her. In situations like these, where everything was further fraught by issues she *did* understand, like the Rogues' completely valid fear of the McKays, who were notorious for their cruelty, or the wariness of the immortal Orders' leaders like Aurelia, everything became even harder for Harlow. There were just so many social cues to parse out, and she often didn't understand what was happening in a given moment, but realized her mistakes later—long after the time had passed to do things the way Thea or the twins would have.

The village buildings grew larger as Harlow descended, though she still felt blessedly removed from the reality of the compound. With her enhanced sight, she spotted Riley Quinn and Enzo walking towards the cottage the three of them shared and she swooped down to greet them. Like Thea, Enzo had integrated nicely into the community here at Sanctum, given his relationship with Riley and all his natural charm. People had always liked her best friend. He had an easy way with people that Harlow lacked, because of his empathic abilities.

Riley was the same, and they reassured Harlow that no one hated or feared her. As they put it, "They just need time to get used to you being around."

Harlow shifted as she landed, appearing silently behind Riley and Enzo. Axel, who sat in the window, watching for all of them, gave her away. He stood, scratching rapidly at the glass, meowing. Riley turned, their locs fanning out behind them as they spun. "Harlow! You're all right. We were worried when you and Sam didn't come back with Tomy."

Harlow tried for a smile, though she felt the way it only pulled at her lips and cheeks, as she took the chameleon shifter's gloved hand, giving it a quick kiss. Enzo pressed another to her forehead. "Glad you're back. We heard about the trouble from Sam, just now."

Harlow nodded, following them through the garden gate. The three of them had elected to share a small house in the village with Cian, rather than breaking up into one of the tiny ski cottages further out.

"I need to get to the Dairy, but I can pick up our grocery allotment on the way home, if you want," she offered.

The two of them held up the canvas bags that held the week's allotment of food for their house. Luckily, Sanctum had been operating off the grid for a long time. While their generators weren't powerful enough to light each of the village's buildings, the greenhouse had priority of power and the human hedge-witches had made quick work of using their newfound access to aether to encourage winter growth.

The human practitioners astonished Harlow. She'd been taught in school that humans were capable of doing magic, but that they would struggle with it terribly, given their inaptitude for it. Since the breach under the catacombs had been released, and aether flowed freely into the threads of the world now, she'd found something quite different from what the Illuminated had taught them.

"Oh, you got them already," Harlow said, taking a bag from Riley and another from Enzo.

Riley wrinkled their nose. "You smell of Vespae guts."

Enzo's face matched Riley's. "I'll get your gear cleaned up while you wash your hair. You've definitely got Vespae goo in your braids."

Harlow glanced at the dark mess in her honey-blonde hair and shrugged. It was a part of fighting the Vespae she'd learned to ignore. Thinking about it for too long turned her stomach. As they entered the little stone house, Axel wound around their legs, chirruping and purring, as everyone took the groceries to the tiny kitchen at the back of the cottage. Each of the village cottages was furnished in a similar beige and cream palette that had been all the rage when the resort was built, and was equipped with a minuscule, but functional kitchen. Though the refrigerator was all but useless except for storage, the rest of the amenities worked well enough most of the time.

Enzo picked Axel up, kissing his head as he filled his bowl with fresh kibble. "I'll start the water heater for your shower, if you want to send your gear down."

Harlow nodded, then simply undressed in the kitchen. Enzo shook his head, smirking. "Cheeky," he murmured as she shot through the house and up the stairs in only her bra and underwear.

She hadn't wanted to stink up the house, though. Some combination of citrus, rosemary and vanilla infused the air here, making it smell homey and comforting, while Vespae blood carried the distinct smell of death. Enzo, who was adept with any magic regarding garments, would have her gear fresh in no time.

It took a few minutes to assess the damage she'd taken in the fight in Austvanger, but there was nothing that needed attention. *Surely the water heater had filled by now*, she thought. But she didn't really know how long it had been. It was hard to keep track of that kind of thing these days. Harlow had never been good with time to begin with, and without the constant aid of her phone, she was often adrift. She tried the shower water, pleased to find it was the perfect temperature, but it wouldn't be for long, so she hurried to rinse herself off before the hot water ran out.

The tiny bathroom had enough room for a sink, a toilet, and a tub, which had a clever showerhead on the ceiling that Harlow stood under, closing her eyes against the sight of the blood washing away. Quickly, she scrubbed with some of the faintly herbal smelling soap that Selene had brought over last week. She had been working with the human hedgewitches, sharing knowledge—learning together about the different ways to use magic.

Harlow couldn't deny she was proud of Mama—how quickly Selene had adapted to the idea of humans using magic. Though she was loath to admit it, she was proud of Aurelia too. Mother had volunteered to share all she knew with the Rogue Order's governing Council in the spirit of cooperation between immortals and humans.

They'd always been told the Rogues were mostly unhappy immortal outcasts, but in truth, humans were primary in leadership. Samira hadn't been exaggerating when she'd said Kate's title as "Queen" was largely nominal. While Kate was the immortal liaison for the Rogues, her title was little more than a nickname here. She was a member of the Council, which was run in an egalitarian fashion, with each member having an important role.

Each of the immortal Orders had representation on the Council, along with representatives of all ancestries that organized committees for necessities like food, combat training and education of Sanctum's children. While the Rogue Order took in anyone who didn't want to be a part of the Illuminated's strict social structures, there was a fair amount of wariness regarding anyone who'd had heavy involvement in the governing bodies of the Immortal Orders, so people like the Kranes, or any of the Knights of Serpens, weren't privy to the inner workings of the Rogue Order.

Until coming to Sanctum, Harlow hadn't realized how much Aurelia's position in the Order of Mysteries had affected her life. Now, she and her family were just like everyone else, citizens who were expected to pull their weight. All of her concerns about finding Larkin and Finn were forced to be secondary to whatever the entire Rogue Order needed. She understood it, but it infuriated her all the same, and in moments like these, when she was alone in the shower, she let it make her as angry as she actually was.

Furious sobs wracked through her as she raged against the futility of showing she was trustworthy on missions like the one she'd been on today, when her sister and Finn were out there somewhere, alone, fending for themselves. She didn't know how she was expected to carry on, and pretending like she was handling things was almost more than she could manage.

Cian had made it clear to her that the Council's choices were appropriate a thousand times, that she needed to grit her teeth and prove herself—as the rest of her family had done. She'd tried to understand, but after being ostracized by the sorcière for being with Mark, she was tired of not having community. Tired and lonely—especially without Larkin and Finn, who'd always understood her best.

Harlow rinsed her hair one more time for good measure, breathing in the lingering steam to calm her fury. The water was starting to cool. Finn would love the way the Rogues approached hierarchy, as it was the same as how he ran the Knights. Leaders ate last and fought first, running the most dangerous missions and taking care of their people first and foremost. A stray tear slipped down her cheek as she tipped her head back and shut off the water before it got cold.

Another sob threatened to break free from her chest, but she didn't have time for her tears—for the aching void inside her where Finn and Larkin should be. She dried off quickly, padding down the hallway to the room she and Cian shared. The air was cold, but the room itself was cozy, decorated in calm, creamy whites. It was out of vogue to decorate with such bland colors, but they soothed Harlow's mind, which was a riot of thoughts and fears these days.

Harlow dressed in thick leggings and an ancient sweater that was somehow completely soft, rather than itchy wool. Enzo and Riley had been careful with the fibers they'd chosen for her when they were allowed to procure clothing for their house. Harlow was struggling with irritating textures, or fits that felt as though they were too close to her neck. Since there weren't many choices for everyone, she had few things, and Enzo often altered them for her so that her senses wouldn't be overwhelmed.

No one was sure why Harlow had grown so sensitive to things like light, sound, and fabrics. It had always been like this for her to a certain extent, but now it was worse. When she'd expressed horror at strong scents, Selene forced her to take a pregnancy test, despite the fact that Finn was protected.

She wasn't pregnant, which had been both a relief and a strange sadness. Finn didn't want children, and neither did she, but in that moment, knowing she might never see him again, there had been a sharp pain in her chest. It faded, but a child would have been part of him, a continuation of *them*.

Axel jumped onto the bed next to her as she pulled on a pair of heavy snow boots and laced them up. He purred loudly as he bumped his head hard on her arm. She scooped him onto her shoulders as she went downstairs and he curled around her neck like a scarf, rubbing his face against hers happily.

Downstairs, Enzo and Riley made a richly herbed wild rice soup together in the kitchen. The way they moved comfortably around one another elicited an ache in Harlow's chest as she settled into a kitchen chair. Axel stepped off her shoulders and sprawled out on the tiny kitchen table, blinking slowly at everyone and purring. After glancing at the kitchen clock, she determined she had a few minutes before she had to go debrief and she wanted to soak in as much of this domestic bliss as possible.

Despite their glamorous lives in the real world, Riley and Enzo were domestic deities here at Sanctum. Riley baked bread and arranged branches of various winter foliage into vases that cheered the entire compound. Enzo took in mending and restyled clothes for folks who had differing needs like Harlow's, and he could often be found by the fire, knitting hats and gloves made from the yarn the Rogues crafted from the wool harvested from their herd of hardy mountain sheep.

He said he liked to do it by hand, but he'd devised a way of making three of the same at once, knitting needles clacking softly next to him, floating in the air in concert with his hands. "Hush please. This is my meditation," he'd say if anyone interrupted him.

The comfort she got from sitting in the kitchen as they cooked made her ache for home. For Aurelia and Selene on Friday nights in the kitchen, making big bowls of pasta and drinking wine. The tears she tried to keep in leaked silently from her eyes. But even as she stifled her sobs, she couldn't hide from Enzo and Riley's empathy.

Both turned as a ghost seemingly emerged from the useless refrigerator, attracted to the intensity of her sadness. Harlow was familiar with it by now, as it seemed comfortable here: a former fox-shifter, who spent most of its time as a decomposing vulpine atrocity that often screamed wildly when she cried. It didn't matter that it couldn't actually make noise on this plane—it was disturbing.

Riley handed her a cloth napkin, smiling sadly. "You have to let some of the grief out, love."

They ignored the ghost entirely, which was what nearly everyone did. It wasn't so easy for Harlow. Axel faced the rotting fox, arching his back, his fur poofing out in an attempt to intimidate the ghost. It simply opened its mouth and maggots fell out. Harlow winced. They weren't real, of course. They weren't even solid, but it was disgusting all the same. Axel hissed at the creature. Perhaps it was intimidated, or just bored, but it dissipated into a little poof of smoke.

Enzo nodded, stirring the soup, completely oblivious to the drama that had taken place behind him. "If you don't, it's going to come out in a storm eventually."

Harlow glanced at the clock, and then let out the sobs choking her in a soft torrent, desperately praying to Akatei to not let the ghost return. Neither Riley or Enzo comforted her with touches or words, but went back to making soup and focaccia, waves of love and acceptance washing over her as she cried.

She was safe to cry. She had plenty of time for her grief. She was held. Harlow repeated these ideas to herself several times, but they didn't take, not really. No matter how hard she tried, she did not feel safe, nor did she have enough time. The only thing she knew for sure was that here, in this house, she was most definitely held. That did ease her pain somewhat.

As her sobs slowed and her breath came more naturally, Riley handed her a cool cloth, which she pressed to her face. It smelled of rosemary and well water. She smiled up at them, her mouth still shaky and stretched-feeling from her sobs.

"Thank you," she whispered.

Riley glanced at the clock, then pressed a kiss to her forehead. "You'd better go, or you'll be late for your debriefing."

CHAPTER 4

Harlow's meltdown made her late, despite her best efforts. She made it across the village, to the Dairy, with haste, but Audata was still waiting at the split door with a vaguely impatient look on her face. The Strider was the only one of the Feriant Legion without a Ventyr partner, and though some people found her to be prickly, Harlow liked her immensely.

Audata always said exactly what she meant. She was herself in a way that made Harlow envious. The tiny sorcière was just tall enough to rest her elbows on the half-door. As Harlow approached, relief flickered across her serious face.

"We got started fifteen minutes ago."

"I know," Harlow replied. "I'm sorry."

Audata stood up, stretching her spine to her full height, which was still nearly eight inches shorter than Harlow. Like Harlow's, her hair was braided into two jet black fishtails that hung down her back. This was standard for the Warbirds with long hair.

Audata searched her face. Though her expression didn't change much, her eyes softened. "You've been crying."

Harlow rubbed her runny nose with the back of her hand, sniffling a little. "Yes."

It was always best to be honest with Audata. Sometimes the tiny witch didn't understand subterfuge, even if it was self-protecting. She was like a walking lie detector, and when she couldn't determine *why* someone was lying, Harlow sensed that it caused her deep distress. Harlow had no desire to confuse or upset Audata. She was one of the few people who'd taken her at face value—who believed what Harlow said about herself without question, so long as she was honest. Harlow thought they might even be friends.

"Are you all right now?" Audata asked.

Harlow nodded. "May I come in?"

Audata looked vaguely surprised for a moment, as though she'd forgotten she was blocking Harlow from entering the Dairy, and then stepped out of the way. She held the door for Harlow, who followed her inside. The Dairy was enormous, having housed dozens of cows when the resort was operational, as well as an artisanal cheese store. Now it was the Warbirds training facility and home base.

There really wasn't any difference between the common room and the training area—the inside of the Dairy was one open room, its gorgeous wide-planked floors its only real luxury. But the common area had a semi-circle of couches and upholstered chairs they'd taken from the cafe that abutted the former cheese shop. The seating area surrounded a giant board that everyone called Audata's "string wall"—the place where she'd pinned up everything they'd collected from the Vespae, since Audata began to notice a pattern.

Small cards with Audata's precise handwriting on them affixed to each of the items and actual string connected them in a pattern that only Audata understood. The tiny Strider carried the little scrap of paper that Samira found, along with the bag of rocks, and another one of her cards. Everyone else was seated already, chatting amiably and drinking various beverages.

Audata pinned the things Harlow and Sam had brought back from Aust-vanger to the board. The manila envelope they'd retrieved lay unopened on the enormous stone coffee table in front of her. Samira beckoned, having saved her a seat on one of the couches. Tomyris was sitting on the floor in front of her, reclining against Sam's knee, piling three plates high with the various goodies everyone had brought from home.

Harlow had forgotten to pick up one of the loaves of focaccia Enzo made. The sting of having made yet another social misstep pierced her chest. Debriefings were usually pleasant, with beverages and food to accompany any of the information they'd gained on their enemy, and Harlow should have remembered the bread. She tried to distract herself from her emerging guilt by watching Audata pin her new treasures to the center of the board. Harlow saw their importance immediately as Audata connected a piece of string to each of the other items on the board.

"This is what we've been looking for," Audata explained as everyone quieted. Tomyris handed Harlow a plate of food. She plucked out a globe of cheddar from the selection and nibbled at it, savoring the sharp taste on her tongue as she listened carefully to everything Audata said. "Each of these items was a piece of information about the same thing— I just didn't know what. But I'm sure now— the Vespae are looking for *this* place." She pointed to the observatory in the figure.

"Do we have any ideas about where—or what—it is?" Max asked. He'd changed back into his human alternae. Now he was a tall, dark-haired man, with soulful brown eyes and burnt umber skin that glowed in the lamplight.

Audata shook her head. "Not yet, but I think each of these is a clue." She gestured to the other pins. "They're like pieces of a puzzle, but they all connect, and that envelope may hold the rest of what we need to know."

Mirai's hands fluttered impatiently. "Okay. So let's open it already."

Several glances shifted towards Harlow. They'd been waiting for her. Guilt over inconveniencing them, when they still didn't like or trust her much, seeped through her so virulently that her hands ached with the power of her emotion. Lest she attract another ghast, Harlow breathed deeply, attempting to calm herself.

Audata watched Harlow closely. Harlow knew from talking with her about such moments that she was processing every detail of the room. The furtive glances, the flush of annoyance at her lateness, and Harlow's reaction to it all. What she gleaned from connecting the dots, Harlow didn't know, but Audata stepped forward and carefully tore the sealed envelope open, pulling out a thin stack of papers.

Audata's eyes darted over the information quickly, discarding page after page in a neat pile on the table. A blonde Strider with a heavy, muscular figure stretched across the table, picking a few of the pages up and glancing through them.

"What do they say?" Mirai asked.

The blonde, Vero, shook her head. "Beats me. It's some kind of technical report."

"It is a detailed survey of a mine," Audata corrected, placing the last sheet face down on the table. "An iridium mine, to be precise."

"Iridium?" Max asked.

Audata went to the board and removed the little bag of rocks. She dumped them onto the table. "Pick them up," she suggested when Max leaned forward to examine them.

He did so, and just as Samira had done, he dropped them immediately. "What the fuck is wrong with those things?"

Then everyone had to try it. The eighteen remaining Striders and Ventyr all picked up the iridium, each having a similar reaction, though they passed the handful of rocks between them, rather than dropping them. When Tomyris had her turn, she calmly put them back in their bag, with barely even a wince. She'd held them longer than anyone else.

Harlow hid a smile behind her hands. Tomy was like that, braver than everyone, with a better poker face too. Audata's face didn't change, but again, there was a softening around her eyes that let Harlow know she too was pleased.

"What does this have to do with the observatory?" Vero asked.

Audata took a long moment to look at the board, then back at the papers she'd discarded. "I believe the observatory is near the minefields. Where that is —I don't know, as much of the report has been redacted. But it's a distinctive landmark, wouldn't you say?"

She pulled the illustration down and passed it around. Each of the Warbirds committed it to memory. The building was built from stone, with a top floor that looked to be an elegant glass solarium, and a solid, rounded dome that likely hid a powerful telescope. It sat atop a range of peaks that jutted out into a valley, surrounded by higher, more imposing mountains. In the distance, beyond the valley, lay a fjord. The perspective was a little off, as though an amateur might have drawn it, but none of the landmarks looked familiar to Harlow.

As she watched the Warbirds react, she understood that like her, none of them immediately recognized the location. Audata sat in front of her board, facing the group. In the light of the oil lamp that was placed near her board, her rosy copper skin glowed. She shook her head finally, as though ruling something out.

"It has to be here. There's no fjords in Avignonne."

Everyone looked as though she'd spoken in some language they didn't understand. Audata's eyes flew to the ceiling. She was often mildly frustrated that no one kept up with her ability to both remember vast amounts of disparate information and put it together in a meaningful way. "Avignonne has the only other mountain range where iridium has been found on Okairos, but it doesn't have fjords. Wherever this is, it's *here* somewhere." When no one spoke, she clarified. "In Falcyra."

Tomyris fought back a smile. "Yes, love. I think we're all wondering why we haven't found it yet, with all the patrols and searches we've done over the past months. We must've flown everywhere by now."

"Especially looking for that portal," Peyton complained.

The sturdy Ventyr was one of the Warbirds who liked Harlow the least, and didn't mind showing it. She was never cruel, but she'd made it clear that she and her partner Vance didn't trust Harlow. They'd asked to be taken off searches for Finn and Larkin, long before the portal had disappeared completely.

Harlow took an even breath, reminding herself of the maggot-vomiting fox ghast in her kitchen. Now was not the time to get upset. She'd been teased enough by the Warbirds for the way the ghasts followed her around.

Audata shrugged. "Unless you've been flying in a precise grid pattern, which you have not been, there is no way you've seen the whole of this country yet. Or even the mountain range we're located in. There's only twenty one of you. Twenty-two if you count Cian. It would take about—"

"We get it," Peyton interrupted. Then a bit more gently. "I just meant…"

"I know what you meant, Peyton," Audata replied.

There was no softness around her eyes now. Audata despised being chastised for her tendency to elaborate on the finer details of the things. Thea had a similar reaction at times, and it only endeared Audata to Harlow further.

"I think we're done for tonight," Audata said. "It suffices to say that the Vespae are looking for this observatory, though we cannot yet say why."

The group of twenty-one Warbirds all nodded, one by one. To her credit, Peyton looked guilty. Harlow couldn't hate her, or even dislike her. She wasn't mean, only protective of this special group of people. Harlow hoped that someday she would be accepted fully among them.

"So we keep looking," Samira said. "We keep an eye out for the observatory on patrols, and we stay careful about searching bodies after a skirmish." Samira was a great diplomat. Often her words ended conversations like this, smoothing over the rough edges of the group's many strong personalities.

Audata nodded. "Yes, I think at this point we must be close to something. And the Vespae certainly think they're close to finding the observatory—because these types of items aren't being found elsewhere."

"No?" Max asked.

"No," Kate Spencer said from the doorway. "I've had my people searching since Audata started the string wall, and nothing like this has been found in Nytra or Castel des Rêves."

Kate strode over to the group. "Sorry I'm late, Aud. Petra said to bring you these."

Kate set a stack of three crates of wine down on the table. Petra had just returned from a supply run to her parents' obscenely well-stocked mountain house a few hundred miles away, with all sorts of goodies, as well as essentials. Peyton stood up, heading for the kitchen for glasses and a wine opener as the Warbirds combed through the wine.

Harlow got up, taking a bottle for herself. Kate watched, mouth open, looking as though she'd like to say something. Harlow stuck a shadow dagger into the cork, pulling it out in one fell swoop as Kate watched, aghast. A few other immortals trickled in, all bringing booze and more food—it wasn't unusual for the Warbirds' friends to join them after a debriefing for parties. The Dairy was big, and far enough outside the residential area of the village to not be a nuisance.

A small team of the Warbirds left to join the ground forces for guard duty, but everyone else clearly meant to let off some steam, and for once, Harlow planned to join them. She pushed through the little crowd forming, tossing words over her shoulder as she went. "Tell Petra thanks for the wine."

CHAPTER 5

Harlow made her way to the little conservatory off the back of the Dairy as more people filled the open space. The tiny glass room used to be a greenhouse for fresh herbs used in the artisanal cheese, back in the days before the vampires had turned the village into a resort, but was now used as a meditation room. The big fireplace connecting the conservatory to the main Dairy was used to heat the entire building.

Harlow dragged one of the beanbags that dotted the room towards the fire and plopped into it, listening to the sounds of a party starting up in the common room. Someone had brought a battery-operated boombox, and music was playing. It was old music from thirty years ago, clearly a dance mix that had been played at parties up at the main Lodge, which the Council used for offices now. Not long ago, this would have been Harlow's cue to leave. She and Finn would have gone home and cozied up the cottage, where she'd be sharing a room with him, rather than Cian.

She wasn't sure if she was going to actually *drink* the wine she'd placed in her lap until she was gulping it down, straight from the bottle. Not one person had asked her if she was all right. If being pursued by the Dominavus had scared her. If she was worried that they'd come so close to taking her.

It was certainly more than Harlow could handle. She'd avoided thinking about it the entire trip back, and until the meeting had wound down. But now, it all rushed back—how close she'd come to being taken. She looked through the glass fireplace at the Warbirds dancing in the Dairy. None of these people would have come after her if the Dominavus had taken her. Not even Tomy or Sam, much as they cared for her.

It wasn't that she thought they *should*. If she'd been taken, it would have been foolish for *anyone* to try to get her back. The Dominavus were that formidable. But Finn would have. Finn, who followed her little sister through a breach between worlds, who would have destroyed *this* world and any other to get to her. Who was still out there somewhere, maybe hurt, maybe even dying. Finn would have come for her, and she couldn't do the same for him.

A little voice inside her whispered that Cian would have come for her, but her body was eager for relief from the rage that coursed through her. She took another long gulp of wine, letting the warmth it elicited washed over her. The edges of everything happening in the present got fuzzy as she drank again and again.

The leads had all dried up when the portal closed. It had been nearly a month since the Council had approved a search. Cian still looked, she knew, but she'd been strictly forbidden from going out on her own. When she'd railed against the idea, screaming at the Council that she'd never back down, they'd had the nerve to threaten her with a Binding to stop her from leaving.

It was too dangerous for her to go out on her own, with all she knew about Sanctum—and the Warbirds were needed for missions like the one to Austvanger. The worst part was, she understood. She didn't even disagree, not really. She'd learned so much about leadership from Finn's example that she got why they'd slowed the physical searches, hoping that magical searches might yield better, safer results.

At least they'd kept their word about that. Harlow brought the bottle to her lips again, almost draining the last of the expensive white wine. It had a slightly floral scent, with a buttery finish that was intoxicating. She laughed bitterly to herself. Of course it was intoxicating. It was wine.

Someone tapped Harlow's shoulder and she twisted in the beanbag chair to find Kate, looking concerned. "Are you drinking?"

"Obviously," Harlow replied, shaking the bottle at Kate. It was an excellent vintage, and she hoped it made Kate sick to see her gulping it down like it was water.

"Slow down," Kate pleaded. "You'll be wasted."

Harlow laughed. "That's sort of the point, Kate."

Kate dragged a beanbag next to Harlow's, clearly meaning to sit down and talk to her. That wouldn't do. They weren't in as bad a place as they'd been when they'd first arrived here, but they hadn't made up either, which put a strain on her relationship with Petra, given that they were living together now.

Harlow took another long pull from the bottle—it was almost gone. Had she really drunk nearly the whole thing already? She stood, and the room spun a little, though she righted herself quickly. There was no way she was staying here to spill all her feelings to Kate, of all people. Harlow pushed past her ex, who followed her back into the seating area in the main Dairy. Max and Mirai were setting up rows of shot glasses, pouring a clear, sparkling liquid into each vessel on the coffee table.

Harlow squeezed back in between Tomyris and Sam. Kate followed, frowning. "She doesn't drink."

Tomyris raised an eyebrow at Kate. "Are you the boss of Harlow, Majesty?"

Kate sighed, exasperated. She pushed a hand through her short reddish-brown hair in obvious frustration. "No, but…"

Sam tilted her head as she turned to Harlow. "And do you have a problem with drinking too much that we don't know about?"

Harlow shook her head, choosing lies over the truth to get her way. Audata wasn't here right now, she reasoned. It was just a little lie, anyway. "I don't like the way it makes me feel anymore."

"And you're still choosing to drink tonight?" Sam asked.

Harlow nodded.

Sam shrugged as Kate opened her mouth to say something else. She knew Harlow was lying, and she didn't care. "Stay out of it, Kate. We've got her."

Harlow swiped three shot glasses from Max and Mirai's rows, downing each in rapid succession. Kate's mouth fell open, this time in shock. "They've got me, Kate," she said with a smile.

Tomyris and Sam each took their own trio of shots and then stood, dragging Harlow onto the dance floor. "Be careful, okay?" Sam shouted into her ear over the music. "I know today was bad, and you're hurting, but don't hurt yourself, okay?"

Harlow nodded. "I just need to forget for a little while."

Tomyris spun her around. "We all need that sometimes, babe."

The booze hit her bloodstream hard and she found herself coasting on waves of music, high off her friends, liquor and the strength of her pain that simply would not relent. She didn't forget—she remembered more, the drunker she got.

Fragments of time and memory wove together in a symphony of torment that beat in time with the rhythm of the music, pulsing through her in agonizing clarity. The room had faded to a blur of color and sound, but her memories were all too clear, and all of Finn. Every touch that passed between him. The flex of the lilacs on the tattoo that covered his arm. The lilacs that were for her. The reminder of what he'd lost. And now what she'd lost. What they'd both lost.

Her heart cried out for him. *Where was he? Why hadn't he found her? Why couldn't she find him?* Harlow knew she was drunk, and that things were about to get ugly, but she couldn't seem to stop herself from going down this path.

Vaguely, she knew Kate had parked herself in a chair, and was monitoring her, but when she looked back to glare at her, she'd finally gone. Harlow danced for so many songs, she lost track, trying to drown her pain in the thumping bass. The music pumped hard, and someone passed a bottle of Lethe around, a rare and legendary brew that was rumored to erase sorrow for an evening.

She had no idea where it came from, but she found it pressed into her hands and she took a long swig before passing it on to someone else. Sam and Tomyris glanced at one another. Tomyris slipped into the crowd, while Harlow danced with Sam. Her body felt lighter than air, and she was sure she could fly. She *could* fly. She could become a giant bird.

That thought made Harlow smile. A slow song came on and Tomyris returned, taking Sam into her arms. Harlow's heart hurt more than she could bear, though she wasn't sure she remembered why now, though she knew who'd caused the pain. She turned to find a tall Ventyr standing before her, backlit by the candles in the chandelier.

"Finn?" she whispered as arms went around her.

"Sorry, love. Just me."

Harlow looked up into Petra's onyx eyes. Her wings spread out behind her. Petra was using her true form. In the dim light of the Dairy, Harlow made out a dusky rose tone to her skin, and hair the color of deepest fuchsia. Of course, Petra was pink in her true form—this was the first time she'd ever seen it.

Harlow began to laugh, until tears streamed down her face. Petra held her closer. "I miss him so much," Harlow sobbed into her friend's shoulder.

"I know," Petra replied. "I do too."

"Why aren't you hanging out with Kate tonight?" Harlow asked, swaying gently to the music with Petra. It was playing softer now, so it was easier to talk. It must be getting late, if someone was turning the music down.

"I wanted to hang out with you."

"Liar," Harlow said, choking on a sob. She was too drunk.

"Am not," Petra insisted. "You never want to hang out with me anymore, so I had to wait for you to make an epically bad choice."

"You're always with *her*."

Petra sighed, taking a swig of Lethe herself, as the bottle was being passed again. "Yeah, that's true. You're gonna make up with Kate eventually, right?"

Harlow nodded, reaching for the bottle.

"Nope," Petra said, passing it on. "Absolutely not."

"You had some!" Harlow whined.

"So did you," Petra argued back.

"Are you drunk too?"

Petra grinned. "Yep. Kate sent me to get you."

"Were you about to have a big romantic night?"

"Absolutely not," Petra lied, grinning. "We were definitely *not* going to stay up all night drinking my parents' nicest sparkling wine and fucking."

Harlow laughed, twirling her friend around. "Take me home so you can get back to your night."

Petra shook her head, twirling Harlow in what was likely an ill-advised spin. When Harlow was safe again in her arms, and hadn't vomited, she said, "No, you need me."

Harlow threw her arms around Petra, hugging her tightly. "I needed you. You came." She pushed her friend away, shaking her shoulders a little. Petra was *so* tall in her true form. Harlow giggled, though she didn't know why. It was time to go. "Will you take me home?"

The Ventyr woman who'd once been her bully, and was now one of her closest friends, nodded solemnly. Harlow let Petra lead her out of the Dairy and into the quiet streets. Most of Sanctum had gone to bed, or was up at the Lodge, socializing at the bar there, or in one of the libraries that was used for games in the evenings. Petra took her hand and they walked home arm in arm, in complete silence. Harlow still felt the music vibrating in her ears and her chest. At the garden gate, she hugged Petra again.

"Thank you," she said, her words slurring slightly.

Petra shook her head, opening the gate and striding across the garden quickly.

"Your true form is soooo pretty," Harlow cooed as Petra went.

Petra glanced back, then did a little spin, her wings spreading out behind her. "I know, right? I'm gorgeous." She knocked on the front door. No one answered, and so she knocked harder.

"Riley and Enzo are out," Harlow remembered. Loudly. She was shouting.

Cian opened the door. "But I am here." They wrinkled their nose. "And the two of you are drunk."

"Her more so than me," Petra said with a grin, shooting into the air. "Night, babe!"

Cian sighed, as though they had never been so tired. "Come inside."

Harlow followed them into the living room, where Cian pushed her into a chair near the fire. "Stay put."

Axel snored softly on the little couch across from her. The arrangement of pillows and blankets told her Cian had been sleeping there, or maybe reading a book. There was one on the floor. She leaned forward, trying to read the title, and fell out of the chair. Axel opened one eye, seeming disappointed at her state. He closed both eyes tighter.

Harlow pointed an unsteady finger at the cat. "Don't be so judgy."

Cian appeared out of nowhere, with a tall glass that smelled of bitter herbs. They sat cross legged on the floor in front of her. "Drink this, please."

In their other hand, they held two thick slices of toast, oozing with butter. "You can have this when you've finished that," Cian promised.

Harlow drank the whole glass in a few long gulps. The liquid was cool and fragrant, but also sharp. "What is that?" she asked, her head feeling a little less spinny right away.

"Something Finn needed frequently when he drank too much as a teenager. He always liked the toast too."

Harlow stared at Cian. Their face was drawn and they looked older than they ever had, as though stress had turned them ancient. The sadness of losing Finn and Larkin was eating at them as much as it was her, and through her drunken haze, she regretted forcing them to care for her.

"Eat your toast. I'll get you some water," the firedrake said, kissing the top of her head.

Harlow munched on her toast, feeling sleepier by the second, but enjoying the idea that Finn liked toast too. Something about the thought was cozy, like he was just in the other room, though of course that made no sense. She didn't make it to the second piece, setting the plate on the floor under the couch. Her heavy head fell on the couch next to Axel, who purred gently as he slept. Harlow was asleep as well when Cian scooped her into their arms and carried her to bed.

CHAPTER 6

Harlow woke before dawn, some disturbance in the threads bothering her. Axel was asleep curled against her, snoring loudly, but otherwise all was well. She stumbled out of bed, peeking out the window. The last flares of a beautiful aurorae display were dying in the sky, the feeling that had woken her fading as the lights did. She let the curtains fall shut. Remarkably, she didn't feel as terrible as she expected to. Her head wasn't even fuzzy, just slightly sore.

She glanced over at Cian's bed, which for the first time in a long time actually had the firedrake in it. Their silver eyes opened, glowing faintly with celestial light.

"You slept," she said.

"Yes," Cian murmured. "I need to rest for a few days, I believe."

Cian had been as restless as she had, and since they were not restricted by the Rogue Order, they'd run themselves ragged searching for Finn and Larkin. As much as she wanted to find them both, she didn't want Cian destroying their health to do it—and they had been. There were dark bruises under the Argent's bloodshot eyes again, which had become an altogether too common state for them.

"That would be good for you," Harlow replied. "Can I get you anything?"

Cian shook their head, but sadness infused every motion with a dull heaviness she felt in her bones. She was shivering by the window. The cottage got chilly overnight, despite the heating spells that kept the fireplace smoldering. When she'd tucked herself into bed next to Cian, a heavy thump signaled that Axel had joined them, settling in behind the shifter's back. Harlow laced her fingers through Cian's, kissing them.

"You were *very* drunk last night." There wasn't a trace of judgment on their face, only the tiny wrinkle between their eyes that appeared when they were worried.

"Yes," Harlow agreed. "Not something I plan to do again anytime soon, but it's been a lot lately."

Cian's eyes glazed over, as though they saw something far away that she did not. "It has. I am so grateful the Dominavus were not successful yesterday, sweet girl."

The pain in Cian's voice nearly broke her. "I love you," she whispered, unable to speak at full volume without sobbing. "You know that, right?"

Cian nodded. "I made so many mistakes."

"We all have."

The Argent growled, a low rumble in their chest. "You haven't forgiven your mother as easily."

"That's different," Harlow reasoned.

"It isn't," Cian said, squeezing her hand. "But I appreciate you all the same."

"We'll find them," Harlow said, sounding more confident than she felt. "I'm on another patrol today, and I'll keep a close eye out."

"You always do." Cian's voice was flat.

Harlow wasn't sure how to respond. They were both exhausted from the highs of hope that only crashed when they didn't find them. "You'll rest?"

"I'll rest," Cian promised, kissing her fingers the same way she'd done.

"Okay, when you're ready, we found something interesting for Audata's string wall. I'd like you to take a look."

But Cian had already fallen back asleep. She could tell them about it later. Harlow fumbled in the dark, donning her clean fighting gear, grateful for Enzo's magic that left it smelling fresh and kept the lining soft against her skin. The old Harlow, before she lost Finn, would have hated herself for getting drunk last night. She would have gone over every moment in her head, worrying that she'd embarrassed herself. And that impulse was there, but she firmly set it aside.

Many nights since coming to Sanctum someone got a little too drunk, a little too sad, or even sometimes a little too angry. It was against the rules to cause repeated issues, but there was a lot of leeway and acceptance here for people grieving the loss of so many Okairons deeply. Nearly everyone at Sanctum had lost someone they cared for in the Vespae's initial surge, and people needed a variety of ways to work through that grief. What she was feeling wasn't special, or unusual. Harlow did her best to let it go. She'd needed to let off a little steam, and that was that.

When she'd finished braiding her hair, Harlow kissed Axel's head. He let out a sleepy little squeak, following her as she crept out of the bedroom. Everyone would be asleep for hours still as the compound was deeply settled into their winter routine. The Rogue Council knew everyone was drained from what they'd endured, and it was common knowledge that spring's arrival would mean the start of an unrelenting conflict.

Axel nearly tripped her, winding through her feet as she made her way to the kitchen to feed him. Absently, she scooped food into his bowl, going through the motions of her morning routine as she obsessed. She turned on the battery operated radio on a low volume in the kitchen. Everyone had one, and the batteries got recharged weekly by humans learning to channel aethereal power.

Sanctum had a very localized radio channel, blocked from the outside by their magical wards, and there were as many updates to what was going on in the outside world as the Council would allow, playing on the hour each day. As the human who read the updates gave the weather report, Harlow zoned out, watching Axel eat. She wanted to hear the overnight report—to find out if the Dominavus had been spotted anywhere outside Austvanger. The host would go through the weather, and then the schedule of volunteer activities for the day, before they got to any of that.

The Rogue Order had every intention of offering an ultimatum to the Illuminated, come spring: join forces to fight the Vespae, and agree to a complete reformation of the way Okairos was governed, or there would be open war. No one expected them to agree to collaboration. It would be war.

War. With the Illuminated—the Ventyr and the Vespae both, on two fronts, at the same time. They didn't have the numbers or the firepower, but there was little other choice at this point. The Vespae were ravaging Okairos, and the Illuminated were holding all the resources hostage. War was inevitable, if only for survival. It was a terrifying notion, but it was still a way off. Deep winter had descended on them here in the high reaches of Falcyra, and it was hard to imagine the season ever ending. The Council encouraged residents to recuperate, to sleep whenever they could, to read books, and to congregate for recreation.

Life here in the Falcyran wilderness was hard, and rest was integral to making certain Sanctum ran smoothly. But Harlow couldn't rest. She couldn't sleep for longer than four hours at a time, most nights. Lately, she was sure to be up long before the sun. But there was someone else in her family who'd be up at this early hour—she knew that much, as she slipped out of the house.

Thea. Her sister would be awake, performing locator spell after locator spell in the little workshop attached to the cottage she shared with Alaric and the maters. Harlow jogged through the frigid morning air, making her way across the steep hills of the village quickly, and let herself into the cozy workshop.

Thea sat at a rustic table, sipping tea. She barely acknowledged Harlow's entrance as she stared at the topographical map in front of her. Blood-red sand was scattered across the table. Thea's slender right palm was covered in the sand used for the locator spell, as though she had slammed her hand down on the table in frustration.

"Nothing still?" Harlow asked as she poured herself a mug of tea, stirring honey into it as she sat across the table. The witchlights in the workshop put off the perfect balance of light. Not so bright that Harlow's eyes strained, but a warm glow that filled the little room entirely.

"Not a godsdamn thing," Thea answered. She tucked her dark brown hair behind her ears. It had grown since her summertime bob, but still didn't quite graze her shoulders. "I don't know why it's not working. I can track you all over creation. I know where Connor is. Where Pasiphae spends her days… But *them*. I can't find them."

Thea's talent with locator spells had been a surprise. But Selene's mother had been adept in this kind of magic, too. Selene hadn't inherited her skill, but talents often skipped generations. Before the twins left, they'd tried, but were only decent at them. Thea had proven to be the gifted one.

Harlow missed the twins. She'd been grateful when Arebos and Meline had joined them at Sanctum, but they'd left again with Indigo and Nox almost as soon as they'd arrived. The Wraiths were needed elsewhere, and the twins were now a part of their unit, running intense intelligence missions for the Rogue Order in both Falcyra and Nytra.

"What about Rakul and Vivia?" Harlow asked.

They'd tried to find the leader of the Dominavus and his wife, as well. The two of them likely knew more about the Vespae and the Illuminated combined, given their age and the fact that Vivia Woolf was the Empress Lofrata's daughter. She was a living legend—a firedrake who'd known the world before the Illuminated came. She'd fought the Vespae alongside her mother, and the other Heraldic shifters, before Okairos was forever changed by the Ventyr's arrival. Vivia and Rakul knew things that could change the Rogue Order's standing in the world order, if only they could find them. But so far, they'd had no luck.

Thea shook her head. "It's the same. I can't find them either. People with access to some of the most sophisticated magical cloaking on Okairos, I can find, but the people we need to find most…" Thea's voice broke over her words.

"Hey," Harlow said, rising to hug her elder sister. "Hey, it's not your fault. We don't know what's going on."

Thea nodded, her chin quivering. She pulled a few threads rapidly, and the sand piled itself up, the map curling around it to contain it as she scowled. "It makes me so *angry*."

Thea truly hated not knowing something. It was one of her best qualities, but also the one that tortured her most. It wasn't unusual for her to fall down tunnels of information for weeks, only emerging sporadically for rest and sustenance— until her curiosity was satisfied. But these last few months, between the Merkhov book, the Scroll of Akatei, and now Finn and Larkin's absence, was about more than serving her own desire to know. It was the cornerstones of her world at stake. Harlow had watched as her eldest sister descended, slowly at first, and quicker since they'd arrived in Falcyra, into obsessively ferreting out the root of things.

Thea got up from the table, pulling a few more threads to clean up her mess. It was a trick that made Harlow endlessly jealous, as cleaning wasn't something she could manage with her own magic, and it made things so convenient for her sister. A metal rack that was probably meant for sorting mail held several of Thea's projects in organized rows on the buffet behind them. Thea plucked a little book from one of the slots. She handed it to Harlow.

It was *The Warden*—the story of how Finn's ancient ancestor Ashbourne had come to guard the most dangerous elemental creatures the universe had ever known—the Ravagers. The story read more like a love story than anything else, a tragedy really, but there were several pages missing that might hold the key to something more substantial about the Ventyr. Harlow couldn't help but wonder if Larkin and Finn might know those secrets after traveling through the limen with Ashbourne, but the dull ache that spread from her chest to the tips of her fingers when she thought about it too hard was enough motivation to shove the thought into a deep hole in her mind.

Thea's eyes narrowed, watching Harlow struggle. "I failed here as well. I can't find anything else out about the missing pages, or the person who wrote this."

"That's okay. It was a long shot since we don't really have access to archives of any kind here."

Thea hummed in affirmation, but her beautiful face clouded with worry. Harlow noticed the hollow in her sister's cheeks, the dark circles under her eyes, and the sallow tone of her skin. Thea didn't look well. In fact, she looked downright queasy. And then she lurched for a trash can, heaving several times before vomiting. Harlow moved quickly, kneeling behind her sister, pulling her hair back from her face. She said nothing, but focused instead on the threads between them, sending cool aethereal light through them to soothe Thea.

"Thank you." Thea slumped next to the trash can, her back resting against the buffet. "That's a neat trick."

"You're sick. We should get you to bed."

Thea's smile was wan, but happy. "I'm not sick, pal."

Harlow bit her lip, a frown crowding her face for a brief moment. Then, as she put the pieces together, the first genuine smile she'd had in weeks stretched her cheeks. "Are you…"

Thea nodded. "Twins."

Harlow threw her arms around her sister, tears pricking at her eyes. "I am so happy for you."

Thea squeezed her back. "Thank you. We're thrilled."

Harlow pulled back a little. "I am too. Congratulations."

Thea stroked Harlow's cheek. "I wish you'd try to hear Aurelia out."

"Please. This is a happy moment. Let's not ruin it."

Thea frowned. "She was trying to protect us."

Harlow groaned. They'd been over this dozens of times since the catacombs. Her shoulders slumped and her head fell into her hands. "But if she'd told us what was going on, Larkin never would have been there—I never would have brought her—and Finn wouldn't have followed her through the breach."

Thea was silent for a moment. When she spoke, her voice shook a little. "Are you angry with Aurelia, or *yourself*, for bringing her with you on such a dangerous mission?"

"So now you're blaming me?"

"No!" Thea insisted. "I'm not blaming anyone. What happened in the catacombs was terrible—but I'm not sure it's anyone's *fault*."

Thea. Always the peacemaker. Harlow sighed, searching her sister's face. For what, she didn't know, but what she found worried her. Thea was too upset, too overwrought about all this. It couldn't be good for the twins.

"You shouldn't be out here doing these spells," she scolded. Magic was safe enough during pregnancy, but like anything, it took energy. Energy Thea clearly didn't have right now. "Let's get you to bed."

Thea began to protest, but the door to the workshop flung open, interrupting her. It was Alaric, and though his usual calm demeanor was firmly in place, his eyes were wide. He rushed to help Thea up off the floor. "We talked about this," he murmured. "And you snuck out here anyway."

Guilt flickered in Thea's eyes. "I had to try out a theory…" she whispered back. "But I was wrong."

Alaric didn't seem to be listening to what she was saying, only waiting for her to stop speaking—too polite to interrupt his wife, even if he had something important to say. As soon as she was quiet, he looked pointedly at Harlow. "A swarm is mounting an attack against Sanctum. You've got to go. They'll be ringing the alarm any minute."

Harlow sprang up, tucking *The Warden* into her jacket. "Get her and the maters to the Lodge."

Alaric nodded. They'd worried this was coming for a few months, especially when Audata obsessed over the objects they'd found. She'd been concerned at first that the Vespae were searching for humans, specifically, like vampires might. But they learned quickly that the Vespae didn't feed off humans, or any animal matter at all. They ate a strictly plant-based diet, despite having evolved into what appeared to be apex predators.

Now, Harlow worried that the advanced wards on Sanctum might actually be working against them. If the Vespae were looking for that observatory, and it was somewhere in this mountain range, they might believe it was hiding behind the wards that obscured the village from view. If they overran Sanctum, everyone here would be dead in a matter of hours.

She kissed her sister and made a split second decision to teleport home. Inside her own cottage, everyone was still asleep. Quickly, she opened the door to Enzo and Riley's room. They were curled up together in their big bed, covered by a fluffy linen duvet.

"It's happening," she hissed, her voice suddenly choked with fear. Enzo, likely feeling her terror, woke immediately, sitting up as Riley woke more slowly.

"The Vespae?" Enzo asked, eyes worried. She nodded, noticing only now that Axel was asleep between them. Harlow scooped him into her arms, kissing his fuzzy cheeks as he purred, a low thrum of comfort.

"I've got to go. Don't worry about taking anything—there's plenty of supplies. Get Cian up, and get to the Lodge. Now. They're going to ring the alarm any moment."

"I love you," Enzo said, her terror reflected in his eyes. He knew exactly how much danger they were in, just as she did.

"I love you too," she said. "Get them out of here. Now."

Riley grabbed her hand. "See you in a few."

It was exactly what she needed to hear. She nodded, and teleported straight to the Dairy, which was abuzz with activity. Audata outfitted everyone. As the only Strider amongst them who hadn't paired with one of the Ventyr yet, she couldn't transform into her Feriant form, but in addition to being their resident genius, she was also the armorer—and she took the job of kitting everyone out for a fight seriously.

"How many?" Harlow asked as soon as Audata spotted her and went to work fitting a pack of something around Harlow's left thigh.

"This is Tomyris' venom. Drop out of the fight to inject yourself if you're stung, okay?"

"How many?" Harlow asked again. Audata was avoiding her eyes.

"A whole swarm."

Harlow's heart sank. That was too many for the Warbirds to fight on their own. They would inevitably come here—and then they'd find out if Sanctum's wards would hold. They weren't meant to keep the Vespae out. Their force was largely in averting perception. If they didn't hold… well, Harlow wasn't going to entertain that thought.

She wished desperately that there were more aerial fighters available—that they'd been able to find more of the Heraldic shifters. As it was, the ones they had found were children. None were older than twelve, and they had no place in a fight like this. As she thought this, she felt a distinct disturbance in the threads around her.

Slowly, she turned. Cian stood in the middle of the barn, looking tired, but alert. Their eyes met and her head began to shake. "No," she insisted, stepping towards them. "No. You haven't been well."

Peyton scoffed. "They've been on patrols, and guarding the children. We *need* them, Krane."

Harlow stepped forward, ready to give Peyton a piece of her mind. More than a piece, actually, a whole damn diatribe. How fucking dare she try to insert herself into this conversation?

"Harlow." It was just one word, but it was a subtle command. Cian outranked her, and loyal as she was to the Warbirds, the Knights were her first affiliation.

Cian took her hands in theirs. "I am well enough for this fight. The Vespae will feel my fire."

She couldn't lose Cian though. If Finn returned and she'd allowed Cian to be harmed, he'd never recover. *When* Finn returned, she corrected herself. When he returned, he would be devastated *if* he found his closest confidant and mentor had been harmed. These little corrections were important for staving off despair.

"I will be fine, Harlow. More than fine. You'll see." Silver flame flickered in the limenal space between them. Harlow felt it, more than saw it.

"What *is* that?" Harlow breathed.

"That's a beast the Vespae won't soon forget," Max said, clapping a hand to Cian's shoulder. "My gran'da fought with the Heraldic in the Great War. I heard stories of your kind my whole life."

All of the Ventyr here were descendants of Ventyr who'd fought in the War of the Orders—they had never been "Illuminated," only ever devoted to the cause of freeing Okairos from oppression. It was the reason the Rogue Order trusted them. Their ancestors hadn't been Knights of Serpens, of course, since all of the Ventyr Knights had been executed, but rather the Ventyr that had been less important to Connor and Pasiphae, the ones who'd gotten away and never returned to Illuminated society.

Cian smiled. "And today I'll give you a story to tell your children."

Mirai wrapped her arms around Max's waist. "Thank you, Cian. I'll feel better if you're with us."

"It will be like the old days," Cian murmured.

Harlow still didn't like it, but she knew better than to argue further. In truth, she didn't want to fight. She wanted to go home. Home to Nuva Troi, not back to the cottage. To a year ago, before any of this had happened. She'd thought that was the worst time in her life, right after she and Mark had split up, but so much of everything that had happened since had been terrible. Not reconnecting with Finn, of course, but the world had changed in ways it would never recover from, and a part of her wanted nothing more than to return to the days when her worst problems were what Section Seven had to say about her.

Audata clapped once, returning everyone's attention to her. "We need a quick briefing on strategy, and then we need to get out there."

The Warbirds quieted, surrounding Cian and Harlow, who still held hands. Cian dropped one hand, so they could turn to face the group. The other, they held to their heart. "Thank you for having me with you today. I am honored to fight with you."

Despite the fact that she didn't want Cian to fight in their exhausted state, she was proud of them. There was no doubt that they were brave. Braver than she could ever be, and an obvious example for everyone in this room, who idolized the Heraldic shifters—firedrakes especially. Once, Okairos had been ruled by what Cian described as a servant-monarchy of Argent, dynasties of silver firedrakes whose only function was to protect humans. Cian was a mythological protector to them, not one of their closest friends. Harlow bit her bottom lip and tried to focus.

Audata spoke about needing an adaptive strategy to beat the Vespae back. Though many of the refugees at Sanctum had survived swarm attacks, most had been too busy fleeing for their lives to stop and analyze how the Vespae were so coordinated and effective in the face of magical wards. The Rogues were going in without vital information about how to win, and would have to bank on the element of surprise with Cian's presence.

They would pull the village's wards back from the edge of the compound to surround the Lodge, while the Legion and the ground divisions would hide inside various strategic points in the village to block the Vespae's approach. Since their numbers were so much greater, a more covert approach was necessary. Everyone was fitted with battery operated walkie-talkies, with old-school headphones. They only worked in close range to one another, but they would allow for the Legion and the ground fighters to adapt as needed during the fight.

It was a risky, terrible plan, as plans went. Harlow hated it. She was so frightened she thought she might have circled back around to bravery, numbness over the unreality of what they were about to do settling over her, as it did before every mission she went on. First came the fear, then the period of feeling absolutely nothing at all.

"Find the queen," Mirai reminded everyone, as the Legion split up. They had minutes until the wards would withdraw from the edges of the village. "The

Council thinks that if you take her out, their telepathy will be damaged, and their efforts less coordinated. It should make them easier to deal with."

Everyone nodded. There was nothing left to discuss.

"See you on the other side," Audata said, her voice solemn.

"On the other side," the Warbirds echoed back.

CHAPTER 7

Harlow peeked out the dormer window of the stables at the edge of town. The animals were sheltering at the Lodge, with everyone else, and it was odd not to hear the chickens chatting to one another, or the soft sounds of the goats and cows as they moved through their days. Harlow had always been a city girl, and it surprised her how quickly she'd grown accustomed to the sounds of livestock in the village.

The stillness was ominous, the feeling made worse by the waiting. She slumped back against Samira's shoulder, shaking her head. Nothing had changed since the last time she looked. There was no sign of Max or Mirai, who were scouting the Vespae's approach. The rest of the Legion was scattered throughout the first ring of rooftops behind them, Cian another few streets closer to the Lodge. The Argent was their secret weapon, their big surprise for when they were overwhelmed by the Vespae's numbers.

Not if. *When*. A whole swarm was more than anyone had ever fought and lived through outside of the big cities, as far as any of them knew. Harlow had to believe that today would be different though. A crackle came over her walkie talkie, and then Max was speaking in her ear. "Harlow?"

She hit the button that allowed her to speak. "Yeah, I'm here." She was surprised Max had contacted her, and not Tomyris.

"No one else's walkies are working. Something's interfering with the signal," Max explained.

Harlow swore quietly, whispering the news to Audata, who sat next to her. The little Strider glowered, furious that her plan had been foiled. She was already scrambling towards the tech supply table she'd set up here in the attic, fiddling with various instruments and radios that Harlow didn't understand. Obviously, she was trying to figure out what was wrong, but as she didn't have answers, Harlow turned her attention back to Max.

"Audata's trying to figure it out," she replied. Sam handed her a pad of paper and a pencil so she could write down whatever Max said next.

"We have a problem…" A crackle interrupted the Ventyr. Harlow caught one last fragment of his news, "…two swarms, not one…" a high pitched whine filled Harlow's ears. "…locate one queen though… not with… guard…" Static took over and then a series of muffled buzzes and clicks.

Harlow frowned at Sam, shaking her head. She'd been trying to listen and write down what Max was saying. "He's gone." Sam removed the headphones from her ears and the buzzing grew louder, overwhelming in volume.

Tomyris peeked out the window now, quickly returning. "There's got to be two swarms. Max is right. This is bad."

Audata shook her head, pushing one of her radios hard in frustration. "The noise they're making. It interferes with the signal. We won't be able to communicate with the ground forces that way."

Tomyris stood. "We're going to have to shift sooner, trap their focus."

Audata nodded. "I'll get the messengers ready. See if you can give us some cover to make up time."

Harlow followed Sam and Tomyris to the roof. Once all the Striders shifted into their Feriant forms, the group would be able to communicate telepathically. They wouldn't need the walkies, but it had been a good way to coordinate their defenses, and a more covert approach with the ground forces.

Sam winced as they climbed onto the roof. "Hope that noise they're making doesn't block our abilities."

Tomyris' mouth twisted with worry. She didn't respond. Sam and Harlow shifted at the same time. There was no time like the present to try it out.

Can you hear me? Sam asked.

Yes, Harlow answered, relieved that one thing was going as planned.

The other Striders checked in as they shifted, all but Mirai, which was understandable. They'd gone behind enemy lines, and it was tough to say what was happening. Harlow said a swift prayer to Akatei for their safety, and then poised herself to launch when commanded.

Vespae drones approached slowly, crawling out of the wooded mountains surrounding Sanctum on all fours. Behind them, the more elite queensguard walked upright, surrounding a queen. Unlike some of the other queens Harlow had encountered, this one's wings were in more than decent shape—they were beautiful.

When another queen joined her, stepping out of the woods to take the first queen's hand, Harlow frowned. The drones surrounded the village, but did not begin the attack. Harlow used her enhanced Feriant vision to hone in on the queens. The second queen's wings, like the first, were in good shape.

Harlow wondered, briefly, if it might indicate that they were younger. There was not another way to tell with the Vespae, as far as Harlow knew. But, of course, they knew so little about them. It was impossible to even tell how many had surged from the breach in Nea Sterlis. The release of magic when the Vascularity collapsed had spit them out into the world in such a way that had obscured all but the fact that they were there.

Not that anyone could miss that fact. They'd barely waited three days before systematically attacking every village, town and city in their way. They'd appeared everywhere, in every nation, all over the planet. If the Illuminated knew how they were doing it, how many there were, or anything that would help the people of Okairos, they never said. They just locked themselves in their cities, and kept the lights firmly turned off for everyone else. The message was clear: *ab ordine libertas*. From Order comes freedom. Submit to the Illuminated Order, or stay victim to an increasingly dangerous world.

This dangerous world, where innocent people would die today, all because people like Connor McKay needed to have all the power. Harlow clucked her giant raptor's tongue, agitated by the thought as she watched the queens, who appeared to be talking to one another, assessing something about the village itself. The second queen scanned the rooftops, looking at each of the Legion in turn. When she came to Harlow, she pointed, making a high-pitched noise.

"What in seventeen hells is she pointing at Harlow for?" Tomyris muttered.

Sam trilled in response. There was no need to translate; Harlow understood. She didn't like it either.

The Vespae still didn't approach. The second queen walked through the drones, and they parted for her, making a pathway towards the village. The queen made direct eye contact with Tomyris—apparently she'd identified her as the leader, which Harlow couldn't blame her for. While Tomy wasn't the largest of the Ventyr present, she carried an aura of absolute authority.

The queen spoke, making a series of buzzes and clicking noises. Of course, no one could understand her as she pointed over and over at Harlow. Finally, obviously frustrated, she threw her long, pale hands in the air. She was graceful as a dancer, and just as beautiful, her long, white hair plaited in a complex braid that used more than three strands. The first queen hissed, a low menacing sound in response. The second hissed back, and then turned to try again.

Tomyris stepped forward, holding up a hand before calling out. "I am sorry we cannot understand you. But your interest in Harlow Krane must go unsatisfied. There is no circumstance in which we'd allow you to take her, or any of our people."

Sam, Harlow insisted. *Tell Tomy I can go with them, if it will stop them from attacking the village.*

There was a long pause, while Sam relayed the information.

Tomyris placed her hand on Harlow's wing. "No," she murmured. "We don't know the terms, so you stay."

Across the telepathic link, the rest of the Legion agreed. Even Peyton, who'd been one of Harlow's least favorite people for the past few months, was absolute in her stance. Something about that surety that she belonged with them soothed her, afraid as she was.

The first queen hissed again, and the noise rippled through the drones. The second queen's brow furrowed, and while Harlow knew little about the Vespae, she recognized frustration easily enough. The second queen looked directly at Harlow, then made a low noise. One that sounded like a plea.

She was cut off by one of the drones that stood, yanking on her arm, dragging her back to the first queen, who struck her across the face. The blow was brutal in force, her taloned fingers dragging across the second queen's face and sending her to her knees. The gashes were deep; the first queen hadn't held back in the slightest.

Harlow had the sinking feeling that whatever they couldn't understand had been the second queen's attempt at something she *could*—she'd tried to find a way to do things differently—and now she was being punished for it. Harlow shifted back into her humanoid form without thinking.

"Stop," she cried. "Stop hurting her."

The first queen turned towards Harlow, then let out an ear splitting screech. As the drones raced forward, Harlow caught sight of the second queen's face as her own people dragged her back into the forest. Though her alien features made it difficult for Harlow to know for certain, she thought she saw regret on the second queen's face.

Around her, the Legion was launching into the air. Harlow had no choice but to shift and follow. The Firestarters in the ground forces, a combination of sorcières and humans with a talent for the fire element, moved their hands in coordinated motion, pulling threads so rapidly Harlow couldn't track them. Dozens of sigils flamed to life. These were Sanctum's secondary wards, a series of tangible, magical barriers. White-hot flame shot into the air as the sigils connected to one another, creating a wall of fire that the drones simply ran through. Some caught fire and died, nearly instantly, but others streamed through the holes their dying comrades made.

Harlow dove with the other Feriant, using the force of their giant wings to skim through the waves of Vespae surging forward, sending dozens to the ground with each subsequent plunge into the fray. Behind them, the Ventyr used celestial fire to burn the fallen before they could rise. It was an effective strategy and if there had been more of them, it might have stopped the Vespae's attack— but there were almost two thousand drones, and only nine pairs of Striders and Ventyr in the air, and Harlow.

They weren't holding them back. The ground forces were making progress, with magic and weapons alike, but they were only slowing the Vespae down, not stopping them. Fighting had moved into the village. The most terrible, wonderful noise Harlow had ever heard—Cian's roar—rose above the sounds of battle, drowning out the Vespae's buzzing. No, not drowning it out, *stopping* it. The Vespae froze, in some kind of vestigial fear, as though some ancient instinct reminded them that firedrakes were their enemies.

Tomyris didn't miss a beat. She headed straight for the queen, who was the only one not affected by the sound of Cian's draconic fury. The queen was pulling threads rapidly, her hands glowing with some power that was neither celestial, nor aethereal in nature. Harlow could hear the wards around the Lodge weakening. This was how they managed it in other places—how they'd gotten past the last barrier in the breach under Nea Sterlis. The Vespae were ward-breakers.

Sam and Harlow plummeted low, ahead of Tomyris, to clear the way of drones. Quickly, they shifted into their humanoid forms to engage with the queensguard, who were less affected by Cian than the drones, but who were sluggish as they fought. Above them, Cian had risen in the air and was now clearing the perimeter of the village of approaching Vespae, with long sweeps of white-hot flame, very similar to what the Firestarters used.

The queen snarled in frustration, but only momentarily, as Tomyris wasted no time: her sword of celestial fire pierced the queen's rib cage, jamming through her back as Tomyris twisted her head in one nearly effortless-looking motion, breaking her neck, then slicing her head off completely as soon as she freed her sword. As the Council had assumed, this created chaos in both the remaining queensguard and the drone ranks.

Harlow shifted back into her Feriant form, tearing the guards who tried to escape apart with her talons and beak. Swiftly, she shifted back into her humanoid form to use her shadows to pick off the drones, now fleeing the village with arrows. She was running through her energy stores like water, but they had one chance to quell the attack. Slowing down meant death, not just for herself, but for everyone she cared for.

She, Sam and the other Striders got as many as they could with their shadow arrows, while the Ventyr of the Feriant Legion followed the ones escaping into the forest. A shout went up in the village, then a horn sounded. It was the signal that they'd turned the tide—to go after the ones escaping, rather than press back towards the Lodge.

Harlow followed her fellow Striders into the air, combing the forest for stragglers. They worked for a solid hour, coordinating kill after kill. No one could find the second queen though, the one the first queen had injured. They'd proven for certain that killing the queen meant disabling the coordination of the drones. It wasn't wise to let the stray queen go—she'd only find another swarm to lead.

Finally after nearly ninety minutes of searching, with snow beginning to fall in heavy sheets, Harlow and Sam shifted in a clearing to talk with Tomyris, who'd just returned from the village. The rest of the Legion was headed back to help the cleanup and medical crews, and they were to find Max and Mirai, and try to hunt the final queen down. Apparently, the Council didn't think finding her was a "true priority," according to Audata. Their mission was finding Max and Mirai.

Sam sat down on the forest floor, closing her eyes. She took one of Harlow's hands, and one of Tomyris', searching the threads for signs of their friends. She was nearly out of energy, like the rest of them. Harlow and Tomyris lent her as much power as they could spare. When her eyes fluttered open, she pointed into the trees. "They're that way—Max is injured. I can't communicate with them, but I think Mirai is with him."

Tomyris nodded. "She was probably stung. Vespae poison has to be some kind of blocker."

Harlow helped Sam up, and then followed her and Tomyris into the thick forest. They moved quietly, not knowing if there were still lingering Vespae hiding, and not daring to shift forms or teleport now. They'd all used too much magic, and if they weren't careful they might not be able to fight off any stray drones. Max and Mirai weren't calling out for help, and there was no telling why they might not be. Exercising caution was best now.

Sam pointed to two sets of footsteps that appeared in front of them. "They went that way."

Snow fell in heavy sheets now, almost like rain, dampening the sounds of the surrounding forest. When Tomyris turned, pushing both Harlow and Samira behind a tree, she clamped a hand to each of their mouths, shaking her head.

Unlike Samira and Harlow, Tomyris' eyesight was supernaturally enhanced, made more so because she stayed in her Ventyr body at all times. When Harlow and Samira both nodded, indicating they understood, Tomyris released them, peeking around the tree again. She made several hand signals, requesting that Harlow and Sam follow her closely, but quietly. They skirted a path through the trees, heading towards a clearing Harlow could see in the distance.

She spotted Max and Mirai, crouched behind an enormous spruce. Both glanced back at the same time. Max motioned for them to join the two of them, his wings flexing, full of tension. He held a gash in his side, which was bleeding through a makeshift bandage that wasn't even coming close to covering the mortal wound. If he didn't get help immediately, Max would die.

"There's Vespae in a cave ahead—and they have someone captive," he whispered as they approached, not addressing his wound, or need for aid.

"How many?" Tomyris asked, keeping her voice quiet.

Tomy and Max conversed softly, while Sam and Harlow looked Mirai over for injury. She was obviously in shock.

Mirai's eyes were wide with fear. "I'm fine—I was stung, but I'm fine," she whispered to Harlow. "Help him, *please.*"

Harlow glanced at Max who nodded, taking Mirai's hand.

"Okay," Harlow whispered. She didn't even bother to glance at Sam, who tensed at Mirai's plea. There was no way that she'd ask her to do this, not in front of Tomy. This would be an extraordinarily intimate moment, and if she could manage it, it would save Max's life, but she couldn't imagine doing something of the sort in front of Finn, even though he'd understand it completely.

Just as she could use Tomyris' venom to heal herself, she could heal Max with hers, since Mirai's link to the aether was incapacitated by the Vespae poison. The Claim was fueled not by magic, but the aether itself. This wouldn't be easy, but it could work. Harlow squeezed Mirai's hands, feeling the bonds between the Strider and Max, her partner. Their Claim was strong, and it stirred deep, jealous feelings in Harlow.

The threads between them sung with their love for one another, which made her ache for Finn. The deeper she fell into their bond, the more agitated she became by their Claim. Her fangs protruded, somewhat reluctantly, but she honed in on Mirai's deep love for Max, her desperation at his injury. Still, no venom came.

Harlow brought Mirai's hands around her waist, turning so she stood in the other woman's arms, then guided her forward. Perhaps she needed to feel Mirai's desire for Max to do this, needed to channel their connection to make it work. It was harder for Striders to force their venom than it was for the Ventyr.

She didn't look at Max, as her body pressed against his, but beyond him, focusing only on Mirai as her fangs slowly cooperated.

One of Mirai's hands spread over Harlow's abdomen, pinning her to her chest. This was easier if Harlow focused on her, not Max. The Strider's lips grazed her ear. "Thank you," Mirai purred, her hand pressing harder into Harlow's abdomen.

In another life, one without Finn, Harlow thought she would have been interested in Mirai, which made this easier, but also more confusing. It took some sort of attraction to elicit a Strider's venom, but not necessarily romantic feelings. Mirai was trying to help her along, but it wasn't working.

And then it hit her: she cared for these two. Despite their reluctance to let her in all the way, they'd never hesitated to help her look for Finn and Larkin. They'd always been as kind as they could manage, while protecting themselves. This moment wasn't about any kind of romantic attraction. It was about love and community. Whether they were sure about her or not, these were her people, and she could help save them.

Venom hit Harlow's tongue and she struck quickly, biting Max in the neck as Mirai breathed a ragged sigh of relief. He winced beneath her, but when she drew back, he looked better. Mirai hadn't let go of her—she sobbed softly against her shoulder now.

Harlow turned, placing both her hands on the girl's face. "I'm sorry," she mouthed, worried that the other Strider might be angry with her for having bitten her Claimed. Even though it was the only way to save him, even though she'd had their consent, Harlow still worried. Mirai shook her head as all of the intensity of the moment drained away.

"Thank you," she whispered, hugging Harlow tightly. "You saved him."

When she released her, Harlow stepped away, letting Max go about the business of biting Mirai himself. She didn't look back at the two of them, knowing they must need any privacy the rest of them could give. Sam took her hand, drawing Harlow into a hug.

"You're a good friend, you know that?" Sam whispered in her ear.

Tomyris patted her cheeks, nodding as she unfastened her med kit from the pack strapped to her massive left thigh. "That was a hard thing to do."

Tomyris was one of the Legion's field medics, and she left Sam and Harlow to look both Max and Mirai over. Harlow took a few deep breaths. The day had been dizzying so far, and they still had to deal with the Vespae in the cave.

<h1 style="text-align:center">CHAPTER 8</h1>

When Tomyris was sure that both Max and Mirai could manage another fight, they moved quickly towards the cave they'd mentioned, about a half a mile away. They stayed hidden and quiet as they approached on foot, but there were no sentries in the forest.

Huge boulders surrounded the cave, so they had significant cover to take stock of the situation. Tomyris took a sharp breath in, pulling Harlow to her side.

"Is that your sister?" she murmured, nearly silently against Harlow's ear. The quiver of both fear and hope reverberated in her ear.

Harlow couldn't see what everyone else was looking at; the cave was too far for her to make out clearly. Harlow tried her best to engage her Feriant vision, but she hadn't mastered the ability to shift parts of her without the whole yet, so she pushed her second sight through the clearing and into the cave, looking for her connection to Larkin in the threads of aether.

Two Vespae guards held a humanoid figure between them as a Vespae queen stung her, shoving her wretched spine into her prisoner's neck. To Harlow's surprise, it wasn't the queen that had tried to communicate with them in the field, but another. *They'd had a third queen with them?*

Harlow winnowed her focus, but couldn't sense the identity of the Vespae's prisoner until the girl screamed. The Vespae poison could block their connection, as it did with most aethereal power, but it couldn't mask what twenty years of jump scares and tickle fights had etched into her mind and heart: the sound of Larkin's voice.

Harlow didn't think, didn't ask permission, didn't stop to make a plan. She simply shifted, shooting into the air above the treeline. Mirai and Samira were right behind her, their dark wings mirroring hers as she dove towards the cave.

You take the queen, Harlow, Samira said.

We'll get the guards and Max and Tomyris will pull Larkin out, Mirai added.

Neither scolded her for acting rashly. The Feriant Legion had little hierarchy among them, and they often acted on instinct, rather than constructing meticulous plans. Harlow felt no guilt for launching into action. It was Larkin, after all.

In a matter of moments, her talons sunk into the Vespae queen's flesh, ripping her wings from her back as she howled in pain. But she released Larkin, who fell to the ground in a limp heap. Harlow tore the queen's head from her shoulders in one clean bite, as Mirai and Sam made short work of the guards and Tomyris and Max spirited Larkin away.

That was too easy. Mirai said, her raptorial eyes blinking as her head tilted to the side, examining the cave. *Why didn't they guard the queen better?*

Harlow picked at the queen's body with her talons, and Sam's giant head dipped, cocking to and fro as she took in the body. *She wasn't their queen. That's why they didn't try harder—either the one they dragged away, or the one we killed must've been their queen.*

Then what was this all about? Harlow asked.

Maybe they left her here to guard your sister? Mirai mused.

Another swarm—smaller this time— is flooding the village. The queen that got away is leading them. Samira replied. *Tomyris got a call on the walkie—the signal's working again. The wards are down, but Cian's doing a lot of damage. We'll win, but they need reinforcements.*

Go. Harlow insisted. She wouldn't dream of letting the Rogues fight without the rest of them. *I'll get there as soon as I'm sure she's stable.*

Sam bumped her raptor's head against Harlow's, showing her a vision of where Larkin lay unconscious, but safe. She bobbed her giant head once, showing that she understood. Communicating in her Feriant form was much simpler than as a humanoid. Sam and Mirai took off, disappearing into the storm.

Harlow followed, but dove for the tree where her sister lay unconscious. She'd barely shifted as she fell to the ground, immediately examining Larkin for broken bones and other serious injuries. The urge to squeeze Larkin was hard to resist, but until she regained consciousness, she should move her as little as possible.

Still, Larkin was *here*. After months of looking, and their family's despair at losing her, she was here. Her baby sister. She refused to think about Finn. She wouldn't until she knew Larkin was going to be okay. A tear fell onto Larkin's face, splashing onto her little sister's cheek.

"Harlow?" Larkin asked. Her eyes were heavy, and her movements shaky as she wiped Harlow's tear off her face. Her forehead wrinkled in confusion, but then she'd been stung. She was likely groggy from the poison.

"It's me. How hurt are you?"

Larkin shook her head, trying to sit up. She touched the wound at her neck, wincing a little. It was already knitting together, but slowly. "Other than my neck, I'm okay. Where is Vivia?"

"Vivia? Vivia Woolf?" Her sister struggled to sit up. Harlow pressed a hand to her shoulder as her mind spun. Why was Larkin talking about Rakul Kimaris' wife? "Rest for me."

"Yes, Vivia Woolf. I was traveling with her. Where is she?" Larkin's eyes watered, full of fear. Harlow shoved aside the stab of pain ricocheting through her chest. Larkin didn't seem all that happy to see her after all this time.

"There was no one else in the cave with you," Harlow explained, wondering how Larkin came to be traveling with the Argent who'd been the battery for the Illuminated's Vascularity spell in Nea Sterlis.

All new reports from Nuva Troi indicated that Rakul had returned to the Dominavus—that he still commanded them—and yet Larkin acted like Vivia was a friend. It was true that the firedrake had tried to stop her husband from cutting her down, but still. If Rakul had gone back to the Dominavus, how could they trust Vivia?

"Look for her. Please. She was injured. The queen took her first…" Whatever Larkin said next was obscured by her sobs.

"We'll figure it out."

There was no way she could leave Larkin here alone to look for, of all people, a potential enemy, but Larkin was crying so hard she was afraid of what might happen if she didn't. She pulled the pistol the Feriant Legion were required to carry from her shoulder holster. "Take this," Harlow said, pressing the gun into Larkin's hands. "It's loaded with adamantine bullets. Shoot any Vespae who comes near and then run like your life depends on it, okay?"

Larkin's fingers closed around the gun, but her chest still shook with sobs. She was likely in shock and hysterical.

"It won't kill them, but it will slow them down enough to buy you some time 'til I get back."

The promise that she was coming back calmed her little sister. Larkin dragged herself off the ground, into a seated position, with her back resting against the trunk of the pine tree. "I lost track of her about a half a mile back, to the north."

Harlow raised her eyebrows. Her little sister had never been outdoorsy, or any good with directions. Neither had she, for that matter, but the past months with the Feriant Legion had changed things.

"Vivia taught me how to navigate," Larkin said, her voice soft. "Please find her. She's saved me so many times since Finn and I were separated."

Harlow's heart beat out of her chest. "Is he alive?"

Larkin nodded. "The last I saw him, he was. Another swarm got him, though. They didn't kill him…"

Though Larkin trailed off, Harlow guessed what she was thinking. If she'd been out here in the Falcyran wilderness, she knew what the Rogue Order did: the Vespae didn't take prisoners. The fact that they'd taken Finn rather than kill him outright was strange—as strange as the Vespae queen's obvious interest in her—but she didn't have time to think of that now. Her chest constricted as her mind raced towards hope.

Harlow pressed a kiss to Larkin's forehead, calming herself as much as her sister. There was no need to get ahead of themselves, or for Larkin to upset herself more than was necessary. "Tell me about it when I get back, pal."

"Okay," Larkin whispered. "I'll be fine by myself."

The wind shifted, and so did Harlow, launching herself into the sky. She flew north, the blizzard obscuring her view of the ground. As she flew, she found the threads that connected her to Larkin, though the connection was muddied—obscured. *Could the Vespae poison, in blocking access to the aether, also be blocking her connection to Larkin?*

That might explain why Thea hadn't been able to find either of them. A cloud hit Harlow in the face, surprising her. She refocused her attention on the ground, looking for any evidence of Vivia Woolf. She flew for miles, circling back in an expanding grid, but came up short.

Snow fell harder now, and Harlow worried Larkin might not be warm enough. Getting her back to the village was a priority. Just as she was about to turn back, the faintest whiff of something metallic scented the wind. Her raptor's sense of smell was keen for a few things, and the scent of fresh blood was one. Somewhere nearby, someone was bleeding profusely.

Her enhanced vision helped her to find the scuffs in the snow below that were quickly disappearing under the accumulation of snow pouring from the sky. Someone had tried to cover their tracks. Harlow dove, flying above the treeline, her hearing honing in on the ground below. Whoever was down there was attempting to muffle the sound of their breathing, probably with their hands. Their inhalations were ragged and as Harlow drifted closer, looking for a place to land in the trees, she heard their heartbeat, erratic and weak.

Whether it was Vivia or not, whoever was down there was hurt and scared. Harlow shifted, using her shadows to slow her fall. She was still learning the ins and outs of using pure aethereal power, rather than manipulating threads the way most sorcière did, and her last step to the ground fell short, causing her to tumble a little as she met the ground.

A soft chuckle rang out from under the tree where she'd sensed the wounded party. Harlow looked up to find a silver-haired Argent, with a beauty so other-worldly it was breathtaking, clutching her side as she laughed. A mass of pale hair fell around her sharply planed face as she doubled over in pain.

Vivia winced as she shifted positions. "You've almost got a handle on your power now, don't you? It won't be long 'til you've mastered it. Your kind are so adaptable."

Harlow squared her shoulders. It was high praise, considering this woman was, in some ways, the reason she had the power she did. She'd likely seen her own granddaughter go through the same learning process with her powers. Harlow was grateful to the firedrake for helping her sister, and she certainly respected her position in history, but she couldn't trust her on Larkin's word alone, especially given Rakul's position with the Illuminated. "Why didn't you shift?"

Vivia shook her head, wincing. "You're smart to ask. I can't shift—not yet anyway—powering the Vascularity left my ability to connect to the aether damaged."

Harlow nodded; though she'd have to have Enzo confirm that for her, it sounded logical. "And why aren't you with Rakul? Or were you taking my sister to him?"

Vivia gritted her teeth, her narrow eyes closing for a brief moment, tempting Harlow to ask if she was all right. Her hands glowed slightly with the same dark light that Harlow's shadows sometimes had. *Did she have the ability to heal herself?*

From the little Cian had told her about Heraldic's power, Harlow knew that while they couldn't do spells or work threads like sorcière, they were capable of some things that more mundane shifters could not accomplish. Cian had been secretive about it, and Harlow respected their privacy, but now she wished she'd pushed harder.

A bit of the pain on Vivia's face receded. "The Illuminated think I'm healing at our villa on Santos Island. Rakul's gone back to them—to win their trust—and I set out to find Finn and Larkin."

"To win their trust?" Harlow asked, suspicious.

Vivia nodded. "Yes. The Dominavus are the Illuminated's best weapon. If we can divide them, we can break the Illuminated from within. We're trying to help you."

Harlow's mind raced. In Nea Sterlis, Vivia had not wanted to be cut down; she'd begged Rakul not to go through with his plan. And for his part, Rakul Kimaris had seemed genuinely sorry to have created this situation. It was plausible that they'd try to help now, but Harlow couldn't make that decision. The Council would have to decide. For once, she was glad to let them take control, not to have to do this on her own. Their purpose clarified for her in that moment. They made the awful decisions by vote, so individuals didn't have to.

A spot of relief came over Harlow. "Larkin says you kept her safe. How did you find her?"

The Argent struggled to her feet. She was a little unsteady, but the scent of blood was fading. She wasn't bleeding any longer. "I may not be able to shift, but I am the oldest firedrake on this planet, Harlow Krane. I am descended from *queens.*" The statement sent a chill through Harlow. Vivia Woolf was the Empress Lofrata's daughter. If Okairos still had a monarchy, she would be Empress now. "I can do things with aether you've never dreamed of—or I could before the Vascularity. Suffice to say, I was able to find your sister, and I've done my best to help her learn to survive as we made our way to you."

"All right." Harlow was willing to accept that she could trust Vivia Woolf. All she said made sense, and certainly the firedrake had reason to oppose the Illuminated. They killed her *entire* family. "You healed yourself. Can you heal others?"

Vivia nodded. "Was Larkin harmed?"

"She's okay, but she needs your help." Harlow sighed, hating what she was going to say next. "I'll carry you to her, hop on." She shifted before she could think too long on the indignity of being ridden like a horse. Harlow would do anything to help her sister, including this.

CHAPTER 9

Vivia was able to finish healing Larkin quickly, and once that was done, Harlow carried them both to one of the Rogue's safehouses just outside the village. She didn't want to leave her sister so quickly—she wanted to smother her with attention, to hear every word of what had happened since she'd lost her in Nea Sterlis—but there was a strange distance between them.

Larkin stood near Vivia, closer than she usually did with people outside their family. They'd obviously been through a lot together, but it made Harlow feel self-conscious about being too affectionate toward Larkin. She tried to brush it off. Larkin had only been back for an hour, and she was likely in shock from the attack. The best thing to do was give her space to calm down, and *then* Harlow could hover like the busybody she was tempted to transform into right now.

The safehouse had been one of a few private cabins the former resort had maintained for staff. An auburn-haired human named Piper Winslow, the Education Councillor, was there with a mix of human and immortal children. The Councillor was about the same age as Harlow, and though she was friendly with many of the Warbirds, she'd always behaved with cold indifference towards Harlow.

Today, as the wiry human's eyes ran over Harlow's body, there was clear disgust in her eyes. Harlow didn't remember the last time she'd felt so *disliked*. Many of the Rogues reacted to her with wariness, but most weren't unkind. Piper's expression softened as they entered the safehouse, as she looked at the children. She was a fierce kind of person, older-seeming at times than she actually was because of how much responsibility she'd taken on. Today was one such example; being out here with a group of Sanctum's littlings had to have been tremendously frightening. Harlow couldn't blame her for being on edge.

The main room's furniture had been pushed to the periphery in favor of a complicated pillow and blanket fort at the center. The children ran haphazardly around the big room. Their energy was buoyant, despite the situation. Unfortunately, they were accompanied by half a dozen shifter ghasts, who were all changing into gruesome creatures to make the children scream with laughter. Harlow shuddered at the sight of them playing together. Why were children *like this?*

"We were on a hike to see the early morning aurorae when the call came over the radio," Piper said, interrupting Harlow's train of thought. Her voice was curt and she avoided eye contact with Harlow. "I brought the children here. The Vespae have never gotten so close before…"

Harlow squeezed Larkin's hand, steering her away from a ghast of a rabbit shifter, whose ribs and entrails were showing as it hopped across the common space of the cabin. Three children followed it, shrieking with delight at the horrific thing. Harlow felt Piper's eyes on her. She was clearly confused by Harlow's reaction to the ghasts. It was odd for sorcière to be disturbed by the spirits, and humans often found it curious that Harlow was repelled by them.

She spoke first, hoping to move things along quickly. Though she was confident the Warbirds didn't need her to triumph over the second wave of Vespae attacking the village, she needed to get back all the same. "We'll take care of it. This is my sister, Larkin, and Vivia Woolf. She has news for the Council."

Larkin smiled at the human, offering her hand. "So nice to meet you. Can Vivia and I help you strengthen the wards?"

Piper nodded—though it was clear she wanted to say no. When she spotted Vivia she inclined her head in a show of respect, and there was relief and reverence in her green eyes. "Your Majesty."

Vivia hugged the human, to Harlow's surprise. "There are no more queens, dear child. No more of my kind. I am only here to help, the best way I know how."

Harlow thought the prickly Education Councillor would react with disdain, as she was so suspicious of outsiders. But she underestimated the power of Vivia's heritage. Piper Winslow's eyes widened with reverence.

"The way you always have," Piper whispered. "We have our stories about you, about the sacrifices you and your ancestors made for us."

Vivia kissed Piper's forehead. "It was our duty, as it is mine now, to help the Rogue Order. I'm no one's empress, no one's queen. Just a woman who needs to make things right."

Harlow glanced at Larkin, whose eyes shone with pride. Jealousy stirred in her, but she got it. Vivia was impressive, beautiful, regal, and so genuinely humble it made Harlow's head spin. She radiated the kind of goodness that was hard to deny, inspiring the kind of deep trust that only came from training. As Lofrata's daughter, she'd likely spent her entire life learning to serve Okairos on a level the Illuminated would never understand. Of course, Larkin was having major hero worship. If Harlow weren't so jealous that she was taking Larkin's attention, she probably would be too.

"Just wait til you get to know her," Larkin whispered. "Vivia is *amazing.*"

That was big praise from Larkin. Harlow squeezed her hand. Despite her mixed feelings, she was happy her little sister was safe. And the veneration Piper

Winslow showed for the Argent made sense. If history had gone differently, Vivia would be her ultimate protector, the humans' leader, though not their ruler. Before the Illuminated came, there had been democratic governments for that, and this was what the Rogue Order proposed they return to now. That the Immortal Orders shift into protective roles, rather than extractive ones, with elected governments to work everything else out.

It had sounded like a dream to Harlow since she'd learned of it, one too good to be true at first; but now, watching the objectively untrusting Piper Winslow talk with Vivia Woolf, she couldn't help but feel inspired. Okairos had been different once, with immortals and humans working together in everyone's best interests. It could happen again, if the Illuminated would just loosen their hold on power—and if they could find a way to deal with the Vespae.

Piper turned away from Vivia, who bent to talk to a sorcière child about the picture she was drawing. The human took Larkin's arm, gesturing towards some children who were busy drawing pictures and reading in the cabin's living room. "Thank you for your offer to help with the wards. I didn't want to ask the children to help, though some of them have an aptitude for magic… I didn't want to frighten them."

Harlow was pleased that Piper's attitude towards Larkin had warmed, but when she smiled at her, the human's freckled face tightened. Harlow averted her eyes immediately, the smile dropping from her face. Inwardly, she cringed. *How had she offended this human so easily?* Sometimes it felt like everyone knew a set of rules she didn't. For fear that the horde of ghasts would turn their attention towards her, Harlow worked on calming herself.

The four adults watched another group of three children chase a ghast-rabbit into a wall, where it disappeared, eliciting even more shrieks of delight. Piper had done an excellent job of keeping them from being frightened. None of them comprehended what was outside their door right now. Harlow had to get back to the fight—she couldn't stall here any longer. She squeezed Larkin's hand again and let go.

Larkin brushed a kiss to Harlow's cheek. "Be careful. We'll help keep them safe."

Harlow watched with ambivalence, as a look passed between her sister and Vivia. They were obviously used to working together, and there was a great deal of trust between them. Still, she was reluctant to leave Larkin alone.

"Okay, I'll see you in a bit," Harlow said, kissing Larkin's forehead.

Harlow shivered as she passed through Larkin's strengthening wards. Maybe Vivia being here would change things for the Rogue Order. They could certainly use a win.

The trip back to the village was quick, her mind racing with new information. Harlow dropped out of the sky as soon as she reached the continued battle for Sanctum. The ground squads were holding the last of the swarm off well enough, but another soldier wouldn't hurt. Harlow joined Sam and Mirai in sweeping through, dragging their razor sharp talons through the second wave of soldier-drones.

Your sister okay? Mirai asked as they made a second pass, using their wings to knock the drones down for their Ventyr counterparts again. It was almost too easy now. Either someone had already killed the queen, or these drones weren't bonded with her, because they lacked the coordinated viciousness that typically made the Vespae so dangerous.

Yes. Vivia Woolf was helping her, she wants to join us. Piper Winslow was at the safehouse with some kids—she had a weird reaction to seeing her.

Sam did a fancy loop-de-loop. They were just playing now. The battle was all but won. *Humans have a lot of respect for the Argent. It's why they're not more suspicious of you, Harls. They love Cian.*

Harlow would have laughed if she were in her humanoid form. It sure *felt* like everyone was suspicious of her. But perhaps "felt" was the key word. Maybe she was being too sensitive. She turned her attention back to the task at hand. They'd almost subdued the last of the Vespae.

Shit, Sam swore. *Three are getting away.*

There's another group headed towards the Lodge, Mirai called.

I'll get the stragglers, you go for the others, Harlow replied. Mirai and Sam headed the opposite direction, with only a quick goodbye.

The escapees headed back into the forest, booking it back over the mountain. They were far enough ahead that she had to increase her speed in order to catch up to them, and that was a push for Harlow. She was nearing the end of her energy. They were headed vaguely in the direction of the safehouse and Harlow could stop them before they got there.

The creatures changed course slightly. They would miss the safehouse by half a mile. Harlow lost track of time as she pursued the stray Vespae, flying faster than she'd ever tried to go before. Her mind and body both strained under the effort. Several times, she lost sight of the Vespae through the trees. She took a moment to look around, and was surprised to find she'd entered territory she didn't recognize.

In her humanoid form, that might not be obvious, but her Feriant perception marked landscapes quite differently. Audata had been right: it wasn't possible they'd seen all of this part of the mountain range. Not that Harlow had doubted her, but here was hard evidence. Below her, the Vespae crested a sharp ridge.

Harlow followed, quite suddenly pulled by some unknown force that carried her over the ridge. It felt like being sent through a tiny hole with a slingshot. She paused, banking hard to come about—almost impossibly, she'd gotten ahead of the Vespae. Behind her, the Vespae were still heading in the direction she'd already come. Strange magic pulsed around her, almost as though it were pushing her away from the ridge: more evidence the Vespae might be warding experts.

Audata had warned the Council several times not to think of them as "creatures" because they moved and acted differently than Okairons. To manipulate aether so purposefully, you needed a hard grasp on reason, on logic. Underestimating the Vespae had been a mistake, one Harlow hoped they wouldn't continue making now that there was evidence of their abilities.

Harlow rose higher, soaring into the cloud cover of the storm. She swept in and out of the clouds, observing the little farm below. It was overrun with

Vespae, more than she'd ever seen gathered, but she was too tired to get an accurate count. Her energy was flagging severely. She wouldn't be able to maintain her Feriant form for much longer.

What were these Vespae doing here? Her Feriant body carried her upward, as she swept back towards the scouts she'd followed. She needed to take care of them before reporting back about this place. They were headed straight for the farm, no doubt to reveal Sanctum's location, if the Vespae weren't already aware of it. While it was possible the farm was the origin of the swarm that attacked, she couldn't know.

She hesitated, watching the scouts move closer to the farm, thinking of the queen who'd tried to communicate. It didn't ever feel *right* to kill the Vespae, but she had little choice. If she let these two return to the farm, they'd be fighting Vespae again in mere days. They'd done well this time, but Cian's presence had been a surprise, one they wouldn't get a second time. Sanctum had been compromised, but killing these two might give them more time to figure out what to do next. Harlow dove into the trees to stop the scouts before they got any closer to the farm.

Once she'd dropped the bodies into a crevasse, she let the storm do the work of hiding their trail. She turned back toward Sanctum, flying fast as she could manage with diminishing energy. As she went, she both saw and felt the wards she'd passed through before, that alien, repellant feeling again. It reminded her a little of the iridium they'd found on the Vespae bodies.

Once on the other side of the wards, she tried to find any remarkable feature in the landscape to mark for return with the rest of the Warbirds. There were none. The sameness of this place was menacing; everywhere she turned, the view was the same as the last. The magic of the wards, combined with her low energy, clouded her head. She couldn't hold her Feriant form for much longer.

Harlow dropped to the ground to avoid losing her grip on her alternae in midair, shifting as she went. She walked back in the direction she'd come, and found the wards easily enough, though she could not pass through them in her humanoid form. Trying gave her a little shock, a warning that going through would likely result in a bigger shock.

This farm was so close to Sanctum it turned her stomach. As she examined the wards, she began to understand how they'd missed it on routine patrols. The ward itself repelled her, which was usual for warding, though this was stronger than she was used to. The repulsion instilled fear—and then an extra layer of confusion and a strong desire to forget she'd ever seen this place.

It reminded her of having a nightmare. *You wake, and your mind's first instinct is to forget the horror of the dream—to distance yourself from it.* This was the same, her mind scrambling desperately to forget she'd seen the Vespae. She wasn't as good at discerning spellwork as Thea or Enzo, but she was almost positive that if she turned around now and flew away, she might actually forget the farm was here.

Snow fell heavier and faster now, and the magic of the strange wards pressed on her, making her sleepy and slow. The feeling was familiar, but she couldn't put her finger on it. All she wanted to do was lay down, forget all of this and sleep. Harlow shook her head. She had to get away from here, but not before she made sure she could get back. Harlow was exhausted, but she fumbled with the zipper to her jacket, fishing out the phone inside.

It felt like forever since she'd used a phone, but Nox and Indigo had ensured before they left that each member of patrols had one, charged by generator, that hacked into a satellite that provided detailed geo-location services. The phones were only to be turned on in a dire emergency.

Harlow switched hers on now, and as it flared to life she pulled up the geolocator and noted her exact coordinates, sending them over encrypted text back to base with a note about what she'd found. Audata replied instantly. *Recorded. Vespae threat eliminated. Return to Haven. Developments in Nytra to report.* Harlow replied with her acquiescence, and shut off the phone. She stumbled away from the wards, feeling better the further away she got.

CHAPTER 10

Harlow rushed into the Dairy upon return, expecting to find a debriefing happening, and hopefully information on where Larkin and Vivia were, as they weren't at the medical station. Larkin was nowhere to be found, but Vivia stood at the center of the Warbirds' attention, their eyes alight with interest as they asked her questions.

Much like with Piper, the Warbirds were eager to talk to Vivia, and while they were obviously watching what they said, they were enthusiastic about the Argent. The ache in her chest was nearly unbearable. Part loneliness, part jealousy, it was all ugly.

"You okay?" Audata asked, having appeared out of nowhere.

"Why is it so easy for them to like everyone but me?" The words were out before she could think about the wisdom of them. She was too tired to hide her real feelings.

Audata stared at the Warbirds for a long moment before answering. "Besides the obvious reasons?"

Harlow nodded, even though she wasn't sure she wanted to hear what Audata had to say. The Strider was brutally honest, and Harlow didn't know if she could stand the truth right now.

"Look at Vivia, she's probably exhausted, but she's over there talking to people like she's a beauty queen at a mixer." Audata's expression was even, as she glanced up at Harlow. "You don't make things easy for people. They can tell you're feeling things, even when you try to hide it. You're unpredictable for them."

Harlow swallowed hard. She wasn't sure how to respond, but that wasn't what she'd expected Audata to say.

"You make people uncomfortable—just like I do, because I don't show enough feelings. Most people like a happy medium, and we're too much and not enough."

Harlow looked down into Audata's brown eyes, and though the Strider's expression didn't change, Harlow felt the truth in her words. They both felt too much—felt everything, but expressed it differently.

"You don't make *everyone* uncomfortable," Harlow replied. If Audata liked to be touched, she would take her hand, but she didn't, so Harlow stayed still but for a slight flex of her hands.

A small smile curled at the corners of Audata's mouth as her eyes tracked the movement of Harlow's fingers. "Neither do you."

Harlow was overcome with gratitude for Audata's mere existence. Lately, she'd felt far too edgy, as though her ability to navigate social situations had evaporated, but Audata never appeared to care about any of that. It wasn't that she didn't care about any social mores—the lone Strider hated when people lied, or were cruel—but Harlow's rough edges, that typically frustrated others, didn't faze Audata.

"Did you get the coordinates for the farm plotted? There were so many of them, Aud. If we could take them by surprise, we might make a dent in this mess."

Audata hummed, a quiet noise she made when she was busy thinking or overwhelmed. "I found it. Once the team finishes their hellos, we'll get started on a plan. Kate and Cian are coming as well. They should be here any minute."

Harlow nodded. "Have you told my parents that Larkin is home?"

The Strider nodded. "Yes. She's with them now." Audata paused, her eyes narrowing. "I apologize. I don't believe I explained the way things are between you and your parents very well."

Harlow didn't bother to ask what she'd told Larkin. Thea would catch their little sister up soon enough. "Larkin is very perceptive. She knows me better than anyone—except maybe Thea."

"And me," Cian's voice purred at her shoulder. "I just hugged our girl. I'm so proud of you for finding her, my dar—" Harlow looked back at her friend, who was now staring at Vivia, mouth open, silver eyes full of tears.

"Vivia!" Cian rushed towards the other Argent. She opened her arms, smiling wide.

They exchanged quick words, Vivia explaining the same things she'd told Harlow, about Rakul and the Dominavus. Cian nodded, believing it all so easily. Harlow was immediately frustrated, and far more jealous over Cian's acceptance of the firedrake than she had been about the Warbirds.

In her irritation, she engaged her second sight, searching the threads between Vivia and Cian to find out why the usually shrewd Argent was acting like there was nothing to worry about with Vivia. There were literally hundreds of threads connecting the two of them, ones that spoke of friendship, family, and shared culture. Ones Harlow didn't even have the ability to understand, they ran so deep.

Harlow felt as though she'd pushed too far, in that moment, intruding on things that were Cian's private business. She pulled her awareness of the threads back, and though she could still sense the connection between them, the finer points were less obvious now. Refining her boundaries around her talent might prove to be more complicated than she'd first assumed.

Audata sighed, the noise edged with her own frustration, though her face remained smooth and emotionless. "We may have to continue the debriefing later."

Harlow was tempted to protest that they needed to make a plan for how to deal with the farm full of Vespae. But it was obvious that no one was going to get much done. The Warbirds crowded around Cian and Vivia, talking with the two of them excitedly about the battle, each person trying to impress the firedrakes with their prowess. Vivia was an exciting distraction—but weren't there priorities?

A glint of annoyance flashed in Audata's eyes as she watched her meeting end without her say-so. The tiny Strider finally shrugged and walked out of the Dairy, pulling her jacket off a hook by the door as she went. Harlow followed close behind, the frigid air hitting her face with an unpleasant bite.

"Can we go talk out our plan?" Harlow asked Audata as Tomyris and Sam sidled up alongside them. "There were more Vespae than I've ever seen at that place. Something big is going on there."

Tomyris took her hand and squeezed. "We should wait til we're all together and work things out. Besides, maybe Cian can help Vivia with her shifting—maybe they know something we don't about how to help her. We should let them talk."

That made sense, but it was still frustrating. Harlow's fists clenched as she wrapped her arms tightly around her body.

"Tell us what you saw," Audata said as she latched the Dairy's garden gate and walked towards the village proper. "We should begin research on the abnormal wards tonight."

Tomyris rolled her eyes. "Research. Ugh. I need a nap."

Sam kissed her lover's cheek as they walked through the village of stone houses. Snow was piling up in the cobblestone streets, covering the mess of the fight. The Vespae had made it all the way into the village, though the ground forces had fought them back.

The thought was chilling, seeping deep into Harlow's bone marrow. The Vespae had broken through their wards, and could do it again. There was no precedent for any settlement or town surviving an attack like the one that occurred here, and nobody knew what the implications of this were. Uncertainty hung in the air.

The village wasn't quiet as they walked—there was too much going on for silence—but there was a deeply unsettling lack of voices. The usual sounds of gossip and friendly chatting in the streets was notably absent, people's faces gray with fear. Audata noticed this as well, and pulled Harlow into an alley, Samira and Tomyris following close behind. The four of them huddled together, out of the wind.

"Tell us what you saw," Audata commanded.

It felt a little like a clandestine meeting, here in the narrow alleyway, shadows already falling as the sun sank below the horizon. The stone of the village buildings, which was normally cozy and friendly, suddenly gave off an air of menace. Harlow kept her voice low as she recounted what she'd seen and felt following the Vespae, a warm feeling of belonging buzzing through her as her friends listened.

These *were* her friends, she realized as they nodded thoughtfully at her story. Was it really so important that everyone like her, if people like Audata, Tomy and Sam did? If her family loved her, messy as that was. If Finn loved her, wherever he might be… Did it actually matter that some people thought she wasn't trustworthy?

Harlow didn't quite register that Audata, Sam and Tomy had started discussing what she'd seen in the mountains. Her discovery felt profound, monumental, despite the smallness of it in comparison to what was happening in their community at large.

It was okay for people to misunderstand her. It was okay for them not to like her, or even trust her—so long as she wasn't doing things to directly cause that distrust. The only thing she needed to concern herself with was doing her best to live in alignment with her values, and to be open to hearing she was wrong, when someone gifted her with the knowledge she'd done something out of line. She couldn't *actually* spend her life trying to anticipate everyone's reactions to her. That was an enormous waste of time and energy.

"I have things I'd like to look up," Audata replied, interrupting Harlow's epiphany. "Samira, will you come with me?"

Sam nodded. "Yes, are you wondering about the possibility that the Vespae use threads differently?"

Audata nodded as Tomyris yawned. "I'm going to go get a snack and take a nap. Sounds like tomorrow is going to be a big day." She kissed Harlow's cheek as they departed. None of them asked her to come along, or for her help, *and it was all right*. They hadn't abandoned her. Very likely, they expected that she'd want to see Larkin now. That she'd be *excited* to see her youngest sister.

And shouldn't she be?

The thought brought an unexpected weight pressing down over the buoyancy of her epiphany. The all-too-familiar dull numbness of the past few months descended over her like a heavy curtain, falling slowly. Soon she'd be covered in it, all her emotions smothered but the barest hint of despair that could never quite be banished. The hopelessness would set in next, the thoughts she tried to block, the ones that whispered that she'd never feel joy or happiness again.

Harlow tried to shake it off. Larkin was back. She would go to Selene's to see her. Now. But Aurelia would be there—and she *couldn't*. Her breath came in short gasps, and she clutched her chest. Panic. That's what this was. She was emotionally and physically spent, and now she was having some kind of panic attack.

"Slow, breathe slow."

Kate. Where had she come from? She did as the vampire asked though, breathing in and out slowly until the blood roaring in her veins calmed. It had been a wretched day, despite their win. Despite getting Larkin back, which she couldn't seem to face at the moment. Her emotions felt as though they were on a horrific roller-coaster she couldn't control.

"I'm fine," Harlow said as her breath returned to a normal pace.

"Clearly not," Kate said as she led Harlow out of the alley, towards a group of people who were restacking a pile of firewood that must have been knocked asunder during the attack on the village. She handed Harlow a pair of gloves and they joined in the efforts. Despite what Tomy had said, it seemed wise to do something with herself, at least until she pulled herself together.

"So, Audata says you found Larkin?" Kate's voice was tentative. After their last encounter, Harlow couldn't really blame her.

"Yes," she answered, trying to keep things short and focus on stacking the wood. Kate meant well, trying to help her, but the gap between them was too wide. Harlow didn't know how to close it.

They stacked wood in silence for a long while. Harlow was surprised when the job was done. As people moved on to find other things to do, Kate simply stood staring at her. She was dressed like an average human, wearing a sweater and a pair of thick leggings and snow boots, her short hair pushed back from her pretty face.

"You can't stay mad forever, Lo." The use of the nickname hurt. "Does it help to be angry with all of us?"

"Shut up," Harlow snapped, showing her anger exactly as it was. She barely felt the cold, she was so hot with the fury bubbling out of her.

She'd spent months convincing herself she was dispassionate. That she simply didn't trust Kate anymore. The truth was that she *was* angry, and it *did* help. Staying mad staved off the void inside her since she lost Finn. The deep insecurity that she'd let herself get so lost in a partner that she didn't feel whole without him.

The vampire sighed so deeply that Harlow felt Kate's exasperation in her own chest. Everyone wanted her to stop being angry, to forgive and forget, but she *couldn't*. She didn't blame the people she loved for wanting better for her, nor could she tame the rage inside her, or make it smaller for their comfort, no matter how much she wanted to. For a moment, it looked like Kate might walk away in the face of Harlow's open fury. It was what nearly everyone else had done, and it was what Harlow expected now.

Instead, Kate stepped forward and wrapped her arms around Harlow, pulling her head down to her shoulder. It brought Harlow back into the moment, back into her body as Kate spoke. "Be mad then. Don't keep shutting us out."

Harlow felt the eyes on them, people watching to see what they'd both do next, and it reminded her of Nuva Troi, of Section Seven. As much as she wanted her earlier epiphany to have changed the way she'd act in this moment, that wasn't how it worked. It would take time, and right now she was angry. She took a few steps away from Kate and the people nearby, her boots crunching on the snow. "Petra told you to come talk to me, didn't she?"

Kate followed, steering Harlow towards a more private part of the street.

"What if she did? She loves you, and she knows something about being estranged from the people you love."

That hurt. Harlow had been a terrible friend, avoiding Petra because she was with Kate. The roller coaster of emotions stopped abruptly, crashing to a halt as the last of Harlow's energy drained from her. Not even the heat of her anger kept her going now—she was empty, bereft. How had she missed all of these important truths about herself? About *life?*

She sunk down into a crouch, then plopped down on a bench. Snow fell in big fluffy flakes, as she buried her face in her hands. "Oh, I fucked this all up."

Kate sat next to her. "That's the way to do it."

Harlow peeked out at her. "What?"

Kate leaned back on the bench, stretching her legs out in front of her, her usual careless smile gracing her face. "You're as bad as Finn. Why don't the two of you ever get it? Life is a series of fuckups, and then you die… Or, if you're us, you don't."

Harlow raised an eyebrow incredulously, but she couldn't stop the smile pulling at the corner of her mouth. Kate opened her mouth, stuck out her tongue and a huge snowflake landed on it. Harlow couldn't help but smile.

"Made you smile," Kate said, bumping her shoulder to Harlow's.

Harlow tipped her head back to watch the flakes floating out of the sky. They were clumping together now, resembling pixies from her favorite faery stories. "That snowflake was a paid actor."

Kate snorted. "Seriously, Lo, life is all about mistakes. If we don't learn from them, then what's the point of immortality?"

Vampires thought a lot more about "the point" of immortality than the rest of the Orders, who simply took it for granted. This was the first time Harlow had really felt the depth of the idea. What *was* the point of immortality, if they just kept doing harm?

Harlow let out a frustrated sigh. "I don't know, Kate. You tell me." Her words carried more sting than she'd intended, but she was tired of all this. Tired of feeling bad, tired of being lonely and scared. Tired of pretending like she was anything but mad all the time.

"Well, I sure as hells don't think carrying all this outrage around helps anything. Your family owns a bookstore. Don't you know better than this?"

Harlow face contorted. "What's that supposed to mean?"

"All this anger. Seems like a perfect villain's origin story to me." Kate's voice was light. She was making fun of her.

Harlow groaned. "You are the *worst*." But when she met Kate's wide eyes, her perception altered. Kate wasn't making fun of her, she was teasing her— teasing her back to a reality where Harlow didn't take every single thing so seriously.

That was a reality she knew Finn would want her to live in. It struck her that this was not what Finn had ever wanted for her. When he'd left her, messy as that had been, he'd always felt he was doing it in service of her happiness. He'd wanted her to have a good life, even if he wasn't there to enjoy it with her.

Harlow took a few deep breaths, the frigid air brightening her outlook and cooling her temper some. Maybe she could let some of this anger go. Kate spoke again. "You have to work things out with your parents at some point. Or are you going to spend eternity being pissed at Aurelia?"

Harlow's anger returned at full force—a wave of dry, crackling heat that scorched the back of her throat. Couldn't Kate be happy that she'd warmed to the idea of moving past her anger at her?

"Maybe I will," Harlow growled. "She lied."

"So did I," Kate pleaded.

"And I'm mad at you too." Harlow's voice was shrill, nearly a wail. Heads turned on the street, so she lowered her volume to a harsh whisper. "I hate all of you. Don't you understand? I hate you for coming out of this unscathed after you deceived everyone. And now you get everything you want while I'm alone again." The words came out in a tumble, and like always, Harlow wasn't sure how much of it she actually meant.

"You're alone because you're *choosing* to be alone," Kate shot back, her voice low and cool. "We've all tried to be there for you, but you're shutting everyone out again. When are you going to grow the fuck up?"

Kate's words hung between them. Sharp barbs played on the tip of Harlow's tongue. There were so many things she could say to hurt Kate right now, so many buttons she knew exactly how to push, and if she did, they'd be screaming at one another like poltergeists, here in full hearing of the whole village.

Nothing is as draining as staying mad. The thought appeared as if from nowhere, but she knew from working with both Enzo and Riley that this was the process of healing, even in deep grief. Progress was slow, and she moved backwards as often as she did forwards, but maybe after weeks of feeling like she was in perpetual reverse, she was finally allowed to advance again.

Harlow surprised herself when she spoke. "You're right."

The truth was hard; she didn't know if she'd ever see Finn again. But she was lucky: her entire family was alive and safe. Everyone she loved had made it out, except him. Thousands, maybe millions, of families across Okairos couldn't say the same right now. She'd lost one man, and it hurt more than she could bear, but Kate was right: she wasn't alone.

"I am?" Kate asked.

Harlow laughed, tears streaming down her face now that she let her grip on her rage loosen. "Yeah."

"Wow, that's a new one," Kate muttered, awe in her voice. "I'm right."

Harlow pulled her ex in for a hug. "You shouldn't have started a relationship with Petra if you wanted to be right much," she said as she hugged Kate.

A snort was her answer, and a hug so tight Harlow gasped as Kate asked, "Will you go see your parents now?"

Harlow nodded. "Yeah. I'll go. You go see Lou, okay?"

Kate looked confused. "Why?"

Harlow took her hand for a brief moment. "Because we're lucky, Katie. We're so fucking lucky to be here."

Kate's eyes widened, watery around the edges. Kate rarely cried, but something in Harlow's tone must have reached her. "*Fuck, Lo,*" she muttered over her shoulder as she turned towards her sire's house.

Harlow turned in the opposite direction, heading towards Selene's home. Her heart was still heavy with missing Finn, with the grief over the possibility of never seeing him again, but she had no intention of giving up. She was afraid of what Larkin might tell her about him—that she might be wrong to hope—but it was time to find out.

CHAPTER 11

Selene's tiny cottage was blessedly warm when Harlow walked in. A fire blazed in the hearth, and she heard the sounds of Thea and Larkin talking in the kitchen. Selene was probably in there as well: the delightful scent of pumpkin pasties baking drifted in, filling her nostrils. At home, Selene rarely had time to cook much, with her full social calendar, but she was an excellent chef.

Harlow discarded her boots and hung her coat up on one of the wood pegs in the entryway. When she turned, Aurelia stood behind her, silver hair tucked behind her ears, a pair of glasses pushed back onto the top of her head. She wore a rumpled wool sweater and a pair of ill-fitting jeans. Her usually stylish mother, quite frankly, looked a mess. Her eyes were rimmed red from crying, and her gaze held sheer terror.

In fact, she looked to be frozen in place, staring at Harlow. Aurelia was afraid of *her*. Of what she might say. When they'd first arrived in Sanctum, Harlow had said a lot—things she now wished she would have tempered better. They were all true, but as she got older, she'd realized that perhaps every true thing didn't need to be said. Selene had been angry as well, but Harlow knew that in the past month Aurelia had been sleeping here. And if she was, then the two of them were on their way back to themselves.

If Selene could forgive Aurelia, could she? Harlow wasn't sure if she could. Not if Finn never came back. But in this moment, looking at her terrified mother, she knew she would never stop loving her. Harlow believed Aurelia thought she'd been doing the right things, keeping her family safe. And she knew beyond a shadow of a doubt that Aurelia was sorry for all the pain she'd caused her family. Maybe that was a start.

"Hi," she said, not knowing what else to say.

The fear in Aurelia's eyes receded to mere wariness. "Hello, my darling."

Conversation in the kitchen stopped. They knew she was here. Harlow closed her eyes and remembered dozens of winter weekends at the lake, so similar to this one. There were two brief years after the twins left for college, but Larkin wasn't yet out of secondary, when only she and Thea came home for winter holidays and it had been the five of them. Harlow loved the twins, beyond all measure, but those had been special times.

Her bottom lip quivered as she opened her eyes. Aurelia stood in front of her now. Tentatively, she took Harlow's hands. Harlow didn't draw back. "Thank you for bringing her home, Harlow. I am sorry. So, so sorry for everything else."

Aurelia's head dipped in shame. Selene stepped into the back hallway, and Harlow gave Mama a small, reassuring smile. She was ready to defend Aurelia, that much was clear. But Harlow had no intention of attacking. This hurt so much, and she had no words to reply to that, so she drew Aurelia into her arms and said the only thing she knew in her heart. "I love you, Mommy."

Selene had always been and would always be Mama to her girls, but Aurelia had turned into Mother when the girls got older. She'd always been so elegant and self-assured—so in control—it had fit her better. Here, at what felt like the end of the world, Harlow wanted her Mommy.

Aurelia clung to her, shoulders shaking. "I love you too."

Selene's hands flew over her face as she suppressed a sob. Larkin and Thea both wrapped their arms around her from behind. Harlow dragged Aurelia down the hall and into the embrace of the rest of her family. For long moments everyone cried, holding each other so tightly Harlow thought they might break their hands from clutching onto one another so hard.

When they finally let go, Aurelia's hands cupped her face. "From the moment you were born, and for all eternity, you will always be my darling girl."

Harlow sniffled as Selene pulled a hanky from her pocket, wiping her eyes and nose like she was a toddler. "I know... I said things—"

Aurelia shook her head. "I let you all down."

Selene sniffled now, her forehead wrinkling. Thea and Larkin leaned on one another. Harlow hugged Aurelia again. "I suppose it had to happen sometime."

Aurelia laughed through her tears, gazing lovingly at Selene. They shared a private thought between them. Selene squeezed Harlow's hand. "It's hard to grow up and find out your parents are people, isn't it?"

That was exactly what it was. Aurelia had always been up on such a pedestal for her that she'd never seen it that way before. The maters were people, like anyone else. They made mistakes, just like she did, and would continue to do so.

"The pasties are done, Mama," Thea said, sniffing the air. "If you leave them in for much longer, they'll burn."

Selene bustled about as everyone else worked in quiet tandem to put pasties onto plates and pour mugs of tea. The Kranes piled onto the overstuffed linen-covered couches in the cottage's living room and ate quietly. Harlow was torn. She wanted to ask Larkin about Finn, but Larkin had already told her what she knew, and Harlow didn't know how to push for more information.

She didn't realize she wasn't eating until Larkin's hand brushed hers. "I wish I had more to tell you about Finn." Larkin's eyes glossed with tears.

Harlow took Larkin's hand and squeezed hard. "It's enough to know he was alive the last time you saw him."

Selene glanced between her girls. The look she gave Harlow was clear: *That's enough.* Harlow's head inclined slightly, a subtle acknowledgement that she understood that Larkin needed rest and time with her family to recover. When Aurelia pulled a puzzle out from a stack of games under the coffee table, each of the Kranes fell into a familiar routine. Larkin turned the puzzle pieces over, as Aurelia sought out the edges, while Thea and Selene began matching middle pieces.

Harlow spread out onto the couch, waiting for her turn at the puzzle. She and the twins typically had the job of grappling with the pieces that seemed like they were in the wrong puzzle. Conversation started up, slowly, focusing on catching Larkin up with the dynamics of Sanctum's social ecosystem. Stories and memories from childhood snuck in, everyone sticking to comfortable topics and family jokes.

When Selene and Larkin got into an intense discussion of how to wash vintage wool, Aurelia moved Harlow's feet. Her touch was ginger at first, but Harlow drew her feet back slowly, smiling at her mother. Like Aurelia, her feelings were still raw, but she craved something normal, despite the feeling that even in this good moment, something was *wrong.*

When Aurelia was settled, Harlow shifted direction on the couch, piling pillows up next to Aurelia so that their heads were close together.

"What's going on in your busy head, darling?"

It was a question Aurelia asked her thousands of times in her life. Harlow smiled as she felt her mother's long fingers rake through strands of her tangled hair. The feeling was so familiar, she hated to ruin it. "Nothing."

"Liar," Aurelia chided.

The admonition felt *good.* It was such a blessing to be known. To be understood when she lied to make others comfortable. For someone to know her, without all her awkward ways of trying to fit.

"I keep having these doom-y feelings," Harlow explained. "Any time things are good, I'm tense, waiting for something to go wrong. I feel ridiculous."

Aurelia's fingers paused, and Harlow glanced up at her mother, who wore a pensive look. "Have you considered that perhaps it's not ridiculous, but perfectly logical?"

Harlow shrugged. Enzo and Riley had said something similar before. Lots of bad things had happened—and Finn *was* still missing. It was natural that she'd expect for things to go wrong.

"I guess. I wish I could feel a little less desperate about things."

Aurelia's eyes narrowed slightly. "That's not exactly what I meant, love. I meant your Strider's talent for sensing connections between people—"

Aurelia was interrupted by Larkin's wide yawn, accompanied by a stretch that morphed into the youngest Krane wedging her body between Aurelia and Harlow. "I'm exhausted," she said as she yawned again.

Aurelia and Selene cleared the plates from their meal as Thea joined her sisters on the couch, taking Aurelia's place. The three of them wound around one another, an inextricably linked pile of limbs and sleepy comfort. Larkin's eyes fell closed nearly as soon as her body relaxed.

On the other side of her, Thea too was falling asleep, pulling Larkin into her lap. A million questions spun in Harlow's head, but as Aurelia covered them with blankets they floated away. The comfortable sounds of the maters washing dishes and talking softly in the kitchen was a balm for her battered heart. There was so much to work out still, but tonight, she could have this.

CHAPTER 12

Harlow woke to Larkin pulling the blanket off her, or so she thought, until she fully opened her eyes. Larkin was sitting up with her eyes open, but she clearly wasn't awake. Harlow glanced at the clock above the fireplace—it was past midnight and the cottage was quiet. She shook Thea awake, pressing a finger to her sister's mouth, gesturing to their little sister, who was now perched on the edge of the couch. Larkin's eyes were wide and unfocused, back ramrod straight.

"How long has she been like that?" Thea asked.

Harlow shook her head. "Not long, I don't think. She woke me, moving."

Thea got up, stealing upstairs to the maters' bedroom. Harlow moved to sit on the heavy rustic coffee table. An ember in the fireplace popped, and Harlow realized she was chilly. She got up, adding another log to the fire, stoking it until it crackled to life.

When she turned back, Larkin was still staring straight ahead, and Thea came downstairs grimacing. "They were…."

Harlow rolled her eyes. "Please don't say it."

Thea shook her head. "I couldn't even if I wanted to."

She sat next to Harlow on the coffee table. "Should we shake her?"

Harlow shrugged. "Wait and see what the maters say, I guess."

Aurelia came down first, wearing a silk robe that was obviously Selene's. "Don't wake her," Aurelia said, after checking Larkin's vital signs. "I believe she's walking the spirit paths. We need to wait for her to return." She pushed her youngest back onto the couch very gently, covering her with the discarded blanket. "I'm going to make some coffee."

Harlow and Thea both nodded, still staring at Larkin.

"The two of you can move," Selene said from the stairs. "It might take her a while to return. You might as well get comfortable."

Thea pulled Harlow into one of the oversized chairs that flanked the couch. "She's kind of creepy like that," Thea whispered.

Harlow glanced back at her, giggling. "Are you ten?"

Thea smiled. "It kind of feels like it tonight." She wrapped her arms around Harlow, pulling her younger sister back against her chest.

Harlow settled against Thea's sharp angular body. "You're so bony," she complained.

"Are *you* ten?" Thea's laugh cut short. She stared at Larkin. "Look at her eyes."

Larkin's eyes darted to and fro in such rapid succession that it looked like it might hurt. Harlow took her youngest sister's wrist into her hands, pressing to feel her pulse. "Her heart is beating really fast."

Aurelia peeked out of the kitchen. "Is something wrong?"

Thea's face twisted with worry. "Come look at her."

Aurelia rushed into the living room. "Something's not right." She glanced at Harlow. "You've traveled to the paths before… To Nihil."

Harlow nodded. "I have. But never on purpose."

Larkin shivered, making a small whimpering noise, her eyes moving faster now, as though she was watching something distressing. Harlow took her hands, focusing on the threads that flowed between them, their affinity shining in her mind's eye with golden light. She traced Larkin's threads, the magic that made her littlest sister *her*. And then she spotted the threads that went to the same tiny eye in her own heart, straight into the limen.

She wasn't ever able to explain with words how it felt to sense the threads with her second sight. It was both like seeing things with her eyes, and completely unlike it at the same time. Harlow followed the slender bundle of threads through that eye, stringing a path back out for herself and Larkin as she went. Outside of her second sight, she felt Thea's fingers lace through hers, grounding her to the waking world.

Beyond that, she felt Aurelia and Selene both. She was anchored, solid in her family's perfectly-imperfect love. They would make it out, she was sure of it. That surety wobbled slightly as she was cast into Nihil, the limen crystallizing around her, more real now that she was no longer following the threads.

Harlow found herself in the chamber where she'd first seen Ashbourne and the generals, the wardens of Nihil, over the summer. Instead of the quiet pulse of the limen's heart, the room was in chaos. Not one of the generals were in their stasis chambers. The heart of the aether boomed erratically, shaking the room.

Someone bumped into her astral body, pushing her hard, though she wasn't sure how that was possible. She turned to find Ashbourne, his heavy brow furrowed with concern.

"You should not be here," he said. "Go home."

"I followed Larkin here," she explained as he took hold of her elbow.

"Larkin?" It was both question and answer. He dragged her now and she moved her spirit body's feet, desperate to keep up. They traveled down what appeared to be a long glass hallway. The clear walls were ornately carved, and beyond them, aether swirled, lit by the storm at the heart of the limen. Harlow could make out shapes in the aether—hundreds, maybe thousands, of screaming faces. She recognized some as humanoid, others creatures she could hardly imagine.

"What is happening here?" Harlow slowed down, unwilling to go further until she understood the situation better.

Ashbourne slowed, but continued to drag her forward. "The Ravagers have escaped."

"Escaped?" Harlow repeated, the idea too big for her to process all at once.

She knew one Ravager had escaped before, and that was the reason for Morgaine Yarlo's visit to Okairos. The creature was wreaking havoc on the human girl's planet, and she'd been sent to try and stop its progress. If the other two Ravagers were loose, what did that mean? Harlow's throat went dry, but she shouldn't be aware of physical sensations here. Not like this. She yanked hard on Ashbourne's arm to get him to stop.

The tall Ventyr turned and the frustrated concern on his face reminded her that he was Finn's uncle. They were so similar, and yet very different at the same time. Ashbourne was, no doubt, more handsome—though Harlow wasn't sure how that was possible. But while Finn's eyes always held warm humor behind the darkness that lurked there, Ashbourne was only cold power, ancient and fierce. "Someone let them out."

Harlow stumbled, though she wasn't sure how it was possible to be clumsy in her spirit body—something in the limen had gone off balance. What Ashbourne said made no sense. Letting the Ravagers loose was unthinkable. Their uncontrolled elemental energy had nearly destroyed worlds before. Harlow's mind spun out, her perception blurring.

Ashbourne dragged her up again, pulling her along. "Stay focused. You must not lose yourself here."

"Who would do something like that?" Harlow asked.

Ashbourne turned. His jaw clenched tightly, his brow creased into deep furrows. "I don't know. The Ravagers cannot be allowed free reign…" His deep voice broke a little then hardened once more. "Please, you must find Larkin and go."

He felt protective over her sister. Cared for her in some way, that was clear. But that care was not something she recognized. Even Connor McKay had emotions she understood. Whoever—whatever—Ashbourne the Warden had become after an eternity in this prison, she could not comprehend it.

And yet, he'd stopped, his grip on her arm gentling. It hadn't hurt her spirit body, but even so, he realized how hard he'd been holding onto her and his face softened a measure.

"Where did the Ravagers go?"

Ash didn't answer her question. His eyes narrowed in intensity. "You must get out, *now*. The structure that holds Nihil together is disintegrating."

Harlow pointed to the screaming faces in the aether. "And that?"

Ash didn't answer, but began walking again. He didn't run, but his stride was quick and purposeful. "Come this way—there is a place your sister often meets me outside Nihil." They turned a corner and the walls became thicker and more textured, like stone.

Ash glanced back as they descended into darkness, a ball of light illuminating in front of him. "Step carefully. This part of Nihil is not an aethereal construction. It is real, and you too shall become more real here."

The metaphysical mechanics of that were baffling, but Harlow didn't have time to think. They'd entered a maze of some kind. "What is this place?"

"The Labyrinth," Ash said. "It has always been here. Like much of the limen, it is but an echo of a real place. But it is…more corporeally inclined. Your sister often appears here. Come."

Harlow looked back, remembering the long glass hallway and the screaming faces. Ashbourne's mouth pressed into a grim line, as though annoyed she'd remembered.

"Do you know so little of the aether? Of what made the Ravagers?" His voice was curt.

Harlow shrugged. "I'm sure you can imagine that Connor and the rest of your kind haven't made that kind of information readily available."

Ashbourne snorted, something nearing a laugh as he moved on, walking quickly through turn by turn of the Labyrinth. "I should have considered that." His face smoothed into thoughtfulness. "There are two kinds of power that allow magic to be used. You understand this, yes?"

Harlow nodded, following Ashbourne. This place was dizzying in its complexity. The Ventyr's steps were sure, but she wondered how she'd ever find her way out. In the distance, there were sounds of something breaking apart, erratic crashes and otherworldly screams.

Ashbourne was trying to keep her calm by talking to her. Harlow recognized the strategy immediately, and appreciated it. Fear had her heart in its cold vice-grip, and she needed to stay moving and sharp. She wouldn't lose Larkin again. "Celestial and aethereal, right? The glowing light—your people use that, rather than aether, right?"

Ashbourne made a "hmm" noise, tilting his head in a raptorial fashion that reminded her of the Feriant. "Not 'rather than.' I would say primarily. Celestial power comes from the universe itself, from all that is outward, while aether comes from within. The Ventyr use both, but we fare better with celestial power." He held out the glowing golden orb in front of him for emphasis. "Aether, because of its nature, is more sentient than starfire. It is prone to individuation—which makes it dangerous."

Harlow had no idea what Ashbourne might mean by that. Somewhere ahead of them, she heard a voice calling out for help. "That's Larkin!"

"Yes," Ash replied, grabbing her hand and rushing them forward. Harlow allowed herself to be dragged.

When she spotted Larkin, she broke free of the Ventyr and ran to her sister's side. Larkin's eyes were unfocused, her expression disoriented. She fell into Harlow's arms. "Harlow?"

"It's me," Harlow answered. "Let's get you out of here."

Ashbourne placed a hand on Larkin's back. "I am so glad you are all right, littling," he said softly.

Harlow glanced up, and finally understood why the ancient immortal had been so interested in her sister. Though there were no threads here, something was missing. Some*one* was missing, and Larkin reminded him of that someone.

"You have a sister," she guessed.

The ancient being—in all ways that counted, a god—bowed his head. "Yes. Thalia was much like Larkin."

There was great sadness in the past tense of the statement. Despite the Ventyr's long lives, Harlow knew immediately that Thalia was gone, and Ashbourne had treated Larkin like his own ever since she was a child. In the distance, something rumbled and creaked. The shrieking increased now, making Harlow want to cover her ears.

"The prison is coming apart," Ashbourne said. "Go. Now."

But Harlow didn't know how. He'd been right. She was more real here, less connected to the aether, and that made all the difference. "Before, when I was here, you sent me back. Can you do that now?"

Ash nodded. "Be careful, little bird. The Ravager you spoke to knows you. It speaks of you often. I fear it will find you when it makes its way to your world."

In the din of Nihil breaking apart, everything stopped for Harlow. Her ears rung with the reality of Ashbourne's words. What he was saying couldn't be true. It just *couldn't*. She hadn't *meant* to draw the creature's attention when she'd first traveled to Nihil. Was this her fault?

Next to her, Larkin stilled. "They've escaped?"

Harlow wouldn't accept this. It was too much. Her world had endured enough. "*No*."

"Yes." Ashbourne's reply was fierce, unyielding as adamantine.

Beyond the Labyrinth, the hideous creaking noise dissolved into an infernal groan. Small stones came loose from the Labyrinth walls, floating in the air, suspended.

"And the other?" Harlow was stalling, trying to wrap her mind around yet another unsolvable problem, one she feared she might have caused.

Ashbourne shook his head. "The other I must follow to Sirin, which is where I believe it has gone. It is the worst of the two—and I must find it, and bring it back."

So he would not help them. Next to her, Larkin's body tensed. She was as scared as Harlow was.

"What about the one that's gone to Okairos?" Harlow's voice came out in a high-pitched shriek.

"You must find a way to vanquish it, or bring it back here." Ashbourne said it so simply that for a moment it sounded *possible*. But how could it be? How could they vanquish it on their own?

More stones came loose from the Labyrinth. The whole thing pitched, like an unstable ship upon a roiling sea.

"Your brethren," Harlow gripped Larkin's arm, trying to steady them both.

It felt as though the limen itself might break apart, but if she'd caused this problem, she had to try to solve it. "The generals. Will they help us?"

Ashbourne laughed, the sound dry and bitter. Unlike Larkin and Harlow, he had no trouble keeping his balance. The world-between-worlds was breaking apart and he was steady as a rock. "The generals will not come to our aid."

"But… I have to…" Harlow couldn't find the words to express what she needed to say. That she couldn't be the cause of this, and return to Okairos with no solution.

He sensed the source of her struggle. "There is nothing you could have done differently. Some things are woven into the tapestry, and cannot be unraveled. This is one such thing." The Ventyr's dark eyes were solemn. "You must go."

"Come with us," Harlow begged, as she and Larkin stumbled into one another again. Larkin ducked to avoid a stone from the Labyrinth hitting her in the head. "We'll need your help."

Ashbourne shook his head. "You have my brother to help you. He was there at the beginning."

Harlow wanted to scream. They didn't have time for this conversation anymore, but he was seriously out of touch if he thought Connor would help them. Ashbourne pushed a loose stone the size of a boulder away from them. At least the Labyrinth was breaking apart slowly, though the noises that came from Nihil increased in pitch and frequency.

"And my nephew. I must do my duty elsewhere, and you must go home." Ash pressed fingers to Larkin and Harlow's foreheads, respectively, and before Harlow could ask another question, she felt her body lose its modicum of corporeality and slide back along the threads so fast it was dizzying. When she opened her eyes, she was in the cottage once more, staring into Larkin's eyes.

CHAPTER 13

Aurelia, Selene, and Thea sat frozen for a fraction of a second, before launching themselves at Larkin and Harlow. When hugs and assurances were given that they were both all right, Larkin announced, "The Ravagers are loose. Nihil has been destroyed."

"What?" Aurelia gasped. "How?"

Harlow shook her head. "We didn't have time to find out. Ash sent us back."

"What were you doing there to begin with, bun?" Aurelia's words were slow and careful.

Larkin sighed. "I wanted to see how Ash was doing. It was never safe enough with Vivia to dream-walk."

Everyone was silent. No one wanted to get into a fight about safety on Larkin's first night back, but it was obvious from the identical tight-lipped expressions on Selene, Aurelia, and Thea's faces they were suppressing the urge to chide. Harlow hid a smile. It was no wonder the twins had thousands of nicknames for Thea that all indicated that she was their third mother.

Finally Selene spoke. "Where have they gone? Did Ash know?"

Larkin glanced at Harlow. "He thought the one that was interested in Harlow might come here. He's gone after the other."

Harlow's cheeks flushed. The creature's interest in her elicited shame. A log in the fireplace popped, sending sparks everywhere. Everyone jumped.

Aurelia put a hand on Harlow's arm. "It is not your fault, darling. We don't even know if it's here."

Harlow wasn't so sure about that, even after all that nonsense Ash had spouted in Nihil about the tapestry not being unraveled.

"What about the other Wardens?" Thea asked. "Won't they come here?"

A hysterical laugh bubbled up from Harlow's belly. "They're gone. No one is coming to help us. Ash says we have Connor to help us. And Finn." Her voice shuddered around Finn's name, her hands fluttering around her face.

"Slow down," Aurelia urged, her tone gentle. "We'll figure this out."

But Harlow couldn't see how. The doom-feeling was coming true. War with the Illuminated was imminent, on the horizon. The Vespae had overrun the planet. They were a rag-tag group of refugees, hiding in desolation, and Finn was *still* missing. How, *how* did anyone expect her to slow her thinking down or figure anything out?

The scream Harlow had been repressing since Nihil burbled out of her in a feral noise. "It never stops," she cried, strangled desperation breaking over her in waves. "Why can't we catch a break?"

Why can't I catch a break?

"We have," Selene said, her voice steady and calm. "We got Larkin back. *You* got Larkin back."

Everyone was silent for a long moment. Harlow saw the panic in the maters' eyes. She inhaled slowly, Thea's fingers still wound around hers, and she gripped them tighter for support. Thea squeezed back, a silent reassurance that she understood, that she wasn't going anywhere.

"I'm sorry," Harlow whispered, her eyes falling into her lap.

Selene stroked her cheek. "There's no need for apologies. Sometimes when situations are at their worst, we can't see the progress we're making."

Aurelia nodded, gazing at her wife. "When the hits keep coming, and it feels like they won't stop, it's hard to remember that we keep getting up." Her eyes slid to Harlow's. "We underestimate the strength it takes to rise."

Harlow wanted desperately to feel comfort in her mother's words, but she could not. But she wouldn't add to anyone else's troubles.

Larkin's head tilted. "There was something else, before, when Finn and I were in the limen with Morgaine... The Ravagers can't function in corporeal realms easily. They need a body. A human body. Morgaine said she doesn't know if immortals make good hosts..."

"So it will inhabit a human?" Thea asked.

From the look on Thea's face, it was clear her question was for herself, not the group, but Larkin answered anyway. "I think so."

The Kranes sat in silence, letting both the depth and breadth of the problems closing in on them sink in. Harlow waited for someone to say something. For a brilliant solution to pop out of one of their mouths, but nothing came. Every moment of respite came paired with something terrible—some new twist of fate that made everything worse. *How were people meant to bear the weight of so much going wrong?*

The front door banged open, cold air flooding the living room of the cottage, a burst of snow swirling in with the wind. Alaric stepped inside, pulling the door hard against the howling storm raging outside. As he pushed his hood back, Thea stood, her movements sharp in reaction to her bondmate's emotions.

Alaric's dark eyes were wide with panic until he counted them. He didn't bother to take off his boots and coat, but strode across the room, pulling Thea into his side, tucking her beneath his arm, as though protecting her from something. For a moment, he hesitated. When he spoke, Harlow could tell he was making every attempt to keep his voice even and calm. "The Vespae broke the wards. They took Petra. You're needed at Kate's."

The air in the room went from heavy desperation to outright panic in the space of a moment. Everyone moved quickly, going for their coats and boots, talking at once, as was the way with the Kranes in a crisis.

"The Vespae don't take prisoners," Thea murmured.

"They do," Larkin replied, searching for her socks under the coffee table. "They took Finn. They didn't kill him. They *took* him. I watched it happen." Larkin turned to Harlow. "In the attack, before you found me, didn't they act like they wanted you?"

Harlow nodded. Pieces of the puzzle were starting to take shape in her mind, but she didn't know what the picture was. *Why hadn't they come here? Why hadn't they come after her, if they'd wanted her?* She glanced at Alaric. "When did they take her?"

Alaric met her eyes, his shrewd sense of duty in a crisis narrowing in on her. "About twenty minutes ago."

Nihil. They'd been in Nihil twenty minutes ago. Not their bodies, but their spirits. *Had that kept the Vespae from finding her, or had they simply not wanted her anymore?*

Larkin's jaw clenched as she thought. "It's like they're looking for something specific."

Harlow nodded as she slid into her jacket. "They are. Audata's put it together. They're looking for a building, an observatory. But I don't know what that would have to do with Finn, or me—or Petra, for that matter."

"An *observatory*?" Aurelia's skin went white, all blood draining from her face. "Let's go."

"What is it, darling?" Selene asked.

Aurelia had never looked so grim. "I know why they're taking them. Let's go."

Unreasonable hope bloomed in Harlow's chest. She took Aurelia's hand, clasping it hard. She didn't know what her mother had put together, but she had to ask. "Could *these* Vespae—the ones who took Petra—have Finn?"

Aurelia's hands went to Harlow's cheeks. "I don't know, love. They might."

Harlow fought to keep her thoughts linear, but didn't succeed. Her mind raced. She'd been right there, at that farm, and he might have been below— needing her. She couldn't think of that now. One thing at a time. They didn't know anything more than they had before, not really, but the hope blossoming in her chest didn't absorb the reason she tried to impose on it. It opened in hundreds of tiny buds—buds that if Harlow could pull them from inside her, she knew would be shaped like lilacs.

Harlow closed her eyes against the tears that threatened, pushing thoughts of Finn deep down inside her, until she could breathe again. When she opened them, Thea's boots were on, but she had lost her coat. When she turned, Alaric was holding it open for her, his face grave. Harlow knew where the glint of protectiveness in her brother-in-law's eyes came from. If the Vespae were attacking and taking people, his priorities were with Thea, no matter how much he loved Petra.

Harlow's heart swelled. Alaric glanced her way, and she nodded at him, and he at her. They understood one another. Thea and the twins she carried would be protected at all costs. Harlow wondered how long she had left with her eldest sister. They couldn't stay here—not if the Vespae knew where they were and were able to break through the village's wards so easily. She and Larkin dressed quickly for the cold and their little party set out into the cold night, towards Kate's house.

~

KATE'S COTTAGE was no bigger than Selene's and decorated in nearly identical linen-colored furniture. It was packed so full of people they were spilling out into the garden. All the top Rogue officials were here. At the center of everything, Kate sat on the couch, head in her hands, rocking back and forth. Lou was next to her, trying and failing to comfort her daughter.

Harlow went to Lou's side. Lou had already been in her seventies when she was turned, and though the transformation had smoothed some of her wrinkles, she still wore more age than most vampires. Her salt and pepper hair was short and she was a stout woman with pale skin and a hard face, with gentle eyes. Those eyes were worried now. Kate did not lose control. *Ever.*

So Kate wasn't dallying with Petra; she was deeply in love with her. Harlow knew they'd fallen hard for one another, but this was news to her. *Maybe it wouldn't be if you'd been talking to your friends,* a nasty voice in the back of her head chided.

Enzo and Riley rushed in from the storm, leaving snowshoes at the door, as Harlow touched Lou's shoulder. "Let me try?"

Lou nodded, rising. "Help her, Harlow. We need her to tell us what happened. All I got out of her was that they took her."

"Get everyone out of here," Harlow replied. "Aurelia has something to tell us —something important."

Lou nodded and cleared the cottage of all but the most important Rogue officials. When only a few were left, they went into the dining room, leaving Harlow alone with Kate.

Harlow wondered if it wouldn't have been better for Enzo or Riley to help. They were both empaths and could probably do a better job than her. But as she sat, Kate reached for her hand, pressing it to her chest. "I can't breathe without her," she gasped.

Terror gripped Kate Spencer like nothing Harlow had ever seen. She squeezed Kate's hand. "I know."

"You don't!" Kate screamed in her face.

Harlow gripped Kate's hand harder, so hard it probably hurt. "I *do,*" she hissed, then softer, "Katie—I do."

Kate's eyes widened and she slowed her rocking. She breathed deeper. "Oh," she said, her bottom lip shaking. "You do."

Harlow nodded again. "Tell me what happened. Was she out when you and I were stacking wood?"

Kate nodded. "Yes, yes… She was burning the bodies… But they were waiting when we got back tonight… Waiting here…. I tried to stop them, Lo."

Kate wheezed between words, her panic rising again. "Breathe," Harlow said, keeping her voice low and soothing. She touched her friend's face. "Breathe and tell me what happened so we can help her."

"They didn't attack like before. They just took her and left. They were so fast… I tried to follow, but… I…. I got lost."

Harlow nodded. "I know you did. It's okay."

"No!" Kate insisted. "It's not. I didn't have my emergency phone. I can't track it back."

"Kate," Harlow said firmly. "It's okay. I know where they took her, and when you're ready, Aurelia says she knows why."

Kate's eyes lost some of the wild panic and she drew breath after shuddering breath. "Okay," she said, after a long pause. Kate's fists clenched tightly as she regained control of herself. "I'm ready."

Harlow took Kate's arm and led her into the dining room, where almost two dozen people were crowded into chairs and corners. The room wasn't big enough for this kind of thing, but it didn't really matter at this point. They were all together.

Kate's arm wound tightly around hers. Something about it made her proud. After everything they'd been through, they were still friends. Right now, her friend wasn't the Rogue Queen, she was a woman whose heart was in pieces. Harlow helped her to sit, and spoke. "Kate says that when she and Petra got home, the Vespae were waiting. They took Petra and left—"

"Why are you telling us this?" a human asked. "Why isn't Kate telling us?"

Harlow's heart sank to see the compact frame and auburn hair of Piper Winslow, the Education Councillor.

"*Please*," Kate managed to say, her voice shaking.

The human woman's eyes narrowed at Kate, and then Harlow. Vivia was sitting next to Piper, and she put a hand on her arm. "I believe Harlow has some pertinent information about what's happened here, don't you, Harlow?"

Harlow nodded, looking around for Cian—she saw them standing towards the back with Alaric and Thea. None of them would typically be allowed in a meeting like this—maybe Cian, but not the rest of them.

Harlow felt like an outsider and a bit of an imposter, but she nodded and continued. "When Kate tried to follow the Vespae, she found the same thing I did earlier today—they've taken over a small farm. There's thousands of them gathered there, and they have some unique warding. It's nearly invisible, hiding the farm entirely…"

"We have that kind of warding here. How is that unique?" Piper interrupted. The way she looked at Harlow felt resentful, and personal. Though Harlow had tried to dismiss her attitude in the past, tonight it was clear that whatever issue Piper had with her, it was more than being wary of her close relationship with Finn.

Harlow took a deep breath, thinking of Finn, and the way she'd watched him navigate thorny moments like this early on during their summer in Nea

Sterlis, with various important people in the lower Orders. He always stayed calm and empathetic, rather than impatient.

"Right," she said after she'd collected herself. Piper looked vaguely surprised to be agreed with. *Had she been expecting Harlow to fight with her?* "We do, you're right. But these were different. They made it hard to think as I passed through them—and I *could* pass through, but only in my Feriant form."

Vivia nodded now, her face thoughtful. Harlow would bet money she had a theory working—all of her sisters made the exact same face when they puzzled something together. Her resentment towards the Argent dissipated a little more. It wasn't Vivia's fault that people automatically liked her, and not Harlow.

She turned her attention back to explaining herself, feeling calmer. "After breaking the wards in my alternae, I started to feel excessively confused when I dropped into my humanoid form. So I marked the geolocation and sent it back to base." Harlow glanced at Kate, who still clung to her. "The exact same thing happened to Kate when she tried to follow Petra's captors."

Piper looked to Aurelia. "You said you know something."

How had the Education Councillor defaulted to running this meeting? Harlow wondered. *Shouldn't Lou be running it, if Kate can't? She's the former queen after all.*

Aurelia bowed her head respectfully to the human. "I have a guess as to why they're taking certain prisoners."

Piper Winslow's face didn't move a muscle, she simply made an imperious gesture with her hand for Aurelia to continue. The atmosphere in the room was tense. Many of the eyes on Aurelia were suspicious, wary. Harlow wasn't the only outsider; it felt like her whole family was intruding on something that wasn't meant for them.

Because it wasn't. The Rogue Order wasn't made for them. It was made for people who could not function in the Orders and the world they'd built—and they'd all done so fairly easily, always. Kate squeezed her hand and when their eyes met, the vampire nodded. Kate always had an uncanny way of following Harlow's trains of thought without her having to say much.

Aurelia cleared her throat as all eyes focused on her. Harlow's heart hurt to see her mother move so uncomfortably in her chair. Apparently she sensed the same discomfort Harlow did, but she steeled herself quickly and spoke. "It's possible these Vespae have Finn McKay, and it's likely he knows where the observatory they are searching for is."

Audata, who sat next to Piper, sat up straight. "Why would he know that?"

Aurelia took a deep breath. "The Illuminated have secret caches of information all over Okairos. Mostly in remote areas. We know they're constantly watching us, but we're not all they're watching. They also monitor the stars closely, and the occurrence of the portals. They track them."

Most of the people around the table nodded. While they hadn't known this explicitly, theories about secret locations of Illuminated information had been posited a number of times.

Aurelia spoke again. "I believe they think Petra and Finn have knowledge of the observatory."

Piper pursed her lips momentarily, then her eyebrows lifted above the frames of her glasses. "They know he's Connor's child… And Petra, well she would have as much of a chance of knowing where the observatory was as he would, wouldn't she?"

Aurelia nodded as the human woman trailed off.

"Why are they interested in Harlow, then?" Piper asked. It came out like a challenge, raising Harlow's hackles, but Aurelia didn't miss a beat.

"As all of you know, I've been privy to many of the Illuminated's secrets over the years. I assume they believe she might know things that I do."

Whispers spun about the room, weaving webs of discord. People weren't sure what to think, or if they could trust what Aurelia said. Harlow heard whispered questions about why they hadn't tried to take Thea, or even Larkin.

"Why wouldn't they just take *you* then?" Piper asked, her voice rising above the quiet chaos. "Why do they want these children?"

Vivia cleared her throat. "If I may, Piper?"

The human nodded, her expression morphing into pleasantness. She looked younger at that moment, more like she was Harlow's age than she had for the whole conversation. The responsibility of her role, whatever it actually was, obviously weighed heavily on Piper Winslow. Harlow didn't believe for a moment that the human was only the Education Councillor.

Vivia spoke, and the room fell completely silent. "It's my belief that Aurelia is onto something pertinent. However, I also believe we should keep an open mind here. The Vespae tried to talk with us, for the first time *ever*, before they attacked us."

Someone, Harlow didn't see who, spoke up from the crowd. "They still tried to wipe us out."

Vivia nodded. "Yes. They are brutal in their methods. But they have an aim of some kind, and I believe we'd be wise to find out what that is. It might help us solve things between our people with less bloodshed."

The room erupted into loud conversation. Not even Vivia Woolf, with her iconic status among the Rogues, could suggest such a thing without evoking controversy. Vivia ran a hand through her long, silver hair, which caught the light with a silken sheen. The firedrake waited, as though thinking deeply, before holding a hand up to silence the room. It only served to give her words more gravitas. Vivia Woolf knew *exactly* how to work a crowd. "Before the Illuminated came, we had a theory that they attacked so viciously because they were very territorial, like wasps…"

"Thus the name…" Piper murmured appreciatively.

Vivia nodded, obviously pleased that Piper had mentioned it. "Yes, exactly. My point is only that we should avoid thinking of their motivations as though they are Okairons. My mother used to say that though their actions were difficult to understand, she didn't believe they were evil…"

More whispers filled the room at the mention of the ancient Empress—the one the Illuminated had eventually overthrown after they helped to rid Okairos of the Vespae originally. It was a reminder of how dire the situation truly was.

"They've killed so many," Cian mused. They were likely the only person who would dare counter Vivia's point.

"I don't suggest that their actions are excusable, or that we should not fight them. Only that measuring evil by Okairos' standards might not be the best way to understand their motivations." The ancient firedrake didn't falter for a moment. This was what immortality could look like if it weren't spent in pursuit of power over others.

Vivia stood. "The best thing we can do now is get our people back and work on fortifying our wards, but of course we'll leave this to a vote." She looked at Cian then, and the rest of Harlow's family in turn. "Come, let's allow the Council some room to talk without the rest of us."

Kate hugged Harlow. "Thank you."

"We'll get her back, okay?" Harlow promised.

"Finn too," Kate replied, her chin quivering a little. "We'll get them both back."

They hugged again, before Lou pulled Kate into a conversation with a few of the Council members and Vivia Woolf. Harlow slipped out the front door, looking for her family. People filed out of the cottage, going their separate ways in small whispering groups. The storm had stopped, for the time being. Harlow's family huddled around Aurelia and Selene, watching the crowd disperse.

Harlow joined them, as Cian took one of Aurelia's hands. "Do you really think it's possible that the Vespae who took Petra have Finn too?"

Aurelia nodded at the firedrake. "I do." She turned to Alaric. "What about the caches in Nuva Troi? Do you know where they are?"

Harlow understood why Aurelia hadn't brought this up in the meeting. She glanced at the cottage. The Council was gathering around the dining room table again. She noticed that while Vivia had said "they" should let the Council speak, that she herself had stayed. This was how power worked; even wonderful people like Vivia worked to have more of it.

Alaric ushered the family along, to keep them moving away from the crowd. When they reached the maters' yard, he moved quickly and quietly, wrapping his own coat around Thea as they all settled into chairs. Everyone was waiting for him to speak, but his focus was on his bondmate.

Harlow hid a smile. Thea was annoyed with the attention. She pulled her handsome husband towards her. "I'm fine," she muttered. "Tell them about the caches."

Alaric rolled his eyes slightly at Thea's admonition. Harlow was glad to see he wasn't offended by her sister's grumpiness. "There's a cache in Nuva Troi. In Connor's office, beneath the Illuminated Order's building. There's one in every major city on the planet—the Knights have been trying to get into one for years."

Cian nodded, rubbing their hands together to warm them. "We've never had any luck. The one in Nuva Troi is the most heavily guarded. But if this observatory is here in Falcyra… That might be a different story. Do you know where it is, Alaric?"

"No," he answered. "I'm sorry."

Thea shivered. Alaric gestured towards the house they shared with the maters. "Could we head inside? Thea is cold."

Selene's keen eyes darted between Thea and Alaric. Aurelia watched her wife, then watched the direction of Selene's gaze. The two of them made eye contact, hope and careful joy lighting their eyes. Despite the difficult nature of the past months, they were connected as they ever were, it seemed.

"Yes," Selene said, standing to take her eldest's arm, dragging her up from her chair. "Let's get you inside."

Thea rolled her eyes. "Don't start treating me like a fragile thing. I won't have it."

Larkin's mouth twisted into a little knot. "What does everyone know that I don't?"

The entire family huddled together as they walked inside, filling Larkin in on the good news that she was about to be an auntie. The aching void inside Harlow's chest shrunk a tiny bit as the cold air stung her cheeks.

CHAPTER 14

Harlow spent an hour with her family, before she and Cian joined the rest of the Warbirds at the Dairy, which was abuzz with activity as they arrived. Vivia, who'd apparently left the Council meeting, broke away from gear prep to hug Cian. Harlow listened while they spoke, but apparently she'd left shortly after they had. Nothing had been decided yet, but she was optimistic that they'd approve a rescue mission.

Harlow went about setting her gear up. None of them would dress until it was time to go; their fighting gear was too well-insulated to wear inside. Enzo had designed it carefully, weaving spells into the seams that made it warmer and more protective.

There wasn't a lot left to do to prepare. Until the Council officially approved their mission, all they could do was rest. Harlow joined the majority of the Warbirds in finding a place to nap until word came through. Tomyris and Sam made room for her on one of the big couches and she soon dozed off.

She woke to Audata's return from the Council meeting. They had approved what Audata called "fast, exploratory action." The Warbirds were sanctioned to rescue Petra, and anyone else they could find, in a targeted, quick attack that would be focused on rescue and information gathering, and nothing else.

The Warbirds spurred into action with this news. Claimed partners ran through drills as they geared up, while Sam and Tomyris were sent on a surveillance mission to get a better idea of the farm itself. Yet another blizzard had fallen over the area overnight, and the day was dark and gloomy, with low visibility. Harlow was sipping a big mug of bone broth with Cian when Sam and Tomyris returned. Once they'd dried off, they joined Harlow and the others on the floor in the training room to finalize the plan.

"There's a big farmhouse," Sam explained as the Warbirds stretched their muscles in a circle around Sam and Tomyris. "Looks like that's where the queen is staying with her guard. They don't let anyone in there."

Tomyris nodded. "And there's a bunch of outbuildings and sheds, but the barn is where they're keeping Petra."

Harlow reached for Cian's hand, her heart beating so hard it hurt. "You saw her?"

Sam's smile was grim. "Yes. She was knocked out, and they were moving her from the farmhouse to the barn. Looks like they had their queen dose her."

Murmurs spread through the room. Audata had a theory that a swarm's queen might be more poisonous than her drones. If she was right, Petra would be incapable of doing much to help when they got her out.

Sam sketched a map of the farm on a piece of paper, while Tomyris continued. "We also saw them carry in more food than was necessary for one person, though it was hard to tell how much they had. It looks like at least one other person is being kept in the barn."

Harlow's heart thumped so hard she thought it might bruise her ribcage. Was Finn there? A few of the Warbirds glanced her way. Mirai and Peyton both shot her sympathetic looks. If anyone could understand how she felt right now, it was this group of people.

Audata looked at the map Sam drew first, then handed it to Vivia to look over. Apparently, the firedrake was being treated as one of their leaders now. Harlow was grateful. The Argent had more experience with Vespae than any of them did. Her knowledge was invaluable.

The Warbirds crouched together, watching as Vivia explained the plan. "The blizzard gives us some cover, but our strongest ally is speed. We need to do this in under ten minutes, if possible."

Everyone nodded along as she explained their flight path, and the formation they'd surround the barn in. Cian would cover them from above, but would stay hidden for as long as possible. "Sam, Tomy—I want you to go in with Harlow and get the prisoners. Teleport them out immediately, and if there are more prisoners than just Petra, pull anyone off the line that you need to help you, okay?"

Sam and Tomyris nodded. Harlow had questions though. "Do *you* think there's more than just Petra at the farm?"

Vivia's silver eyes met hers. "You're asking me if I think Finn's there?" The Dairy went so silent that the wind's howling outside filled Harlow's ears. "I don't know, Harlow. But whoever they've taken, we have to get them back and find out what's been going on at that farm."

Harlow nodded, but Cian spoke. "Of course, I think we should rescue whoever's there…What do you think they're doing to the prisoners? They can't talk to them, right?"

The look of utter helplessness on Vivia's face sent a visible chill through everyone in the room, and her words did nothing to reassure anyone. "In all the time I've been dealing with the Vespae, no one has ever been able to communicate with them. Until the other day, I've never even seen an attempt to talk to us. Not *ever*. And they weren't successful, were they? They can't speak as we do."

Vivia stared at the ceiling for a long time. Her silver hair was braided into two thick braids, like the rest of the Warbirds, and she played with the ends of one as her face scrunched up in thought. Finally she spoke. "I think we have to come to terms with the idea that it's possible someone else is helping the Vespae. Someone who could potentially talk to their prisoners."

Audata's eyes widened in a way that Harlow knew meant that she had a theory. "Someone could be using them as a weapon."

Vivia shrugged. "That's certainly a possibility, but we won't know until we get whoever is there out. It's our best chance to gain vital intelligence on their motivations."

A dry, hollow laugh rasped through Harlow's lungs. "That's why we get to rescue them, isn't it?"

Audata and Vivia exchanged a look. Vivia sighed, her eyes falling closed. "I don't know what you want us to say, Harlow."

Cian answered for her. "The truth."

Audata turned to Harlow, sliding the map to Vivia. "Yes, that's why they're approving the mission. They don't care about rescuing Petra, but they did care about the possibility that the Vespae might have Finn."

Harlow pushed up off the floor, anger filling her. "But not because they trust him, or *us*, right?"

Each of the Warbirds tensed.

Audata's face didn't move, nor did her tone turn conciliatory. "Correct. They want Finn to give information about Connor, and the cache of information in Nuva Troi. That is the reason we're being allowed to go."

Peyton was the first to speak, surprising Harlow with her words. "That's fucked up. He's her Claimed. One of *us*." The Ventyr woman made eye contact with her partner, Vance, a tall redheaded Strider. He nodded, his freckled face clouding with regret.

Peyton turned to Harlow. "I know we've given you a hard time." Many of the Warbirds nodded; it was obvious they'd talked about this. "A lot of us have baggage about the McKays. They've gone after a lot of our families over the years."

Harlow couldn't look up as tears threatened to fall on her cheeks. She knew how bad it felt to have Connor and Aislin McKay come after your family. Peyton cleared her throat. "But you and Finn both are different. You're ours now."

Harlow glanced around as Peyton stood, pulling her to her feet as the rest of the Warbirds, and Cian, did the same thing. "You're one of us, Krane. And whatever the Council's intentions, ours are to get our people home safe."

"Thank you," Harlow whispered.

Peyton dragged her into a hug and a cheer went up. "Let's go get your man."

CHAPTER 15

The group broke up to make their final preparations for the mission. Cian hugged Harlow hard, followed by Sam, Tomyris and each of the Warbirds in turn. The show of affection calmed her wild heartbeat, but only slightly. It was good to finally have the Warbirds' full support, and feel as though she belonged, but as it lessened the anger and frustration she'd been carrying with her, it made way for fear.

Harlow busied herself with tying up a pair of insulated knee-high boots. Enzo had been working with Audata to create thicker gear that the Vespae's poisonous stingers wouldn't be able to penetrate so quickly. The new clothing wasn't as flexible as the old had been, but the loss of a tiny bit of mobility would be worth it, if it stopped the Vespae from being able to incapacitate their magical abilities.

As Harlow was finishing gearing up, Audata handed her a small round device that looked a little like a black elevator button. She'd been passing them out to everyone, clipping them onto their gear somewhere prominent. When she stepped aside she explained to the group. "Nox developed these before she left, and I've finished them the best I could." Audata's mouth twisted in unusual uncertainty. "I'm not sure if they'll work, but Nox thought she'd found a frequency that might disorient the Vespae. Use these when they close in to give yourselves a way out. Since we haven't tested them—"

Tomyris clapped a hand on the solemn Strider's shoulder. "We know, love. It's a risk, you don't know if they'll work." The Ventyr's words were gentle.

Samira smiled at Audata. "They'll work."

Audata's eyes slid to Harlow's. Harlow only shrugged. She had no idea what would work and what wouldn't, and Audata wanted honesty. "We're bringing them home, regardless."

"Hells yes, we are," Max agreed.

When Harlow looked around the circle, she saw nothing but reassurance. Every face reflected the same confidence. No one was holding anything back. They'd rescue Petra, and Finn if he was there.

"Thank you," Harlow said, bowing her head in gratitude. There was nothing else for her to say.

~

THE FERIANT CROSSED the wards with their Ventyr partners on their backs. Harlow carried Vivia, who used a momentary shielding that mimicked the Feriants' biofrequency for a short amount of time. "I'm all right," Vivia called to Harlow as soon as they crossed the ward. "It worked."

Through their telepathic link, they checked in with the other pairs. All were well. Four pairs broke off with Cian, who carried Audata. The six of them would try to bring down the Vespae's odd wards so that everyone could teleport out, if need be. The Ventyr flew on their own now, moving into formation now that they were past the wards.

When the Warbirds broke through the cloud cover above the farm, there were Vespae in the barnyard, huddled together in small clumps against the storm. The vast numbers Harlow had seen before weren't present now. A quick survey revealed two or three dozen in the barnyard.

Where are the rest of them? Sam asked.

I don't know, Harlow answered. *Wherever it is, it can't be good.*

Let's make this fast and we won't have to find out, Mirai added as their formation tightened up, dropping to the ground around the barn in a dive so fast it happened almost without notice.

The Vespae appeared mildly sedated, almost hibernating. They didn't immediately react to the Warbirds' arrival, and Harlow wondered if they hadn't seen them. The Warbirds surrounded the barn, staying close to one another, covering Harlow and Sam as they shifted.

Now the Vespae woke, buzzing between themselves. Tomyris pushed Harlow and Sam toward the barn door. "I think the queen is elsewhere, maybe with the rest of them. This is what they were like at Sanctum when we killed the queen."

Tomyris turned away from the Vespae to open the heavy barn door in one hard shove, and as expected it made a loud creaking noise. The rest of the Vespae in the yard turned their attention to the Warbirds. Their buzzing grew louder. Tomyris shouted, "Get going. We need to get this done even faster—we caught a lucky break. I'll cover you."

"Ten minutes," Samira whispered as she and Harlow slipped inside. "That's all we've got."

Harlow nodded, mirroring Sam as she formed long daggers from her shadows. Outside, the Vespae in the yard sprang to action, clashing with the Warbirds guarding the barn. Harlow's eyes took a moment to adjust to the dim light inside. It didn't smell as though animals lived here, which Harlow found to be a comforting scent. Instead, it smelled like bodily refuse and rotting food. Harlow tried her best not to gag as Samira tensed next to her.

A low groan sounded in a stall to their left. Samira and Harlow crouched in defense, but none of their enemy's strange, pale forms sprung at them from the darkness. There were no Vespae here—not in this part of the barn, anyway. They moved cautiously toward the stall, where they found Petra, bound and groggy on the dirt floor.

Samira untied her, while Harlow began to search what seemed like endless dark, narrow stalls. There was no one else so far, just junk, covered in dust and cobwebs. When she glanced back at Sam, Petra was slumped against her. "Sorry," the Ventyr murmured as she drifted off. "Don't think I'm going to be much… help…"

Outside, the sounds from the fight between the Vespae and the Warbirds were intensifying. They didn't have long to find Finn, if he was here. Harlow resisted the urge to grit her teeth, and kept searching. Her breath came in short, shallow gasps as she moved, acutely aware that they were running out of time.

"Returning scouts," Tomyris shouted from the barn door. A heavy thud accompanied Tomy's growl as she fought off an incoming drone. "The rest of them aren't back yet, but the scouts turned tail."

They'd gone back to report to the larger force. And if they were already mobilized, then they had even less time to find Finn. Harlow fought the urge to rush, forcing her attention to focus on her search. She couldn't afford to make a mistake. Not if there was even the slightest possibility Finn might be here.

The stalls were deep and narrow, stuffed full of old furniture and appliances, covered in threadbare blankets. She had to remove each blanket to look for Finn, worrying he'd been hidden somewhere.

"You're okay," Samira reassured Petra, dragging her towards the barn door. Harlow shot a look down the center of the barn just in time to see Tomyris sweep out the barn door, clearing the way of encroaching Vespae with a violent swipe of celestial fire.

They had a path out, which meant Harlow needed to move faster. Her ears rung slightly with the rush of her blood. Every moment was painfully slow, her awareness that she was failing pounding with every beat of her heart.

"She can't fight or fly," Sam said, pushing Petra toward Tomyris. "Get her out."

Harlow searched another stall. She could feel herself getting careless as the bloom of hope she'd felt before waned. So careless, she almost missed the figure huddled in the corner of the stall she searched. It moved, and she rushed forward, pulling the blanket off it.

Her heart dropped out of her chest. The figure was as tall as Finn, and similarly built, but blonde. A bruised face lifted to hers. "Jareth?"

The vampire nodded. It was one of the Humanist leaders, Jareth Sanvier. The one they'd seen on the video of the Governor's Mansion over the summer. She didn't have time to wonder what he was doing here, or how they'd hit him hard enough that he'd stayed wounded; she had to keep looking.

Harlow stepped out of the stall. "Sam, come here. It's Jareth."

Samira retrieved the vampire, who like Petra was barely conscious. "We've gotta go, Harlow. It's bad out there. Time's almost up."

Harlow's chest ached as she searched another stall and another. Tomyris called to her. "Harlow, he's not here. Come *on*." She adjusted her hold on Petra, who muttered something indistinguishable.

Harlow stilled, standing in the middle of the barn, refusing to take another step until she was sure. There was nowhere else to look, but it was obvious Petra was trying to tell them something. "What did she say?"

Tomyris shrugged, tossing Petra over her shoulder. "Doesn't matter. We're going."

"Finn!" Petra screeched, her voice shrill over the din of the battle outside. Her eyes flew open, panicked. "Don't leave him."

Time slowed as Harlow watched Petra's hand fling out, towards the back of the barn. She'd searched back there already. But then she saw it: the flimsy rope ladder that led to the hayloft. Before anyone could tell her no, Harlow was scrambling up into the hayloft, hoping the rope would hold her weight..

It was darker up here than it had been below. There were no windows in this part of the barn, and she had to adjust to the lack of light again. She blinked desperately, trying to hurry her vision along, but it would not cooperate. Time slowed as her brain processed the lump of solid darkness in front of her. Her hands shook as she stepped forward, acknowledging the terrible reality inside her mind: part of her had given up, the pain of hoping to see him again almost too much to bear.

And now... *Now*... Now Finbar McKay sat slumped in the corner of the hayloft, not even bound. His face was sliced open in several places, his body obviously battered, but whole. As his storm blue eyes opened, he cracked a grin, his half-healed bottom lip splitting open, blood trickling out.

"Hey, Harls." He grinned that lopsided, wicked grin that she loved and her heart flipped twenty times in a mere second. *He was really here.* "Come to play?"

It was an odd thing to say. Time rushed forward, and so did she, hauling his heavy body up off the floor. He didn't help.

"Oh," he laughed. "So it's an escape day?"

"Yeah," she said, playing along, though she didn't know what he meant. It didn't matter. He was here, in her arms, and she'd go along with any silliness he wanted to engage in to keep him calm. It was obvious he'd been dosed with Vespae poison, likely the queen's. "Time to escape."

"Sounds good, babygirl." He laughed again, throwing his body against the wall, away from her. "You wanna tussle again? Like last time, or the time before?"

Now he was resisting her? They didn't have time for this. Harlow tried to grab him, but he was surprisingly quick, given how injured he'd appeared a moment ago.

Finn shook his head, wagging his finger at her like she was a naughty child. "I'll give it to you, you're getting better at this. How'd you manage to smell like her? You even got the Claim right." His face darkened dangerously. "Is she here? Do you have her?"

What in seventeen hells was he talking about? "I'm right here," she soothed.

He lunged at her, using his full strength to pin her against the wall, his hand around her neck. "I'll fucking kill you if you laid a hand on her."

Harlow struggled, not understanding who Finn thought she was. She had to act fast, so she kneed him hard in the groin, wincing in anticipation of his pain. His grip on her slipped, and she concentrated as hard as she could, pressing herself against him, making full body contact in an attempt to engage the Claim's connection through the haze of Vespae poison lingering in his blood.

The poison. That was it. The Vespae poison blocked their connection, but *their* venom would revive it. Finn's body reacted to hers, as if by instinct, and though he still groaned in pain, she felt his arms tighten around her as she wrapped her legs around him, letting her mouth graze his neck.

This wasn't the time she'd have chosen for an arousing reunification, but he needed to *feel* the Claim, to heal and come back to himself. She'd seen it work dozens of times with the other Claimed pairs in the Warbirds. So she focused on his hard, warm body, heaving against hers in violent, confused frustration. Her hips tilted against his and she felt his cock stir.

"You are evil, you know that?" His face turned towards hers. "But you smell so godsdamn good. Fuck it."

His mouth crashed into hers as he slammed her against the wall, his hands sliding up her body. She tasted his blood in her mouth and her own body sprang to life, warmth flooding her abdomen, pooling between her legs as her fangs protracted.

As much as she wanted this moment to last, past any sense of reason, sounds of fighting reached her ears, someone calling her name. It was time to go. She pulled back from Finn's kiss, and struck hard, clamping her mouth around his neck, her fangs sinking deep into him as her venom dripped into his bloodstream. His body went slack against hers, affixing her to the wall.

For a moment, she wondered if something had gone wrong. Then he sprang away from her, his face healing quickly, the split in his lip almost disappearing. His eyes filled with tears. "It's *you*."

Harlow had no idea what Finn had been through. Whatever it was, it had obviously taken its toll. "Of course it is, McKay."

Finn's mouth fell open and he stepped forward, incredulously reaching for her. He stopped, hearing the fight below. "We've gotta get out of here."

"Let's go home," she said, her voice husky with unshed tears.

Finn nodded, looking around at the hayloft as though seeing it for the first time. "There's a rope ladder," she said.

Finn grinned that wicked grin again, but the smile didn't reach his eyes. He swept her into his arms, shifting as he took three long strides towards the open loft. They were on the ground safely before Harlow could think, running for the front of the barn, where Tomyris, Sam, and Jareth fought nearly a dozen of the queensguard who had pushed their way inside. They were alone, which meant everyone else was overwhelmed outside.

So the queen had returned. These elite Vespae soldiers weren't like the rest of the hive drones. They were better fighters, stronger, more independent. And they had their friends cornered.

Finn was like nothing she'd ever seen, cutting through them with the grace of a dancer and the strength of a lyon. He fought with precise, feline grace and she followed his moves, the shadow to the glow of his celestial force. There was no sign of his imprisonment in his body's movements, but when he glanced back to check on her, there was exhaustion in his eyes. He didn't have long to fight at this level; he was giving it everything he had.

Harlow was paying too much attention to Finn. One of the drones' stingers grazed her cheek as she ducked its attack, rolling away as she sent long shadow darts through its eyes. The thing fell, but its poison wove through her, even through the tiniest scratch.

Harlow decapitated the last of the queensguard coming at her and then the way cleared as they pushed outside, moving into tight formation with the rest of the Warbirds, who'd clustered around the barn door.

Tomyris nodded once to Finn. "Good to meet you, McKay." She hauled Petra, who'd passed out, over her shoulder again. "You know the best way out of here?"

More drones descended on them. The Warbirds were holding on, but they were losing ground quickly as the Vespae's numbers increased.

Finn nodded. "I do. Can you call your forces back? Unless you've got another wave coming, we can't fight them all."

"This is all of us," Harlow explained. She made eye contact with Sam. "Did we get the wards?"

"Yeah, but we've only a got a minute or two. It's time." Sam grabbed Jareth's arm, causing him to wince. "We're going to teleport in a second. Hold on tight."

They hit the little buttons Audata had given them. A high-pitched shriek filled the air. Harlow could barely hear it, but she felt it deep in her bones. Around her, the rest of the Warbirds hit their own devices, both the sound and the feeling increasing pitch and intensity. The Vespae screamed, falling to the ground—it had worked better than Audata thought it might.

The Warbirds blinked out, almost at once. When they did, Harlow knew the Vespae sting had done its work, dulling her ability to teleport enough to keep her from leaving with Finn. She could still shift though, and fly back.

A logical voice in her head told her to let him bite her, to let the Claim heal her. But the exhaustion in his eyes, the slump of his shoulders, kept her from asking him. He'd been healed by her bite, but he'd been dosed for Akatei knew how long. The Claim was an exchange of energy, and he had none to share with her. He couldn't take her with him either.

She felt sure she could shift. *This wasn't a problem. They'd both make it out, she'd just be a little slower.* "There's a little village, south of here, on a fjord. Do you know it?"

"The haunted ski resort from that old documentary?" Finn asked, incredulous. Of course he knew about a decades-old documentary about Sanctum's fake destruction. That was Finn.

Harlow nodded, wishing she had a moment more to appreciate that he was still *him*. They'd have time for that later. "Go," she insisted. "I'll be right behind you."

"You all right?" he asked, a frown wrinkling his brow.

"Yep," she said, pulling a small explosive device from a pack at her thigh. "It's my job to set this though, so you go on." It was half true, she had been tasked with setting the bomb, but she could have done it already. He didn't need to know that though.

Finn brushed a kiss to her lips as he vanished, his words echoing as he disappeared. "See you there."

Harlow closed her eyes to follow, tracking the threads that connected them. It would be easy to follow him now, to make sure he got there all right. She gathered her strength. Cian would be here any minute to sweep the battlefield with draconic fire; they must be waiting for her to set the bomb. Harlow had to get out before the fallen Vespae came around, but her body wasn't cooperating. She couldn't shift.

"Hey there, dollface." A chill slipped down Harlow's spine. She turned to face Mark Easton. He grinned at her, sending her into a sick panic. Bile rose in her throat and the world spun as he stepped towards her, that evil smile reaching into the deepest parts of her. Something wasn't right. Mark had been deranged at the end, corrupted by jealousy and Olivia Sanvier's motivations, but he'd never looked like this. He'd been bad, but the thing before her was something else. Something much, much worse.

Whatever the thing that stalked towards her now was, it wasn't Mark. She was sure of it as it spoke. "It's been so long, darling girl. I'd almost forgotten how sweet you smell."

Mark had never spoken to her like that in his life, but this feeling was all too familiar. The fuzziness in her head, the emotions she couldn't affect or control, rising up in her. Now she understood Finn's confusion completely. Her feet, which had felt frozen a moment ago, moved now. "Why are you doing this, Alain?"

The incubus shot forward. "You killed my son. You and McKay."

Harlow was still stuck. Mark's father was using his power as an incubus to make her think she couldn't move. If she could focus, she could break his hold on her, but she needed to buy time. "I did, but only because he tried to kill me first."

Alain's appearance changed, melting into Aurelia. "He wasn't trying to kill you, you fool. He tried to elevate you. Make you more than this filthy *thing* you've become."

"Fine," Harlow agreed. Her toes wiggled in her boots. If she could just eke out a bit more time, she'd be able to move. "I get why you want to kill us. But why are you with the Vespae?"

Alain's Aurelia-face darkened. "You killed my child, Harlow. I have nothing left to live for."

Harlow's feet tingled. Just one more moment and she'd have it. "So the entire world has to pay?"

"This is not a good world. It could use remaking." Before her eyes, the vision of Mark blurred, and cleared into a mirror image of herself. "I had such a good time with your boy," Alain hissed, sounding just like her. Cold dread pooled in her belly. "And I'll have an even better time with you."

"Eat shit," Harlow spat at the incubus. She was back in control, and shoved the bomb in her hand at him—hard. The movement engaged it as Harlow's body cooperated.

She wished she had time to rip Alain Easton apart for hurting Finn, but she knew when the risks were too high. As she shifted, leaping into the air, she spotted him throwing the bomb away from himself as it exploded. Cian would be here soon to clear the battlefield. It was too much to wish for—she knew that —but Harlow hoped the firedrake's flame burned Alain Easton to a crisp.

CHAPTER 16

The flight home was long, and rather than feeling jubilant at finding Finn, Harlow felt mixed up in her mind, twisted by Alain Easton's horrific influence. He was stronger than Mark had ever been. The sickness he'd wrought in her in just a few moments made her nauseous.

To calm herself, she felt into the threads, and when she was finally able to find Finn, a little of Easton's influence drained away. Harlow landed in the village, a few blocks away from where he'd ended up. She needed a moment to breathe—she couldn't face Finn like this, a shaking mess.

People crowded the streets, rushing to meet the returning Warbirds. Harlow ducked into an alleyway and dropped into crouch, burying her head in her hands. The tight, thick fabric of her gear stretched uncomfortably against her skin as she curled into herself. Harlow unzipped the high funnel neck of her jacket, which now felt as though it was choking her. Her breath came in sharp gasps as tears streamed down her face.

"Harlow?" a voice called out from the end of the alley. "What are you doing back here? Finn's this way!"

It was Thea, and she sounded so damn *happy*. *Why could Thea feel happy and she couldn't?* Harlow tucked her head further into her chest, covering her ringing ears. The vision of Mark—no, Alain—shifting into *her*, played over and over in her mind. How had *that* happened? She knew incubi could affect your emotions, but he'd done something like shapeshifting. And what was he doing with the Vespae?

Her skin prickled, heat flushing through her. She heard voices at the end of the alley, and prayed they'd leave. *Couldn't everyone leave her alone?*

"Babygirl." *Finn.*

Harlow couldn't look up. He shouldn't have to see her crying like this. Not when he just got back. She took several quick deep breaths, wiped her face and

600

stood quickly. So quickly she ran into a wall of muscle. Her face smoothed as an eerie calm came over her.

"Hey," she said, looking up. "Teleported in wrong and got kind of sick to my stomach. Just needed a second to recover."

Finn's stormy eyes narrowed, then his face smoothed too as he called down the alleyway. "She's fine. Just a little portal-sickness."

He knew she was lying, and he'd covered for her. That tiny fact seeped into her. Finn knew her by heart. Her hand slipped into his, her fingers lacing through his, as she blinked back tears.

Thea nodded, waving. "We'll give the two of you some space." Her sister winked, calling out to whoever had been following her that Finn and Harlow found one another. She disappeared into the crowd that was gathering in the street.

"Is everyone okay?" Harlow asked, trying to keep her voice light. Finn's hand tightened around hers.

"Everyone else is fine," he said. "You're not."

Harlow couldn't look up. She couldn't burden him with this. He hadn't been back for even a minute, and what Alain had done to her was nothing in comparison with what he'd obviously been doing to Finn.

Cool fingers gripped her chin, tipping her head up until her eyes met his. They were glowing with rage. "You saw him. *Alain.* He fucked with you."

Harlow's eyes fell. "Yes."

"Please look at me," he pleaded.

She would give him anything, painful as it was to make eye contact with him. Her gaze dragged up his body as she tried to ignore the terrible shape his clothes were in. Desperately, she tried to keep her breath even. He would *not* comfort her right now. She wouldn't allow it.

"You lied about being able to teleport," he said. His voice was flat. Not even, not calm. Devoid of emotion.

She nodded. His grip on her chin loosened as his hand swept over her face, his palm grazing her cheek as he stroked her skin. Harlow's eyes fell closed. This was unreal. Finn was *here.* "I saw how tired you were."

"Please don't lie to me." His head lowered towards hers and she could feel the heat of his body as he stepped closer to her, his hands tentative as they slid around her waist. "Please, Harlow."

The plea in his voice broke her. He'd been lied to, manipulated, and then the first thing she'd done was trick him. It had been for all the right reasons, and she knew he knew it. But she couldn't, *wouldn't* do it again.

"I'm sorry," she said, lifting her eyes. A true smile crept onto her lips. "You're *here.*"

Her words woke the reality of the moment in them both. Whatever else had happened, they were finally together again. They crashed towards each other, clinging to one another as their breath ripped through them, hearts beating out of their chests. Neither cried, though she felt their desperation coursing through the threads that bound them. That would come later.

Now there was no room for anything but this deep need to hold onto one another. To hold on hard enough to make up for a tiny fraction of every time they'd missed each other. For every moment either of them had given up hope. When they finally loosened their grip on one another, both their hands shook as they clasped them together.

"So," Harlow said, trying to sound halfway normal. "Do you want to take advantage of some alone time?"

Finn caught onto her game and nodded, speaking in an exaggeratedly calm tone that he often called "broadcast journalism voice." "That would be great."

Harlow couldn't help but snicker as she leaned against him. He was making jokes. Here, in the village, making jokes. She almost hated to hide away with him. Part of her wanted to shove him in front of everyone, yelling, "Look here. It's Finn fucking-McKay!"

But only he would laugh at that, because it's what she used to say when they were teenagers and he got too big for his britches, thinking he was cooler than he was. She'd look up at him and sneer, laying the snark on thick. "Look here. It's Finn fucking-McKay," she'd say and he'd calm right down, going back to being his sweet, goofy self again.

His hand tightened around hers as they made their way out of the alley. They slipped by the crowds that were gathering at the center of the village to hear what had happened at the farm. They walked in silence, which was comfortable at first. But as they got further away from the crowds, Harlow wasn't sure what to say to Finn. She'd been imagining this moment for months, and now that it was here, she was lost.

Finally, when they were about a block away from home, he stopped. The street was empty. "I'm not going to break, Harls."

She turned to face him. "I just don't know where to start."

He took a deep breath. "Let's start with this: I'm happy to see you."

A shuddery breath shook her chest. "I'm happy to see you too... But that doesn't seem like enough for this moment." He stepped towards her and she let her forehead crash against his chest as he drew her in. "I'm fucking this up."

A low laugh rumbled through him, sending comforting vibrations through her. He scooped her up into his arms, lifting her a few inches off the ground. "*Fuck me up forever.* That's what you said in Nea Sterlis, remember?"

Harlow nodded. The feeling of his body against hers, the ease with which he held her aloft, the smell of him, even unwashed as he was, it was all exactly what she wanted. "I remember."

"You can't mess this up, babygirl," he murmured against her mouth as his lips met hers. The kiss was sweet, almost chaste in its gentleness. She couldn't tell if he was being gentle for her sake or his, but she matched his energy, giving him only what he gave her. When he lowered her to the ground there was a warm glow on his skin. He looked a little less tired than he had in the barnyard.

"Come on," she insisted, suddenly wanting to be inside with him, away from any prying eyes. "We're almost there."

They stepped forward, holding hands and leaning against one another. She felt him thinking, but neither of them spoke. They'd been apart for too long, and that was too big to talk about right now. They just needed to *be* for a little while. When the cottage came into sight, Axel was in the front window, napping.

"There's my boy," Finn murmured.

Even a half a block away, Axel heard him. The cat's eyes flew open, and he stood, scratching wildly at the window, howling for his dad. Finn laughed, but it sounded more like a sob and the two of them jogged forward, using the last of their energy to get into the cottage, where they were bombarded by cat purrs. Axel attached himself to his cat-dad, as Finn pulled Harlow into his side.

And then he fell to his knees, clinging to them both, sobs finally shaking through them both. His mouth met hers and their tears combined. Axel purred between them. The kiss was long and slow, but no heat built between them as they fulfilled their longing for one another, slowly as thick honey pouring from a jug. Axel jumped down, rubbing against Finn, yowling with indignation over his abandonment.

Harlow stood slowly, feeling old as time as she held her hand out to Finn so she could drag him off the foyer floor. "I think you're going to have to prove you know where the food is. Reassert yourself as the cat dad extraordinaire."

Finn nodded, his eyes watery but noble as he stretched an arm toward the kitchen. "Show me to the bin."

He followed her through the cottage to the kitchen, where she pointed to the metal bin where they kept Axel's food. Finn scooped a heaping bit out into the food bowl, which was obviously placed near a larger bowl of water. The black cat purred loudly as he ate, looking back at Finn every few moments to make sure he was still there.

Finn turned to Harlow, searching her for signs of injury. When he found none, he lifted her onto the tiled kitchen counter, fitting himself between her legs. His eyes roamed over every bit of her, hungrily now, lingering on her thick, muscular thighs, and the subtle bulge in her arms. For a brief moment, the old Harlow panicked, wondering if the way she took up more space would matter— if it would make him want her less. The worry was fleeting, gone before she had time to consider it too deeply.

"I've been training," she explained, flexing as he squeezed her bicep. "A lot. Everything kind of got… bigger."

"I noticed," he said, his chest heaving with increasing desire. Finn's breath caressed her ear as he bent slowly toward her, his hands sliding down her sides and under her seat. He lifted her off the counter for a moment, squeezing her ass cheeks hard. "It's fucking phenomenal."

Harlow's breath hitched as the motion brought the core of her in contact with the hard length growing in his pants. Finn's mouth crashed into hers, his tongue caressing hers slowly, with the kind of intensity and pressure that made promises. His fingers closed around one of her braids, then the other, and he pulled her head back, looking into her eyes.

"Should we talk?" Harlow asked, without much conviction.

"We can talk later." He lifted her, then walked towards the stairs.

"I'm covered in Vespae blood," she warned. "It's gross."

Finn cleared the staircase in a flash of Ventyr speed. "Then I'll bathe you."

Heat whipped through her as her heartbeat raced in anticipation, but she laughed. "Someone has to turn on the water heater. This place is *vintage*."

Finn set her down, a wicked sparkle in his eye. "Where is it?"

She told him and he disappeared, returning quickly. Harlow had never been so grateful for Illuminated speed. "Now," he said, "Where were we?"

Harlow lowered her voice to a mock-sexy purr. "Thinking about cleaning me up. I'm *dirty*."

She felt Finn's laugh in her bones as he kicked the bathroom door open. "I'm counting on it, babygirl."

Inside the bathroom, they got to work tearing each other's clothes off while the water heater filled. Harlow pushed the pile of their dirty things outside the door. Neither of them smelled very good, and he was coated in a layer of grime that was unusual for him. Whatever had happened in the weeks he'd been captured, they hadn't allowed him to bathe.

Though she hungered for him, they needed to take this slowly. Harlow paused to turn the water on. She wasn't sure how Finn had been hurt, or how the Vespae or Alain Easton had messed with him. She unraveled her braids, stepping into the shower, which was unusually luxurious with its double shower-heads. But of course, this had been a posh resort once, so features like this in the otherwise humble cottages were the norm.

She stepped under one shower head, and he the other. Layers of dirt washed off him as he rinsed, his cock growing with every passing second that he watched her. His eyes took in every curve of her belly, drinking in the heavy swell of her breasts, and the hard muscle she'd gained. She held out her hand, trying to draw him closer now.

"Let me look at you," he murmured. His eyes were feverish with desire, and his cock was at full attention, but his voice was hesitant. "I just…" His smile was watery. "I wasn't sure I'd ever see you again. Please, can I just watch you?"

Harlow nodded, letting the water flow over her skin. She washed her hair slowly, rinsing it and then moved onto her body. As evidence of the fight slid off them both, his muscles relaxed. He washed, never taking his eyes off her as he cleaned every inch of himself.

Harlow slid one hand down her abdomen as he spread soap over his chest. Her breath quickened to a pant as the slide of her hand against her slick skin dipped lower. Finn rinsed, watching her, his lips parting as her fingers reached between her legs.

He leaned forward, one hand moving to the tile wall behind her. He was close, but not yet touching her, as she stroked slow, deliberate circles, teasing herself. Their eyes locked as his free hand traced her spine. His lips met hers, though his body stayed maddeningly far from her own.

He deepened the kiss, and then he was kissing her neck, sucking and licking her wet skin as she teased herself, refusing to dip her fingers inside, or to rub the throbbing bundle of nerves that begged for attention. Finn's mouth traced her collarbones, between her breasts, and then lower, licking the curves of her belly, then back up to capture each of her nipples. His mouth was the only thing touching her, aside from the hand that steadied her back.

He knelt, both hands gripping her ass as she spread her legs for him. Harlow's breath caught as she ran fingers through Finn's wet hair, tipping his head back so his eyes met hers. "You're here," she whispered.

Finn's smile was bittersweet. "I am."

The hurt of their time apart showed, but he needed this. She needed it too. Maybe it was the Claim that drove them, or the trauma of the past months, but they needed this now, not words and explanations.

Finn's eyes dragged away from hers as he pressed his face into her. His mouth met her clit in a long, slow kiss. Harlow spread her legs wider as he buried his face between her thighs. He squeezed her cheeks hard as he licked and sucked, moaning against her as she braced herself against the tile wall.

"I need you inside me," she begged.

He slid up her body, their wet skin finally making contact as he pinned her against the cold tile of the shower wall. Steam curled around them as she wrapped her legs around his waist. The head of his cock nudged at her entrance, sliding in easily.

As he entered her, he gazed into her eyes. "I love you."

"I love you," she replied.

It wasn't an elegant speech, but it was everything either of them needed. They were here, together, now. Later, there would be talking—so much talking—but now there were those three words, and their bodies moving against one another.

She gasped as he thrust harder, filling her completely. At the same time, he shifted into his true form, the base of his cock vibrating slightly as he moved slowly in her. Water from both shower heads cooled. The hot water heater had run its course.

"It's going to get downright frigid in here, in just a second," Harlow said, hating to interrupt.

Finn gripped her with one hand, turning one shower head off, while she did the other. "Bedroom?" he asked.

She nodded. He tried to move, but they were stuck. Harlow laughed. His wings and his true form had wedged them into the small space. "You're too big."

He grinned wickedly. "Say it again."

Harlow moved her hips, rocking against him, so her clit ground against his pelvic bone. "You're too big."

He shifted, setting her down momentarily so she could step out of the shower. He wrapped her in a towel and then scooped her into his arms. "Bedroom."

Harlow pointed, and a moment later he deposited her onto her bed, pulling the towel from her as he spread her legs. In the dim light of the blizzard that still raged on outside, his eyes glowed as his fingers spread her open, caressing her clit, before dipping deep inside her.

He lowered himself next to her as he fingered her, pulling her tight against his body as his mouth closed over her nipples, sucking each into stiff peaks as his fingers thrust into her. Her hips bucked against his hands, her orgasm mounting as his mouth and body slid lower and lower. When his mouth closed around her clit, his fingers thrusting deep inside her, she saw light.

Immediately, she pulled him upwards, dragging his body over hers until his cock slid easily into her. He shifted again, his true form filling her nearly to the point of pain, he was so large. He moved slowly at first, kissing her, whispering how much he'd missed her, how much he needed her, as she moaned.

Her hips moved against his, encouraging him to move faster, harder. He obliged, as if by instinct, feeling her soak his cock with her desire. Above her, his fangs protracted.

"Yes," she cried, pulling his head to her neck.

When his fangs pierced her skin, there was a brief moment of pain, and then euphoria, lighting every nerve in her with celestial fire. Harlow's orgasm burst from her in waves of light and shadow, as she clenched around his cock. She pushed his shoulders, using her legs to guide him, flipping them over. His wings spread out under him on the bed, his hands moving from her hips to her breasts as she rode him, leaning backwards to guide his cock to the place inside her that was most sensitive, as she rubbed her clit.

He rose into a seated position, his wings creating a cocoon of warmth and light around them as she writhed against him, rubbing every part of her against him in a fever of wet heat and long kisses. When her own fangs appeared, she pulled his head back, digging her fingers into his hair.

"Bite me, babygirl" he said. "Claim me."

The heat that roared through her at his words was all the encouragement she needed. Her fangs sunk into his neck, her venom sliding down her throat with his blood as she sucked his neck. Deep inside her, his cock moved slower, but harder now as he came, roaring her name as he gripped her.

Golden light and dark shadow intertwined, writhing as their bodies did. When their movement slowed, drowsiness overtook her. Her eyes flickered to Finn's, which watched her carefully. "I love you," she murmured, barely able to stay awake.

His eyes drooped as well, his exhaustion taking over as he shifted positions. There was the mess of their encounter to clean up, but Harlow could hardly function. He slipped from the bed, returning with a warm, wet cloth and new sheets. As he washed her, she protested, "I should be taking care of you."

His smile was sleepy, but happy. "I need to do normal things. Please."

It was true that he was typically in charge of their aftercare, but he'd been imprisoned. She had no idea what he'd endured these past months. Shouldn't she be the one to care for him right now?

"Stop thinking so much, and sleep," he murmured as he lifted her, easily as if she were a feather to change the sheets beneath her. "Just sleep."

Her body took over, the comedown from the stress of battle coupled with the heady rush of re-engaging the Claim taking over. By the time he crawled into bed next to her, his wings creating a canopy of warmth in the chilly cottage bedroom, Harlow was fast asleep.

CHAPTER 17

When Harlow woke, it was dark still, the house silent save for the tiny feline snores by her head. Axel was tucked under the covers, sharing her pillow. The heavy weight of Finn's arm around her waist reminded her of the beautiful new reality she lived in. *Finn.*

Behind Axel's small symphony of sleep, there was the deep, even rhythm of Finn's breath, and beyond that, his heart, beating soft and slow. Part of her wanted to stay here, revel in this feeling of safety for as long as possible. But as she was already awake, the perpetual feeling of being late immediately overtook her. She'd imagined this would disappear when she got Finn back, but here it was. They were buried under an almost unimaginable load of problems that continued to compound by the moment.

A flicker of opalescent light distracted her from her thoughts. "You're thinking so loud you could wake the dead," Finn murmured, sleep still lacing the deep timbre of his voice.

She rotated to face him, wrapping her arms around his neck. He pulled her closer, one hand darting out behind her head to scratch Axel's ear. "This feels like a dream come true."

Harlow wasn't sure what to say, and hated herself a little for it. He always knew how to comfort her, but her mind just wouldn't work fast enough. The only thing she could think to ask was, "Are you okay?"

Finn answered with a long, rumbling noise. "Physically, yes…. Otherwise…" He paused, and Harlow didn't rush to finish his sentence, or prompt him. She just breathed against him, slow and steady, sending waves of love through the dozens of threads between them. "That is amazing," he breathed. "I bet you have all kinds of new tricks."

Before, that statement would have opened up a wave of lust between them, but now that the fervor had abated, they felt something quieter. Desire, yes. But also the deep comfort of simply being together. This moment was peaceful, filled with love and room for whatever he needed. Harlow let his need guide them, hugging him tightly for a moment, then relaxing gently as they both sunk deeper into the bed. His wings lit with a soft glow around them.

"There you are," she said with a smile. Her fingers traced over the harsher lines of his face in its true form. He was still her Finn, still immediately recognizable, but more rugged and beautiful at the same time.

"I know we need to talk about what happened…" he trailed off. "And I can give you the basics. I need to be debriefed." Finn, always the dutiful leader.

He quieted, but she felt there was more. "You need time to process the feelings though," she said, tipping his chin so his eyes met hers.

Finn nodded. "Yes, can you give me a little time?"

Harlow answered with a kiss. "All the time in the world."

Finn and Axel looked up at the same time, both hearing a noise downstairs. "Enzo's trying to sneak in," he murmured, before calling out, "We're awake."

There were footsteps on the stairs and then a soft knock at the door. "I know you're probably both all wrapped up in reunification bliss. I just wanted to bring Finn some clothes. They're outside the door. No rush."

Harlow pulled the blanket around her and sat up. "Thank you."

"We'll be down in a few minutes," Finn added. "You can tell Riley they can come in the house."

Enzo laughed. "All right. I think Cian would like to see you as well." Footsteps disappeared back downstairs, followed by the comfortable sounds of Enzo and Riley moving around in the kitchen.

Finn looked at the ceiling, as though he could see the firedrake above. "Cian is *flying*."

Harlow smiled. "That they are. Gloriously so, in fact. How did you know?"

Finn hopped up from bed, moving quickly as he picked up the clothes Enzo had left outside the door. "It feels like all my senses are working better."

Harlow grinned, watching him slip into a pair of thick joggers and a heavy sweater. "It's the Claim. The longer we're together, the stronger both our natural talents will become. It's what happened with the other pairs in the Warbirds. Some can even share their magic."

He glanced up at her, grinning as he pulled on a thick pair of socks. His hair fell into his face. *Stupid, floppy hair*, Harlow thought to herself, remembering how angry she'd been last spring when she'd discovered he was back in Nuva Troi. That felt like it was worlds away now, but she still loved that hair, and it had grown even longer now with the months apart.

She got up from bed, as he sat in the little chair next to the window. Axel hopped onto his lap. They didn't speak as she dressed, but the quiet was cozy, rather than tense. She looked up from pulling on a pair of leggings and a long v-neck sweater to see him smiling.

"How do you get more beautiful by the minute?"

She leaned over the chair, pressing a kiss to his lips. The fact that he was here, asking her silly questions, watching her dress—was surreal. His expression shifted to something like fear, though she wasn't sure. He was trying to hide it, but he looked at her like she might disappear.

Her head tilted slightly as she pulled away. There was distress written in the way his shoulders hunched, and his brow furrowed. She didn't want to push, but she needed to know before they talked to anyone else, so she could protect him from probing questions, if need be. "Did Alain torture you?"

Finn looked beyond her and his voice dropped deeper and flatter, sending a chilling rumble through her. He stared at some point on the wall behind her. "I'm not sure it qualifies as torture, if you can't even manage Connor's cruelty."

Harlow's heart nearly shattered. Connor McKay was a monster, and while she knew he'd exposed Finn to all kinds of awful things as a child and teenager, she hadn't known he'd actually tortured him. Her jaw clenched hard, and her shadows billowed around her hands, her fingers staining inky midnight blue almost immediately.

Finn's eyes softened, and he took one of her balled fists in his much larger hand, unfurling her fingers with the other. "Stand down, soldier," he murmured, kissing her palm. "My time with Alain was short. Confusing, yes, but not so bad in the scheme of things. Mostly the Vespae just left me alone."

Harlow let out a shudder of a breath. "Are you saying that to make me feel better?"

He looked up at her, his eyes filling with love. "No. Being taken by the Vespae and then getting stuck with Alain was unpleasant. But the real torment was not knowing if I would see you again. The long, lonely hours of fretting were the real torture."

"What is he doing with them?" Harlow asked, not able to keep her curiosity at bay any longer.

Finn shook his head. "I don't know, but it can't be good. They respect him." His stomach growled loudly before she had to think about it further.

"Let's get you some breakfast," Harlow said, relieved not to have to think of what to say next.

Axel jumped down at the word "breakfast" and meowed plaintively at the bedroom door. The three of them made their way downstairs to the sound of family in the kitchen. When Axel ran ahead of them, the chatter stopped. The entire family was crowded into the cottage's tiny kitchen. Harlow couldn't help it, she burst into tears, turning to bury her face in Finn's sweater. He hugged her tightly, his heart making erratic little thumps that let her know how moved he was.

"Hi," he said, his voice shaking a little.

Larkin ran forward, and he scooped her into a hug, pressing her against Harlow's side. Cian was next, and soon Harlow and Finn were surrounded by nearly everyone they loved, weeping softly. No one had words for what the past few months had been like or what they were feeling in the moment, but if it was anything like the riot of emotions in Harlow's heart, it was happiness and bitter-sweet grief, all at once.

Joy for the fact that they were together again, grief for all they lost getting here. Nothing would ever be the same. But for the first time since she'd lost Finn,

Harlow thought that might be a good thing. That they might all be able to move forward, grounded in a kind of integrity that she hadn't known was missing until she found it in this moment.

From the outer edge of the circle, Riley said, "We have coffee and sausage rolls ready to go, but we need to be at the Dairy in ten."

The family drifted apart, everyone putting on coats and boots and gathering up breakfast and to-go mugs from the kitchen. Harlow caught sight of Aurelia murmuring something that looked like an apology to Finn, who interrupted her with a giant hug. She made eye contact with Harlow over his shoulder, tears streaming down her face again. Harlow couldn't help it—sobs wracked her chest. She continued to dress for the cold, but could not stop crying.

The floodgates of everything she'd been suppressing were open, and now she was a mess. Ghasts gathered in the living room and kitchen, too many to count. Harlow squeezed her eyes shut against them as Finn watched, helpless against them as they moved through him and the others to get to Harlow. It had to be a disturbing sight, watching them swarm her. The more that approached, the more distraught Harlow became.

"What's happening to her?" Larkin asked.

Aurelia tried to explain, while Selene murmured softly in Harlow's ear. "Calm down, dearest, and they'll leave you alone. You know how it works."

When she didn't calm, Selene sighed. "Harlow, stop this now."

The admonition didn't help. Harlow was overwhelmed. Finn pushed through her sisters and the maters, kneeling in front of her. He glanced back at Riley, who nodded immediately.

"We'll meet the rest of you there," Riley said as Enzo ushered everyone but Finn out.

Enzo bent down next to Finn, taking Harlow's hands. She felt his gentle presence in her mind. He didn't try to stop the tidal wave of emotion rolling over her, instead riding it alongside her. "You have to let more of this out," he whispered. "You can't keep it all in."

She nodded, but even as the tears slowed more ghasts gathered around her, pressing towards her, their ghostly fingers feeling more corporeal by the moment. When she looked down, the rotting hand that clasped her shoulder was real, bruising her shoulder with its intensity.

"What's happening?" Finn asked, trying desperately to pry the ghast's hand from her shoulder, to no avail.

Enzo crouched down next to Harlow, murmuring a few words, his hands moving rapidly in the air pulling the threads. An aethereal sigil appeared and the ghast's now-corporeal hand faded first into incorporeality, and then disappeared altogether. He and Riley shared one of their private looks.

"Harlow's emotions seem to be drawing the ghasts to her, which is not uncommon for Striders," Enzo explained. "All sorcière are limenal creatures, but Striders especially, who are more connected to the limen, where most ghasts come from."

Harlow groaned, a soft noise, under her breath. This was the absolute last thing she needed right now. Ghasts being attracted to her—becoming corporeal —*and* having to listen to long explanations about it.

Enzo expressed his exasperation with her attitude by flicking her softly on the forehead. "Hush. I'm trying to explain."

She flicked him back, causing him to snicker. Riley and Finn exchanged a look that clearly said they didn't understand the dynamic. But this was how it had been since they were children. Enzo was as much Harlow's sibling as any of her sisters, and sometimes their interactions devolved into this kind of behavior.

"*Anyway*," Enzo said, drawing the word's syllables out for emphasis. "But this corporeality thing—it's unusual."

Enzo glanced at Riley who sighed before speaking. "After Harlow showed me The Warden, there wasn't much I could do with the text. We have some records here, but our digital archives aren't accessible. But I started talking to some of the human elders. Especially the Falcyrans."

Riley's voice dropped to nearly a whisper. It was clear they'd uncovered something they found disturbing. "The Falcyrans have an old tale about creatures that sound very similar to the Ravagers. There is a winter tale about ghasts crossing the limen—becoming real—when the Ravagers return."

Finn nodded. "I remember a story like that from the Knights' archive. I don't think it's the same one. Maybe from Avignonne?"

"We could ask Kate and Lou…" Harlow murmured. "See what they know."

"We'll handle it," Riley assured Harlow. "You two focus on what's next with the Warbirds."

Enzo rose, smiling as he pressed a kiss to the top of Harlow's head. "Riley's right. We'll figure out this *ghastly* problem."

Harlow's face flushed as she broke into hysterical laughter at the same time Enzo did. They were still laughing as they walked out the front door. Axel followed them, weaving between their legs as they walked through the village, heading towards the Dairy.

Finn shook his head, offering Riley his arm as they walked over a slick spot on the cobbled street. "I never get punny humor."

Riley snickered, which sent Enzo and Harlow into further peals of laughter.

"What?" Finn asked as the three of them leaned against one another for support.

"*Punny* humor?" Harlow said, raising her eyebrows. "As in 'that's punny.'"

Finn shrugged, clearly lost. He picked Axel up, pressing a kiss to the cat's forehead, before the creature squirmed out of his arms, and ran towards the Dairy, chasing shadows. Harlow hugged Finn, whispering, "Punny rhymes with funny."

When she pulled away he smiled, and then laughed. "Oh," he said simply, taking her hand. It wasn't his usual witty banter, but she'd take it.

Riley and Enzo walked ahead of them. The air was cold, but the clouds that threatened more snow kept it from being utterly frigid. Harlow had learned that a sunny day in this part of Falcyra meant terrifyingly low temperatures, not warmth. The clouds were gloomy, but she feared the cold.

Finn was quiet as they walked through the village, which appeared to be sleeping in this morning. Hardly anyone was about. As Riley and Enzo disappeared inside the Dairy with Axel, who'd been waiting at the door, Finn paused, pulling gently on Harlow's arm.

"My dad…" His face crumpled into a deep frown.

Harlow waited. Sometimes it took Finn a little while to talk about his parents. Even though everyone was expecting them, she wouldn't rush him.

"The torture. It wasn't to be cruel."

Harlow waited, biting back all the words she wanted to say about how much she hated Connor—how there was no excuse for torturing a child.

Finn looked at his feet, rather than her face. "I'm not excusing it. My father's parenting philosophy was…terrible. But he didn't do any of it for pleasure."

Harlow opened her mouth to interrupt, but Finn shook his head. Those blue-gray eyes widened, begging her to hear him out. Her mouth closed and she nodded.

"I admit freely, there are things he does for pleasure that are cruel. But the way he raised me was because he was afraid, Harlow. Afraid of his own people coming here, finding us. Afraid of what they might do to not only me, but this whole planet. I'm not saying he's good, or even right. But he isn't evil. He's *scared*."

Harlow's eyes fell closed. She believed what Finn said, but still couldn't make sense of it. "Fine," she finally said. "I can believe that. But it doesn't make the power-hoarding any better."

Finn sighed. "Of course it doesn't. I just want you to understand that horrific as it was, it made me able to do things now that I might not be able to otherwise. It's fucked up. I spent years talking to James Quinn about this shit, and I still don't have it worked out."

Harlow nodded. "What about your mom?" He never talked about Aislin's role in his childhood.

Finn shrugged. "There's nothing to say about Aislin. She wasn't there. Either she was drunk, gone, or arguing with Connor. Mostly, she wasn't there."

His words unlocked a memory for Harlow. Aurelia had been interviewed by a human lifestyle magazine when she was in primary school. The interviewer had asked what she and Selene did to give themselves a break from their "brood of children." Aurelia's answer had been, "Immortals are children for so little time in comparison to the span of their lives, Selene and I choose not to miss a moment of it."

The maters hadn't been perfect parents, not by a long shot, but they'd been there, cherishing their children every step of the way, and Harlow had to appreciate that. She threw her arms around Finn, hugging him so tightly she felt his lungs expand in reaction to her.

"Thank you for telling me," she whispered as he lifted her off the ground an inch or two, returning her embrace.

"Thank you for being the person I can tell."

He grabbed her hand, and Harlow led him into the Dairy. "Prepare yourself," she warned. "They're a lot."

CHAPTER 18

Inside the Dairy, the couple was immediately surrounded by both the Feriant Legion and several Council representatives, Piper Winslow included, who talked all at once. Harlow wasn't sure how Finn was handling things so well, but he'd simply taken a long, even breath and responded calmly, guiding the group towards the seating area and Audata's string board. Questions peppered him from all sides, and Harlow could barely keep track of who'd asked.

"How long were you with the Vespae?" someone asked.

"I'm not sure. I'd have to look at a calendar, but Larkin and I were only together outside the breach for four days... after that I was with them the whole time."

"Do you have any idea what they're searching for?"

"No, no clue."

Finn sat, which caused everyone to try to find seats of their own. There was no room for Harlow, so she stood behind the group, as near to Finn as she could get. She was happy to see that they were responding to him differently than they had to her.

Her happiness, in itself, was a relief. She wasn't resentful in the slightest that the Warbirds' acceptance of her and Finn both carried on to the Council as well, though Piper stood with her arms crossed tightly across her chest and a sour expression as everyone else pelted Finn with questions.

"Do they have language?"

"I think so. But they don't seem to need it because of the——"

"Hive mind." That was Audata, who'd come to stand next to Harlow.

The group asked about a dozen other questions about the structure of the hive, but Finn's answers were all things they'd already known. It was confirmation at least that the Vespae had a complex social hierarchy based on their relationship with the queen, and that they had some sort of communication rooted in shared knowledge.

When the questions finally slowed, Finn noticed the string board. As the group talked over what he'd found, versus what they knew, he wandered over to it. Harlow and Audata followed. Mirai and Max brought out food then, which lent a more congenial air to the debriefing as everyone dug into the various loaves of bread and wheels of cheese.

"Where did you find all this?" Finn asked Audata.

"On the Vespae," Audata explained. "We believe they're searching for that building in the middle."

Harlow had already tracked Finn's gaze; he'd barely looked at the other items, but was zeroed in on the figure of the observatory. He tapped it and said, "Do you know where this is?"

Audata shook her head. "No, do you?"

Everyone quieted, sensing Finn was about to say something important. He turned to the group. "Yes, that's ORAIS."

"That's a strange name," Max said, mouth full of bread.

Finn picked up a marker and went to the giant pad of paper on the easel next to Audata's board. "May I?" he asked.

She nodded. "Of course."

He wrote the name he'd just said on it, but it wasn't a word, as Harlow had assumed, but an acronym. Behind each capital letter he wrote a word: Organization for Research in Alien Intelligence and Societies. He turned, then tapped the words he'd written slowly. "This is what you're looking for, and if you have a topographical map of this area, I can probably show you where it is."

A slow, amazed smile spread over Harlow's face. He'd been back less than a day, and he was already solving problems. This was what he was good at, bringing threads of information, and people, together. She'd missed his easy ability to figure this kind of thing out. Harlow was the emotional compass. He was the ship that brought everyone to where they needed to be. They were finally back in their element.

Several people moved quickly, searching for the right maps. Mirai brought several to Finn; he discarded three or four, then nodded at one. Vivia spread the one he chose out on the coffee table, which had been cleared. She weighed it down with plates and empty mugs. Finn pointed to the fjord, and the valley where Sanctum sat. "We're here, right?"

Audata nodded as Finn traced his fingers along the map, over several high peaks in the mountain range. "ORAIS is around here, above this fjord."

A few of the Legion exchanged looks with one another. "When you were a kid, did your dad teleport you in?" Max asked.

Finn's laugh was sardonic as he sat back on the couch, his arm going around Harlow's shoulders. "No, of course not. We hiked through the mountains. It was training."

Max and Mirai both nodded. "You're dad's an asshole," Mirai said. "But there was a reason for the hike."

Tomyris groaned. "Gale Alley."

Sam leaned forward to look at the map. "Shit, that's right."

Finn glanced at Harlow, a question in his eyes.

Vero, who'd grown up in Falcyra, answered. "Gale Alley is where the wind buffets the peaks so hard that you can't fly through. You also can't teleport in the area at all."

"Because of the iridium," Audata said. "Of course. Why didn't I think of Gale Alley?"

Vero shrugged. "I mean, I think most people figured it was a legend. It's so remote and the weather's so terrible. It's a good location for a secret facility. Nobody goes the other way into that valley either, because of all the stories about the Gate of Lithraea."

"Connor definitely made us do the hike," Finn said. "Even my mom. Which is wild when I think of it now."

Vero grimaced. "It's wild for *all* of us to think of your mom hiking, Finn." Everyone laughed at Vero's easy way of talking, and Aislin McKay's incredible reputation for being prissy. Vero was one of the Warbirds Harlow had especially hoped would like her eventually, so it was nice that she was being friendly now. "Seriously though, there's a lot of legends about the Gate. About creatures called vvyk in the forest, and an old human ritual. Real weird stuff."

"I'd like to know more about that," Finn replied with his signature focused seriousness that made people feel like they were the center of the world. "Hiking in is unpleasant. It feels wrong. Repellent."

"Like the Vespae's wards," Audata mused.

Finn nodded. "Yeah. You think they're amplifying iridium?"

Audata wore her thinking face. "Mmm, they might be. More likely they're mimicking it."

Finn glanced at Harlow, concern forming in the wrinkle between his eyes. She squeezed his hand, a silent reassurance that Audata wasn't being dismissive, or offended. He clearly worried he'd offended her, as she walked off without another word.

"She's just thinking over what you said," Harlow explained.

Finn's smile was tentative as he watched the tiny Strider walk away. "Okay," he said finally, the cloud of worry clearing.

They turned back toward the group, who were having an animated discussion about Gale Alley. Vivia shifted her weight a little, adjusting the very full cup of tea she held in her lap so it wouldn't spill. "So if we want to get to ORAIS, we'll have to hike in."

"Why would we want to get there?" Mirai asked. "I mean, I get that the Vespae are looking for it. But what is it?"

Everyone looked to Finn. "It's both an observatory and an archive of information the elder Illuminated, from the original envoy, have on what's beyond Okairos."

"Beyond Okairos?" Max asked. "I mean, I know we came from elsewhere, my parents made that clear, but does anyone actually know much about where the Ventyr are from?"

Each of the Ventyr in the room shook their heads. Finn was quiet for a long moment, making eye contact with Cian, and then Harlow, an apology on his face. "I know a little. Not a name, or anything like that, but only that where our parents came from there was endless war, royal families fighting with one another, but also… Conquering whole planets for resources."

"Resources…" Audata's eyes widened as she drifted back towards the group.

"Yes," Finn said. "People, unfortunately, were counted as resources by our ancestors."

"They still are," Mirai replied, though she took Max's hand when she said it.

"That's true," Finn said. "And I don't claim that the Illuminated treat the people of this planet well… But it is still better than what they left behind."

The room was silent for a long while. Sam finally spoke up. "So ORAIS was used to monitor what, then? It's an observatory."

Finn shrugged. "I don't really know. I was a teenager the last time I was there. But I know what I'd use the equipment there for *now*, if I were given access to it." The room was so quiet it seemed no one was so much as breathing, waiting for Finn to continue. "I'd be watching for evidence that the Ventyr have found us, especially now that technology here has advanced so much. We would be a valuable commodity for the empire now, much more valuable than when the envoy originally arrived."

Harlow shivered, her body going cold just thinking about what it would be like for more Ventyr to be on Okairos, when the small number of them that had lived here for two thousand years were so powerful.

"I think it would be worth the hike to see what information ORAIS holds, though it may be a dangerous trip to get there, especially if the Vespae are honing in on the location," Audata said after a long pause. "We need to know what they're looking for, and why they think that the children of the original Ventyr envoy will help them find it."

"But it wasn't just the Ventyr that they took," Max reasoned. "They also took Jareth Sanvier. Or did all that have to do with the fact that Alain was angry with him for making that video at the end of summer?"

Finn shrugged. "I'm not sure. We didn't have much of a chance to talk in there. Where is he now?"

"Being debriefed by the rest of Council," Piper replied. "We'll convene later to discuss what to do with you all."

Vivia sat next to the human. The firedrake pulled a strand of her silver hair, twisting it tight around her tiny fingers, then let it go, a thoughtful look on her face. "The Vespae took Jareth, Petra and Finn, and they tried to take Larkin…" she trailed off her brow furrowing further.

Cian leaned toward her. "What are you thinking?"

Vivia gazed at Cian appraisingly. Their relationship had developed in an odd way, as she obviously thought of them as a littling in comparison to herself. It was as if she might be seeing them as more now. Harlow glanced at Finn whose eyebrows had raised in awe or amusement—maybe both. Cian had always seemed so wise to both of them. To see them treated as something of a novice was disorienting.

After a pause that felt awkwardly long for everyone but Vivia and Cian, Vivia explained. "All the people they've taken are children of the leaders of the Immortal Orders."

"Right," Harlow interjected. "Jareth is Berith's natural son." Nearly everyone in the room cringed visibly at the terrible faux pas of Berith having given his child a rhyming name. Harlow ignored them. "Aurelia thought it was because they believed they might have knowledge of the information caches…"

Vivia sat forward, looking hard at both Finn and Harlow, as though trying to discern what was so special about them. "Yes, and it might be that, but in the same vein, your parents all had knowledge of how to create the Vascularity that imprisoned them."

Harlow had leaned towards Vivia as she spoke, and now she fell backwards, into the crook of Finn's arm. He played absently with her hair, both of them thinking hard. "Let's say that was part of it," Finn said, his voice so soft and slow at first it was almost a whisper, as though he were thinking aloud. "Why would they want to know about that? They were eager to enter our world."

"It's their home," Max reasoned. "Why wouldn't they want to come back?"

No one had an answer for that at first. But then Sam turned to Vivia. "*Are the Vespae actually from here?*"

Vivia locked eyes with Cian. "Shortly before my mother was executed, she told me that she wondered if perhaps the Vespae had come to us the way the Illuminated had. She was terrified, grieving the terrible loss of our way of life. I didn't think much of it at the time, but it certainly seems possible they could be from somewhere else. They weren't always a problem—" The Argent's eyes misted, and she seemed unable to continue.

Cian took over. "The theory had been that they had simply outgrown whatever remote territory they originated in. The world was very different back then. There were places we'd never seen, never even imagined existed."

Several people nodded, and the group fell silent once more. Between the Ravagers, the Vespae, and the Illuminated, their problems became more unmanageable by the minute.

Audata turned to the rest of the Council members. "This gives us all a lot to think about. Finn, will you come with us? It might make things easier if you could answer some questions in real time."

Finn looked to Harlow. "I'd like it if Harlow could come too."

Piper Winslow looked ready to argue. Harlow shook her head, meeting the human's eyes with steely grace. "No, love. It will go easier if it's just you."

Finn looked between the two women, saw the tension between them and wisely nodded. "All right." He stood, kissing her deeply before following Audata and the Council out of the Dairy.

A few of the Warbirds let out low whistles of approval as Harlow blushed, gathering around with questions of their own about how their first night back together had gone. Harlow watched as Finn paused by the door, an odd feeling overcoming her as the Warbirds gossiped around her. It was a combination of hope, belonging, and new confidence that she wasn't quite sure she'd ever felt. It was okay that he was going to his meeting, and she was staying here to chat with her friends.

He blew her a kiss as he disappeared out the door, and Harlow turned to the Warbirds. There were questions she had about levitating in intimate moments that needed answers, and she finally had a group of people to ask. She wasn't about to let this moment go to waste.

<h1 style="text-align:center">CHAPTER 19</h1>

The days after Finn's return were full—sometimes wonderful, and sometimes hard. Each morning when Harlow woke up next to him, she had to fight to believe he was real. She could tell he was struggling with what he'd been through, and though she tried to let him know she was there for him, she couldn't quite manage to break through.

They trained with the Warbirds each day, keeping busy, and that was gratifying. Finn was in his element with fellow warriors, exchanging knowledge and techniques that pushed the entire Legion into what felt like a renaissance of learning about their abilities, and what they could do together as Claimed pairs. Harlow was proud of Finn—he was a born leader and teacher, and he seemed in his element.

But when they were alone, he was quiet. Too quiet sometimes, and Harlow worried about the growing distance between them. Nothing was bad, exactly— they got along well—but there was space between them she hadn't expected. Space he'd asked for, she reminded herself, though she wasn't sure she was giving it the right way. He needed rest, and so did she, but knowing that didn't stop her from worrying she'd made the wrong choice.

Harlow hated being worried all the time. She'd thought it would stop when she got him back, but here were her anxieties about *everything*, smacking her in the face, over and over. She frequently realized that a lot of what she thought she perceived was just that, her *thoughts*. But it wasn't so easy to shut off the worrying she'd grown used to in Finn and Larkin's absence.

A week after Finn's rescue, on the day after the Humanist delegation arrived in Sanctum, he was so quiet at breakfast with Cian, Enzo and Riley that she became truly concerned. When he washed his dishes without speaking to anyone and disappeared out the back door, she scrambled to get her boots on.

"I'll speak with him," Cian said, setting their coffee down. The worry in her heart echoed in every thread that connected Cian and Finn. "You stay here."

Cian left so fast Harlow didn't have time to object. Riley poured her another cup of tea, while Enzo frothed milk with a whisk. "He's just processing," Riley said.

Harlow watched Enzo pour the frothed milk into her black tea, making a little design on the top, just like in a cafe. Her best friend smiled at her. "How are things going with him and the Warbirds?"

"Really well," Harlow replied. "He's in his element with them. But at home —with me…" she trailed off, trying not to feel sorry for herself. A ghast peeped out at her from behind the refrigerator, looking as though someone had called its name. It was so excited to do something gruesome that it struck Harlow as funny. She burst into laughter, which must have offended it, because it disappeared instantly.

"They are not to be laughed at, apparently," Enzo said with a grin.

Harlow shook her head. "It just looked so silly. Like, *hello, are you going to cry about it?*" She laughed again with Enzo, but it didn't seem as funny when her worry for Finn crept back in.

"It really is just him adjusting," Riley said as the laughter died down. "I get the sense he's not ready to talk yet. Give him some time."

Enzo nodded as he slid onto the bench seat where Riley was curled up with Axel. "He knows you're there for him when he's ready. You just have to be patient."

That was reassuring to hear, but Harlow couldn't say she actually felt better. "Turn the radio on," she said, settling into her chair. "The meeting's about to start."

Riley turned their battery-powered radio on, and the announcement portion of the meeting was already in progress. Lou Spencer explained that the leaders of the Humanist movement had not known their silent investor was Alain Easton. Nor had they any idea that Easton was working with the Vespae. No additional information had been uncovered about that.

It sounded like the vampire was reading from something she'd written and Harlow's mind drifted while Lou explained that the Humanists also had not carried out the terrorist attacks in Nuva Troi over the summer. Apparently, the working theory was that the Illuminated had faked them to generate hatred for the Humanists. It was a clever idea, but Harlow's mind wouldn't focus.

Larkin slipped in the back door. "Hi," she mouthed, taking a seat next to Harlow after pouring herself a cup of coffee. "Finn and Cian went to Vivia's place for the announcement," she whispered to Harlow. "I saw them on my way over here."

Harlow nodded, pretending like she was listening. A stab of disappointment went through her. She hated to feel clingy, and she knew that without the convenience of their phones that there was little reason to expect to be informed about a casual change of plans like this one. But the fact that he'd just walked off and left her for the morning rankled.

Lou spoke now about the Humanist leaders being very amenable to allying with the Rogue Order. Harlow turned her attention to the radio.

"...have generously offered to help us move our population to their compound north of here, called the Grove. We will begin organizing for this move in the next few weeks. With the Vespae having breached our location, it is only a matter of time before a larger problem arises.

"You will receive household instructions on your move, along with any organizations you are affiliated with. After the conclusion of these announcements, we ask that everyone report into their org leaders for more information..."

Lou continued speaking—about how great the Humanists appeared to be, something about them actually having found a white ash grove, how that would be an asset for the inevitable fight with the Illuminated's forces. The certainty that there would never be an end to this conflict took root in Harlow's gut. The War of the Orders had lasted for years, and they hadn't been dealing with the Vespae or Ravagers. It had only been a few months and Harlow felt as though she'd aged decades.

Next to her, Larkin sighed with relief. "Good. I hope Thea and Alaric will get to go, don't you?"

It took Harlow a moment to comprehend that Larkin was speaking to her. She'd spaced out completely, unable to focus on anything, her anxiety about what was going on with Finn at a fever-pitch with this new twist in the path ahead of them. A few deep breaths brought her back into the moment. "Yeah, I hope Thea will agree to go."

Larkin searched her face, obviously using her sisterly instinct to try and detect what was wrong. "You'll go wherever the Warbirds go, won't you?"

Harlow glanced at Enzo and Riley, who wore matching expressions, both filled with the ache in Larkin's eyes. "Yeah, I guess Finn and I will have to."

Larkin nodded, then turned to Enzo and Riley. "What about you?"

Enzo smiled. "We're not aligned with any particular organization..." He looked to Riley, who took his hand as they answered Larkin. "We'll be headed to the Grove with the rest of Sanctum."

Larkin nodded slowly, thinking things over. "Will Cian go with the Warbirds?"

"Probably," Harlow answered.

"What about Axel?"

"If we go somewhere else with the Warbirds, he'll go with the maters, or Enzo and Riley." Harlow watched closely as Larkin nodded, swiping a bacon and cheddar scone off the plate at the center of the kitchen table. Her sister was perseverating on something. "You've got a lot of questions, pal. Everything okay?"

Larkin shrugged. "I hate being apart. And I'm tired of *resting*."

Everyone laughed, relief edging the threads that bound them to one another. It was such a typical Larkin thing to say. Unlike Finn, she seemed more or less back to herself after her experience through the limen and traveling with Vivia. After several discussions with the maters, Larkin revealed that her adventure had been mostly limited to actually traveling through the limen itself, and the day she'd been rescued. As she'd put it, "Everything else was hiking."

Harlow glanced at the clock on the wall in the kitchen. "I need to get to the Dairy. We're probably meeting about what's next. Wanna come with, Larkin?"

The youngest Krane nodded, getting up to find her jacket. Riley and Enzo stayed put. Harlow felt uneasy at the upcoming changes. "You're sure you'll go to the Grove?"

Riley nodded. "Yes, they'll need empaths. The more refugees we take in, the more counselors are needed, and there just aren't enough."

"Okay," Harlow said, pulling on her boots. "I'm guessing we're not coming with you, not at first anyway."

They'd been lucky so far, given that they were voluntarily separated from the twins and the Wraiths. But this felt bigger. Some of them might not make it to the Grove, and there was every possibility that if the Warbirds were going into combat, she and Finn might not return.

Enzo took her hand. "We have time. You heard what Lou said. We're not saying goodbye today."

"Right," Harlow replied. She knew that, but her brain skipped ahead in moments like these, preparing for the worst immediately. It was all she knew how to do. Larkin handed her coat to her and she zipped herself in, planting a quick kiss on Axel's head. It would be torture to leave him.

Riley looked up at her. "Stay present, Harlow. It will help."

She tried for a smile, even knowing that Riley would see right through it, then followed Larkin out into the brisk morning air. The sky was clear today, the kind of crystalline blue that didn't occur in Nuva Troi, which meant it was so cold that Harlow felt the tiny hairs in her nose freeze.

Larkin shivered, hugging Harlow's arm for extra warmth as they walked through the village. "I feel like I'll never be warm again."

People were bustling about after the announcement. Harlow watched the crowd for Finn and Cian, but didn't see them until they were halfway to the Dairy. Strangely, they were headed in the opposite direction.

Finn pressed a kiss to Harlow's forehead as he tugged on Larkin's ponytail. "Hey, kiddo," he said.

"Yo-ho, buddy-boy," Larkin replied.

Finn raised an eyebrow at her. Larkin shrugged. "If you're going to call me kiddo, I'm insisting on calling you some truly weird shit back."

Harlow snickered, while Finn just nodded. "Fair."

"Where are you two headed?" Harlow asked.

"The meeting's in the bathhouse," Cian said, grinning wickedly.

Larkin raised an eyebrow, as Cian and Finn turned them back in the direction they'd come from.

"You were just complaining about the cold," Harlow said.

Larkin shrugged. "It's fine with me. It just doesn't seem like a very *professional* place for a meeting."

Cian took her arm as they turned the corner that led to the bathhouse. "We're not running a corporation, silly."

They entered the bathhouse through an inconspicuous wooden door in an alley, walking down several flights of stone stairs. Soothing harp music floated up towards them. The geothermal heat that made building a village in such a remote location possible was combined here with an underground mineral spring, and the original owners of the resort had converted the space into a gorgeous spa.

There were several more public pools, but Harlow knew the private one Audata had procured for the meeting. She'd done this before when she thought the Warbirds needed to relax and recharge. The vampire working the front desk smiled at Harlow and Cian, then blushed when she caught sight of Finn.

Harlow kept her smile to herself. This had been happening a lot and she found it strangely adorable. Denizens of Nuva Troi were perpetually cool about their celebrity worship, but here in Sanctum, people were from everywhere. Some people had harbored crushes on Finn since they were teenagers, as he'd always been in the news, gossips and on socials. Meeting him in person was often overwhelming for some of them.

"Your party is in the D'vor pool, Ms. Krane," the vampire said.

"Thank you, Clara," Harlow replied, motioning for the others to follow her. They walked around the edge of the public pools to the softly lit changing rooms, which were full of wooden lockers to store clothes in. The four of them found lockers next to one another and undressed. The textured limestone floors were deliciously heated beneath their feet and Harlow relished the warmth as she waited for everyone else outside the changing area, watching the people doing laps in the exercise pool.

The water in the pools appeared to be a dark blue in the low light of the public area. Witchlights danced on the ceiling, which was painted like the night sky, reflecting in the six public pools. Steam rose from the more heated of the group, and immortals sat chatting amiably, drinking tea in the warmer pools. This was a common place to socialize and warm up.

Not many humans frequented the bathhouses, as human culture had a different view of nudity that confused many immortals. Privately, Harlow thought it prudish, but humans had many ideas about sexual attraction that she didn't always understand. To her, and to most immortals, bodies of all shapes and sizes were simply art to adorn with more art. But to humans, nudity often embarrassed them, making them think immediately of sex.

Once everyone was undressed and had towels, Harlow showed them to the D'vor room, named after one of the vampires that had originally owned the resort. At the center of the room was one long, extra heated pool. The gilt on the domed ceiling made the water appear to be molten gold. Steam clouded the room, which was full of naked Warbirds, splashing in the water and chatting amiably.

On one of the wide steps that surrounded the pool, Piper Winslow sat wrapped up tight in a towel. Next to her, Audata reclined on a cushion, naked as the day she was born, a look of supreme serenity on her face. When her eyes met Harlow's, they sparkled. The little Strider had endured many hours of Piper's prickly company since Finn's return, and Harlow had a feeling this was her subtle revenge.

Larkin stepped into the water, grinning as she sunk into its heated depths. "This is bliss," she said, slapping Harlow's shoulder. "Why haven't we been here every day?"

Harlow flicked water at her sister as Finn immersed himself next to her. When his body brushed hers under the water she empathized with Piper's discomfort. It *was* hard not to think about sex sometimes. But, for her, the only body arousing her was Finn's, his arms going around her waist as he pulled her into the depths of the pool.

Cian, Vivia, and Larkin sat near Sam and Tomy. Vivia poured them tea from a large pitcher as they chatted. Relaxation emanated through the threads in the room. There was a subtle green floral scent in the air that combined with a hint of something woody. As Finn hugged her close, she leaned back against his chest.

"I'm sorry I walked out this morning," he said softly, his mouth against her ear. "Most of the time I feel okay, but some mornings, I wake up and I can't stop worrying that someone will take you from me. That I might lose you."

They weren't alone, and the amount of preternatural hearing in the room meant that this wasn't the place to have this conversation, but everyone was busy with themselves. Even Piper looked like she was relaxing, sipping tea with Audata and chatting somewhat amiably.

"You can talk to me," Harlow replied, keeping things simple.

"I know," he murmured. "I just don't know what to tell you. I don't want to relive the things Alain tricked me into seeing, and the rest of it was just me in my head, worrying about all of you. But especially you."

Harlow didn't much care who heard or saw them at that point. She turned in Finn's arms, wrapping her legs around his waist. Yes, she understood full well why Piper might be uncomfortable now. Pressed against Finn's body, the soft water causing them to slip deliciously against one another, she could think of nothing but having him inside her. Not that she would, but it might be fun to talk about later.

"That's a wicked look," he murmured in her ear as he pulled her closer.

"I love you." She kissed his cheeks. "I was just so anxious while you were gone. I lost myself in grief."

He pushed damp hair from her face, his eyes glowing with love. "And that's what *I* worried about most."

Floating here, facing him, it felt like they were alone. But soft snippets of others' conversations reached her ears, perfectly clear. She felt the relaxed expression slide off her face, locking her gaze on Finn's. He'd done this on purpose. Talked with her about this in front of the others so they'd hear them, empathize more deeply with them as a couple. The evidence was in the shrewd glint in his eyes, combined with his love for her.

Nothing about what they'd said had been false. That was the beauty of it. She just wasn't sure she liked the way he'd maneuvered them into this conversation here, for strategy. His brows pulled together slightly, his expression begging her to understand. This was who he was, a strategist, always thinking a few moves ahead. Steam clouded around them, hiding their faces from the others.

Harlow shook her head once, closing her eyes and leaning back in the water, letting herself float. She would take this slightly confusing moment any day over what she'd endured while he was away. From across the pool, Audata called them in. The Warbirds quieted down, gathering around Audata and Piper to listen.

When the noise died down, Audata nodded to the human. "Piper is joining us to talk about a special mission, but first, I'm sure some of you may already have guessed what we'll be doing next."

"Guard duty!" Rian shouted from the back of the pool. The big Ventyr grinned, their dimples making their dark face even cuter than usual. Their partner Eliana grinned along with them, splashing them.

Audata smiled at the Warbirds' resident goofs as she slid into the water. "Essentially. We'll be partnering with the Humanists' envoy of soldiers to accompany the civilian population to the Grove."

"The usual teams?" Tomyris asked, winking at Harlow and Finn.

"For the most part—" Audata started to say.

Piper pulled her towel around her more tightly as she interrupted. "The Humanists have some issues working with the Knights of Serpens."

The Warbirds fell silent. To their credit, every single face wore some version of the same grim look. They'd accepted Finn and the Knights, and resented that the Council and the Humanists hadn't followed suit.

Finn sighed as he pushed out of the pool. Water dripped down every gorgeous nook and cranny of his abdomen. "I'm sorry. It's me, isn't it?"

Piper Winslow stared at him as he grabbed a towel, her eyes going wide as saucers before she looked quickly away, scowling. "Don't be so fucking dramatic, McKay. *We've* barely finished vetting the Knights, you can't blame them for being worried. They don't want any of you coming and going." She glared at Harlow. "Your sister and her bondmate are welcome at the Grove, but they'll stay put until we're sure of the rest of you."

Tomyris leaned back against the edge of the pool, water beading on her graceful collarbones as she flexed her muscles, her wings stretching out behind her. She saw what Finn had done, and now she obviously wanted in on the fun. She too had abs to show off. "So what's that mean for Harlow and Finn? You want to lock them up at the Grove?" The Ventyr's eyes sparkled dangerously as Piper's eyes went wide again.

Audata stepped in front of Tomyris, a look of vague annoyance crossing her face. Her brood was messing with the poor human more than she'd intended. "No. They're only asking that Alaric and Thea stay put and not leave—"

"And that Finn and Harlow not be a part of the accompaniment," Piper interrupted. She'd obviously lost ground though.

Harlow bit the inside of her cheek to avoid smiling. She felt sorry for Piper until the human spoke again, her confidence returned, apparently. "But fear not, we have another mission for the two of you."

Finn looked up from the glass of tea he'd just poured. "You want us to go to ORAIS, right?"

Piper shot a finger at him. "Ding, ding, ding. You got it, McKay."

The cringe that rippled through the pool was practically audible. The human's tone was discomfiting. Harlow hadn't spent much around the Education Councillor, so she wasn't sure how to take this kind of behavior. Every muscle in Audata's body was tense, as though Piper's performance made her incredibly uncomfortable.

Larkin moved to stand next to Harlow in the pool, nudging her first, then covering her mouth to whisper. "What's up with her?"

Harlow didn't answer, or move a muscle. Piper was looking straight at them, as though she'd heard Larkin perfectly, which was impossible for a human. The woman had a preternatural sense that others were talking about her, apparently.

"The mission to ORAIS is too dangerous to send a large team. You can choose two others to accompany you," Piper continued. "But no one we find vital to our mission to align closely with the Humanists will be given clearance, nor will anyone we need for vital missions elsewhere."

There it was. They'd tipped their hat. The Council was sending them because it was dangerous, and they didn't much care what happened to Finn and Harlow. They didn't hate them, but if they were killed, it wouldn't matter to their overall goals. On the other hand, if they brought back valuable information, it would be a bonus. They'd prioritized aligning with the Humanists, which frankly, made all the sense in the world.

Harlow glanced at Finn, who wore his best diplomat face. She'd seen him use it dozens of times over the summer in Nea Sterlis. He'd assessed the situation the same way she had, then. "Great. I'd like to call Arebos Flynn back to join us. Will that be a problem?"

His tone wasn't challenging in the slightest, but Harlow sensed the misstep immediately. He should have *asked* the human if he could take Ari, not *told* her that he wanted to. Finn didn't seem to see the mistake.

Piper's jaw clenched tightly. "I suppose not. Take anyone from your own team you like, except Cian. They're with us."

Cian visibly tensed. They didn't like being ordered about any better than Finn did. For his part, Finn's forehead crinkled. Harlow knew Cian would have been his first pick, but that he could recognize the Argent was in high demand. Still, he wasn't used to being thwarted like this, and though the others might not see it, Harlow knew he was seething, ever so slightly.

Harlow jumped in before his arrogant mouth could dig them a deeper hole. "That's okay. We'll be good with Ari, and maybe one other person."

Piper shook her head, laughing. The sound was dry and just as arrogant as any noise Finbar McKay could produce. "Let me know when you decide. I'll need a full briefing on your plans before you go. I'm your Council contact point and I'll approve or deny any move you make on the Fifth Order's behalf."

It was the first time Harlow had heard anyone use the term for the combined group of the Rogues and Humanists. Despite the fact that the tension was thick as claggy, over-baked cake, she was pleased to hear it used. Finn had no such reaction. She didn't need to look at him to feel him carefully considering his next words.

"We'll be happy to let you know our plans," Harlow said, before Finn could speak again. "Let us talk about who else might be best on the mission and we'll meet soon."

Piper nodded, obviously curt, but the vitality had gone out of her attitude. "Great. Let me know as soon as possible."

The human woman stood, turning on her heel to stalk out of the pool. Everyone was silent as she went. When the door closed, everyone was silent for long moments. Everyone waited for Piper to reappear, like a monster in a horror film. They always had one more jump scare in them, but apparently Piper did not.

Rian stuck a tongue out at the door, and Eliana raised their brows. "What a bit—"

Eliana's curse was cut off by Audata shaking her finger. "None of that, please. Piper was elected as one of the team leaders for the missions ahead."

"She's the *Education* Councillor," Harlow said, unable to stop herself. "What qualifies her for something like this?" Surely someone could explain what in seventeen hells was so special about the woman.

Vivia stood, gliding out of the pool like a nymph from a faery story. "Enough. The Council has made their decisions. We don't need to know more. Audata, you get everyone here briefed on their teams. Finn, Harlow, you're with us. We'll meet you in the tea room."

Cian followed, and the two of them exited the D'vor lounge. Harlow turned to Larkin. "I'll come over to the maters' later, okay?"

Larkin grabbed her arm. "I want to come to ORAIS with you."

"No!" she and Finn said in unison. A few of the Warbirds looked their way.

Larkin spoke quietly, averting her eyes from the rest of the group. "Can you just let me come talk before you say no?"

"Fine," Finn said, as though his word was final.

Harlow glared at him. "No, pal. Go home. There's nothing you can say that will change *my* mind. And if my mind can't be changed, what do you think Selene and Aurelia are going to say?"

Finn's voice was even and quiet. "She's not a child."

Harlow didn't want to make a scene. "Let's talk privately."

Larkin grinned, making a beeline out of the pool. Harlow followed Finn outside of the lounge, then grabbed his arm when they were outside the heavy doors. "She's not coming with us, Finn. I won't have it."

They stood alone in the hallway outside the private lounge. Finn looked down at where she gripped his arm. "Harlow."

The way he said her name rolled over her, cold as a plunge in an iced over lake. She stepped back, her emotions roiling under the surface of her skin.

Finn's head cocked slightly. "I said she could *talk to us* about why she thinks she needs to go, not that she could come." His arms folded over his chest. "Do you really want to create an environment where Larkin feels as though she can't come to us about her thoughts and feelings?"

Harlow's cheeks flushed hot and her eyes fell to the floor. "No, of course not, but…"

"Then let her talk, for Raia's sake. It won't hurt you to listen to her."

He was exasperated with her, that much was clear, and before she said things that went too far, she needed space. "I need some air," she murmured as she took several big steps away from the staircase. "You can talk without me."

CHAPTER 20

Outside the bathhouse, the sunny day had turned cloudy. Weather was moving in as Harlow broke into a slow jog. She didn't want to talk to Enzo and Riley, or any of the Warbirds. What Harlow wanted right now was her parents. A block away from the maters' house, she nearly ran into them. They were both dressed nicely and coming from the direction of the Council house. They'd probably been to pick up their orders.

Harlow stopped quickly, trying not to knock either of her parents over. "They're sending us to find ORAIS." Selene and Aurelia glanced at one another. Of course, they already knew this. "Larkin wants to go."

"Oh dear," Selene said. "Why don't you come back to the cottage and have a cup of tea with us."

"Yes," Aurelia added. "Have some tea and we can talk about this."

Harlow drew back. "You're not thinking of *letting her go*, are you?"

Selene's mouth drew downward as her eyes widened. "Darling, she's an adult. If she wants to go, and Finn thinks she'd be an asset to the mission, who are we to tell her no?"

It felt as though all the air had been knocked out of her lungs. "Are you kidding?"

Aurelia's shoulders hunched, whether from the cold or emotion, Harlow couldn't tell. "We aren't in the habit of telling our adult children what they can and cannot do with their lives."

Harlow backed away. "Well, maybe if you did every once in a while, we wouldn't end up in such a mess all the time."

The maters protested, but Harlow had already turned, jogging again, but this time she wasn't sure where to go. If no one saw what she did, that Larkin didn't belong on a mission like this—that even after the months of training she had, *she* barely belonged on a mission like this—then what use was there in talking to anyone?

Without thinking about it, she'd jogged up the biggest hill in the village. At the top, there was an excellent view of what had been a park when Sanctum was a resort. Now, they used it for various group activities, including defense classes for civilians. At this time of day, the experienced fighters should be teaching a group of children the basics of escaping a hold and working in groups to subvert enemies larger than themselves. It was gruesome training, but given their circumstances, it was the best way to ensure the children had their best chances of survival.

But the kids were nowhere to be seen. Instead, strangers—Humanists—filled the field, running through a set of drills. They started with a set of postures that reminded Harlow of the mind-body practices Cian had tried to educate her in last summer. But these were different, more obviously aligned with preparing the body for fighting.

There was something about the quality of movements that felt familiar to her. She was so entranced watching the Humanists begin their training that she didn't notice Jareth Sanvier's approach. "You want to join us?" he asked.

She looked down at the fighters moving in unison. They were repeating the same set of movements several times before moving onto a new set. She wasn't sure she could keep up, but unlike the methods Cian had tried to teach her that required a great deal of flexibility and coordination, these were more succinct. Utilitarian.

Harlow nodded, curious, despite the fact that apparently the Humanists didn't trust her. She followed Jareth to the field, finding places in the back of the group. He stood behind her as she watched the people in front of her and then began to move, mimicking the motions of their bodies as best she could. Jareth spoke quietly behind her, instructing her, like a teacher in an exercise class might. His words made sense to her, and she caught on quickly.

With Jareth's help, she realized that there were just a few sets of movements and the fighters cycled through them several times. She was surprised by how quickly she picked up the sequences, how natural they felt to her. Something shifted below her, undulating in time with the movements. Her shadows. They'd emerged.

She nearly stopped, but behind her, Jareth murmured. "There's nothing wrong. You're moving with the aether. That's what these postures are meant to do, align us more closely with aethereal power."

Harlow used her second sight then, pushing it out into the threads. In her mind's eye, the threads danced along with the fighters on the field. They were a surreal picture, thousands of infinitesimal threads of dark-light flowing around them in a sea of coordinated waves.

Her eyes closed, so she could better feel the movement of the magic within the threads, her shadows moving in time with the threads themselves. When they opened, she stood on the spirit paths. She was in the limen. Faint echoes of the people on the field surrounded her.

She walked around, looking at them from all angles. They were here, but they weren't. It was like the vision she'd seen with Ashbourne, of the women on other worlds, the night Connor beat Finn in Nea Sterlis. But she had seen those women's faces and figures clearly. These were mere impressions.

Your people are fascinating, a terrible voice said.

Cold fear gripped her. There was no mistaking who that voice belonged to—the Ravager she'd spoken to last summer. She spun around, but there was no giant entity anywhere. Only the echoes of the people on the field, and the clouds of aether at her feet.

Oh, I am not here, the creature said. *I suppose that's not quite accurate. I am here, but not here.*

Was it talking to her, or itself?

I have no interest in harming you, little bird. Right now, I am only watching.

"Watching?"

Yes, watching. My brethren spent their imprisonment plotting the havoc they wished to wreak when set loose. I have never been much of a planner.

Harlow wasn't sure what to say. If she knew how to run, how to escape, she might. But she wasn't sure that was wise. She wasn't sure of anything at all. "So, you're just watching us?"

No, not just *watching. But yes, watching.*

Maybe it was best to keep it talking. "What else are you doing?"

The creature, the Ravager, laughed. Or at least Harlow thought it did. The sound was more like shrieking, and Harlow wanted to cover her ears, except that wouldn't help. The Ravager's voice was in her head, whatever that meant in her incorporeal state.

Something brushed against her legs, both in the real world, and here in the limen. She looked down to find the auburn cat Axel made friends with over the summer—Morgaine Yarlo's cat. Larkin said his name was Bayun, and that he was incredible.

"Hello," she whispered, crouching to speak to the cat. Bayun was in his corporeal body. "Better get out of here."

Not without you, said another voice in her mind. This voice was different from the Ravager's. Imperious, and distinctly feline.

"Did you just *talk*?" Harlow tried to pet the cat. She wasn't sure if that was possible in her incorporeal form, but his fur was so fluffy and soft, it was worth a try.

The cat lifted his chin to be rubbed, his throat vibrating with purrs. *It is dangerous for you here,* Bayun said. *It is not safe. Not with* them *afoot.*

Who are you talking to, little bird? The Ravager demanded, its terrible voice raising to the pitch of thousands of Vespae buzzing. *Why can't I see you any longer?*

Follow me. The cat beckoned. *Quickly.*

Harlow did as the cat asked. There wasn't time for questions. The aether surrounded them in thick clouds. Within it, there were echoes of voices and strange shapes that looked like faces. As soon as one took shape, and she began to make out its features, it disappeared.

Don't fall behind, the cat commanded.

"What is wrong with the aether?"

The cat looked over its shoulder. *The aether is troubled here.*

"Troubled how?" Harlow asked. Aether was thought to be semi-sentient, but neutral.

Once, someone drew too much power from this place. Misused it. Are disturbed entities on your side?

"Yes," Harlow said, thinking of the ghasts.

When aether is disturbed, its ways of knowing are troubled. It attempts to understand what has happened, which causes it to individuate. Once it does, the result is rarely anything good.

The clouds of pure aether pressed into her body. She felt hands pulling at her hair. Not to harm, but too curious, too invasive all the same. The huge feline hissed and the aether backed off. Harlow looked down at her hands. They were real. She was corporeal.

"Am I really here?"

Yes, unfortunately so. The aether had pulled you in, but just up here, you should be able to return the way you came.

"The way I came?" Harlow asked, feeling utterly confused. The aether cleared, forming more normally. She saw the vague outline of the Dairy, the loft, in particular. Cian, Vivia, Larkin and Finn sat talking, though she couldn't hear what they were saying.

Through the portal within.

"Within?"

Perhaps you think of it as being located in your heart. I believe my girl has mentioned this valve is significant to your kind.

His girl. Echo. Morgaine's Echo. Harlow bent down. "Did Morgaine get home okay? Did she find Echo? Are they together again?"

You are a good person, Harlow Krane, the cat said. *Much like my Echo. Perhaps a bit less... violent.* The cat seemed amused now, as though thinking about his violent human friend pleased him. *We do not have time to tarry, though I would like to speak with you more. Get her home. Now!*

Harlow wasn't sure who the cat was speaking to, but his tone had turned urgent. Bayun bumped her once with his head, and the contact pushed her back into herself, where she had the sense she was being sucked inward. Deeper and deeper she went, into the inner place she called her heart, where she found the tiny pinprick of reality beyond this place. Without really knowing how she was doing it, operating on pure instinct, Harlow dove into the pinprick, guided by some unknown force.

The only way to describe the sensation was that it was as though she'd turned herself inside out, and then back right again. She hit the floor hard. "Oof," she groaned, picking herself up off the hardwood. Her head spun wildly. Hardwood? She'd been on the field before. Axel nudged her face with his, purring loudly. Where had he come from?

"Harlow?" Larkin shouted, panicked for some reason.

Harlow's vision was blurry, and she felt as though she might vomit. She had the vague impression that Finn was sitting next to her, steadying her against his chest. "Breathe, babygirl," he said. "Just try to breathe."

"Where is the cat?" she asked, rubbing her eyes. Her vision was improving, and she felt slightly less like she might lose her breakfast, but she was utterly confused about where she was and how she'd gotten here.

"Axel's right here, darling." That was Cian.

"No, not Axel. Bayun. Where did he go?" Harlow was nearly frantic with worry now.

Finn's arms tightened around her. "Bayun's not here, Harlow. You and Axel just appeared out of nowhere."

Harlow's vision cleared, just as Axel climbed on top of her, purring loudly. She was in one of the private tea rooms, above the bathhouse. She rested against Finn's chest, his arms caging her.

"Hey," he said as she blinked several times.

"Hey," she replied. Her mind swirled, trying to make sense of what happened. There were footsteps on the stairs, which Cian stopped.

"Have any of you seen Harlow?" It was Jareth Sanvier. "She was hanging out with us at the field, and she walked off. I lost track of her, but she was acting kind of strange."

Finn pulled Harlow to her feet, giving her a look that she interpreted to mean, "Follow my lead." She nodded, setting Axel on the floor in front of her.

"She's here," Finn said, stepping forward, motioning behind his back for her to follow.

Harlow peeked around Finn's shoulder. "Hi!" she said, a flush coming to her cheeks.

Jareth looked genuinely concerned. "You're okay."

She smiled, taking Finn's hand. He squeezed hard, once in what she'd consider a quick, staccato note, if it were a noise. *Keep your answers short.* "I'm fine."

Everyone stepped back to allow Jareth into the lofted room. Each of the private tea rooms at the bathhouse looked over the main pools, though they were curtained and most had privacy sigils that could be activated upon arrival. There was an awkward split second of silence. Jareth's eyes narrowed slightly. Harlow spoke. "Sorry to worry you. Axel got out of the house."

"And came to a bathhouse?" Jareth asked, obviously incredulous.

Harlow gestured to Larkin, who now held the cat.

Jareth's eyes softened immediately when he saw Axel. "Can I pet him?"

Harlow was surprised by the reaction, but she couldn't see what the harm was. "Of course."

Larkin let Axel down, and he wound around Harlow's legs, allowing Jareth to crouch down to pet him. As he did, he said casually, "Sometimes people struggle with the energetic aspects of raotham—some have reported strange experiences. You didn't have anything like that happen, did you?"

"Raotham?" Larkin asked from the couch, where she'd folded herself back up. It was a clear deterrent, meant to give Harlow time to think of what to say.

Jareth glanced up. "A mind-body alignment practice that the humans in our organization have practiced for hundreds of years. Some consider it a lost art, as the civilization that it originated from, near present-day Avignonne, simply disappeared without a trace."

The story reminded Harlow of the Alabaster Spire, which had similarly disappeared from Nea Sterlis. It was an odd connection, one that seemed mysteriously tied up with all of this. Jareth looked to Harlow, his pointed expression indicating that he expected an answer to his original question.

"Nothing weird happened with me. Axel just came to find me."

"And you came here, rather than taking him home?" Jareth asked.

He knew. He *knew* she hadn't chased after Axel, and that something else had happened. But they knew so little about what the Humanists' goals were. The Rogue Order might trust them, but this was something more, and she wasn't sure she was even willing to have the Feriant Legion know about it yet.

Harlow shrugged. "I needed to get to this meeting anyway, there was no reason he couldn't come."

Jareth stood. "Look, I get it. You don't know if you can trust me. But know when you're ready to talk about the limen—the aether—and the Ravagers, I'm here."

Finn was perfectly still. Harlow wasn't even sure he was breathing. He looked like Axel, right before he pounced on a bug. Focused, and deadly. Jareth noted this as well, apparently, because he threw his hands up in the air, in a mock-defensive position.

Jareth's tone was light, but his words were serious as he backed towards the stairs. "It's a good faith offer, and I won't push or tell anyone else what I think might have happened out there."

No one said a word, or moved a muscle. Harlow held up a hand. Jareth paused, waiting for her to speak. "Why should we trust you, when your people so clearly don't trust us?" She gestured to herself and Finn. "*Specifically* us."

Finn moved then, crossing his arms and shifting his stance. Something in Harlow swelled. He was intimidating as a god, beautiful and stalwart. Maybe Jareth Sanvier saw a brutal temper, or a spoiled bad boy, but all she saw was a hero. When he spoke, she was even prouder. "You know they're sending us on what's likely a deadly, impossible mission because your higher ups don't like me."

Jareth nodded. "I do. I offered to go with you. They said no, but I'll offer you the same, bring me with you to ORAIS. You get to pick your team. Pick me."

Larkin snorted softly, a delicate noise. Everyone turned her way. She shrugged. "Kinda desperate, that's all."

Harlow raised an eyebrow at her little sister. "And what are *you* up here doing?"

Larkin rolled her eyes. "It's not the same. I've proven to be an essential part of ill-advised, very likely deadly missions in the past. What's *he* done?"

Jareth scoffed, then pulled a face at Larkin. "*I* burned down the governor's mansion. Heard you have some experience watching houses burn, little witch."

There wasn't a trace of malice in Jareth's words. The banter felt familiar, even fun. Like he'd fit right in with all of them. Harlow hated that she liked him so well, so quickly. Larkin snickered. "I like him. Let him come, McKay."

Finn and Cian both rolled their eyes. "We'll think about it," Cian said.

Jareth nodded. "That's all I ask. Thanks."

He left then, whistling an old Falcyran folk song as he went down the stairs two at a time.

Cian turned to her. "Come sit, and tell us everything that happened."

Harlow joined her people on the couch, where Larkin activated the privacy sigil so they could strategize in private.

CHAPTER 21

Harlow felt certain she would scream if she had to consider another minor detail. They talked over Harlow's experience in the limen, and who to choose to go to ORAIS, from an infuriating number of angles. For three days, they talked it over, again and again. This was all made more complicated by the fact that Ari returned from Nuva Troi with a detailed report, which he'd spent the morning giving to the Council, and now Harlow and Finn. There had been rumors, and news from refugees of the outside world, but not a lot of specific information about Nuva Troi until Ari arrived.

The Wraith lay flat on his back in front of the fire, claiming he'd never get warm again, much as Larkin often did. Axel climbed onto his chest, purring happily and making biscuits on Ari's muscled chest while he talked. Apparently, the Illuminated's wards were holding against the Vespae. It had taken them time to get them up, and much of the city had been damaged in the initial onslaught of the Vespae. Harlow listened in horror as Ari described all the places she loved that had been destroyed. She might never see the city she loved again—because it might not ever exist that way again.

Finn was none too happy that the Council had Ari's report before he did, but they were still determined to shut the Knights of Serpens out. The Fifth Order might be progressive in many ways, but just like most of Okairon society, they held grudges deeply. Finn and Alaric's proximity to their parents made them permanently untrustworthy, though it did seem the Council had finally acknowledged that the Knights were not a danger to them. They just didn't want them as a part of their governing body.

Someone knocked at the front door. Harlow got up to answer it, leaving Finn and Ari to talk. A teenage griffyn shifter stood outside, just shifting back into their humanoid form, a lanky young person with a puff of short curly hair and luminous golden eyes.

636

"Piper wants to see you in her office," they said before turning fast and shifting on the run, a streak of gold fur disappearing out the front gate at full speed.

"Do we know that child?" Finn asked from behind her, laughing.

"That's Kym," Harlow replied. "Their claim is that they're the fastest shifter in the village, and they take every chance they can to prove it."

Finn went to let Ari know that they were going to the Lodge, but he was already asleep. He and Harlow dressed for the cold without talking, then made their way out into yet another frigid day. Harlow was well and truly sick of winter.

Finn was chatty, apparently, now that they'd left the house. "Why don't they fly? Kym, I mean."

"Their wings aren't developed enough to carry them aloft. The Heraldic mature very slowly. Cian is only considered to be *nearing* middle age now," Harlow explained. Finn hadn't had the benefit of learning more about the Heraldic, as she had in the past months.

Everything about Finn lit with interest. Like many of the Ventyr, he could be acquisitional in nature, but what Finn loved to collect most was knowledge—knowing things relaxed him. The cogs turned in his mind, as he pieced together all he did know about the rare shifters. The moment his thoughts turned to the task at hand, his body tensed again. "She's going to ask who we're taking."

Harlow wanted to groan, but that wouldn't help things. They were still locked in a perpetual argument about this. Larkin desperately wanted to come to ORAIS with them, so much so that she'd had Vivia vouch for her survival skills and stamina.

"What do you think about Jareth?" Harlow asked. It was easier than trying to tackle the Larkin issue first.

"I think we should take him," Finn replied.

Harlow nodded, slipping her hand into his. "I agree. Even if it's just to watch him—to learn more about the Humanists. I think we'd be smart to suss them out a bit more."

"Agreed," he said, his tone going curt. His hand tensed around hers.

"You still think we should let Larkin come?"

Finn sighed. "I don't want to argue about this."

Harlow was so tempted to fight. To give all her reasons that Larkin shouldn't come again. But she remembered something Aurelia had said—about not clipping the Krane girls' wings when they were ready to fly. She wasn't the boss of her sisters. As much as she wanted to keep them all safe, she knew that wasn't possible. They were all going into danger, and there was no stopping that.

She'd prefer Larkin go to the Grove with the rest of the civilians, but she wasn't really a civilian anymore. Harlow hated that she was about to agree to this, but if it was what her sister wanted, she didn't see how she could stand in her way. "Fine, she can come. But she has to carry Axel. Just for being a brat about the whole thing."

Finn stopped short. "Wait, who said Axel was coming?"

Harlow threw her hands in the air. "Where do you suppose he's going to go? I'd planned to have Larkin take him to the Grove."

Finn grabbed her arm. His grip was loose, but insistent. "Harlow. We can't bring a *cat* with us to ORAIS. Do you have any idea how ridiculous that sounds?"

She stared at him. They'd been doing so well and now he was getting imperious with her? *Where the fuck did he get off? He was getting his way. She'd said yes to Larkin coming.* "I guess you should have thought of that before you agreed to let my baby sister come on another potentially deadly mission. Now we have to take our cat too." She stomped forward, pushing past him. They'd nearly reached the Council building. "Plan better next time," she called over her shoulder.

He caught up to her, fury radiating off him. "We're not bringing Axel, Harlow. Someone else can take him. Petra—we don't know where she's off to yet, do we?"

Harlow sighed, drawing the noise out into a groan. She was being purposely aggravating—she wasn't lying to herself about it. Of course they weren't going to take their cat on a dangerous mission to a secret Illuminated compound that the Vespae were desperate to find. Her anxiety would never recover from that kind of bullshit. But she felt like he hadn't listened to her about why she didn't want Larkin coming along, acting like she was trying to exclude her, rather than keep her safe. And now, rather than being an adult about the whole thing, she was being petty.

"Just tell Piper that we're bringing Larkin, Jareth, Ari, her, and our cat. She'll understand."

They stood in front of the Council office doors now. Finn looked mad enough to shoot fire from his ears, like a dragon. And then he stomped his foot, like a small child. Tears gathered in the corners of his eyes. "Please," he choked out.

Fuck. She was being shitty, and instead of just irritating him, it had actually made him upset. Harlow's eyes fell closed, her shadows dancing around her fingers in a soothing fashion. She took a long, deep breath, banishing her frustration as best she could.

"I'm sorry," she said, feeling every syllable of her apology in her bones. "We'll find somewhere else for him to go." Finn started to nod, and it just slipped out of her mouth, without a thought: "*Of course.*"

Inwardly, she cringed at her tone. Why did she have to add that?

His eyes widened, and his jaw clenched. "Did you actually say all that just to piss me off? I *love* that fucking cat."

"Because you are being such a fucking dick about this Larkin thing."

They were lucky no one was in the square. The two of them were shouting now.

"She's an adult." Finn shook his fists in the air to punctuate each word. It would be comical if she weren't so mad at him.

"The two of you *disappeared*, Finbar. You haven't asked me once how it was for me when you were gone. When the two of you vanished through a breach in reality that I couldn't follow you through."

"I asked," he insisted. "You were vague."

He had asked, and she had been vague. But they were on an epic roll now, both of them stubbornly not backing down. "You could have asked again."

"You could have followed us," he spit out. "You just didn't."

Her mouth fell open. She'd thought they were blowing off steam, but that was below the belt. Harlow was too shocked to cry, and that was saying something. The silence that filled the space between them was pregnant with regret. They stared at one another, both of them obviously fighting with their pride.

Just as she was about to apologize, he reached for her, pulling her towards him, but not quite embracing her. "I'm so fucking sorry. I didn't mean that."

Harlow stared up at him. They'd pushed each other too far. Her eyes fell to her boots. "We can't do this," she murmured. "We can't fight like this. I don't want this to be how we solve things."

He hugged her then, so tight she could hardly speak, but she apologized anyway. "I'm sorry too."

Finn's fingers stroked her hair. "I should have talked to you about why you didn't want Larkin to come."

Harlow nodded, taking in the smell of him. "I shouldn't have screwed with you about Axel."

They'd apologized, and she believed they both meant it sincerely, but she didn't feel better. In fact, all she wanted to do was crawl in bed for a week with Thea and cry. With ice cream. And *Pretty Little Firestarters* reruns. But that was all a lifetime away from the present reality. Now *she* wanted to stomp her foot.

Instead, she drew in a sharp breath and tried to compose herself. "We need to go in. We're in agreement about who's coming?"

He nodded, his face as solemn and exhausted as she felt. They were all so tired these days. "Let's go then."

~

PIPER'S OFFICE WAS TINY, crowded with furniture, and a lot of books. Novels from what Harlow could tell, and an odd variety, including a wide range of comics. Piper caught Harlow's confused look as she dragged a finger over a stack of vintage romance novels, mixed with books about ancient history and biographies of famous immortals. Most of it was popular stuff, fluff, not the kinds of books she'd recommend to anyone who was serious about history, and not what she'd expect the Education Councillor to be reading.

"I like a wide range of genres," Piper said, snatching the stack away from Harlow.

"Of course. *The Parapsych Triad* was very good. I liked it a lot."

Piper looked at her like she'd said she thought cats might fly. She had no idea what Harlow was talking about, which was strange, since it was the most famous series in the pile Piper had just defended. Perhaps she'd forgotten she had it, or maybe she was one of those people who stubbornly didn't keep up with things like trendy books. If so, that was another point against her. Harlow hated reading snobs.

Finn cut to the chase, explaining who they'd like to have come along to ORAIS. Piper nodded absently. She was obviously distracted. Finn shot a glance at Harlow. It was clear neither of them knew what to say, or how to even attempt to handle the human.

"Are you sure you want to meet today, Councillor?" Finn asked, his tone cautious. "We can come back another time."

"I'll be fine," Piper snapped. "You're not taking Sanvier, though. His higher-ups said no. *Again*."

Finn tried to explain why it would be a good idea, but Piper shook her head. "The Humanists were clear with both of you, Sanvier isn't going to ORAIS."

Finn glanced at Harlow, who nodded. "Okay," he said. "That's fine, I guess. Do you want us to replace him? We know he's a good fighter. We might need someone like him along."

Piper began writing on a notepad. "No, you have Arebos Flynn. That will be good enough. You'll leave in three days, so you'd best get about your preparations."

"I'll let Sanvier know then," Finn said.

"Focus your attention on preparing for your journey, McKay. Sanvier is a big boy. He's been told he's not going. The two of you don't need to be colluding behind your superiors' backs. If you make us look bad in all this, I promise I'll make things difficult for you."

Harlow tensed, waiting for Finn to argue again, but he didn't. He just nodded, his jaw clenching as he stood. Piper raised her eyebrows at Finn, daring him to speak again. When he didn't, she continued writing on her notepad.

Harlow recognized the dismissal and stood to leave as well, but Piper spoke as she stood. "I'd like a word with you, Krane."

Finn's eyes widened nearly imperceptibly, but Harlow noted the frustration winding through his shoulders as they tensed. "I'll wait for you outside."

When he'd gone, Piper continued staring at Harlow for an uncomfortably long few moments. "The two of you really don't remember me, do you?"

A shiver of anxiety slipped down Harlow's throat, settling low in her belly until it felt a lot like dread. She did not remember ever having met the human before. All she could do was shake her head in embarrassment. "I'm sorry, I don't."

The human's resulting laugh was entirely without humor. "Of course you don't. I sat next to you or behind you in a total of eight classes in secondary, ten for Finn."

The dread in Harlow's stomach curdled. She struggled to find words. When she came up with nothing, she apologized. "I am so sorry I don't remember you, Piper. Secondary was a difficult time in my life."

There was that humorless laugh again. "Right. What with the rich and powerful immortal parents who adored you, and a group of equally rich and powerful friends. It must have been *terrible* for you."

Indignation rose in Harlow's throat. "We don't know each other, Piper, so I can't compare our lives. But make no mistake, things have not been easy for me —especially not lately."

Piper rolled her eyes. "You're serious, aren't you? A little trouble with a boyfriend and a few tussles through the gossips, and you're sure you've got it bad."

"That doesn't seem fair," Harlow replied, trying hard to keep the whine that edged her voice to a minimum. "I *am* sorry I don't remember you from school, but my life hasn't been as easy as you seem to believe it to be."

The human sat back in her chair, her eyes narrowing. "Have you ever had to work for any of the opportunities you've had, Krane? You bought a fucking *penthouse* when Easton kicked you out, for fuck's sake. Do you know where I lived when my shitty ex did the same?"

Of course she didn't. The puzzle of why Piper had been so unfriendly to both she and Finn made sense now, but she didn't like knowing she was at fault.

"A tiny attic room I rented from a vampire who expected a 'donation' weekly, as part of my rent. That wasn't made clear until I'd moved in, and by that time, I'd spent my entire savings on the security deposit. I had no influence, no network to fall back on. No one to ask for help."

The contrast, which was so obvious to Piper, and had been less so to Harlow, slammed into her. It wasn't that she didn't know that she was more fortunate than most humans—she did. But it wasn't usually brought to her attention in such sharp relief to her own experience.

Harlow wasn't sure what to say. Her mind raced, as her sense of empathy reframed her entire life through this human's perspective. Every muscle in her body contracted painfully. It was impossible to close her mouth, which gaped open as she struggled to find the right words.

When she saw herself the way that Piper must... The Monas and the maters, hundreds of thousands of followers on socials she barely used, money —even if it had been a paltry amount to her. She'd always had everything she needed, even if she'd refused to access the help that was *always* offered to her. This human, and most humans, didn't automatically have that kind of support.

"That's fucked up, Piper," she said, finally. "Nothing like that should ever happen—to anyone."

Piper made a little snorting noise, derisive, but affirmative. "You know all the right things to say, don't you?" The human sat forward, leaning on her desk as she made intense eye contact with Harlow. "But do you know how to *do* the right thing? When it counts, are you going to be able to step aside and let the people who've always been vulnerable take the lead? Is Finn?"

"I—" Harlow was interrupted by the door to Piper's office opening. Harlow glanced back. Finn. He'd been listening on the other side of the door.

For the first time since he'd returned, his eyes were free of burden. Clear, unwavering purpose shone there. "When all of this is over—or as soon as I can get access to my accounts—I will sign over my personal fortune to the Fifth Order. If my parents are killed in the coming days, I will sign over everything they have to you as soon as I inherit. The Fifth Order will be funded by the greatest fortune on Okairos."

Piper's eyebrows raised slightly. "In return for what? A seat on the Council?"

Finn's face went smooth as a becalmed sea, his shoulder squaring. "In return for nothing."

The human shook her head. "Not even our trust?"

Finn crossed his arms, smirking. "I don't believe for one second I could buy your trust, Councillor. Not yours or any other human's. You asked if we would do what's right, didn't you?"

Piper nodded. Finn looked down at Harlow. "Do you agree with me—that this is what we should do? You won't be bonding with rich, powerful Finn McKay; you'll lose everything too."

Harlow stood, taking Finn's hand in her own. "I won't lose anything. Give it all away." She looked down at Piper, waiting for a response.

Though Piper's laugh was curt as she stood, Harlow swore she felt the human open up a little. "The two of you are still assholes, but this is a step in the right direction. I'll let the rest of the Council know."

Finn turned to go, leading Harlow out of the office. Once they were in the hallway, he paused, stepping back inside the door for a moment. "I do actually have a request."

Piper looked up from the piece of paper she was writing on. "What is it?"

"That we'll be allowed to live in safety when this is over. That you won't enact violent punishments for immortals who've wronged you."

Piper slammed her pen down hard, crossing her arms tightly over her chest. "We're not like the Illuminated, Finbar McKay. That was never even a consideration. Agreements about reparative justice will be made when things are settled."

He bowed his head. "And for that, I am grateful. Thank you."

Finn turned, blocking Harlow's view of Piper's office as he led her out of the building. They didn't speak the entire way home, but he held Harlow's hand so tightly she thought it might be crushed, and there was new determination in every line of his body. Whatever else had happened in that office, Finn had dramatically changed the course of the Fifth Order. If their efforts were successful, the world would finally transform.

CHAPTER 22

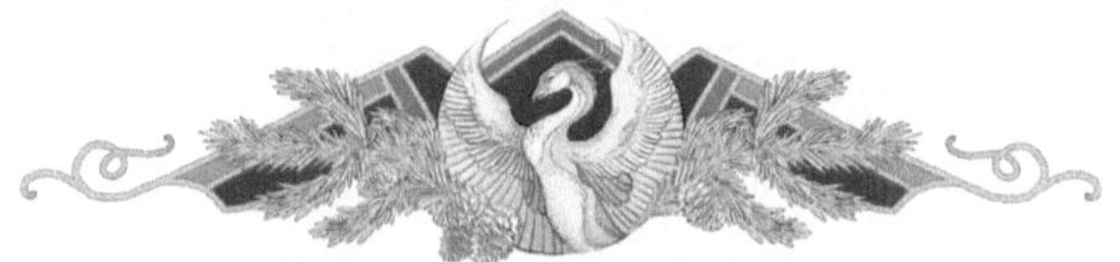

A whirlwind of activity took over their lives, leaving little time for Harlow to worry about the journey ahead. Their little group would teleport as close to ORAIS's location as they could, then make the rest of the journey on foot. As such, Harlow and Larkin began research on the Gate of Lithraea, and Lithraea's Way. They were lucky enough to have a whole host of Falcyran humans in the village to talk to, which Larkin loved.

It was odd to talk to elderly humans, who'd aged so much more than their parents, and yet were younger by hundreds of years than most of the people they knew. Taking the time to hear their stories was special, more than just research. For Harlow, it further shaped her new understanding of the ways simply being immortal had changed everything about her life. It wasn't that she'd never spent time with humans. She'd spent two years with human friends, Mark's friends. But they'd all been the same age as her, and some were even wealthier than her family.

These people were different, and while Harlow was careful not to treat them like means to an end, she understood that they were giving her so much more than an expanded understanding of archaic lore. The lore itself was disturbing though. Stories about Lithraea and her helpers, the vvyk, were varied. She was a trickster goddess, like Voltos, and her role in every story obscured her motives. The takeaway was that their route wouldn't be easy, but it was the fastest way to ORAIS.

Harlow and Finn barely had a moment alone together, let alone time to talk about what had happened in Piper's office. They fell into bed each night exhausted, both physically and emotionally. On their last day in Sanctum, Harlow rolled over in bed, tired upon waking, to find Finn already wide awake.

"What time is it?" she mumbled.

Finn illuminated the witchlights that hung over their bed with celestial fire, dim enough to be pleasant, not so bright as to be harsh. Neither of them seemed able to tolerate harsh lighting these days. Cian had been staying over in Vivia's extra room a lot, after talking late into the night. They were alone in the bedroom. "It's not even five."

"What's wrong?" Harlow asked, moving Axel from his position in the exact center of the bed so she could cuddle up to Finn.

His head fell back against the headboard. "Did I make the right choice? Giving up the money?"

Harlow rolled onto her back. "I think so. Why are you worried?"

He shook his head. "Not about the reality of living without it."

He didn't elaborate, but every muscle in his face and neck were taught, so she curled back into him, hoping to distract him from the storm of worry raging inside him. "Do you ever picture what our lives will be like when all this is over? When we get to start living again, I mean?"

Though Harlow couldn't see Finn's face, she felt his eyes on her. The pause was long—too long. She swallowed hard, fear pooling in her chest. There had been a subtle push and pull between them since he got back that she wasn't used to. They'd always bantered back and forth, disagreeing with one another, but this was different. Harlow struggled to figure out if it was natural, given the stress they were under, or if something was actually wrong.

"No," he said finally. "I don't."

His tone was flat, devoid of any emotion. Harlow recoiled, shame blooming through her, though she couldn't understand *why*. When she drummed up the courage to drag her eyes to his, there was an icy distance coursing through his entire demeanor that pushed her out of bed.

"Oh," she replied, not knowing what else to say. She was tempted to simply start her morning routine, to shut him out the way he was shutting her out. Her mind raced through a series of catastrophic thoughts, immobilizing her.

Finn wasn't looking at her anymore. He was staring at a spot on the wall, just behind her head, and to the untrained eye it would probably seem like he was looking right at her. He'd looked beyond her that way before. A long, long time ago—when they were just seventeen.

And when they'd been seventeen, she'd taken that very personally. After all, it had been directed *at her*. It made all the sense in the world for her to walk away as a teenager, to put her armor on, rather than risk getting even more vulnerable than she already felt. But as an adult—one who was trying to trust that he loved her—she had to risk it.

"What's going on?"

His gaze slid from the wall to meet her eyes. Something almost imperceptible shifted from that icy chill to a softer, fearfulness. His jaw twitched as he held eye contact with her, and he clutched the blankets so hard his knuckles turned white. "I'm having a hard time imagining that things will ever be okay again—that we'll make it out of this."

Why hadn't she just asked him what was going on before? Her fear of rejection was a powerful thing, and the more it was allowed to fester the more it grew. She'd taken his request for time to process too literally.

644

Harlow's attention snapped back to Finn as he buried his face in his hands, shoulders heaving. She scrambled onto the bed, straddling his lap, pulling him into her arms. His arms went around her as he wept against the thin sweater she'd worn to bed.

"Shit," he swore, clinging to her. "I promised myself I wouldn't make this your problem. I'm just so fucking scared that this will all end the way the War of the Orders did. That we'll end up like the last Feriant Legion did."

They'd been separated by the Illuminated. Tortured. Executed. And then the Striders had been exterminated. It was a legitimate fear, especially since they were about to leave the safety Sanctum had provided them. Once they left, the risk of the Dominavus finding them would increase exponentially.

She hugged him tighter, but he pushed her away, holding her at arms' length. "I get it. Why Rakul did what he did in the catacombs. Why he went to so much trouble to save Vivia."

For a moment, Harlow was confused about what this had to do with anything. But then she saw the steel in his eyes. The hard warrior's face she'd seen dozens of times over the summer. "I'd ruin the world for you. If this goes sideways—if they take you—*nothing* will stop me from getting you back."

The shake in his voice was gone now, ironclad conviction replacing it. *Finn McKay would burn worlds down to get to her.* She remembered thinking that months ago. Why she'd doubted it for even a second was beyond her.

"I wish I could be as good as you are, babygirl," he whispered, stroking a piece of hair away from her face, his fingers tracing her softly curved jawline as his eyes fell.

"Good as *me?*" Harlow said, pulling his chin up so his eyes met hers. "You're the one who's given up their fortune and power, for a group of people who don't have much respect for us—because it's the right thing to do. Some would demand that respect, or at least a show of it, in exchange for doing the right thing. I wish I was as good as *you*."

"I had to do it," he murmured. "The resources my parents amassed. No one should have that much while others suffer."

"No," she agreed. "They shouldn't. You *are* a good man."

Heat flared between them, Finn's skin warming against hers, emitting a faint glow. She was acutely aware that she'd only worn a slouchy sweater to bed—one that barely covered her ass—and nothing else. Finn noticed this at the same time she did, the heat intensifying between her legs. His soft pajama pants were thin, doing nothing to disguise the fact that his body had already responded to hers, his erection pressing hard against her.

Finn pulled her closer, his tone deepening as his fingers gripped her hips. "You make me want to be less ruthless than the men who came before me, but I'd throw all semblance of 'good' away if anyone took you from me."

As he spoke, his grip tightened, both their breathing quickening to short, shallow pants. Harlow's hips swiveled, leaning into his hard length, growing thicker by the second beneath the soft, wet core of her. She reached between her legs, yanking his pajama pants down to expose his cock.

She eased him into her now-dripping core, Finn groaning softly as he watched her work. His fingers wound into the hair at the base of her neck. "I will destroy anyone who takes you from me. Do you understand?"

Harlow froze. Fear lanced through her, unbidden and unwanted. She knew what he was trying to say, but someone had wanted to keep her too close before, and it had ended badly. She tried to banish thoughts of Mark, but it wasn't so easy.

His eyes met hers. Love warmed them to a glow. "Unless you *wanted* to go."

A little smile pulled at her lips. He understood. He understood how to make sure the parts of her mind that were trying to protect her didn't scramble his words, or make them into something they weren't, without her permission. They were back in sync, on solid ground.

Finn pulled her body against his, as he looked into her eyes. "I will never cage you, Harlow. You are always free to fly away. But I will *never* let anyone hurt you again."

A little moan unfurled from her lips. *Away?* There was nowhere she wanted to be but here. She pushed down on him, pulling him deeper into her, the movement smooth and torturously slow.

Harlow rolled her hips, taking him deeper and harder with each thrust. He pushed her sweater up, exposing her breasts to the frigid air in the bedroom. His hands slid to cup her breasts, his thumbs swirling around her pebbled nipples.

"Yes," she urged him on, her back arching as he captured one nipple in his mouth, sucking on it as he thrust harder into her, their bodies grinding together where they met in a slippery friction.

This was all she needed, this promise that he would never abandon her. There was no fortune waiting for them on the other side of this war, no castle awaiting their victorious return. If all they had was this, it was all she needed.

Finn's mouth left her breast, in what felt like utter betrayal. "Shhh," he whispered. "You don't want to wake Riley and Enzo, do you?"

She shook her head, and his hands slid to her ass and he pulled her off him, another cruel betrayal of her pleasure. He pulled her close, sliding his cock against her, teasing her as he whispered into the shell of her ear. "Turn around for me."

She did so immediately, turning onto all fours, then backing up into his lap, where he pulled her up so her back rested against his chest as he slowly entered her. He shifted at the same time, his cock growing longer and thicker as they moved. She rested her head against his shoulder, lifting her face to be kissed.

Finn's mouth captured hers as his hands roamed over her, one cupping her face as his tongue slid against hers, the other playing with her nipples. Despite facing away from him, the position made her feel exposed. There was nowhere for her to shy away from his hands that explored every roll and curve of her body.

To her surprise, this heightened the sensation of every touch. Her back arched at the thought of being completely vulnerable to Finn, letting him have her body and trust. Trust that he was here for good. That they would die together before living apart ever again.

His wings wrapped around them, trapping the wet heat they gave off. Finn broke their kiss, dragging his mouth along her jaw, then behind her ear, every breath stimulating the sensitive shell of her ear as the hand that had cupped her face wrapped gently around her neck, applying light pressure to her throat that elicited a primal sound from deep inside her.

This pleased him. "You feel so damn good." The hand that played with her nipples strayed lower, stroking her belly as his cock drove deeper inside her.

"*Fuck.*" His fingers gripped her soft flesh as he growled, "I need you."

Harlow whimpered with pleasure as the pressure of his hand on her curved stomach increased the pleasure of his cock inside her. She clenched hard around him, wanting *more*.

She brought her fingers between her legs. Within moments, her vision went blank, her body exploding in a rush of wet heat. The hand around her neck went over her mouth, his second hand pressing even harder on her belly, causing his cock to hit the spot inside her that sent her so far over the edge that her shadows flooded the cocoon of his wings.

As her orgasm seemed just about to peak, his fangs sunk into her neck, sending her into new heights of pleasure. The hand on her belly slid lower now, replacing her own on her clit as he moved his wrist into her mouth.

"I need you inside me," he whispered into her ear. His words were a plea, a deep need begging to be filled. Her fangs protracted and she sunk them into his wrist, pulling his blood into her mouth, the taste of it sweet and thick as it mixed with her venom.

"Yes," he hissed.

Golden light twined with her shadows as light bloomed behind her eyes. Everything clenched hard for a moment. She fell to all fours and he met her on her knees, thrusting hard into her as she came apart around him, burying her face in a pillow as she silently screamed. All was undone and remade as he came inside her, their magic twisting in time with their bodies—singing for the moment of pure grace their love wrought in the darkness.

Finn's body fell against hers, his arms tightening around her, even as he pulled out. She rotated in his arms, tangling her legs with his. They stayed like that for a while, dozing until Axel woke them, wanting breakfast. Finn went to feed him and turn on the water heater while Harlow packed the last of their clothes. They were traveling light.

Harlow dug in her dresser until she found *The Warden*, tucked underneath some sweaters she was giving back to the community. Finn's arms snaked around her waist after setting a steaming cup of coffee on the dresser for her.

"*The Warden*?" he asked.

"I think we should take it to ORAIS. If we can access the archive there, maybe we can learn more about it."

He kissed the top of her head. "It's a good idea. Bring it."

Harlow set the book on top of the rest of their clothes, only to find Axel snuggled between the scant piles of items they were bringing. The black cat looked up at her, purring loudly, blinking several times in slow succession at both Harlow and Finn.

"What are we going to do with him?" Harlow asked.

"You take a shower," Finn suggested. "I'll have it worked out by the time you're out, I promise."

Harlow started to protest, but he was already gone, the water already running. She kissed the top of the cat's head and took advantage of the last hot shower she could expect for a while.

~

WHEN HARLOW CAME DOWNSTAIRS, Petra was waiting in the living room. She hugged Harlow as soon as she entered the room. The past few days had been hard. Since they were the ones leaving first, they had to say goodbye to everyone they loved. Petra had been in talks about where she was going for nearly two straight days, and this was the first time Harlow had seen her.

As she had in each of her goodbyes, Harlow tried hard not to think about what might happen when the people she considered her family were separated. Instead, she clung to Petra, breathing her in. How she smelled expensive when she hadn't had access to perfume in months baffled Harlow, but maybe Petra was just made from different stuff than other people—perhaps her flesh was cut from couture. For some reason, that thought grew a lump in Harlow's throat.

They sat on the couch together. Finn excused himself to make tea. "Lou, Kate and I are going to Castel des Rêves," Petra explained. The little island nation was located south of Nea Sterlis and was considered wine country. "Lou's sire was from there, you know?"

Harlow hadn't known that, but it wasn't too surprising, given her experience with vineyards.

"Anyway, the Council wants to see if we can get the vampires there to align with us."

Castel des Rêves was largely populated by vampires and humans with a hands-off Illuminated governor, Nephele Ostralios. Unlike Falcyra, they'd lived together in near-perfect harmony for hundreds of years. Harlow had heard whispered rumors about Castel des Rêves, and the mythic levels of peaceful coexistence there, since coming to Sanctum. It made sense to see if they would help, but the Castel des Rêves vampires were notoriously avoidant regarding Illuminated politics, preferring to stay on their island, in peace.

"Have the Vespae made it to Castel des Rêves?" Harlow asked. If they had, it might be the only reason the vampires would help.

Petra shook her head. "Not yet, they got their wards up sooner than other nations, and they've held. We know it's a long shot, but the Council thinks it's worth it to ask before we decide when to make our next move. I've been friends with Nephele for years. She hates the Illuminated—it's why she vied for the position. I think I can convince her and the other Ventyr there to help us, even if the vampires won't."

"Makes sense. When do you go?"

"This afternoon, in an hour, actually… How do you feel about Audata?"

It was a strange question. Harlow wasn't sure why Petra asked. "I love her. Why?"

Pink flushed in Petra's cheeks. "She's coming with us too. I just wondered if you liked her."

Harlow narrowed her eyes. "Why? Do *you* like her?"

Petra fingers fluttered. She clasped them together. "I… I mean. Of course. She's so smart… And pretty."

Harlow giggled. "Being pretty is a real asset in a dangerous mission."

Petra sighed. "I've never been in a position like this before."

"What does Kate say?"

The flush in Petra's cheeks deepened. "She likes her too."

Harlow smiled, but something pulled on her heart. "Be careful, Petra. Audata is a sensitive person, and she hasn't found her Claimed yet."

Petra nodded. "I take that really seriously, and Kate and I have discussed it. We're not trying to force anything. Promise."

"Okay," Harlow said. "Well, for what it's worth, I love her."

Petra let out a giddy breath. "Thank you. One last thing, can I take Axel with me? He'll be safe in Castel des Rêves."

Relief washed over Harlow. "You have somewhere to stay where he'll be welcome?"

Petra nodded. As though summoned, Axel jumped onto Petra's lap. He stood, rubbing his face against hers, then flopped down to take a bath. The cat loved Petra more than just about anyone other than Larkin, Finn, and Harlow, primarily because she loved him so much in return. If Larkin couldn't take him, then this was the perfect solution.

"Thank you," Harlow whispered. Petra glanced at her watch. "You have to go now, don't you?"

"Yes," Petra said, her chin wobbling.

"Don't," Harlow whispered. "If you cry, I will too."

Petra blinked hard a few times, averting her eyes. "We'll be together again soon," she murmured.

"We will," Harlow promised.

Finn came in, holding Axel's backpack. He picked the black cat up and held him close, kissing his head before handing him to Harlow. Her throat closed, watching him turn away, his shoulders shaking with tears. She knew he wasn't ashamed, but was trying not to set her off.

"I love you, buddy," she whispered, big teardrops splashing on his fur. He purred, nuzzling her. "You'll be safe with Petra, and I'll see you again soon."

Something in the threads between them crackled. She'd never thought to make a connection like this with the cat before. For the briefest moment, she thought she heard a voice in her head, the same as she had with Morgaine's cat, Bayun.

We'll be together again soon.

Harlow stared at Axel, wondering, her heart beating fast, but the crackle disappeared, and no more words came through in her head. He jumped into his backpack with not even a peep of resistance.

"See you soon," she said, hugging Petra one more time.

"Love you both," Petra said as she squeezed Finn's hands one last time.

After they left, Harlow sat on the couch, trying not to think about the way her chest felt hollow, as though someone had scooped her out like a squash for roasting. Enzo and Riley would be home soon, and she needed to pack, but every part of her ached.

"Why don't you go over to the maters?" Finn said, interrupting her angst-fueled reverie. "Send Larkin over here with her stuff, and Ari and I'll finish the packing. We can have a late dinner with Enzo and Riley. I invited Sam and Tomy too, so you don't have to try to catch them."

Harlow nodded, grateful for his foresight. But he'd done this type of thing before, sent people he loved on missions they might not come back from, parted ways with the ones he cared for too many times.

"Thank you," she said, as she dressed for the cold. "I'll be back."

THE WALK across the village was a blur of people stopping her to hug and say goodbye. Harlow was surprised by how many people were genuinely sad to see her go. After years of being practically shunned by the sorcières in Nuva Troi, as well as this summer in Nea Sterlis, this was a different feeling. She was a little overwhelmed by the time she got to the maters, and found they were all out back in the garden, a little bonfire going in their firepit.

Aurelia met her at the garden gate. "Hello, love, we were about to send Larkin to get you and Finn. Join us by the bonfire?"

It was a little cold for a bonfire, but it sounded festive, and Aurelia was holding a fuzzy blanket. Harlow smiled. "I'd love to."

Aurelia stepped aside, revealing that the backyard was full of Finn and Harlow's family and friends. "Surprise," Aurelia said softly.

Fingers closed around hers, and Harlow leaned into Finn's steady bulk as he whispered in her ear. "I thought you needed at least half a day with your people."

"What about the packing?"

Finn's arms went around her waist, pulling her tightly against him. "It's handled, nothing to worry about but enjoying yourself." He pushed her towards the little crowd of people, then sped past her to hug Cian and Vivia both.

The next few hours were a pleasant haze of hugging and chatting. She argued with Thea and Alaric about baby names, and listened to Riley and Enzo tell stories about their adventures in domesticity, all with the satisfaction of knowing that the people she loved were cared for. She had no idea what the future held, if all of them would make it through this safely, but knowing they loved one another this deeply helped ease that anxiety.

A sinking sadness crept over her as she thought about the twins and Nox. As if by instinct, Ari was at her side. The shifter loomed over her, his jet-black hair falling into his eyes. "Nox gave this to me, to give to you. I shared one with your parents, as well as Thea and Larkin."

He passed her a nearly paper-thin tablet, which she switched on with a swipe up. There was only one file icon on the home screen. She tapped it and a video filled the screen, showing Indigo, Meline, and Nox. The three of them smiled and waved. They looked phenomenal, happy. Nox's sweet face brightened as she kissed Indi's cheek and then popped out of frame, leaving just the twins.

Indi's dark hair was cut short, just below her chin, in a sleek bob, and Meline's honey-blonde hair was thrown into her signature messy bun. Both wore eyeglasses, though Meline's were more classically "fashion," while Indi's were heavy black, horn-rimmed frames. They didn't look alike anymore, but in all the ways that counted, they were exactly the same as they'd ever been.

"Hi sissy," Meli said. "We can't say much…"

"Except that we love you," Indi finished.

"And that we're doing okay," Meline continued.

Indigo leaned on Meline, and there were tears in both her sisters' eyes as Indi said, "We'll be together again before you know it."

Meli looked about to burst into tears, but she smiled, nodding furiously. The video ended, and Harlow's heart had the feeling of a nearly-healed bruise being knocked about. The video was meant to make her feel better, but it didn't. Until everyone was safe, nothing would be better.

Sam and Tomyris walked in, just in time to distract her from spiraling into worry. "We just came off patrol," Sam said, after brushing a kiss to Harlow's cheek.

"But we wanted to stop by, before we head to Samira's aunties' gathering," Tomyris explained.

Sam and Tomyris both had far more experience with this kind of thing than she did. Tomyris' parents were in Castel des Rêves, and while some of Sam's family was here, a lot were gone, though Harlow didn't know where, as the Strider was extremely private about her family.

The Ventyr's eyes narrowed, assessing Harlow. "Are you doing okay?"

Harlow nodded.

"Good," Sam said. "We can do this. We'll see each other again soon."

All over the village, Harlow assumed similar gatherings were taking place.

She surprised herself by wondering where Piper was—whether the human had family to go to, or friends. A part of her resented the woman, but mostly, she regretted not knowing more about her, or a way to make things right between them. They'd have time enough for that, she supposed. She rejoined the party, wearing herself out on all the love she could take in.

When most everyone had gone home, or inside to use their two hours of generator power for the evening to watch an old movie, Harlow joined the maters and Thea by the fire. Inside the house, Larkin was talking animatedly, moving her hands as she explained something to Ari, who laughed with his whole body.

Thea hugged her from behind; her baby bump was just starting to appear. The bruised feeling in Harlow's heart intensified. She had no idea how long it would be before she saw Thea again. Their mission to ORAIS was open-ended; everything about where they went after depended on what they found. Harlow hated the uncertainty, but they might be gone for days, or even months.

"Let's just be us for the rest of the night," Thea murmured, pulling Harlow towards the circle of chairs around the fire.

Harlow sunk into a chair, her entire body going limp as Selene tucked a blanket around her knees. She fetched Harlow a mug of hot chocolate from the thermos by her own chair, and then sat back down. Thea and Aurelia chatted casually for a while about a novel they'd both been reading, a literary retelling of an old faery story.

"Is that the one about the courts in the labyrinth?" Selene asked.

Aurelia nodded. "Yes, it's a brilliant retelling. The labyrinth and the challenges are a symbol for the main character's inner turmoil."

Harlow smiled at Thea, both of them listening to their parents debate about whether or not it was effective to use folkloric elements as symbols. If Harlow closed her eyes, she could imagine she was back in the Monas, shelving books while Selene and Aurelia debated the merit of literary tropes. She could practically smell the books. Her ache for home filled her the longer Selene and Aurelia talked.

The story itself wasn't one Harlow remembered well, but it was about a character she did, Rhiannon, a warrior-queen of the faery, whose companions could shift into birds. She smiled, wondering if she'd liked stories about Rhiannon so much as a child because of who she was.

"Do you think stories about Rhiannon are actually about Striders?" Harlow interrupted, though she kept her voice low. Thea had dozed off in her chair, her hands resting on her bump.

Aurelia sipped her hot chocolate, smiling first at Thea, then at Selene. "You thought the same once, didn't you, love?"

Selene nodded. "Yes, because of my grandmother, I wondered if stories about Rhiannon were actually ways to talk about the Feriant. I researched the issue thoroughly in my youth—to my family's great surprise."

Selene and Aurelia rarely talked about their families. Unlike most sorcière families, whose many generations were alive and well, theirs had both fallen prey to many tragedies, and as a result, the Kranes had grown up without grandparents, aunties, uncles or cousins. Harlow had always thought that was why Selene and Aurelia wanted so many children, to make up for the tragic loss of both their families.

"Why was it a surprise to your family?" Harlow asked, her curiosity piqued.

Aurelia grinned. "Because your mother was near constant trouble until she met me."

Selene grinned back, a wicked glint in her eye. "And then I got into an entirely different kind of trouble."

Harlow made a silent gagging motion, enjoying feeling like a child for the moment. Adult concerns were looming. For the rest of tonight, she wanted to pretend. "Please move on. What did you find out about Rhiannon?"

Selene reached out and took Aurelia's hand, pressing a kiss to her wife's palm. Harlow was fairly sure she saw her use tongue and rolled her eyes. When Selene tucked Aurelia's hand back into her jacket pocket, Harlow's heart warmed. They always took care of one another.

"That the origin of the Rhiannon stories predated the Immortal Orders entirely. They were human folklore long before the Illuminated arrived. The Books of the Fey were all derived from ancient human lore. The story of the courts and the labyrinth is one of the oldest."

"I've never read it," Harlow said, hoping Selene would tell it to her. She had a wonderful memory for stories, and as children she'd often told tales from memory before bed.

But Selene merely shrugged. "It's been a while since I read it. You girls loved the Violet book best when you were little, and I think it was in the Red. What's it about, love?"

Aurelia sighed. "The idea that the faery courts gather each century for a battle of wits and prowess in a giant labyrinth. Rhiannon is the hero, of course."

"Why?" Harlow asked. When Aurelia raised her brows, she clarified, "Why did they have 'a battle for wits and prowess' in a big maze? What was the point?"

It was Aurelia's turn to shrug. "Honor, I believe. Most of the stories about Rhiannon are about her proving her honor, aren't they?"

Selene launched into a lecture about how Aurelia was confusing Rhiannon with stories of Aphora's consort Pallas, and that they were similar characters in mythological tales, but not the same. Harlow closed her eyes, drifting off to the lovely sound of her parents debating and flames crackling in the background. When Finn came to carry her home, she faintly heard Aurelia say, "Take good care of our girl, Finbar. I believe the past year has worn her out entirely."

"With my last breath," Finn promised. Vaguely, Harlow thought he sounded like one of the chevaliers from faery stories before drifting off to sleep in his arms.

CHAPTER 23

The next day, Harlow and Finn said one last round of goodbyes. They'd promised to keep things short, and the sun was just coming up when they met Ari at the Lodge, where he'd been staying in guest quarters. Larkin was running a little late, as usual. The three of them were dressed for extremely cold weather with a compact pack strapped to their back. As a part of their gear, each person had a light block of adamantine for Harlow to form into skis, crampons, or snowshoes as the situation called for.

They would make three carefully plotted teleports before reaching Gale Alley, where they would have to hike the rest of the way to ORAIS. The route to get there was treacherous at best, and Harlow had been doing her best not to think about it. As they waited for Larkin, Harlow noticed that she'd lost the scarf she'd tucked into the strap of her pack on the walk over. She'd been too hot after her shower and hadn't needed it, but she certainly would in a little while.

She looked around and didn't see it. "Hey," she said softly to Finn, who was going over charts with Ari one last time. "I dropped my scarf on the way over. I'm going to track back and look for it."

He nodded. Ari was asleep on the couch next to him, snoring lightly, his feet in Finn's lap. Finn looked as though he might drop into a nap as well. Harlow left them to it with a small smile. She was glad it would be just them—just family—on this trip.

The village was bustling with activity and Harlow wound through the streets until she spotted her scarf, just outside one of the popular bakeries, stuck to a snow-covered bush. She grabbed it, wishing she had time to wait in the long line forming outside for something else to eat.

As she turned back towards the Lodge, someone stepped out of line to greet her. She smiled at Jareth Sanvier as he fell into stride next to her. "You'll lose your place in line."

He grinned. "Maurice has a special spot in his heart for me."

Maurice was the lead baker, and Harlow imagined he *did* have a special spot in his heart for Jareth. She'd seen the two of them making eyes at one another. Again, she smiled, wishing a little that Jareth, with all his charm, was coming along with them. He would have made a good addition to the team.

"Hey," Jareth's tone was hesitant, as he paused in the street. "I should have explained my motives better. I'm sorry."

Harlow frowned. "What do you mean?"

Jareth sighed. "I'm not always very good at explaining myself and I wish I'd tried a little harder to get Finn to like me."

Harlow was completely confused. She stopped in the street, just outside the Lodge. "Finn likes you just fine."

Now Jareth frowned in confusion. "Then why doesn't he want me to come on this mission?"

Harlow's heart skipped a beat. "He did. We requested that you come with us."

Jareth stepped back, his mouth opening and closing, before he glanced at the Lodge, and then around for anyone in their proximity. Harlow did the same. People were filling the square as the village's day got started. With so many people leaving, it was busy. Anyone might hear them. Jareth shook his head once, and Harlow understood. They were likely being watched.

He gripped her arm, pressing gently, but firmly. His voice lowered to an almost inaudible decibel, his lips barely moving. "Something's off with the Council."

Jareth really was far, far too charming to be trusted. Harlow wasn't sure what to say, or how to say it, so she kept it simple. "What?"

"The Education Councillor, in particular. Something's off about her."

Harlow's heart stilled. Since meeting the woman, she'd thought the same thing. Something was *strange* about her. Harlow pulled Jareth into an archway that led to the Lodge gardens. The little tunnel was likely lovely in the summer, covered as it was in thorny wild roses. They would be somewhat hidden here. She did her best with a muffling spell, though they were not her specialty and her shadows begged to be let out. But if someone saw them, they'd know she was doing magic, and she didn't want to draw attention.

"We still have to be very quiet," she whispered when the threads finally snapped into place for her spell. "I'm not very good at working magic this way."

Jareth nodded. "I overheard my superior officer talking to one of the other Council members a few days ago. The human that helped Finn and Larkin make it through the limen, Morgaine Yarlo, did you know her?"

A lump rose in Harlow's throat at the thought of the human, and losing Finn and Larkin in Nea Sterlis. "Yes."

"When she was with the Council, apparently she brought up some of the signs of someone being possessed by a Ravager."

Every muscle in Harlow's body stilled, her lungs stopped moving, and it felt as though her head might be crushed with the weight of her fear.

"It starts with them acting erratic, out of character and even forgetting things, then moves on to hallucinations and paranoia. Apparently, Morgaine actually talked to the one on her world a few times—and get this—the Ravagers choose someone in power to inhabit."

He raised his eyebrows, and Harlow had to admit that the theory sort of fit. Piper did have an odd amount of power for being the Education Councillor.

"What happens after the hallucinations and paranoia?"

Jareth lowered his voice even further. "I only caught part of what was said. Something about the Ravager *ascending*."

Harlow was certain she didn't want to know what that meant. "That doesn't sound good."

"It really doesn't."

Harlow took a deep breath. "But it also doesn't mean that Piper is the Ravager's host."

Jareth sighed. "I just keep thinking that it doesn't make sense. There's something really off about her."

There *had* been times when Piper had behaved erratically, like the way she was ignorant of the bestselling Wesley Arden series in her office. No one hadn't heard of those books—they'd been made into shows, movies, everything. Literally millions of people had read them. For a moment, Harlow let her imagination run away with her. *Could* the human be the host for the elemental? And if she was possessed, did that mean that the real Piper didn't hate her?

Rational thought crashed back in: they had no evidence, and Jareth's theory seemed far-fetched, even though Harlow was inclined to trust that what he said about Morgaine was true. What reason would he have to lie? Neither of them knew the human well enough to make such a claim against her. Harlow could just imagine how approaching the Council with an accusation that the Education Councillor had been possessed by an elemental being hellsbent on destroying the world would go. It would be a bloodbath, and she would be the loser.

Jareth was still speaking. "I don't have a lick of proof, Harlow. But I have a bad feeling about Piper Winslow. Why did she lie about me not coming with you to us both? I was told you didn't want me along."

Harlow let out a puff of air. This was a lot, right before they were supposed to leave. "We asked for you to come. She said your people denied us."

He shook his head, seeming to come down off the high of his own theory. "Listen, I don't want to jump to conclusions. It's just as likely that the Rogue Council doesn't want the Humanists allying too closely with the Knights. That's the most obvious answer."

It was. It was an incredibly logical answer. Her spell was wearing thin. If she put too much more energy into it, she'd be tired before teleporting and that wasn't ideal. She grabbed Jareth's hands. "Go to my sister Thea about this. Tell no one else. She'll know if any of this sounds like it might hold water."

"She'll tell Cian and Alaric," Jareth reasoned, looking concerned.

Harlow nodded as the muffling spell dissipated. "She will. And that's a *good* thing."

Jareth nodded as they walked in silence back towards the square, but Harlow couldn't help but notice that he seemed disappointed. It occurred to her that it was possible that Piper Winslow just didn't like Jareth, and that was probably something he wasn't used to. The woman had an irritating way about her, but she was also rightfully frustrated with immortals' incredible lack of self-awareness. Harlow wasn't foolish enough to dismiss the vampire's ideas outright, but this theory was far-fetched at best, and outright offensive to Piper in many ways.

There was a brief awkward moment, and then the vampire's arms were around her. He was a good hugger, and the feeling that wrapped around her heart reminded her of how she felt when she was with Enzo. Jareth could be a good friend. Maybe they'd get that chance someday.

"Be careful, Harlow," he said as he pulled away. "I want you to show me the sights of Antiquity Row when all this is over."

The muscles in her throat tensed. "It's a date."

They walked away from each other, Harlow's mind scrambling to put the pieces of all Jareth had said together, and in truth, she didn't come up with much that made her believe he was right. It did worry her that she didn't have the time to follow up on this, but Thea could more than handle it. Harlow smiled to herself as she entered the Lodge; the mystery of it all would give Thea something to distract her from the worry that she was being treated like an incubator.

Larkin had arrived while she was fetching her scarf. Likely, it was better to talk about what Jareth had said after they'd made the necessary jumps for the day. She didn't want any of them distracted.

"So, who's jumping with who?" Ari asked as Harlow joined the group.

"Larkin and I are together. Ari, you're with Finn." Harlow explained.

Finn tapped the map open on the coffee table. They'd all seen it dozens of times now, but it was a good reminder to help them get the location fixed in their minds. "We'll jump to this location first—it's a Humanist safehouse about thirty miles north of here. Then we'll break, patrol, and make our next jump."

Larkin's face scrunched together. "I still wish we could do it all at once."

Ari shook his head. "I know. But it's safer to do it in three parts so no one gets overly tired."

Larkin hugged Ari's arm. It was sweet how close they were. "I know, buddy. I'm just scared."

The big shifter shot her a serious look. "Me too. We can do this though."

Harlow took a deep breath, trying to banish all worries about being immediately tracked by the Vespae, or worse, the Dominavus.

They geared up. Finn checked all their packs, making sure they were safely closed and that they'd brought all they needed to. He examined Harlow's last, pressing a kiss to her lips. "See you at the safehouse."

She nodded, then turned to Larkin. "You're good?"

Her sister nodded. "I am. I got lots of practice teleporting with Vivia. I'm good at it. *Promise.*"

Harlow knew her sister was good. Vivia had spent hours in the last few days going over what Larkin was capable of after their travels together, and the list of what Vivia had to teach was impressive. She wished she'd gotten to spend more time with the firedrake.

Finn pulled Harlow aside to adjust the adamantine block on her pack again. It wasn't necessary, they both knew that, but he clearly needed an extra moment with her. "You remember the alternate for jump two if anything goes wrong?"

Harlow nodded, knowing she wasn't supposed to say it. There were protocols around this kind of thing, even here, among people they assumed were friends. The Knights took even more precautions than the Feriant Legion did. All three jumps had alternate locations that had never been spoken about aloud.

Finn and Ari threw their arms around one another in a dramatic hug, laughing, and Harlow took Larkin's hands. There was no going back now. She was terrified to take her little sister out into the unknown, but this was what she wanted. Harlow had to try to trust that it would be okay. A little tug on her shadows indicated that Larkin's magic was merging with hers, making their power to teleport stronger.

When it hit a crescendo, Larkin nodded to Finn, who murmured, "Now."

They jumped. The teleportation process always took a beat longer with someone in tow, and even with Larkin helping, the drag was longer than Harlow had ever experienced. They tumbled out of the between-space involved in teleportation. Harlow was nauseous, but she didn't throw up.

An acrid scent filled her nose as her blurred vision clarified. The safehouse was on fire. Part of Finn's plan had been to be open about the first jump, and slightly more secretive about the second two, while keeping the alternates completely locked down. While they'd anticipated there was a possibility they'd be followed when they left, no one had thought *this* was possible.

Someone had eliminated their first resting spot. Immediately, Harlow thought of Piper Winslow and Jareth's accusations. The Education Councillor was one of the few people who'd known they would stop here. Harlow hadn't put much stock in what Jareth had said before, but now... Finn shouted, breaking her train of thought. "Alternate two. *Now.*"

Harlow swiveled, checking that Larkin was all right. Her younger sister's eyes were wide with fear. She'd been terrified of fire since the night of the Solstice Gala, when Finn and Harlow's home had been burned to the ground.

"You okay?" Harlow shouted, stepping towards Larkin.

Larkin didn't answer. She'd frozen, staring at the fire. They didn't have time for this. Finn grabbed Larkin and sandwiched her between himself and Ari. Ari held her sister tight, pressing his cheek to hers for closer contact, nodding once to Harlow as they blinked out.

He was making sure she had enough power to get to the alternate location, farther away. Harlow tried to jump, but her magic sputtered, not connecting her to the between—movement distracted her. She couldn't catch sight of whatever was lurking, but it was moving fast, towards her.

It was now or never. Harlow jumped smoothly to the second alternate location, then fell to her knees on a black sand beach, her entire body retching as it tried to expel the stress of the teleportation. Larkin sat next to her, shaking and pale, but in one piece.

Columns of rock protruded from the angry gray ocean, taking a beating from the enormous waves. The scent of salt air hit her face, combining with something metallic and wet. Finn pulled Ari and Larkin back, further ashore. He shouted something, but Harlow couldn't hear what he said over the sound of the crashing waves. Finn appeared before her, panic in his eyes as he grabbed her.

They blinked out, appearing further up the beach, away from the dark water, just in time to see the biggest wave she'd ever seen crashing onto the exact spot Harlow had been standing moments before. Everyone watched as the waves compounded onto one another, getting closer and closer with each increase in size. Harlow had never seen the sea look so sinister, not even in Nea Sterlis' hurricane season, or Nuva Troi's depressing winters. Something about the combination of the dark rocks and sand with the monster waves gave Harlow the impression of looming menace.

"We have to move further in," Ari shouted above the noise of the water. "A storm is brewing at sea. This beach won't be safe for long."

Larkin raised her voice. "Why don't we go to our next location?"

Harlow glanced at Finn, who shook his head. "We can't," she yelled back. "Everyone has to rest first."

There was fear in Larkin's eyes, but she nodded, rather than arguing further. They started picking through the steep rocky shoreline, climbing ever higher. It was a touch warmer here than it had been inland, but not by much. The Apennine Mountain range ended here at this shore, and its jagged peaks crested above them, casting long shadows onto the cold beach.

Finn took last in line, making sure that no one fell behind, while Ari tracked a path through the treacherous rocks. Everything was coated in ice. Harlow winced every time her feet almost slipped. The wind whipped through them, feeling as though it lashed every inch of exposed skin.

Every second in this environment was painful, which was why Finn chose it. Everyone knew this location was one of the most dangerous in Falcyra—unpredictable waves, avalanche-prone mountains, and predatory shades that were only found in the darkest of regions. When evening came, they would have to be careful not to step beyond the light of their fire.

It wasn't an ideal place to rest, but if they were going to make the last jump to Lithraea's Gate tomorrow, they would have to make it through the night.

CHAPTER 24

Ari found a tiny cave safely above the water. He and Finn both worked to gather wood for a fire, while Harlow tended to Larkin, who was still not saying much. When she had Larkin wrapped in her blanket, sipping water, Harlow crouched in front of her.

"Hey, pal. You okay?"

Larkin nodded, but her eyes were still wide with fear. "I shouldn't have come. I'm sorry. I'm the reason we can't jump again."

It was true, and it wasn't. Taking both Larkin and Ari had drained Finn too much to safely make another jump, but emphasizing that wouldn't be helpful. Besides, Larkin didn't need to hear any of that right now. She needed to think about why she was here, and if she wanted to stay. "Do you want to go back?"

Larkin's eyes met Harlow's. "To Sanctum?"

Harlow nodded. "I could take you back. You could go to Nuva Troi with the maters."

Larkin shook her head, then sighed. "Maybe you *should* take me back."

"Why do you want to be here so much?" Larkin hadn't ever really explained what this was all about to Harlow. She'd talked to Finn, but Harlow hadn't pressed him for answers, knowing her little sister had spoken to him in confidence.

Harlow kept hold of Larkin's hand as she snuggled closer to her, tucking herself into her sister's blanket cocoon. Ari and Finn both disappeared to find firewood.

"I wasn't sure why I felt like I needed to come at first," Larkin explained. "But I started having dreams about ORAIS shortly after I arrived in Sanctum."

"Why didn't you tell me?" Harlow asked.

Larkin leaned against Harlow, snuggling into the crook of her arm, like she had when she was small. "I didn't know that's what they were at first, until I

660

talked to Finn. And by the time I knew, you were so against the whole thing… I just…"

"Didn't feel like you could talk to me." Finn had tried to warn her that this was the environment she was creating, but she hadn't listened.

"I know you just want me to be safe. I also know I'm meant to be here. There's a room inside ORAIS that appears in all my dreams."

Harlow was about to ask Larkin to describe it to her, but Larkin started coughing. Harlow slipped out of the blanket's warmth to fetch her sister more water. Finn and Ari returned with wood. Soon, they had a small fire going. Finn sat down next to Harlow, while Ari brought a few energy bars out of his bag, unwrapping them and passing them out. They were terrible, but packed with calories, and Harlow felt better almost immediately.

"Who burned the safehouse?" Harlow finally asked, when the last of the sticky goo of the energy bar was rinsed from her teeth.

Finn shook his head. "There was no time to investigate."

"Something came at me when I was on my way out. It was moving fast."

Ari sipped his water thoughtfully. "Could have been one of the Dominavus, or another Illuminated."

"Or a vampire," Larkin added.

Finn nodded. "Or an incubus."

That was a possibility. Alain Easton would have the ability to move as quickly as one of the Illuminated or a vampire. And he was almost certainly still looking for them. And unfortunately those weren't the only options.

"Jareth Sanvier had a theory that Piper might be the Ravager's host."

Everyone looked up, as though startled. Harlow stared at the little fire, stretching her fingers toward it. "He heard his commander talking about the signs of a Ravager possession, and thought it fit. I didn't believe him, but she knew where we were going."

Finn's eyebrows raised so high he looked like one of those wrinkly face dogs for a brief second. "That's a big accusation." He glanced at Ari. "Arebos here got his hands on the same intel."

"It was all Nox," Ari said with a faint smile for his sister. "But yeah, we've seen it. Doesn't track with the Education Councillor though…"

As the Wraith trailed off, Finn picked up his train of thought. "Unless the Council just wants us dead. Nobody had to be possessed by an elemental for that to be the case."

Harlow's heart fluttered erratically. *Her family.*

Finn caught her expression and grabbed her hand. "I don't actually think it's them, babygirl."

Ari lay back on his pack. "Finn's right. More likely, it's the Dominavus or Easton. From a tactical standpoint, they have a vested interest in us and they'd wait until we separated from the larger group to pick us off. Too much risk with so many elite fighters at Sanctum, and I'm not convinced the Illuminated can even find the place. If I hadn't had the exact coordinates, I wouldn't have been able to."

Oddly, that did make Harlow feel better, awful as it was that there were so many possibilities for who might want to kill them.

"We have too many enemies," Larkin said, with a sad little laugh that didn't make it to her eyes.

Harlow hated the way the past months had changed her sweet little sister into someone who'd experienced more trauma in a few short months than anyone should in a lifetime. She shouldn't have to laugh shit like this off.

Finn grimaced at Larkin. "Everything really does just keep getting worse, doesn't it?"

Larkin laughed, wagging her eyebrows. "Like a psychological thriller. The twists and turns just keep coming."

"You'd better hope not," Ari said with a smirk. "You don't have 'final girl' chops."

Larkin gasped dramatically. "How dare you say that? I do. And that's for horror, I'm the heroine of a *thriller*, Arebos."

The two of them bantered back and forth as Finn scooted behind Harlow, pulling her body between his legs to wrap her in his warmth. The cave was small enough to hold some heat, and Harlow was grateful it wasn't the start to some awful tunnel that subterranean horrors could crawl out of at night. Ari and Larkin's discussion of horror films wasn't helping her frame of mind.

Still, the cave wasn't exactly cozy and Finn's body heat comforted her. "What will happen when night comes?"

Rekyvaar had been plastered all over socials for years as "the most dangerous beach in Falcyra." In some ways, it was iconic, as much for the deadly waves as the shades that haunted the black sand shores.

Larkin's voice was soft. "We'll die."

Harlow smacked her sister's leg. This was no time to joke. Larkin glanced at her, grimacing. "I'm not kidding. Shades kill people here every year. We don't have enough wood to keep a fire going. We *could* die here."

Ari shifted uncomfortably, making eye contact with Finn. "She's right, man. This wasn't ever supposed to be an overnight stop, and there's no more wood out there unless we head toward the forest…"

"Which we're not doing," Finn replied.

The forest at the base of the mountains was the source of the aberrant shades. It was nowhere any breathing creature should be past sunset.

Finn checked his watch. "We have six hours 'til sunset. Ari, can you keep watch? The three of us need to sleep if we're going to make the jump to the next spot before dark."

Ari stretched his legs. "I've got this."

Finn nodded once, then lay down, pulling Harlow into the crook of his arm. Behind her, Larkin snuggled up so they were back to back.

"Wake us in five hours, all right?" Finn said.

Harlow didn't even hear Ari's answer—sleep took her immediately.

∼

HARLOW WOKE TO PITCH-DARKNESS, but for the dying embers of the fire. She sat straight up. Finn was next to her, fast asleep, as was Larkin. Night had fallen and outside the moons had risen, sending silver light through the mouth of the cave.

Where was Ari?

The air was cold and still; all was silent. She shook Finn's shoulder, but he didn't wake. She knew better than to make noise. That would only draw shades. She shook Finn again, harder this time, but he still didn't wake. She tried Larkin, who didn't wake either.

Whatever was happening, it wasn't natural sleep. Finn was one of the lightest sleepers she knew. Harlow didn't want to leave Finn and Larkin, but Ari was nowhere to be seen. She crept silently to the front of the cave and found him slumped just outside the mouth, his head sticky with blood. Someone had hit him. He was breathing, and when she felt for his heartbeat, it was strong.

She shook him gently, and his eyes fluttered open. He winced when he saw her. Harlow pressed her finger to his lips. He saw the moons, and Harlow read the panic in his face. They were supposed to be long gone by now.

His eyes were unfocused and drooping, so she dragged him back towards Finn and the others. Ari squeezed her hand hard, shaking his head. He didn't know what had happened. Then he went deadly still, staring at something behind her.

Harlow felt the shade first: she was already cold, but it felt as though someone dragged an icicle down her spine. She turned to the front of the cave, slowly, pushing Ari behind her. He was injured and she was not.

Shades weren't like ghasts, or even poltergeists, both of which could affect the corporeal world only in small ways. Instead, shades were violent, predatory spirits, prone to killing people. This one was tall and shrouded in darkness, but it had been a sorcière in life. Its eyes glowed with telltale dark aethereal light.

Harlow wasn't sure what she was going to do, but she was the only one capable of protecting the group, so she'd do whatever it took. It was strange that it hadn't killed them already, though. From everything she knew about shades, they killed quickly, feeding on the life force of their victims. She summoned her shadows and stepped forward. When she opened her mouth to ask what it wanted, futile though that might be, she found she couldn't speak.

The shade sent inky, aethereal power flowing into her mouth, silencing her. This was another danger with Shades—they could siphon magic—and this one was using hers.

Silence, the shade cautioned inside her head. *You are being hunted.*

Harlow couldn't believe the shade could communicate with her. She took another step forward, trying to make out its features. At first, she thought it wore a cloak of feathers, but now that she was closer, she practically gasped. The "cloak" was the shade's wings. It had dark, feathered wings that sprung from its back. And they looked familiar, like her own wings in her Feriant form.

A shade's manifestation could be odd; they didn't always appear as they did in life. Sometimes they morphed into strange hybrid creatures, like this one had done.

Were you like me in life? she tried asking it. *A Strider?*

No, child, the shade answered, its eyes glowing with that aethereal light once more. *I was a Feriant.*

Rakul and Vivia's child Inasa had been, as Cian said, "pure shadow, a creature of the limen." If this shade were Inasa's spirit, it might explain why it was helping them. *Inasa Kimaris? Were you Inasa in life?*

Inside her head, Harlow heard laughter. *No, I told you, I am a Feriant. Inasa Kimaris was a witch. Sleep now. I'll keep watch.*

The shade's logic made no sense. The Feriant was a Strider's alternae, a side effect of Striders being a combination of sorcière, Illuminated and draconic heritage, through Vivia, Rakul, and their many progeny. A Feriant was a part of a witch, not something independent. The shade waved a hand, and Harlow stumbled into Ari, who helped her to the ground. Sleep took over almost instantly. Harlow tried her best to fight it, but could not keep her eyes open.

CHAPTER 25

"... **I**t seemed like the shade was *speaking* to her, and we both fell back asleep."

Harlow opened her eyes slowly. Ari and Finn were huddled together by the fire, whispering. She sat up. "Where's Larkin?"

Finn held out a hand to her, pulling her into a seated position. "Doing her business. Right outside the cave." He grimaced, letting her know that he could hear Larkin perfectly well. "Ari says a shade got to us last night. What happened?"

Harlow didn't know. That was the problem. "It was the spirit of a Feriant, or at least that's what it said." She looked to Ari for confirmation.

The Wraith shook his head. "I didn't hear a word it said. I could barely make out its shape."

Larkin stepped into the mouth of the cave. It was obvious she'd been listening, but she didn't comment as she sat down next to Harlow.

"The shade was the spirit of a Feriant," Harlow repeated. "But it didn't appear as any of the Striders I've ever met. It had wings, but retained humanoid attributes..."

"Like the Ventyr?" Larkin asked.

Harlow ran a hand over one of her braids, and finding it messy, began the work of unraveling it as she spoke. "Sort of, except it had bird wings."

"And you're sure it was a shade?" Finn asked.

Ari nodded vigorously. "Yes, the creature had all the hallmarks of a shade. It was able to use magic, appeared to be intact, unlike ghasts, and it was capable of complex thought and speech."

"It wasn't violent or angry though..." Larkin's words came out somewhere between a statement and a question, as she rummaged through her pack for breakfast. "But of course, shades don't actually have to be violent or angry."

She found the energy bars she'd been searching for and handed them out.

"It's just that they usually are. They have to have a strong motivation for being here, and things like anger and revenge are the typical motivators."

"Then what was this Strider's motivation?" Finn asked.

Harlow cleared her throat, needing to clarify. "Actually, the shade was very specific that it wasn't a Strider. It said it wasn't a witch."

Larkin's eyes widened. "Was it Inasa Kimaris?"

Harlow shook her head. "It said it wasn't. It also said we were being hunted, and then put me back to sleep."

Finn and Ari exchanged a look. Harlow glared pointedly at them until Finn spoke. "There's evidence of that outside. Footprints. They circle around the entire area, then head south. But they never came close to the cave."

Harlow's skin prickled and her hands felt clammy. Nausea rose in her throat. She handed her energy bar back to Larkin. "I think I'm going to skip breakfast, until after we've teleported."

Larkin nodded solemnly. "Makes sense."

Harlow stood, needing to stretch her legs. "Are we sticking with the plan and making three jumps?"

Finn shook his head. "Seems pointless now. We know we're being tracked. We might as well get on with things."

"So, straight to the Gate of Lithraea?" Larkin asked.

Ari scrunched his face at the sound of the name. "Seventeen hells, is that what it's called?"

Harlow nodded as she repacked her blanket. "Yes, the Gate's name is an old human word."

Now Ari was curious, which wasn't a surprise. Ari was always curious. "For what?"

Harlow looked up. "Not what. *Who.* Lithraea was a human goddess of death and poison, in this part of the world." She glanced at Finn. "Before the Ventyr came." Finn looked as though he might apologize, but Harlow kept speaking. "The Gate was built by an ancient human society as an entrance to the 'rocks of Lithraea,' which are a deep canyon that was once the bottom of an ocean. The cult of Lithraea believed the ritual of traveling through them was a rite of passage."

"I've never heard of Lithraea," Ari murmured. Shifters were notoriously more religious than other immortals, and Ari was obviously disturbed there were deities he hadn't heard of.

"Then you haven't heard of her nasty little servants, the vvyk," Harlow added. She and Finn had talked about their path once, and only once, because while it was technically safe, it would not be pleasant. "They're said to put travelers through an existential crisis. It's what made getting through the Gate a ritual."

Ari's glared at Finn. "That's what you were talking about? When you mentioned the possibility of hallucinations?" Finn nodded as Ari's mouth fell open. Harlow saw it coming—the adventure junkie in Ari had taken over. The shifter loved a challenge. "How have I never heard of this place?"

Larkin glanced at him, then shot an apologetic look to Finn. "You wouldn't have. It's all human lore. The Illuminated would have most people believe humans were without culture before their arrival."

Finn shrugged. "Hopefully, that's all going to change when the Fifth Order can get Connor and Pasiphae to sit down and talk."

"Does anyone really think that's gonna work?" Ari asked.

"Don't start this again," Finn cautioned. "I can't today, Arebos."

The Wraith nodded, but Harlow sensed this was a sore subject between them. Finn tended to believe his father was more inclined towards peaceful resolutions than almost anyone else. Harlow didn't argue with him over it. "We should go."

"I'm going to pee real quick," Ari said.

How Harlow had missed her body screaming to relieve herself, she didn't know, but she did actually have to go. "Me too," Harlow and Larkin said in unison.

"You just went," Harlow chided, pushing Larkin toward the cave's opening.

"I have to go again," Larkin whined, sounding like she was ten.

Finn made an "ick" face when they all walked out together. It wasn't as though they were watching each other, but it felt safer to go together now that they'd confirmed that someone had tracked them to this location. When Harlow was finished, she waited for Larkin. The sound of the waves on the shoreline below filled Harlow's ears. The wind was so cold all of her appendages had gone numb.

She only heard Larkin's footsteps when she was nearly upon her, which signaled to her just how careful they needed to be. Harlow looked around, carefully feeling through the threads for any signs of disturbance. It wasn't her talent to track aethereal power that way, but Sam had given her a few hints. She found Ari easily, but only their connection, not how near or far he might be. Trying to find anyone who might be watching them, or worse, hunting them, would likely be impossible at this juncture. She tucked her arm in Larkin's as they waited for Ari.

When he rounded the corner he'd disappeared behind, there was an intense look in his eyes Harlow could not identify. As he approached, his voice was low. "Laugh at what I'm saying and continue moving back towards the cave. We're being watched."

Larkin laughed, and Harlow thought she looked completely natural. Harlow did her best to smile, but thoughts of the burning safehouse invaded her ability to pretend. Whoever, or whatever, was following them had certainly tracked them now that they'd all left the cave. They were in danger now, perhaps more than they'd been overnight, with the shade's unlikely protection.

When they returned to the cave, Ari whispered what he'd tracked to Finn, who nodded. They huddled close to him, listening carefully as he explained the jump they'd have to make to get to the Gates of Lithraea at the same time.

"We'll be tracked," he explained. "I don't see how we can get around that."

Larkin's face pulled together into an unpleasant knot. She was thinking, not unhappy. "How does one track teleportation? Does the jump itself leave a signature?"

Harlow wasn't sure what her sister was getting at, but it was an excellent question. Finn appeared to be thinking along the same lines, because instead of blowing past the question, he paused to give it thought. "Yes, and no. You'd have to be aware that someone had teleported and be well versed in recognizing teleportation signatures. It's not exactly easy to do, but not hard or rare either."

Larkin nodded thoughtfully. "So, if say, you didn't have a clear line of sight on the people you were trying to follow, you might not immediately know they'd jumped."

A slow smile came over Finn's face. "Exactly. And the trail gets harder to follow by the minute, after the jump is made."

Vivia had been correct—Larkin was skilled as both a strategist and an adventurer. Harlow asked, "So we trick whoever's watching into thinking we're still here?" She looked to the back of the cave, where several small boulders stood away from the wall, and walked towards them, thoughtful. Finn followed close behind.

"Could you move these?" she asked.

"Easily," he answered.

"Then sit," she ordered. "I need a model to work with and some cover at the front of the cave."

Larkin and Ari both moved, piling the last of their wood onto the dying embers from the previous night's fire. Harlow's shadows danced around her fingers, thrilled to be put to work. She transformed the first boulder to look like Finn. It wasn't perfect, but from a few steps away, it was a good approximation. The fire was roaring now and each of the members of the party took their turn posing for Harlow as she created stone versions of them.

Finn moved each around the fire, and they surveyed their handiwork from the back of the cave.

Larkin laughed, her shoulders shaking giddily. "I think it might work… but…" She frowned a little, her pretty face scrunching unpleasantly again. "What about the sound? It will be silent here when we leave."

An air of apprehension clouded Finn's countenance. "I can help with that." Swiftly, his fingers moved, glowing with celestial light as he pulled threads.

Harlow had no idea he could weave illusions. The Illuminated had the capability, of course, to work with threads as sorcière did, but the fact was that they typically *didn't*. They had so much power otherwise that it was atypical to see them actually do magic of any kind, unless it was violent.

When Finn's fingers stilled, she understood why. For all intents and purposes, it sounded as though a lively conversation was happening around the fire about human folklore. A continuation of what they'd talked about before. The effect was nearly flawless. If people knew the Illuminated could do such spells, they'd never trust them again.

"We should go now," Finn murmured, picking up his pack. He avoided Harlow's questioning eyes. "It will loop in about five minutes. I'm not sure how obvious it will be. I've never woven something quite so complex."

Harlow's heart felt as though it would skip a beat. She grabbed Finn's arm. "I didn't know you could do that."

Under her fingers, the muscles in his forearm tensed. "I know. It's not easy to do, Harlow. And I have a knack for it, but I rarely use the skill. It's a struggle to maintain."

There was a film of sweat beading on his forehead as he spoke. He was already struggling to maintain it. She felt guilty, but her first reaction was relief. The Ventyr were powerful enough without being capable of effortless illusion.

After adjusting her pack, Larkin pulled a few threads. Harlow's second sight revealed the spell itself as she worked. Larkin was adding to Finn's work, adjusting it little by little, giving it strength as she went. She was making it so he didn't have to work so hard to maintain it, but also something else.

When her fingers stilled, she smiled. "Now when it loops, it will do so with variation. If someone is paying close attention to what's being said, it will sound like we're going over old ground, circling back to old topics, so to speak."

Ari chuckled. "Typical sorcière and Illuminated."

Larkin snorted her agreement, taking her place at the center of the tight knot Finn and Harlow made. Ari joined her, his arms wrapping tightly around Larkin's waist as Finn and Harlow joined hands, pressing their bodies close to Larkin and Ari's. This was the safest way to assure they arrived at the Gate at the exact same time. They'd leave a stronger trail, but with the illusion, it might buy them some time.

The jump was quicker than the previous had been. Combining their power made it smoother, as well. When they were assured everyone was all right, Finn urged them on. It was a shame they were in such a hurry; the Gate of Lithraea was situated in the heart of a primeval forest of trees so tall the sky was nearly obscured in their evergreen canopy. Snow dusted the ground here, in places, showing evidence of winter, but it was barely enough for them to leave footprints behind.

A breeze blew a few snowflakes into Harlow's hair, carrying the scent of pine in the abnormally warm air. The whole place would be pleasant, if not for the eerie silence. A forest like this should be full of birdsong and squirrels chattering at one another, but there was nothing. It was as though the forest had swallowed sound itself. And the air was so warm. Too warm—Harlow unzipped her jacket a bit.

Ari bent down to press his palm to the ground. "It's *hot*."

Larkin looked back at him. "There are hot springs here, just beneath the ground. Lithraea's Way will be even warmer."

Finn fished a compass from his pack and then nodded once he got his bearings. Without another word, the group tightened their formation, Larkin and Harlow at the center, Ari taking rear guard.

The tiny hairs on the back of Harlow's neck raised as a pall of foreboding seeped deep into her bones. All around them, she felt eyes boring into her from the shadows.

Finn glanced back at her, nodding once. *You feel it?*

Yes, she replied. *We're not alone here.*

This is why Dad didn't come this way before, he added as he faced forward. *Even he had the sense to be afraid of this place.*

Finn, she called out to him in her mind. *Do you know what the vvyk are?*

His head turned slightly, and she saw the grim line of his mouth, the intense glow of focus in his eyes as his free hand reached back for hers. He squeezed it once, but didn't answer her, shaking his head just once.

Next to her, Larkin had gone pale, her skin turning a sickly gray that made the light sprinkle of freckles across her nose appear as a livid rash. "They're *here*. The vvyk." Larkin's voice shook as she spoke the gnarled, guttural word. Her eyes went wide and vacant, words tumbling from her lips in a mesmerizing rhythm:

"Boughs above and flame below
(silent are the watchers' moans)
No currency, no seed to sow
(writhing beasts ne'er overthrown.)

Walk softly on the forest floor
(secret songs no longer known)
Lest thou stay here evermore
(though together, still alone.)"

They'd all stopped to listen to Larkin's eldritch words, weirdly entranced by the soft cadence of the awkward verses. Ari snapped out of the fog first, clapping a hand over Larkin's mouth. The movement brought the rest of the group around.

Larkin blinked, then pushed Ari's hand away. "What in seventeen hells was that?"

There was real fear in Finn's eyes. "The vvyk. They influence your mind."

"But what *are* they?" Ari insisted. "How do we fight them?"

Finn's answer confirmed what Harlow had suspected. "We don't. No one's ever seen the vvyk and lived to tell about it. We need to move quickly. They won't follow through the Gate."

"No, they won't. Even *they* are afraid of that path." Larkin blinked a few times, shaking her head. "What are we going to do?

Harlow was solemn. "We're going to go as fast as we can through the canyon. The vvyk will whisper all through the Way—the path through the Gate. There's no preparing for it, no trick out of it. There's only getting through it as fast as we can."

Larkin's dreamy look returned. "The verses are the warning. The vvyk capture those unworthy to enter the Gate, and their whispers… They're the test."

Harlow tried to ignore that whatever the eldritch creatures were, they were sending information through her sister.

Ari frowned. "And we don't know what happens after? There have to be accounts of people who've made it through."

"There are," Harlow replied, thankful that she had this much information from talking with the human elders. "But no one is able to speak of it after-wards... *Though together, still alone.*"

Larkin bit her bottom lip. "That's *one* interpretation."

"We don't have time to discuss interpretations," Finn spit, panic filling his eyes. "They vvyk—"

"Are the least of our worries," Ari interrupted. "Our pursuers are here."

Everyone fell silent, but Harlow heard nothing amiss. The forest was still eerily silent. Finn, however, nodded, lowering his voice to barely a whisper. "They must've guessed where we'd go—but they're off course. We've got to move, now."

Harlow's hands shook as they jogged forward, keeping their feet as quiet on the forest floor as they could. Giving into fear wasn't an option, and she'd assumed this journey would be dangerous, but she hadn't known what they'd be up against.

Somewhere, deep in the forest behind them, a sharp scream pierced the silence. "Run," Ari commanded as they entered a clearing.

Ahead, the Gate of Lithraea loomed. It was an arch carved into the stone outcropping that rose out of the forest floor, likely a hundred feet high and intri-cately sculpted with writhing shapes. As they approached, Harlow's eyes ran over the carvings. If the creatures depicted were meant to be representations of the vvyk or their whispers, she deeply regretted their choice of paths. The scenes depicted on the Gate were terrifying, depraved, and beyond anything Harlow could have previously imagined.

"We are so fucked," Larkin murmured as they passed through the Gate.

No one answered, but Harlow was glad to hear her sounding more like herself. Once inside the Gate, the carvings gave way to a narrow, twisting path. It was easy to believe this had once been a deep oceanic canyon, an abyss at the bottom of the sea.

Deep grooves were worn into the rock walls that towered above them. Once, an underwater current had carved this path out over millennia. The Way was dark, narrow, and twisting. Sometimes they could walk two or three across, and others the path narrowed to such a tight space that they had to go single file, turning to the side to squeeze their way through.

Finn set a punishing pace, and for a while, Harlow wondered if the only thing threatening them here was their fear. Perhaps that was the secret of Lithraea's Way. Fear of the unknown, stoked to a fever-pitch by rumor, surrounded by a forest full of unseen horrors.

Harlow glanced at a narrow sliver of sky, and wondered briefly if she could shift and fly above the canyon, but already the winds of Gale Alley howled above them, sending alien echoes skittering through the rocky corridors below. Those echoes combined with the soft sound of moving water, though Harlow could not see a river or stream.

For a while, no one spoke. The little group seemed lost in their thoughts and the echoes of the Way. Harlow's thoughts drowned in the whisper of water. She became sure, after a time, that a river must run parallel to the canyon they traversed. Several times, she opened her lips to ask what the others thought or if they heard it too, but could not seem to form words. This, she chalked up to exhaustion, and the wicked pace that Finn set for them. Ari still drove them from behind. Any time one of them slowed, he gently pushed them forward, saying nothing.

When Harlow glanced back at him, his eyes were as glassy as she imagined her own were. She tried to speak to him, but the words formed in her mind and died on her tongue before she could get them out. There was nothing for it; this place was an enigma.

An enigma that had to be governed by magic.

Harlow engaged her second sight, trying to see into the threads that made up Lithraea's Way. Much like when she'd tried to see into the waters of the Pyriphle, the magical river that flowed through Okairos' underworld, she found no threads in these rocks—only pure aethereal power made up the canyon.

The water she heard was the Pyriphle. She was sure of it now. This canyon had been cut by the river of dark power that ran through the deep vaults of the world, and into the limen, the world between. No wonder that they could not speak, that they could do little but forge ahead. The way the canyon walls rose above them would only amplify the aethereal river that flowed beneath them, around them, and perhaps, now, through them.

Harlow closed her eyes, attempting to use only her second sight to navigate. What she found was very like the limen itself. There was the canyon, and the dim glow of the others around her, but she also saw *more*. In her second sight, she saw the Pyriphle's true form. Not a river of water, but of pure aether, flowing like liquid rather than its usual mists or clouds. Her shadows sang at the sight, longing to join with it.

In her corporeal form, she moved with the group, regulating her breath, putting one foot in front of the other. In her aethereal form, she was freer. She rose above her body, above the mouth of the narrow canyon, trying to see beyond the Gate. Deep within the ancient forest, there were disturbances. Something fought with the vvyk, unseen as the creatures themselves, obscured by the trees.

Their pursuers had not yet entered the canyon, and at this point, had lost nearly an hour of travel time. Harlow calmed at the thought and pulled back towards her corporeal form, though she did not engage her primary sight. Movement to her left caught her attention. A figure materialized in Harlow's second sight—it was the shade from the previous night.

Harlow's mouth still wouldn't form words, so she tried speaking with her mind, as she did with Finn. *Can you hear me?*

The sound the shade made sounded like laughter. *Yes, I suppose you'd call it that.*

What are you doing here? Harlow asked, trying to get a better look at the shade in the daylight. The shade was tall and shapely, with wide curvaceous hips and broad shoulders, across which a pair of giant wings hung like a mantle. Its face was sharply planed, with high cheekbones, an aquiline nose and generous mouth that curved into a smile.

Its features were both familiar and alien. Something about the proportions of its body was different from Okairon humanoids, and even the Ventyr. Harlow could not quite lay a finger on it until she saw the shade's ears, visible in front of its long plaited hair. They were very similar to Ari and Nox's arched ears, but more dramatically pointed. Like the Ventyr, its limbs were longer than the typical Okairon, and its movements graceful and fluid, as though it were made of nothing at all. Like all shades, its entire form was the same midnight blue as the aether.

Rhiannon? Harlow whispered in her mind. The shade looked a bit like the illustrations from her favorite faery lore.

Again, the shade laughed. *I have heard that name before, but it is not my own. I don't remember if I've ever had one.*

How do you know you're not Rhiannon then? Harlow figured if she was going to hallucinate, for this was certainly what was happening, she might as well ask questions. Their proximity to the Pyriphle and the canyon's ability to amplify the supernatural would likely cause hallucinations, which aligned perfectly with the ancient human practice of using the canyon as a coming of age ritual. Combined with the fear of the forest, and the vvyk, it would be a powerful spiritual experience.

An interesting question, the shade mused. *I suppose I do not know if I am or am not for certain, but those names are not familiar to me.*

But you know you are a Feriant? Harlow asked, trying to tease apart what her unconscious mind was trying to tell her.

Of course, the shade answered. *That is not something I could forget.* Its wings flexed, and in Harlow's second sight they caught the light, their feathers iridescent as an oil slick.

Harlow tried another tack. There was some logic here her mind wanted to impart, some collection of information just at the precipice of revelation. *What is a Feriant then?*

The shade's smile turned devious. *You think this is a game, child. A conjure of your mind, due to the river or the canyon. Make no mistake, Harlow Krane, I am real as you are.*

The shade's form began to dissolve. Harlow reached out, though she knew it was futile to try to touch a shade, or a figment of her imagination. To her surprise, her fingers closed around flesh and bone. The shade's luminous eyes widened, its lips parting to reveal a set of wickedly sharp canines.

How interesting you are. Seek the truth of this world and your place in it and perhaps I shall enlighten you. The creature slipped out of her grip, dissolving into nothing more than shadow. Harlow shook her head as her second sight receded, her primary sight returning to show the canyon widening ahead.

CHAPTER 26

Ahead of her, Finn broke into a jog. They'd been walking quickly, and now Harlow caught sight of the state her companions were in. Each was in a state of confusion and disarray, their eyes clouded and their lips moving, though no sound came out. When Finn ran, they ran, and Harlow followed.

The canyon widened further, the dark rocks opening to a snowy scene. Outside the canyon, a cyclone of snow raged, limiting visibility severely. Finn skidded to a halt, throwing his arms out wide to stop Harlow and the others from passing him. Larkin's feet slid, and she let out a panicked shriek, but Ari pulled her back before she fell.

A sudden change of the wind's direction revealed what Larkin had seen when she slipped. The canyon had abruptly opened onto the edge of a gouge in the earth. Harlow's mind tried to make sense of what she saw amidst the snow, but it took Larkin's shuddering words to clarify it for her. "Would we call that a crevasse?"

"It's more of a ravine, I think," Ari said, his usual humor returning now that he had Larkin righted and secure.

Finn's head tilted to the side as he appraised. "Seems like a gorge to me."

"What in seventeen hells is wrong with all of you?" Harlow sputtered. They'd nearly ran straight off the edge of what very much looked like a cliff.

Larkin raised her eyebrows. "I forgot. Harlow is scared of heights."

Her little sister said it like it explained a hissy fit, rather than a completely natural reaction to finding oneself unexpectedly at the edge of a cliff in a storm, while being pursued by an unknown enemy through dangerous territory. And she wasn't scared of heights. Not technically, anyway, especially not since she gained the ability to shift forms.

What Harlow *was* afraid of was her humanoid body's natural proclivity towards clumsiness. That she would step wrong and fall to her death. After slipping on the Ledge of Wishes beneath the Order of Mysteries as a child, it was a reasonable fear, despite her new ability to turn into a giant bird. Harlow let her gaze follow Larkin's, only to find a nightmare waiting for her.

"I'm sorry, Harls," Finn murmured as he moved to stand by her side. He stared across a narrow stone bridge that crossed the ravine. It was ancient, without side rails or handholds of any kind, and looked to be falling apart. Harlow watched as he looked in every direction, knowing his Ventyr eyes saw more than hers. He was looking for another way. The instant he came to the conclusion that this was the only way across, he spoke. "I could carry you."

She did want him to, but the looks on both Larkin and Ari's faces deterred her, different as they were. Ari's eyes were full of pity. The graceful shifter had probably never been afraid of something like an old bridge in his whole life. He was utterly fearless. She hated the idea of Ari thinking she was so weak that she couldn't make it across the bridge. Harlow knew very well that he didn't think her fear was shameful, but both he and Finn would think about her differently if she couldn't master it.

Larkin, on the other hand, looked hopeful. Hopeful that her sister would make her proud. Harlow couldn't let her down. "No," she said, her words firm and steady. "I can do this."

"Okay." Finn pulled his hunk of adamantine from his pack. "Harlow, can you form crampons for us? We'll need them now."

To keep from slipping to our deaths, a voice inside her warned. She ignored it, letting her shadows loose to reform each hunk of metal to form the correct size crampon for each of her companions' boots. When they'd affixed the spiky contraptions to their feet, Finn went first.

"Step slowly and carefully," he warned.

The bridge wasn't so narrow that most people would be truly afraid. Of course, the drop was harrowing. But even at its narrowest, the structure was at least two to three feet wide. The trouble was that as soon as Harlow thought about how easy it would be to slip over the edge, the more unsteady she felt.

Despite her growing fear, she dutifully put one foot in front of the other, staring a few feet ahead, refusing to let her eyes wander right or left. They made good progress, and ahead of her, Finn, and Larkin had all finished the crossing when a low rumble sounded behind her. Harlow startled, and her crampon skidded off the rock directly beneath her next step. She fell to her knees, her body freezing with fear.

Behind her, Ari called out. "It's just a rock slide below. You okay, Harlow?"

She nodded, but couldn't speak. Ari didn't get closer, but he spoke in low and soothing tones, trying to help her get up. "Just clear your mind," the shifter soothed. "You can do this."

But she couldn't *just clear her mind*. She'd never been able to manage such a feat. That was the problem.

"Harlow," Larkin called. "You have to try to get up."

Did she think Harlow didn't know that? Did she really think that every single bit of her wasn't battling to rise and keep going? But her sister kept yelling, and Finn joined her, along with Ari. They were trying to cheer her on, cajole her into just being fine. But that had never worked for Harlow. She'd always needed a little more time, a bit more patience, and had a steeper learning curve than everyone else.

Every shouted word made her flinch, and every flinch shifted her closer to the edge of the bridge as the wind picked up, buffeting her about. In her peripheral vision, she saw Finn making motions to shut everyone up. His silence was the worst, his clear calculation of how he was going to save her showing in every move he made. A part of her mind, that nasty part that had always been with her, whispered terrible things.

Things that tortured her late at night about the mistakes she'd made. The waste of space and talent she obviously was. Deeper and deeper her shame went, until she was at the bottom of the abyss. In her mind's eye, she stood alone at the back door of an apartment building in Nuva Troi, the only being that loved her being taken away from her, while she beat uselessly at the door.

Useless. That was a good word. *Useless.* Why was she even here? Tears pricked the corners of her eyes as her skin flushed, and that word repeated over and over, an erratic, panicked beat.

Useless.

Useless.

Useless.

A dark presence appeared next to her. The words slowed as the shade appeared. *What are you doing, little witch?*

"Baking a tart," she murmured.

Humor, it replied. *So you are not so far gone.*

It made a certain kind of sense. Her companions were silent, still figuring out what to do with her, she assumed, while she hallucinated.

Useless.

No more of that, the shade pleaded. *You are making my head hurt with your misery. The last thing you need is to draw the ghasts. The ones in these mountains are hideous.*

Again, it made a point. Harlow would hate for the last thing she saw before she tumbled to her death to be a ghast. The shade crouched down in front of her, craning its oddly beautiful face so that it looked straight into her own. *Why do you not use your wings?*

A gust of wind howled through the ravine, sending snowflakes flying. "Shifting now would be suicide," she murmured. "I would just get blown into the rocks."

It is not required that you shift the entire way, the shade explained, gesturing to its own magnificent feathers. *Manifest your wings, and use them to keep you balanced.*

Again, this figment of her imagination made sense, and if she could do it, she would. Harlow choked on a sob. "I don't know how to do that. I've only ever shifted fully."

Is that so? Its tone was less incredulous, and more probing.

Because of course, the thing was her, and she was it, and it knew what she did. When she'd made contact with the Pyriphle in Nea Sterlis, she'd partially shifted. That was before she'd made the Claim and initiated her Feriant side.

She'd been able to do it then, albeit without her control, but if she could do it then, why couldn't she do it now? The truth was, she'd never tried.

"I'm different from you," Harlow argued, afraid of trying and failing, being stuck here forever, or falling.

Yes, the shade argued back. *But we are also much the same. Would it hurt to try?*

All Harlow ever did was try. She tried and failed. Over and over... until things worked. *Until they worked.* Yes, that was it. Harlow wasn't the kind of person who got things right on the first try, and she often struggled, but she stuck with things—and when she did, she excelled.

Harlow closed her eyes and thought about how she made the shift the first few times after the Claim. She concentrated on only her wings. Nothing happened. She opened her eyes to ask the shade what it thought she should do, but the creature had disappeared, which startled Harlow further. Just like a figment of her imagination to disappear when she needed the advice most. She appreciated her brain's addled attempt to help her, but she wished it wouldn't be quite so jarring in its efforts.

Still. She could try again. Perhaps something was wrong with what she'd done before. A slight pressure on her back reminded her that her pack was there. That shouldn't matter, but at the back of Harlow's mind, a list of the things she'd lose in the pack if she simply shifted wings through it played like a ticker-tape.

Harlow closed her eyes and slipped out of her pack, moving it slowly to the front of her body. Then she searched out the rest of the worries she had about this idea, letting them all gather in front of her, rather than trying to tamp them down.

Her body wasn't technically engineered to have wings, as it was. It wasn't anatomically possible. But that's where science met magic, because it definitely wasn't anatomically possible for her body parts to turn into a giant bird's body parts. So maybe she could manifest her wings now. She would have to hold them tight to her body at first, until she gauged the direction of the wind.

But that too would be easier with her wings. Their feathers were sensitive, sending messages to her brain about her surroundings in the air in her Feriant form. It would be the same in this form, in this way. Her wings belonged to her, no matter if she kept her humanoid form, or shifted fully into the Feriant.

One by one, her doubts and logical concerns rose and then floated away, acknowledged, validated and addressed. It wasn't the quickest way to go about things, but it was her way. Thinking things through if she had to, even if it was frustrating and annoying. *That* was what worked for her.

A loud rip and a rush of cold wind on her back told Harlow *something* was happening. Soft feathers brushed the skin of her cheek. She opened her eyes; her wings had appeared. There was no pain, no drama. Just her wings, cradling her in their safety as she stood, perfectly balanced for the first time in her life. Each step she took forward was subtly steadier than any step she'd ever taken in her humanoid form.

Harlow didn't realize how off-balance she often was until this very moment. Her wings flexed and contracted with the wind, moving by instinct, just as they did in her Feriant form. Before she knew it, her feet were on a wider path and steps later she was in Finn's arms.

He kissed her hard, clinging to her. "I knew you could figure it out."

When he pulled away, Ari was standing behind them. "The shade," he breathed. "She helped you."

Harlow's breath caught in her lungs. "What?"

Finn frowned. "Didn't you see the winged woman talking to you?"

Harlow searched his face, then Larkin and Ari's. It was obvious they'd all seen the shade. "You saw her too?"

Larkin nodded. "Very clearly. Why wouldn't we?"

Harlow's heart beat faster. "Did you see her in the Way?"

Larkin spoke up first. "I think we were all lost in our own… thoughts. I wasn't aware any of you even existed."

Finn stroked her cheek, concerned. "You saw her there too?"

Harlow nodded. "But I assumed she was a hallucination, a part of the magic of the place. What did the rest of you see?"

No one answered. Their eyes averted. Whatever they'd seen and heard, it was like the legends. They couldn't talk about it. They'd experienced something she hadn't. The wind howled louder now, the cyclone in the ravine worsening by the minute. Across the ravine, four tall figures exited the Way.

"Can you make them out?" Ari asked Finn, all talk of the shade and Harlow's crossing forgotten. He had to raise his voice above the storm.

"No," Finn shouted, grabbing Harlow's hand. "I'm sorry," he said softly.

Before she could ask what for, his arm stretched out in front of him, glowing with both aethereal and celestial light. The ground beneath them shook, the tremor radiating towards the narrow pathway they'd just crossed. Harlow felt her wings disappear, and saw the stone bridge crumble with their pursuers on it as her vision went completely black.

∾

HER EYES OPENED to the world upside down. Finn carried her, thrown over his shoulders like a sack of flour. She looked around—they were on a rocky path, snow swirling wildly around them. Someone had wrapped her in a blanket so she couldn't move.

"Finn?" she shouted, after calling his name in a normal tone didn't yield results. The wind was very loud, after all.

"We're almost there," he shouted. "Just let me carry you the rest of the way."

Behind them, Ari grinned, waving at her through the quickly drifting snow. She'd never live it down if Ari knew she'd let Finn carry her after waking.

"Put me *down!*" she yelled, squirming wildly.

Finn obliged, simply letting her fall into the bank of snow in front of him. Harlow spluttered, breaking free of her blanket. When she manifested her wings again, it was easier—they sprung free from her back, casting the blanket into the screaming storm.

"Thanks," Finn yelled. "That was *my* blanket."

He was smiling though, and pointing to the reason why it didn't really matter. Harlow turned. Rising above them was the observatory, and just a few feet ahead of them, at the base of the mountain, was a gondola lift. Ari ran towards the little shed at the base of the lift. As the rest of them trudged through the snow, the cars began to move, one making its way towards them. They'd made it to ORAIS.

CHAPTER 27

Though it had hardly been two days since they left Sanctum, it *felt* like years since Harlow had been indoors. She hadn't realized how much the sound of the wind's incessant howling had plagued her until it went silent. The ride in the gondola had been a pleasant break, but being inside the actual observatory was blissfully quiet.

They'd entered ORAIS through the glass front doors, which popped open with a simple scan of Finn's left retina. Now, he and Larkin were standing in front of a podium at the center of an enormous atrium, arguing about the logic of code breaking, which was yet another of Larkin's hidden talents. When Harlow expressed surprise at how much she knew about the subject, she'd just shrugged and said it felt like reading music.

The podium at the center of the room, which Finn kept calling a "terminal," housed a computer that could be used to open the facility. Though the retinal scan had remained the same as the last time Finn had been here, the code to enter the building itself had changed. Granted, being out of the wind and snow was a blessing, but every door out of the atrium of ORAIS was locked, and the room was nearly as cold as it was outside—and Finn and Larkin's argument echoed off the glass walls and marble floors. Worse, when Ari had volunteered to run a perimeter patrol, more to escape Finn and Larkin's argument than anything else, they'd found they were now also locked *inside* the foyer.

Harlow and Ari considered setting up their tents. "We'd be warmer inside them, I think," Ari reasoned.

Harlow agreed, looking around the atrium. "We'll be warmer if we try to insulate them." She pointed to the cushions on half a dozen upholstered benches. "If we set up the tent, then build a cushion fort around it, it'll insulate the tent. Maybe we should put some on the floor beneath the tent as well?"

"For cush?" Ari asked, a sparkle in his eye. "Your old bones are tired after the hike?"

Harlow snickered. "For cush—and extra insulation. These floors are like ice."

"Let's do it. Let's build a pillow fort." Ari waved his hand in front of his body dramatically, deepening his voice. "The most epic pillow fort on Okairos."

"The pillow fort at the end of the world," Harlow added.

It was amazing how much Ari felt like family and how good it felt to be joking right now. There was something comforting about the fact that they'd had a harrowing two days, and yet they were still making jokes about pillow forts. If this really was the end of the world for them, at least she'd die laughing.

"Come on. If we get this done quickly, we have a delicious dinner of...." Harlow pointed to Larkin, who'd glanced over at them, a little look of jealousy creeping into her eyes at the fun Harlow and Ari had been having.

"Energy bars!" Larkin chimed in, smiling now.

"Energy bars," Harlow repeated as she collected cushions. "Yes, we have another delicious dinner of energy bars to look forward to."

"But not too many," Ari called from across the room. "Because we are running dangerously low on food."

Finn had gone quiet, watching them gather cushions. He was somewhere else entirely, lost in thought. Suddenly, his eyes lit up, and he typed something else into the terminal. The crystal chandeliers above them lit, but slowly, like they were on a dimmer. Inside the observatory, more lights came on, as the sound of mechanical humming purred through the building. The unmistakable sound of doors unlocking surrounded them.

Ari threw down the pillows he carried and rushed to the doors that led outside. He pulled them, found they opened, and then closed each of them in turn, bolting the manual lock as he went.

"No need for anyone to follow us inside," he murmured to Larkin as she helped.

The four of them gathered their packs, leaving the bench cushions and the unassembled tent on the floor. Finn reached out for the double doors that opened onto the main entryway to the observatory. As he did, a voice spoke. "Welcome back, Finbar."

"Hello, Stella," Finn replied as he walked into the front hall. He turned, spinning easily on the beautiful marble floors. "Aren't you coming?"

"Who, exactly, was that?" Ari asked.

Finn looked around. "Oh, that's Stella, the AI that runs the observatory. If you get lost or need help, you can just ask her."

Everyone just stared at Finn, not moving a muscle to enter the building.

"Like in a science fiction movie?" Larkin asked.

Finn shrugged. "I guess. Except Stella is real. Stella, meet Larkin and Harlow Krane and Arebos Flynn."

"Welcome, friends of Finbar," the disembodied voice said.

Finn cringed at the use of his full name. "Stella, my dad isn't here. Can you just call me Finn?"

The voice answered. "If Connor McKay is not here, then I may do as you ask, Finn."

Finn smiled at the group. "She can't hear you unless you say her name. It's not as creepy as it seems, I promise."

"How do you know?" Larkin asked, stepping gingerly inside the lobby.

"Know what?" Finn asked as everyone followed him down the front hallway and into a lounge with a panoramic view of the storm outside. If the sky ever cleared, the window would provide a gorgeous view of the mountaintops surrounding them.

"That she's stopped listening," Larkin explained as she peeled off her coat. It was warming up inside the lounge. Finn picked up a tablet off a long, rustic wooden console table that stretched across the back of a tailored beige sectional that faced the semi-circle of floor to ceiling windows. The room was beautiful, with a vaulted wood ceiling that peaked at the center of the circular room. A long rectangular dining table, heavily built with clean lines and surrounded by upholstered white chairs, sat at the opposite end of the room.

The center of the room was sunken, a fireplace at its center, surrounded by a circular couch, covered in plush cream-colored cushions and throw blankets. A bar at the back of the room lit up as Finn tapped several buttons on the tablet he'd picked up. Next, the fireplace lit, crackling merrily. Everything was done in a luxurious style that had been popular about seventy years ago, with clean lines and what architects and designers of the time had called a "modern" style. Now, it was charmingly retro, preserved beautifully, as all things ruled by the Illuminated were.

Finn set the tablet down momentarily to take off his jacket. "Might as well get comfortable. It will take Stella a bit to procure food for us, but we can make coffee now, if you'd like."

Harlow's mouth fell open as her eyes fell on the espresso machine at the bar. She suddenly wanted a latte more than anything in the entire world.

"But there's no milk, of course," she whispered, unzipping her jacket. She left it on one of the stools in front of the bar, with her pack. "Stella," she whispered. "You don't have milk for the espresso bar, do you? Or coffee beans for that matter?"

"Yes, Harlow Krane. I do," the voice replied. "You will find beans in the cabinet next to the espresso machine, and I will retrieve milk for you now."

Harlow found the beans, exactly where Stella said they would be, and went about grinding them and preparing the espresso machine. It appeared to be in working order as she busied herself making her first shot. When she opened the door to the stainless steel refrigerator, she found exactly one glass bottle of milk inside, and nothing more. The expiration date on the bottle was ten days from the current day.

"Stella," she asked, her mind reeling. "Where did you get this milk?"

"I made it," the voice replied. "I regret that it is a plant milk, but it has been calibrated to steam well for your latte, Harlow Krane."

"Just Harlow, Stella," Harlow murmured, taking a small sip of the milk. It was perfectly fresh. "You can just call me Harlow."

"As you wish, Harlow."

The work of making the perfect latte distracted her from what felt like a surreal change. They'd gone from burning safe houses to extreme weather to haunted forests and crumbling bridges. Now *this*. Some kind of retro-futuristic resort the Illuminated had created to—what? Hang out in? She'd thought ORAIS would be more like a lab, spare and utilitarian.

As she took the first sip of her latte, she wasn't sure why she was surprised. She stared at the luxurious wood that paneled the walls. It was a rare variety, a rich and creamy pale shade that made her chest ache with nostalgia for something she'd never seen, a time she'd never lived through, but seen in photos of the maters before they'd decided to have children.

"Are you staring at the wall, Harls?" Finn asked from the bar.

Harlow turned slowly, taking the lounge in again. The others were gathered in the center of the room, drinking water from tall glasses and popping popcorn in foil bubbles in the fireplace. It could be Yule, as festive as it was. Light jazz played quietly from a speaker as the afternoon sun dimmed in the sky. Lamps cast glowing pools of light on the marble floors.

"Why didn't you explain that it was like this?" Harlow asked, keeping her voice low.

Finn shrugged. "I wasn't sure what it would be like now. Turns out, it's exactly like it was when I was a kid."

Harlow couldn't muster words. She was too tired.

"I also didn't want to get any of our hopes up that there might be conveniences like food and beds here. For all I knew, my father had this place torn apart."

"Did you say *beds*?" Harlow asked. "If there are showers, I will die happy."

Finn smiled. "There's all of that and more." He called down to the others. "Come take a little tour of ORAIS with me, everyone."

They followed him back through the front entryway through a large archway and into a smaller vestibule, where two long hallways forked into two diverging paths.

Finn pointed left. "Down there are the living quarters. Every room is essentially the same, so pick anywhere. For now, let me show you the observatory and the offices and labs."

They took the right-hand passage, a glass skyway that led to another building entirely. The domed observatory was visible from this angle, as was the steep drop down the mountainside. Harlow's wings had disappeared, leaving her back open to the cool air of the skyway. She'd have to see if there were extra clothes anywhere here later on.

They saw the observatory first, which was home to an enormous telescope and a veritable command center of computers. "Stella won't be able to fire this up for another day or two, probably," Finn explained. He'd been telling them about the way ORAIS's generator worked in the kind of detail that had Harlow thinking about other things.

"Stella," Finn prompted. "What's the progress on the perimeter wards?"

"It is ninety-two percent complete, Finn. I will inform you upon completion, as you asked," the AI replied.

They followed Finn out of the observatory and into another atrium, decorated similarly to the one they'd entered through. Finn pointed to three hallways in succession. "Offices and archives that way, another kitchen and lounge, and then the labs. I think we probably all need some rest. We can get started going through things tomorrow."

Everyone was quiet as they moved back towards the lounge. Finn explained that the fridge should be filling up with the food he'd asked for, and what they could expect from Stella's capabilities. She was a combination of state-of-the-art tech and magic, with the ability to replicate nearly any food, though some things took longer and her generators were still charging.

Harlow hoped she could find a replacement for her sweater. There hadn't been room in the packs for extra clothes, and Harlow would be cranky if she had to darn her damaged sweater herself. Of course, she'd use magic to do it, but still, it was a tedious idea and would take nearly the same amount of time doing it by hand would, since she wasn't talented with textiles like Enzo was.

She missed him and Riley intensely. They'd have loved to see ORAIS. Enzo had made Harlow watch every vintage spy movie they could get their hands on as kids, and there was an Auvray DeVille classic where the titular spy came to an observatory much like this one, only to find the villain was training an army of lingerie models to be super soldiers.

Auvray had seduced at least three of them before the film was over, of course. She *was* an international super-spy, after all. Harlow laughed softly thinking about it. They'd reached the lounge once more, the sun having set quickly below the jagged mountains that encircled the observatory. Ari and Larkin were busy asking Stella about the different kinds of foods she could provide. They played off one another's suggestions in a comfortable way that made it feel like being home.

"I need a new sweater," Harlow told Finn, catching his arm. "And I think I need to lay down before I eat, if that's okay."

One hand curved over the back of her head, tender as he searched her face. "You need some alone time? Or would you rather talk about what happened today?"

Harlow definitely did not want to talk. "I need to fix my sweater and lay down."

He nodded. "You remember the way to the bedrooms?"

It was her turn to nod. "I do."

He pressed a kiss to her forehead. "I know I said they were essentially all the same, but the last door on the left has my favorite view. There should be extra clothes in the closet at the end of the hall. My mom always kept extra stuff in there. Or there's ORAIS sweaters in the front hall."

Harlow narrowed her eyes at Finn, suspiciously. "Who made those?"

Finn shrugged. "Aislin, I guess. She had an idea that this would be a world-class scientific research station someday, but you know Connor…"

There was no doubt in Harlow's mind that whatever Connor McKay's vision for the future of ORAIS had been, he'd had no issue disappointing his wife. It was hard to understand how the two of them had stayed together for so long or how they maintained the fiction of an aligned relationship when in private they were almost permanently at odds. She kissed Finn quickly, grateful for the fact that they would not end up in a similar position.

CHAPTER 28

The ORAIS sweaters were unsurprisingly done in good taste. Aislin had an excellent sense of style, and they had a kind of timeless quality to them that made the slightly retro look eternal. But the crewneck on them was unworkable for Harlow. Just looking at the neck made her feel as though she was being choked.

The closet in the sleeping quarters was Harlow's next stop. She'd had no expectations when Finn mentioned "the closet"—but this was a whole godsdamned *room*. It rivaled the editor's closet at *Ordinas* magazine, which she, like everyone else in Nuva Troi, had seen dozens of videos of over the years. When she and Enzo were estranged, she'd enjoyed the cameos he'd made on the magazine's web series called "The *Ordinas* Closet."

This closet would blow her best friend's mind. Not only for its size, which was impressive, but for its curation. The closet was a meticulously organized study of couture ski and après-ski fashion throughout the past six or seven decades. Harlow marveled at the selection of items, almost fearing to touch any of it; every piece was such high quality. The room itself was illuminated softly from lights positioned behind the racks and racks of sweaters, snowsuits, and various leggings. As she moved toward the back of the room, she found a wall of boots and an enormous freestanding dresser that contained undergarments and gloves.

"What *is* this place?"

Harlow recognized Larkin's voice, and stuck her head out from the back to let her sister know where she was. "Hi, I'm back here."

Larkin's mouth was slightly open as she wandered through the closet. Harlow had begun trying on sweaters after finding a section of folded items that turned out to be a collection of half-zips. She'd gathered a small wardrobe's worth of items that would fit her when Larkin arrived.

"This is excessive," Larkin announced when she reached Harlow's pile of clothes.

Harlow cast her eyes down at her pile. "I don't think anyone else here wears the same size as me—"

"I didn't mean your selection," Larkin interrupted. Her tone was curt, which was unusual. Sometimes Larkin got cranky when she was tired and overstimulated, though—all the Kranes did. Harlow tried not to read too much into it, especially as Larkin continued in a much gentler tone, "I meant this entire place. What is this all *for*?"

Harlow had been wondering the same thing. "I don't know. It's not what I was expecting."

"It's not?" Larkin's eyebrows raised, but the look in her eyes was hopeful, as though she were relieved to find she wasn't the only one astounded by ORAIS's ostentatious luxury. Of all the Kranes, she'd spent the least amount of time with the Illuminated.

"No, I expected it to be nice. I've seen Finn's parents' house in Nuva Troi… But I wasn't expecting—" she gestured to the whole place. "Whatever this is."

Finn had appeared in the doorway. "This is all Aislin," he explained. "She used to come here for her 'little escapes' when I was a child." He lifted Harlow's enormous pile of clothes with little effort, allowing her to stack three pairs of boots onto the top before disappearing without another word.

Larkin's eyebrows raised again. "What's he gonna do with your clothes, pal?"

Harlow laughed. "He's going to go organize it all. Like, in a really, really anal way that will include color-coding."

"That's so Finn," Larkin said, smiling.

In that one sentence, Harlow heard all the ways Finn had become Larkin's family too. She was so proud of Larkin, and who she'd become. It had been terrifying to think of taking her on this mission, but it all made sense now.

"So, does this place feel familiar?" Harlow asked. "Have you seen the room from your dreams?"

Larkin shook her head as she ran a finger along a row of puffy snow boots that had surged in popularity in the last few years after being thought of as old-fashioned for a while. "No, not yet." She selected a bright red pair and sat next to Harlow to try them on. "I keep thinking about Piper being the Ravager's host."

"Yeah," Harlow said, watching her sister pull the boots on. "Me too. It seems less likely to me the more I think of it."

Larkin stuck her feet out, admiring the boots. "Really? The more I think about it the more likely it seems."

"Really?" Harlow asked. "Why?"

A sigh hissed from Larkin's lips. "So many people seem to like her, which makes me think at some point, she must have been really nice. But to us… or you and Finn, I guess, she's been awful. The way she acted in the bathhouse was gross."

Harlow wasn't sure she'd call it "gross," but it hadn't been Piper's best moment. Usually she and Larkin had similar takes on people, but they obviously disagreed about this. "She's human, we're immortal, and that dynamic is a lot more complicated than I ever imagined."

Larkin shrugged, rolling her eyes a bit. "It seems more personal than that, and the Ravager was super interested in you, wasn't it? She seems weirdly obsessed with being mean to you."

Harlow wanted to hug her sister for being so defensive of her. "I think the more likely explanation is that Finn and I were rude to her in secondary, without meaning to be, and that experience wasn't unique for her. But we're the only people she went to school with at Sanctum, so it *looks* like she's singling us out."

Harlow sighed, as Larkin grimaced at her. She couldn't believe she was defending Piper Winslow this staunchly either. "With everything the way it is... I think she's just really angry with us. There's going to be war, and she's responsible for a lot."

Larkin wore a distant look Harlow had seen on her face several times in the past few days. "Humans live such short lives. So many won't see this resolved."

That wasn't something she hadn't considered. The long life she'd been blessed with meant that she had time to see the world change. Her urgency to get things solved was lessened by that factor, as well as the ones Piper had pointed out to her. The defensiveness she'd felt in the Education Councillor's office, which lingered still, dissipated. The humans' resentment of the lower Orders was warranted. What Harlow had read as Piper's rudeness was actually exhaustion, fear, and the knowledge that she—and her people—would bear the brunt of every mistake immortals made trying to solve things. Just like they always had.

Just like everyone on Okairos had when Connor McKay and the convoy leaders had decided to stay on the planet and rule as they saw fit. The pieces of how they'd conquered, even after the battles were over, spun around in her head.

For the first time in her entire life, Harlow thought about the fact that sorcière were part human. Of course, this was something she knew—everyone learned it in school. But she'd never really taken the time to *think* about the fact that the lower Orders had all been human at one time. In fact, she'd never thought about the fact that most vampires had been human in their lifetimes.

"Look," Harlow said softly. "I don't know how we fix this, but I know once we do our part here, we keep following Finn's example. We let the humans lead. They know more than we do about what they need."

Larkin's eyebrows shot up. "You really believe that?"

"Don't you?" Harlow asked, getting up.

"Yeah," Larkin said softly. "I do, but it surprises me a little that you do."

Harlow sighed, more from needing a breath than frustration. "I know I can be pretty focused on myself sometimes, but I do think about the wider world."

Larkin glanced up, shaking her head, as though shaking something off. "That's not... I mean... I know you care about things."

Harlow brushed a kiss on her sister's cheek. "It's okay, pal. I get it. You've always been so much further ahead on stuff like this than me. I'll make you proud. Promise."

Larkin grabbed her hand. "I'm already proud of you, Harlow."

In that moment, Larkin sounded ancient, as though she'd been waiting eons to hear Harlow admit all that. She wished she'd talked about these things sooner. Larkin was so savvy about all this, and probably could have helped Harlow see her way through the spots she'd been missing sooner. But there was time now—the door was open and Harlow wouldn't lose these types of opportunities again.

"Goodnight," she said as she crossed the closet.

"Nighty-night," Larkin replied.

Her sister's tone struck a dissonant note. Harlow spun to look at her, but Larkin was happily sorting through sweaters, touching the cashmere with a reverence Harlow deeply related to. Part of her wanted to be left alone with the closet for the evening, but the day was catching up to her and she needed to rest.

Across the hall, she found the door to the bedroom Finn preferred standing open. It wasn't even really a bedroom, but more of a suite. Rich woods graced the vaulted ceiling, with another panoramic view of the mountains. All Harlow saw now was darkness and snow, of course. She sank into a chair in front of the delightfully retro, conically shaped fireplace, her mind racing.

Somewhere, in the recesses of the room, the soft sound of Finn hanging clothes comforted her, reminding her of the few brief weeks of peace they'd had last spring. It stung to think of the house he'd built for her, especially after the fire, but what stung more now was that while she'd been amazed that he'd gone to such lengths for her, the fact that he'd been able to do so was not a surprise.

It had been special because it was done for her, not because the finishes of the house had been particularly out of the ordinary. A deep crease formed in Harlow's forehead as more of her life sharpened within the context of her recent realizations. Deeper and deeper she went, examining facets of her life she rarely considered. The sound of Finn's footsteps and the soft whoosh of the door shutting brought her back to herself. He sank into the chair next to her, a contrast of dark and light, his tousled hair shadowy against his pale skin.

When he smiled at her, offering his hand, she took it, allowing herself to be pulled from her own chair, into his lap. "You're thinking hard," he said, stroking her hair.

"How much time have you spent thinking about how differently humans live than we do?"

The hitch in his breath startled her. "A lot," he said after a long pause. "Last year, while we were finishing key aspects of the Haven Project, I spent about six months just interviewing humans about what they needed."

Harlow sensed he would say more, so she didn't respond, or ask questions. She let her arms slide around his neck, digging her fingers into his silky soft hair as he spoke.

"It was a humbling experience to come to terms with the fact that I am not, in fact, a relatable person whatsoever."

A low laugh escaped Harlow's lips. "No. You really aren't."

He looked up at her. "Do you hate it?"

"What? The fact that you're not relatable?"

He nodded, gesturing to their surroundings. "All this is just a tiny portion of what I grew up with. When I look at it in comparison to what the humans at Sanctum had before they came to the Rogue Order…"

Harlow finished for him, "It makes you a little ill."

He nodded. "It does. It's why I offered to sign it all away. I don't think I can live in the shadow of what Connor's done any longer."

Harlow hugged him tightly, not knowing what to say next, but letting the words come anyway. "We still have a lot to learn about the way the world actually works, don't we?"

Finn's eyes were sad when they met hers. "We do—in some ways. But in others, we probably know far too much."

CHAPTER 29

Over the next few days, Harlow and Ari worked to sort through the offices they could get into, while Larkin and Finn worked on unlocking Connor's office and the command center in the observatory. Ari, Finn, and Harlow took turns patrolling as well, though Stella's perimeter surveillance was one of the first things they were able to restore, and was reassuringly boring to watch. Periodically, the cameras caught sight of wildlife, but even that was rare in these windy climes.

Perhaps the best thing about ORAIS though was that because there was so little to do outside of searching the station, there was time to rest. Furthermore, because Harlow finally had Finn and Larkin back, her mind began to recover from the stress of the past few months. She was fully rested for the first time in months, and she'd never felt more mentally agile. If only they could get into Connor's office; she was sure it held some sort of information that would tie together the central problems Okairos faced.

On the eighth day at ORAIS, as Harlow woke from her afternoon nap to yet another blizzard outside, movement in the corner of the bedroom caught her eye. Sleepily, she turned over, reaching for Finn.

"Come here," she called, barely opening her eyes. "Come kiss me."

I don't think we have reached such a level of intimacy.

Harlow sat straight up. The shade was back.

"Stella," Harlow called, keeping her voice low. "Who is in my room?"

The AI responded quickly. "Yourself only, Harlow."

The shade stared out the windows, apparently watching the snow. *I am here, but not here. It is an odd existence.*

One thing they'd been able to uncover in ORAIS's general archives was lore about the Ravagers, which confirmed that a powerful elemental's presence on a planet would disturb the more paranormal elements, like spirits. The author's hypothesis was that on planets like Okairos, which derived much of their magical force from aethereal power, a Ravager would possibly change other spirits' essential nature. Finn guessed this might be why the ghasts, and this shade in particular, seemed so attracted to Harlow.

"Where did you live when you were alive?" Harlow asked. "Do you remember?"

The shade turned. *You are still trying to figure out who I am then.*

Harlow nodded. "Shades typically haunt people they have a personal connection with."

The creature smiled, which was a fearsome expression, given its otherworldly beauty and its sharp canines. *These are not the right questions, Harlow.*

The shade dissolved, to her frustration. What had it said to her in Lithraea's Way? *Seek the truth of this world, and your place in it.* Well, she was trying, but until they got into Connor's office and the command center, she doubted she'd have much more success.

Someone knocked at her door. "Come in. I'm up."

Larkin stuck her head inside. "Good. Thought you'd want to come see. I got Connor's office open—*and* Stella and I got the internet working."

"That is correct," the AI added. "I was integral in helping Larkin establish an internet connection, but we have not yet activated the link."

Harlow could swear the AI's flat voice sounded affectionate. If anyone could kindle feelings in a robot, it was Larkin. Harlow dressed quickly, which was easy because Finn had organized all the clothes she'd chosen from Aislin's closet by color.

Larkin shook her head when she emerged from the bathroom. "You look like one of those vintage fashion photos in that outfit. Like you belong in an apres-ski photoshoot."

Harlow glanced down at the monochromatic ensemble of champagne boots, combined with her beige sweater and leggings. She did look like she'd chosen clothes out of an *Ordinas* winter photo spread. She shrugged—it was fun to look put together and feel warm and comfortable at the same time.

"It wasn't a dig," Larkin said, her voice gentle as they made their way down the hall. "You look like yourself for the first time in a long, long time."

Harlow stopped in the lounge to make a quick latte. She'd become a bit addicted to them, here at ORAIS. "What does that mean?"

Larkin hoisted herself onto the counter while Harlow busied herself making them both a drink. "It's like you've come into your own or something. You seem more comfortable being yourself, ever since the bridge. Did the shade help you?"

Harlow made a noise she hoped would be interpreted as affirmative, concentrating on making a pretty design in Larkin's foam.

"Awww, a heart." Larkin grinned.

Harlow tweaked her nose. "Love you, sissy."

Larkin wrinkled her nose, rubbing it. "Don't call me that."

Harlow kissed her cheeks in apology. "I do love you though, Larkin." They set off for Connor's office once more, mugs in hand. Harlow bumped her sister's shoulder lightly. "I'm glad you're here."

Larkin just smiled. "Me too."

Outside, for the first time in days, the blizzard had slowed to flurries. The long hallway that connected the residential section of the facility with the research wing allowed a dazzling view of the surrounding peaks through its floor to ceiling windows.

Larkin slowed down, squinting at something off in the distance. "What is that?"

It was the first time since they'd arrived at ORAIS that there was a clear view of the landscape. Harlow stopped behind her sister, trying to find what she saw. There it was, just beyond the perimeter boundary, skirting it closely. Movement. Harlow's heart thumped with anxiety. Whatever was out there wasn't an animal. It was moving too quickly for that.

"Stella," she called. "Can you bring up the cameras on the north peaks on the main research terminal?"

"Of course, Harlow," the AI answered.

They rushed to the terminal, only to find Finn staring at the screen. "It's not the Vespae," he said as they approached.

Harlow and Larkin crowded next to him. The movement was gaining momentum, and the way it skirted the trigger for the perimeter alarms was reason for concern.

"Could be the Dominavus," Larkin reasoned.

"It's not," Ari said, entering the small foyer that led to the various offices and labs. He was damp, his cheeks flushed from the cold. "We wouldn't see the Dominavus coming until they hit a vulnerable point in the wards. I've studied their tactics. This isn't like them. Whoever that is wants us to know they're there—my sense is that they want us to be afraid."

"That's messed up," Larkin murmured.

Above her head, Harlow and Finn made eye contact. She knew instantly they thought the same name: Alain Easton. It was the only thing that made sense.

"Stella, bring up the wards' force," Finn commanded. "Full strength, please."

"It is done," Stella replied, after a long pause.

Ari watched Finn carefully. "I think it would be better if I ran patrol for a few days, since I can move unseen. The rest of you should stay in."

Harlow looked around for Larkin, who'd disappeared, while Finn thought Ari's proposal through. For a moment, he looked as though he might argue, but eventually he nodded. "We need to finish here and leave quickly. Tangling with whoever's out there isn't worth it."

Larkin emerged from the observatory. "In that case, what I just discovered might be of use." Everyone turned towards her. "I think I unlocked one of the terminals in the command center."

Ari grimaced. "Fill me in? I need a shower and a meal after my run. It's fucking cold out there."

Finn clapped a hand on his friend's shoulder. "Of course."

Harlow followed Larkin into the observatory, while Finn and Ari exchanged information. Harlow looked back over her shoulder. Though she couldn't make out Finn's words, she read "Alain Easton" on his lips. She kept walking, lest she be accused of eavesdropping. Finn would be desperate to keep everyone here safe, and Ari was his trusted second when Cian wasn't around. It was best to let them talk things out.

In the observatory, Larkin sat in a rolling chair, hunched toward a computer screen. "I wanted to see if I could get the command center online. Its sensors could tell us more about whoever is out there. But I couldn't access that part of the system, not yet anyway. The decryptions I was running last night gave me access to this…"

Harlow laughed when she got close enough to read the screen. It was a radar projection for the next two days. Larkin had managed to turn the weather on. Her sister gave her a withering look that shut her up immediately. Harlow pulled up another chair, while Larkin paused the radar progression that played on loop. "See those blue sections?"

Harlow nodded, grateful to have escaped a sisterly scolding for laughing at an inappropriate time.

"Watch them," Larkin ordered, playing the loop again, clearly still peeved that Harlow had laughed at her. On the screen, the blue splotches went from being tiny dots to covering the area surrounding ORAIS for a very brief amount of time, minutes probably.

Larkin paused the projection again, right when the blue dots covered ORAIS. "In two days, there will be a storm that should generate a rare kind of lightning—I don't really know how to explain it other than that it won't be a weather phenomenon, but a magical one. The lightning will be pure celestial energy, pulled through the limen. When it strikes, it will counter the effects of the iridium deposits for about two minutes."

Harlow nodded, touching the screen as the timelapse projection started over. "Here, right?"

Larkin nodded. "Yes, that's it. If we calibrate the computer, we should be able to track it more accurately. I think Ari will be able to do that. It's a little beyond me, but Nox taught him how."

"What is this phenomenon?" Harlow asked.

Larkin stared up at the ceiling, as though she could see the sky, or maybe the limen. "I don't really understand it, but there are times when the limen sort of aligns more closely to us than others, and it pulls celestial power into the world."

"So what does that mean?" Harlow asked, not understanding why this mattered.

Larkin shook her head. "Not much beyond the iridium being temporarily neutralized. We should be able to teleport out, if we want to."

"That will make us vulnerable to Alain and whoever he has with him," Finn remarked, coming to stand behind Harlow. His arms wrapped around her shoulders as he watched the radar projection again.

Larkin sighed. "It's a risk. For sure." Her shoulders slumped a little as she bit her bottom lip, obviously racing to think through alternatives.

"We'll do it," Finn said. "But don't turn on the internet until shortly before we leave, okay? There's a real possibility my dad has that kind of thing tracked. I don't want him to know we've been here, if we can help it."

Larkin nodded. "Great. Let's go plunder his office for secret information." Harlow got up to go, but Larkin pulled her back into her chair. "Hold on, I just want to check if the rest of the terminal unlocked. There's some cool old planetary tracking systems in here that I want to check out."

Her fingers flew over the keyboard. The radar screen disappeared, and another appeared. Harlow didn't understand what she was looking at. The screen was split in two, showing what she assumed were tracking outputs. One showed deep space and a tiny pinprick of a planet; the other looked like some sort of terrain, though it was largely topographical lines and dots, changing features all the time.

"What is that?" Finn asked, pointing to the screen.

At the bottom of the page, in a pop-up window, was a message, dated several weeks prior to the current date. Larkin clicked the button labeled, "OPEN." Finn and Harlow both leaned closer to read. A chat window appeared. It started with a string of numbers and dots, followed by the words: *Population prepared for conquer.* Underneath it, in a message time-stamped only fifteen minutes ago, was a reply. *Received. Delegation assembling.*

Finn froze, his skin turning a deathly shade of gray. He staggered backwards, swallowing hard, his eyes glazing with panic. "The Ventyr are coming."

The room was silent, but Harlow's ears rang with the terror coursing through her. "Did Connor send this?"

Finn stumbled into a chair and slumped into it, covering his face with his hands. He didn't seem capable of answering her.

Larkin shrugged. "I don't know how to tell."

Finn shook his head. "He wouldn't. Believe me."

Larkin looked as though she wanted to argue, but Harlow raised a finger as an indignant expression darkened her sister's face. "Finn knows his dad, pal. He has no illusions about Connor's honor or goodness."

Again, Larkin looked like she might argue. Harlow sighed. "Connor doesn't like to share power."

Larkin's expression softened. "But with things the way they are, mightn't he think the others could help him get the Vespae under control?"

Finn's tone was gentle. "You really don't know my dad, and I'm so glad for that, but he'd let the whole world get eaten by those creatures before he let the Emperor have this world. He sees it, and everything in it, as *his.*"

As that disturbing idea rocketed through them, Harlow watched the topographical map change abruptly. What looked like ancient ruins formed and disappeared in a mere moment. An idea occurred to her. "Is that the limen?"

Finn glanced at it, his eyes narrowing to a squint. He needed his glasses, badly. "It very well could be." He sat back, thoughtful, then asked, "Stella, who's logged into ORAIS for the past three months?"

"I'm sorry, Finn. That information is not available at your clearance level." The AI sounded apologetic. Whoever programmed her had taught her good inflection and emotional reaction—she was likable.

"Worth a try," he muttered, standing. "Our approach is two pronged, then. Someone needs to set up the algorithm to track the storm. Larkin, can you get started?"

Larkin pulled a hair tie off her wrist, yanking her hair into a ponytail as she turned back towards the computer. "Yep. You'll send Ari to help me?"

Finn nodded, motioning to Harlow. "We'd better get started on Connor's office."

CHAPTER 30

Connor's office was exactly how Harlow pictured it would be: decorated in heavy, dark woods, shelves lined with books, uncomfortable leather furniture. Apparently, Aislin's vision for a luxurious, comfortable research station had not extended to his space. A massive set of windows looked out on the mountain range below. Harlow tried not to stare outside, watching for Alain.

"This place has 'villain's lair' written all over it," Harlow said with a curl of her upper lip.

Finn's laugh was dry. He obviously agreed.

They got to work. Harlow took to the bookshelves, Finn took his father's desk. After only a few hours, the room was a mess, and they'd found nothing of interest.

"I'm going to check on Ari and Larkin," Finn said. "Want more coffee?"

Harlow flopped onto the stiff leather chesterfield, grimacing at the hard surface, and nodded. When Finn had gone, she laid back, staring at the ceiling. "There's got to be something here," she reasoned out loud. Sometimes talking to herself helped her visualize a problem better. "Otherwise, why would the door have been so difficult to unlock?"

They'd been through everything. Finn had even searched the desk for hidden compartments and found none. Harlow sat up to perch on the edge of the chesterfield, staring at the shelves. The place really did look like a villain's lair. Like something out of an Auvray Deville film. A spark of an idea lit in Harlow's mind. She dropped onto her hands and knees, crawling around the perimeter of the room, staring at the floor.

As she did so, Finn returned. "What are you doing?"

"Looking for the villain's lair. Like a Deville film."

Finn caught on. "Like the one on the mountain, with the lingerie models?"

"Not that one," Harlow murmured, concentrating. "That would be too obvious for Connor. The one with the casino and the evil professor. Did you see that one?"

She didn't hear Finn's answer over the thrill of discovery rushing through her. There it was: a deep scratch in the floor that arced out from the bookshelf.

"Aces," Harlow breathed, using the iconic spy's catchphrase. "Look what we have here."

"Seventeen hells," Finn murmured. "A fucking secret door. I don't know whether to be impressed or cringe."

Harlow snickered. "Right? It's so predictable."

They rushed to and fro, pulling every book from the shelf, trying to trigger the secret door. Nothing worked. Finn paused, assessing the scene again. His eyes drifted back to the scratch on the floor, then back to his father's desk several times, like he was trying to catch hold of a fleeting thought.

"Why didn't I think of that?" he murmured, searching through the debris he'd scattered on the desk. He pulled what looked like a library card out of a book, then began pulling books from the shelves opposite the door itself. He let out a pleased little grunt, which brought a smile to Harlow's lips.

She stepped back from the shelf, whispering, "It's going to open."

Finn slid the card into a nearly invisible sliver, right at the base of one of the shelves. The way the shadows hit the corner, she never would have seen it. But as the device that read the card made a soft clicking noise, the shelf she had searched first popped open, revealing concrete stairs that delved deep into the bowels of the observatory.

Sconces on the walls lit the way. Harlow started down, but Finn shook his head. "Wait a sec, okay?" He didn't wait for an answer, but jogged out of the room with the card. When he returned, he grinned and waved a walkie talkie. "Better not disappear into a secret passage without telling anyone where we're headed. Ari will keep an ear out for us."

"Where'd you find that?" Harlow asked, pointing to the walkie talkie as he led the way down the stairs.

"Under all the ORAIS sweaters. My mom and I used to use them to play hide and seek when I was really little." He sounded wistful. "Before my dad started training me, we'd come here as a family once a year. I didn't know what this place was—it just felt like an adventure. We took snowmobiles to get here, and it was just the three of us."

The stairs were steep, and Harlow had to watch every step carefully. The stairwell gave her the terrible feeling she was going to topple over. Before she gave it a second thought, she'd manifested her wings, just as she'd done on the bridge. Her shadows danced happily around her fingers, as though thrilled to see her wings. The fabric of the lovely sweater she'd chosen ripped, regrettably, but Harlow didn't feel as though she was going to fall, and she could concentrate on Finn's words.

"I don't know why Connor paired with Aislin. He's never had any interest in her as a person. When I was little, she was magical. Fun."

He paused for a moment. The stairs spiraled ever downward, and now, the smooth wood-paneled walls gave way to rough stone. The sconces were fewer and farther between, with just enough light to keep them from plunging into pitch black darkness. "Careful here, the steps turn to stone as well. They're narrower."

As she followed Finn down, he spoke absently, as though he'd forgotten Harlow was there with him. "When Connor decided I was old enough to train, it was like she disappeared. I never saw the version of Aislin that told stories or played games again. It felt like she blamed me for choosing Connor's side."

Harlow wondered if it was all right to ask him anything, or if she should just let him speak. She decided it was better to interact, especially as he'd trailed off. "So, she didn't approve of Connor's methods?"

Ahead of her, Finn shrugged. "I don't know that she necessarily disapproved of his methods, but she acted as though I'd betrayed her." His head hung.

Surely he didn't feel shame for that? Harlow burned with anger. Of course Finn had taken that on. She caught his elbow, stopping him. "You were a child, and she was the adult. You did nothing wrong."

Finn didn't look back at her, but he nodded once before continuing on down the steps. He didn't say anything else. They walked for what felt like forever, until Finn paused, turning. His laugh was dry, as though he was frustrated with himself for just figuring something out. "We could make this faster, you know?"

Harlow shook her head. "Noooo, it makes me motion sick when you whoosh me around…"

"Come on," Finn cajoled. It was easy to see he was trying to banish the sad thoughts about his mother. He turned motioning to his backside. "Hop on my back."

Harlow couldn't deny him. She retracted her wings, letting them dissolve into nothing, then hopped on to Finn's back. With nothing more than a brief hiss of air, they arrived at the bottom of the staircase. Harlow gasped, feeling a little woozy as she caught her balance.

The staircase opened onto a wood deck that jutted out into a lake. Bioluminescent jellyfish undulated within it, casting a soft blue glow up from the water. Behind the deck, a glass enclosure held what they'd been looking for: shelves of books and maps, and rows of wood filing cabinets. This was Connor's cache of information.

In the distance, Harlow made out an outcropping of rocks, where water flowed slowly down into pools that rose with steam. "Hot springs?"

Finn grinned, leaning towards her to whisper in her ear. "Yes, and they're the perfect temperature for skinny dipping. We'll have to come back later." He raised his eyebrows, a wicked gleam in his eyes.

While Harlow deeply appreciated the warmth licking through her abdomen elicited by that gleam, in the back of her mind she worried. He was always rushing in to help someone, always setting aside his own pain to make things comfortable for someone else. She was concerned about how long he could reasonably keep putting his needs after others.

They still hadn't really talked about what had happened to him when he was with the Vespae. She knew the basics, of course, but he'd never opened up. Though she'd tried to make space for him to talk to her, especially since coming here, he was so deft at moving the conversation in other directions she often didn't notice that he'd evaded her until they were deep into another subject entirely.

The ease with which he put her off was troubling, but she didn't want to push him. After all, when he did talk to her, he told her things like the story about Aislin he'd remembered in the stairwell. His timeline for what to share was different than hers, and that wasn't always easy to respect.

Harlow took Finn's hands in hers. "Do you feel like you can talk to me?"

Confusion clouded his eyes. "Of course. Why would you ask that?"

"Because you don't always talk about the things that hurt very much. All that stuff about your mom? You've never told me any of that…"

One of Finn's hands flew to her face, his thumb grazing her jawline. "I love you so much, Harlow. You're so good to me."

He was doing it now, changing the subject. In moments, they'd decide it was time to go search through Connor's books and files, and he'd be forgotten again.

"You don't have to do that," she murmured. "We can talk about you."

His eyes slid to Connor's office. It was obvious he thought they needed to move on. "I know," he said before pressing his lips to hers. "Thank you."

"Okay." It wasn't what she wanted to say, but she understood. It was often confusing for her to understand how someone else processed their feelings, but she wanted to respect Finn's timelines, even if they weren't comprehensible to her. She changed the subject, gazing into the cavern pool. "Where do the jelly-fish come from?"

Finn shook his head, moving towards the glass room. "I honestly don't know. I've never been down here before."

The large glass doors to the archive were unlocked, but sealed tightly enough that they took a big push from Finn to open. Soft reading lamps turned on as they entered. Inside, the warm humidity of the cave turned to simply warm air. The archive was obviously climate controlled and operated on its own sensors. Finn tried several times to access Stella, but she did not respond.

The archive was organized in a large "U" formation. The windows to the cave were empty, but the sides and back wall were layered three stacks deep in shelves. The biggest old fashioned card catalogue Harlow had ever seen sat against the back wall of the archive. Directly in front of it, in the center of the room, sat a round, elegantly constructed counter height table, with stools tucked under it. A huge, softly lit drum shade was suspended on a gold wire from the ceiling. At the center of the table was a small electronic device, accompanied by a tablet.

"What's that?" Harlow asked, pointing to the tablet and device.

"A holographic projector," Finn answered.

"Okay," Harlow replied. "You should try it out, obviously. What's our strategy here?"

Finn thought for a moment before answering. "Let's spend an hour or so just getting the lay of things. Explore what's here, then we can start honing in on what might be important. I can start with the projector."

Harlow nodded. "That works perfectly. I'm probably better off with the books."

Her first order of business was to search the card catalogue to see what system had been used to organize the books and various documents. It was none of the alpha-numeric systems she recognized, but instead a simple chronological numbering. Subjects could be cross-referenced, but obviously, whoever had created the sections knew their significance by heart. Harlow would have to struggle through the catalogue, or would have to search the stacks manually. She fought the urge to grumble. This was the kind of thing she'd been raised to understand.

After some close examination and a few basic cross-references, she started to recognize a pattern. Searching for a broader topic like "The Order of Mysteries" yielded several sections, and in each, she found accounts of different Okarion cities. She searched several more basic topics and found the same thing each time. The numbered sections were based on location.

This made things tricky, as she wasn't even sure where to start, or what they might be looking for. She sat down in the stacks to let her mind wander. It was a good feeling, one she was familiar with, and enjoyed. The smell of the books, the satisfying feeling of being surrounded by different colored spines. It was all very, very pleasing. But she did wish there were a better system of organization, and she couldn't resist a moment of self-indulgent grumpiness, missing the librarians at the Temple of Akatei library in Nea Sterlis. It would be so convenient if someone could just fetch her what they thought she might need.

She laughed at herself, but stopped short. *The Warden.* She had the copy Morgaine had given her upstairs. The human girl had suggested she look for the missing pages... She'd hoped they'd find them here, but what if she'd been too literal, looking for the actual pages? What if there was a copy of *The Warden* here?

Harlow rushed to the card catalogue, nearly tripping over her feet as she went. There was no luck, but she wasn't discouraged, because in looking, she discovered something else. The card catalogue did not reference *any* book titles, only topics. She started a manual search, scanning up and down each shelf. It was tedious work, and she missed having her headphones and phone to keep her company while she scanned the seemingly endless spines. But after a half-hour of searching, she found it, sitting as though it had been waiting for her.

Connor had a copy of *The Warden.* Though she was tempted to jump into the book, her first order of business had to be to determine where *The Warden* had been shelved—what was the location this section was based around? There were several journals here, many discussing similar topics to what she remembered from *The Warden,* a planet where the industry of war had reigned for centuries, so much so that the entire culture of the place had been based on it. She might not know the name for the place, but she was certain now that this was the section for the Ventyr's home planet. *Now* she felt comfortable satisfying her urge to examine *The Warden.*

She pulled it out carefully, holding it open just enough to examine the pages without endangering the spine, as she assessed the book's fragility. It was a good copy, with no apparent damage, or anything that might make the book susceptible to damage from normal use. In fact, it looked almost new, so she flipped straight to the page where Ashbourne and Lumina's story had left off. It continued here, but not at all how Harlow had expected.

She forced herself to read the story again, reminding herself of the war between the Ventyr houses, and the star-crossed lovers, Ashbourne—the Ash she knew—and his former lover, Lumina. The sadness of the story drew her in, tugging at her heart.

It seemed, for a time, that the two Houses had come to a stalemate. Soon though, Notus devised a devious plan to end this diplomatic conflict so that the great Houses might return to the nobler enterprise of eternal war. As Lumina valued her freedom so highly, second only to her love for Ashbourne, Notus suggested she be exiled to the realm of Sirin—a dark world, populated by creatures so ingenious that the Ventyr could not conquer them. And so Lumina and Ashbourne were separated for all time.

This was where the story had been redacted in the copy she'd received in Nea Sterlis, but here, it was whole. Eagerly, she read on.

To ensure that their punishment continues for all eternity, if Fate allows them to find their way back to one another, House Anemoi's mages were forced to lay a most devious curse upon them. Should the star cross'd lovers ever meet again, they will not recognize one another. The curse was woven so skillfully, so cruelly, that even the desire—should they have it—to speak of their shared past to the other will be hidden from them. As such, the two do not even know they are cursed. They might search for one another still, in fact. But in this plot to separate Ashbourne and his Lumina, I have found one significant flaw.

The thumping in Harlow's chest beat harder, especially now that she knew that Ashbourne was Connor's younger brother—Finn's uncle. He'd said the Ravager he was following was headed to Sirin—but she'd forgotten that's where Lumina would be. She had no way of warning him about what he faced now. What followed confirmed for Harlow that whoever had written *The Warden* must have been well-versed in spellwork:

A curse cannot be crafted without a loophole, though I cannot determine what this one might be. It would be deeply personal to both parties, that much is certain. A bright spot, however, may lie in the fact that Lumina was sent to Sirin, specifically. There she may find help of a different kind, for Sirin is the home of the Vilhar, more specifically, the remnants of the spacecraft Aval-onne. The line of House Feriant lives on—on Sirin, and those fey creatures may have the power to break this curse, once and for all.

If they cannot, the Oscarovi and their devices built to channel elemental power may be able to help her…

Harlow skimmed through the rest of the pages that were missing from her copy of the book, but only found the author's brief history of how the people called the Oscarovi obtained the ability to channel aethereal power, after a prolonged adjustment period to living with the more advanced Vilhar. She could hardly focus on that information though, returning again and again to the sentence, *The line of House Feriant lives on—on Sirin.*

She clutched the book to her chest, rushing to the center of the archive. Finn had the holographic projector working and was examining a truly stunning model of a star system she didn't recognize. She set the book down, opening it to the page in question, tapping the relevant section.

"You found *The Warden.*" He began to read the new portion immediately, his eyes squinting at the tiny print.

When he looked up, she asked, "Have you ever heard anything like this before?"

He shook his head, but gestured towards the projector. "No, but this might be able to help."

He typed a few things into multiple search fields on the tablet's screen. They reminded Harlow of research databases, allowing you to search for multiple factors, rather than just one. Immediately, three results appeared as links on the screen.

Finn tapped the first, and the star system dissolved, replaced by several figures. All had different humanoid qualities, and were in various stages of turning into a very familiar looking giant bird, the Feriant. Their features were intensely familiar to Harlow now.

They looked just like the shade. Similar to the humanoids on Okairos, but sharper in their facial features, a bit taller, and a touch longer in limb.

Harlow let out a low whistle. "Who are they?"

Finn had been scanning through the text on the screen. As Harlow leaned towards him, she saw the pages he was reading weren't typed text, but images of handwritten notes. Now, he read aloud, "The Feriant are one House that comprises the Court of Winds. Though we do not know much about the fey courts, as they are a secretive and ancient society, we learned from Sirin to avoid any world they may have populated or are currently visiting. We made a mistake on Sirin, in thinking that they, like us, were interested in ventures of colonization.

"That mistake was our downfall. The Vilhar and the Oscarovi do not agree on much, but on one thing they adamantly held to: Sirin is theirs and theirs alone. We trapped them on Sirin as retribution, closing all portals to the limen. It is likely they will find ways to open them again, but it gave us time to retreat and recuperate."

Finn and Harlow were silent for a long moment, letting the information sink in. Finally, Harlow said what they must both be thinking. "So the Feriant aren't even a result of being part Ventyr."

Finn shook his head. "I don't know how it's possible. There's nothing else here about it, but my parents *knew.* They must have known." He stared at her, his eyes wide, almost awestruck. "You're part fey, and they wanted us," he gestured between them, "to *breed* the kind of warriors that could resist their own people." Finn's lip curled in disgust at the thought.

So many things made more sense now, they'd only had part of the puzzle before, with the Scroll of Akatei, and the revelations they'd found about the Heraldic and the Feriant. There were so many ancient layers to all this, it might take years to pull them apart and understand them completely. One thing was clear right now: the Illuminated had gone about things all wrong, but they'd done so thinking they were doing good—that they were protecting Okairos from their own kind. From a world of endless wars and conquering. She couldn't quite wrap her mind around the idea.

To help make sense of things, Harlow asked, "Who wrote that?"

Finn swallowed hard. "My mother. This is her handwriting." His grip on the tablet shook.

Harlow took it from him, setting it aside. They needed to talk about Aislin, that much was clear. "I don't mean to be rude, but your mother has always seemed very uninterested in things like politics. Why would she have been writing things like this?"

Finn's jaw twitched. "The woman you know—it's a shadow of the person she was when I was little, who I believe she was before I was born."

"I'm so sorry," Harlow replied, without missing a beat. She didn't need to know the particulars of this. It was obvious he mourned the loss of the mother Aislin had been, at least for a little while, when he was young.

"Thank you," Finn said, his shaking hands steadying. "I've always blamed myself."

"I don't think it was you, sweet boy," she replied, keeping her voice soft. Slowly, his eyes drifted to hers. "I think the more obvious answer here is that Connor is to blame."

He nodded. "I know. I just…" He paused, letting out a huff of air. "Before my parents came to Okairos, my mother was a diplomat. She was also one of the Emperor's mistresses. It wasn't uncommon for a woman of their culture to be both, and she was powerful in her own right. When the Emperor took a new territory, he sent her into smooth relations with the home governments, easing them into the Empire, so to speak."

Harlow grimaced; it sounded like uncomfortable work. Finn laughed at her reaction, seeming to know exactly what she thought. "Awful, isn't it? But she was a proud woman, and good at what she did. I believe she thought she could do the same here, but when the situation changed, when Pasiphae and my dad altered the trajectory of the envoy's plans, she lost her status, even though she and my father shared the Claim."

A hiss of air released from Harlow's lungs. "He Claimed her to control her. To cut her out."

Finn nodded. "That seems like my dad. He might have loved her, or at the very least admired her, but she was loyal to the Emperor. I doubt he trusted her."

Harlow realized why Finn had resisted Claiming her now. She deeply regretted how hard she'd pushed, but of course, she hadn't known any of this. The openness on Finn's face closed. Harlow was beginning to understand the push and pull of his disclosures; he needed breaks after sharing something so raw.

She looked back at the figures of the Feriant. "What else did you find?"

Finn clicked an arrow that functioned as a "back" button and the Feriant dissolved. Now schematics for something that looked like a spaceship appeared. The Illuminated forbade the construction of any such thing, but scientists believed they had the capability to build them, and they were an intense focus in literature and film. This was unlike anything Harlow had ever seen, however. It was like a train, a city, and a spacecraft, all at once. Beautiful in its gothic construction, elegant beyond belief, and enormous.

"This is an artist's rendering of what the Avalonne might have looked like before it was irreparably damaged on Sirin," Finn explained, after reading through what looked like some complicated schematics. "Nearly four thousand years ago, it crashed on Sirin. Or rather, it made an emergency landing, and never left. It carried with it a host of people, the Vilhar, space travelers…" he squinted, then pinched the screen to make the text larger.

Harlow didn't bother to hide her smile. Finn was adorable with his glasses, but he was even cuter without them.

"Stop laughing at my obvious farsightedness," he said with a cocky grin. His cheeks flushed, revealing that he was a little embarrassed by the attention. Harlow was glad to see him acting like himself.

"Okay, so the Vilhar were explorers, from far outside our solar system. The Ventyr really aren't sure where they're from, but they landed on Sirin a long-ass time ago and never left. The planet has been in a certain degree of turmoil ever since. Nothing else about how they might have gotten here, or the Feriant."

"What's the last link show?" Harlow asked.

Finn clicked it, the ship dissolving now, replaced with another star map, though this one showed several solar systems, with four planets highlighted in red. One was Okairos. Finn scrolled through them, a different highlighted planet showing with each swipe of his fingers. They were labeled: Okairos, Sirin, Interra and Earth.

"These are all the populated planets the Ventyr have occupied or interfered with, though not a record of everywhere they've visited. Interra is supposedly their home planet—where my parents came from. They never told me the name…"

Harlow now had a label for the section she'd found *The Warden* in. "Oh," she breathed, as her thoughts came together. "Oh."

Finn waited, knowing she was having an epiphany.

"This place. ORAIS. It's to monitor all the places the Ventyr have been. To keep the elder Illuminated informed about their potential whereabouts."

Finn's head slowly bobbed up and down. "Yes. *Yes.*"

Harlow's eyes drifted back to the planets in the projection. "Did the Ventyr conquer all these places?"

Finn shook his head. "No, these are the planets deemed close enough to Interra to investigate colonizing. Obviously, my parents were involved with the Okairos envoy. It says here that the Earth envoy was to leave shortly after they did, but nothing about how it went. I guess when they cut off contact with the Emperor, they never found out."

"So it's possible the Ventyr have Earth's citizens under their control—the way they wanted to do with us?" Harlow asked.

Finn nodded. "It's possible. Though, of course, they failed with Sirin, so maybe Earth wasn't a successful venture either. It's really hard to know."

"It doesn't matter," Harlow said. "I hate to agree with anything Connor has ever done, but he was right to stop them from coming here, and I agree with you that he's not the one who contacted them. Who else had access to these facilities besides your parents?"

Finn thought for a moment. "All four of the elder Velariuses, Alaric's parents and Petra's. Beyond that, I don't really know. Alaric and Petra never came here as kids, but I know their parents did."

Harlow groaned. "The Rogue Order was monitoring Leopold Velarius' movements. Did Alaric tell you?"

Finn shook his head. "No, we mostly spent time talking about how happy he was about being a father."

Harlow's chest ached at the thought of her sister's bondmate being excited for the baby. She squeezed Finn's hand. "I guess he's expressed a lot of dissatisfaction with both Pasiphae and Connor. The Rogues were always worried about your parents and Pasiphae, but they thought they were predictable. They think Leopold and Petra's parents might want more than what we've always assumed Connor and Pasiphae do."

"They want total domination—of humans, of the lower Orders." Finn sighed, his cheeks blowing out like a balloon. "That tracks with what the Knights have gathered, though I'll admit, I haven't taken the reports very seriously. The three of them have always been so... *uninvolved*."

Harlow shrugged; he would know better than she did. She was only reporting what Thea had told her. "The problem is, they have nearly unlimited resources..."

Finn covered his face with his hands. When he looked up, a muscle in his jaw twitched slightly. "We have to go to Nuva Troi and tell Connor. He's the only one who'd know where the Ventyr will come through—and how to stop it."

The room was quiet for a long moment, before Harlow nodded. "I really wish I didn't agree, but I do."

CHAPTER 31

Larkin and Ari made incredible progress, setting up an algorithm that predicted when the celestial lightning strikes in the incoming storm would be intense enough to disrupt the magical dampening field caused by the iridium deposits. Their estimation was that they'd have three to five minutes notice before the conditions would be perfect, and that they'd narrowed down their appearance to a two-hour window, coming only a day from now.

After talking things over for nearly an hour with Larkin and Ari, they'd ended up in the same place. They were headed to Nuva Troi. Because of the intense wards on the city, they would not be teleporting directly in, but would use the moments before they jumped to connect to Nox, via the dark web. It would be traceable back to ORAIS, but they'd be gone before anyone could track them more closely. Nox should be able to tell them exactly where to teleport in, how to get into the city safely, and the rest wouldn't be *easy*, but it would hopefully be fairly straightforward.

After the decision was made, everyone got to work on their own tasks. Harlow returned to the archives to look for more information about the origins of House Feriant and the Vilhar. After a long hour of searching, both the stacks and the card catalog, she gave up on finding more about those specific terms. Perhaps she needed to widen her search. Going back to *The Warden*, she hit again on the word "fey"—which she'd always understood to be associated with fictional heroes like Rhiannon, and her warrior companions, the Adar.

While the winged warriors had seemed fanciful to her as a child, after seeing the shade—and learning to manifest her Feriant form in various ways—she couldn't deny that this word had to be associated with her, and the Striders, and she wanted to know more. So she began again. The card catalogue yielded only one result, which was familiar to her: *The Violet Book of the Fey*. It was shelved in an anomalous section, tucked deep in a corner where she hadn't had the opportunity to spend much time. This bookcase was dedicated not to one location, but to various folklore.

As she ran her hand over the cover of *The Violet Book of Fey*, nostalgia hit her hard. The embossed gold illustrations of the faeries on the cover nearly had her in tears. They'd had this series of books as children—Selene had read to Thea and Harlow from it nearly every night when the twins were babies.

Harlow was transported back to her and Thea's attic bedroom in Nuva Troi, witchlights dimly lit, bobbing on the ceiling, as Selene's melodious voice carried stories of the many fey courts over their sleepy heads. Harlow missed Nuva Troi fiercely, and though she knew she'd find the city changed, she was ready to go home. She was ready to see her family again, and fight with them for the world that could be.

As she turned to walk back to the projector, something caught her eye—a volume stuck behind the various colors in the "Books of the Fey" series. Harlow pulled it out carefully; she only had to look at it to know it was very old, and not a facsimile or reproduction. A very careful look inside revealed Aislin's handwriting. This journal didn't find its way into what Connor likely considered the most useless part of the archive on accident—surely his wife had hidden it.

Harlow picked up *The Violet Book of Fey* and the journal, and brought them to the table at the center of the archive, powering up the holographic projector with the tablet. It took a few moments for everything to load, and Harlow looked carefully through the journal. The book was remarkably well preserved, and after a cursory glance Harlow strongly suspected Aislin had written much of it before coming to Okairos. It described the Ventyr's many missions into the limen once they had the means to travel there. There was only one reference to how they'd formed the first portal, and it was disturbing:

> *Ouriel will never forgive Lucien for stealing the starfire from her. I fear this will come back to haunt us. I warned Boreas time and again about turning his children against one another, but he would not listen. My influence on him wanes, and I will be sent with the envoy to Okairos— away from him, and more importantly, away from Orynthia, who hates me. I cannot blame her, and if Boreas cannot see the cuckolding beneath his nose, her utter devotion to her people and the insufferable General Ithaina, then hells take him.*

Aislin had been a woman scorned before she met Connor. Against her own better judgment, she wondered what Finn's father had been like back then. She turned pages, looking for information.

> *Conoch is a good leader, and his points about the tiresome nature of always being at war are well taken. I believe Pasiphae will align with him, as will Penemue and Leopold. As for myself, I find I do not care either way. Return or stay. Conquer for Boreas or ourselves. What does any of it matter? I will never have a child of my own. If I can bear a beast for my husband, the babe will be his from the moment it leaves my breast.*

That stung to read. Part of Harlow hated sympathizing with Aislin. She'd done so many terrible things, and was the source of so much of Finn's pain, but here it was in clear letters: she'd known Connor would take Finn from her, turn him against her. There was something deeply sad about that. The whole situation was terrible.

The projector was ready to use now, but Harlow skimmed through more of the journal. At first, she didn't know what she was looking for, but quickly realized that she wanted to find something redeeming in Aislin. She wanted to find any point at which Aislin was someone Harlow could admire, or at least respect. But there was no evidence of any such thing in this journal: it was page after page of heartless commentary on conquering Okairos. The woman had thought little of the people who'd been here when she arrived. As Harlow read, she became certain Finn's mother hadn't seen them as people at all, but tools.

Her stomach turned at the thought. She'd thought she might show this to Finn, but now she was tempted to put it back where she found it and forget she'd ever seen it. Just as she resolved to do so, her eye caught the word "Vespae," and a chill ran through her as she read on.

> *… and they call the creatures Vespae, believing them to be demons of a sort, sent to punish them for their wickedness. The humans on this planet are insufferably naive, but it serves a purpose. They are weakened, and will soon be vulnerable enough to accept our help.*
>
> *I must admit, this was a bit of genius on Pasiphae's part. Conoch wanted to simply strongarm our way in, but she is a clever one. Letting the creatures into this world while we build strongholds in the remotest regions has proven to be wise. When the Heraldic dynasties fall, we will rule them easily. The trouble will be sending the Vespae back, as their world was destroyed, pulled into a dying star shortly after we let them into the limen. Pasiphae suggested finding them a new world, but we have only enough pure starfire to open one last portal, and we've agreed we'll only do so in the direst of circumstances, if our project here fails.*
>
> *Pasiphae's cleverness shall likely save us again, as she and Penemue have devised an advanced Vascularity that shall act as a net, trapping the creatures in the limen…*

Everything past that discussed what Harlow already knew. What she'd already lived, watching Rakul Kimaris cut the love of his life down from the wretched Vascularity in Nea Sterlis. He'd had to do that because the Illuminated had let the Vespae into Okairos to begin with… *on purpose.*

Hot, furious tears slipped down her cheeks. They'd started all of this, created all of this death and destruction. And the Vespae? They were horrible, vicious creatures, but they too were victims of the Illuminated. Harlow grabbed the tablet, typing, "Vespae home world" into the search bar. The projector whirred to life, making a quiet little noise as it showed her a 3D model of something named "Planet 2361: DESTROYED." The caption said only, "Planet 2361, origin of Vespae, destroyed."

This had to be why the Vespae were searching for ORAIS: they wanted to know how to get home. They would not find the answers they sought here. And though she felt deep sympathy for their loss, and the cruelty the Ventyr had shown them, Harlow could not fathom what the creatures might do if they learned they could never return to their home.

She wondered if Alain Easton knew about this place, if with all his resources, he'd found out the same things they had in the past few months: that the Illuminated were not who, or what, they'd portrayed themselves to be. If, in his own way, Alain thought he was changing things for the better. A stab of guilt for killing Mark pierced her, like an arrow through the heart. Not because she was sorry she'd done it, she wasn't. It had been entirely necessary, but because it had only made things worse—if she'd just found another way—if Mark had... Maybe it would all be different now. Maybe they could have helped each other.

The idea broke something inside her, just a little. There had been a time she'd truly loved Mark, and she thought he'd probably loved her too, twisted as he'd been. If Alain had been on the same trail of information they were on for all this time, or longer, it would explain why Mark had tried so hard to get access to the Order of Mysteries' secrets. Her mind spun with the myriad possibilities, trying to weave them in everything else she'd just uncovered.

Harlow didn't know how long she sat staring at the projection of Planet 2361. Her mind couldn't make sense of the problems they faced, the enormity of what stood in front of them. After everything Connor, Aislin, and the elder Illuminated had done, she despised the thought of allying with them. But the Vespae weren't a foe the Fifth Order could fight.

And if the imperial Ventyr were also on their way here... There was no choice. There was nothing else they could do. They would have to ally with Connor and Pasiphae again to make the world safe. She hated to think of what they would ask for in return.

Someone touched her arm, their fingers feather light, but she startled anyway, shrieking. Finn grabbed her before she could tumble off her stool. "I'm so sorry. I called your name three times. You didn't hear me." He motioned to a plate of food. "I brought you lunch."

Hysterical laughter bubbled out of her. "Thank you."

He nodded. "You were thinking hard. What about?"

Now that he was here, and she had a plate of food in front of her, she realized she was starving. She motioned towards the journal, still open to the page she'd left it on, and the projection. As he read, she comforted herself with the sandwich in front of her. It was the only thing to do.

CHAPTER 32

Finn called Ari and Larkin down the moment he'd seen the depth of their problems. They went over everything Harlow had found, and when she'd spent her last word, showing them how deep their problems went, they too simply stared at the projection of Planet 2361.

Ari paced. "This doesn't even touch the issue of the Ravager. We still don't know where it is, or what it might do."

Larkin's eyes followed her friend. "And, we don't know the true extent of what an incubus can do. So we don't know what Alain is capable of. "

Harlow spent a few minutes trying to find information on both those subjects, both in the card catalogue and in the projector's database. Nothing came up, but that didn't surprise her. She had a growing theory that Connor had siloed various caches of information by topic in different locations, so that even if someone he hadn't authorized got into one cache, they would not have access to all his machinations or secrets.

She sat back down. "Nothing here. My guess is anything on the Ravagers or the incubi would be kept somewhere else. Locked down where Connor could keep an eye on it."

Finn didn't seem to hear her. "We are, I'm afraid, well and truly fucked." And then he laughed. "This is literally chaos. What are we going to do?"

She'd never seen him behave this way before. Finn always had an answer. He always had some way to take a step in the right direction to solving a problem. It was one of the things she found so comforting about him. But here he was admitting that this was all too much, that he didn't know what to do next. That he, Finn McKay, commander of the Knights of Serpens, was out of ideas.

Both Ari and Larkin stilled, each as perplexed by this reaction as Harlow. Someone needed to say something, think of something, because their little group was on the verge of spiraling into despair. Harlow took a few deep breaths, rewinding her thoughts some, going back to the moments before Finn had declared them well and truly fucked.

"We need access to another cache," she reasoned aloud. "If we're going to get the Fifth Order all the information they'll need to mount a defense of any kind, or at the very least some kind of bargaining chip, they'll need the full picture. We have to find out more about the Ravagers and the incubi."

Finn's eyes darted to her, the despair that clouded them clearing. "Yes," he murmured. "Yes, of course." He took her hand, squeezing it gratefully. "The Fifth Order can bargain with Connor and Pasiphae, their fighting force to align with the Illuminated's, in exchange for a more equal world."

"They'll agree to reform," Ari snapped, looking as resentful as Harlow felt. "They'll never agree to destroy what they've built for humans and the lower Orders."

"We'll end up right back where we are now," Larkin said, her eyes unfocused. "Right back in this terrible place, over and over."

Harlow didn't necessarily disagree with her sister, but her tone was so strange, so hopeless. So unlike *Larkin*. She worried that more had happened to her sister while they were separated than she was letting on. Harlow reassured herself with the fact that Enzo and Riley would be able to help with that soon. In fact, it could be even sooner.

"You're not coming with us to Nuva Troi," she said.

Larkin startled. "What?"

"You and Ari need to go to the Grove and tell the Council all of what we've found out here, *and* that we're going to find out the rest, everything Connor knows about the Ravagers and the incubi, in Nuva Troi."

Ari nodded. "His office. If you can get in—"

Finn interrupted. "Nox can get a message to the Fifth Order. They can come to the table with all the relevant information, and make a deal with the Illuminated on equal footing at least." He pulled Harlow into a giant hug. "Good job, babygirl. You figured it all out."

Harlow snorted. "It's just our next step."

He kissed her, his lips lingering over hers long past what was appropriate for the fact that they were still with Larkin and Ari. When he pulled away, he smiled, his eyes clear and confident once more. "We only ever need one more step. That's how you solve a problem this big, one bit at a time."

"Okay," Ari said. "I'm going to get back to my nap then. I have a feeling there won't be much sleep in my near future, and you all don't need me, do you?"

Finn shook his head. "I'm going to get us packed. We'll need to move fast, and travel light since we can't teleport into Nuva Troi."

When they'd gone upstairs, Harlow turned to Larkin. "Are you okay with this? With us separating?"

Her sister wore that same faraway look as before, as though she were lost in a world of her own. But she nodded. "Yeah, sure."

Harlow reached out, touching Larkin's cheek. "What's going on up there?"

Larkin smiled at her. "Nothing, sissy. I'm fine."

Harlow wanted to smile, but her lips wouldn't move. "Are you? You're acting strange."

Larkin shrugged, her mouth turning down in a frown. "It's an apocalypse, Harls, and I've been through it these past few months. What do you *want* me to act like?"

Harlow wasn't sure how to respond to that, but she felt instantly terrible about having pressured Larkin. "I'm sorry." Her words were so quiet she was certain Larkin hadn't heard them, because she was already walking away.

"I'm going to go make sure the tracker Ari and I set up is doing okay," Larkin called from the stairs. She didn't sound mad at all, in fact, she grinned at Harlow, blowing her a very Larkin-like kiss from the stairs.

Harlow got up, searching through the desk near the door for paper, pen, and envelopes. She sat down to write a letter to Enzo, letting him know that something seemed wrong with Larkin. He could help her figure things out. They were close, and Larkin might be able to hear him and Riley in a different way than she could her big sister. She tucked the letter into her back pocket to give to Ari later. The thought of going behind Larkin's back was unpleasant, but protecting her was what was most important.

CHAPTER 33

The next morning was hard. The closer their teleport window got, the more afraid Harlow became that splitting up was the wrong choice. Finn found her pacing in their bedroom.

"You know Ari won't let anything happen to her, right?" he said, gently trying to stop her from wearing a hole in the plush rug.

"I trust Ari," Harlow said. "Did you give him the letter for Enzo?"

He hugged her tightly. "Of course."

He hadn't quite understood why she felt so compelled to send it, but he hadn't questioned her either. Harlow got the sense that he was remaining as neutral as possible in all this, which made her feel a tiny bit patronized, even though she was certain that wasn't Finn's intent. The trouble was, Harlow wasn't sure she was being rational. She had no evidence that something was *wrong* with Larkin, just a feeling that something wasn't quite *right*.

Harlow buried her face in the sweater-clad muscles of Finn's chest. He smelled like comfort and strength. "Do you think I'm being overprotective?"

"Probably," he murmured into her hair. "But it's completely justified. I feel the same, and talking to Enzo could only do her good."

She raised her face to be kissed, and he happily obliged, his hands sliding up her back and into her hair. He deepened the kiss, and just as the tension that had knotted through her shoulders and spine began to loosen, Stella interrupted. "You have one hour until the way opens."

"Thanks, Stella," Finn replied. "I wish we had more time for this. It was nice to be here, wasn't it?"

Harlow nodded, pulling away from him to put her hiking boots on. They would not be able to teleport directly into the city, and there would be a walk through the suburbs to get to one of the locations where there were guarded openings in the wards for refugees. If they could get through to Nox, she would get them a more specific location. If they couldn't, Ari had given them the last coordinates he'd had, with the warning that Connor was rotating them at random intervals to keep the Vespae from predicting where the wards might open. It was a smart strategy, but it did make their journey difficult.

When she was laced up, Finn handed her a much lighter pack than the one she'd brought from Sanctum. In just a few hours, if all went the way it was supposed to, she'd be home. Or at the very least, back in Nuva Troi. As was becoming their family's parting custom, she and Larkin had spent time together last night, playing cards late into the evening, but today they were focused.

Ari and Larkin had spent the morning monitoring the incoming celestial storm. As Finn and Harlow made their way to the observatory, Harlow sensed something in the threads.

"I think I can feel the storm," she said softly, falling behind Finn to look at the sky. There was nothing there but a gloomy, gray day, and snow on the craggy peaks. Finn looked back at her, over his shoulder, waiting. "Feels like the aurorae."

He held a hand out for her, which she took. "The lightning that's coming is similar to what causes the aurorae, the clash of celestial power with our atmosphere. It's just a slightly different manifestation."

A bolt of lightning hit one of the peaks, illuminating the clouds across the narrow valley ORAIS was positioned in. It was followed by a roll of thunder unlike any she'd ever heard. Rather than a low, rolling vibration, this thunder was a high-pitched crack, and then a skittering hiss that hurt her ears.

On the peak the lightning-kissed snow began to crack and move. Finn's eyes followed it for half a second and then he yanked her arm as he started to run. "Move. Now. The storm is going to create a series of avalanches."

Harlow let herself be dragged, casting her gaze back over her shoulder to see the first rush of snow fall down the mountain. It was far enough away not to concern them, but she saw the problem. The storm would move right over them, meaning there was every chance that ORAIS would be hit, even though it sat lower than the nearest peak. There wasn't time to figure out if that would be safe, or if the building could withstand the pressure of falling snow, and possibly rock.

This might be their only chance out.

"It's starting," Ari shouted.

They rushed into the observatory, where Larkin typed furiously on a computer screen that hadn't been on the last time Harlow checked. She was getting in touch with Nox, or trying anyway.

Larkin shook her head. "She's not answering. I started early because of that." She flung her hand at several terrain maps.

"The storm's been causing avalanches, all across the range. They're more massive than anything I've ever seen," Ari explained. "We've gotta get out the minute we can."

"How long?" Finn asked, watching another avalanche in real time on the terrain map. Because it was little more than lines, it was hard for Harlow to envision how bad it actually was, but the tension in Finn's shoulders told her this wasn't a mere inconvenience.

Larkin's typing paused as she clicked into another screen. "Six minutes until it's directly overhead. From what I'm seeing, we'll have moments to get out before we're buried. Look, they're picking up in frequency." She pointed to something on the screen, a series of numbers that were rapidly increasing. Harlow had no clue what she was looking at, but she believed her sister.

"Okay," she replied. "Then let's get ready."

Stella's voice broke in as the lights in the observatory turned from their usual pleasant golden glow to flashing red. "Southwest perimeter ward, broken. Hostiles moving at speed toward the facility."

"Stella, lock all glass down," Finn ordered. "Clearance code 412-alpha-1018."

"Code accepted," Stella replied. "Hostiles still incoming. Count six."

"Can you determine their species?" Finn asked.

Stella didn't answer.

"Four minutes," Ari murmured, pulling Larkin up from her chair. "If you haven't got her yet, you're not getting her. Get to the center of the room."

Larkin nodded, distress clouding her features. She strapped her pack on, then hugged Harlow tight. "Ari will open the observatory top in a second, which will give us the clearance to teleport out. Love you. See you soon, okay?"

Harlow kissed her sister's face. "Love you," was all she could manage, she was shaking so hard.

"Hostiles on the roof," Stella said. "Five Vespae drones and an incubus. They are moving quickly toward your location, Finn."

"Shit," Ari swore, running his hands through his long hair. He stood next to the command center, ready to enter the code to open the roof. "If we open it, they'll get in."

Finn shook his head at his friend. "It's the only way, Ari. We'll be out before they can get in. When it's time, do it, and get your ass over here."

Ari nodded. Finn hugged Larkin. "Love you, kiddo. Keep the big guy safe, okay?"

Larkin nodded, grinning. "I can do that." She glanced down at her watch. "Thirty seconds." Ari made eye contact with Larkin and in unison they nodded.

At the same moment, heavy footsteps scrambled over the roof. Harlow's heart beat out of her chest. She hugged Finn tighter, tempted to close her eyes until it was all over, but something caught her eye by the door to the observatory.

The shade leaned against the doorway, smiling. *Have you figured it out yet? Do you know who you are? Do you know who I am?*

Finn couldn't hear it, but he saw the shade at the same moment she did. And then everything happened at once, in a muffled blur.

Ari yelled, "Time!" and ran for Larkin.

The roof opened, moving so slowly Harlow worried they wouldn't make it.

A message appeared on the screen Larkin had been typing on—Nox had responded, but it was too far away for Harlow to see, and there wasn't time to run to the terminal. Finn stared intently at the screen—perhaps he could see it. He only struggled to read things that were close without his glasses.

Six dark figures appeared, their faces obscured by the incredible show the celestial lighting put on in the sky above.

"Now!" Ari bellowed. "Go now."

The shade moved as the Wraith gave the signal. It smiled at Harlow, then disappeared inside her sister. Harlow lurched, not knowing if Finn saw what she had. But it was too late—his arms were wound tightly around her as she struggled—they were jumping.

See you soon, little bird, the shade murmured in her head as the world dissolved, and Harlow finally recognized its voice.

The Ravager had taken her sister. It had Larkin.

SHE HAD no sense of anything other than her rage. That *thing* had tricked her, made her think it was some sort of distant relation to her, made her trust it, and now it was inside her sister. Harlow didn't know how it was possible, but she'd seen it with her own eyes, heard it call her "little bird," just as the Ravager had. There was nothing but pain and fury, her shadows curling around her, concealing the world from her. And, she had the vague sense she was making noise, howling like an animal in pain.

Hands shot through the shadows, followed quickly by Finn's face. He took hold of her shoulders, shaking her hard. "Stop screaming," he hissed, rotating her body by force and clapping one hand over her mouth and the other around her abdomen. She was pinned to his chest, and he was murmuring something in her ear, something soft and comforting, but she could not hear it.

Harlow slumped against him, sobbing silently. Her shadows retreated, licking at her fingers, trying to soothe her pain. Finn took a few steps, though she couldn't see where they were through her tears. Vaguely, she heard a door opening and closing. Finn let her go, whispering for her to stay put.

There was nowhere to go. She was immobilized by the knowledge that she'd lost Larkin again. Already, the shock of what had happened receded in her mind. Harlow worried she was getting far too good at accepting the terrible things that happened to her. She forced air through her lungs, then scanned her body, bringing her attention to each muscle group. In the first days after losing Larkin and Finn, Sam and Tomyris had been the ones who'd coached her back into the present moment, not allowing her to spin out, or panic, promising her that she'd do her loved ones more good with her head on straight than she would by languishing in her despair.

They weren't here now, but they were just a short distance away, along with the rest of her family. The maters would know what to do. Nox would be able to contact the Grove. This wasn't as hopeless as it seemed, though it certainly wasn't good. It was like Finn said, they had to just keep chipping away at the behemoth pile of shit that kept piling up in front of them.

Something about that image made her laugh. Tears still slid down her cheeks, but the world crept back in. She stood in a desolate back hallway of a miserably sparse home. The furniture she could see from where she stood was sleek and modern, and everything was gray. Gray cushions on the couch, gray tile on the floor, gray baseboards, walls, and ceiling. The place was oppressive in its grayness.

Finn stood in front of her, keying in a code on a lock that led to the basement. The lock opened and he leaned down. A red laser scanned his eye, and the door popped softly open. When it did, Harlow was surprised to find that it was not the normal household door it had looked like from the outside; it was metal and nearly eight inches thick.

"Where are we?" she whispered, remembering that Finn had begged her to be quiet.

"Lemosyne Estates," Finn replied, naming a popular human enclave in the suburbs of Nuva Troi. That, at least, explained all the gray. Humans had gone through a period of loving the color in recent years, seemingly a reaction to the vivid color palettes immortals typically favored.

Finn took her hand, pulling her into the stairwell. He pushed her forward, urging her down the stairs, before closing them in, the heavy door shutting with a soft click, followed by the sound of several bolts snicking into place.

When soft lights lit beneath their feet, Harlow replied. "The suburbs?"

Finn pushed gently past her, guiding her down the stairs. "Yes. This is a safe house. Nox directed us here..." He trailed off. The muscles in his shoulders contracted.

The staircase went down three flights, but Harlow could see another door at the bottom. "Did you see it?" she asked as Finn moved a bit quicker.

When they stood in front of the next door, he finally looked back. "Yes. What did it say to you?"

"See you soon, little bird."

This door took another code, and this time, a tiny bit of blood from his thumb. When the door opened, he said, "The Ravager."

Harlow only nodded. There was nothing to say. She needed to keep working on getting herself under control, so she focused on her breath, as sconces, low to the ground, lit the shining wood floors beneath their feet. These, at least, were not gray, but pale bleached wood.

"Petra got to decorate this place about five years ago," he murmured. "She was into a 'beachy' look at the time."

Beyond yet another door, and another coded lock, the hall finally gave way to a large room, with a window that looked out onto a view of Ambracia Bay. Harlow couldn't understand it. She was utterly turned around, trying to remember where Lemosyne Estates actually was. It *did* overlook the bay from some sections, the houses here small but costly.

The bay was blanketed in winter gloom, the sapphire water churning angrily far below. The windows were obscured by rock, set back far enough that it was doubtful anyone below could see them, but they let one of Nuva Troi's most impressive views into the little room.

When Harlow tore her eyes away from the sea, she found two white couches, covered in soft linen fabric, facing one another. An enormous driftwood coffee table with a glass top sat between them. Beyond them was a fireplace, a refrigerator, an open door that led to a small bathroom, and a bed covered in the same white linen as the couches.

Finn held the only thing of value: a phone. He already had it powered up and was sending text messages as he made himself comfortable on one of the couches. He glanced up. "This will take a while, with the wards up. I've gotta hack through a bunch of shit before I'll get to Nox. You should rest."

She stared at him. "Are we going to talk about it?"

He looked back down at the phone, his fingers flying across its touchscreen. "We shouldn't have taken her with us. You were right."

"Is that what you think I want? For you to tell me I was *right*?"

Finn didn't look back up. "Isn't it?"

He was shutting her out. "No," she replied, ice in her voice. "It actually isn't. I'm not your mother."

That got his attention. Anger flashed in his eyes as they glowed, and then immediately receded, softening as he saw her—really saw her. "I know." He set the phone down and got up, taking three long strides to get to her. "I just… fucking lost her again, Harlow. Why can't I keep any of you safe?"

The way his voice crackled over each subsequent word melted the icy anger she'd felt only moments before. As his arms went around her, and she hugged him in return, she sifted through the moments she'd shared with Larkin for the past few days, full of little inconsistencies. Her strange moods, the time she'd called her sissy when Larkin knew she hated it, and then further back to the shade, all it had said to her at ORAIS—one remembered phrase slamming into her.

I am here but not here. The shade had said it to her, and so had the Ravager. It had given her clues, and she missed them all. But why, why had it been kind? Why had it helped her on the bridge? Why did it want her to find the truth of who she was, the origins of the Feriant? And why in seventeen fucking hells had it taken her sister?

Finn kissed her forehead. "I need to get back to this. The sooner we get to Nox, the sooner she can get in touch with the Grove and we can find out where Larkin is." Harlow nodded. Her limbs felt heavy, weighed down by exhaustion. "Babygirl, you're crashing," Finn said as he guided her to the bed. "Lay down for a bit and I'll have news when you wake."

He bent down when she was seated, untying her boots like she was a small child. With every passing moment, she felt the shock of what had happened take over. She was not doing as well as she'd thought.

"Maybe I'm not cut out for this kind of thing," she mumbled, her words feeling thick in her mouth. "I'm not a hero."

Finn stood, then unzipped her jacket, gently peeling it from her shoulders. When he had her free of it, he steered her towards the pillows, lifting her feet to tuck her into the soft blankets.

"There are no heroes, Harlow," he murmured, climbing in next to her.

She cuddled in next to him, watching as he typed and typed on the phone, glad he'd gotten in bed with her, rather than going back to the couch.

"There's you," she breathed as sleep took her.

CHAPTER 34

They didn't hear back from Nox for several hours. It was just after dawn when the phone buzzed, a sound that Harlow had forgotten existed. She was awake, watching the sea, but Finn slept. In fact, he was so asleep he didn't hear the phone. There was no identifying number on the screen, but Harlow assumed that only people who were trustworthy had the number.

"Hello," she said softly.

"Harlow?" It was Nox.

"Yes," she breathed. "Finn is sleeping. We made it to the safehouse in Lemosyne."

"Thank all gods," the shifter breathed. There was a small ruckus in the background as Nox whispered to whomever was with her, "They're safe."

"Are we good to talk?" Harlow asked, curling up on the couch.

"For a few minutes. I sent Finn the information he asked for."

"Okay," Harlow said, slowly, drawing the syllables out as she thought. Nox was usually so specific about things, precise to a fault, at times. The fact that she'd been vague meant she was worried the line could be compromised. Harlow proceeded with the caution, though she had to ask about Larkin. "Have you heard from Larkin and Ari? Did they make it to the Grove?"

Nox was so quiet Harlow worried she'd lost the connection. "Nox?"

"I'm still here." The shifter seemed to be thinking.

"We know, Nox," Harlow murmured. "What happened?"

The Wraith made a small humming noise, apparently relieved she didn't have to try to break the bad news to Harlow. "She completed the jump safely. Then said, *I'll keep her safe*, before disappearing."

Harlow let out a long breath. "Thank gods."

"You trust it?" Nox asked. Whispers in the background let Harlow know that at least some of her family was probably listening in.

"Hi everyone," she said before answering.

"Just me and Mother," Indi's voice chirped softly.

"No," Harlow said, relieved Selene wasn't there. "I don't, but if it wanted her dead, it could have killed her a thousand times."

There was a long pause, and again, Harlow worried they'd lost connection. "Ari said the same," Aurelia replied, sounding distant. "It's not much comfort, but it's some."

"We're going to lose you in a sec," Nox interjected. "We'll talk about this more tomorrow."

"Okay," Harlow replied. "Love you."

A chorus of "love yous" got cut off as the line really did go dead. She would see her family tomorrow and find a way to fix this.

Harlow resisted the urge to begin listing all the things that had gone wrong at this point. Instead, as Finn slept, she clicked into the folder icon on the screen of the phone. It was the only icon, besides the usual ones for settings, text, and compass. There wasn't even music, news, or any of the gossips' apps on this thing, and those usually came standard with phones.

Inside the folder was a complete write-up of the Knights' progress in Nuva Troi, as well as a time and geolocation for the ward's opening. They had until this evening, which was awful, because the wards would open inside Nuva Troi's biggest nekropoleis. Ghasts, poltergeists, and shades would all be coming out, at exactly the same time. Harlow repressed the urge to protest; there was no other option. Instead, she shut the screen off.

She felt a little guilty for having pried into what she considered Finn's private business, but reasoned that it had been necessary to determine if it was all right for him to continue sleeping. She glanced briefly at Finn's slumbering form, wondering if she should wake him, then decided against it. They both needed as much rest as possible today. While she loved their family, being surrounded by them again would take precious energy reserves to navigate, and they both were running low.

Harlow fetched a bottled iced latte from the fridge, checking its expiration date. It was still good. As she walked back towards the couch, Finn stirred— sometime in the night, he'd let his glamour go and he rested in his true form, his wings spread out behind him, spilling over the side of the bed at awkward angles. Much like the many ways Axel slept that looked impossibly uncomfortable, Harlow couldn't imagine how he slept that way, but his face was the picture of peace.

His eyes fluttered open, dark in his true form. "Did Nox call yet?"

Harlow leaned on the bed, laying her head on the pillow close to his. "Yes. Larkin jumped Ari to the Grove, and then disappeared. The Ravager promised to keep her safe—whatever that means."

Finn nodded, his eyelids heavy. He yawned. "What about us?"

He was obviously exhausted, fighting his urge to be Knights' commander. "We don't go 'til tonight," she explained, stroking his brow, which was more prominent in this form. The opalescent, almost blue skin that covered his body glowed softly with her comforting touch. "Nox sent over the coordinates and her report."

Finn nodded sleepily, snuggling deeper into the covers. The room was pleasantly dim, cozy and soft. "You read it, okay? Get caught up on what's going on."

Harlow's eyes widened, just a little. "Really?"

"Yeah, could you?" He buried his face in the pillow, but his arm snaked out to pull her into a hug. "Love you," he mumbled before falling back into what Harlow hoped was a deeply restorative sleep.

She watched him sleep with fascination—he'd never slept so deeply in the entire time they'd been back in each other's lives. As she extricated herself from his heavy embrace, she thought of the thick doors and many locks that separated them from the outside world. It took all that to make him feel safe. That wasn't just the stark fact that the world had gone to shit, it was how Finn lived.

And now he was trusting her to read Nox's report for him. Harlow flexed her hands as she stood, staring at the engagement ring that she never, ever removed. Spending her life with Finn had always been something of a blurry, happy thought, until now. Now, it felt real. The shift between them since she'd gotten him back was nearly imperceptible, but it had made their relationship real in a way it had never been before. Raw, messy, even ugly sometimes. But they just kept trying.

They'd *keep* trying. They'd keep having each other's backs, and fighting when they didn't agree. It wouldn't be a perfect picture; they weren't some ideal. They were a perfect mess—and they were going to make it through this. She knew enough about stories to know this was meant to be her darkest hour—the point when she should feel unable to go on. The odds were certainly stacked against them, in nearly every way possible. There were no clean solutions left to any of their problems, and worse, disaster lurked around every corner.

But for the first time in months, that didn't make her feel unbearably heavy. She was terrified about what might happen to Larkin, but even the tiniest grain of hope was enough. Harlow didn't know what the Ravager wanted, but if she was right that it had been with them, watching them, since its release from Nihil, she wondered—really wondered—if what it wanted was utter destruction.

Harlow pulled a throw blanket from the arm of the couch and tucked herself into a corner where she could see the ocean, sipping her iced coffee, opening the file Nox had sent Finn to update him on what they'd learned so far in Nuva Troi. She assumed the most important information wouldn't be here: Nox might be confident in her ability to hide digital trails, but she'd never risk their operation when she and Finn would be in the same place in a few hours.

As expected, not much in the report was shocking or a secret. The first item was a long list of important places that had been destroyed in the fighting when the first wave of Vespae had come through the city, before the Order of Mysteries had gotten the wards to hold. She was sad to see that the streets surrounding the Monas had taken so much damage. It had been mostly residential, and longtime family friends had lost their homes.

There were also lists of places Nox had tracked the five rings symbol they'd seen marking certain windows last summer. They were cropping up more now, as a beacon of hope, but also an indicator that help for humans could be found within. That was, perhaps, the most depressing news. Humans had a curfew, and had been strictly forbidden from trying to use any aethereal power. They were expelled from the protective wards that surrounded Nuva Troi if they refused to comply.

Hives of Vespae had been tracked carefully. They were surrounding the city, gathering in the suburbs. In fact, there was one not far from Lemosyne Estates. They would have to pass near it, and through the city's outer ring nekropoleis to get to the ward opening later. Harlow shuddered thinking of it. She'd been blessedly free of ghasts for nearly two weeks and had no desire to have them chase her down again.

But by far, the worst news was that all of the gossips were back up and running, and they were calling the gathering of refugees in Nuva Troi, "the winter season." Harlow glanced through a few of the low points Nox had pulled out, shaking her head. The fact that there were members of the lower Orders socializing right now showed just how far removed they were from the realities of the world.

A sorcière Harlow had known since childhood had been quoted as saying, "As long as the wards hold, we're gonna party like the world is ending." At that, Harlow groaned aloud. A year ago she might have rolled her eyes, but she'd have moved on quickly, distracting herself with other pursuits and the idea that there was nothing she could do. Everything was different now.

Finn sat up, his head tilting. She'd woken him reacting to the foolish witch's words. "What time is it?"

Harlow looked at the clock on the end table. "A little past noon. Are you hungry?"

He leaned forward, his wings tensing behind him. "I might be."

Heat flushed through Harlow. His skin glowed softly as he looked her over. "Don't you want me to tell you what Nox sent over?"

"Not particularly," he said, swinging his legs over the side of the bed.

When he stood, the sheets fell away to reveal his naked body. In his true form, he was taller, broader, even more muscular than his humanoid alternae, and he was clearly not interested in hearing about anything other than her from the looks of things.

He strode into the bathroom, giving her a show of his sculpted behind. "Why don't we see about a bath for you?"

Harlow rose without another word, compelled by the rippling movement in his wings, the clenched muscles of his ass, and the sound of water running. They had time—for a little while longer, they had time.

CHAPTER 35

Ari had described the devastation in Nuva Troi, but there weren't words to prepare Harlow for *this*. The damage in the suburbs had been light; the horror here was the profound emptiness. There were no children playing on the streets, no sledders in the parks, and no one was out shoveling snow. Typically, Harlow loved the city best, with its crowded, glittering glory. But in deep winter, the suburbs were always her favorite because of the sheer amount of people making the best of the cold.

Now, as she and Finn quietly made their way through the empty streets, the devastation of Okairos seeped into Harlow. Where were all the people who lived here? Her heart knew the answer, and it shuddered erratically as she followed Finn through back alleys. Traveling inconspicuously here was difficult, as even back alleys were wider than in the city, leaving room for trash trucks and Harlow's ultimate favorite: weekend garage sales. Harlow had never felt so exposed in Lemosyne Estates, which had been one of her favorite places to search for treasures on hot summer weekends.

The journey was quiet at first, and then the buzzing noise of thousands of Vespae seeped in. They were everywhere, essentially unavoidable the closer they got to the nekropoleis. But the day had been bright, sunny, and cold, and it seemed to have lent them a bit of luck so far. As the Vespae did not enjoy sunlight, most they encountered were in a dull stasis, huddled in groups, facing one another.

A mere hint of movement caught Harlow's attention in a deserted playground. She and Finn both froze. It was only a suggestion of pursuit, no footsteps, no brush of fabric, nothing more than a ghost of a sound. But it stopped when they stopped, and moved when they moved. A harsh wind kicked up, sending fresh snow flying in the air, the metal swings creaking back and forth.

Can you tell where they're coming from? Harlow asked, hoping that Finn's hyper-sensitive hearing might be able to discern more than she could.

We've got two tails, he replied. *Both moving alone.*

As he communicated this to her, a single drone crashed through the doors of the little visitors' center next to the playground. Its movements were erratic, as though it weren't moving on its own will. It made straight for Finn, who shouted, "Run! I'll meet you at the nekropoleis."

Harlow hesitated. They'd talked about what to do if something like this happened, but she didn't want to leave him. The logic of letting him fight the drone alone was solid. It was just one. He could use his speed if he had to, though they'd avoided both that and teleporting to keep a lower profile, not wanting to be tracked if the Illuminated were using CCTV or other monitoring devices to locate refugees—or seditionists.

"Harlow," he growled between punches. The drone wasn't fighting particularly well, but it was slippery, seeming to evade and pester, more than attack. He was distracted by her presence, unable to fight well if he knew she was standing there just watching.

Better to be a moving target, she remembered. She forced herself into a jog, out of the park, glancing back only once as she exited the park, but Finn had disappeared from sight, though she could still hear him fighting in the distance. Harlow got the strong sense they were being purposely separated, and she didn't like it. She decided to make one lap through the block she was on and go back for Finn.

Halfway around a block of nearly identical homes, movement in her peripheral vision caught her attention. She turned slowly, hoping to find Finn, but instead came face to face with a Vespae queen. Her wings were beautiful, whole rather than ragged, though her clothes fared no better than any of her counterparts. They were in tatters, looking like they'd been spun from spider-silk. Her face was freshly scarred, as though someone had dragged talons across it recently. It was the queen who'd tried to communicate with Harlow at the attack on Sanctum.

The queen's head tilted, and Harlow braced for the clicking noise that would call her swarm, but there was nothing. The queen moved slowly, carefully, as though she didn't want to startle Harlow. Her rigid brow tightened a little, as though she might be frowning.

Harlow couldn't make sense of what was happening, and her instinct was to run. But the queen's eyes searched hers, bright and intelligent. There wasn't a hint of the Vespae's usual menace in her demeanor. She'd tried to communicate before—might she try again? Harlow kept her voice low and even, putting effort into trying to replicate the buzzing noise the Vespae made when they were resting. "What do you want?"

The queen's head tilted further, her eyes widening some as she looked closely at Harlow's mouth. Despite her disheveled state, Harlow was surprised to find that the creature smelled like spring—like a field of wildflowers and sweet grass. She made a few soft noises, ones utterly different from the calls Harlow had heard in the past. They didn't sound like words, but there was no denying they were language. The Vespae queen *was* trying to communicate with her.

Harlow nodded, hoping to indicate that she was trying to understand. The queen nodded back, her eyes lighting. But then she shook her head no, repeating the same phrase again and again, pausing to nod then shake her head after each time. She was asking if Harlow understood her.

Harlow shook her head no, finally. The queen's shoulders slumped in obvious frustration. Harlow remembered that Alain Easton had somehow been communicating with the Vespae, and wondered how. "Do you understand me?"

The queen's eyes lit up again. She nodded vigorously.

Harlow looked around, thinking quickly. Did she have a pen in her pack? She wasn't sure, but she also didn't want to startle the queen with movement she might mistake as hostile. "Can you read our words? Write?"

This time the queen thought for a moment. She held up a finger as she spoke, which Harlow took to mean "I'm answering your first question." The queen nodded.

Harlow smiled. "You can read our words."

The queen looked horrified by the smile, staring at Harlow's teeth. Harlow stopped. "My apologies. I am happy you understand me."

When the queen looked confused, Harlow tried again. "It brings me joy that you understand my words." Still confusion. Maybe happiness and joy weren't clear concepts for the Vespae. She tried another approach, on a hunch. "It brings me peace that you understand me."

The queen nodded, pressing her hands to her chest, a low comforting buzz emitting from her mouth. Her eyes glazed over with bliss. Peace was a concept the queen understood, and obviously she found it as positive as Harlow did. Harlow kept her mouth closed this time, but nodded as she smiled, pointing to her mouth, then said, "Peace."

The queen nodded again, then held up two fingers. She was answering Harlow's second question about writing. Now she moved her head in an odd fashion, it wasn't a nod, or a shake, but somewhere in between. Then she pointed to her long fingers and curved talons.

"Oh!" Harlow exclaimed. "It's hard for you to write."

The queen nodded. She said several things, her buzzes and clicks repeating softly, as though she were talking to herself. A muscle in her face twitched.

"There's something you want to tell me," Harlow intuited aloud. "But it's complicated."

The queen nodded.

Harlow didn't know what they were going to do. A crash nearby startled them both. She heard Finn cry out, followed by the sounds of fighting. The queen let out a shrill noise, then a series of clicks. The queen looked at the sky in a way that obviously expressed frustration with her swarm but there were sounds of retreat. Finn called her name now, though Harlow didn't want to answer. It wouldn't matter if she said she was all right, he would come, and he would scare the queen off, or try to fight her.

Harlow took a risk and touched the queen's arm. "They'll be here soon, but I want to talk to you. What do your people want? Can you try to tell me?"

The queen nodded, crouching down. Her forehead moved again, this time expressing intense concentration. The snow was dirty, but the queen made big letters in it. The one word she wrote was not a surprise, it confirmed what Harlow had supposed at ORAIS.

"You want to go home."

The queen nodded, making several noises of distress, and movements with her body that indicated pain, then a motion with her hands that looked like a fish swimming along a straight path, followed by the noises that meant peace.

"It's painful to be here," Harlow translated. "You want to go home."

The queen made her "sort of" head motion again, then repeated the fish hand motions and the peace noise. Harlow tried again. "It's painful to be here, and you're looking for a way home."

Now the queen nodded, waiting expectantly. Harlow did what she knew no one else probably would, she took the queen's hands in her own. This did startle the creature, but she did not react violently; she made a lower noise than the peace noise, but similar. Harlow decided this meant it was all right.

She couldn't tell the queen that her world had been destroyed. Not when she was asking for help and Harlow had none. It felt like a betrayal, but their communication was so tenuous that she couldn't tell the whole truth, not until she had a solution that wouldn't devastate them both.

Harlow looked up into the queen's eyes, and told the best truth she could. "I will find the way. It's what I'm here to do." The queen nodded, then slid one of her hands out of Harlow's to write in the snow again. Her letters were messy, but they spelled out ORAIS. The queen pointed to Harlow, then herself several times.

"You were with Alain at ORAIS."

The queen nodded, she made a noise that was unmistakably angry, hitting her chest, but pointing away from Harlow. Then she pointed to Harlow, making the low noise that didn't quite mean peace again.

"Alain?" Harlow breathed, wondering if she was catching on.

The angry noise.

"Harlow," she said, pointed to herself.

The queen made a slightly less pleasant noise now, but it still resembled the positive noises the Vespae made. Harlow took it to mean, "You're not my favorite, but you're fine enough."

"Did you see what I found out about your planet?"

The queen nodded, squeezing her hand. There was no mistaking the sorrow on her face. She needn't have worried about lying. The queen already knew. She spoke quickly, moving her hands in ways Harlow couldn't make out. Then, she drug her talons across her face. Harlow remembered the way the first queen at Sanctum had hurt her.

"The others don't want to work with us?"

The queen shook her head. Finn and the queen's drone were getting closer. Harlow had to think fast. The queen had been to ORAIS, seen what Harlow had and she was reminding Harlow of the discord between herself and the other queen.

"They don't believe you. The others don't believe you that your planet was destroyed."

The queen nodded, making the noise Harlow now associated with Alain.

"Because Alain told them something else."

The queen nodded, dragging a finger across her throat. It was just a guess, but Harlow thought the queen meant that Alain had killed her people, the ones that had been with her. Likely, he'd done so to keep them from telling. Harlow wondered how the queen had escaped. There wasn't time to discuss that now. Footsteps approached from all directions: Finn's and the queen's drones, or perhaps her guard. They'd been found.

Harlow tightened her grip on the queen's hand. "We don't have to fight. Let me try to help."

The queen nodded, pointing to the word "HOME" in the snow. Finn was close now, and so were the queen's people. They were out of time. There would be a fight if they stayed.

"Go," Harlow said, releasing the queen. "I'll do everything I can to help."

The queen pressed a hand to her chest again, and made the full peace noise, as she looked up, into an upstairs window of the house. A figure stood watching —one Harlow would know anywhere.

"Larkin," she shouted.

Her sister stepped away from the window, and the queen shot into the air, calling to her approaching guards. Harlow rushed through the shattered glass of the kitchen door, racing towards the stairs at the center of the house. Larkin stood on the landing, but from the unnatural set of her shoulders, Harlow knew the Ravager had her.

"Please let my sister go," Harlow begged. "I'll do anything you want."

"You're already doing what I want," the Ravager said, with Larkin's voice. "And besides, I'm not hurting her."

Harlow knew better than to rush the stairs. The Ravager would just use Larkin's ability to teleport away. "Why did you help me? Why did you help Ari?"

Larkin's head shook. "The time for questions is over, little bird. We will see each other again when there are answers."

"Wait," Harlow cried out, desperate. "Are you going to kill her? Please. Just tell me the truth. Are you going to kill my sister?"

The Ravager inside her sister sighed deeply. "I am so very tired. Aren't you?" Larkin disappeared.

Harlow was still staring at the spot she'd stood when Finn crashed through the front door. Her entire body felt as though it might go limp. "Larkin was here."

Finn's head swiveled wildly, searching for Larkin. Noise from outside suggested another swarm had found them. The keening cry that threatened to build in Harlow's throat died as Finn grabbed her hand. "We have to go."

CHAPTER 36

Outside, the air vibrated with the noise of approaching Vespae. Finn glanced down at Harlow, whose hand shook in his. "We have to take a risk now, okay?"

She nodded, too upset to think. He took hold of her and they blinked out, reappearing inside a gas station. The electricity was off and across the street, Harlow spotted the entrance to Nuva Troi's largest nekropoleis.

"Are you all right?" he asked as he searched the empty gas station. The shelves had been ransacked.

Harlow shook off the moment with Larkin as best she could. "Yes. But before you found me, the Vespae queen that tried to talk to me at Sanctum, before I found you…"

Finn glanced up from a few aisles away. In a flash, he was next to her, hugging her. "Hey," he murmured into her hair. "Keep talking to me while I see if I can find some salt. We have to keep moving."

Outside, the sun was going down. They didn't have long until the ward opening. "The queen. She was at ORAIS with Alain. They found the information we did. She knows their planet was destroyed, but the other queens don't believe her. I think Alain is lying to them, manipulating them into helping him cause chaos."

Finn nodded. He held a bag of rock salt aloft, smiling. "In case the shades or poltergeists get too frisky." His cheer was fake, but she smiled back in kind. It was all they could do. "He's not causing chaos, Harls. He's making a power play. I have a feeling he wants the Illuminated's reign of power ended as much as we do —he just wants to be on top when it ends."

A sharp pain shot through Harlow's chest. She'd been holding her breath while Finn spoke, and her heart was beating in an uneven rhythm, her lungs pulling sharp gasps of air in. The ceiling felt as though it was lowering for a moment. Harlow closed her eyes, crouching down and unzipping her jacket so her neck and chest could get some air.

Finn crouched next to her, breathing slowly. "We're going to get through this, babygirl. One step at a time, okay?"

Harlow let her eyes drag up from the dirty tile floor to his. "Do you actually think we can do this? Can we win against all these odds?"

"The truth?" he asked.

She nodded, even though she wasn't sure she wanted it. Finn's analytical take on things was most likely grim right now.

"When I look at it objectively, no. We don't stand a fucking chance." Tears sprung in Harlow's eyes. Deep down, she knew this. "I don't know though, Harls…" he trailed off, his stormy eyes sparkling. Here in this dark, abandoned gas station, outside the city they both loved, at what felt like the end of everything, Finn's eyes were sparkling. "I know we can do this. It's not even a question for me. We're going to win—*because we have to.*"

Outside the gas station, ghasts appeared, and at least one poltergeist, attracted to Harlow's grief. Expensive sigils on the door kept them out, but as soon as they went out there, the ghasts would be all over them. Finn stood, pulling Harlow to her feet. He didn't pick the bag of salt back up as he stared at the growing crowd of unquiet spirits.

"If they're using the tracking equipment I'd use, they may already know we're here," he said softly. He wasn't talking to her, but to himself. He glanced down at his watch. "The wards are opening soon. We're blinking in."

Harlow's head tilted as her mouth opened, though to say what, she didn't know. Before she could think of anything to say, he covered her mouth with his, and they disappeared between.

They reappeared in the nekropoleis, along a row of impressive crypts, but Harlow didn't have time to admire the scenery. Ghasts streamed out of every crypt, attracted not only to Harlow, but apparently to the wards themselves. There was nothing to see, but Harlow felt the massive amount of magic being used to keep the wards up, a dome of power over Nuva Troi. She'd never seen anything like it before. The biggest spell she'd ever witnessed was the Vascularity in Nea Sterlis, and though the wards were less complex, the sheer area they covered was impressive.

Finn held her to his chest, his arm tight around her waist. The ghasts solidified as they neared Harlow, her fear growing by the moment. At Sanctum, one had been able to touch her, and now there were hundreds of them, filling the narrow lane between crypts. They were no longer silent, noise accompanying the hideous feats they performed with their rotting bodies.

Across the lane, the wards opened, a sliver of light that shimmered in the threads. "Fuck," Finn swore. "I miscalculated."

Finn grabbed her hand, pulling her towards the sliver of opening in the wards. They had less than a minute to get through. Several vampire ghasts, who'd likely died a hundred years ago from the vintage of their clothing, hissed at them. Their rotting flesh was livid with dark, oozing liquid. The pack of vampire ghasts were closing in on them, though the others materializing mostly milled about, terrifying, but not necessarily violent.

The vampires, however, obviously intended to inflict harm. Their ravenous howls attracted shades, who crept out from several crypts, their hollow eyes roving over the living flesh in their midst. Harlow had no idea how she'd mistaken the Ravager for a shade. Her fear of the dead had kept her from observing them too closely, but she saw the difference easily now.

Finn pushed her behind him. "Get on my back," he growled as he shifted into his true form.

He was going to barrel through them. Every second that passed, the ward-opening grew smaller. She did as he asked, holding tight as he sped through the creatures surrounding them, using his head as a battering ram and his wings as a barrier between her and the spirits they plough through. He shifted back as they crossed through the opening, just as it closed.

It was a bit like teleporting. There was a moment of blank contraction and then they were inside a crypt, gasping for air, both of them sweating from the side effects of having passed through the opening just a tiny bit too late. Inside the crypt, there were four huge Illuminated guards, armed to the teeth with human-made weaponry. It was the kind of tech Alaric called "terrifying in its genius," and was beyond illegal to even speak about, though of course the dark web was full of schematics. Apparently, Connor had found a way to actually produce them.

One of the guards, a redhead, sneered as she stepped forward. "Look what we have here. Finn Fucking McKay."

Harlow glanced from guard to guard. None wore even a shred of empathy on their faces. Which was supposed to help them? They all wore vicious expressions, and she found it hard to believe that even one of them might get them out of this. Finn stepped in front of Harlow.

The redhead took out a pair of zip ties and waved them in Finn's face. "Put these on her, and then on yourself. Kimaris is gonna promote me to the Dominavus for this."

Harlow's heart sung at the mention of Rakul's name. Maybe they'd take them to him, and this nightmare would end. Vivia had to have made it back by now, and the two of them could help Finn and Harlow escape.

The tallest of the guards shook his head. "Fuck that, Marshall. You're not even close to a promotion. I've been shortlisted for the Dominavus twice."

Marshall rolled her eyes. "All the more reason to let me take them in."

Harlow suspected Marshall was the one who was meant to help them, but she worried about Nox's choice in guards. The Illuminated woman was rude, and not particularly convincing. Even Harlow thought it was a stretch that the other guards would just let her take them in. She held out her hands for the zip ties though, the faster they got this over with, the better.

Finn held eye contact with her for a moment longer than necessary, flicking his eyes to Marshall as she and the tall guard argued. He pulled the zip tie closed, but not too tight. Harlow lowered her head in a slow nod. They agreed, Marshall was their best bet, whether she was the person who was supposed to help them or not. At the very least, they could overpower her easily when they were alone.

Marshall was a distracted mess, arguing with the tall guard, rather than watching them tie one another up. "C'mon Penemue, you're a nepo-baby and you'll get any position you want, eventually. Don't be an asshole. Let me take them in."

Finn's eyes widened at the use of the tall guard's name. This was Alix Penemue, the only son of Rosamund Penemue, the former governor of Falcyra. After spending months in Falcyra, Harlow had heard her fair share of rumors about his cruelty. They couldn't go with him. He was too well matched with Finn as a fighter, for one thing.

The other two guards appeared to have lost interest. They'd taken their places on watch. One by the door, one watching a dimly lit computer screen, which appeared to show a heat map of the nekropoleis. There were several Vespae moving through the graves, hot on Finn and Harlow's trail, but the ghasts and shades had disappeared. Harlow wondered about the Vespae. If the queen had called them off, why were they still following? But, of course, there was more than one swarm in the area.

Alix Penemue shook his head. "I'm not arguing about this with you, Marshall. I outrank you. Get back to work."

Harlow held her breath, waiting for Marshall to form another, more clever argument, but nothing came. The redhead grumbled a bit, then went back to a post by the window. Harlow's heart sank. She made eye contact with Finn just as Alix Penemue drew the butt of his gun back, then slammed it into the back of Finn's head so hard, he crumpled to the ground.

Harlow screamed and Penemue grabbed her roughly, tearing the zip ties off her, replacing them with metal cuffs. The second they were on, Harlow knew they were in trouble. The cuffs were made of iridium. She wouldn't be able to shift.

A long whimper escaped her lips as he clamped another set onto Finn. The other guards laughed, even Marshall.

"Gets 'em every time, doesn't it?" the redhead said. "We give shits like you a minute to think of all the ways you're gonna escape, and then you feel the death metal and…" she drew her finger across her throat, making a choking noise. "Makes doing this drudgery bearable, honestly."

The other two laughed again, obviously agreeing. Alix Penemue didn't laugh. His face didn't move one stony muscle as he dragged Finn towards a door at the back of the crypt. He opened it, revealing a dark staircase that only had one possible outcome: the catacombs under Nuva Troi.

"Follow," he commanded.

Harlow did as she was told, though everything in her screamed that if she went down those stairs, she wouldn't surface again. She wasn't sure she had another choice.

Marshall stepped forward as she went, gripping Harlow's arm hard. "I hear it goes better if you don't fight him too hard." She waggled her eyebrows at Harlow suggestively.

Harlow spit in her face. The redhead punched her. Pain bloomed across the bridge of Harlow's nose, sending her to her knees. Ahead of her, Penemue pushed Finn down the stairs, his body thumping the entire way down. He turned, pushing Marshall back, who was spooling up for another punch.

"Don't spoil her face," Penemue said with a smirk.

Marshall laughed harder now, and Harlow knew that laugh. It was one she'd used, the one that held no humor, but relief. Relief it wasn't going to be her that got hurt. She'd used that laugh when Mark got mean with other people in front of her. It was something she'd regret her entire life, laughing when someone else was about to be hurt, rather than herself. But at least she understood.

As Alix Penemue pulled Harlow off the floor she looked Marshall directly in the eyes. "I'm glad it's me this time, instead of you," she whispered. "Maybe someday you'll forgive yourself for this."

The anger fell off the woman's face like a mask. Only shock remained. Behind her, Penemue laughed into her ear, low and cold. "There'll be plenty left for Marshall, don't you worry."

Harlow stared into the redhead's eyes as Penemue dragged her away. It was the only thing that gave her strength, knowing that even for a few moments, she was giving *that* woman relief, even if she hated her. The other two guards kept their eyes carefully ahead, as they had for the entire interaction, pretending not to see. As the darkness of the staircase closed around her, she shut her eyes.

When she opened them again, they were standing by a golf cart, deep in the catacombs. It was an odd sight, so out of place for the surroundings, but it did make sense, she supposed. Penemue was loading Finn into the back, and then shoved Harlow forward. "Get in."

There was a bit less cruelty in his voice now, but Harlow wasn't lulled into complacency. She'd fight every single second of this. She didn't move.

"I'd rather you not be passed out for this," Penemue growled. "Get in the cart."

He glanced back up the stairs, as though watching for the other guards. Was he hoping they'd peek in and see his cruelty? Or was he just satisfied that they'd hear him, whatever he was about to do, with their preternatural hearing. Her stomach turned, and every step was painful, but once she was seated in the cart, Penemue didn't lay a finger on her. So it was worse then; he had some secret lair down here, likely where no one would hear her scream.

She considered trying it anyway, just to stall for more time, but the cart lurched forward and she had to spend all her energy staying upright. There were no lights down here, and the golf cart's headlights were weak, so Harlow could see very little as they sped along. There were forks in the maze of tunnels every twenty to thirty feet, and Harlow didn't know how Penemue knew where to go until she noticed the red lines painted on the path.

Unconsciously, she began watching the lines, focusing all her attention on them. When they took an unmarked turn, her stomach dropped. She'd started to convince herself that Penemue was probably all talk, and that Connor would want them brought back in good condition. Who would risk making him mad? Not even Rosamund Penemue's heir.

But then, Finn was only knocked out. He was probably already healing. And he was who Connor would care about, not her. Her suspicion that Alix had a lair of his own down here seemed more likely to be true with every passing moment. They'd picked up speed, so when the cart slammed to a halt, Harlow lurched forward.

Penemue kept her from flying out of the cart, his arm slamming into her chest. "Get out," he ordered, his voice a murmur.

Harlow didn't move. She was frozen by her own fear. Penemue shook his head, then began unlocking the heavy wooden door in front of them with several combination locks. Harlow struggled against the iridium manacles around her wrists, to no avail, then tried her best to summon her shadows. Nothing worked. The iridium muffled her access to the aether, and Finn was still out cold.

She was a little surprised that when Penemue had the door open, he dragged Finn in first. Harlow jumped out of the cart, rushing to follow Finn, to try to stop whatever Penemue would do next. Finn lay in a heap in front of her, but Penemue was nowhere to be seen. The door slammed shut, the sound of whirling locks sinking her spirits even further. Harlow spun to face Penemue, determined to be brave.

The Illuminated grinned at her, opening his arms. "I'm so fucking glad to see you."

Harlow took several steps backward, in horror, nearly tripping over Finn's body. A ward went up around the door, a strong, sorcière-made ward. And then Penemue's face began to melt. Harlow's vision blurred. She blinked several times and when her sight cleared, Meline stood in front of her.

"Sorry!" her sister cried. Meline grabbed her, hugging her hard, kissing her cheeks. "That was *so* messed up. I'm sorry."

Harlow stood stock-still, completely stunned. The illusion had been *perfect*. Her mouth fell open as Meline pulled away from her. She didn't know whether to laugh or sob.

Meline ran to a spiral staircase that grew out of one corner of the room. The floral carving on the alabaster stone reminded her of something, some*where* familiar. "Are we under the Order of Mysteries?" Harlow breathed.

"Yes," Meline said, before calling up the stairs. "I have them, come quick."

Sam and Tomyris rushed down, and Harlow thought she would lose her mind with relief. Tears fell on her cheeks as her breath shuddered through her. Tomyris gave her a quick, fierce hug, before beginning work on Finn, celestial power flowing through her hands. It took Harlow a moment to register that Tomyris was using her alternae. Instead of the curvaceous, muscular Ventyr woman Harlow was used to seeing, she watched as a woman with all of Tomyris' sharp, angular features, with umber skin and long, ebony hair tied back in a bouncy ponytail, worked to revive Finn.

"Who did her ponytail?" Harlow asked as Sam hugged her tightly.

Her friend's grin was wide. "She did it herself. Your sisters have been giving her tutorials. All her idea—when she found out they used to be influencers."

"Used to be?" Harlow murmured.

Sam nodded, watching as Meline handed things to Tomyris from a duffel bag that served as her medical kit. "Those two are great friends... But yeah, your sisters refused to get back on socials. They've quit."

It wasn't so surprising, she guessed, given all they'd been through, but it was a little odd. The twins had been public figures since they were in their teens. The second the maters let them have social media, they'd already had brand identities planned. An era had ended in Nuva Troi society if they weren't going to be the perpetual "it" girls that everyone looked to for fashion and beauty advice.

But Meline was wearing completely practical clothes even now: a black, funnel neck winter coat, sensible thick leggings, and tall, compact snow boots. She looked stunning, as always, but there wasn't an accessory on her. Her sister had changed. Harlow didn't know if it was for the better, but she looked well. Happy, even. Some of the shock of the past hour wore off and Harlow was able to give Sam a rundown of what the last few days had been like and what they'd found at ORAIS.

When her story wound down, Finn was awake. He sat up, rubbing the back of his head. He looked at Meline, narrowed his eyes and then shook his head. "You hit me, huh?"

She grimaced. "I had to make it look real!"

He shook his head, but started to laugh, pulling Meline into a hug. "You had me fooled. That was great work."

Meline hugged back, and Harlow thought her heart might burst. When she replied with, "Love you, big brother," Harlow burst into tears.

"Aww, Harls," Tomyris bellowed. "Don't start on the waterworks." Tears pricked her big brown eyes though, and she stood, wrapping Harlow and Sam both into a giant hug.

"I missed the two of you so much," Harlow blubbered as Finn and Meline both wedged their way into the group hug.

They didn't stand that way for long. Meline hurried them upstairs. "Go on, I have to go handle Alix's demise. I have a trick up my sleeve to make Connor believe you've escaped back to the suburbs."

Finn, who was halfway into the first spiral, turned. "Is Alix Penemue still alive?"

Meline rolled her eyes. "I didn't become an assassin while you were gone. He's knocked out in a broom closet in their headquarters under the Temple of Raia offices. He won't wake up for another four hours, and I'll be three hours gone by then."

Finn nodded. "You have it all figured out then."

Tomyris clapped a hand on his shoulder. "She's good at this. Really good."

Harlow hugged Meline. "Love you to the moons," she whispered in her sister's ear. "See you wherever home is later?"

Meline cupped Harlow's face in her hands. "You sure will, pal."

Then her sister shifted back into the enormous Illuminated asshole, Alix Penemue, who shook his rump like an agitated chicken and clucked a few times. Meline laughed in Alix's voice. "I just love making dudes like this look like incompetent fucks."

Meline-as-Alix disappeared back through the door, and Harlow stood watching, speechless at the effortlessness of it all. Sam smiled at her. "She can expand her illusion now to others. Up to about a half hour, which is all she should need."

Finn looked down the stairs at Sam. "What do you mean?"

Tomyris grinned, her white teeth shining in that feral way that reminded Harlow that she was an expert fighter. "She's got two of the sorcière we're sending into the 'burbs on recon gussied up as the two of *you*. They're about to go put on a little show for the cameras. 'Harlow and Finn' are about to escape the great Alix Penemue and stuff him in a closet."

Harlow was impressed; she caught Finn's eye and his head shook in amazement. "Why'd we even come back?" he said with a wry smile. "You all have everything handled."

Sam took Harlow's hand. "Come on, your moms are waiting upstairs. They've been staying here for the past few weeks, instead of Alaric's."

Harlow followed Sam upstairs, bringing up the rear, while Tomyris explained, "Aurelia and Selene have been looking for everything we can find on the Ravagers. As soon as we found out how Larkin was taken, we came here."

"And have the maters found anything?" Finn asked.

"A bit," Sam answered, turning to wink at Harlow.

Harlow shook her head. If anyone could work this out, it was Selene and Aurelia. It felt like it took forever, and about twenty spirals, but Finn opened a door into a back hallway so familiar it brought back Harlow's childhood.

The Order of Mysteries smelled of cedarwood, wax, paper, and the merest hint of vanilla absolut, which was an odd change, but pleasant. It was less odd when Selene wrapped her arms around Harlow, surrounding her with her own sultry scent. Vanilla absolut was one of Selene's favorite perfumes, and she smelled of it now.

"Darling," Mama whispered in her ear.

"Let me hug our girl," Aurelia interrupted.

Sam and Tomyris backed away, smiling at the happy reunion. "See you tomorrow," Sam mouthed. "Morning run?"

Harlow shook her head, shooting Sam a mock-glare, mouthing back, "Not a chance."

Tomyris blew her a kiss as they walked off. Selene threw herself at Finn, who'd apparently just been hugged by Aurelia, as he still looked slightly bewildered by the parental attention. Bewildered, but pleased. Harlow was pleased as well. Seeing her entire family just as excited to see him as they were to see her was just the balm she needed after the day she'd had.

CHAPTER 37

Walking down the halls of the Order of Mysteries brought back all kinds of memories, and not just because she'd spent so much time here as a kid, but because nearly everyone her parents trusted most was *here*. Their friends, and their friends' children, and sometimes their children as well.

"What are they all doing here?" Harlow asked as the maters led her and Finn to Aurelia's apartments.

All of the Order of Mysteries' representatives and their staff had quarters in the Order itself for times when there were multi-day rituals, or events. As the Order operated as much as an academic unit and artists' atelier as anything else, their compound in Nuva Troi was nearly the size of the Alcaia liberal arts college next door.

"We're safer together," Aurelia answered. "As well, we decided to come back here to help the administration at Alcaia."

The Order and the university had a close relationship, so that didn't surprise Harlow. "Are things all right there?"

Selene smiled. "The students protested a lot at the beginning. They argued for letting more refugees in…" Mama's eyes got misty.

Aurelia finished. "There was a massacre."

Finn stopped cold. "The Vespae?"

Aurelia placed her hand on Finn's arm, deep empathy in her eyes. "No, darling."

His jaw clenched as his eyes fell to his feet, his cheeks flushing red as people passed.

Aurelia took his hand in both of hers. "No one here blames you, Finn."

Selene added her hand to her wife's. They were making a scene in the hallway, and from the performance Selene was putting on, this was utterly strategic. They were quite a picture, the penitent Knight and the wise sorcière matriarchs.

It was working; people looked on them with sympathy as they passed. A few spared a glance for Harlow, but not one person said hello.

Their eyes slid past her as they had for the past two years. Harlow shook her head. She knew the way to her family's rooms here, and she wasn't going to ruin what Selene and Aurelia were trying to do. She waited until a few people came to speak to Finn and the maters before slipping away. She looked back over her shoulder to find Selene's eyes following her.

Selene's smile spoke of understanding. She knew how unfair it was that they could accept Finn, but were still holding a grudge against Harlow for dating Mark. Selene had been the subject of similar treatment when she was young, and apparently a bit of a rake. As family lore went, Mama had broken the wrong heart right before she met Aurelia, and it took several decades to build their reputation with the Order of Mysteries again.

Harlow's people were wonderful, but sorcière were slow to forgive. As she made her way through the arched limestone hallways, she ignored every curious look, and the accompanying freeze out. Just as she pressed her palm to the electronic lock at the Krane's quarters, a voice called out her name.

She turned to find Avery Hargrove jogging after her. The curvaceous, beautiful witch was another of Mark Easton's exes, and a close friend of Larkin's. Avery, who was usually elegant and reserved, threw her arms around Harlow.

"I heard about Larkin," she murmured, before pulling away. "Not many people know, don't worry. But your moms asked me to help look through the archives for information on the Ravagers."

So they were jumping right in. Still, Harlow was glad for the hug, and glad for Avery's hand slipping into hers. "I'm so glad you're okay, Harlow."

"You are?" The words slipped out before Harlow could think better of them.

But it was clear Avery understood. "I know everyone's still deep in the habit of freezing you out. It took three years for me. Given everything you've done for them, I'd say you have a few more days, tops." Avery's round cheeks lifted towards her sparkling brown eyes in a smile. "And if I'm wrong, fuck 'em. You have Finn and your family, the Knights, the Feriant Legion… and me."

Harlow hugged Avery again. They'd never been friends, never even tried, but she was grateful for this moment. It felt like coming full circle.

Avery made it a few steps before turning back. "He deserved to die, Harlow. Thank you for what you did."

Harlow's heart stopped. She had no idea Avery knew what she'd done last spring. The other woman pressed her hand to her heart. "There are others of us —women he hurt before he found you. Every one of us is grateful to you, Harlow. You are our hero."

Harlow stood there for a long time after Avery disappeared around a corner, stunned by what Avery had said. She stood there so long, in fact, that Selene and Finn rounded the corner. They'd lost Aurelia, apparently. As arch-chancellor, she was likely needed for some Order business.

"What are you doing out here still?" Selene asked, pushing through the door. "Mommy and I have a dinner we're committed to this evening, and Nox and Indi are on patrol 'til ten, so the two of you are on your own."

Harlow laughed. "We literally came through a wasp's nest of danger to get here, and you all have *plans*?"

Selene let out a frustrated little breath. "Scoff all you want, but it's taken a lot for Lili and me to pull the Order together."

Harlow softened her expression. She hadn't meant to sound so harsh. "I know. I was being silly—or trying anyway."

Selene's brows furrowed slightly. "I didn't catch that." Selene really was just like her sometimes. Harlow had the same trouble catching humor, occasionally. Selene's brow smoothed and she hugged Harlow. "I'm just so glad you're here. There's food in the fridge, and we'll talk about what we've learned tomorrow over breakfast. You two get some rest." And then she was gone.

"In and out like a whirlwind," Harlow remarked.

Finn was staring at the living room, just beyond the foyer, surrounded on three sides by books and arched stone windows that looked out on a courtyard. A giant overstuffed sofa in the living room was covered in a dark tapestry fabric depicting unicorns frolicking in a forest. The wood floors were covered in plush patterned rugs in cool jewel tones, and the chairs that flanked the couch were all a lush eggplant velvet. Several oil portraits of animals dressed in historical dress graced the wall opposite them and Finn seemed perplexed by the whimsy of it all.

It was nothing like the retro-minimalism of ORAIS, or the opulent, serious furniture his parents had in their estate. This was Selene at her weirdest. At home, above the Monas, things were colorful, but understated in comparison to this. Lush wallpaper covered the hallway walls, depicting mythical creatures, lurking amongst the flowers in an ancient garden.

"This is something," Finn said, clearly at a loss for words.

Harlow nodded. "See why I wanted to decorate in all neutrals?"

He laughed. "I like this, but yes."

She took him down the hall to the kitchen, where the cabinets were painted a high gloss emerald green with gold hardware. The tile was shaped like dragon scales or arches, depending on how you looked at it.

"Really?" she asked. "You like this?"

Finn smiled, picking up a framed photo of Harlow and Thea when they were five and seven, respectively. They were dressed in little pallyras, for a Solstice ritual. "I *love* this. It feels like home."

She nodded. "This has always been our second home. I just haven't been here much since Mark. Come on, I'll show you to my room."

"You have your own room here?" Finn seemed astonished. He solved his own disbelief moments later. "Because Aurelia is arch-chancellor?"

Harlow shook her head. "No, everyone has room for their whole family."

Finn frowned, his analytical mind working overtime. "But... the building isn't big enough for that."

Harlow raised her eyebrows. "This is the Order of *Mysteries*, Finbar." She began walking down the hall, towards her bedroom. "The building has had a life of its own since its inception. So much magic, all in one place, it defies logic a lot of the time."

"That's not possible," Finn said, following close behind. "That's not how magic works. There's a science to it."

Harlow stopped in front of the door to her room, smirking. "That's what the *Illuminated* believe. Again, we are the Order of Mysteries. Where did you think the name came from?"

He shrugged, frowning so deeply she worried he might crack his forehead. "It's just that…"

The door to her room opened. Her hand wasn't on the doorknob. In fact, both of her hands were clasped firmly in front of her body. Finn's eyes widened as he entered the room. "What is this? I had no idea you had the talent for illusion."

"I don't." There was nothing in her bedroom but a giant bed, a crystal chandelier, and clouds that were slowly changing colors from a deep sapphire to an even deeper emerald green, giving the fantasy of a dark, duotone daydream. They hung from the ceiling, and puffed up from the floors.

"First, it's not an illusion." Harlow sat down on the bed, looking around, pleased to be back after so long. She hadn't known what she'd find when she opened the door. The sorcière had rejected her thoroughly for the past two years, but apparently the Order of Mysteries *itself* had not. "And second, this is a little different from what it was like when I was younger. Back then, the colors were lighter, and there were some posters on the wall."

Finn sat next to her, staring at the clouds as they shifted in slow motion. The chandelier dimmed to a low glow. He laughed, a deep belly laugh that rumbled through her. "Is it… reacting to us?"

Harlow raised her eyebrows and lowered her voice, as she climbed onto his lap. His arms went around her, his hands gripping her hips, drawing her closer to him. "What would it be reacting to?"

His answer was a kiss, his lips pressing to hers, gently at first, then harder as the chandelier lowered the lights further.

Finn wrapped one arm around her, his fingers splaying out across her back as his tongue slid against hers. His other hand dug into her hair, pulling hard at the nape of her neck, eliciting a whimper of pure bliss.

She broke their kiss, tracing the lines of his face with her fingers. "Today was pretty messed up." Finn's smile was sad. He nodded once. Harlow brushed kisses on his brow and his lips. "Will you help me forget it?"

Now his smile reached his eyes, his arms tightening around her as he scooted back on the bed. Soon, he was resting against the upholstered headboard, his knees cradling her smaller body against his. Nestled between her legs, his desire for her grew, but Harlow was in no rush.

She kissed him again, tasting lust on his lips as her hips moved slowly, tantalizingly. She pulled her sweater off, then unclasped her bra. He moaned at the sight of her nipples stiffening in the cool air of the room. Her hips ground against his harder now as she leaned back against his knees, guiding his hands to her breasts.

"You are so beautiful," he murmured, his words sweet as he pinched her nipples, sending a delicious bite of pain through her.

"I need to remember what we're fighting for," Harlow insisted, punctuating her words with another roll of her hips. He stared at her for a moment, wonder in his eyes. Her arms twined around his neck, and she whispered in his ear, "Show me. Fill me with it."

When she pulled back, his eyes glowed faintly, and his fangs emerged. The Claim was brutal in some ways, but it was also pure energy, the combination of both aethereal and celestial force. *Life.*

Finn maneuvered her quickly, lowering her back to the bed as he pulled her leggings smoothly off her, and then the rest of his clothes in quick succession. He kissed his way down her abdomen, slowly, his tongue making a languorous journey towards the pulsing core of her. There was nothing in the world she wanted so much as his mouth on her, now, but he teased her, skipping to her thighs, which he showered with attention. His mouth, his fingers, his face, all caressing her skin in a fever of missing the spot she wanted him most.

Beneath his ministrations, she writhed, attempting to guide him to her preferred location for his efforts. Still, he teased her, his fingers sliding into the legs of her panties, pulling them away from her body enough that air hit her sensitive flesh. Air, but not his touch.

His mouth fell over the fabric covering the slick heat gathering at the apex of her thighs, his tongue sucking and caressing her through the fabric of her panties, stoking both her pleasure and frustration to an inferno.

And then he stopped, yanking the fabric from her as he slid up her body to kiss her mouth. He sank into her, the head of his cock spreading her wide.

"I love you," he murmured as he moved slowly inside her, sliding inch by tantalizing inch. "And if you and I are all that's left at the end of this, I will have everything I need."

She pulled him deeper inside her as her mouth crashed into his, their movements frantic and desperate. Venom filled her mouth as her fangs protracted, and when her mouth fitted against his neck, he mirrored the motion, piercing her skin at the same moment she sank into him.

Finn roared against her neck, his cry muffled as his venom flowed into her. Euphoria lit her from within, and her entire body burst into dark, inky flames. Wings sprung out from her back as her fangs released from Finn's neck. They were levitating several inches above the bed, and she felt the difference in her body, the strength of her Feriant form flowing through her as her pleasure crested.

As the moment passed, they fell back to the bed, crashing awkwardly into one another, laughing. Finn pushed her hair back as he adjusted slightly to lay beside her, rather than atop her. "Your ears…"

She felt them, and though they were fading back to their usual rounded tips, she felt the arch that had been there. "Did I shift completely?" she asked.

He shook his head. "No, not into whatever the shade was, but a little bit like it."

"Weird," she breathed, smiling. "Bath or food next?"

He scooped her into his arms. "Bath."

CHAPTER ¿8

Breakfast was a whirlwind of catching up amongst piles of food, all of Harlow's Nuva Troi favorites, in fact. Chocolate croissants from Lupin, coffee from Cerberus, and all the family chatter she could wish for. As she watched her sisters and the maters orbit around one another in the kitchen, grazing on the spread of fruit, cheeses, and pastries, her heart ached for Thea and Larkin.

Harlow tried to apologize for what had happened to Larkin, but no one would hear it. In fact, the maters thought the whole thing might be good, rather than an utter failure on her part. Finn squeezed her hand to reassure her, seeing that the explanation hadn't helped with the guilt she felt. Instead, they urged she and Finn to catch them up on all that happened since they separated.

The maters were most interested in hearing about the Vespae queen, and Harlow wished she could tell them more. Selene pulled her blonde hair into a tight bun, and Harlow knew instantly that her mind was already spun out in a million different directions, cataloging search terms for later. Nox, who had buzzed off all her ebony hair, jotted several things down in her phone as she listened to Harlow. The quiet shifter fit into their family life seamlessly.

Harlow watched as she and Indigo interacted, so deeply in love they were like extensions of one another. It was a different kind of love than the one she and Finn shared. They were so similar, dressing in the same edgy, stylish clothes that were as utilitarian as they were fashionable, and even speaking in a similar cadence that had Harlow wondering how Meline felt about things. She and Indigo had always been so close.

The longer she watched them, the less she worried. It was obvious the three of them were the best of friends. Harlow noticed that Meline's face went carefully blank every time Ari's name was mentioned. He was settling in all right, from the little they'd heard from the Grove. Nox and Meline loaded the dishwasher as Nox reported out to Finn. It was a little like being in a cross between a family meeting and confabulation of all the organizations they were affiliated with.

Harlow stopped listening to it all, happy to be sitting on a countertop, safe in a kitchen she'd been in thousands of times over her life. She pulled Indigo into her arms, wrapping her legs around her sister's slender body and kissing her short, dark hair. "I missed you," she murmured in her sister's ear. Nox and Meli were talking so animatedly to Finn she risked a question. "What's going on with Meli and Ari?"

Indi glanced over her shoulder, her eyes rolling. "All drama, all the time."

Harlow suppressed a smile, at the same time her heart ached. "They're a couple of big personalities."

Indi nodded. "I'm glad I get to *stop* being a big personality now."

"I heard you retired from the it-girl life."

Indi leaned back, her head falling on Harlow's shoulder. "It was always more Meli's thing than mine, but it just got to be too much. Neither of us meant for it to take over our lives. It was better to delete and move on."

"You deleted your accounts?" Harlow asked, incredulous.

Indi broke free of her embrace, grabbing her twin's hand. Even with their different styling now, they were so alike. "We deleted everything. It's just the Monas' socials for us now. We're going to use our savvy to make it better than ever when all this over."

Meline nodded. "We are. It's gonna be epic."

"I wish we didn't have to go," Indigo said. "But we all have shifts to get to, and the maters need to get you up to date on the Chandelnuit plan."

Harlow was thoroughly confused. Chandelnuit was a ritual to celebrate the return of the light, not a party, at least for the sorcière.

Finn looked as though he might have an idea of what was going on. "They're not actually having their annual party, are they?"

Selene nodded, kissing Meline goodbye as she slung a messenger bag over her shoulders. "See you after I'm done with the kiddos," Meline said.

She was off to teach the sorcière children how to teach their human friends magic. It was a strangely brilliant plan: because the Illuminated valued children so much, they weren't monitoring them in the slightest compared to the adults. So the sorcière taught their own children how to help their human friends learn to use aethereal power, and the human children taught their parents.

Nox and Indigo had a lab, where they monitored the gossips, socials, and the dark web for useful information. They weren't coming up with much more than they'd already reported to Finn, but they were in the middle of decrypting a video missive from the Fifth Order, and they were eager to get back to it.

When the others were gone, Finn and Harlow followed the maters to Aurelia and Selene's office. Outside the glass doors that led to the courtyard, a flock of dark-eyed juncos fought for spots at the feeder. This had long been Harlow's favorite room in the Order of Mysteries' residence. It felt like the Monas, with

744

the same white bookshelves, a similar celestial fresco painted on the ceiling, and a chandelier fashioned to look like a golden orrery that depicted their solar system.

Harlow stared at the chandelier as Selene brought up a folder labeled "Ravagers" on the digital whiteboard. It was hard to imagine just how far away planets like Interra, Sirin, and Earth must be, when they weren't even in their solar system. There weren't any comfortable chairs here, only Selene and Aurelia's desks and room for pacing, so the four of them stood in front of the whiteboard.

The old-fashioned telephone on Aurelia's desk rang, nearly scaring Harlow out of her skin. Aurelia answered, said "mmhmm" a few times, then "I'll be right down." She hung up, and turned back to the group. "Nox forgot to tell you that she has phones ready for the two of you. You'll need them, so I'm going to pick them up."

"What else are you up to?" Selene asked with a wicked smile.

"You can explain things to the children, darling. Apparently, Merhart Locklear is on his way over as well. The Order of Masks may finally have agreed to join us."

Harlow was relieved to hear that. "What about the Order of Night?"

Selene shook her head as Aurelia kissed her goodbye and disappeared. "Most of them are with the Illuminated. Athan is leading the charge now that Berith is gone. Kate and the others had luck though—if the Illuminated don't agree to our terms, the Avignonne vampires will join us, as will Castel des Rêves."

Finn's face opened up into the happiest smile Harlow had seen since he'd returned. "Really? That's wonderful."

Selene smiled. "It seems we have a chance. Our alliances are stronger than they were in the Great War. We won't fail this time."

"Show us what you found," Finn said, stepping closer to Selene.

Harlow tracked the files as Selene scanned through them, noting citations from dozens of books about the origins of aethereal power and theorems regarding elemental beings. She stopped on a scan of an ancient book with an unusual foldout that expanded the page to three times its usual size. The drawings on the foldout were precise, nearly architectural in nature, though the written language was not one Harlow recognized.

"What is this?" Harlow breathed, stepping closer to the screen as Selene enlarged the image.

"The Santvara Manuscript," Selene said, as though that explained everything.

Finn looked to Harlow for a clue, as wonder caused her mouth to gape open. "This is it? You found it? Where?"

Selene looked like a cat who'd swallowed a bird whole. "Some of the children found it tucked in with a skeleton."

Harlow snorted. "In the crypt?"

"Yes," Selene laughed. "They were playing—"

"Hide and Freak," Harlow finished. The lost look on Finn's face deepened.

"It's like 'hide and seek' but in the crypt—and the Santvara Manuscript is practically a legend, said to show the origins of the aether."

She stepped forward examining the image, then pointed to a section that clearly depicted symbols for limenal space. "See here, these symbols are kind of universal to indicate something about the limen, the aether in particular."

Finn tilted his head slightly, then pointed to some of the smaller depictions of cities. "Is this meant to represent the way the limen sometimes replicates real places?"

"Yes!" Selene nodded. "And these symbols are common alchemical markings that show how aether gives way to life, and those who use magic give back to the aether." She pointed to each of the symbols as she described them. "It's like a formula."

Finn glanced at Harlow. "This is stuff you already knew about?"

Harlow smiled. "Identifying this kind of 'stuff' used to be part of my *job*, Finn."

It was ages since she'd thought about her work at what had felt like a completely mundane job, identifying occult texts and archiving them for both the Monas and the Order of Mysteries. She and Thea both. Harlow bit her bottom lip to keep from tearing up. That all seemed so unreal now. Like it was lifetimes ago.

Finn didn't say anything, just took her hand and squeezed. Selene watched, a look of satisfaction passing over her face. Finn had passed a test with her, one neither of them had expected he'd take today, but from the look on Selene's face, it had been an important one.

"So," Selene continued. "This is the part we're interested in, though really, the entire book is fascinating—this is what's relevant."

She enlarged part of the image to show intricately detailed clouds of aether moving into screaming faces, much like the ones Harlow had seen in Nihil when the Ravagers escaped. She didn't recognize the symbols the author had used now, except for the ones that referred to "limen" and "aether."

"What is this?" she asked Selene.

Selene's face was drawn and serious now. "A disturbance—the aether is sentient, as you know. It operates as a whole, a collective of ideas connected to all worlds. It is meant to be infinite and regenerative. But if it's disturbed, the author theorizes here that sometimes it individuates."

Selene zoomed in on another part of the image that depicted an angry, monstrous creature stepping out of the cloud of faces. Above its head was a luridly drawn alchemical symbol Harlow knew all too well.

"That represents the isolation of an element," Harlow explained. "Though I don't think I've ever seen it look so—"

"Angry," Finn finished, squeezing her hand.

Selene took a deep breath. "It's not a particularly positive depiction, but we believe this is meant to represent the way a Ravager is created. It would appear that when first isolated, the aethereal energy is often quite distressed."

"And powerful," Finn mused.

Selene nodded. "You can see how it might be mistaken for an Elemental."

"Technically it is," Harlow said. "Aether is the primary element in all things."

Selene reached towards her face, stroking Harlow's cheek with her knuckle. "My smart girl."

Finn let go of Harlow's hand. "So what about this makes you optimistic about Larkin?"

Selene still stared at Harlow as she answered. "The Elementals your father's people imprisoned are not young. The rest of the images here indicate that the first period of isolation is the worst for the creatures; after that, they develop as people would, as individuals."

"And what would make you think this one isn't angry with us? Why wouldn't it be after what Connor's family did?"

Selene raised her eyebrows at Harlow. "You know the answer, don't you, darling?"

"Judge people by what they've done," Harlow said, tilting her head at her mother. "Not by what you think they might do."

Finn watched them carefully. Harlow hugged Selene with one arm. "It's one of Mama's big life lessons."

"One I learned the hard way as a young woman," Selene explained. "Several times, in fact. I used to jump to many conclusions—and it never failed to get me into trouble."

"It took Larkin without her permission, without telling us why," Finn said, looking at the two of them as though they were taking a bizarre leap of logic.

"I didn't say it made perfect choices, Finbar," Selene said. "But it's reassured us twice now that it will not hurt her and that she's safe. You said she looked well when you encountered her yesterday."

Harlow nodded. "That's true. And it helped me, on the bridge, and with figuring things out about the Vilhar—and the House of Feriant. It's actually given us quite a bit to use against your parents—not to mention the incident with the queen yesterday."

For a brief moment Finn looked as though he wanted to return to the point that the Ravager had stolen Larkin. Eventually, he shook his head. "You're right. We don't even know that it completely understands why just taking her might be a problem for us."

Harlow had another idea. "Or it does understand, but it needs *her*, specifically her. She's a dream walker, Finn, and if the information we have about it is right, it may not have much time before its presence here starts changing Okairos."

Selene clapped a hand over her mouth. "And it knows her, Harlow. How many times has she been to the limen over the years, visiting Ash? We have no idea how its senses work. It could know her."

It all made sense now. The Elemental's immediate recognition of who and what she was, its selection of Larkin as its host. "But what is it here to do?" Harlow asked.

Finn grimaced. "I can't believe I'm about to say this after everything we've been through—but do you think it's trying to *help* us?"

"Help us do what?" Harlow mused.

Finn shook his head. "I don't know—but I have a feeling Larkin might."

Harlow stared at the whiteboard screen as Selene closed the file, and opened another. "I really wish we could ask her."

"At least there's reason to hope," Selene said. "Now, let's talk about the plan for the Chandelnuit party. We're going to need to be precise—and the two of you are going to have to play your parts perfectly, or this won't work."

CHAPTER 39

After lunch from Gastro Lupo, Harlow looked through her new phone. Nox had set everything up so that Harlow's socials were all ready to go. Finn sat with her on the couch in the Order of Mysteries apartment, her feet on his lap. On the surface it looked like he was catching up on Nuva Troi news channels, but Harlow knew better. He was going over every facet of the maters' plan, trying to figure out if it was a good one.

"I know you don't like it," she said, after watching him pretend to scroll for a half hour.

His jaw did that little twitchy thing. "It's *not* the same as before."

"No," she said, poking him in the belly with her toe. "It's safer."

He sighed. That much was true. "You don't need my permission—"

"I don't," she interrupted. "But I'd like to know if you think it's a solid plan."

He dragged her onto his lap, in one fell swoop. "It's a solid plan. Much as I hate the gossips, they're our best tool right now. Go forth and be photographed."

Harlow popped the last of her parm fries in her mouth and grinned. "This is going to be *really* weird."

"It is," he agreed. "Call if you need anything."

HARLOW'S TASK for the day was to retrieve what they'd need to crash an Illuminated party, from home and Enzo's atelier. Nox had it on good authority that Connor believed Harlow and Finn had escaped Penemue, back into the suburbs. He'd sent troops into the wasted neighborhoods, searching for them, and the real Alix was enduring hours of "questioning" with a Dominavus intelligence officer. Harlow was to get into the atelier, and then the Monas, bringing all the jewels and dresses they'd need home with her.

Rakul had been in touch, and he would keep the Dominavus off her trail for the day, leaving Harlow to be caught sneaking around Nuva Troi by the gossips. As they had no idea when the Imperial Ventyr might arrive, they didn't have time to have quiet, never ending talks with Connor about the logic of banding together with the Fifth Order. The Illuminated needed to *see* the tides had turned against them before they presented their plan, and the information about the incoming threat.

The maters had come up with an ingenious plan with the twins, who might have retired from living their lives in public, but who definitely knew how to work the gossips to their own advantage. Harlow's trip out was practical, but it was also an opportunity. Sam was coming with her, to help transport the items back, and Harlow was glad for the company as they stepped past the light wards on the Order of Mysteries.

It felt a little like stepping onto a battlefield, except now the battle would be fought in ways that had typically been used against Harlow. She and Finn had manipulated the gossips a few times over the summer, but nothing quite as calculated as this. All Harlow could do was be grateful that while Nuva Troi winters were cold, they were marginally better than Falcyra.

Winter in Nuva Troi was one of Harlow's least favorite times of year. The sky was a heavy, dreary gray, and the plows had piled snow over and over all winter, making it gray as well. But today, big fluffy flakes had been falling all morning and her walk with Sam felt magical. An added bonus was that Harlow's toes were warm, something that was literally impossible to achieve in Falcyra. Both her and Samira's moods were lifted by the warmer temperatures alone.

The other Strider hadn't spent much time in Nuva Troi, so Harlow pointed out her favorite shops and cafes as they walked. The streets weren't as busy as they usually were this time of day, and the amount of buildings that had been destroyed in the fighting before the wards went up was distressing. Harlow tried hard not to stare, as it would mark her as having just arrived, and there were soldiers patrolling in pairs on every street.

With everyone bundled up against the cold, Harlow and Sam were just another couple of girls in ball caps, sunnies, furry boots, and puffy jackets. The soldiers weren't looking for them—that was the Dominavus' purview. Still, Harlow did have to at least try to look like she was attempting to sneak around. To help this pantomime, Meline had dressed the two of them in what she called "dime a dozen" gear for the winter season, and no one had spared them a second look.

They stopped for coffee at Cerberus, and while Harlow kept her sunnies on in the coffee shop, she caught a few people looking at her longer than was polite. The coffee shop was busy, and for all intents and purposes, life was going on like it always had. After months without reliable power, it was bizarre to be standing in the white-tiled, posh coffee shop, listening to jazz.

She started to sweat a little and unzipped her jacket a little, taking off her gloves and shoving them in her pocket. Her sapphire engagement ring caught the light. A blonde swan shifter at a nearby table stared at the ring, before getting out their phone. Harlow kept her sigh quiet. This was all part of the plan. The ring had been photographed dozens of times over the summer, and it was just one of a few opportunities the twins had suggested for her to be caught—and turned in to Section Seven. When both she and Sam had lattes in their trendy insulated mugs, she slipped her gloves back on.

Outside Cerberus, Sam took a long drink of her latte. "I am never going back to Falcyra. Did you ever notice how awful Audata's coffee is?"

Harlow snickered as they walked towards the atelier. "Yeah."

When they were a few blocks away, their boots crunching on the snowy paths of Riverside Park, Sam asked, "Did it work?"

Harlow shrugged. "Hard to know. The blonde shifter definitely clocked my ring."

Sam nodded. "And did you see the redheaded vampire?"

"No," Harlow replied, feeling almost like they were gossiping, having a totally normal girls day out.

"He was filming you under the table," Samira said. "Is this what your life is always like?"

Harlow thought about how normalized it had been to simply be *watched*. Everywhere she went, someone took photos or videos. "Yes."

Sam's eyebrows raised. "When did it start?"

Harlow shrugged. "Always. Since I was a kid. Even before Aurelia's position with the Order, the maters were always a big deal in the lower Orders."

"Wow, that must have been really hard."

Harlow paused, watching the river for a moment, trying to figure out if Sam was being sarcastic. The fresh snow, combined with the river, the familiar wrought iron light posts, and the cobbled paths made the afternoon seem like something out of an old movie. "Do you mean that?"

Sam laughed, stopping next to Harlow to watch the river. "Yeah. What a fucking trip to have someone watching you all the time. Most kids don't grow up like that."

"No," Harlow mused as they kept walking. "I guess they don't."

They crossed through the park and made it to Enzo's without any more attention. Stopping at Cerberus had been a wise idea.

"How close is the Monas?" Sam asked as they entered the atelier.

"Just a couple blocks away," Harlow murmured absently.

The sight of the atelier's blue walls and plush patterned rugs elicited an ache in Harlow's chest for Enzo. Sam's mouth fell open as she wandered between the rich handcrafted wooden racks, staring at the clothes. "This is all so beautiful. I mean, I've seen his work in magazines, of course, but in person…"

"You didn't go to social stuff much growing up?" Harlow asked.

The Strider laughed. "No, my mother was an Ultima, and her mother before her, and so on. Social events are rarely a thing for us. Don't get me wrong, I've never minded it. I love my lineage, but I think we should party more, if it means wearing stuff like this!"

Harlow laughed. "Then change it. When everything else changes, tell them you want to go to more parties—*have* more parties."

"Oh, we have parties," Sam said, waggling her eyebrows at Harlow. "Just not fancy-dress."

Harlow watched as her friend tried on several dresses, all of which looked beautiful on her. But she settled on a tuxedo for herself in a neon pink velvet that would contrast beautifully with her dark skin, and another in a sleek black satin for Tomyris.

"What are you going to wear?" Sam asked as Harlow bagged her clothes and what she'd gathered for the maters, Finn, her sisters, and Nox.

Harlow looked around. "I honestly don't know. Nothing feels right. Enzo always helps me."

Sam grimaced. "I'm not much help, am I?"

"It's not that," Harlow said, sinking into a chair by Enzo's collection of fashion books, the ones Thea had helped him put together before his grand opening, the ones that had put his business on the map. "I just miss them all so much. I miss our lives before all of this happened, even though I wouldn't go back, even if I could."

Sam wandered between the racks again, admiring the clothes. "I know just how you feel. I don't want to go back either, but the last few months have been a lot."

Harlow stood, remembering that there was one more room. "Come see Enzo's vintage reserve," she called.

Sam followed her into Enzo's office, which was painted the same blue as the main showroom. Back here, he kept some of his most special items—ones his mother had worn to events—preserved behind huge glass frames, like a giant catalogue of her life.

"He must really miss her," Sam said, looking at the clothes.

Harlow fought back tears, thinking of Clarissa Weraka. "She was amazing. The most talented witch I've ever known, and one of the kindest people in the world. She'd be so proud of him—of us. And she'd *love* you and Tomy. She was Selene's best friend growing up."

Sam had paused behind her, staring at something. Harlow stepped closer to her as her friend turned. She wheeled out a covered garment rack, grinning at Harlow. "This has your name on it."

Harlow looked at the tag, and indeed, it did. She turned the tag over and her breath caught. "It's my wedding clothes."

Sam looked over her shoulder. "Oh my gods. Are you sure you want to look?"

Harlow's chin trembled. She didn't really want to, not without Enzo. But she'd wanted his help, his advice about what to wear to a big fancy event, and here was her answer. She unzipped the cloth that covered the rack. Inside were several hanging bags, each carefully labeled in Enzo's precise handwriting. *Engagement party, options one and two. Bridal shower, options one through three. Bachelorette party, only one option. Wedding day casual, one and two. Wedding day robe, antique.* Harlow stopped at her wedding gown. She wouldn't look at it. Not without her best friend.

There were two more bags after that, one was her "Going away suit" and the other read, "reception, one and two." She pulled those out, zipping the rack back up.

Sam nodded, seeming to understand. "You'll do the rest when he gets back."

Harlow tried to agree. She'd felt so hopeful for the past few days, despite everything, but all of a sudden the danger of the situation they were in crashed into her. *What if it all went wrong?*

Sam hugged her. "Hey, it'll be okay. I'm going to take this stuff back to the Order okay? I'll meet you at the Monas?"

"Okay," Harlow said as Sam teleported out.

They'd agreed to walk here, and teleport back for convenience. Harlow opened the first reception option and sighed. She and Enzo fundamentally disagreed on whether blush was a beautiful nude for her, his very wrong opinion, or ugly, her correct assertion. She set the floor length sheath dress aside, which was unfortunate, as the cut was gorgeous, but likely hard to walk in without alterations.

She took a deep breath and stared at the ceiling as she unzipped the second option. "Enzo, please know exactly what I would have said yes to."

When she looked down, she gasped. It was nothing short of phenomenal— and perfect for the occasion. She drew the jumpsuit out first. It was a beautiful shade of midnight blue, cut simply in a halter style with a plunging neckline and a high waist, with wide legs that would allow for freedom of movement. The jacket was the stunner of the ensemble though: a floor length cape with sparkling raptors embroidered into it.

She looked closer at them, realizing Enzo had done the work himself. They were a perfect representation of her Feriant form. She zipped the suit back up and put her jacket back on. There wasn't time to try the suit on, but knowing Enzo, it would fit perfectly.

Harlow took the back alleyways to the Monas, carrying the suit carefully so as to keep it out of the mud. Every step closer to their back courtyard set her heart racing faster. The street behind theirs was sad, the house directly behind the Monas especially, as it had been a part of the courtyard's landscape, and now the gorgeous old townhome was crumbling. It had been a rental for many years, so they hadn't known any of the tenants well, but the building itself had been so familiar to Harlow that seeing it in this state broke her heart.

When the back door unlocked, she stood in the threshold of the doorway for a long moment. Going inside was sure to feel strange. She moved slowly, hanging her coat and the suit in the mud room. As tempting as it was to linger, she forced herself to run upstairs, moving through the apartment quickly, not stopping to look at the photos in the living room, or go upstairs to her and Thea's bedroom.

If she started down memory lane, she was likely to get lost, so she went directly to the giant safe in the maters' vibrant peach bedroom. When she'd gathered all the requested jewels and handbags, she began the work of carrying them downstairs in Aurelia's gigantic canvas shopping bags. It took far too much effort to get them all ready to go somewhere, she decided on her last trip upstairs.

Somewhere in the back of the apartment, something stirred. "Sam?" Harlow called out. Maybe the Strider had misjudged her jump back. The noise stopped abruptly, but no one answered.

Harlow felt for her connection to Sam in the threads, but it led across the city. She was still at the Order, not here. Harlow found another connection instead. Larkin.

"Larkin?" she whispered, then out loud. "Pal, are you here?"

Larkin stepped out of her bedroom. She'd changed clothes, and there was a long scratch on her cheek.

"Gods," Harlow cried out, shooting forward. "Are you okay?"

Larkin stepped back, her eyes wide and glassy. "Don't," she whispered. "It will come back."

"Are you okay?" Harlow whispered.

Larkin didn't make eye contact with her, it was as though she were purposely trying to avoid looking her way. "I am." She touched her cheek. "I ran into a branch. No fighting."

Her little sister didn't sound like herself. Her voice was flat, but not tired.

"Trying not to catch its attention," Larkin said. "It's nearby—reading."

Harlow thought fast. "Downstairs."

Larkin didn't answer, so she took it as a no. There were plenty of other book stores on the Row though, so it could be anywhere.

"Staying here, so it can read, and I can be somewhere familiar," Larkin's voice was so quiet Harlow could hardly hear her. "Thought you were at the Order with the others."

If the Ravager was coming back anyway, they didn't have time for this. She took the risk and teleported the short distance down the hall, and grabbed Larkin. She was prepping for a second jump when Larkin shook her.

"You can't," she hissed. "I have to stay. I have to help."

"You *want* to help it?" Harlow asked.

Larkin smiled, and though she looked tired, the expression was genuine. "Yes…" She stared at something behind Harlow now. "Couldn't we just tell her?"

Harlow spun. The shade stood behind her now, shaking its head. And then it disappeared. When Harlow turned back to her sister, she knew the Ravager had taken her again.

"Why can't you tell me what you're up to?" Harlow demanded.

"It's not all worked out," the Ravager answered, shaking her hands off her sister's shoulders. "You'll have to trust that Larkin trusts me."

Harlow stepped back, trying to at least give the illusion that she was respecting the creature's space. "That's difficult to do. She doesn't seem much like herself."

The creature said nothing for a moment and then Larkin's eyes cleared. "I can't tell you what's happening. I promised."

"But why?" Harlow pleaded.

Larkin threw her hands up helplessly. It wasn't a "typical" Larkin move, but it was recognizable and natural. The creature wasn't puppeteering her. "To be honest, I don't completely understand its logic, but I do understand what it *wants*."

"What?" Harlow shrieked, infuriated.

Larkin shook her head. "I *promised* I wouldn't say… But it isn't bad, okay? Don't you trust that I know the difference between right and wrong?"

Harlow gritted her teeth. "Yes, but I'm worried it's influencing you. That it's been watching you your whole life, visiting Ash in Nihil, and it knows how to manipulate you."

Larkin smiled sweetly, a sad look in her eyes. "I know why you'd think that—and I get it. But that's not what's happening." She took Harlow's hands in her own. "Can you understand why it wouldn't trust Mother, or any of the Illuminated?"

Harlow nodded, unable to speak without screaming. When she got a hold of herself she asked. "So what do you want me to do?"

"Whatever you're planning for Chandelnuit. Just go with the plan."

"You know what the plan is?" Harlow asked, incredulous. Larkin shrugged in response. More secrets then. "And when this is over, I get you back?"

Her sister smiled. "Of course."

"No," Harlow replied. "I want to hear it say it. I want its word."

Harlow wasn't sure why she insisted, but Larkin had emphasized that she *promised* the Ravager so many times now, it stood to reason that promises meant something to the thing.

Larkin's eyes changed again. "You want my word?"

Harlow thought carefully. The amount of times Larkin had said the word promise was odd. Her sister was like a walking thesaurus. "No, I want your promise."

The Ravager inside Larkin smiled. "You are learning, aren't you, little bird? The importance of nuance, the dance of words. Your ancestors knew the power of semantics. Of promises." It gazed beyond Harlow now, to some faraway place. "So many of your kind have wound words like weapons, twisting the bonds between us the wrong way."

Harlow wasn't sure what it spoke of now, but she wondered. "Did the Vilhar create you? Were they responsible for your individuation?"

The Ravager smiled at her again, speaking in unfamiliar terms and circles. "You are right to wonder, but no. Not me, but another, younger part of me. Even now, it calls to us." It took Harlow's hand in Larkin's. "I told you the truth before, little bird. I don't remember who I am any longer. Now, you must go."

Harlow started to walk away. It would probably be better to meet Sam downstairs. She spun on her heel. "You didn't promise that you'd return Larkin to me safe."

"As I said, clever. I promise you, Harlow Krane. I will not harm Larkin, and she will be returned to you." It paused, as though thinking. "She is my friend. Perhaps my only one, unless you are as well?"

Harlow raised her eyebrows. "I suppose all that depends on how things turn out."

"An exchange then," the Ravager said, clapping Larkin's hands together in apparent delight.

Harlow thought of the stories in *The Violet Book of the Fey*. If the Ravager was anything like the foes Rhiannon often encountered, making bargains was a bad idea. "Let's just stick to your promise about my sister, and we'll see where we end up."

"Clever and wise," the Ravager said, obviously pleased. "Your friend has arrived." And then it disappeared, taking all traces of her little sister along with it. Harlow's eyes fell closed, her heart thumping hard. She hadn't even realized she was sweating, or how hard her heart had been beating, she was so focused on the Ravager.

Harlow had no idea if what she'd learned was good or bad news. She was as confused as she'd been before, but it was a small comfort that it promised not to hurt Larkin. She hoped she'd read her sister's signals correctly, and that assurance was binding.

"Harls?" Sam called from the mud room. "Need help up there?"

"No," Harlow yelled back. "I'm ready to go."

CHAPTER 40

Harlow had never been to an event at the Illuminated Order, the main headquarters, offices, and archives for Connor, Pasiphae and the other ruling Illuminated, and their staff. She hadn't known there even was a place for events in the building. She sat in Aurelia's office, after reporting her encounter with the Ravager, examining schematics for the Illuminated Order building.

Merhart Locklear had brought them the day before, as an act of good faith and commitment to the Fifth Order's cause. One of Nuva Troi's rare dolphin shifters, who also happened to be an architect, had made the drawing for them, after using their echolocation to map the building, down to its sub-basement levels. Harlow was nearly startled into dropping her cup of Duke and Duchess tea when Indigo rushed into the room.

"Have you seen it?" Indigo looked and sounded so much like Thea in that moment that Harlow had to blink a few times to clear the image from her head.

"What are you talking about?"

Indigo picked up Harlow's new phone, unlocked it, and brought up the Section Seven app. Harlow rolled her eyes. "Are you serious?"

"It seems strange to me that you *wouldn't* be monitoring it," Indigo chided.

"Really?" Harlow laughed. She was a little annoyed by how fast her sister had forgotten the way the gossips had bullied her. "I'm not actually looking forward to this part."

Indigo sighed. "I know they're cruel to you—and I am sorry to tell you that hasn't changed—but… just look."

Harlow did as her sister asked, and there it was: the pinned story was about her, with a photo taken from outside the front window of Enzo's atelier yesterday. The caption read, *Harlow Krane returns to the city, looking like a drowned kitten, as she ransacks Enzo Weraka's gorgeous atelier.*

She braced herself for the sinking feeling of dread that came with a Section Seven encounter. It didn't come. In fact, she felt nothing at all. Worried she might be dissociating, she moved through her body awareness exercises—she didn't need a meltdown of any kind today. Chandelnuit was tomorrow, and she needed the rest of the day to be calm and quiet so she could optimize her focus and her reserves of power.

She found it wasn't exactly true that she felt nothing; she felt slightly annoyed about being called a "drowned kitten." She looked objectively adorable in the photos. But there was no real sting to it. Section Seven was doing what they'd expected them to. Harlow read the story. It was as they'd planned—they'd been spotted at Cerberus, and Section Seven tracked them to the atelier.

Finn rushed in, his cheeks flushed. He'd been sparring with a few of the sorcière when she returned from her trip out, and she hadn't wanted to bother him. "Are you okay?"

She looked up from her phone, nodding. "I'm fine. It's just Section Seven being Section Seven. It worked just how we planned, so that's good."

Finn shook his head. "Not that—though that's good—the Ravager. Selene just told me."

Harlow nodded. "Yes, I'm fine."

Finn sat in Aurelia's desk chair, rolling it over to where Harlow sat at Selene's desk. "Why didn't you come tell me?"

"I'll let you two talk," Indigo said. "But Harlow, we need to talk next-steps." Harlow and Finn both nodded as Indigo left.

"You were having a nice time," she said slowly, wondering if she'd hurt his feelings. "I wasn't hiding it from you, I just—things have been hard lately."

He took her hands, kissing them. "Thank you for thinking of me that way. You can tell me anything though, okay?"

The last thing she wanted to do was make him feel bad. "I know I can. But I really was okay."

He paused, his eyes searching hers. "You changed while I was gone." Seeing that she was about to explain herself, he shook his head. "It's not a bad thing, I just didn't understand 'til now. You don't need me to guide you through all this rebellious intrigue stuff anymore."

Harlow let a deep breath cleanse any remaining tension from her abdomen. "It's not that I don't need you. I just know more than I used to. I'm intermediate now. You're still the expert…" She nudged his knee with hers. "But I'm catching up fast."

He smiled as he cupped her face in his hands. "You never cease to amaze me, you know that? The way you learn things and adapt so fast. You're incredible."

"Thank you," she replied. "Do you want to look over these schematics Locklear brought over and tell me if you feel like they're accurate?"

He nodded, moving straight into examining the building. As he peered at the pages of the rolled out paper on Selene's desk, Harlow let the compliment he'd given her sink in. She'd never been with anyone else who saw her quite how Finn did—who saw how smart she was and liked it as much as anything else about her. She didn't think Kate had minded that part of her, but she'd never said so. Mark had hated it, and tried to squash it every chance he'd gotten. It's why she hadn't applied to grad school after graduation.

Her eyes rested on the Alcaia brochures Aurelia had brought her, after her return from Enzo's. Finn looked up from the schematics. "These look very accurate to me, I don't see any potential mistakes."

His eye followed her gaze, landing on the brochures. "Are you thinking of applying?"

Harlow shrugged.

He scooted his chair closer to her again. "I think you should—if you want to, that is."

"We have to get through all of this," she waved her hand at the schematics, "before I can even think about that."

"You want to though," he urged.

"Maybe," she replied.

She was spared from having to discuss it further. Selene and Aurelia entered, followed by Nox, Indigo and Meline. Selene pulled up the internet on the whiteboard, swiftly opening window after window of sites that had picked up the Section Seven story about Harlow.

"So what's next?" Selene asked the twins.

They looked at one another, both of them grinning the same wide, dimpled grin. "Now we craft the narrative," Indigo said.

Meline added, "We tell everyone you're back, and why."

"How?" Harlow asked.

Indigo moved to the whiteboard, her hands flying over the screen, bringing up all of Harlow's social accounts. She had nearly a million more followers than she'd had before.

Harlow's mouth gaped. She hadn't had the courage to open her social apps, even though she'd known they'd use them at some point in all this. "What is this?"

Meline held out her hand to Indigo. "You owe me. I told you she didn't know."

Indigo reached into her pocket and handed her sister a flat, shiny rock that the two of them had been passing back and forth since they were children— whoever had it had some kind of privileges between them, one of their mysterious twin rituals.

When that was taken care of, Indigo explained, pushing her glasses back up her nose. "It started around Yule. People wondered what had happened to you, and when we left socials, a lot of our followers followed you instead."

Meline nodded. "It's been a big topic on message boards. A lot of people are just waiting to find out where you are and what you're up to."

Harlow glanced at Finn. "You're sure this is going to work? Don't you think they'd rather hear all this from him?" Finn had always been the popular one between the two of them, and she didn't resent it.

Indigo picked up Harlow's phone and handed it to Meline, who started scanning through various windows. "*You* were romantically involved with a human, *you* have been targeted unfairly over and over by the immortal-idolizing gossips. Believe it or not, they want to hear from you—not us, or Finn, or anyone else. They'll believe what you say, because you never try to spin shit."

It made sense, but it was still a little hard to believe.

Meline shook her head. "If you don't believe her, you should read the comments on this Section Seven story. People are defending you, saying that you and Finn are the "couple of the century" and Section Seven should stop bullying you."

Harlow could hardly believe that. Making fun of her had been something of a pastime. Meline handed her phone to her, pointing at the story. Harlow braced herself, but her sister was right. There were seven hundred comments already, and the vast majority of them defended her.

"This is super weird," she said after a few minutes of reading. She locked her phone. "What changed their minds? People used to love to rag on me."

Indigo sighed. "That was before the Illuminated showed their asses, Harlow. I'm not defending how people acted before, but the context has changed. After all this is over, it will change again."

"You don't have to do this forever," Meline added, seeing that Indigo's tirade had made Harlow more worried, not less. "People are looking for someone to trust in all this. I know it looks like people are just going about their normal lives, but they're messed up inside."

Nox smiled in her quiet way, pushing the sleeves of her hoodie up. "They're looking for a way to help. You can give that to them."

Finn smiled at her, nodding. The maters both looked anxious, but nodded as well. They were all on the same page then. Harlow took a deep breath. "Okay. What should I say? Or post?" They hadn't planned this part. The twins said it was better to wait and see what the gossips posted, and what the response was. Now they had it.

Indi grinned. "I have the best idea, do you trust me?"

Harlow mirrored her sister's grin. "Always."

～

THEY ENDED up in the crumbling ruin of the townhouse behind the Monas, with a pizza and a half-burned dining room chair. Snow drifted on the floor of the burned out dining room. Indigo dressed Harlow in a vintage Gastro Lupo t-shirt, and nothing else.

The chain had been hit hard before the wards went up, and the Illuminated had refused to help rebuild, even though it was hands down everyone's favorite pizza, immortals and humans alike. An odd coalition had sprung up around the restaurant, a mix of Okairons from all walks of life who just wanted their parm fries and MeatLovers Classic.

They'd started reproducing the vintage style of the Gastro Lupo tshirt to make money, and had been able to open two of the restaurants back up, both of which had the five link chain that had come to represent the five groups of people who lived on Okairos—and equality—on their doors. Gastro Lupo had become the unofficial restaurant of a growing movement in Nuva Troi calling for change. Not necessarily the kind of change the Fifth Order sought, but their supporters at least believed that the ways they'd been doing things weren't working, and they were quite outspoken about it.

It was mostly very, very powerful people, who were in no danger from the Illuminated, but plenty of average folks, immortal and human alike, were picking up their Friday night pie from Gastro Lupo, and their social media accounts had *millions* of followers. Of course, Indigo knew their social media manager, and she'd let the shifter know that Harlow was about to tag them.

The photo was eerie: Harlow sitting cross-legged in the destroyed dining room, untouched snow drifted around her, in just her Gastro Lupo t-shirt, taking a big bite of the pie. The caption read, "I'm back. If you believe, like I do, that we can't go on like this, meet me outside the Illuminated Order tomorrow night at dusk for Chandelnuit. Let's show the Illuminated what a unified Okairos could look like."

She posted it when they got back to the Order of Mysteries, worried they hadn't given people enough time as she set her phone down. Effective protests took time to organize, she knew from listening to the Rogue Council, but time wasn't a luxury they had. They could only hope this would be enough. That having eyes on them would remind the Illuminated that the rest of the people on Okairos far outnumbered them, even with the vampires on their side.

Harlow dressed quickly in the clothes Meline had left out for her, a lavender cropped wrap sweater and a pair of gray joggers with the puffy boots she'd worn home from ORAIS, and ran downstairs to meet Finn in the lobby of the Order. They were headed to the Three Besoms for what would look like a date, but was actually an opportunity for the world to see them.

He was leaned up against a huge marble statue of Akatei. Like her, he was wearing gray joggers, a hoodie, and a puffer jacket. He was looking at his phone when she walked up holding her jacket. When he caught wind of her, he looked up, his eyes taking in the outfit.

"Holy shit," he breathed, as she walked up.

"It's just sweats," she murmured as he took her hand, twirling her around.

His laugh was sultry. "It's not. Gods, you are so fucking hot."

Her heart fluttered as her cheeks warmed.

He helped her into her coat, brushing kisses over her face as he zipped her up. "Can we please go back upstairs?" He took her hand. They had to do this, and it was possible it would be fun, but it wasn't a real date, and they both knew it.

The evening air was cold, snow falling harder than it had earlier in the day.

All over the city, lights came on in the dark, setting the snow aglow as they walked towards the bar, hand in hand. Snow caught on Harlow's eyelashes. Meline had done her face, so there was no danger of her makeup smudging.

Something called "fresh face makeup" was apparently all the rage right now, along with the casual dancer-off-duty style she wore. The usual tendency to dress up to go out had gone out of style over the winter, as people saw dressing to the nines as a bit gauche, considering all they'd lost. It looked too much like a celebration, apparently.

Someone had hung strings of faery lights across the street the Three Besoms was on, and it was so simple and beautiful, Harlow's breath caught. Finn stopped, looking down at her. A little laugh fell out of her, as tears sprang to her eyes. The Three Besoms' building was half destroyed. Tonight was a fundraiser for the bar, and the street was crowded with shifters playing music with humans. Vampires danced with humans.

Harlow turned, holding her phone up as she clicked into her stories, raising her phone to show both her and Finn's faces. "Hey, Nuva Troi," Harlow said. "Wanna meet me and Finn at the Three Besoms for a drink?"

Harlow locked her phone, not bothering to look at the post from earlier. She needed to concentrate on what came next. She searched the crowd for Sam and Tomy. Eyes that strayed to her and Finn were wary at first, then friendly when Finn started saying hi to everyone and shaking hands.

"I'll get us some drinks," he said. "There's Sam. Go do your thing."

Sam waved at her. She was standing near two elderly sorcière, with graying hair: Holly and Tori Suvari, the sisters who owned the bar. Harlow hugged them both. They'd been friends of her parents forever.

"What happened?" Harlow asked.

Holly shrugged. "Same thing that happened everywhere. The bombs hit the bar, instead of the bugs."

Tori added bitterly, "No one's allowed to use weapons for years, and then the Illuminated try to train humans in a couple of days. Things went like shit."

Harlow nodded slowly. "Would it be okay if me and Sam helped with the bar?"

Tori threw her hands in the air playfully, obviously trying to have a sense of humor about the situation. "I don't know what you can do, unless Finn's going to pay for a new bar."

Sam winked at her, as Harlow laughed. "We have something a little different in mind, but it'll probably be a bit of a spectacle."

The sisters shrugged. Sam and Harlow took their jackets off, handing them to Holly, who looked like she wanted to tell them they were going to catch cold.

Sam stepped forward with Harlow, towards the building. "This is a little bigger than the tomb in Austvanger."

Harlow raised her eyebrows at her friend. "Think you can handle it?"

Sam grabbed her hand. "I know *we* can."

They pressed their free hands to the building. Behind them, a slow hush came over the crowd in the street. The music stopped playing, all eyes on them. Sam whispered a countdown. "Three, two… one."

Harlow put everything she had into this. Later, Finn would help her regain her energy, but this was an important step in their plan. People had to see a taste of what the Striders could do. Indigo had leaked rumors about the mysterious Striders and their talents, leaving out the fact that they turned into giant birds that could kill the Illuminated. Just a bit of mystery to get people interested, and the hint that Harlow and the friend she'd been spotted out with were both Striders.

The building had collapsed inward onto itself, which meant most of its parts were still there. Harlow and Sam had spent the afternoon examining the original plans for the building's construction, as well as all the improvements the sisters had filed with the Building Commission over the years. They'd come up with a version they thought they could bring the Three Besoms back to without exhausting themselves completely.

Now, Harlow's shadows mingled with Sam's. It was nothing like when she and Finn made love. This was platonic love, strong and steady, fueled by all the things that made Harlow and Sam's friendship great. Slowly, as sweat beaded on each of their foreheads, the building went back up, its bricks rearranging above their heads.

Perspiration beaded on Harlow's chest and lower back. Sam hummed one low note, which helped her concentrate. She was sensing the inside of the building, watching it go back up from the inside out in her second sight.

"It's done," she breathed, pulling Harlow into a hug.

When they turned to look at their work, the Three Besoms looked as it had a hundred years ago. It was missing the rooftop conservatory Holly and Tori had added fifty years ago, but otherwise, it looked much the same as it always had. A cheer went up behind them, the roar startling Harlow.

She'd completely forgotten they had an audience. They turned to find Holly and Tori rushing for them. And then there was a crowd, hugging them, thanking them. The music started back up, and Harlow spotted Finn by the bar. His eyes shone with pride, but he waited to hug her until people had the chance to say thank you, that they would come to the Chandelnuit event tomorrow.

A big bear shifter Finn had invited approached the sisters. "I'm Max Persad," he said. "Finn said you might need a building inspector tonight." He pulled some hard hats out of a bag he carried. "Shall we go check things out?"

The sisters nodded. Tori shouted, "Drinks are on the house. We'll donate the money to someone else!"

Holly hugged Harlow. "Thank you for this. I know people have been hard on you since your fling with that human boy. No one who drinks here will keep on with that."

Harlow was speechless. The Three Besoms was an Order of Mysteries institution, as were the sisters who owned it; what they said went. While Harlow hadn't expected this reaction, she appreciated it. This action had been calculated to get people to come to Chandelnuit, not for Harlow's benefit—but as she made her way through the crowd, it sounded like it had worked on both fronts.

Sam and Tomy had moved nearer to the musicians and started dancing.

When Finn found her in the crowd, he took her hand. "Hey, Krane. Do you wanna dance?"

It was the exact way he'd asked her to dance at their primary school graduation. There was only one thing to do: answer in kind. She punched his shoulder and nodded. "Sure, McKay. Nobody else is asking."

As he twirled her around in the snowy night air, he grinned. "You're the girl of my dreams, Harls. Always have been." He pulled her close. "Always will be."

CHAPTER 41

Finn and Harlow stayed up until the wee hours, recouping Harlow's powers in multiple ways. Afterwards, Harlow slept for most of the day. Finn was off making sure that all their plans were on the right track, and she was starting to get ready. Just as she was about to dress, Meline burst into Harlow's bedroom. "Have you seen your post from yesterday?"

Harlow picked up her phone. There were over five hundred thousand likes, and the comments continued to roll in by the thousands. Most said versions of "see you there." Many told the story about what she'd done at the Three Besoms, though Harlow noted a fair amount of the people telling the story hadn't even been there.

Harlow could hardly believe it. She'd been avoiding her socials because she didn't want to face potential failure. But she hadn't failed. It had all worked.

Finn returned, as Meline was choosing comments for Harlow to respond to.

Meline's phone rang. She held up a finger and answered, murmuring "mhmm" a few times before hanging up. "They're coming, on foot, with candles. A *lot* of them."

Finn grabbed the jacket for his tux. "Is everything else in place?"

Meline nodded, glancing back at her phone, which buzzed wildly in her hand. "The others are here too. Sam's bringing them up."

Harlow fought back tears. She hadn't known if this part would happen, it was such a risk—but they were going all in, all cards on the table. Their people on the ground were ready, and now, so were they. Everyone had arrived from the Grove. In minutes, all of Harlow's family and friends would be reunited for the first time in months.

Finn slipped his jacket on and stared at her. "You look amazing. You *are* amazing. No matter what happens tonight, I am so proud of us."

Harlow took Finn's hand and kissed his palm. "Let's go greet our guests. We have a party to get to."

The Order of Mysteries was nearly empty but for the group standing in the ballroom. Aside from the children, who were all in protective care, everyone else was already headed to the Illuminated Order. From Nox's reports, the streets were full.

Harlow watched with mixed feelings as Meline hugged Ari, then Cian. Everywhere Harlow looked, there were faces of people she loved. Petra had already taken Axel down to where the children were, and he was happily playing with his new entourage of fans. She hugged Kate and Audata, and the rest of the Striders. Riley kissed her cheek, before heading for Finn.

"You found it," Enzo said, pushing through the crowd. His hug was so tight and warm, she nearly forgot to be scared. "You didn't look at the rest did you?"

Harlow shook her head. "Just this and the blush dress."

He laughed, then seeing something behind her, kissed her cheeks. "Look who it is."

Harlow turned, hoping, and then burst into tears at the sight of her pregnant sister. "You are perfect," she sobbed as Thea moved towards her, looking every bit the picture of Aphora in her "Mother" aspect. "You shouldn't be here though."

Thea pulled her into a hug, her pregnant belly between them. "I am *exactly* where I need to be."

Alaric materialized behind them, making eye contact with Harlow. "The slightest hint of danger—"

"And you get her out," Harlow agreed. "I don't want you two going in." She shook Thea's shoulders gently. "Do you understand? They'll have wards up to keep people from teleporting."

Thea nodded, exasperated with both Harlow and Alaric. "But when Pasiphae sees me…" she patted her stomach, which was a sizable bump now.

"She's gonna flip," Harlow said. "So you know the plan then?"

Thea nodded. "Yep. I can't believe I'm going to speak for us all."

"You're the swan of the season," Harlow said.

"*You're* the one they're coming for," Thea replied as she took Harlow's hand.

Everyone had gathered around them and they moved into the agreed upon formation, Harlow and Thea behind Finn and Alaric, their friends and family surrounding them.

Harlow made eye contact with Cian, who looked at their phone and then nodded. Then Aurelia, who also nodded.

"Let's go," she said.

The entire group teleported at once. There was a brief moment of darkness, and they appeared in a clear spot in a huge crowd of people. They were standing in front of the Illuminated Order's enormous building, with its harsh curving lines, imposing and forceful as the Illuminated themselves.

Inside the building, in the elegant lobby, the Chandelnuit party was already going strong, despite the crowds gathered out front. Sequins and satin glittered in light from the hundreds of tapers that lit the room. From the street, Harlow could see piles of food on the buffet tables, amongst ice sculptures and fountains of sparkling wine.

People outside the wards were starving, and not one person stood near the buffet table. Harlow glanced at Finn, whose face was so drawn with anger, she thought he might burst into flames. His eyes glowed with cold fury as he stared at the Dominavus, who stood guard out front. She knew he was wondering what she was: had Rakul managed to turn any of them to their cause? They hadn't had much communication with Rakul and Vivia, as their involvement was part of their element of surprise.

They'd let so much be open, let so much be known, so that the world would see the Illuminated for what they were. If not the world, at least all of Nuva Troi. For twelve blocks the city streets were full of people, all carrying candles or flashlights, ready to be lit. Harlow nodded to Alaric and Ari, who gave the signal to light their candles. As the dark streets filled with pinpricks of light, a hush came over the crowd. No one spoke for long minutes, letting their silent vigil speak for them. Harlow watched as the shifters who played music in the corner of the lobby turned. Each of them stopped playing, staring outside at the people gathered.

The noise from the party died, meeting the silence that waited for them in the street. Vampires and Illuminated alike stopped to stare, first at the musicians, and then at the crowd. Harlow spotted Connor, who grabbed hold of Rakul Kimaris' arm. Behind them, Vivia was dressed in an elegant silver velvet gown. Her eyes met Cian's and she nodded once. They were ready.

Connor pointed to the crowd, still speaking angrily to Rakul, who stayed very calm. The Ventyr took his Argent wife's hand, and together they left the party, walking through the lobby as the crowd inside parted for them.

When they came outside, Rakul spoke in a booming voice that carried over the crowd. "Go home. It's cold, and you should all be inside."

Finn stepped forward. "Tell my father to come out. I'd like a word with him."

Inside the building, the crowd of Illuminated and vampire party-goers shifted. Connor McKay emerged on one end, and Pasiphae the other. Both stared out the windows at their sons. Connor was obviously furious, but Pasiphae merely looked concerned.

"No," Rakul said, staying preternaturally calm. "You may come in, but no one is coming out."

Finn looked back at Harlow. Thea squeezed her hand. She was ready. Alaric and Ari parted to let the two of them through. Inside, Pasiphae clapped her hands over her mouth at the sight of Thea's round belly. In the candlelight, Harlow's eldest sister, dressed in a flowing white gown, looked like Raia the Mother incarnate.

A cry went up over the crowd as Thea and Harlow walked up exactly three steps, just enough so the entire crowd could see her. She held up her hands and they fell silent. "Thank you for coming tonight, all of you. My sister's call was quite compelling, wasn't it?"

There was laughter in the crowd. They liked Thea.

"Like Harlow, I've spent the last few months with the Fifth Order. And while you don't know them now, you will soon. We are here tonight to demand the Illuminated give over their stranglehold on power, and help us usher in a new age of democracy."

Thea touched her belly. "I want my twins born in a world where they're safe. A world where the Illuminated don't decide what they deserve."

Someone in the crowd called out, "And what does Alaric want?"

Thea smiled. "Alaric and I, along with Finn McKay and Petra Velarius, signed over our personal fortunes to the Fifth Order this evening, just before we got here. We want to live in a new world together, as equals—a world where humans have an equal voice to immortals. Where we decide things together, from here on out."

The crowd whispered to one another. This wasn't what they'd expected. Thea turned towards Pasiphae, who stood with one hand pressed to the window. "Will you come and talk with me about this future?"

Connor rushed towards Pasiphae, shouting something at her, but the crowd inside was too thick and she had been moving towards the door the entire time Thea was speaking, her eyes on her daughter-in-law's pregnant belly.

Pasiphae stepped outside, pushing past Rakul to meet Thea on the steps. "Yes, I'll come hear you out."

The crowd sent up a cheer, and Thea guided her towards Alaric, and the three of them teleported out. Harlow rejoined Finn, who stood on the bottom step. "One down," he murmured as she took her hand.

Connor finally made it out onto the steps and the rest of the party streamed out behind him. "Pasiphae doesn't speak for all of us," he shouted.

The crowd behind Harlow was displeased by this proclamation, but the Illuminated and vampires on the steps looked smug.

Connor spoke again. "Go home, all of you, before this turns ugly."

Finn shook his head. "Perhaps you should take your own advice, dad."

Connor stared at his son, aghast that he would speak out against him so directly, in front of so many people. Harlow looked down at Meline, who had her phone out and nodded up at her. This was streaming on all the gossips, *and* on Harlow's livestream. Millions of people were watching.

Finn spoke again. "Happy Chandelnuit, dad."

It was the signal. Lights shone on the rooftops of the buildings surrounding the Illuminated Order, and then came the sound of glass shattering—hundreds of windows breaking as sorcière in the audience broke every window in the square, directing the shards into the empty fountain behind them. It was a spectacular sight on its own, but what happened next sent chills down Harlow's spine, despite the fact that she'd known it would happen.

In each broken window appeared Fifth Order snipers, and a rush of air from above caused everyone to look up. The Feriant legion came first, sweeping low over the crowd. Then came the griffins and alicorns, the flying chimera, and the cockatrice. Last were the wyverns and the firedrakes, all of whom landed on the rooftops, staring down at the crowd below like gargoyles.

These were what the Humanists had brought them, the reason why the

Rogue Council had so readily agreed to align with them: the Humanists had been manufacturing weapons that rivaled those of the Illuminated, and they had a full force of trained Heraldic adults among them.

The aerial units and snipers were not all the Fifth Order had to reveal. At the front of the crowd, the lyons, tygres, stags, and pantheroi shifted, their Heraldic forms much larger than their mundane animal counterparts. Civilians in the crowd surrounding the immediate vicinity of the Illuminated Order building shed their coats, revealing more weapons and fully armored soldiers. While the Rogue Order had been a sanctuary for refugees, the Humanists had built a small army, and joined with the fighters the Rogues had gathered, they were an impressive show of force.

They stood silently in the dark. Further off, Fifth Order volunteers helped the true civilians to get off the street. If fighting was to follow, they wouldn't risk children and the elderly. Many adults stayed though, standing at the back of the trained forces of the Fifth Order, obviously willing to fight for the new world Thea had spoken about.

Connor had the good sense to be stunned into silence, as did the rest of the Illuminated. The maters had planned this with the Order of Mysteries and the Fifth Order down to the second, and so far it had gone off without a hitch. Every piece had fallen into place, and now all they could do was wait. If Connor would agree to talk, they could move forward in relative peace. If not, the war would begin here—tonight. Someone showed Connor their phone, likely telling him that they were still broadcasting, despite the fact that the crowd was thinning.

He stepped forward, coming down several steps, glaring at Finn. "You've made a good show, boy. Now come inside, and let's talk reasonably about this."

Finn lowered his voice. "Send the rest of them home, dad, and I will. You don't want anyone else to hear what I have to say. And you won't be talking to me about what happens next, you'll be talking to *them*."

The First Council of the Fifth Order stepped forward, with representatives from each immortal Order, as well as several humans, including Piper Winslow, who looked very, very satisfied right now. They were flanked by the Feriant Legion, their official guard.

Connor looked back at Rakul. "Arrest them all."

An expression of extreme satisfaction crept over Rakul's face as the Dominavus shifted positions to reveal Petra Velarius at their head, geared up and armed just as they were. She grinned wickedly at Connor as she directed the Dominavus to stand in front of the Council, which was now surrounded by the world's most elite soldiers. Petra stepped forward to stand next to Finn as the realization of what had happened dawned on Connor.

Rakul had turned his most elite fighting force against the Illuminated, and what was more, he'd turned over their leadership to Petra Velarius, whose estrangement from her powerful parents was well known. Harlow tamped down the urge to feel smug. They hadn't won yet.

Connor looked back, his face a mask of horror as Vivia Woolf transformed before his eyes. She was the oldest, and therefore the strongest of the Argent, longer than a city bus, and nearly three stories tall. "Know when you are beaten, McKay," she said as her alternae solidified.

She lowered her head, turning it slowly towards Rakul, which gave Connor an up close look at the inside of her mouth, which she opened slightly now, showing her rows of razor sharp teeth. A tiny wisp of smoke curled from her nostrils before a dart of flame shot through her teeth, singeing Connor's shoes.

He leapt back from the flame, stifling a yelp, his eyes wide. It was as though he'd just remembered that he'd killed her children and grandchildren, not to mention her mother. The arrogant prick had really believed that she'd forgiven him until this very moment. Harlow looked forward to hearing how Vivia had managed to convince him of that, but having seen her way with people at Sanctum, she'd fully believed in her ability to do it.

Rakul hopped onto his wife's lowered neck. He was still spellbound, unable to shift into anything other than his canine form, which wouldn't help him now. "You really shouldn't have fucked with my marriage, Connor. Or given me my own elite crew of soldiers to make unfailingly loyal to me, and me alone… I have a feeling your son is about to enlighten you regarding several other mistakes you've made. We have bigger problems to deal with than your pride."

Connor fumed, clearly not knowing what to say as Vivia lifted her husband away from him. She growled once for emphasis, and Harlow was pleased to see Connor shove his hands in his jacket pockets to hide their shaking from the crowd. The Argent leapt into the air to join the rest of the Heraldic, who peered down at the Illuminated and vampires.

Harlow had been watching the interaction between Vivia, Rakul, and Connor so closely that she'd stopped paying attention to the rest of Connor's people. Some backed away, likely planning to disappear into the building, and out the back; many had already gone. Those who were left were spun up with fury. The vampires hissed and growled, their fangs bared.

"Don't let them do this, Dad," Finn warned. "So few of you can't stand against us."

Athan Sanvier stepped out from behind his people, snarling, "We'll kill you all."

The House of Remiel streamed into the crowd, screaming. Finn shook his head, as several of the younger Illuminated shifted into their true forms, following their vampire friends. The Council was teleported out immediately, as this had been something they'd planned for.

The ground force surged forward to meet the Illuminated and the House of Remiel, meeting in a clash of fangs and claws. Harlow shed her cape, her shadows surrounding her, her wings spread out behind her in a dark blaze of glory. A vampire lunged for her, and she met him, two shadow blades springing from her hands, crossing in front of her as she sliced his head from his shoulders in one clean, quick motion.

Connor stared at her like he'd never seen her before. Harlow grinned at him as she stepped forward to fight another vampire, shoving one of her blades into her chest. Another she decapitated as it screamed, launching itself at her in an erratic fashion that revealed its lack of training. She remembered a time when vampires like this had terrified her, when Athan Sanvier had kidnapped her and menaced her with people just like this, from the House of Remiel.

Now, it was almost comical how amateur they seemed. She had learned to fight truly dangerous creatures, and while she might not be an expert at it, these city vampires were no longer something she had to fear. Her wings beat with the pleasure of this realization as she rose a few feet above the steps. The others coming toward her turned and fled. It had all happened in a matter of moments, she realized, as she caught sight of Connor's shock, alongside Finn's pride.

"They're easier to fight than the Vespae," she remarked as Connor stumbled away from her.

"You are so hot," Finn growled, before grabbing his father's arm. Connor had been trying to get away. He dragged him up the steps, Harlow following close behind. While the others fought, their next task was figuring out how the Imperial Ventyr might enter, and *when*. Finding out who had called them was another problem, but not high on their list of things to take care of immediately.

"Forget about them," Finn hissed as Connor looked toward the crowd. "The Fifth Order will slaughter your people in minutes."

Even now, the Heraldic were holding their own and gaining ground on the Illuminated. The vampires were easier to kill, and there were hardly any left as it was. They'd either fled or had been turned to dust.

Connor laughed. "So you have the Dominavus. I have troops everywhere, being called into duty at this very moment. This fight is far from over."

Finn drew his father close. "You won't want to waste them on us, Dad. Boreas is coming, with an envoy. Where will they enter?"

Connor went deathly pale. "What did you say?"

Harlow stepped closer to Finn's father. "You heard him. Where will they come through? They're coming—we don't know when, but someone sent them a message from ORAIS. We need to do whatever it takes to make sure they can't get in."

Connor shook his head. "They can't get in—the portal is—" His eyes went wide, as though he'd realized something horrible. His eyes met Finn's, wild and furious. "Where the fuck is your mother?"

He swung around, rushing into the building. Finn ran after him, Harlow close behind. Connor stood next to the elevator, pushing the button repeatedly.

"Dad," Finn said, touching his father's shoulder. "Dad, that won't make it come faster."

Connor's breath heaved through him in panicked shudders. "She's going to let them in, boy."

CHAPTER 42

Aislin had signaled the Ventyr. Of course she had. It all made sense. Harlow nearly groaned. "Can we teleport down there?" The portal had to be in the basement archives.

"No," Connor snapped. "Of course not."

All the ground they'd gained, the way everything had come together, began to slip apart in Harlow's mind. They hadn't known exactly when the Imperial Ventyr would arrive. They'd assumed it would be soon, but neither of them had assumed it would be *tonight*. Harlow glanced at Finn, who took her hand. His brow furrowed, and his jaw clenched. He felt it too, the unraveling of their progress, the way the plan was unspooling away from them, the threads pulled in directions they hadn't predicted.

The elevator opened and the three of them rushed in. Connor opened a panel next to the usual buttons and pressed his left thumb to it, swearing. "I never should have trusted her. Two thousand years together and she's still a fucking snake."

"Or unhappy," Harlow murmured.

Connor glared at her, his chest puffing up. Finn stepped between them. "She's right. Maybe if you'd tried a little harder with her she wouldn't have betrayed you."

Connor shook his head. "Us. She betrayed *us*. Hate me all you want, call for reform or my head with your Fifth Order, but do you know what the first thing Boreas' people will do when they get here?"

Harlow and Finn were silent. Smooth jazz played in the background as the elevator slowly descended into the bowels of the building.

"They'll string me, you, *her*," Connor pointed at Harlow, "and every single one of the people you love up first. If you think I fucked this all up, you may well be right, but what happens next—I promise you, Finbar, you can't even *imagine* what the Ventyr are capable of."

Harlow wondered when Connor McKay had shrunk. He'd always seemed taller than her, but for the first time ever, she realized that wasn't true. They had only moments to pull their shit together and he was focusing on the wrong things. "How do we stop them from getting in?"

Connor's head swiveled, as though he were shocked she was speaking to him directly. "What?"

"You said Aislin is going to let them in. How do we *stop it*? What's the mechanism to close the portal—I assume she has a way of opening a portal down here —right?"

Connor sighed, pinching the bridge of his nose. "Once she opens it, it can't be closed without a weapon capable of wielding pure starfire. That's why we didn't open it. It was meant for us to use when we had the population subdued."

"There's no way to close the portal once she opens it?" Finn asked.

"Right," Connor said.

Words Connor didn't need to say hung in the air: this was their only chance. They had moments to change everything, to get the world set right again, or at least get it back on track. They'd all come this far, with vastly different motives, only to have underestimated the foe that could actually beat them. They'd all ignored Aislin for years, assuming she was vapid and uninterested, and it had come back to bite them all.

The elevator dinged, and the doors opened into an enormous room, filled with archways of heavy wooden shelves filled with books and scrolls. Each arch was a long hallway. Connor marched down the center, Finn and Harlow at his heels. Behind them, the elevator door closed, called back up. Harlow couldn't help but wonder where it was going, and who might be headed their way next.

The room opened up to reveal freestanding metal safes, with more shelving along the walls containing glass boxes, full of curious items. Beyond the metal safes, a single desk stood in front of a primordial stone arch. Inside the arch, a silver liquid swirled. There was something menacing about it that turned Harlow's stomach. Something was *wrong* about the magic of the liquid. She felt into the threads and found no connection to aethereal power, nor any celestial power either. The liquid was something else, something awful.

Finn stared at it. "The blood of the universe."

"What?" Harlow didn't know what that was.

"It's what's left when you rip a hole in reality the wrong way," Connor growled, stalking forward. "Sometimes they're like a howling storm. We got the quiet kind. Don't worry, she hasn't got it open yet."

Aislin sat at the desk, swearing at the computer in front of her. She'd managed to get the screen unlocked, but was apparently having trouble with some aspect of whatever came next. She spun in Connor's chair, saw them, and continued typing.

Connor reached her in a burst of speed, dragging her from the computer by her hair. He slammed her against the eldritch archway. "You couldn't even open the portal right, could you?"

Blood oozed out of her mouth, and as angry as Harlow was with Finn's mother, this was abhorrent. She stepped forward, meaning to stop him, but Finn pulled her back, shaking his head. "Don't go near it. It's worse than the barrier in Nea Sterlis. You won't just end up in the limen, it will destroy you."

"Why the fuck would you do this, Aislin?" Connor screamed at his wife.

She laughed, spitting blood in his face. "Why the fuck wouldn't I?"

Next to her, Finn's chin jutted out. Harlow grabbed his hand, her stomach roiling.

"I should kill you," Connor screamed in her face, holding her inches from the terrifying liquid.

"Go ahead," she said, her eyes dead. "It won't stop them from coming."

"We've already stopped you, Mother," Finn said, stepping forward. He held out his hand, towards his father. "We stopped her, Dad. You don't have to kill her."

Connor moved backwards a hair, taking them both to slightly safer ground. He pushed Aislin to the floor, where she collapsed. Harlow thought at first she was crying, but she wasn't. She was laughing.

"You haven't stopped anything, you fools. I took the wards down while you were in the elevator. This city will be cleansed by the five swarms that I called here a week ago." She turned to Harlow. "Your people are already dying."

Before Harlow could do anything, Aislin moved, using her own burst of speed. She pressed three buttons on the computer, and the silver liquid cleared. The way was open, directly into the limen, a swirling maw of dark clouds. Somewhere in the distance, deep within them, the sound of a force marching in lockstep echoed through the archives.

The portal was open, and there was no way to close it. Harlow's face threatened to crumple. They'd come so close, but they'd lost. There was no escaping the fact that the Imperial Ventyr would stream into this world, a plague worse than the Vespae had ever been. But they could run. Retreat now, and live to fight another day. They could regroup, find a way to fight them. They could, couldn't they?

She turned to Finn, her eyes pleading. "We can fight them," Harlow said, her chin trembling. "Let's go get our people and start clearing the city."

Finn nodded, taking her hand. He turned to his father. "What do you say, dad? Can we work together?"

Connor's face changed then, and Harlow saw the father Finn might have had. The one he'd needed all these years. He clapped his hands on each of their shoulders. "Yes." He moved to the computer. "You won't be surprised to know that I have a missile aimed at the building. It's on a satellite."

He was wrong—that *did* surprise Harlow—but apparently not Finn, who nodded.

"It won't close the portal, but it will slow them down a bit. We're going to need to evacuate the city quickly."

Finn started to argue, which they didn't have time for. Still, Harlow whipped out her phone, frustrated to find she had no service.

On the floor, Aislin laughed. "The three of you, against the Empire. You're fools."

Finn glared at her. "And you are my *mother*. You should be ashamed of yourself."

Aislin stood, smiling. "I am not ashamed of anything but you." She stepped over to the computer, placing her hand on Connor's arm. "I disabled your satellite missile days ago. Stop this now and meet your fate with honor."

Connor McKay looked as though he might cry. It was the first time Harlow had ever seen him look sad. "I loved you once," he said, his voice low, as though he meant his words for only her.

"Don't spend your last breath on lies," Aislin spat.

The elevator rang in the distance, curtailing Aislin's words. Footsteps rushed towards them from two directions. Harlow just stared at Finn. They'd been grasping at straws for the last few minutes, but there was no way forward.

She took Finn's hand. "Remember the bridge?"

He nodded once to her—he understood. The day on the bridge, just outside Lithraea's Way, he'd taken her power, channeling it through the Claim. They'd whispered about it in the dark in the days after, wondering what would happen if they tried it again. It had all been theories, playing with ideas in the dark of night.

Tonight, they would do the same, only she would channel *his* power, all of it. It would destroy them both, but also this room, this building. It wouldn't close the portal—she didn't think she and Finn could conjure pure starfire—but they might get close enough to damage it and slow the Imperial Ventyr down enough to give the Fifth Order time to regroup.

Harlow's heart ached to think of all they'd miss. Seeing Alaric and Thea's children. Watching Enzo and Riley grow old together and Petra and Kate defy all odds, and change the world. Seeing what Cian would do next, with their precious, beautiful life. Tears slipped down Harlow's face, as she thought of never seeing Axel again. She hated that the maters wouldn't know what happened, that she wouldn't get to see the twins become the women they were meant to grow into, but most of all, she was sorry she didn't get to tell Larkin any of the thousands of things she needed her to know.

In Finn's eyes, she saw all her hopes and dreams begin and end. They would die together, and for all she'd wanted more, this was a good way to go. Harlow never feared death the way others did. She'd always walked a little too close to it. For years, she'd thought that was a flaw in her construction, something she needed to fix. But now she was at peace.

They would die, but they would not go easily, and they would go together. Whatever was beyond this life, they would meet it as one.

And then Alain Easton emerged from the stacks, followed by five Vespae queens. "The portal is open," he said, with a satisfied smile. "And you've brought me your son, and Harlow Krane. Very good, Aislin. Very good indeed." He turned to the queens. "Take them."

Two of them broke off, tearing Finn from her grip, while just one caught Harlow in her grip. The other two took Connor. Harlow didn't even have time to cry out. She glanced towards the portal. The aether was parting, and in the distance she saw the enormity of what Aislin had done. What looked like an entire army of Ventyr marched towards them. They were still so far off, and something about the perspective within the limen was distorting.

"What are you doing, Alain?" Finn asked, struggling against the queens who held him.

"Winning," Alain Easton said with a grin. "Humans will be treated differently when the Empire arrives, and I'll be given the resources to create more children. More incubi."

Connor rolled his eyes. Unlike Finn, he didn't struggle. "You're a fool to believe that," his eyes fell to the floor. Almost to himself, he muttered, "We're all such fools."

Harlow didn't think she'd live to see the day she completely agreed with Connor McKay, but she did now. Behind her, the queen that held her made a soft noise that sounded like a purr. Harlow twisted in her grip, tearing her eyes from Finn and Connor. It was her queen, the one she'd made friends with. "Did you tell them?"

She shook her head, but spoke to the others. The other queens made noises, and the one that held her responded. Harlow couldn't be sure, but she thought they might be arguing.

Aislin, who now stood next to Alain Easton, cringed. "What are they saying?"

Alain shrugged. "I can hardly understand them. They're brutes, really."

Harlow struggled. "They're not. Tell them the truth, Alain."

The queens quieted, staring first at her, then at Alain.

He scoffed. "What truth?"

Behind Harlow, her queen made a version of the low purring noise, shaking Harlow slightly. Harlow glanced back at her. She nodded—Harlow was being allowed to speak.

"That their world is gone. Destroyed." The queen let go of her. Harlow pointed to Alain. "You told them they could go home if they helped you, didn't you? Tell them the truth, Connor."

He nodded. "It's true. Your world was destroyed shortly after we let you into this one." He had the decency not to apologize, or explain further.

She turned. "I am so sorry. You've been used, horribly. You can never go home."

Harlow wasn't sure how much of the nuance the queens understood. The one who held her, the one Harlow had started to think of as *hers*, placed a hand on her shoulder, her talons sharp, but gentle on Harlow's bare skin. She spoke to her sistren, quickly. They released Finn and Connor immediately, each going into a momentary silence.

Alain and Aislin both had the sense to look nervous. "What's going on?" Alain asked.

The queen that had held Harlow pressed a hand to her chest and buzzed the word that meant "peace." Harlow smiled at her friend. "Get out of here. Get your people out." She lowered her voice. "Finn and I are going to destroy the building, and hopefully the portal. I won't see you again. Please, look for a way to find peace here, with our people."

The queen nodded, and then hugged Harlow tightly, smelling like the freshest spring day, and then they were gone, running for the elevator. Finn and Harlow rushed toward one another. Alain shifted, his incubus form monstrous as he sprang for Finn, and Aislin for Harlow. Connor dove for his wife, but missed as she ducked him, shoving his head hard against the corner of the desk.

Aislin lunged for Harlow, grappling with her. She was much stronger than she looked, and within moments she had Harlow's arms pinned to her side. Harlow wasn't sure why she didn't just shift into her true form. Connor did, and he was on his wife in moments, but he couldn't seem to pry her off Harlow.

"Help Finn!" Harlow screamed.

Connor looked as though he would argue, but he did as he was asked.

Aislin laughed. "The Emperor is going to love breaking you."

Harlow stopped fighting, letting Aislin's grip tighten around her. "Does that scare you, little girl?" Aislin murmured in her ear. "I hope it does. You took my son from me when he was a child. You replaced me as his confidant. I *never* would have let you live, and now I will get the pleasure of watching you die slowly, in glorious pain."

Harlow sighed. "Why do people like you always need to make some big, awful speech?"

Aislin sputtered, her grip on Harlow loosening slightly.

"Seriously, do you ever think it just gives people like me the time to kick your ass?" Harlow didn't wait for an answer; she just shifted, using her beak to toss Aislin against the wall hard enough to kill a human, but only hard enough to send the Illuminated woman into unconsciousness. Harlow was somewhat relieved. She would die in moments with the rest of them, but Harlow preferred not to have killed Finn's mother.

She turned to join Finn's fight, trying to find the place to insert herself where she wouldn't accidentally hurt him. He and Connor were losing to Alain, and quickly. She had to figure something out. Alain punched into Connor's chest. He crumpled to the ground, his heart in Alain's hand. A hole gaped in Connor McKay's chest, but somehow he still gasped for air.

"Dad!" Finn screamed.

Now was her moment. Alain and Finn were separated. She dove forward, taking Finn gently in her beak and tossed him away from the incubus. He slid across the room, towards his mother, but was already running back. She had moments, and Alain was already reaching for her, wrapping his horrible arms around her neck. It worked—her airways were beginning to constrict, despite her strength as the Feriant.

She shifted back into her humanoid form, slipping out of Alain's grip and behind him in a quick and surprising movement, a shadow sword in her hand. She shoved it through his rib cage, willing it to lengthen until it was a longsword growing out of his brain. She yanked it out, swiftly. He was still conscious, but unlike Mark, or Aislin, Harlow didn't take any time to spout off arrogant words. She just shifted back into her full Feriant form and ripped the head from Alain

Easton's miserable body, tossing it into the breach between worlds. It rolled towards the Ventyr and she let out a fierce cry, hissing into the aether.

They were still so far away, but they stopped as the head rolled towards them. Harlow shifted back. She would end this in her humanoid form, though she kept her wings. Finn crouched near his father, who was still breathing, but barely, and who whispered something she couldn't hear before he shuddered and stilled completely.

"I'm sorry," she said softly. "We have to do this now, or we won't be able to do it at all."

Finn kissed his father's forehead and stood, coming to stand with her. "He's gone."

They didn't need words. They'd said them all. She took the power he offered her, her shadows multiplying around her in dark, inky flames, the feathers of her wings shining with dark light that amplified into something bigger, brighter, the more it grew inside her.

"My goddess," Finn said as he fell to his knees before her, wrapping his arms around her waist. "May we meet again in the next world."

The power in her grew, like a dark star imploding. She wondered if that was how this would work. If the portal would survive, but when she was at full capacity she'd draw everything, including the approaching Ventyr, into whatever void she and Finn were headed for. She closed her eyes and held Finn tight, focusing on the pinprick within her heart, the one that would suck them all into oblivion.

"Not so fast," said a familiar voice.

Harlow nearly jumped out of her skin, she was so startled. It was a dangerous time to be distracted. Finn pulled back a little from her, lessening the sense that they were about to hurtle the world into a hungry, cosmic maw. She and Finn turned to find Larkin, standing next to the shade—or rather, the Ravager.

"I told you they'd be willing to sacrifice everything for their people. Is that enough for you? Do they pass your stupid test?" Larkin crossed her arms, looking supremely annoyed.

"They did well," the shade said aloud. It took the form of the Feriant again. "I am sorry we didn't get here sooner. The wards blocking this place were more serious than I anticipated."

"We could have just taken the elevator," Larkin sniped. "But no, you wanted to make an entrance."

Harlow still burned with the combination of celestial and aethereal power. "We don't have time for this. Get my sister out of here. Now."

"I can close the portal for you," the Ravager said. "And take the Vespae with me. I know a place where they will be happy."

Finn stood. "We truly do not have time for this bullshit. The Ventyr are coming, or don't you see them?"

The shade shrugged. "We have time."

"You *know* a place?" Harlow sputtered, still stuck on that turn of phrase. What in seventeen hells was going on?

"Yes," the shade insisted. "A world full of plants to eat and some nasty incorporeal creatures that they can fight if they want to. They can have the whole world to themselves. Here—let's ask them if they want to go."

The shade reached out and pulled Harlow's favorite queen out of thin air. It was one of the most disturbing displays of magic she'd ever seen. The shade spoke in the Vespae's language. The queen nodded vigorously, turning to Harlow with what Harlow thought was her try at a smile.

"See," the shade said. "They want to go."

"You told her about the nasty incorporeal creatures?" Harlow asked, hardly believing they were discussing this. Finn watched, stunned speechless.

"Of course," the shade replied. "She says they need something to make life interesting, or someone to murder—something along those lines. I admit, I don't really understand some of the nuances of their language."

This was, without a doubt, the strangest thing that had ever happened to Harlow, but she wasn't about to let a good turn of events go to waste. "You can actually do this?" she asked. "And you'll just help us? Why?"

The Ravager took Larkin's hand, their eyes softening to a glow as they looked at her. "Because I want to go home. I have not enjoyed being an individual. Your sister helped me to find a way to rejoin the aether. I will deliver the Vespae to their new planet, and then cease to be… this."

The Ravager looked at Larkin as though she were the only person who'd ever understood them. Harlow got it. Larkin made a lot of people feel that way. It didn't make it any less incredible.

"You don't want to destroy everything?" Finn asked, somewhat incredulous.

The Ravager reached out, putting a hand to Finn's cheek. "As Larkin's television shows have taught me to say, 'take the win,' McKay."

Larkin snickered and the Ravager turned to her. "Was that the right way to use that phrase?"

She nodded. "Yes, you finally got an idiomatic phrase right!"

"Just in time." The shade wrapped its arms around Larkin, pressing its forehead to hers as it spoke. "Thank you for everything, little Walker. Visit us soon. You know the place."

Again, Larkin nodded. For reasons Harlow could not comprehend, she was overtaken by emotion. The Ravager *had* called Larkin its friend; perhaps it was hers as well. Inside the aether, the Ventyr were moving again, gaining ground. They were close enough now that they would breach the portal shortly.

"Perhaps you should release some of that power into there," the Ravager suggested, waving a long arm at the shadow flames licking at her fingers. "I don't think it will make you feel very good to keep it inside. Give me a moment to fetch our friends."

Harlow stepped towards the portal, careful to stay away from the transparent barrier. Though the "blood of the universe" or whatever that had been was gone, she'd learned a valuable lesson in Nea Sterlis about the way such breaches could suck a person in, and she'd had quite enough of being separated from Finn. She glanced back at him. "Hold onto me?"

He nodded, steadying himself as he wrapped his arms around her waist, whispering in her ear, "I can't believe this is happening."

"Right?" she breathed. She was grateful, but she felt as though someone had spun her in circles for hours and then sat her down and told her not to puke. Finn's arms tightened around her as she leaned forward, feeling the pull of the barrier.

Harlow's arms shot through the barrier. The first of the Ventyr were close enough now that she could make out their features. They looked like people she knew and loved, but they were not here to help—they were here to conquer.

Still, they looked like Finn, Petra, and Tomyris—and the rest of her Ventyr friends, so much that she knew they were likely related, even if distantly. So Harlow shouted, "Run," into the breach, before letting her power go.

To the warriors' credit, they did, scattering as her dark flames licked at their feet. When she and Finn turned back, the shade had returned and there was a slit in the fabric of reality, different from the portal; more like a window to another part of the world. Again, Harlow was stunned by the magnitude of power the Ravager wielded.

"It will heal," the shade said, as though that explained everything. "This will hurt a little," it added, before time itself twisted.

It did not hurt a little. It was excruciating. Harlow's ears and eyes both began to bleed, as did Larkin and Finn's, all three of them sent to their knees as the Vespae streamed out of the hole in reality into the breach in a painful fast-forward. There was no other way for Harlow to describe it.

If humans had thought the Illuminated were gods when they arrived on Okairos, Harlow now understood the feeling completely. They'd never stood a chance against this being. They were only lucky it hadn't wanted to stay on this planet. The amount of magic it used to manipulate time was horrifying. Harlow felt the aether being sucked directly from the breach to power this feat.

The hole in reality shut as the last of the Vespae stepped through. It was Harlow's queen and as time slowed to a normal pace, she gave Harlow one last farewell, her dark eyes glowing with the joy of going someplace where her people would thrive.

"Goodbye, Larkin Krane," the shade said as it stepped through the breach, following the queen.

"See you later," Larkin said, wiping her face.

The portal closed, as though it had never existed at all. Finn took her hand, then Larkin's. "Are all our problems—solved?"

Larkin shrugged. "Seems like we saved the world."

Harlow rolled her eyes, wiping blood from her cheeks. She probably looked horrific right now. "I can't believe the two of you are *joking* right now."

That was a lie. She could believe it quite easily. They walked towards the elevator, arm in arm. "Wait," Finn said. "Where's Aislin?"

Harlow looked around. She was gone, but she'd been injured in her fight with Harlow, and there were bloody smudges leading to the elevator.

"Guess we have one more thing to do before we throw a pizza party," Larkin said as they stepped onto the elevator.

CHAPTER 43

They found Aislin at the top of the building, in Pasiphae's office. She stood near the blown out windows, looking out on Nuva Troi. Plumes of smoke rose everywhere, and the sound of fighting still rose from the streets. Harlow briefly thought that they needed to get downstairs and fight, before she stumbled. Finn caught her, his hands trembling, just as hers had done.

They'd almost burned themselves out in the basement. Neither of them were going anywhere to fight. This was their last stop for the day.

Larkin squeezed Harlow's hand, her eyes full of concern. "I think I'd better go find someone to tell about all this."

Harlow nodded, staying back while Finn moved slowly towards his mother. She opened her phone and dialed Nox's secure comm line. "Go tell them it's over, pal. You can wait in the assistant's office if you want."

Larkin hugged her. "See you in a few."

Harlow waited until her sister was closed into the inner office on the floor, never so glad to see her sister shut into a room with no windows. Cold winter winds whipped through the building. Falcyrans called this last bit of winter, "the brutal season." Harlow thought it was the perfect name for it.

"So, you ruined everything," Aislin said. She stood too close to the edge of the broken windows, but Harlow wasn't worried. She was one of the Ventyr, after all.

Finn moved slowly towards her, as though he worried she might fall. "Step back from there, please."

"Why?" Aislin shrieked. "So you can punish me? Send me to some prison for the rest of my life? I've spent my entire life in prison. This is the end."

Harlow didn't understand. Being married to Connor couldn't have been easy, but it wasn't a *prison*. Was Aislin really this delusional?

Finn's mother laughed. "Oh, she doesn't know. You didn't tell her."

"No," Finn said. "I made a promise to you, didn't I? I didn't break *my* promises."

Aislin took another step towards the open air. "I release you from secrecy. Tell that girl what kind of family she's marrying into—what your legacy is, Finbar. Tell your precious Harlow who you're destined to become."

Finn turned to Harlow. "Connor spellbound my mother when I was a child. She tried to leave with me, tried to open the portal and take me back to Interra, so he kept her from ever using magic again."

Harlow's mouth fell open in horror. Spellbinding was terrible magic. She held a hand out to Aislin. "Come with us. My mother can help you."

"No," Aislin said.

She stepped into thin air. Harlow screamed. Finn stood still, frozen in fear. It took a moment, but Harlow crept to the edge to look over. Finn couldn't move, but she had to look, she had to be able to tell him his mother was gone.

And she was. Gone, but not dead. There was no trace of a body below. It was dark, but there was still enough light to see that much. Harlow frowned, and then remembered: the horrible thing about spellbinding was that in order to curse someone else so deeply, you bound your life force to the spell. Which meant if you died, the spellbinding wouldn't survive either. Which meant that somewhere, Rakul Kimaris was also free.

Had Aislin known when she jumped? If so, it was a cruel thing to do to Finn. *Finn.*

Harlow scrambled back from the edge. "She isn't dead. Connor's death broke the binding. I don't know if she teleported, or flew aw—"

He grabbed her and hugged her so tightly she couldn't breathe. They clung to one another, alive. Alive and whole. Battered, blood all over their beautiful clothes, but *alive.* Larkin was right, after months of trying to figure out how to overcome what had seemed insurmountable odds, everything had worked out.

Finn's grip on her loosened. "We made it."

"Yeah," she said, a laugh bubbling out of her.

He looked out over the city they loved. "It's a mess out there."

Larkin poked her head through Pasiphae's office door. "The word is out. Indigo says you should post on your story to tell people."

Harlow grimaced, but she sat down on the floor, pulling Larkin and Finn next to her. "If I have to go live to be an apocalyptic influencer, so do the two of you."

"Maybe you should clean your face up?" Finn suggested as he reached up to turn a lamp on. He brought it down to sit in front of them. "It's not the best lighting, but…"

Larkin shook her head. "No, the twins said you should look awful."

"Well?" Harlow asked. "Do I look awful?"

"Yes," Finn and Larkin answered in unison.

The two of them were never going to let her live this down. She hit the "go live" button in revenge. "Hi, Nuva Troi," she waved at the screen. People were popping on by the dozens. "It's me, Harlow."

CHAPTER 44

In the days that followed the Battle for Nuva Troi, there were massive losses to contend with. Hundreds of people had lost their lives. Again, Harlow was shocked by how lucky she'd been. Her entire family was safe, though some were having a harder time adjusting than others.

The Illuminated had scattered, leaving the world to pick up the pieces, though for the time being, they were mostly picking up the mess the Vespae had left. It wasn't perfect, but the Fifth Order took over, as a provisional government in Okairos and Falcyra, allowing Avignonne and Castel des Reves time to discuss how they wanted to proceed in international cooperation. It was a complex set of politics, and Harlow was happy she didn't have any part of it.

Pasiphae would go to trial, but she had already entered a guilty plea, and had turned over her own fortune, in exchange for leaving a little to Alaric, "for the babies." He didn't take it, and the Fifth Order held it in trust for him, starting a generous scholarship fund for students who wanted to learn music, the way he'd wanted to when he was a young man. Now, he took up the guitar, and played every day for Thea and the twins that grew inside her. They were blissfully happy.

For about a month after the Battle for Nuva Troi, the Kranes, the Knights, and most of their friends stayed at the Order of Mysteries together. It was as though they needed the comfort of seeing one another every day. Soon though, people drifted slowly back into their old lives. Enzo and Riley to the apartment above the atelier. The maters and Meline went back to the Monas, which had opened back up. Nox and Indi moved into Harlow's penthouse until they found a place of their own. Kate and Petra moved in together, and Audata was moving to Nuva Troi for good.

Cian left for Avignonne with Vivia and Rakul, on an extended trip to their homeland. They sent postcards frequently, and Harlow enjoyed hearing about their travels. Only Harlow and Finn stayed at the Order of Mysteries with Alaric and Thea.

One morning, just as spring took hold of Nuva Troi for good, Harlow stopped into Selene and Aurelia's office in their quarters at the Order of Mysteries. Finn was in there with Axel asleep on his lap, typing away at a spreadsheet. He was dressed casually, in slouchy gray sweatpants and his My Girlfriend is a Witch t-shirt. His hair had gotten long again, and it was falling in his eyes as he tapped away at the keys of his laptop.

Finn pushed his glasses back up his nose as he looked up. He was so beautiful it hurt to look at him sometimes. "Have time for a walk?" she asked.

"Sure," he replied with a smile. "You break the news to buddy though."

Harlow kissed Axel as she pulled him off Finn, setting him down in a patch of sunshine. He barely even woke, letting out a small mew in protest.

Out in the sunshine, Finn smiled down at her. "You look beautiful today."

Harlow blushed a little.

"The ballet-core look you've pioneered is really catching on," he said, bumping his hip to hers.

It was true, she'd sort of re-popularized athleisure. Section Seven loved it, for now anyway. Harlow kept hoping she'd get to stop with the influencer life soon, but so many people reached out to her in legitimate need, and she'd been able to coordinate help for them. She saw now why the twins had a hard time giving it up. It was hard to believe that had all been just a year ago. That the season had just been a year ago. There would be no official season this year, or ever again. No one needed it anymore.

She and Finn walked in quiet peace for a while, her feet moving without thinking. The path they walked was a familiar one for her. The cherry blossoms were just blooming, and the air was hazy and sweet with spring. While the Fifth Order worked to figure out how the world would be governed, everyone was just muddling through the frequent changes in rules and regulations. Still, in many ways, life had gone back to something similar to what it had been before.

Except now their planet was lonelier. They'd lost so many people. Cities sat half empty, and people were finding their footing with one another. When Harlow had spoken to Piper Winslow, a few days prior, at their now-weekly coffee date, the human told her she thought it would be years before Okairos recovered from this one year. It had been strange the first time Piper asked her to meet, and they spent most of their time arguing, but she thought someday they might actually be friends.

"Where's my girl?" Finn asked, pulling her back to reality. She hadn't realized she'd stopped—but they'd reached their destination, so it was okay.

"Right here," she said, pointing to the house. "This is where I wanted you to come with me."

Finn stared at the house they'd taken her first "influencer" photo in. It was just behind the Monas. "I'm confused."

"Welcome home!" Harlow said, grinning.

Finn was perplexed. "What?"

"I sold the penthouse to Nox and bought this," Harlow explained.

Finn grimaced. "Why? We could have lived in the penthouse. I don't think anyone can live here—ever."

Harlow pushed through the garden gate. "Well… not now, but with some work…"

He smiled at her, looking like he was going to call her his sweet summer child. "We have no money, babygirl."

Harlow tapped his nose. "We actually do. As a part of the home-grant program Piper's heading up with Cian, destroyed homes in residential areas are very cheap. You know they want people to move back to the cities, to help improve infrastructure and efficiency."

"Yes," Finn said. "But even if it were dirt cheap—"

"Which it was!" Harlow interjected.

"Even so, it wouldn't be enough to do the renovations needed to make this place safe," he explained. It was clear he was trying to be gentle with her.

"Finn," she insisted, using his name as a plea for him to just shut up and listen. He stopped staring at the crumbling building in front of them to look at her. She pulled out the blueprints in her bag and spread them out on the stone front porch.

"These are a set of architectural directions, okay? When I applied for the grant, I talked with the architect Cian hired to guide people like us."

"People like us?" Finn asked.

Harlow grinned. "People who are going to renovate."

Finn sighed again. "I—"

"Finn!" Harlow yelled. He shut his mouth as she dragged him up the steps, and into the front hallway. "Did you forget I could do this?"

Her shadows flowed out of her, winding around the broken staircase, mending and weaving the wood back together. In a few moments, Harlow had broken out in a mild sweat, but the stairs were whole and gleaming again.

He broke out into a laugh. "I—yeah. I did sort of forget that. Gods, you are brilliant, and I'm a bit distracted…" He nuzzled her neck, murmuring all the apology she needed.

She grabbed his hand, dragging him away from her neck. "With our powers combined, I think we can get a roof on this place in no time, Mr. McKay."

He laughed. "Okay, babygirl. Let's do it, but what are we gonna do with all this space? There's five floors. This place is a literal mansion."

Harlow's eyes sparkled as she told him her plans for a family home: Alaric and Thea on the top floors, Haven's offices in the middle, and them on the ground floor walkout. She used her shadows to build a little model out of the wood splinters and dust on the floor.

"Do you love it?" she asked when she was done painting her picture.

"I do," he said, wrapping his arms around her, as the model fell back to dust. "And I love you, Harlow Krane. Let's get married."

"We are getting married," she said with a smile.

Finn shook his head. "No, I mean today. Let's get married today. Tonight. I don't want to wait for a better time. There is no better time than right now."

Harlow pulled out her phone and began typing.

"What are you doing?" Finn asked. "I just asked you to marry me now."

Harlow smiled up at him. "I know. I just told the group text. Should be set up in an hour. What do you want to do 'til the wedding?"

Finn shrugged. "Maybe get a roof on this place."

Harlow grinned. "You'd better kiss me first."

And he did.

EPILOGUE
FOUR YEARS LATER

Harlow's sneakers crunched on the dried leaves that covered the cobblestone walkway on Antiquity Row. Summer's heat had finally drained away, and the crisp breeze that ruffled her hair smelled faintly of roasted chestnuts and caramel apples. Fall blew into Nuva Troi with cold nights, softening light, and an air of possibility. It was the start of a new cycle, and in Harlow's opinion, the most magical time of the year.

The golden afternoon sun cast a glow on the shiny "I Voted" button pinned to her sweatshirt. She'd squeezed her vote in right after her final for HIST 4423: The Rectification of Historic Inequality in Nytra. It had been the most brutal of her exams, but she was grateful not to have another paper to write. Dissertation topics beat a slow drumbeat in her mind, thrumming for attention. She'd have to narrow things down soon, and the thought of choosing drove her to distraction.

It wouldn't hurt to check the election results one more time. At the very least it was a good way to turn her busy mind away from her dissertation. There were at least four hours until the polls closed, but she was desperate to know who'd win Nytra's election for representatives to the planetary parliament. She let her feet carry her towards the Monas as she refreshed commentary on the results so far, her phone's notifications going wild as she took it off "do not disturb."

A wall of muscle sprang up before her, taking her by surprise. Strong hands caught both her arms and her phone as it went flying.

"Watch where you're going, Krane," a deep voice rumbled.

Harlow mock-glared into stormy, slate blue eyes, before snatching her phone back. "Don't act like you didn't run into me on purpose."

Finn grinned, brushing a kiss to her temple, his dark hair falling into his eyes. "Damn right I did." He inhaled as he bent to brush another kiss to her ear. "Why do you smell so good?" One hand, free now that she'd recovered her phone, slipped under her sweatshirt, as he pulled her into a hug.

Canvas grocery bags hit her in the leg as Finn nipped at her ear. Harlow glanced down. "Did you go shopping *again*?"

He sighed, a little growl vibrating through him. "No one is following my spreadsheet."

Harlow suppressed a laugh. Finn had added a spreadsheet to their friends and family sharedrive that was *supposed* to govern what everyone brought to their Election Day celebration party. Apparently, he'd caught wind that everyone was going rogue, bringing dips when they signed up for hot appetizers, and generally mocking his attempt at organization.

She raised up on her tiptoes to kiss his cheek. "Sorry, sweet boy."

A chill breeze ruffled some papers sticking out of Finn's grocery bags. Harlow snatched them out, as they walked arm in arm towards the Monas. The pile of papers were get-out-the-vote flyers, stuck to a clipboard attachment on Finn's tablet. She peeked at the tshirt he was wearing under his leather jacket, which read "ASK ME HOW TO REGISTER TO VOTE."

"Any luck getting Nuva Troi's youth to register?" she asked with a sly grin. He was the Election Office's top registry volunteer, exponentially blowing his quotas every week by simply getting out and about with his flyers, tablet, and a wide variety of novelty t-shirts.

He nodded, checking his watch. "There's still a few more hours…"

Harlow sighed as they pushed the doors to the Monas open. The smell of books and Selene's signature perfume hit her nose all at once. The store was uncharacteristically empty for this time of day.

"Hello, darlings!" Selene called from atop one of the brass ladders that ran the gamut of white painted shelves on this level. "Could you flip the 'open' sign over and lock the door?"

Finn reached back and did as Selene asked immediately—he was always eager to please her, a fact that brought a bittersweet ache to Harlow's chest. They still hadn't heard a peep from Aislin, though there were rumors everywhere that she and Petra's parents were mounting a secret campaign against democracy. The world was changing rapidly, but some of the Illuminated were still holding onto the past with an iron grip. Aislin obviously hadn't come to Connor's funeral four years ago. Not many had, other than their friends and family.

Aurelia poked her head out from the back. "Finn! Could you share your spreadsheet with me again? I can't remember what we signed up for…"

"We're the chips and dips, darling," Selene interjected as she glided down the ladder.

Finn sighed. "Actually…"

Selene raised an eyebrow and Finn's mouth shut. He took his tablet from Harlow, handing her the grocery bags. "Could you take these home for me? I'm going to go see if I can get a few more registrations."

Harlow smiled. "Of course." As he leaned in for a kiss, she added, "And you're going to the store again, aren't you?"

His face was a mask of innocence as he unlocked the door to the Monas and disappeared down the street in a flash of speed. Harlow locked the door, shaking her head at the maters. They'd signed up to bring dessert and Harlow knew neither of them had forgotten. "Did you *have* to mess with him that way?"

Selene snorted. "Yes, bun. We absolutely did."

Aurelia leaned against the doorframe to the back office, shrugging. "It is a rite of passage."

Harlow sighed. "It has been *four years*."

Aurelia pushed off the doorframe and crossed the store in a few long strides, snaking her long arms around Selene's waist. "The blink of an eye."

Selene nodded, tears pricking at the corner of her eyes. "A happy blink, though, and we love that boy."

Harlow walked towards her parents, pausing to be squeezed and kissed as she made her way towards the back of the store. Her parents absolutely did love Finn, and despite her chiding, it thrilled her that they teased him the same as they did their daughters. He, Alaric, and Nox were treated just exactly as the girls had always been: endless cups of tea and an ear to listen when they needed something—coupled with the gentle ribbing and pranks that the maters had been notorious for, before what most people now referred to as the Conflict.

Four years later, and the Kranes, along with the rest of the world, were still recovering. So many people were lost, so many lives shattered in ways that simply rebuilding didn't make up for. But most people made the effort anyway, even when no one seemed to agree about how to solve their problems. Piper Winslow, at once of their recent coffee dates, had opined that it would likely be decades before any real recovery was possible.

It had surprised Harlow when the former Education Councillor, who now headed up a task force in Nytran Intelligence, asked her to coffee three years ago. After the Conflict ended, she assumed she'd never hear from the woman again. But Piper had called when they had Haven up and running again, wanting to form a better relationship—and strange as it was to think about, they had. The human's insight was invaluable to Haven's progress, and she'd introduced Finn and Harlow to several of their board members.

Thinking of Piper, Harlow spotted the new Wesley Arden book. She chuckled, thinking of the way that Piper had messed with her by pretending she'd never heard of the last bestselling series from the author. Those days seemed like a dream now. She took the book and rang it up at the register, filling out the form that would have it sent to Piper's uptown flat.

While she finished scrawling a wry note to the human, the maters finished their end-of-day routine. Meline and Indigo emerged from their upstairs offices to help close down the shop for the day. They were running the shop with the maters full time now, and the four of them made a splendid team.

"How'd the midterms go?" Meli asked as she trudged down the stairs. Her eyes were rimmed red and puffy. She and Ari had broken up a month ago, and she was still in the crying-and-ice-cream phase.

"Good," Harlow replied. She had the feeling her sister wanted to ask something else, but was hesitating.

Indi squeezed her twin's hand. "She wants to know if Ari's coming tonight."

Harlow glanced between the two of them and then the maters, who were pretending not to listen. "No. He and Larkin took the Woody on a road trip up to the lake for the long weekend."

Meli nodded, tears welling in her eyes. "That's good. I'm glad he has his best friend."

Indi hugged Meline, their fair and dark hair mingling as Meli's shoulders shook. It was hard to watch. Meline and Ari were both too good natured to have had a dramatic breakup. They'd fallen out of love, and held on for too long, not knowing how to be apart after everything they'd been through together. Larkin had texted before the dreaded HIST 4423 final, letting Harlow know the Woody was fine, and that Ari was as much of a mess as Meline.

Finn thought they'd be friends again in a few months, but Harlow hesitated to make that prediction. They'd always be family to each other—but *friends* might take a while longer than that. It was good, in her opinion, that they were taking a little time to process. And no one would be a better balm for Ari's heart than Larkin, who had become his best friend.

Harlow gave her sisters a long hug, kissing both their foreheads in turn. Their arms went around her and she felt the maters' eyes on them, the heavy feeling of savoring even the sad moments with one another filling her heart with the bittersweet pulse of living, rather than only surviving.

In her pocket, her phone buzzed. She stepped away from her sisters to check it. It was Enzo, sending a photo to both her and Finn in their group message of the baby, who had Riley's luminous eyes and Enzo's wicked smile. Her nose crinkled as she smiled, sending a barrage of hearts with the message that said, *Kiss Sarai a million times for me!* She clicked out of the group message and opened a new one between only her and Enzo: *Please check Finn's spreadsheet before you come. He's freaking out.*

A photo of several bags of cupcakes came through almost immediately. *Riley would never pull the shenanigans Lili and Selene have been.*

Thank you, she responded, after sending another barrage of 3D hearts.

Of course Riley would never. They were too considerate for that. She glanced up. Meli was wiping her eyes, smiling a watery smile. "I won't cry through Election Night. Promise."

Harlow reached out and tugged Meli's long blonde braid. "It's okay if you do. Everyone understands."

Meline took a deep breath, then nodded. "I actually think I'm going to give Ari a quick call."

Selene looked as though she wanted to argue, but Aurelia shook her head slightly and her mouth shut. After Meline disappeared upstairs Indi squeezed Selene's arm. "Believe it or not, they're actually helping each other with this. They know they're not getting back together—they just have to find a way to move forward—and it's hard."

Selene nodded, kissing Indi's forehead. "Okay, bun-bun. You know best."

Indi shook her head. "I don't believe that for a second, Mama. I've gotta run home before the party. See you all in a bit."

Aurelia smiled, placid as a bovine on a cool spring day as Indigo rushed out the back door. The three of them went to watch her, as Nox zoomed up on her motorcycle.

"They're going to be late," Selene said with a pleased smile. She loved the fact that three of her children were so happily paired. "Do you know she told me Nox wants to have children when they're forty or fifty? Won't that be lovely?"

Harlow nodded, grinning at Selene. "Just a steady stream of babies for you to love."

Selene cupped Harlow's face in one hand. "I don't mind about you and Finn, darling."

"I know," Harlow replied, making brief eye contact with Aurelia. Selene did mind a little, but she tried hard to hide it. Still, she had the twins, Sarai, and another baby on the way right now, and Harlow knew it would be enough. "I've gotta run. See you soon?"

The maters both nodded and Harlow made her way out the back door and across the courtyard to the garden gate that connected their backyards. When she passed through the arched gate, a little body rushed towards her, attaching themselves to her legs.

River. "Auntie!"

Harlow crouched down. "Hey, pal."

"Phaedra's in the treehouse and said I can't come up," the littling said, voice muffled, as their face was buried in the stretchy fabric of her leggings.

"Oh no," Harlow said softly, glancing up at Thea, who reclined across the yard in a hammock under the big oak tree that spread over the entire yard. She pulled the blanket River had clearly cast off when Harlow had arrived over her swelling belly. She shrugged, shaking her head, but she didn't get up—she was on bed rest for the last month of her pregnancy. Besides, whenever the twins fought there wasn't much anyone could do—they just had to work things out on their own.

Harlow abandoned the grocery bags and picked the four year old up. They were getting a little too big to be carried around, but it made them feel better to be held. She walked under the tree to stand under the treehouse she and Phaedra had built together. "Hey, chicken," she called up. "Why isn't Riv allowed up with you?"

Phaedra's dark head popped out, her great brown eyes the same as her twin's and Alaric's. "They do not have wings," she explained. "It isn't safe."

"I would be careful," River replied with a pout. "Don't boss me so much."

Phaedra's Strider abilities had manifested when she was two, and River's had not. It had been something of a struggle between them. Thea watched, a faint smile on her lips. She was so beautiful when she was pregnant, and *happy*. Harlow was excited for another baby, despite the resurgence of Selene's reassurances that it was all right for her and Finn not to procreate.

"If you can't share the treehouse, Phae, then you'll need to come down," Thea called from the hammock.

The little girl stepped onto the front porch of the treehouse, spread dark wings behind her, and glided down to the ground, holding her hand out to her twin. "Want me to take you up?"

River nodded vigorously, scrambling out of Harlow's arms and into their sister's, who teleported them both into the treehouse the second Riv's hands met hers. Phaedra was generous with her magic, and soon the sound of laughter suffused the yard. Thea's phone dinged and Harlow looked over as she read a text message.

"Cian's staying in Avignonne with Rakul and the others for another week," she murmured.

The firedrake had been training young Heraldic shifters with the Dominavus all over the world for the past few months, and it was long past time for them all to come home, in Harlow's opinion. She missed them. Thea turned her phone around to show Harlow a photo of Cian with Kate, Petra, and a very pregnant Audata—the firedrake had their arms around Audata's cousin Fernando. Everyone was grinning like wild, laughing their asses off about something.

"Oh," she said softly, handing the phone back to her sister.

"They'll be home soon enough," Thea said with a smile, then slapped her leg playfully. "You're something of a mother hen, you know that?"

Harlow slid into the hammock next to her sister, laying her head on Thea's shoulder as they swung in the warm afternoon sunlight. "I've been feeling a little wistful lately."

"Mmmmm," Thea responded. "You get that way in autumn. Always have."

Axel jumped onto the hammock, mewing loudly at the two of them before settling in between them for belly rubs. Thea adjusted her blanket over her big belly and then proceeded to scratch the cat's chin with her long nails, while Harlow gave the required belly rubs. In moments, the cat was asleep.

"Do you think it'll show this year?" Harlow murmured, not wanting the twins to hear her. The moons were waxing, and the veil between Okairos and the limen was at its thinnest.

"The shade?" Thea whispered back. "It hasn't for two years. Maybe it's gone. Larkin can't find it when she walks."

Harlow glanced up at Thea, who had half her mind in the treehouse, monitoring what the twins were up to. "I think that's on purpose, don't you?"

Thea's smile was wan. "You think she visited too much after things ended and wore out her welcome?"

Harlow shrugged. "I think maybe it sensed she wasn't moving on." The shade visited Harlow for the first two autumns after the Conflict, checking in to find out how Larkin was doing, but avoiding her. It had never stayed long enough for Harlow to find out why it was avoiding her sister, but maybe this year she would.

Thea pointed to a stain on her sweatshirt. "Is that coffee?"

Harlow laughed. She'd spilled on herself during her final. "Yeah, I should go change."

Alaric came down the back steps from the Haven office, located on the first floor of the townhouse they shared, carrying two huge folding tables across his broad shoulders. "When's Finn coming home?"

"When he's bought the grocery store out, I assume," Harlow called back.

Alaric set up the tables, then came to give his wife a kiss. When he was finished with that, he pointed to the stain on Harlow's sweatshirt. "After you change out of that, could you take a quick look at the Lilac House plans?"

Harlow got up, letting Alaric replace her in the hammock. Axel woke with a grumpy chirp and jumped down, obviously prepared to follow Harlow into the house. "Sure, did you email them?"

Alaric shook his head, pulling his wife into his arms. "No, they haven't been scanned yet. The architect's office dropped them off earlier. They're in the office on the conference table."

Harlow nodded. "Okay." She walked across the yard, gathering up the grocery bags and appreciating the bright autumnal foliage. The leaves had finally all turned—the year was going dormant in a blaze of glorious color that warmed her to her toes. Everything about fall was magic.

Axel purred loudly, rubbing his face against her legs as she walked into the ground-level apartment she and Finn shared. Harlow deposited the groceries on the giant antique island, salvaged from one his parents' country homes that had been half burned to the ground in the Conflict. The kitchen, as it turned out, had been one of the only rooms to survive, this island his only keepsake from any of his parents' homes. Everything else had been turned over to the Fifth Order, and soon would be property of the planetary parliament.

When she'd asked why he wanted this, he'd told her the story of his first memory of Cian, bandaging a skinned knee on this very island, and many memories after that of talks with the firedrake in the country cottage. His parents had rarely gone there, but sent him there often with Cian. Four years into their marriage, and Harlow still didn't know all of Finn's stories. She mused over the thought as Axel hopped up to the island and rolled onto his back on the rustic hunk of wood.

The house was quiet, everyone either outside or getting ready for the party. She watched Thea and Alaric in the hammock, keeping an eye on the twins as they played. Her own twin sisters were coming through the garden gate, laughing, though Meline's eyes were red. Nox trailed behind Indi, eyes glued to her phone, but laughing at whatever the twins were. Behind them, the maters seemed to have forgotten something and were bickering over who'd go back to get it. From her kitchen window, Harlow snapped a photo and sent it to Larkin.

Miss you. Love you. Hug Ari for me.

The response was nearly instantaneous. *Happy Election Day. Love you.* Then, a selfie of Larkin and Ari at the lake. They were in a canoe, with a cheeseboard between them. They were fine. Everyone was okay.

Then why was her heart beating so irregularly? Why did she feel like at any moment, the peace she felt might simply dissipate? Axel rubbed his head against her arm on his way to the little bay in the kitchen window, behind the sink. It was one of his favorite afternoon spots, as the sun would shine through soon.

Tears filled her eyes as she watched him flop over. She bit her lip, trying hard not to cry. Today was a happy day, not a sad one.

You have been through much. I am told that it takes humans a long time to process grief and sadness as great as yours.

Harlow spun. Behind her stood the shade, though its form was barely corporeal. "You're here."

Yes, the shade responded, coming to stand next to her. *How long has it been since we last saw one another?*

"Two years."

That long? The shade's eyebrows raised. It still took the form of the fey woman, the Feriant, with elegant, dark-feathered wings wrapped around its shoulders like a cape.

"Why do you appear like that?" Harlow asked. She'd never gotten the chance to ask before.

The shade's incorporeal body rested impossibly against the quartz of the kitchen counter, its wings parting a little to reveal a beautiful gown, cut low between its breasts and flowing to the floor. It wore a pendant with a complex pattern that Harlow couldn't quite make out. *To remind you that the universe is wide. That this world is not alone. That there were beginnings and endings before, and that there will be many more before the end.*

"Going with cryptic, then?" Harlow said with a wry laugh.

I suppose you would think so, the shade said with a sly smile. *But I didn't come to talk of the war. Your part in that is done. I came to see how you fare.*

Harlow didn't miss the implication that a greater war still raged, outside of Okairos' bounds. She was glad to hear her part was done, but wondered if she asked… would it tell her? She'd long puzzled over the piece of the prophecy that Morgaine Yarlo had given her in Nea Sterlis: *Awaken the Fifth Order and the seventh ward shall break, and in so doing balance returns. The terror of the Ravagers ends when gods walk the earth as mere denizens.*

The Fifth Order had awoken, but what about the "seventh ward" and gods walking the earth? She'd searched all the archives she could for two years after the Conflict, needing to make sure nothing else was coming for them. But she'd never come up with an answer. This might be her only chance to find out. "What happened to Ashbourne? And the imperial Ventyr? And what about all that stuff about 'gods walking the earth' and wards breaking?"

The shade stared out at the yard for such a long time that Harlow thought it might not answer. *I told you Harlow, you've played your part. You will not see them again. This world is safe, and I, its guardian.*

The shade's words held a note of finality to them, and she knew by instinct that it would say no more on the matter of the prophecy. But it did explain the terror of the Ravagers ending, she supposed. It had been a while since things felt this big—she'd grown used to her mundane life. It struck her that she was glad of it. Glad to be done, and even glad to be protected by the shade, the Ravager —whatever it was now.

"Why?" Harlow breathed. "Why would you do that?"

Because the people here still try. They still strive for better. They have not given up. It paused. *Because Larkin still lives. Because you do.*

"And do your brethren feel the same?" Harlow asked, a sheen of sweat breaking out on her back at the thought of the other Ravagers.

Their focus is elsewhere. The shade touched her arm, nothing more than a memory of touch, rather than actual pressure. *You have not answered me. How do you fare?*

Harlow sighed, understanding the shade wasn't going to tell her more. "Some days are better than others, though objectively the world is moving on."

The shade nodded, a sage look in its dark eyes. *You cannot forget all you had to do to get here.*

Harlow nodded. She'd thought she'd handled things so well, from killing Mark to everything that had happened after. But when regular life started up again, the dreams started. The nightmares she woke from screaming. The hollow look that haunted Finn, and the eyes of everyone she loved from time to time. The days got easier, and the dreams were less frequent. But even now, there was still the pervasive feeling that it might all disappear.

"Will it ever stop?" she asked. "The remembering?"

The shade's sharp features narrowed. *No. But your life shall be long, and it will become easier to bear.*

"Thank you," she whispered. The shade's form was loosening.

You will recover, Harlow Krane. And you will thrive.

The shade's words held the weight of a portent, and once more, she was grateful. "Will I ever see you again?"

No, the shade said. *Tell Larkin that I said goodbye.* It took one of her hands, its touch like a whisper.

"I will," Harlow promised.

I wish you well, it said as it disappeared, a smile on its incorporeal lips. This time it did not fade into limenal space, as it had done in the past. It broke apart, as though dissolving into tiny pieces. Harlow used her second sight to watch it go. On the other side of the veil, in the limen, pieces of the creature that had once been an Elemental force so terrifying it had to be locked up for centuries floated into clouds of aether.

We will not meet again, voices said, a chorus in her head.

Harlow's spirit body rose above the maze at the center of the limen. All that was Nihil was gone now, but the labyrinth remained. Harlow returned to her side of the veil. When every trace of the shade was gone, Harlow turned to look at Axel, who was snoring in the window. He had fallen asleep during the shade's visit. She bent over the kitchen sink and sobbed, not really knowing why, just that it felt better to let the excess emotion out than force it to stay inside. When her chest stopped shuddering, a slow calm came over her.

She splashed cold water onto her face, movement in the yard catching her eye. Enzo and Riley had arrived and Riley was passing the baby to Selene. Enzo was headed her way. He poked his head in the kitchen door. "Hey—" he took a long look at her face. "Were you crying?"

Harlow didn't want to explain about the shade. "Today just felt like a lot."

He took two long strides across the slate floor and hugged her tight. "I did the same earlier. Cried over my kitchen sink, I mean. Just to get all my big feelings out."

She pulled her face away from the cashmere of his ochre sweater. "I'll get snot on you."

He smiled, his brown eyes sparkling. "Can't have that. Want help picking something out?"

She nodded and he followed her through the large room that made up their dining and living room space, decorated in her favorite cream and beige textures. The space was a combination of rustic and elegant, with art covering the walls, all Finn's selections, and some of the paintings he'd been making in the studio.

Enzo selected a sweater dress in the same cozy cashmere as what he wore, though in a dark gray, rather than ochre. Both sweaters were from a collaboration between himself and a Falcyran sheep farm. Then tall boots and thick socks. She changed quickly, while listening to gossip he'd picked up in the atelier, laughing softly at the mundanity of it all, at the pleasure of telling tales about their friends—Jareth Sanvier was dating one of Riley's exes and there was some salacious rumors about the lyon shifter and one of the press secretaries for Nuva Troi's gubernatorial candidates.

When she was dressed, they walked arm in arm out to the kitchen. Finn had just returned and was organizing massive amounts of food on the tables in the yard, with both sets of twins' help. Alaric was setting up the holo-projector and election counts flickered as he got the settings just right for an outdoor evening.

Harlow leaned her head on Enzo's shoulder. "Are you sad about giving up the arch-chancellor position?"

Enzo shook his head. "No, Aurelia was right. The Orders should have elections as well, and I didn't want it. My mom would be proud, don't you think?"

Harlow nodded, thinking of the Werakas. "Both your parents would be. They always talked about the idea of elections when we were kids, don't you remember?"

Enzo's smile betrayed the ache he must be feeling as well. "I do." He hugged her hard. "I'm glad you do too."

They clasped hands, walking out into the chill air of the early evening, Axel weaving between their feet. It was already getting dark, and friends trickled into the yard. Sam and Tomy waved as they dragged in their portable stove for a bonfire. Finn turned away from his mountain of food. Harlow had to admit, she was impressed with his vision.

He grinned when he saw her, hugging Enzo for a brief moment before Phaedra and River dragged him away. "Well, what do you think?" He asked, turning her towards the party. He'd strung lights across the yard and Sam had just gotten the bonfire crackling merrily. A group of shifters who worked with Haven's building group played folk music on string instruments.

"It looks great… Oh, I forgot to look at the plans the architect brought over for Lilac House."

Finn kissed the top of her head. "I reviewed them. You're going to love them —it's everything we talked about."

Lilac House was the biggest of five multi-generational, secure housing complexes that Haven was building for people who were still displaced from the Conflict, or who were experiencing hardship due to immortal retaliation. It was an unfortunate reality, but not everyone was excited about democracy, and some vampires and Illuminated were not reacting well to its implementation. Haven was Finn, Cian, and Alaric's full-time business now. It would be the real legacy of the Knights of Serpens. When Harlow was done with school, she planned to split her time between The Monas and Haven, like Thea did.

"A life of service and books," Finn had called it when she applied for Alcaia the year after Larkin's conservatory acceptance. It was an accurate description, and she didn't intend to waver from it. She had long years ahead of her, and she couldn't think of a better way to spend them than helping those that would shape the world into a better place for everyone.

Finn's arms tightened around her waist as they watched Axel play with River and Phaedra, who had conjured silvery moths for him to chase around the yard. The sounds of their friends and family chatting as election results rolled in were comforting. Twilight descended and Finn pulled Harlow into a chaise with him to watch the moons rise. She rested her back against his chest as he cradled her in his arms.

People clapped as Nytra's candidate was announced, but to Harlow's surprise she hardly noticed, she was so entranced by the moons. She glanced back at Finn to find him staring at the sky as well.

When he caught her eye, he smiled, one finger twitching to point at the waxing crescents above. "A new beginning," he murmured.

A smile spread slowly over her face as Axel hopped into her lap. "It's perfect."

A chill wind cooled her face, as Axel settled in for a nap and Finn relaxed behind her. Harlow's second sight showed the connections between every person at the party, strong and glowing with love. The smell of leaves and magic floated on the breeze. Just above the Monas, the moons rose in the sky. It was going to be a beautiful night

While The Immortal Orders technically ends here, Meline Krane's story picks up right after these events in the novella *At The White Wolf,* which you can get for free by joining my newsletter.

ALSO BY
ALLISON CARR WAECHTER

THE IMMORTAL ORDERS

Dark Night Golden Dawn

Beneath the Alabaster Spire

Awaken the Fifth Order

At the White Wolf (sequel novella)

"The Hart & The Krane" (prequel story, available in *The Tenth Muse Anthology*)

"The Sculptor" (prequel story, available via Allison's newsletter)

THE AETHEREALS

The Hollow Plane

The Ravaged Dark

"Chevalier, First Class" (prequel story, first published in the *Queer & Cute Anthology*, now available via Allison's newsletter)

THE IMMORTAL EMPIRE QUARTET

"HYMN" (prequel story, published in *The Bookish Box Anthology Volume II*)

SCION (2025)

THE WORLD OF THE ORPHIUM MAERE

The Consulate

The Swan (2025)

The Angel (TBA)

"The Stanley Files" (sequel story to *The Consulate*, available via Allison's newsletter)

ALL THE THANK YOUS

The series you just read changed my life. There are too many people to thank here for all of that, but you know who you are.

Please know that every page read, every share on socials, every time you tell a friend, you change an author's life. You've all certainly changed mine. So while all the individuals who helped this series become what it has been can't all be named here, I can thank with certainty the most important people in this process: *you*.

Authors are nothing without readers, and mine are the best in all universes. Thank you for making it possible for me to do the best job in the world—and thank you for loving these books.

Once and for all: pineapple is delicious. If you love it on pizza, I salute you, but prefer mine in a smoothie.

xoxo,
ACW

ABOUT THE AUTHOR

Allison Carr Waechter is probably feeding a monster cat right now. She lives in Minnesota with two enormous felines and one very supportive Book Daddy.

All she ever wanted was for there to be plenty of kissy bits and found family in her fantasy stories. So whether you call that romantasy, fantasy romance, or something else, that's what she writes.

Join Allison's newsletter at www.allisoncarrwaechter.com for things like:

- Exclusive access to full color maps and sneak peeks at character art, covers, and everything else!
- News about new books, special editions and translations
- The latest news about works in progress
- Exclusive access to Allison's limited eARCs

Otherwise, find Allison on Instagram @allisoncarrwaechter